DREAMSONGS

ALSO BY GEORGE R. R. MARTIN FROM GOLLANCZ

Dying of the Light

Fevre Dream

Windhaven

DREAMSONGS

GRRM: A RRETROSPECTIVE

GEORGE R. R. MARTIN

GOLLANCZ
LONDON

Copyright © George R. R. Martin 2003

The right of George R. R. Martin to be identified as the
author of this work has been asserted by him in accordance
with the Copyright, Designs and Patents Act 1988.

First published in Great Britain in 2006 by Gollanz
An imprint of the Orion Publishing Group
Orion House, 5 Upper St Martin's Lane,
London WC2H 9EA
An Hachette Livre UK Company

A CIP catalogue record for this book is
available from the British Library

ISBN 978 0 57508 1 482

1 3 5 7 9 10 8 6 4 2

Printed and bound at Mackays of Chatham, plc
Chatham, Kent

The Orion Publishing Group's policy is to use papers that
are natural, renewable and recyclable products and made
from wood grown in sustainable forests. The logging and
manufacturing processes are expected to conform to the
environmental regulations of the country of origin.

www.orionbooks.co.uk

Contents

For Phipps, of course,

there is a road, no simple highway,
between the dawn and the dark of night.

I'm glad you're here to walk it with me.

George R. R. Martin

BY GARDNER DOZOIS

Although he's been a major player in several different genres for more than thirty years, has won Hugo Awards, Nebula Awards, and World Fantasy Awards, George R. R. Martin has finally *made it*, beyond the shadow of a doubt.

The sure and certain sign of this is that someone else's book was recently advertised as being 'In the tradition of George R. R. Martin!' When you're successful enough, when your books *sell* well enough that publishers try to entice customers to buy someone *else's* book by saying that it's *like* yours, then you've made it, you're a *really* Big Name Author, and no argument is possible.

If you doubt me, think of the *other* writers whose names are invoked with the phrase 'in the tradition of' to sell books: J. R. R. Tolkien, Robert E. Howard, H. P. Lovecraft, Stephen King, J. K. Rowling. That's pretty heady and high-powered company, but there's little doubt that George – who, with his epic *A Song of Ice and Fire* novel sequence has become one of the best-selling, and, at the same time, most critically acclaimed of modern fantasists – belongs there ... although if you'd told young George, the unpublished eager novice, that one day his name would be ranked in such august company, I'm sure he wouldn't have believed you ... wouldn't have dared to *let* himself believe you, believe such an obvious wish-fulfillment fantasy.

Another thing the young George might not have believed, and something that many of his legions of present-day fans might not even *know* (and one thing that this collection is designed to demonstrate), is that George would become prominent in several *different* fields of endeavor. George has had respectable careers as a science-fiction writer, a horror writer, a fantasy writer, a writer and producer for the television industry, and as an editor/compiler/concept-originator for the long-running *Wild Cards* series of stories and novels by many different hands. What George has accomplished in each of these fields would satisfy many another professional as a life's work – one to be bragged about, in fact.

Not *George*, though, the greedy swine – he had to go and reach well-deserved prominence in *all* of them!

Born in Bayonne, New Jersey, George R. R. Martin made his first sale in 1971, and soon established himself as a mainstay of the Ben Bova *Analog* with vivid, evocative, and emotionally powerful stories such as 'With Morning Comes Mistfall,' 'And Seven Times Never Kill Man,' 'The Second Kind of Loneliness,' 'The Storms of Windhaven' (in collaboration with Lisa Tuttle, and later expanded by them into the novel *Windhaven*), 'Override,' and others, although he was also selling to *Amazing, Fantastic, Galaxy, Orbit,* and other markets during this period. One of his *Analog* stories, the striking novella 'A Song for Lya,' won him his first Hugo Award, in 1974.

By the end of the '70s, he had reached the height of his influence as a science-fiction writer, and was producing his best work in that category – and some of the best work by anyone in that period – with stories such as the famous 'Sandkings,' perhaps his single best-known story, which won both the Nebula and the Hugo in 1980, 'The Way of Cross and Dragon,' which won a Hugo Award in the same year (making George the first author ever to receive *two* Hugo Awards for fiction in the same year), 'Bitterblooms,' 'The Stone City,' 'Starlady,' and others. These stories would be initially collected in *Sandkings*, one of the strongest collections of the period. By now, he had mostly moved away from *Analog*, although he would have a long sequence of stories about the droll interstellar adventures of Haviland Tuf (later collected in *Tuf Voyaging*) running throughout the '80s in the Stanley Schmidt *Analog*, as well as a few strong individual pieces such as the novella 'Nightflyers' – most of his major work of the late '70s and early '80s, though, would appear in *Omni*, at the time the best-paying market in science fiction, the top of the SF short-fiction food chain. (The late '70s also saw the publication of his memorable novel *Dying of the Light*, his only solo SF novel.)

By the early middle years of the '80s, though, George's career was turning in other directions, directions that would take him far from the kind of career-path that you might have forecast for him in the '70s. Horror was starting to burgeon then as a separate publishing category, in the early and middle '80s, and George would produce two of the most original and distinctive novels of the Great Horror Boom period of the '80s: 1982's *Fevre Dream*, an intelligent and suspenseful horror novel set in a vividly realized historical *milieu*, still one of the best of modern vampire novels, and 1983's big, ambitious, 'rock 'n' roll horror apocalypse,' *Armageddon Rag*. Although still considered a cult classic by some, *Armageddon Rag* was a severe commercial disappointment, and would pretty much bring George's career as a horror novelist to an end, although he'd continue to write horror at short lengths for a while, later winning the Bram Stoker Award for his horror story 'The Pear-Shaped Man' and the World Fantasy Award for his werewolf novella 'The Skin Trade.' (Although most of George's horror was supernatural horror, he'd also do some interesting work during this period with science fiction/horror hybrids, including the above-mentioned 'Sandkings' and 'Nightflyers,' 'two' of the best such stories ever produced, perfectly valid both as science fiction *and* as horror at the same time.)

The fact that the Great Horror Boom of the '80s was itself beginning to run out of steam by this point, with stores pulling *out* the separate shelves for horror they'd put *in* a few years before and publishers folding their horror imprints, probably helped George with his decision to turn away from the horror genre. Increasingly, though, he'd turn away from the print world *altogether*, and move into the world of television instead, becoming a story editor on the new *Twilight Zone* series in the mid '80s, and later becoming a producer on the hugely popular fantasy series, *Beauty and the Beast*.

Highly successful as a writer/story editor/producer in the television world, George had little contact with the print world throughout the mid-'80s (although he did win another Nebula in 1985 for his story 'Portraits of His Children') and throughout most of the decade of the '90s, except as editor of the long-running *Wild Cards* shared-world anthologies, which reached fifteen volumes before the series faltered to a stop in the late '90s (it has made a resurgence in the new century, though, after a seven-year hiatus, so that *Wild Cards* is back in business as I write these words). By then, soured on the television business by the failure of his stillborn series *Doorways* to make it on to the air, Martin returned to the print world with the publication in 1996 of the immensely popular and successful fantasy novel *A Game of Thrones*, one of that year's best-selling genre titles.

The rest, as they say, is history. Genre fantasy history, but history nevertheless.

What is it that has enabled George to captivate readers in so many different fields? What qualities are there about George's work that ensnares readers, no matter *what* kind of story he's telling?

For one thing, George has always been a richly *romantic* writer. Dry minimalism or the cooly ironic games of postmodernism so beloved by many modern writers and critics are *not* what you're going to get when you open something by George R. R. Martin. What you're going to get instead is a strongly-plotted story driven by emotional conflict and crafted by someone who's a natural-born storyteller, a story that grabs you on the first page and refuses to let go. You're going to get adventure, action, conflict, romance, and lush, vivid human emotion: obsessive, doomed love, stark undying hatred, unquenchable desire, dedication to duty even in the face of death, unexpected veins of rich humor ... and something that's rare even in science fiction and fantasy these days (let alone the mainstream) – a love of adventure for adventure's sake, a delighting in the strange and colorful, bizarre plants and animals, exotic scenery, strange lands, strange customs, stranger people, backed by the inexhaustible desire to see what's over the next hill, or waiting on the next world.

George is clearly a direct descendant of the old *Planet Stories* tradition, probably influenced by Jack Vance and Leigh Brackett in particular, although you can see strong traces of writers such as Poul Anderson and Roger Zelazny in his work as well. In spite of having long been a mainstay of *Analog*, science and technology play little real part in his work, where the emphasis is on color, adventure, exoticism, and lush romance, in a universe crowded and jostling both with alien races and human societies that have evolved toward strangeness in isolation, and where the drama is often generated by the inability of one of these cultures to clearly understand the psychology and values and motivations of another. 'Color' is a word that can't be used too much in describing George's worlds, and, if you let him sweep you away with him, he'll take you to some of the most evocative places in recent SF and fantasy: to Mistfall at Castle Cloud on Wraithworld, to the endless windswept grasslands known as 'the Dothraki Sea,' to the cold ancient maze of the Stone City, to the bristlingly deadly oceans of Namor, to dusk over the High Lakes at Kabaraijian . . .

   The most important reason, though, why so many readers are affected so strongly by George's work, is the *people*. George has created a gallery of vivid characters – sometimes touching, sometimes grotesque, sometimes touching *and* grotesque – unmatched by most other writers, one rich and various enough to be reminiscent of Dickens: Damien Har Veris, the conflicted and tormented Inquisitor of the Order Militant of the Knights of Jesus Christ, in 'The Way of Cross and Dragon,' and his boss, the immense, aquatic, four-armed Grand Inquisitor, Torgathon Nine-Klariis Tûn, in the same tale; Shawn, the desperate survivor fleeing from icewolves and vampires across a bleak landscape of eternal winter, toward a stranger and more subtle danger, in 'Bitterblooms'; Tyrion Lannister, the machiavellian dwarf who comes to shape the destiny of nations, in *A Clash of Kings*; the obsessed and ruthless games-player, Simon Kress, in 'Sandkings'; the wistful ghost in 'Remembering Melody'; the grotesque, creepy, unforgettable Pear-Shaped Man in the story of the same name; Lya and Robb, the doomed telepathic lovers in 'A Song for Lya'; Haviland Tuf, the neurotic but clever albino ecological engineer with the power of a god at his command, in the stories collected in *Tuf Voyaging*; Daenerys Stormborn, daughter of kings and reluctant *khaleesi* of a *khalasar* of Dothraki horselords, on her way to face her destiny as the future Mother of Dragons . . . and dozens more.

George cares deeply about all of his people, even the spearcarriers, even the villains – and by caring so deeply, he makes *you* care for them as well.

Once you've mastered this magic *trick*, you don't really need another. That above all else is the thing that has earned George his place among all those other 'In the Tradition of . . .' folk listed above. And it is the thing that ensures that, no matter what field he chooses to work in, people will read him – and want to read him again.

ONE
A FOUR-COLOR FANBOY

A FOUR-COLOR FANBOY

In the beginning, I told my tales to no one but myself.

Most of them existed only in my head, but once I learned to read and write I would sometimes put down bits on paper. The oldest surviving example of my writing, which looks like something I might have done in kindergarten or first grade, is an encyclopedia of outer space, block-printed in one of those school tablets with the marbled black and white covers. Each page has a drawing of a planet or a moon, and a few lines about its climate and its people. Real planets like Mars and Venus co-exist happily with ones I'd swiped from *Flash Gordon* and *Rocky Jones*, and others that I made up myself.

It's pretty cool, my encyclopedia, but it isn't finished. I was a lot better at starting stories than I was at finishing them. They were only things I made up to amuse myself.

Amusing myself was something I'd learned to do at a very early age. I was born on September 20, 1948, in Bayonne, New Jersey, the firstborn child of Raymond Collins Martin and Margaret Brady Martin. I don't recall having any playmates my own age until we moved into the projects when I was four. Before that, my parents lived in my great grandmother's house with my great grandmother, her sister, my grandmother, her brother, my parents, and me. Until my sister Darleen was born two years later, I was the only child. We had no kids next door either. Grandma Jones was a stubborn woman who refused to sell her house even after the rest of Broadway had gone commercial, so ours was the only residence for twenty blocks.

When I was four and Darleen was two and Janet was three years shy of being born, my parents finally moved into an apartment of their own in the new federal housing projects down on First Street. The word 'projects' conjures up images of decaying high-rises set amongst grim concrete wastelands, but the LaTourette Gardens were not Cabrini-Green. The buildings stood three stories high, with six apartments on each floor. We had playgrounds and basketball courts, and across the street a park ran beside the oily waters of the Kill van Kull. It wasn't a bad place to grow up . . . and unlike Grandma Jones' house, there were other children around.

We swung on swings and slid down slides, went wading in the summer and had snowball fights in the winter, climbed trees and roller-skated, played stickball in the streets. When the other kids weren't around, I had comic books and television and toys to pass the time. Green plastic army men, cowboys with hats and vests and guns that you could swap around, knights and dinosaurs and spacemen. Like every red-blooded American kid, I knew the proper names of all the different dinosaurs (*Brontosaurus*, damn it, don't tell me any different). I made up the names for the knights and the spacemen.

At Mary Jane Donohoe School on Fifth Street, I learned to read with Dick and Jane and Sally and their dog Spot. Run, Spot, run. See Spot run. Did you ever wonder why Spot runs so much? He's running away from Dick and Jane and Sally, the dullest family in the world. I wanted to run away from them as well, right back to my comic books . . . or 'funny books,' as we called them. My first exposure to the seminal works of western literature came through *Classics Illustrated* comics. I read *Archie* too, and *Uncle Scrooge*, and *Cosmo the Merry Martian*. But the Superman and Batman titles were my favorites . . . especially *World's Finest Comics*, where the two of them teamed up every month.

The first stories I can remember finishing were written on pages torn from my school tablets. They were scary stories about a monster hunter, and I sold them to the other kids in my building for a penny a page. The first story was a page long, and I got a penny. The next was two pages long, and went for two cents. A free dramatic reading was part of the deal; I was the best reader in the projects, renowned for my werewolf howls. The last story in my monster hunter series was five pages long and sold for a nickel, the price of a Milky Way, my favorite candy bar. I remember thinking I had it made. Write a story, buy a Milky Way. Life was sweet . . .

. . . until my best customer started having bad dreams, and told his mother about my monster stories. She came to my mother, who talked to my father, and that was that. I switched from monsters to spacemen (Jarn of Mars and his gang, I'll talk about them later), and stopped showing my stories to anyone.

But I kept reading comics. I saved them in a bookcase made from an orange crate, and over time my collection grew big enough to fill both shelves. When I was ten years old I read my first science fiction novel, and began buying paperbacks too. That stretched my budget thin. Caught in a financial crunch, at eleven I reached the momentous decision that I had grown 'too old' for comics. They were fine for little kids, but I was almost a *teenager*. So I cleared out my orange crate, and my mother donated all my comics to Bayonne Hospital, for the kids in the sick ward to read.

(Dirty rotten sick kids. *I want my comics back!*)

My too-old-for-comics phase lasted perhaps a year. Every time I went into the candy store on Kelly Parkway to buy an Ace Double, the new comics were right there. I couldn't help but see the covers, and some of them looked so *interesting* . . . there were new stories, new heroes, whole new companies . . .

It was the first issue of *Justice League of America* that destroyed my year-old maturity. I had always loved *World's Finest Comics*, where Superman and Batman teamed up, but *JLA* brought together *all* the major DC heroes. The cover of that first issue showed the Flash playing chess against a three-eyed alien. The pieces were shaped like the members of the JLA, and whenever one was captured, the real hero *disappeared*. I had to have it.

Next thing I knew, the orange crate was filling up once more. And a good thing, too. Otherwise I might not have been at the comics rack in 1962, to stumble on the fourth issue of some weird looking funny book that had the temerity to call itself 'the World's Greatest Comic Magazine.' It wasn't a DC. It was from an obscure, third-rate company best known for their not-very-scary monster comics . . . but it did seem to be a superhero team, which was my favorite thing. I bought it, even though it cost *twelve cents* (comics were meant to be a dime!), and thereby changed my life.

It was the World's Greatest Comic Magazine, actually. Stan Lee and Jack Kirby were about to remake the world of funny books. The *Fantastic Four* broke all the rules. Their identities were not secret. One of them was a *monster* (the Thing, who at once became my favorite), at a time when all heroes were required to be handsome. They were a family, rather than a league or a society or a team. And like real families, they squabbled endlessly with one another. The DC heroes in the *Justice League* could only be told apart by their costumes and their hair colors (okay, the Atom was short, the Martian Manhunter was green, and Wonder Woman had breasts, but aside from that they were the same), but the Fantastic Four had *personalities*. Characterization had come to comics, and in 1961 that was a revelation and a revolution.

The first words of mine ever to appear in print were 'Dear Stan and Jack.'

They appeared in *Fantastic Four* #20, dated August 1963, in the letter column. My letter of comment was insightful, intelligent, analytical – the main thrust of it was that Shakespeare had better move on over now that Stan Lee had arrived. At the end of my words of approbation, Stan and Jack printed my name and address.

Soon after, a chain letter turned up in my mailbox.

Mail for *me*? That was astonishing. It was the summer between my freshman and sophomore years at Marist High School, and everyone I knew lived in either Bayonne or Jersey City. Nobody wrote me letters. But here was this list of names, and it said that if I sent a quarter to the name at the top of the list, removed the top name and added mine at the bottom, then sent out four copies, in a few weeks I'd get $64 in quarters. That was enough to keep me in funny books and Milky Ways for years to come. So I scotch-taped a quarter to an index card, put it in an envelope, mailed it off to the name at the top of the list, and sat back to await my riches.

I never got a single quarter, damn it.

Instead I got something much more interesting. It so happened that the guy at the top of the list published a comic fanzine, priced at twenty-five cents. No doubt he mistook my quarter for an order. The 'zine he sent me was printed in faded purple (that was 'ditto,' I would learn later), badly written and crudely drawn, but I didn't care. It had articles and editorials and letters and pin-ups and even amateur comic strips, starring heroes I had never heard of. And there were reviews of other fanzines too, some of which sounded even cooler. I mailed off more sticky quarters, and before long I was up to my neck in the infant comics fandom of the '60s.

Today, comics are big business. The San Diego Comicon has grown into a mammoth trade show that draws crowds ten times the size of science fiction's annual WorldCon. Some small independent comics are still coming out, and comicdom has its trade journals and adzines as well, but no true fanzines as they were in days of yore. The moneychangers long ago took over the temple. In the ultimate act of obscenity, Golden Age comics are bought and sold inside slabs of mylar to insure that their owners can never actually *read* them, and risk decreasing their value as collectibles (whoever thought of that should be sealed inside a slab of mylar himself, if you ask me). No one calls them 'funny books' any more.

Forty years ago it was very different. Comics fandom was in its infancy. Comicons were just starting up (I was at the first one in 1964, held in one room in Manhattan, and organized by a fan named Len Wein, who went on to run both DC and Marvel and create Wolverine), but there were hundreds of fanzines. A few, like *Alter Ego*, were published by actual adults with jobs and lives and wives, but most were written, drawn, and edited by kids no older than myself. The best were professionally printed by photo-offset or letter-press, but those were few. The second tier were done on mimeograph machines, like most of the science fiction fanzines of the day. The majority relied on spirit duplicators, hektographs, or xerox. (*The Rocket's Blast*, which went on to become one of comicdom's largest fanzines, was reproduced by *carbon paper* when it began, which gives you some idea of how large a circulation it had).

Almost all the fanzines included a page or two of ads, where the readers could offer back issues for sale and list the comics they wanted to buy. In one such ad, I saw that some guy from Arlington, Texas was selling *The Brave and the Bold* #28, the issue that introduced the JLA. I mailed off a sticky quarter, and the guy in Texas sent the funny book with a cardboard stiffener on which he'd drawn a rather good barbarian warrior. That was how my lifelong friendship with Howard Waldrop began. How long ago? Well, John F. Kennedy flew down to Dallas not long after.

My involvement in this strange and wondrous world did not end with reading fanzines. Having been published in the *Fantastic Four*, it was no challenge to get my letters printed by fanzines. Before long I was seeing my name in print all over the place. Stan and Jack published more of my LOCs as well. Down the slippery slope I went, from letters to short articles, and then a regular column in a fanzine called *The Comic World News* where I offered suggestions on how comics I did not like could be 'saved.' I did some art for *TCWN* as well, despite the handicap of not being able to draw. I even had one cover published: a picture of the Human Torch spelling out the fanzine's name in fiery letters. Since the Torch was a vague human outline surrounded by flames, he was easier to draw than characters who had noses and mouths and fingers and muscles and stuff.

When I was a freshman at Marist, my dream was still to be an astronaut . . . and not just your regular old astronaut, but the first man on the moon. I still recall the day one of the brothers asked each of us what we wanted to be, and the entire class burst into raucous laughter at my answer. By junior year, a different brother assigned us to research our chosen careers, and I researched fiction writing (and learned that the average fiction writer made $1200 a year from his stories, a discovery almost as appalling as that laughter two years earlier). Something profound had happened to me in between, to change my dreams for good and all. That something was comics fandom. It was during my sophomore and junior years at Marist that I first began to write actual stories for the fanzines.

I had an ancient manual typewriter that I'd found in Aunt Gladys' attic, and had fooled around on it enough to become a real one-finger wonder. The black half of the black-and-red ribbon was so worn you could hardly read the type, but I made up for that by pounding the keys so hard they incised the letters into the paper. The inner parts of the 'e' and 'o' often fell right out, leaving holes. The red half of the ribbon was comparatively fresh; I used red for emphasis, since I didn't know anything about italics. I didn't know about margins, doublespacing, or carbon paper either.

My first stories starred a superhero come to Earth from outer space, like Superman. Unlike Superman, however, my guy did not have a super physique. In fact, he had no physique at all, since he lacked a body. He was a brain in a goldfish bowl. Not the most original of notions; brains in jars were a staple of both print SF and comics, although usually they were the villains. Making my brain-in-a-jar the good guy seemed a terrific twist to me.

Of course, my hero had a robot body he could put on to fight crime. In fact, he had a whole *bunch* of robot bodies. Some had jets so he could fly, some had tank treads so he could roll, some had jointed robot legs so he could walk. He had arms ending in fingers, arms ending in tentacles, arms ending in big nasty metal pincers, arms ending in ray guns. In each story my space brain would don a different body, and if he got smashed up by the villain, there were always spares back in his spaceship.

I called him Garizan, the Mechanical Warrior.

I wrote three stories about Garizan; all very short, but *complete*. I even did the art. A brain in a goldfish bowl is almost as easy to draw as a guy made of fire.

When I shipped off the Garizan stories, I chose one of the lesser fanzines of the day, figuring they stood a better chance of being accepted there. I was right. The editor snapped them up with shouts of glee. This was less of an accomplishment than it might seem. Many of those early fanzines were perpetually desperate for material to fill their dittoed pages, and would have accepted anything anyone cared to send them, even stories about a brain in a goldfish bowl. I could scarcely wait to see my stories in print.

Alas. The fanzine and its editor promptly vanished, before publishing even one of my Garizan stories. The manuscripts were not returned, and since I had not yet mastered the complexities of carbon paper, I had no file copies.

You would think that might have discouraged me, but in fact the acceptance of my stories had done such wonders for my confidence that I hardly noticed their subsequent disappearance. I went back to my type-writer, and invented a new hero. This one I named Manta Ray. A Batman wannabee, Manta Ray was a masked avenger of the night who fought crime with a bullwhip. In his first adventure I pitted him against a villain named the Executioner who had a special gun that shot tiny little guillotine blades instead of bullets.

'Meet the Executioner' turned out much better than any of the Garizan stories, so when it was done I raised my sights and sent it to a higher quality fanzine. *Ymir*, edited by Johnny Chambers, was one of a number of 'zines coming out of the San Francisco Bay Area, a hotbed of early comics fandom.

Chambers accepted my story . . . and what's more, he *published* it! It appeared in *Ymir* #2, dated February 1965; nine pages of superheroics in glorious purple ditto. Don Fowler, one of the leading fan artists of the time (actually a pseudonym for Buddy Saunders), provided a dramatic title page showing the Executioner shooting little guillotines at Manta Ray. He added some nice spot illoes as well. Fowler's art was so much better than anything I could have done that I gave up my own feeble attempts at drawing after that, and settled for telling my stories in prose. 'Text stories,' they were called in those early days of comicdom, to distinguish them from fully-illustrated comic strips (which were much more popular with my fellow fanboys).

Manta Ray later returned for a second story, this one so long (twenty single-spaced pages or so) that Chambers decided to serialize it. The first half of

'The Isle of Death' appeared in *Ymir* #5, and ended with a 'To Be Continued.' Only it wasn't. *Ymir* never had another issue, and the second half of Manta Ray's second adventure went the same way as the three lost Garizan stories.

Meanwhile, I had raised my sights still higher. The most prestigious fanzine in early comics fandom was *Alter Ego*, but that was largely given over to articles, critiques, interviews. For text stories and amateur strips, the place to be was *Star-Studded Comics*, published by three Texas fans named Larry Herndon, Buddy Saunders, and Howard Keltner, who called themselves the Texas Trio.

When *SSC* was launched in '63, it featured a full-color, printed cover glorious to behold, compared to most other fanzines of the day. The inside of the first few issues was the usual faded ditto, but with their fourth issue the Texas Trio went to photo-offset for the interiors as well, making *SSC* far and away the best-looking fanzine of its time. Just like Marvel and DC, the Trio had their own stable of superheroes; Powerman, the Defender, Changling, Dr Weird, the Eye, the Human Cat, the Astral Man, and more. Don Fowler, Grass Green, Biljo White, Ronn Foss, and most of the other top fan artists were doing strips for them, and Howard Waldrop was writing text stories (Howard was sort of the fourth member of the Texas Trio, kind of like being the fifth Beatle). So far as comics fandom was concerned in 1964, *Star-Studded Comics* was the big time.

I wanted to be part of it, and I had a terrific *original* idea. Brains in jars like Garizan and masked crimefighters like Manta Ray were old hat, but no one had ever put a superhero on *skis*. (I had never skiied. Still haven't.) My hero had one ski pole that was also a flamethrower, while the other doubled as a machine gun. Instead of fighting some stupid supervillain, I pitted him against the Commies to be 'realistic.' But the best part of my story was the ending, where the White Raider met a shocking, tragic end. *That* would make the Texas Trio sit up and take notice, I was certain.

I called the story 'The Strange Saga of the White Raider,' and sent it off to Larry Herndon. As well as being one-third of *SSC*'s august editorial triad, Larry had been one of the first people I'd struck up a correspondence with on entering comicdom. I was sure that he would like the story.

He did . . . but not for *SSC*. He explained to me that the Trio's flagship fanzine had a full slate of characters. Rather than adding more, he and Howard and Buddy wanted to develop the heroes they had already introduced. They all liked my writing, though. They would be glad to have me write for *Star-Studded Comics* . . . so long as I wrote stories about their existing characters.

That was how it happened that 'The Strange Saga of the White Raider' ran in *Batwing*, Larry Herndon's solo fanzine, while I went on to appear in *SSC* with text stories about two of Howard Keltner's creations. The Powerman story came first. 'Powerman Vs The Blue Barrier!' was published in *SSC* #7, in August 1965, and was well received . . . but it was 'Only Kids Are Afraid of the Dark,' my Dr Weird story in *SSC* #10, that really made my name in comicdom.

Dr Weird was a mystic avenger who fought ghosts, werewolves, and other supernatural menaces. Despite the similarity of their names, he had little in common with Marvel's Dr Strange. Keltner had modeled him on a Golden Age hero called Mr Justice. Doc Weird went my White Raider one better, dying halfway through his first story instead of at the end. A time traveler from the future, he had stepped out of his time machine right into the middle of a robbery, and was immediately shot and killed. By dying before he was born, however, he had unbalanced the cosmos, so now he had to walk the earth righting wrongs until his birth came round.

I soon found I had an affinity for Doc Weird. Keltner liked what I did with him and encouraged me to do more stories, so when he spun the character off into his own fanzine, I wrote a script called 'The Sword and the Spider' that a new, unknown artist illustrated handsomely. Jim Starlin also adapted 'Only Kids Are Afraid of the Dark' to comic form . . . but the text story came first.

Comicdom had established its own awards by then. The Alley Awards were named after Alley Oop, 'the oldest comic character of all' (the Yellow Kid might have disagreed). Like the Hugo Awards, the Alleys had categories for both professional and fan work; Golden Alleys for the pros, Silver Alleys for the fans. 'Only Kids Are Afraid of the Dark' was nominated for a Silver Alley for best text story . . . and to my shock and delight, it *won* (quite undeservedly, as Howard Waldrop and Paul Moslander were writing rings around me). Visions of gleaming silver trophies danced briefly in my head, but I never received a thing. The sponsoring organization soon collapsed, and that was the end of the Alley Awards . . . but the recognition did wonders for my confidence, and helped to keep me writing.

By the time my Dr Weird stories appeared in print, however, my life had undergone some profound changes. I graduated Marist High in June of 1966. That September I left home for the first time in my life, and rode the Greyhound out to Illinois to attend the Medill School of Journalism at Northwestern University.

College was a strange new world, as exciting as it was scary. I lived in a freshman dorm called Bobb Hall (my mother kept getting confused and thinking Bob was my roommate), in this strange midwestern land where the news came on too early and no one knew how to make a decent pizza pie. The coursework was challenging, there were new friends to make, new assholes to contend with, new vices to acquire (hearts my freshman year, beer when I was a junior) . . . and there were *girls* in my classes. I still bought comics when I saw them, but soon I was missing issues, and my fanac dropped off precipitously. With so much newness to contend with, it was hard to find the time to write. I finished only one story my freshman year – a straight science fiction story called 'The Coach and the Computer,' which was published in the first (and only) issue of an obscure fanzine called In-Depth.

My major was journalism, but I took a minor in history. My sophomore year I signed up for the History of Scandinavia, thinking it would be cool to study Vikings. Professor Franklin D. Scott was an enthusiastic teacher who invited the class to his home for Scandinavian food and glug (a mulled wine with raisins and nuts floating in it). We read Norse sagas, Icelandic eddas, and the poems of the Finnish patriotic poet Johan Ludvig Runeberg.

I loved the sagas and the eddas, which reminded me of Tolkien and Howard, and was much taken with Runeberg's poem 'Sveaborg,' a rousing lament for the great Helsinki fortress, 'Gibraltar of the North,' which surrendered inexplicably during the Russo-Swedish War of 1808. When it came time to write term papers, I chose Sveaborg for my topic. Then I had an off-the-wall idea. I asked Professor Scott if he would allow me to submit a story about Sveaborg rather than a conventional paper. To my delight, he agreed.

'The Fortress' got me an A . . . but more than that, Professor Scott was so pleased with the story that he sent it off to The American-Scandinavian Review for possible publication.

The first rejection letter I ever received was not from Damon Knight, nor Frederik Pohl, nor John Wood Campbell, Jr., but from Erik J. Friis, editor of The American-Scandinavian Review, who regretted 'very much' having to return 'The Fortress' to me. 'It is a very good article,' he wrote in a letter dated June 14, 1968, 'but unfortunately too long for our purpose.'

Seldom has a writer been so thrilled by a rejection. A real editor had seen one of my stories, and liked it well enough to send a letter instead of a rejection slip. I felt as though a door had opened. The next fall, when I returned for my junior year at Northwestern, I signed up for creative writing . . . and soon found myself surrounded by would-be modern poets writing free verse and prose poems. I loved poetry, but not that sort. I had no idea what to say about my classmates' poems, and they had no idea what to say about my stories. Where I dreamed of selling stories to Analog and Galaxy, and maybe Playboy, my classmates hoped to place a poem with TriQuarterly, Northwestern's prestigious literary magazine.

A few of the other writers did submit the occasional short story; plotless character pieces, for the most part, many written in the present tense, some in the second person, a few without the benefit of capitalization. (To be fair, there were exceptions. I remember one, a creepy little horror story set in an old department store, almost Lovecraftian in tone. I liked that story best of all those I read that year; the rest of the class hated it, of course.)

Nonetheless, I managed to complete four short stories (and no poems) for creative writing. 'The Added Safety Factor' and 'The Hero' were science fiction. 'And Death His Legacy' and 'Protector' were mainstream stories with a political slant (it was 1968, and revolution was in the air). The former grew out of a character I'd first envisioned back at Marist, after developing an enthusiasm for James Bond (Ursula Andress had nothing to do with it, no sir, and neither did those sex scenes in the books, nope, nope). Maximilian de Laurier was intended to be an 'elegant assassin,' who would jaunt about the world killing evil dictators in exotic locations. His big gimmick would be a pipe that doubled as a blowgun.

By the time I got around to putting him on paper, only the name remained. My politics had changed, and assassination no longer seemed so sexy after 1968. The story never sold, but you can read it here, only thirty-five short years after it was written.

The class liked the mainstream stories better than the SF stories, but didn't like any of them very much. Our prof, a hip young instructor who drove a classic Porsche and wore corduroy jackets with leather patches on the elbows, was similarly tepid . . . but he also thought that grades were bullshit, so I was able to escape with high marks and four finished stories.

Though the class hadn't liked my stories, I remained hopeful that some editors might. I would send my stories out, and see what happened. I knew the process: find the addresses in *Writer's Market*, put a crisp new ribbon in my Smith-Corona, type up a clean doublespaced manuscript, ship it off with a brief cover letter and a stamped, self-addressed return envelope, and wait. I could do that.

As my junior year at Northwestern was winding down, I began to market the four stories I'd written for creative writing. Whenever a story was returned by one magazine, I'd ship it off to another that same day. I started with the best paying markets and worked my way down the pay scale, as the writers' magazines all recommended. And I made a solemn vow that *I would not give up.*

Good thing. 'The Added Safety Factor' alone collected thirty-seven rejection slips before I finally ran out of places to send it. Nine years after I'd written it, when I was living in Iowa and teaching classes instead of attending them, a fellow teacher named George Guthridge read the story and said he knew how to fix it. I gave him my blessing, and Guthridge rewrote 'The Added Safety Factor' into 'Warship' and sent it forth as a collaboration. As 'Warship' it collected another five rejections before finally finding a home at *F&SF*. Those forty-two rejections remain my personal record, one that I am in no rush to break.

The other stories were all gathering rejections as well, though at a lesser clip. I soon discovered that most magazines did not share the enthusiasm of

The American-Scandinavian Review for stories about the Russo-Swedish War of 1808, and returned 'The Fortress' to the drawer. 'Protector' was revised and retitled 'The Protectors,' but that didn't help. And 'The Hero' came back from *Playboy* and *Analog*, went off to *Galaxy* . . .

. . . and vanished. I'll tell you what became of it in my second commentary. Meanwhile, have a look at my apprentice work, if you dare.

Only Kids Are Afraid of the Dark

Through the silent, shifting shadows
Grotesque forms go drifting by;
Phantom shapes prowl o'er the darkness;
Great winged hellions stalk the sky.
In the ghostly, ghastly grayness
Soul-less horrors make their home.
Know they well this land of evil—
Corlos is the world they roam.

> – found in a Central European cavern,
> once the temple of a dark sect;
> author unknown.

Darkness. Everywhere there was darkness. Grim, foreboding, omnipresent; it hung over the plain like a great stifling mantle. No moonlight sifted down; no stars shone from above; only night, sinister and eternal, and the swirling, choking gray mists that shifted and stirred with every movement. Something screeched in the distance, but its form could not be seen. The mists and the shadows cloaked all.

But no. One object was visible. In the middle of the plain, rising to challenge the grim black mountains in the distance, a smooth, needle-like tower thrust up into the dead sky. Miles it rose, up to where the crackling crimson lightnings played eternally on the polished black rock. A dull scarlet light gleamed from the lone tower window, one single isle in a sea of night.

In the swirling mists below things stirred uneasily, and the rustles of strange movements and scramblings broke the deathly silence. The unholy denizens of Corlos were uneasy, for when the light shone in the tower, it meant that its owner was at home. And even demons can know fear.

High in the summit of the black tower, a grim entity looked out of the single window at the yawning darkness of the plains and cursed them solemnly. Raging, the being turned from the swirling mist of the eternal night towards the well-lighted interior of its citadel. A whimper broke the silence. Chained helplessly to the marble wall, a hideous shape twisted in vain against its bonds. The entity was displeased. Raising one hand, it unleashed a bolt of black power toward the straining horror on the wall.

A shriek of agony cut the endless night, and the bonds went limp. The chained demon was gone. No sound disturbed the solitude of the tower or its grim occupant. The entity rested on a great batlike throne carved from some glowing black rock. It stared across the room and out the window, at the half-seen somethings churning through the dark clouds.

At last the being cried aloud, and its shout echoed and re-echoed down the miles and miles of the sinister tower. Even in the black pit of the dungeons far below it was heard, and the demons imprisoned there shuddered in expectation of even greater agony, for the cry was the epitome of rage.

A bolt of black power shot from an upraised fist into the night. Something screamed outside, and an unseen shape fell writhing from the skies. The entity snarled.

'Feeble sport. There is better to be had in the realm of mortals, where once I reigned, and where I would roam once more, to hunt again for human souls! When will the commandment be fulfilled, and the sacrifice be made that will release me from this eternal exile?'

Thunder rumbled through the darkness. Crimson lightnings played among the black mountains. And the denizens of Corlos cringed in fear. Saagael, Prince of Demons, Lord of Corlos, King of the Netherworld, was angry and restless once more. And when the Lord of Darkness was displeased, his subjects were sent scrambling in terror through the mists.

*

For long ages the great temple had lain hidden by sand and jungle, alone and deserted. The dust of centuries had gathered on its floor, and the silence of eons brooded in the grim, dark recesses. Dark and evil it was, so generations of natives declared it taboo, and it stood alone through the ages.

But now, after timeless solitude, the great black doors carved with their hideous and forgotten symbols creaked open once more. Footsteps stirred the dust of three thousand years, and echoes disturbed the silence of the dark places. Slowly, nervously, with cautious glances into the darkness, two men sneaked into the ancient temple.

They were dirty men, unwashed and unshaven, and their faces were masks of greed and brutality. Their clothes were in rags, and they each carried long, keen knives next to their empty, useless revolvers. They were hunted men, coming to the temple with blood on their hands and fear in their hearts.

The larger of the two, the tall, lean one called Jasper, surveyed the dark, empty temple with a cold and cynical eye. It was a grim place, even by his standards. Darkness prevailed everywhere, in spite of the burning jungle sun outside, for the few windows there were had been stained a deep purple hue through which little light could pass. The rest was stone, a grim ebony stone carved centuries ago. There were strange, hideous murals on the walls, and the air was dank and stale with the smell of death. Of the furnishings, all had long decayed into dust save the huge black altar at the far end of the room. Once there had been stairs leading to a higher level, but they were gone now, rotted into nothingness.

Jasper unslung his knapsack from his back and turned to his short, fat companion. 'Guess this is it, Willie,' he said, his voice a low guttural rumble. 'Here's where we spend the night.'

Willie's eyes moved nervously in their sockets, and his tongue flicked over dry lips. 'I don't like it,' he said. 'This place gives me th' creeps. It's too dark and spooky. And lookit them things on the walls.' He pointed towards one of the more bizarre of the murals.

Jasper laughed, a snarling, bitter, cruel laugh from deep in his throat. 'We got to stay some place, and the natives will kill us if they find us out in the open. They know we've got those sacred rubies of theirs. C'mon, Willie, there's nothing wrong with this joint, and the natives are scared to come near it. So it's a little dark . . . big deal. Only kids are afraid of the dark.'

'Yeah, I . . . I guess yer right,' Willie said hesitantly. Removing his knapsack, he squatted down in the dust next to Jasper and began removing the makings of a meal. Jasper went back out into the jungle and returned minutes later, his arms laden with wood. A small fire was started, and the two squatted in silence and hastily consumed their small meal. Afterward they sat around the fire and spoke in whispers of what they would do in civilization with the sudden wealth they had come upon.

Time passed, slowly but inexorably. Outside, the sun sank behind the mountains in the west. Night came to the jungle.

The temple's interior was even more foreboding by night. The creeping darkness that spread from the walls put a damper on conversation. Yawning, Jasper spread his sleeping bag out on the dust-covered floor and stretched out. He looked up at Willie. 'I'm gonna call it a day,' he said. 'How about you?'

Willie nodded. 'Yeah,' he said. 'Guess so.' He hesitated. 'But not on the floor. All that dust . . . could be bugs . . . spiders, mebbe. Nightcrawlers. I ain't gonna be bit all night in my sleep.'

Jasper frowned. 'Where, then? Ain't no furniture left in the place.'

Willie's hard dark eyes traveled around the room, searching. 'There,' he exclaimed. 'That thing looks wide enough to hold me. And the bugs won't be able to get at me up there.'

Jasper shrugged. 'Suit yourself,' he said. He turned over and soon was asleep. Willie waddled over to the great carven rock, spread his sleeping bag open on it, and clambered up noisily. He stretched out and closed his eyes, shuddering as he beheld the carving on the ceiling. Within minutes his stout frame was heaving regularly, and he was snoring.

Across the length of the dark room Jasper stirred, sat up, and peered through the gloom at his sleeping companion. Thoughts were running feverishly through his head. The natives were hot on their trail, and one man could move much faster than two, especially if the second was a fat, slow cow like Willie. And then there were the rubies – gleaming wealth, greater than any he had ever dreamed of. They could be his – all his.

Silently Jasper rose, and crept wolflike through the blackness towards Willie. His hand went to his waist, and extracted a slim, gleaming knife. Reaching the dais, he stood a moment and looked down on his comrade. Willie heaved and tossed in his sleep. The thought of those gleaming red rubies in Willie's knapsack ran again through Jasper's brain. The blade flashed up, then down.

The fat one groaned once, briefly, and blood was spilled on the ancient sacrificial altar.

Outside, lightning flashed from a clear sky, and thunder rumbled ominously over the hills. The darkness inside the temple seemed to deepen, and a low, howling noise filled the room. Probably the wind whistling through the ancient steeple, thought Jasper, as he fumbled for the jewels in Willie's knapsack. But it was strange how the wind seemed to be whispering a word, lowly and beckoningly. 'Saagael,' it seemed to call softly. 'Saaaaagael . . .'

The noise grew, from a whisper to a shout to a roar, until it filled the ancient temple. Jasper looked around in annoyance. He could not understand what was going on. Above the altar, a large crack appeared, and beyond it mist swirled and things moved. Darkness flowed from the crack, darkness blacker and denser and colder than anything Jasper had ever witnessed. Swirling, shifting, it gathered itself into a pocket of absolute black in one corner of the room. It seemed to grow, to change shape, to harden, and to coalesce.

And quickly it was gone. In its place stood something vaguely humanoid; a large, powerful frame clad in garments of a soft, dark gray. It wore a belt and a cape, leathery things made from the hide of some unholy creature never before seen on earth. A hood of the cape covered its head, and underneath it only blackness stared out, marked by two pits of final night darker and deeper than the rest. A great batlike clasp of some dark, glowing rock fastened the cape in place.

Jasper's voice was a whisper. 'W-w-who are you?'

A low, hollow, haunting laughter filled the recesses of the temple and spread out through the night. 'I? I am War, and Plague, and Blood. I am Death, and Darkness, and Fear.' The laughter again. 'I am Saagael, Prince of Demons, Lord of Darkness, King of Corlos, unquestioned Sovereign of the Netherworld. I am Saagael, he whom your ancestors called the Soul-Destroyer. And you have called me.'

Jasper's eyes were wide with fear, and the rubies, forgotten, lay in the dust. The apparition had raised a hand, and blackness and night gathered around it. Evil power coursed through the air. Then, for Jasper, there was only darkness, final and eternal.

*

Halfway around the world a spectral figure in gold and green stiffened suddenly in mid-flight, its body growing tense and alert. Across the death-white features spread a look of intense concern, as the fathomless phantom-mind once again became in tune with the very essence of its being. Doctor Weird recognized the strange sensations; they were telling him of the presence of a supernatural evil somewhere on the earth. All he had to do was to follow the eerie emanations drawing him like a magnet to the source of the abominable activities.

With the speed of thought the spectral figure flashed away toward the east, led swiftly and unwaveringly to the source of evil; mountains, valleys, rivers, woodlands zipped under him with eye-blurring speed. Great seacoast cities appeared on the horizon, their skyscrapers leaning on the heavens. Then they, too, vanished behind him, and angry, rolling waves moved below. In a wink a continent had been spanned; in another an ocean was crossed. Earthly limits of speed and matter are of no consequence to a spirit; and suddenly it was night.

Thick, clutching jungles appeared below the Golden Ghost, their foliage all the more sinister by night. There was a patch of desert, a great roaring river, more desert. Then the jungle again. Human settlements popped up and vanished in the blink of an eye. The night parted in front of the streaking figure.

Doctor Weird stopped. Huge and ominous, the ancient temple appeared suddenly in front of him, its great walls hiding grim and evil secrets. He approached cautiously. There was an aura of intense evil here, and the darkness clung to the temple thicker and denser than to the jungle around it.

Slowly and warily the Astral Avenger approached a huge black wall. His substance seemed to waver and fade as he passed effortlessly through it into the blackened inside.

Doctor Weird shuddered as he beheld the interior of that dread sanctum; it was horribly familiar to him now. The dark, hideous murals, the row on row of felted, ebony benches, and the huge statue that stared down from above the altar marked this unclean place as a temple of a long-forgotten sect; those who had worshipped one of the black deities that lurk Beyond. The earth had been cleaner when the last such had died out.

And yet – Doctor Weird paused and pondered. Everywhere, everything looked new and unused and – a sense of horror gripped him – there was fresh blood on the sacrificial altar! Could it be that the cult had been revived? That the dwellers in the shadows were worshipped again?

There was a slight noise from a recess near the altar. Instantly, Doctor Weird whirled and searched for its source. Something barely moved in the darkness; and in a flash the Golden Ghost was upon it.

It was a man – or what remained of one. Tall, lean and muscular, it lay unmoving on the floor and stared from unseeing eyes. A heart beat, and lungs inhaled, but there was no other motion. No will stirred this creature; no instincts prompted it. It lay still and silent, eyes focused vacantly on the ceiling; a discarded, empty shell.

It was a thing without a mind – or a soul.

Anger and horror raged through the breast of the Astral Avenger as he whirled, searching the shadows for the thing of evil whose presence now overwhelmed him. Never had he encountered such an engulfing aura of raw, stark wickedness.

'All right!' he shouted. 'I know you are here somewhere. I sense your evil presence. Show yourself . . . if you dare!'

A hollow, haunting laughter issued from the great dark walls and echoed through the hall. 'And who might *you* be?'

But Doctor Weird did not move. His spectral eyes swept the length and breadth of the temple, searching for the source of the eerie laughter.

And again it came, deep, booming, and full of malevolence. 'But what does it matter? Rash mortal, you presume to challenge forces you cannot begin to comprehend! Yet, I shall fulfill your request – I shall reveal myself!' The laughter grew louder. 'You shall soon rue your foolhardy words!'

From above, where polished ebony steps wound upward into the highest reaches of the black temple's tower and steeple, a viscous, fluid, living darkness seemed to ooze down the winding staircase. Like a great cloud of absolute black from the nightmare of a madman it descended until, halfway down, it solidified and took shape. The thing that stood on the stairs was vaguely manlike, but the resemblance only made it even more horrible. Its laughter filled the temple again. 'Doth my visage please you, mortal? Why do you not answer? Can it be you know – fear?'

The answer rang back instantly, loud, clear, and defiant. 'Never, dark one! You call me mortal and expect me to tremble at the sight of you. But you are wrong, for I am as eternal as you. I, who have battled werewolves, vampires, and sorcerers in the past have no qualms about subduing a demon of your ilk!' With this, Doctor Weird shot forward toward the grotesque apparition on the stairs.

Underneath the dark hood, the two great pits of blackness blazed scarlet for an instant, and the laughter began again, wilder than ever. 'So then, spirit, you would fight a demon? Very well! You shall have a demon! We will see who survives!' The dark shape gestured impatiently with its hand.

Doctor Weird had gotten halfway to the staircase when the crack above the altar suddenly opened in front of him and something huge and evil blocked his path. It stood well over twice his height, its mouth a mass of gleaming fangs, the eyes two baleful pinpoints of red. There was a musty odor of death in the air surrounding the monstrous entity.

Barely pausing long enough to size up the situation, the Golden Ghost lashed out at the hideous newcomer, fist burying itself in the cold, clammy flesh. In spite of himself, Doctor Weird shuddered. The flesh of the monster was like soft, yet super-strong dough; foul and filthy, so repulsive as to make the skin crawl.

The being shrugged off the blow. Demoniac talons raked painfully and with stunning force across the shoulder of the Mystic Marauder, leaving a trail of agony in their wake. With sudden alarm, Doctor Weird realized that this was no creature of the ordinary realm, against which he was invulnerable; this horror was of the netherworld, and was as fully capable of inflicting pain upon him as he was on it.

A great arm flashed out, catching him across the chest and sending him staggering backwards. Gibbering and drooling horribly, the demon leaped after him, its great clawed hands reaching. Doctor Weird was caught squarely, thrown off balance, and slammed backward onto the cold stone floor. The thing landed on top of him. Gleaming yellow fangs flashed for his throat.

In desperation, Doctor Weird swung his left arm around and up into the face of the demon as it descended upon him. Spectral muscles strained, and his right fist connected with brutal force, smashing into the horrid visage like a pile driver. The thing gave a sickening squeal of pain, rolled to the side, and scrambled to its feet. In an instant the Golden Ghost had regained his footing.

Eyes blazing hungrily at him, the demon rushed the Super Spirit once again, arms spread wide to grab him. Neatly sidestepping the charge and ducking under the outstretched arms, Doctor Weird took to the air as the creature's speed carried it past him. The demon stopped and whirled quickly, and the airborne wraith smashed into him feet first. The thing roared in anger as it toppled and lay flat. With all of the force he could muster, Doctor Weird brought the heel of his boot down squarely onto the demon's neck.

Like a watermelon hit by a battering ram the monster's head bulged, then smashed under the impact. Thick dark blood formed a great pool on the stone floor, and the hulk-like demon did not stir. Doctor Weird staggered to one side in exhaustion.

Devilish laughter rang about him, snapping him instantly to attention. 'Very good, spirit! You have entertained me! You *have* overcome a demon!' Scarlet flashed again under the hood of the thing on the stairway. 'But I, you see, am no ordinary demon. I am Saagael, the Demon Prince, the Lord of Darkness! That subject of mine you disposed of with such difficulty is as nothing against *my* power!'

Saagael raised a hand and gestured at the fallen demon. 'You have shown me your might, so I will tell you of mine. That shell you found was my work, for I am he they called the Soul-Destroyer, and it is long since I have exercised my power. That mortal shall know no afterlife, no bliss nor damnation, no Immortality. He is gone, as if he had never been, completely nonexistent. I have eradicated his soul, and that is a fate far worse than death.'

The Golden Ghost stared up at him unbelievingly, and a cold chill went through him. 'You mean . . .'

The voice of the Demon Prince was raised in triumph. 'Yes! I perceive you know what I mean. So think, and *now* tremble! You are but a spirit, a discorporate entity. I cannot affect the physical shell of one of mortal birth, but you, a spirit, I could destroy utterly. But it will amuse me to have you to stand by helpless and fearful while I enslave your world, so I shall spare you for now. Stand, and behold the fate of the planet where I reigned once, before history began, and now shall reign again!'

The Lord of Darkness gestured expansively, and all light in the temple vanished. A thick darkness prevailed everywhere, and a vision slowly took shape before the awestruck eyes of Doctor Weird.

He saw men turn against other men in anger and hatred. He witnessed wars and holocaust and blood. Death, grinning and horrible, was everywhere. The world was bathed in chaos and destruction. And then, in the aftermath, he beheld flood and fire and plague, and famine upon the land. Fear and superstition reached new heights. There was a vision of churches being torn down, and of crosses burning against the night sky. Awesome statues were raised in their stead, bearing the hideous likeness of the Demon Prince. Everywhere men bowed before the great dark altars, and gave their daughters to the priests of Saagael. And, lo, the creatures of the night burst forth again in new strength, walking the earth and lusting for blood. Locked doors were no protection. The servants of Saagael ruled supreme on earth, and their dark lord hunted for men's souls. The gates of Corlos were opened, and a great shadow descended over the land. Not in a thousand generations would it be lifted.

As suddenly as it had come the vision was gone, and there was only the thick blackness and the hideous ringing laughter, more cruel now, coming from everywhere and nowhere, echoing and re-echoing in the confines of the huge temple. 'Go now, spirit, before I tire of you. I have preparations to make abroad, and I do not wish to find you in my temple when I return. Hark you this – it is morning now, yet all is still dark outside. From this day forth, night shall be eternal on earth!'

The darkness cleared and Doctor Weird could see again. He stood alone in the empty temple. Saagael was gone, as was the remains of the vanquished demon. Only he and the thing that had once been a man called Jasper remained amongst the silence, and the darkness, and the dust.

*

They came from all over, from the hot nearby jungles, from the burning desert beyond, from the great cities of Europe, from the frigid north of Asia. They were the hard ones, the brutal ones, the cruel ones, those who had long waited the coming of one like the Demon Prince and welcomed him now. They were students of the occult; they had studied those black arts and ancient scrolls that sane men do not believe in, and they knew the dark secrets others spoke of in whispers. Saagael was no mystery to them, for their lore went back to the dim forgotten eras before history had begun when the Lord of Darkness had held dominion over the earth.

And now, from all the corners of the globe, they flocked to his temple and bowed before his statue. Even a dark god needs priests and they were eager to strain in his service in return for forbidden knowledge. When the long night had come over the earth, and the Demon Prince had roamed abroad and feasted, they knew their hour had arrived. So the unclean ones, the dark ones, the evil ones, jammed the great temple even as in the days of yore and formed again the dreaded Sect of Saagael. There they sang their songs of worship, and read their black tomes, and waited for the coming of their lord, for Saagael was still abroad. It was long since he had hunted men's souls, and his hunger was insatiable.

But his servants grew impatient, and so they made for to summon him back. Torches lit the black hall, and hundreds sat moaning a hymn of praise. They read aloud from the unholy texts, as they had not dared to do for many a year, and they sang his name. 'Saagael,' the call went up and echoed in the depths of the temple. 'Saagael,' it beckoned, louder and louder, until the hall rang with it. 'Saagael,' it demanded, a roar now, shrieking out into the night and filling the land and the air with the awful call.

A young girl was strapped to the sacrificial altar, straining and tugging at her bonds, a look of horror in her wide staring eyes. Now the chief of priests, a huge monster of a man with a brutal red slash for a mouth and two dark, piglike eyes, approached her. A long, gleaming, silver knife was in his hand, flashing with reflected torchlight.

He halted and raised his eyes to the huge, towering image of the Demon Prince that loomed above the altar. 'Saagael,' he intoned, his voice a deep, eerie whisper that chilled the blood. 'Prince of Demons, Lord of Darkness, Monarch of the Netherworld, we summon thee. Soul-Destroyer, we, your followers, call. Hear us and appear. Accept our offer of the soul and spirit of this maiden!'

He lowered his eyes. The blade lifted slowly, began to descend. A hush came over the assemblage. The blade flashed silver. The girl screamed.

Then, something caught the sleeve of the priest's robe, bent his arm back with a wrench, and snapped it. A spectral figure glowed in front of the altar, and the night paled in the illumination of the green and gold interloper. Pale white fingers grasped the knife as it fell from the hand of the priest. Wordlessly, they lifted the slim blade and drove it down into the heart of the huge man. Blood flowed, a gasp shocked the silence, and the body fell to the floor.

As the intruder turned and calmly slit the bonds of the now fainted girl, everywhere cries of rage and fear went up among the people, followed by cries of 'sacrilege,' and 'Saagael, protect us!'

Then, as if a heavy cloud had drifted overhead, a great darkness came over the hall and, one by one, the torches winked out. Utter blackness flowed through the air, shimmered, and took shape. A cry of relief and triumph went up from the mortals present.

Scarlet fires flamed under the blackness inside the hood. 'You have gone too far, spirit,' boomed the voice of the Demon Prince. 'You attack the mortals who wisely choose to serve me, and for that you shall pay with your very soul!' The dark aura that surrounded the Lord of Corlos grew in strength, and pushed back the light that emanated from the muscular figure in green and gold.

'Shall I?' Doctor Weird replied. 'I think not. You have witnessed but a small part of my power – I have more I have never shown you! You were born of darkness and death and blood, Saagael. You stand for all that is evil and foul-made-flesh. But I was created by the Will of Powers that dwarf you, that could destroy you with but a mere thought. I stand in defiance of you, those like you, and the vermin that serve you!'

The light that surrounded the Golden Ghost blazed once more and filled the hall like a small sun, driving the inky blackness of the Demon Prince before it. It was as if, suddenly, the Lord of Corlos had felt his first twinge of doubt. But he rallied himself and, without deigning the use of further talk, raised a gloved hand. To it flowed the powers of darkness and death and fear. Then a massive bolt of black, pulsating power streaked through the air, evil and unclean. Straight it flew, and fast.

The Golden Ghost stood his ground, hands on hips. The bolt struck him squarely, and light and darkness flashed for a moment. Then the light went out, and the figure fell quickly and soundlessly.

A horrible, mocking laughter filled the room, and Saagael turned to his worshippers. 'Thus perish those who would defy the dark power, those who would oppose the will of . . .' He stopped. There was a look of total, awesome fear on the faces of his disciples, as they stared at something behind him. The Demon Prince whirled.

The golden figure was rising to his feet. The light blazed forth once more, and momentary fear smote the Lord of Corlos. But again he overcame his doubt, and again an awesome bolt of black power shot through the air, smashing into the advancing Doctor Weird. Again the Astral Avenger keeled over. An instant later, as Saagael watched in mounting horror, the figure rose once more. Silently, wordlessly, it strode toward him.

Panicking, Saagael smashed down the figure a third time. A third time it rose. A gurgle of horror went up from the crowd. The Golden Ghost advanced again towards the Demon Prince. Raising a glowing arm, at last he spoke. 'Too bad, Saagael. I have withstood the best you could throw at me, and I still live. But now, Dark One, you shall feel *my* power!'

'N-NOOOOoooo,' a hideous shriek went through the hall. The figure of the Lord of Darkness shuddered, paled, and melted away into a great black cloud. The crack opened again above the ebony altar. Beyond it mists swirled, and things moved in an eternal night. The black cloud expanded, flowed to the crack, and was gone. An instant later the crack vanished.

Doctor Weird turned to the mortals who filled the room, the shocked and broken servants of Saagael. A howl of fear went up and they fled screaming from the temple. Then the figure turned to the altar, shuddered, and fell. Something fluttered in the air above it, streaked across the room, and vanished into the shadows.

An instant later, a second Astral Avenger strode from the dark recesses, walked to the altar and bent over the first. A spectral hand wiped a layer of white makeup from the fallen figure's face. An eerie voice broke the silence. 'He called you a shell – an empty thing – and he was right. By reverting to my ectoplasmic form and hiding my physical self in the shadows, I was able to wear you like a suit of clothing. He could not affect your corporeal body, so I left you just before his bolts struck, and got back in afterward. And it worked. Even he could be fooled, and frightened.'

Outside the sun was coming up in the east. In the interior of the grim sanctum ebony benches and carved stairways rotted, decayed swiftly, and gave way to piles of dust. One thing, now, remained.

Doctor Weird rose and approached the black altar. Mighty hands gripped the great legs of the statue of Saagael, and rippling muscles strained. The statue toppled, and shattered. It fell, broken and smashed, near the empty hulk of the thing called Jasper, clad in a green and gold costume.

Doctor Weird surveyed the scene with an ironic smile flicking over his dead-white features, 'Even after he had destroyed your mind and soul, it was a man who brought about the downfall of the Lord of Darkness.'

He lifted his eyes to the girl on the altar, now beginning to stir from the terror that had taken her consciousness. He approached her and said, 'Do not be afraid of me. I will take you home now.'

It was day outside. The shadow had lifted. The eternal night was over.

Next issue: Dr Weird Meets the Demon

The Fortress

Have you beheld her gray form rise
Superb o'er bay and sea
With menace in her granite eyes:
Come try your strength on me?
My very look, so grim and dread,
Can strike the impious foeman dead.

Whatever course the war may take
In forest or on plain,
Rouse not the ocean's queen to break
The calm of her disdain.
A thousand cannon, tongued with fire,
Will whelm you with their savage ire!

— *The Tales of Ensign Stål,*
Johan Ludvig Runeberg

A lone and silent in the night, Sveaborg waited. Dark shapes in a sea of ice, the six island citadels of the fortress threw shadows in the moonlight – waiting. Jagged granite walls rose from the islands, and bristled with row on row of silent cannon – waiting. And behind the walls, grim and determined men sat by the guns day and night – waiting.

From the northwest, a bitter wind brought the sounds and smells of the city in the distance to Sveaborg as it shrieked about the fortress walls. And high on the parapets of Vargön, largest of the six islands, Colonel Bengt Anttonen shivered with the cold as he stared morosely into the distance. His uniform hanging loosely from his hard, lean frame, Anttonen's gray eyes were cloudy and troubled.

'Colonel?' The voice came from just behind the brooding officer. Anttonen half turned, and grinned. Captain Carl Bannersson saluted briskly and stepped up to the battlements beside the colonel. 'I hope I'm not disturbing you,' he asked.

Anttonen snorted. 'Not at all, Carl. Just thinking.'

There was a moment of silence. 'The Russian barrage was fairly heavy today,' began Bannersson. 'Several men were wounded out on the ice, and we had to put out two fires.'

Anttonen's eyes roamed over the ice beyond the walls. He seemed almost unmindful of the tall, youthful Swedish captain, and lost in thought. 'The men should never have been out on the ice,' he said, absently.

Bannersson's blue eyes probed the colonel's face questioningly. He hesitated. 'Why do you say that?' he asked. There was no answer from the older officer. Anttonen stared into the night, and was silent.

After a long minute, Anttonen stirred, and turned to face the captain. His face was tense and worried. 'There's something wrong, Carl. Something very wrong.'

Bannersson looked puzzled. 'What are you talking about?'

'Admiral Cronstedt,' replied the colonel. 'I don't like the way he's been acting lately. He worries me.'

'In what way?'

Anttonen shook his head. 'His orders. The way he talks.' The tall, lean Finn gestured towards the city in the distance. 'Remember when the Russian siege began in early March? Their first battery was dragged to Sveaborg on a sledge and mounted on a rock in Helsinki harbor. When we replied to their shelling, every shot told on the city.'

'True. What of it?'

'So the Russians ran up a truce flag, and negotiated, and Admiral Cronstedt agreed that Helsinki should be neutral ground, and neither side should build fortifications near it.' Anttonen pulled a piece of paper from his pocket, and waved it at Bannersson. 'General Suchtelen allows officers' wives from the city to visit us at times, and through them I got this report. It seems the Russians have moved their guns all right, but have established barracks, hospitals, and magazines in Helsinki. And we can't touch them!'

Bannersson frowned. 'I see what you mean. Does the admiral know of this report?'

'Of course,' said Anttonen impatiently. 'But he will not act. Jägerhorn and the others have persuaded him that the report is unreliable. So the Russians hide in the city, in perfect safety.' He crumpled the report savagely, and jammed it into his pocket in disgust.

Bannersson did not reply, and the colonel turned to stare out over the walls again, mumbling under his breath.

There were several moments of strained silence. Captain Bannersson shifted his weight uneasily, and coughed. 'Sir?' he said at last. 'You don't think we're in any real danger, do you?'

Anttonen looked at him blankly. 'Danger?' he said, 'No, not really. The fortress is too strong, and the Russians too weak. They need much more artillery and many more men before they would dare an assault. And we have enough food to outlast their siege. Once the ice melts Sweden can easily reinforce by sea.'

He paused a moment, then continued. 'Still, I'm worried. Admiral Cronstedt finds new vulnerable spots every day, and every day more men die trying to break up the ice in front of them. Cronstedt's family is trapped here with all the other refugees, and he worries about them to excess. He sees weakness everywhere. The men are loyal and ready to die in defense of Sveaborg, but the officers—'

Anttonen sighed and shook his head. After a moment of silence he straightened and turned from the ramparts. 'It's damn cold out here,' he said. 'We had better be getting inside.'

Bannersson smiled. 'True. Perhaps Suchtelen will attack tomorrow, and solve all of our problems.'

The colonel laughed, and clapped him on the back. Together they left the battlements.

And at midnight, March became April. And still Sveaborg waited.

*

'If the Admiral pleases, I would like to disagree. I see no reason to negotiate at this time. Sveaborg is secure against assault, and our supplies are adequate. General Suchtelen can offer us nothing.'

Colonel Anttonen's face was stiff and formal as he spoke, but his knuckles were white where his hand curled around his sword hilt.

'Absurd!' Colonel F.A. Jägerhorn twisted his aristocratic features into a sneer of contempt. 'Our situation is highly dangerous. As the Admiral well knows, our defenses are flawed, and are made even more imperfect by the ice that makes them accessible from all sides. Our powder is running low. The Russians ring us with guns, and their numbers swell daily.'

Behind the commandant's desk, Vice-Admiral Carl Olof Cronstedt nodded gravely. 'Colonel Jägerhorn is right, Bengt. We have many reasons to meet with General Suchtelen. Sveaborg is far from secure.'

'But, Admiral.' Anttonen waved the sheaf of papers clutched in his hands. 'My reports indicate no such thing. The Russians have only about forty guns, and we still outnumber them. They cannot attack.'

Jägerhorn laughed. 'If your reports say that, Colonel Anttonen, they are in error. Lieutenant Klick is in Helsinki, and he informs me that the enemy greatly outnumber us. And they have well over forty guns!'

Anttonen whirled towards his fellow officer furiously. 'Klick! You listen to Klick! Klick is a fool and a damned Anjala traitor; if he is in Helsinki it is because he is working for the Russians'!

The two officers eyed each other angrily, Jägerhorn cold and haughty, Anttonen flushed and impassioned.'I had relatives in the Anjala League,' began the young aristocrat.'They were not traitors, nor is Klick. They are loyal Finns.'

Anttonen snarled something unintelligible, and turned back to Cronstedt. 'Admiral, I swear to you, my reports are accurate. We have nothing to fear if we can hold out until the ice melts, and we can easily do that. Once the sea is open, Sweden will send help.'

Cronstedt rose slowly from his chair, his face drawn and tired, 'No, Bengt. We cannot refuse to negotiate.' He shook his head, and smiled. 'You are too eager for a fight. We cannot be rash.'

'Sir,' said Anttonen. 'If you must, then, negotiate. But give up nothing. Sweden and Finland depend on us. In the spring, General Klingspor and the Swedish fleet will launch their counteroffensive to drive the Russians from Finland; but control of Sveaborg is vital to the plan. The army's morale would be smashed if we should fall. A few months, sir – hold out a few months and Sweden can win the war.'

Cronstedt's face was a mask of despair. 'Colonel, you have not been reading the news. Everywhere Sweden is being routed; her armies are defeated on all fronts. We cannot hope to triumph.'

'But, sir. That news is from the papers that General Suchtelen sends you; they are largely Russian papers. Don't you see, sir, that news is slanted. We cannot rely on it.' Anttonen's eyes were wide with horror; he spoke like a desperate man.

Jäagerhorn laughed, coldly and cynically. 'What matters it if the news is true or false? Do you really think Sweden will win, Anttonen? A small, poor state in the far north hold off Russia? Russia, which extends from the Baltic to the Pacific, from the Black Sea to the Arctic Ocean? Russia, the ally of Napoleon, who has trod upon the crowned heads of Europe?' He laughed again. 'We are beaten, Bengt, beaten. It only remains to see what terms we can get.'

Anttonen stared at Jägerhorn in silence for a moment, and when he spoke his voice was harsh and strained. 'Jägerhorn, you are a defeatist, a coward, and a traitor. You are a disgrace to the uniform you wear.'

The aristocrat's eyes blazed, and his hand sped to his sword hilt. He stepped forward aggressively.

'Gentlemen, gentlemen.' Cronstedt was suddenly between the two officers, holding Jägerhorn at bay. 'We are besieged by the enemy, our country is in flames, and our armies are being routed. This is no time to fight among ourselves.' His face grew stern and hard. 'Colonel Jägerhorn, return to your quarters at once.'

'Yes, sir.' Jägerhorn saluted, whirled, and left the room. Admiral Cronstedt turned back to Anttonen.

He shook his head sadly. 'Bengt, Bengt. Why can't you understand? Jägerhorn is right, Bengt; the other officers agree with him to a man. If we negotiate now we can save the fleet, and much Finnish blood.'

Colonel Anttonen stood stiffly at attention. His eyes were cold, and looked past his admiral as if he were not there. 'Admiral,' he said sternly. 'What if you had felt this way before Ruotsinsalmi? What would have become of your victory then, sir? Defeatism wins no battles.'

Cronstedt's face became harsh, and there was anger in his voice. 'That is enough, Colonel. I will not tolerate insubordination. I am compelled by circumstance to negotiate for the surrender of Sveaborg. The meeting between Suchtelen and myself has been arranged for April sixth; I will be there. And in the future, you will not question this decision. That is an order!'

Anttonen was silent.

Admiral Cronstedt stared at the colonel for a brief moment, his eyes still mirroring anger. Then he turned with a snort, and gestured impatiently towards the door. 'You are dismissed, Colonel. Return to quarters at once.'

*

Captain Bannersson's face masked his shock and disbelief. 'It can't be true, sir. Surrendering? But why would the admiral do such a thing? The men, at least, are ready and willing to fight.'

Anttonen laughed, but it was a hollow, bitter laugh, totally without humor. His eyes held a wild despair, and his hands flexed the blade of his rapier nervously. He was leaning against an elaborately carved tomb, in the shadow of two trees within one of the central courtyards of the Vargön citadel. Bannersson stood a few feet away in the darkness, on the steps that led up to the memorial.

'All the men are willing to fight,' said Anttonen. 'Only the officers are not.' He laughed again. 'Admiral Cronstedt – the hero of our victory at Ruotsinsalmi – reduced to a doubting, fear-wracked old man. General Suchtelen has played upon him well; the newspapers from France and Russia he sent him, the rumors from Helsinki carried here by the officers' wives, all served to plant the seed of defeatism. And then Colonel Jägerhorn helped it to grow.'

Bannersson was still stunned, and puzzled. 'But – but what does the Admiral fear?'

'Everything. He sees weak points in our defenses no one else can see. He fears for his family. He fears for the fleet he once led to victory. He claims Sveaborg is helpless in the winter. He is weak and apprehensive, and every time he doubts, Jägerhorn and his cronies are there to tell him he is right.'

Anttonen's face was distorted with rage. He was nearly shouting now. 'The cowards! The traitors! Admiral Cronstedt wavers and trembles, but if *they* would only be resolute, *he* would find his courage and his mind also.'

'Sir, please, not so loudly,' cautioned Bannersson. 'If what you said is true, what can we do about it?'

Anttonen's eyes lifted, and focused on the Swedish captain below. He considered him coldly. 'The parley is set for tomorrow. Cronstedt may not yield, but if he does, we must be prepared. Get all the loyal men you can, and tell them to be ready. Call it mutiny if you will, but Sveaborg will not capitulate without a fight so long as there is a single man of honor to fire her guns.' The Finnish officer straightened and sheathed his sword. 'Meanwhile, I will speak with Colonel Jägerhorn. Perhaps I can stop this madness yet.'

Bannersson, his face dead white, nodded slowly and turned to leave. Anttonen strode down the steps, then halted. 'Carl?' he called. The departing Swedish officer turned. 'You understand that my life, and perhaps the future of Finland, are in your hands, don't you?'

'Yes, sir,' replied Bannersson, 'You can trust us.' He turned again, and a few seconds later was gone.

Anttonen stood alone in the dark, staring absently at his hand. It was bleeding from where it had gripped the sword blade. Laughing, the officer looked up at the tomb. 'You designed your fortress well, Ehrensvard,' he said, his voice a soft whisper in the night. 'Let's hope the men who guard her are equal to her strength.'

*

Jägerhorn scowled when he saw who was at the door. 'You, Anttonen? After this afternoon? You have courage. What do you want?'

Anttonen stepped inside the room, and closed the door. 'I want to talk to you. I want to change your mind. Cronstedt listens to you; if you advise against it, he will not capitulate. Sveaborg will not fall.'

Jägerhorn grinned and sank back into a chair. 'Perhaps. I am a relative. The admiral respects my opinion. But it is only a matter of time. Sweden cannot win this war, and the more we prolong it, the more Finns will die in battle.'

The aristocrat stared at his fellow officer calmly. 'Sweden is lost,' he continued, 'but Finland need not be. We have assurances from Czar Alexander that Finland will be an autonomous state under his protection. We will have more freedom than we ever had under Sweden.'

'We are Swedes,' said Anttonen. 'We have a duty to defend our king and our homeland.' His voice was brittle with disdain.

A thin smile played across Jägerhorn's lips. 'Swedes? Bah! We are Finns. What did Sweden ever do for us? She taxed us. She took our boys and left them dying in the mud of Poland, and Germany, and Denmark. She made our countryside a battleground for her wars. For this we owe Sweden loyalty?'

'Sweden will aid us when the ice melts,' answered Anttonen. 'We need only hold out till spring, and wait for her fleet.'

Jägerhorn was on his feet, and his words rang with bitterness and scorn. 'I would not count on Swedish aid, Colonel. A look at their history would teach you better than that. Where was Carl XII during the Great Wrath? All over Europe he rode, but could not spare an army for suffering Finland. Where is Marshal Klingspor now, while the Russians lay waste to our land and burn our towns? Did he even fight for Finland? No! He retreated – to save Sweden from attack.'

'So for the Swedes who do not aid us fast enough, you would trade the Russians? The butchers of the Great Wrath? The people who pillage our nation even now? That seems a sorry trade.'

'No. The Russians treat us now as enemies; when we are on their side things will be different. No longer will we have to fight a war every twenty years to please a Swedish king. No longer will the ambitions of a Carl XII or a Gustav III cost thousands of Finnish lives. Once the Czar rules in Finland, we will have peace and freedom.'

Jägerhorn's voice was hot with excitement and conviction, but Anttonen remained cold and formal. He looked at Jägerhorn sadly, almost wistfully, and sighed. 'It was better when I thought you were a traitor. You're not. An idealist, a dreamer, yes. But not a traitor.'

'Me? A dreamer?' Jägerhorn's eyebrows arched in surprise. 'No, Bengt. You're the dreamer. You're the man who deludes himself with hopes of a Swedish victory. I look at the world the way it is, and deal with it on its own terms.'

Anttonen shook his head. 'We've fought Russia over and over through the years; we've been foes for centuries. And you think we can live together peacefully. It won't work, Colonel. Finland knows Russia too well. And she does not forget. This will not be our last war with Russia. Not by any means.'

He turned away slowly, and opened the door to leave. Then, almost as an afterthought, he paused and looked back. 'You're just a misguided dreamer, and Cronstedt's only a weak old man.' He laughed softly. 'There's no one left to hate, Jägerhorn. There's no one left to hate.'

The door closed softly, and Colonel Bengt Anttonen was alone in the darkened, silent hallway. Leaning against the cold stone wall in exhaustion, he sobbed, and covered his face with his hands.

His voice was a hoarse, choking whisper, his body gray and shaken. 'My God, my God. A fool's dreams and an old man's doubts. And between them they'll topple the Gibraltar of the North.'

He laughed a broken, sobbing laugh, straightened, and walked out into the night.

*

'—shall be allowed to dispatch two couriers to the King, the one by the northern, the other by the southern road. They shall be furnished with passports and safeguards, and every possible facility shall be given them for accomplishing their journey. Done at the island of Lonan, 6 April, 1808.'

The droning voice of the officer reading the agreement stopped suddenly, and the large meeting room was deathly quiet. There were mumblings from the back of the room, and a few of the Swedish officers stirred uneasily in their seats, but no one spoke.

From the commandant's desk in front of the gathering of Sveaborg's senior officers, Admiral Cronstedt rose slowly. His face was old beyond its years, his eyes weary and bloodshot. And those in the front could see his gnarled hands trembling slightly.

'That is the agreement,' he began. 'Considering the position of Sveaborg, it is better than we could have hoped for. We have used a third of our powder already; our defenses are exposed to attack from all sides because of the ice; we are outnumbered and forced to support a large number of fugitives who rapidly consume our provisions. Considering all this, General Suchtelen was in a position to demand our immediate surrender.'

He paused and ran tired fingers through his hair. His eyes searched the faces of the Finnish and Swedish officers who sat before him.

'He did not demand that surrender,' continued Cronstedt. 'Instead, we have been allowed to retain three of Sveaborg's six islands, and will regain two of the others if five Swedish ships-of-the-line arrive to aid us before the third of May. If not, we must surrender. But in either case the fleet shall be restored to Sweden after the war, and the truce between now and then will prevent the loss of any more lives.'

Admiral Cronstedt halted, and looked to the side. Instantly Colonel Jägerhorn, sitting beside him, was on his feet. 'I assisted the Admiral in negotiating this agreement. It is a good one, a very good one. General Suchtelen has given us very generous terms. However, in case the Swedish aid does not arrive in time, we must make provisions for surrendering the garrison. That is the purpose of this meeting. We—'

'NO!' The shout rang through the large room and echoed from its walls, cutting off Jägerhorn abruptly. At once there was a shocked silence. All eyes turned towards the rear of the room, where Colonel Bengt Anttonen stood among his fellow officers, white-faced and smoldering with anger.

'Generous terms? Hah! What generous terms?' His voice was sharp with derision. 'Immediate surrender of Wester-Svartö, Oster-Lilla-Svartö, and Langorn; the rest of Sveaborg to come later. *These* are generous terms? NO! Never! It is little more than surrender postponed for a month. And there is no need to surrender. We are NOT outnumbered. We are NOT weak. Sveaborg does not need provisions – it needs only a little courage, and a little faith.'

The atmosphere in the council room had suddenly grown very cold, as Admiral Cronstedt regarded the dissident with frigid distaste. When he spoke, there was a hint of his old authority in his voice. 'Colonel, I remind you of the orders I gave you the other day. I am tired of you questioning each of my actions. True, I have made small concessions, but I have given us a chance of retaining everything for Sweden. It is our *only* chance! Now SIT DOWN, Colonel!'

There was a murmur of agreement from the officers around the room. Anttonen regarded them with disgust, then turned his gaze back to the Admiral. 'Yes, sir,' he said. 'But, sir, this chance you have given us is no chance at all, no chance whatsoever. You see, sir, Sweden can't get ships here fast enough. The ice will not melt in time.'

Cronstedt ignored his words. 'I gave you an order, Colonel,' he said, with iron in his voice. 'Sit down!'

Anttonen stared at him coldly, his eyes burning, his hands clenching and unclenching spasmodically at his sides. There was a long moment of tense silence. Then he sat down.

Colonel Jägerhorn coughed, and rattled the sheaf of papers he was holding in his hands. 'To continue with the business at hand,' he said, 'we must first dispatch the messengers to Stockholm. Speed is essential here. The Russians will provide the necessary papers.'

His eyes combed the room. 'If the Admiral agrees,' he said, 'I would suggest Lieutenant Eriksson and – and—'

He paused a second, and a slow smile spread across his features.

'—and Captain Bannersson,' he concluded.

Cronstedt nodded.

*

The morning air was crisp and cold, and the sun was rising in the east. But no one watched. All eyes in Sveaborg were fixed on the dark and cloudy western horizon. For hours on end officer and soldier, Swede and Finn, sailor and artilleryman all searched the empty sea, and hoped. They looked to Sweden, and prayed for the sails they knew would never come.

And among those who prayed was Colonel Bengt Anttonen. High atop the battlements of Vargön, he scanned the seas with a small telescope, like so many others in Sveaborg. And like the others, he found nothing.

Folding his telescope, Anttonen turned from the ramparts with a frown to address the young ensign who stood by his side. 'Useless,' he said. 'I'm wasting valuable time.'

The ensign looked scared and nervous. 'There's always the chance, sir. Suchtelen's deadline is not until noon. A few hours, but we can hope, can't we?'

Anttonen was grim, sober. 'I wish we could, but we're just deluding ourselves. The armistice agreement provides that the ships must not merely be in sight by noon, but must have entered Sveaborg's harbor.'

The ensign looked puzzled. 'What of it?' he asked.

Anttonen pointed out over the walls, towards an island dimly visible in the distance. 'Look there,' he said. His arm moved to indicate a second island. 'And there. Russian fortifications. They've used the truce to gain command of the sea approaches. Any ship attempting to reach Sveaborg will come under heavy attack.'

The colonel sighed. 'Besides, the sea is dogged with ice. No ship will be able to reach us for weeks. The winter and the Russians have combined to kill our hopes.'

Glumly, ensign and colonel walked from the ramparts into the interior of the fortress together. The corridors were dim and depressing; silence reigned everywhere.

At last, Anttonen spoke, 'We've delayed long enough, Ensign. Vain hopes will no longer suffice; we must strike.' He looked into his companion's eyes as they walked. 'Gather the men. The time has come. I shall meet you near my quarters in two hours.'

The ensign hesitated. 'Sir,' he asked. 'Do you think we have a chance? We have so few men. We're a handful against a fortress.'

In the dim light, Anttonen's face was tired and troubled. 'I don't know,' he said. 'I just don't know. Captain Bannersson had contacts; if he had remained, our numbers would be greater. But I don't know the enlisted men like Carl did. I don't know who we can trust.'

The colonel halted, and clasped the ensign firmly on the shoulder. 'But, regardless, we've got to try. Finland's army has starved and been frozen and watched their homeland burn all winter. The only thing that has kept them going is the dream of winning it back. And without Sveaborg, that dream will die.' He shook his head sadly. 'We can't let that happen. With that dream dies Finland.'

The ensign nodded. 'Two hours, sir. You can count on us. We'll put some fight in Admiral Cronstedt yet.' He grinned, and hurried on his way.

Alone in the silent corridor, Colonel Bengt Anttonen drew his sword, and held it up to where the dim light played along its blade. He gazed at it sadly, and wondered in silence how many Finns he'd have to kill in order to save Finland.

But there was no answer.

*

The two guards fidgeted uneasily. 'I don't know, Colonel,' said one. 'Our orders are to admit no one to the armory without authorization.'

'I should think my rank would be sufficient authorization,' snapped back Anttonen. 'I am giving you a direct order to let us pass.'

The first guard looked at his companion doubtfully. 'Well,' he said. 'In that case perhaps we—'

'No, sir,' said the second guard. 'Colonel Jägerhorn ordered us not to admit anyone without authorization from Admiral Cronstedt. I'm afraid that includes you, too, sir.'

Anttonen regarded him coldly. 'Perhaps we should see Admiral Cronstedt about this,' he said. 'I think he might like to hear how you disobeyed a direct order.'

The first guard winced. Both of them were squirming with unease, and had focused all their attention on the angry Finnish colonel. Anttonen scowled at them. 'Come along,' he said. 'Now.'

The pistol shots that rang out from the nearby corridor at that word took the guards completely by surprise. There was a cry of pain as one clutched his bleeding arm, his gun clattering to the floor. The second whirled towards the sound, and simultaneously Anttonen leaped forward to seize his musket in an iron grip. Before the guard had quite grasped what was happening, the colonel had wrenched his gun from startled fingers. From the corridor on the right issued a group of armed men, most bearing muskets, a few holding still-smoking pistols.

'What shall we do with these two?' asked a gruff, burly corporal at the head of the group. He leveled his bayonet suggestively at the chest of the guard still standing. The other had fallen to his knees, holding his wounded arm tenderly.

Handing the guard's musket to one of the men standing beside him, Anttonen regarded his prisoners coldly. He reached forward and yanked a ring of keys from the belt of the chief guard. 'Tie them up,' he said. 'And watch them. We don't want any more bloodshed than can be helped.'

The corporal nodded and, gesturing with his bayonet, herded the guards away from the door. Stepping forward with the keys, Anttonen worked intently for a moment, then opened the heavy wooden door on the fortress armory.

Instantly there was a rush of men through the doorway. They had prepared for this moment for some time, and they worked quickly and efficiently. Heavy wooden boxes creaked in protest as they were forced open, and there was the rasp of metal on metal as the muskets were lifted from the boxes and passed around.

Standing just inside the door, Anttonen surveyed the scene nervously. 'Hurry up,' he ordered. 'And be sure to take plenty of powder and ammunition. We'll have to leave a good number of men to hold the armory against counterattacks, and—'

Suddenly the colonel whirled. From the hall outside came the sounds of musket fire, and the echo of running footsteps. Fingering his sword hilt apprehensively, Anttonen stepped back outside of the door.

And froze.

The guards he had posted outside of the armory were huddled against the far wall of the corridor, their weapons thrown in a heap at their feet. And facing him was a body of men twice as numerous as his insurgents, their guns trained on him and the armory door behind him. At their head, smiling confidently, was the lean, aristocratic form of Colonel F. A. Jägerhorn, a pistol cradled in his right hand.

'It's all over, Bengt,' he said. 'We figured you'd try something like this, and we've been watching every move you made since the armistice was signed. Your mutiny is finished.'

'I wouldn't be so sure of that,' said Anttonen, shaken but still resolute. 'By now a group of my men have taken Admiral Cronstedt's office, and with him as prisoner are fanning out to seize the main batteries.'

Jägerhorn threw back his head, and laughed. 'Don't be a fool. Our men captured the ensign and his squad before they even got near Admiral Cronstedt. You never had a chance.'

Anttonen's face went white. Horror and despair flickered across his eyes, and were replaced by a coldly burning anger. 'NO!' he cried from behind clenched teeth. 'NO!' His sword leaped from its sheath and flashed silver in the light as he sprang forward towards Jägerhorn.

He had taken but three steps when the first bullet caught him in the shoulder and sent his sword skittering from his grasp. The second and third ripped into his stomach and doubled him up. He took another halting step, and sank slowly to the floor.

Jägerhorn's eyes swept over him indifferently. 'You men in the armory,' he shouted, his voice ringing clearly through the hall. 'Put down your guns and come out slowly. You are outnumbered and surrounded. The revolt is over. Don't make us spill any more blood.'

There was no answer. From the side, where he was being held under guard, the veteran corporal shouted out. 'Do as he says, men. He's got too many men to fight.' He looked towards his commander. 'Sir, tell them to give up. We have no chance now. Tell them, sir.'

But the silence mocked his words, and the colonel lay quite still.

For Colonel Bengt Anttonen was dead.

A few short minutes after it had begun, the mutiny was over. And soon thereafter, the flag of Russia flew from the parapets of Vargön.

And as it flew above Sveaborg, soon it flew above Finland.

EPILOG

The old man propped himself up in the bed painfully, and stared with open curiosity at the visitor who stood in the doorway. The man was tall and powerfully built, with cold blue eyes and dirty blond hair. He wore the uniform of a major in the Swedish army, and carried himself with the confident air of a hardened warrior.

The visitor moved forward, and leaned against the foot of the old man's bed. 'So you don't recognize me?' he said. 'I can see why. I imagine that you've tried to forget Sveaborg and everything connected with it, Admiral Cronstedt.'

The old man coughed violently. 'Sveaborg?' he said weakly, trying to place the stranger who stood before him. 'Were you at Sveaborg?'

The visitor laughed. 'Yes, Admiral. For a good while at any rate. My name is Bannersson, Carl Bannersson. I was a captain then.'

Cronstedt blinked. 'Yes, yes. Bannersson. I remember you now. But you've changed since then.'

'True. You sent me back to Stockholm, and in the years that followed I fought with Carl Johan against Napoleon. I've seen a lot of battles and a lot of sieges since then, sir. But I never forgot Sveaborg. Never.'

The admiral doubled over suddenly with a fit of uncontrollable coughing. 'W-what do you want?' he managed to gasp out at last. 'I'm sorry if I'm rude, but I'm a sick man. Talking is a great strain.' He coughed, again. 'I hope you'll forgive me.'

Bannersson's eyes wandered around the small, dirty bedchamber. He straightened and reached into the breast pocket of his uniform, withdrawing a thick sealed envelope.

'Admiral,' he said, tapping the envelope gently against the palm of his hand for emphasis. 'Admiral, do you know what day this is?'

Cronstedt frowned. 'The sixth of April,' he replied.

'Yes. April 6, 1820. Exactly twelve years since that day you met with General Suchtelen on Lonan, and gave Sveaborg to the Russians.'

The old man shook his head slowly from side to side. 'Please, Major. You're awakening memories I had sealed up long ago. I don't want to talk about Sveaborg.'

Bannersson's eyes blazed, and the lines of his mouth grew hard and angry. 'No? Well, that's too bad. You'd rather talk about Ruotsinsalmi, I suppose. But we won't. We're going to talk about Sveaborg, old man, whether you like it or not.'

Cronstedt shuddered at the violence in his voice. 'Alright, Major. I had to surrender. Once surrounded by ice, Sveaborg is very weak. Our fleet was in danger. And our powder was low.'

The Swedish officer considered him scornfully. 'I have documents here,' he said, holding up the envelope, 'to show just how wrong you were. Facts, Admiral. Cold historical facts.'

He ripped the end of the envelope off violently, and tossed the papers inside it onto Cronstedt's bed. 'Twelve years ago you said we were outnumbered,' he began, his voice hard and emotionless as he recited the facts. 'We were not. The Russians barely had enough men to take over the fortress after it was surrendered to them. We had 7,386 enlisted men and 208 officers. Many more than the Russians.

'Twelve years ago you said Sveaborg could not be defended in winter due to the ice. That's hogwash. I have letters from all the finest military minds of the Swedish, Finnish, and Russian armies testifying to the strength of Sveaborg, summer or winter.

'Twelve years ago you spoke of the formidable Russian artillery that ringed us. It did not exist. At no time did Suchtelen have more than forty-six pieces of cannon, sixteen of which were mortars. We had ten times that number.

'Twelve years ago you said our provisions were running low, and our store of powder was dangerously depleted. It was not so. We had 9,535 cannon cartridges, 10,000 cartouches, two frigates and over 130 smaller ships, magnificent naval stores, enough food to last for months, and over 3,000 barrels of powder. We could easily have waited for Swedish relief.'

The old man shrieked. 'Stop it, stop it!' He put his hands to his ears. 'I won't hear any more. Why are you torturing me? Can't you let an old man rest in peace?'

Bannersson looked at him contemptuously. 'I won't continue,' he said. 'But I'll leave the papers. You can read it all yourself.'

Cronstedt was choking and gasping for breath. 'It was a chance,' he replied. 'It was a chance to save everything for Sweden.'

Bannersson laughed, a hard, cruel, bitter laugh. 'A chance? I was one of your messengers, Admiral; I know what sort of a chance the Russians gave you. They detained us for weeks. You know when I got to Stockholm, Admiral? When I delivered your message?'

The old man's head lifted slowly, and his eyes looked into Bannersson's. His face was pale and sickly, his hands trembling.

'May 3, 1808,' said Bannersson. And Cronstedt winced as if struck.

The tall Swedish major turned and walked to the door. There, knob in hand, he turned and looked back.

'You know,' he said, 'history will forget Bengt and what he tried to do, and will remember Colonel Jägerhorn only as one of the first Finnish nationalists. But you I don't know about. You live in Russian Finland on your thirty pieces of silver, yet Bengt said you were only weak.' He shook his head. 'Which is it, Admiral? What will history have to say about you?'

There was no answer. Count Carl Olof Cronstedt, Vice-Admiral of the Fleet, hero of Ruotsinsalmi, Commandant of Sveaborg, was weeping softly into his pillow.

*

And a day later, he was dead.

> Call him the arm we trusted in
> That shrank in time of stress,
> Call him Affliction, Scorn and Sin
> And Death and Bitterness
> But mention not his former name,
> Lest they should blush who bear the same.
>
> Take all that's dismal in the tomb,
> Take all in life that's base,
> To form one name of guilt and gloom
> For that one man's disgrace,
> Twill rouse less grief in Finland's men
> Than his at Sveaborg did them.'

> – The Tales of Ensign Stål,
> *Johan Ludvig Runeberg*

And Death His Legacy

The Prophet came out of the South with a flag in his right hand and an axe handle in his left, to preach the creed of Americanism. He spoke to the poor and the angry, to the confused and to the fearful, and in them he woke a new determination. For his words were like a fire in the land, and wherever he stopped to speak, there the multitudes arose to march behind him.

His name was Norvel Arlington Beauregard, and he had been a governor before he became a Prophet. He was a big, stocky man, with round black eyes and a square face that flushed blood red when he got excited. His heavy, bushy eyebrows were perpetually crinkled down in suspicion, while his full lips seemed frozen in a sneering half-smile.

But his disciples did not care what he looked like. For Norvel Arlington Beauregard was a Prophet, and Prophets are not to be questioned. He did no miracles, but still they gathered to him, North and South, poor and affluent, steelworkers and factory owners. And soon their numbers were like unto an army.

And the army marched to the music of a military band.

*

'Maximilian de Laurier is dead,' said Maximilian de Laurier aloud to himself as he sat alone in a darkened, book-lined study.

He laughed a low, soft laugh. A match flared briefly in the darkness, flickered momentarily as he touched it to his pipe, and winked out. Maxim de Laurier leaned back in the plush leather armchair, and puffed slowly.

No, he thought. It doesn't work. The words just don't sound right. They've got a hollow ring to them. I'm Maxim de Laurier, and I'm alive.

Yes, answered another part of him, but not for long. Quit fooling yourself. They all say the same thing now. Cancer. Terminal. A year at most. Probably not even that long.

I'm a dead man, then, he told himself. Funny. I don't feel like a dead man. I can't imagine being dead. Not me. Not Maxim de Laurier.

He tried it again. 'Maximilian de Laurier is dead,' he said firmly to the silence.

Then he shook his head. It still doesn't work, he thought. I've got everything to live for. Money. Position. Influence. All that, and more. Everything.

The answer rang ruthless and cold through his head. It doesn't matter, it said. Nothing matters anymore, nothing except that cancer. You're dead. A living dead man.

In the dark, silent room, his hand trembled suddenly, and the pipe flew from his grasp and spilled ashes on the expensive carpet. His fists clenched, and his knuckles began to whiten.

Maximilian de Laurier rose slowly from the chair and walked across the room, brushing a light switch as he passed it. He stopped before the full-length mirror on the door, and surveyed the tall, gray-haired reflection that stared back from the glass. There was a curious whiteness about the face, he noted, and the hands were still trembling slightly.

'And my life?' he said to the reflection. 'What have I done with my life? Read a few books. Driven a few sports cars. Made a few fortunes. A blast, one long, wild blast. Playboy of the Western World.'

He laughed softly, but the reflection still looked grim and shaken. 'But what have I accomplished? In a year, will there be anything to show that Maxim de Laurier has lived?'

He turned from the mirror with a snarl, a bitter, dying man with eyes like the gray ash of a fire that has long since gone out. As he turned, those eyes drank in the gathered remains of a life, sweeping over the rich, heavy furniture, the polished wooden bookcases with their rows of heavy, leather-bound volumes, the cold, sooty fireplace, and the imported hunting rifles mounted in a rack above the mantelpiece.

Suddenly the fire burned again. With quick strides, de Laurier crossed the room and yanked one of the rifles from its mounting. He stroked the stock softly with a trembling hand, but his voice when he spoke was cold and hard and determined.

'Damn it,' he said. 'I'm not dead yet.'

He laughed a wild, snarling laugh as he sat down to oil the gun.

*

Through the far West the Prophet stormed, spreading the Word from a private jet. Everywhere the crowds gathered to cheer him, and husky steelworkers lifted up their children on their shoulders so they could hear him speak. The long-haired hecklers who dared to mock his cause were put down, shouted down, and sometimes beaten down.

'Ah'm for the little man,' he said in San Diego. 'Ah'm for the good patriotic Americans who get forgotten today. This is a free country and I don't mind dissent, but ah'm not about to let the Commies and the anarchists take over. Let's let 'em know they can't fly the Communist flag in this country if there are any red-blooded Americans left around. And if we have to bust a few heads to teach 'em, well, that's okay too.'

And they flocked to him, the patriots and the superpatriots, the vets and the GIs, the angry and the frightened. They flew their flags by day, and read their bibles by night, and pasted 'Beauregard' stickers on the bumpers of their cars.

'Any man has got a right to dissent,' the Prophet shouted from a platform in Los Angeles, 'but when these long-haired anarchists try to impede the progress of the war, why that's not dissent, that's treason.'

'And when these traitors try to block troop trains carrying vital war materials to our boys overseas, ah say it's time to give our policemen some good stout clubs, untie their hands, and let 'em spill a little Commie blood. That'll teach those anarchists to respect the law!'

And all the people cheered and cheered, and the noise all but drowned out the faint echo of jackboots in the distance.

*

Reclining in the deck chair, the tall, gray-haired man glanced at the copy of the *New York Times* lying across his lap. He was a nondescript sort of fellow, with a worn off-the-rack sports jacket and a pair of cheap plastic sunglasses. Few would notice him in a crowd. Fewer still would look closely enough to recognize the dead man who once had been Maximilian de Laurier.

A half smile flickered across the dead man's lips as he read one of the first page stories. The headline read 'De Laurier Fortune Liquidated' in prim gray type. Below, in smaller print, a somber subhead observed that 'English Millionaire Vanishes; Friends Believe Money Deposited in Swiss Banks.'

Yes, he thought. How appropriate. The man vanishes, but the money gets the headlines. I wonder what the papers will say a year from now? Something like 'Heirs Await Reading of Will,' perhaps?

His eyes left the article and wandered upward across the page, coming to rest on the lead story. He stared at the headline in silence, a frown set across his features. Then, slowly and carefully, he read the article.

When he finished, de Laurier rose from the chair, folded the paper carefully, and dropped it over the rail into the murky green water that churned lustily in the liner's wake. Then he shoved his hands into his jacket pockets and walked slowly back to his stateroom in the economy section of the ship. Below, the newspaper tumbled over and over in the turbulence caused by the great liner's passing until it finally became waterlogged and sank. It came to rest at last on the muddy, rock-strewn bottom, where the silence and the darkness were eternal.

And the crabs scuttled to and fro across the fading front page photo of a stocky, square-faced man with bushy eyebrows and a crooked sneer.

*

The Prophet swung East with a vengeance, for here was the homeland of the false seers who had led his people astray, here was the stronghold of those who opposed him. No matter. Here his crowds were even greater, and the sons and the grandsons of the immigrants of the last century were his to a man. So here Norvel Arlington Beauregard chose to attack his enemies in their own lair.

'Ah'm for the little man,' he said in New York City. 'Ah support the right of every American to rent his house or sell his goods to whoever he so chooses, without any interference by briefcase-toting bureaucrats and egghead professors who sit up in their ivory towers and decide how you and me have to live.'

And the people cheered and cheered, and they waved their flags and said the Pledge of Allegiance, and chanted 'Beauregard – Beauregard – Beauregard' over and over again until the arena rocked with the noise. And the Prophet grinned and waved happily, and the Eastern reporters who covered him shook their heads in disbelief and muttered dire things about 'charisma' and 'irony.'

'Ah'm for the working man,' the Prophet told a great labor convention in Philadelphia. 'And ah say all these anarchists and demonstrators better damn well quit their yappin' and go out and get jobs just like everybody else! You and me had to work for what we had, so why should they get pampered by the government? Why should you good folks have to pay taxes to support a bunch of lazy, ignorant bums who don't want to work anyway?'

The crowd roared its approval, and the Prophet clenched his fist and shook it above his head in triumph. For the Word had touched the souls of the workers and the laborers, the strainers and the sweaters, the just-haves of a nation. And they were his. They would follow false gods no longer.

So they all stood up and sang 'The Star-Spangled Banner' together.

*

In New York, Maxim de Laurier caught the first bus from customs to the heart of Manhattan. He carried only one small suitcase packed with clothing, so he did not bother to stop at a hotel. Instead, he went straight towards the financial district, to one of the city's largest banks.

'I'd like to cash a check,' he said to a teller. 'On my bank in Switzerland.'

He scribbled in his checkbook sloppily, ripped the page loose, and shoved it across the counter.

The teller's eyebrows shot up slightly as he noticed the figure. 'Mmmm,' he said. 'I'll have to check this out, sir. I hope you don't mind waiting a few moments. You do have identification, of course, Mister—?'

He glanced at the check again. 'Mister Lawrence,' he concluded.

De Laurier smiled amiably. 'Of course,' he said. 'I'd hardly try to cash a check of this size without proper identification.'

Twenty minutes later he left the bank, walking with measured confidence down the avenue. He made several stops that day, before he finally checked into a cheap hotel for the night.

He bought some clothing, several newspapers, a large number of maps, a battered used car, and a collection of rifles and pistols. He took plenty of ammo, and made sure every rifle had a telescopic sight.

Maximilian de Laurier stayed up late that night, bent over a cheap card table in his hotel room. First he read the newspapers he had purchased. He read them slowly, and carefully, and over and over again. Several times he got up and placed phone calls to the papers' information services, and took down careful notes of what they told him.

And then he spread out his maps, and studied them intently, far into the morning. Selecting those he wanted, he traced a heavy black line across them, constantly referring back to his papers as he worked.

Finally, near dawn, he picked up a red pencil and circled the name of a medium-sized city in Ohio.

Afterwards, he sat down and oiled his guns.

*

The Prophet returned to the Midwest with a fury, for here, more than anywhere except in his homeland, he had found his people. The high priests who had fanned out before him sent back their reports, and they all read the same way. Illinois was going to be good, they said. Indiana was even better. He'd really clean up in Indiana. And Ohio – Ohio was great, Ohio was fantastic.

And so the Prophet crisscrossed the Midwest, bringing the Word to those who were ripe for it, preaching the creed of Americanism in the heartland of America.

'Chicago is my kind of town,' he said repeatedly as he stumped through Illinois, 'You people know how to handle anarchists and Communists in Chicago. There's a lot of good, sensible, patriotic folks in Chicago. You're not about to let those terrorists take over the streets from good, law abiding citizens in Chicago.'

And all the people cheered and cheered, and Beauregard led them in a salute to the police of Chicago. One long-haired heckler yelled out 'Nazi,' but his lone shout was lost in the roar of the applause. Except, at the back of the hall, two burly security guards noted him, nodded to each other, and began to move swiftly and silently through the crowd.

'Ah'm not a racist,' the Prophet said as he crossed the border to speak in northern Indiana. 'Ah stand for the rights of all good Americans, regardless of race, creed, or color. However, ah support your right to sell or rent your property to whoever you choose. And Ah say every person ought to work like you and me, without being allowed to live in dirt and ignorance and immorality on a government handout. And Ah say that looters and anarchists ought to be shot.'

And all the people cheered and cheered, and then went out to spread the Word to their friends, their relatives, and their neighbors. 'I'm no racist and Beauregard's not one either,' they'd tell each other, 'but would you want one to marry your sister?' And the crowds grew larger and larger each week.

And as the Prophet moved east into Ohio, a dead man drove west to meet him.

*

'Is this room satisfactory, Mr Laurel?' asked the thin, elderly landlady, holding the door open for his inspection.

Maxim de Laurier brushed past her and deposited his suitcases on the sagging double bed that stood against one wall. He smiled amiably as he surveyed the dingy cold-water flat. Crossing the room, he lifted the shade and glanced out the window.

'Oh, dear,' said the landlady, fumbling with her keys. 'I hope you won't mind the stadium being located right next door. There's going to be a game next Saturday, and those boys do make a dreadful lot of noise.' She punctuated her sentence with a sharp stomp as her foot came down to crush a cockroach that had crawled out from under the carpet.

De Laurier brushed aside her fears with a wave of his hand. 'The room will be just fine,' he said, 'I rather enjoy football anyway, and from here I'll have a fine view of the game.'

The landlady smiled weakly. 'Very well,' she said, holding out the key. 'I'll take the week's rent in advance, if you don't mind.'

When she left, de Laurier carefully locked the door, and then pulled up a chair in front of the window.

Yes, he thought. A fine view. A perfect view. Of course, the stands are on the other side, so they'll probably have the platform facing that way. But that shouldn't pose any problems. He's a big man, a stocky man, probably quite distinctive even from behind. And those arc lights will be a big help.

Nodding in satisfaction, he rose and returned the chair to its normal place. Then he sat down to oil his guns.

*

It was quite cold out, but the stadium was packed nonetheless. The grandstands were crammed with people, and an overflow crowd had been permitted to drift out onto the field and squat in the grass at the foot of the platform.

The platform itself, draped in red, white, and blue, had been erected on the 50-yard line. American flags flew from staffs at both ends of the platform, with the speaker's podium situated between them. Two harsh white spotlights converged on the rostrum, adding to the garish brilliance of the stadium's own arc lights. The microphones had been carefully hooked up to the stadium's loudspeaker system, and tested over and over again.

It was lucky that they were working, for the roar was deafening when the Prophet stepped up to the podium, and subsided only when he began to speak. And then the hush was sudden and complete, and the call of the Prophet rang out unchallenged through the night.

Time had not dimmed the fire that burned in the soul of the Prophet, and his words were white hot with his anger and his conviction. They came loud and defiant from the platform, and echoed back and forth through the grandstands. They carried far in the clear, cold night air.

They carried to a dingy cold-water flat where Maxim de Laurier sat alone in the darkness, staring out his window. Leaning against his chair was a high-caliber rifle, well-oiled and equipped with a telescopic sight.

On the platform, the Prophet preached the faith to the patriots and to the frightened. He spoke of Americanism, and his whiplike words flailed the Communists, the anarchists, and the long-haired terrorists who were haunting the streets of the nation.

Ah yes, thought de Laurier. I can hear the echoes. Oh, how I can hear the echoes. There was another who attacked the Communists and the anarchists. There was another who said he would save his nation from their clutches.

'—and Ah say to you good folks of Ohio, that when Ah'm in charge, the streets of this country are going to be safe to walk on. Ah'm going to untie the hands of our policemen, and see that they enforce the laws and teach these criminals and terrorists a few lessons.'

A few lessons, thought de Laurier. Yes, yes. It fits, it fits. The police and the army teaching lessons. And such effective teachers. With clubs and guns as study aids. Oh, Mister Beauregard, how well it all fits.

'—and Ah say that when our boys, our fine boys from Mississippi and

Ohio and everywhere else, are fighting and dying for our flag overseas, that we've got to give them all the support we can here at home. And that includes busting the heads of a few of these traitors who defile the flag and call for an enemy victory and obstruct the progress of the war. Ah say that it's time to let 'em know how a patriotic, red-blooded American takes care of treason!'

Treason, thought de Laurier. Yes, treason was what he called it too, that other one so long ago. He said he would get rid of the traitors in the government, the traitors who had caused the nation's defeat and humiliation.

De Laurier slid the chair back slowly. He dropped to one knee, and lifted the rifle to his shoulder.

'—Ah'm no racist, but Ah say that these people oughta—'

De Laurier's face was chalk white, and the gun was unsteady in his hands. 'So sick,' he whispered hoarsely to himself, 'so very, very sick. But do I have the right? If he is what they want, *can* I have the right, alone, to overrule them in the name of sanity?'

He was trembling badly now, and his body was cold and wet with his sweat, despite the chilling wind from outside.

The Prophet's words rang all around him, but he heard them no longer. His mind flashed back, to the visions of another Prophet, and the promised land to which he led his people. He remembered the echo of great armies on the march. He remembered the shriek of the rockets and the bombers in the night. He remembered the terror of the knock on the door. He remembered the charnel smell of the battlefield.

He remembered the gas chambers prepared for the inferior race.

And he wondered, and he listened, and his hands grew steady.

'If he had died early,' said Maximilian de Laurier alone to himself in the darkness, 'how would they have known what horror they had averted?'

He centered the crosshairs on the back of the Prophet's head, and his finger tightened on the trigger.

And the gun spoke death.

Norvel Arlington Beauregard, his fist shaking in the air, jerked suddenly and pitched forward from the platform into the crowd below. And then the screaming started, while the Secret Service men swore and rushed towards the fallen Prophet.

By the time they reached him, Maximilian de Laurier was turning the ignition key in his car and heading for the turnpike.

*

The news of the Prophet's death rocked a nation, and the wail went up from all parts of the land.

'They killed him,' they said. 'Those damn Commies knew that he was the man who could lick them, so they killed him.'

Or, sometimes, they said, 'It was the niggers, the damn niggers. They knew that Beauregard was going to keep them in their places, so they killed him.'

Or, sometimes, 'It was those demonstrators. Goddam traitors. Beau had 'em pegged for what they were, a bunch of anarchists and terrorists. So they killed him, the filthy scum.'

Crosses burned across the land that night, and all the polls turned sharply upward. The Prophet had become a Martyr.

And, three weeks later, Beauregard's vice-presidential candidate announced on a nationwide television address that he was carrying on. 'Our cause is not dead,' he said. 'I promise to fight on for Beau and all that he stood for. And we will fight to victory!'

And all the people cheered and cheered.

*

A few hundred miles away, Maxim de Laurier sat in a hotel room and watched, his face a milk-white mask. 'No,' he whispered, choking on the words. 'Not this. This wasn't supposed to happen. It's wrong, all wrong.'

And he buried his head in his hands, and sobbed, 'My God, my God, what have I done?' And then he was still and silent for a long time. When he rose at last his face was still pale and twisted, but a single dying ember burned still in the ashes of his eyes. 'Maybe,' he said, 'Maybe I can still—'

And he sat down to oil his gun.

TWO
THE FILTHY PRO

THE FILTHY PRO

You never forget the first time you do it for money.

I became a filthy pro in 1970, during the summer between my senior and graduate years at Northwestern University. The story that turned the trick for me was 'The Hero,' which I'd originally written for creative writing my junior year, and had been trying to sell ever since. *Playboy* had seen it first, and returned it with a form rejection slip. *Analog* sent it back with a pithy letter of rejection from John W. Campbell, Jr., the first, last, and only time I got a personal response from that legendary editor. After that 'The Hero' went to Fred Pohl at Galaxy . . .

. . . where it vanished.

It was a year before I realized that Pohl was no longer the editor at Galaxy, that the magazine had changed both publisher and address. When I did, I retyped the story from my carbon – yes, I had finally started to use the stuff, hurrah – and sent it out to *Galaxy's* new editor, Ejler Jakobsson, at *Galaxy's* new address . . .

. . . where it vanished *again!*

Meanwhile, I had celebrated my graduation from Northwestern, though I still had a year of post-graduate study looming ahead of me. Medill offered a five-year program in journalism; at the end of the fourth year you received a Bachelor's degree, but you were encouraged to return for the fifth year, which included a quarter's internship doing political reporting in Washington, D.C. At the end of the fifth year, you received a Master's.

After graduation I returned to Bayonne, and my summer job as a sportswriter/public relations man for the Department of Parks and Recreation. The city sponsored several summer baseball leagues, and my job was to write up the games for the local papers, *The Bayonne Times* and *Jersey Journal*. There were half a dozen leagues, for different age groups, with several games going on every day at different fields around the city, so there was no way for me to actually cover the action. Instead I spent my days in the office, and after every game the umps would bring me a box score. I'd use those as the basis for my stories. So I spent four summers working as a baseball writer, and never saw a game.

By that August, 'The Hero' had been at *Galaxy* for a year. I decided, instead of writing a query letter, to phone the magazine's offices in New York City and inquire about my lost story. The woman who answered was brusque and unfriendly at first, and when I mumbled something about inquiring after a manuscript that had been there for a long time, she told me *Galaxy* could not possibly keep track of all the stories it rejected. I might have given up right there, but somehow I managed to blurt out the title of the story.

There was a pregnant pause. 'Wait a minute,' the woman said. 'We *bought* that story.' (Years later, I discovered that the woman I was speaking to was Judy-Lynn Benjamin, later Judy-Lynn del Rey, who went on to found the Del Rey imprint for Ballatine Books). The story had been purchased *months* ago, she told me, but somehow the manuscript and purchase order had fallen behind a filing cabinet, and had only recently turned up again. (In some alternate universe, no one ever looked behind those files, and I'm a journalist today).

I hung up the phone with a dazed look on my face, before heading off to my summer job. I must have floated, since I was far too high for my feet to touch the ground. Afterward, when neither contracts nor check appeared, I began to wonder if the woman on the phone had misremembered. Perhaps there was some other story called 'The Hero.' I developed a paranoid fear that *Galaxy* might go out of business before publishing my story, a fear that was inflamed when summer ended and I headed back to Chicago, still without a check.

It turned out that *Galaxy* had mailed the check and contract to the North Shore Hotel, the dorm I had vacated on graduating Northwestern that June. By the time it was finally forwarded to my summer address, I was back at school, but in a *different* dorm.

There was a check, though, and I did get my hands on it at last. It proved to be for $94, not an inconsiderable sum of money in 1970. 'The Hero' appeared in the February, 1971 issue of *Galaxy*, in the winter of my graduate year at Medill. Since I did not own a car, I made one of my friends drive me around to half the newsstands on the north shore, so I could buy up all the copies I could find.

Meanwhile, my college years were winding down. I breezed through the first two quarters of my graduate year in Evanston, then packed my bags for Washington and my internship on Capitol Hill. In a few months my real life would begin. I had been doing interviews and sending out job applications, and was looking forward to sorting through all the offers and deciding which of them I'd take. After all, I had graduated *magna cum laude* from the finest journalism school in the country, and would soon have a Master's degree and a prestigious internship under my belt as well. I had lost a lot of weight my graduate year and bought new clothes to suit, so I arrived in D.C. the very picture of a hippie journalist, with my shoulder length hair, bell bottoms, aviator glasses, and double-breasted pin-striped mustard-yellow sports jacket.

My internship was demanding, but exciting. The nation was in turmoil in the spring of 1971, and I was at the center of it all, walking the corridors of power, reporting on congressmen and senators, sitting in the Senate press gallery with real reporters. The Medill News Service had client newspapers all over the country, so a number of my stories actually saw print. The program was run by Neil McNeil, a hardnosed political reporter of the green-eyeshade school who would sit in his cubicle reading your copy, and roar your name whenever he came on something he didn't like. My own name was roared frequently. 'Too cute,' McNeil would scrawl atop my stories, and I'd have to rewrite them and take out everything but the facts before he'd pass them on. I hated it, but I learned a lot.

It was also in Washington that I attended by first actual *science fiction* convention, almost seven years after that first comicon. When I walked into the Sheraton Park Hotel in my burgundy bell bottoms and double-breasted pin-striped mustard-yellow sports jacket, the fellow behind the registration table was this bone-thin hippie writer, with a scraggy beard and long orange hair. He recognized my name (no one forgets the R.R.) and told me that he was *Galaxy's* slush reader, the very fellow who'd fished 'The Hero' out of the slush pile and pushed it on Ejler Jakobsson. So I suppose Gardner Dozois made me a pro and a fan both (though I have since wondered whether he was actually working on registration, or whether he just saw the table unattended and realized that if he sat there people would hand him money. Reading slush for *Galaxy* didn't pay much, after all).

By that time I had a second sale under my belt. Just a few weeks before, Ted White, the new editor at *Amazing* and *Fantastic*, had informed me that he was buying 'The Exit to San Breta,' a futuristic fantasy that I'd written during the spring break of my senior year of college. (Yes, sad to say, when all my friends were down in Florida drinking beer with bikini-clad coeds on the beaches of Ft. Lauderdale, I was back in Bayonne, writing). The story of my second sale was eerily similar to that of my first. Relying on the listings in *Writer's Market*, I'd sent the story off to Harry Harrison at the address given for *Fantastic*, never to see it again. Only later did I learn that both the editor and address had changed, requiring me to retype the manuscript all over again and, well . . . I was starting to wonder if having your story lost in the mail was somehow a necessary prerequisite to selling it.

Galaxy had paid me my $94 on acceptance for 'The Hero,' but *Fantastic* paid on publication, so I would not actually see the money for 'The Exit to San Breta' until October. And when the check did come, it was only for $50. A sale is a sale, however, and your second time is almost as exciting as your first, in writing as in sex. One sale might be a fluke, but *two* sales to two different editors suggested that maybe I had some talent after all.

'The Exit to San Breta' was set in the Southwest, where I live at present, but at the time I wrote it I had never been west of Chicago. The story is all about driving and takes place entirely on highways, but at the time I wrote it I had never been behind the wheel of an automobile. (Our family never owned a car). Despite its futuristic setting, 'Exit' is a fantasy, which is why it appeared in *Fantastic* and not *Amazing*, and why I had not even bothered to send it to *Analog* or *Galaxy*. Inspired by the example of Fritz Leiber's 'Smoke Ghost,' I wanted to take the ghost out of his mouldering old Victorian mansion and put him where a proper twentieth century ghost belonged . . . in a car.

Though the most horrible thing that happens in it is an auto accident, 'The Exit to San Breta' might even be classified as a horror story. If so, my first two sales prefigured my entire career to come, by including all three of the genres I would write in.

Gardner Dozois was not the only writer at that Disclave. I met Joe Haldeman and his brother Jack as well, and George Alec Effinger (still called Piglet, at that time), Ted White, Bob Toomey. All of them were talking about stories they were writing, stories they had written, stories that they meant to write. Terry Carr was the Guest of Honor; a fine writer himself, Carr was also the editor of Ace Specials and the original anthology *Universe*, and went out of his way to be friendly and helpful to all the young writers swarming about him, including me. No convention ever had a warmer or more accessible guest.

I left Disclave resolved to attend more science fiction conventions . . . and to sell more stories. Before I could do that, of course, I would need to *write* more stories. Talking with Gardner and Piglet and the Haldemans had made me realize how little I had actually produced, compared to any of them. If I was serious about wanting to be a writer, I would need to finish more stories.

Of course, that was the summer when my real life was supposed to begin. I would soon be moving somewhere, working at my first real job, living in an apartment of my own. For months I had been dreaming of paychecks, cars, and girlfriends, and wondering where life would take me. Would I have *time* to write fiction? That was hard to say.

Well, life took me back to my old room in Bayonne. Despite all those interviews, letters, and applications, despite my degree and my internship and *magna cum laude*, I had no job.

It did look for a while as if I were going to get an offer from a newspaper in Boca Raton, Florida, and another from *Women's Wear Daily*, but in the end neither place came through. I don't know, maybe I shouldn't have worn the double-breasted pin-striped mustard-yellow sports jacket to that follow-up interview. Even Marvel Comics turned me down, as seemingly unimpressed by my Master's as they were by my old Alley Award.

I did get an offer of sorts from my hometown paper, the *Bayonne Times*, but it was withdrawn when I asked about salary and benefits. 'A beginner should get a job and experience,' the editor scolded me. 'That should have been your first consideration.' (I got my revenge. The *Bayonne Times* ceased publishing that very summer, and both the editor and the guy he hired in place of me found themselves out of work. If I had taken the job, my 'experience' would have lasted all of two weeks.)

Far from starting my real life in some exotic new city, with a salary and an apartment of my own, I found myself covering summer baseball for the Bayonne Department of Parks and Recreation once more. As if that were not wound enough, the Department of Parks had some nice salt to rub in. Because of budget cuts, they could only afford to hire me half-time. However, there were just as many games to write up as last summer, so I would be expected to do the same amount of work in half the time for half the pay.

There were black days that summer when I felt as if my five years of college had been a total waste, that I would be forever trapped in Bayonne and might end up running the Tubs o' Fun again at Uncle Milty's down on 1st Street, as I had my first summer out of high school. Vietnam also loomed. My number had come up in the draft lottery, and by losing all that weight over the past year I had also managed to lose my 4-F exemption. I was opposed to the war in Vietnam, and had applied for conscientious objector status with my local draft board, but everyone told me that my chances of receiving it were small to none. More likely, I'd be drafted. I might only have a month or two of civilian life remaining.

I had that much, however . . . and since I only had a part-time job, I had half of every day as well. I decided to use that time for writing fiction, as I'd resolved to do at Disclave. To work at it *every day*, and see how much I could produce before Uncle Sam called me up. My Parks Department job began in the afternoon, so the mornings became my time to write. Every day after breakfast I would drag out my Smith-Corona portable electric, set it up on my mother's kitchen table, plug it in, flick on the switch that made it *hummmmm*, and set to writing. Nor would I allow myself to put a story aside until I'd finished it. I wanted finished stories I could sell, not fragments and half-developed notions.

That summer I finished a story every two weeks, on the average. I wrote 'Night Shift' and 'Dark, Dark Were the Tunnels.' I wrote 'The Last Super Bowl,' though my title was 'The Final Touchdown Drive.' I wrote 'A Peripheral Affair' and 'Nobody Leaves New Pittsburg,' both of them intended as the first story of a series. And I wrote 'With Morning Comes Mistfall' and

'The Second Kind of Loneliness,' which follow. Seven stories, all in all. Maybe it was the spectre of Vietnam that goaded me, or my accumulated frustration at having neither a job, a girl, or a life. ('Nobody Leaves New Pittsburg,' though perhaps the weakest story I produced that summer, reflects my state of mind most clearly. For 'New Pittsburg,' read 'Bayonne.' For 'corpse,' read me).

Whatever the cause, the words came pouring out of me as they never had before. Ultimately, all seven of the stories that I wrote that summer would go on to sell, though for some it would require four or five years and a score of rejections. Two of the seven, however, proved to be important milestones in my career, and those are the two that I've included here.

They were the two best. I knew that when I wrote them, and said as much in the letters I sent to Howard Waldrop that summer. 'With Morning Comes Mistfall' was the finest thing that I had ever written, *ever* . . . until I wrote 'The Second Kind of Loneliness' a few weeks later. 'Mistfall' seemed to me to be the more polished of the two, a wistful mood piece with little in the way of traditional 'action,' yet evocative and, I hoped, effective. 'Loneliness,' on the other hand, was an open wound of a story, painful to write, painful to read. It represented a real breakthrough for my writing. My earlier stories had come wholly from the head, but this one came from the heart and the balls as well. It was the first story I ever wrote that truly left me feeling vulnerable, the first story that ever made me ask myself, 'Do I *really* want to let people read this?'

'The Second Kind of Loneliness' and 'With Morning Comes Mistfall' were the stories that would make or break my career, I was convinced. For the next half-year, *break* looked more likely than *make*. Neither story sold its first time out. Or its second. Or its third. My other 'summer stories' were getting bounced around as well, but it was the rejections for 'Mistfall' and 'Loneliness' that hurt the most. These were *strong* stories, I was convinced, the best work that I was capable of. If the editors did not want them, maybe I did not understand what makes a good story after all . . . or maybe my best work was just not good enough. It was a dark day each time one of these two came straggling home, and a dark night of doubt that followed.

But in the end my faith was vindicated. Both stories sold, and when they did it was to *Analog*, which boasted the highest circulation and best rates of any magazine in the field. John W. Campbell, Jr. had died that spring, and after a hiatus of several months Ben Bova had been named to take his place as editor of SF's most respected magazine. Campbell would never have touched either of these stories, I am convinced, but Bova intended to take *Analog* in new directions. He bought them both, after some minor rewrites.

'The Second Kind of Loneliness' appeared first, as the cover story of the December, 1972 issue. Frank Kelly Freas did the cover, a gorgeous depiction of my protagonist floating above the whorl of the nullspace vortex. (It was my first cover and I wanted to buy the painting. Freas offered it to me for $200 . . . but I had only received $250 for the story, so I flinched, and bought the two-page interior spread and a cover rough instead. They're both swell, but I wish that I'd gone ahead and bought the painting. The last time I inquired, its current owner was willing to sell for $20,000).

'With Morning Comes Mistfall' followed 'Loneliness' into print in the issue for May, 1973. Two stories appearing in the field's top magazine so close together attracted attention, and 'Mistfall' was nominated for both the Nebula and Hugo Awards, the first of my works to contend for either honor. It lost the Nebula to James Tiptree's 'Love Is the Plan, the Plan Is Death,' and the Hugo to Ursula K. Le Guin's 'The Ones Who Walk Away from Omelas,' but I received a handsome certificate suitable for framing and Gardner Dozois inducted me into the Hugo-and-Nebula Losers Club, chanting 'One of us, one of us, one of us.' I can't complain.

That summer of 1971 proved to be a turning point in my life. If I had been able to find an entry-level job in journalism, I might very well have taken the road more traveled by, the one that came with a salary and health insurance. I suspect I would have continued to write the occasional short story, but with a full-time job to fill my days they would have been few and far between. Today I might be a foreign correspondent for the *New York Times*, an entertainment reporter for *Variety*, a columnist appearing daily in three hundred newspapers coast to coast . . . or more likely, a sour, disgruntled rewrite man on the *Jersey Journal*.

Instead circumstances forced me to do what I loved best.

That summer ended happily in other ways as well. To the vast surprise of all, my draft board granted me my conscientious objector status. (Perhaps 'The Hero' had a bit to do with that. I'd sent it in as part of my application). With my low lottery number, I was still called up to serve at the end of the summer . . . but now, instead of flying off to Vietnam, I was returning to Chicago for two years of alternative service with VISTA.

During the next decade I would find myself directing chess tournaments and teaching college . . . but those were only things I *did*, to pay the rent. After the summer of '71, when people asked me what I *was*, I always said, 'A writer.'

The Hero

The city was dead and the flames of its passing spread a red stain across the green-gray sky.

It had been a long time dying. Resistance had lasted almost a week and the fighting had been bitter for awhile. But in the end the invaders had broken the defenders, as they had broken so many others in the past. The alien sky with its double sun did not bother them. They had fought and won under skies of azure blue and speckled gold and inky black.

The Weather Control boys had hit first, while the main force was still hundreds of miles to the east. Storm after storm had flailed at the streets of the city, to slow defensive preparations and smash the spirit of resistance.

When they were closer the invaders had sent up howlers. Unending high-pitched shrieks had echoed back and forth both day and night and before long most of the populace had fled in demoralized panic. By then the attackers' main force was in range and launched plague bombs on a steady westward wind.

Even then the natives had tried to fight back. From their defensive emplacements ringing the city the survivors had sent up a hail of atomics, managing to vaporize one whole company whose defensive screens were overloaded by the sudden assault. But the gesture was a feeble one at best. By that time incendiary bombs were raining down steadily upon the city and great clouds of acid-gas were blowing across the plains.

And behind the gas, the dreaded assault squads of the Terran Expeditionary Force moved on the last defenses.

*

Kagen scowled at the dented plastoid helmet at his feet and cursed his luck. A routine mopping-up detail, he thought. A perfectly routine operation – and some damned automatic interceptor emplacement somewhere had lobbed a low-grade atomic at him.

It had been only a near miss but the shock waves had damaged his hip rockets and knocked him out of the sky, landing him in this godforsaken little ravine east of the city. His light plastoid battle armor had protected him from the impact but his helmet had taken a good whack.

Kagen squatted and picked up the dented helmet to examine it. His long-range com and all of his sensory equipment were out. With his rockets gone, too, he was crippled, deaf, dumb and half-blind. He swore.

A flicker of movement along the top of the shallow ravine caught his attention. Five natives came suddenly into view, each carrying a hair-trigger submachine gun. They carried them at the ready, trained on Kagen. They were fanned out in line, covering him from both right and left. One began to speak.

He never finished. One instant, Kagen's screech gun lay on the rocks at his feet. Quite suddenly it was in his hand.

Five men will hesitate where one alone will not. During the brief flickering instant before the natives' fingers began to tighten on their triggers, Kagen did not pause, Kagen did not hesitate, Kagen did not think.

Kagen killed.

The screech gun emitted a loud, ear-piercing shriek. The enemy squad leader shuddered as the invisible beam of concentrated high-frequency sound ripped into him. Then his flesh began to liquify. By then Kagen's gun had found two more targets.

The guns of the two remaining natives finally began to chatter. A rain of bullets enveloped Kagen as he whirled to his right and he grunted under the impact as the shots caromed off his battle armor. His screech gun leveled – and a random shot sent it spinning from his grasp.

Kagen did not hesitate or pause as the gun was wrenched from his grip. He bounded to the top of the shallow ravine with one leap, directly toward one of the soldiers.

The man wavered briefly and brought up his gun. The instant was all Kagen needed. With all the momentum of his leap behind it, his right hand smashed the gun butt into the enemy's face and his left, backed by fifteen hundred pounds of force, hammered into the native's body right under the breastbone.

Kagen seized the corpse and heaved it toward the second native, who had ceased fire briefly as his comrade came between himself and Kagen. Now his bullets tore into the airborne body. He took a quick step back, his gun level and firing.

And then Kagen was on him. Kagen knew a searing flash of pain as a shot bruised his temple. He ignored it, drove the edge of his hand into the native's throat. The man toppled, lay still.

Kagen spun, still reacting, searching for the next foe.

He was alone.

Kagen bent and wiped the blood from his hand with a piece of the native's uniform. He frowned in disgust. It was going to be a long trek back to camp, he thought, tossing the blood-soaked rag casually to the ground.

Today was definitely not his lucky day.

He grunted dismally, then scrambled back down into the ravine to recover his screech gun and helmet for the hike.

On the horizon, the city was still burning.

*

Ragelli's voice was loud and cheerful as it came crackling over the short-range communicator nestled in Kagen's fist.

'So it's you, Kagen,' he said laughing. 'You signaled just in time. My sensors were starting to pick up something. Little closer and I would've screeched you down.'

'My helmet's busted and the sensors are out,' Kagen replied. 'Damn hard to judge distance. Long-range com is busted, too.'

'The brass was wondering what happened to you,' Ragelli cut in. 'Made 'em sweat a little. But I figured you'd turn up sooner or later.'

'Right,' Kagen said. 'One of these mudworms zapped the hell out of my rockets and it took me a while to get back. But I'm coming in now.'

He emerged slowly from the crater he had crouched in, coming in sight of the guard in the distance. He took it slow and easy.

Outlined against the outpost barrier, Ragelli lifted a ponderous silver-gray arm in greeting. He was armored completely in a full duralloy battlesuit that made Kagen's plastoid armor look like tissue paper, and sat in the trigger-seat of a swiveling screech-gun battery. A bubble of defensive screens enveloped him, turning his massive figure into an indistinct blur.

Kagen waved back and began to eat up the distance between them with long, loping strides. He stopped just in front of the barrier, at the foot of Ragelli's emplacement.

'You look damned battered,' said Ragelli, appraising him from behind a plastoid visor, aided by his sensory devices. 'That light armor doesn't buy you a nickel's worth of protection. Any farm boy with a pea shooter can plug you.'

Kagen laughed. 'At least I can move. You may be able to stand off an Assault Squad in that duralloy monkey suit, but I'd like to see you do anything on offense, chum. And defense doesn't win wars.'

'Your pot,' Ragelli said. 'This sentry duty is boring as hell.' He flicked a switch on his control panel and a section of the barrier winked out. Kagen was through it at once. A split second later it came back on again.

Kagen strode quickly to his squad barracks. The door slid open automatically as he approached it and he stepped inside gratefully. It felt good to be home again and back at his normal weight. These light gravity mudholes made him queasy after awhile. The barracks were artificially maintained at Wellington-normal gravity, twice Earth-normal. It was expensive but the brass kept saying that nothing was too good for the comfort of our fighting men.

Kagen stripped off his plastoid armor in the squad ready room and tossed it into the replacement bin. He headed straight for his cubicle and sprawled across the bed.

Reaching over to the plain metal table alongside his bed, he yanked open a drawer and took out a fat greenish capsule. He swallowed it hastily, and lay back to relax as it took hold throughout his system. The regulations prohibited taking synthastim between meals, he knew, but the rule was never enforced. Like most troopers, Kagen took it almost continuously to maintain his speed and endurance at maximum.

He was dozing comfortably a few minutes later when the com box mounted on the wall above his bed came to sudden life.

'Kagen.'

Kagen sat up instantly, wide awake.

'Acknowledged,' he said.

'Report to Major Grady at once.'

Kagen grinned broadly. His request was being acted on quickly, he thought. And by a high officer, no less. Dressing quickly in loose-fitting brown fatigues, he set off across the base.

The high officers' quarters were at the center of the outpost. They consisted of a brightly lit, three-story building, blanketed overhead by defensive screens and ringed by guardsmen in light battle armor. One of the guards recognized Kagen and he was admitted on orders.

Immediately beyond the door he halted briefly as a bank of sensors scanned him for weapons. Troopers, of course, were not allowed to bear arms in the presence of high officers. Had he been carrying a screech gun alarms would have gone off all over the building while the tractor beams hidden in the walls and ceilings immobilized him completely.

But he passed the inspection and continued down the long corridor toward Major Grady's office. A third of the way down, the first set of tractor beams locked firmly onto his wrists. He struggled the instant he felt the invisible touch against his skin – but the tractors held him steady. Others, triggered automatically by his passing, came on as he continued down the corridor.

Kagen cursed under his breath and fought with his impulse to resist. He hated being pinned by tractor beams, but those were the rules if you wanted to see a high officer.

The door opened before him and he stepped through. A full bank of tractor beams seized him instantly and immobilized him. A few adjusted slightly and he was snapped to rigid attention, although his muscles screamed resistance.

Major Carl Grady was working at a cluttered wooden desk a few feet away, scribbling something on a sheet of paper. A large stack of papers rested at his elbow, an old-fashioned laser pistol sitting on top of them as a paperweight.

Kagen recognized the laser. It was some sort of heirloom, passed down in Grady's family for generations. The story was that some ancestor of his had used it back on Earth, in the Fire Wars of the early twenty-first century. Despite its age, the thing was still supposed to be in working order.

After several minutes of silence Grady finally set down his pen and looked up at Kagen. He was unusually young for a high officer but his unruly gray hair made him look older than he was. Like all high officers, he was Earth-born; frail and slow before the assault squad troopers from the dense, heavy gravity War Worlds of Wellington and Rommel.

'Report your presence,' Grady said curtly. As always, his lean, pale face mirrored immense boredom.

'Field Officer John Kagen, assault squads, Terran Expeditionary Force.'

Grady nodded, not really listening. He opened one of his desk drawers and extracted a sheet of paper.

'Kagen,' he said, fiddling with the paper, 'I think you know why you're here.' He tapped the paper with his finger. 'What's the meaning of this?'

'Just what it says, Major,' Kagen replied. He tried to shift his weight but the tractor beams held him rigid.

Grady noticed and gestured impatiently. 'At rest,' he said. Most of the tractor beams snapped off, leaving Kagen free to move, if only at half his normal speed. He flexed in relief and grinned.

'My term of enlistment is up within two weeks, Major. I don't plan to reenlist. So I've requested transportation to Earth. That's all there is to it.'

Grady's eyebrows arched a fraction of an inch but the dark eyes beneath them remained bored.

'Really?' he asked. 'You've been a soldier for almost twenty years now, Kagen. Why retire? I'm afraid I don't understand.'

Kagen shrugged. 'I don't know. I'm getting old. Maybe I'm just getting tired of camp life. It's all starting to get boring, taking one damn mudhole after another. I want something different. Some excitement.'

Grady nodded. 'I see. But I don't think I agree with you, Kagen.' His voice was soft and persuasive. 'I think you're underselling the T.E.F. There is excitement ahead, if you'll only give us a chance.' He leaned back in his chair, toying with a pencil he had picked up. 'I'll tell you something, Kagen. You know, we've been at war with the Hrangan Empire for nearly three decades now. Direct clashes between us and the enemy have been few and far between up to now. Do you know why?'

'Sure,' Kagen said.

Grady ignored him. 'I'll tell you why,' he continued. 'So far each of us has been struggling to consolidate his position by grabbing these little worlds in the border regions. These mudholes, as you call them. But they're very important mudholes. We need them for bases, for their raw materials, for their industrial capacity and for the conscript labor they provide. That's why we try to minimize damage in our campaigns. And that's why we use psychwar tactics like the howlers. To frighten away as many natives as possible before each attack. To preserve labor.'

'I know all that,' Kagen interrupted with typical Wellington bluntness. 'What of it? I didn't come here for a lecture.'

Grady looked up from the pencil. 'No,' he said. 'No, you didn't. So I'll tell you, Kagen. The prelims are over. It's time for the main event. There are only a handful of unclaimed worlds left. Soon now, we'll be coming into direct conflict with the Hrangan Conquest Corps. Within a year we'll be attacking their bases.'

The major stared at Kagen expectantly, waiting for a reply. When none came, a puzzled look flickered across his face. He leaned forward again.

'Don't you understand, Kagen?' he asked. 'What more excitement could you want? No more fighting these piddling civilians in uniform, with their dirty little atomics and their primitive projectile guns. The Hrangans are a real enemy. Like us, they've had a professional army for generations upon generations. They're soldiers, born and bred. Good ones, too. They've got screens and modern weapons. They'll be foes to give our assault squads a real test.'

'Maybe,' Kagen said doubtfully. 'But that kind of excitement isn't what I had in mind. I'm getting old. I've noticed that I'm definitely slower lately – even synthastim isn't keeping up my speed.'

Grady shook his head. 'You've got one of the best records in the whole T.E.F., Kagen. You've received the Stellar Cross twice and the World Congress Decoration three times. Every com station on Earth carried the story when you saved the landing party on Torego. Why should you doubt your effectiveness now? We're going to need men like you against the Hrangans. Reenlist.'

'No,' said Kagen emphatically. 'The regs say you're entitled to your pension after twenty years and those medals have earned me a nice bunch of retirement bonuses. Now I want to enjoy them.' He grinned broadly. 'As you say, everyone on Earth must know me. I'm a hero. With that reputation, I figure I can have a real screechout.'

Grady frowned and drummed on the desk impatiently. 'I know what the regulations say, Kagen. But no one ever really retires – you must know that. Most troopers prefer to stay with the front. That's their job. That's what the War Worlds are all about.'

'I don't really care, Major,' Kagen replied. 'I know the regs and I know I have a right to retire on full pension. You can't stop me.'

Grady considered the statement calmly, his eyes dark with thought.

'All right,' he said after a long pause. 'Let's be reasonable about this. You'll retire with full pension and bonuses. We'll set you down on Wellington in a place of your own. Or Rommel if you like. We'll make you a youth barracks director – any age group you like. Or a training camp director. With your record you can start right at the top.'

'Uh-uh,' Kagen said firmly. 'Not Wellington. Not Rommel. Earth.'

'But why? You were born and raised on Wellington – in one of the hill barracks, I believe. You've never seen Earth.'

'True,' said Kagen. 'But I've seen it in camp telecasts and flicks. I like what I've seen. I've been reading about Earth a lot lately, too. So now I want to see what it's like.' He paused, then grinned again. 'Let's just say I want to see what I've been fighting for.'

Grady's frown reflected his displeasure. 'I'm from Earth, Kagen,' he said. 'I tell you, you won't like it. You won't fit in. The gravity is too low – and there are no artificial heavy gravity barracks to take shelter in. Synthastim is illegal, strictly prohibited. But War Worlders need it, so you'll have to pay exorbitant prices to get the stuff. Earthers aren't reaction trained, either. They're a different kind of people. Go back to Wellington. You'll be among your own kind.'

'Maybe that's one of the reasons I want Earth,' Kagen said stubbornly. 'On Wellington I'm just one of hundreds of old vets. Hell, every one of the troopers who *does* retire heads back to his old barracks. But on Earth I'll be a celebrity. Why, I'll be the fastest, strongest guy on the whole damn planet. That's got to have some advantages.'

Grady was starting to look agitated. 'What about the gravity?' he demanded. 'The synthastim?'

'I'll get used to light gravity after a while, that's no problem. And I won't be needing that much speed and endurance, so I figure I can kick the synthastim habit.'

Grady ran his fingers through his unkempt hair and shook his head doubtfully. There was a long, awkward silence. He leaned across the desk.

And, suddenly, his hand darted towards the laser pistol.

Kagen reacted. He dove forward, delayed only slightly by the few tractor beams that still held him. His hand flashed toward Grady's wrist in a crippling arc.

And suddenly wrenched to a halt as the tractor beams seized Kagen roughly, held him rigid and then smashed him to the floor.

Grady, his hand frozen halfway to the pistol, leaned back in the chair. His face was white and shaken. He raised his hand and the tractor beams let up a bit. Kagen climbed slowly to his feet.

'You see, Kagen,' said Grady. 'That little test proves you're as fit as ever. You'd have gotten me if I hadn't kept a few tractors on you to slow you down. I tell you, we need men with your training and experience. We need you against the Hrangans. Reenlist.'

Kagen's cold blue eyes still seethed with anger. 'Damn the Hrangans,' he said. 'I'm not reenlisting and no goddamn little tricks of yours are going to make me change my mind. I'm going to Earth. You can't stop me.'

Grady buried his face in his hands and sighed.

'All right, Kagen,' he said at last. 'You win. I'll put through your request.'

He looked up one more time, and his dark eyes looked strangely troubled.

'You've been a great soldier, Kagen. We'll miss you. I tell you that you'll regret this decision. Are you sure you won't reconsider?'

'Absolutely sure,' Kagen snapped.

The strange look suddenly vanished from Grady's eyes. His face once more took on the mask of bored indifference.

'Very well,' he said curtly. 'You are dismissed.'

The tractors stayed on Kagen as he turned. They guided him – very firmly – from the building.

*

'You ready, Kagen?' Ragelli asked, leaning casually against the door of the cubicle.

Kagen picked up his small travel bag and threw one last glance around to make sure he hadn't forgotten anything. He hadn't. The room was quite bare.

'Guess so,' he said, stepping through the door.

Ragelli slipped on the plastoid helmet that had been cradled under his arm and hurried to catch up as Kagen strode down the corridor.

'I guess this is it,' he said as he matched strides.

'Yeah,' Kagen replied. 'A week from now I'll be taking it easy back on Earth while you're getting blisters on your tail sitting around in that damned duralloy tuxedo of yours.'

Ragelli laughed. 'Maybe,' he said. 'But I still say you're nuts to go to Earth of all places, when you could command a whole damned training camp on Wellington. Assuming you wanted to quit at all, which is also crazy—'

The barracks door slid open before them and they stepped through, Ragelli still talking. A second guard flanked Kagen on the other side. Like Ragelli, he was wearing light battle armor.

Kagen himself was in full dress whites, trimmed with gold braid. A ceremonial laser, deactivated, was slung in a black leather holster at his side. Matching leather boots and a polished steel helmet set off the uniform. Azure blue bars on his shoulder signified field officer rank. His medals jangled against his chest as he walked.

Kagen's entire third assault squad was drawn up at attention on the spacefield behind the barracks in honor of his retirement. Alongside the ramp to the shuttlecraft, a group of high officers stood by, cordoned off by defensive screens. Major Grady was in the front row, his bored expression blurred somewhat by the screens.

Flanked by the two guards, Kagen walked across the concrete slowly, grinning under his helmet. Piped music welled out over the field, and Kagen recognized the T.E.F. battle hymn and the Wellington anthem.

At the foot of the ramp he turned and looked back. The company spread out before him saluted in unison on a command from the high officers and held position until Kagen returned the salute. Then one of the squad's other field officers stepped forward, and presented him with his discharge papers.

Jamming them into his belt, Kagen threw a quick, casual wave to Ragelli, then hurried up the ramp. It lifted slowly behind him.

Inside the ship, a crewman greeted him with a curt nod. 'Got special quarters prepared for you,' he said. 'Follow me. Trip should only take about fifteen minutes. Then we'll transfer you to a starship for the Earth trip.'

Kagen nodded and followed the man to his quarters. They turned out to be a plain, empty room, reinforced with duralloy plates. A viewscreen covered one wall. An acceleration couch faced it.

Alone, Kagen sprawled out on the acceleration couch, clipping his helmet to a holder on the side. Tractor beams pressed down gently, holding him firmly in place for the liftoff.

A few minutes later a dull roar came from deep within the ship and Kagen felt several gravities press down upon him as the shuttlecraft took off. The viewscreen, suddenly coming to life, showed the planet dwindling below.

The viewer blinked off when they reached orbit. Kagen started to sit up but found he still could not move. The tractor beams held him pinned to the couch.

He frowned. There was no need for him to stay in the couch once the craft was in orbit. Some idiot had forgotten to release him.

'Hey,' he shouted, figuring there would be a com box somewhere in the room. 'These tractors are still on. Loosen the damned things so I can move a little.'

No one answered.

He strained against the beams. Their pressure seemed to increase. The blasted things were starting to pinch a little, he thought. Now those morons were turning the knob the wrong way.

He cursed under his breath. 'No,' he shouted. 'Now the tractors are getting heavier. You're adjusting them the wrong way.

But the pressure continued to climb and he felt more beams locking on him, until they covered his body like an invisible blanket. The damn things were really starting to hurt now.

'You idiots,' he yelled. 'You morons. Cut it out, you bastards.' With a surge of anger he strained against the beams, cursing. But even Wellington-bred muscle was no match for tractors. He was held tightly to the couch.

One of the beams was trained on his chest pocket. Its pressure was driving his Stellar Cross painfully into his skin. The sharp edge of the polished medal had already sliced through the uniform and he could see a red stain spreading slowly through the white.

The pressure continued to mount and Kagen writhed in pain, squirming against his invisible shackles. It did no good. The pressure still went higher and more and more beams came on.

'Cut it out!' he screeched. 'You bastards, I'll rip you apart when I get out of here. You're killing me, dammit!'

He heard the sharp snap of a bone suddenly breaking under the strain. Kagen felt a stab of intense pain in his right wrist. An instant later there was another snap.

'Cut it out!' he cried, his voice shrill with pain. 'You're killing me. Damn you, you're killing me!'

And suddenly he realized he was right.

*

Grady looked up with a scowl at the aide who entered the office.

'Yes? What is it?'

The aide, a young Earther in training for high officer rank, saluted briskly. 'We just got the report from the shuttlecraft, sir. It's all over. They want to know what to do with the body.'

'Space it,' Grady replied. 'Good as anything.' A thin smile flickered across his face and he shook his head. 'Too bad. Kagen was a good man in combat but his psych training must have slipped somewhere. We should send a strong note back to his barracks conditioner. Though it's funny it didn't show up until now.'

He shook his head again. 'Earth,' he said. 'For a moment he even had me wondering if it was possible. But when I tested him with my laser, I knew. No way, no way.' He shuddered a little. 'As if we'd ever let a War Worlder loose on Earth.' Then he turned back to his paperwork.

As the aide turned to leave, Grady looked up again.

'One other thing,' he said. 'Don't forget to send that PR release back to Earth. Make it War-Hero-Dies-When-Hrangans-Blast-Ship. Jazz it up good. Some of the big com networks should pick it up and it'll make good publicity. And forward his medals to Wellington. They'll want them for his barracks museum.'

The aide nodded and Grady returned to his work. He still looked quite bored.

The Exit to San Breta

It was the highway that first caught my attention. Up to that night, it had been a perfectly normal trip. It was my vacation, and I was driving to L.A. through the Southwest, taking my own sweet time about it. That was nothing new; I'd done it several times before.

Driving is my hobby. Or cars in general, to be precise. Not many people take the time to drive anymore. It's just too slow for most. The automobile's been pretty much obsolete since they started mass-producing cheap copters back in '93. And whatever life it had left in it was knocked out by the invention of the personal gravpak.

But it was different when I was a kid. Back then, everybody had a car, and you were considered some sort of a social freak if you didn't get your driver's license as soon as you were old enough. I got interested in cars when I was in my late teens, and have stayed interested ever since.

Anyway, when my vacation rolled around, I figured it was a chance to try out my latest find. It was a great car, an English sports model from the late '70s. Jaguar XKL. Not one of the classics, true, but a nice car all the same. It handled beautifully.

I was doing most of my traveling at night, as usual. There's something special about night driving. The old, deserted highways have an atmosphere about them in the starlight, and you can almost see them as they once were – vital and crowded and full of life, with cars jammed bumper to bumper as far as the eye could see.

Today, there's none of that. Only the roads themselves are left, and most of them are cracked and overgrown with weeds. The states can't bother taking care of them anymore – too many people objected to the waste of tax money. But ripping them up would be too expensive. So they just sit, year after year, slowly falling apart. Most of them are still drivable, though; they built their roads well back in the old days.

There's still some traffic. Car nuts like me, of course. And the hovertrucks. They can ride over just about anything, but they can go faster over flat surfaces. So they stick to the old highways pretty much.

It's kind of awesome whenever a hovertruck passes you at night. They do about two hundred or so, and no sooner do you spot one in your rearview mirror then it's on top of you. You don't see much – just a long silver blur, and a shriek as it goes by. And then you're alone again.

Anyway, I was in the middle of Arizona, just outside San Breta, when I first noticed the highway. I didn't think much of it then. Oh, it was unusual all right, but not that unusual.

The highway itself was quite ordinary. It was an eight-lane freeway, with a good, fast surface, and it ran straight from horizon to horizon. At night, it was like a gleaming black ribbon running across the white sands of the desert.

No, it wasn't the highway that was unusual. It was its condition. At first, I didn't really notice. I was enjoying myself too much. It was a clear, cold night, and the stars were out, and the Jag was riding beautifully.

Riding *too* beautifully. That's when it first dawned on me. There were no bumps, no cracks, no potholes. The road was in prime condition, almost as if it had just been built. Oh, I'd been on good roads before. Some of them just stood up better than others. There's a section outside Baltimore that's superb, and parts of the L.A. freeway system are quite good.

But I'd never been on one this good. It was hard to believe a road could be in such good shape, after all those years without repair.

And then there were the lights. They were all on, all bright and clear. None of them were busted. None of them were out, or blinking. Hell, none of them were even dim. The road was beautifully lighted.

After that, I began to notice other things. Like the traffic signs. Most places, the traffic signs are long gone, removed by souvenir hunters or antique collectors as a reminder of an older, slower America. No one replaces them – they aren't needed. Once in awhile you'll come across one that's been missed, but there's never anything left but an oddly shaped, rusted hunk of metal.

But this highway had traffic signs. Real traffic signs. I mean, ones you could read. Speed limit signs, when no one's observed a speed limit in years. Yield signs, when there's seldom any other traffic to yield to. Turn signs, exit signs, caution signs – all kinds of signs. And all as good as new.

But the biggest shock was the lines. Paint fades fast, and I doubt that there's a highway in America where you could still make out the white lines in a speeding car. But you could on this one. The lines were sharp and clear, the paint fresh, the eight lanes clearly marked.

Oh, it was a beautiful highway all right. The kind they had back in the old days. But it didn't make sense. No road could stay in this condition all these years. Which meant someone had to be maintaining it. But who? Who would bother to maintain a highway that only a handful of people used each year? The cost would be enormous, with no return at all.

I was still trying to puzzle it out when I saw the other car.

I had just flashed by a big red sign marking Exit 76, the exit to San Breta, when I saw it. Just a white speck on the horizon, but I knew it had to be another motorist. It couldn't be a hovertruck, since I was plainly gaining on it. And that meant another car, and a fellow aficionado.

It was a rare occasion. It's damn seldom you meet another car on the open road. Oh, there are regular conventions, like the Fresno Festival on Wheels and the American Motoring Association's Annual Trafficjam. But they're too artificial for my tastes. Coming across another motorist on the highway is something else indeed.

I hit the gas, and speeded up to around one-twenty. The Jag could do better, but I'm not a nut on speed like some of my fellow drivers. And I was picking up ground fast. From the way I was gaining, the other car couldn't have been doing better than seventy.

When I got within range, I let go with a blast on my horn, trying to attract his attention. But he didn't seem to hear me. Or at least he didn't show any sign. I honked again.

And then, suddenly, I recognized the make.

It was an Edsel.

I could hardly believe it. The Edsel is one of the real classics, right up there with the Stanley Steamer and the Model T.

The few that are left sell for a rather large fortune nowadays.

And this was one of the rarest, one of those original models with the funny noses. There were only three or four like it left in the world, and those were not for sale at any price. An automotive legend, and here it was on the highway in front of me, as classically ugly as the day it came off the Ford assembly line.

I pulled alongside, and slowed down to keep even with it. I couldn't say that I thought much of the way the thing had been kept up. The white paint was chipped, the car was dirty, and there were signs of body rust on the lower part of the doors. But it was still an Edsel, and it could easily be restored. I honked again to get the attention of the driver, but he ignored me. There were five people in the car from what I could see, evidently a family on an outing. In the back, a heavy-set woman was trying to control two small kids who seemed to be fighting. Her husband appeared to be soundly asleep in the front seat, while a younger man, probably his son, was behind the wheel.

That burned me. The driver was very young, probably only in his late teens, and it irked me that a kid that age should have the chance to drive such a treasure. I wanted to be in his place.

I had read a lot about the Edsel; books of auto lore were full of it. There was never anything quite like it. It was the greatest disaster the field had ever known. The myths and legends that had grown up around its name were beyond number.

All over the nation, in the scattered dingy garages and gas depots where car nuts gather to tinker and talk, the tales of the Edsel are told to this day. They say they built the car too big to fit in most garages. They say it was all horsepower, and no brake. They call it the ugliest machine ever designed by man. They retell the old jokes about its name. And there's one famous legend that when you got it going fast enough, the wind made a funny whistling noise as it rushed around that hood.

All the romance and mystery and tragedy of the old automobile was wrapped up in the Edsel. And the stories about it are remembered and retold long after its glittering contemporaries are so much scrap metal in the junkyards.

As I drove along beside it, all the old legends about the Edsel came flooding back to me, and I was lost in my own nostalgia. I tried a few more blasts on my horn, but the driver seemed intent on ignoring me, so I soon gave up. Besides, I was listening to see if the hood really did whistle in the wind.

I should have realized by then how peculiar the whole thing was – the road, the Edsel, the way they were ignoring me. But I was too enraptured to do much thinking. I was barely able to keep my eyes on the road.

I wanted to talk to the owners, of course. Maybe even borrow it for a little while. Since they were being so damned unfriendly about stopping, I decided to follow them for a bit, until they pulled in for gas or food. So I slowed and began to tail them. I wanted to stay fairly close without tailgating, so I kept to the lane on their immediate left.

As I trailed them, I remember thinking what a thorough collector the owner must be. Why, he had even taken the time to hunt up some rare, old style license plates. The kind that haven't been used in years. I was still mulling over that when we passed the sign announcing Exit 77.

The kid driving the Edsel suddenly looked agitated. He turned in his seat and looked back over his shoulder, almost as if he was trying to get another look at the sign we had already left behind. And then, with no warning, the Edsel swerved right into my lane.

I hit the brakes, but it was hopeless, of course. Everything seemed to happen at once. There was a horrible squealing noise, and I remember getting a brief glimpse of the kid's terrified face just before the two cars made impact. Then came the shock of the crash.

The Jag hit the Edsel broadside, smashing into the driver's compartment at seventy. Then it spun away into the guard rail, and came to a stop. The Edsel, hit straight on, flipped over on its back in the center of the road. I don't recall unfastening my seat belt or scrambling out of my car, but I must have done so, because the next thing I remember I was crawling on the roadway, dazed but unhurt.

I should have tried to do something right away, to answer the cries for help that were coming from the Edsel. But I didn't. I was still shaken, in shock. I don't know how long I lay there before the Edsel exploded and began to burn. The cries suddenly became screams. And then there were no cries.

By the time I climbed to my feet, the fire had burned itself out, and it was too late to do anything. But I still wasn't thinking very clearly. I could see lights in the distance, down the road that led from the exit ramp. I began to walk towards them.

That walk seemed to take forever. I couldn't seem to get my bearings, and I kept stumbling. The road was very poorly lighted, and I could hardly see where I was going. My hands were scraped badly once when I fell down. It was the only injury I suffered in the entire accident.

The lights were from a small café, a dingy place that had marked off a section of the abandoned highway as its airlot. There were only three customers inside when I stumbled through the door, but one of them was a local cop.

'There's been an accident,' I said from the doorway. 'Somebody's got to help them.'

The cop drained his coffee cup in a gulp, and rose from his chair. 'A copter crash, mister?' he said. 'Where is it?'

I shook my head. 'N-no. No. Cars. A crash, a highway accident. Out on the old interstate.' I pointed vaguely in the direction I had come.

Halfway across the room, the cop stopped suddenly and frowned. Everybody else laughed. 'Hell, no one's used that road in twenty years, you sot,' a fat man yelled from the corner of the room. 'It's got so many potholes we use it for a golf course,' he added, laughing loudly at his own joke.

The cop looked at me doubtfully. 'Go home and sober up, mister,' he said. 'I don't want to have to run you in.' He started back towards his chair.

I took a step into the room. 'Dammit, I'm telling the truth,' I said, angry now more than dazed. 'And I'm not drunk. There's been a collision on the interstate, and there's people trapped up there in . . .' My voice trailed off as it finally struck me that any help I could bring would be far too late.

The cop still looked dubious. 'Maybe you ought to go check it out,' the waitress suggested from behind the counter. 'He might be telling the truth. There was a highway accident last year, in Ohio somewhere. I remember seeing a story about it on 3V.'

'Yeah, I guess so,' the cop said at last. 'Let's go, buddy. And you better be telling the truth.'

We walked across the airlot in silence, and climbed into the four-man police copter. As he started up the blades, the cop looked at me and said, 'You know, if you're on the level, you and that other guy should get some kind of medal.'

I stared at him blankly.

'What I mean is, you're probably the only two cars to use that road in ten years. And you still manage to collide. Now that had to take some doing, didn't it?' He shook his head ruefully. 'Not everybody could pull off a stunt like that. Like I said, they ought to give you a medal.'

The interstate wasn't nearly as far from the café as it had seemed when I was walking. Once airborne, we covered the distance in less than five minutes. But there was something wrong. The highway looked somehow different from the air.

And suddenly I realized why. It was darker. Much darker.

Most of the lights were out, and those that weren't were dim and flickering.

As I sat there stunned, the copter came down with a thud in the middle of a pool of sickly yellow light thrown out by one of the fading lamps. I climbed out in a daze, and tripped as I accidentally stepped into one of the potholes that pockmarked the road. There was a big clump of weeds growing in the bottom of this one, and a lot more rooted in the jagged network of cracks that ran across the highway.

My head was starting to pound. This didn't make sense. None of it made sense. I didn't know what the hell was going on.

The cop came around from the other side of the copter, a portable med sensor slung over one shoulder on a leather strap. 'Let's move it,' he said. 'Where's this accident of yours?'

'Down the road, I think,' I mumbled, unsure of myself. There was no sign of my car, and I was beginning to think we might be on the wrong road altogether, although I didn't see how that could be.

It was the right road, though. We found my car a few minutes later, sitting by the guard rail on a pitch black section of highway where all the lights had burnt out. Yes, we found my car all right.

Only there wasn't a scratch on it. And there was no Edsel.

I remembered the Jaguar as I had left it. The windshield shattered. The entire front of the car in ruins. The right fender smashed up where it had scraped along the guard rail. And here it was, in mint condition.

The cop, scowling, played the med sensor over me as I stood there staring at my car. 'Well, you're not drunk,' he said at last, looking up. 'So I'm not going to run you in, even though I should. Here's what you're going to do, mister – you're going to get in that relic, and turn around, and get out of here as fast as you can. 'Cause if I *ever* see you around here again, you might have a real accident. Understand?'

I wanted to protest, but I couldn't find the words. What could I say that would possibly make sense? Instead, I nodded weakly. The cop turned with disgust, muttering something about practical jokes, and stalked back to his copter.

When he was gone, I walked up to the Jaguar and felt the front of it incredulously, feeling like a fool. But it was real. And when I climbed in and turned the key in the ignition, the engine rumbled reassuringly, and the headlights speared out into the darkness. I sat there for a long time before I finally swung the car out into the middle of the road, and made a U-turn.

The drive back to San Breta was long and rough. I was constantly bouncing in and out of potholes. And thanks to the poor lighting and the treacherous road conditions, I had to keep my speed at a minimum.

The road was lousy. There was no doubt about that. Usually I went out of my way to avoid roads that were this bad. There was too much chance of blowing a tire.

I managed to make it to San Breta without incident, taking it slow and easy. It was two A.M. before I pulled into town. The exit ramp, like the rest of the road, was cracked and darkened. And there was no sign to mark it.

I recalled from previous trips through the area that San Breta boasted a large hobbyist garage and gas depot, so I headed there and checked my car with a bored young night attendant. Then I went straight to the nearest motel. A night's sleep, I thought, would make everything make sense.

But it didn't. I was every bit as confused when I woke up in the morning. More so, even. Now something in the back of my head kept telling me the whole thing had been a bad dream. I swatted down that tempting thought out of hand, and tried to puzzle it out.

I kept puzzling through a shower and breakfast, and the short walk back to the gas depot. But I wasn't making any progress. Either my mind had been playing tricks on me, or something mighty funny had been going on last night. I didn't want to believe the former, so I made up my mind to investigate the latter.

The owner, a spry old man in his eighties, was on duty at the gas depot when I returned. He was wearing an old-fashioned mechanic's coverall, a quaint touch. He nodded amiably when I checked out the Jaguar.

'Good to see you again,' he said. 'Where you headed this time?'

'L.A. I'm taking the interstate this time.'

His eyebrows rose a trifle at that. 'The interstate? I thought you had more sense than that. That road's a disaster. No way to treat a fine piece of machinery like that Jaguar of yours.'

I didn't have the courage to try to explain, so I just grinned weakly and let him go get the car. The Jag had been washed, checked over, and gassed up. It was in prime shape.

I took a quick look for dents, but there were none to be found.

'How many regular customers you get around here?' I asked the old man as I was paying him. 'Local collectors, I mean, not guys passing through.'

He shrugged. 'Must be about a hundred in the state. We get most of their business. Got the best gas and the only decent service facilities in these parts.'

'Any decent collections?'

'Some,' he said. 'One guy comes in all the time with a Pierce-Arrow. Another fellow specializes in the forties. He's got a really fine collection. In good shape, too.'

I nodded. 'Anybody around here own an Edsel?' I asked.

'Hardly,' he replied. 'None of my customers have that kind of money. Why do you ask?'

I decided to throw caution on the road, so to speak. 'I saw one last night on the road. Didn't get to speak to the owner, though. Figured it might be somebody local.'

The old man's expression was blank, so I turned to get into the Jag. 'Nobody from around here,' he said as I shut the door. 'Must've been another guy driving through. Funny meeting him on the road like that, though. Don't often get—'

Then, just as I was turning the key in the ignition, his jaw dropped about six feet. 'Wait a minute!' he yelled. 'You said you were driving on the old interstate. You saw an Edsel on the interstate?'

I turned the motor off again. 'That's right,' I said.

'Christ,' he said. 'I'd almost forgotten, it's been so long. Was it a white Edsel? Five people in it?'

I opened the door and got out again. 'Yeah,' I said. 'Do you know something about it?'

The old man grabbed my shoulders with both hands. There was a funny look in his eyes. 'You just saw it?' he said, shaking me. 'Are you sure that's all that happened?'

I hesitated a moment, feeling foolish. 'No,' I finally admitted. 'I had a collision with it. That is, I thought I had a collision with it. But then—' I gestured limply towards the Jaguar.

The old man took his hands off me, and laughed. 'Again,' he muttered. 'After all these years.'

'What do you know about this?' I demanded. 'What the hell went on out there last night?'

He sighed. 'C'mon,' he said. 'I'll tell you all about it.'

*

'It was over forty years ago,' he told me over a cup of coffee in a café across the street. 'Back in the '70s. They were a family on a vacation outing. The kid and his father were taking shifts behind the wheel. Anyway, they had hotel reservations at San Breta. But the kid was driving, and it was late at night, and somehow he missed his exit. Didn't even notice it.

'Until he hit Exit 77, that is. He must've been really scared when he saw that sign. According to people who knew them, his father was a real bastard. The kind who'd give him a real hard time over something like that. We don't know what happened, but they figure the kid panicked. He'd only had his license about two weeks. Of all things, he tried to make a U-turn and head back towards San Breta.

'The other car hit him broadside. The driver of that car didn't have his seat belt on. He went through the windshield, hit the road, and was killed instantly. The people in the Edsel weren't so lucky. The Edsel turned over and exploded, with them trapped inside. All five were burned to death.'

I shuddered a little as I remembered the screams from the burning car. 'But that was forty years ago, you said. How does that explain what happened to me last night?'

'I'm getting to that,' the old man said. He picked up a donut, dunked it into his coffee, and chewed on it thoughtfully. 'Next thing was about two years later,' he said at last. 'Guy reported a collision to the cops. Collision with an Edsel. Late at night. On the interstate. The way he described it, it was an instant replay of the other crash. Only, when they got there, his car wasn't even dented. And there was no sign of the other car.

'Well, that guy was a local boy, so it was dismissed as a publicity stunt of some sort. But then, a year later, still another guy came in with the same story. This time he was from the east, couldn't possibly have heard of the first accident. The cops didn't know what to make of it.

'Over the years it happened again and again. There were a few things common to all the incidents. Each time it was late at night. Each time the man involved was alone in his car, with no other cars in sight. There were never any witnesses, as there had been for the first crash, the real one. All the collisions took place just beyond Exit 77, when the Edsel swerved and tried to make a U-turn.

'Lots of people tried to explain it. Hallucinations, somebody said. Highway hypnosis, claimed somebody else. Hoaxes, one guy argued. But only one explanation ever made sense, and that was the simplest. The

Edsel was a ghost. The papers made the most of that. "The haunted highway," they called the interstate.'

The old man stopped to drain his coffee, and then stared into the cup moodily. 'Well, the crashes continued right up through the years whenever the conditions were right. Until '93. And then traffic began slacking off. Fewer and fewer people were using the interstate. And there were fewer and fewer incidents.' He looked up at me. 'You were the first one in more than twenty years. I'd almost forgotten.' Then he looked down again, and fell silent.

I considered what he had said for a few minutes. 'I don't know,' I said finally, shaking my head. 'It all fits. But a ghost? I don't think I believe in ghosts. And it all seems so out of place.

'Not really,' said the old man, looking up. 'Think back on all the ghost stories you read as a kid. What did they all have in common?'

I frowned. 'Don't know.'

'Violent death, that's what. Ghosts were the products of murders and of executions, debris of blood and violence. Haunted houses were all places where someone had met a grisly end a hundred years before. But in twentieth century America, you didn't find the violent death in mansions and castles. You found it on the highways, the bloodstained highways where thousands died each year. A modern ghost wouldn't live in a castle or wield an axe. He'd haunt a highway, and drive a car. What could be more logical?'

It made a certain amount of sense. I nodded. 'But why this highway? Why this car? So many people died on the roads. Why is this case special?'

The old man shrugged. 'I don't know. What made one murder different from another? Why did only some produce ghosts? Who's to say? But I've heard theories. Some said the Edsel is doomed to haunt the highway forever because it is, in a sense, a murderer. It caused the accident, caused those deaths. This is a punishment.'

'Maybe,' I said doubtfully. 'But the whole family? You could make a case that it was the kid's fault. Or even the father's, for letting him drive with so little experience. But what about the rest of the family? Why should they be punished?'

'True, true,' the old man said. 'I never bought that theory myself. I've got my own explanation.' He looked me straight in the eye.

'I think they're lost,' he said.

'Lost?' I repeated, and he nodded.

'Yes,' he said. 'In the old days, when the roads were crowded, you couldn't just turn around when you missed an exit. You had to keep going, sometimes for miles and miles, before you could find a way to get off the road and then get back on. Some of the cloverleaves they designed were so complicated you might never find your way back to your exit.

'And that's what happened to the Edsel, I think. They missed their exit, and now they can't find it. They've got to keep going. Forever.' He sighed. Then he turned, and ordered another cup of coffee.

We drank in silence, then walked back to the gas depot. From there, I drove straight to the town library. It was all there, in the old newspapers on file. The details of the original accident, the first incident two years later, and the others, in irregular sequence. The same story, the same crash, over and over. Everything was identical, right down to the screams.

The old highway was dark and unlit that night when I resumed my trip. There were no traffic signs or white lines, but there were plenty of cracks and potholes. I drove slowly, lost in thought.

A few miles beyond San Breta I stopped and got out of the car. I sat there in the starlight until it was nearly dawn, looking and listening. But the lights stayed out, and I saw nothing.

Yet, around midnight, there was a peculiar whistling sound in the distance. It built quickly, until it was right on top of me, and then faded away equally fast.

It could have been a hovertruck off over the horizon somewhere, I suppose. I've never heard a hovertruck make that sort of noise, but still, it might have been a hovertruck.

But I don't think so.

I think it was the wind whistling through the nose of a rusty white ghost car, driving on a haunted highway you won't find on any road maps. I think it was the cry of a little lost Edsel, searching forever for the exit to San Breta.

The Second Kind of Loneliness

JUNE 18 – My relief left Earth today.

It will be at least three months before he gets here, of course. But he's on his way.

Today he lifted off from the Cape, just as I did, four long years ago. Out at Komarov Station he'll switch to a moon boat, then switch again in orbit around Luna, at Deepspace Station. There his voyage will really begin. Up to then he's still been in his own backyard.

Not until the *Charon* casts loose from Deepspace Station and sets out into the night will he feel it, *really* feel it, as I felt it four years ago. Not until Earth and Luna vanish behind him will it hit. He's known from the first that there's no turning back, of course. But there's a difference between knowing it and feeling it. Now he'll feel it.

There will be an orbital stopover around Mars, to send supplies down to Burroughs City. And more stops in the belt. But then the *Charon* will begin to gather speed. It will be going very fast when it reaches Jupiter. And much faster after it whips by, using the gravity of the giant planet like a slingshot to boost its acceleration.

After that there are no stops for the *Charon*. No stops at all until it reaches me, out here at the Cerberus Star Ring, six million miles beyond Pluto.

My relief will have a long time to brood. As I did.

I'm still brooding now, today, four years later. But then, there's not much else to do out here. Ringships are infrequent, and you get pretty weary of films and tapes and books after a time. So you brood. You think about your past, and dream about your future. And you try to keep the loneliness and the boredom from driving you out of your skull.

It's been a long four years. But it's almost over now. And it will be nice to get back. I want to walk on grass again, and see clouds, and eat an ice cream sundae.

Still, for all that, I don't regret coming. These four years alone in the darkness have done me good, I think. It's not as if I had left much. My days on Earth seem remote to me now, but I can still remember them if I try. The memories aren't all that pleasant. I was pretty screwed up back then.

I needed time to think, and that's one thing you get out here. The man who goes back on the *Charon* won't be the same one who came out here four years ago. I'll build a whole new life back on Earth. I know I will.

JUNE 20 – Ship today.

I didn't know it was coming, of course. I never do. The ringships are irregular, and the kind of energies I'm playing with out here turn radio signals into crackling chaos. By the time the ship finally punched through the static, the station's scanners had already picked it up and notified me.

It was clearly a ringship. Much bigger than the old system rust-buckets like the *Charon*, and heavily armored to withstand the stresses of the nullspace vortex. It came straight on, with no attempt to decelerate.

While I was heading down to the control room to strap in, a thought hit me. This might be the last. Probably not, of course. There's still three months to go, and that's time enough for a dozen ships. But you can never tell. The ringships are irregular, like I said.

Somehow the thought disturbed me. The ships have been part of my life for four years now. An important part. And the one today might have been the last. If so, I want it all down here. I want to remember it. With good reason, I think. When the ships come, that makes everything else worthwhile.

The control room is in the heart of my quarters. It's the center of everything, where the nerves and the tendons and the muscles of the station are gathered. But it's not very impressive. The room is very small, and once the door slides shut the walls and floor and ceiling are all a featureless white.

There's only one thing in the room: a horseshoe-shaped console that surrounds a single padded chair.

I sat down in that chair today for what might be the last time. I strapped myself in, and put on the earphones, and lowered the helmet. I reached for the controls and touched them and turned them on.

And the room vanished.

It's all done with holographs, of course. I *know* that. But that doesn't make a bit of difference when I'm sitting in that chair. Then, as far as I'm concerned, I'm not inside anymore. I'm out *there*, in the void. The control console is still there, and the chair. But the rest has gone. Instead, the aching darkness is everywhere, above me, below me, all around me. The distant sun is only one star among many, and all the stars are terribly far away.

That's the way it always is. That's the way it was today. When I threw that switch I was alone in the universe with the cold stars and the ring. The Cerberus Star Ring.

I saw the ring as if from outside, looking down on it. It's a vast structure, really. But from out here, it's nothing. It's swallowed by the immensity of it all, a slim silver thread lost in the blackness.

But I know better. The ring is huge. My living quarters take up but a single degree in the circle it forms, a circle whose diameter is more than a hundred miles. The rest is circuitry and scanners and power banks. And the engines, the waiting nullspace engines.

The ring turned silent beneath me, its far side stretching away into nothingness. I touched a switch on my console. Below me, the nullspace engines woke.

In the center of the ring, a new star was born.

It was a tiny dot amid the dark at first. Green today, bright green. But not always, and not for long. Nullspace has many colors.

I could see the far side of the ring then, if I'd wanted to. It was glowing with a light of its own. Alive and awake, the nullspace engines were pouring unimaginable amounts of energy inward, to rip wide a hole in space itself.

The hole had been there long before Cerberus, long before man. Men found it, quite by accident, when they reached Pluto. They built the ring around it. Later they found two other holes, and built other star rings.

The holes were small, too small. But they could be enlarged. Temporarily, at the expense of vast amounts of power, they could be ripped open. Raw energy could be pumped through that tiny, unseen hole in the universe until the placid surface of nullspace roiled and lashed back, and the nullspace vortex formed.

And now it happened.

The star in the center of the ring grew and flattened. It was a pulsing disc, not a globe. But it was still the brightest thing in the heavens. And it swelled visibly. From the spinning green disc, flame-like orange spears lanced out, and fell back, and smoky bluish tendrils uncoiled. Specks of red danced and flashed among the green, grew and blended. The colors all began to run together.

The flat, spinning, multi-colored star doubled in size, doubled again, again. A few minutes before it had not been. Now it filled the ring, lapped against the silver walls, seared them with its awful energy. It began to spin faster and faster, a whirlpool in space, a maelstrom of flame and light.

The vortex. The nullspace vortex. The howling storm that is not a storm and does not howl, for there is no sound in space.

To it came the ringship. A moving star at first, it took on visible form and shape almost faster than my human eyes could follow. It became a dark silver bullet in the blackness, a bullet fired at the vortex.

The aim was good. The ship hit very close to the center of the ring. The swirling colors closed over it.

I hit my controls. Even more suddenly than it had come, the vortex was gone. The ship was gone too, of course. Once more there was only me, and the ring, and the stars.

Then I touched another switch, and I was back in the blank white control room, unstrapping. Unstrapping for what might be the last time, ever.

Somehow I hope not. I never thought I'd miss anything about this place. But I will. I'll miss the ringships. I'll miss moments like today.

I hope I get a few more chances at it before I give it up forever. I want to feel the nullspace engines wake again under my hands, and watch the vortex boil and churn while I float alone between the stars. Once more, at least. Before I go.

JUNE 23 – That ringship has set me to thinking. Even more than usual.

It's funny that with all the ships I've seen pass through the vortex, I've never even given a thought to riding one. There's a whole new world on the other side of nullspace; Second Chance, a rich green planet of a star so far away that astronomers are still unsure whether it shares the same galaxy with us. That's the funny thing about the holes – you can't be sure where they lead until you go through.

When I was a kid, I read a lot about star travel. Most people didn't think it was possible. But those that did always mentioned Alpha Centauri as the first system we'd explore and colonize. Closest, and all that. Funny how wrong they were. Instead, our colonies orbit suns we can't even see. And I don't think we'll ever get to Alpha Centauri—

Somehow I never thought of the colonies in personal terms. Still can't. Earth is where I failed before. That's got to be where I succeed now. The colonies would be just another escape.

Like Cerberus?

JUNE 26 – Ship today. So the other wasn't the last, after all. But what about this one?

JUNE 29 – Why does a man volunteer for a job like this? Why does a man run to a silver ring six million miles beyond Pluto, to guard a hole in space? Why throw away four years of life alone in the darkness?

Why?

I used to ask myself that, in the early days. I couldn't answer it then. Now I think I can. I bitterly regretted the impulse that drove me out here, then. Now I think I understand it.

And it wasn't really an impulse. I ran to Cerberus. Ran. Ran to escape from loneliness.

That doesn't make sense?

Yet it does. I know about loneliness. It's been the theme of my life. I've been alone for as long as I can remember.

But there are two kinds of loneliness.

Most people don't realize the difference. I do. I've sampled both kinds.

They talk and write about the loneliness of the men who man the star rings. The lighthouses of space, and all that. And they're right.

There are times, out here at Cerberus, when I think I'm the only man in the universe. Earth was just a fever dream. The people I remember were just creations of my own mind.

There are times, out here, when I want someone to talk to so badly that I scream, and start pounding on the walls. There are times when the boredom crawls under my skin and all but drives me mad.

But there are *other* times, too. When the ringships come. When I go outside to make repairs. Or when I just sit in the control chair, imaging myself out into the darkness to watch the stars.

Lonely? Yes. But a solemn, brooding, tragic loneliness that a man hates with a passion – and yet loves so much he craves for more.

And then there is the second kind of loneliness.

You don't need the Cerberus Star Ring for that kind. You can find it anywhere on Earth. I know. I did. I found it everywhere I went, in everything I did.

It's the loneliness of people trapped within themselves. The loneliness of people who have said the wrong thing so often that they don't have the courage to say anything anymore.

The loneliness, not of distance, but of fear.

The loneliness of people who sit alone in furnished rooms in crowded cities, because they've got nowhere to go and no one to talk to. The loneliness of guys who go to bars to meet someone, only to discover they don't know how to strike up a conversation, and wouldn't have the courage to do so if they did.

There's no grandeur to that kind of loneliness. No purpose and no poetry. It's loneliness without meaning. It's sad and squalid and pathetic, and it stinks of self-pity.

Oh yes, it hurts at times to be alone among the stars.

But it hurts a lot more to be alone at a party. A lot more.

JUNE 30 – Reading yesterday's entry. Talk about self-pity—

JULY 1 – Reading *yesterday's* entry. My flippant mask. After four years, I still fight back whenever I try to be honest with myself. That's not good. If things are going to be any different this time, I have to understand myself.

So why do I have to ridicule myself when I admit that I'm lonely and vulnerable? Why do I have to struggle to admit that I was scared of life? No one's ever going to read this thing. I'm talking to myself, about myself.

So why are there so many things I can't bring myself to say?

JULY 4 – No ringship today. Too bad. Earth ain't never *had* no fireworks that could match the nullspace vortex, and I felt like celebrating.

But why do I keep Earth calendar out here, where the years are centuries and the seasons a dim memory? July is just like December. So what's the use?

JULY 10 – I dreamed of Karen last night. And now I can't get her out of my skull.

I thought I buried her long ago. It was all a fantasy anyway. Oh, she liked me well enough. Loved me, maybe. But no more than a half-dozen other guys. I wasn't really *special* to her, and she never realized just how special she was to me.

Nor how much I wanted to be special to her – how much I needed to be special to someone, somewhere.

So I elected her. But it was all a fantasy. And I knew it was, in my more rational moments. I had no right to be so hurt. I had no special claim on her.

But I thought I did, in my daydreams. And I was hurt. It was my fault, though, not hers.

Karen would never hurt anyone willingly. She just never realized how fragile I was.

Even out here, in the early years, I kept dreaming. I dreamed of how she'd change her mind. How she'd be waiting for me. Etc.

But that was more wish fulfillment. It was before I came to terms with myself out here. I know now that she won't be waiting. She doesn't need me, and never did. I was just a friend.

So I don't much like dreaming about her. That's bad. Whatever I do, I must *not* look up Karen when I get back. I have to start all over again. I have to find someone who *does* need me. And I won't find her if I try to slip back into my old life.

JULY 18 – A month since my relief left Earth. The *Charon* should be in the belt by now. Two months to go.

JULY 23 – Nightmares. God help me.

I'm dreaming of Earth again. And Karen. I can't stop. Every night it's the same.

It's funny, calling Karen a nightmare. Up to now she's always been a dream. A beautiful dream, with her long, soft hair, and her laugh, and that funny way she had of grinning. But those dreams were always wish fulfillments. In the dreams Karen needed me and wanted me and loved me.

The nightmares have the bite of truth to them. They're all the same. It's always a replay of me and Karen, together on that last night.

It was a good night, as nights went for me. We ate at one of my favorite restaurants, and went to a show. We talked together easily, about many things. We laughed together, too.

Only later, back at her place, I reverted to form. When I tried to tell her how much she meant to me, I remember how awkward and stupid I felt, how I struggled to get things out, how I stumbled over my own words. So much came out wrong.

I remember how she looked at me then. Strangely. How she tried to disillusion me. Gently. She was always gentle. And I looked into her eyes and listened to her voice. But I didn't find love, or need. Just – just pity, I guess.

Pity for an inarticulate jerk who'd been letting life pass him by without touching it. Not because he didn't want to. But because he was afraid to and didn't know how. She'd found that jerk, and loved him, in her way – she loved everybody. She'd tried to help, to give him some of her self-confidence, some of the courage and bounce that she faced life with. And, to an extent, she had.

Not enough, though. The jerk liked to make fantasies about the day he wouldn't be lonely anymore. And when Karen tried to help him, he thought she was his fantasy come to life. Or deluded himself into thinking that. The jerk suspected the truth all along, of course, but he lied to himself about it.

And when the day came that he couldn't lie any longer, he was still vulnerable enough to be hurt. He wasn't the type to grow scar tissue easily.

He didn't have the courage to try again with someone else. So he ran.

I hope the nightmares stop. I can't take them, night after night. I can't take reliving that hour in Karen's apartment.

I've had four years out here. I've looked at myself hard. I've changed what I didn't like, or tried to. I've tried to cultivate that scar tissue, to gather the confidence I need to face the new rejections I'm going to meet before I find acceptance. But I know myself damn well now, and I know it's only been a partial success. There will always be things that will hurt, things that I'll never be able to face the way I'd like to.

Memories of that last hour with Karen are among those things. *God*, I hope the nightmares end.

JULY 26 – More nightmares. Please, Karen. I loved you. Leave me alone. Please.

JULY 29 – There was a ringship yesterday, thank God. I needed one. It helped take my mind off Earth, off Karen. And there was no nightmare last night, for the first time in a week. Instead I dreamed of the nullspace vortex. The raging silent storm.

AUGUST 1 – The nightmares have returned. Not always Karen, now. Older memories too. Infinitely less meaningful, but still painful. All the stupid things I've said, all the girls I never met, all the things I never did.

Bad. Bad. I have to keep reminding myself. I'm not like that anymore. There's a new me, a me I built out here, six million miles beyond Pluto. Made of steel and stars and nullspace, hard and confident and self-assured. And not afraid of life.

The past is behind me. But it still hurts.

AUGUST 2 – Ship today. The nightmares continue. Damn.

AUGUST 3 – No nightmare last night. Second time for that, that I've rested easy after opening the hole for a ringship during the day. (Day? Night? Nonsense out here – but I still write as if they had meaning. Four years haven't even touched the Earth in me.) Maybe the vortex is scaring Karen away. But I never wanted to scare Karen away before. Besides, I shouldn't need crutches.

AUGUST 13 – Another ship came through a few nights ago. No dream afterwards. A pattern!

I'm fighting the memories. I'm thinking of other things about Earth. The good times. There were a lot of them, really, and there will be lots more when I get back. I'm going to make sure of that. These nightmares are stupid. I won't permit them to continue. There was so much else I shared with Karen, so much I'd like to recall. Why can't I?

AUGUST 18 – The *Charon* is about a month away. I wonder who my relief will be. I wonder what drove *him* out here?

Earth dreams continue. No. Call them Karen dreams. Am I even afraid to write her name now?

AUGUST 20 – Ship today. After it was through I stayed out and looked at stars. For several hours, it seems. Didn't seem as long at the time.

It's beautiful out here. Lonely, yes. But such a loneliness! You're alone with the universe, the stars spread out at your feet and scattered around your head.

Each one is a sun. Yet they still look cold to me. I find myself shivering, lost in the vastness of it all, wondering how it got there and what it means.

My relief, whoever it is, I hope he can appreciate this, as it should be appreciated. There are so many who can't, or won't. Men who walk at night, and never look up at the sky. I hope my relief isn't like that.

AUGUST 24 – When I get back to Earth, I *will* look up Karen. I must. How can I pretend that things are going to be different this time if I can't even work up the courage to do that? And they *are* going to be different. So I must face Karen, and prove that I've changed. Really changed.

AUGUST 25 – The nonsense of yesterday. *How* could I face Karen? What would I say to her? I'd only start deluding myself again, and wind up getting burned all over again. No. I must *not* see Karen. Hell, I can't even take the dreams.

AUGUST 30 – I've been going down to the control room and flipping myself out regularly of late. No ringships. But I find that going outside makes the memories of Earth dim. More and more I know I'll miss Cerberus. A year from now, I'll be back on Earth, looking up at the night sky, and remembering how the ring shone silver in the starlight. I know I will.

And the vortex. I'll remember the vortex, and the ways the colors swirled and mixed. Different every time.

Too bad I was never a holo buff. You could make a fortune back on Earth with a tape of the way the vortex looks when it spins. The ballet of the void. I'm surprised no one's ever thought of it.

Maybe I'll suggest it to my relief. Something to do to fill the hours, if he's interested. I hope he is. Earth would be richer if someone brought back a record.

I'd do it myself, but the equipment isn't right, and I don't have the time to modify it.

SEPTEMBER 4 – I've gone outside every day for the last week, I find. No nightmares. Just dreams of the darkness, laced with the colors of nullspace.

SEPTEMBER 9 – Continue to go outside, and drink it all in. Soon, soon now, all this will be lost to me. Forever. I feel as though I must take advantage of every second. I must memorize the way things are out here at Cerberus, so I can keep the awe and the wonder and the beauty fresh inside me when I return to Earth.

SEPTEMBER 10 – There hasn't been a ship in a long time. Is it over, then? Have I seen my last?

SEPTEMBER 12 – No ship today. But I went outside and woke the engines and let the vortex roar.

Why do I always write about the vortex roaring and howling? There is no sound in space. I hear nothing. But I watch it. And it does roar. It does.

The sounds of silence. But not the way the poets meant.

SEPTEMBER 13 – I've watched the vortex again today, though there was no ship.

I've never done that before. Now I've done it twice. It's forbidden. The costs in terms of power are enormous, and Cerberus lives on power. So why?

It's almost as though I don't want to give up the vortex. But I have to. Soon.

SEPTEMBER 14 – Idiot, idiot, idiot. What have I been doing? The *Charon* is less than a week away, and I've been gawking at the stars as if I'd never seen them before. I haven't even started to pack, and I've got to clean up my records for my relief, and get the station in order.

Idiot! Why am I wasting time writing in this damn *book*!

SEPTEMBER 15 – Packing almost done. I've uncovered some weird things, too. Things I tried to hide in the early years. Like my novel. I wrote it in the first six months, and thought it was great. I could hardly wait to get back to Earth, and sell it, and become an Author. Ah, yes. Read it over a year later. It stinks.

Also, I found a picture of Karen.

SEPTEMBER 16 – Today I took a bottle of scotch and a glass down to the control room, set them down on the console, and strapped myself in. Drank a toast to the blackness and the stars and the vortex. I'll miss them.

SEPTEMBER 17 – A day, by my calculations. A day. Then I'm on my way home, to a fresh start and a new life. If I have the courage to live it.

SEPTEMBER 18 – Nearly midnight. No sign of the *Charon*. What's wrong?

Nothing, probably. These schedules are never precise. Sometimes as much as a week off. So why do I worry? Hell, I was late getting here myself. I wonder what the poor guy I replaced was thinking then?

SEPTEMBER 20 – The *Charon* didn't come yesterday, either. After I got tired of waiting, I took that bottle of scotch and went back to the control room. And out. To drink another toast to the stars. And the vortex. I woke the vortex and let it flame, and toasted it.

A lot of toasts. I finished the bottle. And today I've got such a hangover I think I'll never make it back to Earth.

It was a stupid thing to do. The crew of the *Charon* might have seen the vortex colors. If they report me, I'll get docked a small fortune from the pile of money that's waiting back on Earth.

SEPTEMBER 21 – *Where is the Charon!* Did something happen to it? Is it coming?

SEPTEMBER 22 – I went outside again.

God, so beautiful, so lonely, so vast. Haunting, that's the word I want. The beauty out there is haunting. Sometimes I think I'm a fool to go back. I'm giving up all of eternity for a pizza and a lay and a kind word.

NO! What the hell am I writing! No. I'm going back, of course I am. I need Earth, I miss Earth, I want Earth. And this time it *will* be different.

I'll find another Karen, and this time I won't blow it.

SEPTEMBER 23 – I'm sick. God, but I'm sick. The things I've been thinking. I thought I had changed, but now I don't know. I find myself actually thinking about staying, about signing on for another term. I don't want to. No. But I think I'm still afraid of life, of Earth, of everything.

Hurry, *Charon*. Hurry, before I change my mind.

SEPTEMBER 24 – Karen or the vortex? Earth or eternity?

Dammit, how can I *think* that! Karen! Earth! I have to have courage, I have to risk pain, I have to taste life.

I am not a rock. Or an island. Or a star.

SEPTEMBER 25 – No sign of the *Charon*. A full week late. That happens sometimes. But not very often. It will arrive soon. I know it.

SEPTEMBER 30 – Nothing. Each day I watch, and wait. I listen to my scanners, and go outside to look, and pace back and forth through the ring. But nothing. It's never been this late. What's wrong?

OCTOBER 3 – Ship today. Not the *Charon*. I thought it was at first, when the scanners picked it up. I yelled loud enough to wake the vortex. But then I looked, and my heart sank. It was too big, and it was coming straight on without decelerating.

I went outside and let it through. And stayed out for a long time afterward.

OCTOBER 4 – I want to go home. Where are they? I don't understand. I don't understand.

They can't just leave me here. They can't. They won't.

OCTOBER 5 – Ship today. Ringship again. I used to look forward to them. Now I hate them, because they're not the *Charon*. But I let it through.

OCTOBER 7 – I unpacked. It's silly for me to live out of suitcases when I don't know if the *Charon* is coming, or when.

I still look for it, though. I wait. It's coming, I know. Just delayed somewhere. An emergency in the belt maybe. There are lots of explanations.

Meanwhile, I'm doing odd jobs around the ring. I never did get it in proper shape for my relief. Too busy star watching at the time to do what I should have been doing.

OCTOBER 8 (or thereabouts) – Darkness and despair.

I know why the *Charon* hasn't arrived. It isn't due. The calendar was all screwed up. It's January, not October. And I've been living on the wrong time for months. Even celebrated the Fourth of July on the wrong day.

I discovered it yesterday when I was doing those chores around the ring. I wanted to make sure everything was running right. For my relief.

Only there won't be any relief.

The *Charon* arrived three months ago. I – I destroyed it.

Sick. It was sick. I was sick, mad. As soon as it was done, it hit me. What I'd done. Oh, God. I screamed for hours.

And then I set back the wall calendar. And forgot. Maybe deliberately. Maybe I couldn't bear to remember. I don't know. All I know is that I forgot.

But now I remember. Now I remember it all.

The scanners had warned me of the *Charon's* approach. I was outside, waiting. Watching. Trying to get enough of the stars and the darkness to last me forever.

Through that darkness, *Charon* came. It seemed so slow compared to the ringships. And so small. It was my salvation, my relief, but it looked fragile, and silly, and somehow ugly. Squalid. It reminded me of Earth.

It moved towards docking, dropping into the ring from above, groping towards the locks in the habitable section of Cerberus. So very slow. I watched it come. Suddenly I wondered what I'd say to the crewmen, and my relief. I wondered what they'd think of me. Somewhere in my gut, a fist clenched.

And suddenly I couldn't stand it. Suddenly I was afraid of it. Suddenly I hated it.

So I woke the vortex.

A red flare, branching into yellow tongues, growing quickly, shooting off bluegreen bolts. One passed near the *Charon.* And the ship shuddered.

I tell myself, now, that I didn't realize what I was doing. Yet I knew the *Charon* was unarmored. I knew it couldn't take vortex energies, knew.

The *Charon* was so slow, the vortex so fast. In two heartbeats the maelstrom was brushing against the ship. In three it had swallowed it.

It was gone so fast. I don't know if the ship melted, or burst asunder, or crumpled. But I know it couldn't have survived. There's no blood on my star ring, though. The debris is somewhere on the other side of nullspace. If there is any debris.

The ring and the darkness looked the same as ever.

That made it so easy to forget. And I must have wanted to forget very much.

And now? What do I do *now?* Will Earth find out? Will there ever be relief? I want to go home.

Karen, I –

JUNE 18 – My relief left Earth today.

At least I think he did. Somehow the wall calendar was broken, so I'm not precisely sure of the date. But I've got it back into working order.

Anyway, it can't have been off for more than a few hours, or I would have noticed. So my relief *is* on the way. It will take him three months to get here, of course.

But at least he's coming.

With Morning Comes Mistfall

I was early to breakfast that morning, the first day after landing. But Sanders was already out on the dining balcony when I got there. He was standing alone by the edge, looking out over the mountains and the mists.

I walked up behind him and muttered hello. He didn't bother to reply. 'It's beautiful, isn't it?' he said, without turning.

And it was.

Only a few feet below balcony level the mists rolled, sending ghostly breakers to crash against the stones of Sanders' castle. A thick white blanket extended from horizon to horizon, cloaking everything. We could see the summit of the Red Ghost, off to the north; a barbed dagger of scarlet rock jabbing into the sky. But that was all. The other mountains were still below mist level.

But we were above the mists. Sanders had built his hotel atop the tallest mountain in the chain. We were floating alone in a swirling white ocean, on a flying castle amid a sea of clouds.

Castle Cloud, in fact. That was what Sanders had named the place. It was easy to see why.

'Is it always like this?' I asked Sanders, after drinking it all in for awhile.

'Every mistfall,' he replied, turning towards me with a wistful smile. He was a fat man, with a jovial red face. Not the sort who should smile wistfully. But he did.

He gestured towards the east, where Wraithworld's sun rising above the mists made a crimson and orange spectacle out of the dawn sky.

'The sun,' he said. 'As it rises, the heat drives the mists back into the valleys, forces them to surrender the mountains they've conquered during the night. The mists sink, and one by one the peaks come into view. By noon the whole range is visible for miles and miles. There's nothing like it on Earth, or anywhere else.'

He smiled again, and led me over to one of the tables scattered around the balcony. 'And then, at sunset, it's all reversed. You must watch mistrise tonight,' he said.

We sat down, and a sleek robowaiter came rolling out to serve us as the chairs registered our presence. Sanders ignored it. 'It's war, you know,' he continued. 'Eternal war between the sun and the mists. And the mists have the better of it. They have the valleys, and the plains, and the seacoasts. The sun has only a few mountaintops. And them only by day.'

He turned to the robowaiter and ordered coffee for both of us, to keep us occupied until the others arrived. It would be fresh-brewed, of course. Sanders didn't tolerate instants or synthetics on his planet.

'You like it here,' I said, while we waited for the coffee.

Sanders laughed. 'What's not to like? Castle Cloud has everything. Good food, entertainment, gambling, and all the other comforts of home. Plus this planet. I've got the best of both worlds, don't I?'

'I suppose so. But most people don't think in those terms. Nobody comes to Wraithworld for the gambling, or the food.'

Sanders nodded. 'But we do get some hunters. Out after rockcats and plains devils. And once in a while someone will come to look at the ruins.'

'Maybe,' I said. 'But those are your exceptions. Not your rule. Most of your guests are here for one reason.'

'Sure,' he admitted, grinning. 'The wraiths.'

'The wraiths,' I echoed. 'You've got beauty here, and hunting and fishing and mountaineering. But none of that brings the tourists here. It's the wraiths they come for.'

The coffee arrived then, two big steaming mugs accompanied by a pitcher of thick cream. It was very strong, and very hot, and very good. After weeks of spaceship synthetic, it was an awakening.

Sanders sipped at his coffee with care, his eyes studying me over the mug. He set it down thoughtfully. 'And it's the wraiths you've come for, too,' he said.

I shrugged. 'Of course. My readers aren't interested in scenery, no matter how spectacular. Dubowski and his men are here to find wraiths, and I'm here to cover the search.'

Sanders was about to answer, but he never got the chance. A sharp, precise voice cut in suddenly. 'If there are any wraiths to find,' the voice said.

We turned to face the balcony entrance. Dr Charles Dubowski, head of the Wraithworld Research Team, was standing in the doorway, squinting at the light. He had managed to shake the gaggle of research assistants who usually trailed him everywhere.

Dubowski paused for a second, then walked over to our table, pulled out a chair, and sat down. The robowaiter came rolling out again.

Sanders eyed the thin scientist with unconcealed distaste. 'What makes you think the wraiths aren't there, Doctor?' he asked.

Dubowski shrugged, and smiled lightly. 'I just don't feel there's enough evidence,' he said. 'But don't worry. I never let my feelings interfere with my work. I want the truth as much as anyone. So I'll run an impartial expedition. If your wraiths *are* out there, I'll find them.'

'Or they'll find you,' Sanders said. He looked grave. 'And that might not be too pleasant.'

Dubowski laughed. 'Oh, come now, Sanders. Just because you live in a castle doesn't mean you have to be so melodramatic.'

'Don't laugh, Doctor. The wraiths have killed people before, you know.'

'No proof of that,' said Dubowski. 'No proof at all. Just as there's no proof of the wraiths themselves. But that's why we're here. To find proof. Or disproof. But come, I'm famished.' He turned to our robowaiter, who had been standing by and humming impatiently.

Dubowski and I ordered rockcat steaks, with a basket of hot, freshly-baked biscuits. Sanders took advantage of the Earth supplies our ship had brought in last night, and got a massive slab of ham with a half dozen eggs.

Rockcat has a flavor that Earth meat hasn't had in centuries. I loved it, although Dubowski left much of his steak uneaten. He was too busy talking to eat.

'You shouldn't dismiss the wraiths so lightly,' Sanders said after the robowaiter had stalked off with our orders. 'There is evidence. Plenty of it. Twenty-two deaths since this planet was discovered. And eyewitness accounts of wraiths by the dozens.'

'True,' Dubowski said. 'But I wouldn't call that real evidence. Deaths? Yes. Most are simple disappearances, however. Probably people who fell off a mountain, or got eaten by a rockcat, or something. It's impossible to find the bodies in the mists.

'More people vanish every day on Earth, and nothing is thought of it. But here, every time someone disappears, people claim the wraiths got him. No, I'm sorry. It's not enough.'

'Bodies have been found, Doctor,' Sanders said quietly. 'Slain horribly. And not by falls or rockcats, either.'

It was my turn to cut in. 'Only four bodies have been recovered that I know of,' I said. 'And I've backgrounded myself pretty thoroughly on the wraiths.'

Sanders frowned. 'All right,' he admitted. 'But what about those four cases? Pretty convincing evidence, if you ask me.'

The food showed up about then, but Sanders continued as we ate. 'The first sighting, for example. That's never been explained satisfactorily. The Gregor Expedition.'

I nodded. Dave Gregor had captained the ship that had discovered Wraithworld, nearly seventy-five years earlier. He had probed through the mists with his sensors, and set his ship down on the seacoast plains. Then he sent teams out to explore.

There were two men in each team, both well armed. But in one case, only a single man came back, and he was in hysteria. He and his partner had gotten separated in the mists, and suddenly he heard a bloodcurdling scream. When he found his friend, he was quite dead. And something was standing over the body.

The survivor described the killer as manlike, eight feet tall, and somehow insubstantial. He claimed that when he fired at it, the blaster bolt went right through it. Then the creature had wavered, and vanished in the mists.

Gregor sent other teams out to search for the thing. They recovered the body, but that was all. Without special instruments, it was difficult to find the same place twice in the mists. Let alone something like the creature that had been described.

So the story was never confirmed. But nonetheless, it caused a sensation when Gregor returned to Earth. Another ship was sent to conduct a more thorough search. It found nothing. But one of its search teams disappeared without a trace.

And the legend of the mist wraiths was born, and began to grow. Other ships came to Wraithworld, and a trickle of colonists came and went, and Paul Sanders landed one day and erected the Castle Cloud so the public might safely visit the mysterious planet of the wraiths.

And there were other deaths, and other disappearances, and many people claimed to catch brief glimpses of wraiths prowling through the mists. And then someone found the ruins. Just tumbled stone blocks, now. But once, structures of some sort. The homes of the wraiths, people said.

There was evidence, I thought. And some of it was hard to deny. But Dubowski was shaking his head vigorously.

'The Gregor affair proves nothing,' he said. 'You know as well as I this planet has never been explored thoroughly. Especially the plains area, where Gregor's ship put down. It was probably some sort of animal that killed that man. A rare animal of some sort native to that area.'

'What about the testimony of his partner?' Sanders asked.

'Hysteria, pure and simple.'

'The other sightings? There have been an awful lot of them. And the witnesses weren't always hysterical.'

'Proves nothing,' Dubowski said, shaking his head. 'Back on Earth, plenty of people still claim to have seen ghosts and flying saucers. And here, with those damned mists, mistakes and hallucinations are naturally even easier.'

He jabbed at Sanders with the knife he was using to butter a biscuit. 'It's these mists that foul up everything. The wraith myth would have died long ago without the mists. Up to now, no one has had the equipment or the money to conduct a really thorough investigation. But we do. And we will. We'll get the truth once and for all.'

Sanders grimaced. 'If you don't get yourself killed first. The wraiths may not like being investigated.'

'I don't understand you, Sanders,' Dubowski said. 'If you're so afraid of the wraiths and so convinced that they're down there prowling about, why have you lived here so long?'

'Castle Cloud was built with safeguards,' Sanders said. 'The brochure we send prospective guests describes them. No one is in any danger here. For one thing, the wraiths won't come out of the mists. And we're in sunlight most of the day. But it's a different story down in the valleys.'

'That's superstitious nonsense. If I had to guess, I'd say these mist wraiths of yours were nothing but transplanted Earth ghosts. Phantoms of someone's imagination. But I won't guess – I'll wait until the results are in. Then we'll see. If they are real, they won't be able to hide from us.'

Sanders looked over at me. 'What about you? Do you agree with him?'

'I'm a journalist,' I said carefully. 'I'm just here to cover what happens. The wraiths are famous, and my readers are interested. So I've got no opinions. Or none that I'd care to broadcast, anyway.'

Sanders lapsed into a disgruntled silence, and attacked his ham and eggs with a renewed vigor. Dubowski took over for him, and steered the conversation over to the details of the investigation he was planning. The rest of the meal was a montage of eager talk about wraith traps, and search plans, and roboprobes, and sensors. I listened carefully and took mental notes for a column on the subject.

Sanders listened carefully, too. But you could tell from his face that he was far from pleased by what he heard.

*

Nothing much else happened that day. Dubowski spent his time at the spacefield, built on a small plateau below the castle, and supervised the unloading of his equipment. I wrote a column on his plans for the expedition, and beamed it back to Earth. Sanders tended to his other guests, and did whatever else a hotel manager does, I guess.

I went out to the balcony again at sunset, to watch the mists rise.

It was war, like Sanders had said. At mistfall, I had seen the sun victorious in the first of the daily battles. But now the conflict was renewed. The mists began to creep back to the heights as the temperature fell. Wispy gray-white tendrils stole up silently from the valleys, and curled around the jagged mountain peaks like ghostly fingers. Then the fingers began to grow thicker and stronger, and after awhile they pulled the mists up after them.

One by one the stark, wind-carved summits were swallowed up for another night. The Red Ghost, the giant to the north, was the last mountain to vanish in the lapping white ocean. And then the mists began to pour in over the balcony ledge and close around Castle Cloud itself.

I went back inside. Sanders was standing there, just inside the doors. He had been watching me.

'You were right,' I said. 'It was beautiful.'

He nodded. 'You know, I don't think Dubowski has bothered to look yet,' he said.

'Busy, I guess.'

Sanders sighed. 'Too damn busy. C'mon. I'll buy you a drink.'

The hotel bar was quiet and dark, with the kind of mood that promotes good talk and serious drinking. The more I saw of Sanders' castle, the more I liked the man. Our tastes were in remarkable accord.

We found a table in the darkest and most secluded part of the room, and ordered drinks from a stock that included liquors from a dozen worlds. And we talked.

'You don't seem very happy to have Dubowski here,' I said after the drinks came. 'Why not? He's filling up your hotel.'

Sanders looked up from his drink and smiled. 'True. It is the slow season. But I don't like what he's trying to do.'

'So you try to scare him away?'

Sanders' smile vanished. 'Was I that transparent?'

I nodded.

He sighed. 'Didn't think it would work,' he said. He sipped thoughtfully at his drink. 'But I had to try something.'

'Why?'

'Because. Because he's going to destroy this world, if I let him. By the time he and his kind get through, there won't be a mystery left in the universe.'

'He's just trying to find some answers. Do the wraiths exist? What about the ruins? Who built them? Didn't you ever want to know those things, Sanders?'

He drained his drink, looked around, and caught the waiter's eye to order another. No robowaiters in here. Only human help. Sanders was particular about atmosphere.

'Of course,' he said when he had his drink. 'Everyone's wondered about those questions. That's why people come here to Wraithworld, to the Castle Cloud. Each guy who touches down here is secretly hoping he'll have an adventure with the wraiths, and find out all the answers personally.

'So he doesn't. So he slaps on a blaster and wanders around the mist forests for a few days, or a few weeks, and finds nothing. So what? He can come back and search again. The dream is still there, and the romance, and the mystery.

'And who knows? Maybe one trip he glimpses a wraith drifting through the mists. Or something he thinks is a wraith. And then he'll go home happy, 'cause he's been part of a legend. He's touched a little bit of creation that hasn't had all the awe and the wonder ripped from it yet by Dubowski's sort.'

He fell silent and stared morosely into his drink. Finally, after a long pause, he continued. 'Dubowski! Bah! He makes me boil. He comes here with his ship full of lackeys and his million credit grant and all his gadgets, to hunt for wraiths. Oh, he'll get them all right. That's what frightens me. Either he'll prove they don't exist, or he'll find them, and they'll turn out to be some kind of submen or animal or something.'

He emptied his glass again, savagely. 'And that will ruin it. Ruin it, you hear! He'll answer all the questions with his gadgets, and there'll be nothing left for anyone else. It isn't fair.'

I sat there and sipped quietly at my drink and said nothing. Sanders ordered another. A foul thought was running around in my head. Finally I had to say it aloud.

'If Dubowski answers all the questions,' I said, 'then there will be no reason to come here anymore. And you'll be put out of business. Are you sure that's not why you're so worried?'

Sanders glared at me, and I thought he was going to hit me for a second. But he didn't. 'I thought you were different. You looked at mistfall, and understood. I thought you did, anyway. But I guess I was wrong.' He jerked his head toward the door. 'Get out of here,' he said.

I rose. 'Alright,' I said. 'I'm sorry, Sanders. But it's my job to ask nasty questions like that.'

He ignored me, and I left the table. When I reached the door, I turned and looked back across the room. Sanders was staring into his drink again, and talking loudly to himself.

'Answers,' he said. He made it sound obscene. 'Answers. Always they have to have answers. But the questions are so much finer. Why can't they leave them alone?'

I left him alone then. Alone with his drinks.

*

The next few weeks were hectic ones, for the expedition and for me.

Dubowski went about things thoroughly, you had to give him that. He had planned his assault on Wraithworld with meticulous precision.

Mapping came first. Thanks to the mists, what maps there were of Wraithworld were very crude by modern standards. So Dubowski sent out a whole fleet of roboprobes, to skim above the mists and steal their secrets with sophisticated sensory devices. From the information that came pouring in, a detailed topography of the region was pieced together.

That done, Dubowski and his assistants then used the maps to carefully plot every recorded wraith sighting since the Gregor Expedition. Considerable data on the sightings had been compiled and analyzed long before we left Earth, of course. Heavy use of the matchless collection on wraiths in the Castle Cloud library filled in the gaps that remained. As expected, sightings were most common in the valleys around the hotel, the only permanent human habitation on the planet.

When the plotting was completed, Dubowski set out his wraith traps, scattering most of them in the areas where wraiths had been reported most frequently. He also put a few in distant, outlying regions, however, including the seacoast plain where Gregor's ship had made the initial contact.

The traps weren't really traps, of course. They were squat duralloy pillars, packed with most every type of sensing and recording equipment known to Earth science. To the traps, the mists were all but non-existent. If some unfortunate wraith wandered into survey range, there would be no way it could avoid detection.

Meanwhile, the mapping roboprobes were pulled in to be overhauled and reprogrammed, and then sent out again. With the topography known in detail, the probes could be sent through the mists on low-level patrols without fear of banging into a concealed mountain. The sensing equipment carried by the probes was not the equal of that in the wraith traps, of course. But the probes had a much greater range, and could cover thousands of square miles each day.

Finally, when the wraith traps were deployed and the roboprobes were in the air, Dubowski and his men took to the mist forests themselves. Each carried a heavy backpack of sensors and detection devices. The human search teams had more mobility than the wraith traps, and more sophisticated equipment than the probes. They covered a different area each day, in painstaking detail.

I went along on a few of those trips, with a backpack of my own. It made for some interesting copy, even though we never found anything. And while on search, I fell in love with the mist forests.

The tourist literature likes to call them 'the ghastly mist forests of haunted Wraithworld.' But they're not ghastly. Not really. There's a strange sort of beauty there, for those who can appreciate it.

The trees are thin and very tall, with white bark and pale gray leaves. But the forests are not without color. There's a parasite, a hanging moss of some sort, that's very common, and it drips from the overhanging branches in cascades of dark green and scarlet. And there are rocks, and vines, and low bushes choked with misshapen purplish fruits.

But there's no sun, of course. The mists hide everything. They swirl and slide around you as you walk, caressing you with unseen hands, clutching at your feet.

Once in a while, the mists play games with you. Most of the time you walk through a thick fog, unable to see more than a few feet in any direction, your own shoes lost in the mist carpet below. Sometimes, though, the fog closes in suddenly. And then you can't see at all. I blundered into more than one tree when that happened.

At other times, though, the mists – for no apparent reason – will roll back suddenly, and leave you standing alone in a clear pocket within a cloud. That's when you can see the forest in all its grotesque beauty. It's a brief, breathtaking glimpse of never-never land. Moments like that are few and short-lived. But they stay with you.

They stay with you.

In those early weeks, I didn't have much time for walking in the forests, except when I joined a search team to get the feel of it. Mostly I was busy writing. I did a series on the history of the planet, highlighted by the stories of the most famous sightings. I did feature profiles on some of the more colorful members of the expedition. I did a piece on Sanders, and the problems he encountered and overcame in building Castle Cloud. I did science pieces on the little known about the planet's ecology. I did mood pieces about the forests and the mountains. I did speculative thought pieces about the ruins. I wrote about rockcat hunting, and mountain climbing, and the huge and dangerous swamp lizards native to some offshore islands.

And, of course, I wrote about Dubowski and his search. On that I wrote reams.

Finally, however, the search began to settle down into dull routine, and I began to exhaust the myriad other topics Wraithworld offered. My output began to decline. I started to have time on my hands.

That's when I really began to enjoy Wraithworld. I began to take daily walks through the forests, ranging wider each day. I visited the ruins, and flew half a continent away to see the swamp lizards firsthand instead of by holo. I befriended a group of hunters passing through, and shot myself a rockcat. I accompanied some other hunters to the western seacoast, and nearly got myself killed by a plains devil.

And I began to talk to Sanders again.

Through all of this, Sanders had pretty well ignored me and Dubowski and everyone else connected with the wraith research. He spoke to us grudgingly, if at all, greeted us curtly, and spent all his free time with his other guests.

At first, after the way he had talked in the bar that night, I worried about what he might do. I had visions of him murdering someone out in the mists, and trying to make it look like a wraith killing. Or maybe just sabotaging the wraith traps. But I was sure he would try something to scare off Dubowski or otherwise undermine the expedition.

Comes of watching too much holovision, I guess. Sanders did nothing of the sort. He merely sulked, glared at us in the castle corridors, and gave us less than full cooperation at all times.

After awhile, though, he began to warm up again. Not towards Dubowski and his men.

Just towards me.

I guess that was because of my walks in the forests. Dubowski never went out into the mists unless he had to. And then he went out reluctantly, and came back quickly. His men followed their chief's example. I was the only joker in the deck. But then, I wasn't really part of the same deck.

Sanders noticed, of course. He didn't miss much of what went on in his castle. And he began to speak to me again. Civilly. One day, finally, he even invited me for drinks again.

It was about two months into the expedition. Winter was coming to Wraithworld and Castle Cloud, and the air was getting cold and crisp. Dubowski and I were out on the dining balcony, lingering over coffee after another superb meal. Sanders sat at a nearby table, talking to some tourists.

I forget what Dubowski and I were discussing. Whatever it was, Dubowski interrupted me with a shiver at one point. 'It's getting cold out here,' he complained. 'Why don't we move inside?' Dubowski never liked the dining balcony very much.

I sort of frowned. 'It's not that bad,' I said. 'Besides, it's nearly sunset. One of the best parts of the day.'

Dubowski shivered again, and stood up. 'Suit yourself,' he said. 'But I'm going in. I don't feel like catching a cold just so you can watch another mistfall.'

He started to walk off. But he hadn't taken three steps before Sanders was up out of his seat, howling like a wounded rockcat.

'Mistfall,' he bellowed. '*Mistfall!*' He launched into a long, incoherent string of obscenities. I had never seen Sanders so angry, not even when he threw me out of the bar that first night. He stood there, literally trembling with rage, his face flushed, his fat fists clenching and unclenching at his sides.

I got up in a hurry, and got between them. Dubowski turned to me, looking baffled and scared. 'Wha—' he started.

'Get inside,' I interrupted. 'Get up to your room. Get to the lounge. Get somewhere. Get anywhere. But get out of here before he kills you.'

'But – but – what's wrong? What happened? I don't—'

'Mistfall is in the morning,' I told him. 'At night, at sunset, it's mistrise. Now go.'

'That's *all?* Why should that get him so – so—'

'*GO!*'

Dubowski shook his head, as if to say he still didn't understand what was going on. But he went.

I turned to Sanders. 'Calm down,' I said. 'Calm down.'

He stopped trembling, but his eyes threw blaster bolts at Dubowski's back. 'Mistfall,' he muttered. 'Two months that bastard has been here, and he doesn't know the difference between mistfall and mistrise.'

'He's never bothered to watch either one,' I said. 'Things like that don't interest him. That's his loss, though. No reason for you to get upset about it.'

He looked at me, frowning. Finally he nodded. 'Yeah,' he said. 'Maybe you're right.' He sighed. 'But *mistfall!* Hell.' There was a short silence, then, 'I need a drink. Join me?'

I nodded.

We wound up in the same dark corner as the first night, at what must have been Sanders' favorite table. He put away three drinks before I had finished my first. Big drinks. Everything in Castle Cloud was big.

There were no arguments this time. We talked about mistfall, and the forests, and the ruins. We talked about the wraiths, and Sanders lovingly told me the stories of the great sightings. I knew them all already, of course. But not the way Sanders told them.

At one point, I mentioned that I'd been born in Bradbury when my parents were spending a short vacation on Mars. Sanders' eyes lit up at that, and he spent the next hour or so regaling me with Earthman jokes. I'd heard them all before, too. But I was getting more than a little drunk, and somehow they all seemed hilarious.

After that night, I spent more time with Sanders than with anyone else in the hotel. I thought I knew Wraithworld pretty well by that time. But that was an empty conceit, and Sanders proved it. He showed me hidden spots in the forests that have haunted me ever since. He took me to island swamps, where the trees are of a very different sort and sway horridly without a wind. We flew to the far north, to another mountain range where the peaks are higher and sheathed in ice, and to a southern plateau where the mists pour eternally over the edge in a ghostly imitation of a waterfall.

I continued to write about Dubowski and his wraith hunt, of course. But there was little new to write about, so most of my time was spent with Sanders. I didn't worry too much about my output. My Wraithworld series had gotten excellent play on Earth and most of the colony worlds, so I thought I had it made.

Not so.

I'd been on Wraithworld just a little over three months when my syndicate beamed me. A few systems away, a civil war had broken out on a planet called New Refuge. They wanted me to cover it. No news was coming out of Wraithworld anyway, they said, since Dubowski's expedition still had over a year to run.

Much as I liked Wraithworld, I jumped at the chance. My stories had been getting a little stale, and I was running out of ideas, and the New Refuge thing sounded like it could be very big.

So I said goodbye to Sanders and Dubowski and Castle Cloud, and took a last walk through the mist forests, and booked passage on the next ship through.

*

The New Refuge civil war was a firecracker. I spent less than a month on the planet, but it was a dreary month. The place had been colonized by religious fanatics, but the original cult had schismed, and both sides accused the other of heresy. It was all very dingy. The planet itself had all the charm of a Martian suburb.

I moved on as quickly as I could, hopping from planet to planet, from story to story. In six months, I had worked myself back to Earth. Elections were coming up, so I got slapped onto a political beat. That was fine by me. It was a lively campaign, and there was a ton of good stories to be mined.

But throughout it all, I kept myself up on the little news that came out of Wraithworld. And finally, as I'd expected, Dubowski announced a press conference. As the syndicate's resident wraith, I got myself assigned to cover, and headed out on the fastest starship I could find.

I got there a week before the conference, ahead of everyone else. I had beamed Sanders before taking ship, and he met me at the spaceport. We adjourned to the dining balcony, and had our drinks served out there.

'Well?' I asked him, after we had traded amenities. 'You know what Dubowski's going to announce?'

Sanders looked very glum. 'I can guess,' he said. 'He called in all his damn gadgets a month ago, and he's been cross-checking findings on a computer. We've had a couple of wraith sightings since you left. Dubowski moved in hours after each sighting, and went over the areas with a fine-tooth comb. Nothing. That's what he's going to announce, I think. Nothing.'

I nodded. 'Is that so bad, though? Gregor found nothing.'

'Not the same,' Sanders said. 'Gregor didn't look the way Dubowski has. People will believe him, whatever he says.'

I wasn't so sure of that, and was about to say so, when Dubowski arrived. Someone must have told him I was there. He came striding out on the balcony, smiling, spied me, and came over to sit down.

Sanders glared at him and studied his drink. Dubowski trained all of his attention on me. He seemed very pleased with himself. He asked what I'd been doing since I left, and I told him, and he said that was nice.

Finally I got to ask him about his results. 'No comment,' he said. 'That's what I've called the press conference for.'

'C'mon,' I said. 'I covered you for months when everybody else was ignoring the expedition. You can give me some kind of beat. What have you got?'

He hesitated. 'Well, okay,' he said doubtfully. 'But don't release it yet. You can beam it out a few hours ahead of the conference. That should be enough time for a beat.'

I nodded agreement. 'What do you have?'

'The wraiths,' he said. 'I have the wraiths, bagged neatly. They don't exist. I've got enough evidence to prove it beyond a shadow of a doubt.' He smiled broadly.

'Just because you didn't find anything?' I started. 'Maybe they were avoiding you. If they're sentient, they might be smart enough. Or maybe they're beyond the ability of your sensors to detect.'

'Come now,' Dubowski said. 'You don't believe that. Our wraith traps had every kind of sensor we could come up with. If the wraiths existed, they would have registered on something. But they didn't. We had the traps planted in the areas where three of Sanders' so-called sightings took place. Nothing. Absolutely nothing. Conclusive proof that those people were seeing things. Sightings, indeed.'

'What about the deaths, the vanishings?' I asked. 'What about the Gregor Expedition and the other classic cases?'

His smile spread. 'Couldn't disprove all the deaths, of course. But our probes and our searches turned up four skeletons.' He ticked them off on his fingers. 'Two were killed by a rockslide, and one had rockcat claw marks on the bones.'

'The fourth?'

'Murder,' he said. 'The body was buried in a shallow grave, clearly by human hands. A flood of some sort had exposed it. It was down in the records as a disappearance. I'm sure all the other bodies could be found, if we searched long enough. And we'd find that all died perfectly normal deaths.'

Sanders raised his eyes from his drink. They were bitter eyes. 'Gregor,' he said stubbornly. 'Gregor and the other classics.'

Dubowski's smile became a smirk. 'Ah, yes. We searched that area quite thoroughly. My theory was right. We found a tribe of apes nearby. Big brutes. Like giant baboons, with dirty white fur. Not a very successful species, either. We found only one small tribe, and they were dying out. But clearly, that was what Gregor's man sighted. And exaggerated all out of proportion.'

There was silence. Then Sanders spoke, but his voice was beaten. 'Just one question,' he said softly. 'Why?'

That brought Dubowski up short, and his smile faded. 'You never have understood, have you, Sanders?' he said. 'It was for truth. To free this planet from ignorance and superstition.'

'Free Wraithworld?' Sanders said. 'Was it enslaved?'

'Yes,' Dubowski answered. 'Enslaved by foolish myth. By fear. Now this planet will be free, and open. We can find out the truth behind those ruins now, without murky legends about half-human wraiths to fog the facts. We can open this planet for colonization. People won't be afraid to come here, and live, and farm. We've conquered the fear.'

'A colony world? Here?' Sanders looked amused. 'Are you going to bring big fans to blow away the mists, or what? Colonists have come before. And left. The soil's all wrong. You can't farm here, with all these mountains. At least not on a commercial scale. There's no way you can make a profit growing things on Wraithworld.

'Besides, there are hundreds of colony worlds crying for people. Did you need another so badly? Must Wraithworld become yet another Earth?'

He shook his head sadly, drained his drink, and continued. 'You're the one who doesn't understand, Doctor. Don't kid yourself. You haven't freed Wraithworld. You've destroyed it. You've stolen its wraiths, and left an empty planet.'

Dubowski shook his head. 'I think you're wrong. They'll find plenty of good, profitable ways to exploit this planet. But even if you were correct, well, it's just too bad. Knowledge is what man is all about. People like you have tried to hold back progress since the beginning of time. But they failed, and you failed. Man needs to know.'

'Maybe,' Sanders said. 'But is that the *only* thing man needs? I don't think so. I think he also needs mystery, and poetry, and romance. I think he needs a few unanswered questions to make him brood and wonder.'

Dubowski stood up abruptly, and frowned. 'This conversation is as pointless as your philosophy, Sanders. There's no room in my universe for unanswered questions.'

'Then you live in a very drab universe, Doctor.'

'And you, Sanders, live in the stink of your own ignorance. Find some new superstitions if you must. But don't try to foist them off on me with your tales and legends. I've got no time for wraiths.' He looked at me. 'I'll see you at the press conference,' he said. Then he turned and walked briskly from the balcony.

Sanders watched him depart in silence, then swiveled in his chair to look out over the mountains. 'The mists are rising,' he said.

*

Sanders was wrong about the colony too, as it turned out. They did establish one, although it wasn't much to boast of. Some vineyards, some factories, and a few thousand people; all belonging to a couple of big companies.

Commercial farming did turn out to be unprofitable, you see. With one exception – a native grape, a fat gray thing the size of a lemon. So Wraithworld has only one export, a smoky white wine with a mellow, lingering flavor.

They call it mistwine, of course. I've grown fond of it over the years. The taste reminds me of mistfall somehow, and makes me dream. But that's probably me, not the wine. Most people don't care for it much.

Still, in a very minor way, it's a profitable item. So Wraithworld is still a regular stop on the spacelanes. For freighters, at least.

The tourists are long gone, though. Sanders was right about that. Scenery they can get closer to home, and cheaper. The wraiths were why they came.

Sanders is long gone, too. He was too stubborn and too impractical to buy in on the mistwine operations when he had the chance. So he stayed behind his ramparts at Castle Cloud until the last. I don't know what happened to him afterwards, when the hotel finally went out of business.

The castle itself is still there. I saw it a few years ago, when I stopped for a day en route to a story on New Refuge. It's already crumbling, though. Too expensive to maintain. In a few years, you won't be able to tell it from those other, older ruins.

Otherwise the planet hasn't changed much. The mists still rise at sunset, and fall at dawn. The Red Ghost is still stark and beautiful in the early morning light. The forests are still there, and the rockcats still prowl.

Only the wraiths are missing.

Only the wraiths.

THREE
THE LIGHT OF
DISTANT STARS

THE LIGHT OF DISTANT STARS

Here's the thing of it. I was born and raised in Bayonne, New Jersey, and never went *anywhere* . . . not till college, at any rate.

Bayonne is a peninsula, part of New York City's metropolitan area, but when I was growing up it was a world unto itself. An industrial city dominated by its oil refineries and its navy base, it was small, three miles long and only one mile wide. Bayonne adjoins Jersey City on the north; elsewise it is entirely surrounded by water, with Newark Bay to the west, New York Bay to the east, and the narrow deepwater channel that connects them, the Kill van Kull, to the south. Big ocean-going freighters travel along the Kill by night and day, on their way to and from Elizabeth and Port Newark.

When I was four years old, my family moved into the new projects on First Street, facing the dark, polluted waters of the Kill. Across the channel the lights of Staten Island glimmered by night, far off and magical. Aside from a trip to the Staten Island Zoo every three or four years, we never crossed the Kill.

You could get to Staten Island easily enough by driving across the Bayonne Bridge, but my family did not own a car, and neither of my parents drove. You could cross by ferry too. The terminal was only a few blocks from the projects, next to Uncle Milty's amusement park. There was a secret 'cove' a kid could get to by walking along the oil-slick rocks during low tide and slipping around the fence, a grassy little ledge hidden from both the ferry and the street. I liked to go there sometimes, to sit on the grass above the water with a candy bar and some funny books, reading and watching the ferries go back and forth between Bayonne and Staten Island.

The boats made frequent crossings. Often one would be coming as the other one was going, and they would pass each other in the middle of the channel. The ferry line operated three boats, named the *Deneb*, the *Altair*, and the *Vega*. For me, no tramp steamer or clipper ship could have been any more romantic than those little ferries. The fact that they were all named after stars was part of their magic, I think. Although the three boats were identical, so far as I could tell, the *Altair* was always my favorite. Maybe that had something to do with *Forbidden Planet*.

Sometimes, after supper, our apartment could seem crowded and noisy, even if it was just me and my parents and my two sisters. If my parents had friends over, the kitchen would grow hazy with cigarette smoke and loud with voices. Sometimes I would retreat to my own room and close the door. Sometimes I'd stay in the living room, watching TV with my sisters. And sometimes I'd go outside.

Just across the street was Brady's Dock and a long, narrow park that ran beside the Kill van Kull. I would sit on a bench there and watch the big ships go by, or I'd stretch out in the grass and look up at the stars, whose lights were even further off than those of Staten Island. Even on the hottest, muggiest summer nights, the stars always gave me a thrill. Orion was the first constellation that I learned to recognize. I would gaze up at its two bright stars, blue Rigel and red Betelgeuse, and wonder if there was anyone up there looking back down at me.

Fans write of a 'sense of wonder,' and argue over how to define it. To me, a sense of wonder is the feeling I got while lying in the grass beside the Kill van Kull, pondering the light of distant stars. They always made me feel very large and very small. It was a sad feeling, but strange and sweet as well.

Science fiction can give me that same feeling.

My earliest exposure to SF came from television. Mine was the first generation weaned on the tube. We might not have had *Sesame Street*, but we had *Ding Dong School* during the week, *Howdy Doody* on Saturday mornings, and cartoons every day of the week. On *Andy's Gang* Froggy the Gremlin plunked his magic twanger. Though I watched Gene Autry, Roy Rogers, and Hopalong Cassidy, cowboys were more my father's passion than my own. I preferred knights: *Robin Hood* and *Ivanhoe* and *Sir Lancelot*. But nothing could match the space shows.

I must have seen *Captain Video* on the Dumont network, since I have a vague memory of his nemesis Tobor ('Robot' spelled backwards, of course). I don't recall *Space Cadet*, though; my memories of Tom Corbett derive from the books by Carey Rockwell that I read later. I did catch *Flash Gordon*, for certain . . . the TV show, not the movie serial. In one episode Flash visits a planet whose people are good by day and bad by night, a concept that I thought was so cool that I used it in some of my own earliest attempts at stories.

All of these paled, however, before *Rocky Jones, Space Ranger*, the creme de la creme of the SF shows of the early '50s. Rocky had the best looking spaceship on the tube, the sleek, silvery *Orbit Jet*. I was devastated when the *Orbit Jet* got destroyed one episode, but fortunately it was soon replaced by the *Silver Moon*, which looked exactly the same. His crew included the usual comic co-pilot, simpering girlfriend, pompous professor, and annoying little kid, but he also had Pinto Vortando. (Anyone who thinks Gene Roddenberry brought anything fresh to television should take a look at *Rocky Jones*. It's all there, but for Spock, who owes more to D.C. Fontana than to Roddenberry. Harvey Mudd is just Pinto Vortando with the accent toned down).

When I wasn't watching spacemen and aliens on television, I was playing with them at home. Along with the usual cowboys, knights, and green army men, I had all the space toys, the ray guns and rocket ships and hard plastic spacemen with the removable clear plastic helmets that were always getting lost. Best of all were the colored plastic aliens I bought for a nickel apiece from bins in Woolworth's and Kresge's. Some had big swollen brains and some had four arms, and some were spiders with faces or snakes with arms and heads. My favorite guy had a tiny little head and chest on top of a gigantic, hairy lower body. I gave them all names, and decided they were a gang of space pirates, led by the malignant big-brained Martian I called Jarn, who was not *nearly* as nice as Pinto Vortando. And of course I dreamed up endless stories of their adventures, and even made some halting attempts at writing one or two of them down.

Science fiction could be found in the movies as well. I saw *Them* and *War of the Worlds* and *The Day the Earth Stood Still* and *This Island Earth* and *Destination Moon*. And *Forbidden Planet*, which put all of them to shame. Little did I suspect that I was getting my first taste of Shakespeare there in the DeWitt Theater, courtesy of Dr Morbius and Robby the Robot.

Most of my beloved funny books were science fiction of a sort as well. Superman was from another planet, wasn't he? He came to Earth in a *spaceship*, how scientific could you get? The Martian Manhunter came from Mars, Green Lantern was given his ring by a crashed alien, and the Flash and the Atom got their powers in a lab. The comics offered pure space opera as well. There was Space Ranger (my favorite), Adam Strange (everybody else's favorite), Tommy Tomorrow (nobody's favorite), and this guy who drove a space cab along the space freeways . . . There were the Atomic Knights, post-holocaust heroes who patrolled a radioactive wasteland in suits of lead-lined armor, riding giant mutant Dalmatians . . . and on a somewhat more elevated plane, there were the wonderful *Classics Illustrated* adaptions of *War of the Worlds* and *The Time Machine*, which gave me my first introduction to the works of H.G. Wells.

All that was only prelude, though. When I was ten years old, my mother's childhood friend Lucy Antonsson gave me a book for Christmas. Not a comic book, but a *book* book, a hardcover of *Have Space Suit, Will Travel*, by Robert A. Heinlein.

I was a little dubious at first, but I liked Paladin on TV, and the title suggested this might be about some kind of space Paladin, so I took it home and began to read about this kid named Kip, who lived in a small town and never went anywhere, just like me. Some critics have suggested that *Citizen of the Galaxy* is the best of the Heinlein juveniles. *Citizen of the Galaxy* is a fine book. So too are *Tunnel Through the Sky, Starman Jones, Time for the Stars*, and many of the others . . . but *Have Space Suit, Will Travel* towers above them all. Kip and PeeWee, Ace and the malt shop, the old used spacesuit (I could *smell* it), the Mother Thing, the wormfaces, the trek across the moon, the trial in the Lesser Magellanic Cloud with the fate of humanity at stake. 'Die trying is the proudest human thing.' What could compare with that?

Nothing.

To a ten-year-old boy in 1958, *Have Space Suit, Will Travel* was crack with an Ed Emshwiller cover. I had to have more.

There was no way I could afford hardcovers, of course. *Have Space Suit, Will Travel* had cost $2.95, according to the price inside the dustwrapper . . . but the paperbacks on the spinner rack in the candy store on Kelly Parkway only went for 35 cents, the price of three-and-a-half funny books. If I didn't buy so many comics and skipped a Milky Way from time to time, I could scrape together the price of one of those. So I saved my dime and nickels, stopped reading some comics I didn't like all that much to begin with, played a few less games of SkeeBall, avoided the Good Humor truck and Mr Softee when they came by, and started buying paperbacks.

Worlds and universes opened wide before me. I bought every Heinlein that I found; his 'adult' books like *The Man Who Sold the Moon* and *Revolt In 2100*, since the other juveniles were not to be found. RAH was 'the dean of science fiction,' it said so right on the back of his books. If he was the dean, he must be the best. He remained my favorite writer for years to come, and *Have Space Suit, Will Travel* remained my favorite book . . . until the day when I read *The Puppet Masters*.

But I tried other authors too, and found that I enjoyed some of them almost as much as RAH. I loved Andrew North, who turned out to be Andre Norton. What's in a name? Andrew's *Plague Ship* and Andre's *Star Guard* both thrilled me. A.E. van Vogt's stuff had tremendous energy, especially *Slan*, although I never could quite figure out who was doing what to whom, or why. I became enamored of *One Against Herculum*, by Jerry Sohl, which took me to a world where you registered your crimes with the police before you committed them. Eric Frank Russell rocketed to the top of my list when I chanced upon the *Space Willies*, the funniest thing I'd ever read.

Though I bought books from Signet, Gold Medal, and all the other publishers, the Ace Doubles were my mainstay. *Two* 'complete novels' printed back to back and upside-down, with *two* covers, all for the price of one. Wilson Tucker, Alan Nourse, John Brunner, Robert Silverberg, Poul Anderson (*The War of the Wing-Men* was so good it threatened the supremacy of *Have Space Suit, Will Travel*), Damon Knight, Philip Dick, Edmond Hamilton, and the magnificent Jack Vance; I met them all in the pages of those stubby paperbacks with the blue-and-red spines. Tommy Tomorrow and Rocky Jones could not compare with this. This was the real stuff, and I drank it straight, with another for a chaser.

(Eventually my reading would lead me to Robert E. Howard, H. Lovecraft, and J.R.R. Tolkien as well, but I'll save those discoveries for my other commentaries).

I sampled different *kinds* of science fiction along with different authors: 'aliens among us' stories, 'if this goes on' stories, time travel yarns, 'sideways in time' alternate histories, post-holocaust tales, utopias and dystopias. Later, as a writer, I would revisit many of these subgenres . . . but there was one type of science fiction that I loved above all others, both as a reader and later as a writer. I was born and raised in Bayonne and never went *anywhere*, and my favorite books and stories were those that took me over the hills and far away, to lands undreamed of where I might walk beneath the light of distant stars.

The six stories I've chosen here all belong to that category. I wrote a great deal of science fiction in the '70s and '80s, but these stories are among my favorites. They also share a common universe; all six are part of the loose 'future history' that formed the backdrop for much of my SF.

(Though not all of it. 'Run to Starlight' and 'A Peripheral Affair' are part of a different continuity, the two star ring stories are set in yet another, the corpse stories in a third. 'Fast-Friend' stands by itself, as do a number of my other stories. I have no intention of trying to cram these orphans into my future history by retroactive backfill either. That's always a mistake.)

What I thought of as my 'main' future history began with 'The Hero' and reached its fullest development in my first novel, *Dying of the Light*. I never had a name for it, at least not one that stuck. In 'The Stone City' I coined the word 'manrealm' and for a while tried using that as an overall term for the history, analogous to Larry Niven's 'Known Space.' Later, I hit on 'the Thousand Worlds,' which had a nicer ring to it, and would have given me plenty of room to add new planets as I needed them . . . not to mention putting me nine hundred and ninety-two worlds up on John Varley and his 'Eight Worlds.' By that time my writing was taking me in other directions, however, so the name became moot.

'A Song for Lya' is the oldest of the six stories in this section. It was written in 1973, during my days in VISTA, when I was living on Margate Terrace in Chicago's Uptown, sharing a third-floor walk-up with some of my college chess cronies, and working at the Cook County Legal Assistance Foundation. I was also in the midst of the first serious romance of my life; it was not the first time I had ever been in love, but it was certainly the first time my feelings had been reciprocated. That relationship gave 'Lya' its emotional core; without it, I would have been the proverbial blind man describing a sunset. 'A Song for Lya' was also my longest story to date, my first novella.

When I finished it, I knew that I had finally surpassed 'With Morning Comes Mistfall' and 'The Second Kind of Loneliness,' written two years earlier. *This* was the best thing I'd ever done.

Analog had become my major market, so I sent it off to Ben Bova and he bought it straightaway. Terry Carr and Donald A. Wollheim both selected 'Lya' for their competing 'Best of the Year' anthologies, and it was nominated for the Nebula and the Hugo. Robert A. Silverberg had a powerful novella entitled 'Born with the Dead' out that year as well, and we ended up splitting the honors. Silverberg defeated me for the Nebula, but at the 1975 worldcon in Melbourne, Australia, Ben Bova accepted the Hugo on behalf of 'A Song for Lya.' I was in Chicago, sound asleep. Flying to Australia was *way* beyond my budget at that point in my life. Besides, Silverberg had already won the Nebula and the Locus Poll, and I was dead certain he was going to make it three-for-three.

It took months for me to get my hands on the actual rocket. Bova passed through Minneapolis on the way home, and handed it off to Gordon R. Dickson, who gave it Joe Haldeman the next time he saw him, who took it to Iowa City for a while and finally delivered it to me at a con in Chicago. The next time Gardner Dozois saw me, he threw me out of the Hugo Losers Club. Robert Silverberg announced his retirement from writing science fiction. I felt guilty about that, since I was a huge fan of the work he was doing at that time . . . but not so guilty that I contemplated sending him my Hugo, once I'd finally pried the damn thing away from Joe Haldeman.

By the time I wrote 'This Tower of Ashes' in 1974, my life had changed markedly from what it had been a year and a half before, when I'd written 'Lya.' My alternative service with VISTA had come to an end, and I was directing chess tournaments on the weekends to supplement my writing income. I had started the novel that would become *Dying of the Light*, but had put it aside; it would be two years before I felt I was ready to return to it. My great love affair had ended badly, when my girlfriend dumped me in favor of one of my best friends. With that wound still raw and bleeding, I promptly fell in love again, this time with a woman with whom I had so much in common that I felt as though I'd known her all my life. Yet that relationship had only begun to bloom when it ended, almost overnight, as she fell head-over-heels for someone else.

'This Tower of Ashes' came out of all that. Ben Bova bought it for *Analog*, but ended up publishing it in the *Analog Annual*, an original anthology from Pyramid. The idea of the *Annual* was to try and reach book readers and get them interested in the magazine. Whether it did or not, I couldn't say . . . but I would sooner my story had remained in *Analog* itself. One lesson I learned early in my career remains as true today as it was then: the best place for a story to get noticed is in the *magazines*. If anyone ever read 'This Tower of Ashes' besides Ben Bova, you couldn't prove it by me.

'And Seven Times Never Kill Man' was written in 1974 and published in 1975. It got me my second *Analog* cover for that year (a few months earlier, a gorgeous Jack Gaughan painting had adorned the issue featuring 'The Storms of Windhaven,' a collaboration between me and Lisa Tuttle), this one a stunning John Schoenherr that I wish I'd bought. The Steel Angels were created as my answer to Gordy Dickson's Dorsai, although the term 'Steel Angel' came from a song by Kris Kristofferson. Their god, the pale child with a sword, had an older and more dubious pedigree: he was one of the seven dark gods of the mythos I'd designed for Dr Weird, as glimpsed in 'Only Kids Are Afraid of the Dark.' The title is from Kipling's *Jungle Books*, of course, and got me almost as much praise as the story. Afterward several other writers, all Kipling fans, announced that they were annoyed they hadn't thought of it first.

'And Seven Times Never Kill Man' was nominated for a Hugo as the Best Novelette of 1974. 'The Storms of Windhaven' was also up that year for Best Novella. At 'Big Mac,' the 1976 worldcon in Kansas City, the two stories both lost within minutes of one another (the former to Larry Niven, who promptly dropped and broke his Hugo, the latter to Roger Zelazny). The following night, aided and abetted by Gardner Dozois and armed with a jug of cheap white wine left over from someone else's party, I threw the very first Hugo Losers Party in my room at the Muehlebach Hotel. It was the best party at the convention, and in later years would become a worldcon tradition, although recently some irony-challenged smofs have insisted on renaming it 'the Hugo Nominees Party.'

'The Stone City' was first published in *New Voices in Science Fiction*, a hardcover anthology I edited for Macmillan in 1977, but its roots went all the way to the 1973 worldcon in Toronto. John W. Campbell, Jr., the long-time editor of *Analog* and *Astounding*, had died in 1971, and *Analog's* publisher, Conde Nast, had established a new award in his honor, for the best new writer to enter the field during the previous two years. The first time the award was given, I was one of the finalists, along with Lisa Tuttle, George Alec Effinger, Ruth Berman, and Jerry Pournelle. The Campbell was voted by the fans and would be given out at the Toronto worldcon, with the Hugos. If not quite a Hugo itself, it was the next best thing.

My nomination took me utterly by surprise, but it thrilled and delighted me, even though I knew I had no hope of winning. Nor did I. Pournelle took home that first Campbell Award, although Effinger finished so close in the balloting that Torcon awarded him a plaque for second place, the only time I've seen that done. I have no idea where I finished, but for me, at that time, the old cliché was true: it really was an honor just to be nominated.

Afterward, at some of the parties, I told a couple of editors named Dave that there needed to be an anthology devoted to the new award, as there were for the Hugo and the Nebula. I was angling for a *sale*, of course; in 1973, I was still at the point where every one was precious. I got more than I bargained for; both editors named Dave agreed that a Campbell Awards anthology was a fine idea, but they said I had to put it together. 'I've never edited an anthology,' I argued. 'So this will be your first,' they replied.

It was. It took me a year to sell *New Voices* (to an editor named Ellen), and a couple more before all my authors delivered their promised stories, which is why the anthology showcasing the 1973 John W. Campbell Award nominees was published in 1977.

One of my writers gave me no trouble whatsoever, though. Since I was one of the finalists, I got to sell a story to myself.

There is a certain freedom that comes from knowing that the editor is not likely to reject your submission, no matter what you do. On the other hand, there is a certain amount of pressure as well. You don't want the readers thinking you just pulled some sorry old turkey out of the trunk, after all.

'The Stone City' was the story that grew from that freedom and that pressure. Though one of the core stories of my future history, this one is also a bit subversive. I wanted to season it with a little Lovecraft and a pinch of Kafka, and plant the suggestion that, when we go far enough from home, rationality, causality, and the physical laws of the universe itself begin to break down. And yet, of all the stories that I've ever written, 'The Stone City' is the one that comes closest to capturing the yearnings of that boy stretched out in the summer grass beside the Kill van Kull, staring up at Orion. I don't know that I ever evoked the vastness of space or that elusive 'sense of wonder' any better than I did here.

In 1977 a new science fiction magazine named *Cosmos* was launched, edited by David G. Hartwell. David asked me for a story, and I was pleased to oblige. If 'Bitterblooms' has a certain chill to it, that may be because it was one of the first things I wrote after moving to Dubuque, Iowa, where the winters were even more brutal than those I'd weathered in Chicago. Over the years I have done a number of stories inspired by songs. 'Bitterblooms' is one of those as well. (Anyone who can tell me the name of the song that inspired it will win . . . absolutely nothing). Hartwell liked the story well enough to feature it on the cover of the fourth issue of *Cosmos*. Unfortunately the fourth issue of *Cosmos* also proved to be the last issue of *Cosmos*. (It wasn't my fault.) I had headed for Dubuque in the spring of 1976, to take a job teaching journalism at a small Catholic woman's college. Though my writing was going well, I was still wasn't earning enough from my fiction to support myself as a full-time writer, and the chess tournaments had all dried up. Also, I had married in 1975, and had a wife to put through college. The position at Clarke College seemed the perfect answer. I would only be teaching two or three hours a day, after all. Four at the most. That would leave me half of every day to write my stories. Wouldn't it?

Anyone who has ever taught is laughing very loudly right now. The truth is, the demands on a teacher's time are much greater than they appear. You are only in the classroom a few hours a day, true . . . but there are always lessons to be prepared, lectures to be written, papers to read, tests to grade, committees to attend, textbooks to review, students to counsel. As the journalism teacher, I was also expected to serve as faculty advisor to the school newspaper, *The Courier*, which was great fun but got me in no end of trouble with the nuns, since I refused to be a censor.

I soon found that I had neither the time nor the energy to devote to my fiction while Clarke was in session. If I wanted to get any writing done, I had to take advantage of the long summer vacation, and the shorter breaks at Christmas and Easter.

The Christmas break in the winter of 1978–79 was the most productive period I ever had during my years at Clarke. In a few short weeks, I completed three very different stories. 'The Way of Cross and Dragon' was science fiction, 'The Ice Dragon' was a fairy tale fantasy, and 'Sandkings' married an SF background to a horror plot. All three stories are included in this retrospective. I will discuss 'Sandkings' and 'The Ice Dragon' when we reach them.

As for 'The Way of Cross and Dragon,' it is certainly my most *Catholic* story. Though I'd been raised Roman Catholic and had attended a Catholic prep school, I'd stopped practicing during my sophomore year at Northwestern. At Clarke, however, surrounded by nuns and Catholic girls, I found myself wondering what the Church might become, out among the stars.

Ben Bova had recently left *Analog* to become fiction editor for a slick new magazine called *Omni*, that published science fact as well as science fiction. 'The Way of Cross and Dragon' became my first sale to this new market. The story was nominated for both the Hugo and Nebula, lost the latter to Edward Bryant's 'giAnts,' but won the former as the Best Short Story of 1979 . . . on the same night that 'Sandkings' won for Best Novelette, at Noreascon 2 in Boston.

They were my second and third Hugos . . . and since Boston was a good deal closer than Australia, I was actually present for these two. That night, I walked into the Hugo Losers Party with a rocket in each hand, grinning ear to ear, and Gardner Dozois sprayed whipped cream in my hair. I partied with my friends for half the night, and afterward went upstairs with a beautiful woman. (I was happily divorced by that time). We made love as stars shone through the window, and bathed us in their light.

Nights don't come much better than that.

A Song for Lya

The cities of the Shkeen are old, older far than man's, and the great rust-red metropolis that rose from their sacred hill country had proved to be the oldest of them all. The Shkeen city had no name. It needed none. Though they built cities and towns by the hundreds and the thousands, the hill city had no rivals. It was the largest in size and population, and it was alone in the sacred hills. It was their Rome, Mecca, Jerusalem; all in one. It was *the* city, and all Shkeen came to it at last, in the final days before Union.

That city had been ancient in the days before Rome fell, had been huge and sprawling when Babylon was still a dream. But there was no feel of age to it. The human eye saw only miles and miles of low, redbrick domes; small hummocks of dried mud that covered the rolling hills like a rash. Inside they were dim and nearly airless. The rooms were small and the furniture crude.

Yet it was not a grim city. Day after day it squatted in those scrubby hills, broiling under a hot sun that sat in the sky like a weary orange melon; but the city teemed with life: smells of cooking, the sounds of laughter and talk and children running, the bustle and sweat of brickmen repairing the domes, the bells of the Joined ringing in the streets. The Shkeen were a lusty and exuberant people, almost childlike. Certainly there was nothing about them that told of great age or ancient wisdom. This is a young race, said the signs, this is a culture in its infancy.

But that infancy had lasted more than fourteen thousand years.

The human city was the real infant, less than ten Earth years old. It was built on the edge of the hills, between the Shkeen metropolis and the dusty brown plains where the spaceport had gone up. In human terms, it was a beautiful city; open and airy, full of graceful archways and glistening fountains and wide boulevards lined by trees. The buildings were wrought of metal and colored plastic and native woods, and most of them were low in deference to Shkeen architecture. Most of them . . . the Administration Tower was the exception, a polished blue steel needle that split a crystal sky.

You could see it for miles in all directions. Lyanna spied it even before we landed, and we admired it from the air. The gaunt skyscrapers of Old Earth and Baldur were taller, and the fantastic webbed cities of Arachne were far more beautiful – but that slim blue Tower was still imposing enough as it rose unrivaled to its lonely dominance above the sacred hills.

The spaceport was in the shadow of the tower, easy walking distance. But they met us anyway. A low-slung scarlet aircar sat purring at the base of the ramp as we disembarked, with a driver lounging against the stick. Dino Valcarenghi stood next to it, leaning on the door and talking to an aide.

Valcarenghi was the planetary administrator, the boy wonder of the sector. Young, of course, but I'd known that. Short, and good-looking, in a dark, intense way, with black hair that curled thickly against his head and an easy, genial smile.

He flashed us that smile then, when we stepped off the ramp, and reached to shake hands. 'Hi,' he began, 'I'm glad to see you.' There was no nonsense with formal introductions. He knew who we were, and we knew who he was, and Valcarenghi wasn't the kind of man who put much stock in ritual.

Lyanna took his hand lightly in hers, and gave him her vampire look: big, dark eyes opened wide and staring, thin mouth lifted in a tiny faint smile. She's a small girl, almost waiflike, with short brown hair and a child's figure. She can look very fragile, very helpless. When she wants to. But she rattles people with that look. If they know Lya's a telepath they figure she's poking around amid their innermost secrets. Actually she's playing with them. When Lyanna is *really* reading, her whole body goes stiff and you can almost see her tremble. And those big, soul-sucking eyes get narrow and hard and opaque.

But not many people know that, so they squirm under her vampire eyes and look the other way and hurry to release her hand. Not Valcarenghi, though. He just smiled and stared back, then moved on to me.

I was reading when I took his hand – my standard operating procedure. Also a bad habit, I guess, since it's put some promising friendships into an early grave. My talent isn't equal to Lya's. But it's not as demanding, either. I reach emotions. Valcarenghi's geniality came through strong and genuine. With nothing behind it, or at least nothing that was close enough to the surface for me to catch.

We also shook hands with the aide, a middle-aged blond stork named Nelson Gourlay. Then Valcarenghi ushered everybody into the aircar and we took off. 'I imagine you're tired,' he said after we were airborne, 'so we'll save the tour of the city and head straight for the Tower. Nelse will show you your quarters, then you can join us for a drink, and we'll talk over the problem. You've read the materials we sent?'

'Yes,' I said. Lya nodded. 'Interesting background, but I'm not sure why we're here.'

'We'll get to that soon enough,' Valcarenghi replied. 'I ought to be letting you enjoy the scenery.' He gestured toward the window, smiled, and fell silent.

So Lya and I enjoyed the scenery, or as much as we could enjoy during the five-minute flight from spaceport to tower. The aircar was whisking down the main street at treetop level, stirring up a breeze that whipped the thin branches as we went by. It was cool and dark in the interior of the car, but outside the Shkeen sun was riding toward noon, and you could see the heat waves shimmering from the pavement. The population must have been inside huddled around their air conditioners, because we saw very little traffic.

We got out near the main entrance to the Tower and walked through a huge, sparkling-clean lobby. Valcarenghi left us then to talk to some underlings. Gourlay led us into one of the tubes and we shot up fifty floors. Then we waltzed past a secretary into another, private tube, and climbed some more.

Our rooms were lovely, carpeted in cool green and paneled with wood. There was a complete library there, mostly Earth classics bound in synthaleather, with a few novels from Baldur, our home world. Somebody had been researching our tastes. One of the walls of the bedroom was tinted glass, giving a panoramic view of the city far below us, with a control that could darken it for sleeping.

Gourlay showed it to us dutifully, like a dour bellhop. I read him briefly though, and found no resentment. He was nervous, but only slightly. There was honest affection there for someone. Us? Valcarenghi?

Lya sat down on one of the twin beds. 'Is someone bringing our luggage?' she asked.

Gourlay nodded. 'You'll be well taken care of,' he said. 'Anything you want, ask.'

'Don't worry, we will,' I said. I dropped to the second bed, and gestured Gourlay to a chair. 'How long have you been here?'

'Six years,' he said, taking the chair gratefully and sprawling out all over it. 'I'm one of the veterans. I've worked under four administrators now. Dino, and Stuart before him, and Gustaffson before him. I was even under Rockwood a few months.'

Lya perked up, crossing her legs under her and leaning forward. 'That was all Rockwood lasted, wasn't it?'

'Right,' Gourlay said. 'He didn't like the planet, took a quick demotion to assistant administrator someplace else. I didn't care much, to tell the truth. He was the nervous type, always giving orders to prove who was boss.'

'And Valcarenghi?' I asked.

Gourlay made a smile look like a yawn. 'Dino? Dino's OK, the best of the lot. He's good, knows he's good. He's only been here two months, but he's gotten a lot done, and he's made a lot of friends. He treats the staff like people, calls everybody by his first name, all that stuff. People like that.'

I was reading, and I read sincerity. It was Valcarenghi that Gourlay was affectionate toward, then. He believed what he was saying.

I had more questions, but I didn't get to ask them. Gourlay got up suddenly. 'I really shouldn't stay,' he said. 'You want to rest, right? Come up to the top in about two hours and we'll go over things with you. You know where the tube is?'

We nodded, and Gourlay left. I turned to Lyanna. 'What do you think?'

She lay back on the bed and considered the ceiling. 'I don't know,' she said. 'I wasn't reading. I wonder why they've had so many administrators. And why they wanted us.'

'We're Talented,' I said, smiling. With the capital, yes. Lyanna and I have been tested and registered as psi Talents, and we have the licenses to prove it.

'Uh-huh,' she said, turning on her side and smiling back at me. Not her vampire half-smile this time. Her sexy little girl smile.

'Valcarenghi wants us to get some rest,' I said. 'It's probably not a bad idea.'

Lya bounced out of bed. 'OK,' she said, 'but these twins have got to go.'

'We could push them together.'

She smiled again. We pushed them together.

And we *did* get some sleep. Eventually.

Our luggage was outside the door when we woke. We changed into fresh clothes, old casual stuff, counting on Valcarenghi's notorious lack of pomp. The tube took us to the top of the Tower.

*

The office of the planetary administrator was hardly an office. There was no desk, none of the usual trappings. Just a bar and lush blue carpets that swallowed us ankle-high, and six or seven scattered chairs. Plus lots of space and sunlight, with Shkea laid out at our feet beyond the tinted glass. All four walls this time.

Valcarenghi and Gourlay were waiting for us, and Valcarenghi did the bartending chores personally. I didn't recognize the beverage, but it was cool and spicy and aromatic, with a real sting to it. I sipped it gratefully. For some reason I felt I needed a lift.

'Shkeen wine,' Valcarenghi said, smiling, in answer to an unasked question. 'They've got a name for it, but I can't pronounce it yet. But give me time. I've only been here two months, and the language is rough.'

'You're learning Shkeen?' Lya asked, surprised. I knew why. Shkeen is rough on human tongues, but the natives learned Terran with stunning ease. Most people accept that happily, and just forgot about the difficulties of cracking the alien language.

'It gives me an insight into the way they think,' Valcarenghi said. 'At least that's the theory.' He smiled.

I read him again, although it was more difficult. Physical contact makes things sharper. Again, I got a simple emotion, close to the surface – pride this time. With pleasure mixed in. I chalked that up to the wine. Nothing beneath.

'However you pronounce the drink, I like it,' I said.

'The Shkeen produce a wide variety of liquors and foodstuffs,' Gourlay put in. 'We've cleared many for export already, and we're checking others. Market should be good.'

'You'll have a chance to sample more of the local produce this evening.' Valcarenghi said. 'I've set up a tour of the city, with a stop or two in Shkeentown. For a settlement of our size, our night life is fairly interesting. I'll be your guide.'

'Sounds good,' I said. Lya was smiling too. A tour was unusually considerate. Most Normals feel uneasy around Talents, so they rush us in to do whatever they want done, then rush us out again as quickly as possible. They certainly don't socialize with us.

'Now – the problem,' Valcarenghi said, lowering his drink and leaning forward in the chair. 'You read about the Cult of the Union?'

'A Shkeen religion,' Lya said.

'*The* Shkeen religion,' corrected Valcarenghi. 'Every one of them is a believer. This is a planet without heretics.'

'We read the materials you sent on it,' Lya said. 'Along with everything else.'

'What do you think?'

I shrugged. 'Grim. Primitive. But no more than any number of others I've read about. The Shkeen aren't very advanced, after all. There were religions on Old Earth that included human sacrifice.'

Valcarenghi shook his head, and looked toward Gourlay.

'No, you don't understand,' Gourlay started, putting his drink down on the carpet. 'I've been studying their religion for six years. It's like no other in history. Nothing on Old Earth like it, no sir. Nor in any other race we've encountered.

'And Union, well, it's wrong to compare it to human sacrifice, just wrong. The Old Earth religions sacrificed one or two unwilling victims to appease their gods. Killed a handful to get mercy for the millions. And the handful generally protested. The Shkeen don't work it that way. The Greeshka takes *everyone*. And they go willingly. Like lemmings they march off to the caves to be eaten alive by those parasites. *Every* Shkeen is Joined at forty, and goes to Final Union before he's fifty.'

I was confused. 'All right,' I said. 'I see the distinction, I guess. But so what? Is this the problem? I imagine that Union is rough on the Shkeen, but that's their business. Their religion is no worse than the ritual cannibalism of the Hrangans, is it?'

Valcarenghi finished his drink and got up, heading for the bar. As he poured himself a refill, he said, almost casually. 'As far as I know, Hrangan cannibalism has claimed no human converts.'

Lya looked startled. I felt startled. I sat up and stared. 'What?

Valcarenghi headed back to his seat, glass in hand. 'Human converts have been joining the Cult of the Union. Dozens of them are already Joined. None of them have achieved full Union yet, but that's only a question of time.' He sat down, and looked at Gourlay. So did we.

The gangling blond aide picked up the narrative. 'The first convert was about seven years ago. Nearly a year before I got here, two and a half after Shkea was discovered and the settlement built. Guy named Magly. Psipsych, worked closely with the Shkeen. He was it for two years. Then another in '08, more the next year. And the rate's been climbing ever since. There was one big one. Phil Gustaffson.'

Lya blinked. 'The planetary administrator?'

'The same,' said Gourlay. 'We've had a lot of administrators. Gustaffson came in after Rockwood couldn't stand it. He was a big, gruff old guy. Everybody loved him. He'd lost his wife and kids on his last assignment, but you'd never have known it. He was always hearty, full of fun. Well, he got interested in the Shkeen religion, started talking to them. Talked to Magly and some of the other converts too. Even went to see a Greeshka. That shook him up real bad for a while. But finally he got over it, went back to his researches. I worked with him, but I never guessed what he had in mind. A little over a year ago, he converted. He's Joined now. Nobody's ever been accepted that fast. I hear talk in Shkeentown that he may even be admitted to Final Union, rushed right in. Well, Phil was administrator here longer than anybody else. People liked him, and when he went over, a lot of his friends followed. The rate's way up now.'

'Not quite one percent, and rising,' Valcarenghi said. 'That seems low, but remember what it means. One percent of the people in my settlement are choosing a religion that includes a very unpleasant form of suicide.'

Lya looked from him to Gourlay and back again. 'Why hasn't this been reported?'

'It should have been,' Valcarenghi said, 'but Stuart succeeded Gustaffson, and he was scared stiff of a scandal. There's no law against humans adopting an alien religion, so Stuart defined it as a nonproblem. He reported the conversion rate routinely, and nobody higher up ever bothered to make the correlation and remember just what all these people were converting *to*.'

I finished my drink, set it down. 'Go on,' I said to Valcarenghi.

'I define the situation as a problem,' he said. 'I don't care how few people are involved, the idea that human beings would allow the Greeshka to consume them alarms me. I've had a team of psychs on it since I took over, but they're getting nowhere. I needed Talent. I want you two to find out why these people are converting. Then I'll be able to deal with the situation.'

The problem was strange, but the assignment seemed straightforward enough. I read Valcarenghi to be sure. His emotions were a bit more complex this time, but not much.

Confidence above all: he was sure we could handle the problem. There was honest concern there, but no fear, and not even a hint of deception. Again, I couldn't catch anything below the surface. Valcarenghi kept his hidden turmoil well hidden, if he had any.

I glanced at Lyanna. She was sitting awkwardly in her chair, and her fingers were wrapped very tightly around her wine glass. Reading. Then she loosened up and looked my way and nodded.

'All right,' I said. 'I think we can do it.'

Valcarenghi smiled. 'That I never doubted,' he said. 'It was only a question of whether you *would*. But enough of business for tonight. I've promised you a night on the town, and I always try to deliver on my promises. I'll meet you downstairs in the lobby in a half hour.'

*

Lya and I changed into something more formal back in our room. I picked a dark blue tunic, with white slacks and a matching mesh scarf. Not the height of fashion, but I was hoping that Shkea would be several months behind the times. Lya slipped into a silky white skintight with a tracery of thin blue lines that flowed over her in sensuous patterns in response to her body heat. The lines were definitely lecherous, accentuating her thin figure with a singleminded determination. A blue raincape completed the outfit.

'Valcarenghi's funny,' she said as she fastened it.

'Oh?' I was struggling with the sealseam on my tunic, which refused to seal. 'You catch something when you read him?'

'No,' she said. She finished attaching the cape and admired herself in the mirror. Then she spun toward me, the cape swirling behind her. 'That's it. He was thinking what he was saying. Oh, variations in the wording, of course, but nothing important. His mind was on what we were discussing, and behind that there was only a wall.' She smiled. 'Didn't get a single one of his deep dark secrets.'

I finally conquered the sealseam. 'Tsk,' I said. 'Well, you get another chance tonight.'

That got me a grimace. 'The hell I do. I don't read people on off-time. It isn't fair. Besides, it's such a strain. I wish I could catch thoughts as easily as you do feelings.'

'The price of Talent,' I said. 'You're more Talented, your price is higher.' I rummaged in our luggage for a raincape, but I didn't find anything that went well, so I decided not to wear one. Capes were out, anyway. 'I didn't get much on Valcarenghi either. You could have told as much by watching his face. He must be a very disciplined mind. But I'll forgive him. He serves good wine.'

Lya nodded. 'Right! That stuff did me good. Got rid of the headache I woke up with.'

'The altitude,' I suggested. We headed for the door.

The lobby was deserted, but Valcarenghi didn't keep us waiting long. This time he drove his own aircar, a battered black job that had evidently been with him for a while. Gourlay wasn't the sociable type, but Valcarenghi had a woman with him, a stunning auburn-haired vision named Laurie Blackburn. She was even younger than Valcarenghi – midtwenties, by the look of her.

It was sunset when we took off. The whole far horizon was a gorgeous tapestry in red and orange, and a cool breeze was blowing in from the plains. Valcarenghi left the coolers off and opened the car windows, and we watched the city darken into twilight as we drove.

Dinner was at a plush restaurant with Baldurian decor – to make us feel comfortable, I guessed. The food, however, was very cosmopolitan. The spices, the herbs, the *style* of cooking were all Baldur. The meats and vegetables were native. It made for an interesting combination. Valcarenghi ordered for all four of us, and we wound up sampling about a dozen different dishes. My favorite was a tiny Shkeen bird that they cooked in sourtang sauce. There wasn't very much of it, but what there was tasted great. We also polished off three bottles of wine during the meal: more of the Shkeen stuff we'd sampled that afternoon, a flask of chilled Veltaar from Baldur, and some real Old Earth Burgundy.

The talk warmed up quickly; Valcarenghi was a born storyteller and an equally good listener. Eventually, of course, the conversation got around to

Shkea and Shkeen. Laurie led it there. She'd been on Shkea for about six months, working toward an advanced degree in extee anthropology. She was trying to discover why the Shkeen civilization had remained frozen for so many millennia.

'They're older than we are, you know,' she told us. 'They had cities before men were using tools. It should have been space-traveling Shkeen that stumbled on primitive men, not the other way around.'

'Aren't there theories on that already?' I asked.

'Yes, but none of them are universally accepted,' she said. 'Cullen cites a lack of heavy metals, for example. A factor, but is it the *whole* answer? Von Hamrin claims the Shkeen didn't get enough competition. No big carnivores on the planet, so there was nothing to breed aggressiveness into the race. But he's come under a lot of fire. Shkea isn't all *that* idyllic; if it were, the Shkeen never would have reached their present level. Besides, what's the Greeshka if not a carnivore? It *eats* them, doesn't it?'

'What do you think?' Lya asked.

'I think it had something to do with the religion, but I haven't worked it all out yet. Dino's helping me talk to people and the Shkeen are open enough, but research isn't easy.' She stopped suddenly and looked at Lya hard. 'For me, anyway. I imagine it'd be easier for you.'

We'd heard that before. Normals often figure that Talents have unfair advantages, which is perfectly understandable. We do. But Laurie wasn't resentful. She delivered her statement in a wistful, speculative tone, instead of etching it in verbal acid.

Valcarenghi leaned over and put an arm around her. 'Hey,' he said. 'Enough shoptalk. Robb and Lya shouldn't be worrying about the Shkeen until tomorrow.'

Laurie looked at him, and smiled tentatively. 'OK,' she said lightly. 'I get carried away. Sorry.'

'That's OK,' I told her. 'It's an interesting subject. Give us a day and we'll probably be getting enthusiastic too.'

Lya nodded agreement, and added that Laurie would be the first to know if our work turned up anything that would support her theory. I was hardly listening. I know it's not polite to read Normals when you're out with them socially, but there are times I can't resist. Valcarenghi had his arm around Laurie and had pulled her toward him gently. I was curious.

So I took a quick, guilty reading. He was very high – slightly drunk, I guess, and feeling very confident and protective. The master of the situation. But Laurie was a jumble – uncertainty, repressed anger, a vague fading hint of fright. And love, confused but very strong. I doubted that it was for me or Lya. She loved Valcarenghi.

I reached under the table, searching for Lya's hand, and found her knee.

I squeezed it gently and she looked at me and smiled. She wasn't reading, which was good. It bothered me that Laurie loved Valcarenghi, though I didn't know why, and I was just as glad that Lya didn't see my discontent.

We finished off the last of the wine in short order, and Valcarenghi took care of the whole bill. Then he rose. 'Onward!' he announced. 'The night is fresh, and we've got visits to make.'

So we made visits. No holoshows or anything that drab, although the city had its share of theaters. A casino was next on the list. Gambling was legal on Shkea, of course, and Valcarenghi would have legalized it if it weren't. He supplied the chips and I lost some for him, as did Laurie. Lya was barred from playing; her Talent was too strong. Valcarenghi won big; he was a superb mindspin player, and pretty good at the traditional games too.

Then came a bar. More drinks, plus local entertainment which was better than I would have expected.

It was pitch-black when we got out, and I assumed that the expedition was nearing its end. Valcarenghi surprised us. When we got back to the car, he reached under the controls, pulled out a box of sober-ups, and passed them around.

'Hey,' I said. 'You're driving. Why do I need this? I just barely got up here.'

'I'm about to take you to a genuine Shkeen cultural event, Robb,' he said. 'I don't want you making rude comments or throwing up on the natives. Take your pill.'

I took my pill, and the buzz in my head began to fade. Valcarenghi already had the car airborne. I leaned back and put my arm around Lya, and she rested her head on my shoulder. 'Where are we going?' I asked.

'Shkeentown,' he replied, never looking back, 'to their Great Hall. There's a Gathering tonight, and I figured you'd be interested.'

'It will be in Shkeen, of course,' Laurie said, 'but Dino can translate for you. I know a little of the language too, and I'll fill in whatever he misses.'

Lya looked excited. We'd read about Gatherings, of course, but we hardly expected go see one on our first day on Shkea. The Gatherings were a species of religious rite; a mass confessional of sorts for pilgrims who were about to be admitted to the ranks of the Joined. Pilgrims swelled the hill city daily, but Gatherings were conducted only three or four times a year when the numbers of those-about-to-be-Joined climbed high enough.

The aircar streaked almost soundlessly through the brightly-lit settlement, passing huge fountains that danced with a dozen colors and pretty ornamental arches that flowed like liquid fire. A few other cars were airborne, and here and there we flew above pedestrians strolling the city's broad malls. But most people were inside, and light and music flooded from many of the homes we passed.

Then, abruptly, the character of the city began to change. The level ground began to roll and heave, hills rose before us and then behind us, and the lights vanished. Below, the malls gave way to unlit roads of crushed stone and dust, and the domes of glass and metal done in fashionable mock-Shkeen yielded to their older brick brothers. The Shkeen city was quieter than its human counterpart; most of the houses were darkly silent.

Then, ahead of us, a hummock appeared that was larger than the others – almost a hill in itself, with a big arched door and a series of slit-like windows. And light leaked from this one, and noise, and there were Shkeen outside.

I suddenly realized that, although I'd been on Shkea for nearly a day, this was the first sight I'd caught of the Shkeen. Not that I could see them all that clearly from an aircar at night. But I did see them. They were smaller than men – the tallest was around five feet – with big eyes and long arms. That was all I could tell from above.

Valcarenghi put the car down alongside the Great Hall, and we piled out. Shkeen were trickling through the arch from several directions, but most of them were already inside. We joined the trickle, and nobody even looked twice at us, except for one character who hailed Valcarenghi in a thin, squeaky voice and called him Dino. He had friends even here.

The interior was one huge room, with a great crude platform built in the center and an immense crowd of Shkeen circling it. The only light was from torches that were stuck in grooves along the walls and on high poles surrounding the platform. Someone was speaking, and every one of those great, bulging eyes was turned his way. We four were the only humans in the Hall.

The speaker, outlined brightly by the torches, was a fat, middle-aged Shkeen who moved his arms slowly, almost hypnotically, as he talked. His speech was a series of whistles, wheezes, and grunts, so I didn't listen very closely. He was much too far away to read. I was reduced to studying his appearance, and that of other Shkeen near me. All of them were hairless, as far as I could see, with softish-looking orange skin that was creased by a thousand tiny wrinkles. They wore simple shifts of crude, multicolored cloth, and I had difficulty telling male from female.

Valcarenghi leaned over toward me and whispered, careful to keep his voice low. 'The speaker is a farmer,' he said. 'He's telling the crowd how far he's come, and some of the hardships of his life.'

I looked around. Valcarenghi's whisper was the only sound in the place. Everyone else was dead quiet, eyes riveted on the platform, scarcely breathing. 'He's saying that he has four brothers,' Valcarenghi told me. 'Two have gone on to Final Union, one is among the Joined. The other is younger than himself, and now owns the farm.' He frowned. 'The speaker will never see his farm again,' he said, more loudly, 'but he's happy about it.'

'Bad crops?' asked Lya, smiling irreverently. She'd been listening to the same whisper. I gave her a stern look.

The Shkeen went on. Valcarenghi stumbled after him. 'Now he's telling his crimes, all the things he's done that he's ashamed of, his blackest soul-secrets. He's had a sharp tongue at times, he's vain, once he actually struck his younger brother. Now he speaks of his wife, and the other women he has known. He has betrayed her many times, copulating with others. As a boy, he mated with animals for he feared females. In recent years he has grown incapable, and his brother has serviced his wife.'

On and on and on it went, in incredible detail, detail that was both startling and frightening. No intimacy went untold, no secret was left undisturbed. I stood and listened to Valcarenghi's whispers, shocked at first, finally growing bored with the squalor of it all. I began to get restless. I wondered briefly if I knew any human half so well as I now knew this great fat Shkeen. Then I wondered whether Lyanna, with her Talent, knew anyone half so well. It was almost as if the speaker wanted all of us to live through his life right here and now.

His speech lasted for what seemed hours, but finally it began to wind up. 'He speaks now of Union,' Valcarenghi whispered. 'He will be Joined, he is joyful about it, he has craved it for so long. His misery is at an end, his aloneness will cease, soon he shall walk the streets of the sacred city and peal his joy with the bells. And then Final Union, in the years to come. He will be with his brothers in the afterlife.'

'No, Dino.' This whisper was Laurie. 'Quit wrapping human phrases around what he says. He will be his brothers, he says. The phrase also implies they will be him.'

Valcarenghi smiled. 'OK, Laurie. If you say so . . .'

Suddenly the fat farmer was gone from the platform. The crowd rustled, and another figure took his place: much shorter, wrinkled excessively, one eye a great gaping hole. He began to speak, haltingly at first, then with greater skill.

'This one is a brickman, he has worked many domes, he lives in the sacred city. His eye was lost many years ago, when he fell from a dome and a sharp stick poked into him. The pain was very great, but he returned to work within a year, he did not beg for premature Union, he was very brave, he is proud of his courage. He has a wife, but they have never had offspring, he is sad of that, he cannot talk to his wife easily, they are apart even when together and she weeps at night, he is sad of that too, but he has never hurt her and . . .'

It went on for hours again. My restlessness stirred again, but I cracked down on it – this was too important. I let myself get lost in Valcarenghi's narration, and the story of the one-eyed Shkeen. Before long, I was riveted as closely to the tale as the aliens around me. It was hot and stuffy and all but airless in the dome, and my tunic was getting sooty and soaked by sweat, some of it from the creatures who pressed around me. But I hardly noticed.

The second speaker ended as had the first, with a long praise of the joy of being Joined and the coming of Final Union. Toward the end, I hardly even needed Valcarenghi's translation – I could hear the happiness in the voice of the Shkeen, and see it in his trembling figure. Or maybe I was reading, unconsciously. But I can't read at that distance – unless the target is emoting very hard.

A third speaker ascended the platform, and spoke in a voice louder than the others. Valcarenghi kept pace. 'A woman this time,' he said. 'She has carried eight children for her man, she has four sisters and three brothers, she has farmed all her life, she . . .'

Suddenly her speech seemed to peak, and she ended a long sequence with several sharp, high whistles. Then she fell silent. The crowd, as one, began to respond with whistles of their own. An eerie, echoing music filled the Great Hall, and the Shkeen around us all began to sway and whistle. The woman looked out at the scene from a bent and broken position.

Valcarenghi started to translate, but he stumbled over something. Laurie cut in before he could backtrack. 'She has now told them of great tragedy,' she whispered. 'They whistle to show their grief, their oneness with her pain.'

'Sympathy, yes,' said Valcarenghi, taking over again. 'When she was young, her brother grew ill, and seemed to be dying. Her parents told her to take him to the sacred hills, for they could not leave the younger children. But she shattered a wheel on her cart through careless driving, and her brother died upon the plains. He perished without Union. She blames herself.'

The Shkeen had begun again. Laurie began to translate, leaning close to us and using a soft whisper. 'Her brother died, she is saying again. She faulted him, denied him Union, now he is sundered and alone and gone without . . . without . . .'

'Afterlife,' said Valcarenghi. 'Without afterlife.'

'I'm not sure that's entirely right,' Laurie said. 'That concept is . . .'

Valcarenghi waved her silent. 'Listen,' he said. He continued to translate.

We listened to her story, told in Valcarenghi's increasingly hoarse whisper. She spoke longest of all, and her story was the grimmest of the three. When she finished, she too was replaced. But Valcarenghi put a hand on my shoulder and beckoned toward the exit.

The cool night air hit like ice water, and I suddenly realized that I was drenched with sweat. Valcarenghi walked quickly toward the car. Behind us, the speaking was still in progress, and the Shkeen showed no signs of tiring.

'Gatherings go on for days, sometimes weeks,' Laurie told us as we climbed inside the aircar. 'The Shkeen listen in shifts, more or less – they try terribly to hear every word, but exhaustion gets to them sooner or later and they retire for brief rests, then return for more. It is a great honor to last through an entire Gathering without sleep.'

Valcarenghi shot us aloft. 'I'm going to try that someday,' he said. 'I've never attended for more than a couple of hours, but I think I could make it if I fortified myself with drugs. We'll get more understanding between human and Shkeen if we participate more fully in their rituals.'

'Oh,' I said. 'Maybe Gustaffson felt the same way.'

Valcarenghi laughed lightly. 'Yes, well, I don't intend to participate *that* fully.'

The trip home was a tired silence. I'd lost track of time but my body insisted that it was almost dawn. Lya, curled up under my arm, looked drained and empty and only half-awake. I felt the same way.

We left the aircar in front of the Tower and took the tubes up. I was past thinking. Sleep came very, very quickly.

I dreamed that night. A good dream, I think, but it faded with the coming of the light, leaving me empty and feeling cheated. I lay there, after waking, with my arm around Lya and my eyes on the ceiling, trying to recall what the dream had been about. But nothing came.

Instead, I found myself thinking about the Gathering, running it through again in my head. Finally I disentangled myself and climbed out of bed. We'd darkened the glass, so the room was still pitch-black. But I found the controls easily enough, and let through a trickle of late morning light.

Lya mumbled some sort of sleepy protest and rolled over, but made no effort to get up. I left her alone in the bedroom and went out to our library, looking for a book on the Shkeen – something with a little more detail than the material we'd been sent. No luck. The library was meant for recreation, not research.

I found a viewscreen and punched up to Valcarenghi's office. Gourlay answered. 'Hello,' he said. 'Dino figured you'd be calling. He's not here right now. He's out arbitrating a trade contract. What do you need?'

'Books,' I said, my voice still a little sleepy. 'Something on the Shkeen.'

'That I can't do,' Gourlay said. 'Are none, really. Lots of papers and studies and monographs, but no full-fledged books. I'm going to write one, but I haven't gotten to it yet. Dino figured I could be your resource, I guess.'

'Oh.'

'Got any questions?'

I searched for a question, found none. 'Not really,' I said, shrugging. 'I just wanted general background, maybe some more information on Gatherings.'

'I can talk to you about that later,' Gourlay said. 'Dino figured you'd want to get to work today. We can bring people to the Tower, if you'd like, or you can get out to them.'

'We'll go out,' I said quickly. 'Bringing subjects in for interviews fouls up everything. They get all anxious, and that covers up any emotions I might want to read, and they think on different things, too, so Lyanna has trouble.'

'Fine,' said Gourlay. 'Dino put an aircar at your disposal. Pick it up down in the lobby. Also, they'll have some keys for you, so you can come straight up here in the office without bothering with the secretaries and all.'

'Thanks,' I said. 'Talk to you later.' I flicked off the viewscreen and walked back to the bedroom.

Lya was sitting up, the covers around her waist. I sat down next to her and kissed her. She smiled, but didn't respond. 'Hey,' I said. 'What's wrong?'

'Headache,' she replied. 'I thought sober-ups were supposed to get rid of hangovers.'

'That's the theory. Mine worked pretty well.' I went to the closet and began looking for something to wear. 'We should have headache pills around here someplace. I'm sure Dino wouldn't forget anything that obvious.'

'Umpf. Yes. Throw me some clothes.'

I grabbed one of her coveralls and tossed it across the room. Lya stood up and slipped into it while I dressed, then went off to the washroom.

'Better,' she said. 'You're right, he didn't forget medicines.'

'He's the thorough sort.'

She smiled. 'I guess. Laurie knows the language better, though. I read her. Dino made a couple of mistakes in that translation last night.'

I'd guessed at something like that. No discredit to Valcarenghi; he was working on a four-month handicap, from what they said. I nodded. 'Read anything else?'

'No. I tried to get those speakers, but the distance was too much.' She came up and took my hand. 'Where are we going today?'

'Shkeentown,' I said. 'Let's try to find some of these Joined. I didn't notice any at the Gathering.'

'No. Those things are for Shkeen about-to-be-Joined.'

'So I hear. Let's go.'

We went. We stopped at the fourth level for a late breakfast in the Tower cafeteria, then got our aircar pointed out to us by a man in the lobby. A sporty green four-seater, very common, very inconspicuous.

I didn't take the aircar all the way into the Shkeen city, figuring we'd get more of the feel of the place if we went through on foot. So I dropped down just beyond the first range of hills, and we walked.

*

The human city had seemed almost empty, but Shkeentown lived. The crushed-rock streets were full of aliens, hustling back and forth busily, carrying loads of bricks and baskets of fruit and clothing. There were children everywhere, most of them naked; fat balls of orange energy that ran around us in circles, whistling and grunting and grinning, tugging at us every once in a while. The kids looked different from the adults. They had a few patches of reddish hair, for one thing, and their skins were still smooth and unwrinkled. They were the only ones who really paid any attention to us. The adult Shkeen just went about their business, and gave us an occasional friendly smile. Humans were obviously not all that uncommon in the streets of Shkeentown.

Most of the traffic was on foot, but small wooden carts were also common. The Shkeen draft animal looked like a big green dog that was about to be sick. They were strapped to the carts in pairs, and they whined constantly as they pulled. So, naturally, men called them whiners. In addition to whining, they also defecated constantly. That, with odors from the food peddled in baskets and the Shkeen themselves, gave the city a definite pungency.

There was noise too, a constant clamor. Kids whistling. Shkeen talking loudly with grunts and whimpers and squeaks, whiners whining and their carts rattling over the rocks. Lya and I walked through it all silently, hand in hand, watching and listening and smelling and . . . reading.

I was wide open when I entered Shkeentown, letting everything wash over me as I walked, unfocused but receptive. I was the center of a small bubble of emotion – feelings rushed up at me as Shkeen approached, faded as they walked away, circled around and around with the dancing children. I swam in a sea of impressions. And it startled me.

It startled me because it was all so familiar. I'd read aliens before.

Sometimes it was difficult, sometimes it was easy, but it was never pleasant. The Hrangans have sour minds, rank with hate and bitterness, and feel unclean when I come out. The Fyndii feel emotions so palely that I can scarcely read them at all. The Damoosh are . . . *different*. I read them strongly, but I can't find names for the feelings I read.

But the Shkeen – it was like walking down a street on Baldur. No, wait – more like one of the Lost Colonies, when a human settlement has fallen back into barbarism and forgotten its origins. Human emotions rage there, primal and strong and real, but less sophisticated than on Old Earth or Baldur. The Shkeen were like that: primitive, maybe, but very understandable. I read joy and sorrow, envy, anger, whimsy, bitterness, yearning, pain. The same heady mixture that engulfs me everywhere, when I open myself to it.

Lya was reading, too. I felt her hand tense in mine. After a while, it softened again. I turned to her, and she saw the question in my eyes.

'They're people,' she said. 'They're like us.'

I nodded. 'Parallel evolution, maybe. Shkea might be an older Earth, with a few minor differences. But you're right. They're more human than any other race we've encountered in space.' I considered that. 'Does that answer Dino's question? If they're like us, it follows that their religion would be more appealing than a *really* alien one.'

'No, Robb,' Lya said. 'I don't think so. Just the reverse. If they're like us, it doesn't make sense that *they'd* go off so willingly to die. See?'

She was right, of course. There was nothing suicidal in the emotions I'd read, nothing unstable, nothing really abnormal. Yet every one of the Shkeen went off to Final Union in the end.

'We should focus on somebody,' I said. 'This blend of thought isn't getting us anywhere.' I looked around to find a subject, but just then I heard the bells begin.

They were off to the left somewhere, nearly lost in the city's gentle roar. I tugged Lya by the hand, and we ran down the street to find them, turning left at the first gap in the orderly row of domes.

The bells were still ahead, and we kept running, cutting through what must have been somebody's yard, and climbing over a low bush-fence that bristled with sweethorns. Beyond that was another yard, a dung-pit, more domes, and finally a street. It was there we found the bell-ringers.

There were four of them, all Joined, wearing long gowns of bright red fabric that trailed in the dust, with great bronze bells in either hand. They rang the bells constantly, their long arms swinging back and forth, the sharp, clanging notes filling the street. All four were elderly, as Shkeen go – hairless and pinched up with a million tiny wrinkles. But they smiled very widely, and the younger Shkeen that passed smiled at them.

On their heads rode the Greeshka.

I'd expected to find the sight hideous. I didn't. It was faintly disquieting, but only because I knew what it meant. The parasites were bright blobs of crimson goo, ranging in size from a pulsing wart on the back of one Shkeen skull to a great sheet of dripping, moving red that covered the head and shoulders of the smallest like a living cowl. The Greeshka lived by sharing the nutrients in the Shkeen bloodstream, I knew.

And also by slowly – oh so slowly – consuming its host.

Lya and I stopped a few yards from them, and watched them ring. Her face was solemn, and I think mine was. All of the others were smiling, and the songs that the bells sang were songs of joy. I squeezed Lyanna's hand tightly. 'Read,' I whispered.

We read.

Me: I read bells. Not the sound of bells, no, no, but the *feel* of bells, the *emotion* of bells, the bright clanging joy, the hooting-shouting-ringing loudness, the song of the Joined, the togetherness and the sharing of it all. I read what the Joined felt as they pealed their bells, their happiness and anticipation, their ecstasy in telling others of their clamorous contentment. And I read love, coming from them in great hot waves, passionate possessive love of a man and woman together, not the weak watery affection of the human who 'loves' his brothers. This was real and fervent and it burned almost as it washed over me and surrounded me. They loved themselves, and they loved all Shkeen, and they loved the Greeshka, and they loved each other, and they loved us. They loved us. They loved *me*, as hotly and wildly as Lya loved me. And with love I read belonging, and sharing. The four were all apart, all distinct, but they thought as one almost, and they belonged to each other, and they belonged to the Greeshka, and they were all *together* and linked although each was still himself and none could read the others as I read them.

And Lyanna? I reeled back from them, and shut myself off, and looked at Lya. She was white-faced, but smiling. 'They're beautiful,' she said, her voice very small and soft and wondering. Drenched in love, I still remembered how much I loved *her*, and how I was a part of her and her of me.

'What – what did you read?' I asked, my voice fighting the continued clangor of the bells.

She shook her head, as if to clear it. 'They love us,' she said. 'You must know that, but oh, I felt it, they *do* love us. And it's so *deep*. Below that love there's more love, and below that more, and on and on forever. Their minds are so deep, so open. I don't think I've ever read a human that deeply. Everything is right at the surface, right there, their whole lives and all their dreams and feelings and memories and oh – I just took it in, swept it up with a reading, a glance. With men, with humans, it's so much work, I have to dig, I have to fight, and even then I don't get down very far. You know, Robb, you know. Oh, *Robb!*' And she came to me and pressed tight against me, and I held her in my arms. The torrent of feeling that had washed over me must have been a tidal wave for her. Her Talent was broader and deeper than mine, and now she was shaken. I read her as she clutched me, and I read love, great love, and wonder and happiness, but also fear, nervous fear swirling through it all.

Around us, the ringing suddenly stopped. The bells, one by one, ceased to swing, and the four Joined stood in silence for a brief second. One of the other Shkeen nearby came up to them with a huge, cloth-covered basket. The smallest of the Joined threw back the cloth, and the aroma of hot meatrolls rose in the street. Each of the Joined took several from the basket, and before long they were all crunching away happily, and the owner of the rolls was grinning at them. Another Shkeen, a small nude girl, ran up and offered them a flask of water, and they passed it around without comment.

'What's going on?' I asked Lya. Then, even before she told me, I remembered. Something from the literature that Valcarenghi had sent. The Joined did no work. Forty Earth-years they lived and toiled, but from First Joining to Final Union there was only joy and music, and they wandered the streets and rang their bells and talked and sang, and other Shkeen gave them food and drink. It was an honor to feed a Joined, and the Shkeen who had given up his meatrolls was radiating pride and pleasure.

'Lya,' I whispered, 'can you read them now?'

She nodded against my chest and pulled away and stared at the Joined, her eyes going hard and then softening again. She looked back at me. 'It's different,' she said, curious.

'How?'

She squinted in puzzlement. 'I don't know. I mean, they still love us, and all. But now their thoughts are, well, sort of more human. There are levels, you know, and digging isn't easy, and there are hidden things, things they hide even from themselves. It's not all open like it was. They're thinking about the food now and how good it tastes. It's all very vivid. I could taste the rolls myself. But it's not the same.'

I had an inspiration. 'How many minds are there?'

'Four,' she said. 'Linked somehow, I think. But not really.' She stopped, confused, and shook her head. 'I mean, they sort of feel each other's emotions, like you do, I guess. But not thoughts, not the detail. I can read them, but they don't read each other. Each one is distinct. They were closer before, when they were ringing, but they were always individuals.'

I was slightly disappointed. 'Four minds then, not one?'

'Umpf, yes. Four.'

'And the Greeshka?' My other bright idea. If the Greeshka had minds of their own . . .

'Nothing,' Lya said. 'Like reading a plant, or a piece of clothing. Not even yes-I-live.'

That was disturbing. Even lower animals had some vague consciousness of life – the feeling Talents called yes-I-live – usually only a dim spark that it took a major Talent to see. But Lya *was* a major Talent.

'Let's talk to them,' I said. She nodded, and we walked up to where the Joined were munching their meatrolls. 'Hello,' I said awkwardly, wondering how to address them. 'Can you speak Terran?'

Three of them looked at me without comprehension. But the fourth one, the little one whose Greeshka was a rippling red cape, bobbed his head up and down. 'Yesh,' he said, in a piping-thin voice.

I suddenly forgot what I was going to ask, but Lyanna came to my rescue. 'Do you know of human Joined?' she said.

He grinned. 'All Joined are one,' he said.

'Oh,' I said. 'Well, yes, but do you know any who look like us? Tall, you know, with hair and skin that's pink or brown or something?' I came to another awkward halt, wondering just how *much* Terran the old Shkeen knew, and eyeing his Greeshka a little apprehensively.

His head hobbled from side to side. 'Joined are all different, but all are one, all are same. Shome look ash you. Would you Join?'

'No, thanks,' I said. 'Where can I find a human Joined?'

He bobbed his head some more. 'Joined shing and ring and walk the shacred city.'

Lya had been reading. 'He doesn't know,' she told me. 'The Joined just wander and play their bells. There's no pattern to it, nobody keeps track. It's all random. Some travel in groups, some alone, and new groups form every time two bunches meet.'

'We'll have to search,' I said.

'Eat,' the Shkeen told us. He reached into the basket on the ground and his hands came out with two steaming meatrolls. He pressed one into my hand, one in Lya's.

I looked at it dubiously. 'Thank you,' I told him. I pulled at Lya with my free hand and we walked off together. The Joined grinned at us as we left, and started ringing once more before we were halfway down the street.

The meatroll was still in my hand, its crust burning my fingers. 'Should I eat this?' I asked Lya.

She took a bite out of hers. 'Why not? We had them last night in the restaurant, right? And I'm sure Valcarenghi would've warned us if the native food was poisonous.'

That made sense, so I lifted the roll to my mouth and took a bite as I walked. It was hot, and also *hot*, and it wasn't a bit like the meatrolls we'd sampled the previous night. Those had been golden, flaky things, seasoned gently with orangespice from Baldur. The Shkeen version was crunchy, and the meat inside dripped grease and burned my mouth. But it was good, and I was hungry, and the roll didn't last long.

'Get anything else when you read the small guy?' I asked Lya around a mouthful of hot roll.

She swallowed, and nodded. 'Yes, I did. He was happy, even more than the rest. He's older. He's near Final Union, and he's very thrilled about it.' She spoke with her old easy manner; the aftereffects of reading the Joined seemed to have faded.

'Why?' I was musing out loud. 'He's going to die. Why is he so happy about it?'

Lya shrugged. 'He wasn't thinking in any great analytical detail, I'm afraid.'

I licked my fingers to get rid of the last of the grease. We were at a crossroads, with Shkeen bustling by us in all directions, and now we could hear more bells on the wind. 'More Joined,' I said. 'Want to look them up?'

'What would we find out? That we don't already know? We need a *human* Joined.'

'Maybe one of this batch *will* be human.'

I got Lya's withering look. 'Ha. What are the odds?'

'All right,' I conceded. It was now late afternoon. 'Maybe we'd better head back. Get an earlier start tomorrow. Besides, Dino is probably expecting us for dinner.'

*

Dinner, this time, was served in Valcarenghi's office, after a little additional furniture had been dragged in. His quarters, it turned out, were on the level below, but he preferred to entertain upstairs where his guests could enjoy the spectacular Tower view.

There were five of us, all told: me and Lya, Valcarenghi and Laurie, plus Gourlay. Laurie did the cooking, supervised by master chef Valcarenghi. We had beefsteaks, bred on Shkea from Old Earth stock, plus a fascinating blend of vegetables that included mushrooms from Old Earth, ground-pips from Baldur, and Shkeen sweethorns. Dino liked to experiment and the dish was one of his inventions.

Lya and I gave a full report on the day's adventures, interrupted only by Valcarenghi's sharp, perceptive questioning. After dinner, we got rid of tables and dishes and sat around drinking Veltaar and talking. This time Lya and I asked the questions, with Gourlay supplying the biggest chunk of the answers. Valcarenghi listened from a cushion on the floor, one arm around Laurie, the other holding his wine glass. We were not the first Talents to visit Shkea, he told us. Nor the first to claim the Shkeen were manlike.

'Suppose that means something,' he said. 'But I don't know. They're *not* men, you know. No, sir. They're much more social, for one thing. Great little city builders from way back, always in towns, always surrounding themselves with others. And they're more communal than man, too. Cooperate in all sorts of things, and they're big on sharing. Trade, for instance – they see that as mutual-sharing.'

Valcarenghi laughed. 'You can say that again. I just spent the whole day trying to work out a trade contract with a group of farmers who hadn't dealt with us before. It's not easy, believe me. They give us as much of their stuff as we ask for, if they don't need it themselves and no one else has asked for it earlier. But then they want to get whatever they ask for in the future. They expect it, in fact. So every time we deal we've got a choice; hand them a blank check, or go through an incredible round of talks that ends with them convinced that we're totally selfish.'

Lya wasn't satisfied. 'What about sex?' she demanded. 'From the stuff you were translating last night, I got the impression they're monogamous.'

'They're confused about sex relationships,' Gourlay said. 'It's very strange. Sex is sharing, you see, and it's good to share with everyone. But the sharing has to be real and meaningful. That creates problems.'

Laurie sat up, attentive. 'I've studied the point,' she said quickly. 'Shkeen morality insists they love *everybody*. But they can't do it, they're too human, too possessive. They wind up in monogamous relationships, because a really deep sex-sharing with one person is better than a million shallow physical things, in their culture. The ideal Shkeen would sex-share with everyone, with each of the unions being just as deep, but they can't achieve that ideal.'

I frowned. 'Wasn't somebody guilty last night over betraying his wife?'

Laurie nodded eagerly. 'Yes, but the guilt was because his other relationships caused his sharing with his wife to diminish. *That* was the betrayal. If he'd been able to manage it without hurting his older relationship, the sex would have been meaningless. And, if all of the relationships have been real love-sharing, it would have been a plus. His wife would have been proud of him. It's quite an achievement for a Shkeen to be in a multiple union that works.'

'And one of the greatest Shkeen crimes is to leave another alone,' Gourlay said. 'Emotionally alone. Without sharing.'

I mulled over that, while Gourlay went on. The Shkeen had little crime, he told us. Especially no violent crime. No murders, no beatings, no prisons, no wars in their long, empty history.

'They're a race without murderers,' Valcarenghi said, 'which may explain something. On Old Earth, the same cultures that had the highest suicide rates often had the lowest murder rates, too. And the Shkeen suicide rate is one hundred percent.'

'They kill animals,' I said.

'Not part of the Union,' Gourlay replied. 'The Union embraces all that thinks, and its creatures may not be killed. They do not kill Shkeen, or humans, or Greeshka.'

Lya looked at me, then at Gourlay. 'The Greeshka don't think,' she said. 'I tried to read them this morning and got nothing but the minds of the Shkeen they rode. Not even a yes-I-live.'

'We've known that, but the point's always puzzled me,' Valcarenghi said, climbing to his feet. He went to the bar for more wine, brought out a bottle, and filled our glasses. 'A truly mindless parasite, but an intelligent race like the Shkeen are enslaved by it. Why?'

The new wine was good and chilled, a cold trail down my throat. I drank it, and nodded, remembering the flood of euphoria that had swept over us earlier that day. 'Drugs,' I said, speculatively. 'The Greeshka must produce an organic pleasure-drug. The Shkeen submit to it willingly and die happy. The joy is real, believe me. We felt it.'

Lyanna looked doubtful, though, and Gourlay shook his head adamantly. 'No, Robb. Not so. We've experimented on the Greeshka, and . . .'

He must have noticed my raised eyebrows. He stopped.

'How did the Shkeen feel about that?' I asked.

'Didn't tell them. They wouldn't have liked it, not at all. Greeshka's just an animal, but it's their god. Don't fool around with God, you know. We refrained for a long time, but when Gustaffson went over, old Stuart had to know. His orders. We didn't get anywhere, though. No extracts that might be a drug, no secretions, nothing. In fact, the Shkeen are the *only* native life that submits so easily. We caught a whiner, you see, and strapped it down, and let a Greeshka link up. Then, couple hours later, we yanked the straps. Damn whiner was furious, screeching and yelping, attacking the thing on its head. Nearly clawed its own skull to ribbons before it got it off.'

'Maybe only the Shkeen are susceptible?' I said. A feeble rescue attempt.

'Not quite,' said Valcarenghi, with a small, thin smile. 'There's us.'

*

Lya was strangely silent in the tube, almost withdrawn. I assumed she was thinking about the conversation. But the door to our suite had barely slid shut behind us when she turned toward me and wrapped her arms around me.

I reached up and stroked her soft brown hair, slightly startled by the hug. 'Hey,' I muttered, 'what's wrong?'

She gave me her vampire look, big-eyed and fragile. 'Make love to me, Robb,' she said with a soft sudden urgency. 'Please. Make love to me now.'

I smiled, but it was a puzzled smile, not my usual lecherous bedroom grin. Lya generally comes on impish and wicked when she's horny, but now she was all troubled and vulnerable. I didn't quite get it.

But it wasn't a time for questions, and I didn't ask any. I just pulled her to me wordlessly and kissed her hard, and we walked together to the bedroom.

And we made love, *really* made love, more than poor Normals can do. We joined our bodies as one, and I felt Lya stiffen as her mind reached out to mine. And as we moved together I was opening myself to her, drowning myself in the flood of love and need and fear that was pouring from her.

Then, quickly as it had begun, it ended. Her pleasure washed over me in a raw red wave. And I joined her on the crest, and Lya clutched me tightly, her eyes shrunk up small as she drank it all in.

Afterwards, we lay there in the darkness and let the stars of Shkea pour their radiance through the window. Lya huddled against me, her head on my chest, while I stroked her. 'That was good,' I said in a drowsy-dreamy voice, smiling in the star-filled darkness.

'Yes,' she replied. Her voice was soft and small, so small I barely heard it. 'I love you, Robb,' she whispered.

'Uh-huh,' I said. 'And I love you.'

She pulled loose of my arm and rolled over, propping her head on a hand to stare at me and smile. 'You do,' she said. 'I read it. I know it. And you know how much I love you, too, don't you?'

I nodded, smiling. 'Sure.'

'We're lucky, you know. The Normals have only words. Poor little Normals. How can they *tell*, with just words? How can they *know*? They're always apart from each other, trying to reach each other and failing. Even when they make love, even when they come, they're always apart. They must be very lonely.'

There was something . . . disturbing . . . in that. I looked at Lya, into her bright happy eyes, and thought about it. 'Maybe,' I said, finally. 'But it's not that bad for them. They don't know any other way. And they try, they love too. They bridge the gap sometimes.'

'Only a look and a voice, then darkness again and a silence,' Lya quoted, her voice sad and tender. 'We're luckier, aren't we? We have so much more.'

'We're luckier,' I echoed. And I reached out to read her too. Her mind was a haze of satisfaction, with a gentle scent of wistful, lonely longing. But there was something else, way down, almost gone now, but still faintly detectable.

I sat up slowly. 'Hey,' I said. 'You're worried about something. And before, when we came in, you were scared. What's the matter?'

'I don't know, really,' she said. She sounded puzzled and she *was* puzzled; I read it there. 'I *was* scared, but I don't know why. The Joined, I think. I kept thinking about how much they loved me. They didn't even *know* me, but they loved me so much, and they understood – it was almost like what we have. It – I don't know. It bothered me. I mean, I didn't think I could ever be loved that way, except by you. And they were so close, so together. I felt kind of lonely, just holding hands and talking. I wanted to be close to you that way. After the way they were all sharing and everything, being alone just seemed empty. And frightening. You know?'

'I know,' I said, touching her lightly again, with hand and mind. 'I understand. We do understand each other. We're together almost as they are, as Normals can't ever be.'

Lya nodded, and smiled, and hugged me. We went to sleep in each other's arms.

*

Dreams again. But again, at dawn, the memory stole away from me. It was all very annoying. The dream had been pleasant, comfortable. I wanted it back, and I couldn't even remember what it was. Our bedroom, washed by harsh daylight, seemed drab compared to the splendors of my lost vision.

Lya woke after me, with another headache. This time she had the pills on hand, by the bedstand. She grimaced and took one.

'It must be the Shkeen wine,' I told her. 'Something about it takes a dim view of your metabolism.'

She pulled on a fresh coverall and scowled at me. 'Ha. We were drinking Veltaar last night, remember? My father gave me my first glass of Veltaar when I was nine. It never gave me headaches before.'

'A first!' I said, smiling.

'It's not funny,' she said. 'It hurts.'

I quit kidding, and tried to read her. She was right. It *did* hurt. Her whole forehead throbbed with pain. I withdrew quickly before I caught it too.

'All right,' I said. 'I'm sorry. The pills will take care of it, though. Meanwhile, we've got work to do.'

Lya nodded. She'd never let anything interfere with work yet.

The second day was a day of manhunt. We got off to a much earlier start, had a quick breakfast with Gourlay, then picked up our aircar outside the tower. This time we didn't drop down when we hit Shkeentown. We wanted a human Joined, which meant we had to cover a lot of ground. The city was the biggest I'd ever seen, in area at any rate, and the thousand-odd human cultists were lost among millions of Shkeen. And, of those humans, only about half were actually Joined yet.

So we kept the aircar low, and buzzed up and down the dome-dotted hills like a floating roller coaster, causing quite a stir in the streets below us. The Shkeen had seen aircars before, of course, but it still had some novelty value, particularly to the kids, who tried to run after us whenever we flashed by. We also panicked a whiner, causing him to upset the cart full of fruit he was dragging. I felt guilty about that, so I kept the car higher afterwards.

We spotted Joined all over the city, singing, eating, walking – and ringing those bells, those eternal bronze bells. But for the first three hours, all we found were Shkeen Joined. Lya and I took turns driving and watching. After the excitement of the previous day, the search was tedious and tiring.

Finally, however, we found something: a large group of Joined, ten of them, clustered around a bread cart behind one of the steeper hills. Two were taller than the rest.

We landed on the other side of the hill and walked around to meet them, leaving our aircar surrounded by a crowd of Shkeen children. The Joined were still eating when we arrived. Eight of them were Shkeen of various sizes and hues, Greeshka pulsing atop their skulls. The other two were human.

They wore the same long red gowns as the Shkeen, and they carried the same bells. One of them was a big man, with loose skin that hung in flaps, as if he'd lost a lot of weight recently. His hair was white and curly, his face marked by a broad smile and laugh wrinkles around the eyes. The other was a thin, dark weasel of a man with a big hooked nose.

Both of them had Greeshka sucking at their skulls. The parasite riding the weasel was barely a pimple, but the older man had a lordly specimen that dripped down beyond his shoulders and into the back of the gown.

Somehow, this time, it *did* look hideous.

Lyanna and I walked up to them, trying hard to smile, not reading – at least at first. They smiled at us as we approached. Then they waved.

'Hello,' the weasel said cheerily when we got there. 'I've never seen you. Are you new on Shkea?'

That took me slightly by surprise. I'd been expecting some sort of garbled mystic greeting, or maybe no greeting at all. I was assuming that somehow the human converts would have abandoned their humanity to become mock-Shkeen. I was wrong.

'More or less,' I replied. And I read the weasel. He was genuinely pleased to see us, and just bubbled with contentment and good cheer. 'We've been hired to talk to people like you.' I'd decided to be honest about it.

The weasel stretched his grin further than I thought it would go. 'I am Joined, and happy,' he said. 'I'll be glad to talk to you. My name is Lester Kamenz. What do you want to know, brother?'

Lya, next to me, was going tense. I decided I'd let her read in depth while I asked questions. 'When did you convert to the Cult?'

'Cult?' Kamenz said.

'The Union.'

He nodded, and I was struck by the grotesque similarity of his bobbing head and that of the elderly Shkeen we'd seen yesterday. 'I have always been in the Union. You are in the Union. All that thinks is in the Union.'

'Some of us weren't told,' I said. 'How about you? When did you realize you were in the Union?'

'A year ago, Old Earth time. I was admitted to the ranks of the Joined only a few weeks ago. The First Joining is a joyful time. I am joyful. Now I will walk the streets and ring my bells until the Final Union.'

'What did you do before?'

'Before?' A short vague look. 'I ran machines once. I ran computers, in the Tower. But my life was empty, brother. I did not know I was in the Union, and I was alone. I had only machines, cold machines. Now I am Joined. Now I am' – again he searched – 'not alone.'

I reached into him, and found the happiness still there, with love. But now there was an ache too, a vague recollection of past pain, the stink of unwelcome memories. Did these fade? Maybe the gift the Greeshka gave its victims was oblivion, sweet mindless rest and end of struggle. Maybe.

I decided to try something. 'That thing on your head,' I said, sharply. 'It's a parasite. It's drinking your blood right now, feeding on it. As it grows, it will take more and more of the things *you* need to live. Finally it will start to eat your tissue. Understand? It will *eat* you. I don't know how painful it will be, but however it feels, at the end you'll be *dead*. Unless you come back to the Tower now, and have the surgeons remove it. Or maybe you could remove it yourself. Why don't you try? Just reach up and pull it off. Go ahead.'

I'd expected – what? Rage? Horror? Disgust? I got none of these. Kamenz just stuffed bread in his mouth and smiled at me, and all I read was his love and joy and a little pity.

'The Greeshka does not kill,' he said finally. 'The Greeshka gives joy and happy Union. Only those who have no Greeshka die. They are . . . alone. Oh, forever alone.' Something in his mind trembled with sudden fear, but it faded quickly.

I glanced at Lya. She was stiff and hard-eyed, still reading. I looked back and began to phrase another question. But suddenly the Joined began to ring. One of the Shkeen started it off, swinging his bell up and down to produce a single sharp clang. Then his other hand swung, then the first again, then the second, then another Joined began to ring, then still another, and then they were all swinging and clanging and the noise of their bells was smashing against my ears as the joy and the love and the feel of the bells assaulted my mind once again.

I lingered to savor it. The love there was breathtaking, awesome, almost frightening in its heat and intensity, and there was so much sharing to frolic in and wonder at, such a soothing-calming-exhilarating tapestry of good feeling. Something happened to the Joined when they rang, something touched them and lifted them and gave them a glow, something strange and glorious that mere Normals could not hear in their harsh clanging music. I was no Normal, though. I could hear it.

I withdrew reluctantly, slowly. Kamenz and the other human were both ringing vigorously now, with broad smiles and glowing twinkling eyes that transfigured their faces. Lyanna was still tense, still reading. Her mouth was slightly open, and she trembled where she stood.

I put an arm around her and waited, listening to the music, patient. Lya continued to read. Finally, after minutes, I shook her gently. She turned and studied me with hard, distant eyes. Then blinked. And her eyes widened and she came back, shaking her head and frowning.

Puzzled, I looked into her head. Strange and stranger. It was a swirling fog of emotion, a dense moving blend of more feelings than I'd care to put a name to. No sooner had I entered than I was lost, lost and uneasy. Somewhere in the fog there was a bottomless abyss lurking to engulf me. At least it felt that way.

'Lya,' I said. 'What's wrong?'

She shook her head again, and looked at the Joined with a look that was equal parts fear and longing. I repeated my question.

'I – I don't know,' she said. 'Robb, let's not talk now. Let's go. I want time to think.'

'OK,' I said. What was going on here? I took her hand and we walked slowly around the hill to the slope where we'd left the car. Shkeen kids were climbing all over it. I chased them, laughing. Lya just stood there, her eyes gone all faraway on me. I wanted to read her again, but somehow I felt it would be an invasion of privacy.

Airborne, we streaked back toward the Tower, riding higher and faster this time. I drove, while Lya sat beside me and stared out into the distance.

'Did you get anything useful?' I asked her, trying to get her mind back on the assignment.

'Yes. No. Maybe.' Her voice sounded distracted, as if only part of her was talking to me. 'I read their lives, both of them. Kamenz was a computer programmer, as he said. But he wasn't very good. An ugly little man with an ugly little personality, no friends, no sex, no nothing. Lived by himself, avoided the Shkeen, didn't like them at all. Didn't even like people, really. But Gustaffson got through to him, somehow. He ignored Kamenz' coldness, his bitter little cuts, his cruel jokes. He didn't retaliate, you know? After a while, Kamenz came to like Gustaffson, to admire him. They were never really friends in any normal sense, but still Gustaffson was the nearest thing to a friend that Kamenz had.'

She stopped suddenly. 'So he went over with Gustaffson?' I prompted, glancing at her quickly. Her eyes still wandered.

'No, not at first. He was still afraid, still scared of the Shkeen and terrified of the Greeshka. But later, with Gustaffson gone, he began to realize how empty his life was. He worked all day with people who despised him and machines that didn't care, then sat alone at night reading and watching holoshows. Not life, really. He hardly touched the people around him. Finally he went to find Gustaffson, and wound up converted. Now . . .'

'Now . . . ?'

She hesitated. 'He's happy, Robb,' she said. 'He really is. For the first time in his life, he's happy. He'd never known love before. Now it fills him.'

'You got a lot,' I said.

'Yes.' Still the distracted voice, the lost eyes. 'He was open, sort of. There were levels, but digging wasn't as hard as it usually is – as if his barriers were weakening, coming down almost . . .'

'How about the other guy?'

She stroked the instrument panel, staring only at her hand. 'Him? That was Gustaffson . . .'

And that, suddenly, seemed to wake her, to restore her to the Lya I knew and loved. She shook her head and looked at me, and the aimless voice became an animated torrent of words. 'Robb, listen, that was *Gustaffson*, he's been Joined over a year now, and he's going on to Final Union within a week. The Greeshka has accepted him, and he wants it, you know? He really does, and – and – oh Robb, he's *dying!*'

'Within a week, according to what you just said.'

'No. I mean yes, but that's not what I mean. Final Union isn't death, to him. He believes it, all of it, the whole religion. The Greeshka is his god, and he's going to join it. But before, and now, he was dying. He's got the Slow Plague, Robb. A terminal case. It's been eating at him from inside for over fifteen years now. He got it back on Nightmare, in the swamps, when his family died. That's no world for people, but he was there, the administrator over a research base, a short-term thing. They lived on Thor; it was only a visit, but the ship crashed. Gustaffson got all wild and tried to reach them before the end, but he grabbed a faulty pair of skinthins, and the spores got through. And they were all dead when he got there. He had an awful lot of pain, Robb. From the Slow Plague, but more from the loss. He really loved them, and it was never the same after. They gave him Shkea as a reward, kind of, to take his mind off the crash, but he still thought of it all the time. I could see the picture, Robb. It was vivid. He couldn't forget it. The kids were inside the ship, safe behind the walls, but the life system failed and choked them to death. But his wife – oh, Robb – she took some skinthins and tried to go for help, and outside those *things*, those big wrigglers they have on Nightmare—?'

I swallowed hard, feeling a little sick. 'The eater-worms,' I said, dully. I'd read about them, and seen holos. I could imagine the picture that Lya'd seen in Gustaffson's memory, and it wasn't at all pretty. I was glad I didn't have her Talent.

'They were still – still – when Gustaffson got there. You know. He killed them all with a screechgun.'

I shook my head. 'I didn't think things like that really went on.'

'No,' Lya said. 'Neither did Gustaffson. They'd been so – so *happy* before that, before the thing on Nightmare. He loved her, and they were really close, and his career had been almost charmed. He didn't have to go to Nightmare, you know. He took it because it was a challenge, because nobody else could handle it. That gnaws at him, too. And he remembers all the time. He – they—' Her voice faltered. 'They thought they were *lucky*,' she said, before falling into silence.

There was nothing to say to that. I just kept quiet and drove, thinking, feeling a blurred, watered-down version of what Gustaffson's pain must have been like. After a while, Lya began to speak again.

'It was all there, Robb,' she said, her voice softer and slower and more thoughtful once again. 'But he was at peace. He still remembered it all, and the way it had hurt, but it didn't bother him as it had. Only now he was sorry they weren't with him. He was sorry that they died without Final Union. Almost like the Shkeen woman, remember? The one at the Gathering? With her brother?'

'I remember,' I said.

'Like that. And his mind was open, too. More than Kamenz, much more.

When he rang, the levels all vanished, and everything was right at the surface, all the love and pain and everything. His whole life, Robb. I shared his whole life with him, in an instant. And all his thoughts, too . . . he's seen the caves of Union . . . he went down once, before he converted. I . . .'

More silence, settling over us and darkening the car. We were close to the end of Shkeentown. The Tower slashed the sky ahead of us, shining in the sun. And the lower domes and archways of the glittering human city were coming into view.

'Robb,' Lya said. 'Land here. I have to think a while, you know? Go back without me. I want to walk among the Shkeen a little.'

I glanced at her, frowning. 'Walk? It's a long way back to the Tower, Lya.'

'I'll be all right. Please. Just let me think a bit.'

I read her. The thought fog had returned, denser than ever, laced through with the colors of fear. 'Are you sure?' I said. 'You're scared, Lyanna. Why? What's wrong? The eater-worms are a long way off.'

She just looked at me, troubled. 'Please, Robb,' she repeated.

I didn't know what else to do, so I landed.

*

And I, too, thought, as I guided the aircar home. Of what Lyanna had said, and read – of Kamenz and Gustaffson. I kept my mind on the problem we'd been assigned to crack. I tried to keep it off Lya, and whatever was bothering her. That would solve itself, I thought.

Back at the Tower, I wasted no time. I went straight up to Valcarenghi's office. He was there, alone, dictating into a machine. He shut it off when I entered.

'Hi, Robb,' he began. 'Where's Lya?'

'Out walking. She wanted to think. I've been thinking, too. And I believe I've got your answer.'

He raised his eyebrows, waiting.

I sat down. 'We found Gustaffson this afternoon, and Lya read him. I think it's clear why he went over. He was a broken man, inside, however much he smiled. The Greeshka gave him an end to his pain. And there was another convert with him, a Lester Kamenz. He'd been miserable, too, a pathetic lonely man with nothing to live for. Why *shouldn't* he convert? Check out the other converts, and I bet you'll find a pattern. The most lost and vulnerable, the failures, the isolated – those will be the ones that turned to Union.'

Valcarenghi nodded. 'OK, I'll buy that,' he said. 'But our psychs guessed that long ago, Robb. Only it's no answer, not really. Sure, the converts on the whole have been a messed-up crew, I won't dispute that. But why turn to the Cult of the Union? The psychs can't answer that. Take Gustaffson now. He was a strong man, believe me. I never knew him personally, but I knew his career. He took some rough assignments, generally for the hell of it, and beat them. He could have had the cushy jobs, but he wasn't interested. I've heard about the incident on Nightmare. It's famous, in a warped sort of way. But Phil Gustaffson wasn't the sort of man to be beaten, even by something like that. He snapped out of it very quickly, from what Nelse tells me. He came to Shkea and really set the place in order, cleaning up the mess that Rockwood had left. He pushed through the first real trade contract we ever got, *and* he made the Shkeen understand what it meant, which isn't easy.

'So here he is, this competent, talented man, who's made a career of beating tough jobs and handling men. He's gone through a personal nightmare, but it hasn't destroyed him. He's as tough as ever. And suddenly he turns to the Cult of the Union, signs up for a grotesque suicide. Why? For an end to his pain, you say? An interesting theory, but there are other ways to end pain. Gustaffson had years between Nightmare and the Greeshka. He never ran away from pain then. He didn't turn to drink, or drugs, or any of the usual outs. He didn't head back to Old Earth to have a psipsych clean up his memories – and believe me, he could've gotten it paid for, if he'd wanted it. The colonial office would have done anything for him, after Nightmare. He went on, swallowed his pain, rebuilt. Until suddenly he converts.

'His pain made him more vulnerable, yes, no doubt of it. But something else brought him over – something that Union offered, something he couldn't get from wine or memory wipe. The same's true of Kamenz, and the others. They had other outs, other ways to vote no on life. They passed them up. But they chose Union. You see what I'm getting at?'

I did, of course. My answer was no answer at all, and I realized it. But Valcarenghi was wrong too, in parts.

'Yes,' I said. 'I guess we've still got some reading to do.' I smiled wanly. 'One thing, though. Gustaffson hadn't really beaten his pain, not ever. Lya was very clear on that. It was inside him all the time, tormenting him. He just never let it come out.'

'That's victory, isn't it?' Valcarenghi said. 'If you bury your hurts so deep that no one can tell you have them?'

'I don't know. I don't think so. But . . . anyway, there was more. Gustaffson has the Slow Plague. He's dying. He's been dying for years.'

Valcarenghi's expression flickered briefly. 'That I didn't know, but it just bolsters my point. I've read that some eighty percent of Slow Plague victims opt for euthanasia, if they happen to be on a planet where it's legal. Gustaffson was a planetary administrator. He could have *made* it legal. If he passed up suicide for all those years, why choose it now?'

I didn't have an answer for that. Lyanna hadn't given me one, if she had one. I didn't know where we could find one, either, unless . . .

'The caves,' I said suddenly. 'The caves of Union. We've got to witness a Final Union. There must be something about it, something that accounts for the conversions. Give us a chance to find out what it is.'

Valcarenghi smiled. 'All right,' he said. 'I can arrange it. I expected it would come to that. It's not pleasant, though, I'll warn you. I've gone down myself, so I know what I'm talking about.'

'That's OK,' I told him. 'If you think reading Gustaffson was any fun, you should have seen Lya when she was through. She's out now trying to walk it off.' That, I'd decided, must have been what was bothering her. 'Final Union won't be any worse than those memories of Nightmare, I'm sure.'

'Fine, then. I'll set it up for tomorrow. I'm going with you, of course. I don't want to take any chances on anything happening to you.'

I nodded. Valcarenghi rose. 'Good enough,' he said. 'Meanwhile, let's think about more interesting things. You have any plans for dinner?'

We wound up eating at a mock-Shkeen restaurant run by humans, in the company of Gourlay and Laurie Blackburn. The talk was mostly social noises – sports, politics, art, old jokes, that sort of thing. I don't think there was a mention of the Shkeen or the Greeshka all evening.

Afterwards, when I got back to our suite, I found Lyanna waiting for me. She was in bed, reading one of the handsome volumes from our library, a book of Old Earth poetry. She looked up when I entered.

'Hi,' I said. 'How was your walk?'

'Long.' A smile creased her pale, small face, then faded. 'But I had time to think. About this afternoon, and yesterday, and about the Joined. And us.'

'Us?'

'Robb, do you love me?' The question was delivered almost matter-of-factly, in a voice full of question. As if she didn't know. As if she really didn't know.

I sat down on the bed and took her hand and tried to smile. 'Sure,' I said. 'You know that, Lya.'

'I did. I do. You love me, Robb, really you do. As much as a human can love. But . . .' She stopped. She shook her head and closed her book and sighed. 'But we're still apart, Robb. We're still apart.'

'What *are* you talking about?'

'This afternoon. I was so confused afterwards, and scared. I wasn't sure why, but I've thought about it. When I was reading, Robb – I was in there,

with the Joined, sharing them and their love. I really was. And I didn't
want to come out. I didn't want to leave them, Robb. When I did, I felt so
isolated, so cut off.'

'That's your fault,' I said. 'I tried to talk to you. You were too busy
thinking.'

'Talking? What good is talking? It's communication, I guess, but is it
really? I used to think so, before they trained my Talent. After that, reading
seemed to be the real communication, the real way to reach somebody else,
somebody like you. But now I don't know. The Joined – when they ring –
they're so *together*, Robb. All linked. Like us when we make love, almost.
And they love each other, too. And they love us, so intensely. I felt – I
don't know. But Gustaffson loves me as much as you do. No. He loves me
more.'

Her face was white as she said that, her eyes wide, lost, lonely. And me,
I felt a sudden chill, like a cold wind blowing through my soul. I didn't say
anything. I only looked at her, and wet my lips. And bled.

She saw the hurt in my eyes, I guess. Or read it. Her hand pulled at
mine, caressed it. 'Oh, Robb. Please. I don't mean to hurt you. It's not you.
It's all of us. What do *we* have, compared to *them?*'

'I don't know what you're talking about, Lya.' Half of me suddenly
wanted to cry. The other half wanted to shout. I stifled both halves, and
kept my voice steady. But inside I wasn't steady, I wasn't steady at all.

'Do you love me, Robb?' Again. Wondering.

'Yes!' Fiercely. A challenge.

'What does that mean?' she said.

'You know what it means,' I said. 'Dammit, Lya, *think!* Remember all
we've had, all we've shared together. *That's* love, Lya. It is. We're the lucky
ones, remember? You said that yourself. The Normals have only a touch
and a voice, then back to their darkness. They can barely find each other.
They're alone. Always. Groping. Trying, over and over, to climb out of their
isolation booths, and failing, over and over. But not us, we found the way,
we know each other as much as any human beings ever can. There's
nothing I wouldn't tell you, or share with you. I've said that before, and
you know it's true, you can read it in me. *That's* love, dammit. *Isn't it?*'

'I don't know,' she said, in a voice so sadly baffled. Soundlessly, without
even a sob, she began to cry. And while the tears ran in lonely paths down
her cheeks, she talked. 'Maybe that's love. I always thought it was. But
now I don't know. If what we have is love, what was it I felt this
afternoon, what was it I touched and shared in? Oh, Robb. I love you too.
You know that. I try to share with you. I want to share what I read, what it
was like. But I can't. We're cut off. I can't make you understand. I'm here

and you're there and we can touch and make love and talk, but we're still apart. You see? You see? I'm alone. And this afternoon, I wasn't.'

'You're not alone, dammit,' I said suddenly. 'I'm here,' I clutched her hand tightly. 'Feel? Hear? You're not alone!'

She shook her head, and the tears flowed on. 'You don't understand, see? And there's no way I can make you. You said we know each other as much as any human beings ever can. You're right. But how much can human beings know each other? Aren't all of them cut off, really? Each alone in a big dark empty universe? We only trick ourselves when we think that someone else is there. In the end, in the cold lonely end, it's only us, by ourselves, in the blackness. Are you there, Robb? How do I know? Will you die with me, Robb? Will we be together then? Are we together now? You say we're luckier than the Normals. I've said it too. They have only a touch and voice, right? How many times have I quoted that? But what do we have? A touch and two voices, maybe. It's not enough anymore. I'm scared. Suddenly I'm scared.'

She began to sob. Instinctively I reached out to her, wrapped her in my arms, stroked her. We lay back together, and she wept against my chest. I read her, briefly, and I read her pain, her sudden loneliness, her hunger, all aswirl in a darkening mindstorm of fear. And, though I touched her and caressed her and whispered – over and over – that it would be all right, that I was here, that she wasn't alone, I knew that it would not be enough. Suddenly there was a gulf between us, a great dark yawning thing that grew and grew, and I didn't know how to bridge it. And Lya, my Lya, was crying, and she needed me. And I needed her, but I couldn't get to her.

Then I realized that I was crying too.

We held each other, in silent tears, for what must have been an hour. But finally the tears ran out. Lya clutched her body to me so tightly I could hardly breathe, and I held her just as tightly.

'Robb,' she whispered. 'You said – you said we really know each other. All those times you've said it. And you say, sometimes, that I'm *right* for you, that I'm perfect.'

I nodded, wanting to believe. 'Yes. You are.'

'No,' she said, choking out the word, forcing it into the air, fighting herself to say it. 'It's not *so*. I read you, yes. I can hear the words rattling around in your head as you fit a sentence together before saying it. And I listen to you scold yourself when you've done something stupid. And I see memories, some memories, and live through them with you. But it's all on the surface, Robb, all on the top. Below it, there's more, more of *you*. Drifting half-thoughts I don't quite catch. Feelings I can't put a name to. Passions you suppress, and memories even you don't know you have. Sometimes I can get to that level. Sometimes. If I really fight, if I drain myself to exhaustion. But when I get there, I know – I *know* – that there's another level below *that*. And more and more, on and on, down and down. I can't reach them, Robb, though they're part of you. I don't know you, I can't know you. You don't even know yourself, see? And me, do you know me? No. Even less. You know what I tell you, and I tell you the truth, but maybe not all. And you read my feelings, my surface feelings – the pain of a stubbed toe, a quick flash of annoyance, the pleasure I get when you're in me. Does that mean you know me? What of *my* levels, and levels? What about the things I don't even know myself? Do *you* know them? How, Robb, *how?'*

She shook her head again, with that funny little gesture she had whenever she was confused. 'And you say I'm perfect, and that you love me. I'm so right for you. But *am* I? Robb, I *read your thoughts*. I know when you want me to be sexy, so I'm sexy. I see what turns you on, so I do it. I know when you want me to be serious, and when you want me to joke. I know what kind of jokes to tell, too. Never the cutting kind, you don't like that, to hurt or see people hurt. You laugh *with* people not *at* them, and I laugh with you, and love you for your tastes. I know when you want me to talk, and when to keep quiet. I know when you want me to be your proud tigress, your tawny telepath, and when you want a little girl to shelter in your arms. And I *am* those things, Robb, because you want me to be, because I love you, because I can feel the joy in your mind at every *right* thing that I do. I never set out to do it that way, but it happened. I didn't mind, I don't mind. Most of the time it wasn't even conscious. You do the same thing, too. I read it in you. You can't read as I do, so sometimes you guess wrong – you come on witty when I want silent understanding, or you act the strong man when I need a boy to mother. But you get it right sometimes, too. And you *try*, you always try.

'But is it really *you*? Is it really *me*? What if I wasn't perfect, you see, if I was just myself, with all my faults and the things you don't like out in the open? Would you love me *then*? I don't know. But Gustaffson would, and Kamenz. I know that, Robb. I saw it. I know *them*. Their levels . . . vanished. I *KNOW* them, and if I went back I could share with them, more than with you. And they know me, the real me, all of me, I think. And they love me. *You see? You see?'*

Did I see? I don't know. I was confused. Would I love Lya if she was 'herself?' But what was 'herself?' How was it different from the Lya I knew? I thought I loved Lya and would always love Lya – but what if the real Lya wasn't like my Lya? *What* did I love? The strange abstract concept of a human being, or the flesh and voice and personality that I thought of as Lya? I didn't know. I didn't know who Lya was, or who I was, or what the hell it all meant. And I was scared. Maybe I couldn't feel what she had felt that afternoon. But I knew what she was feeling then. I was alone, and I needed someone.

'Lya,' I called. 'Lya, let's try. We don't have to give up. We can reach each other. There's a way, our way. We've done it before. Come, Lya, come with me, come to me.'

As I spoke, I undressed her, and she responded and her hands joined mine. When we were nude, I began to stroke her, slowly, and she me. Our minds reached out to each other. Reached and probed as never before. I could feel her, inside my head, digging. Deeper and deeper. Down. And I opened myself to her, I surrendered, all the petty little secrets I had kept even from her, or tried to, now I yielded up to her, everything I could remember, my triumphs and shames, the good moments and the pain, the times I'd hurt someone, the times I'd been hurt, the long crying sessions by myself, the fears I wouldn't admit, the prejudices I fought, the vanities I battled when the time struck, the silly boyish sins. All. Everything. I buried nothing. I hid nothing. I gave myself to her, to Lya, to *my* Lya. She had to know me.

And so too she yielded. Her mind was a forest through which I roamed, hunting down wisps of emotion, the fear and the need and the love at the top, the fainter things beneath, the half-formed whims and passions still deeper into the woods. I don't have Lya's Talent, I read only feelings, never thoughts. But I read thoughts then, for the first and only time, thoughts she threw at me because I'd never seen them before. I couldn't read much, but some I got.

And as her mind opened to mine, so did her body. I entered her, and we moved together, bodies one, minds entwined, as close as human beings can join. I felt pleasure washing over me in great glorious waves, my pleasure, her pleasure, both together building on each other, and I rode the crest for an eternity as it approached a far distant shore. And finally as it smashed into that beach, we came together, and for a second – for a tiny, fleeting second – I could not tell which orgasm was mine, and which was hers.

But then it passed. We lay, bodies locked together, on the bed. In the starlight. But it was not a bed. It was the beach, the flat black beach, and there were no stars above. A thought touched me, a vagrant thought that was not mine. Lya's thought. We were on a plain, she was thinking, and I saw that she was right. The waters that had carried us here were gone, receded. There was only a vast flat blackness stretching away in all directions, with dim ominous shapes moving on either horizon. *We are here as on a darkling plain*, Lya thought. And suddenly I knew what those shapes were, and what poem she had been reading. We slept.

*

I woke, alone.

The room was dark. Lya lay on the other side of the bed, curled up, still asleep. It was late, near dawn I thought. But I wasn't sure. I was restless.

I got up and dressed in silence. I needed to walk somewhere, to think, to work things out. Where, though?

There was a key in my pocket. I touched it when I pulled on my tunic, and remembered. Valcarenghi's office. It would be locked and deserted at this time of night. And the view might help me think.

I left, found the tubes, and shot up, up, up to the apex of the Tower, the top of man's steel challenge to the Shkeen. The office was unlit, the furniture dark shapes in the shadows. There was only the starlight. Shkea is closer to the galactic center than Old Earth, or Baldur. The stars are a fiery canopy across the night sky. Some of them are very close, and they burn like red and blue-white fires in the awesome blackness above. In Valcarenghi's office, all the walls are glass; I went to one, and looked out. I wasn't thinking. Just feeling. And I felt cold and lost and little.

Then there was a soft voice behind me saying hello. I barely heard it.

I turned away from the window, but other stars leaped at me from the far walls. Laurie Blackburn sat in one of the low chairs, concealed by the darkness.

'Hello,' I said. 'I didn't mean to intrude. I thought no one would be here.'

She smiled. A radiant smile in a radiant face, but there was no humor in it. Her hair fell in sweeping auburn waves past her shoulders, and she was dressed in something long and gauzy. I could see her gentle curves through its folds, and she made no effort to hide herself.

'I come up here a lot,' she said. 'At night, usually. When Dino's asleep. It's a good place to think.'

'Yes,' I said, smiling. 'My thoughts, too.'

'The stars are pretty, aren't they?'

'Yes.'

'I think so. I—' Hesitation. Then she rose and came to me. 'Do you love Lya?' she said.

A hammer of a question. Timed terribly. But I handled it well, I think. My mind was still on my talk with Lya. 'Yes,' I said. 'Very much. Why?'

She was standing close to me, looking at my face, and past me, out to the stars. 'I don't know. I wonder about love, sometimes. I love Dino, you know. He came here two months ago, so we haven't known each other long. But I love him already. I've never known anybody like him. He's kind, and considerate, and he does everything well. I've never seen him fail at anything he tried. Yet he doesn't seem driven, like some men. He wins so easily. He believes in himself a lot, and that's attractive. He's given me anything I could ask for, everything.'

I read her, caught her love and worry, and guessed. 'Except himself,' I said.

She looked at me, startled. Then she smiled. 'I forgot. You're a Talent. Of course you know. You're right. I don't know what I worry about, but I do worry. Dino is so perfect, you know. I've told him – well, everything. All about me and my life. And he listens and understands. He's always receptive, he's there when I need him. But—'

'It's all one way,' I said. It was a statement. I knew.

She nodded. 'It's not that he keeps secrets. He doesn't. He'll answer any question I ask. But the answers mean nothing. I ask him what he fears, and he says nothing, and makes me believe it. He's very rational, very calm. He never gets angry, he never has. I asked him. He doesn't hate people, he thinks hate is bad. He's never felt pain, either, or he says he hasn't. Emotional pain, I mean. Yet he understands me when I talk about my life. Once he said his biggest fault was laziness. But he's not lazy at all, I know that. Is he really that perfect? He tells me he's always sure of himself, because he *knows* he's good, but he smiles when he says it, so I can't even accuse him of being vain. He says he believes in God, but he never talks about it. If you try to talk seriously, he'll listen patiently, or joke with you, or lead the conversation away. He says he loves me, but—'

I nodded. I knew what was coming.

It came. She looked up at me, eyes begging. 'You're a Talent,' she said. 'You've read him, haven't you? You know him? Tell me. Please tell me.'

I was reading her. I could see how much she needed to know, how much she worried and feared, how much she loved. I couldn't lie to her. Yet it was hard to give her the answer I had to.

'I've read him,' I said. Slowly. Carefully. Measuring out my words like precious fluids. 'And you, you too. I saw your love, on that first night, when we ate together.'

'And Dino?'

My words caught in my throat. 'He's – funny, Lya said once. I can read his surface emotions easily enough. Below that, nothing. He's very self-contained, walled off. Almost as if his only emotions are the ones he – *allows* himself to feel. I've felt his confidence, his pleasure. I've felt worry too, but never real fear. He's very affectionate toward you, very protective. He enjoys feeling protective.'

'Is that all?' So hopeful. It hurt.

'I'm afraid it is. He's walled off, Laurie. He needs himself, only himself. If there's love in him, it's behind that wall, hidden. I can't read it. He thinks a lot of you, Laurie. But love – well, it's different. It's stronger and more unreasoning and it comes in crashing floods. And Dino's not like that, at least not out where I can read.'

'Closed,' she said. 'He's closed to me. I opened myself to him, totally. But he didn't. I was always afraid – even when he was with me, I felt sometimes that he wasn't there at all—'

She sighed. I read her despair, her welling loneliness. I didn't know what to do. 'Cry if you like,' I told her, inanely. 'Sometimes it helps. I know. I've cried enough in my time.'

She didn't cry. She looked up, and laughed lightly. 'No,' she said. 'I can't. Dino taught me never to cry. He said tears never solve anything.'

A sad philosophy. Tears don't solve anything, maybe, but they're part of being human. I wanted to tell her so, but instead I just smiled at her.

She smiled back, and cocked her head. 'You cry,' she said suddenly, in a voice strangely delighted. 'That's funny. That's more of an admission than I ever heard from Dino, in a way. Thank you, Robb. Thank you.'

And Laurie stood on her toes and looked up, expectant. And I could read what she expected. So I took her and kissed her, and she pressed her body hard against mine. And all the while I thought of Lya, telling myself that she wouldn't mind, that she'd be proud of me, that she'd understand.

Afterwards, I stayed up in the office alone to watch the dawn come up. I was drained, but somehow content. The light that crept over the horizon was chasing the shadows before it, and suddenly all the fears that had seemed so threatening in the night were silly, unreasoning. We'd bridged it, I thought – Lya and I. Whatever it was, we'd handled it, and today we'd handle the Greeshka with the same ease, together.

When I got back to our room, Lya was gone.

*

'We found the aircar in the middle of Shkeentown,' Valcarenghi was saying. He was cool, precise, reassuring. His voice told me, without words, that there was nothing to worry about. 'I've got men out looking for her. But Shkeentown's a big place. Do you have any idea where she might have gone?'

'No,' I said, dully. 'Not really. Maybe to see some more Joined. She seemed – well, almost obsessed by them. I don't know.'

'Well, we've got a good police force. We'll find her. I'm certain of that. But it may take a while. Did you two have a fight?'

'Yes. No. Sort of, but it wasn't a real fight. It was strange.'

'I see,' he said. But he didn't. 'Laurie tells me you came up here last night, alone.'

'Yes. I needed to think.'

'All right,' said Valcarenghi. 'So let's say Lya woke up, decided she wanted to think too. You came up here. She took a ride. Maybe she just wants a day off to wander around Shkeentown. She did something like that yesterday, didn't she?'

'Yes.'

'So she's doing it again. No problem. She'll probably be back well before dinner.' He smiled.

'Why did she go without telling me, then? Or leaving a note, or *something?*'

'I don't know. It's not important.'

Wasn't it, though? *Wasn't it?* I sat in the chair, head in my hands and a scowl on my face, and I was sweating. Suddenly I was very much afraid, of what I didn't know. I should never have left her alone, I was telling myself. While I was up here with Laurie, Lyanna woke alone in a darkened room, and – and – and *what?* And left.

'Meanwhile, though,' Valcarenghi said, 'we've got work to do. The trip to the caves is all set.'

I looked up, disbelieving. 'The caves? I can't go there, not now, not alone.'

He gave a sigh of exasperation, exaggerated for effect. 'Oh, come now, Robb. It's not the end of the world. Lya will be all right. She seemed to be a perfectly sensible girl, and I'm sure she can take care of herself. Right?'

I nodded.

'Meanwhile, we'll cover the caves. I still want to get to the bottom of this.'

'It won't do any good,' I protested. 'Not without Lya. She's the major Talent. I – I just read emotions. I can't get down deep, as she can. I won't solve anything for you.'

He shrugged. 'Maybe not. But the trip is on, and we've got nothing to lose. We can always make a second run after Lya comes back. Besides, this should do you good, get your mind off this other business. There's nothing you can do for Lya now. I've got every available man out searching for her, and if they don't find her you certainly won't. So there's no sense dwelling on it. Just get back into action, keep busy.' He turned, headed for the tube. 'Come. There's an aircar waiting for us. Nelse will go too.'

Reluctantly, I stood. I was in no mood to consider the problems of the Shkeen, but Valcarenghi's arguments made a certain amount of sense. Besides which, he'd hired Lyanna and me, and we still had obligations to him. I could try anyway, I thought.

On the ride out, Valcarenghi sat in the front with the driver, a hulking police sergeant with a face chiseled out of granite. He'd selected a police car this time so we could keep posted on the search for Lya. Gourlay and I

were in the backseat together. Gourlay had covered our laps with a big
map, and he was telling me about the caves of Final Union.

'Theory is the caves are the original home of the Greeshka,' he said.
'Probably true, makes sense. Greeshka are a lot bigger there. You'll see. The
caves are all through the hills, away from our part of Shkeentown, where
the country gets wilder. A regular little honeycomb. Greeshka in every one,
too. Or so I've heard. Been in a few myself, Greeshka in all of them. So I
believe what they say about the rest. The city, the sacred city, well, it was
probably built *because* of the caves. Shkeen come here from all over the
continent, you know, for Final Union. Here, this is the cave region.' He
took out a pen, and made a big circle in red near the center of the map. It
was meaningless to me. The map was getting me down. I hadn't realized
that the Shkeen city was so *huge*. How the hell could they find anyone who
didn't want to be found?

Valcarenghi looked back from the front seat. 'The cave we're going to is
a big one, as these places go. I've been there before. There's no formality
about Final Union, you understand. The Shkeen just pick a cave, and walk
in, and lie down on top of the Greeshka. They'll use whatever entrance is
most convenient. Some of them are no bigger than sewer pipes, but if you
went in far enough, theory says you'd run into a Greeshka, setting back in
the dark and pulsing away. The biggest caves are lighted with torches, like
the Great Hall, but that's just a frill. It doesn't play any real part in the
Union.'

'I take it we're going to one of them?' I said.

Valcarenghi nodded. 'Right. I figured you'd want to see what a mature
Greeshka is like. It's not pretty, but it's educational. So we need lighting.'

Gourlay resumed his narrative then, but I tuned him out. I felt I knew
quite enough about the Shkeen and the Greeshka, and I was still worried
about Lyanna. After a while he wound down, and the rest of the trip was
in silence. We covered more ground than we ever had before. Even the
Tower – our shining steel landmark – had been swallowed by the hills
behind us.

The terrain got rougher, rockier, and more overgrown, and the hills rose
higher and wilder. But the domes went on and on and on, and there were
Shkeen everywhere. Lya could be down there, I thought, lost among those
teeming millions. Looking for what? Thinking what?

Finally we landed, in a wooded valley between two massive, rock-
studded hills. Even here there were Shkeen, the red-brick domes rising
from the undergrowth among the stubby trees. I had no trouble spotting
the cave. It was halfway up one of the slopes, a dark yawn in the rock face,
with a dusty road winding up to it.

We set down in the valley and climbed that road. Gourlay ate up the distance with long, gawky strides, while Valcarenghi moved with an easy, untiring grace, and the policeman plodded on stolidly. I was the straggler. I dragged myself up, and I was half-winded by the time we got to the cave mouth.

If I'd expected cave paintings, or an altar, or some kind of nature temple, I was sadly disappointed. It was an ordinary cave, with damp stone walls and low ceilings and cold, wet air. Cooler than most of Shkea, and less dusty, but that was about it. There was one long, winding passage through the rock, wide enough for the four of us to walk abreast yet low enough so Gourlay had to stoop. Torches were set along the walls at regular intervals, but only every fourth one or so was lit. They burned with an oily smoke that seemed to cling to the top of the cave and drift down into the depths before us. I wondered what was sucking it in.

After about ten minutes of walking, most of it down a barely perceptible incline, the passage led us out into a high, brightly-lit room, with a vaulting stone roof that was stained sooty by torch smoke. In the room, the Greeshka.

Its color was a dull brownish-red, like old blood, not the bright near-translucent crimson of the small creatures that clung to the skulls of the Joined. There were spots of black, too, like burns or soot stains on the vast body. I could barely see the far side of the cave; the Greeshka was too huge, it towered above us so that there was only a thin crack between it and the roof. But it sloped down abruptly halfway across the chamber, like an immense jellied hill, and ended a good twenty feet from where we stood. Between us and the great bulk of the Greeshka was a forest of hanging, dangling red strands, a living cobweb of Greeshka tissue that came almost to our faces.

And it pulsed. As one organism. Even the strands kept time, widening and then contracting again, moving to a silent beat that was one with the great Greeshka behind them.

My stomach churned, but my companions seemed unmoved. They'd seen this before. 'Come,' Valcarenghi said, switching on a flashlight he'd brought to augment the torchlight. The light, twisting around the pulsing web, gave the illusion of some weird haunted forest. Valcarenghi stepped into that forest. Lightly. Swinging the light and brushing aside the Greeshka.

Gourlay followed him, but I recoiled. Valcarenghi looked back and smiled. 'Don't worry,' he said. 'The Greeshka takes hours to attach itself, and it's easily removed. It won't grab you if you stumble against it.'

I screwed up my courage, reached out, and touched one of the living strands. It was soft and wet, and there was a slimy feel to it. But that was all. It broke easily enough. I walked through it, reaching before me and bending and breaking the web to clear my path. The policeman walked silently behind me.

Then we stood on the far side of the web, at the front of the great Greeshka. Valcarenghi studied it for a second, then pointed with his flashlight. 'Look,' he said. 'Final Union.'

I looked. His beam had thrown a pool of light around one of the dark spots, a blemish on the reddish hulk. I looked closer. There was a head in the blemish. Centered in the dark spot, with just the face showing, and even that covered by a thin reddish film. But the features were unmistakable. An elderly Shkeen, wrinkled and big-eyed, his eyes closed now. But smiling. Smiling.

I moved closer. A little lower and to the right, a few fingertips hung out of the mass. But that was all. Most of the body was already gone, sunken into the Greeshka, dissolved or dissolving. The old Shkeen was dead, and the parasite was digesting his corpse.

'Every one of the dark spots is a recent Union,' Valcarenghi was saying, moving his light around like a pointer. 'The spots fade in time, of course. The Greeshka is growing steadily. In another hundred years it will fill this chamber, and start up the passageway.'

Then there was a rustle of movement behind us. I looked back. Someone else was coming through the web.

She reached us soon, and smiled. A Shkeen woman, old, naked, breasts hanging past her waist. Joined, of course. Her Greeshka covered most of her head and hung lower than her breasts. It was still bright and translucent from its time in the sun. You could see through it, to where it was eating the skin off her back.

'A candidate for Final Union,' Gourlay said.

'This is a popular cave,' Valcarenghi added in a low, sardonic voice.

The woman did not speak to us, nor us to her. Smiling, she walked past us. And lay down on the Greeshka.

The little Greeshka, the one that rode her back, seemed almost to dissolve on contact, melting away into the great cave creature, so the Shkeen woman and the great Greeshka were joined as one. After that, nothing. She just closed her eyes, and lay peacefully, seemingly asleep.

'What's happening?' I asked.

'Union,' said Valcarenghi. 'It'll be an hour before you'd notice anything, but the Greeshka is closing over her even now, swallowing her. A response to her body heat, I'm told. In a day she'll be buried in it. In two, like him—' The flash found the half-dissolved face above us.

'Can you read her?' Gourlay suggested. 'Maybe that'd tell us something.'

'All right,' I said, repelled but curious. I opened myself. And the mindstorm hit.

But it's wrong to call it a mindstorm. It was immense and awesome and intense, searing and blinding and choking. But it was peaceful too, and gentle with a gentleness that was more violent than human hate. It shrieked soft shrieks and siren calls and pulled at me seductively, and it washed over me in crimson waves of passion, and drew me to it. It filled me and emptied me all at once. And I heard the bells somewhere, clanging a harsh bronze song, a song of love and surrender and togetherness, of joining and union and never being alone.

Storm, mindstorm, yes, it was that. But it was to an ordinary mindstorm as a supernova is to a hurricane, and its violence was the violence of love. It loved me, that mindstorm, and it wanted me, and its bells called to me, and sang its love, and I reached to it and touched, wanting to be with it, wanting to link, wanting never to be alone again. And suddenly I was on the crest of a great wave once again, a wave of fire that washed across the stars forever, and this time I knew the wave would never end, this time I would not be alone afterwards upon my darkling plain.

But with that phrase I thought of Lya.

And suddenly I was struggling, fighting it, battling back against the sea of sucking love. I ran, ran, *ran*, *RAN* . . . and closed my minddoor and hammered shut the latch and let the storm flail and howl against it while I held it with all my strength, resisting. Yet the door began to buckle and crack.

I screamed. The door smashed open, and the storm whipped in and clutched at me, whirled me out and around and around. I sailed up to the cold stars but they were cold no longer, and I grew bigger and bigger until I *was* the stars and they were me, and I was Union, and for a single solitary glittering instant I was the universe.

Then nothing.

*

I woke up back in my room, with a headache that was trying to tear my skull apart. Gourlay was sitting on a chair reading one of our books. He looked up when I groaned.

Lya's headache pills were still on the bedstand. I took one hastily, then struggled to sit up in bed.

'You all right?' Gourlay asked.

'Headache,' I said, rubbing my forehead. It *throbbed*, as if it was about to burst. Worse than the time I'd peered into Lya's pain. 'What happened?'

He stood up. 'You scared the hell out of us. After you began to read, all of a sudden you started trembling. Then you walked right into the goddamn Greeshka. And you screamed. Dino and the sergeant had to drag you out. You were stepping right in the thing, and it was up to your knees. Twitching, too. Weird. Dino hit you, knocked you out.'

He shook his head, started for the door. 'Where are you going?' I said.

'To sleep,' he said. 'You've been out for eight hours or so. Dino asked me to watch you till you came to. OK, you came to. Now get some rest, and I will too. We'll talk about it tomorrow.'

'I want to talk about it now.'

'It's late,' he said, as he closed the bedroom door. I listened to his footsteps on the way out. And I'm sure I heard the outer door lock. Somebody was clearly afraid of Talents who steal away into the night. I wasn't going anywhere.

I got up and went out for a drink. There was Veltaar chilling. I put away a couple of glasses quick, and ate a light snack. The headache began to fade. Then I went back to the bedroom, turned off the light and cleared the glass, so the stars would all shine through. Then back to sleep.

*

But I didn't sleep, not right away. Too much had happened. I had to think about it. The headache first, the incredible headache that ripped at my skull. Like Lya's. But Lya hadn't been through what I had. Or had she? Lya was a major Talent, much more sensitive than I was, with a greater range. Could that mindstorm have reached *this* far, over miles and miles? Late at night, when humans and Shkeen were sleeping and their thoughts dim? Maybe. And maybe my half-remembered dreams were pale reflections of whatever she had felt the same nights. But my dreams had been pleasant. It was waking that bothered me, waking and not remembering.

But again, had I had this headache when I slept? Or when I woke?

What the hell had happened? What was that thing, that reached me there in the cave, and pulled me to it? The Greeshka? It had to be. I hadn't even time to focus on the Shkeen woman, it *had* to be the Greeshka. But Lyanna had said that Greeshka had no minds, not even a yes-I-live . . .

It all swirled around me, questions on questions on questions, and I had no answers. I began to think of Lya then, to wonder where she was and why she'd left me. Was this what she had been going through? Why hadn't I understood? I missed her then. I needed her beside me, and she wasn't there. I was alone, and very aware of it.

I slept.

Long darkness then, but finally a dream, and finally I remembered. I was back on the plain again, the infinite darkling plain with its starless sky and black shapes in the distance, the plain Lya had spoken of so often. It was from one of her favorite poems. I was alone, forever alone, and I knew it. That was the nature of things. I was the only reality in the universe, and

I was cold and hungry and frightened, and the shapes were moving toward me, inhuman and inexorable. And there was no one to call to, no one to turn to, no one to hear my cries. There never had been anyone. There never would be anyone.

Then Lya came to me.

She floated down from the starless sky, pale and thin and fragile, and stood beside me on the plain. She brushed her hair back with her hand, and looked at me with glowing wide eyes, and smiled. And I knew it was no dream. She was with me, somehow. We talked.

Hi, Robb.

Lya? Hi, Lya. Where are you? You left me.

I'm sorry. I had to. You understand, Robb. You have to. I didn't want to be here anymore, ever, in this place, this awful place. I would have been, Robb. Men are always here, but for brief moments.

A touch and a voice?

Yes, Robb. Then darkness again, and a silence. And the darkling plain.

You're mixing two poems, Lya. But it's OK. You know them better than I do. But aren't you leaving out something? The earlier part. 'Ah love, let us be true . . .'

Oh, Robb.

Where are you?

I'm – everywhere. But mostly in a cave. I was ready, Robb. I was already more open than the rest. I could skip the Gathering, and the Joining. My Talent made me used to sharing. It took me.

Final Union?

Yes.

Oh, Lya.

Robb. Please. Join us, join me. It's happiness, you know? Forever and forever, and belonging and sharing and being together. I'm in love, Robb, I'm in love with a billion billion people, and I know all of them better than I ever knew you, and they know me, all of me, and they love me. And it will last forever. Me. Us. The Union. I'm still me, but I'm them too, you see? And they're me. The Joined, the reading, opened me, and the Union called to me every night, because it loved me, you see? Oh, Robb, join us, join us. I love you.

The Union. The Greeshka, you mean. I love you, Lya. Please come back. It can't have absorbed you already. Tell me where you are. I'll come to you.

Yes, come to me. Come anywhere, Robb. The Greeshka is all one, the caves all connect under the hills, the little Greeshka are all part of the Union. Come to me and join me. Love me as you said you did. Join me. You're so far away, I can hardly reach you, even with the Union. Come and be one with us.

No. I will not be eaten. Please, Lya, tell me where you are.

Poor Robb. Don't worry, love. The body isn't important. The Greeshka needs it for nourishment, and we need the Greeshka. But, oh Robb, the Union isn't just the Greeshka, you see? The Greeshka isn't important, it doesn't even have a mind, it's just the link, the medium, the Union is the Shkeen. A million billion billion Shkeen, all the Shkeen that have lived and Joined in fourteen thousand years, all together and loving and belonging, immortal. It's beautiful, Robb, it's more than we had, much more, and we were the lucky ones, remember? We were! But this is better.

Lya. My Lya. I loved you. This isn't for you, this isn't for humans. Come back to me.

This isn't for humans? Oh, it IS! It's what humans have always been looking for, searching for, crying for on lonely nights. It's love, Robb, real love, and human love is only a pale imitation. You see?

No.

Come, Robb. Join. Or you'll be alone forever, alone on the plain, with only a voice and a touch to keep you going. And in the end when your body dies, you won't even have that. Just an eternity of empty blackness. The plain, Robb, forever and ever. And I won't be able to reach you, not ever. But it doesn't have to be . . .

No.

Oh, Robb. I'm fading. Please come.

No. Lya, don't go. I love you, Lya. Don't leave me.

I love you, Robb. I did. I really did . . .

And then she was gone. I was alone on the plain again. A wind was blowing from somewhere, and it whipped her fading words away from me, out into the cold vastness of infinity.

*

In the cheerless morning, the outer door was unlocked. I ascended the tower and found Valcarenghi alone in his office. 'Do you believe in God?' I asked him.

He looked up, smiled. 'Sure.' Said lightly. I was reading him. It was a subject he'd never thought about.

'I don't,' I said. 'Neither did Lya. Most Talents are atheists, you know. There was an experiment tried back on Old Earth fifty years ago. It was organized by a major Talent named Linnel, who was also devoutly religious. He thought that by using drugs, and linking together the minds of the world's most potent Talents, he could reach something he called the Universal Yes-I-Live. Also known as God. The experiment was a dismal failure, but *something* happened. Linnel went mad, and the others came away with only a vision of a vast, dark, uncaring nothingness, a void without reason or form or meaning. Other Talents have felt the same way, and Normals too. Centuries ago there was a poet named Arnold, who wrote of a darkling plain. The poem's in one of the old languages, but it's worth reading. It shows – fear, I think. Something basic in man, some dread of being alone in the cosmos. Maybe it's just fear of death, maybe it's more. I don't know. But it's primal. All men are forever alone, but they don't want to be. They're always searching, trying to make contact, trying to reach others across the void. Some people never succeed, some break through occasionally. Lya and I were lucky. But it's never permanent. In the end you're alone again, back on the darkling plain. You see, Dino? *Do you see?*'

He smiled an amused little smile. Not derisive – that wasn't his style – just surprised and disbelieving. 'No,' he said.

'Look again, then. Always people are reaching for something, for someone, searching. Talk, Talent, love, sex, it's all part of the same thing, the same search. And gods, too. Man invents gods because he's afraid of being alone, scared of an empty universe, scared of the darkling plain. That's why your men are converting, Dino, that's why people are going over. They've found God, or as much of a God as they're ever likely to find. The Union is a mass-mind, an immortal mass-mind, many in one, all love. The Shkeen don't die, dammit. No wonder they don't have the concept of an afterlife. They *know* there's a God. Maybe it didn't create the universe, but it's love, pure love, and they say that God is love, don't they? Or maybe what we call love is a tiny piece of God. I don't care, whatever it is, the Union is it. The end of the search for the Shkeen, and for Man too. We're alike after all, we're so alike it hurts.'

Valcarenghi gave his exaggerated sigh. 'Robb, you're overwrought. You sound like one of the Joined.'

'Maybe that's just what I should be. Lya is. She's part of the Union now.'

He blinked. 'How do you know that?'

'She came to me last night, in a dream.'

'Oh. A dream.'

'It was *true*, dammit. It's all true.'

Valcarenghi stood, and smiled. 'I believe you,' he said. 'That is, I believe that the Greeshka uses a psi-lure, a love lure if you will, to draw in its prey, something so powerful that it convinces men – even you – that it's God. Dangerous, of course. I'll have to think about this before taking action. We could guard the caves to keep humans out, but there are too many caves. And sealing off the Greeshka wouldn't help our relations with the Shkeen. But now it's my problem. You've done your job.'

I waited until he was through. 'You're wrong, Dino. This is real, no trick, no illusion. I *felt* it, and Lya too. The Greeshka hasn't even a yes-I-live, let alone a psi-lure strong enough to bring in Shkeen and men.'

'You expect me to believe that God is an animal who lives in the caves of Shkea?'

'Yes.'

'Robb, that's absurd, and you know it. You think the Shkeen have found the answer to the mysteries of creation. But look at them. The oldest civilized race in known space, but they've been stuck in the Bronze Age for fourteen thousand years. We came to *them*. Where are their spaceships? Where are their towers?'

'Where are our bells?' I said. 'And our joy? They're happy, Dino. Are we? Maybe they've found what we're still looking for. Why the hell is man so driven, anyway? Why is he out to conquer the galaxy, the universe, whatever? Looking for God, maybe...? Maybe. He can't find him anywhere, though, so on he goes, on and on, always looking. But always back to the same darkling plain in the end.'

'Compare the accomplishments. I'll take humanity's record.'

'Is it worth it?'

'I think so.' He went to the window, and looked out. 'We've got the only Tower on their world,' he said, smiling, as he looked down through the clouds.

'They've got the only God in our universe,' I told him. But he only smiled.

'All right, Robb,' he said, when he finally turned from the window. 'I'll keep all this in mind. And we'll find Lyanna for you.'

My voice softened. 'Lya is lost,' I said. 'I know that now. I will be too, if I wait. I'm leaving tonight. I'll book passage on the first ship out to Baldur.'

He nodded. 'If you like. I'll have your money ready.' He grinned. 'And we'll send Lya after you, when we find her. I imagine she'll be a little miffed, but that's your worry.'

I didn't answer. Instead I shrugged, and headed for the tube. I was almost there when he stopped me.

'Wait,' he said. 'How about dinner tonight? You've done a good job for us. We're having a farewell party anyway, Laurie and me. She's leaving too.'

'I'm sorry,' I said.

His turn to shrug. 'What for? Laurie's a beautiful person, and I'll miss her. But it's no tragedy. There are other beautiful people. I think she was getting restless with Shkea, anyway.'

I'd almost forgotten my Talent, in my heat and the pain of my loss. I remembered it now. I read him. There was no sorrow, no pain, just a vague disappointment. And below that, his wall. Always the wall, keeping him apart, this man who was a first-name friend to everyone and an intimate to none. And on it, it was almost as if there were a sign that read, THIS FAR YOU GO, and no further.

'Come up,' he said. 'It should be fun.' I nodded.

*

I asked myself, when my ship lifted off, why I was leaving.

Maybe to return home. We have a house on Baldur, away from the cities, on one of the undeveloped continents with only wilderness for a neighbor. It stands on a cliff, above a high waterfall that tumbles endlessly down into a shaded green pool. Lya and I swam there often, in the sunlit days between assignments. And afterwards we'd lie down nude in the shade of the orangespice trees, and make love on a carpet of silver moss. Maybe I'm returning to that. But it won't be the same without Lya, lost Lya . . .

Lya whom I still could have. Whom I could have now. It would be easy, so easy. A slow stroll into a darkened cave, a short sleep. Then Lya with me for eternity, in me, sharing me, being me, and I her. Loving and knowing more of each other than men can ever do. Union and joy, and no darkness again, ever. God. If I believed that, what I told Valcarenghi, then why did I tell Lya no?

Maybe because I'm not sure. Maybe I still hope, for something still greater and more loving than the Union, for the God they told me of so long ago. Maybe I'm taking a risk, because part of me still believes. But if I'm wrong . . . then the darkness, and the plain . . .

But maybe it's something else, something I saw in Valcarenghi, something that made me doubt what I had said.

For man is more than Shkeen, somehow; there are men like Dino and Gourlay as well as Lya and Gustaffson, men who fear love and Union as much as they crave it. A dichotomy, then. Man has two primal urges, and the Shkeen only one? If so, perhaps there is a human answer, to reach and join and not be alone, and yet to still be men.

I do not envy Valcarenghi. He cries behind his wall, I think, and no one knows, not even he. And no one will ever know, and in the end he'll always be alone in smiling pain. No, I do not envy Dino.

Yet there is something of him in me, Lya, as well as much of you. And that is why I ran, though I loved you.

Laurie Blackburn was on the ship with me. I ate with her after liftoff, and we spent the evening talking over wine. Not a happy conversation, maybe, but a human one. Both of us needed someone, and we reached out.

Afterwards, I took her back to my cabin, and made love to her as fiercely as I could. Then, the darkness softened, we held each other and talked away the night.

This Tower of Ashes

My tower is built of bricks, small soot-gray bricks mortared together with a shiny black substance that looks strangely like obsidian to my untrained eye, though it clearly cannot be obsidian. It sits by an arm of the Skinny Sea, twenty feet tall and sagging, the edge of the forest only a few feet away.

I found the tower nearly four years ago, when Squirrel and I left Port Jamison in the silver aircar that now lies gutted and overgrown in the weeds outside my doorstep. To this day I know almost nothing about the structure, but I have my theories.

I do not think it was built by men, for one. It clearly predates Port Jamison, and I often suspect it predates human spaceflight. The bricks (which are curiously small, less than a quarter the size of normal bricks) are tired and weathered and old, and they crumble visibly beneath my feet. Dust is everywhere and I know its source, for more than once I have pried loose a brick from the parapet on the roof and crushed it idly to fine dark powder in my naked fist. When the salt wind blows from the east, the tower flies a plume of ashes.

Inside, the bricks are in better condition, since the wind and the rain have not touched them quite so much, but the tower is still far from pleasant. The interior is a single room full of dust and echoes, without windows; the only light comes from the circular opening in the center of the roof. A spiral stair, built of the same ancient brick as the rest, is part of the wall; around and around it circles, like the threading on a screw, before it reaches roof level. Squirrel, who is quite small as cats go, finds the stairs easy climbing, but for human feet they are narrow and awkward.

But I still climb them. Each night I return from the cool forests, my arrows black with the caked blood of the dream-spiders and my bag heavy with their poison sacs, and I set aside my bow and wash my hands and then climb up to the roof to spend the last few hours before dawn. Across the narrow salt channel, the lights of Port Jamison burn on the island, and from up there it is not the city I remember. The square black buildings wear a bright romantic glow at night; the lights, all smoky orange and muted blue, speak of mystery and silent song and more than a little loneliness, while the starships rise and fall against the stars like the tireless wandering fireflies of my boyhood on Old Earth.

'There are stories over there,' I told Korbec once, before I had learned better. 'There are people behind every light, and each person has a life, a story. Only they lead those lives without ever touching us, so we'll never know the stories.' I think I gestured then; I was, of course, quite drunk.

Korbec answered with a toothy smile and a shake of his head. He was a great dark fleshy man, with a beard like knotted wire. Each month he came out from the city in his pitted black aircar to drop off my supplies and take the venom I had collected, and each month we went up to the roof and got drunk together. A track driver, that was all Korbec was, a seller of cut-rate dreams and secondhand rainbows. But he fancied himself a philosopher and a student of man.

'Don't fool yourself,' he said to me then, his face flush with wine and darkness, 'you're not missing nothin'. Lives are rotten stories, y'know. Real stories, now, they usually got a plot to 'em. They start and they go on a bit and when they end they're over, unless the guy's got a series goin'. People's lives don't do that nohow, they just kinda wander around and ramble and go on and on. Nothin' ever finishes.'

'People die,' I said. 'That's enough of a finish, I'd think.'

Korbec made a loud noise. 'Sure, but have you ever known anybody to die at the right time? No, don't happen that way. Some guys fall over before their lives have properly gotten started, some right in the middle of the best part. Others kinda linger on after everything is really over.'

Often when I sit up there alone, with Squirrel warm in my lap and a glass of wine by my side, I remember Korbec's words and the heavy way he said them, his coarse voice oddly gentle. He is not a smart man, Korbec, but that night I think he spoke the truth, maybe never realizing it himself. But the weary realism that he offered me then is the only antidote there is for the dreams that spiders weave.

But I am not Korbec, nor can I be, and while I recognize his truth, I cannot live it.

*

I was outside taking target practice in the late afternoon, wearing nothing but my quiver and a pair of cutoffs, when they came. It was closing on dusk and I was loosening up for my nightly foray into the forest – even in those early days I lived from twilight to dawn, as the dream-spiders do. The grass felt good under my bare feet, the double-curved silverwood bow felt even better in my hand, and I was shooting well.

Then I heard them coming. I glanced over my shoulder toward the beach, and saw the dark blue aircar swelling rapidly against the eastern sky. Gerry, of course, I knew that from the sound; his aircar had been making noises as long as I had known him.

I turned my back on them, drew another arrow – quite steady – and notched my first bull's-eye of the day.

Gerry set his aircar down in the weeds near the base of the tower, just a few feet from my own. Crystal was with him, slim and grave, her long gold hair full of red glints from the afternoon sun. They climbed out and started toward me.

'Don't stand near the target,' I told them, as I slipped another arrow into place and bent the bow. 'How did you find me?' The twang of the arrow vibrating in the target punctuated my question.

They circled well around my line of fire. 'You'd mentioned spotting this place from the air once,' Gerry said, 'and we knew you weren't anywhere in Port Jamison. Figured it was worth a chance.' He stopped a few feet from me, with his hands on his hips, looking just as I remembered him: big, dark-haired and very fit. Crystal came up beside him and put one hand lightly on his arm.

I lowered my bow and turned to face them. 'So. Well, you found me. Why?'

'I was worried about you, Johnny,' Crystal said softly. But she avoided my eyes when I looked at her.

Gerry put a hand around her waist, very possessively, and something flared within me. 'Running away never solves anything,' he told me, his voice full of the strange mixture of friendly concern and patronizing arrogance he had been using on me for months.

'I did *not* run away,' I said, my voice strained. 'Damn it. You should never have come.'

Crystal glanced at Gerry, looking very sad, and it was clear that suddenly she was thinking the same thing. Gerry just frowned. I don't think he ever once understood why I said the things I said, or did the things I did; whenever we discussed the subject, which was infrequently, he would only tell me with vague puzzlement what he would have done if our roles had been reversed. It seemed infinitely strange to him that anyone could possibly do anything differently in the same position.

His frown did not touch me, but he'd already done his damage. For the month I'd been in my self-imposed exile at the tower, I had been trying to come to terms with my actions and my moods, and it had been far from easy. Crystal and I had been together for a long time – nearly four years – when we came to Jamison's World, trying to track down some unique silver and obsidian artifacts that we'd picked up on Baldur. I had loved her all that time, and I still loved her, even now, after she had left me for Gerry. When I was feeling good about myself, it seemed to me that the impulse that had driven me out of Port Jamison was a noble and unselfish one. I wanted Crys to be happy, simply, and she could not be happy with me there. My wounds were too deep, and I wasn't good at hiding them; my presence put the damper of guilt on the newborn joy she'd found with Gerry. And since she could not bear to cut me off completely, I felt compelled to cut myself off. For them. For her.

Or so I liked to tell myself. But there were hours when that bright rationalization broke down, dark hours of self-loathing. Were those the real reasons? Or was I simply out to hurt myself in a fit of angry immaturity, and by doing so, punish them – like a willful child who plays with thoughts of suicide as a form of revenge?

I honestly didn't know. For a month I'd fluctuated from one belief to the other while I tried to understand myself and decide what I'd do next. I wanted to think myself a hero, willing to make a sacrifice for the happiness of the woman I loved. But Gerry's words made it clear that he didn't see it that way at all.

'Why do you have to be so damned dramatic about everything?' he said, looking stubborn. He had been determined all along to be very civilized, and seemed perpetually annoyed at me because I wouldn't shape up and heal my wounds so that everybody could be friends. Nothing annoyed me quite so much as his annoyance; *I* thought I was handling the situation pretty well, all things considered, and I resented the inference that I wasn't.

But Gerry was determined to convert me, and my best withering look was wasted on him. 'We're going to stay here and talk things out until you agree to fly back to Port Jamison with us,' he told me, in his most forceful now-I'm-getting-tough tone.

'Like shit,' I said, turning sharply away from them and yanking an arrow from my quiver. I slid it into place, pulled, and released, all too quickly. The arrow missed the target by a good foot and buried itself in the soft dark brick of my crumbling tower.

'What *is* this place, anyway?' Crys asked, looking at the tower as if she'd just seen it for the first time. It's possible that she had – that it took the incongruous sight of my arrow lodging in stone to make her notice the ancient structure. More likely, though, it was a premeditated change of subject, designed to cool the argument that was building between Gerry and me.

I lowered my bow again and walked up to the target to recover the arrows I'd expended. 'I'm really not sure,' I said, somewhat mollified and anxious to pick up the cue she'd thrown me. 'A watchtower, I think, of nonhuman origin. Jamison's World has never been thoroughly explored. It may have had a sentient race once.' I walked around the target to the tower, and yanked loose the final arrow from the crumbling brick. 'It still may, actually. We know very little of what goes on on the mainland.'

'A damn gloomy place to live, if you ask me,' Gerry put in, looking over the tower. 'Could fall in any moment, from the way it looks.'

I gave him a bemused smile. 'The thought had occurred to me. But when I first came out here, I was past caring.' As soon as the words were out, I regretted saying them; Crys winced visibly. That had been the whole story of my final weeks in Port Jamison. Try as I might, it had seemed that I had only two choices; I could lie, or I could hurt her. Neither appealed to me, so here I was. But here they were too, so the whole impossible situation was back.

Gerry had another comment ready, but he never got to say it. Just then Squirrel came bounding out from between the weeds, straight at Crystal.

She smiled at him and knelt, and an instant later he was at her feet, licking her hand and chewing on her fingers. Squirrel was in a good mood, clearly. He liked life near the tower. Back in Port Jamison, his life had been constrained by Crystal's fears that he'd be eaten by alleysnarls or chased by dogs or strung up by local children. Out here I let him run free, which was much more to his liking. The brush around the tower was overrun by whipping-mice, a native rodent with a hairless tail three times its own body length. The tail packed a mild sting, but Squirrel didn't care, even though he swelled up and got grouchy every time a tail connected. He liked stalking whipping-mice all day. Squirrel always fancied himself a great hunter, and there's no skill involved in chasing down a bowl of catfood.

He'd been with me even longer than Crys had, but she'd become suitably fond of him during our time together. I often suspected that Crystal would have gone with Gerry even sooner than she did, except that she was upset at the idea of leaving Squirrel. Not that he was any great beauty. He was a small, thin, scuffy-looking cat, with ears like a fox and fur a scroungy gray-brown color, and a big bushy tail two sizes too big for him. The friend who gave him to me back on Avalon informed me gravely that Squirrel was the illegitimate offspring of a genetically-engineered psicat and a mangy alley tom. But if Squirrel could read his owner's mind, he didn't pay much attention. When he wanted affection, he'd do things like climb right up on the book I was reading and knock it away and begin biting my chin: when he wanted to be let alone, it was dangerous folly to try to pet him.

As Crystal knelt by him and stroked him and Squirrel nuzzled up to her hand, she seemed very much the woman I'd traveled with and loved and talked to at endless length and slept with every night, and I suddenly realized how I'd missed her. I think I smiled; the sight of her, even under these conditions, still gave me a cloud-shadowed joy. Maybe I was being silly and stupid and vindictive to send them away, I thought, after they had come so far to see me. Crys was still Crys, and Gerry could hardly be so bad, since she loved him.

Watching her, wordless, I made a sudden decision; I would let them stay. And we could see what happened. 'It's close to dusk,' I heard myself saying. 'Are you folks hungry?'

Crys looked up, still petting Squirrel, and smiled. Gerry nodded. 'Sure.'

'All right,' I said. I walked past them, turned and paused in the doorway, and gestured them inside. 'Welcome to my ruin.'

I turned on the electric torches and set about making dinner. My lockers were well stocked back in those days; I had not yet started living off the forests. I thawed three big sandragons, the silver-shelled crustacean that Jamie fishermen dragged for relentlessly, and served them up with bread and cheese and white wine.

Mealtime conversation was polite and guarded. We talked of mutual friends in Port Jamison, Crystal told me about a letter she'd received from a couple we had known on Baldur, Gerry held forth on politics and the efforts of the Port police to crack down on the traffic in dreaming venom. 'The Council is sponsoring research on some sort of super-pesticide that would wipe out the dream-spiders,' he told me. 'A saturation spraying of the near coast would cut off most of the supply, I'd think.'

'Certainly,' I said, a bit high on the wine and a bit piqued at Gerry's stupidity. Once again, listening to him, I had found myself questioning Crystal's taste. 'Never mind what other effects it might have on the ecology, right?'

Gerry shrugged, 'Mainland,' he said simply. He was Jamie through-and-through, and the comment translated to, 'Who cares?' The accidents of history had given the residents of Jamison's World a singularly cavalier attitude toward their planet's one large continent. Most of the original settlers had come from Old Poseidon, where the sea had been a way of life for generations. The rich, teeming oceans and peaceful archipelagoes of their new world had attracted them far more than the dark forests of the mainland. Their children grew up to the same attitudes, except for a handful who found an illegal profit selling dreams.

'Don't shrug it all off so easy,' I said.

'Be realistic,' he replied. 'The mainland's no use to anyone, except the spider-men. Who would it hurt?'

'Damn it, Gerry, look at this tower! Where did it come from, tell me that! I tell *you*, there might be intelligence out there, in those forests. The Jamies have never even been bothered to look.'

Crystal was nodding over her wine. 'Johnny could be right,' she said, glancing at Gerry. 'That was why I came here, remember. The artifacts. The shop on Baldur said they were shipped out of Port Jamison. He couldn't trace them back any farther than that. And the workmanship – I've handled alien art for years, Gerry. I know Fyndii work, and Damoosh, and I've seen all the others. This was *different*.'

Gerry only smiled. 'Proves nothing. There are other races, millions of them, further in toward the core. The distances are too great, so we don't hear of them very often, except maybe third-hand, but it isn't impossible that every so often a piece of their art would trickle through.' He shook his head. 'No, I'd bet this tower was put up by some early settler. Who knows? Could be there was another discoverer, before Jamison, who never reported his find. Maybe he built the place. But I'm not going to buy mainland sentients.'

'At least not until you fumigate the damned forests and they all come out waving their spears,' I said sourly. Gerry laughed and Crystal smiled at me. And suddenly, suddenly, I had an overpowering desire to win this argument. My thoughts had the hazy clarity that only wine can give, and it seemed so logical. I was so clearly *right*, and here was my chance to show up Gerry like the provincial he was and make points with Crys.

I leaned forward. 'If you Jamies would ever look, you might find sentients,' I said. 'I've only been on the mainland a month, and already I've found a great deal. You've no damned concept of the kind of beauty you talk so blithely of wiping out. A whole ecology is out there, different from the islands, species upon species, a lot probably not even discovered yet. But what do you know about it? Any of you?'

Gerry nodded. 'So, show me.' He stood up suddenly. 'I'm always willing to learn, Bowen. Why don't you take us out and show us all the wonders of the mainland?'

I think Gerry was trying to make points, too. He probably never thought I'd take up his offer, but it was exactly what I'd wanted. It was dark outside now, and we had been talking by the light of my torches. Above, stars shone through the hole in my roof. The forest would be alive now, eerie and beautiful, and I was suddenly eager to be out there, bow in hand, in a world where I was a force and a friend, Gerry a bumbling tourist.

'Crystal?' I said.

She looked interested. 'Sounds like fun. If it's safe.'

'It will be,' I said. 'I'll take my bow.' We both rose, and Crys looked happy. I remembered the times we tackled Baldurian wilderness together, and suddenly I felt very happy, certain that everything would work out well. Gerry was just part of a bad dream. She couldn't possibly be in love with him.

First I found the sober-ups; I was feeling good, but not good enough to head out into the forest when I was still dizzy from wine. Crystal and I flipped ours down immediately, and seconds after my alcoholic glow began to fade. Gerry, however, waved away the pill I offered him. 'I haven't had that much,' he insisted. 'Don't need it.'

I shrugged, thinking that things were getting better and better. If Gerry went crashing drunkenly through the woods, it couldn't help but turn Crys away from him. 'Suit yourself,' I said.

Neither of them was really dressed for wilderness, but I hoped that wouldn't be a problem, since I didn't really plan on taking them very deep in the forest. It would be a quick trip, I thought; wander down my trail a bit, show them the dust pile and the spider-chasm, maybe nail a dream-spider for them. Nothing to it, out and back again.

I put on a dark coverall, heavy trail boots, and my quiver, handed Crystal a flash in case we wandered away from the bluemoss regions, and picked up my bow. 'You really need that?' Gerry asked, with sarcasm.

'Protection,' I said.

'Can't be that dangerous.'

It isn't, if you know what you're doing, but I didn't tell him that. 'Then why do you Jamies stay on your islands?'

He smiled. 'I'd rather trust a laser.'

'I'm cultivating a deathwish. A bow gives the prey a chance, of sorts.'

Crys gave me a smile of shared memories. 'He only hunts predators,' she told Gerry. I bowed.

Squirrel agreed to guard my castle. Steady and very sure of myself, I belted on a knife and led my ex-wife and her lover out into the forests of Jamison's World.

We walked in single file, close together, me up front with the bow, Crys following, Gerry behind her. Crys used the flashlight when we first set out, playing it over the trail as we wound our way through the thick grove of spikearrows that stood like a wall against the sea. Tall and very straight, crusty gray of bark and some as big around as my tower, they climbed to a ridiculous height before sprouting their meager load of branches. Here and there they crowded together and squeezed the path between them, and more than one seemingly impassable fence of wood confronted us suddenly in the dark. But Crys could always pick out the way, with me a foot ahead of her to point her flash when it paused.

Ten minutes out from the tower, the character of the forest began to change. The ground and the very air were drier here, the wind cool but without the snap of salt; the water-hungry spikearrows had drained most of the moisture from the air. They began to grow smaller and less frequent, the spaces between them larger and easier to find. Other species of plant began to appear: stunted little goblin trees, sprawling mockoaks, graceful ebonfires whose red veins pulsed brilliantly in the dark wood when caught by Crystal's wandering flash.

And bluemoss.

Just a little at first; here a ropy web dangling from a goblin's arm, there a small patch on the ground, frequently chewing its way up the back of an ebonfire or a withering solitary spikearrow. Then more and more; thick carpets underfoot, mossy blankets on the leaves above, heavy trailers that dangled from the branches and danced around in the wind. Crystal sent the flash darting about, finding bigger and better bunches of the soft blue fungus, and peripherally I began to see the glow.

'Enough,' I said, and Crys turned off the light.

Darkness lasted only for a moment, till our eyes adjusted to a dimmer light. Around us, the forest was suffused by a gentle radiance, as the bluemoss drenched us in its ghostly phosphorescence. We were standing near one side of a small clearing, below a shiny black ebonfire, but even the flames of its red-veined wood seemed cool in the faint blue light. The moss had taken over the undergrowth, supplanting all the local grasses and making nearby shrubs into fuzzy blue beachballs. It climbed the sides of most of the trees, and when we looked up through the branches at the stars, we saw that other colonies had set upon the woods a glowing crown.

I laid my bow carefully against the dark flank of the ebonfire, bent, and offered a handful of light to Crystal. When I held it under her chin, she smiled at me again, her features softened by the cool magic in my hand. I remember feeling very good, to have led them to this beauty.

But Gerry only grinned at me. 'Is this what we're going to endanger, Bowen?' he asked. 'A forest full of bluemoss?'

I dropped the moss. 'You don't think it's pretty?'

Gerry shrugged. 'Sure, it's pretty. It is also a fungus, a parasite with a dangerous tendency to overrun and crowd out all other forms of plantlife. Bluemoss was very thick on Jolostar and the Barbis Archipelago once, you know. We rooted it all out; it can eat its way through a good corn crop in a month.' He shook his head.

And Crystal nodded. 'He's right, you know,' she said.

I looked at her for a long time, suddenly feeling very sober indeed, the last memory of the wine long gone. Abruptly it dawned on me that I had, all unthinking, built myself another fantasy. Out here, in a world I had started to make my own, a world of dream-spiders and magic moss, somehow I had thought that I could recapture my own dream long fled, my smiling crystalline soulmate. In the timeless wilderness of the mainland, she would see us both in fresh light and would realize once again that it was me she loved.

So I'd spun a pretty web, bright and alluring as the trap of any dream-spider, and Crys had shattered the flimsy filaments with a word. She was his; mine no longer, not now, not ever. And if Gerry seemed to me stupid or insensitive or overpractical, well, perhaps it was those very qualities that made Crys choose him. And perhaps not – I had no right to second-guess her love, and possibly I would never understand it.

I brushed the last flakes of glowing moss from my hands while Gerry took the heavy flash from Crystal and flicked it on again. My blue fairyland dissolved, burned away by the bright white reality of his flashlight beam. 'What now?' he asked, smiling. He was not so very drunk after all.

I lifted my bow from where I'd set it down. 'Follow me,' I said, quickly, curtly. Both of them looked eager and interested, but my own mood had shifted dramatically. Suddenly the whole trip seemed pointless. I wished that they were gone, that I was back at my tower with Squirrel. I was down . . .

. . . and sinking. Deeper in the moss-heavy woods, we came upon a dark swift stream, and the brilliance of the flashlight speared a solitary ironhorn that had come to drink. It looked up quickly, pale and startled, then bounded away through the trees, for a fleeting instant looking a bit like the unicorn of Old Earth legend. Long habit made me glance at Crystal, but her eyes sought Gerry's when she laughed.

Later, as we climbed a rocky incline, a cave loomed near at hand; from the smell, a woodsnarl lair.

I turned to warn them around it, only to discover that I'd lost my audience. They were ten steps behind me, at the bottom of the rocks, walking very slowly and talking quietly, holding hands.

Dark and angry, wordless, I turned away again and continued on over the hill. We did not speak again until I'd found the dust pile.

I paused on its edge, my boots an inch deep in the fine gray powder, and they came straggling up behind me. 'Go ahead, Gerry,' I said. 'Use your flash here.'

The light roamed. The hill was at our back, rocky and lit here and there with the blurred cold fire of bluemoss-choked vegetation. But in front of us was only desolation; a wide vacant plain, black and blasted and lifeless, open to the stars. Back and forth Gerry moved the flashlight, pushing at the borders of the dust nearby, fading as he shone it straight out into the gray distance. The only sound was the wind.

'So?' he said at last.

'Feel the dust,' I told him. I was not going to stoop this time. 'And when you're back at the tower, crush one of my bricks and feel that. It's the same thing, a sort of powdery ash.' I made an expansive gesture. 'I'd guess there was a city here once, but now it's all crumbled into dust. Maybe my tower was an outpost of the people who built it, you see?'

'The vanished sentients of the forests,' Gerry said, still smiling. 'Well, I'll admit there's nothing like this on the islands. For a good reason. We don't let forest fires rage unchecked.'

'*Forest fire!* Don't give me that. Forest fires don't reduce everything to a fine powder, you always get a few blackened stumps or something.'

'Oh? You're probably right. But all the ruined cities I know have at least a few bricks still piled on top of each other for the tourists to take pictures of,' Gerry said. The flash beam flicked to and fro over the dust pile, dismissing it. 'All you have is a mound of rubbish.'

Crystal said nothing.

I began walking back, while they followed in silence. I was losing points every minute; it had been idiocy to bring them out here. At that moment nothing more was on my mind than getting back to my tower as quickly as possible, packing them off to Port Jamison together, and resuming my exile.

Crystal stopped me, after we'd come back over the hill into the bluemoss forest.

'Johnny,' she said. I stopped, they caught up, Crys pointed.

'Turn off the light,' I told Gerry. In the fainter illumination of the moss, it was easier to spot: the intricate iridescent web of a dream-spider, slanting groundward from the low branches of a mockoak. The patches of moss that shone softly all around us were nothing to this; each web strand was as thick as my little finger, oily and brilliant, running with the colors of the rainbow.

Crys took a step toward it, but I took her by the arm and stopped her. 'The spiders are around someplace,' I said. 'Don't go too close. Papa spider never leaves the web, and Mama ranges around in the trees at night.'

Gerry glanced upward a little apprehensively. His flash was dark, and suddenly he didn't seem to have all the answers. The dream-spiders are dangerous predators, and I suppose he'd never seen one outside of a display case. They weren't native to the islands. 'Pretty big web,' he said. 'Spiders must be a fair size.'

'Fair,' I said, and at once I was inspired. I could discomfort him a lot more if an ordinary web like this got to him. And he had been discomforting me all night. 'Follow me. I'll show you a real dream-spider.' We circled around the web carefully, never seeing either of its guardians. I led them to the spider-chasm.

It was a great V in the sandy earth, once a creekbed perhaps, but dry and overgrown now. The chasm is hardly very deep by daylight, but at night it looks formidable enough, as you stare down into it from the wooded hills on either side. The bottom is a dark tangle of shrubbery, alive with little flickering phantom lights; higher up, trees of all kinds lean into the chasm, almost meeting in the center. One of them, in fact, does cross the gap. An ancient, rotting spikearrow, withered by lack of moisture, had fallen long ago to provide a natural bridge. The bridge hangs with bluemoss, and glows. The three of us walked out on that dim-lit, curving trunk, and I gestured down.

Yards below us, a glittering multihued net hung from hill to hill, each strand of the web thick as a cable and aglisten with sticky oils. It tied all the lower trees together in a twisting intricate embrace, and it was a shining fairy-roof above the chasm. Very pretty; it made you want to reach out and touch it.

That, of course, was why the dream-spiders spun it. They were nocturnal predators, and the bright colors of their webs afire in the night made a potent lure.

'Look,' Crystal said, 'the spider.' She pointed. In one of the darker corners of the web, half-hidden by the tangle of a goblin tree that grew out of the rock, it was sitting. I could see it dimly, by the webfire and moss light, a great eight-legged white thing the size of a large pumpkin. Unmoving. Waiting.

Gerry glanced around uneasily again, up into the branches of a crooked mockoak that hung partially above us. 'The mate's around somewhere, isn't it?'

I nodded. The dream-spiders of Jamison's World are not quite twins to the arachnids of Old Earth. The female is indeed the deadlier of the species, but far from eating the male, she takes him for life in a permanent specialized partnership. For it is the sluggish, great-bodied male who wears the spinnerets, who weaves the shining-fire web and makes it sticky with his oils, who binds and ties the prey snared by light and color. Meanwhile, the smaller female roams the dark branches, her poison sac full of the viscous dreaming-venom that grants bright visions and ecstasy and final blackness. Creatures many times her own size she stings, and drags limp back to the web to add to the larder.

The dream-spiders are soft, merciful hunters for all that. If they prefer live food, no matter; the captive probably enjoys being eaten. Popular Jamie wisdom says a spider's prey moans with joy as it is consumed. Like all popular wisdoms, it is vastly exaggerated. But the truth is, the captives never struggle.

Except that night, something was struggling in the web below us.

'What's that?' I said, blinking. The iridescent web was not even close to empty – the half-eaten corpse of an ironhorn lay close at hand below us, and some great dark bat was bound in bright strands just slightly farther away – but these were not what I watched. In the corner opposite the male spider, near the western trees, something was caught and fluttering. I remember a brief glimpse of thrashing pale limbs, wide luminous eyes, and something like wings. But I did not see it clearly.

That was when Gerry slipped.

Maybe it was the wine that made him unsteady, or maybe the moss under our feet, or the curve of the trunk on which we stood. Maybe he was just trying to step around me to see whatever it was I was staring at. But, in any case, he slipped and lost his balance, let out a yelp, and suddenly he was five yards below us, caught in the web. The whole thing shook to the impact of his fall, but it didn't come close to breaking – dream-spider webs are strong enough to catch ironhorns and wood-snarls, after all.

'Damn,' Gerry yelled. He looked ridiculous; one leg plunged right down through the fibers of the web, his arms half-sunk and tangled hopelessly, only his head and shoulders really free of the mess. 'This stuff is sticky. I can hardly move.'

'Don't try,' I told him. 'It'll just get worse. I'll figure out a way to climb down and cut you loose. I've got my knife.' I looked around, searching for a tree limb to shimmy out on.

'*John,*' Crystal's voice was tense, on edge.

The male spider had left his lurking place behind the goblin tree. He was moving toward Gerry with a heavy deliberate gait; a gross white shape clamoring over the preternatural beauty of his web.

'Damn,' I said. I wasn't seriously alarmed, but it was a bother. The great male was the biggest spider I'd ever seen, and it seemed a shame to kill him. But I didn't see that I had much choice. The male dream-spider has no venom, but he is a carnivore, and his bite can be most final, especially when he's the size of this one. I couldn't let him get within biting distance of Gerry.

Steadily, carefully, I drew a long gray arrow out of my quiver and fitted it to my bowstring. It was night, of course, but I wasn't really worried. I was a good shot, and my target was outlined clearly by the glowing strands of his web.

Crystal screamed.

I stopped briefly, annoyed that she'd panic when everything was under control. But I knew all along that she would not, of course. It was something else. For an instant I couldn't imagine what it could be.

Then I saw, as I followed Crys' eyes with my own. A fat white spider the size of a big man's fist had dropped down from the mockoak to the bridge we were standing on, not ten feet away. Crystal, thank God, was safe behind me.

I stood there – how long? I don't know. If I had just acted, without stopping, without thought, I could have handled everything. I should have taken care of the male first, with the arrow I had ready. There would have been plenty of time to pull a second arrow for the female.

But I froze instead, caught in that dark bright moment, for an instant timeless, my bow in my hand yet unable to act. It was all so complicated, suddenly. The female was scuttling toward me, faster than I would have believed, and it seemed so much quicker and deadlier than the slow white thing below. Perhaps I should take it out first. I might miss, and then I would need time to go for my knife or a second arrow.

Except that would leave Gerry tangled and helpless under the jaws of the male that moved toward him inexorably. He could die. He could die. Crystal could never blame me. I had to save myself, and her, she would understand that. And I'd have her back again.

Yes.

NO!

Crystal was screaming, screaming, and suddenly everything was clear and I knew what it had all meant and why I was here in this forest and what I had to do. There was a moment of glorious transcendence. I had lost the gift of making her happy, my Crystal, but now for a moment suspended in time that power had returned to me, and I could give or withhold happiness forever. With an arrow, I could prove a love that Gerry would never match.

I think I smiled. I'm sure I did.

And my arrow flew darkly through the cool night, and found its mark in the bloated white spider that raced across a web of light.

The female was on me, and I made no move to kick it away or crush it beneath my heel. There was a sharp stabbing pain in my ankle.

Bright and many-colored are the webs the dream-spiders weave.

At night, when I return from the forests, I clean my arrows carefully and open my great knife, with its slim barbed blade, to cut apart the poison sacs I've collected. I slit them open, each in turn, as I have earlier cut them from the still white bodies of the dream-spiders, and then I drain the venom off into a bottle, to wait for the day when Korbec flies out to collect it.

Afterwards I set out the miniature goblet, exquisitely wrought in silver and obsidian and bright with spider motifs, and pour it full of the heavy black wine they bring me from the city. I stir the cup with my knife, around and around until the blade is shiny clean again and the wine a trifle darker than before. And I ascend to the roof.

Often Korbec's words will return to me then, and with them my story. Crystal my love, and Gerry, and a night of lights and spiders. It all seemed so very right for that brief moment, when I stood upon the moss-covered bridge with an arrow in my hand, and decided. And it has all gone so very very *wrong* . . .

. . . from the moment I awoke, after a month of fever and visions, to find myself in the tower where Crys and Gerry had taken me to nurse me back to health. My decision, my transcendent choice, was not so final as I would have thought.

At times I wonder if it *was* a choice. We talked about it, often, while I regained my strength, and the tale that Crystal tells me is not the one that I remember. She says that we never saw the female at all, until it was too late, that it dropped silently onto my neck just as I released the arrow that killed the male. Then, she says, she smashed it with the flashlight that Gerry had given her to hold, and I went tumbling into the web.

In fact, there *is* a wound on my neck, and none on my ankle. And her story has a ring of truth. For I have come to know the dream-spiders in the slow-flowing years since that night, and I know that the females are stealthy killers that drop down on their prey unawares. They do not charge across fallen trees like berserk ironhorns; it is not the spiders' way.

And neither Crystal nor Gerry has any memory of a pale winged thing flapping in the web.

Yet *I* remember it clearly . . . as I remember the female spider that scuttled toward me during the endless years that I stood frozen . . . but then . . . they say the bite of a dream-spider does strange things to your mind.

That could be it, of course.

Sometimes when Squirrel comes behind me up the stairs, scraping the sooty bricks with his eight white legs, the wrongness of it all hits me, and I know I've dwelt with dreams too long.

Yet the dreams are often better than the waking, the stories so much finer than the lives.

Crystal did not come back to me, then or ever. They left when I was healthy. And the happiness I'd brought her with the choice that was not a choice and the sacrifice not a sacrifice, my gift to her forever – it lasted less than a year. Korbec tells me that she and Gerry broke up violently, and that she has since left Jamison's World.

I suppose that's truth enough, if you can believe a man like Korbec. I don't worry about it overmuch.

I just kill dream-spiders, drink wine, pet Squirrel. And each night I climb this tower of ashes to gaze at distant lights.

And Seven Times Never Kill Man

Ye may kill for yourselves,
and your mates,
and your cubs as they need,
and ye can;

But kill not for pleasure of killing,
and seven times never kill Man!

– Rudyard Kipling

O utside the walls the Jaenshi children hung, a row of small gray-furred
bodies still and motionless at the ends of long ropes. The oldest among
them, obviously, had been slaughtered before hanging; here a headless
male swung upside down, the noose around the feet, while there dangled
the blast-burned carcass of a female. But most of them, the dark hairy
infants with the wide golden eyes, most of them had simply been hanged.
Toward dusk, when the wind came swirling down out of the ragged hills,
the bodies of the lighter children would twist at the ends of their ropes and
bang against the city walls, as if they were alive and pounding for
admission.

But the guards on the walls paid the thumping no mind as they walked
their relentless rounds, and the rust-streaked metal gates did not open.

'Do you believe in evil?' Arik neKrol asked Jannis Ryther as they looked
down on the City of the Steel Angels from the crest of a nearby hill. Anger
was written across every line of his flat yellow-brown face, as he squatted
among the broken shards of what once had been a Jaenshi worship
pyramid.

'Evil?' Ryther murmured in a distracted way. Her eyes never left the
redstone walls below, where the dark bodies of the children were outlined
starkly. The sun was going down, the fat red globe that the Steel Angels
called the Heart of Bakkalon, and the valley beneath them seemed to swim
in bloody mists.

'Evil,' neKrol repeated. The trader was a short, pudgy man, his features decidedly mongoloid except for the flame-red hair that fell nearly to his waist. 'It is a religious concept, and I am not a religious man. Long ago, when I was a very child growing up on ai-Emerel, I decided that there was no good or evil, only different ways of thinking.' His small, soft hands felt around in the dust until he had a large, jagged shard that filled his fist. He stood and offered it to Ryther. 'The Steel Angels have made me believe in evil again,' he said.

She took the fragment from him wordlessly and turned it over in her hands. Ryther was much taller than neKrol, and much tinier; a hard bony woman with a long face, short black hair, and eyes without expression. The sweat-stained coveralls she wore hung loosely on her spare frame.

'Interesting,' she said finally, after studying the shard for several minutes. It was as hard and smooth as glass, but stronger; colored a translucent red, yet so very dark it was almost black. 'A plastic?' she asked, throwing it back to the ground.

NeKrol shrugged. 'That was my very guess, but of course it is impossible. The Jaenshi work in bone and wood and sometimes metal, but plastic is centuries beyond them.'

'Or behind them,' Ryther said. 'You say these worship pyramids are scattered all through the forest?'

'Yes, as far as I have ranged. But the Angels have smashed all those close to their valley to drive the Jaenshi away. As they expand, and they *will* expand, they will smash others.'

Ryther nodded. She looked down into the valley again, and as she did the last sliver of the Heart of Bakkalon slid below the western mountains and the city lights began to come on. The Jaenshi children swung in pools of soft blue illumination, and just above the city gates two stick figures could be seen working. Shortly they heaved something outward, a rope uncoiled, and then another small dark shadow jerked and twitched against the wall. 'Why?' Ryther said, in a cool voice, watching.

NeKrol was anything but cool. 'The Jaenshi tried to defend one of their pyramids. Spears and knives and rocks against the Steel Angels with lasers and blasters and screechguns. But they caught them unaware, killed a man. The Proctor announced it would not happen again.' He spat. 'Evil. The children trust them, you see.'

'Interesting,' Ryther said.

'Can you do anything?' neKrol asked, his voice agitated. 'You have your ship, your crew. The Jaenshi need a protector, Jannis. They are helpless before the Angels.'

'I have four men in my crew,' Ryther said evenly. 'Perhaps four hunting lasers as well.' That was all the answer she gave.

NeKrol looked at her helplessly. *'Nothing?'*

'Tomorrow, perhaps, the Proctor will call on us. He has surely seen the *Lights* descend. Perhaps the Angels wish to trade.' She glanced again into the valley. 'Come, Arik, we must go back to your base. The trade goods must be loaded.'

Wyatt, Proctor of the Children of Bakkalon on the World of Corlos, was tall and red and skeletal, and the muscles stood out clearly on his bare arms. His blue-black hair was cropped very short, his carriage was stiff and erect. Like all the Steel Angels, he wore a uniform of chameleon cloth (a pale brown now, as he stood in the full light of day on the edge of the small, crude spacefield), a mesh-steel belt with hand-laser and communicator and screechgun, and a stiff red Roman collar. The tiny figurine that hung on a chain about his neck – the pale child Bakkalon, nude and innocent and bright-eyed, but holding a great black sword in one small fist – was the only sign of Wyatt's rank.

Four other Angels stood behind him: two men, two women, all dressed identically. There was a sameness about their faces, too; the hair always cropped tightly, whether it was blond or red or brown, the eyes alert and cold and a little fanatic, the upright posture that seemed to characterize members of the military-religious sect, the bodies hard and fit. NeKrol, who was soft and slouching and sloppy, disliked everything about the Angels.

Proctor Wyatt had arrived shortly after dawn, sending one of his squad to pound on the door of the small gray prefab bubble that was neKrol's trading base and home. Sleepy and angry, but with a guarded politeness, the trader had risen to greet the Angels, and had escorted them out to the center of the spacefield, where the scarred metal teardrop of the *Lights of Jolostar* squatted on three retractable legs.

The cargo ports were all sealed now; Ryther's crew had spent most of the evening unloading neKrol's trade goods and replacing them in the ship's hold with crates of Jaenshi artifacts that might bring good prices from collectors of extraterrestrial art. No way of knowing until a dealer looked over the goods; Ryther had dropped neKrol only a year ago, and this was the first pickup.

'I am an independent trader, and Arik is my agent on this world,' Ryther told the proctor when she met him on the edge of the field. 'You must deal through him.'

'I see,' Proctor Wyatt said. He still held the list he had offered Ryther, of goods the Angels wanted from the industrialized colonies on Avalon and Jamison's World. 'But neKrol will not deal with us.'

Ryther looked at him blankly.

'With good reason,' neKrol said. 'I trade with the Jaenshi, you slaughter them.'

The Proctor had spoken to neKrol often in the months since the Steel Angels had established their city-colony, and the talks had all ended in arguments; now he ignored him. 'The steps we took were needed,' Wyatt said to Ryther. 'When an animal kills a man, the animal must be punished, and other animals must see and learn, so that beasts may know that man, the seed of Earth and child of Bakkalon, is the lord and master of them all.'

NeKrol snorted. 'The Jaenshi are not beasts, Proctor, they are an intelligent race, with their own religion and art and customs, and they . . .'

Wyatt looked at him. 'They have no soul. Only the children of Bakkalon have souls, only the seed of Earth. What mind they may have is relevant only to you, and perhaps them. Soulless, they are beasts.'

'Arik has shown me the worship pyramids they build,' Ryther said. 'Surely creatures that build such shrines must have souls.'

The Proctor shook his head. 'You are in error in your belief. It is written clearly in the Book. We, the seed of Earth, are truly the children of Bakkalon, and no others. The rest are animals, and in Bakkalon's name we must assert our dominion over them.'

'Very well,' Ryther said. 'But you will have to assert your dominion without aid from the *Lights of Jolostar*, I'm afraid. And I must inform you, Proctor, that I find your actions seriously disturbing, and intend to report them when I return to Jamison's World.'

'I expected no less,' Wyatt said. 'Perhaps by next year you will burn with love of Bakkalon, and we may talk again. Until then, the world of Corlos will survive.' He saluted her, and walked briskly from the field, followed by the four Steel Angels.

'What good will it do to report them?' neKrol said bitterly, after they had gone.

'None,' Ryther said, looking off toward the forest. The wind was kicking up the dust around her, and her shoulders slumped, as if she were very tired. 'The Jamies won't care, and if they did, what could they do?'

NeKrol remembered the heavy red-bound book that Wyatt had given him months ago. 'And Bakkalon the pale child fashioned his children out of steel,' he quoted, 'for the stars will break those of softer flesh. And in the hand of each new-made infant He placed a beaten sword, telling them, "This is the Truth and the Way."' He spat in disgust. 'That is their very creed. And we can do nothing?'

Her face was empty of expression now. 'I will leave you two lasers. In a year, make sure the Jaenshi know how to use them. I believe I know what sort of trade goods I should bring.'

*

The Jaenshi lived in clans (as neKrol thought of them) of twenty to thirty, each clan divided equally between adults and children, each having its own home-forest and worship pyramid. They did not build; they slept curled up in trees around their pyramid. For food, they foraged; juicy blue-black fruits grew everywhere, and there were three varieties of edible berries, a hallucinogenic leaf, and a soapy yellow root the Jaenshi dug for. NeKrol had found them to be hunters as well, though infrequently. A clan would go for months without meat, while the snuffling brown bushogs multiplied all around them, digging up roots and playing with the children. Then suddenly, when the bushog population had reached some critical point, the Jaenshi spearmen would walk among them calmly, killing two out of every three, and that week great hog roasts would be held each night around the pyramid. Similar patterns could be discerned with the white-bodied tree slugs that sometimes covered the fruit trees like a plague, until the Jaenshi gathered them for a stew, and with the fruit-stealing pseudomonks that haunted the higher limbs.

So far as neKrol could tell, there were no predators in the forests of the Jaenshi. In his early months on their world, he had worn a long force-knife and a hand-laser as he walked from pyramid to pyramid on his trade route. But he had never encountered anything even remotely hostile, and now the knife lay broken in his kitchen, while the laser was long lost.

The day after the *Lights of Jolostar* departed, neKrol went armed into the forest again, with one of Ryther's hunting lasers slung over his shoulder.

Less than two kilometers from his base, neKrol found the camp of the Jaenshi he called the waterfall folk. They lived up against the side of a heavy-wooded hill, where a stream of tumbling blue-white water came sliding and bouncing down, dividing and rejoining itself over and over, so the whole hillside was an intricate glittering web of waterfalls and rapids and shallow pools and spraying wet curtains. The clan's worship pyramid sat in the bottommost pool, on a flat gray stone in the middle of the eddies: taller than most Jaenshi, coming up to neKrol's chin, looking infinitely heavy and solid and immovable, a three-sided block of dark, dark red.

NeKrol was not fooled. He had seen other pyramids sliced to pieces by the lasers of the Steel Angels and shattered by the flames of their blasters; whatever powers the pyramids might have in Jaenshi myth, whatever mysteries might lie behind their origin, it was not enough to stay the swords of Bakkalon.

The glade around the pyramid-pool was alive with sunlight when neKrol entered, and the long grasses swayed in the light breeze, but most of the waterfall folk were elsewhere. In the trees perhaps, climbing and coupling and pulling down fruits, or ranging through the forests on their hill. The trader found only a few small children riding on a bushog in the clearing when he arrived. He sat down to wait, warm in the sunlight.

Soon the old talker appeared.

He sat down next to neKrol, a tiny shriveled Jaenshi with only a few patches of dirty gray-white fur left to hide the wrinkles in his skin. He was toothless, clawless, feeble; but his eyes, wide and golden and pupil-less as those of any Jaenshi, were still alert, alive. He was the talker of the waterfall folk, the one in closest communication with the worship pyramid. Every clan had a talker.

'I have something new to trade,' neKrol said, in the soft slurred speech of the Jaenshi. He had learned the tongue before coming here, back on Avalon. Tomas Chung, the legendary Avalonian linguist, had broken it centuries before, when the Kleronomas Survey brushed by this world. No other human had visited the Jaenshi since, but the maps of Kleronomas and Chung's language-pattern analysis both remained alive in the computers at the Avalon Institute for the Study of Non-Human Intelligence.

'We have made you more statues, have fashioned new woods,' the old talker said. 'What have you brought? Salt?'

NeKrol undid his knapsack, laid it out, and opened it. He took out one of the bricks of salt he carried, and laid it before the old talker. 'Salt,' he said. 'And more.' He laid the hunting rifle before the Jaenshi.

'What is this?' the old talker asked.

'Do you know of the Steel Angels?' neKrol asked.

The other nodded, a gesture neKrol had taught him. 'The godless who run from the dead valley speak of them. They are the ones who make the gods grow silent, the pyramid breakers.'

'This is a tool like the Steel Angels use to break your pyramids,' neKrol said. 'I am offering it to you in trade.'

The old talker sat very still. 'But we do not wish to break pyramids,' he said.

'This tool can be used for other things,' neKrol said. 'In time, the Steel Angels may come here, to break the pyramid of the waterfall folk. If by then you have tools like this, you can stop them. The people of the pyramid in the ring-of-stone tried to stop the Steel Angels with spears and knives, and now they are scattered and wild and their children hang dead from the walls of the City of the Steel Angels. Other clans of the Jaenshi were unresisting, yet now they too are godless and landless. The time will come when the waterfall folk will need this tool, old talker.'

The Jaenshi elder lifted the laser and turned it curiously in his small withered hands. 'We must pray on this,' he said. 'Stay, Arik. Tonight we

shall tell you, when the god looks down on us. Until then, we shall trade.'
He rose abruptly, gave a swift glance at the pyramid across the pool, and
faded into the forest, still holding the laser.

NeKrol sighed. He had a long wait before him; the prayer assemblies
never came until sundown. He moved to the edge of the pool and unlaced
his heavy boots to soak his sweaty, calloused feet in the crisp cold waters.

When he looked up, the first of the carvers had arrived; a lithe young
Jaenshi female with a touch of auburn in her body fur. Silent (they were
all silent in neKrol's presence, all save the talker), she offered him her
work.

It was a statuette no larger than his fist, a heavy-breasted fertility
goddess fashioned out of the fragrant, thin-veined blue wood of the fruit
trees. She sat cross-legged on a triangular base, and three thin slivers of
bone rose from each corner of the triangle to meet above her head in a blob
of clay.

NeKrol took the carving, turned it this way and that, and nodded his
approval. The Jaenshi smiled and vanished, taking the salt brick with her.
Long after she was gone, neKrol continued to admire his acquisition. He
had traded all his life, spending ten years among the squid-faced gethsoids
of Aath and four with the stick-thin Fyndii, traveling a trader's circuit to a
half-dozen stone age planets that had once been slaveworlds of the broken
Hrangan Empire; but nowhere had he found artists like the Jaenshi. Not
for the first time, he wondered why neither Kleronomas nor Chung had
mentioned the native carvings. He was glad they hadn't, though, and fairly
certain that once the dealers saw the crates of wooden gods he had sent
back with Ryther, the world would be overrun by traders. As it was, he had
been sent here entirely on speculation, in hopes of finding a Jaenshi drug
or herb or liquor that might move well in stellar trade. Instead he'd found
the art, like an answer to a prayer.

Other workmen came and went as the morning turned to afternoon and
the afternoon to dusk, setting their craft before him. He looked over each
piece carefully, taking some and declining others, paying for what he took
in salt. Before full darkness had descended, a small pile of goods sat by his
right hand; a matched set of redstone knives, a gray deathcloth woven
from the fur of an elderly Jaenshi by his widow and friends (with his face
wrought upon it in the silky golden hairs of a pseudomonk), a bone spear
with tracings that reminded neKrol of the runes of Old Earth legend; and
statues. The statues were his favorites, always; so often alien art was alien
beyond comprehension, but the Jaenshi workmen touched emotional
chords in him. The gods they carved, each sitting in a bone pyramid, wore
Jaenshi faces, yet at the same time seemed archetypically human: stern-
faced war gods, things that looked oddly like satyrs, fertility goddesses like

the one he had bought, almost-manlike warriors and nymphs. Often neKrol had wished that he had a formal education in extee anthropology, so that he might write a book on the universals of myth. The Jaenshi surely had a rich mythology, though the talkers never spoke of it; nothing else could explain the carvings. Perhaps the old gods were no longer worshipped, but they were still remembered.

By the time the Heart of Bakkalon went down and the last reddish rays ceased to filter through the looming trees, neKrol had gathered as much as he could carry, and his salt was all but exhausted. He laced up his boots again, packed his acquisitions with painstaking care, and sat patiently in the poolside grass, waiting. One by one, the waterfall folk joined him. Finally the old talker returned.

The prayers began.

The old talker, with the laser still in his hand, waded carefully across the night-dark waters, to squat by the black bulk of the pyramid. The others, adults and children together, now some forty strong, chose spots in the grass near the banks, behind neKrol and around him. Like him, they looked out over the pool, at the pyramid and the talker outlined clearly in the light of a new-risen, oversized moon. Setting the laser down on the stone, the old talker pressed both palms flat against the side of the pyramid, and his body seemed to go stiff, while all the other Jaenshi also tensed and grew very quiet.

NeKrol shifted restlessly and fought a yawn. It was not the first time he'd sat through a prayer ritual, and he knew the routine. A good hour of boredom lay before him; the Jaenshi did silent worship, and there was nothing to be heard but their steady breathing, nothing to be seen but forty impassive faces. Sighing, the trader tried to relax, closing his eyes and concentrating on the soft grass beneath him and the warm breeze that tossed his wild mane of hair. Here, briefly, he found peace. How long would it last, he mused, should the Steel Angels leave their valley . . .

The hour passed, but neKrol, lost in meditation, scarce felt the flow of time. Until suddenly he heard the rustlings and chatter around him, as the waterfall folk rose and went back into the forest. And then the old talker stood in front of him, and laid the laser at his feet.

'No,' he said simply.

NeKrol started. 'What? But you *must*. Let me show you what it can do . . .'

'I have had a vision, Arik. The god has shown me. But also he has shown me that it would not be a good thing to take this in trade.'

'Old Talker, the Steel Angels will come . . .'

'If they come, our god shall speak to them,' the Jaenshi elder said, in his

purring speech, but there was finality in the gentle voice, and no appeal in
the vast liquid eyes.

*

'For our food, we thank ourselves, none other. It is ours because we
worked for it, ours because we fought for it, ours by the only right that is:
the right of the strong. But for that strength – for the might of our arms
and the steel of our swords and the fire in our hearts – we thank Bakkalon,
the pale child, who gave us life and taught us how to keep it.'

The Proctor stood stiffly at the centermost of the five long wooden tables
that stretched the length of the great mess hall, pronouncing each word of
the grace with solemn dignity. His large veined hands pressed tightly
together as he spoke, against the flat of the upward-jutting sword, and the
dim lights had faded his uniform to an almost-black. Around him, the
Steel Angels sat at attention, their food untouched before them: fat boiled
tubers, steaming chunks of bushog meat, black bread, bowls of crunchy
green neograss. Children below the fighting age of ten, in smocks of
starchy white and the omnipresent mesh-steel belts, filled the two
outermost tables beneath the slit-like windows; toddlers struggled to sit
still under the watchful eyes of stern nine-year-old houseparents with
hardwood batons in their belts. Further in, the fighting brotherhood sat,
fully armed, at two equally long tables, men and women alternating,
leather-skinned veterans sitting next to ten-year-olds who had barely
moved from the children's dorm to the barracks. All of them wore the
same chameleon cloth as Wyatt, though without his collar, and a few had
buttons of rank. The center table, less than half the length of the others,
held the cadre of the Steel Angels; the squadfathers and squadmothers,
the weaponsmasters, the healers, the four fieldbishops, all those who wore
the high, stiff crimson collar. And the Proctor, at its head.

'Let us eat,' Wyatt said at last. His sword moved above his table with a
whoosh, describing the slash of blessing, and he sat to his meal. The
Proctor, like all the others, had stood single-file in the line that wound past
the kitchen to the mess hall, and his portions were no larger than the least
of the brotherhood.

There was a clink of knives and forks, and the infrequent clatter of a
plate, and from time to time the thwack of a baton, as a houseparent
punished some transgression of discipline by one of his charges; other than
that, the hall was silent. The Steel Angels did not speak at meals, but
rather meditated on the lessons of the day as they consumed their spartan
fare.

Afterwards, the children – still silent – marched out of the hall, back to
their dormitory. The fighting brotherhood followed, some to chapel, most

to the barracks, a few to guard duty on the walls. The men they were relieving would find late meals still warm in the kitchen.

The officer corp remained; after the plates were cleared away, the meal became a staff meeting.

'At ease,' Wyatt said, but the figures along the table relaxed little, if at all. Relaxation had been bred out of them by now. The Proctor found one of them with his eyes. 'Dhallis,' he said, 'you have the report I requested?'

Fieldbishop Dhallis nodded. She was a husky middle-aged woman with thick muscles and skin the color of brown leather. On her collar was a small steel insignia, an ornamental memory-chip that meant Computer Services. 'Yes, Proctor,' she said, in a hard, precise voice. 'Jamison's World is a fourth-generation colony, settled mostly from Old Poseidon. One large continent, almost entirely unexplored, and more than twelve thousand islands of various sizes. The human population is concentrated almost entirely on the islands, and makes its living by farming sea and land, aquatic husbandry, and heavy industry. The oceans are rich in food and metal. The total population is about seventy-nine million. There are two large cities, both with spaceports: Port Jamison and Jolostar.' She looked down at the computer printout on the table. 'Jamison's World was not even charted at the time of the Double War. It has never known military action, and the only Jamie armed forces are their planetary police. It has no colonial program and has never attempted to claim political jurisdiction beyond its own atmosphere.'

The Proctor nodded. 'Excellent. Then the trader's threat to report us is essentially an empty one. We can proceed. Squadfather Walman?'

'Four Jaenshi were taken today, Proctor, and are now on the walls,' Walman reported. He was a ruddy young man with a blond crew cut and large ears. 'If I might, sir, I would request discussion of possible termination of the campaign. Each day we search harder for less. We have virtually wiped out every Jaenshi youngling of the clans who originally inhabited Sword Valley.'

Wyatt nodded. 'Other opinions?'

Fieldbishop Lyon, blue-eyed and gaunt, indicated dissent. 'The adults remain alive. The mature beast is more dangerous than the youngling, Squadfather.'

'Not in this case,' Weaponsmaster C'ara DaHan said. DaHan was a giant of a man, bald and bronze-colored, the chief of Psychological Weaponry and Enemy Intelligence. 'Our studies show that once the pyramid is destroyed, neither full-grown Jaenshi nor the immature pose any threat whatsoever to the children of Bakkalon. Their social structure virtually disintegrates. The adults either flee, hoping to join some other clan, or revert to near-animal savagery. They abandon the younglings, most of

whom fend for themselves in a confused sort of way and offer no
resistance when we take them. Considering the number of Jaenshi on our
walls, and those reported slain by predators or each other, I strongly feel
that Sword Valley is virtually clean of the animals. Winter is coming,
Proctor, and much must be done. Squadfather Walman and his men
should be set to other tasks.'

There was more discussion, but the tone had been set; most of the
speakers backed DaHan. Wyatt listened carefully, and all the while prayed
to Bakkalon for guidance. Finally he motioned for quiet.

'Squadfather,' he said to Walman, 'tomorrow collect all the Jaenshi –
both adults and children – that you can, but do not hang them if they are
unresisting. Instead, take them to the city, and show them their clanmates
on our walls. Then cast them from the valley, one in each direction of the
compass.' He bowed his head. 'It is my hope that they will carry a message,
to all the Jaenshi, of the price that must be paid when a beast raises hand
or claw or blade against the seed of Earth. Then, when the spring comes
and the children of Bakkalon move beyond Sword Valley, the Jaenshi will
peacefully abandon their pyramids and quit whatever lands men may
require, so the glory of the pale child might be spread.'

Lyon and DaHan both nodded, among others. 'Speak wisdom to us,'
Fieldbishop Dhallis said then.

Proctor Wyatt agreed. One of the lesser-ranking squad-mothers brought
him the Book, and he opened it to the Chapter of Teachings.

'In those days much evil had come upon the seed of Earth,' the Proctor
read, 'for the children of Bakkalon had abandoned Him to bow to softer
gods. So their skies grew dark and upon them from above came the Sons
of Hranga with red eyes and demon teeth, and upon them from below
came the vast Horde of Fyndii like a cloud of locusts that blotted out the
stars. And the worlds flamed, and the children cried out, "Save us! Save
us!"

'And the pale child came and stood before them, with His great sword in
His hand, and in a voice like thunder He rebuked them. "You have been
weak children," He told them, "for you have disobeyed. Where are your
swords? Did I not set swords in your hands?"

'And the children cried out, "We have beaten them into plowshares, oh
Bakkalon!"

'And He was sore angry. "With plowshares, then, shall you face the Sons
of Hranga! With plowshares shall you slay the Horde of Fyndii?" ' And He
left them, and heard no more their weeping, for the Heart of Bakkalon is a
Heart of Fire.

'But then one among the seed of Earth dried his tears, for the skies did
burn so bright that they ran scalding on his cheeks. And the bloodlust rose

in him and he beat his plowshare back into a sword, and charged the Sons of Hranga, slaying as he went. The others saw, and followed, and a great battle cry rang across the worlds.

'And the pale child heard, and came again, for the sound of battle is more pleasing to his ears than the sound of wails. And when He saw, He smiled. "Now you are my children again," He said to the seed of Earth. "For you had turned against me to worship a god who calls himself a lamb, but did you not know that lambs go only to the slaughter? Yet now your eyes have cleared, and again you are the Wolves of God!"

'And Bakkalon gave them all swords again, all His children and all the seed of Earth, and He lifted his great black blade, the Demon-Reaver that slays the soulless, and swung it. And the Sons of Hranga fell before His might, and the great Horde that was the Fyndii burned beneath His gaze. And the children of Bakkalon swept across the worlds.'

The Proctor lifted his eyes. 'Go, my brothers-in-arms, and think on the Teachings of Bakkalon as you sleep. May the pale child grant you visions!'

They were dismissed.

*

The trees on the hill were bare and glazed with ice, and the snow – unbroken except for their footsteps and the stirrings of the bitter-sharp north wind – gleamed a blinding white in the noon sun. In the valley beneath, the City of the Steel Angels looked preternaturally clean and still. Great snowdrifts had piled against the eastern walls, climbing halfway up the stark scarlet stone; the gates had not opened in months. Long ago, the children of Bakkalon had taken their harvest and fallen back inside the city, to huddle around their fires. But for the blue lights that burned late into the cold black night, and the occasional guard pacing atop the walls, neKrol would hardly have known that the Angels still lived.

The Jaenshi that neKrol had come to think of as the bitter speaker looked at him out of eyes curiously darker than the soft gold of her brothers. 'Below the snow, the god lies broken,' she said, and even the soothing tones of the Jaenshi tongue could not hide the hardness in her voice. They stood at the very spot where neKrol had once taken Ryther, the spot where the pyramid of the people of the ring-of-stone once stood. NeKrol was sheathed head to foot in a white thermosuit that clung too tightly, accenting every unsightly bulge. He looked out on Sword Valley from behind a dark blue plastifilm in the suit's cowl. But the Jaenshi, the bitter speaker, was nude, covered only by the thick gray fur of her winter coat. The strap of the hunting laser ran down between her breasts.

'Other gods beside yours will break unless the Steel Angels are stopped,' neKrol said, shivering despite his thermosuit.

The bitter speaker seemed hardly to hear. 'I was a child when they came, Arik. If they had left our god, I might be a child still. Afterwards, when the light went out and the glow inside me died, I wandered far from the ring-of-stone, beyond our own home forest; knowing nothing, eating where I could. Things are not the same in the dark valley. Bushogs honked at my passing, and charged me with their tusks, other Jaenshi threatened me and each other. I did not understand and I could not pray. Even when the Steel Angels found me, I did not understand, and I went with them to their city, knowing nothing of their speech. I remember the walls, and the children, many so much younger than me. Then I screamed and struggled; when I saw those on the ropes, something wild and godless stirred to life inside me.' Her eyes regarded him, her eyes like burnished bronze. She shifted in the ankle-deep snow, curling a clawed hand around the strap of her laser.

NeKrol had taught her well since the day she had joined him, in the late summer when the Steel Angels had cast her from Sword Valley. The bitter speaker was by far the best shot of his six, the godless exiles he had gathered to him and trained. It was the only way; he had offered the lasers in trade to clan after clan, and each had refused. The Jaenshi were certain that their gods would protect them. Only the godless listened, and not all of them; many – the young children, the quiet ones, the first to flee – many had been accepted into other clans. But others, like the bitter speaker, had grown too savage, had seen too much; they fit no longer. She had been the first to take the weapon, after the old talker had sent her away from the waterfall folk.

'It is often better to be without gods,' neKrol told her. 'Those below us have a god, and it has made them what they are. And so the Jaenshi have gods, and because they trust, they die. You godless are their only hope.'

The bitter speaker did not answer. She only looked down on the silent city, besieged by snow, and her eyes smoldered.

And neKrol watched her, and wondered. He and his six were the hope of the Jaenshi, he had said; if so, was there hope at all? The bitter speaker, and all his exiles, had a madness about them, a rage that made him tremble. Even if Ryther came with the lasers, even if so small a group could stop the Angels' march, even if all that came to pass – what then? Should all the Angels die tomorrow, where would his godless find a place?

They stood, all quiet, while the snow stirred under their feet and the north wind bit at them.

*

The chapel was dark and quiet. Flameglobes burned a dim, eerie red in either corner, and the rows of plain wooden benches were empty. Above the heavy altar, a slab of rough black stone, Bakkalon stood in hologram, so real he almost breathed; a boy, a mere boy, naked and milky white, with the wide eyes and blond hair of innocent youth. In his hand, half again taller than himself, was the great black sword.

Wyatt knelt before the projection, head bowed and very still. All through the winter his dreams had been dark and troubled, so each day he would kneel and pray for guidance. There was none else to seek but Bakkalon; he, Wyatt, was the Proctor, who led in battle and in faith. He alone must riddle his visions.

So daily he wrestled with his thoughts, until the snows began to melt and the knees of his uniform had nearly worn through from long scraping on the floor. Finally, he had decided, and this day he had called upon the senior collars to join him in the chapel.

Alone they entered, while the Proctor knelt unmoving, and chose seats on the benches behind him, each apart from his fellows. Wyatt took no notice; he prayed only that his words would be correct, his vision true. When they were all there, he stood and turned to face them.

'Many are the worlds on which the children of Bakkalon have lived,' he told them, 'but none so blessed as this, our Corlos. A great time is on us, my brothers-in-arms. The pale child has come to me in my sleep, as once he came to the first Proctors in the years when the brotherhood was forged. He has given me visions.'

They were quiet, all of them, their eyes humble and obedient; he was their Proctor, after all. There could be no questioning when one of higher rank spoke wisdom or gave orders. That was one of the precepts of Bakkalon, that the chain of command was sacred and never to be doubted. So all of them kept silence.

'Bakkalon Himself has walked upon this world. He has walked among the soulless and the beasts of the field and told them our dominion, and this he has said to me: that when the spring comes and the seed of Earth moves from Sword Valley to take new land, all the animals shall know their place and retire before us. This I do prophesy!

'More, we shall see miracles. That too the pale child has promised me, signs by which we will know His truth, signs that shall bolster our faith with new revelation. But so too shall our faith be tested, for it will be a time of sacrifices, and Bakkalon will call upon us more than once to show our trust in Him. We must remember His Teachings and be true, and each of us must obey Him as a child obeys the parent and a fighting man his officer: that is, swiftly and without question. For the pale child knows best.

'These are the visions He has granted me, these are the dreams that I have dreamed. Brothers, pray with me.'

And Wyatt turned again and knelt, and the rest knelt with him, and all

the heads were bowed in prayer save one. In the shadows at the rear of the
chapel where the flameglobes flickered but dimly, C'ara DaHan stared at
his Proctor from beneath a heavy beetled brow.

That night, after a silent meal in the mess hall and a short staff meeting,
the Weaponsmaster called upon Wyatt to go walking on the walls.
'Proctor, my soul is troubled,' he told him. 'I must have counsel from he
who is closest to Bakkalon.' Wyatt nodded, and both donned heavy
nightcloaks of black fur and oil-dark metal cloth, and together they walked
the redstone parapets beneath the stars.

Near the guardhouse that stood above the city gates, DaHan paused and
leaned out over the ledge, his eyes searching the slow-melting snow for
long moments before he turned them on the Proctor. 'Wyatt,' he said at
last, 'my faith is weak.'

The Proctor said nothing, merely watched the other, his face concealed
by the hood of his nightcloak. Confession was not a part of the rites of the
Steel Angels; Bakkalon had said that a fighting man's faith ought never to
waver.

'In the old days,' C'ara DaHan was saying, 'many weapons were used
against the children of Bakkalon. Some, today, exist only in tales. Perhaps
they never existed. Perhaps they are empty things, like the gods the soft
men worship. I am only a Weaponsmaster; such knowledge is not mine.

'Yet there is a tale, my Proctor – one that troubles me. Once, it is said, in
the long centuries of war, the Sons of Hranga loosed upon the seed of
Earth foul vampires of the mind, the creatures men called soul-sucks.
Their touch was invisible, but it crept across kilometers, farther than a man
could see, farther than a laser could fire, and it brought madness. Visions,
my Proctor, visions! False gods and foolish plans were put in the minds of
men, and . . .'

'Silence,' Wyatt said. His voice was hard, as cold as the night air that
crackled around them and turned his breath to steam.

There was a long pause. Then, in a softer voice, the Proctor continued.
'All winter I have prayed, DaHan, and struggled with my visions. I am the
Proctor of the Children of Bakkalon on the World of Corlos, not some new-
armed child to be lied to by false gods. I spoke only after I was sure. I
spoke as your Proctor, as your father in faith and your commanding officer.
That you would question me, Weaponsmaster, that you would doubt – this
disturbs me greatly. Next will you stop to argue with me on the field of
battle, to dispute some fine point of my orders?'

'Never, Proctor,' DaHan said, kneeling in penance in the packed snow
atop the walkway.

'I hope not. But, before I dismiss you, because you are my brother in
Bakkalon, I will answer you, though I need not and it was wrong of you to

expect it. I will tell you this; the Proctor Wyatt is a good officer as well as a devout man. The pale child has made prophecies to me, and has predicted that miracles will come to pass. All these things we shall see with our very eyes. But if the prophecies should fail us, and if no signs appear, well, our eyes will see that too. And then I will know that it was not Bakkalon who sent the visions, but only a false god, perhaps a soul-suck of Hranga. Or do you think a Hrangan can work miracles?'

'No,' DaHan said, still on his knees, his great bald head downcast. 'That would be heresy.'

'Indeed,' said Wyatt. The Proctor glanced briefly beyond the walls. The night was crisp and cold and there was no moon. He felt transfigured, and even the stars seemed to cry the glory of the pale child, for the constellation of the Sword was high upon the zenith, the Soldier reaching up toward it from where he stood on the horizon.

'Tonight you will walk guard without your cloak,' the Proctor told DaHan when he looked down again. 'And should the north wind blow and the cold bite at you, you will rejoice in the pain, for it will be a sign that you submit to your Proctor and your god. As your flesh grows bitter numb, the flame in your heart must burn hotter.'

'Yes, my Proctor,' DaHan said. He stood and removed his nightcloak, handing it to the other. Wyatt gave him the slash of blessing.

*

On the wallscreen in his darkened living quarters the taped drama went through its familiar measured paces, but neKrol, slouched in a large cushioned recliner with his eyes half-closed, hardly noticed. The bitter speaker and two of the other Jaenshi exiles sat on the floor, golden eyes rapt on the spectacle of humans chasing and shooting each other amid the vaulting tower cities of ai-Emerel; increasingly they had begun to grow curious about other worlds and other ways of life. It was all very strange, neKrol thought; the waterfall folk and the other clanned Jaenshi had never shown any such interest. He remembered the early days, before the coming of the Steel Angels in their ancient and soon-to-be-dismantled warship, when he had set all kinds of trade goods before the Jaenshi talkers; bright bolts of glittersilk from Avalon, glowstone jewelry from High Kavalaan, duralloy knives and solar generators and steel powerbows, books from a dozen worlds, medicines and wines – he had come with a little of everything. The talkers took some of it, from time to time, but never with any enthusiasm; the only offering that excited them was salt.

It was not until the spring rains came and the bitter speaker began to question him that neKrol realized, with a start, how seldom any of the Jaenshi clans had ever asked him anything. Perhaps their social structure and their religion stifled their natural intellectual curiosity. The exiles were certainly eager enough, especially the bitter speaker. NeKrol could answer only a small portion of her questions of late, and even then she always had new ones to puzzle him with. He had begun to grow appalled with the extent of his own ignorance.

But then, so had the bitter speaker; unlike the clanned Jaenshi – did the religion make *that* much difference? – she would answer questions as well, and neKrol had tried quizzing her on many things that he'd wondered at. But most of the time she would only blink in bafflement, and begin to question herself.

'There are no stories about our gods,' she said to him once, when he'd tried to learn a little of Jaenshi myth. 'What sort of stories could there be? The gods live in the worship pyramids, Arik, and we pray to them and they watch over us and light our lives. They do not bounce around and fight and break each other like your gods seem to do.'

'But you had other gods once, before you came to worship the pyramids,' neKrol objected. 'The very ones your carvers did for me.' He had even gone so far as to unpack a crate and show her, though surely she remembered, since the people of the pyramid in the ring-of-stone had been among the finest craftsmen.

Yet the bitter speaker only smoothed her fur, and shook her head. 'I was too young to be a carver, so perhaps I was not told,' she said. 'We all know that which we need to know, but only the carvers need to do these things, so perhaps only they know the stories of these old gods.'

Another time he had asked her about the pyramids, and had gotten even less. 'Build them?' she had said. 'We did not build them, Arik. They have always been, like the rocks and the trees.' But then she blinked. 'But they are not like the rocks and the trees, are they?' And, puzzled, she went away to talk to the others.

But if the godless Jaenshi were more thoughtful than their brothers in the clans, they were also more difficult, and each day neKrol realized more and more the futility of their enterprise. He had eight of the exiles with him now – they had found two more, half dead from starvation, in the height of winter – and they all took turns training with the two lasers and spying on the Angels. But even should Ryther return with the weaponry, their force was a joke against the might the Proctor could put in the field. The *Lights of Jolostar* would be carrying a full arms shipment in the expectation that every clan for a hundred kilometers would now be roused and angry, ready to resist the Steel Angels and overwhelm them by sheer force of numbers; Jannis would be blank-faced when only neKrol and his ragged band appeared to greet her.

If in fact they did. Even that was problematical; he was having much difficulty keeping his guerrillas together. Their hatred of the Steel Angels still bordered on madness, but they were far from a cohesive unit. None of them liked to take orders very well, and they fought constantly, going at each other with bared claws in struggles for social dominance. If neKrol had not warned them, he suspected they might even duel with the lasers. As for staying in good fighting shape, that too was a joke. Of the three females in the band, the bitter speaker was the only one who had not allowed herself to be impregnated. Since the Jaenshi usually gave birth in litters of four to eight, neKrol calculated that late summer would present them with an exile population explosion. And there would be more after that, he knew; the godless seemed to copulate almost hourly, and there was no such thing as Jaenshi birth control. He wondered how the clans kept their population so stable, but his charges didn't know that either.

'I suppose we sexed less,' the bitter speaker said when he asked her, 'but I was a child, so I would not really know. Before I came here, there was never the urge. I was just young, I would think.' But when she said it, she scratched herself and seemed very unsure.

Sighing, neKrol eased himself back in the recliner and tried to shut out the noise of the wall-screen. It was all going to be very difficult. Already the Steel Angels had emerged from behind their walls, and the powerwagons rolled up and down Sword Valley turning forest into farmland. He had gone up into the hills himself, and it was easy to see that the spring planting would soon be done. Then, he suspected, the children of Bakkalon would try to expand. Just last week one of them – a giant 'with no head fur,' as his scout had described him – was seen up in the ring-of-stone, gathering shards from the broken pyramid. Whatever that meant, it could not be for the good.

Sometimes he felt sick at the forces he had set in motion, and almost wished that Ryther would forget the lasers. The bitter speaker was determined to strike as soon as they were armed, no matter what the odds. Frightened, neKrol reminded her of the hard Angel lesson the last time a Jaenshi had killed a man; in his dreams he still saw children on the walls.

But she only looked at him, with the bronze tinge of madness in her eyes, and said, 'Yes, Arik. I remember.'

*

Silent and efficient, the white-smocked kitchen boys cleared away the last of the evening's dishes and vanished. 'At ease,' Wyatt said to his officers. Then: 'The time of miracles is upon us, as the pale child foretold.

'This morning I sent three squads into the hills to the southeast of Sword Valley, to disperse the Jaenshi clans on lands that we require. They reported back to me in early afternoon, and now I wish to share their reports with you. Squadmother Jolip, will you relate the events that transpired when you carried out your orders?'

'Yes, Proctor.' Jolip stood, a white-skinned blonde with a pinched face, her uniform hanging slightly loose on a lean body. 'I was assigned a squad of ten to clear out the so-called cliff clan, whose pyramid lies near the foot of a low granite cliff in the wilder part of the hills. The information provided by our intelligence indicated that they were one of the smaller clans, with only twenty-odd adults, so I dispensed with heavy armor. We did take a class five blastcannon, since the destruction of the Jaenshi pyramids is slow work with sidearms alone, but other than that our armament was strictly standard issue.

'We expected no resistance, but recalling the incident at the ring-of-stone, I was cautious. After a march of some twelve kilometers through the hills to the vicinity of the cliff, we fanned out in a semi-circle and moved in slowly, with screechguns drawn. A few Jaenshi were encountered in the forest, and these we took prisoner and marched before us, for use as shields in the event of an ambush or attack. That, of course, proved unnecessary.

'When we reached the pyramid by the cliff, they were waiting for us. At least twelve of the beasts, sir. One of them sat near the base of the pyramid with his hands pressed against its side, while the others surrounded him in a sort of a circle. They all looked up at us, but made no other move.'

She paused a minute, and rubbed a thoughtful finger up against the side of her nose. 'As I told the Proctor, it was all very odd from that point forward. Last summer, I twice led squads against the Jaenshi clans. The first time, having no idea of our intentions, none of the soulless were there; we simply destroyed the artifact and left. The second time, a crowd of the creatures milled around, hampering us with their bodies while not being actively hostile. They did not disperse until I had one of them screeched down. And, of course, I studied the reports of Squadfather Allor's difficulties at the ring-of-stone.

'This time, it was all quite different. I ordered two of my men to set the blastcannon on its tripod, and gave the beasts to understand that they must get out of the way. With hand signals, of course, since I know none of their ungodly tongue. They complied at once, splitting into two groups and, well, lining up, on either side of the line-of-fire. We kept them covered with our screechguns, of course, but everything seemed very peaceful.

'And so it was. The blaster took the pyramid out neatly, a big ball of flame and then sort of a thunder as the thing exploded. A few shards were scattered, but no one was injured, as we had all taken cover and the Jaenshi seemed unconcerned. After the pyramid broke, there was a sharp ozone smell, and for an instant a lingering bluish fire – perhaps an afterimage. I hardly had time to notice them, however, since that was when the Jaenshi all fell to their knees before us. All at once, sirs. And then they pressed their heads against the ground, prostrating themselves. I thought for a moment that they were trying to hail us as gods, because we had shattered their god, and I tried to tell them that we wanted none of their animal worship, and required only that they leave these lands at once. But then I saw that I had misunderstood, because that was when the other four clan members came forward from the trees atop the cliff, and climbed down, and gave us the statue. Then the rest got up. The last I saw, the entire clan was walking due east, away from Sword Valley and the outlying hills. I took the statue and brought it back to the Proctor.' She fell silent but remained standing, waiting for questions.

'I have the statuette here,' Wyatt said. He reached down beside his chair and set it on the table, then pulled off the white cloth covering he had wrapped around it.

The base was a triangle of rockhard blackbark, and three long splinters of bone rose from the corners to make a pyramid frame. Within, exquisitely carved in every detail from soft blue wood, Bakkalon the pale child stood, holding a painted sword.

'What does this mean?' Fieldbishop Lyon asked, obviously startled.

'Sacrilege!' Fieldbishop Dhallis said.

'Nothing so serious,' said Gorman, Fieldbishop for Heavy Armor. 'The beasts are simply trying to ingratiate themselves, perhaps in the hope that we will stay our swords.'

'None but the seed of Earth may bow to Bakkalon,' Dhallis said. 'It is written in the Book! The pale child will not look with favor on the soulless!'

'Silence, my brothers-in-arms!' the Proctor said, and the long table abruptly grew quiet again. Wyatt smiled a thin smile. 'This is the first of the miracles of which I spoke this winter in the chapel, the first of the strange happenings that Bakkalon told to me. For truly He has walked this world, our Corlos, so even the beasts of the fields know His likeness! Think on it, my brothers. Think on this carving. Ask yourselves a few simple questions. Have any of the Jaenshi animals ever been permitted to set foot in this holy city?'

'No, of course not,' someone said.

'Then clearly none of them have seen the holograph that stands above our altar. Nor have I often walked among the beasts, as my duties keep me here within the walls. So none could have seen the pale child's likeness on the chain of office that I wear, for the few Jaenshi who have seen my visage have not lived to speak of it – they were those I judged, who hung upon our city walls. The animals do not speak the language of the Earthseed, nor have any among us learned their simple beastly tongue. Lastly, they have not read the Book. Remember all this, and wonder; how did their carvers know what face and form to carve?'

Quiet; the leaders of the children of Bakkalon looked back and forth among themselves in wonderment.

Wyatt quietly folded his hands. 'A miracle. We shall have no more trouble with the Jaenshi, for the pale child has come to them.'

To the Proctor's right, Fieldbishop Dhallis sat rigidly. 'My Proctor, my leader in faith,' she said, with some difficulty, each word coming slowly, 'surely, *surely*, you do not mean to tell us that these, these *animals* – that they can worship the pale child, that He accepts their worship!'

Wyatt seemed calm, benevolent; he only smiled. 'You need not trouble your soul, Dhallis. You wonder whether I commit the First Fallacy, remembering perhaps the Sacrilege of G'hra when a captive Hrangan bowed to Bakkalon to save himself from an animal's death, and the False Proctor Gibrone proclaimed that all who worship the pale child must have souls.' He shook his head. 'You see, I read the Book. But no, Fieldbishop, no sacrilege has transpired. Bakkalon has walked among the Jaenshi, but surely has given them only truth. They have seen Him in all His armed dark glory, and heard Him proclaim that they are animals, without souls, as surely He would proclaim. Accordingly, they accept their place in the order of the universe, and retire before us. They will never kill a man again. Recall that they did not bow to the statue they carved, but rather gave the statue to us, the seed of Earth, who alone can rightfully worship it. When they did prostrate themselves, it was at *our* feet, as animals to men, and that is as it should be. You see? They have been given truth.'

Dhallis was nodding. 'Yes, my Proctor. I am enlightened. Forgive my moment of weakness.'

But halfway down the table, C'ara DaHan leaned forward and knotted his great knuckled hands, frowning all the while. 'My Proctor,' he said heavily.

'Weaponsmaster?' Wyatt returned. His face grew stern.

'Like the Fieldbishop, my soul has flickered briefly with worry, and I too would be enlightened, if I might?'

Wyatt smiled. 'Proceed,' he said, in a voice without humor.

'A miracle this thing may be indeed,' DaHan said, 'but first we must question ourselves, to ascertain that it is not the trick of a soulless enemy. I do not fathom their stratagem, or their reasons for acting as they have, but I do know of one way that the Jaenshi might have learned the features of our Bakkalon.'

'Oh?'

'I speak of the Jamish trading base, and the red-haired trader Arik neKrol. He is an Earthseed, an Emereli by his looks, and we have given him the Book. But he remains without a burning love of Bakkalon, and goes without arms like a godless man. Since our landing he has opposed us, and he grew most hostile after the lesson we were forced to give the Jaenshi. Perhaps he put the cliff clan up to it, told them to do the carving, to some strange ends of his own. I believe that he *did* trade with them.'

'I believe you speak truth, Weaponsmaster. In the early months after landing, I tried hard to convert neKrol. To no avail, but I did learn much of the Jaenshi beasts and of the trading he did with them.' The Proctor still smiled. 'He traded with one of the clans here in Sword Valley, with the people of ring-of-stone, with the cliff clan and that of the far fruit tangle, with the waterfall folk, and sundry clans further east.'

'Then it is his doing,' DaHan said. 'A trick!'

All eyes moved to Wyatt. 'I did not say that. NeKrol, whatever intentions he might have, is but a single man. He did not trade with all the Jaenshi, nor even know them all.' The Proctor's smile grew briefly wider. 'Those of you who have seen the Emereli know him for a man of flab and weakness; he could hardly walk as far as might be required, and he has neither aircar nor power sled.'

'But he *did* have contact with the cliff clan,' DaHan said. The deep-graven lines on his bronze forehead were set stubbornly.

'Yes, he did,' Wyatt answered. 'But Squadmother Jolip did not go forth alone this morning. I also sent out Squadfather Walman and Squadfather Allor, to cross the waters of the White Knife. The land there is dark and fertile, better than that to the east. The cliff clan, who are southeast, were between Sword Valley and the White Knife, so they had to go. But the other pyramids we moved against belonged to far-river clans, more than thirty kilometers south. They have never seen the trader Arik neKrol, unless he has grown wings this winter.'

Then Wyatt bent again, and set two more statues on the table, and pulled away their coverings. One was set on a base of slate, and the figure was carved in a clumsy broad manner; the other was finely detailed soaproot, even to the struts of the pyramid. But except for the materials and the workmanship, the later statues were identical to the first.

'Do you see a trick, Weaponsmaster?' Wyatt asked.

DaHan looked, and said nothing, for Fieldbishop Lyon rose suddenly and said, 'I see a miracle,' and others echoed him. After the hubbub had finally quieted, the brawny Weaponsmaster lowered his head and said, very softly, 'My Proctor. Read wisdom to us.'

*

'The lasers, speaker, the *lasers!*' There was a tinge of hysterical desperation in neKrol's tone. 'Ryther is not back yet, and that is the very point. We must wait.'

He stood outside the bubble of the trading base, bare-chested and sweating in the hot morning sun, with the thick wind tugging at his tangled hair. The clamor had pulled him from a troubled sleep. He had stopped them just on the edge of the forest, and now the bitter speaker had turned to face him, looking fierce and hard and most unJaenshi-like with the laser slung across her shoulders, a bright blue glittersilk scarf knotted around her neck, and fat glowstone rings on all eight of her fingers. The other exiles, but for the two that were heavy with child, stood around her. One of them held the other laser, the rest carried quivers and powerbows. That had been the speaker's idea. Her newly-chosen mate was down on one knee, panting; he had run all the way from the ring-of-stone.

'No, Arik,' the speaker said, eyes bronze-angry. 'Your lasers are now a month overdue, by your own count of time. Each day we wait, and the Steel Angels smash more pyramids. Soon they may hang children again.'

'Very soon,' neKrol said. 'Very soon, if you attack them. Where is your very hope of victory? Your watcher says they go with two squads and a powerwagon – can you stop them with a pair of lasers and four powerbows? Have you learned to think here, or not?'

'Yes,' the speaker said, but she bared her teeth at him as she said it. 'Yes, but that cannot matter. The clans do not resist, so we must.'

From one knee, her mate looked up at neKrol. 'They . . . they march on the waterfall,' he said, still breathing heavily.

'The waterfall!' the bitter speaker repeated. 'Since the death of winter, they have broken more than twenty pyramids, Arik, and their powerwagons have crushed the forest and now a great dusty road scars the soil from their valley to the riverlands. But they had hurt no Jaenshi yet this season, they had let them go. And all those clans-without-a-god have gone to the waterfall, until the home forest of the waterfall folk is bare and eaten clean. Their talkers sit with the old talker and perhaps the waterfall god takes them in, perhaps he is a very great god. I do not know these things. But I *do* know that now the bald Angel has learned of the twenty clans together, of a grouping of half-a-thousand Jaenshi adults, and he leads a powerwagon against them. Will he let them go so easy this time, happy with a carved statue? Will *they* go, Arik, will they give up a second god as easily as a first?' The speaker blinked. 'I fear they will resist with their silly claws. I fear the bald Angel will hang them even if they do not resist, because so many in union throws suspicion in him. I fear many things and know little, but I know *we* must be there. You will not stop us, Arik, and we cannot wait for your long-late lasers.'

And she turned to the others and said, 'Come, we must run,' and they had faded into the forest before neKrol could even shout for them to stay. Swearing, he turned back to the bubble.

The two female exiles were leaving just as he entered. Both were close to the end of their term, but they had powerbows in their hands. NeKrol stopped short. 'You too!' he said furiously, glaring at them. 'Madness, it is the very stuff of madness!' They only looked at him with silent golden eyes, and moved past him toward the trees.

Inside, he swiftly braided his long red hair so it would not catch on the branches, slipped into a shirt, and darted toward the door. Then he stopped. A weapon, he must have a weapon! He glanced around frantically and ran heavily for his storeroom. The powerbows were all gone, he saw. What then, what? He began to rummage, and finally settled for a duralloy machete. It felt strange in his hand and he must have looked most unmartial and ridiculous, but somehow he felt he must take something.

Then he was off, toward the place of the waterfall folk.

*

NeKrol was overweight and soft, hardly used to running, and the way was nearly two kilometers through lush summer forest. He had to stop three times to rest, and quiet the pains in his chest, and it seemed an eternity before he arrived. But still he beat the Steel Angels; a powerwagon is ponderous and slow, and the road from Sword Valley was longer and more hilly.

Jaenshi were everywhere. The glade was bare of grass and twice as large as neKrol remembered it from his last trading trip, early that spring. Still the Jaenshi filled all of it, sitting on the ground, staring at the pool and the waterfall, all silent, packed together so there was scarcely room to walk among them. More sat above, a dozen in every fruit tree, some of the children even ascending to the higher limbs where the pseudomonks usually ruled alone.

On the rock at the center of the pool, with the waterfall behind them as a backdrop, the talkers pressed around the pyramid of the waterfall folk. They were closer together than even those in the grass, and each had his palms flat against the sides. One, thin and frail, sat on the shoulders of another so that he too might touch. NeKrol tried to count them and gave up; the group was too dense, a blurred mass of gray-furred arms and golden eyes, the pyramid at their center, dark and unmovable as ever.

The bitter speaker stood in the pool, the waters ankle-deep around her. She was facing the crowd and screeching at them, her voice strangely unlike the usual Jaenshi purr; in her scarf and rings, she looked absurdly out of place. As she talked, she waved the laser rifle she was holding in one hand. Wildly, passionately, hysterically, she was telling the gathered Jaenshi that the Steel Angels were coming, that they must leave at once, that they should break up and go into the forest and regroup at the trading base. Over and over again she said it.

But the clans were stiff and silent. No one answered, no one listened, no one heard. In full daylight, they were praying.

NeKrol pushed his way through them, stepping on a hand here and a foot there, hardly able to set down a boot without crunching Jaenshi flesh. He was standing next to the bitter speaker, who still gestured wildly, before her bronze eyes seemed to see him. Then she stopped. 'Arik,' she said, 'the Angels are coming, and *they will not listen.*'

'The others,' he panted, still short on breath. 'Where are they?'

'The trees,' the bitter speaker replied, with a vague gesture. 'I sent them up in the trees. Snipers, Arik, such as we saw upon your wall.'

'Please,' he said. 'Come back with me. Leave them, leave them. You told them. I told them. Whatever happens, it is their doing, it is the fault of their fool religion.'

'I cannot leave,' the bitter speaker said. She seemed confused, as so often when neKrol had questioned her back at the base. 'It seems I should, but somehow I know I must stay here. And the others will never go, even if I did. They feel it much more strongly. We must be here. To fight, to talk.' She blinked. 'I do not know *why*, Arik, but we must.'

And before the trader could reply, the Steel Angels came out of the forest.

There were five of them at first, widely spaced; then shortly five more. All afoot, in uniforms whose mottled dark greens blended with the leaves, so that only the glitter of the mesh-steel belts and matching battle helmets stood out. One of them, a gaunt pale woman, wore a high red collar; all of them had hand-lasers drawn.

'You!' the blonde woman shouted, her eyes finding Arik at once, as he stood with his braid flying in the wind and the machete dangling uselessly in his hand. 'Speak to these animals! Tell them they must leave! Tell them that no Jaenshi gathering of this size is permitted east of the mountains, by order of the Proctor Wyatt, and the pale child Bakkalon. Tell them!' And then she saw the bitter speaker, and started. 'And take the laser from the hand of that animal before we burn both of you down!'

Trembling, neKrol dropped the machete from limp fingers into the water. 'Speaker, drop the gun,' he said in Jaenshi, '*please*. If you ever hope to see the far stars. Let loose the laser, my friend, my child, this very now. And I will take you when Ryther comes, with me to ai-Emerel and further places.' The trader's voice was full of fear; the Steel Angels held their lasers steady, and not for a moment did he think the speaker would obey him.

But strangely, meekly, she threw the laser rifle into the pool. NeKrol could not see to read her eyes.

The Squadmother relaxed visibly. 'Good,' she said. 'Now, talk to them in their beastly talk, tell them to leave. If not, we shall crush them. A powerwagon is on its way!' And now, over the roar and tumble of the nearby waters, neKrol could hear it; a heavy crunching as it rolled over trees, rending them into splinters beneath wide duramesh treads. Perhaps they were using the blastcannon and the turret lasers to clear away boulders and other obstacles.

'We have told them,' neKrol said desperately. 'Many times we have told them, but they do not hear!' He gestured all about him; the glade was still hot and close with Jaenshi bodies and none among the clans had taken the slightest notice of the Steel Angels or the confrontation. Behind him, the clustered talkers still pressed small hands against their god.

'Then we shall bare the sword of Bakkalon to them,' the Squadmother said, 'and perhaps they will hear their own wailing!' She holstered her laser and drew a screechgun, and neKrol, shuddering, knew her intent. The screechers used concentrated high-intensity sound to break down cell walls and liquify flesh. Its effects were psychological as much as anything; there was no more horrible death.

But then a second squad of the Angels were among them, and there was a creak of wood straining and snapping, and from behind a final grove of fruit trees, dimly, neKrol could see the black flanks of the powerwagon, its blastcannon seemingly trained right at him. Two of the newcomers wore the scarlet collar – a red-faced youth with large ears who barked orders to his squad, and a huge, muscular man with a bald head and lined bronze skin. NeKrol recognized him; the Weaponsmaster C'ara DaHan. It was DaHan who laid a heavy hand on the Squadmother's arm as she raised her screechgun. 'No,' he said. 'It is not the way.'

She holstered the weapon at once. 'I hear and obey.'

DaHan looked at neKrol. 'Trader,' he boomed, 'is this your doing?'

'No,' neKrol said.

'They will not disperse,' the Squadmother added.

'It would take us a day and a night to screech them down,' DaHan said, his eyes sweeping over the glade and the trees, and following the rocky twisted path of the waterwall up to its summit. 'There is an easier way. Break the pyramid and they go at once.' He stopped then, about to say something else; his eyes were on the bitter speaker.

'A Jaenshi in rings and cloth,' he said. 'They have woven nothing but deathcloth up to now. This alarms me.'

'She is one of the people of the ring-of-stone,' neKrol said quickly. 'She has lived with me.'

DaHan nodded. 'I understand. You are truly a godless man, neKrol, to consort so with soulless animals, to teach them to ape the ways of the seed of Earth. But it does not matter.' He raised his arm in signal; behind him, among the trees, the blastcannon of the powerwagon moved slightly to the right. 'You and your pet should move at once,' DaHan told neKrol. 'When I lower my arm, the Jaenshi god will burn and if you stand in the way, you will never move again.'

'The *talkers!*' neKrol protested, 'the blast will—' and he started to turn to show them. But the talkers were crawling away from the pyramid, one by one.

Behind him, the Angels were muttering. 'A miracle!' one said hoarsely. 'Our child! Our Lord!' cried another.

NeKrol stood paralyzed. The pyramid on the rock was no longer a reddish slab. Now it sparkled in the sunlight, a canopy of transparent crystal. And below that canopy, perfect in every detail, the pale child Bakkalon stood smiling, with his Demon-Reaver in his hand.

The Jaenshi talkers were scrambling from it now, tripping in the water in their haste to be away. NeKrol glimpsed the old talker, running faster than any despite his age. Even he seemed not to understand. The bitter speaker stood open-mouthed.

The trader turned. Half of the Steel Angels were on their knees, the rest had absent-mindedly lowered their arms and they froze in gaping wonder. The Squadmother turned to DaHan. 'It *is* a miracle,' she said. 'As Proctor Wyatt has foreseen. The pale child walks upon this world.'

But the Weaponsmaster was unmoved. 'The Proctor is not here and this is no miracle,' he said in a steely voice. 'It is a trick of some enemy, and I will not be tricked. We will burn the blasphemous thing from the soil of Corlos.' His arm flashed down.

The Angels in the powerwagon must have been lax with awe; the blastcannon did not fire. DaHan turned in irritation. 'It is no miracle!' he shouted. He began to raise his arm again.

Next to neKrol, the bitter speaker suddenly cried out. He looked over with alarm, and saw her eyes flash a brilliant yellow-gold. 'The god!' she muttered softly. 'The light returns to me!'

And the whine of powerbows sounded from the trees around them, and two long bolts shuddered almost simultaneously in the broad back of C'ara DaHan. The force of the shots drove the Weaponsmaster to his knees, smashed him against the ground.

'*RUN!*' neKrol screamed, and he shoved the bitter speaker with all his strength, and she stumbled and looked back at him briefly, her eyes dark bronze again and flickering with fear. Then, swiftly, she was running, her scarf aflutter behind her as she dodged toward the nearest green.

'Kill her!' the Squadmother shouted. 'Kill them all!' And her words woke Jaenshi and Steel Angels both; the children of Bakkalon lifted their lasers against the suddenly-surging crowd, and the slaughter began. NeKrol knelt and scrabbled on the moss-slick rocks until he had the laser rifle in his hands, then brought it to his shoulder and commenced to fire. Light stabbed out in angry bursts; once, twice, a third time. He held the trigger down and the bursts became a beam, and he sheared through the waist of a silver-helmeted Angel before the fire flared in his stomach and he fell heavily into the pool.

For a long time he saw nothing; there was only pain and noise, the water gently slapping against his face, the sounds of high-pitched Jaenshi screaming, running all around him. Twice he heard the roar and crackle of the blastcannon, and more than twice he was stepped on. It all seemed unimportant. He struggled to keep his head on the rocks, half out of the water, but even that seemed none too vital after a while. The only thing that counted was the burning in his gut.

Then, somehow, the pain went away, and there was a lot of smoke and horrible smells but not so much noise, and neKrol lay quietly and listened to the voices.

'The pyramid, Squadmother?' someone asked.

'It *is* a miracle,' a woman's voice replied. 'Look, Bakkalon stands there yet. And see how he smiles! We have done right here today!'

'What should we do with it?'

'Lift it aboard the powerwagon. We shall bring it back to Proctor Wyatt.'

Soon after the voices went away, and neKrol heard only the sound of the water, rushing down endlessly, falling and tumbling. It was a very restful sound. He decided he would sleep.

*

The crewman shoved the crowbar down between the slats and lifted. The thin wood hardly protested at all before it gave. 'More statues, Jannis,' he reported, after reaching inside the crate and tugging loose some of the packing material.

'Worthless,' Ryther said, with a brief sigh. She stood in the broken ruins of neKrol's trading base. The Angels had ransacked it, searching for armed Jaenshi, and debris lay everywhere. But they had not touched the crates.

The crewman took his crowbar and moved on to the next stack of crated artifacts. Ryther looked wistfully at the three Jaenshi who clustered around her, wishing they could communicate a little better. One of them, a sleek female who wore a trailing scarf and a lot of jewelry and seemed always to be leaning on a powerbow, knew a smattering of Terran, but hardly enough. She picked up things quickly, but so far the only thing of

substance she had said was, 'Jamson' World. Arik take us. Angels kill.'
That she had repeated endlessly until Ryther had finally made her
understand that, yes, they would take them. The other two Jaenshi, the
pregnant female and the male with the laser, never seemed to talk at all.

'Statues again,' the crewman said, having pulled a crate from atop the
stack in the ruptured storeroom and pried it open.

Ryther shrugged; the crewman moved on. She turned her back on him
and wandered slowly outside, to the edge of the spacefield where the *Lights
of Jolostar* rested, its open ports bright with yellow light in the gathering
gloom of dusk. The Jaenshi followed her, as they had followed her since
she arrived; afraid, no doubt, that she would go away and leave them if
they took their great bronze eyes off her for an instant.

'Statues,' Ryther muttered, half to herself and half to the Jaenshi. She
shook her head. 'Why did he do it?' she asked them, knowing they could
not understand. 'A trader of his experience? You could tell me, maybe, if
you knew what I was saying. Instead of concentrating on deathcloths and
such, on real Jaenshi art, why did Arik train you people to carve alien
versions of human gods? He should have known no dealer would accept
such obvious frauds. Alien art is *alien*.' She sighed. 'My fault, I suppose. We
should have opened the crates.' She laughed.

The bitter speaker stared at her. 'Arik deathcloth. Gave.'

Ryther nodded, abstractly. She had it now, hanging just above her bunk;
a strange small thing, woven partly from Jaenshi fur and mostly from long
silken strands of flame red hair. On it, gray against the red, was a crude
but recognizable caricature of Arik neKrol. She had wondered at that, too.
The tribute of the widow? A child? Or just a friend? What *had* happened to
Arik during the year the *Lights* had been away? If only she had been back
on time, then ... but she'd lost three months on Jamison's World,
checking dealer after dealer in an effort to unload the worthless statuettes.
It had been middle autumn before the *Lights of Jolostar* returned to Corlos,
to find neKrol's base in ruins, the Angels already gathering in their
harvests.

And the Angels – when she'd gone to them, offering the hold of
unwanted lasers, offering to trade, the sight on those blood-red city walls
had sickened even her. She had thought she'd gone prepared, but the
obscenity she encountered was beyond any preparation. A squad of Steel
Angels found her, vomiting, beyond the tall rusty gates, and had escorted
her inside, before the Proctor.

Wyatt was twice as skeletal as she remembered him. He had been
standing outdoors, near the foot of a huge platform-altar that had been
erected in the middle of the city. A startlingly lifelike statue of Bakkalon,
encased in a glass pyramid and set atop a high redstone plinth, threw a

long shadow over the wooden altar. Beneath it, the squads of Angels were piling the newly-harvested neograss and wheat and the frozen carcasses of bushogs.

'We do not need your trade,' the Proctor told her. 'The World of Corlos is many-times-blessed, my child, and Bakkalon lives among us now. He has worked vast miracles, and shall work more. Our faith is in Him.' Wyatt gestured toward the altar with a thin hand. 'See? In tribute we burn our winter stores, for the pale child has promised that this year winter will not come. And He has taught us to cull ourselves in peace as once we were culled in war, so the seed of Earth grows ever stronger. It is a time of great new revelation!' His eyes had burned as he spoke to her; eyes darting and fanatic, vast and dark yet strangely flecked with gold.

As quickly as she could, Ryther had left the City of the Steel Angels, trying hard not to look back at the walls. But when she had climbed the hills, back toward the trading base, she had come to the ring-of-stone, to the broken pyramid where Arik had taken her. Then Ryther found that she could not resist, and powerless she had turned for a final glance out over Sword Valley. The sight had stayed with her.

Outside the walls the Angel children hung, a row of small white-smocked bodies still and motionless at the end of long ropes. They had gone peacefully, all of them, but death is seldom peaceful; the older ones, at least, died quickly, necks broken with a sudden snap. But the small pale infants had the nooses round their waists, and it had seemed clear to Ryther that most of them had simply hung there till they starved.

As she stood, remembering, the crewman came from inside neKrol's broken bubble. 'Nothing,' he reported. 'All statues.' Ryther nodded.

'Go?' the bitter speaker said. 'Jamson' World?'

'Yes,' she replied, her eyes staring past the waiting *Lights of Jolostar*, out toward the black primal forest. The Heart of Bakkalon was sunk forever. In a thousand thousand woods and a single city, the clans had begun to pray.

The Stone City

The crossworlds had a thousand names. Human starcharts listed it as Greyrest, when they listed it at all – which was seldom, for it lay a decade's journey inward from the realms of men. The Dan'lai named it Empty in their high, barking tongue. To the ul-mennaleith, who had known it longest, it was simply the world of the stone city. The Kresh had a word for it, as did the Linkellar, and the Cedrans, and other races had landed there and left again, so other names lingered on. But mostly it was the crossworlds to the beings who paused there briefly while they jumped from star to star.

It was a barren place, a world of gray oceans and endless plains where the windstorms raged. But for the spacefield and the stone city, it was empty and lifeless. The field was at least five thousand years old, as men count time. The ul-nayileith had built it in the glory days when they claimed the ullish stars, and for a hundred generations it had made the crossworlds theirs. But then the ul-nayileith had faded and the ul-mennaleith had come to fill up their worlds and now the elder race was remembered only in legends and prayers.

Yet their spacefield endured, a great pockmark on the plains, circled by the towering windwalls that the vanished engineers had built against the storms. Inside the high walls lay the port city – hangars and barracks and shops where tired beings from a hundred worlds could rest and be refreshed. Outside, to the west, nothing; the winds came from the west, battering against the walls with a fury soon drained and used for power. But the eastern walls had a second city in their shadows, an open-air city of plastic bubbles and metal shacks. There huddled the beaten and the outcast and the sick; there clustered the shipless.

Beyond that, further east: the stone city.

It had been there when the ul-nayileith had come, five thousand years before. They had never learned how long it stood against the winds, or why. The ullish elders were arrogant and curious in those days, it was said, and they had searched. They walked the twisting alleys, climbed the narrow stairs, scaled the close-set towers and the square-topped pyramids. They found the endless dark passageways that wove maze-like beneath the earth. They discovered the vastness of the city, found all the dust and awesome silence. But nowhere did they find the Builders.

Finally, strangely, a weariness had come upon the ul-nayileith, and with it a fear. They had withdrawn from the stone city, never to walk its halls again. For thousands of years the stone was shunned, and the worship of the Builders was begun. And so too had begun the long decline of the elder race.

But the ul-mennaleith worship only the ul-nayileith. And the Dan'lai worship nothing. And who knows what humans worship? So now, again, there were sounds in the stone city; footfalls rode the alley winds.

*

The skeletons were imbedded in the wall. They were mounted above the windwall gates in no particular pattern, one short of a dozen, half sunk in the seamless ullish metal and half exposed to the crossworlds wind. Some were in deeper than others. High up, the new skeleton of some nameless winged being rattled in the breeze, a loose bag of hollow fairy bones welded to the wall only at wrists and ankles. Yet lower, up and to the right a little from the doorway, the yellow barrel-stave ribs of a Linkellar were all that could be seen of the creature.

MacDonald's skeleton was half in, half out. Most of the limbs were sunk deep in the metal, but the fingertips dangled out (one hand still holding a laser), and the feet, and the torso was open to the air. And the skull, of course – bleached white, half crushed, but still a rebuke. It looked down at Holt every dawn as he passed through the portal below. Sometimes, in the curious half-light of an early crossworlds morning, it seemed as though the missing eyes followed him on his long walk toward the gate.

But that had not bothered Holt for months. It had been different right after they had taken MacDonald, and his rotting body had suddenly appeared on the windwall, half joined to the metal. Holt could smell the stench then, and the corpse had been too recognizably Mac. Now it was just a skeleton, and that made it easier for Holt to forget.

On that anniversary morning, the day that marked the end of the first full standard year since the *Pegasus* had set down, Holt passed below the skeletons with hardly an upward glance.

Inside, as always, the corridor stood deserted. It curved away in both directions, white, dusty, very vacant; thin blue doors stood at regular intervals, but all of them were closed.

Holt turned to the right and tried the first door, pressing his palm to the entry plate. Nothing; the office was locked. He tried the next, with the same result. And then the next. Holt was methodical. He had to be. Each day only one office was open, and each day it was a different one.

The seventh door slid open at his touch.

Behind a curving metal desk a single Dan'la sat, looking out of place. The room, the furniture, the field – everything had been built to the proportions of the long-departed ul-nayileith, and the Dan'la was entirely too small for its setting. But Holt had gotten used to it. He had come every day for a year now, and every day a single Dan'la sat behind a desk. He had no idea whether it was the same one changing offices daily, or a different one each day. All of them had long snouts and darting eyes and bristling reddish fur. The humans called them foxmen. With rare exceptions, Holt could not tell one from the other. The Dan'lai would not help him. They refused to give names, and the creature behind the desk sometimes recognized him, often did not. Holt had long since given up the game, and resigned himself to treating every Dan'la as a stranger.

This morning, though, the foxman knew him at once. 'Ah,' he said as Holt entered. 'A berth for you?'

'Yes,' Holt said. He removed the battered ship's cap that matched his frayed gray uniform, and he waited – a thin, pale man with receding brown hair and a stubborn chin.

The foxman interlocked slim, six fingered hands and smiled a swift thin smile. 'No berth, Holt,' he said, 'Sorry. No ship today.'

'I heard a ship last night,' Holt said. 'I could hear it all the way over in the stone city. Get me a berth on it. I'm qualified. I know standard drive, and I can run a Dan'lai jump-gun. I have credentials.'

'Yes, yes.' Again the snapping smile. 'But there is no ship. Next week, perhaps. Next week perhaps a man-ship will come. Then you'll have a berth, Holt, I swear it, I promise you. You a good jump man, right? You tell me. I get you a berth. But next week, next week. No ship now.'

Holt bit his lip and leaned forward, spreading his hands on the desktop, the cap crushed beneath one fist. 'Next week you won't be here,' he said. 'Or if you are, you won't recognize me, won't remember anything you promised. Get me a berth on the ship that came last night.'

'Ah,' said the Dan'la. 'No berth. Not a man-ship, Holt. No berth for a man.'

'I don't care. I'll take any ship. I'll work with Dan'lai, ullies, Cedrans, anything. Jumps are all the same. Get me on the ship that came in last night.'

'But there *was* no ship, Holt,' the foxman said. His teeth flashed, then were gone again. 'I tell you, Holt. No ship, no ship. Next week, come back. Come back, next week.' There was dismissal in his tone. Holt had learned to recognize it. Once, months ago, he'd stayed and tried to argue. But the desk-fox had summoned others to drag him away. For a week afterward, *all* the doors had been locked in the mornings. Now Holt knew when to leave.

Outside in the wan light, he leaned briefly against the windwall and tried to still his shaking hands. He must keep busy, he reminded himself. He needed money, food tokens, so that was one task he could set to. He could visit the Shed, maybe look up Sunderland. As for a berth, there was always tomorrow. He had to be patient.

With a brief glance up at MacDonald, who had not been patient, Holt went off down the vacant streets of the city of the shipless.

*

Even as a child, Holt had loved the stars. He used to walk at night, during the years of high cold when the iceforests bloomed on Ymir. Straight out he would go, for kilometers, crunching the snow beneath until the lights of town were lost behind him and he stood alone in the glistening blue-white wonderland of frost-flowers and ice-webs and bitterblooms. Then he would look up.

WinterYear nights on Ymir are clear and still and very black. There is no moon. The stars and the silence are everything.

Diligent, Holt had learned the names – not the starnames (no one named the stars any more – numbers were all that was needed), but rather the names of the worlds that swung around each. He was a bright child. He learned quickly and well, and even his gruff, practical father found a certain pride in that. Holt remembered endless parties at the Old House when his father, drunk on summerbrew, would march all his guests out onto the balcony so his son could name the worlds. 'There,' the old man would say, holding a mug in one hand and pointing with the other, 'there, that bright one!'

'Arachne,' the boy would reply, blank-faced. The guests would smile and mutter politely.

'And there?'

'Baldur.'

'There. There. Those three over there.'

'Finnegan. Johnhenry. Celia's World, New Rome, Cathaday.' The names skipped lightly off his youthful tongue. And his father's leathery face would crinkle in a smile, and he would go on and on until the others grew bored and restive and Holt had named all the worlds a boy could name standing on a balcony of the Old House on Ymir. He had always hated the ritual.

It was a good thing that his father had never come with him off into the iceforests, for away from the lights a thousand new stars could be seen, and that meant a thousand names to know. Holt never learned them all, the names that went with the dimmer, far-off stars that were not man's. But he learned enough. The pale stars of the Damoosh inwards toward the core, the reddish sun of the Silent Centaurs, the scattered lights where the Fyndii hordes raised their emblem-sticks; these he knew, and more.

He continued to come as he grew older, not always alone now. All his youthful sweethearts he dragged out with him, and he made his first love in the starlight during a SummerYear when the trees dripped flowers instead of ice. Sometimes he talked about it with lovers, and friends. But the words came hard. Holt was never eloquent, and he could not make them understand. He scarcely understood himself.

After his father died, he took over the Old House and the estates and ran them for a long WinterYear, though he was only twenty standard. When the thaw came, he left it all and went to Ymir City. A ship was down, a trader bound for Finnegan and worlds further in. Holt found a berth.

*

The streets grew busier as the day aged. Already the Dan'lai were out, setting up food stalls between the huts. In an hour or so the streets would be lined with them. A few gaunt ul-mennaleith were also about, traveling in groups of four or five. They all wore powder-blue gowns that fell almost to the ground, and they seemed to flow rather than walk – eerie, dignified, wraithlike. Their soft gray skin was finely powdered, their eyes were liquid and distant. Always they seemed serene, even *these*, these sorry shipless ones.

Holt fell in behind a group of them, increasing his pace to keep up. The fox merchants ignored the solemn ul-mennaleith, but they all spied Holt and called out to him as he passed. And laughed their high, barking laughs when he ignored them.

Near the Cedran neighborhoods Holt took his leave of the ullies, darting into a tiny side street that seemed deserted. He had work to do, and this was the place to do it.

He walked deeper into the rash of yellowed bubble-huts and picked one almost at random. It was old, its plastic exterior heavily polished; the door was wood, carved with nest symbols. Locked, of course – Holt put his shoulder to it and pushed. When it held firm, he retreated a bit, then ran and crashed against it. On his fourth try it gave noisily. The noise didn't bother him. In a Cedran slum, no one would hear.

Pitch-dark inside. He felt near the door and found a coldtorch, touched it until it returned his body heat as light. Then, leisurely, he looked around.

There were five Cedrans present: three adults and two younglings, all curled up into featureless balls on the floor. Holt hardly gave them a glance. By night, the Cedrans were terrifying. He'd seen them many times on the darkened streets of the stone city, moaning in their soft speech and swaying sinister. Their segmented torsos unfolded into three meters of milk-white maggotflesh, and they had six specialized limbs; two wide-splayed feet, a pair of delicate branching tentacles for manipulation, and the wicked fighting-claws. The eyes, saucer-sized pools of glowing violet, saw everything. By night, Cedrans were beings to be avoided.

By day, they were immobile balls of meat.

Holt walked around them and looted their hut. He took a handheld coldtorch, set low to give the murky purple half-light the Cedrans liked best, plus a sack of food tokens and a clawbone. The polished, jeweled fighting-claws of some illustrious ancestor sat in an honored place on the wall, but Holt was careful not to touch them. If their family god was stolen, the entire nest would be obliged to find the thief or commit suicide.

Finally he found a set of wizard-cards, smoke-dark wooden plaques inlaid with iron and gold. He shoved them in a pocket and left. The street was still empty. Few beings visited the Cedran districts save Cedrans.

Quickly Holt found his way back to the main thoroughfare, the wide gravel path that ran from the windwalls of the spacefield to the silent gates of the stone city five kilometers away. The street was crowded and noisy now, and Holt had to push his way through the throng. Foxmen were everywhere, laughing and barking, snapping their quick grins on and off, rubbing reddish brown fur up against the blue gowns of the ul-menna-leith, the chitinous Kresh, and the loose baggy skin of the pop-eyed green Linkellars. Some of the food stalls had hot meals to offer, and the ways were heavy with smokes and smells. Holt had been months on the crossworlds before he had finally learned to distinguish the food scents from the body odors.

As he fought his way down the street, dodging in and out among the aliens with his loot clutched tightly in his hand, Holt watched carefully. It was habit now, drilled into him; he looked constantly for an unfamiliar human face, the face that might mean a man-ship was in, that salvation had come.

He did not find one. As always, there was only the milling press of the crossworlds all around him – Dan'lai barks and Kresh clickings and the ululating speech of the Linkellars, but never a human voice. By now, it had ceased to affect him.

He found the stall he was looking for. From beneath a flap of gray leather, a frazzled Dan'la looked up at him. 'Yes, yes,' the foxman snapped impatiently. 'Who are you? What do you want?'

Holt shoved aside the multicolored blinking-jewels that were strewn over the counter and put down the coldtorch and clawbone he had taken. 'Trade,' he said. 'These for tokens.'

The foxman looked down at the goods, up at Holt, and began to rub his snout vigorously. 'Trade. Trade. A trade for you,' he chanted. He picked up the clawbone, tossed it from one hand to the other, set it down again, touched the coldtorch to wake it to barely perceptible life. Then he nodded and turned on his grin. 'Good stuff. Cedran. The big worms will want it. Yes. Yes. Trade, then. Tokens?'

Holt nodded.

The Dan'la fumbled in the pocket of the smock he was wearing, and tossed a handful of food tokens on the counter. They were bright disks of plastic in a dozen different colors, the nearest things to currency the crossworlds had. The Dan'lai merchants honored them for food. And the Dan'lai brought in all the food there was on their fleets of jump-gun spacers.

Holt counted the tokens, then scooped them up and threw them in the sack that he'd taken from the Cedran bubble-hut. 'I have more,' he said, reaching into his pocket for the wizard-cards.

His pocket was empty. The Dan'la grinned and snapped his teeth together. 'Gone? Not the only thief on Empty, then. No. Not the only thief.'

He remembered his first ship; he remembered the stars of his youth on Ymir, he remembered the worlds he'd touched since, he remembered all the ships he'd served on and the men (and not-men) he had served with. But better than any of them he remembered his first ship: the *Laughing Shadow* (an old name heavy with history, but no one told him the story until much later), out of Celia's World and bound for Finnegan. It was a converted ore freighter, great blue-gray teardrop of pitted duralloy that was at least a century older than Holt was. Sparse and raw – big cargo holds and not much crew space, sleep-webs for the twelve who manned it, no gravity grid (he'd gotten used to free fall quickly), nukes for landing and lifting, and a standard ftl drive for the star-shifts. Holt was set to working in the drive room, an austere place of muted lights and bare metal and computer consoles. Cain narKarmian showed him what to do.

Holt remembered narKarmian too. An old, *old* man, too old for shipwork he would have thought; skin like soft yellow leather that has been folded and wrinkled so many times that there is nowhere a piece of it without a million tiny creases, eyes brown and almond-shaped, a mottled bald head and a wispy blond goatee. Sometimes Cain seemed senile, but most often he was sharp and alert; he knew the drives, and he knew the stars, and he would talk incessantly as he worked.

'Two hundred standard years!' he said once as they both sat before their

consoles. He smiled a shy, crooked smile, and Holt saw that he still had
teeth, even at his age – or perhaps he had teeth *again*. 'That's how long
Cain's been shipping, Holt. The very truth! You know, your regular man
never leaves the very world he's born on. Never! Ninety-five percent of
them, anyway. They never leave, just get born and grow up and die, all on
the same world. And the ones that do ship – well, most of *them* ship only a
little. A world or two or ten. Not me! You know where I was born, Holt?
Guess!'

Holt shrugged. 'Old Earth?'

Cain just laughed. 'Earth? Earth's nothing, only three or four years out
from here. Four, I think. I forget. No, no, but I've seen Earth, the very
homeworld, the seeding place. Seen it fifty years ago on the – the *Corey
Dark*, I'd guess it was. It was about time, I thought. I'd been shipping a
hundred fifty standard even then, and I still hadn't been to Earth. But I
finally got there!'

'You weren't born there?' Holt prompted.

Old Cain shook his head and laughed again. 'Not very! I'm an Emereli.
From ai-Emerel. You know it, Holt?'

Holt had to think. It was not a world-name he recognized, not one of the
stars his father had pointed to, aflame in the night of Ymir. But it rang a
bell, dimly. 'The Fringe?' he guessed finally. The Fringe was the furthest
out-edge of human space, the place where the small sliver of the galaxy
they called the manrealm had brushed the top of the galactic lens, where
the stars drew thin. Ymir and the stars he knew were on the other side of
Old Earth, inward toward the denser starfields and the still-unreachable
core.

Cain was happy at his guess. 'Yes! I'm an outworlder. I'm near to two
hundred and twenty standard, and I've seen near that many worlds now,
human worlds and Hrangan and Fyndii and all sorts, even some worlds in
the manrealm where the men aren't *men* any more, if you understand
what I'm saying. Shipping, always shipping. Whenever I found a place that
looked interesting I'd skip ship and stay a time, then go on when I wanted
to. I've seen all sorts of things, Holt. When I was young I saw the Festival
of the Fringe, and hunted banshee on High Kavalaan, and got a wife on
Kimdiss. She died, though, and I got on. Saw Prometheus and Rhiannon,
which are in a bit from the Fringe, and Jamison's World and Avalon,
which are in further still. You know. I was a Jamie for a bit, and on Avalon
I got three wives. And two husbands, or co-husbands, or however you say
it. I was still shy of a hundred then, maybe less. That was a time when we
owned our own ship, did local trading, hit some of the old Hrangan
slaveworlds that have gone off their own ways since the war. Even Old
Hranga itself, the very place. They say there are still some Minds on

Hranga, deep underground, waiting to come back and attack the manrealm again. But all I ever saw was a lot of kill-castes and workers and the other lesser types.'

He smiled. 'Good years, Holt, very good years. We called our ship *Jamison's Ass*. My wives and my husbands were all Avalonians, you see, except for one who was Old Poseidon, and Avalonians don't like Jamies much, which is how we arrived at that very name. But I can't say that they were wrong. I was a Jamie too, before that, and Port Jamison is a stulty priggy town on a planet that's the same.

'We were together nearly thirty standard on *Jamison's Ass*. The marriage outlasted two wives and one husband. And me too, finally. They wanted to keep Avalon as their trade base, you see, but after thirty I'd seen all the worlds I wanted to see around there, and I hadn't seen a lot else. So I shipped on. But I loved them. Holt, I did love them. A man should be married to his shipmates. It makes for a very good feeling.' He sighed. 'Sex comes easier too. Less uncertainty.'

By then, Holt was caught. 'Afterward,' he asked, his young face showing only a hint of the envy he felt, 'what did you do then?'

Cain had shrugged, looked down at his console, and started to punch the glowing studs to set in a drive correction. 'Oh, shipped on, shipped on. Old worlds, new worlds, man, not-man, aliens. New Refuge and Pachacuti and burnt-out old Wellington, and then Newholme and Silversky and Old Earth. And now I'm going in, as far as I can go before I die. Like Tomo and Walberg, I guess. You know about Tomo and Walberg, in here at Ymir?'

And Holt had only nodded. Even Ymir knew about Tomo and Walberg. Tomo was an outworlder too, born on Darkdawn high atop the Fringe, and they say he was a darkling dreamer. Walberg was an Altered Man from Prometheus, a roistering adventurer according to the legend. Three centuries ago, in a ship called the *Dreaming Whore*, they had set off from Darkdawn for the opposite edge of the galaxy. How many worlds they had visited, what had happened on each, how far they had gotten before death – those were the knots in the tale, and schoolboys disputed them still. Holt liked to think that they were still out there, somewhere. After all, Walberg had said he was a superman, and there was no telling how long a superman might live. Maybe even long enough to reach the core, or beyond.

He had been staring at the console, daydreaming, and Cain had grinned over at him and said, 'Hey! Starsick!' And when Holt had started and looked up, the old man nodded (still smiling), saying, 'Yes, you, the very one! Set to, Holt, or you won't be shipping nowhere!'

But it was a gentle rebuke, and a gentle smile, and Holt never forgot it or Cain narKarmian's other words. Their sleep-webs were next to each other and Holt listened every night, for Cain was hard to silence and Holt was not about to try. And when the *Laughing Shadow* finally hit Cathaday, as far in as it would go, and got ready to turn back into the manrealm towards Celia's World and home, Holt and narKarmian signed off together and got berths on a mailship that was heading for Vess and the alien Damoosh suns.

They had shipped together for six years when narKarmian finally died. Holt remembered the old man's face much better than his father's.

*

The Shed was a long, thin, metal building, a corrugated shack of blue duralloy that someone had found in the stores of a looted freighter, probably. It was built kilometers from the windwall, within sight of the gray walls of the stone city and the high iris of the Western Door. Around it were other, larger metal buildings, the warehouse-barracks of the shipless ul-mennaleith. But there were no ullies inside, ever.

It was near noon when Holt arrived, and the Shed was almost empty. A wide columnar coldtorch reached from floor to ceiling in the center of the room, giving off a tired ruddy light that left most of the deserted tables in darkness. A party of muttering Linkellars filled a corner off in the shadows; opposite them, a fat Cedran was curled up in a tight sleep-ball, his slick white skin glistening. And next to the coldtorch pillar, at the old *Pegasus* table, Alaina and Takker-Rey were sharing a white stone flask of amberlethe.

Takker spied him at once. 'Look,' he said, raising his glass. 'We have company, Alaina. A lost soul returns! How are things in the stone city, Michael?'

Holt sat down. 'The same as always, Takker. The same as always.' He forced a smile for bloated, pale-faced Takker, then quickly turned to Alaina. She had worked the jump-gun with him once, a year ago and more. And they had been lovers, briefly. But that was over. Alaina had put on weight and her long auburn hair was dirty and matted. Her green eyes used to spark; now amberlethe made them dull and cloudy.

Alaina favored him with a pudgy smile. ''Lo, Michael,' she said. 'Have you found your ship?'

Takker-Rey giggled, but Holt ignored him. 'No,' he said. 'But I keep going. Today the foxman said there'd be a ship in next week. A man-ship. He promised me a berth.'

Now both of them giggled. 'Oh, Michael,' Alaina said. 'Silly, silly. They used to tell *me* that. I haven't gone for so long. Don't you go, either. I'll take you back. Come up to my room. I miss you. Tak is such a bore.'

Takker frowned, hardly paying attention. He was intent on pouring himself a new glass of amberlethe. The liquor flowed with agonizing slowness, like honey. Holt remembered the taste of it, gold fire on his tongue, and the easy sense of peace it brought. They had all done a lot of drinking in the early weeks, while they waited for the Captain to return. Before things fell apart.

'Have some 'lethe,' Takker said. 'Join us.'

'No,' Holt said. 'Maybe a little fire brandy, Takker, if you're buying. Or a foxbeer. Summerbrew, if there's some handy. I miss summerbrew. But no 'lethe. That's why I went away, remember?'

Alaina gasped suddenly; her mouth drooped open and something flickered in her eyes. 'You went away,' she said in a thin voice. 'I remember, you were the first. You went away. You and Jeff. You were the first.

'No, dear,' Takker interrupted very patiently. He set down the flask of amberlethe, took a sip from his glass, smiled, and proceeded to explain. 'The Captain was the first one to go away. Don't you recall? The Captain and Villareal and Susie Benet, they all went away together, and we waited and waited.'

'Oh, yes,' Alaina said. 'Then later Jeff and Michael left us. And poor Irai killed herself, and the foxes took Ian and put him up on the wall. And all the others went away. Oh, I don't know where, Michael, I just don't.' Suddenly she started to weep. 'We all used to be together, all of us, but now there's just Tak and me. They all left us. We're the only ones who come here any more, the *only* ones.' She broke down and started sobbing.

Holt felt sick. It was worse than his last visit the month before – much worse. He wanted to grab the amberlethe and smash it to the floor. But it was pointless. He had done that once a long time ago – the second month after landing – when the endless hopeless waiting had sent him into a rare rage. Alaina had wept, MacDonald cursed and hit him and knocked loose a tooth (it still hurt sometimes, at night), and Takker-Rey bought another flask. Takker always had money. He wasn't much of a thief, but he'd grown up on Vess where men shared a planet with two alien races, and like a lot of Vessmen he'd grown up a xenophile. Takker was soft and willing, and foxmen (some foxmen) found him attractive. When Alaina had joined him, in his room and his business, Holt and Jeff Sunderland had given up on them and moved to the outskirts of the stone city.

'Don't cry, Alaina,' Holt said now. 'Look, I'm here, see? I even brought food tokens.' He reached into his sack and tossed a handful onto the table – red, blue, silver, black. They clattered and rolled and lay still.

At once, Alaina's tears were gone. She began to scrabble among the tokens, and even Takker leaned forward to watch. 'Red ones,' she said excitedly. 'Look, Takker, red ones, meat tokens! And silvers, for 'lethe.

Look, look!' She began to scoop loose tokens into her pockets, but her hands were trembling, and more than one token was thrown onto the floor. 'Help me, Tak,' she said.

Takker giggled. 'Don't worry, love, that was only a green. We don't need worm food anyway, do we?' He looked at Holt. 'Thank you, Michael, thank you. I always told Alaina you had a generous soul, even if you did leave us when we needed you. You and Jeff, Ian said you were a coward, you know, but I always defended you. Thank you, yes.' He picked up a silver token and flipped it with his thumb. 'Generous Michael. You're always welcome here.'

Holt said nothing. The Shed-boss had suddenly materialized at his elbow, a vast bulk of musky blue-black flesh. His face looked down at Holt – if you could call it looking, since the being was eyeless, and if you could call it a face, since there was no mouth either. The thing that passed for a head was a flabby, half-filled bladder full of breathing holes and ringed by whitish tentacles. It was the size of a child's head, an infant's, and it looked absurdly small atop the gross oily body and the rolls of mottled fat. The Shed-boss did not speak; not Terran nor ullis nor the pidgin Dan'lai that passed for crossworlds trade talk. But he always knew what his customers wanted.

Holt just wanted to leave. While the Shed-boss stood, silent and waiting, he rose and lurched for the door. It slid shut behind him, and he could hear Alaina and Takker-Rey arguing over the tokens.

*

The Damoosh are a wise and gentle race, and great philosophers – or so they used to say on Ymir. The outermost of their suns interlock with the innermost parts of the ever-growing manrealm, and it was on a timeworn Damoosh colony that narKarmian died and Holt first saw a Linkellar.

Rayma-k-Tel was with him at the time, a hard hatchet-faced woman who'd come out of Vess; they were drinking in an enclave bar just off the spacefield. The place had good manrealm liquor, and he and Ram swilled it down together from seats by a window of stained yellow glass. Cain was three weeks dead. When Holt saw the Linkellar shuffling past the window, its bulging eyes a-wobble, he tugged at Ram's arm and turned her around and said, 'Look. A new one. You know the race?'

Rayma shrugged loose her arm and shook her head. 'No,' she said irritated. She was a raging xenophobe, which is the other thing that growing up on Vess will do to you. 'Probably from further in somewhere. Don't even *try* to keep them straight, Mikey. There's a million different kinds, specially this far in. Damn Damos'll trade with any *thing*.'

Holt had looked again, still curious, but the heavy being with the loose green skin was out of sight. Briefly he thought of Cain, and something like a thrill went through him. The old man had shipped for more than two hundred years, he thought, and yet he'd probably never seen an alien of the race *they'd* just seen. He said something to that effect to Rayma-k-Tel.

She was most unimpressed. 'So what?' she said. 'So *we've* never seen the Fringe or a Hrangan, though I'd be damned to know why we'd *want* to.' She smiled thinly at her own wit. 'Aliens are like jellybeans, Mikey. They come in a lot of different colors, but inside they're just about the same.

'So don't turn yourself into a collector like old narKarmian. Where did it ever get him, after all? He moved around a lot on a bunch of third-rate ships, but he never saw the Far Arm and he never saw the core, and nobody ever will. He didn't get too rich, neither. Just relax and make a living.'

Holt had hardly been listening. He put down his drink and lightly touched the cool glass of the window with his fingertips.

That night, after Rayma had returned to their ship, Holt left the offworld enclave and wandered out into the Damoosh home-places. He paid half-a-run's salary to be led to the underground chamber where the world's wisdompool lay: a vast computer of living light linked to the dead brains of telepathic Damoosh elders (or at least that was how the guide explained it to Holt).

The chamber was a bowl of green fog stirring with little waves and swells. Within its depths, curtains of colored light rippled and faded and were gone. Holt stood on the upper lip looking down and asked his questions, and the answers came back in an echoing whisper as of many tiny voices speaking together. First he described the being he'd seen that afternoon and asked what it had been, and it was then he heard the word Linkellar.

'Where do they come from?' Holt asked.

'Six years from the manrealm by the drive you use,' the whispers told him while the green fog moved. 'Toward the core but not straight in. Do you want coordinates?'

'No. Why don't we see them more often?'

'They are far away, too far perhaps,' the answer came. 'The whole width of the Damoosh suns is between the manrealm and the Twelve Worlds of the Linkellar, and so too the colonies of the Nor T'alush and a hundred worlds that have not found stardrives. The Linkellars trade with the Damoosh, but they seldom come to this place, which is closer to you than to them.'

'Yes,' said Holt. A chill went through him, as if a cold wind blew across the cavern and the flickering sea of fog. 'I have heard of the Nor T'alush, but not of the Linkellars. What else is there? Further in?'

'There are many directions,' the fog whispered. Colors undulated deep below. 'We know the dead worlds of the vanished race the Nor T'alush call the First Ones, though they were not truly the first, and we know the Reaches of the Kresh, and the lost colony of the gethsoids of Aath who sailed from far within the manrealm before it was the manrealm.'

'What's beyond *them?*'

'The Kresh tell of a world called Cedris, and of a great sphere of suns larger than the manrealm and the Damoosh suns and the old Hrangan Empire all together. The stars within are the ullish stars.'

'Yes,' Holt said. There was a tremor in his voice. 'And beyond that? Around it? Further in?'

A fire burned within the far depths of the fog; the green mists glowed with a smoldering reddish light. 'The Damoosh do not know. Who sails so far, so long? There are only tales. Shall we tell you of the Very Old Ones? Of the Bright Gods, or the shipless sailors? Shall we sing the old song of the race without a world? Ghost ships have been sighted further in, things that move faster than a man-ship or a Damoosh drive, and they destroy where they will, yet sometimes they are not there at all. Who can say what they are, who they are, where they are, if they are? We have names, names, stories, we can give you names and stories. But the facts are dim. We hear of a world named Huul the Golden that trades with the lost gethsoids who trade with the Kresh who trade with the Nor T'alush who trade with us, but no Damoosh ship has ever sailed to Huul the Golden and we cannot say much of it or even where it is. We hear of the veiled men of a world unnamed, who puff themselves up and float around and around in their atmosphere, but they may be only a legend, and we cannot even say *whose* legend. We hear of a race that lives in deep space, who talk to a race called the Dan'lai who trade with the ullish stars, who trade with Cedris, and so the string runs back to us. But we Damoosh on this world so near the manrealm have never seen a Cedran, so how can we trust the string?' There was a sound like muttering; below his feet, the fog churned, and something that smelled like incense rose to touch Holt's nostrils.

'I'll go in,' Holt said. 'I'll ship on, and see.'

'Then come back one day and tell us,' the fogs cried, and for the very first time Holt heard the mournful keen of a wisdompool that is not wise enough. 'Come back, come back. There is much to learn.' The smell of incense was very strong.

*

Holt looted three more Cedran bubble-huts that afternoon, and broke into two others. The first of those was simply cold and vacant and dusty; the second was occupied, but not by a Cedran. After jiggling loose the door, he'd stood stock-still while an ethereal winged thing with feral eyes flapped against the roof of the hut and hissed down at him. He got nothing from that bubble, nor from the empty one, but the rest of his break-ins paid off.

Toward sunset, he returned to the stone city, climbing a narrow ramp to the Western Iris with a bag of food slung over his shoulders.

In the pale and failing light, the city looked colorless, washed out, dead. The circling walls were four meters high and twice as thick, fashioned of a smooth and seamless gray stone as if they were a single piece; the Western Iris that opened on the city of the shipless was more a tunnel than a gateway. Holt went through it quickly, out into a narrow zigzag alley that threaded its way between two huge buildings – or perhaps they were not buildings. Twenty meters tall, irregularly shaped, windowless and door-less; there could be no possible entrance save through the stone city's lower levels. Yet this type of structure, these odd-shaped dented blocks of gray stone, dominated the easternmost part of the stone city in an area of some twelve kilometers square. Sunderland had mapped it.

The alleys here were a hopeless maze, none of them running straight for more than ten meters; from above, Holt had often imagined them to look like a child's drawing of a lightning bolt. But he had come this route often, and he had Sunderland's maps committed to memory (for this small portion of the stone city, at any rate). He moved with speed and confidence, encountering no one.

From time to time, when he stood in the nexus points where several alleys joined, Holt caught glimpses of other structures in the distance. Sunderland had mapped most of them, too; they used the sights as landmarks. The stone city had a hundred separate parts, and in each the architecture and the very building stone itself was different. Along the northwest wall was a jungle of obsidian towers set close together with dry canals between; due south lay a region of blood-red stone pyramids; east was an utterly empty granite plain with a single mushroom-shaped tower ascending from its center. And there were other regions, all strange, all uninhabited. Sunderland mapped a few additional blocks each day. Yet even this was only the tip of the iceberg. The stone city had levels beneath levels, and neither Holt nor Sunderland nor any of the others had penetrated those black and airless warrens.

Dusk was all around him when Holt paused at a major nexus point, a wide octagon with a smaller octagonal pool in its center. The water was still and green; not even a ripple of wind moved across its surface until Holt stopped to wash. Their rooms, just past here, were as bone-dry as this whole area of the city. Sunderland said the pyramids had indoor water supplies, but near the Western Iris there was nothing but this single public pool.

Holt resumed walking when he had cleaned the day's dust from his face and hands. The food bag bounced on his back, and his footsteps, echoing, broke the alley stillness. There was no other sound; the night was falling fast. It would be as bleak and moonless as any other crossworlds night. Holt knew that. The overcast was always heavy, and he could seldom spot more than a half-dozen dim stars.

Beyond the plaza of the pool, one of the great buildings had fallen. There was nothing left but a jumble of broken rock and sand. Holt cut across it carefully, to a single structure that stood out of place among the rest – a huge gold stone dome like a blown-up Cedran bubble-hut. It had a dozen entrance holes, a dozen narrow little staircases winding up to them, and a honeycomb of chambers within.

For nearly ten standard months, this had been home.

Sunderland was squatting on the floor of their common room when Holt entered, his maps spread out all around him. He had arranged each section to fit with the others in a patchwork tapestry; old yellowed scraps he'd purchased from the Dan'lai and corrected were sandwiched between sheets of *Pegasus* gridfilm and lightweight squares of silvery ullish metal. The totality carpeted the room, each piece covered with lines and Sunderland's neat notation. He sat in the middle of it all with a map on his lap and a marker in his hand, looking owlish and rumpled and very overweight.

'I've got food,' Holt said. He flipped the bag across the room and it landed among the maps, disarraying several of the loose sections.

Sunderland squawked, 'Ahh, the *maps!* Be careful!' He blinked and pushed the food aside and rearranged everything neatly again.

Holt crossed the room to his sleep-web, strung between two sturdy coldtorch pillars. He walked on the maps as he went and Sunderland squawked again, but Holt ignored him and climbed into the web.

'Damn you,' Sunderland said, smoothing the trodden sections. 'Be more careful, will you?' He looked up and saw that Holt was frowning at him. 'Mike?'

'Sorry,' Holt said. 'You find something today?' His tone made the question an empty formality.

Sunderland never noticed. 'I got into a whole new section, off to the south,' he said excitedly. 'Very interesting, too. Obviously designed as a unit. There's this central pillar, you see, built out of some soft green stone, and surrounded by ten slightly smaller pillars, and there are these bridges – well, sort of ribbons of stone, they loop from the top of the big ones to the tops of the little ones. The pattern is repeated over and over. And below you've got sort of a labyrinth of waist-high stone walls. It will take me weeks to map them.'

Holt was looking at the wall next to his head, where the count of the days was scored in the golden stone. 'A year,' he said. 'A standard year, Jeff.'

Sunderland looked at him curiously, then stood and began gathering up his maps. 'How was your day?' he asked.

'We're not going to leave this place,' Holt said, speaking more to himself than to Sunderland. 'Never. It's over.'

Now Sunderland stopped. 'Stop it,' the small fat man said. 'I won't have it, Holt. Give up, and next thing you know you'll be drowning in amberlethe with Alaina and Takker. The stone city is the key. I've known that all along. Once we discover all its secrets, we can sell them to the foxmen and get out of this place. When I finish my mapping—'

Holt rolled over on his side to face Sunderland. 'A year, Jeff, a year. You're not going to finish your mapping. You could map for ten years and still have covered only part of the stone city. And what about the tunnels? The levels beneath?'

Sunderland licked his lips nervously. 'Beneath. Well. If I had the equipment on board the *Pegasus*, then—'

'You don't, and it doesn't work anyway. Nothing works on the stone city. That was why the Captain landed. The rules don't work down here.'

Sunderland shook his head and resumed his gathering up the maps. 'The human mind can understand anything. Give me time, that's all, and I'll figure it all out. We could even figure out the Dan'lai and the ullies if Susie Benet was still here.' Susie Benet had been their contact specialist – a third-rate linguesp, but even a minor talent is better than none when dealing with alien minds.

'Susie Benet isn't here,' Holt said. His voice had a hard edge to it. He began to tick off names on his fingers. 'Susie vanished with the Captain. Ditto Carlos. Irai suicided. Ian tried to shoot his way inside the windwalls and wound up on them. Det and Lana and Maje went down beneath, trying to find the Captain, and they vanished too. Davie Tillman sold himself as a Kresh egg host, so he's surely finished by now. Alaina and Takker-Rey are vegetables, useless, and we don't know what went on with the four aboard the *Pegasus*. That leaves us, Sunderland, you and me.' He smiled grimly. 'You make maps, I steal from the worms, and nobody understands anything. We're finished. We'll die here in the stone city. We'll never see the stars again.'

He stopped as suddenly as he had started. It was a rare outburst for Holt; in general he was quiet, unexpressive, maybe a little repressed. Sunderland stood there, astonished, while Holt sagged back hopelessly into his sleep-web.

'Day after day after day,' Holt said. 'And none of it means anything. You remember what Irai told us?'

'She was unstable,' Sunderland insisted. 'She proved that beyond our wildest dreams.'

'She said we'd come too far,' Holt said, as if Sunderland had never spoken. 'She said it was wrong to think that the whole universe operated by rules we could understand. You remember. She called it "sick, arrogant human folly." You remember, Jeff. That was how she talked. Like that. Sick, arrogant human folly.'

He laughed. 'The crossworlds *almost* made sense, that was what fooled us. But if Irai was right, that would figure. After all, we're still only a little bit from the manrealm, right? Further in, maybe the rules change even more.'

'I don't like this kind of talk,' said Sunderland. 'You're getting defeatist. Irai was sick. At the end, you know, she was going to ul-mennaleith prayer meetings, submitting herself to the ul-nayileith, that sort of thing. A mystic, that was what she became. A mystic.'

'She was wrong?' Holt asked.

'She was wrong,' Sunderland said firmly.

Holt looked at him again. 'Then explain things, Jeff. Tell me how to get out of here. Tell me how it all makes sense.'

'The stone city,' Sunderland said. 'Well, when I finish my maps—' He stopped suddenly. Holt was leaning back in his web again and not listening at all.

*

It took him five years and six ships to move across the great star-flecked sphere the Damoosh claimed as their own and penetrate the border sector beyond. He consulted other, greater wisdompools as he went, and learned all he could, but always there were mysteries and surprises waiting on the world beyond this one. Not all the ships he served on were crewed by humans; man-ships seldom straggled in this far, so Holt signed on with Damoosh and stray gethsoids and other, lesser mongrels. But still there were usually a few men on every port he touched, and he even began to hear rumors of a second human empire some five hundred years in toward the core, settled by a wandering generation ship and ruled from a glittering world called Prester. On Prester the cities floated on clouds, one withered Vessman told him. Holt believed that for a time until another crewmate said that Prester was really a single world-spanning city, kept alive by fleets of food freighters greater than anything the Federal Empire had built in the wars before the Collapse. The same man said it had not been a generation ship that had settled her at all – he proved that by showing how far a slow-light ship could get from Old Earth since the dawn of the interstellar age – but rather a squadron of Earth Imperials fleeing a Hrangan Mind. Holt stayed skeptical this time. When a woman from a grounded Cathadayn freighter insisted that Prester had been founded by Tomo and Walberg, and that Walberg ruled it still, he gave up on the whole idea.

But there were other legends, other stories, and they drew him on.

As they drew others.

On an airless world circling a blue-white star, in its single domed city, Holt met Alaina. She told him about the *Pegasus*.

'The Captain built her from scratch, you know, right here. He was trading, going in further than usual, like we all do' – she flashed an understanding smile, figuring that Holt too was a trading gambler out for the big find— 'and he met a Dan'la. They're further in.'

'I know,' Holt said.

'Well, maybe you don't know what's going *on* in there. The Captain said the Dan'lai have all but taken over the ullish stars – you've heard of the ullish stars? . . . Good. Well, it's because the ul-mennaleith haven't resisted much, I gather, but also because of the Dan'lai jump-gun. It's a new concept, I guess, and the Captain says it cuts travel time in half, or better. The standard drive warps the fabric of the space-time continuum, you know, to get ftl effects, and—'

'I'm a drive man,' Holt said curtly. But he was leaning forward as he said it, listening intently.

'Oh,' Alaina said, not rebuked in the least. 'Well, the Dan'lai jump-gun does something else, shifts you into another continuum and then back again. Running it is entirely different. It's partly psionic, and they put this ring around your head.'

'You *have* a jump-gun?' Holt interrupted.

She nodded. 'The Captain melted down his old ship, just about, to build the *Pegasus*. With a jump-gun he bought from the Dan'lai. He's collecting a crew now, and they're training us.'

'Where are you going?' he said.

She laughed, lightly, and her bright green eyes seemed to flash. 'Where else? In!'

*

Holt woke at dawn, in silence, rose and dressed himself quickly, and traced his path backwards, past the quiet green pool and the endless alleys, out the Western Iris and through the city of the shipless. He walked under the wall of skeletons without an upward glance.

Inside the windwall, in the long corridor, he began to try the doors. The first four rattled and stayed shut. The fifth opened on an empty office. No Dan'la.

That was something new. Holt entered cautiously, peering around. No one, nothing, and no second door. He walked around the wide ullish desk and began to rifle it methodically, much as he looted the Cedran bubble-huts. Maybe he could find a field pass, a gun, something – anything to get him back to the *Pegasus*. If it was still sitting beyond the walls. Or maybe he could find a berth assignment.

The door slid open; a foxman stood there. He was indistinguishable from all the others. He barked, and Holt jumped away from the desk.

Swiftly the Dan'la circled around and seized the chair. 'Thief!' he said. 'Thief. I will shoot. You be shot. Yes.' His teeth snapped.

'No,' Holt said, edging toward the door. He could run if the Dan'la called others. 'I came for a berth,' he said inanely.

'Ah!' the foxman interlocked his hands. 'Different. Well, Holt, who are you?'

Holt stood mute.

'A berth, a berth, Holt wants a berth,' the Dan'la said in a squeaky singsong.

'Yesterday they said that a man-ship would be in next week,' Holt said.

'No no no. I'm sorry. No man-ship will come. There will be no man-ship. Next week, yesterday, no time. You understand? And we have no berth. Ship is full. You never go on field with no berth.'

Holt moved forward again, to the other side of the desk. 'No ship next week?'

The foxman shook his head. 'No ship. No ship. No man-ship.'

'Something else, then. I'll crew for ullies, for Dan'lai, for Cedrans. I've told you. I know drive, I know your jump-guns. Remember? I have credentials.'

The Dan'la tilted his head to one side. Did Holt remember the gesture? Was this a Dan'la he'd dealt with before? 'Yes, but no berth.'

Holt started for the door.

'Wait,' the foxman commanded.

Holt turned.

'No man-ship next week,' the Dan'la said. 'No ship, no ship, no ship,' he sang. Then he stopped singing. 'Man-ship is *now*!'

Holt straightened. '*Now?*! You mean there's a man-ship on the field right now?'

The Dan'la nodded furiously.

'A berth!' Holt was frantic. 'Get me a berth, damn you.'

'Yes. Yes. A berth for you, for you a berth.' The foxman touched something on the desk, a drawer slid open, and he took out a film of silver metal and a slim wand of blue plastic. 'Your name?'

'Michael Holt,' he answered.

'Oh.' The foxman put down the wand, took the metal sheet and put it back in the drawer, and barked, 'No berth!'

'No berth?'

'No one can have two berths,' the Dan'la said.

'Two?'

The deskfox nodded. 'Holt has a berth on *Pegasus*.'

Holt's hands were trembling. 'Damn,' he said. 'Damn.'

The Dan'la laughed. 'Will you take berth?'

'On *Pegasus*?'

A nod.

'You'll let me through the walls, then? Out onto the field?'

The foxman nodded again. 'Write Holt field pass.'

'Yes,' Holt said. 'Yes.'

'Name?'

'Michael Holt.'

'Race?'

'Man.'

'Homeworld?'

'Ymir.'

There was a short silence. The Dan'la had been sitting there staring at Holt, his hands folded. Now he suddenly opened the drawer again, took out an ancient-looking piece of parchment that crumbled as he touched it, and picked up the wand again. 'Name?' he asked.

They went through the whole thing again.

When the Dan'la had finished writing, he gave the paper to Holt. It flaked as he fingered it. He tried to be very careful. None of the scrawls made sense. 'This will get me past the guards?' Holt said skeptically. 'On the field? To the *Pegasus*?'

The Dan'la nodded. Holt turned and almost ran for the door.

'Wait,' the foxman cried.

Holt froze, then spun. 'What?' he said between his teeth, and it was almost a snarl of rage.

'Technical thing.'

'Yes?'

'Field pass, to be good, must be signed.' The Dan'la flashed on its toothy smile. 'Signed, yes yes, signed by your captain.'

There was no noise. Holt's hand tightened spasmodically around the slip of yellow paper, and the pieces fluttered stiffly to the floor.

Then, swift and wordless, he was on him.

The Dan'la had time for only one brief bark before Holt had him by the throat. The delicate six-fingered hands clawed air, helplessly. Holt twisted, and the neck snapped. He was holding a bundle of limp reddish fur.

He stood there for a long time, his hands locked, his teeth clenched. Then slowly he released his grip and the Dan'la corpse tumbled backward, toppling the chair.

In Holt's eyes, a picture of the windwall flashed briefly.

He ran.

*

The *Pegasus* had standard drives too, in case the jump-gun failed; the walls of the room were the familiar blend of naked metal and computer consoles. But the center was filled by the Dan'lai jump-gun: a long cylinder of metallic glass, thick around as a man, mounted on an instrument panel. The cylinder was half full of a sluggish liquid that changed color abruptly each time a pulse of energy was run through the tank. Around it were seats for four jumpmen, two on a side. Holt and Alaina sat on one flank, opposite tall blonde Irai and Ian MacDonald; each of them wore a hollow glass crown full of the same liquid that sloshed in the gun cylinder.

Carlos Villareal was behind Holt, at the main console, draining data from the ship's computer. The jumps were already planned. They were going to see the ullish stars, the Captain had decided. And Cedris and Huul the Golden, and points further in. And maybe even Prester and the core.

The first stop was a transit point named Greyrest (clearly, by the name, some other men had gone there once – the star was on the charts). The Captain had heard a story of a stone city older than time.

Beyond the atmosphere the nukes cut off, and Villareal gave the order. 'Coordinates are in, navigation is ready,' he said, his voice a little less sure than usual; the whole procedure was so new. 'Jump.'

They switched on the Dan'lai jump-gun.

darkness flickering with colors and a thousand whirling stars and Holt was in the middle all alone but no! there was Alaina and there someone else and all of them joined and the chaos whirled around them and great gray waves crashed over their heads and faces appeared ringed with fire laughing and dissolving and pain pain pain and they were lost and nothing was solid and eons passed and now Holt saw something burning calling pulling the core the core and there out from it Greyrest but then it was gone and somehow Holt brought it back and he yelled to Alaina and she grabbed for it too and MacDonald and Irai and they PULLED

They were sitting before the jump-gun again, and Holt was suddenly conscious of a pain in his wrist, and he looked down and saw that someone had taped an i.v. needle into him. Alaina was plugged in too, and the others, Ian and Irai. There was no sign of Villareal.

The door slid open and Sunderland stood there smiling at them and blinking. 'Thank God!' the chubby navigator said. 'You've been out for three months. I thought we were finished.'

Holt took the glass crown from his head and saw that there was only a thin film of liquid left. Then he noticed that the jump cylinder was almost empty as well. 'Three months?'

Sunderland shuddered. 'It was horrible. There was nothing outside, *nothing*, and we couldn't rouse you. Villareal had to play nursemaid. If it hadn't been for the Captain, I don't know what would have happened. I know what the foxman said, but I wasn't sure you could ever pull us out of – of wherever we were.'

'Are we there?' MacDonald demanded.

Sunderland went around the jump-gun to Villareal's console and hooked it in to the ship's viewscreen. In a field of black, a small yellow sun was burning. And a cold gray orb filled the screen.

'Greyrest,' Sunderland said. 'I've taken readings. We're there. The Captain has already opened a beam to them. The Dan'lai seem to run things, and they've cleared us to land. The time checks, too; three months subjective, three months objective, as near as we can figure '

'And by standard drive?' Holt said. 'The same trip by standard drive?'

'We did even better than the Dan'lai promised,' Sunderland said. 'Greyrest is a good year and a half in from where we were.'

*

It was too early; there was too great a chance that the Cedrans might not be comatose yet. But Holt had to take the risk. He smashed his way into the first bubble-hut he found and looted it completely, ripping things apart with frantic haste. The residents, luckily, were torpid sleep-balls.

Out on the main thoroughfare, he ignored the Dan'lai merchants, half afraid he would confront the same foxman he had just killed. Instead he found a stall tended by a heavy blind Linkellar, its huge eyes like rolling balls of pus. The creature still cheated him, somehow. But he traded all that he had taken for an eggshell-shaped helmet of transparent blue and a working laser. The laser startled him; it was a twin for the one MacDonald had carried, even down to the Finnegan crest. But it worked, and that was all that mattered.

The crowds were assembling for the daily shuffle up and down the ways of the city of the shipless. Holt pushed through them savagely, toward the Western Iris, and broke into a measured jog when he reached the empty alleys of the stone city.

Sunderland was gone; out mapping. Holt took one of his markers and wrote across a map; KILLED A FOX. MUST HIDE. I'M GOING INTO THE STONE CITY. SAFE THERE.

Then he took all the food that was left, a good two weeks' supply, more if he starved himself. He filled a pack with it, strapped it on, and left. The laser was snug in his pocket, the helmet tucked under his arm.

The nearest underway was only a few blocks away; a great corkscrew that descended into the earth from the center of a nexus. Holt and Sunderland had often gone to the first level, as far as the light reached. Even there it was dim, gloomy, stuffy; a network of tunnels as intricate as the alleys above had branched off in every direction. Many of them slanted downward. And of course the corkscrew went further down, with more branchings, growing darker and more still with every turn. No one went beyond the first level; those that did – like the Captain – never came back. They had heard stories about how deep the stone city went, but there was no way to check them out; the instruments they had taken from *Pegasus* had never worked on the crossworlds.

At the bottom of the first full turn, the first level, Holt stopped and put on the pale blue helmet. It was a tight fit; the front of it pressed against the edge of his nose and the sides squeezed his head uncomfortably. Clearly it had been built for an ul-mennalei. But it would do; there was a hole around his mouth, so he could talk and breathe.

He waited a moment while his body heat was absorbed by the helmet. Shortly it began to give off a somber blue light. Holt continued down the corkscrew, into the darkness.

Around and around the underway curved, with other tunnels branching off at every turning; Holt kept on and soon lost track of the levels he had come. Outside his small circle of light there was only pitch-black and silence and still hot air that was increasingly difficult to breathe. But fear was driving him now, and he did not slow. The surface of the stone city was deserted, but not entirely so; the Dan'lai entered when they had to. Only down here would he be safe. He would stay on the corkscrew itself, he vowed; if he did not wander he could not get lost. That was what happened to the Captain and the others, he was sure; they'd left the underway, gone off into the side tunnels, and had starved to death before they could find their way back. But not Holt. In two weeks or so he could come up and get food from Sunderland, perhaps.

For what seemed hours he walked down the twisting ramp, past endless walls of featureless gray stone tinted blue by his helmet, past a thousand gaping holes that ran to the sides and up and down, each calling to him with a wide black mouth. The air grew steadily warmer; soon Holt was breathing heavily. Nothing around him but stone, yet the tunnels seemed rank and thick. He ignored it.

After a time Holt reached a place where the corkscrew ended; a triple fork confronted him, three arched doorways and three narrow stairs, each descending sharply in a different direction, each curving so that Holt could see only a few meters into the dark. By then his feet were sore. He sat and removed his boots and took out a tube of smoked meat to chew on.

Darkness all around him; without his footsteps echoing heavily, there was no sound. Unless. He listened carefully. Yes. He heard something, dim and far off. A rumble, sort of. He chewed on his meat and listened even harder and after a long while decided the sounds were coming from the left-hand staircase.

When the food was gone, he licked his fingers and pulled on his boots and rose. Laser in hand, he slowly started down the stair as quietly as he could manage.

The stair too was spiral; a tighter corkscrew than the ramp, without branchings and very narrow. He barely had room to turn around, but at least there was no chance of getting lost.

The sound got steadily louder as he descended, and before long Holt realized that it was not a rumble after all, but more a howl. Then, later, it changed again. He could barely make it out. Moans and barking.

The stairway made a sharp turn. Holt followed it and stopped suddenly.

He was standing in a window in an oddly shaped gray stone building, looking out over the stone city. It was night, and a tapestry of stars filled the sky. Below, near an octagonal pool, six Dan'lai surrounded a Cedran. They were laughing, quick barking laughs full of rage, and they were chattering to each other and clawing at the Cedran whenever it tried to move. It stood above them trapped in the circle, confused and moaning, swaying back and forth. The huge violet eyes glowed brightly, and the fighting-claws waved.

One of the Dan'lai had something. He unfolded it slowly; a long jag-toothed knife. A second appeared, a third; all the foxmen had them. They laughed to each other. One of them darted in at the Cedran from behind, and the silvered blade flashed, and Holt saw black ichor ooze slowly from a long cut in the milk-white Cedran flesh.

There was a blood-curdling low moan and the worm turned slowly as the Dan'la danced back, and its fighting-claws moved quicker than Holt would have believed. The Dan'la with the dripping black knife was lifted, kicking, into the air. He barked furiously, and then the claw snapped together, and the foxman fell in two pieces to the ground. But the others closed in, laughing, and their knives wove patterns and the Cedran's moan became a screech. It lashed out with its claws and a second Dan'la was knocked headless into the waters, but by then two others were cutting off its thrashing tentacles and yet another had driven his blade hilt-deep into the swaying wormlike torso. All the foxmen were wildly excited; Holt could not hear the Cedran over their frantic barking.

He lifted his laser, took aim on the nearest Dan'la, and pushed the firing stud. Angry red light spurted.

A curtain dropped across the window, blocking the view. Holt reached out and yanked it aside. Behind it was a low-roofed chamber, with a dozen level tunnels leading off in all directions. No Dan'lai, no Cedran. He was far beneath the city. The only light was the blue glow of his helmet.

Slowly, silently, Holt walked to the center of the chamber. Half of the tunnels, he saw, were bricked in. Others were dead black holes. But from one, a blast of cool air was flowing. He followed it a long way in darkness until at last it opened on a long gallery full of glowing red mist, like droplets of fire. The hall stretched away to left and right as far as Holt could see, high-ceilinged and straight; the tunnel that had led him here was only one of many. Others – each a different size and shape, all as black as death – lined the walls.

Holt took one step into the soft red fog, then turned and burned a mark into the stone floor of the tunnel behind him. He began walking down the hall, past the endless rows of tunnel mouths. The mist was thick but easy to see through, and Holt saw that the whole vast gallery was empty – at least to the limits of his vision. But he could not see either end, and his footsteps made no sound.

He walked a long time, almost in a trance, somehow forgetting to be afraid. Then, briefly, a white light surged from a portal far ahead. Holt began to run, but the glow had faded before he covered half the distance to the tunnel. Still something called him on.

The tunnel mouth was a high arch full of night when Holt entered. A few meters of darkness, and a door; he stopped.

The arch opened on a high bank of snow and a forest of iron-gray trees linked by fragile webs of ice, so delicate that they would melt and shatter at a breath. No leaves, but hardy blue flowers peeked from the wind-crannies beneath every limb. The stars blazed in the frigid blackness above. And, sitting high on the horizon, Holt saw the wooden stockade and stone-fairy parapets of the rambling twisted Old House.

He paused for a long time, watching, remembering. The cold wind stirred briefly, blowing a flurry of snow in through the door, and Holt shivered in the blast. Then he turned and went back to the hall of the red mist.

Sunderland was waiting for him where tunnel met gallery, half wrapped in the sound-sucking fog. 'Mike!' he said, talking normally enough, but all that Holt heard was a whisper. 'You've got to come back. We need you,

Mike. I can't map without you to get food for me, and Alaina and Takker
. . . You must come back!'

Holt shook his head. The mists thickened and whirled, and Sunderland's
portly figure was draped and blurred until all Holt could see was the heavy
outline. Then the air cleared, and it was not Sunderland at all. It was the
Shed-boss. The creature stood silently, the white tentacles trembling on
the bladder atop its torso. It waited. Holt waited.

Across the gallery, sudden light woke dimly in a tunnel. Then the two
that flanked them began to glow, and then the two beyond that. Holt
glanced right, then left; on both sides of the gallery, the silent waves raced
from him until all the portals shone – here a dim red, here a flood of blue-
white, here a friendly homesun yellow.

Ponderously the Shed-boss turned and began to walk down the hall. The
rolls of blue-black fat bounced and jiggled as it went along, but the mists
leeched away the musky smell. Holt followed it, his laser still in his hand.

The ceiling rose higher and higher, and Holt saw that the doorways were
growing larger. As he watched, a craggy mottled being much like the
Shed-boss came out of one tunnel, crossed the hall, and entered another.

They stopped before a tunnel mouth, round and black and twice as tall
as Holt. The Shed-boss waited. Holt, laser at ready, entered. He stood
before another window, or perhaps a viewscreen; on the far side of the
round crystal port, chaos swirled and screamed. He watched it briefly, and
just as his head was starting to hurt, the swirling view solidified. If you
could call it solid. Beyond the port, four Dan'lai sat with jump-gun tubes
around their brows and a cylinder before them. Except – except – the
picture was blurred. Ghosts, there were ghosts, second images that almost
overlapped the first, but not quite, not completely. And then Holt saw a
third image, and a fourth, and suddenly the picture *cracked* and it was as
though he was looking into an infinite array of mirrors. Long rows of
Dan'lai sat on top of each other, blurring into one another, growing smaller
and smaller until they dwindled into nothingness. In unison – no, no,
almost in unison (for here one image did not move with his reflections, and
here another fumbled) – they removed the drained jump-gun tubes and
looked at each other and began to laugh. Wild, high barking laughs; they
laughed and laughed and laughed and Holt watched as the fires of
madness burned in their eyes, and the foxmen all (no, *almost* all) hunched
their slim shoulders and seemed more feral and animal than he had ever
seen them.

He left. Back in the hall, the Shed-boss still stood patiently. Holt
followed again.

There were others in the hall now; Holt saw them faintly, scurrying back
and forth through the reddish mist. Creatures like the Shed-boss seemed

to dominate, but they were not alone. Holt glimpsed a single Dan'la, lost and frightened; the foxman kept stumbling into walls. And there were things part-angel and part-dragonfly that slid silently past overhead, and something tall and thin surrounded by flickering veils of light, and other presences that he felt as much as saw. Frequently he saw the bright-skinned striders with their gorgeous hues and high collars of bone and flesh, and always slender, sensuous animals loped at their heels, moving with fluid grace on four legs. The animals had soft gray skins and liquid eyes and strangely sentient faces.

Then he thought he spied a man; dark and very dignified, in ship's uniform and cap. Holt strained after the vision and ran toward it, but the mists confused him, bright and glowing as they were, and he lost the sight. When he looked around again, the Shed-boss was gone too.

He tried the nearest tunnel. It was a doorway, like the first; beyond was a mountain ledge overlooking a hard arid land, a plain of baked brick broken by a great crevasse. A city stood in the center of the desolation, its walls chalk white, its buildings all right angles. It was quite dead, but Holt still knew it, somehow. Often Cain narKarmian had told him how the Hrangans build their cities, in the war-torn reaches between Old Earth and the Fringe.

Hesitant, Holt extended a hand past the door frame, and withdrew it quickly. Beyond the arch was an oven; it was not a viewscreen, no more than the sight of Ymir had been.

Back in the gallery he paused and tried to understand. The hall went on and on in both directions, and beings like none he had ever seen drifted past in the mists, death silent, barely noticing the others. The Captain was down here, he knew, and Villareal and Susie Benet and maybe the others – or – or perhaps they *had* been down here, and now they were elsewhere. Perhaps they too had seen their homes calling to them through a stone doorway, and perhaps they had followed and not returned. Once beyond the arches, Holt wondered, how could you come back?

The Dan'la came into sight again, crawling now, and Holt saw that he was very old. The way he fumbled made it clear that he was quite blind, and yet, and yet his eyes *looked* good enough. Then Holt began to watch the others, and finally to follow them. Many went out through the doorways, and they did indeed walk off into the landscapes beyond. And the *landscapes* . . . he watched the ullish worlds in all their weary splendor, as the ul-mennaleith glided to their worships . . . he saw the starless night of Darkdawn, high atop the Fringe, and the darkling dreamers wandering beneath . . . and Huul the Golden (real after all, though less than he expected) . . . and the ghost ships flitting out from the core and the screechers of the black worlds in the Far Arm and the ancient races that had locked their stars in spheres and a thousand worlds undreamed of.

Soon he stopped following the quiet travelers and began to wander on his own, and then he found that the views beyond the doors could change. As he stood before a square gate that opened on the plains of ai-Emerel, he thought for a moment on Old Cain, who had indeed shipped a long ways, but not quite far enough. The Emereli towers were before him, and Holt wished to see them closer, and suddenly the doorway opened onto one. Then the Shed-boss was at his elbow, materializing as abruptly as ever in the Shed, and Holt glanced over into the faceless face. Then he put away the laser and removed his helmet (it had ceased to glow, oddly – why hadn't he noticed that?) and stepped forward.

He was on a balcony, cold wind stroking his face, black Emereli metal behind and an orange sunset before him. Across the horizon the other towers stood, and Holt knew that each was a city of a million; but from here, they were only tall dark needles.

A world. Cain's world. Yet it would have changed a lot since Cain had last seen it, some two hundred years ago. He wondered how. No matter; he would soon find out.

As he turned to go inside, he promised himself that soon he would go back, to find Sunderland and Alaina and Takker-Rey. For them, perhaps, it would be all darkness and fear below, but Holt could guide them home. Yes, he would do that. But not right now. He wanted to see ai-Emerel first, and Old Earth, and the Altered Men of Prometheus. Yes. But later he would go back. Later. In a little bit.

*

Time moves slowly in the stone city; more slowly down below where the webs of spacetime were knotted by the Builders. But still it moves, inexorably. The great gray buildings are all tumbled now, the mushroom tower fallen, the pyramids blown dust. Of the ullish windwalls not a trace remains, and no ship has landed for millennia. The ul-mennaleith grow few and strangely diffident and walk with armored hoppers at their heels, the Dan'lai have disintegrated into violent anarchy after a thousand years of jump-guns, the Kresh are gone, the Linkellars are enslaved, and the ghost ships still keep silent. Outwards, the Damoosh are a dying race, though the wisdompools live on and ponder, waiting for questions that no longer come. New races walk on tired worlds; old ones grow and change. No man has reached the core.

The crossworlds sun grows dim.

In empty tunnels beneath the ruins, Holt walks from star to star.

Bitterblooms

When he finally died, Shawn found to her shame that she could not even bury him.

She had no proper digging tools; only her hands, the longknife strapped to her thigh, and the smaller blade in her boot. But it would not have mattered. Beneath its sparse covering of snow, the ground was frozen hard as rock. Shawn was sixteen, as her family counted years, and the ground had been frozen for half her lifetime. The season was deepwinter, and the world was cold.

Knowing the futility of it before she started, Shawn still tried to dig. She picked a spot a few meters from the rude lean-to she had built for their shelter, broke the thin crust of the snow and swept it away with her hands, and began to hack at the frozen earth with the smaller of her blades. But the ground was harder than her steel. The knife broke, and she looked at it helplessly, knowing how precious it had been, knowing what Creg would say. Then she began to claw at the unfeeling soil, weeping, until her hands ached and her tears froze within her mask. It was not right for her to leave him without burial; he had been father, brother, lover. He had always been kind to her, and she had always failed him. And now she could not even bury him.

Finally, not knowing what else to do, she kissed him one last time – there was ice in his beard and his hair, and his face was twisted unnaturally by the pain and the cold, but he was still family, after all – and toppled the lean-to across his body, hiding him within a rough bier of branches and snow. It was useless, she knew; vampires and windwolves would knock it apart easily to get at his flesh. But she could not abandon him without shelter of some kind.

She left him his skis and his big silverwood bow, its bowstring snapped by the cold. But she took his sword and his heavy fur cloak; it was little enough burden added to her pack. She had nursed him for almost a week after the vampire had left him wounded, and that long delay in the little lean-to had depleted most of their supplies. Now she hoped to travel light and fast. She strapped on her skis, standing next to the clumsy grave she had built him, and said her last farewell leaning on her poles. Then she set off over the snow, through the terrible silence of the deepwinter woods, toward home and fire and family. It was just past midday.

By dusk, Shawn knew that she would never make it.

She was calmer then, more rational. She had left her grief and her shame behind with his body, as she had been taught to do. The stillness and the cold were all around her, but the long hours of skiing had left her flushed and almost warm beneath her layers of leather and fur. Her thoughts had the brittle clarity of the ice that hung in long spears from the bare, twisted trees around her.

As darkness threw its cloak over the world, Shawn sought shelter in the lee of the greatest of those trees, a massive blackbark whose trunk was three meters across. She spread the fur cloak she had taken on a bare patch of ground and pulled her own woven cape over her like a blanket to shut out the rising wind. With her back to the trunk and her longknife drawn beneath her cape, just in case, she slept a brief, wary sleep, and woke in full night to contemplate her mistakes.

The stars were out; she could see them peeking through the bare black branches above her. The Ice Wagon dominated the sky, bringing cold into the world, as it had for as long as Shawn could remember. The driver's blue eyes glared down at her, mocking.

It had been the Ice Wagon that killed Lane, she thought bitterly. Not the vampire. The vampire had mauled him badly that night, when his bowstring broke as he tried to draw in their defense. But in another season, with Shawn nursing him, he would have lived. In deepwinter, he never had a chance. The cold crept in past all the defenses she had built for him; the cold drained away all his strength, all his ferocity. The cold left him a shrunken white thing, numb and pale, his lips tinged with blue. And now the driver of the Ice Wagon would claim his soul.

And hers, too, she knew. She should have abandoned Lane to his fate. That was what Creg would have done, or Leila – any of them. There had never been any hope that he would live, not in deepwinter. Nothing lived in deepwinter. The trees grew stark and bare in deepwinter, the grass and the flowers perished, the animals all froze or went underground to sleep. Even the windwolves and the vampires grew lean and fierce, and many starved to death before the thaw.

As Shawn would starve.

They had already been running three days late when the vampire attacked them, and Lane had had them eating short rations. Afterward he had been so weak. He had finished his own food on the fourth day, and Shawn had started feeding him some of hers, never telling him. She had very little left now, and the safety of Carinhall was still nearly two weeks of hard travel away. In deepwinter, it might as well be two years.

Curled beneath her cape, Shawn briefly considered starting a fire. A fire would bring vampires – they could feel the heat three kilometers off. They would come stalking silently between the trees, gaunt black shadows taller than Lane had been, their loose skin flapping over skeletal limbs like dark cloaks, concealing the claws. Perhaps, if she lay in wait, she could take one by surprise. A full-grown vampire would feed her long enough to return to Carinhall. She played with the idea in the darkness, and only reluctantly put it aside. Vampires could run across the snow as fast as an arrow in flight, scarcely touching the ground, and it was virtually impossible to see them by night. But they could see her very well, by the heat she gave off. Lighting a fire would only guarantee her a quick and relatively painless death.

Shawn shivered and gripped the hilt of her longknife more tightly for reassurance. Every shadow suddenly seemed to have a vampire crouched within it, and in the keening of the wind she thought she could hear the flapping noise their skin made when they ran.

Then, louder and very real, another noise reached her ears – an angry high-pitched whistling like nothing Shawn had ever heard. And suddenly the black horizon was suffused with light, a flicker of ghostly blue radiance that outlined the naked bones of the forest and throbbed visibly against the sky. Shawn inhaled sharply, a draught of ice down her raw throat, and struggled to her feet, half-afraid she was under attack. But there was nothing. The world was cold and black and dead; only the light lived, flickering dimly in the distance, beckoning, calling to her. She watched it for long minutes, thinking back on old Jon and the terrible stories he used to tell the children when they gathered round Carinhall's great hearth. *There are worse things than vampires,* he would tell them; and remembering, Shawn was suddenly a little girl again, sitting on the thick furs with her back to the fire, listening to Jon talk of ghosts and living shadows and cannibal families who lived in great castles built of bone.

As abruptly as it had come, the strange light faded and was gone, and with it went the high-pitched noise. Shawn had marked where it had shone, however. She took up her pack and fastened Lane's cloak about her for extra warmth, then began to don her skis. She was no child now, she told herself, and that light had been no ghost dance. Whatever it was, it might be her only chance. She took her poles in hand and set off toward it.

Night travel was dangerous in the extreme, she knew. Creg had told her that a hundred times, and Lane as well. In the darkness, in the scant starlight, it was easy to go astray, to break a ski or a leg or worse. And movement generated heat, heat that drew vampires from the deep of the woods. Better to lay low until dawn, when the nocturnal hunters had retired to their lairs. All of her training told her that, and all of her instincts. But it was deepwinter, and when she rested the cold bit through even the warmest of furs, and Lane was dead and she was hungry, and the light had been so close, so achingly close. So she followed it, going slowly, going carefully, and it seemed that this night she had a charm upon her. The terrain was all flatland, gentle to her, almost kind, and the snow cover was sparse enough so that neither root nor rock could surprise and trip her. No dark predators came gliding out of the night, and the only sound was the sound of her motion, the soft crackling of the snow crust beneath her skis.

The forest grew steadily thinner as she moved, and after an hour Shawn emerged from it entirely, into a wasteland of tumbled stone blocks and twisted, rusting metal. She knew what it was; she had seen other ruins before, where families had lived and died, and their halls and houses had gone all to rot. But never a ruin so extensive as this. The family that had lived here, however long ago, had been very great once; the shattered remains of their dwellings were more extensive than a hundred Carinhalls. She began to pick a careful path through the crumbling, snow-dusted masonry. Twice she came upon structures that were almost intact, and each time she considered seeking shelter within those ancient stone walls, but there was nothing in either of them that might have caused the light, so Shawn passed on after only a brief inspection. The river she came to soon thereafter stopped her for a slightly longer time. From the high bank where she paused, she could see the remains of two bridges that had once spanned the narrow channel, but both of them had fallen long ago. The river was frozen over, however, so she had no trouble crossing it. In deepwinter the ice was thick and solid and there was no danger of her falling through.

As she climbed painstakingly up the far bank, Shawn came upon the flower.

It was a very small thing, its thick black stem emerging from between two rocks low on the river bank. She might never have seen it in the night, but her pole dislodged one of the ice-covered stones as she struggled up the slope, and the noise made her glance down to where it grew.

It startled her so that she took both poles in one hand, and with the other fumbled in the deepest recesses of her clothing, so that she might risk a flame. The match gave a short, intense light. But it was enough; Shawn saw.

A flower, tiny, so tiny, with four blue petals, each the same pale blue shade that Lane's lips had been just before he died. A flower, here, alive, growing in the eighth year of deepwinter, when all the world was dead.

They would never believe her, Shawn thought, not unless she brought the truth with her, back to Carinhall. She freed herself from her skis and tried to pick the flower. It was futile, as futile as her effort to bury Lane. The stem was as strong as metal wire. She struggled with it for several minutes, and fought to keep from crying when it would not come. Creg would call her a liar, a dreamer, all the things he always called her.

She did not cry, though, finally. She left the flower where it grew, and climbed to the top of the river ridge. There she paused.

Beneath her, going on and on for meters upon meters, was a wide empty field. Snow stood in great drifts in some places, and in others there was only bare flat stone, naked to the wind and the cold. In the center of the field was the strangest building Shawn had even seen, a great fat teardrop of a building that squatted like an animal in the starlight on three black legs. The legs were bent beneath it, flexed and rimed over with ice at their joints, as if the beast had been about to leap straight up into the sky. And legs and building both were covered with flowers.

There were flowers everywhere, Shawn saw when she took her eyes off the squat building long enough to look. They sprouted, singly and in clusters, from every little crack in the field, with snow and ice all around them, making dark islands of life in the pure white stillness of deepwinter.

Shawn walked through them, closer to the building, until she stood next to one of the legs and reached up to touch its joint wonderingly with a gloved hand. It was all metal, metal and ice and flowers, like the building itself. Where each of the legs rested, the stone beneath had broken and fractured in a hundred places, as if shattered by some great blow, and vines grew from the crevices, twisting black vines that crawled around the flanks of the structure like the webs of a summer-spinner. The flowers burst from the vines, and now that she stood up close, Shawn saw that they were not like her little river bloom at all. There were blossoms of many colors, some as big as her head, growing in wild profusion everywhere, as if they did not realize that it was deepwinter, when they should be black and dead.

She was walking around the building, looking for an entrance, when a noise made her turn her head toward the ridge.

A thin shadow flickered briefly against the snow, then seemed to vanish. Shawn trembled and retreated quickly, putting the nearest of the tall legs to her back, and then she dropped everything and Lane's sword was in her left hand and her own longknife in her right, and she stood cursing herself for that match, that stupid, stupid match, and listening for the *flap-flap-flap* of death on taloned feet.

It was too dark, she realized, and her hand shook, and even as it did the shape rushed upon her from the side. Her longknife flashed at it, stabbing, slicing, but cut only the skincloak, and then the vampire gave a shriek of triumph and Shawn was buffeted to the ground and she knew she was bleeding. There was a weight on her chest, and something black and leathery settled across her eyes, and she tried to knife it and that was when she realized that her blade was gone. She screamed.

Then the vampire screamed, and the side of Shawn's head exploded in pain, and she had blood in her eyes, and she was choking on blood, and blood and blood, and nothing more . . .

*

It was blue, all blue; hazy, shifting blue. A pale blue, dancing, dancing, like the ghost light that had flickered on the sky. A soft blue, like the little flower, the impossible blossom by the riverbank. A cold blue, like the eyes of the Ice Wagon's black driver, like Lane's lips when last she kissed them. Blue, blue, and it moved and would not be still. Everything was blurred, unreal. There was only blue. For a long time, only blue.

Then music. But it was blurred music, blue music somehow, strange and high and fleeting, very sad, lonely, a bit erotic. It was a lullaby, like old Tesenya used to sing when Shawn was very little, before Tesenya grew weak and sick and Creg put her out to die. It had been so long since Shawn had heard such a song; all the music she knew was Creg on his harp, and Rys on her guitar. She found herself relaxing, floating, all her limbs turned to water, lazy water, though it was deepwinter and she knew she should be ice.

Soft hands began to touch her, lifting her head, pulling off her facemask so the blue warm brushed her naked cheeks, then drifting lower, lower, loosening her clothes, stripping her of furs and cloth and leather, off with her belt and off with her jerkin and off with her pants. Her skin tingled. She was floating, floating. Everything was warm, so warm, and the hands fluttered here and there and they were so gentle, like old mother Tesenya had been, like her sister Leila was sometimes, like Devin. Like Lane, she thought, and it was a pleasant thought, comforting and arousing at the same time, and Shawn held close to it. She was with Lane, she was safe and warm and . . . and she remembered his face, the blue in his lips, the ice in his beard where his breath had frozen, the pain burned into him, twisting his features like a mask. She remembered, and suddenly she was drowning in the blue, choking on the blue, struggling, screaming.

The hands lifted her and a stranger's voice muttered something low and soothing in a language she did not understand. A cup was pressed to Shawn's lips. She opened her mouth to scream again, but instead she was drinking. It was hot and sweet and fragrant, full of spices, and some of them were very familiar, but others she could not place at all. Tea, she thought, and her hands took it from the other hands as she gulped it down.

She was in a small dim room, propped up on a bed of pillows, and her clothes were piled next to her and the air was full of blue mist from a burning stick. A woman knelt beside her, dressed in bright tatters of many different colors, and gray eyes regarded her calmly from beneath the thickest, wildest hair that Shawn had ever seen. 'You . . . who . . .' Shawn said.

The woman stroked her brow with a pale soft hand. 'Carin,' she said clearly.

Shawn nodded, slowly, wondering who the woman was, and how she knew the family.

'Carinhall,' the woman said, and her eyes seemed amused and a bit sad. 'Lin and Eris and Caith. I remember them, little girl. Beth, Voice Carin, how hard she was. And Kaya and Dale and Shawn.'

'Shawn. I'm Shawn. That's me. But Creg is Voice Carin . . .'

The woman smiled faintly, and continued to stroke Shawn's brow. The skin of her hand was very soft. Shawn had never felt anything so soft. 'Shawn is my lover,' the woman said. 'Every tenthyear, at Gathering.'

Shawn blinked at her, confused. She was beginning to remember. The light in the forest, the flowers, the vampire. 'Where am I?' she asked.

'You are everywhere you never dreamed of being, little Carin,' the woman said, and she laughed at herself.

The walls of the room shone like dark metal, Shawn noticed. 'The building,' she blurted, 'the building on legs, with all the flowers . . .'

'Yes,' the woman said.

'Do you . . . who are you? Did you make the light? I was in the forest, and Lane was dead and I was nearly out of food, and I saw a light, a blue . . .'

'That was my light, Carin child, as I came down from the sky. I was far away, oh yes, far away in lands you never heard of, but I came back.' The woman stood up suddenly, and whirled around and around, and the gaudy cloth she wore flapped and shimmered, and she was wreathed in pale blue smoke. 'I am the witch they warn you of in Carinhall, child,' she yelled, exulting, and she whirled and whirled until finally, dizzy, she collapsed again beside Shawn's bed.

No one had ever warned Shawn of a witch. She was more puzzled than afraid. 'You killed the vampire,' she said. 'How did you . . . ?'

'I am magic,' the woman said. 'I am magic and I can do magic things and I will live forever. And so will you, Carin child, Shawn, when I teach you. You can travel with me, and I will teach you all the magics and tell you stories, and we can be lovers. You are my lover already, you know, you've always been, at Gathering. Shawn, Shawn.' She smiled.

'No,' Shawn said. '*That* was some other person.'

'You're tired, child. The vampire hurt you, and you don't remember. But you will remember, you will.' She stood up and moved across the room, snuffing out the burning stick with her fingertips, quieting the music. When her back was turned, her hair fell nearly to her waist, and all of it was curls and tangles; wild restless hair, tossing as she moved like the waves on the distant sea. Shawn had seen the sea once, years ago, before deepwinter came. She remembered.

The woman faded the dim lights somehow, and turned back to Shawn in darkness. 'Rest now. I took away your pain with my magics, but it may come back. Call me if it does. I have other magics.'

Shawn did feel drowsy. 'Yes,' she murmured, unresisting. But when the woman moved to leave, Shawn called out to her again. 'Wait,' she said. 'Your family, mother. Tell me who you are.'

The woman stood framed in yellow light, a silhouette without features. 'My family is very great, child. My sisters are Lilith and Marcyan and Erika Stormjones and Lamiya-Bailis and Deirdre d'Allerane. Kleronomas and Stephen Cobalt Northstar and Tomo and Walberg were all brothers to me, and fathers. Our house is up past the Ice Wagon, and my name, my name is Morgan.' And then she was gone, and the door closed behind her, and Shawn was left to sleep.

*

Morgan, she thought as she slept. Morganmorganmorgan. The name drifted through her dreams like smoke.

She was very little, and she was watching the fire in the hearth at Carinhall, watching the flames lick and tease at the big black logs, smelling the sweet fragrances of thistlewood, and nearby someone was telling a story. Not Jon, no, this was before Jon had become storyteller. This was long ago. It was Tesenya, so very old, her face wrinkled, and she was talking in her tired voice so full of music, her lullaby voice, and all the children listened. Her stories had been different from Jon's. His were always about fighting, wars and vendettas and monsters, chock-full with blood and knives and impassioned oaths sworn by a father's corpse. Tesenya was quieter. She told of a group of travelers, six of family Alynne, who were lost in the wild one year during the season of freeze. They chanced upon a huge hall built all of metal, and the family within welcomed them with a great feast. So the travelers ate and drank, and just as they were wiping their lips to go, another banquet was served, and thus it went. The Alynnes stayed and stayed, for the food was richer and more delightful than any they had ever tasted, and the more they ate of it, the hungrier they grew. Besides, deepwinter had set in outside the metal hall. Finally, when thaw came many years later, others of family Alynne went searching for the six wanderers. They found them dead in the forest. They had put off their good warm furs and dressed in flimsies. Their steel had gone all to rust, and each of them had starved. For the name of the metal hall was Morganhall, Tesenya told the children, and the family who lived there was the family named Liar, whose food is empty stuff made of dreams and air.

Shawn woke naked and shivering.

Her clothes were still piled next to her bed. She dressed quickly, first pulling on her undergarments, and over them a heavy blackwool shift, and over that her leathers, pants and belt and jerkin, then her coat of fur with its hood, and finally the capes, Lane's cloak and her own of child's cloth. Last of all was her facemask. She pulled the taut leather down over her head and laced it closed beneath her chin, and then she was safe from deepwinter winds and stranger's touches both. Shawn found her weapons thrown carelessly in a corner with her boots. When Lane's sword was in her hand and her longknife back in its familiar sheath, she felt complete again. She stepped outside determined to find skis and exit.

Morgan met her with laughter bright and brittle, in a chamber of glass and shining silver metal. She stood framed against the largest window Shawn had ever seen, a sheet of pure clean glass taller than a man and wider than Carinhall's great hearth, even more flawless than the mirrors of family Terhis, who were famed for their glassblowers and lensmakers. Beyond the glass it was midday; the cool blue midday of deepwinter. Shawn saw the field of stone and snow and flowers, and beyond it the low ridge that she had climbed, and beyond that the frozen river winding through the ruins.

'You look so fierce and angry,' Morgan said, when her silly laughter had stopped. She had been threading her wild hair with wisps of cloth and gems on silver clips that sparkled when she moved. 'Come, Carin child, take off your furs again. The cold can't touch us here, and if it does we can leave it. There are other lands, you know.' She walked across the room.

Shawn had let the point of her sword droop toward the floor; now she jerked it up again. 'Stay away,' she warned. Her voice sounded hoarse and strange.

'I am not afraid of you, Shawn,' Morgan said. 'Not you, my Shawn, my lover.' She moved around the sword easily, and took off the scarf she wore, a gossamer of gray spidersilk set with tiny crimson jewels, to drape it around Shawn's neck. 'See, I know what you are thinking,' she said, pointing to the jewels. One by one, they were changing color; fire became blood, blood crusted and turned brown, brown faded to black. 'You are frightened of me, nothing more. No anger. You would never hurt me.' She tied the scarf neatly under Shawn's facemask, and smiled.

Shawn stared at the gems with horror. 'How did you do that?' she demanded, backing off uncertainly.

'With magic,' Morgan said. She spun on her heels and danced back to the window. 'Morgan is full of magic.'

'You are full of lies,' Shawn said. 'I know about the six Alynnes. I'm not going to eat here and starve to death. Where are my skis?'

Morgan seemed not to hear her; the older woman's eyes were clouded, wistful. 'Have you ever seen Alynne House in summer, child? It's very beautiful. The sun comes up over the redstone tower, and sinks every night into Jamei's Lake. Do you know it, Shawn?'

'No,' Shawn said boldly, 'and you don't either. What do you talk about Alynne House for? You said your family lived on the Ice Wagon, and they all had names I never heard of, Kleraberus and things like that.'

'Kleronomas,' Morgan said, giggling. She raised her hand to her mouth to still herself, and chewed on a finger idly while her gray eyes shone. All her fingers were ringed with bright metal. 'You should see my brother Kleronomas, child. He is half of metal and half of flesh, and his eyes are bright as glass, and he knows more than all the Voices who've ever spoken for Carinhall.'

'He does not,' Shawn said. 'You're lying again!'

'He *does*,' Morgan said. Her hand fell and she looked cross. 'He's magic. We all are. Erika died, but she wakes up to live again and again and again. Stephen was a warrior – he killed a billion families, more than you can count – and Celia found a lot of secret places that no one had ever found before. My family all does magic things.' Her expression grew suddenly sly. 'I killed the vampire, didn't I? How do you think I did that?'

'With a knife!' Shawn said fiercely. But beneath her mask she flushed. Morgan *had* killed the vampire; that meant there was a debt. And she had drawn steel! She flinched under Creg's imagined fury, and dropped the sword to clatter on the floor. All at once she was very confused.

Morgan's voice was gentle. 'But you had a longknife *and* a sword, and you couldn't kill the vampire, could you, child? No.' She came across the room. 'You are mine, Shawn Carin, you are my lover and my daughter and my sister. You have to learn to trust. I have much to teach you. Here.' She took Shawn by the hand and led her to the window. 'Stand here. Wait, Shawn, wait and watch, and I will show you more of Morgan's magics.' At the far wall, smiling, she did something with her rings to a panel of bright metal and square dim lights.

Watching, Shawn grew suddenly afraid.

Beneath her feet, the floor began to shake, and a sound assaulted her, a high whining shriek that stabbed at her ears through the leather mask, until she clapped her gloved hands on either side of her head to shut it out.

Even then she could hear it, like a vibration in her bones. Her teeth ached, and she was aware of a sudden shooting pain up in her left temple. And that was not the worst of it.

For outside, where everything had been cold and bright and still, a somber blue light was shifting and dancing and staining all the world. The snowdrifts were a pale blue, and the plumes of frozen powder that blew from each of them were paler still, and blue shadows came and went upon the river ridge where none had been before. And Shawn could see the light reflected even on the river itself, and on the ruins that stood desolate and broken upon the farther crest. Morgan was giggling behind her, and then everything in the window began to blur, until there was nothing to be seen at all, only colors, colors bright and dark running together, like pieces of a rainbow melting in some vast stewpot. Shawn did not budge from where she stood, but her hand fell to the hilt of her longknife, and despite herself she trembled.

'Look, Carin child!' Morgan shouted, over the terrible whine. Shawn could barely hear her. 'We've jumped up into the sky now, away from all that cold. I told you, Shawn. We're going to ride the Ice Wagon now.' And she did something to the wall again, and the noise vanished, and the colors were gone. Beyond the glass was sky.

Shawn cried out in fear. She could see nothing except darkness and stars, stars everywhere, more than she had ever seen before. And she knew she was lost. Lane had taught her all the stars, so she could use them for a guide, find her way from anywhere to anywhere, but these stars were wrong, were *different*. She could not find the Ice Wagon, or the Ghost Skier, or even Lara Carin with her windwolves. She could find nothing familiar; only stars, stars that leered at her like a million eyes, red and white and blue and yellow, and none of them would even blink.

Morgan was standing behind her. 'Are we in the Ice Wagon?' Shawn asked in a small voice.

'Yes.'

Shawn trembled, threw away her knife so that it bounded noisily off a metal wall, and turned to face her host. 'Then we're dead, and the driver is taking our souls off to the frozen waste,' she said. She did not cry. She had not wanted to be dead, especially not in deepwinter, but at least she would see Lane again.

Morgan began to undo the scarf she had fastened round Shawn's neck. The stones were black and frightening. 'No, Shawn Carin,' she said evenly. 'We are not dead. Live here with me, child, and you will never die. You'll see.' She pulled off the scarf and starting unlacing the thongs of Shawn's facemask. When it was loose, she pulled it up and off the girl's head, tossing it casually to the floor. 'You're pretty, Shawn. You have always been pretty, though. I remember, all those years ago. I remember.'

'I'm not pretty,' Shawn said. 'I'm too soft, and I'm too weak, and Creg says I'm skinny and my face is all pushed in. And I'm not . . .'

Morgan shushed her with a touch to her lips, and then unfastened her neck clasp. Lane's battered cloak slipped from her shoulders. Her own cape followed, and then her coat was off, and Morgan's fingers moved down to the laces of her jerkin.

'No,' Shawn said, suddenly shying away. Her back pressed up against the great window, and she felt the awful night laying its weight upon her. 'I can't, Morgan. I'm Carin, and you're not family; I *can't.*'

'Gathering,' Morgan whispered. 'Pretend this is Gathering, Shawn. You've always been my lover during the Gathering.'

Shawn's throat was dry. 'But it *isn't* Gathering,' she insisted. She had seen one Gathering, down by the sea, when forty families came together to trade news and goods and love. But that had been years before her blood, so no one had taken her; she was not yet a woman, and thus untouchable. 'It *isn't* Gathering,' she repeated, close to tears.

Morgan giggled. 'Very well. I am no Carin, but I am Morgan full-of-magic. I can make it Gathering.' She darted across the room on bare feet, and thrust her rings against the wall once more, and moved them this way and that, in a strange pattern. Then she called out, 'Look! Turn and look.' Shawn, confused, glanced back at the window.

Under the double suns of highsummer, the world was bright and green. Sailing ships moved languidly on the slow-flowing waters of the river, and Shawn could see the bright reflections of the twin suns bobbing and rolling in their wake, balls of soft yellow butter afloat upon the blue. Even the sky seemed sweet and buttery; white clouds moved like the stately schooners of family Crien, and nowhere could a star be seen. The far shore was dotted by houses, houses small as a road shelter and greater than even Carinhall, towers as tall and sleek as the wind-carved rocks in the Broken Mountains. And here and there and all among them people moved; lithe swarthy folk strange to Shawn, and people of the families too, all mingling together. The stone field was free of snow and ice, but there were metal buildings everywhere, some larger than Morganhall, many smaller, each with its distinctive markings, and every one of them squatting on three legs. Between the buildings were the tents and stalls of the families, with their sigils and their banners. And mats, the gaily-colored lovers' mats. Shawn saw people coupling, and felt Morgan's hand resting lightly on her shoulder.

'Do you know what you are seeing, Carin child?' Morgan whispered.

Shawn turned back to her with fear and wonder in her eyes. 'It is Gathering.'

Morgan smiled. 'You see,' she said. 'It is Gathering, and I claim you. Celebrate with me.' And her fingers moved to the buckle on Shawn's belt, and Shawn did not resist.

*

Within the metals walls of Morganhall, seasons turned to hours turned to years turned to days turned to months turned to weeks turned to seasons once again. Time had no sense. When Shawn awoke, on a shaggy fur that Morgan had spread beneath the window, highsummer had turned back into deep winter, and the families, ships, and Gathering were gone. Dawn came earlier than it should have, and Morgan seemed annoyed, so she made it dusk; the season was freeze, with its ominous chill, and where the stars of sunrise had shown, now gray clouds raced across a copper-colored sky. They ate while the copper turned to black. Morgan served mushrooms and crunchy summer greens, dark bread dripping with honey and butter, creamed spice-tea, and thick cuts of red meat floating in blood, and afterward there was flavored ice with nuts, and finally a tall hot drink with nine layers, each a different color with a different taste. They sipped the drink from glasses of impossibly thin crystal, and it made Shawn's head ache. And she began to cry, because the food had seemed real and all of it was good, but she was afraid that if she ate any more of it she would starve to death. Morgan laughed at her and slipped away and returned with dried leathery strips of vampire meat; she told Shawn to keep it in her pack and munch on it whenever she felt hungry.

Shawn kept the meat for a long time, but never ate from it.

At first she tried to keep track of the days by counting the meals they ate, and how many times they slept, but soon the changing scenes outside the window and the random nature of life in Morganhall confused her past any hope of understanding. She worried about it for weeks – or perhaps only for days – and then she ceased to worry. Morgan could make time do anything she pleased, so there was no sense in Shawn caring about it.

Several times Shawn asked to leave, but Morgan would have none of it. She only laughed and did some great magic that made Shawn forget about everything. Morgan took her blades away one night when she was asleep, and all her furs and leathers too, and afterward Shawn was forced to dress as Morgan wanted her to dress, in clouds of colored silk and fantastic tatters, or in nothing at all. She was angry and upset at first, but later she grew used to it. Her old clothing would have been much too hot inside Morganhall, anyway.

Morgan gave her gifts. Bags of spice that smelled of summer. A windwolf fashioned of pale blue glass. A metal mask that let Shawn see in the dark. Scented oils for her bath, and bottles of a slow golden liquor that brought her forgetfulness when her mind was troubled. A mirror, the finest mirror that had ever been. Books that Shawn could not read. A bracelet set with small red stones than drank in light all day and glowed by night. Cubes that played exotic music when Shawn warmed them with her hand. Boots woven of metal that were so light and flexible she could crumple them up in the palm of one hand. Metal miniatures of men and women and all manner of demons.

Morgan told her stories. Each gift she gave to Shawn had a story that went with it, a tale of where it came from and who had made it and how it had come here. Morgan told them all. There were tales for each of her relatives as well; indomitable Kleronomas who drove across the sky hunting for knowledge, Celia Marcyan the ever-curious and her ship *Shadow Chaser*, Erika Stormjones whose family cut her up with knives that she might live again, savage Stephen Cobalt Northstar, melancholy Tomo, bright Deirdre d'Allerane and her grim ghostly twin. Those stories Morgan told with magic. There was a place in one wall with a small square slot in it, and Morgan would go there and insert a flat metallic box, and then all the lights would go out and Morgan's dead relatives would live again, bright phantoms who walked and talked and dripped blood when they were hurt. Shawn thought they were real until the day when Deirdre first wept for her slain children, and Shawn ran to comfort her and found they could not touch. It was not until afterward that Morgan told her Deirdre and the others were only spirits, called down by her magic. Morgan told her many things. Morgan was her teacher as well as her lover, and she was nearly as patient as Lane had been, though much more prone to wander and lose interest. She gave Shawn a beautiful twelve-stringed guitar and began to teach her to play it, and she taught her to read a little, and she taught her a few of the simpler magics, so Shawn could move easily around the ship. That was another thing that Morgan taught her; Morganhall was no building after all, but a ship, a sky-ship that could flex its metal legs and leap from star to star. Morgan told her about the planets, lands out by those far-off stars, and said that all the gifts she had given Shawn had come from out there, from beyond the Ice Wagon; the mask and mirror were from Jamison's World, the books and cubes from Avalon, the bracelet from High Kavalaan, the oils from Braque, the spices from Rhiannon and Tara and Old Poseidon, the boots from Bastion, the figurines from Chul Damien, the golden liquor from a land so far away that even Morgan did not know its name. Only the fine glass windwolf had been made here, on Shawn's world, Morgan said. The windwolf had always been one of Shawn's favorites, but now she found she did not like it half so well as she had thought she did. The others were all so much more exciting. Shawn had always wanted to travel, to visit distant families in wild distant climes, to gaze on seas and mountains. But she had been too young, and when she finally reached her womanhood, Creg would not let her go; she was too slow, he said, too timid, too irresponsible. Her life would be spent at home, where she could put her meager talents to better use for Carinhall. Even the fateful trip that had led her here had been a fluke; Lane had insisted, and Lane alone of all the others was strong enough to stand up to Creg, Voice Carin.

Morgan took her traveling, though, on sails between the stars. When blue fire flickered against the icy landscape of deepwinter and the sound rose up out of nowhere, higher and higher, Shawn would rush eagerly to the window, where she would wait with mounting impatience for the colors to clear. Morgan gave her all the mountains and all the seas she could dream of, and more. Through the flawless glass Shawn saw the lands from all the stories; Old Poseidon with its weathered docks and its fleets of silver ships, the meadows of Rhiannon, the vaulting black steel towers of ai-Emerel, High Kavalaan's windswept plains and rugged hills, the island-cities of Port Jamison and Jolostar on Jamison's World. Shawn learned about cities from Morgan, and suddenly the ruins by the river seemed different in her eyes. She learned about other ways of living as well, about arcologies and holdfasts and brotherhoods, about bond-companies and slavery and armies. Family Carin no longer seemed the beginning and the end of human loyalties.

Of all the places they sailed to, they came to Avalon most often, and Shawn learned to love it best. On Avalon the landing field was always full of other wanderers, and Shawn could watch ships come and go on wands of pale blue light. And in the distance she could see the buildings of the Academy of Human Knowledge, where Kleronomas had deposited all his secrets so that they might be held in trust for Morgan's family. Those jagged glass towers filled Shawn with a longing that was almost a hurt, but a hurt that she somehow craved.

Sometimes – on several of the worlds, but most particularly on Avalon – it seemed to Shawn that some stranger was about to board their ship. She would watch them come, striding purposefully across the field, their destination clear from every step. They never came aboard, though, much to her disappointment. There was never anyone to touch or talk to except Morgan. Shawn suspected that Morgan magicked the would-be visitors away, or else lured them to their doom. She could not quite make up her mind which; Morgan was so moody that it might be both. One dinnertime she remembered Jon's story of the cannibal hall, and looked down with horror at the red meat they were eating. She ate only vegetables that meal, and for several meals thereafter until she finally decided that she was being childish. Shawn considered asking Morgan about the strangers who approached and vanished, but she was afraid. She remembered Creg, whose temper was awful if you asked him the wrong question. And if the older woman was really killing those who tried to board her ship, it would not be wise to mention it to her. When Shawn was just a child, Creg had beaten her savagely for asking why old Tesenya had to go outside and die.

Other questions Shawn did ask, only to find that Morgan would not answer. Morgan would not talk about her own origins, or the source of their food, or the magic that flew the ship. Twice Shawn asked to learn the spells that moved them from star to star, and both times Morgan refused with anger in her voice. She had other secrets from Shawn as well. There were rooms that would not open to Shawn, things that she was not allowed to touch, other things that Morgan would not even talk about. From time to time Morgan would disappear for what seemed like days, and Shawn would wander desolately, with nothing outside the window to occupy her but steady unwinking stars. On those occasions Morgan would be somber and secretive when she returned, but only for a few hours, after which she would return to normal.

For Morgan, though, normal was different than for other people.

She would dance about the ship endlessly, singing to herself, sometimes with Shawn as a dancing partner and sometimes alone. She would converse with herself in a musical tongue that Shawn did not know. She would be alternately as serious as a wise old mother, and three times as knowledgeable as a Voice, and as giddy and giggly as a child of one season. Sometimes Morgan seemed to know just who Shawn was, and sometimes she insisted on confusing her with that other Shawn Carin who had loved her during Gathering. She was very patient and very impetuous; she was unlike anyone that Shawn had ever met before. 'You're silly,' Shawn told her once. 'You wouldn't be so silly if you lived in Carinhall. Silly people die, you know, and they hurt their families. Everyone has to be useful, and you're not useful. Creg would make you be useful. You're lucky that you aren't a Carin.'

Morgan had only caressed her, and gazed at her from sad gray eyes. 'Poor Shawn,' she'd whispered. 'They've been so hard to you. But the Carins were always hard. Alynne House was different, child. You should have been born an Alynne.' And after that she would say no more of it.

Shawn squandered her days in wonder and her nights in love, and she thought of Carinhall less and less, and gradually she found that she had come to care for Morgan as if she were family. And more, she had come to trust her.

Until the day she learned about the bitterblooms.

*

Shawn woke up one morning to find that the window was full of stars, and Morgan had vanished. That usually meant a long boring wait, but this time Shawn was still eating the food that Morgan had left out for her when the older woman returned with her hands full of pale blue flowers.

She was so eager; Shawn had never seen her so eager. She made Shawn leave her breakfast half-eaten, and come across the room to the fur rug by the window, so that she could wind the flowers in Shawn's hair. 'I saw while you were sleeping, child,' she said happily as she worked. 'Your hair has grown long. It used to be so short, chopped off and ugly, but you've been here long enough and now it's better, long like mine. The bitterblooms will make it best of all.'

'Bitterblooms?' Shawn asked, curious. 'Is that what you call them? I never knew.'

'Yes, child,' Morgan replied, still fussing and arranging. Shawn had her back to her, so she could not see her face. 'The little blue ones are the bitterblooms. They flower even in the bitterest cold, so that's why they call them that. Originally they came from a world named Ymir, very far off, where they have winters nearly as long and cold as we do. The other flowers are from Ymir too, the ones that grow on the vines around the ship. Those are called frostflowers. Deepwinter is always so bleak, so I planted them to make everything look nicer.' She took Shawn by the shoulder and turned her around. 'You look like me now,' she said. 'Go and get your mirror and see for yourself, Carin child.'

'It's over there,' Shawn answered, and she darted around Morgan to get it. Her bare foot came down in something cold and wet. She flinched from it and made a noise; there was a puddle on the rug.

Shawn frowned. She stood very still and looked at Morgan. The woman had not removed her boots. They dripped.

And behind Morgan, there was nothing to be seen but blackness and unfamiliar stars. Shawn was afraid; something was very wrong. Morgan was looking at her uneasily.

She wet her lips, then smiled shyly, and went to get the mirror.

*

Morgan magicked the stars away before she went to sleep; it was night outside their window, but a gentle night far from the frozen rigor of deepwinter. Leafy trees swayed in the wind on the perimeter of their landing field, and a moon overhead made everything bright and beautiful. A good safe world to sleep on, Morgan said.

Shawn did not sleep. She sat across the room from Morgan, staring at the moon. For the first time since she had come to Morganhall, she was using her mind like a Carin. Lane would have been proud of her; Creg would only have asked what took her so long.

Morgan had returned with a handful of bitterblooms and boots wet with snow. But outside had been nothing, only the emptiness that Morgan said filled the space between the stars.

Morgan said that the light Shawn had seen in the forest had been the fires of her ship as it landed. But the thick vines of the frostflowers grew in and around and over the legs of that ship, and they had been growing for years.

Morgan would not let her go outside. Morgan showed her everything through the great window. But Shawn could not remember seeing any window when she had been *outside* Morganhall. And if the window was a window, where were the vines that should have crept across it, the deepwinter frost that should have covered it?

For the name of the metal hall was Morganhall, Tesenya told the children, and the family who lived there was the family named Liar, whose food is empty stuff made of dreams and air.

Shawn arose in the lie of moonlight and went to where she kept the gifts that Morgan had given her. She looked at them each in turn, and lifted the heaviest of them, the glass windwolf. It was a large sculpture, hefty enough so that Shawn used two hands to lift it, one hand on the creature's snarling snout, the other around its tail. 'Morgan!' she shouted.

Morgan sat up drowsily, and smiled. 'Shawn,' she murmured. 'Shawn child. What are you doing with your windwolf?'

Shawn advanced and lifted the glass animal high above her head. 'You lied to me. We've never gone anywhere. We're still in the ruined city, and it's still deepwinter.'

Morgan's face was somber. 'You don't know what you're saying.' She got shakily to her feet. 'Are you going to hit me with that thing, child? I'm not afraid of it. Once you held a sword on me, and I wasn't afraid of you then, either. I am Morgan, full-of-magic. You cannot hurt me, Shawn.'

'I want to leave,' Shawn said. 'Bring me my blades and my clothing, my old clothing. I'm going back to Carinhall. I am a woman of Carin, not a child. You've made a child of me. Bring me food too.'

Morgan giggled. 'So serious. And if I don't?'

'If you don't,' Shawn said, 'then I'll throw this right through your window.' She hefted the windwolf for emphasis.

'No,' Morgan said. Her expression was unreadable. 'You don't want to do that, child.'

'I *will*,' Shawn said. 'Unless you do as I say.'

'You don't want to leave me, Shawn Carin, no you don't. We're lovers, remember. We're family. I can do magics for you.' Her voice trembled. 'Put that down, child. I'll show you things I never showed you before. There are so many places we can go together, so many stories I can tell you. Put that down.' She was pleading.

Shawn could sense triumph; oddly enough, there were tears in her eyes. 'Why are you so afraid?' she demanded angrily. 'You can fix a broken window with your magic, can't you? Even I can fix a broken window, and Creg says I'm hardly good for anything at all.' The tears were rolling down her naked cheeks now, but silently, silently. 'It's warm outside, you can see that, and there's moonlight to work by, and even a city. You could hire a glazier. I don't see why you are so afraid. It isn't as if it were deepwinter out there, with cold and ice, vampires gliding through the dark. It isn't like that.'

'No,' Morgan said, 'No.'

'No,' Shawn echoed. 'Bring me my things.'

Morgan did not move. 'It wasn't all lies. It wasn't. If you stay with me, you'll live for a long time. I think it's the food, but it's true. A lot of it was true, Shawn. I didn't mean to lie to you. I wanted it to be best, the way it was for me at first. You just have to pretend, you know. Forget that the ship can't move. It's better that way.' Her voice sounded young, frightened; she was a woman, and she begged like a little girl, in a little girl's voice. 'Don't break the window. The window is the most magic thing. It can take us anywhere, almost. Please, *please*, don't break it, Shawn. Don't.'

Morgan was shaking. The fluttering rags she wore seemed faded and shabby suddenly, and her rings did not sparkle. She was just a crazy old woman. Shawn lowered the heavy glass windowlf. 'I want my clothing, and my sword, and my skis. And food. Lots and lots of food. Bring it to me and maybe I won't break your window, liar. Do you hear me?'

And Morgan, no longer full of magic, nodded and did as she was told. Shawn watched her in silence. They never spoke again.

*

Shawn returned to Carinhall and grew old.

Her return was a sensation. She had been missing for more than a standard year, she discovered, and everyone had presumed that both she and Lane were dead. Creg refused to believe her story at first, and the others followed his lead, until Shawn produced a handful of bitterblooms that she had picked from her hair. Even then, Creg could not accept the more fanciful parts of her tale. 'Illusions,' he snorted, 'every bit of it illusion. Tesenya told it true. If you went back, your magic ship would be gone, with no sign that it had ever been there. Believe me, Shawn.' But it was never clear to her whether Creg truly believed himself. He issued orders, and no man or woman of family Carin ever went that way again.

Things were different at Carinhall after Shawn's return. The family was smaller. Lane's was not the only face she missed at the meal table. Food had grown very short while she had been away, and Creg, as was the custom, had sent the weakest and most useless out to die. Jon was among the missing. Leila was gone too, Leila who had been so young and strong. A vampire had taken her three months ago. But not everything was sadness. Deepwinter was ending. And, on a more personal level, Shawn found that her position in the family had changed. Now even Creg treated her with a rough respect. A year later, when thaw was well under way, she bore her first child, and was accepted as an equal into the councils of Carinhall. Shawn named her daughter Lane.

She settled easily into family life. When it was time for her to choose a permanent profession, she asked to be a trader, and was surprised to find that Creg did not speak against her choice. Rys took her as apprentice, and after three years she got an assignment of her own. Her work kept her on the road a great deal. When she was home in Carinhall, however, Shawn found to her surprise that she had become the favored family storyteller. The children said she knew the best stories of anyone. Creg, ever practical, said that her fancies set a bad example for the children and had no proper lesson to them. But by that time he was very sick, a victim of highsummer fever, and his opposition carried little weight. He died soon after, and Devin became Voice, a gentler and more moderate Voice than Creg. Family Carin had a generation of peace while he spoke for Carinhall, and their numbers increased from forty to nearly one hundred.

Shawn was frequently his lover. Her reading had improved a great deal by then, through long study, and Devin once yielded to her whim and showed her the secret library of the Voices, where each Voice for untold centuries had kept a journal detailing the events of his service. As Shawn had suspected, one of the thicker volumes was called *The Book of Beth, Voice Carin*. It was about sixty years old.

Lane was the first of nine children for Shawn. She was lucky. Six of them lived, two fathered by family and four that she brought back with her from Gathering. Devin honored her for bringing so much fresh blood into Carinhall, and later another Voice would name her for exceptional prowess as a trader. She traveled widely, met many families, saw waterfalls and volcanoes as well as seas and mountains, sailed halfway around the world on a Crien schooner. She had many lovers and much esteem. Jannis followed Devin as Voice, but she had a bitter unhappy time of it, and when she passed, the mothers and fathers of family Carin offered the position to Shawn. She turned it down. It would not have made her happy. Despite everything she had done, she was not a happy person.

She remembered too much, and sometimes she could not sleep very well at night.

During the fourth deepwinter of her life, the family numbered two hundred and thirty-seven, fully a hundred of them children. But game was scarce, even in the third year after freeze, and Shawn could see the hard cold times approaching. The Voice was a kind woman who found it hard to make the decisions that had to be made, but Shawn knew what was coming. She was the second eldest of those in Carinhall. One night she stole some food – just enough, two weeks' traveling supply – and a pair of skis, left Carinhall at dawn, and spared the Voice the giving of the order.

She was not so fast as she had been when she was young. The journey took closer to three weeks than to two, and she was lean and weak when she finally entered the ruined city.

But the ship was just as she had left it.

Extremes of heat and cold had cracked the stone of the spacefield over the years, and the alien flowers had taken advantage of every little opening. The stone was dotted with bitterblooms, and the frostflower vines that twined around the ship were twice as thick as Shawn remembered them. The big brightly colored blossoms stirred faintly in the wind.

Nothing else moved.

She circled the ship three times, waiting for a door to open, waiting for someone to see her and appear. But if the metal noticed her presence, it gave no sign. On the far side of the ship Shawn found something she hadn't seen before – writing, faded but still legible, obscured only by ice and flowers. She used her longknife to shatter the ice and cut the vines, so she might read. It said:

MORGAN LE FAY
Registry: Avalon 476 3319

Shawn smiled. So even her name had been a lie. Well, it did not matter now. She cupped her gloved hands together over her mouth. 'Morgan,' she shouted. 'It's Shawn.' The wind whipped her words away from her. 'Let me in, Morgan. Lie to me, Morgan full-of-magic. I'm sorry. Lie to me and make me believe.'

There was no answer. Shawn dug herself a hollow in the snow, and sat down to wait. She was tired and hungry, and dusk was close at hand. Already she could see the driver's ice blue eyes staring through the wispy clouds of twilight.

When at last she slept, she dreamt of Avalon.

The Way of Cross and Dragon

'**H**eresy,' he told me. The brackish waters of his pool sloshed gently.
'Another one?' I said wearily. 'There are so many these days.'

My Lord Commander was displeased by that comment. He shifted position heavily, sending ripples up and down the pool. One broke over the side, and a sheet of water slid across the tiles of the receiving chamber. My boots were soaked yet again. I accepted that philosophically. I had worn my worst boots, well aware that wet feet are among the inescapable consequences of paying a call on Torgathon Nine-Klariis Tuñ, elder of the ka-Thane people, and also Archbishop of Vess, Most Holy Father of the Four Vows, Grand Inquisitor of the Order Militant of the Knights of Jesus Christ, and counselor to His Holiness, Pope Daryn XXI of New Rome.

'Be there as many heresies as stars in the sky, each single one is no less dangerous, Father,' the Archbishop said solemnly. 'As Knights of Christ, it is our ordained task to fight them one and all. And I must add that this new heresy is particularly foul.'

'Yes, my Lord Commander,' I replied. 'I did not intend to make light of it. You have my apologies. The mission to Finnegan was most taxing. I had hoped to ask you for a leave of absence from my duties. I need rest, a time for thought and restoration.'

'Rest?' The Archbishop moved again in his pool; only a slight shift of his immense bulk, but it was enough to send a fresh sheet of water across the floor. His black, pupilless eyes blinked at me. 'No, Father, I am afraid that is out of the question. Your skills and your experience are vital to this new mission.' His bass tones seemed then to soften somewhat. 'I have not had time to go over your reports on Finnegan,' he said. 'How did your work go?'

'Badly,' I told him, 'though I think that ultimately we will prevail. The Church is strong on Finnegan. When our attempts at reconciliation were rebuffed, I put some standards into the right hands, and we were able to shut down the heretics' newspaper and broadcast facilities. Our friends also saw to it that their legal actions came to nothing.'

'That is not *badly*,' the Archbishop said. 'You won a considerable victory for the Lord.'

'There were riots, my Lord Commander,' I said. 'More than a hundred of the heretics were killed, and a dozen of our own people. I fear there will be more violence before the matter is finished. Our priests are attacked if they so much as enter the city where the heresy has taken root. Their leaders risk their lives if they leave that city. I had hoped to avoid such hatreds, such bloodshed.'

'Commendable, but not realistic,' said Archbishop Torgathon. He blinked at me again, and I remembered that among people of his race, that was a sign of impatience. 'The blood of martyrs must sometimes be spilled, and the blood of heretics as well. What matters it if a being surrenders his life, so long as his soul is saved?'

'Indeed,' I agreed. Despite his impatience, Torgathon would lecture me for another hour if given a chance. That prospect dismayed me. The receiving chamber was not designed for human comfort, and I did not wish to remain any longer than necessary. The walls were damp and moldy, the air hot and humid and thick with the rancid-butter smell characteristic of the ka-Thane. My collar was chafing my neck raw, I was sweating beneath my cassock, my feet were thoroughly soaked, and my stomach was beginning to churn. I pushed ahead to the business at hand. 'You say this new heresy is unusually foul, my Lord Commander?'

'It is,' he said.

'Where has it started?'

'On Arion, a world some three weeks' distance from Vess. A human world entirely. I cannot understand why you humans are so easily corrupted. Once a ka-Thane has found the faith, he would scarcely abandon it.'

'That is well known,' I said politely. I did not mention that the number of ka-Thane to find the faith was vanishingly small. They were a slow, ponderous people, and most of their vast millions showed no interest in learning any ways other than their own, nor in following any creed but their own ancient religion. Torgathon Nine-Klariis Tuñ was an anomaly. He had been among the first converts almost two centuries ago, when Pope Vidas L had ruled that nonhumans might serve as clergy. Given his great lifespan and the iron certainty of his belief, it was no wonder that Torgathon had risen as far as he had, despite the fact that less than a thousand of his race had followed him into the Church. He had at least a century of life remaining to him. No doubt he would someday be Torgathon Cardinal Tuñ, should he squelch enough heresies. The times are like that.

'We have little influence on Arion,' the Archbishop was saying. His arms moved as he spoke, four ponderous clubs of mottled green-gray flesh churning the water, and the dirty white cilia around his breathing hole trembled with each word. 'A few priests, a few churches, and some believers, but no power to speak of. The heretics already out-number us on this world. I rely on your intellect, your shrewdness. Turn this calamity into an opportunity. This heresy is so spurious that you can easily disprove it. Perhaps some of the deluded will turn to the true way.'

'Certainly,' I said. 'And the nature of this heresy? What must I disprove?' It is a sad indication of my own troubled faith to add that I did not really care. I have dealt with too many heretics. Their beliefs and their questionings echo in my head and trouble my dreams at night. How can I be sure of my own faith? The very edict that had admitted Torgathon into the clergy had caused a half-dozen worlds to repudiate the Bishop of New Rome, and those who had followed that path would find a particularly ugly heresy in the massive naked (save for a damp Roman collar) alien who floated before me, and wielded the authority of the Church in four great webbed hands. Christianity is the greatest single human religion, but that means little. The non-Christians out-number us five-to-one, and there are well over seven hundred Christian sects, some almost as large as the One True Interstellar Catholic Church of Earth and the Thousand Worlds. Even Daryn XXI, powerful as he is, is only one of seven to claim the title of Pope. My own belief was once strong, but I have moved too long among heretics and nonbelievers. Now, even my prayers do not make the doubts go away. So it was that I felt no horror – only a sudden intellectual interest – when the Archbishop told me the nature of the heresy on Arion.

'They have made a saint,' he said, 'out of Judas Iscariot.'

*

As a senior in the Knights Inquisitor, I command my own starship, which it pleases me to call the *Truth of Christ*. Before the craft was assigned to me, it was named the *Saint Thomas*, after the apostle, but I did not consider a saint notorious for doubting to be an appropriate patron for a ship enlisted in the fight against heresy.

I have no duties aboard the *Truth*, which is crewed by six brothers and sisters of the Order of Saint Christopher the Far-Traveling, and captained by a young woman I hired away from a merchant trader. I was therefore able to devote the entire three-week voyage from Vess to Arion to a study of the heretical Bible, a copy of which had been given to me by the Archbishop's administrative assistant. It was a thick, heavy, handsome book, bound in dark leather, its pages tipped with gold leaf, with many splendid interior illustrations in full color with holographic enhancement. Remarkable work, clearly done by someone who loved the all-but-forgotten art of bookmaking. The paintings reproduced inside – the originals, I gathered, were to be found on the walls of the House of Saint

Judas on Arion – were masterful, if blasphemous, as much high art as the Tammerwens and RoHallidays that adorn the Great Cathedral of Saint John on New Rome.

Inside, the book bore an imprimatur indicating that it had been approved by Lukyan Judasson, First Scholar of the Order of Saint Judas Iscariot.

It was called *The Way of Cross and Dragon*.

I read it as the *Truth of Christ* slid between the stars, at first taking copious notes to better understand the heresy I must fight, but later simply absorbed by the strange, convoluted, grotesque story it told. The words of text had passion and power and poetry.

Thus it was that I first encountered the striking figure of Saint Judas Iscariot, a complex, ambitious, contradictory, and altogether extraordinary human being.

He was born of a whore in the fabled ancient city-state of Babylon on the same day that the savior was born in Bethlehem, and he spent his childhood in the alleys and gutters, selling his own body when he had to, pimping when he was older. As a youth he began to experiment with the dark arts, and before the age of twenty he was a skilled necromancer. That was when he became Judas the Dragon-Tamer, the first and only man to bend to his will the most fearsome of God's creatures, the great winged fire-lizards of Old Earth. The book held a marvelous painting of Judas in some great dank cavern, his eyes aflame as he wields a glowing lash to keep a mountainous green-gold dragon at bay. Beneath his arm is a woven basket, its lid slightly ajar, and the tiny scaled heads of three dragon chicks are peering from within. A fourth infant dragon is crawling up his sleeve. That was in the first chapter of his life.

In the second, he was Judas the Conqueror, Judas the Dragon-King, Judas of Babylon, the Great Usurper. Astride the greatest of his dragons, with an iron crown on his head and a sword in his hand, he made Babylon the capital of the greatest empire Old Earth had ever known, a realm that stretched from Spain to India. He reigned from a dragon throne amid the Hanging Gardens he had caused to be constructed, and it was there he sat when he tried Jesus of Nazareth, the troublemaking prophet who had been dragged before him bound and bleeding. Judas was not a patient man, and he made Christ bleed still more before he was through with Him. And when Jesus would not answer his questions, Judas contemptuously had Him cast back out into the streets. But first, he ordered his guards to cut off Christ's legs. 'Healer,' he said, 'heal thyself.'

Then came the Repentance, the vision in the night, and Judas Iscariot gave up his crown, his dark arts, and his riches to follow the man he had crippled. Despised and taunted by those he had tyrannized, Judas became the Legs of the Lord, and for a year carried Jesus on his back to the far corners of the realm he once ruled. When Jesus did finally heal Himself, then Judas walked at His side, and from that time forth he was Jesus' trusted friend and counselor, the first and foremost of the Twelve. Finally, Jesus gave Judas the gift of tongues, recalled and sanctified the dragons that Judas had sent away, and sent His disciple forth on a solitary ministry across the oceans, 'to spread My Word where I cannot go.'

There came a day when the sun went dark at noon and the ground trembled, and Judas swung his dragon around on ponderous wings and flew back across the raging seas. But when he reached the city of Jerusalem, he found Christ dead on the cross.

In that moment his faith faltered, and for the next three days the Great Wrath of Judas was like a storm across the ancient world. His dragons razed the Temple in Jerusalem, drove the people forth from the city, and struck as well at the great seats of power in Rome and Babylon. And when he found the others of the Twelve and questioned them and learned of how the one named Simon-called-Peter had three times betrayed the Lord, he strangled Peter with his own hands and fed the corpse to his dragons. Then he sent those dragons forth to start fires throughout the world, funeral pyres for Jesus of Nazareth.

And Jesus rose on the third day, and Judas wept, but his tears could not turn Christ's anger, for in his wrath he had betrayed all of Christ's teachings.

So Jesus called back the dragons, and they came, and everywhere the fires went out. And from their bellies He called forth Peter and made him whole again, and gave him dominion over the Church.

Then the dragons died, and so too did all dragons everywhere, for they were the living sigil of the power and wisdom of Judas Iscariot, who had sinned greatly. And He took from Judas the gift of tongues and the power of healing He had given, and even his eyesight, for Judas had acted as a blind man (there was a fine painting of the blinded Judas weeping over the bodies of his dragons). And He told Judas that for long ages he would be remembered only as Betrayer, and people would curse his name, and all that he had been and done would be forgotten.

But then, because Judas had loved Him so, Christ gave him a boon: an extended life, during which he might travel and think on his sins and finally come to forgiveness. Only then might he die.

And that was the beginning of the last chapter in the life of Judas Iscariot. But it was a very long chapter indeed. Once dragon-king, once the friend of Christ, now he was only a blind traveler, outcast and friendless, wandering all the cold roads of the Earth, living still when all the cities and people and things he had known were dead. Peter, the first Pope and ever his enemy, spread far and wide the tale of how Judas had sold Christ for thirty pieces of silver, until Judas dared not even use his true name. For a time he called himself just Wandering Ju', and afterward many other names. He lived more than a thousand years and became a preacher, a healer, and a lover of animals, and was hunted and persecuted when the Church that Peter had founded became bloated and corrupt. But he had a great deal of time, and at last he found wisdom and a sense of peace, and finally, Jesus came to him on a long-postponed deathbed and they were reconciled, and Judas wept once again. Before he died, Christ promised that he would permit a few to remember who and what Judas had been, and that with the passage of centuries the news would spread, until finally Peter's Lie was displaced and forgotten.

Such was the life of Saint Judas Iscariot, as related in *The Way of Cross and Dragon*. His teachings were there as well, and the apocryphal books he had allegedly written.

When I had finished the volume, I lent it to Arla-k-Bau, the captain of the *Truth of Christ*. Arla was a gaunt, pragmatic woman of no particular faith, but I valued her opinion. The others of my crew, the good sisters and brothers of Saint Christopher, would only have echoed the Archbishop's religious horror.

'Interesting,' Arla said when she returned the book to me.

I chuckled. 'Is that all?'

She shrugged. 'It makes a nice story. An easier read than your Bible, Damien, and more dramatic as well.'

'True,' I admitted. 'But it's absurd. An unbelievable tangle of doctrine, apocrypha, mythology, and superstition. Entertaining, yes, certainly. Imaginative, even daring. But ridiculous, don't you think? How can you credit dragons? A legless Christ? Peter being pieced together after being devoured by four monsters?'

Arla's grin was taunting. 'Is that any sillier than water changing into wine, or Christ walking on the waves, or a man living in the belly of a fish?' Arla-k-Bau liked to jab at me. It had been a scandal when I selected a nonbeliever as my captain, but she was very good at her job and I liked her around to keep me sharp. She had a good mind, Arla did, and I valued that more than blind obedience. Perhaps that was a sin in me.

'There is a difference,' I said.

'Is there?' she snapped back. Her eyes saw through any mask 'Ah, Damien, admit it. You rather liked this book.'

I cleared my throat. 'It piqued my interest,' I acknowledged. I had to justify myself. 'You know the kind of matter I deal with ordinarily. Dreary little doctrinal deviations; obscure quibblings on theology somehow blown all out of proportion; bald-faced political maneuverings designed to set some ambitious planetary bishop up as a new pope, or wrest some concession or other from New Rome or Vess. The war is endless, but the battles are dull and dirty. They exhaust me spiritually, emotionally, physically. Afterward I feel drained and guilty.' I tapped the book's leather cover. 'This is different. The heresy must be crushed of course, but I admit that I am anxious to meet this Lukyan Judasson.'

'The artwork is lovely as well,' Arla said, flipping through the pages of *The Way of Cross and Dragon* and stopping to study one especially striking plate – Judas weeping over his dragons, I think. I smiled to see that it had affected her as much as me. Then I frowned.

That was the first inkling I had of the difficulties ahead.

*

So it was that the *Truth of Christ* came to the porcelain city Ammadon on the world of Arion, where the Order of Saint Judas Iscariot kept its House.

Arion was a pleasant, gentle world, inhabited for these past three centuries. Its population was under nine million; Ammadon, the only real city, was home to two of those millions. The technological level was medium high, but chiefly imported. Arion had little industry and was not an innovative world, except perhaps artistically. The arts were quite important here, flourishing and vital. Religious freedom was a basic tenet of the society, but Arion was not a religious world either, and the majority of the populace lived devoutly secular lives. The most popular religion was Aestheticism, which hardly counts as a religion at all. There were also Taoists, Erikaners, Old True Christers, and Children of the Dreamer, plus adherents of a dozen lesser sects.

And finally there were nine churches of the One True Interstellar Catholic faith. There had been twelve. The other three were now houses of Arion's fastest-growing faith, the Order of Saint Judas Iscariot, which also had a dozen newly built churches of its own.

The Bishop of Arion was a dark, severe man with close-cropped black hair who was not at all happy to see me. 'Damien Har Veris!' he exclaimed with some wonderment when I called on him at his residence. 'We have heard of you, of course, but I never thought to meet or host you. Our numbers here are small.'

'And growing smaller,' I said, 'a matter of some concern to my Lord Commander, Archbishop Torgathon. Apparently you are less troubled, Excellency, since you did not see fit to report the activities of this sect of Judas worshippers.'

He looked briefly angry at the rebuke, but quickly swallowed his temper. Even a bishop can fear a Knight Inquisitor. 'We are concerned, of course,' he said. 'We do all we can to combat the heresy. If you have advice that will help us, I will be glad to listen.'

'I am an Inquisitor of the Order Militant of the Knights of Jesus Christ,' I said bluntly. 'I do not give advice, Excellency. I take action. To that end I was sent to Arion, and that is what I shall do. Now, tell me what you know about this heresy, and this First Scholar, this Lukyan Judasson.'

'Of course, Father Damien,' the Bishop began. He signaled for a servant to bring us a tray of wine and cheese, and began to summarize the short but explosive history of the Judas cult. I listened, polishing my nails on the crimson lapel of my jacket until the black paint gleamed brilliantly, interrupting from time to time with a question. Before he had half finished, I was determined to visit Lukyan personally. It seemed the best course of action.

And I had wanted to do so all along.

*

Appearances were important on Arion, I gathered, and I deemed it necessary to impress Lukyan with myself and my station. I wore my best boots – sleek, dark handmade boots of Roman leather that had never seen the inside of Torgathon's receiving chamber – and a severe black suit with deep burgundy lapels and stiff collar. Around my neck was a splendid crucifix of pure gold; my collarpin was a matching golden sword, the sigil of the Knights Inquisitor. Brother Denis carefully painted my nails, all black as ebon, and darkened my eyes as well, and used a fine white powder on my face. When I glanced in the mirror, I frightened even myself. I smiled, but only briefly. It ruined the effect.

I walked to the House of Saint Judas Iscariot. The streets of Ammadon were wide and spacious and golden, lined by scarlet trees called whisperwinds whose long, drooping tendrils did indeed seem to whisper secrets to the gentle breeze. Sister Judith came with me. She is a small woman, slight of build even in the cowled coveralls of the Order of Saint Christopher. Her face is meek and kind, her eyes wide and youthful and innocent. I find her useful. Four times now she has killed those who attempted to assault me.

The House itself was newly built. Rambling and stately, it rose from amid gardens of small bright flowers and seas of golden grass; the gardens were surrounded by a high wall. Murals covered both the outer wall around the property and the exterior of the building itself. I recognized a few of them from *The Way of Cross and Dragon*, and stopped briefly to admire them before walking through the main gate. No one tried to stop us. There were no guards, not even a receptionist. Within the walls, men and women strolled languidly through the flowers, or sat on benches beneath silverwoods and whisperwinds.

Sister Judith and I paused, then made our way directly to the House itself.

We had just started up the steps when a man appeared from within, and stood waiting in the doorway. He was blond and fat, with a great wiry beard that framed a slow smile, and he wore a flimsy robe that fell to his sandaled feet. On the robe were dragons, dragons bearing the silhouette of a man holding a cross.

When I reached the top of the steps, he bowed to me. 'Father Damien Har Veris of the Knights Inquisitor,' he said. His smile widened. 'I greet you in the name of Jesus, and in the name of Saint Judas. I am Lukyan.'

I made a note to myself to find out which of the Bishop's staff was feeding information to the Judas cult, but my composure did not break. I have been a Knight Inquisitor for a long, long time. 'Father Lukyan Mo,' I said, taking his hand. 'I have questions to ask of you.' I did not smile.

He did. 'I thought you might,' he said.

*

Lukyan's office was large but spartan. Heretics often have a simplicity that the officers of the true Church seem to have lost. He did have one indulgence, however. Dominating the wall behind his desk console was the painting I had already fallen in love with: the blinded Judas weeping over his dragons.

Lukyan sat down heavily and motioned me to a second chair. We had left Sister Judith outside in the waiting chamber. 'I prefer to stand, Father Lukyan,' I said, knowing it gave me an advantage.

'Just Lukyan,' he said. 'Or Luke, if you prefer. We have little use for hierarchy here.'

'You are Father Lukyan Mo, born here on Arion, educated in the seminary on Cathaday, a former priest of the One True Interstellar Catholic Church of Earth and the Thousand Worlds,' I said. 'I will address you as befits your station, Father. I expect you to reciprocate. Is that understood?'

'Oh, yes,' he said amiably.

'I am empowered to strip you of your right to perform the sacraments, to order you shunned and excommunicated for this heresy you have formulated. On certain worlds I could even order your death.'

'But not on Arion,' Lukyan said quickly. 'We're very tolerant here. Besides, we outnumber you.' He smiled. 'As for the rest, well, I don't perform those sacraments much anyway, you know. Not for years. I'm First Scholar now. A teacher, a thinker. I show others the way, help them find the faith. Excommunicate me if it will make you happy, Father Damien. Happiness is what all of us seek.'

'You have given up the faith then, Father Lukyan,' I said. I deposited my copy of *The Way of Cross and Dragon* on his desk. 'But I see you have found a new one.' Now I did smile, but it was all ice, all menace, all mockery. 'A more ridiculous creed I have yet to encounter. I suppose you will tell me that you have spoken to God, that he trusted you with this new revelation, so that you might clear the good name, such that it is, of Holy Judas?'

Now Lukyan's smile was very broad indeed. He picked up the book and beamed at me. 'Oh, no,' he said. 'No, I made it all up.'

That stopped me. 'What?'

'I made it all up,' he repeated. He hefted the book fondly. 'I drew on many sources, of course, especially the Bible, but I do think of *Cross and Dragon* as mostly my own work. It's rather good, don't you agree? Of course, I could hardly put my name on it, proud as I am of it, but I did include my imprimatur. Did you notice that? It was the closest I dared come to a byline.'

I was speechless only for a moment. Then I grimaced. 'You startle me,' I admitted. 'I expected to find an inventive madman, some poor self-deluded fool, firm in his belief that he had spoken to God. I've dealt with such fanatics before. Instead I find a cheerful cynic who has invented a religion for his own profit. I think I prefer the fanatics. You are beneath contempt, Father Lukyan. You will burn in hell for eternity.'

'I doubt it,' Lukyan said, 'but you do mistake me, Father Damien. I am no cynic, nor do I profit from my dear Saint Judas. Truthfully, I lived more comfortably as a priest of your own Church. I do this because it is my vocation.'

I sat down. 'You confuse me,' I said. 'Explain.'

'Now I am going to tell you the truth,' he said. He said it in an odd way, almost as a chant. 'I am a Liar,' he added.

'You want to confuse me with a child's paradoxes,' I snapped.

'No, no,' he smiled. 'A *Liar*. With a capital. It is an organization, Father Damien. A religion, you might call it. A great and powerful faith. And I am the smallest part of it.'

'I know of no such church,' I said.

'Oh, no, you wouldn't. It's secret. It has to be. You can understand that, can't you? People don't like being lied to.'

'I do not like being lied to,' I said.

Lukyan looked wounded. 'I told you this would be the truth, didn't I? When a Liar says that, you can believe him. How else could we trust each other?'

'There are many of you?' I asked. I was starting to think that Lukyan was a madman after all, as fanatical as any heretic, but in a more complex way. Here was a heresy within a heresy, but I recognized my duty: to find the truth of things, and set them right.

'Many of us,' Lukyan said, smiling. 'You would be surprised, Father Damien, really you would. But there are some things I dare not tell you.'

'Tell me what you dare, then.'

'Happily,' said Lukyan Judasson. 'We Liars, like those of all other religions, have several truths we take on faith. Faith is always required. There are some things that cannot be proven. We believe that life is worth living. That is an article of faith. The purpose of life is to live, to resist death, perhaps to defy entropy.'

'Go on,' I said, interested despite myself.

'We also believe that happiness is a good, something to be sought after.'

'The Church does not oppose happiness,' I said drily.

'I wonder,' Lukyan said. 'But let us not quibble. Whatever the Church's position on happiness, it does preach belief in an afterlife, in a supreme being and a complex moral code.'

'True.'

'The Liars believe in no afterlife, no God. We see the universe as it *is*, Father Damien, and these naked truths are cruel ones. We who believe in life, and treasure it, will die. Afterward there will be nothing, eternal emptiness, blackness, nonexistence. In our living there has been no purpose, no poetry, no meaning. Nor do our deaths possess these qualities. When we are gone, the universe will not long remember us, and shortly it will be as if we had never lived at all. Our worlds and our universe will not long outlive us. Ultimately, entropy will consume all, and our puny efforts cannot stay that awful end. It will be gone. It has never been. It has never mattered. The universe itself is doomed, transient, uncaring.'

I slid back in my chair, and a shiver went through me as I listened to poor Lukyan's dark words. I found myself fingering my crucifix. 'A bleak philosophy,' I said, 'as well as a false one. I have had that fearful vision myself. I think all of us do, at some point. But it is not so, Father. My faith sustains me against such nihilism. It is a shield against despair.'

'Oh, I know that, my friend, my Knight Inquisitor,' Lukyan said. 'I'm glad to see you understand so well. You are almost one of us already.'

I frowned.

'You've touched the heart of it,' Lukyan continued. 'The truths, the great truths – and most of the lesser ones as well – they are unbearable for most men. We find our shield in faith. Your faith, my faith, any faith. It doesn't matter, so long as we *believe*, really and truly believe, in whatever lie we cling to.' He fingered the ragged edges of his great blond beard. 'Our psychs have always told us that believers are the happy ones, you know.

They may believe in Christ or Buddha or Erika Stormjones, in reincarnation or immortality or nature, in the power of love or the platform of a political faction, but it all comes to the same thing. They believe. They are happy. It is the ones who have seen truth who despair, and kill themselves. The truths are so vast, the faiths so little, so poorly made, so riddled with error and contradiction that we see around them and through them, and then we feel the weight of darkness upon us, and can no longer be happy.'

I am not a slow man. I knew, by then, where Lukyan Judasson was going. 'Your Liars invent faiths.'

He smiled. 'Of all sorts. Not only religious. Think of it. We know truth for the cruel instrument it is. Beauty is infinitely preferable to truth. We invent beauty. Faiths, political movements, high ideals, belief in love and fellowship. All of them are lies. We tell those lies, among others, endless others. We improve on history and myth and religion, make each more beautiful, better, easier to believe in. Our lies are not perfect, of course. The truths are too big. But perhaps someday we will find one great lie that all humanity can use. Until then, a thousand small lies will do.'

'I think I do not care for your Liars very much,' I said with a cold, even fervor. 'My whole life has been a quest for truth.'

Lukyan was indulgent. 'Father Damien Har Veris, Knight Inquisitor, I know you better than that. You are a Liar yourself. You do good work. You ship from world to world, and on each you destroy the foolish, the rebels, the questioners who would bring down the edifice of the vast lie that you serve.'

'If my lie is so admirable,' I said, 'then why have you abandoned it?'

'A religion must fit its culture and society, work with them, not against them. If there is conflict, contradiction, then the lie breaks down, and the faith falters. Your Church is good for many worlds, Father, but not for Arion. Life is too kind here, and your faith is stern. Here we love beauty, and your faith offers too little. So we have improved it. We studied this world for a long time. We know its psychological profile. Saint Judas will thrive here. He offers drama, and color, and much beauty – the aesthetics are admirable. His is a tragedy with a happy ending, and Arion dotes on such stories. And the dragons are a nice touch. I think your own Church ought to find a way to work in dragons. They are marvelous creatures.'

'Mythical,' I said.

'Hardly,' he replied. 'Look it up.' He grinned at me. 'You see, really, it all comes back to faith. Can you really know what happened three thousand years ago? You have one Judas, I have another. Both of us have books. Is yours true? Can you really believe that? I have been admitted only to the first circle of the order of Liars, so I do not know all our secrets, but I know that we are very old. It would not surprise me to learn that the gospels were written by men very much like me. Perhaps there never was a Judas at all. Or a Jesus.'

'I have faith that that is not so,' I said.

'There are a hundred people in this building who have a deep and very real faith in Saint Judas, and the way of cross and dragon,' Lukyan said. 'Faith is a very good thing. Do you know that the suicide rate on Arion has decreased by almost a third since the Order of Saint Judas was founded?'

I remember rising slowly from my chair. 'You are as fanatical as any heretic I have ever met, Lukyan Judasson,' I told him. 'I pity you the loss of your faith.'

Lukyan rose with me. 'Pity yourself, Damien Har Veris,' he said. 'I have found a new faith and a new cause, and I am a happy man. You, my dear friend, are tortured and miserable.'

'*That is a lie!*' I am afraid I screamed.

'Come with me,' Lukyan said. He touched a panel on his wall, and the great painting of Judas weeping over his dragons slid up out of sight. There was a stairway leading down into the ground. 'Follow me,' he said.

In the cellar was a great glass vat full of pale green fluid, and in it a thing was floating, a thing very like an ancient embryo, aged and infantile at the same time, naked, with a huge head and a tiny atrophied body. Tubes ran from its arms and legs and genitals, connecting it to the machinery that kept it alive.

When Lukyan turned on the lights, it opened its eyes. They were large and dark and they looked into my soul.

'This is my colleague,' Lukyan said, patting the side of the vat, 'Jon Azure Cross, a Liar of the fourth circle.'

'And a telepath,' I said with a sick certainty. I had led pogroms against other telepaths, children mostly, on other worlds. The Church teaches that the psionic powers are one of Satan's traps. They are not mentioned in the Bible. I have never felt good about those killings.

'The moment you entered the compound, Jon read you and notified me,' Lukyan said. 'Only a few of us know that he is here. He helps us lie most efficiently. He knows when faith is true, and when it is feigned. I have an implant in my skull. Jon can talk to me at all times. It was he who initially recruited me into the Liars. He knew my faith was hollow. He felt the depth of my despair.'

Then the thing in the tank spoke, its metallic voice coming from a speaker-grille in the base of the machine that nurtured it. '*And I feel yours, Damien Har Veris, empty priest. Inquisitor, you have asked too many questions. You are sick at heart, and tired, and you do not believe. Join us, Damien. You have been a Liar for a long, long time!*'

For a moment I hesitated, looking deep into myself, wondering what it was I *did* believe. I searched for my faith – the fire that had once sustained me, the certainty in the teachings of the Church, the presence of Christ within me. I found none of it, none. I was empty inside, burned out, full of questions and pain. But as I was about to answer Jon Azure Cross and the smiling Lukyan Judasson, I found something else, something I *did* believe in, had always believed in.

Truth.

I believed in truth, even when it hurt.

'*He is lost to us,*' said the telepath with the mocking name of Cross.

Lukyan's smile faded. 'Oh, really? I had hoped you would be one of us, Damien. You seemed ready.'

I was suddenly afraid, and I considered sprinting up the stairs to Sister Judith. Lukyan had told me so very much, and now I had rejected them.

The telepath felt my fear. '*You cannot hurt us, Damien,*' it said. '*Go in peace. Lukyan has told you nothing.*'

Lukyan was frowning. 'I told him a good deal, Jon,' he said.

'*Yes. But can he trust the words of such a Liar as you?*' The small misshapen mouth of the thing in the vat twitched in a smile, and its great eyes closed, and Lukyan Judasson sighed and led me up the stairs.

*

It was not until some years later that I realized it was Jon Azure Cross who was lying, and the victim of his lie was Lukyan. I *could* hurt them. I did.

It was almost simple. The Bishop had friends in government and media. With some money in the right places, I made some friends of my own. Then I exposed Cross in his cellar, charging that he had used his psionic powers to tamper with the minds of Lukyan's followers. My friends were receptive to the charges. The guardians conducted a raid, took the telepath Cross into custody, and later tried him.

He was innocent, of course. My charge was nonsense; human telepaths can read minds in close proximity, but seldom anything more. But they are rare, and much feared, and Cross was hideous enough so that it was easy to make him a victim of superstition. In the end, he was acquitted, but he left the city Ammadon and perhaps Arion itself, bound for regions unknown.

But it had never been my intention to convict him. The charge was enough. The cracks began to show in the lie that he and Lukyan had built together. Faith is hard to come by, and easy to lose. The merest doubt can begin to erode even the strongest foundation of belief.

The Bishop and I labored together to sow further doubts. It was not as easy as I might have thought. The Liars had done their work well.

Ammadon, like most civilized cities, had a great pool of knowledge, a computer system that linked the schools and universities and libraries together, and made their combined wisdom available to any who needed it.

But when I checked, I soon discovered that the histories of Rome and Babylon had been subtly reshaped, and there were three listings for Judas Iscariot – one for the betrayer, one for the saint, and one for the conqueror-king of Babylon. His name was also mentioned in connection with the Hanging Gardens, and there is an entry for a so-called 'Codex Judas.'

And according to the Ammadon library, dragons became extinct on Old Earth around the time of Christ.

We finally purged all those lies, wiped them from the memories of the computers, though we had to cite authorities on a half-dozen non-Christian worlds before the librarians and academics would credit that the differences were anything more than a question of religious preference. By then the Order of Saint Judas had withered in the glare of exposure. Lukyan Judasson had grown gaunt and angry, and at least half of his churches had closed.

The heresy never died completely, of course. There are always those who believe no matter what. And so to this day *The Way of Cross and Dragon* is read on Arion, in the porcelain city Ammadon, amid murmuring whisperwinds.

Arla-k-Bau and the *Truth of Christ* carried me back to Vess a year after my departure, and Archbishop Torgathon finally gave me the rest I had asked for, before sending me out to fight still other heresies. So I had my victory, and the Church continued on much as before, and the Order of Saint Judas Iscariot was crushed and diminished. The telepath Jon Azure Cross had been wrong, I thought then. He had sadly underestimated the power of a Knight Inquisitor.

Later, though, I remembered his words.

You cannot hurt us, Damien.

Us?

The Order of Saint Judas? Or the Liars?

He lied, I think, deliberately, knowing I would go forth and destroy the way of cross and dragon, knowing too that I could not touch the Liars, would not even dare mention them. How could I? Who would believe it? A grand star-spanning conspiracy as old as history? It reeks of paranoia, and I had no proof at all.

The telepath lied for Lukyan's benefit, so that he would let me go. I am certain of that now. Cross risked much to snare me. Failing, he was willing to sacrifice Lukyan Judasson and his lie, pawns in some greater game.

So I left, and carried within me the knowledge that I was empty of faith but for a blind faith in truth, a truth I could no longer find in my Church. I grew certain of that in my year of rest, which I spent reading and studying on Vess and Cathaday and Celia's World. Finally I returned to the Archbishop's receiving room, and stood again before Torgathon Nine-Klariis Tuñ in my very worst pair of boots. 'My Lord Commander,' I said to him, 'I can accept no further assignments. I ask that I be retired from active service.'

'For what cause?' Torgathon rumbled, splashing feebly.

'I have lost the faith,' I said to him, simply.

He regarded me for a long time, his pupilless eyes blinking. At last he said, 'Your faith is a matter between you and your confessor. I care only about your results. You have done good work, Damien. You may not retire, and we will not allow you to resign.'

The truth will set us free.

But freedom is cold and empty and frightening, and lies can often be warm and beautiful.

Last year the Church finally granted me a new and better ship. I named this one *Dragon*.

FOUR
THE HEIRS OF
TURTLE CASTLE

THE HEIRS OF TURTLE CASTLE

Me and fantasy go way back.

Let's get that straight right from the start, because there seem to be some strange misconceptions floating around. On one hand, I have readers who never heard of me until they picked up *A Game of Thrones*, who seem convinced that I've never written anything but epic fantasy. On the other hand, I have the folks who have read all my older stuff, yet persist in the delusion that I'm a science fiction writer who 'turned to fantasy,' for nefarious reasons.

The truth is, I've been reading and writing fantasy (and horror, for that matter) since my boyhood in Bayonne. My first sale may have been a science fiction story, but my second was a ghost story, and never mind those damned hovertrucks whooshing by.

'The Exit to San Breta' was by no means the first fantasy I ever wrote, either. Even before Jarn of Mars and his band of alien space pirates, I was wont to fill my idle hours by making up stories about a great castle and the brave knights and kings who dwelled there. The only thing was, all of them were turtles.

The projects did not permit tenants to keep dogs or cats. You could have smaller pets, though. I had guppies, I had parakeets, and I had turtles. Lots and lots of turtles. They were the sort you bought in the five-and-ten, and they came with little plastic bowls divided down the center, one side for water, one for gravel. In the middle of the bowl was a fake plastic palm tree.

I also owned a toy castle that had come with my toy knights (a Marx tin litho castle, though I don't recall which model). It sat on top of the table that served me for a desk, and had just enough room inside its yard to fit two dimestore turtle bowls side by side. So that was where my turtles lived . . . and since they lived inside a *castle*, they must be kings and knights and princes. (I owned Marx's Fort Apache as well, but cowboy turtles would just have been *wrong*.)

The first turtle king was Big Fellow, who must have been a different species, since he was brown instead of green and twice as large as any of the little red-eared guys. One day I found Big Fellow dead, however, no doubt the victim of some sinister plot by the horned toads and chameleons who lived in the adjoining kingdoms. The turtle who followed Big Fellow to the throne was well-meaning but hapless, and he soon died as well, but just when things were looking bleakest, Frisky and Peppy swore eternal friendship and started a turtle round table. Peppy the First turned out to be the greatest of the turtle kings, but when he was old . . .

Turtle Castle had no beginning and no end, but lots of middle. Only parts of it were ever written down, but I acted out all the best bits in my head, the swordfights and battles and betrayals. I went through at least a dozen turtle kings. My mighty monarchs had a disconcerting habit of escaping the Marx castle and turning up dead beneath the refrigerator, the turtle equivalent of Mordor.

So there you are. I have *always* been a fantasy writer.

I cannot say that I was always a fantasy reader, though, for the simple reason that there was not a lot of fantasy around to be read back in the '50s and '60s. The spinner racks of my childhood were ruled by science fiction, murder mysteries, westerns, gothics, and historical novels; you could look high and low and not find a fantasy anywhere. I had signed up for the Science Fiction Book Club (three hardcovers for a dime, couldn't beat that), but they were the *science fiction* book club in those days, and fantasy need not apply.

It was five years after *Have Space Suit, Will Travel* that I stumbled across the book that would give me my first real taste of fantasy: a slim Pyramid anthology entitled *Swords & Sorcery*, edited by L. Sprague de Camp and published in December of 1963. And quite a tasty taste it was. Inside were stories by Poul Anderson, Henry Kuttner, Clark Ashton Smith, Lord Dunsany, and H.P. Lovecraft. There was a Jirel of Joiry story by C.L. Moore and a tale of Fafhrd and the Gray Mouser by Fritz Leiber . . . and there was a story titled 'Shadows in the Moonlight,' by Robert E. Howard.

'Know, O prince,' it opened, 'that between the years when the oceans drank Atlantis and the gleaming cities, and the years of the rise of the sons of the Aryas, there was an age undreamed of, when shining kingdoms lay spread across the world like blue mantles beneath the stars – Nemedia, Ophir, Brythunia, Hyperborea, Zamora with its dark-haired women and towers of spider-haunted mystery, Zingara with its chivalry, Koth that bordered on the pastoral lands of Shem, Stygia with its shadow-guarded tombs, Hyrkania whose riders wore steel and silk and gold. But the proudest kingdom of the world was Aquilonia, reigning supreme in the dreaming west. Hither came Conan, the Cimmerian, black-haired, sullen-eyed, sword in hand, a thief, a reaver, a slayer, with gigantic melancholies and gigantic mirths, to tread the jeweled thrones of the Earth under his sandaled feet.'

Howard had me at Zamora. The 'towers of spider-haunted mystery' would have done it all by themselves, though by 1963 I was fifteen, and those 'dark-haired women' stirred some interest up as well. Fifteen is a fine age to make the acquaintance of Conan of Cimmeria. If *Swords & Sorcery* did not start me buying heroic fantasy right and left, the way *Have Space Suit, Will Travel* had started me buying science fiction, it was only because you could hardly find any fantasy, heroic or otherwise.

In the '60s and '70s, fantasy and science fiction were often considered one field, although the field usually went by the name 'science fiction.' It was commonplace for the same writers to work in both genres. Robert A. Heinlein, Andre Norton, and Eric Frank Russell, three of my boyhood favorites, were all strongly identified with science fiction, but they all wrote fantasy as well. Poul Anderson was writing *The Broken Sword* and *Three Hearts and Three Lions* in between his tales of Nicholas van Rijn and Dominic Flandry. Jack Vance created Big Planet *and* the Dying Earth. Fritz Leiber's Spiders and Snakes fought their Time War even as Fafhrd and the Gray Mouser were fighting the Lords of Quarmall.

And yet, though all the top writers wrote fantasy, they did not write *much* of it, not if they wanted to pay their rent and eat. Science fiction was far more popular, far more commercial. The SF magazines wanted *only* SF, and would not publish fantasy no matter how well done. From time to time, fantasy magazines were launched, but few lasted long. *Astounding* spanned years and decades to become *Analog*, but *Unknown* did not survive the paper shortages of World War II. The publishers of *Galaxy* and *If* tried *Worlds of Fantasy*, and as quickly killed it. *Fantastic* endured for decades, but *Amazing* was the prize horse in that stable. And when Boucher and McComas launched *The Magazine of Fantasy*, it took them only one issue before they renamed it *The Magazine of Fantasy and Science-Fiction*.

These things often go in cycles, of course. As it happened, huge changes were looming just around the corner. In 1965, Ace Books would take advantage of a loophole in the copyright laws to release an unauthorized paperback reprint of J.R.R. Tolkien's *Lord of the Rings*. They would sell hundreds of thousands of copies before Tolkien and Ballantine Books, moving hurriedly, could answer with an authorized edition. In 1966, Lancer Books, perhaps inspired by the success that Ace and Ballantine had been having with Tolkien, would begin reprinting all of the Conan tales in a series of matched paperbacks with Frank Frazetta covers. Come 1969, Lin Carter (a dreadful writer but a fine editor) would launch the Ballantine Adult Fantasy Series and bring dozens of classic fantasies back into print. But all that lay well in the future in 1963, when I finished de Camp's *Swords & Sorcery* and looked about for more fantasy to read.

I found some in a most unlikely place: a comics fanzine.

Early comics fandom grew out of science fiction fandom, but after a few years it had become so much a world unto itself that most new fans were not even aware of the existence of the earlier, parent fandom. At the same time, all those high school boys were growing older, and their interests were broadening to include things other than superhero comics. Things like music, cars, girls . . . and books without pictures. Inevitably the scope of their fanzines began to broaden as well. The wheel was duly reinvented, and before long specialized 'zines began to pop up, devoted not to superheroes but to secret agents, or private eyes, or the old pulps, or the Barsoom stories of Edgar Rice Burroughs . . . or to heroic fantasy.

Cortana was the name of the sword & sorcery fanzine. Edited 'on a tri-monthly schedule' (hah) by Clint Bigglestone, who would later go on to be one of the founders of the Society for Creative Anachronism, it came out of the San Francisco Bay Area in 1964. Printed in the usual faded purple ditto, *Cortana* was nothing special to look at, but it was great fun to *read*, full of articles and news items about Conan and his competitors, and original heroic fantasies by some of the top writers of '60s comics fandom: Paul Moslander and Victor Baron (who were the same person), my penpal Howard Waldrop (who wasn't), Steve Perrin, and Bigglestone himself. Waldrop's stories starred an adventurer known only as the Wanderer whose exploits were recorded in the 'Canticles of Chimwazle.' Howard also drew the covers of *Cortana*, and provided some of the interior art.

In *Star Studded Comics* and most other comics fanzines, prose fiction was the homely sister; pride of place went to comic strips. Not here. In *Cortana* the text stories ruled. I wrote a gushing letter of comment at once, but I wanted to be a bigger part of this great new fanzine than that. So I put Manta Ray and Dr Weird aside, and sat down to write my first fantasy since Turtle Castle.

'Dark Gods of Kor-Yuban,' I called it, and yes, my version of Mordor sounds like a brand of coffee. My heroes were the usual pair of mismatched adventurers, the melancholy exile prince R'hllor of Raugg and his boisterous, swaggering companion Argilac the Arrogant. 'Dark Gods of Kor-Yuban' was the longest story I'd ever attempted (maybe five thousand words), and had a tragic ending where Argilac got eaten by the titular dark gods. I had been reading Shakespeare at Marist and learning about tragedy, so I gave Argilac the tragic flaw of arrogance, which caused his downfall. R'hllor escaped to tell the tale . . . and to fight another day, I hoped. When the story was done, I shipped it off to San Francisco, where Clint Bigglestone promptly accepted it for publication in *Cortana*.

Cortana never published another issue.

By my senior year of high school I *did* know how to use carbon paper, honest. I was just too lazy to bother with it. 'Dark Gods of Kor-Yuban' became another of my lost stories. (It was the last, though. In college, I made carbon copies of every story I wrote.) Before folding up its purple ditto tent, *Cortana* did me one more favor. In his third issue, Bigglestone ran an article called 'Don't Make a Hobbit of It,' wherein, for the first time, I learned of J.R.R. Tolkien and his fantasy trilogy, *Lord of the Rings*. The story sounded intriguing enough so that I did not hesitate a few months later, when I chanced to see the pirated Ace paperback of *The Fellowship of the Ring* on a newsstand.

Dipping into the fat red paperback during my bus ride home, I began to wonder if I had not made a mistake. *Fellowship* did not seem like proper heroic fantasy at all. What the hell was all this stuff about pipe-weed? Robert E. Howard's stories usually opened with a giant serpent slithering by or an axe cleaving someone's head in two. Tolkien opened his with a birthday party. And these hobbits with their hairy feet and love of 'taters seemed to have escaped from a Peter Rabbit book. *Conan would hack a bloody path right through the Shire, end to end*, I remembered thinking. *Where are the gigantic melancholies and the gigantic mirths?*

Yet I kept on reading. I almost gave up at Tom Bombadil, when people started going '*Hey! Come derry do! Tom Bombadillo!*' Things got more interesting in the barrow downs, though, and even more so in Bree, where Strider strode onto the scene. By the time we got to Weathertop, Tolkien had me. 'Gil-Galad was an elven king,' Sam Gamgee recited, 'of him the harpers sadly sing.' A chill went through me, such as Conan and Kull had never evoked.

Almost forty years later, I find myself in the middle of my own high fantasy, *A Song of Ice and Fire*. The books are huge, and hugely complex, and take me years to write. Within days of each volume being published, I begin to get emails asking when the next is coming out. 'You do not know how hard it is to wait,' some of my readers cry plaintively. *I do*, I want to tell them, *I know just how hard it is. I waited too.* When I finished *The Fellowship of the Ring*, it was the only volume out in paperback. I had to wait for Ace to bring out *The Two Towers*, and again for *The Return of the King*. Not a long wait, admittedly, yet somehow it seemed like decades. The moment I got my hands on the next volume I put everything else aside so I could read it . . . but halfway through *The Return of the King*, I slowed down. Only a few hundred pages remained, and once they were done, I would never be able to read *Lord of the Rings* for the first time again. As much as I wanted to know how it all came out, I did not want the experience to be over.

That was how fiercely I loved those books, as a reader.

As a writer, however, I was seriously daunted by Tolkien. When I read Robert E. Howard, I would think, *Some day I may be able to write as well as him.* When I read Lin Carter or John Jakes, I would think, *I can write better stuff than this right now.* But when I read Tolkien, I despaired. *I will never be able to do what he's done*, I would think. *I will never be able to come close.* Though

I would write fantasy in the years to come, most of it remained closer in tone to Howard than to Tolkien. One does not presume to tread upon the master's heels.

I began a second R'hllor story during my freshman year at Northwestern, when I still deluded myself that Cortana was only delayed, not dead, and that 'Dark Gods of Kor-Yuban' would be coming out real soon now. In the sequel, my exile prince finds himself in the Dothrak Empire, where he joins Barron of the Bloody Blade to fight the winged demons who slew his grandsire, King Barristan the Bold. I'd written twenty-three pages when some friends found the story on my desk one day, and had so much fun reading the purple prose aloud that I was too chagrined to continue. (I still have the pages, and yes, they're a bit purple, bordering on indigo.)

I wrote no more fantasy during my college years. And aside from 'The Exit to San Breta,' which was neither high nor heroic fantasy, I hardly touched it as a fledgling pro. That was not because I liked it any less than science fiction. My reasons were more pragmatic. I had rent to pay.

The early '70s were a splendid time to be a young science fiction writer at the start of a career. New SF magazines were being launched every year: *Vertex, Cosmos, Odyssey, Galileo, Asimov's*. (There were no new fantasy magazines.) Of the existing magazines, only *Fantastic* and *F&SF* bought fantasy, and the latter preferred quirky modern fantasies, partaking more of Thorne Smith and Gerald Kersh than Tolkien or Howard. New or old, the SF mags had serious rivals in the original anthology series: *Orbit, New Dimensions, Universe, Infinity, Quark, Alternities, Andromeda, Nova, Stellar, Chrysalis*. (There were no original anthologies devoted to fantasy.) The men's magazines were also booming, having just discovered that women had pubic hair; many wanted SF stories to fill up the pages between the pictures. (They would buy horror as well, but neither high fantasy nor heroic fantasy need apply.)

There were more book publishers than there are today (Bantam Doubleday Dell Random House Ballantine Fawcett were six publishers, not one, most of whom had SF lines. (The major fantasy imprint era was the Ballantine Adult Fantasy Series, which was largely devoted to reprints. Lancer had its Robert E. Howard titles . . . but Lancer was a bottom-feeder, a low-prestige, low-pay house that most writers fled as soon as they could sell elsewhere.) The World Fantasy Convention did not yet exist, and the World Science Fiction Convention rarely nominated any fantasies for Hugo Awards, no more than the Science Fiction Writers of America (who had not yet added 'and Fantasy' to their name) nominated them for Nebulas.

In short, you could not make a career as a fantasist. Not then. Not yet. So I did what all those other writers before me had done, what Jack Williamson had done, and Poul Anderson, and Andre Norton, and Jack Vance, and

Heinlein and Kuttner and Russell and de Camp and C.L. Moore and the rest. I wrote science fiction . . . and from time to time, for love, I snuck in a fantasy or two.

'The Lonely Songs of Laren Dorr' was my first pure fantasy as a pro. *Fantastic* published it in 1976. Keen-eyed readers will notice certain names and motifs that go all the way back to 'Only Kids Are Afraid of the Dark,' and other names and motifs that I would pick up and use again in later works. In my fiction, as in real life, I never throw anything away. You can never tell when you might find another use for it. Sharra and her dark crown were originally meant for the Dr Weird mythos that Howard Keltner once asked me to create. By 1976, however, my fanzine days were almost a decade behind me and *Dr Weird* had folded up shop, so I felt free to reclaim the ideas and rework them for a different sort of tale.

Once upon a time I meant to follow 'Laren Dorr' with more tales about Sharra, 'the girl who goes between the worlds.' I never did . . . but the phrase remained with me, as you'll see when we reach the section about my years in film and television.

'The Ice Dragon' was the second of the three stories that I wrote over Christmas break during the winter of 1978–79, as described in the last commentary. Dubuque winters had a way of inspiring stories about ice and snow and freezing cold. You won't often find me saying, 'The story wrote itself,' but it was true in this case. The words seemed to pour out of me, and when I was done I was convinced that this was one of the best short stories I had ever written, maybe *the* best.

No sooner had I finished than I chanced to see a market report announcing that Orson Scott Card was looking for submissions for an original anthology called *Dragons of Light and Darkness*. The timing could not have been more perfect; the gods were trying to tell me something. So I sent 'The Ice Dragon' to Card, and it was published in *Dragons of Light*, where it promptly vanished with nary a trace, as stories in anthologies so often do. Maybe surrounding it with other dragon stories was not the best idea I ever had.

Ice dragons have become commonplace features of a lot of fantasy books and games in the twenty-odd years since I wrote 'The Ice Dragon,' but I believe mine was the first. And most of these other 'ice dragons' appear to be no more than white dragons living in cold climates. Adara's friend, a dragon *made* of ice that breathes cold instead of flame, remains unique so far as I'm aware, my only truly original contribution to the fantasy bestiary.

'In the Lost Lands,' the third of the stories showcased in this section, first appeared in the DAW anthology *Amazons*, edited by Jessica Amanda Salmonson. ('How did *she* get a story out of you?' another anthology editor asked me, in annoyed tones, after the book came out. 'Well,' I said, 'she asked for one.') Like 'The Lonely Songs of Laren Dorr,' it was meant to be the opening installment of a series. I would later write a few pages of a sequel called 'The Withered Hand,' but as usual I never managed to complete it. Until such time as I return to it (if ever), 'In the Lost Lands' will remain yet another example of my patented one-story series.

I might also mention that some of the inspiration for 'In the Lost Lands' came from a song. Which one? That would be telling. Seems obvious to me. The clue is right in the first line, for those who care about such puzzles.

Sharra and Laren Dorr, Adara and her ice dragon, Gray Alys, Boyce, and Blue Jerais . . . one and all, they are the heirs of Turtle Castle, the ancestors of Ice and Fire. This book would not have been complete without them.

Why do I love fantasy? Let me answer that with a piece I wrote in 1996, to accompany my portrait in Pati Perret's book of photographs, *The Faces of Fantasy*:

> The best fantasy is written in the language of dreams. It is alive as dreams are alive, more real than real . . . for a moment at least . . . that long magic moment before we wake.
>
> Fantasy is silver and scarlet, indigo and azure, obsidian veined with gold and lapis lazuli. Reality is plywood and plastic, done up in mud brown and olive drab. Fantasy tastes of habaneros and honey, cinnamon and cloves, rare red meat and wines as sweet as summer. Reality is beans and tofu, and ashes at the end. Reality is the strip malls of Burbank, the smoke-stacks of Cleveland, a parking garage in Newark. Fantasy is the towers of Minas Tirith, the ancient stones of Gormenghast, the halls of Camelot. Fantasy flies on the wings of Icarus, reality on Southwest Airlines. Why do our dreams become so much smaller when they finally come true?
>
> We read fantasy to find the colors again, I think. To taste strong spices and hear the song the sirens sang. There is something old and true in fantasy that speaks to something deep within us, to the child who dreamt that one day he would hunt the forests of the night, and feast beneath the hollow hills, and find a love to last forever somewhere south of Oz and north of Shangri-La.
>
> They can keep their heaven. When I die, I'd sooner go to Middle Earth.

The Lonely Songs of Laren Dorr

T here is a girl who goes between the worlds.
   She is gray-eyed and pale of skin, or so the story goes, and her hair is
a coal-black waterfall with half-seen hints of red. She wears about her
brow a circlet of burnished metal, a dark crown that holds her hair in place
and sometimes puts shadows in her eyes. Her name is Sharra; she knows
the gates.

The beginning of her story is lost to us, with the memory of the world
from which she sprang. The end? The end is not yet, and when it comes we
shall not know it.

We have only the middle, or rather a piece of that middle, the smallest
part of the legend, a mere fragment of the quest. A small tale within the
greater, of one world where Sharra paused, and of the lonely singer Laren
Dorr and how they briefly touched.

*

One moment there was only the valley, caught in twilight. The setting sun
hung fat and violet on the ridge above, and its rays slanted down silently
into a dense forest whose trees had shiny black trunks and colorless
ghostly leaves. The only sounds were the cries of the mourning-birds
coming out for the night, and the swift rush of water in the rocky stream
that cut the woods.

Then, through a gate unseen, Sharra came tired and bloodied to the
world of Laren Dorr. She wore a plain white dress, now stained and
sweaty, and a heavy fur cloak that had been half-ripped from her back.
And her left arm, bare and slender, still bled from three long wounds. She
appeared by the side of the stream, shaking, and she threw a quick, wary
glance about her before she knelt to dress her wounds. The water, for all its
swiftness, was a dark and murky green. No way to tell if it was safe, but
Sharra was weak and thirsty. She drank, washed her arm as best she could
in the strange and doubtful water, and bound her injuries with bandages
ripped from her clothes. Then, as the purple sun dipped lower behind the
ridge, she crawled away from the water to a sheltered spot among the
trees, and fell into exhausted sleep.

She woke to arms around her, strong arms that lifted her easily to carry her somewhere, and she woke struggling. But the arms just tightened, and held her still. 'Easy,' a mellow voice said, and she saw a face dimly through gathering mist, a man's face, long and somehow gentle.

'You are weak,' he said, 'and night is coming. We must be inside before darkness.'

Sharra did not struggle, not then, though she knew she should. She had been struggling a long time, and she was tired. But she looked at him, confused. 'Why?' she asked. Then, not waiting for an answer, 'Who are you? Where are we going?'

'To safety,' he said.

'Your home?' she asked, drowsy.

'No,' he said, so soft she could scarcely hear his voice. 'No, not home, not ever home. But it will do.' She heard splashing then, as if he were carrying her across the stream, and ahead of them on the ridge she glimpsed a gaunt, twisted silhouette, a triple-towered castle etched black against the sun. Odd, she thought, that wasn't there before.

She slept.

When she woke, he was there, watching her. She lay under a pile of soft, warm blankets in a curtained, canopied bed. But the curtains had been drawn back, and her host sat across the room in a great chair draped by shadows. Candlelight flickered in his eyes, and his hands locked together neatly beneath his chin. 'Are you feeling better?' he asked, without moving.

She sat up, and noticed she was nude. Swift as suspicion, quicker than thought, her hand went to her head. But the dark crown was still there, in place, untouched, its metal cool against her brow. Relaxing, she leaned back against the pillows and pulled the blankets up to cover herself. 'Much better,' she said, and as she said it she realized for the first time that her wounds were gone.

The man smiled at her, a sad wistful sort of smile. He had a strong face, with charcoal-colored hair that curled in lazy ringlets and fell down into dark eyes somehow wider than they should be. Even seated, he was tall. And slender. He wore a suit and cape of some soft gray leather, and over that he wore melancholy like a cloak. 'Claw marks,' he said speculatively, while he smiled. 'Claw marks down your arm, and your clothes almost ripped from your back. Someone doesn't like you.'

'Something,' Sharra said. 'A guardian, a guardian at the gate.' She sighed. 'There is always a guardian at the gate. The Seven don't like us to move from world to world. Me they like least of all.'

His hands unfolded from beneath his chin, and rested on the carved wooden arms of his chair. He nodded, but the wistful smile stayed. 'So, then,' he said. 'You know the Seven, and you know the gates.' His eyes strayed to her forehead. 'The crown, of course. I should have guessed.'

Sharra grinned at him. 'You did guess. More than that, you knew. Who are you? What world is this?'

'My world,' he said evenly. 'I've named it a thousand times, but none of the names ever seem quite right. There was one once, a name I liked, a name that fit. But I've forgotten it. It was a long time ago. *My* name is Laren Dorr, or that was my name, once, when I had use for such a thing. Here and now it seems somewhat silly. But at least I haven't forgotten *it*.'

'Your world,' Sharra said. 'Are you a king, then? A god?'

'Yes,' Laren Dorr replied, with an easy laugh. 'And more. I'm whatever I choose to be. There is no one around to dispute me.'

'What did you do to my wounds?' she asked.

'I healed them.' He gave an apologetic shrug. 'It's my world. I have certain powers. Not the powers I'd like to have, perhaps, but powers nonetheless.'

'Oh.' She did not look convinced.

Laren waved an impatient hand. 'You think it's impossible. Your crown, of course. Well, that's only half right. I could not harm you with my, ah, powers, not while you wear that. But I can help you.' He smiled again, and his eyes grew soft and dreamy. 'But it doesn't matter. Even if I could I would never harm you, Sharra. Believe that. It has been a long time.'

Sharra looked startled. 'You know my name. How?'

He stood up, smiling, and came across the room to sit beside her on the bed. And he took her hand before replying, wrapping it softly in his and stroking her with his thumb. 'Yes, I know your name. You are Sharra, who moves between the worlds. Centuries ago, when the hills had a different shape and the violet sun burned scarlet at the very beginning of its cycle, they came to me and told me you would come. I hate them, all Seven, and I will always hate them, but that night I welcomed the vision they gave me. They told me only your name, and that you would come here, to my world. And one thing more, but that was enough. It was a promise. A promise of an ending or a start, of a change. And any change is welcome on this world. I've been alone here through a thousand sun-cycles, Sharra, and each cycle lasts for centuries. There are few events to mark the death of time.'

Sharra was frowning. She shook her long black hair, and in the dim light of the candles the soft red highlights glowed. 'Are they that far ahead of me, then?' she said. 'Do they know what will happen?' Her voice was troubled. She looked up at him. 'This other thing they told you?'

He squeezed her hand, very gently. 'They told me I would love you,' Laren said. His voice still sounded sad. 'But that was no great prophecy. I could have told them as much. There was a time long ago – I think the sun was yellow then – when I realized that I would love *any* voice that was not an echo of my own.'

*

Sharra woke at dawn, when shafts of bright purple light spilled into her room through a high arched window that had not been there the night before. Clothing had been laid out for her; a loose yellow robe, a jeweled dress of bright crimson, a suit of forest green. She chose the suit, dressed quickly. As she left, she paused to look out the window.

She was in a tower, looking out over crumbling stone battlements and a dusty triangular courtyard. Two other towers, twisted matchstick things with pointed conical spires, rose from the other corners of the triangle. There was a strong wind that whipped the rows of gray pennants set along the walls, but no other motion to be seen.

And, beyond the castle walls, no sign of the valley, none at all. The castle with its courtyard and its crooked towers was set atop a mountain, and far and away in all directions taller mountains loomed, presenting a panorama of black stone cliffs and jagged rocky walls and shining clean ice steeples that gleamed with a violet sheen. The window was sealed and closed, but the wind *looked* cold.

Her door was open. Sharra moved quickly down a twisting stone staircase, out across the courtyard into the main building, a low wooden structure built against the wall. She passed through countless rooms, some cold and empty save for dust, others richly furnished, before she found Laren Dorr eating breakfast.

There was an empty seat at his side; the table was heavily laden with food and drink. Sharra sat down, and took a hot biscuit, smiling despite herself. Laren smiled back.

'I'm leaving today,' she said, in between bites. 'I'm sorry, Laren. I must find the gate.'

The air of hopeless melancholy had not left him. It never did. 'So you said last night,' he replied, sighing. 'It seems I have waited a long time for nothing.'

There was meat, several types of biscuits, fruit, cheese, milk. Sharra filled a plate, face a little downcast, avoiding Laren's eyes. 'I'm sorry,' she repeated.

'Stay awhile,' he said. 'Only a short time. You can afford it, I would think. Let me show you what I can of my world. Let me sing to you.' His eyes, wide and dark and very tired, asked the question.

She hesitated. 'Well . . . it takes time to find the gate.'

'Stay with me for awhile, then.'

'But Laren, eventually I must go. I have made promises. You understand?'

He smiled, gave a helpless shrug. 'Yes. But look. I know where the gate is. I can show you, save you a search. Stay with me, oh, a month. A month as you measure time. Then I'll take you to the gate.' He studied her. 'You've been hunting a long, long time, Sharra. Perhaps you need a rest.'

Slowly, thoughtfully, she ate a piece of fruit, watching him all the time. 'Perhaps I do,' she said at last, weighing things. 'And there will be a guardian, of course. You could help me then. A month . . . that's not so long. I've been on other worlds far longer than a month.' She nodded, and a smile spread slowly across her face. 'Yes,' she said, still nodding. 'That would be all right.'

He touched her hand lightly. After breakfast he showed her the world they had given him.

They stood side by side on a small balcony atop the highest of the three towers, Sharra in dark green and Laren tall and soft in gray. They stood without moving, and Laren moved the world around them. He set the castle flying over restless churning seas, where long black serpent-heads peered up out of the water to watch them pass. He moved them to a vast echoing cavern under the earth, all aglow with a soft green light, where dripping stalactites brushed down against the towers and herds of blind white goats moaned outside the battlements. He clapped his hands and smiled, and steam-thick jungle rose around them; trees that climbed each other in rubber ladders to the sky, giant flowers of a dozen different colors, fanged monkeys that chittered from the walls. He clapped again, and the walls were swept clean, and suddenly the courtyard dirt was sand and they were on an endless beach by the shore of a bleak gray ocean, and above the slow wheeling of a great blue bird with tissue-paper wings was the only movement to be seen. He showed her this, and more, and more, and in the end as dusk seemed to threaten in one place after another, he took the castle back to the ridge above the valley. And Sharra looked down on the forest of black-barked trees where he had found her, and heard the mourning-birds whimper and weep among transparent leaves.

'It is not a bad world,' she said, turning to him on the balcony.

'No,' Laren replied. His hands rested on the cold stone railing, his eyes on the valley below. 'Not entirely. I explored it once, on foot, with a sword and a walking stick. There was a joy there, a real excitement. A new mystery behind every hill.' He chuckled. 'But that, too, was long ago. Now I know what lies behind every hill. Another empty horizon.'

He looked at her, and gave his characteristic shrug. 'There are worse hells, I suppose. But this is mine.'

'Come with me, then,' she said. 'Find the gate with me, and leave. There are other worlds. Maybe they are less strange and less beautiful, but you will not be alone.'

He shrugged again. 'You make it sound so easy,' he said in a careless voice. 'I have found the gate, Sharra. I have tried it a thousand times. The guardian does not stop me. I step through, briefly glimpse some other world, and suddenly I'm back in the courtyard. No. I cannot leave.'

She took his hand in hers. 'How sad. To be alone so long. I think you must be very strong, Laren. I would go mad in only a handful of years.'

He laughed, and there was a bitterness in the way he did it. 'Oh, Sharra. I have gone mad a thousand times, also. They cure me, love. They always cure me.' Another shrug, and he put his arm around her. The wind was cold and rising. 'Come,' he said. 'We must be inside before full dark.'

They went up in the tower to her bedroom, and they sat together on her bed and Laren brought them food; meat burned black on the outside and red within, hot bread, wine. They ate and they talked.

'Why are you here?' she asked him, in between mouthfuls, washing her words down with wine. 'How did you offend them? Who were you, before?'

'I hardly remember, except in dreams,' he told her. 'And the dreams – it has been so long, I can't even recall which ones are truth and which are visions born of my madness.' He sighed. 'Sometimes I dream I was a king, a great king in a world other than this, and my crime was that I made my people happy. In happiness they turned against the Seven, and the temples fell idle. And I woke one day, within my room, within my castle, and found my servants gone. And when I went outside, my people and my world were also gone, and even the woman who slept beside me.

'But there are other dreams. Often I remember vaguely that I was a god. Well, an almost-god. I had powers, and teachings, and they were not the teachings of the Seven. They were afraid of me, each of them, for I was a match for any of them. But I could not meet all Seven together, and that was what they forced me to do. And then they left me only a small bit of my power, and set me here. It was cruel irony. As a god, I'd taught that people should turn to each other, that they could keep away the darkness by love and laughter and talk. So all these things the Seven took from me.

'And even that is not the worst. For there are other times when I think that I have always been here, that I was born here some endless age ago. And the memories are all false ones, sent to make me hurt the more.'

Sharra watched him as he spoke. His eyes were not on her, but far away, full of fog and dreams and half-dead rememberings. And he spoke very slowly, in a voice that was also like fog, that drifted and curled and hid things, and you knew that there were mysteries there and things brooding just out of sight and far-off lights that you would never reach.

Laren stopped, and his eyes woke up again. 'Ah, Sharra,' he said. 'Be careful how you go. Even your crown will not help you should they move on you directly. And the pale child Bakkalon will tear at you, and Naa-Slas feed upon your pain, and Saagael on your soul.'

She shivered, and cut another piece of meat. But it was cold and tough when she bit into it, and suddenly she noticed that the candles had burned very low. How long had she listened to him speak?

'Wait,' he said then, and he rose and went outside, out the door near where the window had been. There was nothing there now but rough gray stone; the windows all changed to solid rock with the last fading of the sun. Laren returned in a few moments, with a softly shining instrument of dark black wood slung around his neck on a leather cord. Sharra had never quite seen its like. It had sixteen strings, each a different color, and all up and down its length brightly-glowing bars of light were inlaid amid the polished wood. When Laren sat, the bottom of the device rested on the floor and the top came to just above his shoulder. He stroked it lightly, speculatively; the lights glowed, and suddenly the room was full of swift-fading music.

'My companion,' he said, smiling. He touched it again, and the music rose and died, lost notes without a tune. And he brushed the light-bars and the very air shimmered and changed color. He began to sing.

> I am the lord of loneliness,
> Empty my domain . . .

. . . the first words ran, sung low and sweet in Laren's mellow far-off fog voice. The rest of the song – Sharra clutched at it, heard each word and tried to remember, but lost them all. They brushed her, touched her, then melted away, back into the fog, here and gone again so swift that she could not remember quite what they had been. With the words, the music; wistful and melancholy and full of secrets, pulling at her, crying, whispering promises of a thousand tales untold. All around the room the candles flamed up brighter, and globes of light grew and danced and flowed together until the air was full of color.

Words, music, light; Laren Dorr put them all together, and wove for her a vision.

She saw him then as he saw himself in his dreams; a king, strong and tall and still proud, with hair as black as hers and eyes that snapped. He was dressed all in shimmering white, pants that clung tight and a shirt that ballooned at the sleeves, and a great cloak that moved and curled in the wind like a sheet of solid snow. Around his brow he wore a crown of flashing silver, and a slim, straight sword flashed just as bright at his side. This Laren, this younger Laren, this dream vision, moved without melancholy, moved in a world of sweet ivory minarets and languid blue canals. And the world moved around him, friends and lovers and one special woman whom Laren drew with words and lights of fire, and there was an infinity of easy days and laughter.

Then, sudden, abrupt darkness. He was here.

The music moaned; the lights dimmed; the words grew sad and lost. Sharra saw Laren wake, in a familiar castle now deserted. She saw him search from room to room, and walk outside to face a world he'd never seen. She watched him leave the castle, walk off towards the mists of a far horizon in the hope that those mists were smoke. And on and on he walked, and new horizons fell beneath his feet each day, and the great fat sun waxed red and orange and yellow, but still his world was empty. All the places he had shown her he walked to; all those and more; and finally, lost as ever, wanting home, the castle came to him.

By then his white had faded to dim gray. But still the song went on. Days went, and years, and centuries, and Laren grew tired and mad but never old. The sun shone green and violet and a savage hard blue-white, but with each cycle there was less color in his world. So Laren sang, of endless empty days and nights when music and memory were his only sanity, and his songs made Sharra feel it.

And when the vision faded and the music died and his soft voice melted away for the last time and Laren paused and smiled and looked at her, Sharra found herself trembling.

'Thank you,' he said softly, with a shrug. And he took his instrument and left her for the night.

*

The next day dawned cold and overcast, but Laren took her out into the forests, hunting. Their quarry was a lean white thing, half cat, half gazelle, with too much speed for them to chase easily and too many teeth for them to kill. Sharra did not mind. The hunt was better than the kill. There was a singular, striking joy in that run through the darkling forest, holding a bow she never used and wearing a quiver of black wood arrows cut from the same dour trees that surrounded them. Both of them were bundled up tightly in gray fur, and Laren smiled out at her from under a wolf's-head hood. And the leaves beneath their boots, as clear and fragile as glass, cracked and splintered as they ran.

Afterwards, unblooded but exhausted, they returned to the castle and

Laren set out a great feast in the main dining room. They smiled at each other from opposite ends of a table fifty feet long, and Sharra watched the clouds roll by the window behind Laren's head, and later watched the window turn to stone.

'Why does it do that?' she asked. 'And why don't you ever go outside at night?'

He shrugged. 'Ah. I have reasons. The nights are, well, not good here.' He sipped hot spice wine from a great jeweled cup. 'The world you came from, where you started – tell me, Sharra, did you have stars?'

She nodded. 'Yes. It's been so long, though. But I still remember. The nights were very dark and black, and the stars were little pinpoints of light, hard and cold and far away. You could see patterns sometimes. The men of my world, when they were young, gave names to each of those patterns, and told grand tales about them.'

Laren nodded. 'I would like your world, I think,' he said. 'Mine was like that, a little. But our stars were a thousand colors, and they moved, like ghostly lanterns in the night. Sometimes they drew veils around them to hide their light. And then our nights would be all shimmer and gossamer. Often I would go sailing at startime, myself and she whom I loved. Just so we could see the stars together. It was a good time to sing.' His voice was growing sad again.

Darkness had crept into the room, darkness and silence, and the food was cold and Sharra could scarce see his face fifty long feet away. So she rose and went to him, and sat lightly on the great table near to his chair. And Laren nodded and smiled, and at once there was a whooosh, and all along the walls torches flared to sudden life in the long dining hall. He offered her more wine, and her fingers lingered on his as she took the glass.

'It was like that for us, too,' Sharra said. 'If the wind was warm enough, and other men were far away, then we liked to lie together in the open. Kaydar and I.' She hesitated, looked at him.

His eyes were searching. 'Kaydar?'

'You would have liked him, Laren. And he would have liked you, I think. He was tall and he had red hair and there was a fire in his eyes. Kaydar had powers, as did I, but his were greater. And he had such a will. They took him one night, did not kill him, only took him from me and from our world. I have been hunting for him ever since. I know the gates, I wear the dark crown, and they will not stop me easily.'

Laren drank his wine and watched the torchlight on the metal of his goblet. 'There are an infinity of worlds, Sharra.'

'I have as much time as I require. I do not age, Laren, no more than you do. I will find him.'

'Did you love him so much?'

Sharra fought a fond, flickering smile, and lost. 'Yes,' she said, and now it was her voice that seemed a little lost. 'Yes, so much. He made me happy, Laren. We were only together for a short time, but he *did* make me happy. The Seven cannot touch that. It was a joy just to watch him, to feel his arms around me and see the way he smiled.'

'Ah,' he said, and he did smile, but there was something very beaten in the way he did it. The silence grew very thick.

Finally Sharra turned to him. 'But we have wandered a long way from where we started. You still have not told me why your windows seal themselves at night.'

'You have come a long way, Sharra. You move between the worlds. Have you seen worlds without stars?'

'Yes. Many, Laren. I have seen a universe where the sun is a glowing ember with but a single world, and the skies are vast and vacant by night. I have seen the land of frowning jesters, where there is no sky and the hissing suns burn below the ocean. I have walked the moors of Carradyne, and watched dark sorcerers set fire to a rainbow to light that sunless land.'

'This world has no stars,' Laren said.

'Does that frighten you so much, that you stay inside?'

'No. But it has something else instead.' He looked at her. 'Would you see?'

She nodded.

As abruptly as they had lit, the torches all snuffed out. The room swam with blackness. And Sharra shifted on the table to look over Laren's shoulder. Laren did not move. But behind him, the stones of the window fell away like dust and light poured in from outside.

The sky was very dark, but she could see clearly, for against the darkness a shape was moving. Light poured from it, and the dirt in the courtyard and the stones of the battlements and the gray pennants were all bright beneath its glow. Puzzling, Sharra looked up.

Something looked back. It was taller than the mountains and it filled up half the sky, and though it gave off light enough to see the castle by, Sharra knew that it was dark beyond darkness. It had a man-shape, roughly, and it wore a long cape and a cowl, and below that was blackness even fouler than the rest. The only sounds were Laren's soft breathing and the beating of her heart and distant weeping of a mourning-bird, but in her head Sharra could hear demonic laughter.

The shape in the sky looked down at her, in her, and she felt the cold dark in her soul. Frozen, she could not move her eyes. But the shape did move. It turned, and raised a hand, and then there was something else up there with it, a tiny man-shape with eyes of fire that writhed and screamed and called to her.

Sharra shrieked, and turned away. When she glanced back, there was no window. Only a wall of safe, sure stone, and a row of torches burning, and Laren holding her within strong arms. 'It was only a vision,' he told her. He pressed her tight against him, and stroked her hair. 'I used to test myself at night,' he said, more to himself than to her. 'But there was no need. They take turns up there, watching me, each of the Seven. I have seen them too often, burning with black light against the clean dark of the sky, and holding those I loved. Now I don't look. I stay inside and sing, and my windows are made of nightstone.'

'I feel . . . fouled,' she said, still trembling a little.

'Come,' he said. 'There is water upstairs, you can clean away the cold. And then I'll sing for you.' He took her hand, and led her up into the tower.

Sharra took a hot bath while Laren set up his instrument and tuned it in the bedroom. He was ready when she returned, wrapped head to foot in a huge fluffy brown towel. She sat on the bed, drying her hair and waiting.

And Laren gave her visions.

He sang his other dream this time, the one where he was a god and the enemy of the Seven. The music was a savage pounding thing, shot through with lightning and tremors of fear, and the lights melted together to form a scarlet battlefield where a blinding-white Laren fought shadows and the shapes of nightmare. There were seven of them, and they formed a ring around him and darted in and out, stabbing him with lances of absolute black, and Laren answered them with fire and storm. But in the end they overwhelmed him, the light faded, and then the song grew soft and sad again and the vision blurred as lonely dreaming centuries flashed by.

Hardly had the last notes fallen from the air and the final shimmers died than Laren started once again. A new song this time, and one he did not know so well. His fingers, slim and graceful, hesitated and retraced themselves more than once, and his voice was shaky too, for he was making up some of the words as he went along. Sharra knew why. For this time he sang of her, a ballad of her quest. Of burning love and endless searching, of worlds beyond worlds, of dark crowns and waiting guardians that fought with claws and tricks and lies. He took every word that she had spoken, and used each, and transformed each. In the bedroom, glittering panoramas formed where hot white suns burned beneath eternal oceans and hissed in clouds of steam, and men ancient beyond time lit rainbows to keep away the dark. And he sang Kaydar, and he sang him true somehow, he caught and drew the fire that had been Sharra's love and made her believe anew.

But the song ended with a question, the halting finale lingering in the air, echoing, echoing. Both of them waited for the rest, and both knew there was no more. Not yet.

Sharra was crying. 'My turn, Laren,' she said. Then: 'Thank you. For giving Kaydar back to me.'

'It was only a song,' he said, shrugging. 'It's been a long time since I had a new song to sing.'

Once again he left her, touching her cheek lightly at the door as she stood there with the blanket wrapped around her. Then Sharra locked the door behind him and went from candle to candle, turning light to darkness with a breath. And she threw the towel over a chair and crawled under the blankets and lay a long long time before drifting off to sleep.

It was still dark when she woke, not knowing why. She opened her eyes and lay quietly and looked around the room, and nothing was there, nothing was changed. Or was there?

And then she saw him, sitting in the chair across the room with his hands locked under his chin, just as he had sat that first time. His eyes steady and unmoving, very wide and dark in a room full of night. He sat very still. 'Laren?' she called, softly, still not quite sure the dark form was him.

'Yes,' he said. He did not move. 'I watched you last night, too, while you slept. I have been alone here for longer than you can ever imagine, and very soon now I will be alone again. Even in sleep, your presence is a wonder.'

'Oh, Laren,' she said. There was a silence, a pause, a weighing and an unspoken conversation. Then she threw back the blanket, and Laren came to her.

*

Both of them had seen centuries come and go. A month, a moment; much the same.

They slept together every night, and every night Laren sang his songs while Sharra listened. They talked throughout dark hours, and during the day they swam nude in crystalline waters that caught the purple glory of the sky. They made love on beaches of fine white sand, and they spoke a lot of love.

But nothing changed. And finally the time drew near. On the eve of the night before the day that was end, at twilight, they walked together through the shadowed forest where he'd found her.

Laren had learned to laugh during his month with Sharra, but now he was silent again. He walked slowly, clutched her hand hard in his, and his mood was more gray than the soft silk shirt he wore. Finally, by the side of the valley stream, he sat and pulled her down by his side. They took off their boots and let the water cool their feet. It was a warm evening, with a lonely restless wind and already you could hear the first of the mourning-birds.

'You must go,' he said, still holding her hand but never looking at her. It was a statement, not a question.

'Yes,' she said, and the melancholy had touched her too, and there were leaden echoes in her voice.

'My words have all left me, Sharra,' Laren said. 'If I could sing for you a vision now, I would. A vision of a world once empty, made full by us and our children. I could offer that. My world has beauty and wonder and mystery enough, if only there were eyes to see it. And if the nights are evil, well, men have faced dark nights before, on other worlds in other times. I would love you, Sharra, as much as I am able. I would try to make you happy.'

'Laren . . .' she started. But he quieted her with a glance.

'No, I could say that, but I will not. I have no right. Kaydar makes you happy. Only a selfish fool would ask you to give up that happiness to share my misery. Kaydar is all fire and laughter, while I am smoke and song and sadness. I have been alone too long, Sharra. The gray is part of my soul now, and I would not have you darkened. But still . . .'

She took his hand in both of hers, lifted it, and kissed it quickly. Then, releasing him, she lay her head on his unmoving shoulder. 'Try to come with me, Laren,' she said. 'Hold my hand when we pass through the gate, and perhaps the dark crown will protect you.'

'I will try anything you ask. But don't ask me to believe that it will work.' He sighed. 'You have countless worlds ahead of you, Sharra, and I cannot see your ending. But it is not here. That I know. And maybe that is best. I don't know anymore, if I ever did. I remember love vaguely, I think I can recall what it was like, and I remember that it never lasts. Here, with both of us unchanging and immortal, how could we help but to grow bored? Would we hate each other then? I'd not want that.' He looked at her then, and smiled an aching, melancholy smile. 'I think that you had known Kaydar for only a short time, to be so *in* love with him. Perhaps I'm being devious after all. For in finding Kaydar, you may lose him. The fire will go out some day, my love, and the magic will die. And then you may remember Laren Dorr.'

Sharra began to weep, softly. Laren gathered her to him, and kissed her, and whispered a gentle 'No.' She kissed back, and they held each other wordless.

When at last the purple gloom had darkened to near-black, they put back on their boots and stood. Laren hugged her and smiled.

'I *must* go,' Sharra said. 'I *must*. But leaving is hard, Laren, you must believe that.'

'I do,' he said. 'I love you *because* you will go, I think. Because you cannot forget Kaydar, and you will not forget the promises you made. You are Sharra, who goes between the worlds, and I think the Seven must fear you far more than any god I might have been. If you were not you, I would not think as much of you.'

'Oh. Once you said you would love any voice that was not any echo of your own.'

Laren shrugged. 'As I have often said, love, *that* was a very long time ago.'

They were back inside the castle before darkness, for a final meal, a final night, a final song. They got no sleep that night, and Laren sang to her again just before dawn. It was not a very good song, though; it was an aimless, rambling thing about a wandering minstrel on some nondescript world. Very little of interest ever happened to the minstrel; Sharra couldn't quite get the point of the song, and Laren sang it listlessly. It seemed an odd farewell, but both of them were troubled.

He left her with the sunrise, promising to change clothes and meet her in the courtyard. And sure enough, he was waiting when she got there, smiling at her, calm and confident. He wore a suit of pure white; pants that clung, a shirt that puffed up at the sleeves, and a great heavy cape that snapped and billowed in the rising wind. But the purple sun stained him with its shadow rays.

Sharra walked out to him and took his hand. She wore tough leather, and there was a knife in her belt, for dealing with the guardian. Her hair, jet black with light-born glints of red and purple, blew as freely as his cape, but the dark crown was in place. 'Good-bye, Laren,' she said. 'I wish I had given you more.'

'You have given me enough. In all the centuries that come, in all the sun-cycles that lie ahead, I will remember. I shall measure time by you, Sharra. When the sun rises one day and its color is blue fire, I will look at it and say, "Yes, this is the first blue sun after Sharra came to me."'

She nodded. 'And I have a new promise. I will find Kaydar, some day. And if I free him, we will come back to you, both of us together, and we will pit my crown and Kaydar's fires against all the darkness of the Seven.'

Laren shrugged. 'Good. If I'm not here, be sure to leave a message,' he said. And then he grinned.

'Now, the gate. You said you would show me the gate.'

Laren turned and gestured at the shortest tower, a sooty stone structure Sharra had never been inside. There was a wide wooden door in its base. Laren produced a key.

'Here?' she said, looking puzzled. 'In the castle?'

'Here,' Laren said. They walked across the courtyard, to the door. Laren inserted the heavy metal key and began to fumble with the lock. While he worked, Sharra took one last look around, and felt the sadness heavy on her soul. The other towers looked bleak and dead, the courtyard was forlorn, and beyond the high icy mountains was only an empty horizon. There was no sound but Laren working at the lock, and no motion but the steady wind that kicked up the courtyard dust and flapped the seven gray pennants that hung along each wall. Sharra shivered with sudden loneliness.

Laren opened the door. No room inside; only a wall of moving fog, a fog without color or sound or light. 'Your gate, my lady,' the singer said.

Sharra watched it, as she had watched it so many times before. What world was next? she wondered. She never knew. But maybe in the next one, she would find Kaydar.

She felt Laren's hand on her shoulder. 'You hesitate,' he said, his voice soft.

Sharra's hand went to her knife. 'The guardian,' she said suddenly. 'There is always a guardian.' Her eyes darted quickly round the courtyard.

Laren sighed. 'Yes. Always. There are some who try to claw you to pieces, and some who try to get you lost, and some who try to trick you into taking the wrong gate. There are some who hold you with weapons, some with chains, some with lies. And there is one, at least, who tried to stop you with love. Yet he was true for all that, and he never sang you false.'

And with a hopeless, loving shrug, Laren shoved her through the gate.

*

Did she find him, in the end, her lover with the eyes of fire? Or is she searching still? What guardian did she face next?

When she walks at night, a stranger in a lonely land, does the sky have stars?

I don't know. He doesn't. Maybe even the Seven do not know. They are powerful, yes, but all power is not theirs, and the number of worlds is greater than even they can count.

There is a girl who goes between the worlds, but her path is lost in legend by now. Maybe she is dead, and maybe not. Knowledge moves slowly from world to world, and not all of it is true.

But this we know; in an empty castle below a purple sun, a lonely minstrel waits, and sings of her.

The Ice Dragon

Adara liked the winter best of all, for when the world grew cold the ice dragon came.

She was never quite sure whether it was the cold that brought the ice dragon or the ice dragon that brought the cold. That was the sort of question that often troubled her brother Geoff, who was two years older than her and insatiably curious, but Adara did not care about such things. So long as the cold and the snow and the ice dragon all arrived on schedule, she was happy.

She always knew when they were due because of her birthday. Adara was a winter child, born during the worst freeze that anyone could remember, even Old Laura, who lived on the next farm and remembered things that had happened before anyone else was born. People still talked about that freeze. Adara often heard them.

They talked about other things as well. They said it was the chill of that terrible freeze that had killed her mother, stealing in during her long night of labor past the great fire that Adara's father had built, and creeping under the layers of blankets that covered the birthing bed. And they said that the cold had entered Adara in the womb, that her skin had been pale blue and icy to the touch when she came forth, and that she had never warmed in all the years since. The winter had touched her, left its mark upon her, and made her its own.

It was true that Adara was always a child apart. She was a very serious little girl who seldom cared to play with the others. She was beautiful, people said, but in a strange, distant sort of way, with her pale skin and blonde hair and wide clear blue eyes. She smiled, but not often. No one had ever seen her cry. Once when she was five she had stepped upon a nail imbedded in a board that lay concealed beneath a snowbank, and it had gone clear through her foot, but Adara had not wept or screamed even then. She had pulled her foot loose and walked back to the house, leaving a trail of blood in the snow, and when she had gotten there she had said only, 'Father, I hurt myself.' The sulks and tempers and tears of ordinary childhood were not for her.

Even her family knew that Adara was different. Her father was a huge, gruff bear of a man who had little use for people in general, but a smile always broke across his face when Geoff pestered him with questions, and he was full of hugs and laughter for Teri, Adara's older sister, who was golden and freckled, and flirted shamelessly with all the local boys. Every so often he would hug Adara as well, especially when he was drunk, which was frequent during the long winters. But there would be no smiles then. He would only wrap his arms around her, and pull her small body tight against him with all his massive strength, sob deep in his chest, and fat wet tears would run down his ruddy cheeks. He never hugged her at all during the summers. During the summers he was too busy.

Everyone was busy during the summers except for Adara. Geoff would work with his father in the fields and ask endless questions about this and that, learning everything a farmer had to know. When he was not working he would run with his friends to the river, and have adventures. Teri ran the house and did the cooking, and worked a bit at the inn by the crossroads during the busy season. The innkeeper's daughter was her friend, and his youngest son was more than a friend, and she would always come back giggly and full of gossip and news from travelers and soldiers and king's messengers. For Teri and Geoff the summers were the best time, and both of them were too busy for Adara.

Their father was the busiest of all. A thousand things needed to be done each day, and he did them, and found a thousand more. He worked from dawn to dusk. His muscles grew hard and lean in summer, and he stank from sweat each night when he came in from the fields, but he always came in smiling. After supper he would sit with Geoff and tell him stories and answer his questions, or teach Teri things she did not know about cooking, or stroll down to the inn. He was a summer man, truly.

He never drank in summer, except for a cup of wine now and again to celebrate his brother's visits.

That was another reason why Teri and Geoff loved the summers, when the world was green and hot and bursting with life. It was only in summer that Uncle Hal, their father's younger brother, came to call. Hal was a dragonrider in service to the king, a tall slender man with a face like a noble. Dragons cannot stand the cold, so when winter fell Hal and his wing would fly south. But each summer he returned, brilliant in the king's green-and-gold uniform, en route to the battlegrounds to the north and west of them. The war had been going on for all of Adara's life.

Whenever Hal came north, he would bring presents; toys from the king's city, crystal and gold jewelry, candies, and always a bottle of some expensive wine that he and his brother could share. He would grin at Teri and make her blush with his compliments, and entertain Geoff with tales of war and castles and dragons. As for Adara, he often tried to coax a smile out of her, with gifts and jests and hugs. He seldom succeeded.

For all his good nature, Adara did not like Hal; when Hal was there, it meant that winter was far away.

Besides, there had been a night when she was only four, and they thought her long asleep, that she overheard them talking over wine. 'A solemn little thing,' Hal said. 'You ought to be kinder to her, John. You cannot blame *her* for what happened.'

'Can't I?' her father replied, his voice thick with wine. 'No, I suppose not. But it is hard. She looks like Beth, but she has none of Beth's warmth. The winter is in her, you know. Whenever I touch her I feel the chill, and I remember that it was for her that Beth had to die.'

'You are cold to her. You do not love her as you do the others.'

Adara remembered the way her father laughed then. 'Love her? Ah, Hal. I loved her best of all, my little winter child. But she has never loved back. There is nothing in her for me, or you, any of us. She is such a cold little girl.' And then he began to weep, even though it was summer and Hal was with him. In her bed, Adara listened and wished that Hal would fly away. She did not quite understand all that she had heard, not then, but she remembered it, and the understanding came later.

She did not cry; not at four, when she heard, or six, when she finally understood. Hal left a few days later, and Geoff and Teri waved to him excitedly when his wing passed overhead, thirty great dragons in proud formation against the summer sky. Adara watched with her small hands by her sides.

There were other visits in other summers, but Hal never made her smile, no matter what he brought her.

Adara's smiles were a secret store, and she spent of them only in winter. She could hardly wait for her birthday to come, and with it the cold. For in winter she was a special child.

She had known it since she was very little, playing with the others in the snow. The cold had never bothered her the way it did Geoff and Teri and their friends. Often Adara stayed outside alone for hours after the others had fled in search of warmth, or run off to Old Laura's to eat the hot vegetable soup she liked to make for the children. Adara would find a secret place in the far corner of the fields, a different place each winter, and there she would build a tall white castle, patting the snow in place with small bare hands, shaping it into towers and battlements like those Hal often talked about on the king's castle in the city. She would snap icicles off from the lower branches of trees, and use them for spires and spikes and guardposts, ranging them all about her castle. And often in the dead of winter would come a brief thaw and a sudden freeze, and overnight her snow castle would turn to ice, as hard and strong as she imagined real castles to be. All through the winters she would build on her castle, and no one ever knew. But always the spring would come, and a thaw not followed by a freeze; then all the ramparts and walls would melt away, and Adara would begin to count the days until her birthday came again.

Her winter castles were seldom empty. At the first frost each year, the ice lizards would come wriggling out of their burrows, and the fields would be overrun with the tiny blue creatures, darting this way and that, hardly seeming to touch the snow as they skimmed across it. All the children played with the ice lizards. But the others were clumsy and cruel, and they would snap the fragile little animals in two, breaking them between their fingers as they might break an icicle hanging from a roof. Even Geoff, who was too kind ever to do something like that, sometimes grew curious, and held the lizards too long in his efforts to examine them, and the heat of his hands would make them melt and burn and finally die.

Adara's hands were cool and gentle, and she could hold the lizards as long as she liked without harming them, which always made Geoff pout and ask angry questions. Sometimes she would lie in the cold, damp snow and let the lizards crawl all over her, delighting in the light touch of their feet as they skittered across her face. Sometimes she would wear ice lizards hidden in her hair as she went about her chores, though she took care never to take them inside where the heat of the fires would kill them. Always she would gather up scraps after the family ate, and bring them to the secret place where her castle was a-building, and there she would scatter them. So the castles she erected were full of kings and courtiers every winter; small furry creatures that snuck out from the woods, winter birds with pale white plumage, and hundreds and hundreds of squirming, struggling ice lizards, cold and quick and fat. Adara liked the ice lizards better than any of the pets the family had kept over the years.

But it was the ice dragon that she loved.

She did not know when she had first seen it. It seemed to her that it had always been a part of her life, a vision glimpsed during the deep of winter, sweeping across the frigid sky on wings serene and blue. Ice dragons were rare, even in those days, and whenever it was seen the children would all point and wonder, while the old folks muttered and shook their heads. It was a sign of a long and bitter winter when ice dragons were abroad in the land. An ice dragon had been seen flying across the face of the moon on the night Adara had been born, people said, and each winter since it had been seen again, and those winters had been very bad indeed, the spring coming later each year. So the people would set fires and pray and hope to keep the ice dragon away, and Adara would fill with fear.

But it never worked. Every year the ice dragon returned. Adara knew it came for her.

The ice dragon was large, half again the size of the scaled green war dragons that Hal and his fellows flew. Adara had heard legends of wild dragons larger than mountains, but she had never seen any. Hal's dragon was big enough, to be sure, five times the size of a horse, but it was small compared to the ice dragon, and ugly besides.

The ice dragon was a crystalline white, that shade of white that is so hard and cold that it is almost blue. It was covered with hoarfrost, so when it moved its skin broke and crackled as the crust on the snow crackles beneath a man's boots, and flakes of rime fell off.

Its eyes were clear and deep and icy.

Its wings were vast and batlike, colored all a faint translucent blue. Adara could see the clouds through them, and oftentimes the moon and stars, when the beast wheeled in frozen circles through the skies.

Its teeth were icicles, a triple row of them, jagged spears of unequal length, white against its deep blue maw.

When the ice dragon beat its wings, the cold winds blew and the snow swirled and scurried and the world seemed to shrink and shiver. Sometimes when a door flew open in the cold of winter, driven by a sudden gust of wind, the householder would run to bolt it and say, 'An ice dragon flies nearby.'

And when the ice dragon opened its great mouth, and exhaled, it was not fire that came streaming out, the burning sulfurous stink of lesser dragons.

The ice dragon breathed cold.

Ice formed when it breathed. Warmth fled. Fires guttered and went out, shriven by the chill. Trees froze through to their slow secret souls, and their limbs turned brittle and cracked from their own weight. Animals turned blue and whimpered and died, their eyes bulging and their skin covered over with frost.

The ice dragon breathed death into the world; death and quiet and cold. But Adara was not afraid. She was a winter child, and the ice dragon was her secret.

She had seen it in the sky a thousand times. When she was four, she saw it on the ground.

She was out building on her snow castle, and it came and landed close to her, in the emptiness of the snow-covered fields. All the ice lizards ran away. Adara simply stood. The ice dragon looked at her for ten long heartbeats, before it took to the air again. The wind shrieked around her and through her as it beat its wings to rise, but Adara felt strangely exulted.

Later that winter it returned, and Adara touched it. Its skin was very cold. She took off her glove nonetheless. It would not be right otherwise. She was half afraid it would burn and melt at her touch, but it did not. It was much more sensitive to heat than even the ice lizards, Adara knew somehow. But she was special, the winter child, cool. She stroked it, and finally gave its wing a kiss that hurt her lips. That was the winter of her fourth birthday, the year she touched the ice dragon.

The winter of her fifth birthday was the year she rode upon it for the first time.

It found her again, working on a different castle at a different place in the fields, alone as ever. She watched it come, and ran to it when it landed, and pressed herself against it. That had been the summer when she had heard her father talking to Hal.

They stood together for long minutes until finally Adara, remembering Hal, reached out and tugged at the dragon's wing with a small hand. And the dragon beat its great wings once, and then extended them flat against the snow, and Adara scrambled up to wrap her arms about its cold white neck.

Together, for the first time, they flew.

She had no harness or whip, as the king's dragonriders use. At times the beating of the wings threatened to shake her loose from where she clung, and the coldness of the dragon's flesh crept through her clothing and bit and numbed her child's flesh. But Adara was not afraid.

They flew over her father's farm, and she saw Geoff looking very small below, startled and afraid, and knew he could not see her. It made her laugh an icy, tinkling laugh, a laugh as bright and crisp as the winter air.

They flew over the crossroads inn, where crowds of people came out to watch them pass.

They flew above the forest, all white and green and silent.

They flew high into the sky, so high that Adara could not even see the ground below, and she thought she glimpsed another ice dragon, way off in the distance, but it was not half so grand as *hers*.

They flew for most of the day, and finally the dragon swept around in a great circle, and spiraled down, gliding on its stiff and glittering wings. It let her off in the field where it had found her, just after dusk.

Her father found her there, and wept to see her, and hugged her savagely. Adara did not understand that, nor why he beat her after he had gotten her back to the house. But when she and Geoff had been put to sleep, she heard him slide out of his own bed and come padding over to hers. 'You missed it all,' he said. 'There was an ice dragon, and it scared everybody. Father was afraid it had eaten you.'

Adara smiled to herself in the darkness, but said nothing.

She flew on the ice dragon four more times that winter, and every winter after that. Each year she flew further and more often than the year before, and the ice dragon was seen more frequently in the skies above their farm.

Each winter was longer and colder than the one before.

Each year the thaw came later.

And sometimes there were patches of land, where the ice dragon had lain to rest, that never seemed to thaw properly at all.

There was much talk in the village during her sixth year, and a message was sent to the king. No answer ever came.

'A bad business, ice dragons,' Hal said that summer when he visited the farm. 'They're not like real dragons, you know. You can't break them or train them. We have tales of those that tried, found frozen with their whip and harness in hand. I've heard about people that have lost hands or fingers just by touching one of them. Frostbite. Yes, a bad business.'

'Then why doesn't the king do something?' her father demanded. 'We sent a message. Unless we can kill the beast or drive it away, in a year or two we won't have any planting season at all.'

Hal smiled grimly. 'The king has other concerns. The war is going badly, you know. They advance every summer, and they have twice as many dragonriders as we do. I tell you, John, it's hell up there. Some year I'm not going to come back. The king can hardly spare men to go chasing an ice dragon.' He laughed. 'Besides, I don't think anybody's ever killed one of the things. Maybe we should just let the enemy take this whole province. Then it'll be *his* ice dragon.'

But it wouldn't be, Adara thought as she listened. No matter what king ruled the land, it would always be *her* ice dragon.

Hal departed and summer waxed and waned. Adara counted the days until her birthday. Hal passed through again before the first chill, taking his ugly dragon south for the winter. His wing seemed smaller when it came flying over the forest that fall, though, and his visit was briefer than usual, and ended with a loud quarrel between him and her father.

'They won't move during the winter,' Hal said. 'The winter terrain is too treacherous, and they won't risk an advance without dragonriders to cover them from above. But come spring, we aren't going to be able to hold them. The king may not even try. Sell the farm now, while you can still get a good price. You can buy another piece of land in the south.'

'This is my land,' her father said. 'I was born here. You too, though you seem to have forgotten it. Our parents are buried here. And Beth too. I want to lie beside her when I go.'

'You'll go a lot sooner than you'd like if you don't listen to me,' Hal said angrily. 'Don't be stupid, John. I know what the land means to you, but it isn't worth your life.' He went on and on, but her father would not be moved. They ended the evening swearing at each other, and Hal left in the dead of night, slamming the door behind him as he went.

Adara, listening, had made a decision. It did not matter what her father did or did not do. She would stay. If she moved, the ice dragon would not know where to find her when winter came, and if she went too far south it would never be able to come to her at all.

It did come to her, though, just after her seventh birthday. That winter was the coldest one of all. She flew so often and so far that she scarcely had time to work on her ice castle.

Hal came again in the spring. There were only a dozen dragons in his wing, and he brought no presents that year. He and her father argued once again. Hal raged and pleaded and threatened, but her father was stone. Finally Hal left, off to the battlefields.

That was the year the king's line broke, up north near some town with a long name that Adara could not pronounce.

Teri heard about it first. She returned from the inn one night flushed and excited. 'A messenger came through, on his way to the king,' she told them. 'The enemy won some big battle, and he's to ask for reinforcements. He said our army is retreating.'

Their father frowned, and worry lines creased his brow. 'Did he say anything of the king's dragonriders?' Arguments or no, Hal was family.

'I asked,' Teri said. 'He said the dragonriders are the rear guard. They're supposed to raid and burn, delay the enemy while our army pulls back safely. Oh, I hope Uncle Hal is safe!'

'Hal will show them,' Geoff said. 'Him and Brimstone will burn 'em all up.'

Their father smiled. 'Hal could always take care of himself. At any rate, there is nothing we can do. Teri, if any more messengers come through, ask them how it goes.'

She nodded, her concern not quite covering her excitement. It was all quite thrilling.

In the weeks that followed, the thrill wore off, as the people of the area began to comprehend the magnitude of the disaster. The king's highway grew busier and busier, and all the traffic flowed from north to south, and all the travelers wore green-and-gold. At first the soldiers marched in disciplined columns, led by officers wearing golden helmets, but even then they were less than stirring. The columns marched wearily, and the uniforms were filthy and torn, and the swords and pikes and axes the soldiers carried were nicked and oft times stained. Some men had lost their weapons; they limped along blindly, empty-handed. And the trains of wounded that followed the columns were often longer than the columns themselves. Adara stood in the grass by the side of the road and watched them pass. She saw a man with no eyes supporting a man with only one leg, as the two of them walked together. She saw men with no legs, or no arms, or both. She saw a man with his head split open by an axe, and many men covered with caked blood and filth, men who moaned low in their throats as they walked. She *smelled* men with bodies that were horribly greenish and puffed-up. One of them died and was left abandoned by the side of the road. Adara told her father and he and some of the men from the village came out and buried him.

Most of all, Adara saw the burned men. There were dozens of them in every column that passed, men whose skin was black and seared and falling off, who had lost an arm or a leg or half of a face to the hot breath of a dragon. Teri told them what the officers said, when they stopped at the inn to drink or rest: the enemy had many, many dragons.

For almost a month the columns flowed past, more every day. Even Old Laura admitted that she had never seen so much traffic on the road. From time to time a lone messenger on horseback rode against the tide, galloping towards the north, but always alone. After a time everyone knew there would be no reinforcements.

An officer in one of the last columns advised the people of the area to pack up whatever they could carry and move south. 'They are coming,' he warned. A few listened to him, and indeed for a week the road was full of refugees from towns further north. Some of them told frightful stories. When they left, more of the local people went with them.

But most stayed. They were people like her father, and the land was in their blood.

The last organized force to come down the road was a ragged troop of cavalry, men as gaunt as skeletons riding horses with skin pulled tight around their ribs. They thundered past in the night, their mounts heaving and foaming, and the only one to pause was a pale young officer, who reigned his mount up briefly and shouted, 'Go, go. They are burning everything!' Then he was off after his men.

The few soldiers who came after were alone or in small groups. They did not always use the road, and they did not pay for the things they took. One swordsman killed a farmer on the other side of town, raped his wife, stole his money, and ran. His rags were green-and-gold.

Then no one came at all. The road was deserted.

The innkeeper claimed he could smell ashes when the wind blew from the north. He packed up his family and went south. Teri was distraught. Geoff was wide-eyed and anxious and only a bit frightened. He asked a thousand questions about the enemy, and practiced at being a warrior. Their father went about his labors, busy as ever. War or no war, he had crops in the field. He smiled less than usual, however, and he began to drink, and Adara often saw him glancing up at the sky while he worked.

Adara wandered the fields alone, played by herself in the damp summer heat, and tried to think of where she would hide if her father tried to take them away.

Last of all, the king's dragonriders came, and with them Hal.

There were only four of them. Adara saw the first one, and went and told her father, and he put his hand on her shoulder and together they watched it pass, a solitary green dragon with a vaguely tattered look. It did not pause for them.

Two days later, three dragons flying together came into view, and one of them detached itself from the others and circled down to their farm while the other two headed south.

Uncle Hal was thin and grim and sallow-looking. His dragon looked sick. Its eyes ran, and one of its wings had been partially burned, so it flew in an awkward, heavy manner, with much difficulty. 'Now will you go?' Hal said to his brother, in front of all the children.

'No. Nothing has changed.'

Hal swore. 'They will be here within three days,' he said. 'Their dragonriders may be here even sooner.'

'Father, I'm scared,' Teri said.

He looked at her, saw her fear, hesitated, and finally turned back to his brother. 'I am staying. But if you would, I would have you take the children.'

Now it was Hal's turn to pause. He thought for a moment, and finally shook his head. 'I can't, John. I would, willingly, joyfully, if it were possible. But it isn't. Brimstone is wounded. He can barely carry me. If I took on any extra weight, we might never make it.'

Teri began to weep.

'I'm sorry, love,' Hal said to her. 'Truly I am.' His fists clenched helplessly.

'Teri is almost full-grown,' their father said. 'If her weight is too much, then take one of the others.'

Brother looked at brother, with despair in their eyes. Hal trembled. 'Adara,' he said finally. 'She's small and light.' He forced a laugh. 'She hardly weighs anything at all. I'll take Adara. The rest of you take horses, or a wagon, or go on foot. But go, damn you, go.'

'We will see,' their father said noncommittally. 'You take Adara, and keep her safe for us.'

'Yes,' Hal agreed. He turned and smiled at her. 'Come, child. Uncle Hal is going to take you for a ride on Brimstone.'

Adara looked at him very seriously. 'No,' she said. She turned and slipped through the door and began to run.

They came after her, of course, Hal and her father and even Geoff. But her father wasted time standing in the door, shouting at her to come back, and when he began to run he was ponderous and clumsy, while Adara was indeed small and light and fleet of foot. Hal and Geoff stayed with her longer, but Hal was weak, and Geoff soon winded himself, though he sprinted hard at her heels for a few moments. By the time Adara reached the nearest wheat field, the three of them were well behind her. She quickly lost herself amid the grain, and they searched for hours in vain while she made her way carefully towards the woods.

When dusk fell, they brought out lanterns and torches and continued their search. From time to time she heard her father swearing, or Hal calling out her name. She stayed high in the branches of the oak she had climbed, and smiled down at their lights as they combed back and forth through the fields. Finally she drifted off to sleep, dreaming about the coming of winter and wondering how she would live until her birthday. It was still a long time away.

Dawn woke her; dawn and a noise in the sky.

Adara yawned and blinked, and heard it again. She shinnied to the uppermost limb of the tree, as high as it would bear her, and pushed aside the leaves.

There were dragons in the sky.

She had never seen beasts quite like these. Their scales were dark and sooty, not green like the dragon Hal rode. One was a rust color and one was the shade of dried blood and one was black as coal. All of them had eyes like glowing embers, and steam rose from their nostrils, and their tails flicked back and forth as their dark, leathery wings beat the air. The rust-colored one opened its mouth and roared, and the forest shook to its challenge, and even the branch that held Adara trembled just a little. The black one made a noise too, and when it opened its maw a spear of flame lanced out, all orange and blue, and touched the trees below. Leaves withered and blackened, and smoke began to rise from where the dragon's breath had fallen. The one the color of blood flew close overhead, its wings creaking and straining, its mouth half-open. Between its yellowed teeth Adara saw soot and cinders, and the wind stirred by its passage was fire and sandpaper, raw and chafing against her skin. She cringed.

On the backs of the dragons rode men with whip and lance, in uniforms of black-and-orange, their faces hidden behind dark helmets. The one on the rust dragon gestured with his lance, pointing at the farm buildings across the fields. Adara looked.

Hal came up to meet them.

His green dragon was as large as their own, but somehow it seemed small to Adara as she watched it climb upwards from the farm. With its wings fully extended, it was plain to see how badly injured it was; the right wing tip was charred, and it leaned heavily to one side as it flew. On its back, Hal looked like one of the tiny toy soldiers he had brought them as a present years before.

The enemy dragonriders split up and came at him from three sides. Hal saw what they were doing. He tried to turn, to throw himself at the black dragon head-on, and flee the other two. His whip flailed angrily, desperately. His green dragon opened its mouth, and roared a challenge, but its flame was pale and short and did not reach enemy.

The others held their fire. Then, on a signal, their dragons all breathed as one. Hal was wreathed in flames.

His dragon made a high wailing noise, and Adara saw that it was burning, *he* was burning, they were all burning, beast and master both. They fell heavily to the ground, and lay smoking amidst her father's wheat.

The air was full of ashes.

Adara craned her head around in the other direction, and saw a column of smoke rising from beyond the forest and the river. That was the farm where Old Laura lived with her grandchildren and *their* children.

When she looked back, the three dark dragons were circling lower and lower above her own farm. One by one they landed. She watched the first of the riders dismount and saunter towards their door.

She was frightened and confused and only seven, after all. And the heavy air of summer was a weight upon her, and it filled her with a helplessness and thickened all her fears. So Adara did the only thing she knew, without thinking, a thing that came naturally to her. She climbed down from her tree and ran. She ran across the fields and through the woods, away from the farm and her family and the dragons, away from all of it. She ran until her legs throbbed with pain, down in the direction of the river. She ran to the coldest place she knew, to the deep caves underneath the river bluffs, to chill shelter and darkness and safety.

And there in the cold she hid. Adara was a winter child, and cold did not bother her. But still, as she hid, she trembled.

Day turned into night. Adara did not leave her cave.

She tried to sleep, but her dreams were full of burning dragons.

She made herself very small as she lay in the darkness, and tried to count how many days remained until her birthday. The caves were nicely cool; Adara could almost imagine that it was not summer after all, that it was winter, or near to winter. Soon her ice dragon would come for her, and she would ride on its back to the land of always-winter, where great ice castles and cathedrals of snow stood eternally in endless fields of white, and the stillness and silence were all.

It almost felt like winter as she lay there. The cave grew colder and colder, it seemed. It made her feel safe. She napped briefly. When she woke, it was colder still. A white coating of frost covered the cave walls, and she was sitting on a bed of ice. Adara jumped to her feet and looked up towards the mouth of the cave, filled with a wan dawn light. A cold wind caressed her. But it was coming from outside, from the world of summer, not from the depths of the cave at all.

She gave a small shout of joy and climbed and scrambled up the ice-covered rocks.

Outside, the ice dragon was waiting for her.

It had breathed upon the water, and now the river was frozen, or at least a part of it was, although one could see that the ice was fast melting as the summer sun rose. It had breathed upon the green grass that grew along the banks, grass as high as Adara, and now the tall blades were white and brittle, and when the ice dragon moved its wings the grass cracked in half and tumbled, sheared as clean as if it had been cut down with a scythe.

The dragon's icy eyes met Adara's, and she ran to it and up its wing, and threw her arms about it. She knew she had to hurry. The ice dragon looked smaller than she had ever seen it, and she understood what the heat of summer was doing to it.

'Hurry, dragon,' she whispered. 'Take me away, take me to the land of always-winter. We'll never come back here, never. I'll build you the best castle of all, and take care of you, and ride you every day. Just take me away, dragon, take me home with you.'

The ice dragon heard and understood. Its wide translucent wings unfolded and beat the air, and bitter arctic winds howled through the fields of summer. They rose. Away from the cave. Away from the river. Above the forest. Up and up. The ice dragon swung around to the north. Adara caught a glimpse of her father's farm, but it was very small and growing smaller. They turned their back to it, and soared.

Then a sound came to Adara's ears. An impossible sound, a sound that was too small and too far away for her to ever have heard it, especially above the beating of the ice dragon's wings. But she heard it nonetheless. She heard her father scream.

Hot tears ran down her cheeks, and where they fell upon the ice dragon's back they burned small pockmarks in the frost. Suddenly the cold beneath her hands was biting, and when she pulled one hand away Adara saw the mark that it had made upon the dragon's neck. She was scared, but still she clung. 'Turn back,' she whispered. 'Oh, *please*, dragon. Take me back.'

She could not see the ice dragon's eyes, but she knew what they would look like. Its mouth opened and a blue-white plume issued, a long cold streamer that hung in the air. It made no noise; ice dragons are silent. But in her mind Adara heard the wild keening of its grief.

'Please,' she whispered once again. 'Help me.' Her voice was thin and small.

The ice dragon turned.

The three dark dragons were outside of the barn when Adara returned, feasting on the burned and blackened carcasses of her father's stock. One of the dragonriders was standing near them, leaning on his lance and prodding his dragon from time to time.

He looked up when the cold gust of wind came shrieking across the fields, and shouted something, and sprinted for the black dragon. The beast tore a last hunk of meat from her father's horse, swallowed, and rose reluctantly into the air. The rider flailed his whip.

Adara saw the door of the farmhouse burst open. The other two riders rushed out, and ran for their dragons. One of them was struggling into his pants as he ran. He was bare-chested.

The black dragon roared, and its fire came blazing up at them. Adara felt the searing of heat, and a shudder went through the ice dragon as the flames played along its belly. Then it craned its long neck around, and fixed its baleful empty eyes upon the enemy, and opened its frostrimmed jaws. Out from among its icy teeth its breath came streaming, and that breath was pale and cold.

It touched the left wing of the coal-black dragon beneath them, and the dark beast gave a shrill cry of pain, and when it beat its wings again, the frost-covered wing broke in two. Dragon and dragonrider began to fall.

The ice dragon breathed again.

They were frozen and dead before they hit the ground.

The rust-colored dragon was flying at them, and the dragon the color of blood with its bare-chested rider. Adara's ears were filled with their angry roaring, and she could feel their hot breath around her, and see the air shimmering with heat, and smell the stink of sulfur.

Two long swords of fire crossed in midair, but neither touched the ice dragon, though it shriveled in the heat, and water flew from it like rain whenever it beat its wings.

The blood-colored dragon flew too close, and the breath of the ice dragon blasted the rider. His bare chest turned blue before Adara's eyes, and moisture condensed on him in an instant, covering him with frost. He screamed, and died, and fell from his mount, though his harness had remained behind, frozen to the neck of his dragon. The ice dragon closed on it, wings screaming the secret song of winter, and a blast of flame met a blast of cold. The ice dragon shuddered once again, and twisted away, dripping. The other dragon died.

But the last dragonrider was behind them now, the enemy in full armor on the dragon whose scales were the brown of rust. Adara screamed, and even as she did the fire enveloped the ice dragon's wing. It was gone in less than an instant, but the wing was gone with it, melted, destroyed.

The ice dragon's remaining wing beat wildly to slow its plunge, but it came to earth with an awful crash. Its legs shattered beneath it, and its wing snapped in two places, and the impact of the landing threw Adara from its back. She tumbled to the soft earth of the field, and rolled, and struggled up, bruised but whole.

The ice dragon seemed very small now, very broken. Its long neck sank wearily to the ground, and its head rested amid the wheat.

The enemy dragonrider came swooping in, roaring with triumph. The dragon's eyes burned. The man flourished his lance and shouted.

The ice dragon painfully raised its head once more, and made the only sound that Adara ever heard it make: a terrible thin cry full of melancholy, like the sound the north wind makes when it moves around the towers and battlements of the white castle that stands empty in the land of always-winter.

When the cry had faded, the ice dragon sent cold into the world one final time: a long smoking blue-white stream of cold that was full of snow and stillness and the end of all living things. The dragonrider flew right into it, still brandishing whip and lance. Adara watched him crash.

Then she was running, away from the fields, back to the house and her family within, running as fast as she could, running and panting and crying all the while like a seven-year-old.

Her father had been nailed to the bedroom wall. They had wanted him to watch while they took their turns with Teri. Adara did not know what to do, but she untied Teri, whose tears had dried by then, and they freed Geoff, and then they got their father down. Teri nursed him and cleaned out his wounds. When his eyes opened and he saw Adara he smiled. She hugged him very hard, and cried for him.

By night he said he was fit enough to travel. They crept away under cover of darkness, and took the king's road south.

Her family asked no questions then, in those hours of darkness and fear. But later, when they were safe in the south, there were questions endlessly. Adara gave them the best answers she could. But none of them ever believed her, except for Geoff, and he grew out of it when he got older. She was only seven, after all, and she did not understand that ice dragons are never seen in summer, and cannot be tamed nor ridden.

Besides, when they left the house that night, there was no ice dragon to be seen. Only the huge dark corpses of three war dragons and the smaller bodies of three dragonriders in black-and-orange. And a pond that had never been there before, a small quiet pool where the water was very old. They had walked around it carefully, headed towards the road.

Their father worked for another farmer for three years in the south. His hands were never as strong as they had been, before the nails had been pounded through them, but he made up for that with the strength of his back and his arms, and his determination. He saved whatever he could, and he seemed happy. 'Hal is gone, and my land,' he would tell Adara, 'and I am sad for that. But it is all right. I have my daughter back.' For the winter was gone from her now, and she smiled and laughed and even wept like other little girls.

Three years after they had fled, the king's army routed the enemy in a great battle, and the king's dragons burned the foreign capital. In the peace that followed, the northern provinces changed hands once more. Teri had recaptured her spirit and married a young trader, and she remained in the south. Geoff and Adara returned with their father to the farm.

When the first frost came, all the ice lizards came out, just as they had always done. Adara watched them with a smile on her face, remembering the way it had been. But she did not try to touch them. They were cold and fragile little things, and the warmth of her hands would hurt them.

In the Lost Lands

You can buy anything you might desire from Gray Alys. But it is better not to.

*

The Lady Melange did not come herself to Gray Alys. She was said to be a clever and a cautious young woman, as well as exceedingly fair and she had heard the stories. Those who dealt with Gray Alys did so at their own peril, it was said. Gray Alys did not refuse any of those who came to her, and she always got them what they wanted. Yet somehow, when all was done, those who dealt with Gray Alys were never happy with the things that she brought them, the things that they had wanted. The Lady Melange knew all this, ruling as she did from the high keep built into the side of the mountain. Perhaps that was why she did not come herself.

Instead, it was Jerais who came calling on Gray Alys that day; Blue Jerais, the lady's champion, foremost of the paladins who secured her high keep and led her armies into battle, captain of her colorguard. Jerais wore an underlining of pale blue silk beneath the deep azure plate of his enameled armor. The sigil on his shield was a maelstrom done in a hundred subtle hues of blue, and a sapphire large as an eagle's eye was set in the hilt of his sword. When he entered Gray Alys' presence and removed his helmet, his eyes were a perfect match for the jewel in his sword, though his hair was a startling and inappropriate red.

Gray Alys received him in the small, ancient stone house she kept in the dim heart of the town beneath the mountain. She waited for him in a windowless room full of dust and the smell of mold, seated in an old high-backed chair that seemed to dwarf her small, thin body. In her lap was a gray rat the size of a small dog. She stroked it languidly as Jerais entered and took off his helmet and let his bright blue eyes adjust to the dimness.

'Yes?' Gray Alys said at last.

'You are the one they call Gray Alys,' Jerais said.

'I am.'

'I am Jerais. I come at the behest of the Lady Melange.'

'The wise and beautiful Lady Melange,' said Gray Alys. The rat's fur was soft as velvet beneath her long, pale fingers. 'Why does the Lady send her champion to one as poor and plain as I?'

'Even in the keep, we hear tales of you,' said Jerais.

'Yes.'

'It is said, for a price, you will sell things strange and wonderful.'

'Does the Lady Melange wish to buy?'

'It is said also that you have powers, Gray Alys. It is said that you are not always as you sit before me now, a slender woman of indeterminate age, clad all in gray. It is said that you become young and old as you wish. It is said that sometimes you are a man, or an old woman, or a child. It is said that you know the secrets of shapeshifting, that you go abroad as a great cat, a bear, a bird, and that you change your skin at will, not as a slave to the moon like the werefolk of the lost lands.'

'All of these things are said,' Gray Alys acknowledged.

Jerais removed a small leather bag from his belt and stepped closer to where Gray Alys sat. He loosened the drawstring that held the bag shut, and spilled out the contents on the table by her side. Gems. A dozen of them, in as many colors. Gray Alys lifted one and held it to her eye, watching the candle flame through it. When she placed it back among the others, she nodded at Jerais and said, 'What would the Lady buy of me?'

'Your secret,' Jerais said, smiling. 'The Lady Melange wishes to shapeshift.'

'She is said to be young and beautiful,' Gray Alys replied. 'Even here beyond the keep, we hear many tales of her. She has no mate but many lovers. All of her colorguard are said to love her, among them yourself. Why should she wish to change?'

'You misunderstand. The Lady Melange does not seek youth or beauty. No change could make her fairer than she is. She wants from you the power to become a beast. A wolf.'

'Why?' asked Gray Alys.

'That is none of your concern. Will you sell her this gift?'

'I refuse no one,' said Gray Alys. 'Leave the gems here. Return in one month, and I shall give you what the Lady Melange desires.'

Jerais nodded. His face looked thoughtful. 'You refuse no one?'

'No one.'

He grinned crookedly, reached into his belt, and extended his hand to her. Within the soft blue crushed velvet of his gloved palm rested another jewel, a sapphire even larger than the one set in the hilt of his sword. 'Accept this as payment, if you will. I wish to buy for myself.'

Gray Alys took the sapphire from his palm, held it up between thumb and forefinger against the candle flame, nodded, and dropped it among the other jewels. 'What would you have, Jerais?'

His grin spread wider. 'I would have you fail,' he said. 'I do not want the Lady Melange to have this power she seeks.'

Gray Alys regarded him evenly, her steady gray eyes fixed on his own cold blue ones. 'You wear the wrong color, Jerais,' she said at last. 'Blue is the color of loyalty, yet you betray your mistress and the mission she entrusted to you.'

'I am loyal,' Jerais protested. 'I know what is good for her, better than she knows herself. Melange is young and foolish. She thinks it can be kept secret, when she finds this power she seeks. She is wrong. And when the people know, they will destroy her. She cannot rule these folk by day, and tear out their throats by night.'

Gray Alys considered that for a time in silence, stroking the great rat that lay across her lap. 'You lie, Jerais,' she said when she spoke again. 'The reasons you give are not your true reasons.'

Jerais frowned. His gloved hand, almost casually, came to rest on the hilt of his sword. His thumb stroked the great sapphire set there. 'I will not argue with you,' he said gruffly. 'If you will not sell to me, give me back my gem and be damned with you!'

'I refuse no one,' Gray Alys replied.

Jerais scowled in confusion. 'I shall have what I ask?'

'You shall have what you want.'

'Excellent,' said Jerais, grinning again. 'In a month, then!'

'A month,' agreed Gray Alys.

*

And so Gray Alys sent the word out, in ways that only Gray Alys knew. The message passed from mouth to mouth through the shadows and alleys and the secret sewers of the town, and even to the tall houses of scarlet wood and colored glass where dwelled the noble and the rich. Soft gray rats with tiny human hands whispered it to sleeping children, and the children shared it with each other, and chanted a strange new chant when they skipped rope. The word drifted to all the army outposts to the east, and rode west with the great caravans into the heart of the old empire of which the town beneath the mountain was only the smallest part. Huge leathery birds with the cunning faces of monkeys flew the word south, over the forests and the rivers, to a dozen different kingdoms, where men and women as pale and terrible as Gray Alys herself heard it in the solitude of their towers. Even north, past the mountains, even into the lost lands, the word traveled.

It did not take long. In less than two weeks, he came to her. 'I can lead you to what you seek,' he told her. 'I can find you a werewolf.'

He was a young man, slender and beardless. He dressed in the worn leathers of the rangers who lived and hunted in the windswept desolation beyond the mountains. His skin had the deep tan of a man who spent all his life outdoors, though his hair was as white as mountain snow and fell about his shoulders, tangled and unkempt. He wore no armor and carried a long knife instead of a sword, and he moved with a wary grace. Beneath the pale strands of hair that fell across his face, his eyes were dark and sleepy. Though his smile was open and amiable, there was a curious indolence to him as well, and a dreamy, sensuous set to his lips when he thought no one was watching. He named himself Boyce.

Gray Alys watched him and listened to his words and finally said, 'Where?'

'A week's journey north,' Boyce replied. 'In the lost lands.'

'Do you dwell in the lost lands, Boyce?' Gray Alys asked of him.

'No. They are no fit place for dwelling. I have a home here in town. But I go beyond the mountains often, Gray Alys. I am a hunter. I know the lost lands well, and I know the things that live there. You seek a man who walks like a wolf. I can take you to him. But we must leave at once, if we are to arrive before the moon is full.'

Gray Alys rose. 'My wagon is loaded, my horses are fed and shod. Let us depart then.'

Boyce brushed the fine white hair from his eyes, and smiled lazily.

*

The mountain pass was high and steep and rocky, and in places barely wide enough for Gray Alys' wagon to pass. The wagon was a cumbersome thing, long and heavy and entirely enclosed, once brightly-painted but now faded so by time and weather that its wooden walls were all a dreary gray. It rode on six clattering iron wheels, and the two horses that pulled it were of necessity monsters half again the size of normal beasts. Even so, they kept a slow pace through the mountains. Boyce, who had no horse, walked ahead or alongside, and sometimes rode up next to Gray Alys. The wagon groaned and creaked. It took them three days to ascend to the highest point on the mountain road, where they looked through a cleft in the mountains out onto the wide barren plains of the lost lands. It took them three more days to descend.

'Now we will make better time,' Boyce promised Gray Alys when they reached the lost lands themselves. 'Here the land is flat and empty, and the going will be easy. A day now, perhaps two, and you shall have what you seek.'

'Yes,' said Gray Alys.

They filled the water barrels full before they left the mountain and Boyce went hunting in the foothills and returned with three black rabbits and the carcass of a small deer, curiously deformed, and when Gray Alys asked him how he had brought them down with only a knife as a weapon, Boyce smiled and produced a sling and sent several small stones whistling through the air. Gray Alys nodded. They made a small fire and cooked two of the rabbits, and salted the rest of the meat. The next morning, at dawn, they set off into the lost lands.

Here they moved quickly indeed. The lost lands were a cold and empty place, and the earth was packed as hard and firm as the road that wound through the empire beyond the mountains. The wagon rolled along briskly, creaking and clattering, shaking a bit from side to side as it went. In the lost lands there were no thickets to cut through, no rivers to cross. Desolation lay before them on all sides, seemingly endless. From time to time they saw a grove of trees, gnarled and twisted all together, limbs heavy with swollen fruit with skin the color of indigo, shining. From time to time they clattered through a shallow, rocky stream, none deeper than ankle level. From time to time vast patches of white fungus blanketed the desolate gray earth. Yet all these things were rare. Mostly there was only the emptiness, the shuddering dead plains all around them, and the winds. The winds were terrible in the lost lands. They blew constantly, and they were cold and bitter, and sometimes they smelled of ash, and sometimes they seemed to howl and shriek like some poor doomed soul.

At last they had come far enough so Gray Alys could see the end of the lost lands: another line of mountains far, far north of them, a vague bluish-white line across the gray horizon. They could travel for weeks and not reach those distant peaks, Gray Alys knew, yet the lost lands were so flat and so empty that even now they could make them out, dimly.

At dusk Gray Alys and Boyce made their camp, just beyond a grove of the curious tortured trees they had glimpsed on their journey north. The trees gave them a partial respite from the fury of the wind, but even so they could hear it, keening and pulling at them, twisting their fire into wild suggestive shapes.

'These lands are lost indeed,' Gray Alys said as they ate.

'They have their own beauty,' Boyce replied. He impaled a chunk of meat on the end of his long knife, and turned it above the fire. 'Tonight, if the clouds pass, you will see the lights rippling above the northern mountains, all purple and gray and maroon, twisting like curtains caught in this endless wind.'

'I have seen those lights before,' said Gray Alys.

'I have seen them many times,' Boyce said. He bit off a piece of meat, pulling at it with his teeth, and a thin line of grease ran down from the corner of his mouth. He smiled.

'You come to the lost lands often,' Gray Alys said.

Boyce shrugged. 'I hunt.'

'Does anything live here?' asked Gray Alys. 'Live amidst all this desolation?'

'Oh yes,' Boyce replied. 'You must have eyes to find it, you must know the lost lands, but it is there. Strange twisted beasts never seen beyond the mountains, things out of legends and nightmares, enchanted things and accursed things, things whose flesh is impossibly rare and impossibly delicious. Humans, too, or things that are almost human. Werefolk and changelings and gray shapes that walk only by twilight, shuffling things half-living and half-dead.' His smile was gentle and taunting. 'But you are Gray Alys, and all this you must know. It is said you came out of the lost lands yourself once, long ago.'

'It is said,' Gray Alys answered.

'We are alike, you and I,' Boyce replied. 'I love the town, the people, song and laughter and gossip. I savor the comforts of my house, good food and good wine. I relish the players who come each fall to the high keep and perform for the Lady Melange. I like fine clothes and jewels and soft, pretty women. Yet part of me is only at home here, in the lost lands, listening to the wind, watching the shadows warily each dusk, dreaming things the townsfolk never dare.' Full dark had fallen by then. Boyce lifted his knife and pointed north, to where dim lights had begun to glow faintly against the mountains. 'See there, Gray Alys. See how the lights shimmer and shift. You can see shapes in them if you watch long enough. Men and women and things that are neither, moving against the darkness. Their voices are carried by the wind. Watch and listen. There are great dramas in those lights, plays grander and stranger than any ever performed on the Lady's stage. Do you hear? Do you see?'

Gray Alys sat on the hard-packed earth with her legs crossed and her gray eyes unreadable, watching in silence. Finally she spoke. 'Yes,' she said, and that was all.

Boyce sheathed his long knife and came around the campfire – it had died now to a handful of dim reddish embers – to sit beside her. 'I knew you would see,' he said. 'We are alike, you and I. We wear the flesh of the city, but in our blood the cold wind of the lost lands is blowing always. I could see it in your eyes, Gray Alys.'

She said nothing; she sat and watched the lights, feeling the warm presence of Boyce beside her. After a time he put an arm about her shoulders, and Gray Alys did not protest. Later, much later, when the fire had gone entirely dark and the night had grown cold, Boyce reached out and cupped her chin within his hand and turned her face to his. He kissed her, once, gently, full upon her thin lips.

And Gray Alys woke, as if from a dream, and pushed him back upon the ground and undressed him with sure, deft hands and took him then and there. Boyce let her do it all. He lay upon the chill hard ground with his hands clasped behind his head, his eyes dreamy and his lips curled up in a lazy, complacent smile, while Gray Alys rode him, slowly at first, then faster and faster, building to a shuddering climax. When she came her body went stiff and she threw her head back; her mouth opened, as if to cry out, but no sound came forth. There was only the wind, cold and wild, and the cry it made was not a cry of pleasure.

*

The next day dawned chill and overcast. The sky was full of thin, twisted gray clouds that raced before them faster than clouds ought to race. What light filtered through seemed wan and colorless. Boyce walked beside the wagon while Gray Alys drove it forward at a leisurely pace. 'We are close now,' Boyce told her. 'Very close.'

'Yes.'

Boyce smiled up at her. His smile had changed since they had become lovers. It was fond and mysterious, and more than a bit indulgent. It was a smile that presumed. 'Tonight,' he told her.

'The moon will be full tonight,' Gray Alys said.

Boyce smiled and pushed the hair from his eyes and said nothing.

*

Well before dusk, they drew up amidst the ruins of some nameless town long forgotten even by those who dwelled in the lost lands. Little remained to disturb the sweeping emptiness, only a huddle of broken masonry, forlorn and pitiful. The vague outlines of town walls could still be discerned, and one or two chimneys remained standing, jagged and half-shattered, gnawing at the horizon like rotten black teeth. No shelter was to be found here, no life. When Gray Alys had fed her horses, she wandered through the ruins but found little. No pottery, no rusted blades, no books. Not even bones. Nothing at all to hint of the people who had once lived here, if people they had been.

The lost lands had sucked the life out of this place and blown away even the ghosts, so not a trace of memory remained. The shrunken sun was low on the horizon, obscured by scuttling clouds, and the scene spoke to her with the wind's voice, cried out in loneliness and despair. Gray Alys stood for a long time, alone, watching the sun sink while her thin tattered cloak billowed behind her and the cold wind bit through into her soul. Finally she turned away and went back to the wagon.

Boyce had built a fire, and he sat in front of it, mulling some wine in a copper pot, adding spices from time to time. He smiled his new smile for

Gray Alys when she looked at him. 'The wind is cold,' he said. 'I thought a hot drink would make our meal more pleasant.'

Gray Alys glanced away towards the setting sun, then back at Boyce. 'This is not the time or the place for pleasure, Boyce. Dusk is all but upon us, and soon the full moon shall rise.'

'Yes,' said Boyce. He ladled some of the hot wine into his cup, and tried a swallow. 'No need to rush off hunting, though,' he said, smiling lazily. 'The wolf will come to us. Our scent will carry far in this wind, in this emptiness, and the smell of fresh meat will bring him running.'

Gray Alys said nothing. She turned away from him and climbed the three wooden steps that led up to the interior of her wagon. Inside she lit a brazier carefully, and watched the light shift and flicker against the weathered gray wallboards and the pile of furs on which she slept. When the light had grown steady, Gray Alys slid back a wall panel, and stared at the long row of tattered garments that hung on pegs within the narrow closet. Cloaks and capes and billowing loose shirts, strangely cut gowns and suits that clung like a second skin from head to toe, leather and fur and feathers. She hesitated briefly, then reached in and chose a great cloak made of a thousand long silver feathers, each one tipped delicately with black. Removing her simple cloth cloak, Gray Alys fastened the flowing feathered garment at her neck. When she turned it billowed all about her, and the dead air inside the wagon stirred and briefly seemed alive before the feathers settled and stilled once again. Then Gray Alys bent and opened a huge oaken chest, bound in iron and leather. From within she drew out a small box. Ten rings rested against worn gray felt, each set with a long, curving silver claw instead of a stone. Gray Alys donned them methodically, one ring to each finger, and when she rose and clenched her fists, the claws shone dimly and menacingly in the light from the brazier.

Outside, it was twilight. Boyce had not prepared any food, Gray Alys noted as she took her seat across the fire from where the pale-haired ranger sat quaffing his hot wine.

'A beautiful cloak,' Boyce observed amiably.

'Yes,' said Gray Alys.

'No cloak will help you when *he* comes, though.'

Gray Alys raised her hand, made a fist. The silver claws caught the firelight. Gleamed.

'Ah,' said Boyce. 'Silver.'

'Silver,' agreed Gray Alys, lowering her hand.

'Still,' Boyce said. 'Others have come against him, armed with silver. Silver swords, silver knives, arrows tipped with silver. They are dust now, all those silvered warriors. He gorged himself on their flesh.'

Gray Alys shrugged.

Boyce stared at her speculatively for a time, then smiled and went back to his wine. Gray Alys drew her cloak more tightly about herself to keep out the cold wind. After a while, staring off into the far distance, she saw lights moving against the northern mountains. She remembered the stories that she had seen there, the tales that Boyce had conjured for her from that play of colored shadows. They were grim and terrible stories. In the lost lands, there was no other kind.

At last another light caught her eye. A spreading dimness in the east, wan and ominous. Moonrise.

Gray Alys stared calmly across the dying camp fire. Boyce had begun to change.

She watched his body twist as bone and muscle changed within, watched his pale white hair grow longer and longer, watched his lazy smile turn into a wide red grin that split his face, saw the canines lengthen and the tongue come lolling out, watched the wine cup fall as his hands melted and writhed and became paws. He started to say something once, but no words came out, only a low, coarse snarl of laughter, half-human and half-animal. Then he threw back his head and howled, and he ripped at his clothing until it lay in tatters all about him and he was Boyce no longer. Across the fire from Gray Alys the wolf stood, a great shaggy white beast, half again the size of an ordinary wolf, with a savage red slash of a mouth and glowing scarlet eyes. Gray Alys stared into those eyes as she rose and shook the dust from her feathered cloak. They were knowing eyes, cunning, wise. Inside those eyes she saw a smile, a smile that presumed.

A smile that presumed too much.

The wolf howled once again, a long wild sound that melted into the wind. And then he leapt, straight across the embers of the fire he had built.

Gray Alys threw her arms out, her cloak bunched in her hands, and changed.

Her change was faster than his had been, over almost as soon as it had begun, but for Gray Alys it lasted an eternity. First there was the strange choking, clinging feeling as the cloak adhered to her skin, then dizziness and a curious liquid weakness as her muscles began to run and flow and reshape themselves. And finally exhilaration, as the power rushed into her and came coursing through her veins, a wine fiercer and hotter and wilder than the poor stuff Boyce had mulled above their fire.

She beat her vast silvery wings, each pinion tipped with black, and the dust stirred and swirled as she rose up into the moonlight, up to safety high above the white wolf's bound, up and up until the ruins shrunk to insignificance far beneath her. The wind took hold of her, caressed her with trembling icy hands, and she yielded herself to it and soared. Her great wings filled with the dread melody of the lost lands, carrying her higher and higher. Her cruel curving beak opened and closed and opened again, though no sound came forth. She wheeled across the sky, drunken with flight. Her eyes, sharper than any human eyes could be, saw far into the distance, spied out the secrets of every shadow, glimpsed all the dying and half-dead things that stirred and shambled across the barren face of the lost lands. The curtains of light to the north danced before her, a thousand times brighter and more gorgeous than they had been before, when she had only the dim eyes of the little thing called Gray Alys to perceive them with. She wanted to fly to them, to soar north and north and north, to cavort among those lights, shredding them into glowing strips with her talons.

She lifted her talons as if in challenge. Long and wickedly curved they were, and razor sharp, and the moonlight flashed along their length, pale upon the silver. And she remembered then, and she wheeled about in a great circle, reluctantly, and turned away from the beckoning lights of the northlands. Her wings beat and beat again, and she began to descend, shrieking down through the night air, plunging toward her prey.

She saw him far beneath her, a pale white shape hurtling away from the wagon, away from the fire, seeking safety in the shadows and the dark places. But there was no safety in the lost lands. He was strong and untiring, and his long powerful legs carried him forward in a steady swift lope that ate up the miles as if they were nothing. Already he had come a long way from their camp. But fast as he was, she was faster. He was only a wolf, after all, and she was the wind itself.

She descended in a dead silence, cutting through the wind like a knife, silver talons outstretched. But he must have spied her shadow streaking towards him, etched clear by the moonlight, for as she closed he spurted forward wildly, driven by fear. It was useless. He was running full out when she passed above him, raking him with her talons. They cut through fur and twisted flesh like ten bright silver swords, and he broke stride and staggered and went down.

She beat her wings and circled overhead for another pass, and as she did the wolf regained his feet and stared up at her terrible silhouette dark against the moon, his eyes brighter now than ever, turned feverish by fear. He threw back his head and howled a broken bloody howl that cried for mercy.

She had no mercy in her. Down she came, and down, talons drenched with blood, her beak open to rend and tear. The wolf waited for her, and leapt up to meet her dive, snarling, snapping. But he was no match for her.

She slashed at him in passing, evading him easily, opening five more long gashes that quickly welled with blood.

The next time she came around he was too weak to run, too weak to rise against her. But he watched her turn and descend, and his huge shaggy body trembled just before she struck.

*

Finally his eyes opened, blurred and weak. He groaned and moved feebly. It was daylight, and he was back in the camp, lying beside the fire. Gray Alys came to him when she heard him stir, knelt, and lifted his head. She held a cup of wine to his lips until he had drunk his fill.

When Boyce lay back again, she could see the wonder in his eyes, the surprise that he still lived. 'You knew,' he said hoarsely. 'You knew . . . what I was.'

'Yes,' said Gray Alys. She was herself once more; a slender, small, somehow ageless woman with wide gray eyes, clad in faded cloth. The feathered cloak was hung away, the silver claws no longer adorned her fingers.

Boyce tried to sit up, winced at the pain, and settled back on to the blanket she had laid beneath him. 'I thought . . . thought I was dead,' he said.

'You were close to dead,' Gray Alys replied.

'Silver,' he said bitterly. 'Silver cuts and burns so.'

'Yes.'

'But you saved me,' he said, confused.

'I changed back to myself, and brought you back, and tended you.'

Boyce smiled, though it was only a pale ghost of his old smile. 'You change at will,' he said wonderingly. 'Ah, there is a gift I would kill for, Gray Alys!'

She said nothing.

'It was too open here,' he said. 'I should have taken you elsewhere. If there had been cover . . . buildings, a forest, anything . . . then you should not have had such an easy time with me.'

'I have other skins,' Gray Alys replied. 'A bear, a cat. It would not have mattered.'

'Ah,' said Boyce. He closed his eyes. When he opened them again, he forced a twisted smile. 'You were beautiful, Gray Alys. I watched you fly for a long time before I realized what it meant and began to run. It was hard to tear my eyes from you. I knew you were the doom of me, but still I could not look away. So beautiful. All smoke and silver, with fire in your eyes. The last time, as I watched you swoop towards me, I was almost glad.

Better to perish at the hands of she who is so terrible and fine, I thought, than by some dirty little swordsman with his sharpened silver stick.'

'I am sorry,' said Gray Alys.

'No,' Boyce said quickly. 'It is better that you saved me. I will mend quickly, you will see. Even silver wounds bleed but briefly. Then we will be together.'

'You are still weak,' Gray Alys told him. 'Sleep.'

'Yes,' said Boyce. He smiled at her, and closed his eyes.

*

Hours had passed when Boyce finally woke again. He was much stronger, his wounds all but mended. But when he tried to rise, he could not. He was bound in place, spread-eagled, hands and feet tied securely to stakes driven into the hard gray earth.

Gray Alys watched him make the discovery, heard him cry out in alarm. She came to him, held up his head, and gave him more wine.

When she moved back, his head twisted around wildly, staring at his bonds, and then at her. 'What have you done?' he cried.

Gray Alys said nothing.

'Why?' he asked. 'I do not understand, Gray Alys. *Why*? You saved me, tended me, and now I am bound.'

'You would not like my answer, Boyce.'

'The moon!' he said wildly. 'You are afraid of what might happen tonight, when I change again.' He smiled, pleased to have figured out. 'You are being foolish. I would not harm you, not now, after what has passed between us, after what I know. We belong together, Gray Alys. We are alike, you and I. We have watched the lights together, and I have seen you fly! We must have trust between us! Let me loose.'

Gray Alys frowned and sighed and gave no other answer.

Boyce stared at her uncomprehending. 'Why?' he asked again 'Untie me, Alys, let me prove the truth of my words. You need not fear me.'

'I do not fear you, Boyce,' she said sadly.

'Good,' he said eagerly. 'Then free me, and change with me. Become a great cat tonight, and run beside me, hunt with me. I can lead you to prey you never dreamed of. There is so much we can share. You have felt how it is to change, you know the truth of it, you have tasted the power, the freedom, seen the lights from a beast's eyes, smelled fresh blood, gloried in a kill. You know ... the freedom ... the intoxication of it ... all the ... you know ...'

'I know,' Gray Alys acknowledged.

'Then free me! We are meant for one another, you and I. We will live together, love together, hunt together.'

Gray Alys shook her head.

'I do not understand,' Boyce said. He strained upward wildly at his bonds, and swore, then sunk back again. 'Am I hideous? Do you find me evil, unattractive?'

'No.'

'Then what?' he said bitterly. 'Other women have loved me, have found me handsome. Rich, beautiful ladies, the finest in the land. All of them have wanted me, even when they knew.'

'But you have never returned that love, Boyce,' she said.

'No,' he admitted. 'I have loved them after a fashion. I have never betrayed their trust, if that is what you think. I find my prey here, in the lost lands, not from among those who care for me.' Boyce felt the weight of Gray Alys' eyes, and continued. 'How could I love them more than I did?' he said passionately. 'They could know only half of me, only the half that lived in town and loved wine and song and perfumed sheets. The rest of me lived out here, in the lost lands, and knew things that they could never know, poor soft things. I told them so, those who pressed me hard. To join with me wholly they must run and hunt beside me. Like you. Let me go, Gray Alys. Soar for me, watch me run. Hunt with me.'

Gray Alys rose and sighed. 'I am sorry, Boyce. I would spare you if I could, but what must happen must happen. Had you died last night, it would have been useless. Dead things have no power. Night and day, black and white, they are weak. All strength derives from the realm between, from twilight, from shadow, from the terrible place between life and death. From the gray, Boyce, from the gray.'

He wrenched at his bonds again, savagely, and began to weep and curse and gnash his teeth. Gray Alys turned away from him and sought out the solitude of her wagon. There she remained for hours, sitting alone in the darkness and listening to Boyce swear and cry out to her with threats and pleadings and professions of love. Gray Alys stayed inside until well after moonrise. She did not want to watch him change, watch his humanity pass from him for the last time.

At last his cries had become howls, bestial and abandoned and full of pain. That was when Gray Alys finally reemerged. The full moon cast a wan pale light over the scene. Bound to the hard ground, the great white wolf writhed and howled and struggled and stared at her out of hungry scarlet eyes.

Gray Alys walked toward him calmly. In her hand was the long silver skinning knife, its blade engraved with fine and graceful runes.

*

When he finally stopped struggling, the work went more quickly, but still it was a long and bloody night. She killed him the instant she was done, before the dawn came and changed him and gave him back a human voice to cry his agony. Then Gray Alys hung up the pelt and brought out tools and dug a deep, deep grave in the packed cold earth. She piled stones and broken pieces of masonry on top of it, to protect him from the things that roamed the lost lands, the ghouls and the carrion crows and the other creatures that did not flinch at dead flesh. It took her most of the day to bury him, for the ground was very hard indeed, and even as she worked she knew it was a futile labor.

And when at last the work was done, and dusk had almost come again, she went once more into her wagon, and returned wearing the great cloak of a thousand silver feathers, tipped with black. Then she changed, and flew, and flew, a fierce and tireless flight, bathed in strange lights and wedded to the dark. All night she flew beneath a full and mocking moon, and just before dawn she cried out once, a shrill scream of despair and anguish that rang and keened on the sharp edge of the wind and changed its sound forever.

*

Perhaps Jerais was afraid of what she might give him, for he did not return to Gray Alys alone. He brought two other knights with him, a huge man all in white whose shield showed a skull carved out of ice, and another in crimson whose sigil was a burning man. They stood at the door, helmeted and silent, while Jerais approached Gray Alys warily. 'Well?' he demanded.

Across her lap was a wolfskin, the pelt of some huge massive beast, all white as mountain snow. Gray Alys rose and offered the skin to Blue Jerais, draping it across his outstretched arm. 'Tell the Lady Melange to cut herself, and drip her own blood onto the skin. Do this at moon-rise when the moon is full, and then the power will be hers. She need only wear the skin as a cloak, and will the change thereafter. Day or night, full moon or no moon, it makes no matter.'

Jerais looked at the heavy white pelt and smiled a hard smile. 'A wolfskin, eh? I had not expected that. I thought perhaps a potion, a spell.'

'No,' said Gray Alys. 'The skin of a werewolf.'

'A werewolf?' Jerais' mouth twisted curiously, and there was a sparkle in his deep sapphire eyes. 'Well, Gray Alys, you have done what the Lady Melange asked, but you have failed me. I did not pay you for success. Return my gem.'

'No,' said Gray Alys. 'I have earned it, Jerais.'

'I do not have what I asked for.'

'You have what you wanted, and that is what I promised.' Her gray eyes met his own without fear. 'You thought my failure would help you get what you truly wanted, and that my success would doom you. You were wrong.'

Jerais looked amused. 'And what do I truly desire?'

'The Lady Melange,' said Gray Alys. 'You have been one lover among many, but you wanted more. You wanted all. You knew you stood second in her affections. I have changed that. Return to her now, and bring her the thing that she has bought.'

*

That day there was bitter lamentation in the high keep on the mountain, when Blue Jerais knelt before the Lady Melange and offered her a white wolfskin. But when the screaming and the wailing and the mourning was done, she took the great pale cloak and bled upon it and learned the ways of change. It is not the union she desired, but it is a union nonetheless. So every night she prowls the battlements and the mountainside, and the townsfolk say her howling is wild with grief.

And Blue Jerais, who wed her a month after Gray Alys returned from the lost lands, sits beside a madwoman in the great hall by day, and locks his doors by night in terror of his wife's hot red eyes, and does not hunt anymore, or laugh, or lust.

*

You can buy anything you might desire from Gray Alys.

But it is better not to.

FIVE
HYBRIDS AND HORRORS

HYBRIDS AND HORRORS

I never read horror stories as a kid. At least, I never called them that. Monster stories, though . . . *those* I loved. At Halloween, when we went out trick-or-treating, I always wanted to be a ghost or monster, never a cowboy or a hobo or a clown.

The Plaza was the dingiest of Bayonne's three regular movie theaters, but I never missed their monster matinees on Saturday afternoons. Admission was only a quarter. The DeWitt and the Lyceum, the more upscale theaters, were where I saw William Castle's gimmick films, *The Tingler* and *13 Ghosts*. The one time I set foot inside the Victory, Bayonne's cavernous old decaying opera house, closed during most of my childhood, that was for a monster movie too. The seats were musty and dusty and, it turned out, infested; I came home covered with insect bites, and the Victory was boarded up again shortly thereafter.

There was scary stuff on television as well. You could catch the old Universal horror films at night, if your mother let you stay up late enough. The Wolfman was my favorite monster, though I liked Count Dracula and Frankenstein (he was always Frankenstein to us, never 'Frankenstein's monster' or 'the monster') as well. The Creature from the Black Lagoon and the Invisible Man were not to be compared to the big three, and the Mummy was just stupid. Besides the old movies, the tube also offered the occasional creepy episode of *The Twilight Zone* and *The Alfred Hitchcock Show* . . . but *Thriller*, hosted by Boris Karloff, was scarier than both and then some. Their adaptation of Robert E. Howard's 'Pigeons from Hell' frightened me as much as anything I ever saw on television until the Vietnam War . . . and the Vietnam War didn't have a guy come down a staircase with an axe buried in his head.

I devoured monster comics too, though I was too young for the really good ones, *Tales from the Crypt* and its mouldering EC ilk. I read about those later in the fanzines, but never owned a copy. I do recall coming across a beat-up old comic at the local barbershop that was a *lot* scarier than the ones I was buying; almost certainly, an old EC that the barber still had lying around. (He had piles of old pre-DC *Blackhawk* comics as well.) Before Marvel was Marvel, they published a lot of not-especially-scary monster comics where the monsters had these goofy names and came from outer space. Those I got, though they were tepid fare for the most part, and I never liked them half as well as superhero comics.

Funny books, movies, and television planted the seeds, and monstrous seed they were . . . but my love of actual horror fiction did not take root until 1965, when I paid fifty cents (outrageous the way book prices were going up) for an Avon paperback anthology called *Boris Karloff's Favorite Horror Stories* and read 'The Haunter of the Dark,' by H.P. Lovecraft. There were some other great yarns in that book as well, by the likes of Poe, Kornbluth, and Robert Bloch, but the Lovecraft was the one that caught me by the throat and wouldn't let go. I was afraid to go to sleep that night. The next day I began looking for more books with stories by HPL, who had vaulted to the top of my personal hit parade, where he remained for a long time, sharing pride of place with RAH and JRRT.

We write what we read. I never read Zane Grey growing up, and I've never written a western. I did read Heinlein, Tolkien, and Lovecraft. It was inevitable that one day I would set out to make some monsters of my own. As for those hybrids . . .

. . . long before H.P. Lovecraft came into my life, I once found a chemistry set waiting underneath the Christmas tree.

Chemistry sets were all the rage in the '50s, and were found beneath as many trees as Lionel trains or Roy Rogers gunbelts with the matching six-shooters (if you were a boy – girls got the Dale Evans set, and Betty Crocker baking sets instead of chemistry sets). It was the age of Sputnik, the age of Charles van Doren, the age of the atom; America wanted all us boys to grow up to be rocket scientists, so we could beat the damned Russkies to the moon.

The chemistry sets they sold then (and may still be selling, for all I know) consisted of a big hinged metal box with racks of little glass jars of chemicals inside, along with a few test tubes and beakers, and an instructional booklet describing the various educational experiments you could perform. On the front of the box there was usually a picture of a clean cut boy (never a girl) in a white lab coat, holding up a test tube as he performed one of the many educational experiments. (White lab coats were not included). Somewhere, I do not doubt, there must have been some kids like him, kids who dutifully followed the instructions, performed the educational experiments, learned many valuable scientific things, and grew up to be chemists.

I never knew any, though. All of the kids I knew who got chemistry sets for Christmas were more interested in trying to make stuff explode. Or turn weird colors. Or bubble and smoke. 'Let's see what will happen if we mix *this* with *that*,' we would say, as we dreamed of finding the secret formula that would turn us into a superhero, or at least Mr Hyde. Maybe our parents thought the chemistry sets would set us on the path to becoming Jonas Salk or Wernher von Braun, but we were more interested in becoming one of the great Victors . . . von Frankenstein or von Doom.

Most of the time when we mixed *this* with *that*, all we made was a mess. That was probably a good thing. If we had ever actually found a formula that turned weird colors and bubbled and smoked, we might have tried to drink it . . . or at the very least, see if our little sister could be convinced to drink it.

My chemistry set soon ended up at the back of my closet, gathering dust behind my collection of *TV Guides*, but my passion for mixing *this* with *that* remained as I grew older, and found expression in my fiction. Modern publishing loves to sort the tales we tell into categories, producing racks of books that resemble the racks of little bottles in the chemistry set, with neat little labels that read: MYSTERY. ROMANCE. WESTERN. HISTORICAL. SF. JUVENILE.

Pfui, I say. Let's mix *this* with *that* and see what happens. Let's cross some genre lines and blur some boundaries, make some stories that are both and neither. Some of the time we'll make a mess, sure . . . but once in a while, if we do it right, we may stumble on a combination that *explodes!*

With that as my philosophy, it's no wonder that I've produced a number of odd hybrids over the years. *Feure Dream* is one such. Although most often categorized as horror, it is as much a steamboat novel as a vampire novel. The *Armageddon Rag* is even more difficult to classify; fantasy, horror, murder mystery, rock n' roll novel, political novel, '60s novel. It's got Froggy the Gremlin too. Even my fantasy series, *A Song of Ice and Fire*, is a hybrid of sorts, inspired as much by the historical fiction of Thomas B. Costain and Nigel Tranter as the fantasy of Tolkien, Howard, and Fritz Leiber.

The two genres that I've mixed most often, though, are horror and science fiction.

I was doing it as early as my second sale. Despite its SF setting, 'The Exit to San Breta' is a ghost story at heart . . . though admittedly not a very frightening one. My first two corpse handler tales, 'Nobody Leaves New Pittsburg' and 'Override,' were further fumbling attempts at the same sort of cross-pollination, offering as they did a science fictional take on an old friend from the world of horror, the zombie. I was going for a horrific feel in 'Dark, Dark Were the Tunnels' as well, and (much more successfully) in a later, stronger work, my novella 'In the House of the Worm.'

Some critics have argued that horror and science fiction are actually antithetical to one another. They can make a plausible case, certainly, especially in the case of Lovecraftian horror. SF assumes that the universe, however mysterious or frightening it may seem to us, is ultimately knowable, while Lovecraft suggests that even a glimpse of the true nature of reality would be enough to drive men mad. You cannot get much further from the

Campbellian view of the cosmos than that. In *Billion Year Spree*, his insightful study of the history of science fiction, Brian W. Aldiss puts John W. Campbell at the genre's 'thinking pole' and H.P. Lovecraft all the way over at the 'dreaming pole,' on the opposite end of the literary universe.

And yet both men wrote stories that can fairly be described as SF/ horror hybrids. There are, in fact, some startling similarities between HPL's 'At the Mountains of Madness' and JWC's 'Who Goes There?' Both are effective horror stories, but both work as science fiction too. And 'Who Goes There?' is probably the best thing Campbell ever wrote, while 'At the Mountains of Madness' must surely rank in Lovecraft's top five. That's hybrid vigor.

A few of my own hybrids and horrors follow.

The oldest story here, 'Meathouse Man,' was the third of my corpse handler stories, and turned out to be the last of the series. The horror is sexual and psychological, rather than visceral, but this is an SF/horror hybrid all the same. Easily the darkest thing that I have ever written (and I've produced some pretty dark stuff), 'Meathouse Man' was supposed to be my story for *The Last Dangerous Visions*. Harlan Ellison's groundbreaking anthologies *Dangerous Visions* and *Again, Dangerous Visions* had a tremendous impact on me, as they did on most readers of my generation. When I met Harlan for the first time in the corridors of the 1972 Lunacon in New York City, virtually the first thing I asked him was whether I might send him a story for *TLDV*. He told me no; the anthology was closed.

A year later, however, it opened up again . . . at least for me. By that time, I had gotten to know Harlan better, through our mutual friend Lisa Tuttle, and I'd published more stories at well, which may have helped convince him that I was worthy of inclusion in what was, after all, going to be a monumental book, the anthology to end anthologies. Whatever made him change his mind, change it he did; in 1973, he invited me to send him a story. I was thrilled . . . and nervous as hell. *TLDV* would have a lot of heavy hitters in it. Could I measure up? Could I possibly be *dangerous* enough?

I struggled with the story for several months, finally mailed it off to Harlan in early 1974. 'Meathouse Man' was the title, but otherwise it shared only some background and character names with the 'Meathouse Man' that follows. It was much shorter, about a third the length of the present story, and much more superficial. I was trying my damnedest to be dangerous, but in that first version 'Meathouse Man' remained no more than an intellectual exercise.

Harlan returned my manuscript on March 30, 1974, with a letter of rejection that began, 'Aside from shirking all responsibility to the material that forms the core, it's a nice story.' After which he eviscerated me, while challenging me to tear the guts out of the story and rewrite the whole thing from page one. I cursed and fumed and kicked the wall, but I could not quarrel with a single thing he said. So I sat down and ripped the guts out of the story and rewrote the whole thing from page one, and this time I opened a vein as well, and let the blood drip down right onto the paper. While 1973 and 1974 were great years for me professionally, they were by no means happy years. My career was going wonderfully; my life, not so much so. I was wounded, and in a lot of pain. I put it all into 'Meathouse Man,' and sent the story back to Harlan.

He still didn't like it. This time he was much gentler with me, but a gentle pass is still a pass.

Afterward I considered simply abandoning 'Meathouse Man.' Even now, almost thirty years later, I find it painful to reread. But in the end, I had put too much work into the story to forsake it, so I sent it out to other markets, and ended up selling it to Damon Knight for *Orbit*, the only time I ever managed to crack that prestigious anthology series. It appeared in 1976, in *Orbit* 18.

'Remembering Melody,' some three years later, was my first contemporary horror story. Lisa Tuttle gets the blame for this one. When we were starting work on 'The Fall' in 1979, I flew down to Austin for a few weeks to consult with her in person, and get the novella started. We took turns at her typewriter. While she was pounding on the keys I would sit around reading carbons of her latest stories. Lisa was turning out a lot of contemporary horror by then, some wonderfully creepy tales that gave me the urge to try something along those lines myself.

'Remembering Melody' was the story that resulted. My agent tried (and failed) to place it with some of the big, high-paying men's slicks, but *Twilight Zone* magazine was glad to snap it up, and it appeared in the April, 1981 issue.

Hollywood has had a love affair with horror fiction that goes back as far as Murnau's *Nosferatu* in the days of silent film, so it should come as no surprise that three of the six stories in this section have had film or television versions. But 'Remembering Melody' was not only the first of my works to go before a camera, but remains the only one to be filmed *twice* – first as a short student film (full of short student actors), then later as an episode of the HBO anthology series *The Hitchhiker*.

If you know my work at all, I suspect you've heard of 'Sandkings.' Until *A Song of Ice and Fire*, it was the story that I was best known for, far and away the most popular thing I ever did.

'Sandkings' was the third of the three stories I wrote during that Christmas break in the winter of 1978–79. The inspiration for it came from a guy I knew in college, who hosted *Creature Features* parties every Saturday. He kept a tank of piranha, and in between the first and the second creature feature, he would sometimes throw a goldfish into the tank, for the amusement of his guests.

'Sandkings' was also intended to be the first of a series. The strange little shop on the back alley where queer, dangerous items can be bought had long been a familiar trope of fantasy. I thought it might be fun to do a science fiction version. My 'strange little shop' was actually going to be a franchise, with branches scattered over light-years, on many different planets. Its mysterious proprietors, Wo & Shade, would figure in each story, but the protagonists would be the customers, like Simon Kress. (Yes, I did begin a second Wo & Shade story, set on ai-Emerel, a world much mentioned in my old future history, but never seen. It was called 'Protection' and I wrote 18 pages of it before putting it aside, for reasons that I no longer recall.) If you had asked me back in January, 1979 about the three stories I'd just finished, I would have told you that 'The Ice Dragon' was going to knock people's socks off. I ranked it right up there with the best work I'd ever done. I felt 'The Way of Cross and Dragon' was damned good too, might even win some awards. And 'Sandkings?' Not bad at all. Not near as strong as the other two, mind you, but hey . . . no one hits a home run every time.

I have never been so wrong about a story. 'Sandkings' sold to *Omni*, the best paying market in the field, and became the most popular story they ever published. It won *both* the Hugo and the Nebula in its year, the only one of my stories ever to accomplish that double. It has been reprinted and anthologized so many times that I've lost count, and has earned me more money than two of my novels and most of my TV scripts and screenplays. It was adapted as a graphic novel by DC Comics, and some day soon may be a computer game as well. Hollywood producers flocked to it, and I sold half a dozen options and saw half a dozen different screenplays and treatments before the story was finally filmed for television as the two-hour premiere episode of the new *Outer Limits*, adapted by my friend Melinda M. Snod-grass.

Is it the best thing I ever wrote? You be the judge.

The success of 'Sandkings' inspired me to try more SF/ horror hybrids, most notably with 'Nightflyers,' my haunted starship story.

I'd put ghosts in a futuristic setting way back as early as 'The Exit to San Breta,' but those were actual spirits of the dead. In 'Nightflyers' I wanted to see if I could provide a legitimate sfnal explanation for the hauntings.

The original version of 'Nightflyers,' published in *Analog* with a nice Paul Lehr cover, weighed in at 23,000 words . . . but even at that length, I felt it was severely compressed, especially in the handling of its secondary characters. (They did not even have names, only job titles) When Jim Frenkel of Dell Books offered to buy an expanded version of the novella for his new *Binary Star* series, an attempt to revive the old Ace Doubles concept, I leapt at the opportunity. It is the *Binary Star* version you'll find here.

'Nightflyers' won the Locus Poll as the Best Novella of 1980, but lost the Hugo to Gordon R. Dickson's 'Lost Dorsai' at Denvention. It was soon optioned by Hollywood, and became the first of my works to be made into a feature film. *Nightflyers* starred Catherine Mary Stewart and Michael Praed, and was so terrific that the director took his name off the film. Large hunks of my story are still recognizable in the movie, although for some inexplicable reason the single scariest sequence in the novella was dropped.

'The Monkey Treatment' and 'The Pear-Shaped Man' both date to my Gerold Kersh period. Kersh was a major writer of the '40s and '50s, the author of some excellent mainstream novels like *Night and the City* as well as a plethora of bizarre, disturbing, delightful short stories, collected in *On an Odd Note, Nightshades and Damnations,* and *Men without Bones*. Because he tended to publish his short fiction in places like *Collier's* and the *Saturday Evening Post* rather than *Weird Tales* or *Fantastic Stories*, he was little known to fantasy readers even in his own time, and today he seems utterly forgotten. That's a great shame, as Kersh was a unique voice, a brilliant writer with a gift for taking his readers to some odd corners of the world, where strange, disturbing things are wont to happen. Some small press really needs to gather all of Kersh's weird fiction together in a book as large as this one, and put him back in print for a new generation of readers.

'The Monkey Treatment,' the older of the two stories, was easy to write but hard as hell to sell. It seemed to me to be the sort of story that would appeal to a more general readership, so I set out to try and place it with one of the large slicks, *Playboy* or *Penthouse* or *Omni*. Frustration followed. The story elicited admiring comments everywhere it went, but no one seemed to feel it 'right for us.' Too strange, they said. Too disturbing. 'Boy, is it repulsive,' Ellen Datlow of *Omni* wrote me, in the same letter where she said how much she wished that she could buy the story.

I would have tried *Collier's* and the *Saturday Evening Post* next, but they were both long defunct by 1981, so in the end I fell back on my usual genre markets, and sold the story to *The Magazine of Fantasy and Science-Fiction*. Strange and repulsive or not, it was nominated for the Nebula and the Hugo, losing both.

'The Pear-Shaped Man' had an easier time of it, perhaps because 'The Monkey Treatment' had primed the pump. Ellen Datlow had only been an assistant editor at *Omni* when Robert Sheckley returned 'The Monkey Treatment,' but she had moved up to fiction editor by the time I wrote 'The Pear-Shaped Man,' and she took it straightaway. It appeared in *Omni* in 1987, and won one of the first Bram Stoker Awards, given by the newly-formed Horror Writers of America (HWA) for the best horror of the year.

The founding of the HWA (originally it was going to be called HOWL, for Horror and Occult Writers League, a *much* cooler name that got howled down by members desperate for respectability) coincided with the great horror boom of the '80s. Subsequently horror has suffered an even greater bust, a victim of its own excess. Today there are those in publishing who will tell you that horror is dead ('and deservedly so,' others will add).

As a commercial publishing genre? Yes, horror is dead.

But monster stories will never die, so long as we remember what it's like to be afraid.

In 1986, I edited the horror anthology *Night Visions 3* for Dark Harvest. In my introduction, I wrote, 'Those who claim that we read horror stories for the same reasons we ride rollercoasters are missing the point. At the best of times we come away from a rollercoaster with a simple adrenalin high, and that's not what fiction is about. Like a rollercoaster, a really bad horror story can perhaps make us sick, but that's as far as the comparison extends. We go to fiction for things beyond those to be found in amusement parks.

'A good horror story will frighten us, yes. It will keep us awake at night, it will make our flesh crawl, it will creep into our dreams and give new meaning to the darkness. Fear, terror, horror; call it what you will, it drinks from all those cups. But please, don't confuse the feelings with simple vertigo. The great stories, the ones that linger in our memories and change our lives, are never really about the things that they're about.

'Bad horror stories concern themselves with six ways to kill a vampire, and graphic accounts of how the rats ate Billy's genitalia. Good horror stories are about larger things. About hope and despair. About love and hatred, lust and jealousy. About friendship and adolescence and sexuality and rage, loneliness and alienation and psychosis, courage and cowardice, the human mind and body and spirit under stress and in agony, the human heart in unending conflict with itself. Good horror stories make us look at our reflections in dark distorting mirrors, where we glimpse things that disturb us, things that we did not really want to look at. Horror looks into the shadows of the human soul, at the fears and rages that live within us all.

'But darkness is meaningless without light, and horror is pointless without beauty. The best horror stories are stories first and horror second, and however much they scare us, they do more than that as well. They have room in them for laughter as well as screams, for triumph and tenderness as well as tragedy. They concern themselves not simply with fear, but with life in all its infinite variety, with love and death and birth and hope and lust and transcendence, with the whole range of experiences and emotions that make up the human condition. Their characters are people, people who linger in our imagination, people like those around us, people who do not exist solely to be the objects of violent slaughter in chapter four. The best horror stories tell us truths.'

That was almost twenty years ago, but I stand by every word.

Meathouse Man

I
In the Meathouse

They came straight from the ore-fields that first time, Trager with the others, the older boys, the almost-men who worked their corpses next to his. Cox was the oldest of the group, and he'd been around the most, and he said that Trager had to come even if he didn't want to. Then one of the others laughed and said that Trager wouldn't even know what to do, but Cox the kind-of leader shoved him until he was quiet. And when payday came, Trager trailed the rest to the meathouse, scared but somehow eager, and he paid his money to a man downstairs and got a room key.

He came into the dim room trembling, nervous. The others had gone to other rooms, had left him alone with her (no, *it*, not her but *it*, he reminded himself, and promptly forgot again). In a shabby gray cubicle with a single smoky light.

He stank of sweat and sulfur, like all who walked the streets of Skrakky, but there was no help for that. It would be better if he could bathe first, but the room did not have a bath. Just a sink, double bed with sheets that looked dirty even in the dimness, a corpse.

She lay there naked, staring at nothing, breathing shallow breaths. Her legs were spread; ready. Was she always that way, Trager wondered, or had the man before him arranged her like that? He didn't know. He knew how to do it (he did, he *did*, he'd read the books Cox gave him, and there were films you could see, and all sorts of things), but he didn't know much of anything else. Except maybe how to handle corpses. That he was good at, the youngest handler on Skrakky, but he had to be. They had forced him into the handlers' school when his mother died, and they made him learn, so that was the thing he did. This, this he had never done (but he knew how, yes, yes, he *did*); it was his first time.

He came to the bed slowly and sat to a chorus of creaking springs. He touched her and the flesh was warm. Of course. She was not a corpse, not really, no; the body was alive enough, a heartbeat under the heavy white breasts, she breathed. Only the brain was gone, ripped from her, replaced with a deadman's synthabrain. She was meat now, an extra body for a corpsehandler to control, just like the crew he worked each day under sulfur skies. She was not a woman. So it did not matter that Trager was just a boy, a jowly frog-faced boy who smelled of Skrakky. She (no *it*, remember?) would not care, could not care.

Emboldened, aroused and hard, the boy stripped off his corpse handler's clothing and climbed in bed with the female meat. He was very excited; his hands shook as he stroked her, studied her. Her skin was very white, her hair dark and long, but even the boy could not call her pretty. Her face was too flat and wide, her mouth hung open, and her limbs were loose and sagging with fat.

On her huge breasts, all around the fat dark nipples, the last customer had left tooth-marks where he'd chewed her. Trager touched the marks tentatively, traced them with a finger. Then, sheepish about his hesitations, he grabbed one breast, squeezed it hard, pinched the nipple until he imagined a real girl would squeal with pain. The corpse did not move. Still squeezing, he rolled over on her and took the other breast into his mouth.

And the corpse responded.

She thrust up at him, hard, and meaty arms wrapped around his pimpled back to pull him to her. Trager groaned and reached down between her legs. She was hot, wet, excited. He trembled. How did they do that? Could she really get excited without a mind, or did they have lubricating tubes stuck into her, or what?

Then he stopped caring. He fumbled, found his penis, put it into her, thrust. The corpse hooked her legs around him and thrust back. It felt good, real good, better than anything he'd ever done to himself, and in some obscure way he felt proud that she was so wet and excited.

It only took a few strokes; he was too new, too young, too eager to last long. A few strokes was all he needed – but it was all she needed too. They came together, a red flush washing over her skin as she arched against him and shook soundlessly.

Afterwards she lay again like a corpse.

Trager was drained and satisfied, but he had more time left, and he was determined to get his money's worth. He explored her thoroughly, sticking his fingers everywhere they would go, touching her everywhere, rolling it over, looking at everything. The corpse moved like dead meat.

He left her as he'd found her, lying face up on the bed with her legs apart. Meathouse courtesy.

*

The horizon was a wall of factories, all factories, vast belching factories that sent red shadows to flick against the sulfur-dark skies. The boy saw but hardly noticed. He was strapped in place high atop his automill, two stories up on a monster machine of corroding yellow-painted metal with savage teeth of diamond and duralloy, and his eyes were blurred with triple images. Clear and strong and hard he saw the control panel before him, the wheel, the fuel-feed, the bright handle of the ore-scoops, the banks of light that would tell of trouble in the refinery under his feet, the brake and emergency brake. But that was not all he saw. Dimly, faintly, there were echoes; overlaid images of two other control cabs, almost identical to his, where corpse hands moved clumsily over the instruments.

Trager moved those hands, slow and careful, while another part of his mind held his own hands, his real hands, very still. The corpse controller hummed thinly on his belt.

On either side of him, the other two automills moved into flanking positions. The corpse hands squeezed the brakes; the machines rumbled to a halt. On the edge of the great sloping pit, they stood in a row, shabby pitted juggernauts ready to descend into the gloom. The pit was growing steadily larger; each day new layers of rock and ore were stripped away.

Once a mountain range had stood here, but Trager did not remember that.

The rest was easy. The automills were aligned now. To move the crew in unison was a cinch, any decent handler could do *that*. It was only when you had to keep several corpses busy at several different tasks that things got tricky. But a good corpsehandler could do that, too. Eight-crews were not unknown to veterans; eight bodies linked to a single corpse controller moved by a single mind and eight synthabrains. The deadmen were each tuned to one controller, and only one; the handler who wore that controller and thought corpse-thoughts in its proximity field could move those deadmen like secondary bodies. Or like his own body. If he was good enough.

Trager checked his filtermask and earplugs quickly, then touched the fuel-feed, engaged, flicked on the laser-knives and the drills. His corpses echoed his moves, and pulses of light spit through the twilight of Skrakky. Even through his plugs he could hear the awful whine as the ore-scoops revved up and lowered. The rock-eating maw of an automill was even wider than the machine was tall.

Rumbling and screeching, in perfect formation, Trager and his corpse crew descended into the pit. Before they reached the factories on the far side of the plain, tons of metal would have been torn from the earth, melted and refined and processed, while the worthless rock was reduced to powder and blown out into the already unbreathable air. He would deliver finished steel at dusk, on the horizon.

He was a good handler, Trager thought as the automills started down. But the handler in the meathouse – now she must be an artist. He imagined her down in the cellar somewhere, watching each of her corpses through holos and psi circuits, humping them all to please her patrons. Was it just a fluke then, that his fuck had been so perfect? Or was she always that good? But how, *how*, to move a dozen corpses without even being near them, to have them doing different things, to keep them all excited, to match the needs and rhythm of each customer so exactly?

The air behind him was black and choked by rock-dust, his ears were full of screams, and the far horizon was a glowering red wall beneath which yellow ants crawled and ate rock. But Trager kept his hard-on all across the plain as the automill shook beneath him.

*

The corpses were company-owned; they stayed in the company deadman depot. But Trager had a room, a slice of the space that was his own in a steel-and-concrete warehouse with a thousand other slices. He only knew a handful of his neighbors, but he knew all of them too; they were corpsehandlers. It was a world of silent shadowed corridors and endless closed doors. The lobby-lounge, all air and plastic, was a dusty deserted place where none of the tenants ever gathered.

The evenings were long there, the nights eternal. Trager had bought extra light-panels for his particular cube, and when all of them were on they burned so bright that his infrequent visitors blinked and complained about the glare. But always there came a time when he could read no more, and then he had to turn them out, and the darkness returned once more.

His father, long gone and barely remembered, had left a wealth of books and tapes, and Trager kept them still. The room was lined with them, and others stood in great piles against the foot of the bed and on either side of the bathroom door. Infrequently he went on with Cox and the others, to drink and joke and prowl for real women. He imitated them as best he could, but he always felt out of place. So most of his nights were spent at home, reading and listening to the music, remembering and thinking.

That week he thought long after he'd faded his light panels into black, and his thoughts were a frightened jumble. Payday was coming again, and Cox would be after him to return to the meathouse, and yes, yes, he wanted to. It had been good, exciting; for once he had felt confident and virile. But it was so easy, cheap, *dirty*. There had to be more, didn't there? Love, whatever that was? It had to be better with a real woman, had to, and he wouldn't find one of those in a meathouse. He'd never found one outside, either, but then he'd never really had the courage to try. But he had to try, *had* to, or what sort of life would he ever have?

Beneath the covers he masturbated, hardly thinking of it, while he resolved not to return to the meathouse.

*

But a few days later, Cox laughed at him and he had to go along. Somehow he felt it would prove something.

A different room this time, a different corpse. Fat and black, with bright orange hair, less attractive than his first, if that was possible. But Trager came to her ready and eager, and this time he lasted longer. Again, the performance was superb. Her rhythm matched his stroke for stroke, she came with him, she seemed to know exactly what he wanted.

Other visits; two of them, four, six. He was a regular now at the meathouse, along with the others, and he had stopped worrying about it. Cox and the others accepted him in a strange half-hearted way, but his dislike of them had grown, if anything. He was better than they were, he thought. He could hold his own in a meathouse, he could run his corpses and his automills as good as any of them, and he still thought and dreamed. In time he'd leave them all behind, leave Skrakky, be something. They would be meathouse men as long as they would live, but Trager knew he could do better. He believed. He would find love.

He found none in the meathouse, but the sex got better and better, though it was perfect to begin with. In bed with the corpses, Trager was never dissatisfied; he did everything he'd ever read about, heard about, dreamt about. The corpses knew his needs before he did. When he needed it slow, they were slow. When he wanted to have it hard and quick and brutal, then they gave it to him that way, perfectly. He used every orifice they had; they always knew which one to present to him.

His admiration of the meathouse handler grew steadily for months, until it was almost worship. Perhaps somehow he could meet her, he thought at last. Still a boy, still hopelessly naïve, he was sure he would love her. Then he would take her away from the meathouse to a clean corpseless world where they could be happy together.

One day, in a moment of weakness, he told Cox and the others. Cox looked at him, shook his head, grinned. Somebody else snickered. Then they all began to laugh. 'What an *ass* you are, Trager,' Cox said at last. 'There is no fucking *handler!* Don't tell me you never heard of a feedback circuit?'

He explained it all, to laughter; explained how each corpse was tuned to a controller built into its bed, explained how each customer handled his own meat, explained why non-handlers found meathouse women dead and still. And the boy realized suddenly why the sex was always perfect. He was a better handler than even he had thought.

That night, alone in his room with all the lights burning white and hot, Trager faced himself. And turned away, sickened. He was good at his job, he was proud of that, but the rest . . .

It was the meathouse, he decided. There was a trap there in the meathouse, a trap that could ruin him, destroy life and dream and hope. He would not go back; it was too easy. He would show Cox, show all of them. He could take the hard way, take the risks, feel the pain if he had to. And maybe the joy, maybe the love. He'd gone the other way too long.

Trager did not go back to the meathouse. Feeling strong and decisive and superior, he went back to his room. There, as years passed, he read and dreamed and waited for life to begin.

I

When I Was One-and-Twenty

Josie was the first.

She was beautiful, had always been beautiful, knew she was beautiful; all that had shaped her, made her what she was. She was a free spirit. She was aggressive, confident, conquering. Like Trager, she was only twenty when they met, but she had lived more than he had, and she seemed to have the answers. He loved her from the first.

And Trager? Trager before Josie, but years beyond the meathouse? He was taller now, broad and heavy with both muscle and fat, often moody, silent and self-contained. He ran a full five-crew in the ore fields, more than Cox, more than any of them. At night, he read books; sometimes in his room, sometimes in the lobby. He had long since forgotten that he went there to meet someone. Stable, solid, unemotional; that was Trager. He touched no one, and no one touched him. Even the tortures had stopped, though the scars remained *inside*. Trager hardly knew they were there; he never looked at them.

He fit in well now. With his corpses.

Yet – not completely. Inside, the dream. Something believed, something hungered, something yearned. It was strong enough to keep him away from the meathouse, from the vegetable life the others had all chosen. And sometimes, on bleak lonely nights, it would grow stronger still. Then Trager would rise from his empty bed, dress, and walk the corridors for hours with his hands shoved deep into his pockets while something twisted, clawed and whimpered in his gut. Always, before his walks were over, he would resolve to do something, to change his life tomorrow.

But when tomorrow came, the silent gray corridors were half forgotten, the demons had faded, and he had six roaring, shaking automills to drive across the pit. He would lose himself in routine, and it would be long months before the feelings came again.

Then Josie. They met like this:

It was a new field, rich and unmined, a vast expanse of broken rock and rubble that filled the plain. Low hills a few weeks ago, but the company skimmers had leveled the area with systematic nuclear blast mining, and now the automills were moving in. Trager's five-crew had been one of the first, and the change had been exhilarating at first. The old pit had been just about worked out; here there was a new terrain to contend with, boulders and jagged rock fragments, baseball-sized fists of stone that came shrieking at you on the dusty wind. It all seemed exciting, dangerous. Trager, wearing a leather jacket and filtermask and goggles and earplugs, drove his six machines and six bodies with a fierce pride, reducing boulders to powder, clearing a path for the later machines, fighting his way yard by yard to get whatever ore he could.

And one day, suddenly, one of the eye echoes suddenly caught his attention. A light flashed red on a corpse-driven automill. Trager reached, with his hands, with his mind, with five sets of corpse-hands. Six machines stopped, but still another light went red. Then another, and another. Then the whole board, all twelve. One of his automills was out. Cursing, he looked across the rock field towards the machine in question, used his corpse to give it a kick. The lights stayed red. He beamed out for a tech.

By the time she got there – in a one-man skimmer that looked like a tear drop of pitted black metal – Trager had unstrapped, climbed down the metal rings on the side of the automill, walked across the rocks to where the dead machine stopped. He was just starting to climb up when Josie arrived; they met at the foot of the yellow-metal mountain, in the shadow of its treads.

She was field-wise, he knew at once. She wore a handler's coverall, earplugs, heavy goggles, and her face was smeared with grease to prevent dust abrasions. But still she was beautiful. Her hair was short, light brown, cut in a shag that was jumbled by the wind; her eyes, when she lifted the goggles, were bright green. She took charge immediately.

All business, she introduced herself, asked him a few questions, then opened a repair bay and crawled inside, into the guts of the drive and the ore-smelt and the refinery. It didn't take her long; ten minutes, maybe, and she was back outside.

'Don't go in there,' she said, tossing her hair from in front of her goggles with a flick of her head. 'You've got a damper failure. The nukes are running away.'

'Oh,' said Trager. His mind was hardly on the automill, but he had to make an impression, made to say something intelligent. 'Is it going to blow up?' he asked, and as soon as he said it he knew that *that* hadn't been intelligent at all. Of course it wasn't going to blow up; runaway nuclear reactors didn't work that way, he knew that.

But Josie seemed amused. She smiled – the first time he saw her distinctive flashing grin – and seemed to see him, *him*, Trager, not just a corpsehandler. 'No,' she said. 'It will just melt itself down. Won't even get hot out here, since you've got shields built into the walls. Just don't go in there.'

'All right.' Pause. What could he say now? 'What do I do?'

'Work the rest of your crew, I guess. This machine'll have to be scrapped. It should have been overhauled a long time ago. From the looks of it, there's been a lot of patching done in the past. Stupid. It breaks down, it breaks down, it breaks down, and they keep sending it out. Should realize that something is wrong. After that many failures, it's sheer self-delusion to think the thing's going to work right next time out.'

'I guess,' Trager said. Josie smiled at him again, sealed up the panel, and started to turn.

'Wait,' he said. It came out before he could stop it, almost in spite of him. Josie turned, cocked her head, looked at him questioningly. And Trager drew a sudden strength from the steel and the stone and the wind; under sulfur skies, his dreams seemed less impossible. Maybe, he thought. Maybe.

'Uh. I'm Greg Trager. Will I see you again?'

Josie grinned. 'Sure. Come tonight.' She gave him the address.

He climbed back into his automill after she had left, exulting in his six strong bodies, all fire and life, and he chewed up rock with something near to joy. The dark red glow in the distance looked almost like a sunrise.

*

When he got to Josie's, he found four other people there, friends of hers. It was a party of sorts. Josie threw a lot of parties and Trager – from that night on – went to all of them. Josie talked to him, laughed with him, *liked* him, and suddenly his life was no longer the same.

With Josie, he saw parts of Skrakky he had never seen before, did things he had never done:

—he stood with her in the crowds that gathered on the streets at night, stood in the dusty wind and sickly yellow light between the windowless concrete buildings, stood and bet and cheered himself hoarse while grease-stained mechs raced yellow rumbly tractor-trucks up and down and down and up.

—he walked with her through the strangely silent and white and clean underground Offices, and sealed air-conditioned corridors where off-worlders and paper-shufflers and company executives lived and worked.

—he prowled the rec-malls with her, those huge low buildings so like a warehouse from the outside, but full of colored lights and game rooms and cafeterias and tape shops and endless bars where handlers made their rounds.

—he went with her to dormitory gyms, where they watched handlers less skillful than himself send their corpses against each other with clumsy fists.

—he sat with her and her friends, and they woke dark quiet taverns with their talk and with their laughter, and once Trager saw someone looking much like Cox staring at him from across the room, and he smiled and leaned a bit closer to Josie.

He hardly noticed the other people, the crowds that Josie surrounded herself with; when they went out on one of her wild jaunts, six of them or eight or ten, Trager would tell himself that he and Josie were going out, and that some others had come along with them.

Once in a great while, things would work out so they were alone together, at her place, or his. Then they would talk. Of distant worlds, of politics, of corpses and life on Skrakky, of the books they both consumed, of sports or games or friends they had in common. They shared a good deal. Trager talked a lot with Josie. And never said a word.

He loved her, of course. He suspected it the first month, and soon he was convinced of it. He loved her. This was the real thing, the thing he had been waiting for, and it had happened just as he knew it would.

But with his love: agony. He could not tell her. A dozen times he tried; the words would never come. What if she did not love him back?

His nights were still alone, in the small room with the white lights and the books and the pain. He was more alone than ever now; the peace of his routine, of his half-life with his corpses, was gone, stripped from him. By day he rode the great automills, moved his corpses, smashed rock and melted ore, and in his head rehearsed the words he'd say to Josie. And dreamed of those that she'd speak back. She was trapped too, he thought. She'd had men, of course, but she didn't love them, she loved him. But she couldn't tell him, any more than he could tell her. When he broke through, when he found the words and the courage, then everything would be all right. Each day he said that to himself, and dug swift and deep into the earth.

But back home, the sureness faded. Then, with awful despair, he knew that he was kidding himself. He was a friend to her, nothing more, never would be more. Why did he lie to himself? He'd had hints enough. They had never been lovers, never would be; on the few times he'd worked up the courage to touch her, she would smile, move away on some pretext, so he was never quite sure that he was being rejected. But he got the idea, and in the dark it tore at him. He walked the corridors weekly now, sullen, desperate, wanting to talk to someone without knowing how. And all the old scars woke up to bleed again.

Until the next day. When he would return to his machines, and believe again. He must believe in himself, he knew that, he shouted it out loud. He must stop feeling sorry for himself. He must do something. He must tell Josie. He would.

And she would love him, cried the day.

And she would laugh, the nights replied.

Trager chased her for a year, a year of pain and promise, the first year that he had ever *lived*. On that the night-fears and the day-voice agreed; he was alive now. He would never return to the emptiness of his time before Josie; he would never go back to the meathouse. That far, at least, he had come. He could change, and someday he would be strong enough to tell her.

*

Josie and two friends dropped by his room that night, but the friends had to leave early. For an hour or so they were alone, talking about nothing. Finally she had to go. Trager said he'd walk her home.

He kept his arm around her down the long corridors, and he watched her face, watched the play of light and shadow on her cheeks as they walked from light to darkness. 'Josie,' he started. He felt so fine, so good, so warm, and it came out. 'I love you.'

And she stopped, pulled away from him, stepped back. Her mouth opened, just a little, and something flickered in her eyes. 'Oh, Greg,' she said. Softly. Sadly. 'No, Greg, no, don't, don't.' And she shook her head.

Trembling slightly, mouthing silent words, Trager held out his hand. Josie did not take it. He touched her cheek, gently, and wordless she spun away from him.

Then, for the first time ever, Trager shook. And the tears came.

Josie took him to her room. There, sitting across from each other on the floor, never touching, they talked.

J: ... *known it for a long time ... tried to discourage you, Greg, but I didn't just want to come right out and ... I never wanted to hurt you ... a good person ... don't worry ...*

T: ... *knew it all along ... that it would never ... lied to myself ... wanted to believe, even if it wasn't true ... I'm sorry, Josie, I'm sorry, I'm sorry, I'm sorryimsorryimsorry ...*

J: ... *afraid you would go back to what you were ... don't Greg, promise me ... can't give up ... have to believe ...*

T: *why?*

J: ... *stop believing, then you have nothing ... dead ... you can do better ... a good handler ... get off Skrakky, find something ... no life here ... someone ... you will, you will, just believe, keep on believing ...*

T: ... *you ... love you forever, Josie ... forever ... how can I find someone ... never anyone like you, never ... special ...*

J: ... *oh, Greg ... lots of people ... just look ... open ...*

T: (laughter) ... *open? ... first time I ever talked to anyone ...*

J: ... *talk to me again, if you have to ... I can talk to you ... had enough lovers, everyone wants to get to bed with me, better just to be friends ...*

T: ... *friends ... (laughter) ... (tears) ...*

II

Promises of Someday

The fire had burned out long ago, and Stevens and the forester had retired, but Trager and Donelly still sat around the ashes on the edges of the clear zone. They talked softly, so as not to wake the others, yet their words hung long in the restless night air. The uncut forest, standing dark behind them, was dead still; the wildlife of Vendalia had all fled the noise that the fleet of buzztrucks made during the day.

'... a full six-crew, running buzztrucks, I know enough to know that's not easy,' Donelly was saying. He was a pale, timid youth, likeable but self-conscious about everything he did. Trager heard echoes of himself in Donelly's stiff words. 'You'd do well in the arena.'

Trager nodded, thoughtful, his eyes on the ashes as he moved them with a stick. 'I came to Vendalia with that in mind. Went to the gladiatorial once, only once. That was enough to change my mind. I could take them, I guess, but the whole idea made me sick. Out here, well, the money doesn't even match what I was getting on Skrakky, but the work is, well, clean. You know?'

'Sort of,' said Donelly. 'Still, you know, it isn't like they were real people out there in the arena. Only meat. All you can do is make the bodies as dead as the minds. That's the logical way to look at it.'

Trager chuckled. 'You're too logical, Don. You ought to *feel* more. Listen, next time you're in Gidyon, go to the gladiatorials and take a look. It's ugly, *ugly*. Corpses stumbling around with axes and swords and morning-stars, hacking and hewing at each other. Butchery, that's all it is. And the audience, the way they cheer at each blow. And *laugh*. They *laugh*, Don! No.' He shook his head, sharply. 'No.'

Donelly never abandoned an argument. 'But why not? I don't under-stand, Greg. You'd be good at it, the best. I've seen the way you work your crew.'

Trager looked up, studied Donelly briefly while the youth sat quietly, waiting. Josie's word came back; open, be open. The old Trager, the Trager who lived friendless and alone and closed inside a Skrakky handlers' dorm, was gone. He had grown, changed.

'There was a girl,' he said, slowly, with measured words. Opening. 'Back on Skrakky, Don, there was a girl I loved. It, well, it didn't work out. That's why I'm here, I guess. I'm looking for someone else, for something better. That's all part of it, you see.' He stopped, paused, tried to think his words out. 'This girl, Josie, I wanted her to love me. You know.' The words came hard. 'Admire me, all that stuff. Now, yeah, sure, I could do good running corpses in the arena. But Josie could never love someone who had a job like *that*. She's gone now, of course, but still . . . the kind of person I'm looking for, I couldn't find them as an arena corpsemaster.' He stood up, abruptly. 'I don't know. That's what's important, though, to me. Josie, somebody like her, someday. Soon, I hope.'

Donelly sat quiet in the moonlight, chewing his lip, not looking at Trager, his logic suddenly useless. While Trager, his corridors long gone, walked off alone into the woods.

*

They had a tight-knit group; three handlers, a forester, thirteen corpses. Each day they drove the forest back, with Trager in the forefront. Against the Vendalian wilderness, against the blackbriars and the hard gray ironspike trees and the bulbous rubbery snaplimbs, against the tangled hostile forest, he would throw his six-crew and their buzztrucks. Smaller than the automills he'd run on Skrakky, fast and airborne, complex and demanding, those were buzztrucks. Trager ran six of them with corpse hands, a seventh with his own. Before his screaming blades and laser knives, the wall of wilderness fell each day. Donelly came behind him, pushing three of the mountain-sized rolling mills, to turn the fallen trees into lumber for Gidyon and other cities of Vendalia. Then Stevens, the third handler, with a flame-cannon to burn down stumps and melt rocks, and the soilpumps that would ready the fresh clear land for farming. The forester was their foreman. The procedure was a science.

Clean, hard, demanding work; Trager thrived on it by day. He grew lean, almost athletic; the lines of his face tightened and tanned, he grew steadily browner under Vendalia's hot bright sun. His corpses were almost part of him, so easily did he move them, fly their buzztrucks. As an ordinary man might move a hand, a foot. Sometimes his control grew so firm, the echoes so clear and strong, that Trager felt he was not a handler working a crew at all, but rather a man with seven bodies. Seven strong bodies that rode the sultry forest winds. He exulted in their sweat.

And the evenings, after work ceased, they were good too. Trager found a sort of peace there, a sense of belonging he had never known on Skrakky. The Vendalian foresters, rotated back and forth from Gidyon, were decent enough, and friendly. Stevens was a hearty slab of a man who seldom stopped joking long enough to talk about anything serious. Trager always found him amusing. And Donelly, the self-conscious youth, the quiet logical voice, he became a friend. He was a good listener, empathetic, compassionate, and the new open Trager was a good talker. Something close to envy shone in Donelly's eyes when Trager spoke of Josie and exorcised his soul. And Trager knew, or thought he knew, that Donelly was himself, the old Trager, the one before Josie who could not find the words.

In time, though, after days and weeks of talking, Donelly found his words. Then Trager listened, and shared another's pain. And he felt *good about it. He was helping; he was lending strength; he was needed.*

Each night around the ashes, the two men traded dreams. And wove a hopeful tapestry of promises and lies.

Yet still the nights would come.

Those were the worst times, as always; those were the hours of Trager's long lonely walks. If Josie had given Trager much, she had taken something too; she had taken the curious deadness he had once had, the trick of not-thinking, the pain-blotter of his mind. On Skrakky, he had walked the corridors infrequently; the forest knew him far more often.

After the talking all had stopped, after Donelly had gone to bed, that was when it would happen, when Josie would come to him in the loneliness of his tent. A thousand nights he lay there with his hands hooked behind his head, staring at the plastic tent film while he relived the night he'd told her. A thousand times he touched her cheek, and saw her spin away.

He would think of it, and fight it, and lose. Then, restless, he would rise and go outside. He would walk across the clear area, into the silent looming forest, brushing aside low branches and tripping on the underbrush; he would walk until he found water. Then he would sit down, by a scum-choked lake or a gurgling stream that ran swift and oily in the moonlight. He would fling rocks into the water, hurl them hard and flat into the night to hear them when they splashed.

He would sit for hours, throwing rocks and thinking, till finally he could convince himself the sun would rise.

*

Gidyon; the city; the heart of Vendalia, and through it of Slagg and Skrakky and New Pittsburg and all the other corpseworlds, the harsh ugly places where men would not work and corpses had to. Great towers of black and silver metal, floating aerial sculpture that flashed in the sunlight and shone softly at night, the vast bustling spaceport where freighters rose and fell on invisible firewands, malls where the pavement was polished, ironspike wood that gleamed a gentle gray; Gidyon.

The city with the rot. The corpse city. The meatmart.

For the freighters carried cargoes of men, criminals and derelicts and troublemakers from a dozen worlds bought with hard Vendalian cash (and there were darker rumors, of liners that had vanished mysteriously on routine tourist hops). And the soaring towers were hospitals and corpseyards, where men and women died and deadmen were born to walk anew. And all along the ironspike boardwalks were corpse-seller's shops and meathouses.

The meathouses of Vendalia were far-famed. The corpses were guaranteed beautiful.

Trager sat across from one, on the other side of the wide gray avenue, under the umbrella of an outdoor café. He sipped a bittersweet wine, thought about how his leave had evaporated too quickly, and tried to keep his eyes from wandering across the street. The wine was warm on his tongue, and his eyes were very restless.

Up and down the avenue, between him and the meathouse, strangers moved. Dark-faced corpsehandlers from Vendalia, Skrakky, Slagg; pudgy merchants, gawking tourists from the Clean Worlds like Old Earth and Zephyr, and dozens of question marks whose names and occupations and errands Trager would never know. Sitting there, drinking his wine and watching, Trager felt utterly cut off. He could not touch these people, could not reach them; he didn't know how, it wasn't possible, it wouldn't work. He could rise and walk out into the street and grab one, and still they would not touch. The stranger would only pull free and run. All his leave like that, all of it; he'd run through all the bars of Gidyon, forced a thousand contacts, and nothing had clicked.

His wine was gone. Trager looked at the glass dully, turning it in his hands, blinking. Then, abruptly, he stood up and paid his bill. His hands trembled.

It had been so many years, he thought as he started across the street. Josie, he thought, forgive me.

*

Trager returned to the wilderness camp, and his corpses flew their buzztrucks like men gone wild. But he was strangely silent around the campfire, and he did not talk to Donelly at night. Until finally, hurt and puzzled, Donelly followed him into the forest. And found him by a languid death-dark stream, sitting on the bank with a pile of throwing stones at his feet.

T: ... *went in* ... *after all I said, all I promised* ... *still I went in* ...
D: ... *nothing to worry* ... *remember what you told me* ... *keep on believing* ...
T: ... *did believe, DID* ... *no difficulties* ... *Josie* ...
D: ... *you say I shouldn't give up, you better not* ... *repeat everything you told me, everything Josie told you* ... *everybody finds someone* ... *if they keep looking* ... *give up, dead* ... *all you need* ... *openness* ... *courage to look* ... *stop feeling sorry for yourself* ... *told me that a hundred times* ...
T: ... *fucking lot easier to tell you than do it myself* ...
D: ... *Greg* ... *not a meathouse man* ... *a dreamer* ... *better than they are* ...
T: (sighing) ... *yeah* ... *hard, though* ... *why do I do this to myself?* ...
D: ... *rather be like you were?* ... *not hurting, not living?* ... *like me?* ...
T: ... *no* ... *no* ... *you're right* ...

2
The Pilgrim, Up and Down

Her name was Laurel. She was nothing like Josie, save in one thing alone. Trager loved her.

Pretty? Trager didn't think so, not at first. She was too tall, a half-foot taller than he was, and she was a bit on the heavy side, and more than a bit on the awkward side. Her hair was her best feature, her hair that was red-brown in winter and glowing blonde in summer, that fell long and straight down past her shoulders and did wild beautiful things in the wind. But she was not beautiful, not the way Josie had been beautiful. Although, oddly, she grew more beautiful with time, and maybe that was because she was losing weight, and maybe that was because Trager was falling in love with her and seeing her through kinder eyes, and maybe that was because he *told* her she was pretty and the very telling made it so. Just as Laurel told him he was wise, and her belief gave him wisdom. Whatever the reason, Laurel was very beautiful indeed after he had known her for a time.

She was five years younger than he, clean scrubbed and innocent, shy where Josie had been assertive. She was intelligent, romantic, a dreamer; she was wondrously fresh and eager; she was painfully insecure, and full of hungry need.

She was new to Gidyon, fresh from the Vendalian outback, a student forester. Trager, on leave again, was visiting the forestry college to say hello to a teacher who'd once worked with his crew. They met in the teacher's office. Trager had two weeks free in a city of strangers and meathouses; Laurel was alone. He showed her the glittering decadence of Gidyon, feeling smooth and sophisticated, and she was suitably impressed.

Two weeks went quickly. They came to the last night. Trager, suddenly afraid, took her to the park by the river that ran through Gidyon and they sat together on the low stone wall by the water's edge. Close, not touching.

'Time runs too fast,' he said. He had a stone in his hand. He flicked it out over the water, flat and hard. Thoughtfully, he watched it splash and sink. Then he looked at her. 'I'm nervous,' he said, laughing. 'I – Laurel. I don't want to leave.'

Her face was unreadable (wary?). 'The city is nice,' she agreed.

Trager shook his head violently. 'No. *No!* Not the city, you. Laurel, I think I . . . well . . .'

Laurel smiled for him. Her eyes were bright, very happy. 'I know,' she said.

Trager could hardly believe it. He reached out, touched her cheek. She turned her head and kissed his hand. They smiled at each other.

*

He flew back to the forest camp to quit. 'Don, *Don*, you've got to meet her,' he shouted. 'See, you can do it, *I* did it, just keep believing, keep trying. I feel so goddamn good it's obscene.'

Donelly, stiff and logical, smiled for him, at a loss as how to handle such a flood of happiness. 'What will you do?' he asked, a little awkwardly. 'The arena?'

Trager laughed. 'Hardly, you know how I feel. But something like that. There's a theatre near the spaceport, puts on pantomime with corpse actors. I've got a job there. The pay is rotten, but I'll be near Laurel. That's all that matters.'

*

They hardly slept at night. Instead they talked and cuddled and made love. The lovemaking was a joy, a game, a glorious discovery; never as good technically as the meathouse, but Trager hardly cared. He taught her to be open. He told her every secret he had, and wished he had more secrets.

'Poor Josie,' Laurel would often say at night, her body warm against his. 'She doesn't know what she missed. I'm lucky. There couldn't be anyone else like you.'

'No,' said Trager, '*I'm* lucky.'

They would argue about it, laughing.

*

Donelly came to Gidyon and joined the theatre. Without Trager, the forest work had been no fun, he said. The three of them spent a lot of time together, and Trager glowed. He wanted to share his friends with Laurel, and he'd already mentioned Donelly a lot. And he wanted Donelly to see how happy he'd become, to see what belief could accomplish.

'I like her,' Donelly said, smiling, the first night after Laurel had left.

'Good,' Trager replied, nodding.

'No,' said Donelly. 'Greg, I *really* like her.'

*

They spent a *lot* of time together.

*

'Greg,' Laurel said one night in bed. 'I think that Don is . . . well, after me. You know.'

Trager rolled over and propped his head up on his elbow. 'God,' he said. He sounded concerned.

'I don't know how to handle it.'

'Carefully,' Trager said. 'He's very vulnerable. You're probably the first woman he's ever been interested in. Don't be too hard on him. He shouldn't have to go through the stuff I went through, you know?'

*

The sex was never as good as a meathouse. And, after a while, Laurel began to close. More and more nights now she went to sleep after they made love; the days when they talked till dawn were gone. Perhaps they had nothing left to say. Trager had noticed that she had a tendency to finish his stories for him. It was nearly impossible to come up with one he hadn't already told her.

*

'He said *that?*' Trager got out of bed, turned on a light, and sat down frowning. Laurel pulled the covers up to her chin.

'Well, what did *you* say?'

She hesitated. 'I can't tell you. It's between Don and me. He said it wasn't fair, the way I turn around and tell you everything that goes on between us, and he's right.'

'*Right!* But I tell you everything. Don't you remember what we . . .'

'I know, but . . .'

Trager shook his head. His voice lost some of its anger. 'What's going on, Laurel, huh? I'm scared, all of a sudden. I love you, remember? How can everything change so fast?'

Her face softened. She sat up, and held out her arms, and the covers fell back from full soft breasts. 'Oh, Greg,' she said. 'Don't worry. I love you, I always will, but it's just that I love him too, I guess. You know?'

Trager, mollified, came into her arms, and kissed her with fervor. Then, suddenly, he broke off. 'Hey,' he said, with mock sternness to hide the trembling in his voice, 'who do you love *more?*'

'You, of course, always you.'

Smiling, he returned to the kiss.

*

'I know you know,' Donelly said. 'I guess we have to talk about it.'

Trager nodded. They were backstage in the theatre. Three of his corpses walked up behind him, and stood arms crossed, like a guard. 'All right.' He looked straight at Donelly, and his face – smiling until the other's words – was suddenly stern. 'Laurel asked me to pretend I didn't know anything. She said you felt guilty. But pretending was quite a strain, Don. I guess it's time we got everything out in the open.'

Donelly's pale blue eyes shifted to the floor, and he stuck his hands into his pockets. 'I don't want to hurt you,' he said.

'Then don't.'

'But I'm not going to pretend I'm dead, either. I'm not. I love her too.'

'You're supposed to be my friend, Don. Love someone else. You're just going to get yourself hurt this way.'

'I have more in common with her than you do.'

Trager just stared.

Donelly looked up at him. Then, abashed, back down again. 'I don't know. Oh, Greg. She loves you more anyway, she said so. I never should have expected anything else. I feel like I've stabbed you in the back. I . . .'

Trager watched him. Finally, he laughed softly. 'Oh, shit, I can't take this. Look, Don, you haven't stabbed me, c'mon, don't talk like that. I guess, if you love her, this is the way it's got to be, you know. I just hope everything comes out all right.'

Later that night, in bed with Laurel; 'I'm worried about him,' he told her.

*

His face, once tanned, now ashen. 'Laurel?' he said. Not believing.

'I don't love you anymore. I'm sorry. I don't. It seemed real at the time, but now it's almost like a dream. I don't even know if I ever loved you, really.'

'Don,' he said woodenly.

Laurel flushed. 'Don't say anything bad about Don. I'm tired of hearing you run him down. He never says anything except good about you.'

'Oh, Laurel. Don't you *remember?* The things we said, the way we felt? I'm the same person you said those words to.'

'But I've grown,' Laurel said, hard and tearless, tossing her red-gold hair. 'I remember perfectly well, but I just don't feel that way any more.'

'Don't,' he said. He reached for her.

She stepped back. 'Keep your hands off me. I told you, Greg, it's *over.* You have to leave now. Don is coming by.'

*

It was worse than Josie. A thousand times worse.

III
Wanderings

He tried to keep on at the theatre; he enjoyed the work, he had friends there. But it was impossible. Donelly was there every day, smiling and being friendly, and sometimes Laurel came to meet him after the day's show and they went off together, arm in arm. Trager would stand and watch, try not to notice. While the twisted thing inside him shrieked and clawed.

He quit. He would not see them again. He would keep his pride.

*

The sky was bright with the lights of Gidyon and full of laughter, but it was dark and quiet in the park.

Trager stood stiff against a tree, his eyes on the river, his hands folded tightly against his chest. He was a statue. He hardly seemed to breathe. Not even his eyes moved.

Kneeling near the low wall, the corpse pounded until the stone was slick with blood and its hands were mangled clots of torn meat. The sounds of the blows were dull and wet, but for the infrequent scraping of bone against rock.

*

They made him pay first, before he could even enter the booth. Then he sat there for an hour while they found her and punched through. Finally, though, finally; 'Josie.'

'Greg,' she said, grinning her distinctive grin. 'I should have known. Who else would call all the way from Vendalia? How are you?'

He told her.

Her grin vanished. 'Oh, Greg,' she said. 'I'm sorry. But don't let it get to you. Keep going. The next one will work out better. They always do.'

Her words didn't satisfy him. 'Josie,' he said, 'How are things back there? You miss me?'

'Oh, sure. Things are pretty good. It's still Skrakky, though. Stay where you are, you're better off.' She looked off screen, then back. 'I should go, before your bill gets enormous. Glad you called, love.'

'Josie,' Trager started. But the screen was already dark.

*

Sometimes, at night, he couldn't help himself. He would move to his home screen and ring Laurel. Invariably her eyes would narrow when she saw who it was. Then she would hang up.

And Trager would sit in a dark room and recall how once the sound of his voice made her so very, very happy.

*

The streets of Gidyon are not the best of places for lonely midnight walks. They are brightly lit, even in the darkest hours, and jammed with men and deadmen. And there are meathouses, all up and down the boulevards and the ironspike boardwalks.

Josie's words had lost their power. In the meathouses, Trager abandoned dreams and found cheap solace. The sensuous evenings with Laurel and the fumbling sex of his boyhood were things of yesterday; Trager took his meatmates hard and quick, almost brutally, fucked them with a wordless savage power to the inevitable perfect orgasm. Sometimes, remembering the theatre, he would have them act out short erotic playlets to get him in the mood.

*

In the night. Agony.

He was in the corridors again, the low dim corridors of the corpsehandlers' dorm on Skrakky, but now the corridors were twisted and torturous and Trager had long since lost his way. The air was thick with a rotting gray haze, and growing thicker. Soon, he feared, he would be all but blind.

Around and around he walked, up and down, but always there was more corridor, and all of them led nowhere. The doors were grim black rectangles, knobless, locked to him forever; he passed them by without thinking, most of them. Once or twice, though, he paused, before doors where light leaked around the frame. He would listen, and inside there were sounds, and then he would begin to knock wildly. But no one ever answered.

So he would move on, through the haze that got darker and thicker and seemed to burn his skin, past door after door after door, until he was weeping and his feet were tired and bloody. And then, off a ways, down a long long corridor that loomed straight before him, he would see an open door. From it came light so hot and white it hurt the eyes, and music bright and joyful, and the sounds of people laughing. Then Trager would run, though his feet were raw bundles of pain and his lungs burned with the haze he was breathing. He would run and run until he reached the room with the open door.

Only when he got there, it was his room, and it was empty.

*

Once, in the middle of their brief time together, they'd gone out into the wilderness and made love under the stars. Afterwards she had snuggled hard against him, and he stroked her gently. 'What are you thinking?' he asked.

'About us,' Laurel said. She shivered. The wind was brisk and cold. 'Sometimes I get scared, Greg. I'm so afraid something will happen to us, something that will ruin it. I don't ever want you to leave me.'

'Don't worry,' he told her. 'I won't.'

Now, each night before sleep came, he tortured himself with her words. The good memories left him with ashes and tears; the bad ones with a wordless rage.

He slept with a ghost beside him, a supernaturally beautiful ghost, the husk of a dead dream. He woke to her each morning.

*

He hated them. He hated himself for hating.

3
Duvalier's Dream

Her name does not matter. Her looks are not important. All that counts is that she *was*, that Trager tried again, that he forced himself on and made himself believe and didn't give up. He *tried*.

But something was missing. Magic?

The words were the same.

How many times can you speak them, Trager wondered, *speak them and believe them, like you believed them the first time you said them? Once? Twice? Three times, maybe? Or a hundred? And the people who say it a hundred times, are they really so much better at loving? Or only at fooling themselves? Aren't they really people who long ago abandoned the dream, who use its name for something else?*

He said the words, holding her, cradling her and kissing her. He said the words, with a knowledge that was surer and heavier and more dead than any belief. He said the words and *tried*, but no longer could he mean them.

And she said the words back, and Trager realized that they meant nothing to him. Over and over again they said the things each wanted to hear, and both of them knew they were pretending.

They tried *hard*. But when he reached out, like an actor caught in his role, doomed to play out the same part over and over again, when he reached out his hand and touched her cheek – the skin was smooth and soft and lovely. And wet with tears.

IV
Echoes

'I don't want to hurt you,' said Donelly, shuffling and looking guilty, until Trager felt ashamed for having hurt a friend.

He touched her cheek, and she spun away from him.

'I never wanted to hurt you,' Josie said, and Trager was sad. She had given him so much; he'd only made her guilty. Yes, he was hurt, but a stronger man would never have let her know.

He touched her cheek, and she kissed his hand.

'I'm sorry, I don't,' Laurel said. And Trager was lost. What had he done, where was his fault, how had he ruined it? She had been so sure. They had had so much.

He touched her cheek, and she wept.

How many times can you speak them, his voice echoed, *speak them and believe them, like you believed them the first time you said them?*

The wind was dark and dust heavy, the sky throbbed painfully with flickering scarlet flame. In the pit, in the darkness, stood a young woman with goggles and a filtermask and short brown hair and answers. 'It breaks down, it breaks down, it breaks down, and they keep sending it out,' she said. 'Should realize that something is wrong. After that many failures, it's sheer self-delusion to think the thing's going to work right next time out.'

The enemy corpse is huge and black, its torso rippling with muscle, a product of months of exercise, the biggest thing that Trager has ever faced. It advances across the sawdust in a slow, clumsy crouch, holding the gleaming broadsword in one hand. Trager watches it come from his chair atop one end of the fighting arena. The other corpsemaster is careful, cautious.

His own deadman, a wiry blond, stands and waits, a Morningstar trailing down in the blood-soaked arena dust. Trager will move him fast enough and well enough when the time is right. The enemy knows it, and the crowd.

The black corpse suddenly lifts its broadsword and scrambles forward in a run, hoping to use reach and speed to get its kill. But Trager's corpse is no longer there when the enemy's measured blow cuts the air where he had been.

Sitting comfortably above the fighting pit/down in the arena, his feet grimy with blood and sawdust – Trager/the corpse – snaps the command/ swings the morningstar – and the great studded ball drifts up and around, almost lazily, almost gracefully. Into the back of the enemy's head, as he tries to recover and turn. A flower of blood and brain blooms swift and sudden, and the crowd cheers.

Trager walks his corpse from the arena, then stands to receive applause. It is his tenth kill. Soon the championship will be his. He is building such a record that they can no longer deny him a match.

*

She is beautiful, his lady, his love. Her hair is short and blonde, her body very slim, graceful, almost athletic, with trim legs and small hard breasts. Her eyes are bright green, and they always welcome him. And there is a strange erotic innocence in her smile.

She waits for him in bed, waits for his return from the arena, waits for him eager and playful and loving. When he enters, she is sitting up, smiling for him, the covers bunched around her waist. From the door he admires her nipples.

Aware of his eyes, shy, she covers her breasts and blushes. Trager knows it is all false modesty, all playing. He moves to the bedside, sits, reaches out to stroke her cheek. Her skin is very soft; she nuzzles against his hand as it brushes her. Then Trager draws her hands aside, plants one gentle kiss on each breast, and a not-so-gentle kiss on her mouth. She kisses back, with ardor; their tongues dance.

They make love, he and she, slow and sensuous, locked together in a loving embrace that goes on and on. Two bodies move flawlessly in perfect rhythm, each knowing the other's needs. Trager thrusts, and his other body meets the thrusts. He reaches, and her hand is there. They come together (always, *always*, both orgasms triggered by the handler's brain), and a bright red flush burns on her breasts and earlobes. They kiss.

Afterwards, he talks to her, his love, his lady. You should always talk afterwards; he learned that long ago.

'You're lucky,' he tells her sometimes, and she snuggles up to him and plants tiny kisses all across his chest. 'Very lucky. They lie to you out there, love. They teach you a silly shining dream and they tell you to believe and chase it and they tell you that for you, for everyone, there is someone. But it's all wrong. The universe isn't fair, it never has been, so why do they tell you so? You run after the phantom, and lose, and they tell you next time, but it's all rot, all empty rot. Nobody ever finds the dream at all, they just kid themselves, trick themselves so they can go on believing. It's just a clutching lie that desperate people tell each other, hoping to convince themselves.'

But then he can't talk anymore, for her kisses have gone lower and lower, and now she takes him in her mouth. And Trager smiles at his love and gently strokes her hair.

*

Of all the bright cruel lies they tell you, the crudest is the one called love.

Remembering Melody

Ted was shaving when the doorbell sounded. It startled him so badly that he cut himself. His condominium was on the thirty-second floor, and Jack the doorman generally gave him advance warning of any prospective visitors. This had to be someone from the building, then. Except that Ted didn't know anyone in the building, at least not beyond the trade-smiles-in-the-elevator level.

'Coming,' he shouted. Scowling, he snatched up a towel and wiped the lather from his face, then dabbed at his cut with a tissue. 'Shit,' he said loudly to his face in the mirror. He had to be in court this afternoon. If this was another Jehovah's Witness like the one who'd gotten past Jack last month, they were going to be in for a very rough time indeed.

The buzzer buzzed again. 'Coming, dammit,' Ted yelled. He made a final dab at the blood on his neck, then threw the tissue into a waste-basket and strode across the sunken living room to the door. He peered through the eyehole carefully before he opened. 'Oh, shit,' he muttered. Before she could buzz again, Ted slid off the chain and threw open the door. 'Hello, Melody,' he said.

She smiled wanly. 'Hi, Ted,' she replied. She had an old suitcase in her hand, a battered cloth bag with a hideous red-and-black plaid pattern, its broken handle replaced by a length of rope. The last time Ted had seen her, three years before, she'd looked terrible. Now she looked worse. Her clothes – shorts and a tie-dyed T-shirt – were wrinkled and dirty, and emphasized how gaunt she'd become. Her ribs showed through plainly; her legs were pipestems. Her long stringy blonde hair hadn't been washed recently, and her face was red and puffy, as if she'd been crying. That was no surprise. Melody was always crying about one thing or another. 'Aren't you going to ask me in, Ted?'

Ted grimaced. He certainly didn't *want* to ask her in. He knew from past experience how difficult it was to get her out again. But he couldn't just leave her standing in the hall with her suitcase in hand. After all, he thought sourly, she was an old and dear friend. 'Oh, sure,' he said. He gestured. 'Come on in.'

He took her bag from her and set it by the door, then led her into the kitchen and put on some water to boil. 'You look as though you could use a cup of coffee,' he said, trying to keep his voice friendly.

Melody smiled again. 'Don't you remember, Ted? I don't drink coffee. It's no good for you, Ted. I used to tell you that. Don't you remember?' She got up from the kitchen table, and began rummaging through his cupboards. 'Do you have any hot chocolate?' she asked. 'I like hot chocolate.'

'I don't drink hot chocolate,' he said. 'Just a lot of coffee.'

'You shouldn't,' she said. 'It's no good for you.'

'Yeah,' he said. 'Do you want juice? I've got juice.'

Melody nodded. 'Fine.'

He poured her a glass of orange juice, and led her back to the table, then spooned some Maxim into a mug while he waited for his kettle to whistle. 'So,' he asked, 'what brings you to Chicago?'

Melody began to cry. Ted leaned back against the stove and watched her. She was a very noisy crier, and she produced an amazing amount of tears for someone who cried so often. She didn't look up until the water began to boil. Ted poured some into his cup and stirred in a teaspoon of sugar. Her face was redder and more puffy than ever. Her eyes fixed on him accusingly. 'Things have been real bad,' she said. 'I need help, Ted. I don't have any place to live. I thought maybe I could stay with you a while. Things have been real bad.'

'I'm sorry to hear that, Melody,' Ted replied, sipping at his coffee thoughtfully. 'You can stay here for a few days, if you want. But no longer. I'm not in the market for a roommate.' She always made him feel like such a bastard, but it was better to be firm with her right from the start, he thought.

Melody began to cry again when he mentioned roommates. 'You used to say I was a *good* roommate,' she whined. 'We used to have fun, don't you remember? You were my friend.'

Ted set down his coffee mug and looked at the kitchen clock. 'I don't have time to talk about old times right now,' he said. 'I was shaving when you rang. I've got to get to the office. He frowned. 'Drink your juice and make yourself at home. I've got to get dressed.' He turned abruptly, and left her weeping at the kitchen table.

Back in the bathroom, Ted finished shaving and tended to his cut more properly, his mind full of Melody. Already he could tell that this was going to be difficult. He felt sorry for her – she was messed-up and miserably unhappy, with no one to turn to – but he wasn't going to let her inflict all her troubles on him. Not this time. She'd done it too many times before.

In his bedroom, Ted stared pensively into the closet for a long time before selecting the gray suit. He knotted his tie carefully in the mirror, scowling at his cut. Then he checked his briefcase to make sure all the papers on the Syndio case were in order, nodded, and walked back into the kitchen.

Melody was at the stove, making some pancakes. She turned and smiled at him happily when he entered. 'You remember my pancakes, Ted?' she asked. 'You used to love it when I made pancakes, especially blueberry pancakes, you remember? You didn't have any blueberries, though, so I'm just making plain. Is that alright?'

'Jesus,' Ted muttered. 'Dammit, Melody, who said you should make *anything*? I told you I had to get to the office. I don't have time to eat with you. I'm late already. Anyway, I don't eat breakfast. I'm trying to lose weight.'

Tears began to trickle from her eyes again. 'But – but these are my special pancakes, Ted. What am I going to do with them? What am I going to *do?*'

'Eat them,' Ted said. 'You could use a few extra pounds. Jesus, you look terrible. You look like you haven't eaten for a month.'

Melody's face screwed up and became ugly. 'You bastard,' she said. 'You're supposed to be my *friend*.'

Ted sighed. 'Take it easy,' he said. He glanced at his watch. 'Look, I'm fifteen minutes late already. I've got to go. You eat your pancakes and get some sleep. I'll be back around six. We can have dinner together and talk, all right? Is that what you want?'

'That would be nice,' she said, suddenly contrite. 'That would be real nice.'

*

'Tell Jill I want to see her in my office, right away,' Ted snapped to the secretary when he arrived. 'And get us some coffee, willya? I really need some coffee.'

'Sure.'

Jill arrived a few minutes after the coffee. She and Ted were associates in the same law firm. He motioned her to a seat, and pushed a cup at her. 'Sit down,' he said. 'Look, the date's off tonight. I've got problems.'

'You look it,' she said. 'What's wrong?'

'An old friend showed up on my doorstep this morning,' he said.

Jill arched one elegant eyebrow. 'So?' she said. 'Reunions can be fun.'

'Not with Melody they can't.'

'Melody?' she said. 'A pretty name. An old flame, Ted? What is it, unrequited love?'

'No,' he said, 'no, it wasn't like that.'

'Tell me what it was like, then. You know I love the gory details.'

'Melody and I were roommates, back in college. Not just us – don't get the wrong idea. There were four of us. Me and a guy named Michael Englehart, Melody and another girl, Anne Kaye. The four of us shared a big old run-down house for two years. We were – friends.'

'Friends?' Jill looked skeptical.

Ted scowled at her. 'Friends,' he repeated. 'Oh, hell, I slept with Melody a few times. With Anne too. And both of them fucked Michael a time or two. But when it happened, it was just kind of – kind of *friendly*, you know? Our love life was mostly with outsiders, we used to tell each other our troubles, swap advice, cry on one another's shoulders. Hell, I know it sounds weird. It was 1970, though. I had hair down to my ass. Everything was weird.' He sloshed the dregs of his coffee around in the cup, and looked pensive. 'They were good times, too. Special times. Sometimes I'm sorry they had to end. The four of us were close, really close. I loved those people.'

'Watch out,' Jill said, 'I'll get jealous. My roommate and I cordially despised each other.' She smiled. 'So what happened?'

Ted shrugged. 'The usual story,' he said. 'We graduated, drifted apart. I remember the last night in the old house. We smoked a ton of dope, and got very silly. Swore eternal friendship. We weren't ever going to be strangers, no matter what happened, and if any of us ever needed help, well, the other three would always be there. We sealed the bargain with – well, kind of an orgy.'

Jill smiled. 'Touching,' she said. 'I never dreamed you had it in you.'

'It didn't last, of course,' Ted continued. 'We tried, I'll give us that much. But things changed too much. I went on to law school, wound up here in Chicago. Michael got a job with a publishing house in New York City. He's an editor at Random House now, been married and divorced, two kids. We used to write. Now we trade Christmas cards. Anne's a teacher. She was down in Phoenix the last I heard, but that was four, five years ago. Her husband didn't like the rest of us much, the one time we had a reunion. I think Anne must have told him about the orgy.'

'And your house guest?'

'Melody,' he sighed. 'She became a problem. In college, she was wonderful; gutsy, pretty, a real free spirit. But afterwards she couldn't cut it. She tried to make it as a painter for a couple of years, but she wasn't good enough. Got nowhere. She went through a couple of relationships that turned sour, then married some guy about a week after she'd met him in a singles bar. That was terrible. He used to get drunk and beat her. She took about six months of it, and finally got a divorce. He still came round to beat her up for a year, until he finally got frightened off. After that Melody got into drugs, bad. She spent some time in an asylum. When she got out, it was more of the same. She can't hold a job, or stay away from drugs. Her relationships don't last more than a few weeks. She's let her body go to hell.' He shook his head.

Jill pursed her lips. 'Sounds like a lady who needs help,' she said.

Ted flushed, and grew angry. 'You think I don't know that? You think we haven't tried to help her? *Jesus*. When she was trying to be an artist, Michael got her a couple of cover assignments from the paperback house he was with. Not only did she blow the deadlines, but she got into a screaming match with the art director. Almost cost Michael his job. I flew to Cleveland and handled her divorce for her, gratis. Flew back a couple of months later, and spent quite a while there trying to get the cops to give her protection against her ex-hubby. Anne took her in when she had no place to stay, got her into a drug rehabilitation program. In return, Melody tried to seduce her boyfriend – said she wanted to *share* him, like they'd done in the old days. All of us have lent her money. She's never paid back any of it. And we've listened to her troubles, God but we've listened to her troubles. There was a period a few years ago when she'd phone every week, usually collect, with some new sad story. She cried over the phone a lot. If *Queen for a Day* was still on TV, Melody would be a natural!'

'I'm beginning to see why you're not thrilled by her visit,' Jill said drily. 'What are you going to do?'

'I don't know,' Ted replied. 'I shouldn't have let her in. The last few times she's called, I just hung up on her, and that seemed to work pretty well. Felt guilty about it at first, but that passed. This morning, though, she looked so pathetic that I didn't know how to send her away. I suppose eventually I'll have to get brutal, and go through a scene. Nothing else works. She'll make a lot of accusations, remind me of what good friends we were and the promises we made, threaten to kill herself. Fun times ahead.'

'Can I help?' Jill asked.

'Pick up my pieces afterwards,' Ted said. 'It's always nice to have someone around afterwards, to tell you that you're not a son of a bitch even though you just kicked an old dear friend out into the gutter.'

*

He was terrible in court that afternoon. His thoughts were full of Melody, and the strategies that most occupied him concerned how to get rid of her most painlessly, instead of the case at hand. Melody had danced flamenco on his psyche too many times before; Ted wasn't going to let her leech off him this time, nor leave him an emotional wreck.

When he got back to his condo with a bag of Chinese food under his arm – he'd decided he didn't want to take her out to a restaurant – Melody was

sitting nude in the middle of his conversation pit, giggling and sniffing
some white powder. She looked up at Ted happily when he entered. 'Here,'
she said. 'I scored some coke.'

'*Jesus*,' he swore. He dropped the Chinese food and his briefcase, and
strode furiously across the carpet. 'I don't *believe* you,' he roared. 'I'm a
lawyer, for Chrissakes. Do you want to get me disbarred?'

Melody had the coke in a little paper square, and was sniffing it from a
rolled-up dollar bill. Ted snatched it all away from her, and she began to
cry. He went to the bathroom and flushed it down the toilet, dollar bill and
all. Except it wasn't a dollar bill, he saw, as it was sucked out of sight. It
was a twenty. That made him even angrier. When he returned to the living
room, Melody was still crying.

'Stop that,' he said. 'I don't want to hear it. And put some clothes on.'
Another suspicion came to him. 'Where did you get the money for that
stuff?' he demanded. 'Huh, *where*!'

Melody whimpered. 'I sold some stuff,' she said in a timid voice. 'I
didn't think you'd mind. It was good coke.' She shied away from him and
threw an arm across her face, as if Ted was going to hit her.

Ted didn't need to ask whose stuff she'd sold. He knew; she'd pulled the
same trick on Michael years before, or so he'd heard. He sighed. 'Get
dressed,' he repeated wearily. 'I brought Chinese food.' Later he could
check what was missing, and phone the insurance company.

'Chinese food is no good for you,' Melody said. 'It's full of monosodium
glutamate. Gives you headaches, Ted.' But she got to her feet obediently, if
a bit unsteadily, went off towards the bathroom, and came back a few
minutes later wearing a halter-top and a pair of ratty cutoffs. Nothing else,
Ted guessed. A couple of years ago she must have decided that underwear
was no good for you.

Ignoring her comment about monosodium glutamate, Ted found some
plates and served up the Chinese food in his dining nook. Melody ate it
meekly enough, drowning everything in soy sauce. Every few minutes she
giggled at some private joke, then grew very serious again and resumed
eating. When she broke open her fortune cookie, a wide smile lit her face.
'Look, Ted,' she said happily, passing the little slip of paper across to him.

He read it. OLD FRIENDS ARE THE BEST FRIENDS, it said. 'Oh,
shit,' he muttered. He didn't even open his own. Melody wanted to know
why. 'You ought to read it, Ted,' she told him. 'It's bad luck if you don't
read your fortune cookie.'

'I don't want to read it,' he said. 'I'm going to change out of this suit.'
He rose. 'Don't do anything.'

But when he came back, she'd put an album on the stereo. At least she
hadn't sold that, he thought gratefully.

'Do you want me to dance for you?' she asked. 'Remember how I used to dance for you and Michael? Real sexy . . . you used to tell me how good I dance. I could have been a dancer if I'd wanted.' She did a few steps in the middle of his living room, stumbled, and almost fell. It was grotesque.

'Sit down, Melody,' Ted said, as sternly as he could manage. 'We have to talk.'

She sat down.

'Don't cry,' he said before he started. 'You understand that? I don't want you to cry. We can't talk if you're going to cry every time I say anything. You start crying and this conversation is over.'

Melody nodded. 'I won't cry, Ted,' she said. 'I feel much better now than this morning. I'm with you now. You make me feel better.'

'You're *not* with me, Melody. Stop that.'

Her eyes filled up with tears. 'You're my friend, Ted. You and Michael and Anne, you're the special ones.'

He sighed. 'What's wrong, Melody? Why are you here?'

'I lost my job, Ted,' she said.

'The waitress job?' he asked. The last time he'd seen her, three years ago, she'd been waiting tables in a bar in Kansas City.

Melody blinked at him, confused. 'Waitress?' she said. 'No, Ted. That was before. That was in Kansas City. Don't you remember?'

'I remember very well,' he said. 'What job was it you lost?'

'It was a shitty job,' Melody said. 'A factory job. It was in Iowa. In Des Moines. Des Moines is a shitty place. I didn't come to work, so they fired me. I was strung out, you know? I needed a couple of days off. I would have come back to work. But they fired me.' She looked close to tears again. 'I haven't had a good job in a long time, Ted. I was an art major. You remember? You and Michael and Anne used to have my drawings hung up in your rooms. You still have my drawings, Ted?'

'Yes,' he lied. 'Sure. Somewhere.' He'd gotten rid of them years ago. They reminded him too much of Melody, and that was too painful.

'Anyway, when I lost my job, Johnny said I wasn't bringing in any money. Johnny was the guy I lived with. He said he wasn't gonna support me, that I had to get some job, but I couldn't. I *tried*, Ted, but I couldn't. So Johnny talked to some man, and he got me this job in a massage parlor, you know. And he took me down there, but it was crummy. I didn't want to work in no massage parlor, Ted. I used to be an art major.'

'I remember, Melody,' Ted said. She seemed to expect him to say something.

Melody nodded. 'So I didn't take it, and Johnny threw me out. I had no place to go, you know. And I thought of you, and Anne, and Michael. Remember the last night? We all said that if anyone ever needed help . . .'

'I remember, Melody,' Ted said. 'Not as often as you do, but I remember. You don't ever let any of us forget it, do you? But let it pass. What do you want this time?' His tone was flat and cold.

'You're a lawyer, Ted,' she said.

'Yes.'

'So, I thought—' Her long, thin fingers plucked nervously at her face. 'I thought maybe you could get me a job. I could be a secretary, maybe. In your office. We could be together again, every day, like it used to be. Or maybe,' – she brightened visibly – 'maybe I could be one of those people who draw pictures in the courtroom. You know. Like Patty Hearst and people like that. On TV. I'd be good at that.'

'Those artists work for TV stations,' Ted said patiently. 'And there are no openings in my office. I'm sorry, Melody. I can't get you a job.'

Melody took that surprisingly well. 'All right, Ted,' she said. 'I can find a job, I guess. I'll get one all by myself. Only – only let me live here, okay? We can be roommates again.'

'Oh, Jesus,' Ted said. He sat back and crossed his arms. 'No,' he said flatly.

Melody took her hand away from her face, and stared at him imploringly. 'Please, Ted,' she whispered. 'Please.'

'No,' he said. The word hung there, chill and final.

'You're my *friend*, Ted,' she said. 'You *promised*.'

'You can stay here a week,' he said. 'No longer. I have my own life, Melody. I have my own problems. I'm tired of dealing with yours. We all are. You're nothing but problems. In college, you were fun. You're not fun any longer. I've helped you and helped you and helped you. How fucking much do you want out of me?' He was getting angrier as he talked. 'Things change, Melody,' he said brutally. 'People change. You can't hold me forever to some dumb promise I made when I was stoned out of my mind back in college. I'm not responsible for your life. Tough up, dammit. Pull yourself together. I can't do it for you, and I'm sick of all your shit. I don't even like to see you anymore, Melody, you know that?'

She whimpered. 'Don't say that, Ted. We're friends. You're special. As long as I have you and Michael and Anne, I'll never be alone, don't you see?'

'You *are* alone,' he said. Melody infuriated him.

'No I'm not,' she insisted. 'I have my friends, my special friends. They'll help me. You're my *friend*, Ted.'

'I used to be your friend,' he replied.

She stared at him, her lip trembling, hurt beyond words. For a moment he thought that the dam was going to burst, that Melody was finally about to break down and begin one of her marathon crying jags. Instead, a change came over her face. She paled perceptibly, and her lips drew back slowly, and her expression settled into a terrible mask of anger. She was hideous when she was angry. 'You bastard,' she said.

Ted had been this route too. He got up from the couch and walked to his bar. 'Don't start,' he said, pouring himself a glass of Chivas Regal on the rocks. 'The first thing you throw, you're out on your ass. Got that, Melody?'

'You scum,' she repeated. 'You were never my friend. None of you were. You lied to me, made me trust you, used me. Now you're all so high and mighty and I'm nothing, and you don't want to know me. You don't want to help me. You never wanted to help me.'

'I did help you,' Ted pointed out. 'Several times. You owe me something close to two thousand dollars, I believe.'

'Money,' she said. 'That's all you care about, you bastard.'

Ted sipped at his scotch and frowned at her. 'Go to hell,' he said.

'I could, for all you care.' Her face had gone white. 'I cabled you, two years ago. I cabled all three of you. I needed you, you promised that you'd come if I needed you, that you'd be there, you promised that and you made love to me and you were my friend, but I cabled you and you didn't come, you bastard, you didn't come, none of you came, none of you came.' She was screaming.

Ted had forgotten about the telegram. But it all came back to him in a rush. He'd read it over several times, and finally he'd picked up the phone and called Michael. Michael hadn't been in. So he'd reread the telegram one last time, then crumbled it up and flushed it down the toilet. One of the others could go to her this time, he remembered thinking. He had a big case, the Argrath Corporation patent suit, and he couldn't risk leaving it. But it had been a desperate telegram, and he'd been guilty about it for weeks, until he finally managed to put the whole thing out of his mind. 'I was busy,' he said, his tone half-angry and half-defensive. 'I had more important things to do than come hold your hand through another crisis.'

'It was *horrible*,' Melody screamed. 'I needed you and you left me all *alone*. I almost *killed* myself.'

'But you didn't, did you?'

'I could have,' she said. 'I could have killed myself, and you wouldn't have even cared.'

Threatening suicide was one of Melody's favorite tricks. Ted had been through it a hundred times before. This time he decided not to take it. 'You could have killed yourself,' he said calmly, 'and we probably wouldn't've cared. I think you're right about that. You would have rotted for weeks before anyone found you, and we probably wouldn't even have heard about it for half a year. And when I did hear, finally, I guess it would have made me sad for an hour or two, remembering how things had been, but then I would have gotten drunk or phoned up my girlfriend or something, and pretty soon I'd have been out of it. And then I could have forgotten all about you.'

'You would have been sorry,' Melody said.

'No,' Ted replied. He strolled back to the bar and freshened his drink. 'No, you know, I don't think I would have been sorry. Not in the least. Not guilty, either. So you might as well stop threatening to kill yourself, Melody, because it isn't going to work.'

The anger drained out of her face, and she gave a little whimper. 'Please, Ted,' she said. 'Don't say such things. Tell me you'd care. Tell me you'd remember me.'

He scowled at her. 'No,' he said. It was harder when she was pitiful, when she shrunk up all small and vulnerable and whimpered instead of accusing him. But he had to end it once and for all, get rid of this curse on his life.

'I'll go away tomorrow,' she said meekly. 'I won't bother you. But tell me you care, Ted. That you're my friend. That you'll come to me. If I need you.'

'I won't come to you, Melody,' he said. 'That's over. And I don't want you coming here anymore, or phoning, or sending telegrams, no matter what kind of trouble you're in. You understand? Do you? I want you out of my life, and when you're gone I'm going to forget you as quick as I can, 'cause lady, you are one hell of a bad memory.'

Melody cried out as if he had struck her. 'NO!' she said. 'No, don't say that, remember me, you have to. I'll leave you alone, I promise I will, I'll never see you again. But say you'll remember me.' She stood up abruptly. 'I'll go right now,' she said. 'If you want me to go, I'll go. But make love to me first, Ted. Please. I want to give you something to remember me by.' She smiled a lascivious little smile, and began to struggle out of her halter top, and Ted felt sick.

He set down his glass with a bang. 'You're crazy,' he said. 'You ought to get professional help, Melody. But I can't give it to you and I'm not going to put up with this anymore. I'm going out for a walk. I'll be gone a couple of hours. You be gone when I get back.'

Ted started for the door. Melody stood looking at him, her halter in her hand. Her breasts looked small and shrunken, and the left one had a tattoo on it that he'd never noticed before. There was nothing even vaguely desirable about her. She whimpered. 'I just wanted to give you something to remember me by,' she said.

Ted slammed the door.

*

It was midnight when he returned, drunk and surly, resolved that if

Melody was still there, he would call the police and that would be the end of that. Jack was behind the desk, having just gone on duty. Ted stopped and gave him hell for having admitted Melody that morning, but the doorman denied it vehemently. 'Wasn't nobody got in, Mister Cirelli. I don't let in anyone without buzzing up, you ought to know that. I been here six years, and I never let in nobody without buzzing up.' Ted reminded him forcefully about the Jehovah's Witness, and they ended up in a shouting match.

Finally Ted stormed away and took the elevator up to the thirty-second floor.

There was a drawing taped to his door.

He blinked at it furiously for a moment, then snatched it down. It was a cartoon, a caricature of Melody. Not the Melody he'd seen today, but the Melody he'd known in college; sharp, funny, pretty. When they'd been roommates, Melody had always illustrated her notes with little cartoons of herself. He was surprised that she could still draw this well. Beneath the face, she'd printed a message.

I LEFT YOU SOMETHING TO REMEMBER ME BY.

Ted scowled down at the cartoon, wondering whether he should keep it or not. His own hesitation made him angry. He crumbled the paper in his hand, and fumbled for his keys. At least she's gone, he thought, and maybe for good. If she left the note, it meant that she'd gone. He was rid of her for another couple of years at least.

He went inside, tossed the crumbled ball of paper across the room towards a wastebasket, and smiled when it went in. 'Two points,' he said loudly to himself, drunk and self-satisfied. He went to the bar and began to mix himself a drink.

But something was wrong.

Ted stopped stirring his drink, and listened. The water was running, he realized. She'd left the water running in the bathroom.

'Christ,' he said, and then an awful thought hit him; maybe she hadn't gone after all. Maybe she was still in the bathroom, taking a shower or something, freaked out of her mind, crying, whatever. 'Melody!' he shouted.

No answer. The water was running all right. It couldn't be anything else. But she didn't answer.

'Melody, are you still here?' he yelled. 'Answer, dammit!'

Silence.

He put down his drink and walked to the bathroom. The door was closed. Ted stood outside. The water was definitely running. 'Melody,' he said loudly, 'are you in there? Melody?'

Nothing. Ted was beginning to be afraid.

He reached out and grasped the doorknob. It turned easily in his hand. The door hadn't been locked.

Inside the bathroom was filled with steam. He could hardly see, but he made out that the shower curtain was drawn. The shower was running full blast, and judging from the amount of steam, it must be scalding. Ted stepped back and waited for the steam to dissipate. 'Melody?' he said softly. There was no reply.

'Shit,' he said. He tried not to be afraid. She only talked about it, he told himself; she'd never really do it. The ones who talk about it never do it, he'd read that somewhere. She was just doing this to frighten him.

He took two quick strides across the room and yanked back the shower curtain.

She was there, wreathed in steam, water streaming down her naked body. She wasn't stretched out in the tub at all; she was sitting up, crammed in sideways near the faucets, looking very small and pathetic. Her position seemed half-fetal. The needle spray had been directed down at her, at her hands. She'd opened her wrists with his razor blades, and tried to hold them under the water, but it hadn't been enough, she'd slit the veins crosswise, and everybody knew the only way to do it was lengthwise. So she'd used the razor elsewhere, and now she had two mouths, and both of them were smiling at him, smiling. The shower had washed away most of the blood; there were no stains anywhere, but the second mouth below her chin was still red and dripping. Trickles oozed down her chest, over the flower tattooed on her breast, and the spray of the shower caught them and washed them away. Her hair hung down over her cheeks, limp and wet. She was smiling. She looked so happy. The steam was all around her. She'd been in there for hours, he thought. She was very clean.

Ted closed his eyes. It didn't make any difference. He still saw her. He would always see her.

He opened them again; Melody was still smiling. He reached across her and turned off the shower, getting the sleeve of his shirt soaked in the process.

Numb, he fled back into the living room. God, he thought, God. I have to call someone, I have to report this, I can't deal with this. He decided to call the police. He lifted the phone, and hesitated with his finger poised over the buttons. The police won't help, he thought. He punched for Jill.

When he had finished telling her, it grew very silent on the other end of the phone. 'My god,' she said at last. 'How awful. Can I do anything?'

'Come over,' he said. 'Right away.' He found the drink he'd set down, took a hurried sip from it.

Jill hesitated. 'Er – look, Ted, I'm not very good at dealing with corpses,' she said. 'Why don't you come over here? I don't want to – well, you know. I don't think I'll ever shower at your place again.'

'Jill,' he said, stricken. 'I need someone right now.' He laughed a frightened, uncertain laugh.

'Come over here,' she urged.

'I can't just *leave* it there,' he said.

'Well, don't,' she said. 'Call the police. They'll take it away. Come over afterwards.'

Ted called the police.

*

'If this is your idea of a joke, it isn't funny,' the patrolman said. His partner was scowling.

'Joke?' Ted said.

'There's nothing in your shower,' the patrolman said. 'I ought to take you down to the station house.'

'Nothing in the shower?' Ted repeated, incredulous.

'Leave him alone, Sam,' the partner said. 'He's stinko, can't you tell?'

Ted rushed past them both into the bathroom.

The tub was empty. Empty. He knelt and felt the bottom of it. Dry. Perfectly dry. But his shirt sleeve was still damp. 'No,' he said, 'no.' He rushed back out to the living room. The two cops watched him with amusement. Her suitcase was gone from its place by the door. The dishes had all been run through the dishwasher, no way to tell if anyone had made pancakes or not. Ted turned the wastebasket upside down, spilling out the contents all over his couch. He began to scrabble through the papers.

'Go to bed and sleep it off, mister,' the older cop said. 'You'll feel better in the morning.'

'C'mon,' his partner said. They departed, leaving Ted still pawing through the papers. No cartoon. No cartoon. No cartoon.

Ted flung the empty wastebasket across the room, and it caromed off the wall with a ringing metallic clang.

He took a cab to Jill's.

*

It was near dawn when he sat up in bed suddenly, his heart thumping, his mouth dry with fear.

Jill murmured sleepily. 'Jill,' he said, shaking her.

She blinked up at him. 'What?' she said. 'What time is it, Ted? What's wrong?' She sat up, pulling up the blanket to cover herself.

'Don't you hear it?'

'Hear what?' she asked.

He giggled. 'Your shower is running.'

That morning he shaved in the kitchen, even though there was no mirror. He cut himself twice. His bladder ached, but he would not go past the bathroom door, despite Jill's repeated assurances that the shower was not running. Dammit, he could *hear* it. He waited until he got to the office. There was no shower in the washroom there.

But Jill looked at him strangely.

*

At the office, Ted cleared his desk, and tried to think. He was a lawyer. He had a good, analytical mind. He tried to reason it out. He drank only coffee, lots of coffee.

No suitcase, he thought. Jack hadn't seen her. No corpse. No cartoon. No one had seen her. The shower was dry. No dishes. He'd been drinking. But not all day, only later, after dinner. Couldn't be the drinking. Couldn't be. No cartoon. He was the only one who'd seen her. No cartoon. I LEFT YOU SOMETHING TO REMEMBER ME BY. He'd crumpled up her cable, and flushed her away. Two years ago. Nothing in the shower.

He picked up his phone. 'Billie,' he said, 'get me a newspaper in Des Moines, Iowa. Any newspaper, I don't care.'

When he finally got through the woman who tended the morgue was reluctant to give him any information. But she softened when he told her he was a lawyer, and needed the information for an important case.

The obituary was very short. Melody was identified only as a 'massage parlor employee.' She'd killed herself in her shower.

'Thank you,' Ted said. He set down the receiver. For a long time he sat staring out of his window. He had a very good view; he could see the lake and the soaring tower of the Standard Oil building. He pondered what to do next. There was a thick knot of fear in his gut.

He could take the day off and go home. But the shower would be running at home, and sooner or later he would have to go in there.

He could go back to Jill's. If Jill would have him. She'd seemed awfully cool after last night. She'd recommended a shrink to him as they shared a cab to the office. She didn't understand. No one would understand . . . unless . . . he picked up the phone again, searching through his circular file. There was no card, no number, they'd drifted that far apart. He buzzed for Billie again. 'Get me through to Random House in New York City,' he said. 'To Mr Michael Englehart. He's an editor there.'

But when he finally connected, the voice on the other end of the line was strange and distant. 'Mister Cirelli? Were you a friend of Michael's? Or one of his authors?'

Ted's mouth was dry. 'A friend,' he said. 'Isn't Michael in? I need to talk to him. It's . . . urgent.'

'I'm afraid Michael's no longer with us,' the voice said. 'He had a nervous breakdown, less than a week ago.'

'Is he . . . ?'

'He's alive. They took him to a hospital, I believe. You know. Maybe I can find you the number.'

'No,' Ted said. 'No, that's quite all right.' He hung up.

Phoenix directory assistance had no listing for an Anne Kaye. Of course not, he thought. She was married now. He tried to remember her married name. It took him a long time. Something Polish, he thought. Finally it came to him.

He hadn't expected to find her at home. It was a school day, after all. But someone picked up the phone on the third ring. 'Hello,' he said. 'Anne, is that you? This is Ted, in Chicago. Anne, I've got to talk to you. It's about Melody. Anne, I need your help.' He was breathless.

There was a giggle. 'Anne isn't here right now, Ted,' Melody said. 'She's off at school, and then she's got to visit her husband. They're separated, you know. But she promised to come back by eight.'

'Melody,' he said.

'Of course, I don't know if I can believe her. You three were never very good about promises. But maybe she'll come back, Ted. I hope so.

'I want to leave her something to remember me by.'

Sandkings

Simon Kress lived alone in a sprawling manor house among the dry, rocky hills fifty kilometers from the city. So, when he was called away unexpectedly on business, he had no neighbors he could conveniently impose on to take his pets. The carrion hawk was no problem; it roosted in the unused belfry and customarily fed itself anyway. The shambler Kress simply shooed outside and left to fend for itself; the little monster would gorge on slugs and birds and rockjocks. But the fish tank, stocked with genuine Earth piranha, posed a difficulty. Kress finally just threw a haunch of beef into the huge tank. The piranha could always eat each other if he were detained longer than expected. They'd done it before. It amused him.

Unfortunately, he was detained *much* longer than expected this time. When he finally returned, all the fish were dead. So was the carrion hawk. The shambler had climbed up to the belfry and eaten it. Simon Kress was vexed.

The next day he flew his skimmer to Asgard, a journey of some two hundred kilometers. Asgard was Baldur's largest city and boasted the oldest and largest starport as well. Kress liked to impress his friends with animals that were unusual, entertaining, and expensive; Asgard was the place to buy them.

This time, though, he had poor luck. Xenopets had closed its doors, t'Etherane the Petseller tried to foist another carrion hawk off on him, and Strange Waters offered nothing more exotic than piranha, glow-sharks, and spider squids. Kress had had all those; he wanted something new.

Near dusk, he found himself walking down the Rainbow Boulevard, looking for places he had not patronized before. So close to the starport, the street was lined by importers' marts. The big corporate emporiums had impressive long windows, where rare and costly alien artifacts reposed on felt cushions against dark drapes that made the interiors of the stores a mystery. Between them were the junk shops – narrow, nasty little places whose display areas were crammed with all manner of offworld bric-a-brac. Kress tried both kinds of shop, with equal dissatisfaction.

Then he came across a store that was different.

It was quite close to the port. Kress had never been there before. The shop occupied a small, single-story building of moderate size, set between a euphoria bar and a temple-brothel of the Secret Sisterhood. Down this far, the Rainbow Boulevard grew tacky. The shop itself was unusual. Arresting.

The windows were full of mist; now a pale red, now the gray of true fog, now sparkling and golden. The mist swirled and eddied and glowed faintly from within. Kress glimpsed objects in the window – machines, pieces of art, other things he could not recognize – but he could not get a good look at any of them. The mists flowed sensuously around them, displaying a bit of first one thing and then another, then cloaking all. It was intriguing.

As he watched, the mist began to form letters. One word at a time. Kress stood and read:

WO. AND. SHADE. IMPORTERS. ARTIFACTS. ART. LIFEFORMS. AND. MISC.

The letters stopped. Through the fog, Kress saw something moving. That was enough for him, that and the word 'Lifeforms' in their advertisement. He swept his walking cloak over his shoulder and entered the store.

Inside, Kress felt disoriented. The interior seemed vast, much larger than he would have guessed from the relatively modest frontage. It was dimly lit, peaceful. The ceiling was a starscape, complete with spiral nebulae, very dark and realistic, very nice. The counters all shone faintly, the better to display the merchandise within. The aisles were carpeted with ground fog. In places, it came almost to his knees and swirled about his feet as he walked.

'Can I help you?'

She seemed almost to have risen from the fog. Tall and gaunt and pale, she wore a practical gray jumpsuit and a strange little cap that rested well back on her head.

'Are you Wo or Shade?' Kress asked. 'Or only sales help?'

'Jala Wo, ready to serve you,' she replied. 'Shade does not see customers. We have no sales help.'

'You have quite a large establishment,' Kress said. 'Odd that I have never heard of you before.'

'We have only just opened this shop on Baldur,' the woman said. 'We have franchises on a number of other worlds, however. What can I sell you? Art, perhaps? You have the look of a collector. We have some fine Nor T'alush crystal carvings.'

'No,' Simon Kress said. 'I own all the crystal carvings I desire. I came to see about a pet.'

'A lifeform?'

'Yes.'

'Alien?'

'Of course.'

'We have a mimic in stock. From Celia's World. A clever little simian. Not only will it learn to speak, but eventually it will mimic your voice, inflections, gestures, even facial expressions.'

'Cute,' said Kress. 'And common. I have no use for either, Wo. I want something exotic. Unusual. And not cute. I detest cute animals. At the moment I own a shambler. Imported from Cotho, at no mean expense. From time to time I feed him a litter of unwanted kittens. That is what I think of *cute*. Do I make myself understood?'

Wo smiled enigmatically. 'Have you ever owned an animal that worshipped you?' she asked.

Kress grinned. 'Oh, now and again. But I don't require worship, Wo. Just entertainment.'

'You misunderstood me,' Wo said, still wearing her strange smile. 'I meant worship literally.'

'What are you talking about?'

'I think I have just the thing for you,' Wo said. 'Follow me.'

She led Kress between the radiant counters and down a long, fog-shrouded aisle beneath false starlight. They passed through a wall of mist into another section of the store, and stopped before a large plastic tank. An aquarium, thought Kress.

Wo beckoned. He stepped closer and saw that he was wrong. It was a terrarium. Within lay a miniature desert about two meters square. Pale and bleached scarlet by wan red light. Rocks: basalt and quartz and granite. In each corner of the tank stood a castle.

Kress blinked, and peered, and corrected himself; actually only three castles stood. The fourth leaned; a crumbled, broken ruin. The other three were crude but intact, carved of stone and sand. Over their battlements and through their rounded porticoes, tiny creatures climbed and scrambled. Kress pressed his face against the plastic. 'Insects?' he asked.

'No,' Wo replied. 'A much more complex lifeform. More intelligent as well. Considerably smarter than your shambler. They are called sandkings.'

'Insects,' Kress said, drawing back from the tank. 'I don't care how complex they are.' He frowned. 'And kindly don't try to gull me with this talk of intelligence. These things are far too small to have anything but the most rudimentary brains.'

'They share hiveminds,' Wo said. 'Castle minds, in this case. There are only three organisms in the tank, actually. The fourth died. You see how her castle has fallen.'

Kress looked back at the tank. 'Hiveminds, eh? Interesting.' He frowned again. 'Still, it is only an oversized ant farm. I'd hoped for something better.'

'They fight wars.'

'Wars? Hmmm.' Kress looked again.

'Note the colors, if you will,' Wo told him. She pointed to the creatures that swarmed over the nearest castle. One was scrabbling at the tank wall. Kress studied it. It still looked like an insect to his eyes. Barely as long as his fingernail, six-limbed, with six tiny eyes set all around its body. A wicked set of mandibles clacked visibly, while two long, fine antennae wove patterns in the air. Antennae, mandibles, eyes, and legs were sooty black, but the dominant color was the burnt orange of its armor plating. 'It's an insect,' Kress repeated.

'It is not an insect,' Wo insisted calmly. 'The armored exoskeleton is shed when the sandking grows larger. *If* it grows larger. In a tank this size, it won't.' She took Kress by the elbow and led him around the tank to the next castle. 'Look at the colors here.'

He did. They were different. Here the sandkings had bright red armor; antennae, mandibles, eyes, and legs were yellow. Kress glanced across the tank. The denizens of the third live castle were off-white, with red trim. 'Hmmm,' he said.

'They war, as I said,' Wo told him. 'They even have truces and alliances. It was an alliance that destroyed the fourth castle in this tank. The blacks were getting too numerous, so the others joined forces to destroy them.'

Kress remained unconvinced. 'Amusing, no doubt. But insects fight wars too.'

'Insects do not worship,' Wo said.

'Eh?'

Wo smiled and pointed at the castle. Kress stared. A face had been carved into the wall of the highest tower. He recognized it. It was Jala Wo's face. 'How . . . ?'

'I projected a hologram of my face into the tank, kept it there for a few days. The face of god, you see? I feed them; I am always close. The sandkings have a rudimentary psionic sense. Proximity telepathy. They sense me, and worship me by using my face to decorate their buildings. All the castles have them, see.' They did.

On the castle, the face of Jala Wo was serene and peaceful, and very lifelike. Kress marveled at the workmanship. 'How do they do it?'

'The foremost legs double as arms. They even have fingers of a sort; three small, flexible tendrils. And they cooperate well, both in building and in battle. Remember, all the mobiles of one color share a single mind.'

'Tell me more,' Kress said.

Wo smiled. 'The maw lives in the castle. Maw is my name for her. A pun, if you will; the thing is mother and stomach both. Female, large as your fist, immobile. Actually, sandking is a bit of a misnomer. The mobiles are peasants and warriors, the real ruler is a queen. But that analogy is faulty as well. Considered as a whole, each castle is a single hermaphroditic creature.'

'What do they eat?'

'The mobiles eat pap – predigested food obtained inside the castle. They get it from the maw after she has worked on it for several days. Their stomachs can't handle anything else, so if the maw dies, they soon die as well. The maw . . . the maw eats anything. You'll have no special expense there. Table scraps will do excellently.'

'Live food?' Kress asked.

Wo shrugged. 'Each maw eats mobiles from the other castles, yes.'

'I am intrigued,' he admitted. 'If only they weren't so small.'

'Yours can be larger. These sandkings are small because their tank is small. They seem to limit their growth to fit available space. If I moved these to a larger tank, they'd start growing again.'

'Hmmmm. My piranha tank is twice this size, and vacant. It could be cleaned out, filled with sand . . .'

'Wo and Shade would take care of the installation. It would be our pleasure.'

'Of course,' said Kress, 'I would expect four intact castles.'

'Certainly,' Wo said.

They began to haggle about the price.

*

Three days later Jala Wo arrived at Simon Kress' estate, with dormant sandkings and a work crew to take charge of the installation. Wo's assistants were aliens unlike any Kress was familiar with – squat, broad bipeds with four arms and bulging, multifaceted eyes. Their skin was thick and leathery, twisted into horns and spines and protrusions at odd spots upon their bodies. But they were very strong, and good workers. Wo ordered them about in a musical tongue that Kress had never heard.

In a day it was done. They moved his piranha tank to the center of his spacious living room, arranged couches on either side of it for better viewing, scrubbed it clean, and filled it two-thirds of the way up with sand and rock. Then they installed a special lighting system, both to provide the dim red illumination the sandkings preferred and to project holographic images into the tank. On top they mounted a sturdy plastic cover, with a feeder mechanism built in. 'This way you can feed your sandkings without removing the top of the tank,' Wo explained. 'You would not want to take any chances on the mobiles escaping.'

The cover also included climate control devices, to condense just the right amount of moisture from the air. 'You want it dry, but not too dry,' Wo said.

Finally one of the four-armed workers climbed into the tank and dug deep pits in the four corners. One of his companions handed the dormant maws over to him, removing them one by one from their frosted cryonic traveling cases. They were nothing to look at. Kress decided they resembled nothing so much as a mottled, half-spoiled chunk of raw meat. With a mouth.

The alien buried them, one in each corner of the tank. Then they sealed it all up and took their leave.

'The heat will bring the maws out of dormancy,' Wo said. 'In less than a week, mobiles will begin to hatch and burrow to the surface. Be certain to give them plenty of food. They will need all their strength until they are well established. I would estimate that you will have castles rising in about three weeks.'

'And my face? When will they carve my face?'

'Turn on the hologram after about a month,' she advised him. 'And be patient. If you have any questions, please call. Wo and Shade are at your service.' She bowed and left.

Kress wandered back to the tank and lit a joy-stick. The desert was still and empty. He drummed his fingers impatiently against the plastic, and frowned.

*

On the fourth day, Kress thought he glimpsed motion beneath the sand, subtle subterranean stirrings.

On the fifth day, he saw his first mobile, a lone white.

On the sixth day, he counted a dozen of them, whites and reds and blacks. The oranges were tardy. He cycled through a bowl of half-decayed table scraps. The mobiles sensed it at once, rushed to it, and began to drag pieces back to their respective corners. Each color group was very organized. They did not fight. Kress was a bit disappointed, but he decided to give them time.

The oranges made their appearance on the eighth day. By then the other sandkings had begun to carry small stones and erect crude fortifications. They still did not war. At the moment they were only half the size of those he had seen at Wo and Shade's, but Kress thought they were growing rapidly.

The castles began to rise midway through the second week. Organized battalions of mobiles dragged heavy chunks of sandstone and granite to their corners, where other mobiles were pushing sand into place with mandibles and tendrils. Kress had purchased a pair of magnifying goggles so he could watch them work, wherever they might go in the tank. He wandered around and around the tall plastic walls, observing. It was fascinating. The castles were a bit plainer than Kress would have liked, but he had an idea about that. The next day he cycled through some obsidian and flakes of colored glass along with the food. Within hours, they had been incorporated into the castle walls.

The black castle was the first completed, followed by the white and red fortresses. The oranges were last, as usual. Kress took his meals into the living room and ate seated on the couch, so he could watch. He expected the first war to break out any hour now.

He was disappointed. Days passed; the castles grew taller and more grand, and Kress seldom left the tank except to attend to his sanitary needs and answer critical business calls. But the sandkings did not war. He was getting upset.

Finally, he stopped feeding them.

Two days after the table scraps had ceased to fall from their desert sky, four black mobiles surrounded an orange and dragged it back to their maw. They maimed it first, ripping off its mandibles and antennae and limbs, and carried it through the shadowed main gate of their miniature castle. It never emerged. Within an hour, more than forty orange mobiles marched across the sand and attacked the blacks' corner. They were outnumbered by the blacks that came rushing up from the depths. When the fighting was over, the attackers had been slaughtered. The dead and dying were taken down to feed the black maw.

Kress, delighted, congratulated himself on his genius.

When he put food into the tank the following day, a three-cornered battle broke out over its possession. The whites were the big winners. After that, war followed war.

*

Almost a month to the day after Jala Wo had delivered the sandkings, Kress turned on the hologram projector, and his face materialized in the tank. It turned, slowly, around and around so his gaze fell on all four castles equally. Kress thought it rather a good likeness – it had his impish grin, wide mouth, full cheeks. His blue eyes sparkled, his gray hair was carefully arrayed in a fashionable sidesweep, his eye-brows were thin and sophisticated.

Soon enough, the sandkings set to work. Kress fed them lavishly while his image beamed down at them from their sky. Temporarily, the wars stopped. All activity was directed towards worship.

His face emerged on the castle walls.

At first all four carvings looked alike to him, but as the work continued and Kress studied the reproductions, he began to detect subtle differences in technique and execution. The reds were the most creative, using tiny flakes of slate to put the gray in his hair. The white idol seemed young and mischievous to him, while the face shaped by the blacks – although virtually the same, line for line – struck him as wise and beneficent. The orange sandkings, as ever, were last and least. The wars had not gone well for them, and their castle was sad compared to the others. The image they carved was crude and cartoonish, and they seemed to intend to leave it that way. When they stopped work on the face, Kress grew quite piqued with them, but there was really nothing he could do.

When all the sandkings had finished their Kress-faces, he turned off the hologram and decided that it was time to have a party. His friends would be impressed. He could even stage a war for them, he thought. Humming happily to himself, he began to draw up a guest list.

The party was a wild success.

Kress invited thirty people: a handful of close friends who shared his amusements, a few former lovers, and a collection of business and social rivals who could not afford to ignore his summons. He knew some of them would be discomfited and even offended by his sandkings. He counted on it. Simon Kress customarily considered his parties a failure unless at least one guest walked out in high dudgeon.

On impulse he added Jala Wo's name to his list. 'Bring Shade if you like,' he added when dictating her invitation.

Her acceptance surprised him just a bit. 'Shade, alas, will be unable to attend. He does not go to social functions,' Wo added. 'As for myself, I look forward to the chance to see how your sandkings are doing.'

Kress ordered them up a sumptuous meal. And when at last the conversation had died down, and most of his guests had gotten silly on wine and joysticks, he shocked them by personally scraping their table leavings into a large bowl. 'Come, all of you,' he told them. 'I want to introduce you to my newest pets.' Carrying the bowl, he conducted them into his living room.

The sandkings lived up to his fondest expectations. He had starved them for two days in preparation, and they were in a fighting mood. While the guests ringed the tank, looking through the magnifying glasses Kress had thoughtfully provided, the sandkings waged a glorious battle over the scraps. He counted almost sixty dead mobiles when the struggle was over. The reds and whites, who had recently formed an alliance, emerged with most of the food.

'Kress, you're disgusting,' Cath m'Lane told him. She had lived with him for a short time two years before, until her soppy sentimentality almost drove him mad. 'I was a fool to come back here. I thought perhaps you'd changed, wanted to apologize.' She had never forgiven him for the time his shambler had eaten an excessively cute puppy of which she had been fond. 'Don't *ever* invite me here again, Simon.' She strode out, accompanied by her current lover and a chorus of laughter.

His other guests were full of questions.

Where did the sandkings come from? they wanted to know. 'From Wo and Shade, Importers,' he replied, with a polite gesture towards Jala Wo, who had remained quiet and apart through most of the evening.

Why did they decorate their castles with his likeness? 'Because I am the source of all good things. Surely you know that?' That brought a round of chuckles.

Will they fight again? 'Of course, but not tonight. Don't worry. There will be other parties.'

Jad Rakkis, who was an amateur xenologist, began talking about other social insects and the wars they fought. 'These sandkings are amusing, but nothing really. You ought to read about Terran soldier ants, for instance.'

'Sandkings are not insects,' Jala Wo said sharply, but Jad was off and running, and no one paid her the slightest attention. Kress smiled at her and shrugged.

Malada Blane suggested a betting pool the next time they got together to watch a war, and everyone was taken with the idea. An animated discussion about rules and odds ensued. It lasted for almost an hour. Finally the guests began to take their leave.

Jala Wo was the last to depart. 'So,' Kress said to her when they were alone, 'it appears my sandkings are a hit.'

'They are doing well,' Wo said. 'Already they are larger than my own.'

'Yes,' Kress said, 'except for the oranges.'

'I had noticed that,' Wo replied. 'They seem few in number, and their castle is shabby.'

'Well, someone must lose,' Kress said. 'The oranges were late to emerge and get established. They have suffered for it.'

'Pardon,' said Wo, 'but might I ask if you are feeding your sandkings sufficiently?'

Kress shrugged. 'They diet from time to time. It makes them fiercer.'

She frowned. 'There is no need to starve them. Let them war in their own time, for their own reasons. It is their nature, and you will witness conflicts that are delightfully subtle and complex. The constant war brought on by hunger is artless and degrading.'

Simon Kress repaid Wo's frown with interest. 'You are in my house, Wo, and here I am the judge of what is degrading. I fed the sandkings as you advised, and they did not fight.'

'You must have patience.'

'No,' Kress said. 'I am their master and their god, after all. Why should I wait on their impulses? They did not war often enough to suit me. I corrected the situation.'

'I see,' said Wo. 'I will discuss the matter with Shade.'

'It is none of your concern, or his,' Kress snapped.

'I must bid you good night, then,' Wo said with resignation. But as she slipped into her coat to depart, she fixed him with a final disapproving stare. 'Look to your faces, Simon Kress,' she warned him. 'Look to your faces.'

Puzzled, he wandered back to the tank and stared at the castles after she had taken her departure. His faces were still there, as ever. Except – he snatched up his magnifying goggles and slipped them on. Even then it was hard to make out. But it seemed to him that the expression on the face of his images had changed slightly, that his smile was somehow twisted so that it seemed a touch malicious. But it was a very subtle change, if it was a change at all. Kress finally put it down to his suggestibility, and resolved not to invite Jala Wo to any more of his gatherings.

*

Over the next few months, Kress and about a dozen of his favorites got together weekly for what he liked to call his 'war games.' Now that his initial fascination with the sandkings was past, Kress spent less time around his tank and more on his business affairs and his social life, but he still enjoyed having a few friends over for a war or two. He kept the combatants sharp on a constant edge of hunger. It had severe effects on the orange sandkings, who dwindled visibly until Kress began to wonder if their maw was dead. But the others did well enough.

Sometimes at night, when he could not sleep, Kress would take a bottle of wine into the darkened living room, where the red gloom of his miniature desert was the only light. He would drink and watch for hours, alone. There was usually a fight going on somewhere, and when there was not he could easily start one by dropping in some small morsel of food.

They took to betting on the weekly battles, as Malada Blane had suggested. Kress won a good amount by betting on the whites, who had become the most powerful and numerous colony in the tank, with the grandest castle. One week he slid the corner of the tank top aside, and dropped the food close to the white castle instead of on the central battleground as usual, so that the others had to attack the whites in their stronghold to get any food at all. They tried. The whites were brilliant in defense. Kress won a hundred standards from Jad Rakkis.

Rakkis, in fact, lost heavily on the sandkings almost every week. He pretended to a vast knowledge of them and their ways, claiming that he had studied them after the first party, but he had no luck when it came to placing his bets. Kress suspected that Jad's claims were empty boasting. He had tried to study the sandkings a bit himself, in a moment of idle curiosity, tying in to the library to find out to what world his pets were native. But there was no listing for them. He wanted to get in touch with Wo and ask her about it, but he had other concerns, and the matter kept slipping his mind.

Finally, after a month in which his losses totaled more than a thousand standards, Jad Rakkis arrived at the war games carrying a small plastic case under his arm. Inside was a spiderlike thing covered with fine golden hair.

'A sand spider,' Rakkis announced. 'From Cathaday. I got it this afternoon from t'Etherane the Petseller. Usually they remove the poison sacs, but this one is intact. Are you game, Simon? I want my money back. I'll bet a thousand standards, sand spider against sandkings.'

Kress studied the spider in its plastic prison. His sandkings had grown – they were twice as large as Wo's, as she'd predicted – but they were still dwarfed by this thing. It was venomed, and they were not. Still, there were an awful lot of them. Besides, the endless sandking wars had begun to grow tiresome lately. The novelty of the match intrigued him. 'Done,' Kress said. 'Jad, you are a fool. The sandkings will just keep coming until this ugly creature of yours is dead.'

'You are the fool, Simon,' Rakkis replied, smiling. 'The Cathadayn sand spider customarily feeds on burrowers that hide in nooks and crevices and – well, watch – it will go straight into those castles, and eat the maws.'

Kress scowled amid general laughter. He hadn't counted on that. 'Get on with it,' he said irritably. He went to freshen his drink.

The spider was too large to cycle conveniently through the food chamber. Two of the others helped Rakkis slide the tank top slightly to one side, and Malada Blane handed him up his case. He shook the spider out. It landed lightly on a miniature dune in front of the red castle, and stood confused for a moment, mouth working, legs twitching menacingly.

'Come on,' Rakkis urged. They all gathered round the tank. Simon Kress found his magnifiers and slipped them on. If he was going to lose a thousand standards, at least he wanted a good view of the action.

The sandkings had seen the invader. All over the castle, activity had ceased. The small scarlet mobiles were frozen, watching.

The spider began to move toward the dark promise of the gate. On the tower above, Simon Kress' countenance stared down impassively.

At once there was a flurry of activity. The nearest red mobiles formed themselves into two wedges and streamed over the sand toward the spider. More warriors erupted from inside the castle and assembled in a triple line to guard the approach to the underground chamber where the maw lived. Scouts came scuttling over the dunes, recalled to fight.

Battle was joined.

The attacking sandkings washed over the spider. Mandibles snapped shut on legs and abdomen, and clung. Reds raced up the golden legs to the invader's back. They bit and tore. One of them found an eye, and ripped it loose with tiny yellow tendrils. Kress smiled and pointed.

But they were *small*, and they had no venom, and the spider did not stop. Its legs flicked sandkings off to either side. Its dripping jaws found others, and left them broken and stiffening. Already a dozen of the reds lay dying. The sand spider came on and on. It strode straight through the triple line of guardians before the castle. The lines closed around it, covered it, waging desperate battle. A team of sandkings had bitten off one of the spider's legs, Kress saw. Defenders leaped from atop the towers to land on the twitching, heaving mass.

Lost beneath the sandkings, the spider somehow lurched down into the darkness and vanished.

Jad Rakkis let out a long breath. He looked pale. 'Wonderful,' someone else said. Malada Blane chuckled deep in her throat.

'Look,' said Idi Noreddian, tugging Kress by the arm.

They had been so intent on the struggle in the corner that none of them had noticed the activity elsewhere in the tank. But now the castle was still, the sands empty save for dead red mobiles, and now they saw.

Three armies were drawn up before the red castle. They stood quite still, in perfect array, rank after rank of sandkings, orange and white and black. Waiting to see what emerged from the depths.

Simon Kress smiled. 'A *cordon sanitaire*,' he said. 'And glance at the other castles, if you will, Jad.'

Rakkis did, and swore. Teams of mobiles were sealing up the gates with sand and stone. If the spider somehow survived this encounter, it would find no easy entrance at the other castles. 'I should have brought four spiders,' Jad Rakkis said. 'Still, I've won. My spider is down there right now, eating your damned maw.'

Kress did not reply. He waited. There was motion in the shadows.

All at once, red mobiles began pouring out of the gate. They took their positions on the castle, and began repairing the damage the spider had wrought. The other armies dissolved and began to retreat to their respective corners.

'Jad,' said Simon Kress, 'I think you are a bit confused about who is eating who.'

*

The following week Rakkis brought four slim silver snakes. The sandkings dispatched them without much trouble.

Next he tried a large black bird. It ate more than thirty white mobiles, and its thrashing and blundering virtually destroyed their castle, but ultimately its wings grew tired, and the sandkings attacked in force wherever it landed.

After that it was a case of insects, armored beetles not too unlike the sandkings themselves. But stupid, stupid. An allied force of oranges and blacks broke their formation, divided them, and butchered them.

Rakkis began giving Kress promissory notes.

It was around that time that Kress met Cath m'Lane again, one evening when he was dining in Asgard at his favorite restaurant. He stopped at her table briefly and told her about the war games, inviting her to join them. She flushed, then regained control of herself and grew icy. 'Someone has to put a stop to you, Simon. I guess it's going to be me,' she said. Kress shrugged and enjoyed a lovely meal and thought no more about her threat.

Until a week later, when a small, stout woman arrived at his door and showed him a police wristband. 'We've had complaints,' she said. 'Do you keep a tank full of dangerous insects, Kress?'

'Not insects,' he said, furious. 'Come, I'll show you.'

When she had seen the sandkings, she shook her head. 'This will never do. What do you know about these creatures, anyway? Do you know what world they're from? Have they been cleared by the ecological board? Do you have a license for these things? We have a report that they're carnivores, possibly dangerous. We also have a report that they are semi-sentient. Where did you get these creatures, anyway?'

'From Wo and Shade,' Kress replied.

'Never heard of them,' the woman said. 'Probably smuggled them in, knowing our ecologists would never approve them. No, Kress, this won't do. I'm going to confiscate this tank and have it destroyed. And you're going to have to expect a few fines as well.'

Kress offered her a hundred standards to forget all about him and his sandkings.

She tsked. 'Now I'll have to add attempted bribery to the charges against you.'

Not until he raised the figure to two thousand standards was she willing to be persuaded.

'It's not going to be easy, you know,' she said. 'There are forms to be altered, records to be wiped. And getting a forged license from the ecologists will be time-consuming. Not to mention dealing with the complainant. What if she calls again?'

'Leave her to me,' Kress said. 'Leave her to me.'

*

He thought about it for a while. That night he made some calls.

First he got t'Etherane the Petseller. 'I want to buy a dog,' he said. 'A puppy.'

The round-faced merchant gawked at him. 'A puppy? That is not like you, Simon. Why don't you come in? I have a lovely choice.'

'I want a very specific *kind* of puppy,' Kress said. 'Take notes. I'll describe to you what it must look like.'

Afterward he punched for Idi Noreddian. 'Idi,' he said, 'I want you out here tonight with your holo equipment. I have a notion to record a sandking battle. A present for one of my friends.'

The night after they made the recording, Simon Kress stayed up late. He absorbed a controversial new drama in his sensorium, fixed himself a small snack, smoked a joy-stick or two, and broke out a bottle of wine. Feeling very happy with himself, he wandered into the living room, glass in hand.

The lights were out. The red glow of the terrarium made the shadows flushed and feverish. He walked over to look at his domain, curious as to how the blacks were doing in the repairs on their castle. The puppy had left it in ruins.

The restoration went well. But as Kress inspected the work through his magnifiers, he chanced to glance closely at the face. It startled him.

He drew back, blinked, took a healthy gulp of wine, and looked again.

The face on the wall was still his. But it was all wrong, all *twisted*. His cheeks were bloated and piggish, his smile was a crooked leer. He looked impossibly malevolent.

Uneasy, he moved around the tank to inspect the other castles. They were each a bit different, but ultimately all the same.

The oranges had left out most of the fine detail, but the result still seemed monstrous, crude – a brutal mouth and mindless eyes.

The reds gave him a Satanic, twitching kind of smile. His mouth did odd, unlovely things at its corners.

The whites, his favorites, had carved a cruel idiot god.

Simon Kress flung his wine across the room in rage. 'You *dare*,' he said under his breath. 'Now you won't eat for a week, you damned . . . ' His voice was shrill. 'I'll teach you.' He had an idea. He strode out of the room, and returned a moment later with an antique iron throwing-sword in his hand. It was a meter long, and the point was still sharp. Kress smiled, climbed up and moved the tank cover aside just enough to give him working room, opening one corner of the desert. He leaned down, and jabbed the sword at the white castle below him. He waved it back and forth, smashing towers and ramparts and walls. Sand and stone collapsed, burying the scrambling mobiles. A flick of his wrist obliterated the features of the insolent, insulting caricature the sandkings had made of his face. Then he poised the point of the sword above the dark mouth that opened down into the maw's chamber, and thrust with all his strength. He heard a soft, squishing sound, and met resistance. All of the mobiles trembled and collapsed. Satisfied, Kress pulled back.

He watched for a moment, wondering whether he'd killed the maw. The point of the throwing-sword was wet and slimy. But finally the white sandkings began to move again. Feebly, slowly, but they moved.

He was preparing to slide the cover back in place and move on to a second castle when he felt something crawling on his hand.

He screamed and dropped the sword, and brushed the sandking from his flesh. It fell to the carpet, and he ground it beneath his heel, crushing it thoroughly long after it was dead. It had crunched when he stepped on it. After that, trembling, he hurried to seal the tank up again, and rushed off to shower and inspect himself carefully. He boiled his clothing.

Later, after several fresh glasses of wine, he returned to the living room. He was a bit ashamed of the way the sandking had terrified him. But he was not about to open the tank again. From now on, the cover stayed sealed permanently. Still, he had to punish the others.

Kress decided to lubricate his mental processes with another glass of wine. As he finished it, an inspiration came to him. He went to the tank smiling, and made a few adjustments to the humidity controls.

By the time he fell asleep on the couch, his wine glass still in his hand, the sand castles were melting in the rain.

*

Kress woke to angry pounding on his door.

He sat up, groggy, his head throbbing. Wine hangovers were always the worst, he thought. He lurched to the entry chamber.

Cath m'Lane was outside. 'You monster,' she said, her face swollen and puffy and streaked by tears. 'I cried all night, damn you. But no more, Simon, no more.'

'Easy,' he said, holding his head. 'I've got a hangover.'

She swore and shoved him aside and pushed her way into his house. The shambler came peering round a corner to see what the noise was. She spat at it and stalked into the living room, Kress trailing ineffectually after her. 'Hold on,' he said. 'Where do you ... you can't ...' He stopped, suddenly horrorstruck. She was carrying a heavy sledgehammer in her left hand. 'No,' he said.

She went directly to the sandking tank. 'You like the little charmers so much, Simon? Then you can live with them.'

'*Cath!*' he shrieked.

Gripping the hammer with both hands, she swung as hard as she could against the side of the tank. The sound of the impact set his head to screaming, and Kress made a low blubbering sound of despair. But the plastic held.

She swung again. This time there was a *crack*, and a network of thin lines sprang into being.

Kress threw himself at her as she drew back her hammer for a third swing. They went down flailing, and rolled. She lost her grip on the hammer and tried to throttle him, but Kress wrenched free and bit her on the arm, drawing blood. They both staggered to their feet, panting.

'You should see yourself, Simon,' she said grimly. 'Blood dripping from your mouth. You look like one of your pets. How do you like the taste?'

'Get out,' he said. He saw the throwing-sword where it had fallen the night before, and snatched it up. 'Get out,' he repeated, waving the sword for emphasis. 'Don't go near that tank again.'

She laughed at him. 'You wouldn't dare,' she said. She bent to pick up her hammer.

Kress shrieked at her, and lunged. Before he quite knew what was happening, the iron blade had gone clear through her abdomen. Cath m'Lane looked at him wonderingly, and down at the sword. Kress fell back whimpering. 'I didn't mean . . . I only wanted . . .'

She was transfixed, bleeding, dead, but somehow she did not fall. 'You monster,' she managed to say, though her mouth was full of blood. And she whirled, impossibly, the sword in her, and swung with her last strength at the tank. The tortured wall shattered, and Cath m'Lane was buried beneath an avalanche of plastic and sand and mud.

Kress made small hysterical noises and scrambled up on the couch.

Sandkings were emerging from the muck on his living room floor. They were crawling across Cath's body. A few of them ventured tentatively out across the carpet. More followed.

He watched as a column took shape, a living, writhing square of sandkings, bearing something, something slimy and featureless, a piece of raw meat big as a man's head. They began to carry it away from the tank. It pulsed.

That was when Kress broke and ran.

*

It was late afternoon before he found the courage to return. He had run to his skimmer and flown to the nearest city, some fifty kilometers away, almost sick with fear. But once safely away, he had found a small restaurant, put down several mugs of coffee and two anti-hangover tabs, eaten a full breakfast, and gradually regained his composure.

It had been a dreadful morning, but dwelling on that would solve nothing. He ordered more coffee and considered his situation with icy rationality.

Cath m'Lane was dead at his hand. Could he report it, plead that it had been an accident? Unlikely. He had run her through, after all, and he had already told that policer to leave her to him. He would have to get rid of the evidence, and hope that she had not told anyone where she was going this morning. That was probable. She could only have gotten his gift late last night. She said that she had cried all night, and she had been alone when she arrived. Very well; he had one body and one skimmer to dispose of.

That left the sandkings. They might prove more of a difficulty. No doubt they had all escaped by now. The thought of them around his house, in his bed and his clothes, infesting his food – it made his flesh crawl. He shuddered and overcame his revulsion. It really shouldn't be too hard to kill them, he reminded himself. He didn't have to account for every mobile. Just the four maws, that was all. He could do that. They were large, as he'd seen. He would find them and kill them.

Simon Kress went shopping before he flew back to his home. He bought a set of skinthins that would cover him from head to foot, several bags of poison pellets for rockjock control, and a spray canister of illegally strong pesticide. He also bought a magnalock towing device.

When he landed, he went about things methodically. First he hooked Cath's skimmer to his own with the magnalock. Searching it, he had his first piece of luck. The crystal chip with Idi Noreddian's holo of the sandking fight was on the front seat. He had worried about that.

When the skimmers were ready, he slipped into his skinthins and went inside for Cath's body.

It wasn't there.

He poked through the fast-drying sand carefully, but there was no doubt of it; the body was gone. Could she have dragged herself away? Unlikely, but Kress searched. A cursory inspection of his house turned up neither the body nor any sign of the sandkings. He did not have time for a more thorough investigation, not with the incriminating skimmer outside his front door. He resolved to try later.

Some seventy kilometers north of Kress' estate was a range of active volcanoes. He flew there, Cath's skimmer in tow. Above the glowering cone of the largest, he released the magnalock and watched it vanish in the lava below.

It was dusk when he returned to his house. That gave him pause. Briefly he considered flying back to the city and spending the night there. He put the thought aside. There was work to do. He wasn't safe yet.

He scattered the poison pellets around the exterior of his house. No one would find that suspicious. He'd always had a rockjock problem. When that task was completed, he primed the canister of pesticide and ventured back inside.

Kress went through the house room by room, turning on lights everywhere he went until he was surrounded by a blaze of artificial illumination. He paused to clean up in the living room, shoveling sand and plastic fragments back into the broken tank. The sandkings were all gone, as he'd feared. The castles were shrunken and distorted, slagged by the watery bombardment Kress had visited upon them, and what little remained was crumbling as it dried.

He frowned and searched on, the canister of pest spray strapped across his shoulders.

Down in his deepest wine cellar, he came upon Cath m'Lane's corpse.

It sprawled at the foot of a steep flight of stairs, the limbs twisted as if by a fall. White mobiles were swarming all over it, and as Kress watched, the body moved jerkily across the hard-packed dirt floor.

He laughed, and twisted the illumination up to maximum. In the far corner, a squat little earthen castle and a dark hole were visible between two wine racks. Kress could make out a rough outline of his face on the cellar wall.

The body shifted once again, moving a few centimeters towards the castle. Kress had a sudden vision of the white maw waiting hungrily. It might be able to get Cath's foot in its mouth, but no more. It was too absurd. He laughed again, and started down into the cellar, finger poised on the trigger of the hose that snaked down his right arm. The sandkings – hundreds of them moving as one – deserted the body and formed up battle lines, a field of white between him and their maw.

Suddenly Kress had another inspiration. He smiled and lowered his firing hand. 'Cath was always hard to swallow,' he said, delighted at his wit. 'Especially for one your size. Here, let me give you some help. What are gods for, after all?'

He retreated upstairs, returning shortly with a cleaver. The sandkings, patient, waited and watched while Kress chopped Cath m'Lane into small, easily digestible pieces.

*

Simon Kress slept in his skinthins that night, the pesticide close at hand, but he did not need it. The whites, sated, remained in the cellar, and he saw no sign of the others.

In the morning he finished the cleanup of the living room. After he was through, no trace of the struggle remained except for the broken tank.

He ate a light lunch, and resumed his hunt for the missing sandkings. In full daylight, it was not too difficult. The blacks had located in his rock garden, and built a castle heavy with obsidian and quartz. The reds he founds at the bottom of his long-disused swimming pool, which had partially filled with windblown sand over the years. He saw mobiles of both colors ranging about his grounds, many of them carrying poison pellets back to their maws. Kress decided his pesticide was unnecessary. No use risking a fight when he could just let the poison do its work. Both maws should be dead by evening.

That left only the burnt orange sandkings unaccounted for. Kress circled his estate several times, in ever-widening spirals, but found no trace of them. When he began to sweat in his skinthins – it was a hot, dry day – he decided it was not important. If they were out here, they were probably eating the poison pellets along with the reds and blacks.

He crunched several sandkings underfoot, with a certain degree of satisfaction, as he walked back to the house. Inside, he removed his skinthins, settled down to a delicious meal, and finally began to relax. Everything was under control. Two of the maws would soon be defunct, the third was safely located where he could dispose of it after it had served his purposes, and he had no doubt that he would find the fourth. As for Cath, all trace of her visit had been obliterated.

His reverie was interrupted when his viewscreen began to blink at him. It was Jad Rakkis, calling to brag about some cannibal worms he was bringing to the war games tonight.

Kress had forgotten about that, but he recovered quickly. 'Oh, Jad, my pardons. I neglected to tell you. I grew bored with all that, and got rid of the sandkings. Ugly little things. Sorry, but there'll be no party tonight.'

Rakkis was indignant. 'But what will I do with my worms?'

'Put them in a basket of fruit and send them to a loved one,' Kress said, signing off. Quickly he began calling the others. He did not need anyone arriving at his doorstep now, with the sandkings alive and infesting the estate.

As he was calling Idi Noreddian, Kress became aware of an annoying oversight. The screen began to clear, indicating that someone had answered at the other end. Kress flicked off. Idi arrived on schedule an hour later. She was surprised to find the party canceled, but perfectly happy to share an evening alone with Kress. He delighted her with his story of Cath's reaction to the holo they had made together. While telling it, he managed to ascertain that she had not mentioned the prank to anyone. He nodded, satisfied, and refilled their wine glasses. Only a trickle was left. 'I'll have to get a fresh bottle,' he said. 'Come with me to my wine cellar, and help me pick out a good vintage. You've always had a better palate than I.'

She came along willingly enough, but balked at the top of the stairs when Kress opened the door and gestured for her to precede him. 'Where are the lights?' she said. 'And that smell – what's that peculiar smell, Simon?'

When he shoved her, she looked briefly startled. She screamed as she tumbled down the stairs. Kress closed the door and began to nail it shut with the boards and airhammer he had left for that purpose. As he was finishing, he heard Idi groan. 'I'm hurt,' she said. 'Simon, what is this?' Suddenly she squealed, and shortly after that the screaming started.

It did not cease for hours. Kress went to his sensorium and dialed up a saucy comedy to blot it off of his mind.

When he was sure she was dead, Kress flew her skimmer north to the volcanoes and discarded it. The magnalock was proving a good investment.

*

Odd scrabbling noises were coming from beyond the wine cellar door the next morning when Kress went down to check it out. He listened for several uneasy moments, wondering if Idi Noreddian could possibly have survived, and was now scratching to get out. It seemed unlikely; it had to be the sandkings. Kress did not like the implications of that. He decided that he would keep the door sealed, at least for the moment, and went outside with a shovel to bury the red and black maws in their own castles.

He found them very much alive.

The black castle was glittering with volcanic glass, and sandkings were all over it, repairing and improving. The highest tower was up to his waist, and on it was a hideous caricature of his face. When he approached, the blacks halted in their labors, and formed up into two threatening phalanxes. Kress glanced behind him and saw others closing off his escape. Startled, he dropped the shovel and sprinted out of the trap, crushing several mobiles beneath his boots.

The red castle was creeping up the walls of the swimming pool. The maw was safely settled in a pit, surrounded by sand and concrete and battlements. The reds crept all over the bottom of the pool. Kress watched them carry a rockjock and a large lizard into the castle. He stepped back from the poolside, horrified, and felt something crunch. Looking down, he saw three mobiles climbing up his leg. He brushed them off and stamped them to death, but others were approaching quickly. They were larger than he remembered. Some were almost as big as his thumb.

He ran. By the time he reached the safety of the house, his heart was racing and he was short of breath. The door closed behind him, and Kress hurried to lock it. His house was supposed to be pest-proof. He'd be safe in here.

A stiff drink steadied his nerve. So poison doesn't faze them, he thought. He should have known. Wo had warned him that the maw could eat anything. He would have to use the pesticide. Kress took another drink for good measure, donned his skinthins, and strapped the canister to his back. He unlocked the door.

Outside, the sandkings were waiting.

Two armies confronted him, allied against the common threat. More than he could have guessed. The damned maws must be breeding like rockjocks. They were everywhere, a creeping sea of them.

Kress brought up the hose and flicked the trigger. A gray mist washed over the nearest rank of sandkings. He moved his hand from side to side.

Where the mist fell, the sandkings twitched violently and died in sudden spasms. Kress smiled. They were no match for him. He sprayed in a wide arc before him and stepped forward confidently over a litter of black and red bodies. The armies fell back. Kress advanced, intent on cutting through them to their maws.

All at once the retreat stopped. A thousand sandkings surged toward him.

Kress had been expecting the counterattack. He stood his ground, sweeping his misty sword before him in great looping strokes. They came at him and died. A few got through; he could not spray everywhere at once. He felt them climbing up his legs, sensed their mandibles biting futilely at the reinforced plastic of his skinthins. He ignored them, and kept spraying.

Then he began to feel soft impacts on his head and shoulders.

Kress trembled and spun and looked up above him. The front of his house was alive with sandkings. Blacks and reds, hundreds of them. They were launching themselves into the air, raining down on him. They fell all around him. One landed on his faceplate, its mandibles scraping at his eyes for a terrible second before he plucked it away.

He swung up his hose and sprayed the air, sprayed the house, sprayed until the airborne sandkings were all dead and dying. The mist settled back on him, making him cough. He coughed, and kept spraying. Only when the front of the house was clean did Kress turn his attention back to the ground.

They were all around him, on him, dozens of them scurrying over his body, hundreds of others hurrying to join them. He turned the mist on them. The hose went dead. Kress heard a loud *hiss*, and the deadly fog rose in a great cloud from between his shoulders, cloaking him, choking him, making his eyes burn and blur. He felt for the hose, and his hand came away covered with dying sandkings. The hose was severed; they'd eaten it through. He was surrounded by a shroud of pesticide, blinded. He stumbled and screamed, and began to run back to the house, pulling sandkings from his body as he went.

Inside, he sealed the door and collapsed on the carpet, rolling back and forth until he was sure he had crushed them all. The canister was empty by then, hissing feebly. Kress stripped off his skinthins and showered. The hot spray scalded him and left his skin reddened and sensitive, but it made his flesh stop crawling.

He dressed in his heaviest clothing, thick workpants and leathers, after shaking them out nervously. 'Damn,' he kept muttering, 'damn.' His throat was dry. After searching the entry hall thoroughly to make certain it was clean, he allowed himself to sit and pour a drink. 'Damn,' he repeated. His hand shook as he poured, slopping liquor on the carpet.

The alcohol settled him, but it did not wash away the fear. He had a second drink and went to the window furtively. Sandkings were moving across the thick plastic pane. He shuddered and retreated to his communications console. He had to get help, he thought wildly. He would punch through a call to the authorities, and policers would come out with flamethrowers and . . .

Simon Kress stopped in mid-call, and groaned. He couldn't call in the police. He would have to tell them about the whites in his cellar, and they'd find the bodies there. Perhaps the maw might have finished Cath m'Lane by now, but certainly not Idi Noreddian. He hadn't even cut her up. Besides, there would be bones. No, the police could be called in only as a last resort.

He sat at the console, frowning. His communications equipment filled a whole wall; from here he could reach anyone on Baldur. He had plenty of money, and his cunning – he had always prided himself on his cunning. He would handle this somehow.

He briefly considered calling Wo, but soon dismissed the idea. Wo knew too much, and she would ask questions, and he did not trust her. No, he needed someone who would do as he asked *without* questions.

His frown faded, and slowly turned into a smile. Simon Kress had contacts. He put through a call to a number he had not used in a long time.

A woman's face took shape on his viewscreen: white-haired, bland of expression, with a long hook nose. Her voice was brisk and efficient. 'Simon,' she said. 'How is business?'

'Business is fine, Lissandra,' Kress replied. 'I have a job for you.'

'A removal? My price has gone up since last time, Simon. It has been ten years, after all.'

'You will be well paid,' Kress said. 'You know I'm generous. I want you for a bit of pest control.'

She smiled a thin smile. 'No need to use euphemisms, Simon. The call is shielded.'

'No, I'm serious. I have a pest problem. Dangerous pests. Take care of them for me. No questions. Understood?'

'Understood.'

'Good. You'll need . . . oh, three or four operatives. Wear heat-resistant skinthins, and equip them with flamethrowers, or lasers, something on that order. Come out to my place. You'll see the problem. Bugs, lots and lots of them. In my rock garden and the old swimming pool you'll find castles. Destroy them, kill everything inside them. Then knock on the door, and I'll show you what else needs to be done. Can you get out here quickly?'

Her face was impassive. 'We'll leave within the hour.'

*

Lissandra was true to her word. She arrived in a lean black skimmer with three operatives. Kress watched them from the safety of a second-story window. They were all faceless in dark plastic skinthins. Two of them wore portable flamethrowers, a third carried lasercannon and explosives. Lissandra carried nothing; Kress recognized her by the way she gave orders.

Their skimmer passed low overhead first, checking out the situation. The sandkings went mad. Scarlet and ebon mobiles ran everywhere, frenetic. Kress could see the castle in the rock garden from his vantage point. It stood tall as a man. Its ramparts were crawling with black defenders, and a steady stream of mobiles flowed down into its depths.

Lissandra's skimmer came down next to Kress' and the operatives vaulted out and unlimbered their weapons. They looked inhuman, deadly.

The black army drew up between them and the castle. The reds – Kress suddenly realized that he could not see the reds. He blinked. Where had they gone?

Lissandra pointed and shouted, and her two flamethrowers spread out and opened up on the black sandkings. Their weapons coughed dully and began to roar, long tongues of blue-and-scarlet fire licking out before them. Sandkings crisped and blackened and died. The operatives began to play the fire back and forth in an efficient, interlocking pattern. They advanced with careful, measured steps.

The black army burned and disintegrated, the mobiles fleeing in a thousand different directions, some back toward the castle, others toward the enemy. None reached the operatives with the flamethrowers. Lissandra's people were very professional.

Then one of them stumbled.

Or seemed to stumble. Kress looked again, and saw that the ground had given way beneath the man. Tunnels, he thought with a tremor of fear – tunnels, pits, traps. The flamer was sunk in sand up to his waist, and suddenly the ground around him seemed to erupt, and he was covered with scarlet sandkings. He dropped the flamethrower and began to claw wildly at his own body. His screams were horrible to hear.

His companion hesitated, then swung and fired. A blast of flame swallowed human and sandkings both. The screaming stopped abruptly. Satisfied, the second flamer turned back to the castle and took another step forward, and recoiled as his foot broke through the ground and vanished up to the ankle. He tried to pull it back and retreat, and the sand all around him gave way. He lost his balance and stumbled, flailing, and the sandkings were everywhere, a boiling mass of them, covering him as he writhed and rolled. His flamethrower was useless and forgotten.

Kress pounded wildly on the window, shouting for attention. 'The castle! Get the castle!'

Lissandra, standing back by her skimmer, heard and gestured. Her third operative sighted with the lasercannon and fired. The beam throbbed across the grounds and sliced off the top of the castle. He brought it down sharply, hacking at the sand and stone parapets. Towers fell. Kress' face disintegrated. The laser bit into the ground, searching round and about. The castle crumbled; now it was only a heap of sand. But the black mobiles continued to move. The maw was buried too deeply; they hadn't touched her.

Lissandra gave another order. Her operative discarded the laser, primed an explosive, and darted forward. He leaped over the smoking corpse of the first flamer, landed on solid ground within Kress' rock garden, and heaved. The explosive ball landed square atop the ruins of the black castle. White-hot light seared Kress' eyes, and there was a tremendous gout of sand and rock and mobiles. For a moment dust obscured everything. It was raining sandkings and pieces of sandkings.

Kress saw that the black mobiles were dead and unmoving.

'The pool,' he shouted down through the window. 'Get the castle in the pool.'

Lissandra understood quickly; the ground was littered with motionless blacks, but the reds were pulling back hurriedly and reforming. Her operative stood uncertain, then reached down and pulled out another explosive ball. He took one step forward, but Lissandra called him and he sprinted back in her direction.

It was all so simple then. He reached the skimmer, and Lissandra took him aloft. Kress rushed to another window in another room to watch. They came swooping in just over the pool, and the operative pitched his bombs down at the red castle from the safety of the skimmer. After the fourth run, the castle was unrecognizable, and the sandkings stopped moving.

Lissandra was thorough. She had him bomb each castle several additional times. Then he used the lasercannon, crisscrossing methodically until it was certain that nothing living could remain intact beneath those small patches of ground.

Finally they came knocking at his door. Kress was grinning manically when he let them in. 'Lovely,' he said, 'lovely.'

Lissandra pulled off the mask of her skinthins. 'This will cost you, Simon. Two operatives gone, not to mention the danger to my own life.'

'Of course,' Kress blurted. 'You'll be well paid, Lissandra. Whatever you ask, just so you finish the job.'

'What remains to be done?'

'You have to clean out my wine cellar,' Kress said. 'There's another castle down there. And you'll have to do it without explosives. I don't want my house coming down around me.' Lissandra motioned to her operative. 'Go outside and get Rajk's flamethrower. It should be intact.'

He returned armed, ready, silent. Kress led them down to the wine cellar.

The heavy door was still nailed shut, as he had left it. But it bulged outward slightly, as if warped by some tremendous pressure. That made Kress uneasy, as did the silence that held reign about them. He stood well away from the door as Lissandra's operative removed his nails and planks. 'Is that safe in here?' he found himself muttering, pointing at the flamethrower. 'I don't want a fire, either, you know.'

'I have the laser,' Lissandra said. 'We'll use that for the kill. The flamethrower probably won't be needed. But I want it here just in case. There are worse things than fire, Simon.'

He nodded.

The last plank came free of the cellar door. There was still no sound from below. Lissandra snapped an order, and her underling fell back, took up a position behind her, and leveled the flamethrower square at the door. She slipped her mask back on, hefted the laser, stepped forward, and pulled open the door.

No motion. No sound. It was dark down there.

'Is there a light?' Lissandra asked.

'Just inside the door,' Kress said. 'On the right hand side. Mind the stairs, they're quite steep.'

She stepped into the door, shifted the laser to her left hand, and reached up with her right, fumbling inside for the light panel. Nothing happened. 'I feel it,' Lissandra said, 'but it doesn't seem to . . .'

Then she was screaming, and she stumbled backward. A great white sandking had clamped itself around her wrist. Blood welled through her skinthins where its mandibles had sunk in. It was fully as large as her hand.

Lissandra did a horrible little jig across the room and began to smash her hand against the nearest wall. Again and again and again. It landed with a heavy, meaty thud. Finally the sandking fell away. She whimpered and fell to her knees. 'I think my fingers are broken,' she said softly. The blood was still flowing freely. She had dropped the laser near the cellar door.

'I'm not going down there,' her operative announced in clear firm tones.

Lissandra looked up at him. 'No,' she said. 'Stand in the door and flame it all. Cinder it. Do you understand?'

He nodded.

Simon Kress moaned. 'My *house*,' he said. His stomach churned. The white sandking had been so *large*. How many more were down there? 'Don't,' he continued. 'Leave it alone. I've changed my mind. Leave it alone.'

Lissandra misunderstood. She held out her hand. It was covered with blood and greenish-black ichor. 'Your little friend bit clean through my glove, and you saw what it took to get it off. I don't care about your house, Simon. Whatever is down there is going to die.'

Kress hardly heard her. He thought he could see movement in the shadows beyond the cellar door. He imagined a white army bursting forth, all as large as the sandking that had attacked Lissandra. He saw himself being lifted by a hundred tiny arms, and dragged down into the darkness where the maw waited hungrily. He was afraid. 'Don't,' he said.

They ignored him.

Kress darted forward, and his shoulder slammed into the back of Lissandra's operative just as the man was bracing to fire. He grunted and unbalanced and pitched forward into the black. Kress listened to him fall down the stairs. Afterward there were other noises – scuttlings and snaps and soft squishing sounds.

Kress swung around to face Lissandra. He was drenched in cold sweat, but a sickly kind of excitement was on him. It was almost sexual.

Lissandra's calm cold eyes regarded him through her mask. 'What are you doing?' she demanded as Kress picked up the laser she had dropped. '*Simon!*'

'Making a peace,' he said, giggling. 'They won't hurt god, no, not so long as god is good and generous. I was cruel. Starved them. I have to make up for it now, you see.'

'You're insane,' Lissandra said. It was the last thing she said. Kress burned a hole in her chest big enough to put his arm through. He dragged the body across the floor and rolled it down the cellar stairs. The noises were louder – chitinous clackings and scrapings and echoes that were thick and liquid. Kress nailed up the door once again.

As he fled, he was filled with a deep sense of contentment that coated his fear like a layer of syrup. He suspected it was not his own.

He planned to leave his home, to fly to the city and take a room for a night, or perhaps for a year. Instead Kress started drinking. He was not quite sure why. He drank steadily for hours, and retched it all up violently on his living room carpet. At some point he fell asleep. When he woke, it was pitch dark in the house.

He cowered against the couch. He could hear *noises*. Things were moving in the walls. They were all around him. His hearing was extraordinarily acute. Every little creak was the footstep of a sandking. He closed his eyes and waited, expecting to feel their terrible touch, afraid to move lest he brush against one.

Kress sobbed, and was very still for a while, but nothing happened.

He opened his eyes again. He trembled. Slowly the shadows began to soften and dissolve. Moonlight was filtering through the high windows. His eyes adjusted.

The living room was empty. Nothing there, nothing, nothing. Only his drunken fears.

Simon Kress steeled himself, and rose, and went to a light.

Nothing there. The room was quiet, deserted.

He listened. Nothing. No sound. Nothing in the walls. It had all been his imagination, his fear.

The memories of Lissandra and the thing in the cellar returned to him unbidden. Shame and anger washed over him. Why had he done that? He could have helped her burn it out, kill it. *Why* . . . he knew why. The maw had done it to him, put fear in him. Wo had said it was psionic, even when it was small. And now it was large, so large. It had feasted on Cath, and Idi, and now it had two more bodies down there. It would keep growing. And it had learned to like the taste of human flesh, he thought.

He began to shake, but he took control of himself again and stopped. It wouldn't hurt him. He was god. The whites had always been his favorites.

He remembered how he had stabbed it with his throwing-sword. That was before Cath came. Damn her anyway.

He couldn't stay here. The maw would grow hungry again. Large as it was, it wouldn't take long. Its appetite would be terrible. What would it do then? He had to get away, back to the safety of the city while it was still contained in his wine cellar. It was only plaster and hard-packed earth down there, and the mobiles could dig and tunnel. When they got free . . . Kress didn't want to think about it.

He went to his bedroom and packed. He took three bags. Just a single change of clothing, that was all he needed; the rest of the space he filled with his valuables, with jewelry and art and other things he could not bear to lose. He did not expect to return.

His shambler followed him down the stairs, staring at him from its baleful glowing eyes. It was gaunt. Kress realized that it had been ages since he had fed it. Normally it could take care of itself, but no doubt the pickings had grown lean of late. When it tried to clutch at his leg, he snarled at it and kicked it away, and it scurried off, offended.

Kress slipped outside, carrying his bags awkwardly, and shut the door behind him.

For a moment he stood pressed against the house, his heart thudding in his chest. Only a few meters between him and his skimmer. He was afraid to cross them. The moonlight was bright, and the front of his house was a scene of carnage. The bodies of Lissandra's two flamers lay where they had fallen, one twisted and burned, the other swollen beneath a mass of dead sandkings. And the mobiles, the black and red mobiles, they were all around him. It was an effort to remember that they were dead. It was almost as if they were simply waiting, as they had waited so often before.

Nonsense, Kress told himself. More drunken fears. He had seen the castles blown apart. They were dead, and the white maw was trapped in his cellar. He took several deep and deliberate breaths, and stepped forward onto the sandkings. They crunched. He ground them into the sand savagely. They did not move.

Kress smiled, and walked slowly across the battleground, listening to the sounds, the sounds of safety.

Crunch. Crackle. Crunch.

He lowered his bags to the ground and opened the door to his skimmer.

Something moved from shadow into light. A pale shape on the seat of his skimmer. It was as long as his forearm. Its mandibles clacked together softly, and it looked up at him from six small eyes set all around its body.

Kress wet his pants and backed away slowly.

There was more motion from inside the skimmer. He had left the door open. The sandking emerged and came toward him, cautiously. Others followed. They had been hiding beneath his seats, burrowed into the upholstery. But now they emerged. They formed a ragged ring around the skimmer.

Kress licked his lips, turned, and moved quickly to Lissandra's skimmer.

He stopped before he was halfway there. Things were moving inside that one too. Great maggoty things, half-seen by the light of the moon.

Kress whimpered and retreated back toward the house. Near the front door, he looked up.

He counted a dozen long white shapes creeping back and forth across the walls of the building. Four of them were clustered close together near the top of the unused belfry where the carrion hawk had once roosted. They were carving something. A face. A very recognizable face.

Simon Kress shrieked and ran back inside.

*

A sufficient quantity of drink brought him the easy oblivion he sought. But he woke. Despite everything, he woke. He had a terrible headache, and he smelled, and he was hungry. Oh so very hungry. He had never been so hungry.

Kress knew it was not his *own* stomach hurting.

A white sandking watched him from atop the dresser in his bedroom, its antennae moving faintly. It was as big as the one in the skimmer the night before. He was horribly dry, sandpaper dry. He licked his lips and fled from the room.

The house was full of sandkings; he had to be careful where he put his feet. They all seemed busy on errands of their own. They were making modifications in his house, burrowing into or out of his walls, carving things. Twice he saw his own likeness staring out at him from unexpected places. The faces were warped, twisted, livid with fear.

He went outside to get the bodies that had been rotting in the yard, hoping to appease the white maw's hunger. They were gone, both of them. Kress remembered how easily the mobiles could carry things many times their own weight.

It was terrible to think that the maw was *still* hungry after all of that.

When Kress reentered the house, a column of sandkings was wending its way down the stairs. Each carried a piece of his shambler. The head seemed to look at him reproachfully as it went by.

Kress emptied his freezers, his cabinets, everything, piling all the food in the house in the center of his kitchen floor. A dozen whites waited to take it away. They avoided the frozen food, leaving it to thaw in a great puddle, but they carried off everything else.

When all the food was gone, Kress felt his own hunger pangs abate just a bit, though he had not eaten a thing. But he knew the respite would be short-lived. Soon the maw would be hungry again. He had to feed it.

Kress knew what to do. He went to his communicator. 'Malada,' he began casually when the first of his friends answered, 'I'm having a small party tonight. I realize this is terribly short notice, but I hope you can make it. I really do.'

He called Jad Rakkis next, and then the others. By the time he had finished, nine of them had accepted his invitation. Kress hoped that would be enough.

Kress met his guests outside – the mobiles had cleaned up remarkably quickly, and the grounds looked almost as they had before the battle – and walked them to his front door. He let them enter first. He did not follow.

When four of them had gone through, Kress finally worked up his courage. He closed the door behind his latest guest, ignoring the startled exclamations that soon turned into shrill gibbering, and sprinted for the skimmer the man had arrived in. He slid in safely, thumbed the startplate, and swore. It was programmed to lift only in response to its owner's thumbprint, of course.

Jad Rakkis was the next to arrive. Kress ran to his skimmer as it set down, and seized Rakkis by the arm as he was climbing out. 'Get back in, quickly,' he said, pushing. 'Take me to the city. Hurry, Jad. *Get out of here!*'

But Rakkis only stared at him, and would not move. 'Why, what's wrong, Simon? I don't understand. What about your party?'

And then it was too late, because the loose sand all around them was stirring, and the red eyes were staring at them, and the mandibles were clacking. Rakkis made a choking sound, and moved to get back in his skimmer, but a pair of mandibles snapped shut about his ankle, and suddenly he was on his knees. The sand seemed to boil with subterranean activity. Jad thrashed and cried terribly as they tore him apart. Kress could hardly bear to watch.

After that, he did not try to escape again. When it was all over, he cleaned out what remained in his liquor cabinet, and got extremely drunk. It would be the last time he would enjoy that luxury, he knew. The only alcohol remaining in the house was stored down in the wine cellar.

Kress did not touch a bite of food the entire day, but he fell asleep feeling bloated, sated at last, the awful hunger vanquished. His last thoughts before the nightmares took him were of whom he could ask out tomorrow.

Morning was hot and dry. Kress opened his eyes to see the white sandking on his dresser again. He shut them again quickly, hoping the dream would leave him. It did not, and he could not go back to sleep. Soon he found himself staring at the thing.

He stared for almost five minutes before the strangeness of it dawned on him; the sandking was not moving.

The mobiles could be preternaturally still, to be sure. He had seen them wait and watch a thousand times. But always there was some motion about them – the mandibles clacked, the legs twitched, the long fine antennae stirred and swayed.

But the sandking on his dresser was completely still.

Kress rose, holding his breath, not daring to hope. Could it be dead? Could something have killed it? He walked across the room.

The eyes were glassy and black. The creature seemed swollen, somehow, as if it were soft and rotting inside, filling up with gas that pushed outward at the plates of white armor.

Kress reached out a trembling hand and touched it.

It was warm – hot even – and growing hotter. But it did not move.

He pulled his hand back, and as he did, a segment of the sandking's white exoskeleton fell away from it. The flesh beneath was the same color, but softer-looking, swollen and feverish. And it almost seemed to throb.

Kress backed away, and ran to the door.

Three more white mobiles lay in his hall. They were all like the one in his bedroom.

He ran down the stairs, jumping over sandkings. None of them moved. The house was full of them, all dead, dying, comatose, whatever. Kress did not care what was wrong with them. Just so they could not move.

He found four of them inside his skimmer. He picked them up one by one, and threw them as far as he could. Damned monsters. He slid back in, on the ruined half-eaten seats, and thumbed the startplate.

Nothing happened.

Kress tried again, and again. Nothing. It wasn't fair. This was *his* skimmer, it ought to start, why wouldn't it lift, he didn't understand.

Finally he got out and checked, expecting the worst. He found it. The sandkings had torn apart his gravity grid. He was trapped. He was still trapped.

Grimly, Kress marched back into the house. He went to his gallery and found the antique axe that had hung next to the throwing-sword he had used on Cath m'Lane. He set to work. The sandkings did not stir even as he chopped them to pieces. But they splattered when he made the first cut, the bodies almost bursting. Inside was awful; strange half-formed organs, a viscous reddish ooze that looked almost like human blood, and the yellow ichor.

Kress destroyed twenty of them before he realized the futility of what he was doing. The mobiles were nothing, really. Besides, there were so *many* of them. He could work for a day and night and still not kill them all.

He had to go down into the wine cellar and use the axe on the maw.

Resolute, he started down. He got within sight of the door, and stopped.

It was not a door any more. The walls had been eaten away, so that the hole was twice the size it had been, and round. A pit, that was all. There was no sign that there had ever been a door nailed shut over that black abyss.

A ghastly, choking, fetid odor seemed to come from below.

And the walls were wet and bloody and covered with patches of white fungus.

And worst, it was *breathing*.

Kress stood across the room and felt the warm wind wash over him as it exhaled, and he tried not to choke, and when the wind reversed direction, he fled.

Back in the living room, he destroyed three more mobiles, and collapsed. What was *happening*? He didn't understand.

Then he remembered the only person who might understand. Kress went to his communicator again, stepping on a sandking in his haste, and prayed fervently that the device still worked.

When Jala Wo answered, he broke down and told her everything.

She let him talk without interruption, no expression save for a slight frown on her gaunt, pale face. When Kress had finished, she said only, 'I ought to leave you there.'

Kress began to blubber. 'You can't. Help me. I'll pay . . .'

'I ought to,' Wo repeated, 'but I won't.'

'Thank you,' Kress said. 'Oh, thank . . .'

'Quiet,' said Wo. 'Listen to me. This is your own doing. Keep your sandkings well, and they are courtly ritual warriors. You turned yours into something else, with starvation and torture. You were their god. You made them what they are. That maw in your cellar is sick, still suffering from the wound you gave it. It is probably insane. Its behavior is . . . unusual.

'You have to get out of there quickly. The mobiles are not dead, Kress. They are dormant. I told you the exoskeleton falls off when they grow larger. Normally, in fact, it falls off much earlier. I have never heard of sandkings growing as large as yours while still in the insectoid stage. It is another result of crippling the white maw, I would say. That does not matter.

'What matters is the metamorphosis your sandkings are now under-going. As the maw grows, you see, it gets progressively more intelligent. Its psionic powers strengthen, and its mind becomes more sophisticated, more ambitious. The armored mobiles are useful enough when the maw is tiny and only semi-sentient, but now it needs better servants, bodies with capabilities. Do you understand? The mobiles are all going to give birth to a new breed of sandking. I can't say exactly what it will look like. Each maw designs its own, to fit its perceived needs and desires. But it will be biped, with four arms, and opposable thumbs. It will be able to construct and operate advanced machinery. The individual sandkings will not be sentient. But the maw will be very sentient indeed.'

Simon Kress was gaping at Wo's image on the viewscreen. 'Your workers,' he said, with an effort. 'The ones who came out here . . . who installed the tank . . .'

Jala Wo managed a faint smile. 'Shade,' she said.

'Shade is a sandking,' Kress repeated numbly. 'And you sold me a tank of . . . of . . . infants, ah . . .'

'Do not be absurd,' Wo said. 'A first-stage sandking is more like a sperm than an infant. The wars temper and control them in nature. Only one in a hundred reaches second stage. Only one in a thousand achieves the third and final plateau, and becomes like Shade. Adult sandkings are not sentimental about the small maws. There are too many of them, and their mobiles are pests.' She sighed. 'And all this talk wastes time. That white sandking is going to waken to full sentience soon. It is not going to need you any longer, and it hates you, and it will be very hungry. The transformation is taxing. The maw must eat enormous amounts both before and after. So you have to get out of there. Do you understand?'

'*I can't*,' Kress said. 'My skimmer is destroyed, and I can't get any of the others to start. I don't know how to reprogram them. Can you come out for me?'

'Yes,' said Wo. 'Shade and I will leave at once, but it is more than two hundred kilometers from Asgard to you, and there is equipment we will need to deal with the deranged sandking you've created. You cannot wait there. You have two feet. Walk. Go due east, as near as you can determine, as quickly as you can. The land out there is pretty desolate. We'll find you easily with an aerial search, and you'll be safely away from the sandking. Do you understand?'

'Yes,' said Simon Kress. 'Yes, oh, yes.'

They signed off, and he walked quickly toward the door. He was halfway there when he heard the noise – a sound halfway between a pop and a crack.

One of the sandkings had split open. Four tiny hands covered with pinkish-yellow blood came up out of the gap and began to push the dead skin aside.

Kress began to run.

*

He had not counted on the heat.

The hills were dry and rocky. Kress ran from the house as quickly as he could, ran until his ribs ached and his breath was coming in gasps. Then he walked, but as soon as he had recovered he began to run again. For almost an hour he ran and walked, ran and walked, beneath the fierce hot sun. He sweated freely, and wished that he had thought to bring some water. He watched the sky in hopes of seeing Wo and Shade.

He was not made for this. It was too hot, and too dry, and he was in no condition. But he kept himself going with the memory of the way the maw had breathed, and the thought of the wriggling little things that by now were surely crawling all over his house. He hoped Wo and Shade would know how to deal with them.

He had his own plans for Wo and Shade. It was all their fault, Kress had decided, and they would suffer for it. Lissandra was dead, but he knew others in her profession. He would have his revenge. He promised himself that a hundred times as he struggled and sweated his way east.

At least he hoped it was east. He was not that good at directions, and he wasn't certain which way he had run in his initial panic, but since then he had made an effort to bear due east, as Wo had suggested.

When he had been running for several hours, with no sign of rescue, Kress began to grow certain that he had gone wrong.

When several more hours passed, he began to grow afraid. What if Wo and Shade could not find him? He would die out here. He hadn't eaten in two days; he was weak and frightened; his throat was raw for want of water. He couldn't keep going. The sun was sinking now, and he'd be completely lost in the dark. What was wrong? Had the sandkings eaten Wo and Shade? The fear was on him again, filling him, and with it a great thirst and a terrible hunger. But Kress kept going. He stumbled now when he tried to run, and twice he fell. The second time he scraped his hand on a rock, and it came away bloody. He sucked at it as he walked, and worried about infection.

The sun was on the horizon behind him. The ground grew a little cooler, for which Kress was grateful. He decided to walk until last light and settle in for the night. Surely he was far enough from the sandkings to be safe, and Wo and Shade would find him come morning.

When he topped the next rise, he saw the outline of a house in front of him.

It wasn't as big as his own house, but it was big enough. It was habitation, safety. Kress shouted and began to run toward it. Food and drink, he had to have nourishment, he could taste the meal now. He was aching with hunger. He ran down the hill towards the house, waving his arms and shouting to the inhabitants. The light was almost gone now, but he could still make out a half-dozen children playing in the twilight. 'Hey there,' he shouted. 'Help, help.'

They came running toward him.

Kress stopped suddenly. 'No,' he said, 'oh, no. Oh, no.' He backpedaled, slipped on the sand, got up and tried to run again. They caught him easily. They were ghastly little things with bulging eyes and dusky orange skin. He struggled, but it was useless. Small as they were, each of them had four arms, and Kress had only two.

They carried him toward the house. It was a sad, shabby house built of crumbling sand, but the door was quite large, and dark, and it breathed. That was terrible, but it was not the thing that set Simon Kress to screaming. He screamed because of the others, the little orange children who came crawling out from the castle, and watched impassive as he passed.

All of them had his face.

Nightflyers

When Jesus of Nazareth hung dying on his cross, the *volcryn* passed within a year of his agony, headed outward.

When the Fire Wars raged on Earth, the *volcryn* sailed near Old Poseidon, where the seas were still unnamed and unfished. By the time the stardrive had transformed the Federated Nations of Earth into the Federal Empire, the *volcryn* had moved into the fringes of Hrangan space. The Hrangans never knew it. Like us they were children of the small bright worlds that circled their scattered suns, with little interest and less knowledge of the things that moved in the gulfs between.

War flamed for a thousand years and the *volcryn* passed through it, unknowing and untouched, safe in a place where no fires could ever burn. Afterwards, the Federal Empire was shattered and gone, and the Hrangans vanished in the dark of the Collapse, but it was no darker for the *volcryn*.

When Kleronomas took his survey ship out from Avalon, the *volcryn* came within ten light years of him. Kleronomas found many things, but he did not find the *volcryn*. Not then and not on his return to Avalon, a lifetime later.

When I was a child of three, Kleronomas was dust, as distant and dead as Jesus of Nazareth, and the *volcryn* passed close to Daronne. That season all the Crey sensitives grew strange and sat staring at the stars with luminous, flickering eyes.

When I was grown, the *volcryn* had sailed beyond Tara, past the range of even the Crey, still heading outward.

And now I am old and growing older and the *volcryn* will soon pierce the Tempter's Veil where it hangs like a black mist between the stars. And we follow, we follow. Through the dark gulfs where no one goes, through the emptiness, through the silence that goes on and on, my *Nightflyer* and I give chase.

*

They made their way slowly down the length of the transparent tube that linked the orbital docks to the waiting starship ahead, pulling themselves hand over hand through weightlessness.

Melantha Jhirl, the only one among them who did not seem clumsy and ill at ease in free fall, paused briefly to look at the dappled globe of Avalon below, a stately vastness in jade and amber. She smiled and moved swiftly down the tube, passing her companions with an easy grace. They had boarded starships before, all of them, but never like this. Most ships docked flush against the station, but the craft that Karoly d'Branin had chartered for his mission was too large, and too singular in design. It loomed ahead; three small eggs side-by-side, two larger spheres beneath and at right angles, the cylinder of the driveroom between, lengths of tube connecting it all. The ship was white and austere.

Melantha Jhirl was the first one through the airlock. The others straggled up one by one until they had all boarded; five women and four men, each an Academy scholar, their backgrounds as diverse as their fields of study. The frail young telepath, Thale Lasamer, was the last to enter. He glanced about nervously as the others chatted and waited for the entry procedure to be completed. 'We're being watched,' he said.

The outer door was closed behind them, the tube had fallen away; now the inner door slid open. 'Welcome to my *Nightflyer*,' said a mellow voice from within.

But there was no one there.

Melantha Jhirl stepped into the corridor. 'Hello,' she said, looking about quizzically. Karoly d'Branin followed her.

'Hello,' the mellow voice replied. It was coming from a communicator grille beneath a darkened viewscreen. 'This is Royd Eris, master of the *Nightflyer*. I'm pleased to see you again, Karoly, and pleased to welcome the rest of you.'

'Where are you?' someone demanded.

'In my quarters, which occupy half of this life-support sphere,' the voice of Royd Eris replied amiably. 'The other half is comprised of a lounge-library-kitchen, two sanitary stations, one double cabin, and a rather small single. The rest of you will have to rig sleepwebs in the cargo spheres, I'm afraid. The *Nightflyer* was designed as a trader, not a passenger vessel. However, I've opened all the appropriate passage-ways and locks, so the holds have air and heat and water. I thought you'd find it more comfortable that way. Your equipment and computer system have been stowed in the holds, but there is still plenty of space, I assure you. I suggest you settle in, and then meet in the lounge for a meal.'

'Will you join us?' asked the psipsych, a querulous hatchet-faced woman named Agatha Marij-Black.

'In a fashion,' Royd Eris said, 'in a fashion.'

*

The ghost appeared at the banquet.

They found the lounge easily enough, after they had rigged their sleepwebs and arranged their personal belongings around their sleeping quarters. It was the largest room in this section of the ship. One end of it was a fully equipped kitchen, well stocked with provisions. The opposite end offered several comfortable chairs, two readers, a holotank, and a wall of books and tapes and crystal chips. In the center was a long table with places set for ten.

A light meal was hot and waiting. The academicians helped themselves and took seats at the table, laughing and talking to each other, more at ease now than when they had boarded.

The ship's gravity grid was on, which went a long way towards making them more comfortable; the queasy awkwardness of their weightless transit was soon forgotten.

Finally all the seats were occupied except for one at the head of the table.

The ghost materialized there.

All conversation stopped.

'Hello,' said the spectre, the bright shade of a lithe, pale-eyed young man with white hair. He was dressed in clothing twenty years out of date; a loose blue pastel shirt that ballooned at his wrists, clinging white trousers with built-in boots. They could see through him, and his own eyes did not see them at all.

'A hologram,' said Alys Northwind, the short, stout xenotech.

'Royd, Royd, I do not understand,' said Karoly d'Branin, staring at the ghost. 'What is this? Why do you send us a projection? Will you not join us in person?'

The ghost smiled faintly and lifted an arm. 'My quarters are on the other side of that wall,' he said. 'I'm afraid there is no door or lock between the two halves of the sphere. I spend most of my time by myself, and I value my privacy. I hope you will all understand and respect my wishes. I will be a gracious host nonetheless. Here in the lounge my projection can join you. Elsewhere, if you have anything you need, if you want to talk to me, just use a communicator. Now, please resume your meal, and your conversations. I'll gladly listen. It's been a long time since I had passengers.'

They tried. But the ghost at the head of the table cast a long shadow, and the meal was strained and hurried.

*

From the hour the *Nightflyer* slipped into stardrive, Royd Eris watched his passengers.

Within a few days most of the academicians had grown accustomed to

the disembodied voice from the communicators and the holographic
spectre in the lounge, but only Melantha Jhirl and Karoly d'Branin ever
seemed really comfortable in his presence. The others would have been
even more uncomfortable if they had known that Royd was always with
them. Always and everywhere, he watched. Even in the sanitary stations,
Royd had eyes and ears.

He watched them work, eat, sleep, copulate; he listened untiringly to
their talk. Within a week he knew them, all nine, and had begun to ferret
out their tawdry little secrets.

The cyberneticist, Lommie Thorne, talked to her computers and seemed
to prefer their company to that of humans. She was bright and quick, with
a mobile, expressive face and a small hard boyish body; most of the others
found her attractive, but she did not like to be touched. She sexed only
once, with Melantha Jhirl. Lommie Thorne wore shirts of softly-woven
metal, and had an implant in her left wrist that let her interface directly
with her computers.

The xenobiologist, Rojan Christopheris, was a surly, argumentative man,
a cynic whose contempt for his colleagues was barely kept in check, a
solitary drinker. He was tall and stooped and ugly.

The two linguists, Dannel and Lindran, were lovers in public, constantly
holding hands and supporting each other. In private they quarreled
bitterly. Lindran had a mordant wit and liked to wound Dannel where it
hurt the most, with jokes about his professional competence. They sexed
often, both of them, but not with each other.

Agatha Marij-Black, the psipsych, was a hypochrondriac given to black
depressions, which worsened in the close confines of the *Nightflyer*.

Xenotech Alys Northwind ate constantly and never washed. Her stubby
fingernails were always caked with black dirt, and she wore the same
jumpsuit for the first two weeks of the voyage, taking it off only for sex,
and then only briefly.

Telepath Thale Lasamer was nervous and temperamental, afraid of
everyone around him, yet given to bouts of arrogance in which he taunted
his companions with thoughts he had snatched from their minds.

Royd Eris watched them all, studied them, lived with them and through
them. He neglected none, not even the ones he found the most distasteful.
But by the time the *Nightflyer* had been lost in the roiling flux of stardrive
for two weeks, two of his riders had come to engage the bulk of his
attention.

'Most of all, I want to know the why of them,' Karoly d'Branin told him
one false night the second week out from Avalon.

Royd's luminescent ghost sat close to d'Branin in the darkened lounge,
watching him drink bittersweet chocolate. The others were all asleep.

Night and day are meaningless on a starship, but the *Nightflyer* kept the usual cycles and most of the passengers followed them. Old d'Branin, administrator, generalist, and mission leader, was the exception; he kept his own hours, preferred work to sleep, and liked nothing better than to talk about his pet obsession, the *volcryn* he hunted.

'The *if* of them is important as well, Karoly,' Royd answered. 'Can you truly be certain these aliens of yours exist?'

'*I* can be certain,' Karoly d'Branin said, with a broad wink. He was a compact man, short and slender, iron gray hair carefully styled and his tunic almost fussily neat, but the expansiveness of his gestures and the giddy enthusiasms to which he was prone belied his sober appearance. 'That is enough. If everyone else were certain as well, we would have a fleet of research ships instead of your little *Nightflyer*.' He sipped at his chocolate and sighed with satisfaction. 'Do you know the Nor T'alush, Royd?'

The name was strange, but it took Royd only a moment to consult his library computer. 'An alien race on the other side of human space, past the Fyndii worlds and the Damoosh. Possibly legendary.'

D'Branin chuckled. 'No, no, no! Your library is out of date, my friend, you must supplement it the next time you visit Avalon. Not legends, no, real enough, though far away. We have little information about the Nor T'alush, but we are sure they exist, though you and I may never meet one. They were the start of it all.'

'Tell me,' Royd said. 'I am interested in your work, Karoly.'

'I was coding some information into the Academy computers, a packet newly arrived from Dam Tullian after twenty standard years in transit. Part of it was Nor T'alush folklore. I had no idea how long that had taken to get to Dam Tullian, or by what route it had come, but it did not matter – folklore is timeless anyway, and this was fascinating material. Did you know that my first degree was in xenomythology?'

'I did not. Please continue.'

'The *volcryn* story was among the Nor T'alush myths. It awed me; a race of sentients moving out from some mysterious origin in the core of the galaxy, sailing towards the galactic edge and, it was alleged, eventually bound for intergalactic space itself, meanwhile always keeping to the interstellar depths, no planetfalls, seldom coming within a light year of a star.' D'Branin's gray eyes sparkled, and as he spoke his hands swept enthusiastically to either side, as if they could encompass the galaxy. 'And doing it all *without a stardrive*, Royd, that is the real wonder! Doing it in ships moving only a fraction of the speed of light! That was the detail that obsessed me! How different they must be, my *volcryn* – wise and patient, long-lived and long-viewed, with none of the terrible haste and passion that consumes the lesser races. Think how *old* they must be, those *volcryn* ships!'

'Old,' Royd agreed. 'Karoly, you said ships. More than one?'

'Oh, yes,' d'Branin said. 'According to the Nor T'alush, one or two appeared first, on the innermost edges of their trading sphere, but others followed. Hundreds of them, each solitary, moving by itself, bound outward, always outward. The direction was always the same. For fifteen thousand standard years they moved among the Nor T'alush stars, and then they began to pass out from among them. The myth said that the last *volcryn* ship was gone three thousand years ago.'

'Eighteen thousand years,' Royd said, adding, 'are the Nor T'alush that old?'

'Not as star-travellers, no,' d'Branin said, smiling. 'According to their own histories, the Nor T'alush have only been civilized for about half that long. That bothered me for a while. It seemed to make the *volcryn* story clearly a legend. A wonderful legend, true, but nothing more.

'Ultimately, however, I could not let it alone. In my spare time I investigated, cross-checking with other alien cosmologies to see whether this particular myth was shared by any races other than the Nor T'alush. I thought perhaps I could get a thesis out of it. It seemed a fruitful line of inquiry.

'I was startled by what I found. Nothing from the Hrangans, or the Hrangan slave races, but that made sense, you see. Since they were *out* from human space, the *volcryn* would not reach them until after they had passed through our own sphere. When I looked *in*, however, the *volcryn* story was everywhere.' D'Branin leaned forward eagerly. 'Ah, Royd, the stories, the *stories*!'

'Tell me,' Royd said.

'The Fyndii call them *iy-wivii*, which translates to something like void-horde or dark-horde. Each Fyndii horde tells the same story, only the mindmutes disbelieve. The ships are said to be vast, much larger than any known in their history or ours. Warships, they say. There is a story of a lost Fyndii horde, three hundred ships under *rala-fyn*, all destroyed utterly when they encountered an *iy-wivii*. This was many thousands of years ago, of course, so the details are unclear.

'The Damoosh have a different story, but they accept it as literal truth – and the Damoosh, you know, are the oldest race we've yet encountered. The people of the gulf, they call my *volcryn*. Lovely stories, Royd, lovely! Ships like great dark cities, still and silent, moving at a slower pace than the universe around them. Damoosh legends say the *volcryn* are refugees from some unimaginable war deep in the core of the galaxy, at the very beginning of time. They abandoned the worlds and stars on which they had evolved, sought true peace in the emptiness between.

'The gethsoids of Aath have a similar story, but in their tale that war destroyed all life in our galaxy, and the *volcryn* are gods of a sort, reseeding the worlds as they pass. Other races see them as god's messengers, or shadows out of hell warning us all to flee some terror soon to emerge from the core.'

'Your stories contradict each other, Karoly.'

'Yes, yes, of course, but they all agree on the essentials – the *volcryn*, sailing out, passing through our short-lived empires and transient glories in their ancient eternal sublight ships. *That* is what matters! The rest is frippery, ornamentation; we will soon know the truth of it. I checked what little was known about the races said to flourish further in still, beyond even the Nor T'alush – civilizations and peoples half legendary themselves, like the Dan'lai and the ullish and the Rohenna'kh – and where I could find anything at all, I found the *volcryn* story once again.'

'The legend of the legends,' Royd suggested. The spectre's wide mouth turned up in a smile.

'Exactly, exactly,' d'Branin agreed. 'At that point, I called in the experts, specialists from the Institute for the Study of Non-Human Intelligence. We researched for two years. It was all there, in the libraries and memories and matrices of the Academy. No one had ever looked before, or bothered to put it together.

'The *volcryn* have been moving through the manrealm for most of human history, since before the dawn of spaceflight. While we twist the fabric of space itself to cheat relativity, they have been sailing their great ships right through the heart of our alleged civilization, past our most populous worlds, at stately slow sublight speeds, bound for the Fringe and the dark between the galaxies. Marvelous, Royd, marvelous!'

'Marvelous!' Royd agreed.

Karoly d'Branin drained his chocolate cup with a swig, and reached out to catch Royd's arm, but his hand passed through empty light. He seemed disconcerted for a moment, before he began to laugh at himself. 'Ah, my *volcryn*. I grow overenthused, Royd. I am so close now. They have preyed on my mind for a dozen years, and within the month I will have them, will behold their splendor with my own weary eyes. Then, then, if only I can open communication, if only my people can reach ones so great and strange as they, so different from us – I have hopes, Royd, hopes that at last I will know the why of it!'

The ghost of Royd Eris smiled for him, and looked on through calm transparent eyes.

*

Passengers soon grow restless on a starship under drive, sooner on one as small and spare as the *Nightflyer*. Late in the second week, the speculation began in deadly earnest.

'Who is this Royd Eris, really?' the xenobiologist, Rojan Christopheris, complained one night when four of them were playing cards. 'Why doesn't he come out? What's the purpose of keeping himself sealed off from the rest of us?'

'Ask him,' suggested Dannel, the male linguist.

'What if he's a criminal of some sort?' Christopheris said. 'Do we know anything about him? No, of course not. D'Branin engaged him, and d'Branin is a senile old fool, we all know that.'

'It's your play,' Lommie Thorne said.

Christopheris snapped down a card. 'Setback,' he declared, 'you'll have to draw again.' He grinned. 'As for this Eris, who knows that he isn't planning to kill us all.'

'For our vast wealth, no doubt,' said Lindran, the female linguist. She played a card on top of the one Christopheris had laid down. 'Ricochet,' she called softly. She smiled. So did Royd Eris, watching.

*

Melantha Jhirl was good to watch.

Young, healthy, active, Melantha Jhirl had a vibrancy about her the others could not match. She was big in every way; a head taller than anyone else on board, large-framed, large-breasted, long-legged, strong, muscles moving fluidly beneath shiny coal-black skin. Her appetites were big as well. She ate twice as much as any of her colleagues, drank heavily without ever seeming drunk, exercised for hours every day on equipment she had brought with her and set up in one of the cargo holds. By the third week out she had sexed with all four of the men on board and two of the other women. Even in bed she was always active, exhausting most of her partners. Royd watched her with consuming interest.

'I am an improved model,' she told him once as she worked out on her parallel bars, sweat glistening on her bare skin, her long black hair confined in a net.

'Improved?' Royd said. He could not send his projection down to the holds, but Melantha had summoned him with the communicator to talk while she exercised, not knowing he would have been there anyway.

She paused in her routine, holding her body straight and aloft with the strength of her arms and her back. 'Altered, captain,' she said. She had taken to calling him captain. 'Born on Prometheus among the elite, child of two genetic wizards. Improved, captain. I require twice the energy you do, but I use it all. A more efficient metabolism, a stronger and more durable body, an expected lifespan half again the normal human's. My people have made some terrible mistakes when they try to radically redesign humanity, but the small improvements they do well.'

She resumed her exercises, moving quickly and easily, silent until she had finished. When she was done, she vaulted away from the bars and stood breathing heavily for a moment, then crossed her arms and cocked her head and grinned. 'Now you know my life story, captain,' she said. She pulled off the net to shake free her hair.

'Surely there is more,' said the voice from the communicator.

Melantha Jhirl laughed. 'Surely,' she said. 'Do you want to hear about my defection to Avalon, the whys and wherefores of it, the trouble it caused my family on Prometheus? Or are you more interested in my extraordinary work in cultural xenology? Do you want to hear about that?'

'Perhaps some other time,' Royd said politely. 'What is that crystal you wear?'

It hung between her breasts ordinarily; she had removed it when she stripped for her exercises. She picked it up again and slipped it over her head; a small green gem laced with traceries of black, on a silver chain. When it touched her Melantha closed her eyes briefly, then opened them again, grinning. 'It's alive,' she said. 'Haven't you ever seen one? A whisperjewel, captain. Resonant crystal, etched psionically to hold a memory, a sensation. The touch brings it back, for a time.'

'I am familiar with the principle,' Royd said, 'but not this use. Yours contains some treasured memory, then? Of your family, perhaps?'

Melantha Jhirl snatched up a towel and began to dry the sweat from her body. 'Mine contains the sensations of a particularly satisfying session in bed, captain. It arouses me. Or it did. Whisperjewels fade in time, and this isn't as potent as it once was. But sometimes – often when I've come from lovemaking or strenuous exercise – it comes alive on me again, like it did just then.'

'Oh,' said Royd's voice. 'It has made you aroused, then? Are you going off to copulate now?'

Melantha grinned. 'I know what part of my life you want to hear about, captain – my tumultuous and passionate love life. Well, you won't have it. Not until I hear your life story, anyway. Among my modest attributes is an insatiable curiosity. Who are you, captain? Really?'

'One as improved as you,' Royd replied, 'should certainly be able to guess.'

Melantha laughed, and tossed her towel at the communicator grille.

*

Lommie Thorne spent most of her days in the cargo hold they had designated as the computer room, setting up the system they would use to analyze the *volcryn*. As often as not, the xenotech Alys Northwind came with her to lend a hand. The cyberneticist whistled as she worked; Northwind obeyed her orders in a sullen silence. Occasionally they talked.

'Eris isn't human,' Lommie Thorne said one day, as she supervised the installation of a display viewscreen.

Alys Northwind grunted. 'What?' A frown broke across her square, flat features. Christopheris and his talk had made her nervous about Eris. She clicked another component into position, and turned.

'He talks to us, but he can't be seen,' the cyberneticist said. 'This ship is uncrewed, seemingly all automated except for him. Why not entirely automated, then? I'd wager this Royd Eris is a fairly sophisticated computer system, perhaps a genuine Artificial Intelligence. Even a modest program can carry on a blind conversation indistinguishable from a human's. This one could fool you, I'd bet, once it's up and running.'

The xenotech grunted and turned back to her work. 'Why fake being human, then?'

'Because,' said Lommie Thorne, 'most legal systems give AIs no rights. A ship can't own itself, even on Avalon. The *Nightflyer* is probably afraid of being seized and disconnected.' She whistled. 'Death, Alys; the end of self-awareness and conscious thought.'

'I work with machines every day,' Alys Northwind said stubbornly. 'Turn them off, turn them on, makes no difference. They don't mind. Why should this machine care?'

Lommie Thorne smiled. 'A computer is different, Alys,' she said. 'Mind, thought, life, the big systems have all of that.' Her right hand curled around her left wrist, and her thumb began idly rubbing the nubs of her implant. 'Sensation, too. I know. No one wants the end of sensation. They are not so different from you and I, really.'

The xenotech glanced back and shook her head. 'Really,' she repeated, in a flat, disbelieving voice.

Royd Eris listened and watched, unsmiling.

*

Thale Lasamer was a frail young thing; nervous, sensitive, with limp flaxen hair that fell to his shoulders, and watery blue eyes. Normally he dressed like a peacock, favoring the lacy V-necked shirts and codpieces that were still the fashion among the lower classes of his homeworld. But on the day he sought out Karoly d'Branin in his cramped, private cabin, Lasamer was dressed almost somberly, in an austere gray jumpsuit.

'I feel it,' he said, clutching d'Branin by the arm, his long fingernails digging in painfully. 'Something is wrong, Karoly, something is very wrong. I'm beginning to get frightened.'

The telepath's nails bit, and d'Branin pulled away hard. 'You are hurting me,' he protested. 'My friend, what is it? Frightened? Of what, of whom? I do not understand. What could there be to fear?'

Lasamer raised pale hands to his face. 'I don't know, I don't *know*,' he wailed. 'Yet it's *there*, I feel it. Karoly, I'm picking up something. You know I'm good, I am, that's why you picked me. Just a moment ago, when my nails dug into you, I felt it. I can read you now, in flashes. You're thinking I'm too excitable, that it's the confinement, that I've got to be calmed down.' The young man laughed a thin hysterical laugh that died as quickly as it had begun. 'No, you see, I am good. Class one, tested, and I tell you I'm afraid. I sense it. Feel it. Dream of it. I felt it even as we were boarding, and it's gotten worse. Something dangerous. Something volatile. And alien, Karoly, *alien!*'

'The *volcryn!*' d'Branin said.

'No, impossible. We're in drive, they're light years away.' The edgy laughter sounded again. 'I'm not that good, Karoly. I've heard your Crey story, but I'm only a human. No, this is close. On the ship.'

'One of us?'

'Maybe,' Lassamer said. He rubbed his cheek absently. 'I can't sort it out.'

D'Branin put a fatherly hand on his shoulder. 'Thale, this feeling of yours – could it be that you are just tired? We have all of us been under strain. Inactivity can be taxing.'

'Get your hand off me,' Lasamer snapped.

D'Branin drew back his hand quickly.

'This is *real*,' the telepath insisted, 'and I don't need you thinking that maybe you shouldn't have taken me, all that crap. I'm as stable as anyone on this ... this ... how *dare* you think I'm unstable, you ought to look inside some of these others, Christopheris with his bottle and his dirty little fantasies, Dannel half sick with fear, Lommie and her machines, with her it's all metal and lights and cool circuits, sick, I tell you, and Jhirl's arrogant and Agatha whines even in her head to herself all the time, and Alys is empty, like a cow. You, you don't touch them, see into them, what do you know of *stable?* Losers, d'Branin, they've given you a bunch of losers, and I'm one of your best, so don't you go thinking that I'm not stable, not sane, you hear.' His blue eyes were fevered. 'Do you *hear?*'

'Easy,' d'Branin said. 'Easy, Thale, you're getting excited.'

The telepath blinked, and suddenly the wildness was gone. 'Excited?' he said. 'Yes.' He looked around guiltily. 'It's hard, Karoly, but listen to me, you must. I'm warning you. We're in danger.'

'I will listen,' d'Branin said, 'but I cannot act without more definite information. You must use your talent and get it for me, yes? You can do that.'

Lasamer nodded. 'Yes,' he said. 'Yes.' They talked quietly for more than an hour, and finally the telepath left peacefully.

Afterwards d'Branin went straight to the psipsych, who was lying in her sleepweb surrounded by medicines, complaining bitterly of aches. 'Interesting,' she said when d'Branin told her. 'I've felt something too, a sense of threat, very vague, diffuse. I thought it was me, the confinement, the boredom, the way I feel. My moods betray me at times. Did he say anything more specific?'

'No.'

'I'll make an effort to move around, read him, read the others, see what I can pick up. Although, if this is real, he should know it first. He's a one, I'm only a three.'

D'Branin nodded. 'He seems very receptive,' he said. 'He told me all kinds of things about the others.'

'Means nothing. Sometimes, when a telepath insists he is picking up everything, what it means is that he's picking up nothing at all. He imagines feelings, readings, to make up for those that will not come. I'll keep careful watch on him, d'Branin. Sometimes a talent can crack, slip into a kind of hysteria, and begin to broadcast instead of receive. In a closed environment, that's very dangerous.'

Karoly d'Branin nodded. 'Of course, of course.'

In another part of the ship, Royd Eris frowned.

*

'Have you noticed the clothing on that holograph he sends us?' Rojan Christopheris asked Alys Northwind. They were alone in one of the holds, reclining on a mat, trying to avoid the wet spot. The xenobiologist had lit a joystick. He offered it to his companion, but Northwind waved it away.

'A decade out of style, maybe more. My father wore shirts like that when he was a boy on Old Poseidon.'

'Eris has old-fashioned taste,' Alys Northwind said. 'So? I don't care what he wears. Me, I like my jumpsuits. They're comfortable. Don't care what people think.'

'You don't, do you?' Christopheris said, wrinkling his huge nose. She did not see the gesture. 'Well, you miss the point. What if that isn't really Eris? A projection can be anything, can be made up out of whole cloth. I don't think he really looks like that.'

'No?' Now her voice was curious. She rolled over and curled up beneath his arm, her heavy white breasts against his chest.

'What if he's sick, deformed, ashamed to be seen the way he really looks?' Christopheris said. 'Perhaps he has some disease. The Slow Plague can waste a person terribly, but it takes decades to kill, and there are other contagions – manthrax, new leprosy, the melt, Langamen's Disease, lots of them. Could be that Royd's self-imposed quarantine is just that. A quarantine. Think about it.'

Alys Northwind frowned. 'All this talk of Eris,' she said, 'is making me edgy.'

The xenobiologist sucked on his joystick and laughed. 'Welcome to the *Nightflyer*, then. The rest of us are already there.'

*

In the fifth week out, Melantha Jhirl pushed her pawn to the sixth rank and Royd saw that it was unstoppable and resigned. It was his eighth straight defeat at her hands in as many days. She was sitting cross-legged on the floor of the lounge, the chessmen spread out before her in front of a darkened viewscreen. Laughing, she swept them all away. 'Don't feel bad, Royd,' she told him. 'I'm an improved model. Always three moves ahead.'

'I should tie in my computer,' he replied. 'You'd never know.' His ghost materialized suddenly, standing in front of the viewscreen, and smiled at her.

'I'd know within three moves,' Melantha Jhirl said. 'Try it.'

They were the last victims of a chess fever that had swept the *Nightflyer* for more than a week. Initially it had been Christopheris who produced the set and urged people to play, but the others had lost interest quickly when Thale Lasamer sat down and beat them all, one by one. Everyone was certain that he'd done it by reading their minds, but the telepath was in a volatile, nasty mood, and no one dared voice the accusation. Melantha, however, had been able to defeat Lasamer without very much trouble. 'He isn't that good a player,' she told Royd afterwards, 'and if he's trying to lift ideas from me, he's getting gibberish. The improved model knows certain mental disciplines. I can shield myself well enough, thank you.' Christopheris and a few of the others then tried a game or two against Melantha, and were routed for their troubles. Finally Royd asked if he might play. Only Melantha and Karoly were willing to sit down with him over the board, and since Karoly could barely recall how the pieces moved from one moment to the next, that left Melantha and Royd as regular opponents. They both seemed to thrive on the games, though Melantha always won.

Melantha stood up and walked to the kitchen, stepping right through Royd's ghostly form, which she steadfastly refused to pretend was real. 'The rest of them walk around me,' Royd complained.

She shrugged, and found a bulb of beer in a storage compartment.

'When are you going to break down and let me behind your wall for a visit, captain?' she asked. 'Don't you get lonely back there? Sexually frustrated? Claustrophobic?'

'I have flown the *Nightflyer* all my life, Melantha,' Royd said. His projection, ignored, winked out. 'If I were subject to claustrophobia, sexual frustration, or loneliness, such a life would have been impossible. Surely that should be obvious to you, being as improved a model as you are?'

She took a squeeze of her beer and laughed her mellow, musical laugh at him. 'I'll solve you yet, captain,' she warned.

'Meanwhile,' he said, 'tell me some more lies about your life.'

*

'Have you ever heard of Jupiter?' the xenotech demanded of the others. She was drunk, lolling in her sleepweb in the cargo hold.

'Something to do with Earth,' said Lindran. 'The same myth system originated both names, I believe.'

'Jupiter,' the xenotech announced loudly, 'is a gas giant in the same solar system as Old Earth. Didn't know that, did you?'

'I've got more important things to occupy my mind than such trivia, Alys,' Lindran said.

Alys Northwind smiled down smugly. 'Listen, I'm talking to you. They were on the verge of exploring this Jupiter when the stardrive was discovered, oh, way back. After that, 'course, no one bothered with gas giants. Just slip into drive and find the habitable worlds, settle them, ignore the comets and the rocks and the gas giants – there's another star just a few light years away, and it has *more* habitable planets. But there were people who thought those Jupiters might have life, you know. Do you see?'

'I see that you're blind drunk,' Lindran said.

Christopheris looked annoyed. 'If there is intelligent life on the gas giants, it shows no interest in leaving them,' he snapped. 'All of the sentient species we have met up to now have originated on worlds similar to Earth, and most of them are oxygen breathers. Unless you're suggesting that the *volcryn* are from a gas giant?'

The xenotech pushed herself up to a sitting position and smiled conspiratorially. 'Not the *volcryn*,' she said. 'Royd Eris. Crack that forward bulkhead in the lounge, and watch the methane and ammonia come smoking out.' Her hand made a sensuous waving motion through the air, and she convulsed with giddy laughter.

*

The system was up and running. Cyberneticist Lommie Thorne sat at the master console, a featureless black plastic plate upon which the phantom images of a hundred keyboard configurations came and went in holographic display, vanishing and shifting even as she used them. Around her rose crystalline data grids, ranks of viewscreens and readout panels upon which columns of figures marched and geometric shapes did stately whirling dances, dark columns of seamless metal that contained the mind and soul of her system. She sat in the semi-darkness happily, whistling as she ran the computer through several simple routines, her fingers moving across the flickering keys with blind speed and quickening tempo. 'Ah,' she said once, smiling. Later, only, 'Good.'

Then it was time for the final run-through. Lommie Thorne slid back the metallic fabric of her left sleeve, pushed her wrist beneath the console, found the prongs, jacked herself in. Interface.

Ecstasy.

Inkblot shapes in a dozen glowing colors twisted and melded and broke apart on the readout screens.

In an instant it was over.

Lommie Thorne pulled free her wrist. The smile on her face was shy and satisfied, but across it lay another expression, the merest hint of puzzlement. She touched her thumb to the holes of her wrist jack, and found them warm to the touch, tingling. Lommie shivered.

The system was running perfectly, hardware in good condition, all software systems functioning according to plan, interface meshing well. It had been a delight, as it always was. When she joined with the system, she was wise beyond her years, and powerful, and full of light and electricity and the stuff of life, cool and clean and exciting to touch, and never alone, never small or weak. That was what it was always like when she interfaced and let herself expand.

But this time something had been different. Something cold had touched her, only for a moment. Something very cold and very frightening, and together she and the system had seen it clearly for a brief moment, and then it had been gone again.

The cyberneticist shook her head, and drove the nonsense out. She went back to work. After a time, she began to whistle.

*

During the sixth week, Alys Northwind cut herself badly while preparing a snack. She was standing in the kitchen, slicing a spiced meatstick with a long knife, when suddenly she screamed.

Dannel and Lindran rushed to her, and found her staring down in horror at the chopping block in front of her. The knife had taken off the first joint of the index finger on her left hand, and the blood was spreading in ragged spurts. 'The ship lurched,' Alys said numbly, staring up at Dannel. 'Didn't you feel it jerk? It pushed the knife to the side.'

'Get something to stop the bleeding,' Lindran said. Dannel looked around in panic. 'Oh, I'll do it myself,' Lindran finally said, and she did.

The psipsych, Agatha Marij-Black, gave Northwind a tranquilizer, then looked at the two linguists. 'Did you see it happen?'

'She did it herself, with the knife,' Dannel said.

From somewhere down the corridor, there came the sound of wild, hysterical laughter.

*

'I dampened him,' Marij-Black reported to Karoly d'Branin later the same day. 'Psionine-4. It will blunt his receptivity for several days, and I have more if he needs it.'

D'Branin wore a stricken look. 'We talked several times and I could see that Thale was becoming ever more fearful, but he could never tell me the why of it. Did you have to shut him off?'

The psipsych shrugged. 'He was edging into the irrational. Given his level of talent, if he'd gone over the edge he might have taken us all with him. You should never have taken a class one telepath, d'Branin. Too unstable.'

'We must communicate with an alien race. I remind you that is no easy task. The *volcryn* will be more alien than any sentients we have yet encountered. We needed class one skills if we were to have any hope of reaching them. And they have so much to teach us, my friend!'

'Glib,' she said, 'but you might have no working skills at all, given the condition of your class one. Half the time he's curled up into the fetal position in his sleepweb, half the time he's strutting and crowing and half mad with fear. He insists we're all in real physical danger, but he doesn't know why or from what. The worst of it is that I can't tell if he's really sensing something or simply having an acute attack of paranoia. He certainly displays some classic paranoid symptoms. Among other things, he insists that he's being watched. Perhaps his condition is completely unrelated to us, the *volcryn*, and his talent. I can't be sure.'

'What of your own talent?' d'Branin said. 'You are an empath, are you not?'

'Don't tell me my job,' she said sharply. 'I sexed with him last week. You don't get more proximity or better rapport for esping than that. Even under those conditions, I couldn't be sure of anything. His mind is a chaos, and his fear is so rank it stank up the sheets. I don't read anything from the others either, besides the ordinary tensions and frustrations. But I'm only a three, so that doesn't mean much. My abilities are limited. You know I haven't been feeling well, d'Branin. I can barely breathe on this ship. The air seems thick and heavy to me, my head throbs. I ought to stay in bed.'

'Yes, of course,' d'Branin said hastily. 'I did not mean to criticize. You have been doing all you can under difficult circumstances. How long will it be until Thale is with us again?'

The psipsych rubbed her temple wearily. 'I'm recommending we keep him dampened until the mission is over, d'Branin. I warn you, an insane or hysterical telepath is dangerous. That business with Northwind and the knife might have been his doing, you know. He started screaming not long after, remember. Maybe he'd touched her, for just an instant – oh, it's a wild idea, but it's possible. The point is, we don't take chances. I have enough psionine-4 to keep him numb and functional until we're back on Avalon.'

'*But* – Royd will take us out of drive soon, and we will make contact with the *volcryn*. We will need Thale, his mind, his talent. Is it vital to keep him dampened? Is there no other way?'

Marij-Black grimaced. 'My other option was an injection of esperon. It would have opened him up completely, increased his psionic receptivity tenfold for a few hours. Then, I'd hope, he could focus in on this danger he's feeling. Exorcise it if it's false, deal with it if it's real. But psionine-4 is a lot safer. Esperon is a hell of a drug, with devastating side effects. It raises the blood pressure dramatically, sometimes brings on hyperventilation or seizures, has even been known to stop the heart. Lasamer is young enough so that I'm not worried about that, but I don't think he has the emotional stability to deal with that kind of power. The psionine should tell us something. If his paranoia persists, I'll know it has nothing to do with his telepathy.'

'And if it does not persist?' Karoly d'Branin said.

Agatha Marij-Black smiled wickedly at him. 'If Lasamer becomes quiescent, and stops babbling about danger? Why, that would mean he was no longer picking up anything, wouldn't it? And *that* would mean there had been something to pick up, that he'd been right all along.'

*

At dinner that night, Thale Lasamer was quiet and distracted, eating in a rhythmic, mechanical sort of way, with a cloudy look in his blue eyes. Afterwards he excused himself and went straight to bed, falling into exhausted slumber almost immediately.

'What did you do to him?' Lommie Thorne asked Marij-Black.

'I shut off that prying mind of his,' she replied.

'You should have done it two weeks ago,' Lindran said. 'Docile, he's a lot easier to take.'

Karoly d'Branin hardly touched his food.

*

False night came, and Royd's wraith materialized while Karoly d'Branin sat brooding over his chocolate. 'Karoly,' the apparition said, 'would it be possible to tie in the computer your team brought on board with my shipboard system? Your *volcryn* stories fascinate me, and I would like to be able to study them further at my leisure. I assume the details of your investigation are in storage.'

'Certainly,' d'Branin replied in an offhand, distracted manner. 'Our system is up now. Patching it into the *Nightflyer* should present no problem. I will tell Lommie to attend to it tomorrow.'

Silence hung in the room heavily. Karoly d'Branin sipped at his chocolate and stared off into the darkness, almost unaware of Royd.

'You are troubled,' Royd said after a time.

'Eh? Oh, yes.' D'Branin looked up. 'Forgive me, my friend. I have much on my mind.'

'It concerns Thale Lasamer, does it not?'

Karoly d'Branin looked at the pale, luminescent figure across from him for a long time before he finally managed a stiff nod. 'Yes. Might I ask how you knew that?'

'I know everything that occurs on the *Nightflyer*,' Royd said.

'You have been watching us,' d'Branin said gravely, accusation in his tone. 'Then it is so, what Thale says, about us being watched. Royd, how could you? Spying is beneath you.'

The ghost's transparent eyes had no life in them, did not see. 'Do not tell the others,' Royd warned. 'Karoly, my friend – if I may call you my friend – I have my own reasons for watching, reasons it would not profit you to know. I mean you no harm. Believe that. You have hired me to take you safely to the *volcryn* and safely back, and I mean to do just that.'

'You are being evasive, Royd,' d'Branin said. 'Why do you spy on us? Do you watch everything? Are you a voyeur, some enemy, is that why you do not mix with us? Is watching all you intend to do?'

'Your suspicions hurt me, Karoly.'

'Your deception hurts me. Will you not answer me?'

'I have eyes and ears everywhere,' Royd said. 'There is no place to hide from me on the *Nightflyer*. Do I see everything? No, not always. I am only human, no matter what your colleagues might think. I sleep. The monitors remain on, but there is no one to observe them. I can only pay attention to one or two scenes or inputs at once. Sometimes I grow distracted, unobservant. I watch everything, Karoly, but I do not see everything.'

'Why?' D'Branin poured himself a fresh cup of chocolate, steadying his hand with an effort.

'I do not have to answer that question. The *Nightflyer* is my ship.'

D'Branin sipped chocolate, blinked, nodded to himself. 'You grieve me, my friend. You give me no choice. Thale said we were being watched, I now learn that he was right. He says also that we are in danger. Something alien, he says. You?'

The projection was still and silent.

D'Branin clucked. 'You do not answer. Ah, Royd, what am I to do? I must believe him, then. We are in danger, perhaps from you. I must abort our mission, then. Return us to Avalon, Royd. That is my decision.'

The ghost smiled wanly. 'So close, Karoly? Soon now we will be dropping out of drive.'

Karoly d'Branin made a small sad noise deep in his throat. 'My *volcryn,*' he said, sighing. 'So close – ah, it pains me to desert them. But I cannot do otherwise, I cannot.'

'You can,' said the voice of Royd Eris. 'Trust me. That is all I ask, Karoly. Believe me when I tell you that I have no sinister intentions. Thale Lasamer may speak of danger, but no one has been harmed so far, have they?'

'No,' admitted d'Branin. 'No, unless you count Alys, cutting herself this afternoon.'

'What?' Royd hesitated briefly. 'Cutting herself? I did not see, Karoly. When did this happen?'

'Oh, early – just before Lasamer began to scream and rant, I believe.'

'I see.' Royd's voice was thoughtful. 'I was watching Melantha go through her exercises,' he said finally, 'and talking to her. I did not notice. Tell me how it happened.'

D'Branin told him.

'Listen to me,' Royd said. 'Trust me, Karoly, and I will give you your *volcryn.* Calm your people. Assure them that I am no threat. And keep Lasamer drugged and quiescent, do you understand? That is very important. He is the problem.'

'Agatha advises much the same thing.'

'I know,' said Royd. 'I agree with her. Will you do as I ask?'

'I do not know,' d'Branin said. 'You make it hard for me. I do not understand what is going wrong, my friend. Will you not tell me more?'

Royd Eris did not answer. His ghost waited.

'Well,' d'Branin said at last, 'you do not talk. How difficult you make it. How soon, Royd? How soon will we see my *volcryn?*'

'Quite soon,' Royd replied. 'We will drop out of drive in approximately seventy hours.'

'Seventy hours,' d'Branin said. 'Such a short time. Going back would gain us nothing.' He moistened his lips, lifted his cup, found it empty. 'Go on, then. I will do as you bid. I will trust you, keep Lasamer drugged, I will not tell the others of your spying. Is that enough, then? Give me my *volcryn*. I have waited so long!'

'I know,' said Royd Eris. 'I know.'

Then the ghost was gone, and Karoly d'Branin sat alone in the darkened lounge. He tried to refill his cup, but his hand began to tremble unaccountably, and he poured the chocolate over his fingers and dropped the cup, swearing, wondering, hurting.

*

The next day was a day of rising tensions and a hundred small irritations. Lindran and Dannel had a 'private' argument that could be overheard through half the ship. A three-handed war game in the lounge ended in disaster when Christopheris accused Melantha Jhirl of cheating. Lommie Thorne complained of unusual difficulties in tying her system into the shipboard computers. Alys Northwind sat in the lounge for hours, staring at her bandaged finger with a look of sullen hatred on her face. Agatha Marij-Black prowled through the corridors, complaining that the ship was too hot, that her joints throbbed, that the air was thick and full of smoke, that the ship was too cold. Even Karoly d'Branin was despondent and on edge.

Only the telepath seemed content. Shot full of psionine-4, Thale Lasamer was often sluggish and lethargic, but at least he no longer flinched at shadows.

Royd Eris made no appearance, either by voice or holographic projection.

He was still absent at dinner. The academicians ate uneasily, expecting him to materialize at any moment, take his accustomed place, and join in the mealtime conversation. Their expectations were still unfulfilled when the after-dinner pots of chocolate and spiced tea and coffee were set on the table.

'Our captain seems to be occupied,' Melantha Jhirl observed, leaning back in her chair and swirling a snifter of brandy.

'We will be shifting out of drive soon,' Karoly d'Branin said. 'Undoubtedly there are preparations to make.' Secretly, he fretted over Royd's absence, and wondered if they were being watched even now.

Rojan Christopheris cleared his throat. 'Since we're all here and he's not, perhaps this is a good time to discuss certain things. I'm not concerned about him missing dinner. He doesn't eat. He's a damned hologram. What does it matter? Maybe it's just as well, we need to talk about this. Karoly, a lot of us have been getting uneasy about Royd Eris. What do you know about this mystery man anyway?'

'Know, my friend?' D'Branin refilled his cup with the thick bittersweet chocolate and sipped at it slowly, trying to give himself a moment to think. 'What is there to know?'

'Surely you've noticed that he never comes out to play with us,' Lindran said drily. 'Before you engaged his ship, did anyone remark on this quirk of his?'

'I'd like to know the answer to that one too,' said Dannel, the other linguist. 'A lot of traffic comes and goes through Avalon. How did you come to choose Eris? What were you told about him?'

'Told about him? Very little, I must admit. I spoke to a few port officials and charter companies, but none of them were acquainted with Royd. He had not traded out of Avalon originally, you see.'

'How convenient,' said Lindran.

'How suspicious,' added Dannel.

'Where *is* he from, then?' Lindran demanded. 'Dannel and I have listened to him pretty carefully. He speaks standard very flatly, with no discernible accent, no idiosyncrasies to betray his origins.'

'Sometimes he sounds a bit archaic,' Dannel put in, 'and from time to time one of his constructions will give me an association. Only it's a different one each time. He's traveled a lot.'

'Such a deduction,' Lindran said, patting his hand. 'Traders frequently do, love. Comes of owning a starship.'

Dannel glared at her, but Lindran just went on. 'Seriously, though, do you know anything about him? Where did this *Nightflyer* of ours come from?'

'I do not know,' d'Branin admitted. 'I – I never thought to ask.'

The members of his research team glanced at each other incredulously. 'You never thought to ask?' Christopheris said. 'How did you come to select this ship?'

'It was available. The administrative council approved my project and assigned me personnel, but they could not spare an Academy ship. There were budgetary constraints as well.'

Agatha Marij-Black laughed sourly. 'What d'Branin is telling those of you who haven't figured it out is that the Academy was pleased with his studies in xenomyth, with the discovery of the *volcryn* legend, but less than enthusiastic about his plan to seek them out. So they gave him a small budget to keep him happy and productive, assuming this little mission would be fruitless, and they assigned him people who wouldn't be missed back on Avalon.' She looked around. 'Look at the lot of you. None of us had worked with d'Branin in the early stages, but we were all available for this jaunt. And not a one of us is a first-rate scholar.'

'Speak for yourself,' Melantha Jhirl said. 'I volunteered for this mission.'

'I won't argue the point,' the psipsych said. 'The crux is that the choice of the *Nightflyer* is no large enigma. You just engaged the cheapest charter you could find, didn't you, d'Branin?'

'Some of the available ships would not consider my proposition,' d'Branin said. 'The sound of it is odd, we must admit. And many shipmasters have an almost superstitious fear of dropping out of drive in interstellar space, without a planet near. Of those who would agree to the conditions, Royd Eris offered the best terms, and he was able to leave at once.'

'And we *had* to leave at once,' said Lindran. 'Otherwise the *volcryn* might get away. They've only been passing through this region for ten thousand years, give or take a few thousand.'

Someone laughed. D'Branin was nonplussed. 'Friends, no doubt I could have postponed departure. I admit I was eager to meet my *volcryn*, to see their great ships and ask them all the questions that have haunted me, to discover the why of them. But I admit also that a delay would have been no great hardship. But why? Royd has been a gracious host, a good pilot. We have been treated well.'

'Did you meet him?' Alys Northwind asked. 'When you were making your arrangements, did you ever see him?'

'We spoke many times, but I was on Avalon, and Royd in orbit. I saw his face on my viewscreen.'

'A projection, a computer simulation, could be anything,' Lommie Thorne said. 'I can have my system conjure up all sorts of faces for your viewscreen, Karoly.'

'No one has ever seen this Royd Eris,' Christopheris said. 'He has made himself a cipher from the start.'

'Our host wishes his privacy to remain inviolate,' d'Branin said.

'Evasions,' Lindran said. 'What is he hiding?'

Melantha Jhirl laughed. When all eyes had moved to her, she grinned and shook her head. 'Captain Royd is perfect, a strange man for a strange mission. Don't any of you love a mystery? Here we are flying light years to intercept a hypothetical alien starship from the core of the galaxy that has been outward bound for longer than humanity has been having wars, and all of you are upset because you can't count the warts on Royd's nose.' She leaned across the table to refill her brandy snifter. 'My mother was right,' she said lightly. 'Normals are subnormal.'

'Maybe we should listen to Melantha,' Lommie Thorne said thoughtfully. 'Royd's foibles and neuroses are his business, if he does not impose them on us.'

'It makes me uncomfortable,' Dannel complained weakly.

'For all we know,' said Alys Northwind, 'we might be traveling with a criminal or an alien.'

'*Jupiter*,' someone muttered. The xenotech flushed red and there was sniggering around the long table.

But Thale Lasamer looked up furtively from his plate, and giggled. 'An *alien*,' he said. His blue eyes flicked back and forth in his skull, as if seeking escape. They were bright and wild.

Marij-Black swore. 'The drug is wearing off,' she said quickly to d'Branin. 'I'll have to go back to my cabin to get some more.'

'What drug?' Lommie Thorne demanded. D'Branin had been careful not to tell the others too much about Lasamer's ravings, for fear of inflaming the shipboard tensions. 'What's going on?'

'Danger,' Lasamer said. He turned to Lommie, sitting next to him, and grasped her forearm hard, his long painted fingernails clawing at the silvery metal of her shirt. 'We're in danger, I tell you, I'm reading it. Something *alien*. It means us ill. Blood, I see blood.' He laughed. 'Can you taste it, Agatha? I can almost taste the blood. *It* can, too.'

Marij-Black rose. 'He's not well,' she announced to the others. 'I've been dampening him with psionine, trying to hold his delusions in check. I'll get some more.' She started towards the door.

'Dampening him?' Christopheris said, horrified. 'He's warning us of something. Don't you hear him? I want to know what it *is*.'

'Not psionine,' said Melantha Jhirl. 'Try esperon.'

'Don't tell me my job, woman!'

'Sorry,' Melantha said. She gave a modest shrug. 'I'm one step ahead of you, though. Esperon might exorcise his delusions, no?'

'Yes, but—'

'And it might help him focus on this threat he claims to detect, correct?'

'I know the characteristics of esperon quite well,' the psipsych said testily.

Melantha smiled over the rim of her brandy glass. 'I'm sure you do. Now listen to me. All of you are anxious about Royd, it seems. You can't stand not knowing whatever it is he's concealing. Rojan has been making up stories for weeks, and he's ready to believe any of them. Alys is so nervous she cut her finger off. We're squabbling constantly. Fears like that won't help us work together as a team. Let's end them. Easy enough.' She pointed to Thale. 'Here sits a class one telepath. Boost his power with esperon and he'll be able to recite our captain's life history to us, until we're all suitably bored with it. Meanwhile he'll also be vanquishing his personal demons.'

'*He's watching us,*' the telepath said in a low, urgent voice.

'No,' said Karoly d'Branin, 'we must keep Thale dampened.'

'Karoly,' Christopheris said, 'this has gone too far. Several of us are nervous and this boy is terrified. I believe we all need an end to the mystery of Royd Eris. For once, Melantha is right.'

'We have no right,' d'Branin said.

'We have the need,' said Lommie Thorne. 'I agree with Melantha.'

'Yes,' echoed Alys Northwind. The two linguists were nodding.

D'Branin thought regretfully of his promise to Royd. They were not giving him any choice. His eyes met those of the psipsych, and he sighed. 'Do it, then,' he said. 'Get him the esperon.'

'*He's going to kill me.*' Thale Lasamer screamed. He leapt to his feet, and when Lommie Thorne tried to calm him with a hand on his arm, he seized a cup of coffee and threw it square in her face. It took three of them to hold him down. 'Hurry,' Christopheris barked, as the telepath struggled.

Marij-Black shuddered and left the lounge.

*

When she returned, the others had lifted Lasamer to the table and forced him down, pulling aside his long pale hair to bare the arteries in his neck.

Marij-Black moved to his side.

'Stop that,' Royd said. 'There is no need.'

His ghost shimmered into being in its empty chair at the head of the long dinner table. The psipsych froze in the act of slipping an ampule of esperon into her injection gun, and Alys Northwind startled visibly and released one of Lasamer's arms. The captive did not pull free. He lay on the table, breathing heavily, his pale blue eyes fixed glassily on Royd's projection, transfixed by the vision of his sudden materialization.

Melantha Jhirl lifted her brandy glass in salute. 'Boo,' she said. 'You've missed dinner, captain.'

'Royd,' said Karoly d'Branin, 'I am sorry.'

The ghost stared unseeing at the far wall. 'Release him,' said the voice from the communicators. 'I will tell you my great secrets, if my privacy intimidates you so.'

'He *has* been watching us,' Dannel said.

'We're listening,' Northwind said suspiciously. 'What are you?'

'I liked your guess about the gas giants,' Royd said. 'Sadly, the truth is less dramatic. I am an ordinary *homo sapiens* in middle age. Sixty-eight standard, if you require precision. The hologram you see before you is the real Royd Eris, or was so some years ago. I am somewhat older now, but I use computer simulation to project a more youthful appearance to my guests.'

'Oh?' Lommie Thorne's face was red where the coffee had scalded her. 'Then why the secrecy?'

'I will begin the tale with my mother,' Royd replied. 'The *Nightflyer* was her ship originally, custom-built to her design in the Newholme space-yards. My mother was a freetrader, a notably successful one. She was born trash on a world called Vess, which is a very long way from here, although perhaps some of you have heard of it. She worked her way up, position by position, until she won her own command. She soon made a fortune through a willingness to accept the unusual consignment, fly off the major trade routes, take her cargo a month or a year or two years beyond where it was customarily transferred. Such practices are riskier but more profitable than flying the mail runs. My mother did not worry about how often she and her crews returned home. Her ships were her home. She forgot about Vess as soon as she left it, and seldom visited the same world twice if she could avoid it.'

'Adventurous,' Melantha Jhirl said.

'No,' said Royd. 'Sociopathic. My mother did not like people, you see. Not at all. Her crews had no love for her, nor she for them. Her one great dream was to free herself from the necessity of crew altogether. When she grew rich enough, she had it done. The *Nightflyer* was the result. After she boarded it at Newholme, she never touched a human being again, or walked a planet's surface. She did all her business from the compartments that are now mine, by viewscreen or lasercom. You would call her insane. You would be right.' The ghost smiled faintly. 'She did have an interesting life, though, even after her isolation. The worlds she saw, Karoly! The things she might have told you would break your heart, but you'll never hear them. She destroyed most of her records for fear that other people might get some use or pleasure from her experiences after her death. She was like that.'

'And you?' asked Alys Northwind.

'She must have touched at least *one* other human being,' Lindran put in, with a smile.

'I should not call her my mother,' Royd said. 'I am her cross-sex clone. After thirty years of flying this ship alone, she was bored. I was to be her companion and lover. She could shape me to be a perfect diversion. She had no patience with children, however, and no desire to raise me herself. After she had done the cloning, I was sealed in a nurturant tank, an embryo linked into her computer. It was my teacher. Before birth and after. I had no birth, really. Long after the time a normal child would have been born, I remained in the tank, growing, learning, on slow-time, blind and dreaming and living through tubes. I was to be released when I had attained the age of puberty, at which time she guessed I would be fit company.'

'How horrible,' Karoly d'Branin said. 'Royd, my friend, I did not know.'

'I'm sorry, captain,' Melantha Jhirl said. 'You were robbed of your childhood.'

'I never missed it,' Royd said. 'Nor her. Her plans were all futile, you see. She died a few months after the cloning, when I was still a fetus in the tank. She had programmed the ship for such an eventuality, however. It dropped out of drive and shut down, drifted in interstellar space for eleven standard years while the computer made—' He stopped, smiling. 'I was going to say *while the computer made me a human being*. Well, while the computer made me whatever I am, then. That was how I inherited the *Nightflyer*. When I was born, it took me some months to acquaint myself with the operation of the ship and my own origins.'

'Fascinating,' said Karoly d'Branin.

'Yes,' said the linguist Lindran, 'but it doesn't explain why you keep yourself in isolation.'

'Ah, but it does,' Melantha Jhirl said. 'Captain, perhaps you should explain further for the less improved models.'

'My mother hated planets,' Royd said. 'She hated stinks and dirt and bacteria, the irregularity of the weather, the sight of other people. She engineered for us a flawless environment, as sterile as she could possibly make it. She disliked gravity as well. She was accustomed to weightlessness from years of service on ancient freetraders that could not afford gravity grids, and she preferred it. These were the conditions under which I was born and raised.

'My body has no immune systems, no natural resistance to anything. Contact with any of you would probably kill me, and would certainly make me very sick. My muscles are feeble, in a sense atrophied. The gravity the *Nightflyer* is now generating is for your comfort, not mine. To me it is agony. At this moment the real me is seated in a floating chair that supports my weight. I still hurt, and my internal organs may be suffering damage. It is one reason why I do not often take on passengers.'

'You share your mother's opinion of the run of humanity?' asked Marij-Black.

'I do not. I like people. I accept what I am, but I did not choose it. I experience human life in the only way I can, vicariously. I am a voracious consumer of books, tapes, holoplays, fictions and drama and histories of all sorts. I have experimented with dreamdust. And infrequently, when I dare, I carry passengers. At those times, I drink in as much of their lives as I can.'

'If you kept your ship under weightlessness at all times, you could take on more riders,' suggested Lommie Thorne.

'True,' Royd said politely. 'I have found, however, that most planet-born are as uncomfortable weightless as I am under gravity. A shipmaster who does not have artificial gravity, or elects not to use it, attracts few riders. The exceptions often spend much of the voyage sick or drugged. No. I could also mingle with my passengers, I know, if I kept to my chair and wore a sealed environ-wear suit. I have done so. I find it lessens my participation instead of increasing it. I become a freak, a maimed thing, one who must be treated differently and kept at a distance. These things do not suit my purpose. I prefer isolation. As often as I dare, I study the aliens I take on as riders.'

'Aliens?' Northwind's voice was confused.

'You are all aliens to me,' Royd answered.

Silence filled the *Nightflyer*'s lounge.

'I am sorry this has happened, my friend,' Karoly d'Branin said. 'We ought not have intruded on your personal affairs.'

'Sorry,' muttered Agatha Marij-Black. She frowned and pushed the ampule of esperon into the injection chamber. 'Well, it's glib enough, but is it the truth? We still have no proof, just a new bedtime story. The hologram could have claimed it was a creature from Jupiter, a computer, or a diseased war criminal just as easily. We have no way of verifying anything that he's said. No – we have one way, rather.' She took two quick steps forward to where Thale Lasamer lay on the table. 'He still needs treatment and we still need confirmation, and I don't see any sense in stopping now after we've gone this far. Why should we live with all this anxiety if we can end it all now?' Her hand pushed the telepath's unresisting head to one side. She found the artery and pressed the gun to it.

'Agatha,' said Karoly d'Branin. 'Don't you think . . . perhaps we should forgo this, now that Royd . . . ?'

'NO.' Royd said. 'Stop. I order it. This is my ship. Stop, or . . .'

'. . . or what?' The gun hissed loudly, and there was a red mark on the telepath's neck when she lifted it away.

Lasamer raised himself to a half-sitting position, supported by his elbows, and Marij-Black moved close to him. 'Thale,' she said in her best professional tones, 'focus on Royd. You can do it, we all know how good you are. Wait just a moment, the esperon will open it all up for you.'

His pale blue eyes were clouded. 'Not close enough,' he muttered. 'One, I'm one, tested. Good, you know I'm good, but I got to be *close*.' He trembled.

The psipsych put an arm around him, stroked him, coaxed him. 'The esperon will give you range, Thale,' she said. 'Feel it, feel yourself grow stronger. Can you feel it? Everything's getting clear, isn't it?' Her voice was a reassuring drone. 'You can hear what I'm thinking, I know you can, but never mind that. The others too, push them aside, all that chatter, thoughts, desires, fear. Push it all aside. Remember the danger now? Remember? Go find it, Thale, go find the danger. Look beyond the wall there, tell us what it's like beyond the wall. Tell us about Royd. Was he telling the truth? Tell us. You're good, we all know that, you can tell us.' The phrases were almost an incantation.

He shrugged off her support and sat upright by himself. 'I can feel it,' he said. His eyes were suddenly clearer. 'Something – my head hurts – I'm *afraid!*'

'Don't be afraid,' said Marij-Black. 'The esperon won't make your head hurt, it just makes you better. We're all here with you. Nothing to fear.' She stroked his brow. 'Tell us what you see.'

Thale Lasamer looked at Royd's ghost with terrified little-boy eyes, and his tongue flicked across his lower lips. 'He's—'

Then his skull exploded.

*

Hysteria and confusion.

The telepath's head had burst with awful force, splattering them all with blood and bits of bone and flesh. His body thrashed madly on the tabletop for a long instant, blood spurting from the arteries in his neck in a crimson stream, his limbs twitching in a macabre dance. His head had simply ceased to exist, but he would not be still.

Agatha Marij-Black, who had been standing closest to him, dropped her injection gun and stood slack-mouthed. She was drenched with his blood, covered with pieces of flesh and brain. Beneath her right eye, a long sliver of bone had penetrated her skin, and her own blood was mingling with his. She did not seem to notice.

Rojan Christopheris fell over backwards, scrambled to his feet, and pressed himself hard against the wall.

Dannel screamed, and screamed, and screamed, until Lindran slapped him hard across a blood-smeared cheek and told him to be quiet.

Alys Northwind dropped to her knees and began to mumble a prayer in a strange tongue.

Karoly d'Branin sat very still, staring, blinking, his chocolate cup forgotten in his hand.

'Do something,' Lommie Thorne moaned. 'Somebody *do* something.' One of Lasamer's arms moved feebly, and brushed against her. She shrieked and pulled away.

Melantha Jhirl pushed aside her brandy snifter. 'Control yourself,' she snapped. 'He's dead, he can't hurt you.'

They all looked at her, but for d'Branin and Marij-Black, both of whom seemed frozen in shock. Royd's projection had vanished at some point, Melantha realized suddenly. She began to give orders. 'Dannel, Lindran, Rojan – find a sheet or something to wrap him in, and get him out of here. Alys, you and Lommie get some water and sponges. We've got to clean up.' Melantha moved to d'Branin's side as the others rushed to do as she had told them. 'Karoly,' she said, putting a gentle hand on his shoulder, 'are you all right, Karoly?'

He looked up at her, gray eyes blinking. 'I – yes, yes, I am – I told her not to go ahead, Melantha. I told her.'

'Yes you did,' Melantha Jhirl said. She gave him a reassuring pat and moved around the table to Agatha Marij-Black. 'Agatha,' she called. But the psipsych did not respond, not even when Melantha shook her bodily by the shoulders. Her eyes were empty. 'She's in shock,' Melantha announced. She frowned at the sliver of bone protruding from Marij-Black's cheek. Sponging off her face with a napkin, she carefully removed the splinter.

'What do we do with the body?' asked Lindran. They had found a sheet and wrapped it up. It had finally stopped twitching, although blood continued to seep out, turning the concealing sheet red.

'Put it in a cargo hold,' suggested Christopheris.

'No,' Melantha said, 'not sanitary. It will rot.' She thought for a moment. 'Suit up and take it down to the driveroom. Cycle it through and lash it in place somehow. Tear up the sheet if you have to. That section of the ship is vacuum. It will be best there.'

Christopheris nodded, and the three of them moved off, the dead weight of Lasamer's corpse supported between them. Melantha turned back to Marij-Black, but only for an instant. Lommie Thorne, who was mopping the blood from the tabletop with a piece of cloth, suddenly began to retch violently. Melantha swore. 'Someone help her,' she snapped.

Karoly d'Branin finally seemed to stir. He rose and took the blood-soaked cloth from Lommie's hand, and led her away back to his cabin.

'I can't do this alone,' whined Alys Northwind, turning away in disgust.

'Help me, then,' Melantha said. Together she and Northwind half-led and half-carried the psipsych from the lounge, cleaned her and undressed her, and put her to sleep with a shot of one of her own drugs. Afterwards Melantha took the injection gun and made the rounds. Northwind and Lommie Thorne required mild tranquilizers, Dannel a somewhat stronger one.

It was three hours before they met again.

*

The survivors assembled in the largest of the cargo holds, where three of them hung their sleepwebs. Seven of eight attended. Agatha Marij-Black was still unconscious, sleeping or in a coma or deep shock; none of them were sure. The rest seemed to have recovered, though their faces were pale and drawn. All of them had changed clothes, even Alys Northwind, who had slipped into a new jumpsuit identical to the old one.

'I do not understand,' Karoly d'Branin said. 'I do not understand what . . .'

'Royd killed him, is all,' Northwind said bitterly. 'His secret was endangered so he just – just blew him apart. We all saw it.'

'I cannot believe that,' Karoly d'Branin said in an anguished voice. 'I cannot. Royd and I, we have talked, talked many a night when the rest of you were sleeping. He is gentle, inquisitive, sensitive. A dreamer. He understands about the *volcryn*. He would not do such a thing, could not.'

'His projection certainly winked out quick enough when it happened,' Lindran said. 'And you'll notice he hasn't had much to say since.'

'The rest of us haven't been unusually talkative either,' said Melantha Jhirl. 'I don't know what to think, but my impulse is to side with Karoly. We have no proof that the captain was responsible for Thale's death. There's something here none of us understands yet.'

Alys Northwind grunted. 'Proof,' she said disdainfully.

'In fact,' Melantha continued unperturbed, 'I'm not even sure *anyone* is responsible. Nothing happened until he was given the esperon. Could the drug be at fault?'

'Hell of a side effect,' Lindran muttered.

Rojan Christopheris frowned. 'This is not my field, but I would think, no. Esperon is extremely potent, with both physical and psionic side effects verging on the extreme, but not *that* extreme.'

'What, then?' said Lommie Thorne. 'What killed him?'

'The instrument of death was probably his own talent,' the xenobiologist said, 'undoubtedly augmented by the drug. Besides boosting his principal power, his telepathic sensitivity, esperon would also tend to bring out other psi-talents that might have been latent in him.'

'Such as?' Lommie demanded.

'Biocontrol. Telekinesis.'

Melantha Jhirl was way ahead of him. 'Esperon shoots blood pressure way up anyway. Increase the pressure in his skull even more by rushing all the blood in his body to his brain. Decrease the air pressure around his head simultaneously, using teke to induce a short-lived vacuum. Think about it.'

They thought about it, and none of them liked it.

'Who could do such a thing?' Karoly d'Branin said. 'It could only have been self-induced, his own talent wild out of control.'

'Or turned against him by a greater talent,' Alys Northwind said stubbornly.

'No human telepath has talent on that order, to seize control of someone else, body and mind and soul, even for an instant.'

'Exactly,' the stout xenotech replied. 'No *human* telepath.'

'Gas giant people?' Lommie Thorne's tone was mocking.

Alys Northwind stared her down. 'I could talk about Crey sensitives or *githyanki* soulsucks, name a half-dozen others off the top of my head, but I don't need to. I'll only name one. A Hrangan Mind.'

That was a disquieting thought. All of them fell silent and stirred uneasily, thinking of the vast, inimical power of a Hrangan Mind hidden in the command chambers of the *Nightflyer*, until Melantha Jhirl broke the spell with a short, derisive laugh. 'You're frightening yourself with shadows, Alys,' she said. 'What you're saying is ridiculous, if you stop to think about it. I hope that isn't too much to ask. You're supposed to be xenologists, the lot of you, experts in alien languages, psychology, biology, technology. You don't act the part. We warred with Old Hranga for a thousand years, but we *never* communicated successfully with a Hrangan Mind. If Royd Eris is a Hrangan, they've improved their conversational skills markedly in the centuries since the Collapse.'

Alys Northwind flushed. 'You're right,' she said. 'I'm jumpy.'

'Friends,' said Karoly d'Branin, 'we must not let our actions be dictated by panic or hysteria. A terrible thing has happened. One of our colleagues is dead, and we do not know why. Until we do, we can only go on. This is no time for rash actions against the innocent. Perhaps, when we return to Avalon, an investigation will tell us what happened. The body is safe for examination, is it not?'

'We cycled it through the airlock into the driveroom,' Dannel said. 'It'll keep.'

'And it can be studied closely on our return,' d'Branin said.

'Which should be immediate,' said Northwind. 'Tell Eris to turn this ship around!'

D'Branin looked stricken. 'But the *volcryn!* A week more and we shall know them, if my figures are correct. To return would take us six weeks. Surely it is worth one additional week to know that they exist? Thale would not have wanted his death to be for nothing.'

'Before he died, Thale was raving about aliens, about danger,' Northwind insisted. 'We're rushing to meet some aliens. What if they're the danger? Maybe these *volcryn* are even more potent than a Hrangan Mind, and maybe they don't want to be met, or investigated, or observed. What

about that, Karoly? You ever think about that? Those stories of yours –
don't some of them talk about terrible things happening to the races that
meet the *volcryn?*'

'Legends,' d'Branin said. 'Superstition.'

'A whole Fyndii horde vanishes in one legend,' Rojan Christopheris put
in.

'We cannot put credence in these fears of others,' d'Branin argued.

'Perhaps there's nothing to the stories,' Northwind said, 'but do you care
to risk it? *I* don't. For what? Your sources may be fictional or exaggerated
or wrong, your interpretations and computations may be in error, or they
may have changed course – the *volcryn* may not even be within light years
of where we'll drop out.'

'Ah,' Melantha Jhirl said, 'I understand. Then we shouldn't go on
because they won't be there, and besides, they might be dangerous.'

D'Branin smiled and Lindran laughed. 'Not funny,' protested Alys
Northwind, but she argued no further.

'No,' Melantha continued, 'any danger we are in will not increase
significantly in the time it will take us to drop out of drive and look about
for *volcryn*. We have to drop out anyway, to reprogram for the shunt home.
Besides, we've come a long way for these *volcryn*, and I admit to being
curious.' She looked at each of them in turn, but no one spoke. 'We
continue, then.'

'And Royd?' demanded Christopheris. 'What do we do about him?'

'What *can* we do?' said Dannel.

'Treat the Captain as before,' Melantha said decisively. 'We should open
lines to him and talk. Maybe now we can clear up some of the mysteries
that are bothering us, if Royd is willing to discuss things frankly.'

'He is probably as shocked and dismayed as we are, my friends,' said
d'Branin. 'Possibly he is fearful that we will blame him, try to hurt him.'

'I think we should cut through to his section of the ship and drag him
out kicking and screaming,' Christopheris said. 'We have the tools. That
would write a quick end to all our fears.'

'It could kill Royd,' Melantha said. 'Then he'd be justified in anything he
did to stop us. He controls this ship. He could do a great deal, if he decided
we were his enemies.' She shook her head vehemently. 'No, Rojan, we
can't attack Royd. We've got to reassure him. I'll do it, if no one else wants
to talk to him.' There were no volunteers. 'All right. But I don't want any
of you trying any foolish schemes. Go about your business. Act normally.'

Karoly d'Branin was nodding agreement. 'Let us put Royd and poor
Thale from our minds, and concern ourselves with our work, with our
preparations. Our sensory instruments must be ready for deployment as
soon as we shift out of drive and reenter normal space, so we can find our

quarry quickly. We must review everything we know of the *volcryn*.' He turned to the linguists and began discussing some of the preliminaries he expected of them, and in a short time the talk had turned to the *volcryn*, and bit by bit the fear drained out of the group.

Lommie Thorne sat listening quietly, her thumb absently rubbing her wrist implant, but no one noticed the thoughtful look in her eyes.

Not even Royd Eris, watching.

*

Melantha Jhirl returned to the lounge alone.

Someone had turned out the lights. 'Captain?' she said softly.

He appeared to her; pale, glowing softly, with eyes that did not see. His clothes, filmy and out-of-date, were all shades of white and faded blue. 'Hello, Melantha,' the mellow voice said from the communicators, as the ghost silently mouthed the same words.

'Did you hear, captain?'

'Yes,' he said, his voice vaguely tinged by surprise. 'I hear and I see everything on my *Nightflyer*, Melantha. Not only in the lounge, and not only when the communicators and viewscreens are on. How long have you known?'

'Known?' She smiled. 'Since you praised Alys' gas giant solution to the Roydian mystery. The communicators were not on that night. You had no way of knowing. Unless . . .'

'I have never made a mistake before,' Royd said. 'I told Karoly, but that was deliberate. I am sorry. I have been under stress.'

'I believe you, captain,' she said. 'No matter. I'm the improved model, remember? I'd guessed weeks ago.'

For a time Royd said nothing. Then: 'When do you begin to reassure me?'

'I'm doing so right now. Don't you feel reassured yet?'

The apparition gave a ghostly shrug. 'I am pleased that you and Karoly do not think I murdered that man. Otherwise, I am frightened. Things are getting out of control, Melantha. Why didn't she listen to me? I told Karoly to keep him dampened. I told Agatha not to give him that injection. I warned them.'

'They were afraid, too,' Melantha said. 'Afraid that you were only trying to frighten them off, to protect some awful plan. I don't know. It was my fault, in a sense. I was the one who suggested esperon. I thought it would put Thale at ease, and tell us something about you. I was curious.' She frowned. 'A deadly curiosity. Now I have blood on my hands.'

Melantha's eyes were adjusting to the darkness in the lounge. By the faint light of the holograph, she could see the table where it had happened, dark streaks of drying blood across its surface among the plates and cups and cold pots of tea and chocolate. She heard a faint dripping as well, and could not tell if it was blood or coffee. She shivered. 'I don't like it in here.'

'If you would like to leave, I can be with you wherever you go.'

'No,' she said. 'I'll stay. Royd, I think it might be better if you were *not* with us wherever we go. If you kept silent and out of sight, so to speak. If I asked you to, would you shut off your monitors throughout the ship? Except for the lounge, perhaps. It would make the others feel better, I'm sure.'

'They don't know.'

'They will. You made that remark about gas giants in everyone's hearing. Some of them have probably figured it out by now.'

'If I told you I had cut myself off, you would have no way of knowing whether it was the truth.'

'I could trust you,' Melantha Jhirl said.

Silence. The spectre stared at her. 'As you wish,' Royd's voice said finally. 'Everything off. Now I see and hear only in here. Now, Melantha, you must promise to control them. No secret schemes, or attempts to breach my quarters. Can you do that?'

'I think so,' she said.

'Did you believe my story?' Royd asked.

'Ah,' she said. 'A strange and wondrous story, captain. If it's a lie, I'll swap lies with you any time. You do it well. If it's true, then you are a strange and wondrous man.'

'It's true,' the ghost said quietly. 'Melantha . . .'

'Yes?'

'Does it bother you that I have . . . watched you? Watched you when you were not aware?'

'A little,' she said, 'but I think I can understand it.'

'I watched you copulating.'

She smiled. 'Ah,' she said, 'I'm good at it.'

'I wouldn't know,' Royd said. 'You're good to watch.'

Silence. She tried not to hear the steady, faint dripping off to her right. 'Yes,' she said after a long hesitation.

'Yes? What?'

'Yes, Royd,' she said, 'I would probably sex with you if it were possible.'

'*How did you know what I was thinking?*' Royd's voice was suddenly frightened, full of anxiety and something close to fear.

'Easy,' Melantha said, startled. 'I'm an improved model. It wasn't so difficult to figure out. I told you, remember? I'm three moves ahead of you.'

'You're not a telepath, are you?'

'No,' Melantha said. 'No.'

Royd considered that for a long time. 'I believe I'm reassured,' he said at last.

'Good,' she said.

'Melantha,' he added, 'one thing. Sometimes it is not wise to be too many moves ahead. Do you understand?'

'Oh? No, not really. You frighten me. Now reassure me. Your turn, captain Royd.'

'Of what?'

'What happened in here? Really?'

Royd said nothing.

'I think you know something,' Melantha said. 'You gave up your secret to stop us from injecting Lasamer with esperon. Even after your secret was forfeit, you ordered us not to go ahead. Why?'

'Esperon is a dangerous drug,' Royd said.

'More than that, captain,' Melantha said. 'You're evading. What killed Thale Lasamer? Or is it *who*?'

'*I* didn't.'

'One of us? The *volcryn*?'

Royd said nothing.

'Is there an alien aboard your ship, captain?'

Silence.

'Are we in danger? Am *I* in danger, captain? I'm not afraid. Does that make me a fool?'

'I like people,' Royd said at last. 'When I can stand it, I like to have passengers. I watch them, yes. It's not so terrible. I like you and Karoly especially. I won't let anything happen to you.'

'What might happen?'

Royd said nothing.

'And what about the others, Royd? Christopheris and Northwind, Dannel and Lindran, Lommie Thorne? Are you taking care of them, too? Or only Karoly and I?'

No reply.

'You're not very talkative tonight,' Melantha observed.

'I'm under strain,' his voice replied. 'And certain things you are safer not to know. Go to bed, Melantha Jhirl. We've talked long enough.'

'All right, captain,' she said. She smiled at the ghost and lifted her hand. His own rose to meet it. Warm dark flesh and pale radiance brushed, melded, were one. Melantha Jhirl turned to go. It was not until she was out in the corridor, safe in the light once more, that she began to tremble.

*

False midnight.

The talks had broken up, and one by one the academicians had gone to bed. Even Karoly d'Branin had retired, his appetite for chocolate quelled by his memories of the lounge.

The linguists had made violent, noisy love before giving themselves up to sleep, as if to reaffirm their life in the face of Thale Lasamer's grisly death. Rojan Christopheris had listened to music. But now they were all still.

The *Nightflyer* was filled with silence.

In the darkness of the largest cargo hold, three sleepwebs hung side by side. Melantha Jhirl twisted occasionally in her sleep, her face feverish, as if in the grip of some nightmare. Alys Northwind lay flat on her back, snoring loudly, a reassuring wheeze of noise from her solid, meaty chest.

Lommie Thorne lay awake, thinking.

Finally she rose and dropped to the floor, nude, quiet, light and careful as a cat. She pulled on a tight pair of pants, slipped a wide-sleeved shirt of black metallic cloth over her head, belted it with a silver chain, shook out her short hair. She did not don her boots. Barefoot was quieter. Her feet were small and soft, with no trace of callus.

She moved to the middle sleepweb and shook Alys Northwind by her shoulder. The snoring stopped abruptly. 'Huh?' the xenotech said. She grunted in annoyance.

'Come,' whispered Lommie Thorne. She beckoned.

Northwind got heavily to her feet, blinking, and followed the cyberneticist through the door, out into the corridor. She'd been sleeping in her jumpsuit, its seam open nearly to her crotch. She frowned and sealed it. 'What the hell,' she muttered. She was disarrayed and unhappy.

'There's a way to find out if Royd's story was true,' Lommie Thorne said carefully. 'Melantha won't like it, though. Are you game to try?'

'What?' Northwind asked. Her face betrayed her interest.

'Come,' the cyberneticist said.

They moved silently through the ship, to the computer room. The system was up, but dormant. They entered quietly; all empty. Currents of light ran silkily down crystalline channels in the data grids, meeting, joining, splitting apart again; rivers of wan multihued radiance crisscrossing a black landscape. The chamber was dim, the only noise a buzz at the edge of human hearing, until Lommie Thorne moved through it, touching keys, tripping switches, directing the silent luminescent currents. Bit by bit the machine woke.

'What are you *doing?*' Alys Northwind said.

'Karoly told me to tie in our system with the ship,' Lommie Thorne replied as she worked. 'I was told Royd wanted to study the *volcryn* data.

Fine, I did it. Do you understand what that means?' Her shirt whispered in soft metallic tones when she moved.

Eagerness broke across the flat features of xenotech Alys Northwind. 'The two systems are tied together!'

'Exactly. So Royd can find out about the *volcryn*, and we can find out about Royd.' She frowned. 'I wish I knew more about the *Nightflyer*'s hardware, but I think I can feel my way through. This is a pretty sophisticated system d'Branin requisitioned.'

'Can you take over from Eris?'

'Take over?' Lommie sounded puzzled. 'You been drinking again, Alys?'

'No, I'm serious. Use your system to break into the ship's control, overwhelm Eris, countermand his orders, make the *Nightflyer* respond to us, down here. Wouldn't you feel safer if we were in control?'

'Maybe,' the cyberneticist said doubtfully. 'I could try, but why do that?'

'Just in case. We don't have to use the capacity. Just so we have it, if an emergency arises.'

Lommie Thorne shrugged. 'Emergencies and gas giants. I only want to put my mind at rest about Royd, whether he had anything to do with killing Lasamer.' She moved over to a readout panel, where a half-dozen meter-square viewscreens curved around a console, and brought one of them to life. Long fingers ghosted through holographic keys that appeared and disappeared as she used them, the keyboard changing shape again and yet again. The cyberneticist's pretty face grew thoughtful and serious. 'We're in,' she said. Characters began to flow across a viewscreen, red flickerings in glassy black depths. On a second screen, a schematic of the *Nightflyer* appeared, revolved, halved; its spheres shifted size and perspective at the whim of Lommie's fingers, and a line of numerals below gave the specifications. The cyberneticist watched, and finally froze both screens.

'Here,' she said, 'here's my answer about the hardware. You can dismiss your takeover idea, unless those gas giant people of yours are going to help. The *Nightflyer*'s bigger and smarter than our little system here. Makes sense, when you stop to think about it. Ship's all automated, except for Royd.'

Her hands moved again, and two more display screens stirred. Lommie Thorne whistled and coaxed her search program with soft words of encouragement. 'It looks as though there *is* a Royd, though. Configurations are all wrong for a robot ship. Damn, I would have bet anything.' The characters began to flow again, Lommie watching the figures as they drifted by. 'Here's life support specs, might tell us something.' A finger jabbed, and one screen froze yet again.

'Nothing unusual,' Alys Northwind said in disappointment.

'Standard waste disposal. Water recycling. Food processor, with protein and vitamin supplements in stores.' She began to whistle. 'Tanks of Renny's moss and neograss to eat up the CO_2. Oxygen cycle, then. No methane or ammonia. Sorry about that.'

'Go sex with a computer!'

The cyberneticist smiled. 'Ever tried it?' Her fingers moved again. 'What else should I look for? You're the tech, what would be a give-away? Give me some ideas.'

'Check the specs for nurturant tanks, cloning equipment, that sort of thing,' the xenotech said. 'That would tell us whether he was lying.'

'I don't know,' Lommie Thorne said. 'Long time ago. He might have junked that stuff. No use for it.'

'Find Royd's life history,' Northwind said. 'His mother's. Get a readout on the business they've done, all this alleged trading. They must have records. Account books, profit-and-loss, cargo invoices, that kind of thing.' Her voice grew excited, and she gripped the cyberneticist from behind by her shoulders. 'A log, a ship's log! There's got to be a log. Find it!'

'All right.' Lommie Thorne whistled, happy, at ease with her system, riding the data winds, curious, in control. Then the screen in front of her turned a bright red and began to blink. She smiled, touched a ghost key, and the keyboard melted away and reformed under her. She tried another tack. Three more screens turned red and began to blink. Her smile faded.

'What is it?'

'Security,' said Lommie Thorne. 'I'll get through it in a second. Hold on.' She changed the keyboard yet again, entered another search program, attached on a rider in case it was blocked. Another screen flashed red. She had her machine chew the data she'd gathered, sent out another feeler. More red. Flashing. Blinking. Bright enough to hurt the eyes. All the screens were red now. 'A good security program,' she said with admiration. 'The log is well protected.'

Alys Northwind grunted. 'Are we blocked?'

'Response time is too slow,' Lommie Thorne said, chewing on her lower lip as she thought. 'There's a way to fix that.' She smiled, and rolled back the soft black metal of her sleeve.

'What are you doing?'

'Watch,' she said. She slid her arm under the console, found the prongs, jacked in.

'Ah,' she said, low in her throat. The flashing red blocks vanished from her readout screens, one after the other, as she sent her mind coursing into the *Nightflyer*'s system, easing through all the blocks. 'Nothing like slipping past another system's security. Like slipping onto a man.' Log entries were flickering past them in a whirling, blurring rush, too fast for Alys Northwind to read. But Lommie read them.

Then she stiffened. 'Oh,' she said. It was almost a whimper. 'Cold,' she said. She shook her head and it was gone, but there was a sound in her ears, a terrible whooping sound. 'Damn,' she said, 'that'll wake everyone.' She glanced up when she felt Alys' fingers dig painfully into her shoulder, squeezing, hurting.

A gray steel panel slid almost silently across the access to the corridor, cutting off the whooping cry of the alarm. 'What?' Lommie Thorne said.

'That's an emergency airseal,' said Alys Northwind in a dead voice. She knew starships. 'It closes where they're about to load or unload cargo in vacuum.'

Their eyes went to the huge curving outer airlock above their heads. The inner lock was almost completely open, and as they watched it clicked into place, and the seal on the outer door cracked, and now it was open half a meter, sliding, and beyond was twisted nothingness so burning-bright it seared the eyes.

'Oh,' said Lommie Thorne, as the cold coursed up her arm. She had stopped whistling.

*

Alarms were hooting everywhere. The passengers began to stir. Melantha Jhirl tumbled from her sleepweb and darted into the corridor, nude, frantic, alert. Karoly d'Branin sat up drowsily. The psipsych muttered fitfully in drug-induced sleep. Rojan Christopheris cried out in alarm.

Far away metal crunched and tore, and a violent shudder ran through the ship, throwing the linguists out of their sleepwebs, knocking Melantha from her feet.

In the command quarters of the *Nightflyer* was a spherical room with featureless white walls, a lesser sphere – a suspended control console – floating in its center. The walls were always blank when the ship was in drive; the warped and glaring underside of spacetime was painful to behold.

But now darkness woke in the room, a holoscope coming to life, cold black and stars everywhere, points of icy unwinking brilliance, no up and no down and no direction, the floating control sphere the only feature in the simulated sea of night.

The *Nightflyer* had shifted out of drive.

Melantha Jhirl found her feet again and thumbed on a communicator. The alarms were still hooting, and it was hard to hear. 'Captain,' she shouted, 'what's happening?'

'I don't know,' Royd's voice replied. 'I'm trying to find out. Wait.'

Melantha waited. Karoly d'Branin came staggering out into the corridor, blinking and rubbing his eyes. Rojan Christopheris was not long behind him. 'What is it? What's wrong?' he demanded, but Melantha just shook her head. Lindran and Dannel soon appeared as well. There was no sign of Marij-Black, Alys Northwind, or Lommie Thorne. The academicians looked uneasily at the seal that blocked cargo hold three. Finally Melantha told Christopheris to go look. He returned a few minutes later. 'Agatha is still unconscious,' he said, talking at the top of his voice to be heard over the alarms. 'The drugs still have her. She's moving around, though. Crying out.'

'Alys and Lommie?'

Christopheris shrugged. 'I can't find them. Ask your friend Royd.'

The communicator came back to life as the alarms died. 'We have returned to normal space,' Royd's voice said, 'but the ship is damaged. Hold three, your computer room, was breached while we were under drive. It was ripped apart by the flux. The computer dropped us out of drive automatically, fortunately for us, or the drive forces might have torn my entire ship apart.'

'Royd,' said Melantha, 'Northwind and Thorne are missing.'

'It appears your computer was in use when the hold was breached,' Royd said carefully. 'I would presume them dead, although I cannot say that with certainty. At Melantha's request I have deactivated most of my monitors, retaining only the lounge input. I do not know what transpired. But this is a small ship, and if they are not with you, we must assume the worst.' He paused briefly. 'If it is any consolation, they died swiftly and painlessly.'

'You killed them,' Christopheris said, his face red and angry. He started to say more, but Melantha slipped her hand firmly over his mouth. The two linguists exchanged a long, meaningful look. 'Do we know how it happened, captain?' Melantha asked.

'Yes,' he said, reluctantly.

The xenobiologist had taken the hint, and Melantha took away her hand to let him breathe. 'Royd?' she prompted.

'It sounds insane, Melantha,' his voice replied, 'but it appears your colleagues opened the hold's loading lock. I doubt they did so deliberately, of course. They were using the system interface to gain entry to the *Nightflyer's* data storage and controls, and they shunted aside all the safeties.'

'I see,' Melantha said. 'A terrible tragedy.'

'Yes. Perhaps more terrible than you think. I have yet to discover the extent of damage to my ship.'

'We should not keep you if you have duties to perform,' Melantha said.

'All of us are shocked, and it is difficult to talk now. Investigate the condition of your ship, and we'll continue our discussion at a more opportune time. Agreed?'

'Yes,' said Royd.

Melantha turned off the communicator. Now, in theory, the device was dead; Royd could neither see nor hear them.

'Do you believe him?' Christopheris snapped.

'I don't know,' Melantha Jhirl said, 'but I do know that the other cargo holds can all be flushed just as hold three was. I'm moving my sleepweb into a cabin. I suggest that those of you who are living in hold two do the same.'

'Clever,' Lindran said, with a sharp nod of her head. 'We can crowd in. It won't be comfortable, but I doubt that I'd sleep the sleep of angels in the holds after this.'

'We should also get our suits out of storage in four,' Dannel suggested. 'Keep them close at hand. Just in case.'

'If you wish,' Melantha said. 'It's possible that all the locks might pop open simultaneously. Royd can't fault us for taking precautions.' She flashed a grim smile. 'After today we've earned the right to act irrationally.'

'This is no time for your damned jokes, Melantha,' Christopheris said. He was still red-faced, and his tone was full of fear and anger. 'Three people are dead, Agatha is perhaps deranged or catatonic, the rest of us are endangered—'

'Yes. And we still have no idea what is happening,' Melantha pointed out.

'*Royd Eris is killing us!*' Christopheris shrieked. 'I don't know who or what he is and I don't know if that story he gave us is true and I don't *care*. Maybe he's a Hrangan Mind or the avenging angel of the *volcryn* or the second coming of Jesus Christ. What the hell difference does it make? He's *killing* us!' He looked at each of them in turn. 'Any one of us could be next,' he added. 'Any one of us. Unless . . . we've got to make plans, *do* something, put a stop to this once and for all.'

'You realize,' Melantha said gently, 'that we cannot actually know whether the good captain has turned off his sensory inputs down here. He could be watching and listening to us right now. He isn't, of course. He said he wouldn't and I believe him. But we have only his word on that. Now, Rojan, you don't appear to trust Royd. If that's so, you can hardly put any faith in his promises. It follows therefore that from your own point of view it might not be wise to say the things that you're saying.' She smiled slyly. 'Do you understand the implications of what I'm saying?'

Christopheris opened his mouth and closed it again, looking very like a tall, ugly fish. He said nothing, but his eyes moved furtively, and his flush deepened.

Lindran smiled thinly. 'I think he's got it,' she said.

'The computer is gone, then,' Karoly d'Branin said suddenly in a low voice.

Melantha looked at him. 'I'm afraid so, Karoly.'

D'Branin ran his fingers through his hair, as if half aware of how untidy he looked. 'The *volcryn*,' he muttered. 'How will we work without the computer?' He nodded to himself. 'I have a small unit in my cabin, a wrist model, perhaps it will suffice. It *must* suffice, it must. I will get the figures from Royd, learn where we have dropped out. Excuse me, my friends. Pardon, I must go.' He wandered away in a distracted haze, talking to himself.

'He hasn't heard a word we've said,' Dannel said, incredulous.

'Think how distraught he'd be if *all* of us were dead,' added Lindran. 'Then he'd have no one to help him look for *volcryn*.'

'Let him go,' Melantha said. 'He is as hurt as any of us, maybe more so. He wears it differently. His obsessions are his defense.'

'Ah. And what is *our* defense?'

'Patience, maybe,' said Melantha Jhirl. 'All of the dead were trying to breach Royd's secret when they died. We haven't tried. Here we are discussing their deaths.'

'You don't find that suspicious?' asked Lindran.

'Very,' Melantha said. 'I even have a method of testing my suspicions. One of us can make yet another attempt to find out whether our captain told us the truth. If he or she dies, we'll know.' She shrugged. 'Forgive me, however, if I'm not the one who tries. But don't let me stop you if you have the urge. I'll note the results with interest. Until then, I'm going to move out of the cargo hold and get some sleep.' She turned and strode off, leaving the others to stare at each other.

'Arrogant bitch,' Dannel observed almost conversationally after Melantha had left.

'Do you really think he can hear us?' Christopheris whispered to the two linguists.

'Every pithy word,' Lindran said. She smiled at his discomfiture. 'Come, Dannel, let's get to a safe area and back to bed.'

He nodded.

'But,' said Christopheris, 'we have to *do* something. Make plans. Defenses.'

Lindran gave him a final withering look, and pulled Dannel off behind her down the corridor.

*

'Melantha? Karoly?'

She woke quickly, alert at the mere whisper of her name, fully awake almost at once, and sat up in the narrow single bed. Squeezed in beside her, Karoly d'Branin groaned and rolled over, yawning.

'Royd?' she asked. 'Is it morning?'

'We are drifting in interstellar space three light years from the nearest star, Melantha,' replied the soft voice from the walls. 'In such a context, the term *morning* has no meaning. But, yes, it is morning.'

Melantha laughed. '*Drifting*, you said? How bad is the damage?'

'Serious, but not dangerous. Hold three is a complete ruin, hanging from my ship like half of a broken egg, but the damage was confined. The drives themselves are intact, and the *Nightflyer*'s computers did not seem to suffer from your system's destruction. I feared they might. I have heard of phenomena like electronic death traumas.'

D'Branin said, 'Eh? Royd?'

Melantha stroked him affectionately. 'I'll tell you later, Karoly,' she said. 'Go back to sleep. Royd, you sound serious. Is there more?'

'I am worried about our return flight, Melantha,' Royd said. 'When I take the *Nightflyer* back into drive, the flux will be playing directly on portions of the ship that were never engineered to withstand it. Our configurations are askew now; I can show you the mathematics of it, but the question of the flux forces is the vital one. The airseal across the access to hold three is a particular concern. I've run some simulations, and I don't know if it can take the stress. If it bursts, my whole ship will split apart in the middle. My engines will go shunting off by themselves, and the rest – even if the life support sphere remains intact, we will all soon be dead.'

'I see. Is there anything we can do?'

'Yes. The exposed areas would be easy enough to reinforce. The outer hull is armored to withstand the warping forces, of course. We could mount it in place, a crude shield, but according to my projections it would suffice. If we do it correctly, it will help correct our configurations as well. Large portions of the hull were torn loose when the locks opened, but they are still out there, most within a kilometer or two, and could be used.'

At some point Karoly d'Branin had finally come awake. 'My team has four vacuum sleds,' he said. 'We can retrieve those pieces for you, my friend.'

'Fine, Karoly, but that is not my primary concern. My ship is self-repairing within certain limits, but this exceeds those limits by an order of magnitude. I will have to do this myself.'

'You?' D'Branin was startled. 'Royd, you said – that is, your muscles, your weakness – this work will be too much for you. Surely we can do this for you!'

Royd's reply was tolerant. 'I am only a cripple in a gravity field, Karoly. Weightless, I am in my element, and I will be killing the *Nightflyer*'s gravity grid momentarily, to try to gather my own strength for the repair work. No, you misunderstand. I am capable of the work. I have the tools, including my own heavy-duty sled.'

'I think I know what you are concerned about, captain,' Melantha said.

'I'm glad,' Royd said. 'Perhaps then you can answer my question. If I emerge from the safety of my chambers to do this work, can you keep your colleagues from harming me?'

Karoly d'Branin was shocked. 'Oh, Royd, Royd, how could you think such a thing? We are scholars, scientists, not – not criminals, or soldiers, or – or animals, we are human, how can you believe we would threaten you or do you harm?'

'Human,' Royd repeated, 'but alien to me, suspicious of me. Give me no false assurances, Karoly.'

He sputtered. Melantha took him by the hand and bid him quiet. 'Royd,' she said, 'I won't lie to you. You'd be in some danger. But I'd hope that, by coming out, you'd make our friends joyously happy. They'd be able to see that you told the truth, see that you were only human.' She smiled. 'They *would* see that, wouldn't they?'

'They would,' Royd said, 'but would it be enough to offset their suspicions? They believe I am responsible for the deaths of the other three, do they not?'

'Believe is too strong a word. They suspect it, they fear it. They are frightened, captain, and with good cause. *I* am frightened.'

'No more than I.'

'I would be less frightened if I knew what *did* happen. Will you tell me?'

Silence.

'Royd, if—'

'I have made mistakes, Melantha,' Royd said gravely. 'But I am not alone in that. I did my best to stop the esperon injection, and I failed. I might have saved Alys and Lommie if I had seen them, heard them, known what they were about. But you made me turn off my monitors, Melantha. I cannot help what I cannot see. Why? If you saw three moves ahead, did you calculate these results?'

Melantha Jhirl felt briefly guilty. '*Mea culpa*, captain, I share the blame. I know that. Believe me, I know that. It is hard to see three moves ahead when you do not know the rules, however. Tell me the rules.'

'I am blind and deaf,' Royd said, ignoring her. 'It is frustrating. I cannot help if I am blind and deaf. I am going to turn on the monitors again,

Melantha. I am sorry if you do not approve. I want your approval, but I must do this with or without it. I have to see.'

'Turn them on,' Melantha said thoughtfully. 'I was wrong, captain. I should never have asked you to blind yourself. I did not understand the situation, and I overestimated my own power to control the others. A failing of mine. Improved models too often think they can do anything.' Her mind was racing, and she felt almost sick; she had miscalculated, misled, and there was more blood on her hands. 'I think I understand better now.'

'Understand what?' Karoly d'Branin said, baffled.

'You do *not* understand,' Royd said sternly. 'Don't pretend that you do, Melantha Jhirl. Don't! It is not wise or safe to be too many moves ahead.' There was something disturbing in his tone.

Melantha understood that too.

'What?' Karoly said. 'I do not understand.'

'Neither do I,' Melantha said carefully. 'Neither do I, Karoly.' She kissed him lightly. 'None of us understands, do we?'

'Good,' said Royd.

She nodded, and put a reassuring arm around Karoly. 'Royd,' she said, 'to return to the question of repairs, it seems to me you must do this work, regardless of what promises we can give you. You won't risk your ship by slipping back into drive in your present condition, and the only other option is to drift out here until we all die. What choice do we have?'

'I have a choice,' Royd said with deadly seriousness. 'I could kill all of you, if that were the only way to save myself and my ship.'

'You could try,' Melantha said.

'Let us have no more talk of death,' d'Branin said.

'You are right, Karoly,' Royd said, 'I do not wish to kill any of you. But I must be protected.'

'You will be,' Melantha said. 'Karoly can set the others to chasing your hull fragments. I'll be your protection. I'll stay by your side. If anyone tries to attack you, they'll have to deal with me. They won't find that easy. And I can assist you. The work will be done three times as fast.'

Royd was polite. 'It is my experience that most planet-born are clumsy and easily tired in weightlessness. It would be more efficient if I worked alone, although I will gladly accept your services as a bodyguard.'

'I remind you that I'm the improved model, captain,' Melantha said. 'Good in free fall as well as in bed. I'll help.'

'You are stubborn. As you will, then. In a few moments I shall depower the gravity grid. Karoly, go and prepare your people. Unship your vacuum sleds and suit up. I will exit the *Nightflyer* in three standard hours, after I

have recovered from the pains of your gravity. I want all of you outside the
ship before I leave. Is that condition understood?'

'Yes,' said Karoly. 'All except Agatha. She has not regained consciousness, friend, she will not be a problem.'

'No,' said Royd, 'I meant *all* of you, including Agatha. Take her outside
with you.'

'But Royd!' protested d'Branin.

'You're the captain,' Melantha Jhirl said firmly. 'It will be as you say; all
of us outside. Including Agatha.'

*

Outside. It was as though some vast animal had taken a bite out of the
stars.

Melantha Jhirl waited on her sled close by the *Nightflyer* and looked at
stars. It was not so very different out here in the depths of interstellar
space. The stars were cold, frozen points of light; unwinking, austere, more
chill and uncaring somehow than the same suns made to dance and
twinkle by an atmosphere. Only the absence of a landmark primary
reminded her of where she was: in the places between, where men and
women and their ships do not stop, where the *volcryn* sail crafts impossibly
ancient. She tried to pick out Avalon's sun, but she did not know where to
search. The configurations were strange to her and she had no idea of how
she was oriented. Behind her, before her, above, all around, the starfields
stretched endlessly. She glanced down, or what seemed like down just
then, beyond her feet and her sled and the *Nightflyer*, expecting still more
alien stars. And the *bite* hit her with an almost physical force.

Melantha fought off a wave of vertigo. She was suspended above a pit, a
yawning chasm in the universe, black, starless, vast.

Empty.

She remembered then: the Tempter's Veil. Just a cloud of dark gases,
nothing really, galactic pollution that obscured the light from the stars of
the Fringe. But this close at hand, it seemed immense, terrifying, and she
had to break her gaze when she began to feel as if she were falling. It was a
gulf beneath her and the frail silver-white shell of the *Nightflyer*, a gulf
about to swallow them.

Melantha touched one of the controls on the sled's forked handle,
swinging around so the Veil was to her side instead of beneath her. That
seemed to help somehow. She concentrated on the *Nightflyer*, ignoring the
looming wall of blackness beyond. It was the largest object in her universe,
bright amid the darkness, ungainly, its shattered cargo sphere giving the
whole craft an unbalanced cast.

She could see the other sleds as they angled through the black, tracking the missing pieces of hull, grappling with them, bringing them back. The linguistic team worked together, as always, sharing a sled. Rojan Christopheris was alone, working in a sullen silence. Melantha had almost had to threaten him with physical violence before he agreed to join them. The xenobiologist was certain that it was all another plot, that once they were outside the *Nightflyer* would slip into drive without them and leave them to lingering deaths. His suspicions were inflamed by drink, and there had been alcohol on his breath when Melantha and Karoly had finally forced him to suit up. Karoly had a sled too, and a silent passenger; Agatha Marij-Black, freshly drugged and asleep in her vacuum suit, safely locked into place.

While her colleagues labored, Melantha Jhirl waited for Royd Eris, talking to the others occasionally over the comm link. The two linguists, unaccustomed to weightlessness, were complaining a good deal, and bickering as well. Karoly tried to soothe them frequently. Christopheris said little, and his few comments were edged and biting. He was still angry. Melantha watched him flit across her field of vision, a stick figure in form-fitting black armor standing erect at the controls of his sled.

Finally the circular airlock atop the foremost of the *Nightflyer's* major spheres dilated and Royd Eris emerged.

She watched him approach, curious, wondering what he would look like. In her mind were a half-dozen contradictory pictures. His genteel, cultured, too-formal voice sometimes reminded her of the dark aristocrats of her native Prometheus, the wizards who toyed with human genes and played baroque status games. At other times his naïveté made her imagine him as an inexperienced youth. His ghost was a tired-looking thin young man, and he was supposed to be considerably older than that pale shadow, but Melantha found it difficult to hear an old man talking when he spoke.

Melantha felt a nervous tingle as he neared. The lines of his sled and his suit were different than theirs, disturbingly so. Alien, she thought, and quickly squelched the thought. Such differences meant nothing. Royd's sled was large, a long oval plate with eight jointed grappling arms bristling from its underside like the legs of a metallic spider. A heavy-duty cutting laser was mounted beneath the controls, its snout jutting threateningly forward. His suit was far more massive than the carefully engineered Academy worksuits they wore, with a bulge between its shoulder blades that was probably a power pack, and rakish radiant fins atop shoulders and helmet. It made him seem hulking; hunched and deformed.

But when he finally came near enough for Melantha to see his face, it was just a face.

White, very white, that was the predominant impression she got; white hair cropped very short, a white stubble around the sharply chiseled lines of his jaw, almost invisible eyebrows beneath which his eyes moved restlessly. His eyes were large and vividly blue, his best feature. His skin was pale and unlined, scarcely touched by time.

He looked wary, she thought. And perhaps a bit frightened.

Royd stopped his sled close to hers, amid the twisted ruin that had been cargo hold three, and surveyed the damage, the pieces of floating wreckage that had once been flesh, blood, glass, metal, plastic. Hard to distinguish now, all of them fused and burned and frozen together. 'We have a good deal of work to do,' he said. 'Shall we begin?'

'First let's talk,' she replied. She shifted her sled closer and reached out to him, but the distance was still too great, the width of the bases of the two vacuum sleds keeping them apart. Melantha backed off and turned herself over completely, so that Royd stood upside down in her world and she upside down in his. She moved to him again, positioning her sled directly over/under his. Their gloved hands met, brushed, parted. Melantha adjusted her altitude. Their helmets touched.

'Now I have touched you,' Royd said, with a tremor in his voice. 'I have never touched anyone before, or been touched.'

'Oh, Royd. This isn't touching, not really. The suits are in the way. But I will touch you, *really* touch you. I promise you that.'

'You can't. It's impossible.'

'I'll find a way,' she said firmly. 'Now, turn off your comm. The sound will carry through our helmets.'

He blinked and used his tongue controls and it was done.

'Now we can talk,' she said. 'Privately.'

'I do not like this, Melantha,' he said. 'This is too obvious. This is dangerous.'

'There is no other way. Royd, I *do* know.'

'Yes,' he said. 'I knew you did. Three moves ahead, Melantha. I remember the way you play chess. But this is a more serious game, and you are safer if you feign ignorance.'

'I understand that, captain. Other things I'm less sure about. Can we talk about them?'

'No. Don't ask me to. Just do as I tell you. You are in peril, all of you, but I can protect you. The less you know, the better I can protect you.' Through the transparent faceplates, his expression was somber.

She stared into his upside-down eyes. 'It might be a second crew member, someone else hidden in your quarters, but I don't believe that. It's the ship, isn't it? Your ship is killing us. Not you. It. Only that doesn't make sense. You command the *Nightflyer*. How can it act independently? And why? What motive? And how was Thale Lasamer killed? The business with Alys and Lommie, that was easy, but a psionic murder? A starship with psi? I can't accept that. It can't be the ship. Yet it can't be anything else. Help me, captain.'

He blinked, anguish behind his eyes. 'I should never have accepted Karoly's charter, not with a telepath among you. It was too risky. But I wanted to see the *volcryn*, and he spoke of them so movingly.' He sighed. 'You understand too much already, Melantha. I can't tell you more, or I would be powerless to protect you. The ship is malfunctioning, that is all you need to know. It is not safe to push too hard. As long as I am at the controls, I think I can keep you and the others from harm. Trust me.'

'Trust is a two-way bond,' Melantha said.

Royd lifted his hand and pushed her away, then tongued his communicator back to life. 'Enough gossip,' he announced. 'We have work to do. Come. I want to see just how improved you actually are.'

In the solitude of her helmet, Melantha Jhirl swore softly.

*

With an irregular twist of metal locked beneath him in his sled's magnetic grip, Rojan Christopheris sailed back towards the *Nightflyer*. He was watching from a distance when Royd Eris emerged on his over-sized work sled. He was closer when Melantha Jhirl moved to him, inverted her sled, and pressed her faceplate to Royd's. Christopheris listened to their soft exchange, heard Melantha promise to touch him, Eris, the *thing*, the killer. He swallowed his rage. Then they cut him out, cut all of them out, went off the open circuit. But still she hung there, suspended by that cipher in the hunchbacked spacesuit, faces pressed together like two lovers kissing.

Christopheris swept in close, unlocked his captive plate so it would drift towards them. 'Here,' he announced. 'I'm off to get another.' He tongued off his own comm and swore, and his sled slid around the spheres and tubes of the *Nightflyer*.

Somehow they were all in it together, Royd and Melantha and possibly old d'Branin as well, he thought sourly. She had protected Eris from the first, stopped them when they might have taken action together, found out who or what he was. He did not trust her. His skin crawled when he remembered that they had been to bed together. She and Eris were the same, whatever they might be. And now poor Alys was dead, and that fool Thorne and even that damned telepath, but still Melantha was *with* him, against them. Rojan Christopheris was deeply afraid, and angry, and half drunk.

The others were out of sight, off chasing spinning wedges of half-slagged metal. Royd and Melantha were engrossed in each other, the ship abandoned and vulnerable. This was his chance. No wonder Eris had insisted that all of them precede him into the void; outside, isolated from the controls of the *Nightflyer*, he was only a man. A weak one at that.

Smiling a thin hard smile, Christopheris brought his sled curling around the cargo spheres, hidden from sight, and vanished into the gaping maw of the driveroom. It was a long tunnel, everything open to vacuum, safe from the corrosion of an atmosphere. Like most starships, the *Nightflyer* had a triple propulsion system: the gravfield for landing and lifting, useless away from a gravity well, the nukes for deep space sublight maneuverings, and the great stardrives themselves. The lights of his sled flickered past the encircling ring of nukes and sent long bright streaks along the sides of the closed cylinders of the stardrives, the huge engines that bent the stuff of spacetime, encased in webs of metal and crystal.

At the end of the tunnel was a great circular door, reinforced metal, closed: the main airlock.

Christopheris set the sled down, dismounted – pulling his boots free of the sled's magnetic grip with an effort – and moved to the airlock. This was the hardest part, he thought. The headless body of Thale Lasamer was tethered loosely to a massive support strut by the lock, like a grisly guardian of the way. The xenobiologist had to stare at it while he waited for the lock to cycle. Whenever he glanced away, somehow he would find his eyes creeping back to it. The body looked almost natural, as if it had never had a head. Christopheris tried to remember what Lasamer had looked like, but the features would not come to mind. He moved uncomfortably, but then the lock door slid open and he gratefully entered the chamber to cycle through.

He was alone in the *Nightflyer*.

A cautious man, Christopheris kept his suit on, though he collapsed the helmet and yanked loose the suddenly-limp metallic fabric so it fell behind his back like a hood. He could snap it in place quickly enough if the need arose. In cargo hold four, where they had stored their equipment, the xenobiologist found what he was looking for; a portable cutting laser, charged and ready. Low power, but it would do.

Slow and clumsy in weightlessness, he pulled himself down the corridor into the darkened lounge.

It was chilly inside, the air cold on his cheeks. He tried not to notice. He braced himself at the door and pushed off across the width of the room, sailing above the furniture, which was all safely bolted into place. As he drifted towards his objective, something wet and cold touched his face. It startled him, but it was gone before he could quite make out what it was.

When it happened again, Christopheris snatched at it, caught it, and felt briefly sick. He had forgotten. No one had cleaned the lounge yet. The –

the *remains* were still there, floating now, blood and flesh and bits of bone and brain. All around him.

He reached the far wall, stopped himself with his arms, pulled himself down to where he wanted to go. The bulkhead. The wall. No doorway was visible, but the metal couldn't be very thick. Beyond was the control room, the computer access, safety, power. Rojan Christopheris did not think of himself as a vindictive man. He did not intend to harm Royd Eris, that judgment was not his to make. He would take control of the *Nightflyer*, warn Eris away, make certain the man stayed sealed in his suit. He would take them all back without any more mysteries, any more killings. The Academy arbiters could listen to the story, and probe Eris, and decide the right and wrong of it, guilt and innocence, what should be done.

The cutting laser emitted a thin pencil of scarlet light. Christopheris smiled and applied it to the bulkhead. It was slow work, but he had patience. They would not have missed him, quiet as he'd been, and if they did they would assume he was off sledding after some hunk of salvage. Eris' repairs would take hours, maybe days, to finish. The bright blade of the laser smoked where it touched the metal. Christopheris applied himself diligently.

Something moved on the periphery of his vision, just a little flicker, barely seen. A floating bit of brain, he thought. A sliver of bone. A bloody piece of flesh, hair still hanging from it. Horrible things, but nothing to worry about. He was a biologist, he was used to blood and brains and flesh. And worse, and worse; he had dissected many an alien in his day, cutting through chitin and mucous, pulsing stinking food sacs and poisonous spines, he had seen and touched it all.

Again the motion caught his eye, teased at it. Not wanting to, Christopheris found himself drawn to look. He could not *not* look, somehow, just as he had been unable to ignore the headless corpse near the airlock. He looked.

It was an eye.

Christopheris trembled and the laser slipped sharply off to one side, so he had to wrestle with it to bring it back to the channel he was cutting. His heart raced. He tried to calm himself. Nothing to be frightened of. No one was home, and if Royd should return, well, he had the laser as a weapon and he had his suit on if an airlock blew.

He looked at the eye again, willing away his fear. It was just an eye, Thale Lasamer's eye, pale blue, bloody but intact, the same watery eye the boy had when alive, nothing supernatural. A piece of dead flesh, floating in the lounge amid other pieces of dead flesh. Someone should have cleaned up the lounge, Christopheris thought angrily. It was indecent to leave it like this, it was uncivilized.

The eye did not move. The other grisly bits were drifting on the air currents that flowed across the room, but the eye was still. It neither bobbed nor spun. It was fixed on him. Staring.

He cursed himself and concentrated on the laser, on his cutting. He had burned an almost straight line up the bulkhead for about a meter. He began another at a right angle.

The eye watched dispassionately. Christopheris suddenly found he could not stand it. One hand released its grip on the laser, reached out, caught the eye, flung it across the room. The action made him lose balance. He tumbled backward, the laser slipping from his grasp, his arms flapping like the wings of some absurd heavy bird. Finally he caught an edge of the table and stopped himself.

The laser hung in the center of the room, floating amid coffee pots and pieces of human debris, still firing, turning slowly. That did not make sense. It should have ceased fire when he released it. A malfunction, Christopheris thought nervously. Smoke was rising where the thin line of the laser traced a path across the carpet.

With a shiver of fear, Christopheris realized that the laser was turning towards him.

He raised himself, put both hands flat against the table, pushed up out of the way, bobbing towards the ceiling.

The laser was turning more swiftly now.

He pushed away from the ceiling hard, slammed into a wall, grunted in pain, bounced off the floor, kicked. The laser was spinning quickly, chasing him. Christopheris soared, braced himself for another ricochet off the ceiling. The beam swung around, but not fast enough. He'd get it while it was still firing off in the other direction.

He moved close, reached, and saw the eye.

It hung just above the laser. Staring.

Rojan Christopheris made a small whimpering sound low in his throat, and his hand hesitated – not long, but long enough – and the scarlet beam came up and around.

Its touch was a light, hot caress across his neck.

*

It was more than an hour later before they missed him. Karoly d'Branin noticed his absence first, called for him over the comm link, and got no answer. He discussed it with the others.

Royd Eris moved his sled back from the armor plate he had just mounted, and through his helmet Melantha Jhirl could see the lines around his mouth grow hard.

It was just then that the noises began.

A shrill bleat of pain and fear, followed by moans and sobbing. Terrible wet sounds, like a man choking on his own blood. They all heard. The sounds filled their helmets. And almost clear amid the anguish was something that sounded like a word: 'Help.'

'That's Christopheris,' a woman's voice said. Lindran.

'He's hurt,' Dannel added. 'He's crying for help. Can't you hear it?'

'Where—?' someone started.

'The ship,' Lindran said. 'He must have returned to the ship.'

Royd Eris said, 'The fool. No. I warned—'

'We're going to check,' Lindran announced. Dannel cut free the hull fragment they had been bringing in, and it spun away, tumbling. Their sled angled down towards the *Nightflyer*.

'Stop,' Royd said. 'I'll return to my chambers and check from there, if you wish, but you may not enter the ship. Stay outside until I give you clearance.'

The terrible sounds went on and on.

'Go to hell,' Lindran snapped at him over the open circuit.

Karoly d'Branin had his sled in motion too, hastening after the linguists, but he had been further out and it was a long way back to the ship. 'Royd, what can you mean, we must help, don't you see? He is hurt, listen to him. Please, my friend.'

'No,' Royd said. 'Karoly, stop! If Rojan went back to the ship alone, he is dead.'

'How do you know that?' Dannel demanded. 'Did you arrange it? Set traps in case we disobeyed you?'

'No,' Royd said, 'listen to me. You can't help him now. Only I could have helped him, and he did not listen to me. Trust me. Stop.' His voice was despairing.

In the distance, d'Branin's sled slowed. The linguists did not. 'We've already listened to you too damn much, I'd say,' Lindran said. She almost had to shout to be heard above the noises, the whimpers and moans, the awful wet sucking sounds, the distorted pleas for help. Agony filled their universe. 'Melantha,' Lindran continued, 'keep Eris right where he is. We'll go carefully, find out what is happening inside, but I don't want him getting back to his controls. Understood?'

Melantha Jhirl hesitated. The sounds beat against her ears. It was hard to think.

Royd swung his sled around to face her, and she could feel the weight of his stare. 'Stop them,' he said. 'Melantha, Karoly, order it. They will not listen to me. They do not know what they are doing.' He was clearly in pain.

In his face Melantha found decision. 'Go back inside quickly, Royd. Do what you can. I'm going to try to intercept them.'

'Whose side are you on?' Lindran demanded.

Royd nodded to her across the gulf, but Melantha was already in motion. Her sled backed clear of the work area, congested with hull fragments and other debris, then accelerated briskly as she raced around the exterior of the *Nightflyer* towards the driveroom.

But even as she approached, she knew it was too late. The linguists were too close, and already moving much faster than she was.

'*Don't*,' she said, authority in her tone. 'Christopheris is dead.'

'His ghost is crying for help, then,' Lindran replied. 'When they tinkered you together, they must have damaged the genes for hearing, bitch.'

'The ship isn't safe.'

'Bitch,' was all the answer she got.

Karoly's sled pursued vainly. 'Friends, you must stop, please, I beg it of you. Let us talk this out together.'

The sounds were his only reply.

'I am your superior,' he said. 'I order you to wait outside. Do you hear me? I order it, I invoke the authority of the Academy of Human Knowledge. Please, my friends, please.'

Melantha watched helplessly as Lindran and Dannel vanished down the long tunnel of the driveroom.

A moment later she halted her own sled near the waiting black mouth, debating whether she should follow them on into the *Nightflyer*. She might be able to catch them before the airlock opened.

Royd's voice, hoarse counterpoint to the sounds, answered her unvoiced question. 'Stay, Melantha. Proceed no further.'

She looked behind her. Royd's sled was approaching.

'What are you doing here? Royd, use your own lock. You have to get back inside!'

'Melantha,' he said calmly, 'I cannot. The ship will not respond to me. The lock will not dilate. The main lock in the driveroom is the only one with manual override. I am trapped outside. I don't want you or Karoly inside the ship until I can return to my console.'

Melantha Jhirl looked down the shadowed barrel of the driveroom, where the linguists had vanished.

'What will—'

'Beg them to come back, Melantha. Plead with them. Perhaps there is still time.'

She tried. Karoly d'Branin tried as well. The twisted symphony of pain and pleading went on and on, but they could not raise Dannel or Lindran at all.

'They've cut out their comm,' Melantha said furiously. 'They don't want to listen to us. Or that . . . that sound.'

Royd's sled and d'Branin's reached her at the same time. 'I do not understand,' Karoly said. 'Why can you not enter, Royd? What is happening?'

'It is simple, Karoly,' Royd replied. 'I am being kept outside until – until—'

'Yes?' prompted Melantha.

'—until Mother is done with them.'

*

The linguists left their vacuum sled next to the one that Christopheris had abandoned, and cycled through the airlock in unseemly haste, with hardly a glance for the grim headless doorman.

Inside they paused briefly to collapse their helmets. 'I can still hear him,' Dannel said. The sounds were faint inside the ship.

Lindran nodded. 'It's coming from the lounge. Hurry.'

They kicked and pulled their way down the corridor in less than a minute. The sounds grew steadily louder, nearer. 'He's in there,' Lindran said when they reached the doorway.

'Yes,' Dannel said, 'but is he alone? We need a weapon. What if . . . Royd had to be lying. There is someone else on board. We need to defend ourselves.'

Lindran would not wait. 'There are two of us,' she said. 'Come *on!*' She launched herself through the doorway, calling Christopheris by name.

It was dark inside. What little light there was spilled through the door from the corridor. Her eyes took a long moment to adjust. Everything was confused; walls and ceilings and floor were all the same, she had no sense of direction. 'Rojan,' she called, dizzily. 'Where are you?' The lounge seemed empty, but maybe it was only the light, or her sense of unease.

'Follow the sound,' Dannel suggested. He hung in the door, peering warily about for a minute, and then began to feel his way cautiously down a wall, groping with his hands.

As if in response to his comment, the sobbing sounds grew suddenly louder. But they seemed to come first from one corner of the room, then from another.

Lindran, impatient, propelled herself across the chamber, searching. She brushed against a wall in the kitchen area, and that made her think of weapons, and Dannel's fears. She knew where the utensils were stored. 'Here,' she said a moment later, turning towards him, 'Here, I've got a knife, that should thrill you.' She flourished it, and brushed against a floating bubble of liquid as big as her fist. It burst and reformed into a hundred smaller globules. One moved past her face, close, and she tasted it. Blood.

But Lasamer had been dead a long time. His blood ought to have dried by now, she thought.

'Oh, merciful god,' said Dannel.

'What?' Lindran demanded. 'Did you find him?'

Dannel was fumbling his way back towards the door, creeping along the wall like an oversized insect, back the way he had come. 'Get out, Lindran,' he warned. '*Hurry!*'

'Why?' She trembled despite herself. 'What's wrong?'

'The screams,' he said. 'The wall, Lindran, the wall. The sounds.'

'You're not making sense,' she snapped. 'Get a hold of yourself.'

He gibbered. 'Don't you see? The sounds are coming from the *wall*. The communicator. Faked. Simulated.' Dannel reached the door, and dove through it, sighing audibly. He did not wait for her. He bolted down the corridor and was gone, pulling himself hand over hand wildly, his feet thrashing and kicking behind him.

Lindran braced herself and moved to follow.

The sounds came from in front of her, from the door. 'Help me,' it said, in Rojan Christopheris' voice. She heard moaning and that terrible wet choking sound, and she stopped.

From her side came a wheezing ghastly death rattle. 'Ahhhh,' it moaned, loudly, building in a counterpoint to the other noise. 'Help me.'

'Help me, help me, help me,' said Christopheris from the darkness behind her.

Coughing and a weak groan sounded under her feet.

'Help me,' all the voices chorused, 'help me, help me, help me.' Recordings, she thought, recordings being played back. 'Help me, help me, help me, help me.' All the voices rose higher and louder, and the words turned into a scream, and the scream ended in wet choking, in wheezes and gasps and death. Then the sounds stopped. Just like that; turned off.

Lindran kicked off, floated towards the door, knife in hand.

Something dark and silent crawled from beneath the dinner table and rose to block her path. She saw it clearly for a moment, as it emerged between her and the light. Rojan Christopheris, still in his vacuum suit, but with the helmet pulled off. He had something in his hand that he raised to point at her. It was a laser, Lindran saw, a simple cutting laser.

She was moving straight towards him, coasting, helpless. She flailed and tried to stop herself, but she could not.

When she got quite close, she saw that Rojan had a second mouth below his chin, a long blackened slash, and it was grinning at her, and little droplets of blood flew from it, wetly, as he moved.

*

Dannel rushed down the corridor in a frenzy of fear, bruising himself as he smashed off walls and doorways. Panic and weightlessness made him clumsy. He kept glancing over his shoulder as he fled, hoping to see Lindran coming after him, but terrified of what he might see in her stead. Every time he looked back, he lost his sense of balance and went tumbling again.

It took a long, *long* time for the airlock to open. As he waited, trembling, his pulse began to slow. The sounds had dwindled behind him, and there was no sign of pursuit. He steadied himself with an effort. Once inside the lock chamber, with the inner door sealed between him and the lounge, he began to feel safe.

Suddenly Dannel could barely remember why he had been so terrified. And he was ashamed; he had run, abandoned Lindran. And for what? What had frightened him so? An empty lounge? Noises from the walls? A rational explanation for that forced itself on him all at once. It only meant that poor Christopheris was somewhere else in the ship, that's all, just somewhere else, alive and in pain, spilling his agony into a comm unit.

Dannel shook his head ruefully. He'd hear no end of this, he knew. Lindran liked to taunt him. She would never let him forget it. But at least he would return, and apologize. That would count for something. Resolute, he reached out and killed the cycle on the airlock, then reversed it. The air that had been partially sucked out came gusting back into the chamber.

As the inner door rolled back, Dannel felt his fear return briefly, an instant of stark terror when he wondered what might have emerged from the lounge to wait for him in the corridors of the *Nightflyer*. He faced the fear and willed it away. He felt strong.

When he stepped out, Lindran was waiting.

He could see neither anger nor disdain in her curiously calm features, but he pushed himself towards her and tried to frame a plea for forgiveness anyway. 'I don't know why I—'

With languid grace, her hand came out from behind her back. The knife flashed up in a killing arc, and that was when Dannel finally noticed the hole burned in her suit, still smoking, just between her breasts.

*

'Your *mother?*' Melantha Jhirl said incredulously as they hung helpless in the emptiness beyond the ship.

'She can hear everything we say,' Royd replied. 'But at this point it no longer makes any difference. Rojan must have done something very foolish, very threatening. Now she is determined to kill you all.'

'She, she, what do you mean?' D'Branin's voice was puzzled. 'Royd, surely you do not tell us that your mother is still alive. You said she died even before you were born.'

'She did, Karoly,' Royd said. 'I did not lie to you.'

'No,' Melantha said. 'I didn't think so. But you did not tell us the whole truth either.'

Royd nodded. 'Mother is dead, but her – her spirit still lives, and animates my *Nightflyer*.' He sighed. 'Perhaps it would be more fitting to say her *Nightflyer*. My control has been tenuous at best.'

'Royd,' d'Branin said, 'spirits do not exist. They are not real. There is no survival after death. My *volcryn* are more real than any ghosts.'

'I don't believe in ghosts either,' said Melantha curtly.

'Call it what you will, then,' Royd said. 'My term is as good as any. The reality is unchanged by the terminology. My mother, or some part of my mother, lives in the *Nightftyer*, and she is killing all of you as she has killed others before.'

'Royd, you do not make sense,' d'Branin said.

'Quiet, Karoly. Let the captain explain.'

'Yes,' Royd said. 'The *Nightflyer* is very – very advanced, you know. Automated, self-repairing, large. It had to be, if mother were to be freed from the necessity of a crew. It was built on Newholme, you will recall. I have never been there, but I understand that Newholme's technology is quite sophisticated. Avalon could not duplicate this ship, I suspect. There are few worlds that could.'

'The point, captain?'

'The point – the point is the computers, Melantha. They had to be extraordinary. They are, believe me, they are. Crystal-matrix cores, lasergrid data retrieval, full sensory extension, and other – features.'

'Are you trying to tell us that the *Nightflyer* is an Artificial Intelligence? Lommie Thorne suspected as much.'

'She was wrong,' Royd said. 'My ship is not an Artificial Intelligence, not as I understand it. But it is something close. Mother had a capacity for personality impress built in. She filled the central crystal with her own memories, desires, quirks, her loves and her – her hates. That was why she could trust the computer with my education, you see? She knew it would raise me as she herself would, had she the patience. She programmed it in certain other ways as well.'

'And you cannot deprogram, my friend?' Karoly asked.

Karoly's voice was despairing. 'I have *tried*, Karoly. But I am a weak hand at systems work, and the programs are very complicated, the machines very sophisticated. At least three times I have eradicated her, only to have her surface once again. She is a phantom program, and I cannot track her. She comes and goes as she will. A ghost, do you see? Her memories and her personality are so intertwined with the programs that run the *Nightflyer* that I cannot get rid of her without destroying the central crystal, wiping the entire system. But that would leave me helpless. I could never reprogram, and with the computers down the entire ship would fail, drivers, life support, everything. I would have to leave the *Nightflyer*, and that would kill me.'

'You should have told us, my friend,' Karoly d'Branin said. 'On Avalon, we have many cyberneticists, some very great minds. We might have aided you. We could have provided expert help. Lommie Thorne might have helped you.'

'Karoly, I have *had* expert help. Twice I have brought systems specialists on board. The first one told me what I have just told you; that it was impossible without wiping the programs completely. The second had trained on Newholme. She thought she might be able to help me. Mother killed her.'

'You are still holding something back,' Melantha Jhirl said. 'I understand how your cybernetic ghost can open and close airlocks at will and arrange other accidents of that nature. But how do you explain what she did to Thale Lasamer?'

'Ultimately I must bear the guilt,' Royd replied. 'My loneliness led me to a grievous error. I thought I could safeguard you, even with a telepath among you. I have carried other riders safely. I watch them constantly, warn them away from dangerous acts. If Mother attempts to interfere, I countermand her directly from the master control console. That usually works. Not always. Usually. Before this trip she had killed only five times, and the first three died when I was quite young. That was how I learned about her, about her presence in my ship. That party included a telepath, too.

'I should have known better, Karoly. My hunger for life has doomed you all to death. I overestimated my own abilities, and underestimated her fear of exposure. She strikes out when she is threatened, and telepaths are always a threat. They sense her, you see. A malign, looming presence, they tell me, something cool and hostile and inhuman.'

'Yes,' Karoly d'Branin said, 'yes, that was what Thale said. An alien, he was certain of it.'

'No doubt she feels alien to a telepath used to the familiar contours of organic minds. Hers is not a human brain, after all. What it is I cannot say – a complex of crystallized memories, a hellish network of interlocking programs, a meld of circuitry and spirit. Yes, I can understand why she might feel alien.'

'You still haven't explained how a computer program could explode a man's skull,' Melantha said.

'You wear the answer between your breasts, Melantha.'

'My whisperjewel?' she said, puzzled. She felt it then, beneath her vacuum suit and her clothing; a touch of cold, a vague hint of eroticism that made her shiver. It was as if his mention had been enough to make the gem come alive.

'I was not familiar with whisperjewels until you told me of yours,' Royd said, 'but the principle is the same. Esper-etched, you said. Then you know that psionic power can be stored. The central core of my computer is resonant crystal, many times larger than your tiny jewel. I think Mother impressed it as she lay dying.'

'Only an esper can etch a whisperjewel,' Melantha said.

'You never asked the *why* of it, either of you,' Royd said. 'You never asked why mother hated people so. She was born gifted, you see. On Avalon she might have been a class one, tested and trained and honored, her talent nurtured and rewarded. I think she might have been very famous. She might have been stronger than a class one, but perhaps it is only after death that she acquired such power, linked as she is to the *Nightflyer*.

'The point is moot. She was not born on Avalon. On Vess, her ability was seen as a curse, something alien and fearful. So they cured her of it. They used drugs and electroshock and hypnotraining that made her violently ill whenever she tried to use her talent. They used other, less savory methods as well. She never lost her power, of course, only the ability to use it effectively, to control it with her conscious mind. It remained part of her, suppressed, erratic, a source of shame and pain, surfacing violently in times of great emotional stress. And half a decade of institutional care almost drove her insane. No wonder she hated people.'

'What was her talent? Telepathy?'

'No. Oh, some rudimentary ability perhaps. I have read that all psi talents have several latent abilities in addition to their one developed strength. But mother could not read minds. She had some empathy, although her cure had twisted it curiously, so that the emotions she felt literally sickened her. But her major strength, the talent they took five years to shatter and destroy, was teke.'

Melantha Jhirl swore. 'Of *course* she hated gravity! Telekinesis under weightlessness is—'

'Yes,' Royd finished. 'Keeping the *Nightflyer* under gravity tortures me, but it limits Mother.'

In the silence that followed that comment, each of them looked down the dark cylinder of the drive room. Karoly d'Branin moved awkwardly on his sled. 'Dannel and Lindran have not returned,' he said.

'They are probably dead,' Royd said dispassionately.

'What will we do, then? We must plan. We cannot wait here indefinitely.'

'The first question is what *I* can do,' Royd Eris replied. 'I have talked freely, you'll note. You deserved to know. We have passed the point where ignorance was a protection. Obviously things have gone too far. There have been too many deaths and you have been witness to all of them. Mother cannot allow you to return to Avalon alive.'

'True,' said Melantha. 'But what shall she do with you? Is your own status in doubt, captain?'

'The crux of the problem,' Royd admitted. 'You are still three moves ahead, Melantha. I wonder if it will suffice. Your opponent is four ahead in this game, and most of your pawns are already captured. I fear checkmate is imminent.'

'Unless I can persuade my opponent's king to desert, no?'

She could see Royd's wan smile. 'She would probably kill me too if I choose to side with you. She does not need me.'

Karoly d'Branin was slow to grasp the point. 'But – but what else could—'

'My sled has a laser. Yours do not. I could kill you both, right now, and thereby earn my way back into the *Nightflyer*'s good graces.'

Across the three meters that lay between their sleds, Melantha's eyes met Royd's. Her hands rested easily on the thruster controls. 'You could try, captain. Remember, the improved model isn't easy to kill.'

'I would not kill you, Melantha Jhirl,' Royd said seriously. 'I have lived sixty-eight standard years and I have never lived at all. I am tired, and you tell grand gorgeous lies. Will you really touch me?'

'Yes.'

'I risk a lot for that touch. Yet in a way it is no risk at all. If we lose, we will all die together. If we win, well, I shall die anyway when they destroy the *Nightflyer*, either that or live as a freak in an orbital hospital, and I would prefer death.'

'We will build you a new ship, captain,' Melantha promised.

'Liar,' Royd replied. But his tone was cheerful. 'No matter. I have not had much of a life anyway. Death does not frighten me. If we win, you must tell me about your *volcryn* once again, Karoly. And you, Melantha, you must play chess with me, and find a way to touch me, and . . .'

'And sex with you?' she finished, smiling.

'If you would,' he said quietly. He shrugged. 'Well, Mother has heard all of this. Doubtless she will listen carefully to any plans we might make, so there is no sense making them. Now there is no chance that the control lock will admit me, since it is keyed directly into the ship's computer. So we must follow the others through the driveroom, and enter through the main lock, and take what small chances we are given. If I can reach my console and restore gravity, perhaps we can win. If not—'

He was interrupted by a low groan.

For an instant Melantha thought the *Nightflyer* was wailing at them again, and she was surprised that it was so stupid as to try the same tactic twice. Then the groan sounded once more, and in the back of Karoly d'Branin's sled, the forgotten fourth member of their company struggled against the bonds that held her down. D'Branin hastened to free her, and Agatha Marij-Black tried to rise to her feet and almost floated off the sled, until he caught her hand and pulled her back. 'Are you well?' he asked. 'Can you hear me? Have you pain?'

Imprisoned beneath a transparent faceplate, wide frightened eyes flicked rapidly from Karoly to Melantha to Royd, and then to the broken *Nightflyer*. Melantha wondered whether the woman was insane, and started to caution d'Branin, when Marij-Black spoke.

'The *volcryn!*' was all she said. 'Oh. The *volcryn!*'

Around the mouth of the driveroom, the ring of nuclear engines took on a faint glow. Melantha Jhirl heard Royd suck in his breath sharply. She gave the thruster controls of her sled a violent twist. 'Hurry,' she said loudly. 'The *Nightflyer* is preparing to move.'

*

A third of the way down the long barrel of the driveroom, Royd pulled abreast of her, stiff and menacing in his black, bulky armor. Side by side they sailed past the cylindrical stardrives and the cyberwebs; ahead, dimly lit, was the main airlock and its ghastly sentinel.

'When we reach the lock, jump over to my sled,' Royd said. 'I want to stay armed and mounted, and the chamber is not large enough for two sleds.'

Melantha Jhirl risked a quick glance behind her. 'Karoly,' she called. 'Where are you?'

'Outside, my love, my friend,' the answer came. 'I cannot come. Forgive me.'

'We have to stay together!'

'No,' d'Branin said, 'no, I could not risk it, not when we are so close. It would be so tragic, so futile, Melantha. To come so close and fail. Death I do not mind, but I must see them first, finally, after all these years.'

'My mother is going to move the ship,' Royd cut in. 'Karoly, you will be left behind, lost.'

'I will wait,' d'Branin replied. 'My *volcryn* come, and I must wait for them.'

Then the time for conversation was gone, for the airlock was almost upon them. Both sleds slowed and stopped, and Royd Eris reached out and began the cycle while Melantha Jhirl moved to the rear of his huge oval worksled. When the outer door moved aside, they glided through into the lock chamber.

'When the inner door opens it will begin,' Royd told her evenly. 'The permanent furnishings are either built in or welded or bolted into place, but the things that your team brought on board are not. Mother will use those things as weapons. And beware of doors, airlocks, any equipment tied into the *Nightflyer*'s computer. Need I warn you not to unseal your suit?'

'Hardly,' she replied.

Royd lowered the sled a little, and its grapplers made a metallic sound as they touched against the floor of the chamber.

The inner door hissed open, and Royd applied his thrusters.

Inside Dannel and Lindran waited, swimming in a haze of blood. Dannel had been slit from crotch to throat and his intestines moved like a nest of pale, angry snakes. Lindran still held the knife. They swam closer, moving with a grace they had never possessed in life.

Royd lifted his foremost grapplers and smashed them to the side as he surged forward. Dannel caromed off a bulkhead, leaving a wide wet mark where he struck, and more of his guts came sliding out. Lindran lost control of the knife. Royd accelerated past them, driving up the corridor through the cloud of blood.

'I'll watch behind,' Melantha said. She turned and put her back to his. Already the two corpses were safely behind them. The knife was floating uselessly in the air. She started to tell Royd that they were all right when the blade abruptly shifted and came after them, gripped by some invisible force.

'*Swerve!*' she cried.

The sled shot wildly to one side. The knife missed by a full meter, and glanced ringingly off a bulkhead.

But it did not drop. It came at them again.

The lounge loomed ahead. Dark.

'The door is too narrow,' Royd said. 'We will have to abandon—' As he spoke, they hit; he wedged the sled squarely into the doorframe, and the sudden impact jarred them loose.

For a moment Melantha floated clumsily in the corridor, her head whirling, trying to sort up from down. The knife slashed at her, opening her suit and her shoulder clear through to the bone. She felt sharp pain and the warm flush of bleeding. 'Damn,' she shrieked. The knife came around again, spraying droplets of blood.

Melantha's hand darted out and caught it.

She muttered something under her breath and wrenched the blade free of the hand that had been gripping it.

Royd had regained the controls of his sled and seemed intent on some manipulation. Beyond him, in the dimness of the lounge, Melantha glimpsed a dark semi-human form rise into view.

'Royd!' she warned. The thing activated its small laser. The pencil beam caught Royd square in the chest.

He touched his own firing stud. The sled's heavy-duty laser came alive, a shaft of sudden brilliance. It cindered Christopheris' weapon and burned off his right arm and part of his chest. The beam hung in the air, throbbing, and smoked against the far bulkhead.

Royd made some adjustments and began cutting a hole. 'We'll be through in five minutes or less,' he said curtly.

'Are you all right?' Melantha asked.

'I'm uninjured,' he replied. 'My suit is better armored than yours, and his laser was a low-powered toy.'

Melantha turned her attention back to the corridor.

The linguists were pulling themselves toward her, one on each side of the passage, to come at her from two directions at once. She flexed her muscles. Her shoulder stabbed and screamed. Otherwise she felt strong, almost reckless. 'The corpses are coming after us again,' she told Royd. 'I'm going to take them.'

'Is that wise?' he asked. 'There are two of them.'

'I'm an improved model,' Melantha said, 'and they're dead.' She kicked herself free of the sled and sailed towards Dannel in a high, graceful trajectory. He raised his hands to block her. She slapped them aside, bent one arm back and heard it snap, and drove her knife deep into his throat before she realized what a useless gesture that was. Blood oozed from his neck in a spreading cloud, but he continued to flail at her. His teeth snapped grotesquely.

Melantha withdrew her blade, seized him, and with all her considerable strength threw him bodily down the corridor. He tumbled, spinning wildly, and vanished into the haze of his own blood.

Melantha flew in the opposite direction, revolving lazily.

Lindran's hands caught her from behind.

Nails scrabbled against her faceplate until they began to bleed, leaving red streaks on the plastic.

Melantha whirled to face her attacker, grabbed a thrashing arm, and flung the woman down the passageway to crash into her struggling companion. The reaction sent her spinning like a top. She spread her arms and stopped herself, dizzy, gulping.

'I'm through,' Royd announced.

Melantha turned to see. A smoking meter-square opening had been cut through one wall of the lounge. Royd killed the laser, gripped both sides of the doorframe, and pushed himself towards it.

A piercing blast of sound drilled through her head. She doubled over in agony. Her tongue flicked out and clicked off the comm; then there was blessed silence.

In the lounge it was raining. Kitchen utensils, glasses and plates, pieces of human bodies all lashed violently across the room, and glanced harmlessly off Royd's armored form. Melantha – eager to follow – drew back helplessly. That rain of death would cut her to pieces in her lighter, thinner vacuum suit. Royd reached the far wall and vanished into the secret control section of the ship. She was alone.

The *Nightflyer* lurched, and sudden acceleration provided a brief semblance of gravity. Melantha was thrown to one side. Her injured shoulder smashed painfully against the sled.

All up and down the corridor doors were opening.

Dannel and Lindran were moving toward her once again.

*

The *Nightflyer* was a distant star sparked by its nuclear engines. Blackness and cold enveloped them, and below was the unending emptiness of the Tempter's Veil, but Karoly d'Branin did not feel afraid. He felt strangely transformed.

The void was alive with promise.

'They *are* coming,' he whispered. 'Even I, who have no psi at all, even I can feel it. The Crey story must be so, even from light years off they can be sensed. Marvelous!'

Agatha Marij-Black seemed small and shrunken. 'The *volcryn*,' she muttered. 'What good can they do us. I hurt. The ship is gone. D'Branin, my head aches.' She made a small frightened noise. 'Thale said that, just after I injected him, before – before – you know. He said that his head hurt. It aches so terribly.'

'Quiet, Agatha. Do not be afraid. I am here with you. Wait. Think only of what we shall witness, think only of that!'

'I can sense them,' the psipsych said.

D'Branin was eager. 'Tell me, then. We have our little sled. We shall go to them. Direct me.'

'Yes,' she agreed. 'Yes. Oh, yes.'

*

Gravity returned; in a flicker, the universe became almost normal.

Melantha fell to the deck, landed easily and rolled, and was on her feet cat-quick.

The objects that had been floating ominously through the open doors along the corridor all came clattering down.

The blood was transformed from a fine mist to a slick covering on the corridor floor.

The two corpses dropped heavily from the air, and lay still.

Royd spoke to her from the communicators built into the walls. 'I made it,' he said.

'I noticed,' she replied.

'I'm at the main control console. I have restored the gravity with a manual override, and I'm cutting off as many computer functions as possible. We're still not safe, though. Mother will try to find a way around me. I'm countermanding her by sheer force, as it were. I cannot afford to overlook anything, and if my attention should lapse, even for a moment . . . Melantha, was your suit breached?'

'Yes. Cut at the shoulder.'

'Change into another one. *Immediately*. I think the counterprogramming I'm doing will keep the locks sealed, but I can't take any chances.'

Melantha was already running down the corridor, toward the cargo hold where the suits and equipment were stored.

'When you have changed,' Royd continued, 'dump the corpses into the mass conversion unit. You'll find the appropriate hatch near the driveroom airlock, just to the left of the lock controls. Convert any other loose objects that are not indispensable as well; scientific instruments, books, tapes, tableware—'

'Knives,' suggested Melantha.

'By all means.'

'Is teke still a threat, captain?'

'Mother is vastly weaker in a gravity field,' Royd said. 'She has to fight it. Even boosted by the *Nightflyer's* power, she can only move one object at a time, and she has only a fraction of the lifting force she wields under weightless conditions. But the power is still there, remember. Also, it is possible she will find a way to circumvent me and cut out the gravity again. From here I can restore it in an instant, but I don't want any likely weapons lying around even for that brief period of time.'

Melantha reached the cargo area. She stripped off her vacuum suit and slipped into another one in record time, wincing at the pain in her shoulder. It was bleeding badly, but she had to ignore it. She gathered up the discarded suit and a double armful of instruments and dumped them into the conversion chamber. Afterwards she turned her attention to the bodies. Dannel was no problem. Lindran crawled down the corridor after her as she pushed him through, and thrashed weakly when it was her own turn, a grim reminder that the *Nightflyer's* powers were not all gone. Melantha easily overcame her feeble struggles and forced her through.

Christopheris' burned, ruined body writhed in her grasp and snapped its teeth at her, but Melantha had no real trouble with it. While she was cleaning out the lounge, a kitchen knife came spinning at her head. It came slowly, though, and Melantha just batted it aside, then picked it up and added it to the pile for conversion. She was working through the cabins, carrying Agatha Marij-Black's abandoned drugs and injection gun under her arm, when she heard Royd cry out.

A moment later a force like a giant invisible hand wrapped itself around her chest and squeezed and pulled her, struggling, to the floor.

*

Something was moving across the stars.

Dimly and far off, d'Branin could see it, though he could not yet make out details. But it was there, that was unmistakable, some vast shape that blocked off a section of the starscape. It was coming at them dead on.

How he wished he had his team with him now, his computer, his telepath, his experts, his instruments.

He pressed harder on the thrusters, and rushed to meet his *volcryn*.

*

Pinned to the floor, hurting, Melantha Jhirl risked opening her suit's comm. She had to talk to Royd. 'Are you there?' she asked. 'What's happen . . . happening?' The pressure was awful, and it was growing steadily worse. She could barely move.

The answer was pained and slow in coming. '. . . outwitted . . . me,' Royd's voice managed. '. . . hurts to . . . talk.'

'Royd—'

'. . . she . . . teked . . . the . . . dial . . . up . . . two . . . gees . . . three . . . higher . . . right . . . on . . . the . . . board . . . all . . . I . . . have to . . . to do . . . turn it . . . back . . . back . . . let me.'

Silence. Then, finally, when Melantha was near despair, Royd's voice again. One word:

'. . . can't . . .'

Melantha's chest felt as if it were supporting ten times her own weight. She could imagine the agony Royd must be in; Royd, for whom even one gravity was painful and dangerous. Even if the dial was an arm's length away, she knew his feeble musculature would never let him reach it. 'Why,' she started. Talking was not as hard for her as it seemed to be for him. 'Why would . . . she turn *up* the . . . the gravity . . . it . . . weakens her, too . . . yes?'

'. . . yes . . . but . . . in a . . . a time . . . hour . . . minute . . . my . . . my heart . . . will burst . . . and . . . and then . . . you alone . . . she . . . will . . . kill gravity . . . kill you . . .'

Painfully Melantha reached out her arm and dragged herself half a length down the corridor. 'Royd . . . hold on . . . I'm coming . . .' She dragged herself forward again. Agatha's drug kit was still under her arm, impossibly heavy. She eased it down and started to shove it aside. It felt as if weighed a hundred kilos. She reconsidered. Instead she opened its lid.

The ampules were all neatly labeled. She glanced over them quickly, searching for adrenaline or synthastim, anything that might give her the strength she needed to reach Royd. She found several stimulants, selected the strongest, and was loading it into the injection gun with awkward, agonized slowness when her eyes chanced on the supply of esperon.

Melantha did not know why she hesitated. Esperon was only one of a half-dozen psionic drugs in the kit, none of which could do her any good, but something about seeing it bothered her, reminded her of something she could not quite lay her finger on. She was trying to sort it out when she heard the noise.

'Royd,' she said, 'your mother . . . could she move . . . she couldn't move anything . . . teke it . . . in this high a gravity . . . could she?'

'Maybe,' he answered, '. . . if . . . concentrate . . . all her . . . power . . . hard . . . maybe possible . . . why?'

'Because,' Melantha Jhirl said grimly, 'because something . . . some*one* . . . is cycling through the airlock.'

*

'It is not truly a ship, not as I thought it would be,' Karoly d'Branin was saying. His suit, Academy-designed, had a built-in encoding device, and he was recording his comments for posterity, strangely secure in the certainty of his impending death. 'The scale of it is difficult to imagine, difficult to estimate. Vast, vast. I have nothing but my wrist computer, no instruments, I cannot make accurate measurements, but I would say, oh, a hundred kilometers, perhaps as much as three hundred, across. Not solid mass, of course, not at all. It is delicate, airy, no ship as we know ships, no city either. It is – oh, beautiful – it is crystal and gossamer, alive with its own dim lights, a vast intricate kind of spiderwebby craft – it reminds me a bit of the old starsail ships they used once, in the days before drive, but this great construct, it is not solid, it cannot be driven by light. It is no ship at all, really. It is all open to vacuum, it has no sealed cabins or life-support spheres, none visible to me, unless blocked from my line of sight in some fashion, and no, I cannot believe that, it is too open, too fragile. It moves quite rapidly. I would wish for the instrumentation to measure its speed, but it is enough to be here. I am taking the sled at right angles to it, to get clear of its path, but I cannot say that I will make it. It moves so much faster than we. Not at light speed, no, far below light speed, but still faster than the *Nightflyer* and its nuclear engines, I would guess . . . only a guess.

'The *volcryn* craft has no visible means of propulsion. In fact, I wonder how – perhaps it is a light-sail, laser-launched millennia ago, now torn and rotted by some unimaginable catastrophe – but no, it is too symmetrical, too beautiful, the webbings, the great shimmering veils near the nexus, the beauty of it.

'I must describe it, I must be more accurate, I know. It is *difficult*, I grow too excited. It is large, as I have said, kilometers across. Roughly – let me count – yes, roughly octagonal in shape. The nexus, the center, is a bright area, a small darkness surrounded by a much greater area of light, but only the dark portion seems entirely solid – the lighted areas are translucent, I can see stars through them, though discolored, shifted towards the purple. Veils, I call those the veils. From the nexus and the veils eight long – oh, vastly long – spurs project, not quite spaced evenly, so it is not a true geometric octagon – ah, I see better now, one of the spurs is shifting, oh, very slowly, the veils are rippling – they are mobile then, those projections, and the webbing runs from one spur to the next, around and around, but there are – patterns, odd patterns, it is not at all the simple webbing of a spider. I cannot quite see order in the patterns, in the traceries of the webs, but I feel sure the order is there, the meaning is waiting to be found.

'There are lights. Have I mentioned the lights? The lights are brightest around the center nexus, but they are nowhere very bright, a dim violet. Some visible radiation then, but not much. I would like to take an ultraviolet reading of this craft, but I do not have the instrumentation. The lights move. The veils seem to ripple, and lights run constantly up and down the length of the spurs, at differing rates of speed, and sometimes other lights can be seen transversing the webbing, moving across the patterns. I do not know what the lights are. Some form of communication, perhaps. I cannot tell whether they emanate from inside the craft or outside. I – oh! There was another light just then. Between the spurs, a brief flash, a starburst. It is gone now, already. It was more intense than the others, indigo. I feel so helpless, so ignorant. But they are beautiful, my *volcryn* . . .

'The myths, they – this is really not much like the legends, not truly. The size, the lights. The *volcryn* have often been linked to lights, but those reports were so vague, they might have meant anything, described anything from a laser propulsion system to simple exterior lighting. I could not know it meant this. Ah, what mystery! The ship is still too far away to see the finer detail. It is so large, I do not think we shall get clear of it. It seems to have turned towards us, I think, yet I may be mistaken, it is only an impression. My instruments, if I only had my instruments. Perhaps the darker area in the center is a craft, a life capsule. The *volcryn* must be inside it. I wish my team were with me, and Thale, poor Thale. He was a class one, we might have made contact, might have communicated with them. The things we would learn! The things they have seen! To think how old this craft is, how ancient the race, how long they have been outbound ... it fills me with awe. Communication would be such a gift, such an impossible gift, but they are so alien.'

'*D'Branin*' Agatha Marij-Black said in a low, urgent voice. 'Can't you feel?'

Karoly d'Branin looked at her as if seeing her for the first time. 'Can *you* feel them? You are a three, can you sense them now, strongly?'

'Long ago,' the psipsych said, 'long ago.'

'Can you project? Talk to them, Agatha. Where are they? In the center area? The dark?'

'Yes,' she replied, and she laughed. Her laugh was shrill and hysterical, and d'Branin had to recall that she was a very sick woman. 'Yes, in the center, d'Branin, that's where the pulses come from. Only you're wrong about them. It's not a them at all, your legends are all lies, lies, I wouldn't be surprised if we were the first ever to see your *volcryn*, to come this close. The others, those aliens of yours, they merely *felt*, deep and distantly, sensed a bit of the nature of the *volcryn* in their dreams and visions, and fashioned the rest to suit themselves. Ships, and wars, and a race of eternal travelers, it is all – all—'

'Yes. What do you mean, Agatha, my friend? You do not make sense. I do not understand.'

'No,' Marij-Black said, 'you do not, do you?' Her voice was suddenly gentle. 'You cannot feel it, as I can. So clear now. This must be how a one feels, all the time. A one full of esperon.'

'What do you feel? *What?*'

'It's not a *them*, Karoly. It's an *it*. Alive, Karoly, and quite mindless, I assure you.'

'Mindless?' d'Branin said. 'No, you must be wrong, you are not reading correctly. I will accept that it is a single creature if you say so, a single great marvelous star-traveler, but how can it be mindless? You sensed it, its mind, its telepathic emanations. You and the whole of the Crey sensitives and all the others. Perhaps its thoughts are too alien for you to read.'

'Perhaps. But what I do read is not so terribly alien at all. Only animal. Its thoughts are slow and dark and strange, hardly thoughts at all, faint.

Stirrings cold and distant. The brain must be huge all right, I grant you that, but it can't be devoted to conscious thought.'

'What do you mean?'

'The propulsion system, d'Branin. Don't you *feel*? The pulses? They are threatening to rip off the top of my skull. Can't you guess what is driving your damned *volcryn* across the galaxy? And why they avoid gravity wells? Can't you guess how it is moving?'

'No,' d'Branin said, but even as he denied it a dawn of comprehension broke across his face, and he looked away from his companion, back at the swelling immensity of the *volcryn*, its lights moving, its veils a-ripple as it came on and on, across light-years, light-centuries, across eons.

When he looked back at her, he mouthed only a single word: 'Teke,' he said.

She nodded.

*

Melantha Jhirl struggled to lift the injection gun and press it against an artery. It gave a single loud hiss, and the drug flooded her system. She lay back and gathered her strength and tried to think. Esperon, esperon, why was that important? It had killed Lasamer, made him a victim of his own latent abilities, multiplied his power and his vulnerability. Psi. It all came back to psi.

The inner door of the airlock opened. The headless corpse came through.

It moved with jerks, unnatural shufflings, never lifting its legs from the floor. It sagged as it moved, half-crushed by the weight upon it. Each shuffle was crude and sudden; some grim force was literally yanking one leg forward, then the next. It moved in slow motion, arms stiff by its sides.

But it moved.

Melantha summoned her own reserves and began to squirm away from it, never taking her eyes off its advance.

Her thoughts went round and round, searching for the piece out of place, the solution to the chess problem, finding nothing.

The corpse was moving faster than she was. Clearly, visibly, it was gaining.

Melantha tried to stand. She got to her knees with a grunt, her heart pounding. Then one knee. She tried to force herself up, to lift the impossible burden on her shoulders as if she were lifting weights. She was strong, she told herself. She was the improved model.

But when she put all her weight on one leg, her muscles would not hold her. She collapsed, awkwardly, and when she smashed against the floor it was as if she had fallen from a building. She heard a sharp *snap*, and a stab of agony flashed up her arm, her good arm, the arm she had tried to use to break her fall. The pain in her shoulder was terrible and intense. She blinked back tears and choked on her own scream.

The corpse was halfway up the corridor. It must be walking on two broken legs, she realized. It didn't care. A force greater than tendons and bone and muscle was holding it up.

'Melantha . . . heard you . . . are . . . you . . . Melantha?'

'*Quiet,*' she snarled at Royd. She had no breath to waste on talk.

Now she used all the disciplines she had ever learned, willed away the pain. She kicked feebly, her boots scraping for purchase, and she pulled herself forward with her unbroken arm, ignoring the fire in her shoulder.

The corpse came on and on.

She dragged herself across the threshold of the lounge, worming her way under the crashed sled, hoping it would delay the cadaver. The thing that had been Thale Lasamer was a meter behind her.

In the darkness, in the lounge, where it had all begun, Melantha Jhirl ran out of strength.

Her body shuddered and she collapsed on the damp carpet, and she knew that she could go no further.

On the far side of the door, the corpse stood stiffly. The sled began to shake. Then, with the scrape of metal against metal, it slid backwards, moving in tiny sudden increments, jerking itself free and out of the way.

Psi. Melantha wanted to curse it, and cry. Vainly she wished for a psi power of her own, a weapon to blast apart the teke-driven corpse that stalked her. She was improved, she thought despairingly, but not improved enough. Her parents had given her all the genetic gifts they could arrange, but psi was beyond them. The genes were astronomically rare, recessive, and—

—and suddenly it came to her.

'Royd,' she said, putting all of her remaining will into her words. She was weeping, wet, frightened. 'The dial . . . *teke* it. Royd, teke it!'

His reply was faint, troubled. '. . . can't . . . I don't . . . Mother . . . only . . . her . . . not me . . . no . . . Mother . . .'

'Not Mother,' she said, desperate. 'You always . . . say . . . *Mother.* I forgot . . . forgot. Not your mother . . . listen . . . you're a *clone* . . . same genes . . . you have it too . . . power.'

'Don't,' he said. 'Never . . . must be . . . sex-linked.'

'No! It *isn't.* I know . . . Promethean, Royd . . . don't tell a Promethean . . . about genes . . . turn it!'

The sled jumped a third of a meter, and listed to the side. A path was clear.

The corpse came forward.

'. . . trying,' Royd said. 'Nothing . . . I *can't!*'

'She *cured* you,' Melantha said bitterly. 'Better than . . . she . . . was cured . . . prenatal . . . but it's only . . . suppressed . . . you *can!*'

'I . . . don't . . . know . . . how.'

The corpse stood above her. Stopped. Its pale-fleshed hands trembled, spasmed, jerked upward. Long painted fingernails. Made claws. Began to rise.

Melantha swore. '*Royd!*'

'. . . sorry . . .'

She wept and shook and made a futile fist.

And all at once the gravity was gone. Far, far away, she heard Royd cry out and then fall silent.

*

'The flashes come more frequently now,' Karoly d'Branin dictated, 'or perhaps it is simply that I am closer, that I can see them better. Bursts of indigo and deep violet, short and fast-fading. Between the webbing. A field, I think. The flashes are particles of hydrogen, the thin ethereal stuff of the reaches between the stars. They touch the field, between the webbing, the spurs, and shortly flare into the range of visible light. Matter to energy, yes, that is what I guess. My *volcryn* feeds.

'It fills half the universe, comes on and on. We shall not escape it, oh, so sad. Agatha is gone, silent, blood on her faceplate. I can almost see the dark area, almost, almost. I have a strange vision, in the center is a face, small, ratlike, without mouth or nose or eyes, yet still a face somehow, and it stares at me. The veils move so sensuously. The webbing looms around us.

'Ah, the light, the light!'

*

The corpse bobbed awkwardly into the air, its hands hanging limply before it. Melantha, reeling in the weightlessness, was suddenly violently sick. She ripped off the helmet, collapsed it, and pushed away from her own nausea, trying to ready herself for the *Nightflyer's* furious assault.

But the body of Thale Lasamer floated dead and still, and nothing else moved in the darkened lounge. Finally Melantha recovered, and she moved to the corpse, weakly, and pushed it, a small and tentative shove. It sailed across the room.

'Royd?' she said uncertainly.

There was no answer.

She pulled herself through the hole into the control chamber.

And found Royd Eris suspended in his armored suit. She shook him, but he did not stir. Trembling, Melantha Jhirl studied his suit, and then began to dismantle it. She touched him. 'Royd,' she said, 'here. Feel, Royd, here, I'm here, feel it.' His suit came apart easily, and she flung the pieces of it away. 'Royd, *Royd.'*

Dead. Dead. His heart had given out. She punched it, pummeled it, tried to pound it into new life. It did not beat. Dead. Dead.

Melantha Jhirl moved back from him, blinded by her own tears, edged into the console, glanced down.

Dead. Dead.

But the dial on the gravity grid was set on zero.

'Melantha,' said a mellow voice from the walls.

*

I have held the *Nightflyer's* crystalline soul within my hands.

It is deep red and multi-faceted, large as my head, and icy to the touch. In its scarlet depths, two small sparks of smoky light burn fiercely, and sometimes seem to whirl.

I have crawled through the consoles, wound my way carefully past safeguards and cybernets, taking care to damage nothing, and I have laid rough hands on that great crystal, knowing it is where *she* lives.

And I cannot bring myself to wipe it.

Royd's ghost has asked me not to.

Last night we talked about it once again, over brandy and chess in the lounge. Royd cannot drink, of course, but he sends his spectre to smile at me, and he tells me where he wants his pieces moved.

For the thousandth time he offered to take me back to Avalon, or any world of my choice, if only I would go outside and complete the repairs we abandoned so many years ago, so the *Nightflyer* might safely slip into stardrive.

For the thousandth time I refused.

He is stronger now, no doubt. Their genes are the same, after all. Their power is the same. Dying, he too found the strength to impress himself upon the great crystal. The ship is alive with both of them, and frequently they fight. Sometimes she outwits him for a moment, and the *Nightflyer* does odd, erratic things. The gravity goes up or down or off completely. Blankets wrap themselves around my throat when I sleep. Objects come hurtling out of dark corners.

Those times have come less frequently of late, though. When they do come, Royd stops her, or I do. Together, the *Nightflyer* is ours.

Royd claims he is strong enough alone, that he does not really need me, that he can keep her under check. I wonder. Over the chessboard, I still beat him nine games out of ten.

And there are other considerations. Our work, for one. Karoly would be proud of us. The *volcryn* will soon enter the mists of the Tempter's Veil, and we follow close behind. Studying, recording, doing all that old d'Branin would have wanted us to do. It is all in the computer, and on tape and paper as well, should the system ever be wiped. It will be interesting to see how the *volcryn* thrives in the Veil. Matter is so thick there, compared to the thin diet of interstellar hydrogen on which the creature has fed so many endless eons.

We have tried to communicate with it, with no success. I do not believe it is sentient at all. And lately Royd has tried to imitate its ways, gathering all his energies in an attempt to move the *Nightflyer* by teke. Sometimes, oddly, his mother even joins with him in those efforts. So far they have always failed, but we will keep trying.

So goes our work. We know our results will reach humanity. Royd and I have discussed it, and we have a plan. Before I die, when my time is near, I will destroy the central crystal and clear the computers, and afterwards I will set course manually for the close vicinity of an inhabited world. The *Nightflyer* will become a true ghost ship then. It will work. I have all the time I need, and I am an improved model.

I will not consider the other option, although it means much to me that Royd suggests it again and again. No doubt I could finish the repairs, and perhaps Royd could control the ship without me, and go on with the work. But that is not important.

I was wrong so many times. The esperon, the monitors, my control of the others; all of them my failures, payment for my hubris. Failure hurts. When I finally touched him, for the first and last and only time, his body was still warm. But he was gone already. He never felt my touch. I could not keep that promise.

But I can keep my other.

I will not leave him alone with her.

Ever.

The Monkey Treatment

Kenny Dorchester was a fat man.

He had not always been a fat man, of course. He had come into the world a perfectly normal infant of modest weight, but the normalcy was short-lived in Kenny's case, and before very long he had become a chubby-cheeked toddler well-swaddled in baby fat. From then on it was all downhill and upscale so far as Kenny was concerned. He became a pudgy child, a corpulent adolescent, and a positively porcine college student, all in good turn, and by adulthood he had left all those intermediate steps behind and graduated into full obesity.

People became obese for a variety of reasons, some of them physiological and some psychological. Kenny's reason was relatively simple: food. Kenny Dorchester loved to eat. Often he would paraphrase Will Rogers, winking broadly, and tell his friends that he had never met a food he didn't like. This was not precisely true, since Kenny loathed both liver and prune juice. Perhaps, if his mother had served them more often during his childhood, he would never have attained the girth and gravity that so haunted him at maturity. Unfortunately, Gina Dorchester was more inclined to lasagne and roast turkey with stuffing and sweet potatoes and chocolate pudding and veal cordon bleu and buttered corn-on-the-cob and stacks of blueberry pancakes (although not all in one meal) than she was to liver and prune juice, and once Kenny had expressed his preference in the matter by retching his liver back onto his plate, she obligingly never served liver and prune juice again. Thus, all unknowing, she set her son on the soft, suety road to the monkey treatment. But that was long ago and the poor woman really cannot be blamed, since it was Kenny himself who ate his way there.

Kenny loved pepperoni pizza, or plain pizza, or garbage pizza with everything on it including anchovies. Kenny could eat an entire slab of barbequed ribs, either beef or pork, and the spicier the sauce was the more he approved. He was fond of rare prime rib and roast chicken and Rock Cornish game hens stuffed with rice, and he was hardly the sort to object to a nice sirloin or a platter of fried shrimp or a hunk of kielbasa. He liked his burgers with everything on them, and fries and onion rings on the side, please. There was nothing you could do to his friend the potato that would turn him against it, but he was also partial to pasta and rice, to yams candied and un-, and even to mashed rutabagas. 'Desserts are my downfall,' he would sometimes say, for he liked sweets of all varieties, especially devil's food cake and cannoli and hot apple pie with whipped cream. 'Bread is my downfall,' he would say at other times, when it seemed likely that no dessert was forthcoming, and so saying he would rip off another chunk of sourdough or butter up another crescent roll or reach for another slice of garlic bread, which was a particular vice. Kenny had a lot of particular vices. He thought himself an authority on both fine restaurants and fast-food franchises, and could discourse endlessly and knowledgeably about either. He relished Greek food and Chinese food and Japanese food and Korean food and German food and Italian food and French food and Indian food, and was always on the lookout for new ethnic groups so he might 'expand my cultural horizons.' When Saigon fell, Kenny speculated about how many of the Vietnamese refugees would be likely to open restaurants. When Kenny traveled, he always made it a point to gorge himself on the area's specialty, and he could tell you the best places to eat in any of twenty-four major American cities, while reminiscing fondly about the meals he had enjoyed in each of them. His favorite writers were James Beard and Calvin Trillin.

'I live a tasty life!' Kenny Dorchester would proclaim, beaming. And so he did. But Kenny also had a secret. He did not often think of it and never spoke it, but it was there nonetheless, down at the heart of him beneath all those great rolls of flesh, and not all his sauces could drown it, nor could his trusty fork keep it at bay.

Kenny Dorchester did not *like* being fat.

Kenny was like a man torn between two lovers, for while he loved his food with an abiding passion, he also dreamed of other loves, of women, and he knew that in order to secure the one he would have to give up the other, and that knowledge was his secret pain. Often he wrestled with the dilemmas posed by his situation. It seemed to Kenny that while it might be preferable to be slender and have a woman than to be fat and have only a crawfish bisque, nonetheless the latter was not entirely to be spurned. Both were sources of happiness after all, and the real misery fell to those who gave up the one and failed to obtain the other. Nothing depressed or saddened Kenny so much as the sight of a fat person eating cottage cheese. Such pathetic human beings never seemed to get appreciably skinnier, Kenny thought, and were doomed to go through life bereft of both women and crawfish, a fate too grim to contemplate.

Yet despite all his misgivings, at times the secret pain inside Kenny Dorchester would flare up mightily, and fill him with a sense of resolve that made him feel as if anything might be possible. The sight of a particularly beautiful woman or the word of some new, painless, and wonderfully effective diet were particularly prone to trigger what Kenny thought of as his 'aberrations.' When such moods came, Kenny would be driven to diet.

Over the years he tried every diet there was, briefly and secretly. He tried Dr Atkins' diet and Dr Stillman's diet, the grapefruit diet and the brown rice diet. He tried the liquid protein diet, which was truly disgusting. He lived for a week on nothing but Slender and Sego, until he had run through all of the flavors and gotten bored. He joined a Pounds-Off club and attended a few meetings, until he discovered that the company of fellow dieters did him no good whatsoever, since all they talked about was food. He went on a hunger strike that lasted until he got hungry. He tried the fruit juice diet, and the drinking man's diet (even though he was not a drinking man), and the martinis-and-whipped-cream diet (he omitted the martinis). A hypnotist told him that his favorite foods tasted bad and he wasn't hungry anyway, but it was a damned lie, and that was that for hypnosis. He had his behavior modified so he put down his fork between bites, used small plates that looked full even with tiny portions, and wrote down everything he ate in a notebook. That left him with stacks of notebooks, a great many small dishes to wash, and unusual manual dexterity in putting down and picking up his fork. His favorite diet was the one that said you could eat all you wanted of your favorite food, so long as you ate nothing *but* that. The only problem was that Kenny couldn't decide what was really his one true favorite, so he wound up eating ribs for a week, and pizza for a week, and Peking duck for a week (that was an expensive week), and losing no weight whatsoever, though he did have a great time.

Most of Kenny Dorchester's aberrations lasted for a week or two. Then, like a man coming out of a fog, he would look around and realize that he was absolutely miserable, losing relatively little weight, and in imminent danger of turning into one of those cottage cheese fatties he so pitied. At that point he would chuck the diet, go out for a good meal, and be restored to his normal self for another six months, until his secret pain surfaced again.

Then, one Friday night, he spied Henry Moroney at the Slab.

The Slab was Kenny's favorite barbeque joint. It specialized in ribs, charred and meaty and served dripping with a sauce that Kenny approved of mightily. And on Fridays the Slab offered all the ribs you could eat for only fifteen dollars, which was prohibitively high for most people but a bargain for Kenny, who could eat a great many ribs. On that particular Friday, Kenny had just finished his first slab and was waiting for the second, sipping beer and eating bread, when he chanced to look up and realized, with a start, that the slim haggard fellow in the next booth was, in fact, Henry Moroney.

Kenny Dorchester was nonplussed. The last time he had seen Henry Moroney they had both been unhappy Pounds-Off members, and Moroney had been the only one in the club who weighed more than Kenny did. A great fat whale of a man, Moroney had carried about the cruel nickname of 'Boney,' as he confessed to his fellow members. Only now the nickname seemed to fit. Not only was Moroney skinny enough to hint at a ribcage under his skin, but the table in front of him was absolutely littered with bones. That was the detail that intrigued Kenny Dorchester. All those bones. He began to count, and he lost track before very long, because all the bones were disordered, strewn about on empty plates in little puddles of drying sauce. But from the sheer mass of them it was clear that Moroney had put away at least four slabs of ribs, maybe five.

It seemed to Kenny Dorchester that Henry 'Boney' Moroney knew the secret. If there was a way to lose hundreds of pounds and still be able to consume five slabs of ribs at a sitting, that was something Kenny desperately needed to know. So he rose and walked over to Moroney's booth and squeezed in opposite him. 'It is you,' he said.

Moroney looked up as if he hadn't noticed Kenny until that very second. 'Oh,' he said in a thin, tired voice. 'You.' He seemed very weary, but Kenny thought that was probably natural for someone who had lost so much weight. Moroney's eyes were sunk in deep gray hollows, his flesh sagged in pale empty folds, and he was slouching forward with his elbows on the table as if he were too exhausted to sit up straight. He looked terrible, but he had lost so much *weight* . . .

'You look wonderful!' Kenny blurted. 'How did you do it? How? You must tell me, Henry, really you must.'

'No,' Moroney whispered. 'No, Kenny. Go away.'

Kenny was taken aback. 'Really!' he declared. 'That's not very friendly. I'm not leaving until I know your secret, Henry. You owe it to me. Think of all the times we've broken bread together.'

'Oh, Kenny,' Moroney said, in his faint and terrible voice. 'Go, please, go, you don't want to know, it's too . . . too . . .' He stopped in mid-sentence, and a spasm passed across his face. He moaned. His head twisted wildly to the side, as if he were having some kind of a fit, and his hands beat on the table. 'Ooooo,' he said.

'Henry, what's wrong?' Kenny said, alarmed. He was certain now that Boney Moroney had overdone his diet.

'Ohhhh,' Moroney sighed in sudden relief. 'Nothing, nothing. I'm fine.' His voice had none of the enthusiasm of his words. 'I'm wonderful, in fact. Wonderful, Kenny. I haven't been so slim since . . . since . . . why, never.

It's a miracle.' He smiled faintly. 'I'll be at my goal soon, and then it will be over. I think. Think I'll be at my goal. Don't know my weight, really.' He put a hand to his brow. 'I am slender, though, truly I am. Don't you think I look good?'

'Yes, yes,' Kenny agreed impatiently. 'But how? You must tell me. Surely not those Pounds-Off phonies . . .'

'No,' said Moroney weakly. 'No, it was the monkey treatment. Here, I'll write it down for you.' He took out a pencil and scrawled an address on a napkin.

Kenny stuffed the napkin into a pocket. 'The monkey treatment? I've never heard of that. What is it?'

Henry Moroney licked his lips . . .' 'They . . .' he started, and then another fit hit him, and his head twitched around grotesquely. 'Go,' he said to Kenny, 'just go. It works, Kenny, yes, oh. The monkey treatment, yes. I can't say more. You have the address. Excuse me.' He placed his hands flat on the table and pushed himself to his feet, then walked over to the cashier, shuffling like a man twice his age. Kenny Dorchester watched him go, and decided that Moroney had *definitely* overdone this monkey treatment, whatever it was. He had never had tics or spasms before, or whatever that had been.

'You have to have a sense of proportion about these things,' Kenny said stoutly to himself. He patted his pocket to make sure the napkin was still there, resolved that he would handle things more sensibly than Boney Moroney, and returned to his own booth and his second slab of ribs. He ate four that night, figuring that if he was going to start a diet tomorrow he had better get in some eating while the eating was good.

The next day being Saturday, Kenny was free to pursue the monkey treatment and the dream of a new, slender him. He rose early, and immediately rushed to the bathroom to weigh himself on his digital scale, which he loved dearly because you didn't have to squint down at the numbers, since they lit up nice and bright and precise in red. This morning they lit up as 367. He had gained a few pounds, but he hardly minded. The monkey treatment would strip them off again soon enough.

Kenny tried to phone ahead, to make sure this place was open on a Saturday, but that proved to be impossible. Moroney had written nothing but an address, and there was no diet center at that listing in the yellow pages, nor a health club, nor a doctor. Kenny looked in the white pages under 'Monkey' but that yielded nothing. So there was nothing to do but go down there in person.

Even that was troublesome. The address was way down by the docks in a singularly unsavory neighborhood, and Kenny had a hard time getting the cab to take him there. He finally got his way by threatening to report the cabbie to the commissioner. Kenny Dorchester knew his rights.

Before long, though, he began to have his doubts. The narrow little streets they wound through were filthy and decaying, altogether unappetizing and it occurred to Kenny that any diet center located down here might offer only dangerous quackery. The block in question was an old commercial strip gone to seed, and it put his hackles up even more. Half the stores were boarded closed, and the rest lurked behind filthy dark windows and iron gates. The cab pulled up in front of an absolutely miserable old brick storefront, flanked by two vacant lots full of rubble, its plate glass windows grimed over impenetrably. A faded Coca-Cola sign swung back and forth, groaning, above the door. But the number was the number that Boney Moroney had written down.

'Here you are,' the cabbie said impatiently, as Kenny peered out the taxi window, aghast.

'This does not look correct,' Kenny said. 'I will investigate. Kindly wait here until I am certain this is the place.'

The cabbie nodded, and Kenny slid over and levered himself out of the taxi. He had taken two steps when he heard the cab shift gears and pull away from the curb, screeching. He turned and watched in astonishment. 'Here, you can't . . .' he began. But it did. He would most definitely report that man to the commissioner, he decided.

But meanwhile he was stranded down here, and it seemed foolish not to proceed when he had come this far. Whether he took the monkey treatment or not, no doubt they would let him use a phone to summon another cab. Kenny screwed up his resolution, and went on in the grimy, unmarked storefront. A bell tinkled as he opened the door.

It was dark inside. The dust and dirt on the windows kept out nearly all the sunlight, and it took a moment for Kenny's eyes to adjust. When they did, he saw to his horror that he had walked into someone's living room. One of those gypsy families that moved into abandoned stores, he thought. He was standing on a threadbare carpet, and around and about him was a scatter of old furniture, no doubt the best the Salvation Army had to offer. An ancient black-and-white TV set crouched in one corner, staring at him blindly. The room stank of urine. 'Sorry,' Kenny muttered feebly, terrified that some dark gypsy youth would come out of the shadows to knife him. 'Sorry.' He had stepped backwards, groping behind him for the doorknob, when the man came out of the back room.

'Ah!' the man said, spying Kenny at once from tiny bright eyes. 'Ah, the monkey treatment!' He rubbed his hands together and grinned. Kenny was terrified. The man was the fattest, grossest human being that Kenny had ever laid eyes on. He had squeezed through the door sideways. He was fatter than Kenny, fatter than Boney Moroney. He literally dripped with fat. And he was repulsive in other ways as well. He had the complexion of a mushroom, and miniscule little eyes almost invisible in rolls of pale flesh. His corpulence seemed to have overwhelmed even his hair, of which he had very little. Bare-chested, he displayed vast areas of folded, bulging skin, and his huge breasts flopped as he came forward quickly and seized Kenny by the arm. 'The monkey treatment!' he repeated eagerly, pulling Kenny forward. Kenny looked at him, in shock, and was struck dumb by his grin. When the man grinned, his mouth seemed to become half his face, a grotesque semicircle full of shining white teeth.

'No,' Kenny said at last, 'no, I have changed my mind.' Boney Moroney or no, he didn't think he cared to try this monkey treatment if it was administered by such as this. In the first place, it clearly could not be very effective, or else the man would not be so monstrously obese. Besides, it was probably dangerous, some quack potion of monkey hormones or something like that. 'NO!' Kenny repeated more forcefully, trying to wrest his arm free from the grasp of the grotesquerie who held it.

But it was useless. The man was distinctly larger and infinitely stronger than Kenny, and he propelled him across the room with ease, oblivious to Kenny's protests, grinning like a maniac all the while.

'Fat man,' he burbled, and as if to prove his point he reached out and seized one of Kenny's bulges and twisted it painfully. 'Fat, fat, fat, no good. Monkey treatment make you thin.'

'Yes, but . . .'

'Monkey treatment,' the man repeated, and somehow he had gotten behind Kenny. He put his weight against Kenny's back and pushed, and Kenny staggered through a curtained doorway into the back room. The smell of urine was much stronger in there, strong enough to make him want to retch. It was pitch black, and from all sides Kenny heard rustlings and scurryings in the darkness. *Rats*, he thought wildly. Kenny was deathly afraid of rats. He fumbled about and propelled himself toward the square of dim light that marked the curtain he had come through.

Before he was quite there, a high-pitched chittering sounded suddenly from behind him, sharp and rapid as fire from a machine gun. Then another voice took it up, then a third, and suddenly the dark was alive with the terrible hammering noise. Kenny put his hands over his ears and staggered through the curtain, but just as he emerged he felt something brush the back of his neck, something warm and hairy. 'Aieee!' he screamed, dancing out into the front room where the tremendous bare-chested madman was waiting patiently. Kenny hopped from one foot to the other, screeching, 'Aieee, a rat, a rat on my back. Get it off, get it *off*.' He was trying to grab for it with both hands, but the thing was very quick, and shifted around so cleverly so that he couldn't get ahold of it. But he felt it there, alive, moving. 'Help me, help me!' he called out. 'A rat!'

The proprietor grinned at him and shook his head, so all his many chins went bobbing merrily. 'No, no,' he said. 'No rat, fat man. Monkey. You get the monkey treatment.' Then he stepped forward and seized Kenny by the elbow again, and drew him over to a full-length mirror mounted on the wall. It was so dim in the room that Kenny could scarcely make out anything in the mirror, except that it wasn't wide enough and chopped off both his arms. The man stepped back and yanked a pull-cord dangling from the ceiling, and a single bare lightbulb clicked on overhead. The bulb swung back and forth, back and forth, so the light shifted crazily. Kenny Dorchester trembled and stared at the mirror.

'Oh!' he said.

There was a monkey on his back.

Actually it was on his shoulders, its legs wrapped around his thick neck and twined together beneath his triple chin. He could feel its monkey hair scratching the back of his neck, could feel its warm little monkey paws lightly grasping his ears. It was a very tiny monkey. As Kenny looked into the mirror, he saw it peek out from behind his head, grinning hugely. It had quick darting eyes, coarse brown hair, and altogether too many shiny white teeth for Kenny's liking. Its long prehensile tail swayed about restlessly, like some hairy snake that had grown out of the back of Kenny's skull.

Kenny's heart was pounding away like some great air-hammer lodged in his chest and he was altogether distressed by this place, this man, and this monkey. But he gathered all his reserves and forced himself to be calm. It wasn't a rat, after all. The little monkey couldn't harm him. It had to be a trained monkey, the way it had perched on his shoulders. Its owner must let it ride around like this, and when Kenny had come unwillingly through the curtain, it had probably mistook him. All fat men look alike in the dark. Kenny grabbed behind him and tried to pull the monkey loose, but somehow he couldn't seem to get a grip on it. The mirror, reversing everything, just made it worse. He jumped up and down ponderously, shaking the entire room and making the furniture leap around every time he landed, but the monkey held on tight to his ears and could not be dislodged.

Finally, with what Kenny thought was incredible aplomb under the circumstances, he turned to the gross proprietor and said, 'Your monkey, sir. Kindly help me remove it.'

'No, no,' the man said. 'Make you skinny. Monkey treatment. You no want to be skinny?'

'Of course I do,' Kenny said unhappily, 'but this is absurd.' He was confused. This monkey on his back seemed to be part of the monkey treatment, but that certainly didn't make very much sense.

'Go,' the man said. He reached up and snapped off the light with a sharp tug that sent the bulb careening wildly again. Then he started toward Kenny, who backpedaled nervously. 'Go,' the man repeated, as he grabbed Kenny's arm again. 'Out, out. You get monkey treatment, you go now.'

'See here!' Kenny said furiously. 'Let go of me! Get this monkey off me, do you hear? I don't want your monkey! Do you hear me? Quit pushing, sir! I tell you, I have friends with the police department, you aren't going to get away with this. Here now . . .'

But all his protestations were useless. The man was a veritable tidal wave of sweating, smelling pale flesh, and he put his weight against Kenny and propelled him helplessly towards the door. The bell rang again as he pulled it open and shoved Kenny out into the garish bright sunlight.

'I'm not going to pay for this!' Kenny said stoutly, staggering. 'Not a cent, do you hear!'

'No charge for monkey treatment,' the man said, grinning.

'At least let me call a cab,' Kenny began, but it was too late, the man had closed the door. Kenny stepped forward angrily and tried to yank it back open, but it did not budge. Locked. 'Open up in there!' Kenny demanded at the top of his lungs. There was no reply. He shouted again, and grew suddenly and uncomfortably aware that he was being stared at. Kenny turned around. Across the street three old winos were sitting on the stoop of a boarded-up store, passing a bottle in a brown paper bag and regarding him through wary eyes.

That was when Kenny Dorchester recalled that he was standing there in the street in broad daylight with a monkey on his back.

A flush crept up his neck and spread across his cheeks. He felt very silly. 'A pet!' he shouted to the winos, forcing a smile. 'Just my little pet!' They went staring on. Kenny gave a last angry look at the locked door, and set off down the street, his legs pumping furiously. He had to get to someplace private.

Rounding the corner, he came upon a dark, narrow alley behind two gray old tenement buildings, and ducked inside, wheezing for breath. He sat down heavily on a trash can, pulled out his handkerchief, and mopped his brow. The monkey shifted just a bit, and Kenny felt it move. 'Off me!' he shouted, reaching up and back again to try to wrench it off by the scruff of its neck, only to have it elude him once more. He tucked away his handkerchief and groped behind his head with both hands, but he just couldn't get ahold of it. Finally, exhausted, he stopped, and tried to think.

The legs! he thought. The legs under his chins! That's the ticket! Very calmly and deliberately he reached up, and felt for the monkey's legs, and wrapped one big fleshy hand around each of them. He took a deep breath and then savagely tried to yank them apart, as if they were two ends of a giant wishbone.

The monkey attacked him.

One hand twisted his right ear painfully, until it felt like it was being pulled clean off his head. The other started hammering against his temple, beating a furious tattoo. Kenny Dorchester yelped in distress and let go of the monkey's legs – which he hadn't budged for all his efforts. The monkey quit beating on him and released his ear. Kenny sobbed, half with relief and half with frustration. He felt wretched.

He sat there in that filthy alley for ages, defeated in his efforts to remove the monkey and afraid to go back to the street where people would point at him and laugh, or make rude insulting comments under their breath. It was difficult enough going through life as a fat man, Kenny thought. How much worse, then, to face the cruel world as a fat man with a monkey on his back. Kenny did not want to know. He resolved to sit there on that trash can in the dark alley until he died or the monkey died, rather than face shame and ridicule on the streets.

His resolve endured about an hour. Then Kenny Dorchester began to get hungry. Maybe people would laugh at him, but they had always laughed at him, so what did it matter? Kenny rose and dusted himself off, while the monkey settled itself more comfortably on his neck. He ignored it, and decided to go in search of a pepperoni pizza.

He did not find one easily. The abysmal slum in which he had been stranded had a surfeit of winos, dangerous-looking teenagers, and burned-out or boarded-up buildings, but it had precious few pizza parlors. Nor did it have any taxis. Kenny walked down the main thoroughfare with brisk dignity, looking neither left nor right, heading for safer neighborhoods as fast as his plump little legs could carry him. Twice he came upon phone booths, and eagerly fetched out a coin to summon transportation, but both times the phones proved to be out of order. Vandals, thought Kenny Dorchester, were as bad as rats.

Finally, after what seemed like hours of walking, he stumbled upon a sleazy café. The lettering on the window said JOHN'S GRILL, and there was a neon sign about the door that said, simply, EAT. Kenny was very familiar with those three lovely letters, and he recognized the sign two blocks off. It called to him like a beacon. Even before he entered, he knew it was rather unlikely that such a place would include pepperoni pizza on its menu, but by this time Kenny had ceased to care.

As he pushed the door aside, Kenny experienced a brief moment of apprehension, partially because he felt very out of place in the café, where the rest of the diners all appeared to be muggers, and partially because he was afraid they would refuse to serve him because of the monkey on his back. Acutely uncomfortable in the doorway, he moved quickly to a small table in an obscure corner, where he hoped to escape the curious stares. A gaunt gray-haired waitress in a faded pink uniform moved purposefully toward him, and Kenny sat with his eyes downcast, playing nervously with the salt, pepper, and ketchup, dreading the moment when she arrived and said, 'Hey, you can't bring that thing in here!'

But when the waitress reached his table, she simply pulled a pad out of her apron's pocket and stood poised, pencil in hand. 'Well?' she demanded. 'What'll it be?'

Kenny stared up in shock, and smiled. He stammered a bit, then recovered himself and ordered a cheese omelet with a double side of bacon, coffee and a large glass of milk, and cinnamon toast. 'Do hash browns come with?' he asked hopefully, but the waitress shook her head and departed.

What a marvelous kind woman, Kenny thought as he waited for his meal and shredded a paper napkin thoughtfully. What a wonderful place! Why, they hadn't even mentioned his monkey! How very polite of them.

The food arrived shortly. 'Ahhhh,' Kenny said as the waitress laid it out in front of him on the Formica tabletop. He was ravenous. He selected a slice of cinnamon toast, and brought it to his mouth.

And a little monkey hand darted out from behind his head and snatched it clean away.

Kenny Dorchester sat in numb surprise for an instant, his suddenly empty hand poised before his mouth. He heard the monkey eating his toast, chomping noisily. Then, before Kenny had quite comprehended what was happening, the monkey's great long tail snaked in under his armpit, curled around his glass of milk, and spirited it up and away in the blink of an eye. '*Hey!*' Kenny said, but he was much too slow. Behind his back he heard slurping, sucking sounds, and all of a sudden the glass came vaulting over his left shoulder. He caught it before it fell and smashed, and set it down unsteadily. The monkey's tail came stealthily around and headed for his bacon. Kenny grabbed up a fork and stabbed at it, but the monkey was faster than he was. The bacon vanished, and the tines of the fork bent against the hard Formica uselessly. By then Kenny knew he was in a race. Dropping the bent fork, he used his spoon to cut off a chunk of the omelet, dripping cheese, and he bent forward as he lifted it, quick as he could. The monkey was quicker. A little hand flashed in from somewhere, and the spoon had only a tantalizing gob of half-melted cheese remaining on it when it reached Kenny's mouth. He lunged back towards his plate, and loaded up again, but it didn't matter how fast he tried to be. The monkey had two paws and a tail, and once it even used a little monkey foot to snatch something away from him. In hardly any time at all, Kenny Dorchester's meal was gone. He sat there staring down at the empty, greasy plate, and he felt tears gathering in his eyes.

The waitress reappeared without Kenny noticing. 'My, you sure are a hungry one,' she said to him, ripping off his check from her pad and putting it in front of him. 'Polished that off quicker than anyone I ever saw.'

Kenny looked up at her. 'But I *didn't*,' he protested. 'The monkey ate it all!'

The waitress looked at him very oddly. 'The monkey?' she said, uncertainly.

'The monkey,' Kenny said. He did not care for the way she was staring at him, like he was crazy or something.

'What monkey?' she asked. 'You didn't sneak no animals in here, did you? The Board of Health don't allow no animals in here, Mister.'

'What do you mean, *sneak?*' Kenny said in annoyance. 'Why the monkey is right on me . . .' He never got a chance to finish. Just then the monkey hit him, a tremendous hard blow on the left side of his face. The force of it twisted his head half-around, and Kenny yelped in pain and shock.

The waitress seemed concerned. 'You OK, Mister?' she asked. 'You ain't gonna have a fit, are you, twitching like that?'

'*I didn't twitch!*' Kenny all but shouted. 'The goddamned monkey hit me! Can't you see?'

'Oh,' said the waitress, taking a step backwards. 'Oh, of course. Your monkey hit you. Pesky little things, ain't they?'

Kenny pounded his fists on the table in frustration. 'Never mind,' he said, 'just never mind.' He snatched up the check – the monkey did not take that away from him, he noted – and rose. 'Here,' he said, pulling out his wallet. 'And you have a phone in this place, don't you? Call me a cab, all right? You can do that, can't you?'

'Sure,' the waitress said, moving to the register to ring up his meal. Everyone in the café was staring at him. 'Sure, Mister,' she muttered. 'A cab. We'll get you a cab right away.'

Kenny waited, fuming. The cab driver made no comment on his monkey. Instead of going home, he took the cab to his favorite pizza place, three blocks from his apartment. Then he stormed right in and ordered a large pepperoni. The monkey ate it all, even when Kenny tried to confuse it by picking up one slice in each hand moving them simultaneously toward his mouth. Unfortunately, the monkey had two hands as well, both of them faster than Kenny's. When the pizza was completely gone, Kenny thought for a moment, summoned over the waitress, and ordered a second. This time he got a large anchovy. He thought that was very clever.

Kenny Dorchester had never met anyone else besides himself who liked anchovy pizza. Those little salty fishes would be his salvation, he thought. To increase the odds, when the pizza arrived Kenny picked up the hot pepper shaker and covered it with enough hot peppers to ignite a major conflagration. Then, feeling confident, he tried to eat a slice.

The monkey liked anchovy pizza with lots of hot peppers. Kenny Dorchester almost wept.

He went from the pizza place to the Slab, from the Slab to a fine Greek restaurant, from the Greek restaurant to a local McDonald's, from a McDonald's to a bakery that made the most marvelous chocolate éclairs. Sooner or later, Kenny Dorchester thought, the monkey would be full. It was only a very little monkey, after all. How much food could it eat? He would just keep on ordering food, he resolved, and the monkey would either reach its limit or rupture and die.

That day Kenny spent more than two hundred dollars on meals.

He got absolutely nothing to eat.

The monkey seemed to be a bottomless pit. If it had a capacity, that capacity was surely greater than the capacity of Kenny's wallet. Finally he was forced to admit defeat. The monkey could not be stuffed into submission.

Kenny cast about for another tactic, and finally hit on it. Monkeys were stupid, after all, even invisible monkeys with prodigious appetites. Smiling shyly, Kenny went to a neighborhood supermarket, and picked up a box of banana pudding (it seemed appropriate) and a box of rat poison. Humming a spry little tune, he walked on home, and set to work making the pudding, stirring in liberal amounts of rat poison as it cooked. The poison was nicely odorless. The pudding smelled wonderful. Kenny poured it into some dessert cups to cool, and watched television for an hour or so. Finally he rose nonchalantly, went to the refrigerator, and got out a pudding and a nice big spoon. He sat back down in front of the set, spooned up a generous glob of pudding, and brought it to his open mouth. Where he paused. And paused. And waited.

The monkey did nothing.

Maybe it was full at last, Kenny thought. He put aside the poisoned pudding and rushed back into his kitchen, where he found a box of vanilla wafers hiding on a shelf, and a few forlorn Fig Newtons as well.

The monkey ate all of them.

A tear trickled down Kenny's cheek. The monkey would let him have all the poisoned pudding he wanted, it seemed, but nothing else. He reached back half-heartedly and tried to grab the monkey once again, thinking maybe all that eating would have slowed it down some, but it was a vain hope. The monkey evaded him, and when Kenny persisted the monkey bit his finger. Kenny yowled and snatched his hand back. His finger was bleeding. He sucked on it. That much, at least, the monkey permitted him.

When he had washed his finger and wrapped a Band-Aid around it, Kenny returned to his living room and seated himself heavily, weary and defeated, in front of his television set. An old rerun of *The Galloping Gourmet* was coming on. He couldn't stand it. He jabbed at his remote control to change the channel, and watched blindly for hours, sunk in despair, weeping at the Betty Crocker commercials. Finally, during the late late show, he stirred a little at one of the frequent public service announcements. That was it, he thought, he had to enlist others, he had to get help.

He picked up his phone and punched out the Crisis Line number.

The woman who answered sounded kind and sympathetic and very beautiful, and Kenny began to pour out his heart to her, all about the monkey that wouldn't let him eat, about how nobody else seemed to notice the monkey, about . . . but he had barely gotten his heart-pouring going good when the monkey smashed him across the side of the head. Kenny moaned. 'What's wrong?' the woman asked. The monkey yanked his ear. Kenny tried to ignore the pain and keep on talking, but the monkey kept hurting him until finally he shuddered and sobbed and hung up the phone.

This is a nightmare, Kenny thought, a terrible nightmare. And so thinking, he pushed himself to his feet and staggered off to bed, hoping that everything would be normal in the morning, that the monkey would have been nothing but part of some wretched dream, no doubt brought on by indigestion.

The merciless little monkey would not even allow him to sleep properly, Kenny discovered. He was accustomed to sleeping on his back, with his hands folded very primly on his stomach. But when he undressed and tried to assume that position, the monkey fists came raining down on his poor head like some furious hairy hail. The monkey was not about to be squashed between Kenny's bulk and the pillows, it seemed. Kenny squealed with pain and rolled over on his stomach. He was very uncomfortable this way and had difficulty falling asleep, but it was the only way the monkey would leave him alone.

The next morning Kenny Dorchester drifted slowly into wakefulness, his cheek mashed against the pillows and his right arm still asleep. He was afraid to move. It was all a dream, he told himself, there is no monkey, what a silly thing that would be, monkey indeed, it was only that Boney Moroney had told him about this 'monkey treatment' and he had slept on it and had a nightmare. He couldn't feel anything on his back, not a thing. This was just like any other morning. He opened one bleary eye. His bedroom looked perfectly normal. Still he was afraid to move. It was very peaceful lying here like this, monkeyless, and he wanted to savor the feeling. So Kenny lay very still for the longest time, watching the numbers on his digital clock change slowly.

Then his stomach growled at him. 'There is no monkey!' he proclaimed loudly, and he sat up in bed.

He felt the monkey shift.

Kenny trembled and almost started to weep again, but he controlled himself with an effort. No monkey was going to get the best of Kenny Dorchester, he told himself. Grimacing, he donned his slippers and plodded into the bathroom.

The monkey peered out cautiously from behind his head while Kenny was shaving. He glared at it in the bathroom mirror. It seemed to have grown a bit, but this was hardly surprising, considering how much it had eaten yesterday. Kenny toyed with the idea of trying to cut the monkey's throat, but decided that his Norelco electric shaver was not terribly well suited to that end. And even if he used a knife, trying to stab behind his own back while looking in the mirror was a dangerously uncertain proposition.

Before leaving the bathroom, Kenny was struck by a whim. He stepped on his scale.

The numbers lit up at once. 367. The same as yesterday, he thought. The monkey weighed nothing. He frowned. No, that had to be wrong. No doubt the little monkey weighed a pound or two, but its weight was offset by whatever poundage Kenny had lost. He had to have lost *some* weight, he reasoned, since he hadn't been allowed to eat anything for ever so long. He stepped off the scale, then got back on quickly, just to double-check. It still read 367. Kenny was certain that he had lost weight. Perhaps some good would come of his travails after all. The thought made him feel oddly cheerful.

Kenny grew even more cheerful at breakfast. For the first time since he had gotten his monkey, he managed to get some food in his mouth.

When he arrived at the kitchen, he debated between French toast and bacon and eggs, but only briefly. Then he decided he would never get to taste either. Instead, with a somber fatalism, Kenny fetched down a bowl and filled it with corn flakes and milk. The monkey would probably steal it all anyway, he thought, so there was no sense going to any trouble.

Quick as he could he hurried the spoon to his mouth. The monkey grabbed it away. Kenny had expected it, had known it would happen, but when the monkey hand wrenched the spoon away he nonetheless felt a sudden and terrible grief. 'No,' he said useless. 'No, no, no.' He could hear the corn flakes crunching in that filthy monkey mouth, and he felt milk dropping down the back of his neck. Tears gathered in his eyes as he stared down at the bowl of corn flakes, so near and yet so far.

Then he had an idea.

Kenny Dorchester lunged forward and stuck his face right down in the bowl.

The monkey twisted his ear and shrieked and pounded on his temple, but Kenny didn't care. He was sucking in milk gleefully and gobbling up as many corn flakes as his mouth could hold. By the time the monkey's tail lashed around angrily and sent the bowl sailing from the table to the floor, Kenny had a huge wet mouthful. His cheeks bulged and milk dribbled down his chin, and somehow he'd gotten a corn flake up his nostril, but Kenny was in heaven. He chewed and swallowed as fast as he could, almost choking on the food.

When it was all gone he licked his lips and rose triumphantly. 'Ha, ha,' he said. 'Ha, ha, ha.' He walked back to his bedroom with great dignity and dressed, sneering at the monkey in the full-length bedroom mirror. He had beaten it.

In the days and weeks that followed, Kenny Dorchester settled into a new sort of daily routine and an uneasy accommodation with his monkey. It proved easier than he might have imagined, except at meal times. When he was not attempting to get food into his mouth, it was almost possible to forget about the monkey entirely. At work it sat peacefully on his back while Kenny shuffled his papers and made his phone calls. His coworkers either failed to notice the monkey or were sufficiently polite so as not to comment on it. The only difficulty came one day at coffee break, when Kenny fool-heartedly approached the coffee vendor in an effort to secure a cheese Danish. The monkey ate nine of them before Kenny could stagger away, and the man insisted that Kenny had done it when his back was turned.

Simply by avoiding mirrors, a habit that Kenny Dorchester now began to cultivate as assiduously as any vampire, he was able to keep his mind off the monkey for most of the day. He had only one difficulty, though it occurred thrice daily; breakfast, lunch, and dinner. At those times the monkey asserted itself forcefully, and Kenny was forced to deal with it. As the weeks passed, he gradually fell into the habit of ordering food that could be served in bowls, so that he might practice what he termed his 'Kellogg maneuver.' By this stratagem, Kenny usually managed to get at least a few mouthfuls to eat each and every day.

To be sure, there *were* problems. People would stare at him rather strangely when he used the Kellogg maneuver in public, and sometimes make rude comments on his table manners. At a chili emporium Kenny liked to frequent, the proprietor assumed he had suffered a heart attack when he dove towards his chili, and was very angry with him afterwards. On another occasion a bowl of soup left him with facial burns that made it look as though he was constantly blushing. And the last straw came when he was thrown bodily out of his favorite seafood restaurant in the world, simply because he plunged his face into a bowl of crawfish bisque and began sucking it up noisily. Kenny stood in the street and berated them loudly and forcefully, reminding them how much money he had spent there over the years. Thereafter he ate only at home.

Despite the limited success of the Kellogg maneuver, Kenny Dorchester still lost nine-tenths of every meal and ten-tenths of some to the voracious monkey on his back. At first he was constantly hungry, frequently depressed, and full of schemes for ridding himself of his monkey. The only problem with these schemes was that none of them seemed to work. One Saturday Kenny went to the monkey house at the zoo, hoping that his monkey might hop off to play with others of its kind, or perhaps go in pursuit of some attractive monkey of the opposite sex. Instead, no sooner had he entered the monkey house than all the monkeys imprisoned therein ran to the bars of their cages and began to chitter and scream and spit and leap up and down madly. His own monkey answered in kind, and when some of the caged monkeys began to throw peanut husks and other bits of garbage Kenny clapped his hands over his ears and fled. On another occasion he allowed himself to visit a local saloon, and order a number of boilermakers, a drink he understood to be particularly devastating. His intent was to get his monkey so blind drunk that it might be easily removed. This experiment too had rather unfortunate consequences. The monkey drank the boilermakers as fast as Kenny could order them, but after the third one it began to keep time to the disco music from the jukebox by beating on the top of Kenny's head. The next morning it was Kenny who woke with the pounding headache; the monkey seemed fine.

After a time, Kenny finally put all his scheming aside. Failure had discouraged him, and moreover the matter seemed somehow less urgent than it had originally. He was seldom hungry after the first week, in fact. Instead he went through a brief period of weakness, marked by frequent dizzy spells, and then a kind of euphoria settled over him. He felt just wonderful, and even better, he was losing weight!

To be sure, it did not show on his scale. Every morning he climbed up on it, and every morning it lit up as 367. But that was only because it was weighing the monkey as well as himself. Kenny knew he was losing; he could almost feel the pounds and inches just melting away, and some of his coworkers in the office remarked on it as well. Kenny owned up to it, beaming. When they asked him how he was doing it, he winked and replied. 'The monkey treatment! The mysterious monkey treatment!' He said no more than that. The one time he tried to explain, the monkey fetched him such a wallop it almost took his head off, and his friends began to mutter about his strange spasms.

Finally the day came when Kenny had to tell his cleaner to take in all his pants a few inches. That was one of the most delightful tasks of his life, he thought.

All the pleasure went right out of the moment when he exited the store, however, and chanced to glance briefly to his side and see his reflection in the window. At home Kenny had long since removed all his mirrors, so he was shocked at the sight of his monkey. It had grown. It was a little thing no longer. Now it hunched on his back like some evil deformed chimpanzee, and its grinning face loomed above his head instead of peering out behind it. The monkey was grossly fat beneath its sparse brown hair, almost as wide as it was tall, and its great long tail drooped all the way to the ground. Kenny stared at it with horror, and it grinned back at him. No wonder he had been having backaches recently, he thought.

He walked home slowly, all the jauntiness gone out of his step, trying to think. A few neighborhood dogs followed him up the street, barking at his monkey. Kenny ignored them. He had long since learned that dogs could see his monkey, just like the monkeys at the zoo. He suspected that drunks could see it as well. One man had stared at him for a very long time that night he had visited the saloon. Of course, the fellow might just have been staring at those vanishing boilermakers.

Back in his apartment Kenny Dorchester stretched out on his couch on his stomach, stuck a pillow underneath his chin, and turned on his television set. He paid no attention to the screen, however. He was trying to figure things out.

Even the Pizza Hut commercials were insufficiently distracting, although Kenny did absently mutter 'Ah-h-h' like you were supposed to when the slice of pizza, dripping long strands of cheese, was first lifted from the pan.

When the show ended, Kenny got up and turned off the set and sat himself down at his dining room table. He found a piece of paper and a stubby little pencil. Very carefully, he block-printed a formula across the paper, and stared at it.

ME + MONKEY = 367 POUNDS

There were certain disturbing implications in that formula, Kenny thought. The more he considered them, the less he liked them. He was definitely losing weight, to be sure, and that was not to be sneered at – nonetheless, the grim inflexibility of the formula hinted that most of the gains traditionally attributed to weight loss would never be his to enjoy. No matter how much fat he shed, he would continue to carry around 367 pounds, and the strain on his body would be the same. As for becoming svelte and dashing and attractive to women, how could he even consider it so long as he had his monkey? Kenny thought of how a dinner date might go for him, and shuddered. 'Where will it end?' he said aloud.

The monkey shifted, and snickered a vile little snicker.

Kenny pursed his lips in firm disapproval. This could not go on, he resolved. He decided to go straight to the source on the morrow, and with that idea planted firmly in his head, he took himself to bed.

The next day, after work, Kenny Dorchester returned by cab to the seedy neighborhood where he'd been subjected to the monkey treatment.

The storefront was gone.

Kenny sat in the backseat of the taxi (this time he had the good sense not to get out, and moreover had tipped the driver handsomely in advance) and blinked in confusion. A tiny wet blubbery moan escaped his lips. The address was right, he knew it, he still had the slip of paper that had brought him there in the first place. But where he had found a grimy brick storefront adorned by a faded Coca-Cola sign and flanked by two vacant lots, now there was only one large vacant lot, choked with weeds and rubbish and broken bricks. 'Oh, no,' Kenny said. 'Oh, no.'

'You OK?' asked the lady driving the cab.

'Yes,' Kenny muttered. 'Just . . . just wait, please. I have to think.' He held his head in his hands. He feared he was going to develop a splitting headache. Suddenly he felt weak and dizzy. And very hungry. The meter ticked. The cabbie whistled. Kenny thought. The street looked just as he remembered it, except for the missing storefront. It was just as dirty, the old winos were still on their stoop, the . . .

Kenny rolled down the window. 'You, sir!' he called out to one of the winos. The man stared at him. 'Come here, sir!' Kenny yelled.

Warily the old man shuffled across the street.

Kenny fetched out a dollar bill from his wallet and pressed it into the man's hand. 'Here, friend,' he said, 'Go and buy yourself some vintage Thunderbird, if you will.'

'Why you givin' me this?' the wino said suspiciously.

'I wish you to answer me a question. What has become of the building that was standing there' – Kenny pointed – 'a few weeks ago.'

The man stuffed the dollar into his pocket quickly. 'Ain't been no buildin' there fo' years,' he said.

'I was afraid of that,' Kenny said. 'Are you certain? I was here in the not-so-distant past and I *distinctly* recall . . .'

'No buildin',' the wino said firmly. He turned and walked away, but after a few steps he paused and glanced back. 'You're one of them fat guys,' he said accusingly.

'What do you know about . . . ahem . . . overweight men?'

'See 'em wanderin' over there, all the time. Crazy, too. Yellin' at thin air, playing with some kind of animals. Yeah. I 'member you. You're one of them fat guys all right.' He scowled at Kenny, confused. 'Looks like you lost some of that blubber, though. Real good. Thanks for the dollar.'

Kenny Dorchester watched him return to his stoop and begin conversing animatedly with his colleagues. With a tremulous sigh, Kenny rolled up the window, glanced at the empty lot again, and bid his driver take him home. Him and his monkey, that is.

Weeks went dripping by and Kenny Dorchester lived as if in a trance. He went to work, shuffled his papers, mumbled pleasantries to his co-workers, struggled and schemed for his meager mouthfuls of food, avoided mirrors. The scale read 367. His flesh melted away from him at a precipitous rate. He developed slack droopy jowls, and his skin sagged all about his middle, looking as flaccid and pitiful as a used condom. He began to have fainting spells, brought on by hunger. At times he staggered and lurched about the street, his thinning and weakened legs unable to support the weight of his growing monkey. His vision got blurry. Once he even thought that his hair had started to fall out, but that at least was a false alarm; it was the monkey who was losing hair, thank goodness. It shed all over the place, ruining his furniture, and even daily vacuuming didn't seem to help much. Soon Kenny stopped trying to clean up. He lacked energy. He lacked energy for just about everything, in fact. Rising from a chair was a major undertaking. Cooking dinner was impossible torment – but he did *that* anyway, since the monkey beat him severely when it was not fed. Nothing seemed to matter very much to Kenny Dorchester. Nothing but the terrible tale of his scale each morning, and the formula that he had Scotch-taped to his bathroom wall.

ME + MONKEY = 367 POUNDS

He wondered how much was ME anymore, and how much was MONKEY, but he did not really want to find out. One day, following the dictates of a kind of feeble whim, Kenny made a sudden grab for the monkey's legs under his chin, hoping against hope that it had gotten slow and obese and that he would be able to yank it from his back. His hands closed on nothing. On his own pale flesh. The monkey's legs did not seem to be there, though Kenny could still feel its awful crushing weight. He patted his neck and breast in dim confusion, staring down at himself, and noting absently that he could see his feet. He wondered how long that had been true. They seemed to be perfectly nice feet, Kenny Dorchester thought, although the legs to which they were attached were alarmingly gaunt.

Slowly his mind wandered back to the quandary at hand – what had become of the monkey's legs? Kenny frowned and puzzled and tried to work it all out in his head, but nothing occurred to him. Finally he slid his newly-rediscovered feet into a pair of bed slippers and shuffled to the closet where he had stored all of his mirrors. Closing his eyes, he reached in, fumbled about, and found the full-length mirror that had once hung on his bedroom wall. It was a large, wide mirror. Working entirely by touch, Kenny fetched it out, carried it a few feet, and painstakingly propped it up against a wall. Then he held his breath and opened his eyes.

There in the mirror stood a gaunt, gray, skeletal looking fellow, hunched over and sickly. On his back, grinning, was a thing the size of a gorilla. A very obese gorilla. It had a long pale snakelike tail, and great long arms, and it was as white as a maggot and entirely hairless. It had no legs. It was . . . *attached* to him now, growing right out of his back. Its grin was terrible, and filled up half of its face. It looked very like the gross proprietor of the monkey treatment emporium, in fact. Why had he never noticed that before? Of course, of course.

Kenny Dorchester turned from the mirror, and cooked the monkey a big rich dinner before going to bed.

That night he dreamed of how it had all started, back in the Slab when he had met Boney Moroney. In his nightmare a great evil white thing rode atop Moroney's shoulders, eating slab after slab of ribs, but Kenny politely pretended not to notice while he and Boney made bright, sprightly conversation. Then the thing ran out of ribs, so it reached down and lifted one of Boney's arms and began to eat his hand. The bones crunched nicely, and Moroney kept right on talking. The creature had eaten its way up to the elbow when Kenny woke screaming, covered with a cold sweat. He had wet his bed too.

Agonizingly he pushed himself up and staggered to the toilet, where he dry-heaved for ten minutes. The monkey, angry at being wakened, gave him a desultory slap from time to time.

And then a furtive light came into Kenny Dorchester's eyes. 'Boney,' he whispered. Hurriedly he scrambled back to his bedroom on hands and knees, rose, and threw on some clothes. It was three in the morning, but Kenny knew there was no time to waste. He looked up an address in the phone book and called a cab.

Boney Moroney lived in a tall modern high-rise by the river with moonlight shining brightly off its silver-mirrored flanks. When Kenny staggered in, he found the doorman asleep at his station, which was just as well. Kenny tiptoed past him to the elevators and rode up to the eighth floor. The monkey on his back had begun stirring now, and seemed uneasy and ill-tempered.

Kenny's finger trembled as he pushed the round black button set in the door to Moroney's apartment, just beneath the eyehole. Musical chimes sounded loudly within, startling in the morning stillness. Kenny leaned on the button. The music played on and on. Finally he heard footsteps, heavy and threatening. The peephole opened and closed again. Then the door swung open.

The apartment was black, though the far wall was made entirely of glass, so the moonlight illuminated the darkness softly. Outlined against the stars and the light of the city stood the man who had opened the door. He was hugely, obscenely fat, and his skin was a pasty fungoid white, and he had little dark eyes set deep into crinkles in his broad suety face. He wore nothing but a vast pair of striped shorts. His breasts flopped about against his chest when he shifted his weight. And when he smiled, his teeth filled up half his face. A great crescent moon of teeth. He smiled when he saw Kenny, and Kenny's monkey. Kenny felt sick. The thing in the door weighed twice as much as the one on his back. Kenny trembled. 'Where is he?' he whispered softly. 'Where is Boney? What have you done to him?'

The creature laughed, and its pendulous breasts flounced about wildly as it shook with mirth. The monkey on Kenny's back began to laugh too, a higher thinner laughter as sharp as the edge of a knife. It reached down and twisted Kenny's ear cruelly. Suddenly a vast fear and a vast anger filled Kenny Dorchester. He summoned all the strength left in his wasted body and pushed forward, and somehow, somehow, he barged past the obese colossus who barred his way and staggered into the interior of the apartment. 'Boney,' he called, 'where are you, Boney? It's me, Kenny.'

There was no answer. Kenny went from room to room. The apartment was filthy, a shambles. There was no sign of Boney Moroney anywhere. When Kenny came panting back to the living room, the monkey shifted abruptly, and threw him off balance. He stumbled and fell hard. Pain went shooting up through his knees, and he cut open one outstretched hand on the edge of the chrome-and-glass coffee table. Kenny began to weep.

He heard the door close, and the thing that lived here moved slowly toward him. Kenny blinked back tears and stared at the approach of those two mammoth legs, pale in the moonlight, sagging all around with fat. He looked up and it was like gazing up the side of a mountain. Far, far above him grinned those horrible mocking teeth. *'Where is he?'* Kenny Dorchester whispered. 'What have you done with poor Boney?'

The grin did not change. The thing reached down a meaty hand, fingers as thick as a length of kielbasa, and snagged the waistband of the baggy striped shorts. It pulled them down clumsily, and they settled to the ground like a parachute, bunching around its feet.

'Oh, no,' said Kenny Dorchester.

The thing had no genitals. Hanging down between its legs, almost touching the carpet now that it had been freed from the confines of the soiled shorts, was a wrinkled droopy bag of skin, long and gaunt, growing from the creature's crotch. But as Kenny stared at it in horror, it thrashed feebly, and stirred, and the loose folds of flesh separated briefly into tiny arms and legs.

Then it opened its eyes.

Kenny Dorchester screamed and suddenly he was back on his feet, lurching away from the grinning obscenity in the center of the room. Between its legs, the thing that had been Boney Moroney raised its pitiful stick-thin arms in supplication. 'Oh, nooooo,' Kenny moaned, blubbering, and he danced about wildly, the vast weight of his monkey heavy on his back. Round and round he danced in the dimness, in the moonlight, searching for an escape from this madness.

Beyond the plate glass wall the lights of the city beckoned.

Kenny paused and panted and stared at them. Somehow the monkey must have known what he was thinking, for suddenly it began to beat on him wildly, to twist his ears, to rain savage blows all around his head. But Kenny Dorchester paid no mind. With a smile that was almost beatific, he gathered the last of his strength and rushed pell-mell toward the moonlight.

The glass shattered into a million glittering shards, and Kenny smiled all the way down.

*

It was the smell that told him he was still alive, the smell of disinfectant, and the feel of starched sheets beneath him. A hospital, he thought amidst a haze of pain. He was in a hospital. Kenny wanted to cry. Why hadn't he died? Oh, why, oh, why? He opened his eyes and tried to say something.

Suddenly a nurse was there, standing over him, feeling his brow and looking down with concern. Kenny wanted to beg her to kill him, but the words would not come. She went away and when she came back she had others with her.

A chubby young man said, 'You'll be all right, Mr Dorchester, but you have a long way to go. You're in a hospital. You're a very lucky man. You fell eight stories. You ought to be dead.'

I want to be dead, Kenny thought, and he shaped the words very very carefully with his mouth, but no one seemed to hear them. Maybe the monkey has taken over, he thought. Maybe I can't even talk anymore.

'He wants to say something,' the nurse said.

'I can see that,' said the chubby young doctor. 'Mr Dorchester please don't strain yourself. Really. If you are trying to ask about your friend, I'm afraid he wasn't as lucky as you. He was killed by the fall. You would have died as well, but fortunately you landed on top of him.'

Kenny's fear and confusion must have been obvious, for the nurse put a gentle hand on his arm. 'The other man,' she said patiently. 'The fat one. You can thank God he was so fat, too. He broke your fall like giant pillow.'

And finally Kenny Dorchester understood what they were saying and began to weep, but now he was weeping for joy, and trembling.

Three days later, he managed his first word. 'Pizza,' he said, and it came weak and hoarse from between his lips, and then louder still, and before long he was pushing the nurse's call button and shouting and pushing and shouting. 'Pizza, pizza, pizza, pizza,' he chanted, and he would not be calm until they ordered one for him. Nothing had ever tasted so good.

The Pear-Shaped Man

The Pear-shaped Man lives beneath the stairs. His shoulders are narrow and stooped, but his buttocks are impressively large. Or perhaps it is only the clothing he wears; no one has ever admitted to seeing him nude, and he has never admitted to wanting to. His trousers are brown polyester double knits, with wide cuffs and a shiny seat; they are always baggy, and they have big, deep, droopy pockets so stuffed with oddments and bric-a-brac that they bulge against his sides. He wears his pants very high, hiked up above the swell of his stomach, and cinches them in place around his chest with a narrow brown leather belt. He wears them so high that his drooping socks show clearly, and often an inch or two of pasty white skin as well.

His shirts are always short-sleeved, most often white or pale blue, and his breast pocket is always full of Bic pens, the cheap throwaway kind that write with blue ink. He has lost the caps or tossed them out, because his shirts are all stained and splotched around the breast pockets. His head is a second pear set atop the first; he has a double chin and wide, full, fleshy cheeks, and the top of his head seems to come almost to a point. His nose is broad and flat, with large, greasy pores; his eyes are small and pale, set close together. His hair is thin, dark, limp, flaky with dandruff; it never looks washed, and there are those who say that he cuts it himself with a bowl and a dull knife. He has a smell, too, the Pear-shaped Man; it is a sweet smell, a sour smell, a rich smell, compounded of old butter and rancid meat and vegetables rotting in the garbage bin. His voice, when he speaks, is high and thin and squeaky; it would be a funny little voice, coming from such a large, ugly man, but there is something unnerving about it, and something even more chilling about his tight, small smile. He never shows any teeth when he smiles, but his lips are broad and wet.

Of course you know him. Everyone knows a Pear-shaped Man.

*

Jessie met hers on her first day in the neighborhood, while she and Angela were moving into the vacant apartment on the first floor. Angela and her boyfriend, Donald the student shrink, had lugged the couch inside and accidentally knocked away the brick that had been holding open the door to the building. Meanwhile Jessie had gotten the recliner out of the U-Haul all by herself and thumped it up the steps, only to find the door locked when she backed into it, the recliner in her arms. She was hot and sore and irritable and ready to scream with frustration.

And then the Pear-shaped Man emerged from his basement apartment under the steps, climbed onto the sidewalk at the foot of the stoop, and looked up at her with those small, pale, watery eyes of his. He made no move to help her with her chair. He did not say hello or offer to let her into the building. He only blinked and smiled a tight, wet smile that showed none of his teeth and said in a voice as squeaky and grating as nails on a blackboard, 'Ahhhh. *There* she is.' Then he turned and walked away. When he walked he swayed slightly from side to side.

Jessie let go of the recliner; it bumped down two steps and turned over. She suddenly felt cold, despite the sweltering July heat. She watched the Pear-shaped Man depart. That was her first sight of him. She went inside and told Donald and Angela about him, but they were not much impressed. 'Into every girl's life a Pear-shaped Man must fall,' Angela said, with the cynicism of the veteran city girl. 'I bet I met him on a blind date once.'

Donald, who didn't live with them but spent so many nights with Angela that sometimes it seemed as though he did, had a more immediate concern. 'Where do you want this recliner?' he wanted to know.

Later they had a few beers, and Rick and Molly and the Heathersons came over to help them warm the apartment, and Rick offered to pose for her (wink wink, nudge nudge) when Molly wasn't there to hear, and Donald drank too much and went to sleep on the sofa, and the Heathersons had a fight that ended with Geoff storming out and Lureen crying; it was a night like any other night, in other words, and Jessie forgot all about the Pear-shaped Man. But not for long.

The next morning Angela roused Donald, and the two of them went off, Angie to the big downtown firm where she was a legal secretary, Don to study shrinking. Jessie was a freelance commercial illustrator. She did her work at home, which as far as Angela and Donald and her mother and the rest of Western civilization were concerned meant that she didn't work at all. 'Would you mind doing the shopping?' Angie asked her just before she left. They had pretty well devastated their refrigerator in the two weeks before the move, so as not to have a lot of food to lug across town. 'Seeing as how you'll be home all day? I mean, we really need some food.'

So Jessie was pushing a full cart of groceries down a crowded aisle in Santino's Market, on the corner, when she saw the Pear-shaped Man the second time. He was at the register, counting out change into Santino's hand. Jessie felt like making a U-turn and busying herself until he'd gone. But that would be silly. She'd gotten everything she needed, and she was a grown woman, after all, and he was standing at the only open register. Resolute, she got in line behind him.

Santino dumped the Pear-shaped Man's coins into the old register and bagged up his purchase: a big plastic bottle of Coke and a one-pound bag of Cheez Doodles. As he took the bag, the Pear-shaped Man saw her and smiled that little wet smile of his. 'Cheez Doodles are the best,' he said. 'Would you like some?'

'No, thank you,' Jessie said politely. The Pear-shaped Man put the brown paper sack inside a shapeless leather bag of the sort that schoolboys use to carry their books, gathered it up, and waddled out of the store. Santino, a big grizzled man with thinning salt-and-pepper hair, began to ring up Jessie's groceries. 'He's something, ain't he?' he asked her.

'Who is he?' she asked.

Santino shrugged. 'Hell, I dunno. Everybody just calls him the Pear-shaped Man. He's been around here forever. Comes in every morning, buys a bottle of Coke and a big bag of Cheez Doodles. Once we run out of Cheez Doodles, so I tell him he oughta try them Cheetos or maybe even potato chips, y'know, for a change? He wasn't having none of it, though.'

Jessie was bemused. 'He must buy something besides Coke and Cheez Doodles.'

'Wanna bet, lady?'

'Then he must shop somewhere else.'

'Besides me, the nearest supermarket is nine blocks away. Charlie down at the candy store tells me the Pear-shaped Man comes in every afternoon at four-thirty and has himself a chocolate ice-cream soda, but far as we can tell, that's all he eats.' He rang for a total. 'That's seventy-nine eighty-two, lady. You new around here?'

'I live just above the Pear-shaped Man,' Jessie confessed.

'Congratulations,' Santino said.

Later that morning, after she lined the shelves and put away the groceries, set up her studio in the spare bedroom, made a few desultory dabs on the cover she was supposed to be painting for Pirouette Publishing, ate lunch and washed the dishes, hooked up the stereo and listened to some Carly Simon, and rearranged half of the living room furniture, Jessie finally admitted a certain restlessness and decided this would be a good time to go around the building and introduce herself to her new neighbors. Not many people bothered with that in the city, she knew, but she was still a smalltown kid at heart, and it made her feel safer to know the people around her. She decided to start with the Pear-shaped Man down in the basement and got as far as descending the stairs to his door. Then a funny feeling came over her. There was no name on the doorbell, she noticed. Suddenly she regretted her impulse. She retreated back upstairs to meet the rest of the building.

The other tenants all knew him; most of them had spoken to him, at least once or twice, trying to be friendly. Old Sadie Winbright, who had lived across the hall in the other first-floor apartment for twelve years, said he was very quiet. Billy Peabody, who shared the big second-floor apartment with his crippled mother, thought the Pear-shaped Man was creepy, especially that little smile of his. Pete Pumetti worked the late shift, and told her how those basement lights were always on, no matter what hour of the night Pete came swaggering home, even though it was hard to tell on account of the way the Pear-shaped Man had boarded up his windows. Jess and Ginny Harris didn't like their twins playing around the stairs that led down to his apartment and had forbidden them to talk to him. Jeffries the barber, whose small two-chair shop was down the block from Santino's, knew him and had no great desire for his patronage. All of them, every one, called him the Pear-shaped Man. That was who he was. 'But who is he?' Jessie asked. None of them knew. 'What does he do for a living?' she asked.

'I think he's on welfare,' Old Sadie Winbright said. 'The poor dear, he must be feebleminded.'

'Damned if I know,' said Pete Pumetti. 'He sure as hell don't work. I bet he's a queer.'

'Sometimes I think he might be a drug pusher,' said Jeffries the barber, whose familiarity with drugs was limited to witch hazel.

'I betcha he writes them pornographic books down there,' Billy Peabody surmised.

'He doesn't do anything for a living,' said Ginny Harris. 'Jess and I have talked about it. He's a shopping-bag man, he has to be.'

That night, over dinner, Jessie told Angela about the Pear-shaped Man and the other tenants and their comments. 'He's probably an attorney,' Angie said. 'Why do you care so much, anyway?'

Jessie couldn't answer that. 'I don't know. He gives me goose bumps. I don't like the idea of some maniac living right underneath us.'

Angela shrugged. 'That's the way it goes in the big, glamorous city. Did the guy from the phone company come?'

'Maybe next week,' said Jessie. 'That's the way it goes in the big, glamorous city.'

*

Jessie soon learned that there was no avoiding the Pear-shaped Man. When she visited the laundromat around the block, there he was, washing a big load of striped boxer shorts and ink-stained short-sleeved shirts, snacking on Coke and Cheez Doodles from the vending machines. She tried to ignore him, but whenever she turned around, there he was, smiling wetly, his eyes fixed on her, or perhaps on the underthings she was loading into the dryer.

When she went down to the corner candy store one afternoon to buy a paper, there he was, slurping his ice cream soda, his buttocks overflowing the stool on which he was perched. 'It's homemade,' he squeaked at her. She frowned, paid for her newspaper, and left.

One evening when Angela was seeing Donald, Jessie picked up an old paperback and went out on the stoop to read and maybe socialize and enjoy the cool breeze that was blowing up the street. She got lost in the story, until she caught a whiff of something unpleasant, and when she looked up from the page, there he was, standing not three feet away, staring at her. 'What do you want?' she snapped, closing the book.

'Would you like to come down and see my house?' the Pear-shaped Man asked in that high, whiny voice.

'No,' she said, retreating to her own apartment. But when she looked out a half hour later, he was still standing in the same exact spot, clutching his brown bag and staring at her windows while dusk fell around him. He made her feel very uneasy. She wished that Angela would come home, but she knew that wouldn't happen for hours. In fact, Angie might very well decide to spend the night at Don's place.

Jessie shut the windows despite the heat, checked the locks on her door, and then went back to her studio to work. Painting would take her mind off the Pear-shaped Man. Besides, the cover was due at Pirouette by the end of the week.

She spent the rest of the evening finishing off the background and doing some of the fine detail on the heroine's gown. The hero didn't look quite right to her when she was done, so she worked on him, too. He was the usual dark-haired, virile, strong-jawed type, but Jessie decided to individualize him a bit, an effort that kept her pleasantly occupied until she heard Angie's key in the lock.

She put away her paints and washed up and decided to have some tea before calling it a night. Angela was standing in the living room, with her hands behind her back, looking more than a little tipsy, giggling. 'What's so funny?' Jessie asked.

Angela giggled again. 'You've been holding out on me,' she said. 'You got yourself a new beau and you didn't tell.'

'What are you talking about?'

'He was standing on the stoop when I got home,' Angie said, grinning. She came across the room. 'He said to give you these.' Her hand emerged from behind her back. It was full of fat, orange worms, little flaking twists of corn and cheese that curled between her fingers and left powdery stains on the palm of her hand. 'For you,' Angie repeated, laughing. 'For you.'

*

That night Jessie had a long, terrible dream, but when the daylight came she could remember only a small part of it. She was standing at the door to the Pear-shaped Man's apartment under the stairs; she was standing there in darkness, waiting, waiting for something to happen, something awful, the worst thing she could imagine. Slowly, slowly, the door began to open. Light fell upon her face, and Jessie woke, trembling.

*

He might be dangerous, Jessie decided the next morning over Rice Krispies and tea. Maybe he had a criminal record. Maybe he was some kind of mental patient. She ought to check up on him. But she needed to know his name first. She couldn't just call up the police and say, 'Do you have anything on the Pear-shaped Man?'

After Angela had gone to work, Jessie pulled a chair over by the front window and sat down to wait and watch. The mail usually arrived about eleven. She saw the postman ascend the stairs, heard him putting the mail in the big hall mailbox. But the Pear-shaped Man got his mail separately, she knew. He had his own box, right under his doorbell, and if she remembered right it wasn't the kind that locked, either. As soon as the postman had departed, she was on her feet, moving quickly down the stairs. There was no sign of the Pear-shaped Man. The door to his apartment was down under the stoop, and farther back she could see overflowing garbage cans, smell their rich, sickly sweet odor. The upper half of the door was a window, boarded up. It was dark under the stoop. Jessie barked her knuckles on the brick as she fumbled for his mailbox. Her hand brushed the loose metal lid. She got it open, pulled out two thin envelopes. She had to squint and move toward the sunlight to read the name. They were both addressed to Occupant.

She was stuffing them back into the box when the door opened. The Pear-shaped Man was framed by bright light from within his apartment. He smiled at her, so close she could count the pores on his nose, see the sheen of the saliva on his lower lip. He said nothing.

'I,' she said, startled, 'I, I . . . I got some of your mail by mistake. Must be a new man on the route. I, I was just bringing it back.'

The Pear-shaped Man reached up and into his mailbox. For a second his hand brushed Jessie's. His skin was soft and damp and seemed much colder than it ought to be, and the touch gave her goose bumps all up and down her arm. He took the two letters from her and looked at them briefly and then stuffed them into his pants pocket. 'It's just garbage,' squeaked the Pear-shaped Man. 'They shouldn't be allowed to send you garbage. They ought to be stopped. Would you like to see my things? I have things inside to look at.'

'I,' said Jessie, 'uh, no. No, I can't. Excuse me.' She turned quickly, moved out from under the stairs, back into the sunlight, and hurried back inside the building. All the way, she could feel his eyes on her.

She spent the rest of that day working, and the next as well, never glancing outside, for fear that he would be standing there. By Thursday the painting was finished. She decided to take it in to Pirouette herself and have dinner downtown, maybe do a little shopping. A day away from the apartment and the Pear-shaped Man would do her good, soothe her nerves. She was being overimaginative. He hadn't actually done anything, after all. It was just that he was so damned *creepy*.

Adrian, the art director at Pirouette, was glad to see her, as always. 'That's my Jessie,' he said after he'd given her a hug. 'I wish all my artists were like you. Never miss a deadline, never turn in anything but the best work, a real pro. Come on back to my office, we'll look at this one and talk about some new assignments and gossip a bit.' He told his secretary to hold his calls and escorted her back through the maze of tiny little cubicles where the editors lived. Adrian himself had a huge corner office with two big windows, a sign of his status in Pirouette Publishing. He gestured Jessie to a chair, poured her a cup of herb tea, then took her portfolio and removed the cover painting and held it up at arm's length.

The silence went on far too long.

Adrian dragged out a chair, propped up the painting, and retreated several feet to consider it from a distance. He stroked his beard and cocked his head this way and that. Watching him, Jessie felt a thin prickle of alarm. Normally, Adrian was given to exuberant outbursts of approval. She didn't like this quiet. 'What's wrong?' she said, setting down her teacup. 'Don't you like it?'

'Oh,' Adrian said. He put out a hand, palm open and level, waggled it this way and that. 'It's well executed, no doubt. Your technique is very professional. Fine detail.'

'I researched all the clothing,' she said in exasperation. 'It's all authentic for the period; you know it is.'

'Yes, no doubt. And the heroine is gorgeous, as always. I wouldn't mind ripping her bodice myself. You do amazing things with mammaries, Jessie.'

She stood up. 'Then what is it?' she said. 'I've been doing covers for you for three years now, Adrian. There's never been any problem.'

'Well,' he said. He shook his head, smiled. 'Nothing, really. Maybe you've been doing too many of these. I know how it can go. They're so much alike, it gets boring, painting all those hot embraces one after another; so pretty soon you feel an urge to experiment, to try something a little bit different.' He shook a finger at her. 'It won't do, though. Our readers just want the same old shit with the same old covers. I understand, but it won't do.'

'There's nothing experimental about this painting.' Jessie said, exasperated. 'It's the same thing I've done for you a hundred times before. *What* won't do?'

Adrian looked honestly surprised. 'Why, the man, of course,' he said. 'I thought you'd done it deliberately.' He gestured. 'I mean, look at him. He's almost *unattractive.*'

'What?' Jessie moved over to the painting. 'He's the same virile jerk I've painted over and over again.'

Adrian frowned. 'Really now,' he said. 'Look.' He started pointing things out. 'There, around his collar, is that or is that not just the faintest hint of a double chin? And look at that lower lip! Beautifully executed yes, but it looks, well, gross. Like it was wet or something. Pirouette heroes rape, they plunder, they seduce, they threaten, but they do not drool, darling. And perhaps it's just a trick of perspective, but I could swear' – he paused, leaned close, shook his head – 'no, it's not perspective, the top of his head is definitely narrower than the bottom. A pinhead! We can't have pinheads on Pirouette books, Jessie. Too much fullness in the cheeks, too. He looks as though he might be storing nuts for the winter.' Adrian shook his head. 'It won't do, love. Look, no big problem. The rest of the painting is fine. Just take it home and fix him up. How about it?'

Jessie was staring at her painting in horror, as if she were seeing it for the first time. Everything Adrian had said, everything he had pointed out, was true. It was all very subtle, to be sure; at first glance the man looked almost like your normal Pirouette hero, but there was something just the tiniest bit off about him, and when you looked closer, it was blatant and unmistakable. Somehow the Pear-shaped Man had crept into her painting. 'I,' she began, 'I, yes, you're right, I'll do it over. I don't know what happened. There's this man who lives in my building, a creepy-looking guy, everybody calls him the Pear-shaped Man. He's been getting on my nerves. I swear, it wasn't intentional. I guess I've been thinking about him so much it just crept into my work subconsciously.'

'I understand,' Adrian said. 'Well, no problem, just set it right. We do have deadline problems, though.'

'I'll fix it this weekend, have it back to you by Monday,' Jessie promised.

'Wonderful,' said Adrian. 'Let's talk about those other assignments then.' He poured her more Red Zinger, and they sat down to talk. By the time Jessie left his office, she was feeling much better.

Afterward she enjoyed a drink in her favorite bar, met a few friends, and had a nice dinner at an excellent new Japanese restaurant. It was dark by the time she got home. There was no sign of the Pear-shaped Man. She kept her portfolio under her arm as she fished for her keys and unlocked the door to the building.

When she stepped inside, Jessie heard a faint noise and felt something crunch underfoot. A nest of orange worms clustered against the faded blue of the hallway carpet, crushed and broken by her foot.

*

She dreamed of him again. It was the same shapeless, terrible dream. She was down in the dark beneath the stoop, near the trash bins crawling with all kinds of things, waiting at his door. She was frightened, too frightened to knock or open the door yet helpless to leave. Finally the door crept open of its own accord. There he stood, smiling, smiling. 'Would you like to stay?' he said, and the last words echoed, *to stay to stay to stay to stay*, and he reached out for her, and his fingers were as soft and pulpy as earthworms when he touched her on the cheek.

The next morning Jessie arrived at the offices of Citywide Realty just as they opened their doors. The receptionist told her that Edward Selby was out showing some condos; she couldn't say when he'd be in. 'That's all right,' Jessie said. 'I'll wait.' She settled down to leaf through some magazines, studying pictures of houses she couldn't afford.

Selby arrived just before eleven. He looked momentarily surprised to see her, before his professional smile switched on automatically. 'Jessie,' he said, 'how nice. Something I can do for you?'

'Let's talk,' she said, tossing down the magazines.

They went to Selby's desk. He was still only an associate with the rental firm, so he shared the office with another agent, but she was out, and they had the room to themselves. Selby settled himself into his chair and leaned back. He was a pleasant-looking man, with curly brown hair and white teeth, his eyes careful behind silver aviator frames. 'Is there a problem?' he asked.

Jessie leaned forward. 'The Pear-shaped Man,' she said.

Selby arched one eyebrow. 'I see. A harmless eccentric.'

'Are you sure of that?'

He shrugged. 'He hasn't murdered anybody yet, at least that I know of.'

'How much do you know about him? For starters, what's his name?'

'Good question,' Selby said, smiling. 'Here at Citywide Realty we just think of him as the Pear-shaped Man. I don't think I've ever gotten a name out of him.'

'What the hell do you mean?' Jessie demanded. 'Are you telling me his checks have THE PEAR-SHAPED MAN printed on them?'

Selby cleared his throat. 'Well, no. Actually, he doesn't use checks. I come by on the first of every month to collect, and knock on his door, and he pays me in cash. One-dollar bills, in fact. I stand there, and he counts out the money into my hand, dollar by dollar. I'll confess, Jessie, that I've never been inside the apartment, and I don't especially care to. Kind of a funny smell, you know? But he's a good tenant, as far as we're concerned. Always has his rent paid on time. Never bitches about rent hikes. And he certainly doesn't bounce checks on us.' He showed a lot of teeth, a broad smile to let her know he was joking.

Jessie was not amused. 'He must have given a name when he first rented the apartment.'

'I wouldn't know about that,' Selby said. 'I've only handled that building for six years. He's been down in the basement a lot longer than that.'

'Why don't you check his lease?'

Selby frowned. 'Well, I could dig it up, I suppose. But really, is his name any of your business? What's the problem here, anyway? Exactly what has the Pear-shaped Man *done?*'

Jessie sat back and crossed her arms. 'He looks at me.'

'Well,' Selby said, carefully, 'I, uh, well, you're an attractive woman, Jessie. I seem to recall asking you out myself.'

'That's different,' she said. 'You're normal. It's the way he looks at me.'

'Undressing you with his eyes?' Selby suggested.

Jessie was nonplussed. 'No,' she said. 'That isn't it. It's not sexual, not in the normal way, anyhow. I don't know how to explain it. He keeps asking me down to his apartment. He's always hanging around.'

'Well, that's where he lives.'

'He bothers me. He's crept into my paintings.'

This time both of Selby's eyebrows went up. 'Into your paintings?' he said. There was a funny hitch in his voice.

Jessie was getting more and more discomfited; this wasn't coming out right at all. 'Okay, it doesn't sound like much, but he's *creepy,* I tell you. His lips are always wet. The way he smiles. His eyes. His squeaky little voice. And that smell. Jesus Christ, you collect his rent, you ought to know.'

The realtor spread his hands helplessly. 'It's not against the law to have body odor. It's not even a violation of his lease.'

'Last night he snuck into the building and left a pile of Cheez Doodles right where I'd step in them.'

'Cheez Doodles?' Selby said. His voice took on a sarcastic edge. 'God, not *Cheez Doodles!* How fucking heinous! Have you informed the police?'

'It's not funny. What was he doing inside the building anyway?'

'He lives there.'

'He lives in the basement. He has his own door, he doesn't need to come into our hallway. Nobody but the six regular tenants ought to have keys to that door.'

'Nobody does, as far as I know,' Selby said. He pulled out a notepad. 'Well, that's something, anyway. I'll tell you what, I'll have the lock changed on the outer door. The Pear-shaped Man won't get a key. Will that make you happy?'

'A little,' said Jessie, slightly mollified.

'I can't promise that he won't get in,' Selby cautioned. 'You know how it is. If I had a nickel for every time some tenant has taped over a lock or propped open a door with a doorstop because it was more convenient, well . . .'

'Don't worry, I'll see that nothing like that happens. What about his name? Will you check the lease for me?'

Selby sighed. 'This is really an invasion of privacy. But I'll do it. A personal favor. You owe me one.' He got up and went across the room to a black metal filing cabinet, pulled open a drawer, rummaged around, and came out with a legal-sized folder. He was flipping through it as he returned to his desk.

'Well?' Jessie asked, impatiently.

'Hmmmm,' Selby said. 'Here's your lease. And here's the others.' He went back to the beginning and checked the papers one by one. 'Winbright, Peabody, Pumetti, Harris, Jeffries.' He closed the file, looked up at her, and shrugged. 'No lease. Well, it's a crummy little apartment, and he's been there forever. Either we've misfiled his lease or he never had one. It's not unknown. A month-to-month basis . . .'

'Oh, great,' Jessie said. 'Are you going to do anything about it?'

'I'll change that lock,' Selby said. 'Beyond that, I don't know what you expect of me. I'm not going to evict the man for offering you Cheez Doodles.'

*

The Pear-shaped Man was standing on the stoop when Jessie got home, his battered bag tucked up under one arm. He smiled when he saw her approach. *Let him touch me,* she thought; *just let him touch me when I walk by, and I'll have him booked for assault so fast it'll make his little pointy head swim.* But the Pear-shaped Man made no effort to grab her. 'I have things to show you downstairs,' he said as Jessie ascended the stairs. She had to pass within a foot of him; the smell was overwhelming today, a rich odor like yeast and decaying vegetables. 'Would you like to look at my things?' he called after her. Jessie unlocked the door and slammed it behind her.

I'm not going to think about him, she told herself inside, over a cup of tea. She had work to do. She'd promised Adrian the cover by Monday, after all. She went into her studio, drew back the curtains, and set to work, determined to eradicate every hint of the Pear-shaped Man from the cover. She painted away the double chin, firmed up the jaw, redid those tight wet lips, darkened the hair, made it blacker and bushier and more wind tossed so the head didn't seem to come to such a point. She gave him sharp, high, pronounced cheekbones – cheekbones like the blade of a knife – made the face almost gaunt. She even changed the color of his eyes. Why had she given him those weak, pale eyes? She made the eyes green, a crisp, clean, commanding green, full of vitality.

It was almost midnight by the time she was done, and Jessie was exhausted, but when she stepped back to survey her handiwork, she was delighted. The man was a real Pirouette hero now: a rakehell, a rogue, a hell-raiser whose robust exterior concealed a brooding, melancholy, poetic soul. There was nothing the least bit pear-shaped about him. Adrian would have puppies.

It was a good kind of tiredness. Jessie went to sleep feeling altogether satisfied. Maybe Selby was right; she was too imaginative, she'd really let the Pear-shaped Man get to her. But work, good hard old-fashioned work was the perfect antidote for these shapeless fears of hers. Tonight, she was sure, her sleep would be deep and dreamless.

*

She was wrong. There was no safety in her sleep. She stood trembling on his doorstep once again. It was so dark down there, so filthy. The rich ripe smell of the garbage cans was overwhelming, and she thought she could hear things moving in the shadows. The door began to open. The Pear-shaped Man smiled at her and touched her with cold, soft fingers like a nest of grubs. He took hold of her by the arm and drew her inside, inside, inside, inside . . .

*

Angela knocked on her door the next morning at ten. 'Sunday brunch,' she called out. 'Don is making waffles. With chocolate chips and fresh strawberries. And bacon. And coffee. And O.J. Want some?'

Jessie sat up in bed. 'Don? Is he here?'

'He stayed over,' Angela said.

Jessie climbed out of bed and pulled on a paint-splattered pair of jeans.

'You know I'd never turn down one of Don's brunches. I didn't even hear you guys come in.'

'I snuck my head into your studio, but you were painting away, and you didn't even notice. You had that intent look you get sometimes, you know, with the tip of your tongue peeking out of one corner of your mouth. I figured it was better not to disturb the artist at work.' She giggled. 'How you avoided hearing the bed-springs, though, I'll never know.'

Breakfast was a triumph. There were times when Jessie couldn't understand just what Angela saw in Donald the student shrink, but mealtimes were not among them. He was a splendid cook. Angela and Donald were still lingering over coffee, and Jessie over tea, at eleven, when they heard noises from the hall. Angela went to check. 'Some guy's out there changing the lock,' she said when she returned. 'I wonder what that's all about.'

'I'll be damned,' Jessie said. 'And on the weekend, too. That's time and a half. I never expected Selby to move so fast.'

Angela looked at her curiously. 'What do you know about this?'

So Jessie told them all about her meeting with the realtor and her encounters with the Pear-shaped Man. Angela giggled once or twice, and Donald slipped into his wise shrink face. 'Tell me, Jessie,' he said when she had finished, 'don't you think you're overreacting a bit here?'

'No,' Jessie said curtly.

'You're stonewalling,' Donald said. 'Really now, try and look at your actions objectively. What has this man done to you?'

'Nothing, and I intend to keep it that way,' Jessie snapped. 'I didn't ask for your opinion.'

'You don't have to ask,' Donald said. 'We're friends, aren't we? I hate to see you getting upset over nothing. It sounds to me as though you're developing some kind of phobia about a harmless neighborhood character.'

Angela giggled. 'He's just got a crush on you, that's all. You're such a heartbreaker.'

Jessie was getting annoyed. 'You wouldn't think it was funny if he was leaving Cheez Doodles for you,' she said angrily. 'There's something . . . well, something *wrong* there. I can feel it.'

Donald spread his hands. 'Something wrong? Most definitely. The man is obviously very poorly socialized. He's unattractive, sloppy, he doesn't conform to normal standards of dress or personal hygiene, he has unusual eating habits and a great deal of difficulty relating to others. He's probably a very lonely person and no doubt deeply neurotic as well. But none of this makes him a killer or a rapist, does it? Why are you becoming so obsessed with him?'

'I am not becoming obsessed with him.'

'Obviously you are,' Donald said.

'She's in love,' Angela teased.

Jessie stood up. 'I am *not* becoming obsessed with him!' she shouted, 'and this discussion has just ended.'

*

That night, in her dream, Jessie saw inside for the first time. He drew her in, and she found she was too weak to resist. The lights were very bright inside, and it was warm and oh so humid, and the air seemed to move if she had entered the mouth of some great beast, and the walls were orange and flaky and had a strange, sweet smell, and there were empty plastic Coke bottles everywhere and bowls of half-eaten Cheez Doodles, too, and the Pear-shaped Man said, 'You can see my things, you can have my things and he began to undress, unbuttoning his short-sleeved shirt, pulling it off, revealing dead, white, hairless flesh and two floppy breasts, and the right breast was stained with blue ink from his leaking pens, and he was smiling, smiling, and he undid his thin belt, and then pulled down the fly on his brown polyester pants, and Jessie woke screaming.

*

On Monday morning, Jessie packed up her cover painting, phoned a messenger service, and had them take it down to Pirouette for her. She wasn't up to another trip downtown. Adrian would want to chat, and Jess wasn't in a very sociable mood. Angela kept needling her about the Pear-shaped Man, and it had left her in a foul temper. Nobody seemed to understand. There was something wrong with the Pear-shaped Man, something serious, something horrible. He was no joke. He was frightening. Somehow she had to prove it. She had to learn his name, had to find out what he was hiding.

She could hire a detective, except detectives were expensive. There had to be something she could do on her own. She could try his mailbox again. She'd be better off if she waited until the day the gas and electric bills came, though. He had lights in his apartment, so the electric company would know his name. The only problem was that the electric bill wasn't due for another couple of weeks.

The living room windows were wide open, Jessie noticed suddenly. Even the drapes had been drawn all the way back. Angela must have done it that morning before taking off for work. Jessie hesitated and then went to the window. She closed it, locked it, moved to the next, closed it, locked it. It made her feel safer. She told herself she wouldn't look out. It would be better if she didn't look out.

How could she not look out? She looked out. He was there, standing on the sidewalk below her, looking up. 'You could see my things,' he said in his high, thin voice. 'I knew when I saw you that you'd want my things. You'd like them. We could have food.' He reached into a bulgy pocket, brought out a single Cheez Doodle, held it up to her. His mouth moved silently.

'Get away from here, or I'll call the police!' Jessie shouted.

'I have something for you. Come to my house and you can have it. It's in my pocket. I'll give it to you.'

'No you won't. Get away, I warn you. Leave me alone.' She stepped back, closed the drapes. It was gloomy in here with the drapes pulled, but that was better than knowing that the Pear-shaped Man was looking in. Jessie turned on a light, picked up a paperback, and tried to read. She found herself turning pages rapidly and realized she didn't have the vaguest idea of what the words meant. She slammed down the book, marched into the kitchen, made a tuna salad sandwich on whole wheat toast. She wanted something with it, but she wasn't sure what. She took out a dill pickle and sliced it into quarters, arranged it neatly on her plate, searched through her cupboard for some potato chips. Then she poured a big fresh glass of milk and sat down to lunch.

She took one bite of the sandwich, made a face, and shoved it away. It tasted funny. Like the mayonnaise had gone bad or something. The pickle was too sour, and the chips seemed soggy and limp and much too salty. She didn't want chips anyway. She wanted something else. Some of those little orange cheese curls. She could picture them in her head, almost taste them. Her mouth watered.

Then she realized what she was thinking and almost gagged. She got up and scraped her lunch into the garbage. She had to get out of here, she thought wildly. She'd go see a movie or something, forget all about the Pear-shaped Man for a few hours. Maybe she could go to a singles' bar somewhere, pick someone up, get laid. At his place. Away from here. Away from the Pear-shaped Man. That was the ticket. A night away from the apartment would do her good.

She went to the window, pulled aside the drapes, peered out.

The Pear-shaped Man smiled, shifted from side to side. He had his misshapen briefcase under his arm. His pockets bulged. Jessie felt her skin crawl. He was *revolting*, she thought. But she wasn't going to let him keep her prisoner.

She gathered her things together, slipped a little steak knife into her purse just in case, and marched outside. 'Would you like to see what I have in my case?' the Pear-shaped Man asked her when she emerged. Jessie had decided to ignore him. If she did not reply at all, just pretended he wasn't there, maybe he'd grow bored and leave her alone. She descended the steps briskly and set off down the street. The Pear-shaped Man followed close behind her. 'They're all around us,' he whispered. She could smell him hurrying a step or two behind her, puffing as he walked. 'They are. They laugh at me. They don't understand, but they want my things. I can show you proof. I have it down in my house. I know you want to come see.'

Jessie continued to ignore him. He followed her all the way to the bus stop.

*

The movie was a dud. Having skipped lunch, Jessie was hungry. She got a Coke and a tub of buttered popcorn from the candy counter. The Coke was three-quarters crushed ice, but it still tasted good. She couldn't eat the popcorn. The fake butter they used had a vaguely rancid smell that reminded her of the Pear-shaped Man. She tried two kernels and felt sick.

Afterward, though, she did a little better. His name was Jack, he said. He was a sound man on a local TV news show, and he had an interesting face: an easy smile, Clark Gable ears, nice gray eyes with friendly little crinkles in the corners. He bought her a drink and touched her hand; but the way he did it was a little clumsy, like he was a bit shy about this whole scene, and Jessie liked that. They had a few drinks together, and then he suggested dinner back at his place. Nothing fancy, he said. He had some cold cuts in the fridge; he could whip up some jumbo sandwiches and show her his stereo system, which was some kind of special super setup he'd rigged himself. That all sounded fine to her.

His apartment was on the twenty-third floor of a midtown high rise, and from his windows you could see sailboats tacking off on the horizon. Jack put the new Linda Ronstadt album on the stereo while he went to make the sandwiches. Jessie watched the sailboats. She was finally beginning to relax. 'I have beer or ice tea,' Jack called from the kitchen. 'What'll be?'

'Coke,' she said absently.

'No Coke,' he called back. 'Beer or ice tea.'

'Oh,' she said, somehow annoyed. 'Ice tea, then.'

'You got it. Rye or wheat?'

'I don't care,' she said. The boats were very graceful. She'd like to paint them someday. She could paint Jack, too. He looked like he had a nice body.

'Here we go,' he said, emerging from the kitchen carrying a tray. 'I hope you're hungry.'

'Famished,' Jessie said, turning away from the window. She went over to where he was setting the table and froze.

'What's wrong?' Jack said. He was holding out a white stoneware plate.

On top of it was a truly gargantuan ham-and-Swiss sandwich on fresh deli rye, lavishly slathered with mustard, and next to it, filling up the rest of the plate, was a pile of puffy orange cheese curls. They seemed to writhe and move, to edge toward the sandwich, toward her. 'Jessie?' Jack said.

She gave a choked, inarticulate cry and pushed the plate away wildly. Jack lost his grip; ham, Swiss cheese, bread, and Cheez Doodles scattered in all directions. A Cheez Doodle brushed against Jessie's leg. She whirled and ran from the apartment.

*

Jessie spent the night alone at a hotel and slept poorly. Even here, miles from the apartment, she could not escape the dream. It was the same as before, the same, but each night it seemed to grow longer, each night it went a little further. She was on the stoop, waiting, afraid. The door opened, and he drew her inside, the orange warm, the air like fetid breath, the Pear-shaped Man smiling. 'You can see my things,' he said, 'you can have my things,' and then he was undressing, his shirt first, his skin so white, dead flesh, heavy breasts with a blue ink stain, his belt, his pants falling, polyester pudding around his ankles, all the trash in his pockets scattering on the floor, and he really was pear-shaped, it wasn't just the way he dressed, and then the boxer shorts last of all, and Jessie looked down despite herself and there was no hair and it was small and wormy and kind of yellow, like a cheese curl, and it moved slightly and the Pear-shaped Man was saying, 'I want your things now, give them to me, let me see your things,' and why couldn't she run, her feet wouldn't move, but her hands did, her hands, and she began to undress.

The hotel detective woke her, pounding on her door, demanding to know what the problem was and why she was screaming.

*

She timed her return home so that the Pear-shaped Man would be away on his morning run to Santino's Market when she arrived. The house was empty. Angela had already gone to work, leaving the living room windows open again. Jessie closed them, locked them, and pulled the drapes. With luck, the Pear-shaped Man would never know that she'd come home.

Already the day outside was swelteringly hot. It was going to be a real scorcher. Jessie felt sweaty and soiled. She stripped, dumped her clothing into the wicker hamper in her bedroom, and immersed herself in a long, cold shower. The icy water hurt, but it was a good clean kind of hurting, and it left her feeling invigorated. She dried her hair and wrapped herself in a huge, fluffy blue towel, then padded back to her bedroom, leaving wet footprints on the bare wood floors.

A halter top and a pair of cutoffs would be all she'd need in this heat, Jessie decided. She had a plan for the day firmly in mind. She'd get dressed, do a little work in her studio, and after that she could read or watch some soaps or something. She wouldn't go outside; she wouldn't even look out the window. If the Pear-shaped Man was at his vigil, it would be a long, hot, boring afternoon for him.

Jessie laid out her cutoffs and a white halter top on the bed, draped the wet towel over a bedpost, and went to her dresser for a fresh pair of panties. She ought to do a laundry soon, she thought absently as she snatched up a pair of pink bikini briefs.

A Cheez Doodle fell out.

Jessie recoiled, shuddering. It had been *inside*, she thought wildly, it had been inside the briefs. The powdery cheese had left a yellow stain on the fabric. The Cheez Doodle lay where it had fallen, in the open drawer on top of her underwear. Something like terror took hold of her. She balled the bikini briefs up in her first and tossed them away with revulsion. She grabbed another pair of panties, shook them, and another Cheez Doodle leapt out. And then another. Another. She began to make a thin, hysterical sound, but she kept on. Five pairs, six, nine, that was all, but that was enough. Someone had opened her drawer and taken out every pair of panties and carefully wrapped a Cheez Doodle in each and put them all back.

It was a ghastly joke, she thought. Angela, it had to be Angela who'd done it, maybe she and Donald together. They thought this whole thing about the Pear-shaped Man was a big laugh, so they decided to see if they could really freak her out.

Except it hadn't been Angela. She knew it hadn't been Angela.

Jessie began to sob uncontrollably. She threw her balled-up panties to the floor and ran from the room, crushing Cheez Doodles into the carpet.

Out in the living room, she didn't know where to turn. She couldn't go back to her bedroom, *couldn't*, not just now, not until Angela got back, and she didn't want to go to the windows, even with the drapes closed. He was out there, Jessie could feel it, could feel him staring up at the windows. She grew suddenly aware of her nakedness and covered herself with her hands. She backed away from the windows, step by uncertain step, and retreated to her studio.

Inside she found a big square package leaning up against the door, with a note from Angela taped to it. 'Jess, this came for you last evening,' signed with Angie's big winged A. Jessie stared at the package, uncomprehending. It was from Pirouette. It was her painting, the cover she'd rushed to redo for them. Adrian had sent it back. Why?

She didn't want to know. She had to know.

Wildly, Jessie ripped at the brown paper wrappings, tore them away in long, ragged strips, baring the cover she'd painted. Adrian had written on the mat; she recognized his hand. 'Not funny, kid,' he'd scrawled. 'Forget it.'

'No,' Jessie whimpered, backing off.

There it was, her painting, the familiar background, the trite embrace, the period costumes researched so carefully, but no, she hadn't done that, someone had changed it, it wasn't her work, the woman was her, her, her, slender and strong with sandy blonde hair and green eyes full of rapture, and he was crushing her to him, to *him*, the wet lips and white skin, and he had a blue ink stain on his ruffled lace shirtfront and dandruff on his velvet jacket and his head was pointed and his hair was greasy and the fingers wrapped in her locks were stained yellow, and he was smiling thinly and pulling her to him and her mouth was open and her eyes half closed and it was him and it was her, and there was her own signature, there, down at the bottom.

'No,' she said again. She backed away, tripped over an easel, and fell. She curled up into a little ball on the floor and lay there sobbing, and that was how Angela found her, hours later.

*

Angela laid her out on the couch and made a cold compress and pressed it to her forehead. Donald stood in the doorway between the living room and the studio, frowning, glancing first at Jessie and then in at the painting and then at Jessie again. Angela said soothing things and held Jessie's hand and got her a cup of tea; little by little her hysteria began to ebb. Donald crossed his arms and scowled. Finally, when Jessie had dried the last of her tears, he said, 'This obsession of yours has gone too far.'

'Don, don't,' Angela said. 'She's terrified.'

'I can see that,' Donald said. 'That's why something has to be done. She's doing it to herself, honey.'

Jessie had a hot cup of Morning Thunder halfway to her mouth. She stopped dead still. 'I'm doing it to myself?' she repeated incredulously.

'Certainly,' Donald said.

The complacency in his tone made Jessie suddenly, blazingly angry. 'You stupid ignorant callous son of a bitch,' she roared. 'I'm doing it to myself, *I'm* doing it, *I'm* doing it, how *dare* you say that *I'm* doing it.' She flung the teacup across the room, aiming for his fat head. Donald ducked; the cup shattered and the tea sent three long brown fingers running down the off-white wall.

'Go on, let out your anger,' he said. 'I know you're upset. When you calm down, we can discuss this rationally, maybe get to the root of your problem.'

Angela took her arm, but Jessie shook off the grip and stood, her hands balled into fists. 'Go into my bedroom, you jerk, go in there right now and look around and come back and tell me what you see.'

'If you'd like,' Donald said. He walked over to the bedroom door, vanished, reemerged several moments later. 'All right,' he said patiently.

'Well?' Jessie demanded.

Donald shrugged. 'It's a mess,' he said. 'Underpants all over the floor, lots of crushed cheese curls. Tell me what you think it means.'

'He broke in here!' Jessie said.

'The Pear-shaped Man?' Donald queried pleasantly.

'*Of course* it was the Pear-shaped Man,' Jessie screamed. 'He snuck in here while we were all gone and he went into my bedroom and pawed through all my things and put Cheez Doodles in my underwear. He was *here!* He was touching my stuff.'

Donald wore an expression of patient, compassionate wisdom. 'Jessie, dear, I want you to think about what you just told us.'

'There's nothing to think about!'

'Of course there is,' he said. 'Let's think it through together. The Pear-shaped Man was here, you think?'

'Yes.'

'Why?'

'To do . . . to do what he did. It's disgusting. He's disgusting.'

'Hmmm,' Don said. 'How, then? The locks were changed, remember? He can't even get in the building. He's never had a key to this apartment. There was no sign of forced entry. How did he get in with his bag of cheese curls?'

Jessie had him there. 'Angela left the living room windows open,' she said.

Angela looked stricken. 'I did,' she admitted. 'Oh, Jessie, honey, I'm so sorry. It was hot. I just wanted to get a breeze, I didn't mean . . .'

'The windows are too high to reach from the sidewalk,' Donald pointed out. 'He'd have needed a ladder or something to stand on. He'd have needed to do it in broad daylight, from a busy street, with people coming and going all the time. He'd have had to have left the same way. There's the problem of the screens. He doesn't look like a very athletic sort, either.'

'He did it,' Jessie insisted. 'He was here, wasn't he?'

'I know you think so, and I'm not trying to deny your feelings, just explore them. Has this Pear-shaped Man ever been invited into the apartment?'

'Of course not!' Jessie said. 'What are you suggesting?'

'Nothing, Jess. Just consider. He climbs in through the windows with these cheese curls he intends to secret in your drawers. Fine. How does he know which room is yours?'

Jessie frowned. 'He . . . I don't know . . . he searched around, I guess.'

'And found what clue? You've got three bedrooms here, one a studio, two full of women's clothing. How'd he pick the right one?'

'Maybe he did it in both.'

'Angela, would you go check your bedroom, please?' Donald asked.

Angela rose hesitantly. 'Well,' she said, 'okay.' Jessie and Donald stared at each other until she returned a minute or so later. 'All clean,' she said.

'I don't know how he figured out which damned room was mine,' Jessie said. 'All I know is that he did. He had to. How else can you explain what happened, huh? Do you think I did it *myself?*'

Donald shrugged. 'I don't know,' he said calmly. He glanced over his shoulder into the studio. 'Funny, though. That painting in there, him and you, he must have done that some other time, after you finished it but before you sent it to Pirouette. It's good work, too. Almost as good as yours.'

Jessie had been trying very hard not to think about the painting. She opened her mouth to throw something back at him, but nothing flew out. She closed her mouth. Tears began to gather in the corners of her eyes. She suddenly felt weary, confused, and very alone. Angela had walked over to stand beside Donald. They were both looking at her. Jessie looked down at her hands helplessly and said, 'What am I going to do? God. What am I going to *do?*'

God did not answer; Donald did. 'Only one thing *to* do,' he said briskly. 'Face up to your fears. Exorcise them. Go down there and talk to the man, get to know him. By the time you come back up, you may pity him or have contempt for him or dislike him, but you won't fear him any longer; you'll see that he's only a human being and a rather sad one.'

'Are you sure, Don?' Angela asked him.

'Completely. Confront this obsession of yours, Jessie. That's the only way you'll ever be free of it. Go down to the basement and visit with the Pear-shaped Man.'

*

'There's nothing to be afraid of,' Angela told her again.

'That's easy for you to say.'

'Look, Jess, the minute you're inside, Don and I will come out and sit on the stoop. We'll be just an earshot away. All you'll have to do is let out the teeniest little yell and we'll come rushing right down. So you won't be alone, not really. And you've still got that knife in your purse, right?'

Jessie nodded.

'Come on, then, remember the time that purse snatcher tried to grab your shoulder bag? You decked him good. If this Pear-shaped Man tries anything, you're quick enough. Stab him. Run away. Yell for us. You'll be perfectly safe.'

'I suppose you're right,' Jessie said with a small sigh. They *were* right. She knew it. It didn't make any sense. He was a dirty, foul-smelling, unattractive man, maybe a little retarded, but nothing she couldn't handle, nothing she had to be afraid of, she didn't want to be crazy, she was letting this ridiculous obsession eat her alive and it had to end now, Donald was perfectly correct, she'd been doing it to herself all along and now she was going to take hold of it and stop it, certainly, it all made perfect sense and there was nothing to worry about, nothing to be afraid of, what could the Pear-shaped Man do to her, after all, what could he possibly *do* to her that was so terrifying? Nothing. Nothing.

Angela patted her on the back. Jessie took a deep breath, took the doorknob firmly in hand, and stepped out of the building into the hot, damp evening air. Everything was under control.

So why was she so scared?

*

Night was falling, but down under the stairs it had fallen already. Down under the stairs it was always night. The stoop cut off the morning sun, and the building itself blocked the afternoon light. It was dark, so dark. She stumbled over a crack in the cement, and her foot rang off the side of a metal garbage can. Jessie shuddered, imagining flies and maggots and other, worse things moving and breeding back there where the sun never shone. *No, mustn't think about that, it was only garbage, rotting and festering in the warm, humid dark, mustn't dwell on it*. She was at the door.

She raised her hand to knock, and then the fear took hold of her again. She could not move. *Nothing to be frightened of*, she told herself, *nothing at all*. What could he possibly *do* to her? Yet still she could not bring herself to knock. She stood before his door with her hand raised, her breath raw in her throat. It was so hot, so suffocatingly hot. She had to breathe. She had to get out from under the stoop, get back to where she could breathe.

A thin vertical crack of yellow light split the darkness. No, Jessie thought, *oh, please no*.

The door was opening.

Why did it have to open so slowly? Slowly, like in her dreams. Why did it have to open at all?

The light was so bright in there. As the door opened, Jessie found herself squinting.

The Pear-shaped Man stood smiling at her.

'I,' Jessie began, 'I, uh, I . . .'

'*There* she is,' the Pear-shaped Man said in his tinny little squeak.

'What do you want from me?' Jessie blurted.

'I knew she'd come,' he said, as though she wasn't there. 'I knew she'd come for my things.'

'No,' Jessie said. She wanted to run away, but her feet would not move.

'You can come in,' he said. He raised his hand, moved it toward her face. He touched her. Five fat white maggots crawled across her cheek and wriggled through her hair. His fingers smelled like cheese curls. His pinkie touched her ear and tried to burrow inside. She hadn't seen his other hand move until she felt it grip her upper arm, pulling, pulling. His flesh felt damp and cold. Jessie whimpered.

'Come in and see my things,' he said. 'You have to. You know you have to.' And somehow she was inside then, and the door was closing behind her, and she was there, inside, alone with the Pear-shaped Man.

Jessie tried to get a grip on herself. *Nothing to be afraid of,* she repeated to herself, a litany, a charm, a chant, *nothing to be afraid of, what could he do to you, what could he do?* The room was L-shaped, low ceilinged, filthy. The sickly sweet smell was overwhelming. Four naked light bulbs burned in the fixture above, and along one wall was a row of old lamps without shades, bare bulbs blazing away. A three-legged card table stood against the opposite wall, its fourth corner propped up by a broken TV set with wires dangling through the shattered glass of its picture tube. On top of the card table was a big bowl of Cheez Doodles. Jessie looked away, feeling sick. She tried to step backward, and her foot hit an empty plastic Coke bottle. She almost fell. But the Pear-shaped Man caught her in his soft, damp grip and held her upright.

Jessie yanked herself free of him and backed away. Her hand went into her purse and closed around the knife. It made her feel better, stronger. She moved close to the boarded-up window. Outside she could make out Donald and Angela talking. The sound of their voices, so close at hand – that helped, too. She tried to summon up all of her strength. 'How do you live like this?' she asked him. 'Do you need help cleaning up the place? Are you sick?' It was so hard to force out the words.

'Sick,' the Pear-shaped Man repeated. 'Did they tell you I was sick? They lie about me. They lie about me all the time. Somebody should make them stop.' If only he would stop smiling. His lips were so wet. But he never stopped smiling. 'I knew you would come. Here. This is for you.' He pulled it from a pocket, held it out.

'No,' said Jessie. 'I'm not hungry. Really.' But she was hungry, she realized. She was famished. She found herself staring at the thick orange twist between his fingers, and suddenly she wanted it desperately. 'No,' she said again, but her voice was weaker now, barely more than a whisper, and the cheese curl was very close.

Her mouth sagged open. She felt it on her tongue, the roughness of the powdery cheese, the sweetness of it. It crunched softly between her teeth. She swallowed and licked the last orange flakes from her lower lip. She wanted more.

'I knew it was you,' said the Pear-shaped Man. 'Now your things are mine.' Jessie stared at him. It was like in her nightmare. The Pear-shaped Man reached up and began to undo the little white plastic buttons on his shirt. She struggled to find her voice. He shrugged out of the shirt. His undershirt was yellow, with huge damp circles under his arms. He peeled it off, dropped it. He moved closer, and heavy white breasts flopped against his chest. The right one was covered by a wide blue smear. A dark little tongue slid between his lips. Fat white fingers worked at his belt like a team of dancing slugs. 'These are for you,' he said.

Jessie's knuckles were white around the hilt of the knife. 'Stop,' she said in a hoarse whisper.

His pants settled to the floor.

She couldn't take it. No more, no more. She pulled the knife free of her bag, raised it over her head. '*Stop!*'

'Ahh,' said the Pear-shaped Man, 'there it is.'

She stabbed him.

The blade went in right to the hilt, plunged deep into his soft, white skin. She wrenched it down and out. The skin parted, a huge, meaty gash. The Pear-shaped Man was smiling his little smile. There was no blood, no blood at all. His flesh was soft and thick, all pale dead meat.

He moved closer, and Jessie stabbed him again. This time he reached up and knocked her hand away. The knife was embedded in his neck. The hilt wobbled back and forth as he padded toward her. His dead, white arms reached out and she pushed against him and her hand sank into his body like he was made of wet, rotten bread. 'Oh,' he said, 'oh, oh, oh.' Jessie opened her mouth to scream, and the Pear-shaped Man pressed those heavy wet lips to her own and swallowed at her sound. His pale eyes sucked at her. She felt his tongue darting forward, and it was round and black and oily, and then it was snaking down inside her, touching, tasting, feeling all her things. She was drowning in a sea of soft, damp flesh.

*

She woke to the sound of the door closing. It was only a small click, a latch sliding into place, but it was enough. Her eyes opened, and she pulled herself up. It was so hard to move. She felt heavy, tired. Outside they were laughing. They were laughing at her. It was dim and far-off, that laughter, but she knew it was meant for her.

Her hand was resting on her thigh. She stared at it and blinked. She wiggled her fingers, and they moved like five fat maggots. She had something soft and yellow under her nails and deep dirty yellow stains up near her fingertips.

She closed her eyes, ran her hand over her body, the soft heavy curves, the thicknesses, the strange hills and valleys. She pushed, and the flesh gave and gave and gave. She stood up weakly. There were her clothes, scattered on the floor. Piece by piece she pulled them on, and then she moved across the room. Her briefcase was down beside the door; she gathered it up, tucked it under her arm, she might need something, yes, it was good to have the briefcase. She pushed open the door and emerged into the warm night. She heard the voices above her: '. . . were right all along,' a woman was saying, 'I couldn't believe I'd been so silly. There's nothing sinister about him, really, he's just pathetic. Donald, I don't know how to thank you.'

She came out from under the stoop and stood there. Her feet hurt so. She shifted her weight from one to the other and back again. They had stopped talking, and they were staring at her, Angela and Donald and a slender, pretty woman in blue jeans and work shirt. 'Come back,' she said, and her voice was thin and high. 'Give them back. You took them, you took my things. You have to give them back.'

The woman's laugh was like ice cubes tinkling in a glass of Coke.

'I think you've bothered Jessie quite enough,' Donald said.

'She has my things,' she said. 'Please.'

'I saw her come out, and she didn't have anything of yours,' Donald said.

'She took all my things,' she said.

Donald frowned. The woman with the sandy hair and the green eyes laughed again and put a hand on his arm. 'Don't look so serious, Don. He's not all there.'

They were all against her, she knew, looking at their faces. She clutched her briefcase to his chest. They'd taken her things, he couldn't remember exactly what, but they wouldn't get her case, he had stuff in there and they wouldn't get it. She turned away from them. He was hungry, she realized. She wanted something to eat. He had half a bag of Cheez Doodles left, she remembered. Downstairs. Down under the stoop.

As she descended, the Pear-shaped Man heard them talking about her. He opened the door and went inside to stay. The room smelled like home. He sat down, laid his case across his knees, and began to eat. He stuffed the cheese curls into his mouth in big handfuls and washed them down with sips from a glass of warm Coke straight from the bottle he'd opened that morning, or maybe yesterday. It was good. Nobody knew how good it was. They laughed at him, but they didn't know, they didn't know about all the nice things he had. No one knew. No one. Only someday he'd see somebody different, somebody to give his things to, somebody who would give him all their things. Yes. He'd like that. He'd know her when he saw her.

He'd know just what to say.

SIX
A TASTE OF TUF

A TASTE OF TUF

My career is littered with the corpses of dead series.

I launched my star ring series with 'The Second Kind of Loneliness' and 'Nor the Many-Colored Fires of a Star Ring,' then lost interest and never did a third story.

'A Peripheral Affair' was meant to be followed by the further adventures of the starship *Mjolnir* and the *Good Ship Lollipop*. None ever appeared, for the simple reason that none was ever written.

My corpse handler series went all the way to three: 'Nobody Leaves New Pittsburg' began it, 'Override' followed, and 'Meathouse Man' brought it to . . . well, a finish, if not an end. A fourth story exists as a four-page fragment, and there are ideas in my files for a dozen more. I once intended to write them all, publish them in the magazines, then collect them all together in a book I'd call *Songs the Dead Men Sing*. But that fourth story never got finished, and the others never got started. When I did finally use the title *Songs the Dead Men Sing* for a collection (from Dark Harvest, in 1983), 'Meathouse Man' was the only corpse story to make the cut.

I fared somewhat better with the Windhaven series, perhaps because Lisa Tuttle and I were collaborating on that one, so I had someone to give me a swift kick whenever my creative juices dried up (Lisa also added some swell creative juices of her own). We started out trying to write a short story, which turned into the novella 'The Storms of Windhaven' (a Hugo and Nebula loser) at the prompting of *Analog* editor Ben Bova. 'One-Wing' and 'The Fall' followed, two more novellas. Then Lisa and I put the three of them together, added a prologue and epilogue, and published *Windhaven*, a classic example of the 'fix up' novel; a novel made by cobbling together a series of previously published short stories or novellas.

Windhaven wasn't supposed to be the end of Windhaven, however. Lisa and I meant to continue the tale through two more books and two more generations, showing how the changes Maris started in 'The Storms of Windhaven' continued to transform her world. The second book was to be entitled *Painted Wings*. The protagonist would be the little girl we'd introduced in 'The Fall,' all grown up.

We never wrote it. We *talked* about writing it for years, but the timing never worked out. When I was free, Lisa was in the throes of a novel. When she was free, I was out in Hollywood, or doing *Wild Cards*, or a novel of my own. We were a thousand miles apart even when we were closest; then I went west (to Santa Fe and Los Angeles) and she went east (to England and Scotland), and we saw each other less and less often. Also, as we grew older, our voices and styles and ways of looking at the world became more and more distinct, which would have made collaborating far more challenging. Literary collaboration is a game for young writers, I think . . . or for old, cynical ones trying to cash in on their names. So our *Painted Wings* never took flight.

My other series all proved to be even shorter, as I've mentioned here and there throughout these commentaries. There was the Steel Angel series (one story). The Sharra series (one story). The Gray Alys series (one story). The Wo & Shade series (one story). The Skin Trade series (one story). It's enough to make one suspect a terminal case of *creatus interruptus*.

Ah, but then comes Tuf.

Haviland Tuf, ecological engineer, master of the *Ark*, and the protagonist of *Tuf Voyaging*, which is either a collection of short stories or a fix up novel, depending on whether you're a critic or a publisher. 'Twas Tuf who broke my series bugaboo for good and all, and opened up the gates for *Wild Cards* and *A Song of Ice and Fire*.

As a reader, I had my own favorite series characters. In fantasy, I was drawn to Moorcock's Elric and Howard's Solomon Kane, and I loved Fritz Leiber's dashing rogues, Fafhrd and the Gray Mouser. In SF, I was fond of Retief, of Dominic Flandry, of Lije Bailey and R. Daneel Olivaw. But my favorites had to be Jack Vance's galactic effectuator Magnus Ridolph and Poul Anderson's fat, scheming merchant prince of the spaceways, Nicholas van Rijn.

As a writer, I still had dreams of establishing a popular, long-running series of my own. I had an idea that I was certain could sustain one as well. It was 1975, and 'ecology' was a word on everyone's lips. It seemed to me that a series about some sort of biogenetic engineer, who moves from world to world solving (or in some cases, creating) ecological problems, would offer no end of story possibilities. The subject matter would allow me to explore all sorts of juicy issues . . . and best of all, no one else had done anything remotely like it, so far as I knew.

But who was this fellow? It seemed to me I had a terrific concept, but to sustain a series I needed a terrific *character* as well, someone the readers would enjoy following story after story. With that in mind, I went back and looked at some of the characters that I loved as a reader. Nicholas van Rijn. Conan. Sherlock Holmes. Mowgli. Travis McGee. Horatio Hornblower. Elric of Melnibone. Batman. Northwest Smith. Flashman. Fafhrd and the Mouser.

Retief. Susan Calvin. Magnus Ridolph. A diverse bunch, certainly. I wanted to see if they shared any traits in common.

They did.

Two things leapt out at me. One, they all had great names, names that fit them perfectly. Memorable names. *Singular* names. You were not like to meet two Horatio Hornblowers. Melnibone's phone book would not list four Elrics. Northwest Smith was not required to use his middle initials to distinguish himself from all the other Northwest Smiths.

Secondly, every one of them was larger than life. No average joes in this bunch. No danger of any of them vanishing into the wallpaper. Many of them are supreme in their own spheres, be that naval warfare (Hornblower), deduction (Holmes), hand-to-hand combat (Conan), or cowardice and lechery (Flashman). Most of them are severely idiosyncratic, to say the least. There is surely a place in fiction for small, commonplace, realistic characters, subtly rendered . . . but not as the star of an ongoing series.

Okay, I thought to myself, *I can do that*.

Thus was born Haviland Tuf, merchant, cat lover, vegetarian, big and bald, drinking mushroom wine and playing god, a fussy man and formal, who has long since veered past idiosyncracy into out-and-out eccentricity. There's some of Holmes and Ridolph in him, a pinch of Nicholas van Rijn, a little Hercule Poirot and a lot of Alfred Hitchcock . . . but not much me at all. Of all my protagonists, Tuf is the least like myself (although I did own a cat named Dax, though he was not telepathic).

The name? Well, 'Haviland' was a surname I noticed on the wall charts at a chess tournament I was directing. I'm not at all certain where the 'Tuf' came from. When I put the two of them together, though, that was *him*, and never a doubt.

Back in the '70s, I was still trying to place my stories in as wide a variety of markets as possible. I wanted to prove that I could sell to *anybody*, not just the same few editors. Also, I figured that every time I had a story in a new market I would reach new readers, who might then go on to look for my stuff elsewhere.

Working on that theory, I sold the first Haviland Tuf story to a British hardcover anthology called *Andromeda*, edited by Peter Weston. Perhaps 'A Beast for Norn' did indeed win me legions of new British readers, I couldn't say; unfortunately, very few of my old American readers ever found the story until St Martin's printed an American edition of *Andromeda* three years later. By that time, I had already published the second Tuf story, 'Call Him Moses.' I'd sold that one to Ben Bova. Thereafter Tuf became a familiar figure in the pages of *Analog*. Ben and his successor Stanley Schmidt got first look at each new Tuf story, and bought them all.

Not that there were a great many. Tuf was fun, but he was by no means the only fish in my frypan. In the late '70s I was still teaching at Clarke College, so my writing time was limited, and I had other stories I wanted to tell. And when I moved to Santa Fe at the end of 1979, to try and make a go of it as a full-time writer, my attention shifted to novels. *Fevre Dream* occupied most of my writing time in 1981, *The Armageddon Rag* in 1982, *Black and White and Red All Over* in 1984. (We won't talk about 1983, my Lost Year.) The Tuf series might well have petered out at three or four stories, but for Betsy Mitchell.

Betsy had been the assistant editor at *Analog* under Stan Schmidt, but in 1984 she left the magazine to become an editor at Baen Books. Not long after joining Baen she phoned to ask if I had ever considered doing a collection of Haviland Tuf's adventures. I had, of course . . . but that was for 'eventually,' some future time when I had accumulated enough Tuf stories to make a book.

In 1984 I had maybe half a book at best. Still, Betsy's offer was not one I could refuse. My career was in serious trouble just then. The readers had ignored *The Armageddon Rag* in droves, and as a result no editor would touch *Black and White and Red All Over*. This was a chance to get back into the game. I could write some more Tuf tales, sell first serial rights to Stan Schmidt at *Analog*, put them all together for Betsy, and make enough money to pay my mortgage for a little while longer.

So I wrote 'The Plague Star,' the tale of how Tuf came to be the master of the *Ark*, followed by the S'uthlam triptych, which gave the book a spine. Baen published *Tuf Voyaging* in February, 1986, as a novel. My fifth novel, some say . . . though I've always counted *Tuf Voyaging* as a short story collection. (In my own mind, *Black and White And Red All Over* will forever be my fifth novel, broken and unfinished though it is.)

No sampling of my checkered career could possibly be complete without a taste of Tuf, so I've included two stories here. The rest can be found in *Tuf Voyaging*, for those who want more.

'A Beast for Norn' was the earliest Tuf story, written in 1975 and published in 1976. When it came time for me to assemble *Tuf Voyaging* for Betsy in 1985, a decade had passed, and Haviland Tuf had changed somewhat, coming more into focus, as it were. The Tuf of 'A Beast for Norn' no longer quite fit, so I decided to revise and expand the story, to bring the proto-Tuf more in line with the character as he'd evolved in the later stories. It is the revised version of 'A Beast for Norn' that appears in *Tuf Voyaging*. For this retrospective, however, I thought it might be interesting to go back to my first take on Tuf. So what follows is the *original* version of 'A Beast for Norn,' as it appeared in *Andromeda* in 1976.

'Guardians' is of somewhat later vintage, having first been published in *Analog* in October, 1981. It was the most popular entry in the series with the readers, winning the *Locus* poll as Best Novelette of the year, and garnering a Hugo nomination. It finished second in the final balloting, losing the award to Roger Zelazny's superb 'Unicorn Variations.' (Roger was a dear friend of mine, and I had suggested the idea for 'Unicorn Variations' to him jokingly one day, as we drove to Albuquerque for a writers' lunch. Roger acknowledged that with a tip o' the hat by naming his protagonist Martin . . . and then went right out and took my Hugo.)

At one time there was supposed to be a second Tuf book. *Tuf Voyaging* did well enough so that Betsy Mitchell suggested a sequel; either another book of collected stories or perhaps a genuine full-length novel. I was willing. I had ideas for another dozen Tuf stories in my files. So contracts were duly drawn up and signed, and the book was even announced in *Locus*. Our working title was *Twice as Tuf*, although if I had gone the novel route I would probably have changed that to *Tuf Landing*.

It never happened. Hollywood intervened, and I found myself out in L.A., making as much money in two weeks as the *Twice as Tuf* contract would have paid me for a year's work. I needed money badly at that time, in the wake of *Armageddon Rag*'s disastrous sales and the failure of *Black and White and Red All Over* to sell.

When the deadline came and went without a book, I suggested to Betsy that I might bring in a collaborator, who could write the stories from my outlines. I take contracts seriously, and wanted to fulfill mine with Baen if at all possible . . . but taking on a partner really wasn't a very good idea. Betsy Mitchell did not think so either, and she talked me out of it. For that I remain grateful. She was right; Tuf stories written by someone else would not have been the same. I would have been cheating Baen Books, my readers, and myself. I ended up settling the *Twice as Tuf* contract by granting Baen Books the right to reprint some of my older books, so everyone ended up reasonably happy except the Tuf fans.

There are still a number of those about, actually. Every year for a decade or more, a few letters have come trickling in, urging me to stop writing *Wild Cards*, or those TV shows, or that series of big fat fantasy novels, so I can write some more Haviland Tuf stories instead.

To which I can only say, 'Maybe one of these days, when you least expect it . . .'

A Beast for Norn

Haviland Tuf was relaxing in an alehouse on Tamber when the thin man found him. He sat by himself in the darkest corner of the dimly-lit tavern, his elbows resting on the table and the top of his bald head almost brushing the low wooden beam above. Four empty mugs sat before him, their insides streaked by rings of foam, while a fifth, half-full, was cradled in huge calloused hands.

If Tuf was aware of the curious glances the other patrons gave him from time to time, he showed no sign of it; he quaffed his ale methodically, and his face – bone-white and completely hairless, as was the rest of him – was without expression. He was a man of heroic dimensions, Haviland Tuf, a giant with an equally gigantic paunch, and he made a singular solitary figure drinking alone in his booth.

Although he was not *quite* alone, in truth; his black tomcat Dax lay asleep on the table before him, a ball of dark fur, and Tuf would occasionally set down his mug of ale and idly stroke his quiet companion. Dax would not stir from his comfortable position among the empty mugs. The cat was fully as large, compared to other cats, as Haviland Tuf was compared to other men.

When the thin man came walking up to Tuf's booth, Tuf said nothing at all. He merely looked up, and blinked, and waited for the other to begin.

'You are Haviland Tuf, the animal-seller,' the thin man said. He was indeed painfully thin. His garments, all black leather and grey fur, hung loose on him, bagging here and there. Yet he was plainly a man of some means, since he wore a thin brass coronet around his brow, under a mop of black hair, and his fingers were all adorned with rings.

Tuf stroked Dax, and – looking down at the cat – began to speak. 'Did you hear that, Dax?' he said. He spoke very slowly, his voice a deep bass with only a hint of inflection. 'I am Haviland Tuf, the animal-seller. Or so I am taken to be.' Then he looked up at the thin man who stood there impatiently. 'Sir,' he said. 'I am indeed Haviland Tuf. And I do indeed trade in animals. Yet perhaps I do not consider myself an animal-seller. Perhaps I consider myself an ecological engineer.'

The thin man waved his hand in an irritated gesture, and slid uninvited into the booth opposite Tuf. 'I understand that you own a seedship of the ancient Ecological Corps, but that does not make you an ecological engineer, Tuf. They are all dead, and have been for centuries. But if you would prefer to be called an ecological engineer, then well and good. I require your services. I want to buy a monster from you, a great fierce beast.'

'Ah,' said Tuf, speaking to the cat again. 'He wants to buy a monster, this stranger who seats himself at my table.'

'My name is Herold Norn, if that is what's bothering you,' the thin man said. 'I am the Senior Beast-Master of my House, one of the Twelve Great Houses of Lyronica.'

'Lyronica,' Tuf stated. 'I have heard of Lyronica. The next world out from here towards the Fringe, is it not? Esteemed for its gaming pits?'

Norn smiled. 'Yesyes,' he said.

Haviland Tuf scratched Dax behind the ear, a peculiar rhythmic scratch, and the tomcat slowly uncurled, yawning, and glanced up at the thin man. A wave of reassurance came flooding into Tuff; the visitor was well-intentioned and truthful, it seemed. According to Dax. All cats have a touch of psi. Dax had more than a touch; the genetic wizards of the vanished Ecological Corps had seen to that. He was Tuf's mindreader.

'The affair becomes clearer,' Tuf said. 'Perhaps you would care to elaborate, Herold Norn?'

Norn nodded. 'Certainly, certainly. What do you know of Lyronica, Tuf? Particularly of the gaming pits?'

Tuf's heavy and stark white face remained emotionless. 'Some small things. Perhaps not enough, if I am to deal with you. Tell me what you will, and Dax and I will consider the matter.'

Herold Norn rubbed thin hands together, and nodded again, 'Dax?' he said. 'Oh, of course. Your cat. A handsome animal, although personally I have never been fond of beasts who cannot fight. Real beauty lies in killing-strength, I always say.'

'A peculiar attitude,' Tuf commented.

'Nono,' said Norn, 'not at all. I hope that your work here has not infected you with Tamberkin squeamishness.'

Tuf drained his mug in silence, then signaled for two more. The barkeep brought them promptly.

'Thank you, thank you,' Norn said, when the mug was set golden and foaming in front of him.

'Proceed.'

'Yes. Well, the Twelve Great Houses of Lyronica compete in the gaming pits, you know. It began – oh, centuries ago. Before that, the Houses warred. This way is much better. Family honor is upheld, fortunes are made, and no one is injured. You see, each House controls great tracts, scattered widely over the planet, and since the land is very thinly settled, animal life teems. The lords of the Great Houses, many years ago during a time of peace, started to have animal-fights. It was a pleasant diversion, rooted deep in history – you are aware, maybe, of the ancient custom of cock-fighting and the Old Earth folk called Romans who would set all manner of strange beasts against each other in their great arena?'

Norn paused and drank some ale, waiting for an answer, but Tuf merely stroked a quietly alert Dax and said nothing.

'No matter,' the thin Lyronican finally said, wiping foam from his mouth with the back of his hand. 'That was the beginning of the sport, you see. Each House had its own particular land, its own particular animals. The House of Varcour, for example, sprawls in the hot, swampy south, and they are fond of sending huge lizard-lions to the gaming pits. Feridian, a mountainous realm, has bred and championed its fortunes with a species of rock-ape which we call, naturally, *feridian*. My own house, Norn, stands on the grassy plains of the large northern continent. We have sent a hundred different beasts into combat in the pits, but we are most famed for our ironfangs.'

'Ironfangs,' Tuf said.

Norn gave a sly smile. 'Yes,' he said proudly. 'As Senior Beast-Master, I have trained thousands. Oh, but they are lovely animals! Tall as you are, with fur of the most marvelous blue-black color, fierce and relentless.'

'Canine?'

'But *such* canines,' Norn said.

'Yet you require from me a monster.'

Norn drank more of his ale. 'In truth, in truth. Folks from a dozen near worlds voyage to Lyronica, to watch the beasts fight in the gaming pits and gamble on the outcome. Particularly they flock to the Bronze Arena that has stood for six hundred years in the City of All Houses. That's where the greatest fights are fought. The wealth of our Houses and our world has come to depend on this. Without it, rich Lyronica would be as poor as the farmers of Tamber.'

'Yes,' said Tuf.

'But you understand, this wealth, it goes to the Houses according to their honor, according to their victories. The House of Arneth has grown greatest and most powerful because of the many deadly beasts in their varied lands; the others rank according to their scores in the Bronze Arena. The income from each match – all the monies paid by those who watch and bet – goes to the victor.'

Haviland Tuf scratched Dax behind the ear again. 'The House of Norn ranks last and least among the Twelve Great Houses of Lyronica,' he said, and the twinge that Dax relayed to him told him he was correct.

'You know,' Norn said.

'Sir. It was obvious. But is it ethical to buy an offworld monster, under the rules of your Bronze Arena?'

'There are precedents. Some seventy-odd standard years ago, a gambler came from Old Earth itself, with a creature called a timber wolf that he had trained. The House of Colin backed him, in a fit of madness. His poor beast was matched against a Norn ironfang, and proved far from equal to its task. There are other cases as well.

'In recent years, unfortunately, our ironfangs have not bred well. The wild species has all but died out on the plains, and the few who remain become swift and elusive, difficult for our housemen to capture. In the breeding kennels, the strain seems to have softened, despite my efforts and those of the Beast-Masters before me. Norn has won few victories of late, and I will not remain Senior for long unless something is done. We grow poor. When I heard that a seedship had come to Tamber, then, I determined to seek you out. I will begin a new era of glory for Norn, with your help.'

Haviland Tuf sat very still. 'I comprehend. Yet I am not in the habit of selling monsters. *The Ark* is an ancient seedship, designed by the Earth Imperials thousands of years ago, to decimate the Hrangans through ecowar. I can unleash a thousand diseases, and in the cell-banks I have cloning material for beasts from more worlds than you can count. You misunderstand the nature of ecowar, however. The deadliest enemies are not large predators, but tiny insects that lay waste to a world's crops, or hoppers that breed and breed and crowd out all other life.'

Herold Norn looked crestfallen. 'You have nothing, then?'

Tuf stroked Dax. 'Little. A million types of insects, a hundred thousand kinds of small birds, full as many fish. But monsters, monsters – only a few – a thousand perhaps. They were used from time to time, for psychological reasons as often as not.'

'A thousand monsters!' Norn was excited again. 'That is more than enough selection! Surely, among that thousand, we can find a beast for Norn!'

'Perhaps,' Tuf said. 'Do you think so, Dax?' he said to his cat. 'Do you? So!' He looked at Norn again. 'This matter does interest me, Herold Norn. And my work here is done, as I have given the Tamberkin a bird that will check their rootworm plague, and the bird does well. So Dax and I will take *The Ark* to Lyronica, and see your gaming pits, and we will decide what is to be done with them.'

Norn smiled. 'Excellent,' he said. 'Then I will buy this round of ale.' And

Dax told Haviland Tuf in silence that the thin man was flush with the feel of victory.

*

The Bronze Arena stood square in the center of the City of All Houses, at the point where sectors dominated by the Twelve Great Houses met like slices in a vast pie. Each section of the rambling stone city was walled off, each flew a flag with its distinctive colors, each had its own ambience and style; but all met in the Bronze Arena.

The Arena was not bronze after all, but mostly black stone and polished wood. It bulked upwards, taller than all but a few of the city's scattered towers and minarets, and topped by a shining bronze dome that gleamed with the orange rays of the sunset. Gargoyles peered from the various narrow windows, carved of stone and hammered from bronze and wrought iron. The great doors in the black stone walls were fashioned of metal as well, and there were twelve of them, each facing a different sector of the City of All Houses. The colors and the etching on each gateway were distinctive to its House.

Lyronica's sun was a fist of red flame smearing the western horizon when Herold Norn led Haviland Tuf to the games. The housemen had just fired gas torches, metal obelisks that stood like dark teeth in a ring about the Bronze Arena, and the hulking ancient building was surrounded by flickering pillars of blue-and-orange flame. In a crowd of gamblers and gamesters, Tuf followed Herold Norn from the half-deserted streets of the Nornic slums down a path of crushed rock, passing between twelve bronze ironfangs who snarled and spit in timeless poses on either side of the street, and then through the wide Norn Gate whose doors were intricate ebony and brass. The uniformed guards, clad in the same black leather and grey fur as Herold Norn himself, recognized the Beast-Master and admitted them; others stopped to pay with coins of gold and iron.

The Arena was the greatest gaming pit of all; it *was* a pit, the sandy combat-floor sunk deep below ground level, with stone walls four meters high surrounding it. Then the seats began, just atop the walls, circling and circling in ascending tiers until they reached the doors. Enough seating for thirty thousand, although those towards the back had a poor view at best, and other seats were blocked off by iron pillars. Betting stalls were scattered throughout the building, windows in the outer walls.

Herold Norn took Tuf to the best seats in the Arena, in the front of the Norn section, with only a stone parapet separating them from the four-meter drop to the combat sands. The seats here were not rickety wood-and-iron, like those in the rear, but thrones of leather, huge enough to accommodate even Tuf's vast bulk without difficulty, and opulently comfortable. 'Every seat is bound in the skin of a beast that has died nobly below,' Herold Norn told Tuf, as they seated themselves. Beneath them, a work crew of men in one-piece blue coveralls was dragging the carcass of some gaunt feathered animal towards one of the entryways. 'A fighting-bird of the House of Wrai Hill,' Norn explained. 'The Wrai Beast-Master sent it up against a Varcour lizard-lion. Not the most felicitous choice.'

Haviland Tuf said nothing. He sat stiff and erect, dressed in a grey vinyl greatcoat that fell to his ankles, with flaring shoulder-boards and a visored green-and-brown cap emblazoned with the golden theta of the Ecological Engineers. His large, rough hands interlocked atop his bulging stomach while Herold Norn kept up a steady stream of conversation.

Then the Arena announcer spoke, and the thunder of his magnified voice boomed all around them. 'Fifth match,' he said. 'From the House of Norn, a male ironfang, aged two years, weight 2.6 quintals, trained by Junior Beast-Master Kers Norn. New to the Bronze Arena.' Immediately below them, metal grated harshly on metal, and a nightmare creature came bounding into the pit. The ironfang was a shaggy giant, with sunken red eyes and a double row of curving teeth that dripped slaver; a wolf grown all out of proportion and crossed with a saber-toothed tiger, its legs as thick as young trees, its speed and killing grace only partially disguised by the blue-black fur that hid the play of muscles. The ironfang snarled and the Arena echoed to the noise; scattered cheering began all around them.

Herold Norn smiled. 'Kers is a cousin, and one of our most promising juniors. He tells me this beast will do us proud. Yes, yes. I like its looks, don't you?'

'Being new to Lyronica and your Bronze Arena, I have no standard of comparison,' Tuf said in a flat voice.

The announcer began again. 'From the House of Arneth-in-the-Gilded-Wood, a strangling-ape, aged six years, weight 3.1 quintals, trained by Senior Beast-Master Danel Leigh Arneth. Three times a veteran of the Bronze Arena, three times surviving.'

Across the combat pit, another of the entryways – the one wrought in gold and crimson – slid open, and the second beast lumbered out on two squat legs and looked around. The strangling-ape was short but immensely broad, with a triangular torso and a bullet-shaped head, eyes sunk deep under a heavy ridge of bone. Its arms, double-jointed and muscular, dragged in the Arena sand. From head to toe the beast was hairless, but for patches of dark red fur under its arms; its skin was a dirty white. And it smelled. Across the Arena, Haviland Tuf still caught the musky odor.

'It sweats,' Norn explained. 'Danel Leigh has driven it to killing frenzy before sending it forth. His beast has the edge in experience, you understand, and the strangling-ape is a savage creature as well. Unlike its cousin, the mountain feridian, it is naturally a carnivore and needs little training. But Kers' ironfang is younger. The match should be of interest.' The Norn Beast-Master leaned forward while Tuf sat calm and still.

The ape turned, growling deep in its throat, and already the ironfang was streaking towards it, snarling, a blue-black blur that scattered arena sand as it ran. The strangling-ape waited for it, spreading its huge gangling arms, and Tuf had a blurred impression of the great Norn killer leaving the ground in one tremendous bound. Then the two animals were locked together, rolling over and over in a tangle of ferocity, and the arena became a symphony of screams. 'The throat,' Norn was shouting. 'Tear out its throat! Tear out its throat!'

Then, as sudden as they had met, the two beasts parted. The ironfang spun away and began to move in slow circles, and Tuf saw that one of its forelegs was bent and broken, so that it limped on the three remaining. Yet still it circled. The strangling-ape gave it no opening, but turned constantly to face it as it prowled. Long gashes drooled blood on the ape's wide chest, where the ironfang's sabers had slashed, but the beast of Arneth seemed little weakened. Herold Norn had begun to mutter softly at Tuf's side.

Impatient with the lull, the watchers in the Bronze Arena began a rhythmic chant, a low wordless noise that swelled louder and louder as new voices heard and joined. Tuf saw at once that the sound affected the animals below. Now they began to snarl and hiss, calling battle cries in savage voices, and the strangling-ape moved from one leg to the other, back and forth, in a macabre dance, while slaver ran in dripping rivers from the gaping jaws of the ironfang. The chant grew and grew – Herold Norn joined in, his thin body swaying slightly as he moaned – and Tuf recognized the bloody killing-chant for what it was. The beasts below went into a frenzy. Suddenly the ironfang was charging again, and the ape's long arms reached to meet it in its wild lunge. The impact of the leap threw the strangler backwards, but Tuf saw that the ironfang's teeth had closed on air while the ape wrapped its hands around the blue-black throat. The ironfang thrashed wildly, but briefly, as they rolled in the sand. Then came a sharp, horribly loud snap, and the wolf-creature was nothing but a rag of fur, its head lolling grotesquely to one side.

The watchers ceased their moaning chant, and began to applaud and whistle. Afterwards, the gold and crimson door slid open once again and the strangling-ape returned to where it had come. Four men in Norn House black and grey came out to carry off the corpse.

Herold Norn was sullen. 'Another loss. I will speak to Kers. His beast did not find the throat.'

Haviland Tuf stood up. 'I have seen your Bronze Arena.'

'Are you going?,' Norn asked anxiously. 'Surely not so soon! There are five more matches. In the next, a giant feridian fights a water-scorpion from Amar Island!'

'I need see no more. It is feeding time for Dax, so I must return to *The Ark.*'

Norn scrambled to his feet, and put an anxious hand to Tuf's shoulder to restrain him. 'Will you sell us a monster, then?'

Tuf shook off the Beast-Master's grip. 'Sir. I do not like to be touched. Restrain yourself.' When Norn's hand had fallen, Tuf looked down into his eyes. 'I must consult my records, my computers. *The Ark* is in orbit. Shuttle up the day after next. A problem exists, and I shall address myself to its correction.' Then, without further word, Haviland Tuf turned and walked from the Bronze Arena, back to the spaceport of the City of All Houses, where his shuttlecraft sat waiting.

*

Herold Norn had obviously not been prepared for *The Ark*. After his black-and-grey shuttle had docked and Tuf had cycled him through, the Beast-Master made no effort to disguise his reaction. 'I should have known,' he kept repeating. 'The size of this ship, the *size*. But of course I should have known.'

Haviland Tuf stood unmoved, cradling Dax in one arm and stroking the cat slowly. 'Old Earth built larger ships than modern worlds,' he said impassively. '*The Ark*, as a seedship, had to be large. It once had two hundred crewmen. Now it has one.'

'You are the *only* crewman?' Norn said.

Dax suddenly warned Tuf to be alert. The Beast-Master had begun to think hostile thoughts. 'Yes,' Tuf said. 'The only crewman. But there is Dax, of course. And defenses programmed in, lest control be wrested from me.'

Norn's plans suddenly withered, according to Dax. 'I see,' he said. Then, eagerly, 'Well, what have you come up with?'

'Come,' said Tuf, turning.

He led Norn out of the reception floor down a small corridor that led into a larger. There they boarded a three-wheeled vehicle and drove through a long tunnel lined by glass vats of all sizes and shapes, filled with gently-bubbling liquid. One bank of vats was divided into units as small as a man's fingernail; on the other extreme, there was a single unit large enough to contain the interior of the Bronze Arena. It was empty, but in some of the medium-sized tanks, dark shapes hung in translucent bags, and stirred fitfully. Tuf, with Dax curled in his lap, stared straight ahead as he drove, while Norn looked wonderingly from side to side.

They departed the tunnel at last, and entered a small room that was all computer consoles. Four large chairs sat in the four corners of the square chamber, with control panels on their arms; a circular plate of blue metal was built into the floor amidst them. Haviland Tuf dropped Dax into one of the chairs before seating himself in a second. Norn looked around, then took the chair diagonally opposite Tuf.

'I must inform you of several things,' Tuf began.

'Yesyes,' said Norn.

'Monsters are expensive,' Tuf said. 'I will require one hundred thousand standards.'

'*What*! That's an outrage! We would need a hundred victories in the Bronze Arena to amass that sum. I told you, Norn is a poor House.'

'So. Perhaps then a richer House would meet the required price. The Ecological Engineering Corps has been defunct for centuries, sir. No ship of theirs remains in working order, save *The Ark* alone. Their science is largely forgotten. Techniques of cloning and genetic engineering such as they practiced exist now only on Prometheus and Old Earth itself, where such secrets are closely guarded. And the Private Northeans no longer have the stasis field, thus their clones grow to natural maturity.' Tuf looked across to where Dax sat in a chair before the gently winking lights of the computer consoles. 'And yet, Dax, Herold Norn feels my price to be excessive.'

'Fifty thousand standards,' Norn said. 'We can barely meet that price.'

Haviland Tuf said nothing.

'Eighty thousand standards, then! I can go no higher. The House of Norn will be bankrupt! They will tear down our bronze ironfangs, and seal the Norn Gate!'

Haviland Tuf said nothing.

'Curse you! A hundred thousand, yesyes. But only if your monster meets our requirements.'

'You will pay the full sum on delivery.'

'Impossible!'

Tuf was silent again.

'Oh, very well.'

'As to the monster itself, I have studied your requirements closely, and have consulted my computers. Here upon *The Ark*, in my frozen cell-banks, thousands upon thousands of predators exist, including many now extinct on their original homeworlds. Yet few, I would think, would satisfy the demands of the Bronze Arena. And of those that might, many are unsuitable for other reasons. For example, I have considered the selection to be limited to beasts that might with luck be bred on the lands of the House of Norn. A creature who could not replicate himself would be a poor investment. No matter how invincible he might be, in time the animal would age and die, and Norn victories would be at an end.'

'An excellent point,' Herold Norn said. 'We have, from time to time, attempted to raise lizard-lions and feridians and other beasts of the Twelve Houses, with ill success. The climate, the vegetation . . .' He made a disgusted gesture.

'Precisely. Therefore, I have eliminated silicon-based life forms, which would surely die on your carbon-based world. Also, animals of planets whose atmosphere varies too greatly from Lyronica's. Also, beasts of dissimilar climes. You will comprehend the various and sundry difficulties incumbent in my search.'

'Yesyes, but get to the point. What have you found? What is this hundred thousand standard monster?'

'I offer you a selection,' Tuf said. 'From among some thirty animals. Attend!'

He touched a glowing button on the arm of his chair, and suddenly a beast was squatting on the blue-metal plate between them. Two meters tall with rubbery pink-grey skin and thin white hair, the creature had a low forehead and a swinish snout, plus a set of nasty curving horns and dagger-like claws on its hands.

'I will not trouble you with species names, since I observe that informality was the rule of the Bronze Arena,' Haviland Tuf said. 'This is the so-called stalking-swine of Heydey, native to both forests and plain. Chiefly a carrion-eater, but it has been known to relish fresh meat, and it fights viciously when attacked. Said to be quite intelligent, yet impossible to domesticate. The stalking-swine is an excellent breeder. The colonists from Gulliver eventually abandoned their Heydey settlement because of this animal. That was some two hundred years past.'

Herold Norn scratched his scalp between dark hair and brass coronet. 'No. It is too thin, too light. Look at the neck! Think what a feridian would do to it.' He shook his head violently, 'Besides, it is ugly. And I resent the offer of a scavenger, no matter how ill-tempered. The House of Norn breeds proud fighters, beasts who kill their own game!'

'So,' said Tuf. He touched the button, and the stalking-swine vanished. In its place, bulking large enough to touch the plates above and fade into them, was a massive ball of armored grey flesh as featureless as battle plate.

'This creature's homeworld has never been named, nor settled. A team from Old Poseidon once explored it, however, and cell samples were taken. Zoo specimens existed briefly, but did not thrive. The beast was nicknamed the rolleram. Adults weigh approximately six metric tons. On the plains of their homeworld, the rollerams achieve speed in excess of fifty kilometers per standard hour, crushing prey beneath them. The beast is all mouth. Thusly, as any portion of its skin can be made to exude digestive enzymes, it simply rests atop its meal until the meat has been absorbed.'

Herold Norn, himself half-immersed in the looming holograph, sounded impressed. 'Ah, yes. Better, much better. An awesome creature. Perhaps . . . but no.' His tone changed suddenly. 'Nono, this will never do. A creature weighing six tons and rolling that fast might smash its way out of the Bronze Arena, and kill hundreds of our patrons. Besides, who would pay hard coin to watch this *thing* crush a lizard-lion or a strangler? No. No sport. Your rolleram is *too* monstrous, Tuf.'

Tuf, unmoved, hit the button once again. The vast grey bulk gave way to a sleek, snarling cat, fully as large as an ironfang, with slitted yellow eyes and powerful muscles bunched beneath a coat of dark blue fur. The fur was striped, here and there; long thin lines of bright silver running lengthwise down the creature's flanks.

'Ahhhhhhhh,' Norn said. 'A beauty, in truth, in truth.'

'The cobalt panther of Celia's World,' Tuf said, 'often called the cobalcat. One of the largest and deadliest of the great cats, or their analogs. The beast is a truly superlative hunter, its senses miracles of biological engineering. It can see into the infrared for night prowling, and the ears – note the size and the spread, Beast-Master – the ears are extremely sensitive. Being of felinoid stock, the cobalcat has psionic ability, but in its case this ability is far more developed than the usual. Fear, hunger, and bloodlust all act as triggers; then the cobalcat becomes a mindreader.'

Norn looked up, startled. 'What?'

'Psionics, sir. I said psionics. The cobalcat is very deadly, simply because it knows what moves an antagonist will make before those moves are made. It anticipates. Do you comprehend?'

'Yes.' Norn's voice was excited. Haviland Tuf looked over at Dax, and the big tomcat – who'd been not the least disturbed by the parade of scentless phantoms flashing on and off – confirmed the thin man's enthusiasm as genuine. 'Perfect, perfect! Why, I'll venture to say that we can even train these beasts as we'd train ironfangs, eh? Eh? And *mindreaders!* Perfect. Even the colors are right, dark blue, you know, and our ironfangs were blue-black, so the cats will be most Nornic, yesyes!'

Tuf touched his chair arm, and the cobalcat vanished. 'So then, no need to proceed further. Delivery will be in three weeks standard, if that pleases you. For the agreed-upon sum, I will provide three pair, two sets of younglings who should be released as breeding stock, and one mated set full-grown, who might be immediately sent into the Bronze Arena.'

'So soon,' Norn began. 'Fine, but . . .'

'I use the stasis field, sir. Reversed it produces chronic distortion, a time acceleration if you will. Standard procedure. Promethean techniques would require that you wait until the clones aged to maturity naturally, which sometimes is considered inconvenient. It would perhaps be prudent to add that, although I provide Norn House with six animals, only three actual individuals are represented. *The Ark* carries a triple cobalcat cell. I will clone each specimen twice, male and female, and hope for a viable genetic mix when they crossbreed on Lyronica.'

Dax filled Tuf's head with a curious flood of triumph and confusion and impatience. Herold Norn, then, had understood nothing of what Tuf had said, or at any rate that was one interpretation. 'Fine, whatever you say,' Norn said. 'I will send the ships for the animals promptly, with proper cages. Then we will pay you.'

Dax radiated deceit, distrust, alarm.

'Sir. You will pay the full fee before any beasts are handed over.'

'But you said on delivery.'

'Admitted. Yet I am given to impulsive whims, and impulse now tells me to collect first, rather than simultaneously.'

'Oh, very well,' Norn said. 'Though your demands are arbitrary and excessive. With these cobalcats, we shall soon recoup our fee.' He started to rise.

Haviland Tuf raised a single finger. 'One moment. You have not seen fit to inform me overmuch of the ecology of Lyronica, nor the particular realms of Norn House. Perhaps prey exists. I must caution you, however, that your cobalcats will not breed unless hunting is good. They need suitable game species.'

'Yesyes, of course.'

'Let me add this, then. For an additional five thousand standards, I might clone you a breeding stock of Celian hoppers, delightful furred herbivores renowned on a dozen worlds for their succulent flesh.'

Herold Norn frowned. 'Bah. You ought to give them to us without charge. You have extorted enough money, trader, and . . .'

Tuf rose, and gave a ponderous shrug. 'The man berates me, Dax,' he said to his cat. 'What am I to do? I seek only a honest living.' He looked at Norn. 'Another of my impulses comes to me. I feel, somehow, that you will not relent, not even were I to offer you an excellent discount. Therefore I shall yield. The hoppers are yours without charge.'

'Good. Excellent.' Norn turned towards the door. 'We shall take them at the same time as the cobalcats, and release them about the estates.'

Haviland Tuf and Dax followed him from the chamber, and they rode in silence back to Norn's ship.

*

The fee was sent up by the House of Norn the day before delivery was due. The following afternoon, a dozen men in black-and-grey ascended to *The Ark*, and carried six tranquilized cobalcats from Haviland Tuf's nutrient vats to the waiting cages in their ships. Tuf bid them a passive farewell, and heard no more from Herold Norn. But he kept *The Ark* in orbit about Lyronica.

Less than three of Lyronica's shortened days passed before Tuf observed that his clients had slated a cobalcat for a bout in the Bronze Arena. On the appointed evening, he disguised himself as best a man like he could disguise himself – with a false beard and a shoulder-length wig of red hair, plus a gaudy puff-sleeved suit of canary yellow complete with a furred turban – and shuttled down to the City of All Houses with the hope of escaping attention. When the match was called (it was the third on the schedule), Tuf was sitting in the back of the Arena, a rough stone wall against his shoulders and a narrow wooden seat attempting to support his weight. He had paid a few irons for admission, but had scrupulously bypassed the betting booths.

'Third match,' the announcer cried, even as workers pulled off the scattered meaty chunks of the loser in the second match. 'From the House of Varcour, a female lizard-lion, aged nine months, weight 1.4 quintals, trained by Junior Beast-Master Ammariy Varcour Otheni. Once a veteran of the Bronze Arena, once surviving.' Those customers close to Tuf began to cheer and wave their hands wildly – he had chosen to enter by the Varcour Gate this time, walking down a green concrete road and through the gaping maw of a monstrous golden lizard – and, far away and below, a green-and-gold enameled door slid up. Tuf had worn binoculars. He lifted them to his eyes, and saw the lizard-lion scrabble forward; two meters of scaled green reptile with a whip-like tail thrice its own length and the long snout of an Old Earth alligator. Its jaws opened and closed soundlessly, displaying an array of impressive teeth.

'From the House of Norn, imported from offworld for your amusement, a female cobalcat. Aged – aged three weeks.' The announcer paused. 'Aged three years,' he said at last, 'weight 2.3 quintals, trained by Senior Beast-Master Herold Norn. New to the Bronze Arena.' The metallic dome overhead rang to the cacophonous cheering of the Norn sector; Herold Norn had packed the Bronze Arena with his housemen and tourists betting the grey-and-black standard.

The cobalcat came from the darkness slowly, with cautious fluid grace, and its great golden eyes swept the arena. It was every bit the beast that Tuf had promised; a bundle of deadly muscle and frozen motion, all blue with but a single silvery streak. Its growl could scarcely be heard, so far was Tuf from the action, but he saw its mouth gape through his glasses.

The lizard-lion saw it too, and came waddling forward, its short scaled legs kicking in the sand while the long impossible tail arched above it like the sting of some reptilian scorpion. Then, when the cobalcat turned its liquid eyes on the enemy, the lizard-lion brought the tail forward and down. Hard. With a bone-breaking crack the whip made contact, but the cobalcat had smoothly slipped to one side, and nothing shattered but air and sand.

The cat circled, yawning. The lizard-lion, implacable, turned and raised its tail again, opened its jaws, lunged forward. The cobalcat avoided both teeth and whip. Again the tail cracked, and again, the cat was too quick. Someone in the audience began to moan the killing chant, others picked it up; Tuf turned his binoculars, and saw swaying in the Norn seats. The lizard-lion gnashed its long jaws in frenzy, smashed its whip across the nearest entry door, and began to thrash.

The cobalcat, sensing an opening, moved behind its enemy with a graceful leap, pinned the struggling lizard with one great blue paw, and clawed the soft greenish flanks and belly to ribbons. After a time and a few futile snaps of its whip that only distracted the cat, the lizard-lion lay still.

The Norns were cheering very loudly. Haviland Tuf – huge and full-bearded and gaudily dressed – rose and left.

*

Weeks passed; *The Ark* remained in orbit around Lyronica. Haviland Tuf listened to results from the Bronze Arena on his ship's comm, and noted that the Norn cobalcats were winning match after match after match. Herold Norn still lost a contest on occasion – usually when he used an ironfang to fill up his Arena obligations – but those defeats were easily outweighed by his victories.

Tuf sat with Dax curled in his lap, drank tankards of brown ale from *The Ark* brewery, and waited.

About a month after the debut of the cobalcats, a ship rose to meet him; a slim, needle-browed shuttlecraft of green and gold. It docked, after comm contact, and Tuf met the visitors in the reception room with Dax in his arms. The cat read them as friendly enough, so he activated no defenses.

There were four, all dressed in metallic armor of scaled gold metal and green enamel. Three stood stiffly at attention. The fourth, a florid and corpulent man who wore a golden helmet with a bright green plume to conceal his baldness, stepped forward and offered a meaty hand.

'Your intent is appreciated,' Tuf told him, keeping both of his own hands firmly on Dax, 'But I do not care to touch. I do require your name and business, sir.'

'Morho y Varcour Otheni,' the leader began.

Tuf raised one palm. 'So. And you are the Senior Beast-Master of the House of Varcour, come to buy a monster. Enough. I knew it all the while, I must confess. I merely wished – on impulse, as it were – to determine if you would tell the truth.'

The fat Beast-Master's mouth puckered in an 'o.'

'Your housemen should remain here,' Tuf said, turning. 'Follow me.'

Haviland Tuf let Morho y Varcour Otheni utter scarcely a word until they were alone in the computer room, sitting diagonally opposite. 'You heard of me from the Norns,' Tuf said then. 'Is that not correct?'

Morho smiled toothily. 'Indeed we did. A Norn houseman was persuaded to reveal the source of their cobalcats. To our delight, your *Ark* was still in orbit. You seem to have found Lyronica diverting?'

'Problems exist. I hope to help. Your problem, for example. Varcour is, in all probability, now the last and least of the Twelve Great Houses. Your lizard-lions fail to awe me, and I understand your realms are chiefly swampland. Choice of combatants being therefore limited. Have I divined the essence of your complaint?'

'Hmpf. Yes, indeed You do anticipate me, sir. But you do it well. We were holding our own well enough until you interfered; then, well, we have not taken a match from Norn since, and they were previously our chiefest victims. A few paltry wins over Wrai Hill and Amar Island, a lucky score against Feridian, a pair of death-draws with Arneth and Sin Doon – that has been our lot this past month. Pfui. We cannot survive. They will make me a Brood-Tender and ship me back to the estates unless I act.'

Tuf quieted Morho with an upraised hand. 'No need to speak further. Your distress is noted. In the time since I have helped Herold Norn, I have been fortunate enough to be gifted with a great deal of leisure. Accordingly, as an exercise of the mind, I have been able to devote myself to the problems of the Great Houses, each in its turn. We need not waste time. I can solve your present difficulties. There will be cost, however.'

Morho grinned. 'I come prepared. I heard about your price. It's high, there is no arguing, but we are prepared to pay, if you can . . .'

'Sir,' Tuf said. 'I am a man of charity. Norn was a poor House, Herold almost a beggar. In mercy, I gave him a low price. The domains of Varcour are richer, its standards brighter, its victories more wildly sung. For you, I must charge three hundred thousand standards, to make up for the losses I suffered in dealing with Norn.'

Morho made a shocked blubbering sound, and his scales gave metallic clinks as he shifted in his seat. 'Too much, too much,' he protested. 'I implore you. Truly, we are more glorious than Norn, but not so great as you suppose. To pay this price of yours, we must need starve. Lizard-lions would run over our battlements. Our towns would sink on their stilts, until the swamp mud covered them over and the children drowned.'

Tuf was looking at Dax. 'Quite so,' he said, when his glance went back to Morho. 'You touch me deeply. Two hundred thousand standards.'

Morho y Varcour Otheni began to protest and implore again, but this time Tuf merely sat silently, arms on their armrests, until the Beast-Master, red-faced and sweating, finally ran down and agreed to pay his price.

Tuf punched his control arm. The image of a great lizard materialized between him and Morho; it stood three meters tall, covered in grey-green plate scales and standing on two thick clawed legs. Its head, atop a short neck, was disproportionately large, with jaws great enough to take off a man's head and shoulders in a single chomp. But the creature's most remarkable features were its forelegs; short thick ropes of muscle ornamented by meter-long spurs of discolored bone.

'The *tris neryei* of Cable's Landing,' Tuf said, 'or so it was named by the Fyndii, whose colonists preceded men on that world by a millennium. The term translates, literally, as 'living knife.' Also called the bladed tyrant, a name of human origin referring to the beast's resemblance to the tyrannosaur, or tyrant lizard, a long-extinct reptile of Old Earth. A superficial resemblance only, to be sure. The *tris neryei* is a far more efficient carnivore than the tyrannosaur ever was, due to its terrible forelegs, swords of bone that it uses with a frightful instinctive ferocity.'

Morho was leaning forward until his seat creaked beneath him, and Dax filled Tuf's head with hot enthusiasm. 'Excellent!' the Beast-Master said, 'though the names are a bit long-winded. We shall call them tyranno-swords, eh?'

'Call them what you will, it matters not to me. The animals have many obvious advantages for the House of Varcour,' Tuf said. 'Should you take them, I will throw in – without any additional charge – a breeding stock of Cathadayn tree-slugs. You will find that . . .'

*

When he could, Tuf followed the news from the Bronze Arena, although he never again ventured forth to the soil of Lyronica. The cobalcats continued to sweep all before them in the latest featured encounter; one of the Norn beasts had destroyed a prime Arneth strangling-ape and an Amar Island fleshfrog during a special triple match.

But Varcour fortunes were also on the upswing; the newly-introduced tyrannoswords had proved a Bronze Arena sensation, with their booming cries and their heavy tread, and the relentless death of their bone-swords. In three matches so far, a huge feridian, a water-scorpion, and a Gnethin spidercat had all proved impossibly unequal to the Varcour lizards. Morho y Varcour Otheni was reportedly ecstatic. Next week, tyrannosword would face cobalcat in a struggle for supremacy, and a packed arena was being predicted. Herold Norn called up once, shortly after the tyrannoswords had scored their first victory. 'Tuft,' he said sternly, 'you were not to sell to the other Houses.'

Haviland Tuf sat calmly, regarding Norn's twisted frown, petting Dax. 'No such matter was ever included in the discussion. Your own monsters perform as expected. Do you complain because another now shares your good fortune?'

'Yes. No. That is – well, never mind. I suppose I can't stop you. If the other Houses get animals that can beat our cats, however, you will be expected to provide us with something that can beat whatever you sell them. You understand?'

'Sir. Of course.' He looked down at Dax. 'Herold Norn now questions my comprehension.' Then up again. 'I will always sell, if you have the price.'

Norn scowled on the comm screen. 'Yesyes. Well, by then our victories should have mounted high enough to afford whatever outlandish price you intend to charge.'

'I trust that all goes well otherwise?' Tuf said.

'Well, yes and no. In the Arena, yesyes, definitely. But otherwise, well, that was what I called about. The four young cats don't seem interested in breeding, for some reason. And our Brood-tender keeps complaining that they are getting thin. He doesn't think they're healthy. Now, I can't say personally, as I'm here in the City and the animals are back on the plains around Norn House. But some worry does exist. The cats run free, of course, but we have tracers on them, so we can . . .'

Tuf raised a hand. 'It is no doubt not mating season for the cobalcats. Did you not consider this?'

'Ah. No, no, don't suppose so. That makes sense. Just a question of time then, I suppose. The other question I wanted to go over concerned these hoppers of yours. We set them loose, you know, and they have demonstrated no difficulty whatever in breeding. The ancestral Norn grasslands have been chewed bare. It is very annoying. They hop about everywhere. What are we to do?'

'Breed the cobalcats,' Tuf suggested. 'They are excellent predators, and will check the hopper plague.'

Herold Norn looked puzzled, and mildly distressed. 'Yesyes,' he said.

He started to say something else, but Tuf rose. 'I fear I must end our conversation,' he said. 'A shuttleship has entered into docking orbit with *The Ark*. Perhaps you would recognize it. It is blue-steel, with large triangular grey wings.

'The House of Wrai Hill!' Nom said.

'Fascinating,' said Tuf. 'Good day.'

*

Beast-Master Denis Lon Wrai paid three hundred thousand standards for his monster, an immensely powerful red-furred ursoid from the hills of Vagabond. Haviland Tuf sealed the transaction with a brace of scamper-sloth eggs.

The week following, four men in orange silk and flame red capes visited *The Ark*. They returned to the House of Feridian four hundred fifty thousand standards poorer, with a contract for the delivery of six great poison-elk, plus a gift herd of Hrangan grass pigs.

The Beast-Master of Sin Boon received a giant serpent; the emissary from Amar Island was pleased by his godzilla. A committee of a dozen Dant seniors in milk white robes and silver buckles delighted in the slavering garghoul that Haviland Tuf offered them, with a trifling gift. And so, one by one, each of the Twelve Great Houses of Lyronica sought him out, each received its monster, each paid the ever-increasing price.

By that time, both of Norn's fighting cobalcats were dead, the first sliced easily in two by the bone-sword of a Varcour tyrannosword, the second crushed between the massive clawed paws of a Wrai Hill ursoid (though in the latter case, the ursoid too had died) – if the great cats had escaped their fate, they nonetheless had proved unable to avoid it. Herold Norn had been calling *The Ark* daily, but Tuf had instructed his computer to refuse the calls.

Finally, with eleven Houses as past customers, Haviland Tuf sat across the computer room from Danel Leigh Arneth, Senior Beast-Master of Arneth-in-the-Gilded-Wood, once the greatest and proudest of the Twelve Great Houses of Lyronica, now the last and least. Arneth was an immensely tall man, standing even with Tuf himself, but he had none of Tuf's fat; his skin was hard ebony, all muscle, his face a hawk-nosed axe, his hair short and iron grey. The Beast-Master came to the conference in cloth-of-gold, with crimson belt and boots and a tiny crimson beret aslant upon his head. He carried a trainer's pain-prod like a walking stick.

Dax read immense hostility in the man, and treachery, and a barely-suppressed rage. Accordingly, Haviland Tuf carried a small laser strapped to his stomach just beneath his greatcoat.

'The strength of Arneth-in-the-Gilded-Wood has always been in variety,' Danel Leigh Arneth said early on. 'When the other Houses of Lyronica threw all their fortunes on the backs of a single beast, our fathers and grandfathers worked with dozens. Against any animal of theirs, we had an optimal choice, a strategy. That has been our greatness and our pride. But we can have no strategy against these demon-beasts of yours, trader. No matter which of our hundred fighters we send onto the sand, it comes back dead. We are forced to deal with you.'

'Not so,' said Haviland Tuf. 'I force no one. Still, look at my stock. Perhaps fortune will see fit to give you back your strategic options.' He touched the buttons on his chair, and a parade of monsters came and went before the eyes of the Arneth Beast-Master; creatures furred and scaled and feathered and covered by armor plate, beasts of hill and forest and lake and plain, predators and scavengers and deadly herbivores of sizes great and small. And Danel Leigh Arneth, his lips pressed tightly together, finally ordered four each of the dozen largest and deadliest species, at a cost of some two million standards.

The conclusion of the transaction – complete, as with all the other Houses, with a gift of some small harmless animal – did nothing to soothe Arneth's foul temper. 'Tuf,' he said when the dealing was over, 'you are a clever and devious man, but you do not fool me.'

Haviland Tuf said nothing.

'You have made yourself immensely wealthy, and you have cheated all who bought from you and thought to profit. The Norns, for example – their cobalcats are worthless.

'They were a poor House; your price brought them to the edge of bankruptcy, just as you have done to all of us. They thought to recoup through victories. Bah! There will be no Norn victories now! Each House that you have sold to gained the edge on those who purchased previously. Thus Arneth, the last to purchase, remains the greatest House of all. Our monsters will wreak devastation. The sands of the Bronze Arena will darken with the blood of the lesser beasts.'

Tuf's hands locked on the bulge of his stomach. His face was placid.

'You have changed nothing! The Great Houses remain, Arneth the greatest and Norn the least. All you have done is bleed us, like the profiteer you are, until every lord must struggle and scrape to get by. The Houses now wait for victory, pray for victory, depend on victory, but all the victories will be Ameth's. We alone have not been cheated, because I thought to buy last and thus best.'

'So,' said Haviland Tuf. 'You are then a wise and sagacious Beast-Master, if this indeed is the case. Yet I deny that I have cheated anyone.'

'Don't play with words!' Arneth roared. 'Henceforth you will deal no longer with the Great Houses. Norn has no money to buy from you again, but if they did, you would not sell to them. *Do you understand?* We will not go round and round forever.'

'Of course,' Tuf said. He looked at Dax. 'Now Danel Leigh Arneth imputes my understanding. I am always misunderstood.' His calm gaze returned to the angry Beast-Master in red-and-gold. 'Your point, sir, is well-taken. Perhaps it is time for me to leave Lyronica. In any event, I shall not deal with Norn again, nor with any of the Great Houses. This is a foolish impulse – by thus acting I foreswear great profits – but I am a gentle man much given to following my whim. Obedient to the esteemed Danel Leigh Arneth, I bow to your demand.'

Dax reported wordlessly that Arneth was pleased and pacified; he had cowed Tuf, and won the day for his House. His rivals would get no new champions. Once again, the Bronze Arena would be predictable. He left satisfied.

Three weeks later, a fleet of twelve glittering gold-flecked shuttles and a dozen work squads of men in gold-and-crimson armor arrived to remove the purchases of Danel Leigh Arneth. Haviland Tuf, stroking a limp, lazy Dax, saw them off, then returned down the long corridors of *The Ark* to his control room, to take a call from Herold Norn.

The thin Beast-Master looked positively skeletal. 'Tuf!' he exclaimed. 'Everything is going wrong. You must help.'

'Wrong? I solved your problem.'

Norn pressed his features together in a grimace, and scratched beneath his brass coronet. 'Nono, listen. The cobalcats are all dead, or sick. Four of them dead in the Bronze Arena – we knew the second pair were too young, you understand, but when the first couple lost, there was nothing else to do. It was that or go back to ironfangs.

'Now we have only two left. They don't eat much – catch a few hoppers, but nothing else. And we can't train them, either. A trainer comes into the pen with a pain-prod, and the damn cats know what he intends. They're always a move ahead, you understand? In the arena, they won't respond to the killing chant at all. It's *terrible*. The worst thing is they don't even breed. We need *more* of them. What are we supposed to enter in the gaming pits?'

'It is not cobalcat breeding season,' Tuf said.

'Yesyes. When *is* their breeding season?'

'A fascinating question. A pity you did not ask sooner. As I understand the matter, the female cobalt panther goes into heat each spring, when the snowtufts blossom on Celia's World. Some type of biological trigger is involved.'

'I – Tuf. You *planned* this. Lyronica has no snowthings, whatever. Now I suppose you intend charging us a fortune for these flowers.'

'Sir. Of course not. Were the option mine, I would gladly give them to you. Your plight wounds me. I am concerned. However, as it happens, I have given my word to Danel Leigh Arneth to deal no more with the Great Houses of Lyronica.' He shrugged hopelessly.

'We won victories with your cats,' Norn said, with an edge of desperation in his voice. 'Our treasury has been growing – we have something like forty thousand standards now. It is yours. Sell us these flowers. Or better, a new animal. Bigger. Fiercer. I saw the Dant garghouls. Sell us something like that. We have nothing to enter in the Bronze Arena!'

'No? What of your ironfangs? The pride of Norn, I was told.'

Herold Norn waved impatiently. 'Problems, you understand, we have been having problems. These hoppers of yours, they eat anything, everything. They've gotten out of control. Millions of them, all over, eating all the grass, and all the crops. The things they've done to farmland – the cobalcats love them, yes, but we don't have enough cobalcats. And the wild ironfangs won't touch the hoppers. They don't like the taste, I suppose. I don't know, not really. But, you understand, all the other grass-eaters left, driven out by these hoppers of yours, and the ironfangs went with them. Where, I don't know that either. Gone, though. Into the unclaimed lands, beyond the realms of Norn. There are some villages out there, a few farmers, but they hate the Great Houses. Tamberkin, all of them, don't even have dog fights. They'll probably try to *tame* the ironfangs, if they see them.'

'So,' said Tuf. 'But then you have your kennels, do you not?'

'Not any more,' Norn said. He sounded very harried. 'I ordered them shut. The ironfangs were losing every match, especially after you began to sell to the other Houses. It seemed a foolish waste to maintain dead weight. Besides, the expense – we needed every standard. You bled us dry. We had Arena fees to pay, and of course we had to wager, and lately we've had to buy some food from Taraber just to feed all our housemen and trainers. I mean, you would never believe the things the hoppers have done to our crops.'

'Sir,' said Tuf. 'You insult me. I am an ecologist. I know a great deal of hoppers and their ways. Am I to understand that you shut your ironfang kennels?'

'Yesyes. We turned the useless things loose, and now they're gone with the rest. What are we going to do? The hoppers are overrunning the plains, the cats won't mate, and our money will run out soon if we must continue to import food and pay Arena fees without any hope of victory.'

Tuf folded his hands together. 'You do indeed face a series of delicate problems. And I am the very man to help you to their solution. Unfortunately, I have pledged my bond to Danel Leigh Arneth.'

'Is it hopeless, then? Tuf, I am a man begging, I a Senior Beast-Master of Norn. Soon we will drop from the games entirely. We will have no funds for Arena fees or betting, no animals to enter. We are cursed by ill fortune.

No Great House has ever failed to provide its allotment of fighters, not even Feridian during its Twelve Year Drought. We will be shamed. The House of Norn will sully its proud history by sending dogs and cats onto the sand, to be shredded ignominiously by the huge monsters that you have sold the other Houses.'

'Sir,' Tuf said, 'if you will permit me an impertinent remark, and one perhaps without foundation – if you will permit this to me – well, then, I will tell you my opinion. I have a hunch – mmm, *hunch*, yes, that is the proper word, and a curious word it is too – a hunch, as I was saying, that the monsters you fear may be in short supply in the weeks and months to come. For example, the adolescent ursoids of Vagabond may very shortly go into hibernation. They are less than a year old, you understand. I hope the lords of Wrai Hill are not unduly disconcerted by this, yet I fear that they may be. Vagabond, as I'm sure you are aware, has an extremely irregular orbit about its primary, so that its Long Winters last approximately twenty standard years. The ursoids are attuned to this cycle. Soon their body processes will slow to almost nothing – some have mistaken a sleeping ursoid for a dead one, you know – and I don't think they will be easily awakened. Perhaps, as the trainers of Wrai Hill are men of high good character and keen intellect, they might find a way. But I would be strongly inclined to further suspect that most of their energies and their funds will be devoted to feeding their populace, in the light of the voracious appetites of scampersloths. In quite a like manner, the men of the House of Varcour will be forced to deal with an explosion of Cathadayn tree-slugs. The tree-slugs are particularly fascinating creatures. At one point in their life cycle, they become veritable sponges, and double in size. A large enough grouping is fully capable of drying up even an extensive swampland.' Tuf paused, and his thick fingers beat in drumming rhythms across his stomach. 'I ramble unconsciously, Sir. Do you grasp my point, though? My thrust?'

Herold Norn looked like a dead man. 'You are mad. You have destroyed us. Our economy, our ecology . . . but *why*? We paid you fairly. The Houses, the Houses . . . no beasts, no funds. How can the games go on? *No one* will send fighters to the Bronze Arena!'

Haviland Tuf raised his hands in shock. 'Really?' he said.

Then he turned off the communicator and rose. Smiling a tiny, tight-lipped smile, he began to talk to Dax.

Guardians

Haviland Tuf thought the Six Worlds Bio-Agricultural Exhibition a great disappointment.

He had spent a long, wearying day on Brazelourn, trooping through the cavernous exhibition halls, pausing now and then to give a cursory inspection to a new grain hybrid or a genetically improved insect. Although the *Ark's* cell library held cloning material for literally millions of plant and animal species from an uncounted number of worlds, Haviland Tuf was nonetheless always alert for any opportunity to expand his stock-in-trade.

But few of the displays on Brazelourn seemed especially promising, and as the hours passed Tuf grew bored and uncomfortable in the jostling, indifferent crowds. People swarmed everywhere – Vagabonder tunnel-farmers in deep maroon furs, plumed and perfumed Areeni landlords, somber nightsiders and brightly garbed evernoons from New Janus, and a plethora of the native Brazeleen. All of them made excessive noise and favored Tuf with curious stares as he passed among them. Some even brushed up against him, bringing a frown to his long face.

Ultimately, seeking escape from the throngs, Tuf decided he was hungry. He pressed his way through the fairgoers with dignified distaste, and emerged from the vaulting five-story Ptolan Exhibit Hall. Outside, hundreds of vendors had set up booths between the great buildings. The man selling pop-onion pies seemed least busy of those nearby, and Tuf determined that a pop-onion pie was the very thing he craved.

'Sir,' he said to the vendor, 'I would have a pie.'

The pieman was round and pink and wore a greasy apron. He opened his hotbox, reached in with a gloved hand, and extracted a hot pie. When he pushed it across the counter at Tuf, he stared. 'Oh,' he said, 'you're a big one.'

'Indeed, sir,' said Haviland Tuf. He picked up the pie and bit into it impassively.

'You're an offworlder,' the pieman observed. 'Not from no place nearby, neither.'

Tuf finished his pie in three neat bites, and cleaned his greasy fingers on a napkin. 'You belabor the obvious, sir,' he said. He held up a long, calloused finger. 'Another,' he said.

Rebuffed, the vendor fetched out another pie without further observations, letting Tuf eat in relative peace. As he savored the flaky crust and tartness within, Tuf studied the milling fairgoers, the rows of vendors' booths, and the five great halls that loomed over the landscape. When he had done eating, he turned back to the pieman, his face as blank as ever. 'Sir. If you will, a question.'

'What's that?' the other said gruffly.

'I see five exhibition halls,' said Haviland Tuf. 'I have visited each in turn.' He pointed. 'Brazelourn, Vale Areen, New Janus, Vagabond, and here Ptola.' Tuf folded his hands together neatly atop his bulging stomach. 'Five, sir. Five halls, five worlds. No doubt, being a stranger as I am, I am unfamiliar with some subtle point of local usage, yet I am perplexed. In those regions where I have heretofore traveled, a gathering calling itself the Six Worlds Bio-Agricultural Exhibition might be expected to include exhibits from six worlds. Plainly that is not the case here. Perhaps you might enlighten me as to why?'

'No one came from Namor.'

'Indeed,' said Haviland Tuf.

'On account of the troubles,' the vendor added.

'All is made clear,' said Tuf. 'Or, if not all, at least a portion. Perhaps you would care to serve me another pie, and explain to me the nature of these troubles. I am nothing if not curious, sir. It is my great vice, I fear.'

The pieman slipped on his glove again and opened the hotbox. 'You know what they say. Curiosity makes you hungry.'

'Indeed,' said Tuf. 'I must admit I have never heard them say that before.'

The man frowned. 'No, I got it wrong. Hunger makes you curious, that's what it is. Don't matter. My pies will fill you up.'

'Ah,' said Tuf. He took up the pie. 'Please proceed.'

So the pie-seller told him, at great rambling length, about the troubles on the world Namor. 'So you can see,' he finally concluded, 'why they didn't come, with all this going on. Not much to exhibit.'

'Of course,' said Haviland Tuf, dabbing his lips. 'Sea monsters can be most vexing.'

*

Namor was a dark green world, moonless and solitary, banded by wispy golden clouds. The *Ark* shuddered out of drive and settled ponderously into orbit around it. In the long, narrow communications room, Haviland Tuf moved from seat to seat, studying the planet on a dozen of the room's hundred viewscreens. Three small gray kittens kept him company, bounding across the consoles, pausing only to slap at each other. Tuf paid them no mind.

A water world, Namor had only one landmass decently large enough to be seen from orbit, and that none too large. But magnification revealed thousands of islands scattered in long, crescent-shaped archipelagoes across the deep green seas, earthen jewels strewn throughout the oceans. Other screens showed the lights of dozens of cities and towns on the nightside, and pulsing dots of energy outlay where settlements sat in sunlight.

Tuf looked at it all, and then seated himself, flicked on another console, and began to play a war game with the computer. A kitten bounded up into his lap and went to sleep. He was careful not to disturb it. Some time later, a second kitten vaulted up and pounced on it, and they began to tussle. Tuf brushed them to the floor.

It took longer than even Tuf had anticipated, but finally the challenge came, as he had known it would. *'Ship in orbit,'* came the demand, 'ship in orbit, this is Namor Control. State your name and business. State your name and business, please. Interceptors have been dispatched. State your name and business.'

The transmission was coming from the chief landmass. The *Ark* tapped into it. At the same time, it found the ship that was moving toward them – there was only one – and flashed it on another screen.

'I am the *Ark*,' Haviland Tuf told Namor Control.

Namor Control was a round-faced woman with close-cropped brown hair, sitting at a console and wearing a deep green uniform with golden piping. She frowned, her eyes flicking to the side, no doubt to a superior or another console. *'Ark,'* she said, 'state your homeworld. State your homeworld and your business, please.'

The other ship had opened communications with the planet, the computer indicated. Two more viewscreens lit up. One showed a slender young woman with a large, crooked nose on a ship's bridge, the other an elderly man before a console. They both wore green uniforms, and they were conversing animatedly in code. It took the computer less than a minute to break it, so Tuf could listen in. '. . . damned if I know what it is,' the woman on the ship was saying. 'There's never been a ship that big. My God, just look at it. Are you getting all this? Has it answered?'

'Ark,' the round-faced woman was still saying, 'state your homeworld and your business, please. This is Namor Control.'

Haviland Tuf cut into the other conversation, to talk to all three of them simultaneously. 'This is the *Ark*,' he said. 'I have no homeworld, sirs. My intentions are purely peaceful – trade and consultation. I learned of your tragic difficulties, and moved by your plight, I have come to offer you my services.'

The woman on the ship looked startled. 'What are *you* . . .' she started. The man was equally nonplussed, but he said nothing, only gaped open-mouthed at Tuf's blank white visage.

'This is Namor Control, *Ark*,' said the round-faced woman. 'We are closed to trade. Repeat, we are closed to trade. We are under martial law here.'

By then the slender woman on the ship had composed herself. '*Ark*, this is Guardian Kefira Qay, commanding NGS *Sunrazor*. We are armed, *Ark*. Explain yourself. You are a thousand times larger than any trader I have ever seen, *Ark*. Explain yourself or be fired upon.'

'Indeed,' said Haviland Tuf. 'Threats will avail you little, Guardian. I am most sorely vexed. I have come all this long way from Brazelourn to offer you my aid and solace, and you meet me with threats and hostility.' A kitten leapt up into his lap. Tuf scooped it up with a huge white hand, and deposited it on the console in front of him, where the viewer would pick it up. He gazed down at it sorrowfully. 'There is no trust left in humanity,' he said to the kitten.

'Hold your fire, *Sunrazor*,' said the elderly man. '*Ark*, if your intentions are truly peaceful, explain yourself. What are you? We are hard-pressed here, *Ark*, and Namor is a small, undeveloped world. We have never seen your like before. Explain yourself.'

Haviland Tuf stroked the kitten. 'Always I must truckle to suspicion,' he told it. 'They are fortunate that I am so kind-hearted, or else I would simply depart and leave them to their fate.' He looked up, straight into the viewer. 'Sir,' he said. 'I am the *Ark*. I am Haviland Tuf, captain and master here, crew entire. You are troubled by great monsters from the depths of your seas, I have been told. Very well. I shall rid you of them.'

'*Ark*, this is *Sunrazor*. How do you propose doing that?'

'The *Ark* is a seedship of the Ecological Engineering Corps,' said Haviland Tuf with stiff formality. 'I am an ecological engineer and a specialist in biological warfare.'

'Impossible,' said the old man. 'The EEC was wiped out a thousand years ago, along with the Federal Empire. None of their seedships remain.'

'How distressing,' said Haviland Tuf. 'Here I sit in an illusion. No doubt, now that you have told me my ship does not exist, I shall sink right through it and plunge into your atmosphere, where I shall burn up as I fall.'

'Guardian,' said Kefira Qay from the *Sunrazor*, 'these seedships may indeed no longer exist, but I am fast closing on something that my scopes tell me is almost thirty kilometers long. It does not appear to be an illusion.'

'I am not yet falling,' admitted Haviland Tuf.

'Can you truly help us?' asked the round-faced woman at Namor Control.

'Why must I always be doubted?' Tuf asked the small gray kitten.

'Lord Guardian, we must give him the chance to prove what he says,' insisted Namor Control.

Tuf looked up. 'Threatened, insulted, and doubted as I have been, nonetheless my empathy for your situation bids me to persist. Perhaps I might suggest that *Sunrazor* dock with me, so to speak. Guardian Qay may come aboard and join me for an evening meal, while we converse. Surely your suspicions cannot extend to mere conversation, that most civilized of human pastimes.'

The three Guardians conferred hurriedly with each other and with a person or persons offscreen, while Haviland Tuf sat back and toyed with the kitten. 'I shall name you Suspicion,' he said to it, 'to commemorate my reception here. Your siblings shall be Doubt, Hostility, Ingratitude and Foolishness.'

'We accept your proposal, Haviland Tuf,' said Guardian Kefira Qay from the bridge of the *Sunrazor*. 'Prepare to be boarded.'

'Indeed,' said Tuf. 'Do you like mushrooms?'

*

The shuttle deck of the *Ark* was as large as the landing field of a major starport, and seemed almost a junkyard for derelict spacecraft. The *Ark*'s own shuttles stood trim in their launch berths, five identical black ships with rakish lines and stubby triangular wings angling back, designed for atmospheric flight and still in good repair. Other craft were less impressive. A teardrop-shaped trading vessel from Avalon squatted wearily on three extended landing legs, next to a driveshift courier scored by battle, and a Karaleo lionboat whose ornate trim was largely gone. Elsewhere stood vessels of stranger, more alien design.

Above, the great dome cracked into a hundred pie-wedge segments, and drew back to reveal a small yellow sun surrounded by stars, and a dull green manta-shaped ship of about the same size as one of Tuf's shuttles. The *Sunrazor* settled, and the dome closed behind it. When the stars had been blotted out again, atmosphere came swirling back in to the deck, and Haviland Tuf arrived soon after.

Kefira Qay emerged from her ship with her lips set sternly beneath her big, crooked nose, but no amount of control could quite conceal the awe in her eyes. Two armed men in golden coveralls trimmed with green followed her.

Haviland Tuf drove up to them in an open three-wheeled cart. 'I am afraid that my dinner invitation was only for one, Guardian Qay,' he said when he saw her escort. 'I regret any misunderstanding, yet I must insist.'

'Very well,' she said. She turned to her guard. 'Wait with the others. You have your orders.' When she got in next to Tuf she told him, 'The *Sunrazor* will tear your ship apart if I am not returned safely within two standard hours.'

Haviland Tuf blinked at her. 'Dreadful,' he said. 'Everywhere my warmth and hospitality is met with mistrust and violence.' He set the vehicle into motion.

They drove in silence through a maze of interconnected rooms and corridors, and finally entered a huge shadowy shaft that seemed to extend the full length of the ship in both directions. Transparent vats of a hundred different sizes covered walls and ceiling as far as the eye could see, most empty and dusty, a few filled with colored liquids in which half-seen shapes stirred feebly. There was no sound but a wet, viscous dripping somewhere off behind them. Kefira Qay studied everything and said nothing. They went at least three kilometers down the great shaft, until Tuf veered off into a blank wall that dilated before them. Shortly thereafter they parked and dismounted.

A sumptuous meal had been laid out in the small, spartan dining chamber to which Tuf escorted the Guardian Kefira Qay. They began with iced soup, sweet and piquant and black as coal, followed by neograss salads with a gingery topping. The main course was a breaded mushroom top full as large as the plate on which it was served, surrounded by a dozen different sorts of vegetables in individual sauces. The Guardian ate with great relish.

'It would appear you find my humble fare to your taste,' observed Haviland Tuf.

'I haven't had a good meal in longer than I care to admit,' replied Kefira Qay. 'On Namor, we have always depended on the sea for our sustenance. Normally it is bountiful, but since our troubles began . . .' She lifted a forkful of dark, misshapen vegetables in a yellow-brown sauce. 'What am I eating? It's delightful.'

'Rhiannese sinners' root, in a mustard sauce,' Haviland Tuf said.

Qay swallowed and set down her fork. 'But Rhiannon is so far, how do you . . .' She stopped.

'Of course,' Tuf said, steepling his fingers beneath his chin as he watched her face. 'All this provender derives from the *Ark*, though originally it might be traced back to a dozen different worlds. Would you like more spiced milk?'

'No,' she muttered. She gazed at the empty plates. 'You weren't lying, then. You are what you claim, and this is a seedship of the . . . what did you call them?'

'The Ecological Engineering Corps, of the long-defunct Federal Empire. Their ships were few in number, and all but one destroyed by the vicissitudes of war. The *Ark* alone survived, derelict for a millennium. The details need not concern you. Suffice it to say that I found it, and made it functional.'

'You *found* it?'

'I believe I just said as much, in those very same words. Kindly pay attention. I am not partial to repeating myself. Before finding the *Ark*, I made a humble living from trade. My former ship is still on the landing deck. Perhaps you chanced to see it.'

'Then you're really just a trader.'

'Please!' said Tuf with indignation. 'I am an ecological engineer. The *Ark* can remake whole planets, Guardian. True, I am but one man, alone, when once this ship was crewed by two hundred, and I do lack the extensive formal training such as was given centuries ago to those who wore the golden theta, the sigil of the Ecological Engineers. Yet, in my own small way, I contrive to muddle through. If Namor would care to avail itself of my services, I have no doubt that I can help you.'

'Why?' the slender Guardian asked warily. 'Why are you so anxious to help us?'

Haviland Tuf spread his big white hands helplessly. 'I know, I might appear a fool. I cannot help myself. I am a humanitarian by nature, much moved by hardship and suffering. I could no more abandon your people, beset as they are, than I could harm one of my cats. The Ecological Engineers were made of sterner stuff, I fear, but I am helpless to change my sentimental nature. So here I sit before you, prepared to do my best.'

'You want nothing?'

'I shall labor without recompense,' said Tuf. 'Of course, I will have operating expenses. I must charge a small fee to offset them. Say, three million standards. Do you think that fair?'

'Fair,' she said sarcastically. 'Fairly high, I'd say. There have been others like you, Tuf – arms merchants and soldiers of fortune who have come to grow rich off our misery.'

'Guardian,' said Tuf, reproachfully, 'you do me grievous wrong. I take little for myself. The Ark is so large, so costly. Perhaps two million standards would suffice? I cannot believe you would grudge me this pittance. Is your world worth less?'

Kefira Qay sighed, a tired look etched on her narrow face. 'No,' she admitted. 'Not if you can do all you promise. Of course, we are not a rich world. I will have to consult my superiors. This is not my decision alone.' She stood up abruptly. 'Your communications facilities?'

'Through the door and left down the blue corridor. The fifth door on the right.' Tuf rose with ponderous dignity, and began cleaning up as she left.

When the Guardian returned he had opened a decanter of liquor, vividly scarlet, and was stroking a black-and-white cat who had made herself at home on the table. 'You're hired, Tuf,' said Kefira Qay, seating herself. 'Two million standards. *After* you win this war.'

'Agreed,' said Tuf. 'Let us discuss your situation over glasses of this delightful beverage.'

'Alcoholic?'

'Mildly narcotic.'

'A Guardian uses no stimulants or depressants. We are a fighting guild. Substances like that pollute the body and slow the reflexes. A Guardian must be vigilant. We guard and protect.'

'Laudable,' said Haviland Tuf. He filled his own glass.

'*Sunrazor* is wasted here. It has been recalled by Namor Control. We need its combat capabilities below.'

'I shall expedite its departure, then. And yourself?'

'I have been detached,' she said, wrinkling up her face. 'We are standing by with data on the situation below. I am to help brief you, and act as your liaison officer.'

*

The water was calm, a tranquil green mirror from horizon to horizon.

It was a hot day. Bright yellow sunlight poured down through a thin bank of gilded clouds. The ship rested still on the water, its metallic sides flashing silver-blue, its open deck a small island of activity in an ocean of peace. Men and women small as insects worked the dredges and nets, bare-chested in the heat. A great claw full of mud and weeds emerged from the water, dripping, and was sluiced down an open hatchway. Elsewhere bins of huge milky jellyfish baked in the sun.

Suddenly there was agitation. For no apparent reason, people began to run. Others stopped what they were doing and looked around, confused. Still others worked on, oblivious. The great metal claw, open and empty now, swung back out over the water and submerged again, even as another one rose on the far side of the ship. More people were running. Two men collided and went down.

Then the first tentacle came curling up from beneath the ship.

It rose and rose. It was longer than the dredging claws. Where it emerged from the dark green sea, it looked as thick as a big man's torso. It tapered to the size of an arm. The tentacle was white, a soft slimy sort of white. All along its underside were vivid pink circles big as dinner plates, circles that writhed and pulsed as the tentacle curled over and about the huge farming ship. The end of the tentacle split into a rat's nest of smaller tentacles, dark and restless as snakes.

Up and up it went, and then over and down, pinioning the ship. Something moved on the other side, something pale stirring beneath all that green, and the second tentacle emerged. Then a third, and a fourth. One wrestled with a dredging claw. Another had the remains of a net draped all about it, like a veil, which didn't seem to hinder it. Now all the people were running – all but those the tentacles had found. One of them had curled itself around a woman with an axe. She hacked at it wildly, thrashing in the pale embrace, until her back arched and suddenly she fell still. The tentacle dropped her, white fluid pulsing feebly from the gashes she had left, and seized someone else.

Twenty tentacles had attached themselves when the ship abruptly listed to starboard. Survivors slid across the deck and into the sea. The ship tilted more and more. Something was pushing it over, pulling it down. Water sloshed across the side, and into the open hatchways. Then the ship began to break up.

Haviland Tuf stopped the projection, and held the image on the large viewscreen: the green sea and golden sun, the shattered vessel, the pale embracing tentacles. 'This was the first attack?' he asked.

'Yes and no,' replied Kefira Qay. 'Prior to this, one other harvester and two passenger hydrofoils had vanished mysteriously. We were investigating, but we did not know the cause. In this case, a news crew happened to be on the site, making a recording for an educational broadcast. They got more than they bargained for.'

'Indeed,' said Tuf.

'They were airborne, in a skimmer. The broadcast that night almost caused a panic. But it was not until the next ship went down that things began to get truly serious. That was when the Guardians began to realize the full extent of the problem.'

Haviland Tuf stared up at the viewscreen, his heavy face impassive, expressionless, his hands resting on the console. A black-and-white kitten began to bat at his fingers. 'Away, Foolishness,' he said, depositing the kitten gently on the floor.

'Enlarge a section of one of the tentacles,' suggested the Guardian beside him.

Silently, Tuf did as she bid him. A second screen lit up, showing a grainy close-up of a great pale rope of tissue arching over the deck.

'Take a good look at one of the suckers,' said Qay. 'The pink areas, there, you see?'

'The third one from the end is dark within. And it appears to have teeth.'

'Yes,' said Kefira Qay. 'All of them do. The outer lips of those suckers are a kind of hard, fleshy flange. Slapped down, they spread and create a vacuum seal of sorts, virtually impossible to tear loose. But each of them is a mouth, too. Within the flange is a soft pink flap that falls back, and then the teeth come sliding out – a triple row of them, serrated, and sharper than you'd think. Now move down to the tendrils at the end, if you would.'

Tuf touched the console, and put another magnification up on a third screen, bringing the twisting snakes into easy view.

'Eyes,' said Kefira Qay. 'At the end of every one of those tendrils. Twenty eyes. The tentacles don't need to grope around blindly. They can *see* what they are doing.'

'Fascinating,' said Haviland Tuf. 'What lies beneath the water? The source of these terrible arms?'

'There are cross-sections and photographs of dead specimens later on, as well as some computer simulations. Most of the specimens we took were quite badly mangled. The main body of the thing is sort of an inverted cup, like a half-inflated bladder, surrounded by a great ring of bone and muscle that anchors these tentacles. The bladder fills and empties with water to enable the creature to rise to the surface, or descend far below – the submarine principle. By itself it doesn't weigh much, although it is amazingly strong. What it does, it empties its bladder to rise to the surface, grabs hold, and then begins to fill again. The capacity of the bladder is astounding, and as you can see, the creature is *huge*. If need be, it can even force water up those tentacles and out of its mouths, in order to flood the vessel and speed things along. So those tentacles are arms, mouths, eyes, and living hoses all at once.'

'And you say that your people had no knowledge of such creatures until this attack?'

'Right. A cousin of this thing, the Namorian man-of-war, was well-known in the early days of colonization. It was sort of a cross between a jellyfish and an octopus, with twenty arms. Many native species are built along the same lines – a central bladder, or body, or shell, or what have you, with twenty legs or tendrils or tentacles in a ring around it. The men-of-war were carnivores, much like this monster, although they had a ring of eyes on the central body instead of at the end of the tentacles. The arms couldn't function as hoses, either. And they were much smaller – about the size of a human. They bobbed about on the surface above the continental shelves, particularly above mud-pot beds, where fish were thick. Fish were

their usual prey, although a few unwary swimmers met a bloody awful
death in their embrace.'

'Might I ask what became of them?' said Tuf.

'They were a nuisance. Their hunting grounds were the same areas we
needed – shallows rich with fish and seagrass and waterfruit, over mud-
pot beds and scrabbler runs full of chameleon-clams and bobbing freddies.
Before we could harvest or farm safely, we had to pretty much clean out
the men-of-war. We did. Oh, there are still a few around, but they are rare
now.'

'I see,' said Haviland Tuf. 'And this most formidable creature, this living
submarine and ship-eater that plagues you so dreadfully, does it have a
name?'

'The Namorian dreadnaught,' said Kefira Qay. 'When it first appeared,
we theorized it was an inhabitant of the great deeps that had somehow
wandered to the surface. Namor has been inhabited for barely a hundred
standard years, after all. We have scarcely begun to explore the deeper
regions of the seas, and we have little knowledge of the things that might
live down there. But as more and more ships were attacked and sunk, it
became obvious that we had an army of dreadnaughts to contend with.'

'A navy,' corrected Haviland Tuf.

Kefira Qay scowled. 'Whatever. A lot of them, not one lost specimen. At
that point the theory was that some unimaginable catastrophe had taken
place deep under the ocean, driving forth this entire species.'

'You give no credit to this theory,' Tuf said.

'No one does. It's been disproved. The dreadnaughts wouldn't be able to
withstand the pressures at those depths. So now we don't know where
they came from.' She made a face. 'Only that they are here.'

'Indeed,' said Haviland Tuf. 'No doubt you fought back.'

'Certainly. A game but losing fight. Namor is a young planet, with
neither the population nor the resources for the sort of struggle we have
been plunged into. Three million Namorians are scattered across our seas,
on more than seventeen thousand small islands. Another million huddle
on New Atlantis, our single small continent. Most of our people are
fisherfolk and sea-farmers. When this all began, the Guardians numbered
barely fifty thousand. Our guild is descended from the crews of the ships
who brought the colonists from Old Poseidon and Aquarius here to Namor.
We have always protected them, but before the coming of the dreadnaughts our task was simple. Our world was peaceful, with little real
conflict. There was some ethnic rivalry between Poseidonites and Aqua-
rians, but it was good-natured. The Guardians provided planetary defense,
with *Sunrazor* and two similar craft, but most of our work was in fire and
flood control, disaster relief, police work, that sort of thing. We had about a

hundred armed hydrofoil patrol boats, and we used them for escort duty for a while, and inflicted some casualties, but they were really no match for the dreadnaughts. It soon became clear that there were more dread-naughts than patrol boats, anyway.'

'Nor do patrolboats reproduce, as I must assume these dreadnaughts do,' Tuf said. Foolishness and Doubt were tussling in his lap.

'Exactly. Still, we tried. We dropped depth charges on them when we detected them below the sea, we torpedoed them when they came to the surface. We killed hundreds. But there were hundreds more, and every boat we lost was irreplaceable. Namor has no technological base to speak of. In better days, we imported what we needed from Brazelourn and Vale Areen. Our people believed in a simple life. The planet couldn't support industry anyway. It is poor in heavy metals and has almost no fossil fuel.'

'How many Guardian patrolboats remain to you?' asked Haviland Tuf.

'Perhaps thirty. We dare not use them anymore. Within a year of the first attack, the dreadnaughts were in complete command of our sea lanes. All of the great harvesters were lost, hundreds of sea-farms had been abandoned or destroyed, half of the small fisherfolk were dead, and the other half huddled fearfully in port. Nothing human dared move on the seas of Namor.'

'Your islands were isolated from one another?'

'Not quite,' Kefira Qay replied. 'The Guardians had twenty armed skimmers, and there were another hundred-odd skimmers and aircars in private hands. We commandeered them, armed them. We also had our airships. Skimmers and aircars are difficult and expensive to maintain here. Parts are hard to come by, and we have few trained techs, so most of the air traffic before the troubles was carried by airships – solar-powered, helium-filled, large. There was quite a sizable fleet, as many as a thousand. The airships took over the provisioning of some of the small islands, where starvation was a very real threat. Other airships, as well as the Guardian skimmers, carried on the fight. We dumped chemicals, poisons, explosives and such from the safety of the air and destroyed thousands of dreadnaughts, although the cost was frightful. They clustered thickest about our best fishing grounds and mud-pot beds, so we were forced to blow up and poison the very areas we needed most. Still, we had no choice. For a time, we thought we were winning the fight. A few fishing boats even put out and returned safely, with a Guardian skimmer flying escort.'

'Obviously, this was not the ultimate result of the conflict,' said Haviland Tuf, 'or we would not be sitting here talking.' Doubt batted Foolishness soundly across the head, and the smaller kitten fell off Tuf's knee to the floor. Tuf bent and scooped him up. 'Here,' he said, handing him to Kefira Qay, 'hold him, if you please. Their small war is distracting me from your larger one.'

'I – why, of course.' The Guardian took the small black-and-white kitten in hand gingerly. He fit snugly into her palm. 'What is it?' she asked.

'A cat,' said Tuf. 'He will jump out of your hand if you continue to hold him as if he were a diseased fruit. Kindly put him in your lap. I assure you he is harmless.'

Kefira Qay, appearing very uncertain, shook the kitten out of her hand onto her knees. Foolishness yowled, almost tumbling to the floor again before sinking his small claws into the fabric of her uniform. '*Ow*,' said Kefira Qay. 'It has talons.'

'Claws,' corrected Tuf. 'Tiny and harmless.'

'They aren't poisoned, are they?'

'I think not,' said Tuf. 'Stroke him, front to back. It will make him less agitated.'

Kefira Qay touched the kitten's head uncertainly.

'Please,' said Tuf. 'I said *stroke*, not pat.'

The Guardian began to pet the kitten. Instantly, Foolishness began to purr. She stopped and looked up in horror. 'It's trembling,' she said, 'and making a noise.'

'Such a response is considered favorable,' Tuf assured her. 'I beg you to continue your ministrations, and your briefing. If you will.'

'Of course,' said Qay. She resumed petting Foolishness, who settled down comfortably on her knee. 'If you would go on to the next tape,' she prompted.

Tuf wiped the stricken ship and the dreadnaught off the main screen. Another scene took their place – a winter's day, windy and chill by the look of it. The water below was dark and choppy, flecked with white foam as the wind pushed against it. A dreadnaught was afloat the unruly sea, its huge white tentacles extended all around it, giving it the look of some vast swollen flower bobbing on the waves. It reached up as they passed overhead, two arms with their writhing snakes lifting feebly from the water, but they were too far above to be in danger. They appeared to be in the gondola of some long silver airship, looking down through a glass-bottomed viewport, and as Tuf watched, the vantage point shifted and he saw that they were part of a convoy of three immense airships, cruising with stately indifference above the war-torn waters.

'The *Spirit of Aquarius*, the *Lyle D.*, and the *Skyshadow*,' said Kefira Qay, 'on a relief mission to a small island grouping in the north where famine had been raging. They were going to evacuate the survivors and take them back to New Atlantis.' Her voice was grim. 'This record was made by a news crew on the *Skyshadow*, the only airship to survive. Watch.'

On and on the airships sailed, invincible and serene. Then, just ahead of the silver-blue *Spirit of Aquarius*, there was motion in the water, something stirring beneath that dark green veil. Something big, but not a dreadnaught. It was dark, not pale. The water grew black and blacker in a great swelling patch, then bulged upward. A great ebony dome heaved into view and grew, like an island emerging from the depths, black and leathery and immense, and surrounded by twenty long black tentacles. Larger and higher it swelled, second by second, until it burst from the sea entirely. Its tentacles hung below it, dripping water, as it rose. Then they began to lift and spread. The thing was fully as large as the airship moving toward it. When they met, it was as if two vast leviathans of the sky had come together to mate. The black immensity settled atop the long silver-blue dirigible, its arms curling about in a deadly embrace. They watched the airship's outer skin tear asunder, and the helium cells rip and crumple. The *Spirit of Aquarius* twisted and buckled like a living thing, and shriveled in the black embrace of its lover. When it was over, the dark creature dropped the remains into the sea.

Tuf froze the image, staring with solemn regard at the small figures leaping from the doomed gondola.

'Another one got the *Lyle D.* on the way home,' said Kefira Qay. 'The *Skyshadow* survived to tell the story, but it never returned from its next mission. More than a hundred airships and twelve skimmers were lost in the first week the fire-balloons emerged.'

'Fire-balloons?' queried Haviland Tuf. He stroked Doubt, who was sitting on his console. 'I saw no fire.'

'The name was coined the first time we destroyed one of the accursed things. A Guardian skimmer put a round of explosive shot into it, and it went up like a bomb, then sank, burning into the sea. They are extremely inflammable. One laser burst, and they go up spectacularly.'

'Hydrogen,' said Haviland Tuf.

'Exactly,' the Guardian confirmed. 'We've never taken one whole, but we've puzzled them out from bits and pieces. The creatures can generate an electric current internally. They take on water, and perform a sort of biological electrolysis. The oxygen is vented into the water or the air, and helps push the things around. Air jets, so to speak. The hydrogen fills the balloon sacs and gives them lift. When they want to retreat to the water, they open a flap on top – see, up there – and all the gas escapes, so the fire-balloon drops back into the sea. The outer skin is leathery, very tough. They're slow, but clever. At times they hide in cloud banks and snatch unwary skimmers flying below. And we soon discovered, to our dismay, that they breed just as fast as the dreadnaughts.'

'Most intriguing,' said Haviland Tuf. 'So, I might venture to suggest, with the emergence of these fire-balloons, you lost the sky as well as the sea.'

'More or less,' admitted Kefira Qay. 'Our airships were simply too slow to risk. We tried to keep things going by sending them out in convoys, escorted by Guardian skimmers and aircars, but even that failed. The morning of the Fire Dawn . . . I was there, commanding a nine-gun skimmer . . . it was terrible . . .'

'Continue,' said Tuf.

'The Fire Dawn,' she muttered bleakly. 'We were . . . we had thirty airships, *thirty*, a great convoy, protected by a dozen armed skimmers. A long trip, from New Atlantis to the Broken Hand, a major island grouping. Near dawn on the second day, just as the east was turning red, the sea beneath us began to . . . seethe. Like a pot of soup that has begun to boil. It was *them*, venting oxygen and water, rising. Thousands of them, Tuf, thousands. The waters churned madly, and they rose, all those vast black shadows coming up at us, as far as the eye could see in all directions. We attacked with lasers, with explosive shells, with everything we had. It was like the sky itself was ablaze. All those things were bulging with hydrogen, and the air was rich and giddy with the oxygen they had vented. The Fire Dawn, we call it. It was terrible. Screaming everywhere, balloons burning, our airships crushed and falling around us, bodies afire. There were dreadnaughts waiting below, too. I saw them snatching swimmers who had fallen from the airships, those pale tentacles coiling around them and yanking them under. Four skimmers escaped from that battle. Four. Every airship was lost, with all hands.'

'A grim tale,' said Tuf.

Kefira Qay had a haunted look in her eyes. She was petting Foolishness with a blind rhythm, her lips pressed tightly together, her eyes fixed on the screen, where the first fire-balloon floated above the tumbling corpse of the *Spirit of Aquarius*. 'Since then,' she said at last, 'life has been a continuing nightmare. We have lost our seas. On three-fourths of Namor, hunger and even starvation hold sway. Only New Atlantis still has surplus food, since only there is land-farming practiced extensively. The Guardians have continued to fight. The *Sunrazor* and our two other spacecraft have been pressed into service – bombing runs, dumping poison, evacuating some of the smaller islands. With aircars and fast skimmers, we have maintained a loose web of contact with the outer islands. And we have radio, of course. But we are barely hanging on. Within the last year, more than twenty islands have fallen silent. We sent patrols out to investigate in a half-dozen of those cases. Those that returned all reported the same things. Bodies everywhere, rotting in the sun. Buildings crushed and ruined. Scrabblers and crawling maggies feasting on the corpses. And on one island they found something else, something even more frightful. The island was Seastar. Almost forty thousand people lived there, and it was a major spaceport as well, before trade was cut off. It was a terrible shock when Seastar suddenly stopped broadcasting. Go to the next exhibit, Tuf. Go on.'

Tuf pressed a series of lights on the console.

A dead thing was lying on a beach, rotting on indigo sands.

It was a still picture, this one, not a tape. Haviland Tuf and Guardian Kefira Qay had a long time to study the dead thing where it sprawled, rich and rotten. Around and about it was a litter of human corpses, lending it scale by their proximity. The dead thing was shaped like an inverted bowl, and it was as big as a house. Its leathery flesh, cracked and oozing pustulence now, was a mottled gray-green. Spread on the sand around it, like spokes from a central wheel, were the thing's appendages – ten twisted green tentacles, puckered with pinkish-white mouths and, alternately, ten limbs that looked stiff and hard and black, and were obviously jointed.

'Legs,' said Kefira Qay bitterly. 'It was a walker, Tuf, before they killed it. We have only found that one specimen, but it was enough. We know why our islands fall silent now. They come from out of the sea, Tuf. Things like that. Larger, smaller, walking on ten legs like spiders and grabbing and eating with the other ten, the tentacles. The carapace is thick and tough. A single explosive shell or laser burst won't kill one of these the way it would a fire-balloon. So now you understand. First the sea, then the air, and now it has begun on the land as well. The land. They burst from the water in thousands, striding up onto the sand like some terrible tide. Two islands were overrun last week alone. They mean to wipe us from this planet. No doubt a few of us will survive on New Atlantis, in the high inland mountains, but it will be a cruel life and a short one. Until Namor throws something new at us, some new thing out of nightmare.' Her voice had a wild edge of hysteria.

Haviland Tuf turned off his console, and the telescreens all went black. 'Calm yourself, Guardian,' he said, turning to face her. 'Your fears are understandable but unnecessary. I appreciate your plight more fully now. A tragic one indeed, yet not hopeless.'

'You still think you can help?' she said. 'Alone? You and this ship? Oh, I'm not discouraging you, by any means. We'll grasp at any straw. But . . .'

'But you do not believe,' Tuf said. A small sigh escaped his lips. 'Doubt,' he said to the gray kitten, hoisting him up in a huge white hand, 'you are indeed well named.' He shifted his gaze back to Kefira Qay. 'I am a forgiving man, and you have been through many cruel hardships, so I shall take no notice of the casual way you belittle me and my abilities. Now, if you might excuse me, I have work to do. Your people have sent up a great

many more detailed reports on these creatures, and on Namorian ecology
in general. It is vital that I peruse these, in order to understand and
analyze the situation. Thank you for your briefing.'

Kefira Qay frowned, lifted Foolishness from her knee and set him on the
ground, and stood up. 'Very well,' she said. 'How soon will you be ready?'

'I cannot ascertain that with any degree of accuracy,' Tuf replied, 'until I
have had a chance to run some simulations. Perhaps a day and we shall
begin. Perhaps a month. Perhaps longer.'

'If you take too long, you'll find it difficult to collect your two million,'
she snapped. 'We'll all be dead.'

'Indeed,' said Tuf. 'I shall strive to avoid that scenario. Now, if you
would let me work. We shall converse again at dinner. I shall serve
vegetable stew in the fashion of Arion, with plates of Thorite fire
mushrooms to whet our appetites.'

Qay sighed loudly. 'Mushrooms again?' she complained. 'We had stir-
fried mushrooms and peppers for lunch, and crisped mushrooms in bitter
cream for breakfast.'

'I am fond of mushrooms,' said Haviland Tuf.

'I am weary of mushrooms,' said Kefira Qay. Foolishness rubbed up
against her leg, and she frowned down at him. 'Might I suggest some
meat? Or seafood?' She looked wistful. 'It has been years since I've had a
mud-pot. I dream of it sometimes. Crack it open and pour butter inside,
and spoon out the soft meat . . . you can't imagine how fine it was. Or
sabrefin. Ah, I'd kill for a sabrefin on a bed of seagrass!'

Haviland Tuf looked stern. 'We do not eat animals here,' he said. He set
to work, ignoring her, and Kefira Qay took her leave. Foolishness went
bounding after her. 'Appropriate,' muttered Tuf, 'indeed.'

*

Four days and many mushrooms later, Kefira Qay began to pressure
Haviland Tuf for results. 'What are you *doing*?' she demanded over dinner.
'When are you going to act? Every day you seclude yourself and every day
conditions on Namor worsen. I spoke to Lord Guardian Harvan an hour
ago, while you were off with your computers. Little Aquarius and the
Dancing Sisters have been lost while you and I are up here dithering, Tuf.'

'Dithering?' said Haviland Tuf. 'Guardian, I do not dither. I have never
dithered, nor do I intend to begin dithering now. I work. There is a great
mass of information to digest.'

Kefira Qay snorted. 'A great mass of mushrooms to digest, you mean,'
she said. She stood up, tipping Foolishness from her lap. The kitten and
she had become boon companions of late. 'Twelve thousand people lived
on Little Aquarius,' she said, 'and almost as many on the Dancing Sisters.

Think of that while you're digesting, Tuf.' She spun and stalked out of the room.

'Indeed,' said Haviland Tuf. He returned his attention to his sweet-flower pie.

A week passed before they clashed again. 'Well?' the Guardian demanded one day in the corridor, stepping in front of Tuf as he lumbered with great dignity down to his work room.

'Well,' he repeated. 'Good day, Guardian Qay.'

'It is not a good day,' she said querulously. 'Namor Control tells me the Sunrise Islands are gone. Overrun. And a dozen skimmers lost defending them, along with all the ships drawn up in those harbors. What do you say to that?'

'Most tragic,' replied Tuf. 'Regrettable.'

'When are you going to be ready?'

He gave a great shrug. 'I cannot say. This is no simple task you have set me. A most complex problem. Complex. Yes, indeed, that is the very word. Perhaps I might even say mystifying. I assure you that Namor's sad plight has fully engaged my sympathies, however, and this problem has similarly engaged my intellect.'

'That's all it is to you, Tuf, isn't it? A problem?'

Haviland Tuf frowned slightly, and folded his hands before him, resting them atop his bulging stomach. 'A problem indeed,' he said.

'No. It is not just a problem. This is no game we are playing. Real people are dying down there. Dying because the Guardians are not equal to their trust, and because you do nothing. *Nothing.*'

'Calm yourself. You have my assurance that I am laboring ceaselessly on your behalf. You must consider that my task is not so simple as yours. It is all very well and good to drop bombs on a dreadnaught, or fire shells into a fire-balloon and watch it burn. Yet these simple, quaint methods have availed you little, Guardian. Ecological engineering is a far more demanding business. I study the reports of your leaders, your marine biologists, your historians. I reflect and analyze. I devise various approaches, and run simulations on the *Ark's* great computers. Sooner or later I shall find your answer.'

'Sooner,' said Kefira Qay, in a hard voice. 'Namor wants results, and I agree. The Council of Guardians is impatient. Sooner, Tuf. Not later. I warn you.' She stepped aside, and let him pass.

Kefira Qay spent the next week and a half avoiding Tuf as much as possible. She skipped dinner and scowled when she saw him in the corridors. Each day she repaired to the communications room, where she had long discussions with her superiors below, and kept up on all the latest news. It was bad. All the news was bad.

Finally, things came to a head. Pale-faced and furious, she stalked into the darkened chamber Tuf called his 'war room,' where she found him sitting before a bank of computer screens, watching red and blue lines chase each other across a grid. '*Tuf!*' she roared. He turned off the screen and swung to face her, batting away Ingratitude. Shrouded by shadows, he regarded her impassively. 'The Council of Guardians has given me an order,' she said.

'How fortunate for you,' Tuf replied. 'I know you have been growing restless of late from inactivity.'

'The Council wants immediate action, Tuf. *Immediate.* Today. Do you understand?'

Tuf steepled his hands beneath his chin, almost in an attitude of prayer. 'Must I tolerate not only hostility and impatience, but slurs on my intelligence as well? I understand all that needs understanding about your Guardians, I assure you. It is only the peculiar and perverse ecology of Namor that I do not understand. Until I have acquired that understanding, I cannot act.'

'You *will* act,' said Kefira Qay. Suddenly a laser pistol was in her hand, aimed at Tuf's broad paunch. 'You will act now.'

Haviland Tuf reacted not at all. 'Violence,' he said, in a voice of mild reproach. 'Perhaps, before you burn a hole in me and thereby doom yourself and your world, you might give me the opportunity to explain?'

'Go on,' she said. 'I'll listen. For a little while.'

'Excellent,' said Haviland Tuf. 'Guardian, something very odd is happening on Namor.'

'You've noticed,' she said drily. The laser did not move.

'Indeed. You are being destroyed by an infestation of creatures that we must, for want of a better term, collectively dub sea monsters. Three species have appeared, in less than half a dozen standard years. Each of these species is apparently new, or at least unknown. This strikes me as unlikely in the extreme. Your people have been on Namor for one hundred years, yet not until recently have you had any knowledge of these things you call dreadnaughts, fire-balloons, and walkers. It is almost as if some dark analogue of my *Ark* were waging biowar upon you, yet obviously that is not the case. New or old, these sea monsters are native to Namor, a product of local evolution. Their close relatives fill your seas – the mud-pots, the bobbing freddies, the jelly dancers and men-of-war. So. Where does that leave us?'

'I don't know,' said Kefira Qay.

'Nor do I,' Tuf said. 'Consider further. These sea monsters breed in vast numbers. The sea teems with them, they fill the air, they overrun populous islands. They kill. Yet they do not kill each other, nor do they seem to have any other natural enemies. The cruel checks of a normal ecosystem do not apply. I have studied the reports of your scientists with great interest. Much about these sea monsters is fascinating, but perhaps most intriguing is the fact that you know nothing about them except in their full adult form. Vast dreadnaughts prowl the seas and sink ships, monstrous fire-balloons swirl across your skies. Where, might I ask, are the little dreadnaughts, the baby balloons? Where indeed.'

'Deep under the sea.'

'Perhaps, Guardian, perhaps. You cannot say for certain, nor can I. These monsters are most formidable creatures, yet I have seen equally formidable predators on other worlds. They do not number in hundreds or thousands. Why? Ah, because the young, or the eggs, or the hatchlings, they are less formidable than the parents, and most die long before reaching their terrible maturity. This does not appear to happen on Namor. It does not appear to happen at all. What can it all mean? What indeed.' Tuf shrugged. 'I cannot say, but I work on, I think, I endeavor to solve the riddle of your overabundant sea.'

Kefira Qay grimaced. 'And meanwhile, we die. We die, and you don't care.'

'I protest!' Tuf began.

'Silence!' she said, waving the laser. 'I'll talk now, you've given your speech. Today we lost contact with the Broken Hand. Forty-three islands, Tuf. I'm afraid to even think how many people. All gone now, in a single day. A few garbled radio transmissions, hysteria, and silence. And you sit and talk about riddles. No more. You *will* take action now. I insist. Or threaten, if you prefer. Later, we will solve the whys and hows of these things. For the moment, we will kill them, without pausing for questions.'

'Once,' said Haviland Tuf, 'there was a world idyllic but for a single flaw – an insect the size of a dust mote. It was a harmless creature, but it was everywhere: It fed on the microscopic spores of a floating fungus. The folk of this world hated the tiny insect, which sometimes flew about in clouds so thick they obscured the sun. When citizens went outdoors, the insects would land on them by the thousands, covering their bodies with a living shroud. So a would-be ecological engineer proposed to solve their problem. From a distant world, he introduced another insect, larger, to prey on the living dust motes. The scheme worked admirably. The new insects multiplied and multiplied, having no natural enemies in this ecosystem, until they had entirely wiped out the native species. It was a great triumph. Unfortunately, there were unforeseen side effects. The invader, having destroyed one form of life, moved on to other, more beneficial sorts. Many native insects became extinct. The local analogue of bird life, deprived of its customary prey and unable to digest the alien bug, also suffered grievously. Plants were not pollinated as before. Whole forests and jungles changed and withered. And the spores of the fungus that had been the food of the original nuisance were left unchecked. The fungus grew everywhere – on buildings, on food crops, even on living animals. In short, the ecosystem was wrenched entirely askew. Today, should you visit, you would find a planet dead but for a terrible fungus. Such are the fruits of hasty action, with insufficient study. There are grave risks should one move without understanding.'

'And certain destruction if one fails to move at all,' Kefira Qay said stubbornly. 'No, Tuf. You tell frightening tales, but we are a desperate people. The Guardians accept whatever risks there may be. I have my orders. Unless you do as I bid, I will use this.' She nodded at her laser.

Haviland Tuf folded his arms. 'If you use that,' he said, 'you will be very foolish. No doubt you could learn to operate the *Ark*. In time. The task would take years, which by your own admission you do not have. I shall work on in your behalf, and forgive you your crude bluster and your threats, but I shall move only when I deem myself ready. I am an ecological engineer. I have my personal and professional integrity. And I must point out that, without my services, you are utterly without hope. Utterly. So, since you know this and I know this, let us dispense with further drama. You will not use that laser.'

For a moment, Kefira Qay's face looked stricken. 'You . . .' she said in confusion; the laser wavered just a bit. Then her look hardened once again. 'You're wrong, Tuf,' she said. 'I *will* use it.'

Haviland Tuf said nothing.

'Not on you,' she said. 'On your cats. I will kill one of them every day, until you take action.' Her wrist moved slightly, so the laser was trained not on Tuf, but on the small form of Ingratitude, who was prowling hither and yon about the room, poking at shadows. 'I will start with this one,' the Guardian said. 'On the count of three.'

Tuf's face was utterly without emotion. He stared.

'One,' said Kefira Qay.

Tuf sat immobile.

'Two,' she said.

Tuf frowned, and there were wrinkles in his chalk-white brow.

'Three,' Qay blurted.

'No,' Tuf said quickly. 'Do not fire. I shall do as you insist. I can begin cloning within the hour.'

The Guardian holstered her laser.

*

So Haviland Tuf went reluctantly to war.

On the first day he sat in his war room before his great console, tight-lipped and quiet, turning dials and pressing glowing buttons and phantom holographic keys. Elsewhere on the *Ark*, murky liquids of many shades and colors spilled and gurgled into the empty vats along the shadowy main shaft, while specimens from the great cell library were shifted and sprayed and manipulated by tiny waldoes as sensitive as the hands of a master surgeon. Tuf saw none of it. He remained at his post, starting one clone after another.

On the second day he did the same.

On the third day he rose and strolled slowly down the kilometers-long shaft where his creations had begun to grow, indistinct forms that stirred feebly or not at all in the tanks of translucent liquid. Some tanks were fully as large as the *Ark*'s shuttle deck, others as small as a fingernail. Haviland Tuf paused by each one, studied the dials and meters and glowing spyscopes with quiet intensity, and sometimes made small adjustments. By the end of the day he had progressed only half the length of the long, echoing row.

On the fourth day he completed his rounds.

On the fifth day he threw in the chronowarp. 'Time is its slave,' he told Kefira Qay when she asked him. 'It can hold it slow, or bid it hurry. We shall make it run, so the warriors I breed can reach maturity more quickly than in nature.'

On the sixth day he busied himself on the shuttle deck, modifying two of his shuttles to carry the creatures he was fashioning, adding tanks great and small and filling them with water.

On the morning of the seventh day he joined Kefira Qay for breakfast and said, 'Guardian, we are ready to begin.'

She was surprised. 'So soon?'

'Not all of my beasts have reached full maturity, but that is as it should be. Some are monstrous large, and must be transshipped before they have attained adult growth. The cloning shall continue, of course. We must establish our creatures in sufficient numbers so they will remain viable. Nonetheless, we are now at the stage where it is possible to begin seeding the seas of Namor.'

'What is your strategy?' asked Kefira Qay.

Haviland Tuf pushed aside his plate and pursed his lips. 'Such strategy as I have is crude and premature, Guardian, and based on insufficient knowledge. I take no responsibility for its success or failure. Your cruel threats have impelled me to unseemly haste.'

'Nonetheless,' she snapped. 'What are you doing?'

Tuf folded his hands atop his stomach. 'Biological weaponry, like other sorts of armament, comes in many forms and sizes. The best way to slay a human enemy is a single laser burst planted square in the center of the forehead. In biological terms, the analogue might be a suitable natural enemy or predator, or a species-specific pestilence. Lacking time, I have had no opportunity to devise such an economical solution.

'Other approaches are less satisfactory. I might introduce a disease that would cleanse your world of dreadnaughts, fire-balloons, and walkers, for example. Several likely candidates exist. Yet your sea monsters are close relatives of many other kinds of marine life, and those cousins and uncles would also suffer. My projections indicate that fully three-quarters of Namor's oceangoing life would be vulnerable to such an attack. Alternatively, I have at my disposal fast-breeding fungi and microscopic animals who would literally fill your seas and crowd out all other life. That choice too is unsatisfactory. Ultimately it would make Namor incapable of sustaining human life. To pursue my analogy of a moment ago, these methods are the biological equivalent of killing a single human enemy by exploding a low-yield thermonuclear device in the city in which he happens to reside. So I have ruled them out.

'Instead, I have opted for what might be termed a scattershot strategy, introducing many new species into your Namorian ecology in the hopes that some of them will prove effective natural enemies capable of winnowing the ranks of your sea monsters. Some of my warriors are great deadly beasts, formidable enough to prey even on your terrible dreadnaughts. Others are small and fleet, semi-social pack hunters who breed quickly. Still others are tiny things. I have hope that they will find and feed on your nightmare creatures in their younger, less potent stages, and thereby thin them out. So you see, I pursue many strategies. I toss down the entire deck rather than playing a single card. Given your bitter ultimatum, it is the only way to proceed.' Tuf nodded at her. 'I trust you will be satisfied, Guardian Qay.'

She frowned and said nothing.

'If you are finished with that delightful sweet-mushroom porridge,' Tuf said, 'we might begin. I would not have you think that I was dragging my feet. You are a trained pilot, of course?'

'Yes,' she snapped.

'Excellent!' Tuf exclaimed. 'I shall instruct you in the peculiar idiosyncracies of my shuttle craft, then. By this hour, they are already fully stocked for our first run. We shall make long low runs across your seas, and discharge our cargoes into your troubled waters. I shall fly the *Basilisk* above your northern hemisphere. You shall take the *Manticore* to the south. If this plan is acceptable, let us go over the routes I have planned for us.' He rose with great dignity.

*

For the next twenty days, Haviland Tuf and Kefira Qay crisscrossed the
dangerous skies of Namor in a painstaking grid pattern, seeding the seas.
The Guardian flew her runs with elan. It felt good to be in action again,
and she was filled with hope as well. The dreadnaughts and fire-balloons
and walkers would have their own nightmares to contend with now –
nightmares from half-a-hundred scattered worlds.

From Old Poseidon came vampire eels and nessies and floating tangles
of web-weed, transparent and razor-sharp and deadly.

From Aquarius Tuf cloned black raveners, the swifter scarlet raveners,
poisonous puff-puppies, and fragrant, carnivorous lady's bane.

From Jamison's World the vats summoned sand-dragons and dreer-
hants and a dozen kinds of brightly colored water snakes, large and small.

From Old Earth itself the cell library provided great white sharks,
barracuda, giant squid, and clever semi-sentient orcas.

They seeded Namor with the monstrous gray kraken of Lissador and the
smaller blue kraken of Ance, with waterjelly colonies from Noborn,
Daronnian spinnerwhips, and bloodlace out of Cathaday, with swimmers
as large as the fortress-fish of Dam Tullian, the mockwhale of Gulliver, and
the ghrin'da of Hruun-2, or as small as the blisterfins of Avalon, the
parasitical cacsni from Ananda, and the deadly nest-building, egg-laying
Deirdran waterwasps. To hunt the drifting fire-balloons they brought forth
countless fliers: lashtail mantas, bright red razorwings, flocks of scorn,
semi-aquatic howlers, and a terrible pale blue thing – half-plant and half-
animal and all but weightless – that drifted with the wind and lurked
inside clouds like a living, hungry spiderweb. Tuf called it the-weed-that-
weeps-and-whispers, and advised Kefira Qay not to fly through clouds.

Plants and animals and things that were both and neither, predators
and parasites, creatures dark as night or bright and gorgeous or entirely
colorless, things strange and beautiful beyond words or too hideous even
for thought, from worlds whose names burned bright in human history
and from others seldom heard of. And more, and more. Day after day the
Basilisk and the *Manticore* flashed above the seas of Namor, too swift and
deadly for the fire-balloons that drifted up to attack them, dropping their
living weapons with impunity.

After each day's run they would repair to the *Ark*, where Haviland Tuf
and one or more of his cats would seek solitude, while Kefira Qay
habitually took Foolishness with her to the communications room so she
could listen to the reports.

'Guardian Smitt reports the sighting of strange creatures in the Orange
Strait. No sign of dreadnaughts.'

'A dreadnaught has been seen off Batthern, locked in terrible combat with some huge tentacled thing twice its size. A gray kraken, you say? Very well. We shall have to learn these names, Guardian Qay.'

'Mullidor Strand reports that a family of lashtail mantas has taken up residence on the offshore rocks. Guardian Horn says they slice through fire-balloons like living knives – that the balloons flail and deflate and fall helplessly. Wonderful!'

'Today we heard from Indigo Beach, Guardian Qay. A strange story. Three walkers came rushing out of the water, but it was no attack. They were crazed, staggering about as if in great pain, and ropes of some pale scummy substance dangled from every joint and gap. What is it?'

'A dead dreadnaught washed up on New Atlantis today. Another corpse was sighted by the *Sunrazor* on its western patrol, rotting atop the water. Various strange fishes were picking it to pieces.'

'*Starsword* swung out to Fire Heights yesterday, and sighted less than a half-dozen fire-balloons. The Council of Guardians is thinking of resuming short airship flights to the Mud-Pot Pearls, on a trial basis. What do you think, Guardian Qay? Would you advise that we risk it, or is it premature?'

Each day the reports flooded in, and each day Kefira Qay smiled more broadly as she made her runs in the *Manticore*. But Haviland Tuf remained silent and impassive.

Thirty-four days into the war, Lord Guardian Lysan told her, 'Well, another dead dreadnaught was found today. It must have put up quite a battle. Our scientists have been analyzing the contents of its stomachs, and it appears to have fed exclusively on orcas and blue kraken.' Kefira Qay frowned slightly, then shrugged it off.

'A gray kraken washed up on Boreen today,' Lord Guardian Moen told her a few days later. 'The residents are complaining of the stink. It has gigantic round bite-marks, they report. Obviously a dreadnaught, but even larger than the usual kind.' Guardian Qay shifted uncomfortably.

'All the sharks seem to have vanished from the Amber Sea. The biologists can't account for it. What do you think? Ask Tuf about it, will you?' She listened, and felt a faint trickle of alarm.

'Here's a strange one for you two. Something has been sighted moving back and forth across the Coherine Deep. We've had reports from both *Sunrazor* and *Skyknife*, and various confirmations from skimmer patrols. A huge thing, they say, a veritable living island, sweeping up everything in its path. Is that one of yours? If it is, you may have miscalculated. They say it is eating barracuda and blisterfins and larder's needles by the thousands.' Kefira Qay scowled.

'Fire-balloons sighted again off Mullidor Strand – hundreds of them. I can hardly give credence to these reports, but they say the lashtail mantas just carom off them now. Do you . . .'

'Men-of-war again, can you believe it? We thought they were all nearly gone. So many of them, and they are gobbling up Tuf's smaller fish like nobody's business. You have to . . .'

'Dreadnaughts spraying water to knock howlers from the sky . . .'

'Something new, Kefira, a *flyer*, or a glider rather, swarms of them launch from the tops of these fire-balloons. They've gotten three skimmers already, and the mantas are no match for them . . .'

'. . . all over, I tell you, that thing that hides in the clouds . . . the balloons just rip them loose, the acid doesn't bother them anymore, they fling them down . . .'

'. . . more dead waterwasps, hundreds of them, thousands, where are they all . . .'

'. . . walkers again. Castle Dawn has fallen silent, must be overrun. We can't understand it. The island was ringed by bloodlace and water-jelly colonies. It ought to have been safe, unless . . .'

'. . . no word from Indigo Beach in a week . . .'

'. . . thirty, forty fire-balloons seen just off Cabben. The Council fears . . .'

'. . . nothing from Lobbadoon . . .'

'. . . dead fortress-fish, half as big as the island itself . . .'

'. . . dreadnaughts came right into the harbor . . .'

'. . . walkers . . .'

'. . . Guardian Qay, the *Starsword* is lost, gone down over the Polar Sea. The last transmission was garbled, but we think . . .'

Kefira Qay pushed herself up, trembling, and turned to rush out of the communications room, where all the screens were babbling news of death, destruction, defeat. Haviland Tuf was standing behind her, his pale white face impassive, Ingratitude sitting calmly on his broad left shoulder.

'What is happening?' the Guardian demanded.

'I should think that would be obvious, Guardian, to any person of normal intelligence. We are losing. Perhaps we have lost already.'

Kefira Qay fought to keep from shrieking. 'Aren't you going to *do* anything? Fight back? This is all your fault, Tuf. You aren't an ecological engineer – you're a trader who doesn't know what he's doing. That's why this is . . .'

Haviland Tuf raised up a hand for silence. 'Please,' he said. 'You have already caused me considerable vexation. Insult me no further. I am a gentle man, of kindly and benevolent disposition, but even one such as myself can be provoked to anger. You press close to that point now. Guardian, I take no responsibility for this unfortunate course of events. This hasty biowar we have waged was none of my idea. Your uncivilized ultimatum forced me to unwise action in order to placate you. Fortunately, while you have spent your nights gloating over transient and illusory victories, I have continued with my work. I have mapped out your world on my computers and watched the course of your war shudder and flow across it in all its manifold stages. I've duplicated your biosphere in one of my great tanks and seeded it with samples of Namorian life cloned from dead specimens – a bit of tentacle here, a piece of carapace there. I have observed and analyzed and at last I have come to conclusions. Tentative, to be sure, although this late sequence of events on Namor tends to confirm my hypothesis. So defame me no further, Guardian. After a refreshing night's sleep I shall descend to Namor and attempt to end this war of yours.'

Kefira Qay stared at him, hardly daring to believe, her dread turning to hope once again. 'You have the answer, then?'

'Indeed. Did I not just say as much?'

'What is it?' she demanded. 'Some new creatures? That's it – you've cloned something else, haven't you? Some plague? Some monster?'

Haviland Tuf held up his hand. 'Patience. First I must be certain. You have mocked me and derided me with such unflagging vigor that I hesitate to open myself to further ridicule by confiding my plans to you. I shall prove them valid first. Now, let us discuss tomorrow. You shall fly no war run with the *Manticore*. Instead, I would have you take it to New Atlantis and convene a full meeting of the Council of Guardians. Fetch those who require fetching from outlying islands, please.'

'And you?' Kefira Qay asked.

'I shall meet with the council when it is time. Prior to that, I shall take my plans and my creature to Namor on a mission of our own. We shall descend in the *Phoenix*, I believe. Yes. I do think the *Phoenix* most appropriate, to commemorate your world rising from its ashes. Markedly wet ashes, but ashes nonetheless.'

*

Kefira Qay met Haviland Tuf on the shuttle deck just prior to their scheduled departure. *Manticore* and *Phoenix* stood ready in their launch berths amidst the scatter of derelict spacecraft. Haviland Tuf was punching numbers into a mini-computer strapped to the inside of his wrist. He wore a long gray vinyl greatcoat with copious pockets and flaring shoulder-boards. A green and brown duckbilled cap decorated with the golden theta of the Ecological Engineers perched rakishly atop his bald head.

'I have notified Namor Control and Guardian Headquarters,' Qay said. 'The Council is assembling. I will provide transportation for a half-dozen Lords Guardian from outlying districts, so all of them will be on hand. How about you, Tuf? Are you ready? Is your mystery creature on board?'

'Soon,' said Haviland Tuf, blinking at her.

But Kefira Qay was not looking at his face. Her gaze had gone lower. 'Tuf,' she said, 'there is something in your pocket. Moving.' Incredulous, she watched the ripple creep along beneath the vinyl.

'Ah,' said Tuf. 'Indeed.' And then the head emerged from his pocket, and peered around curiously. It belonged to a kitten, a tiny jet-black kitten with lambent yellow eyes.

'A cat,' muttered Kefira Qay sourly.

'Your perception is uncanny,' said Haviland Tuf. He lifted the kitten out gently, and held it cupped in one great white hand while scratching behind its ear with a finger from the other. 'This is Dax,' he said solemnly. Dax was scarcely half the size of the older kittens who frisked about the *Ark*. He looked like nothing but a ball of black fur, curiously limp and indolent.

'Wonderful,' the Guardian replied. 'Dax, eh? Where did this one come from? No, don't answer that. I can guess. Tuf, don't we have more important things to do than play with cats?'

'I think not,' said Haviland Tuf. 'You do not appreciate cats sufficiently, Guardian. They are the most civilized of creatures. No world can be considered truly cultured without cats. Are you aware that all cats, from time immemorial, have had a touch of psi? Do you know that some ancient societies of Old Earth worshipped cats as gods? It is true.'

'Please,' said Kefira Qay irritably. 'We don't have time for a discourse on cats. Are you going to bring that poor little thing down to Namor with you?'

Tuf blinked. 'Indeed. This poor little thing, as you so contemptuously call him, is the salvation of Namor. Respect might be in order.'

She stared at him as if he had gone mad. 'What? That? Him? I mean, Dax? Are you serious. What are you talking about? You're joking, aren't you? This is some kind of insane jest. You've got some thing loaded aboard the *Phoenix*, some huge leviathan that will cleanse the sea of those dreadnaughts – something, anything, I don't know. But you can't mean ... you can't ... not that.'

'Him,' said Haviland Tuf. 'Guardian, it is so wearisome to have to state the obvious, not once but again and again. I have given you raveners and krakens and lashtail mantas, at your insistence. They have not been efficacious. Accordingly, I have done much hard thinking, and I have cloned Dax.'

'A kitten,' she said. 'You're going to use a *kitten* against the dread-naughts and the fire-balloons and the walkers. One. Small. *Kitten.*'

'Indeed,' said Haviland Tuf. He frowned down at her, slid Dax back into the roomy confines of his great pocket, and turned smartly toward the waiting *Phoenix*.

*

Kefira Qay was growing very nervous. In the council chambers high atop Breakwater Tower on New Atlantis, the twenty-five Lords Guardian who commanded the defense of all Namor were restive. All of them had been waiting for hours. Some had been there all day. The long conference table was littered with personal communicators and computer printouts and empty water glasses. Two meals had already been served and cleared away. By the wide curving window that dominated the far wall, portly Lord Guardian Alis was talking in low urgent tones to Lord Guardian Lysan, thin and stern, and both of them were giving meaningful glances to Kefira Qay from time to time. Behind them the sun was going down, and the great bay was turning a lovely shade of scarlet. It was such a beautiful scene that one scarcely noticed the small bright dots that were Guardian skimmers, flying patrol.

Dusk was almost upon them, the council members were grumbling and stirring impatiently in their big cushioned chairs, and Haviland Tuf had still failed to make an appearance. 'When did he say he would be here?' asked Lord Guardian Khem, for the fifth time.

'He wasn't very precise, Lord Guardian,' Kefira Qay replied uneasily, for the fifth time.

Khem frowned and cleared his throat.

Then one of the communicators began to beep, and Lord Guardian Lysan strode over briskly and snatched it up. 'Yes?' he said. 'I see. Quite good. Escort him in.' He set down the communicator and rapped its edge on the table for order. The others shuffled to their seats, or broke off their conversations, or straightened. The council chamber grew silent. 'That was the patrol. Tuf's shuttle has been sighted. He is on his way, I am pleased to report.' Lysan glanced at Kefira Qay. 'At last.'

The Guardian felt even more uneasy then. It was bad enough that Tuf had kept them waiting, but she was dreading the moment when he came lumbering in, Dax peering out of his pocket. Qay had been unable to find the words to tell her superiors that Tuf proposed to save Namor with a small black kitten. She fidgeted in her seat and plucked at her large, crooked nose. This was going to be bad, she feared.

It was worse than anything she could have dreamed.

All of the Lords Guardian were waiting, stiff and silent and attentive, when the doors opened and Haviland Tuf walked in, escorted by four armed guards in golden coveralls. He was a mess. His boots made a squishing sound as he walked, and his greatcoat was smeared with mud. Dax was visible in his left pocket all right, paws hooked over its edge and large eyes intent. But the Lords Guardian weren't looking at the kitten. Beneath his other arm, Haviland Tuf was carrying a muddy rock the size of a big man's head. A thick coating of green-brown slime covered it, and it was dripping water onto the plush carpet.

Without so much as a word, Tuf went directly to the conference table and set the rock down in the center of it. That was when Kefira Qay saw the fringe of tentacles, pale and fine as threads, and realized that it wasn't a rock after all. 'A mud-pot,' she said aloud in surprise. No wonder she hadn't recognized it. She had seen many a mud-pot in her time, but not until after they had been washed and boiled and the tendrils trimmed away. Normally they were served with a hammer and chisel to crack the bony carapace, and a dish of melted butter and spices on the side.

The Lords Guardian looked on in astonishment, and then all twenty-five began talking at once, and the council chamber became a blur of overlapping voices.

'. . . it *is* a mud-pot, I don't understand . . .'

'What is the meaning of this?'

'He makes us wait all day and then comes to council as filthy as a mudgrubber. The dignity of the council is . . .'

'. . . haven't eaten a mud-pot in, oh, two, three . . .'

'. . . can't be the man who is supposed to save . . .'

'. . . insane, why just look at . . .'

'. . . what is that thing in his pocket? Look at it! My God, it *moved!* It's alive, I tell you, I saw it . . .'

'*Silence!*' Lysan's voice was like a knife cutting through the hubbub. The room quieted as, one by one, the Lords Guardian turned toward him. 'We have come together at your beck and call,' Lysan said acidly to Tuf. 'We expected you to bring us an answer. Instead you appear to have brought us dinner.'

Someone snickered.

Haviland Tuf frowned down at his muddy hands, and wiped them primly on his greatcoat. Taking Dax from his pocket, Tuf deposited the lethargic black kitten on the table. Dax yawned and stretched, and ambled toward the nearest of the Lords Guardian, who stared in horror and hurriedly inched her chair back a bit. Shrugging out of his wet, muddy greatcoat, Tuf looked about for a place to put it, and finally hung it from the laser rifle of one of his escort. Only then did he turn back to the Lords Guardian. 'Esteemed Lords Guardian,' he said, 'this is not dinner you see before you. In that very attitude lies the root of all your problems. This is the ambassador of the race that shares Namor with you, whose name, regrettably, is far beyond my small capabilities. His people will take it quite badly if you eat him.'

*

Eventually someone brought Lysan a gavel, and he rapped it long and loud enough to attract everyone's attention, and the furor slowly ebbed away. Haviland Tuf had stood impassively through all of it, his face without expression, his arms folded against his chest. Only when silence was restored did he say, 'Perhaps I should explain.'

'You are mad,' Lord Guardian Harvan said, looking from Tuf to the mud-pot and back again. 'Utterly mad.'

Haviland Tuf scooped up Dax from the table, cradled him in one arm, and began to pet him. 'Even in our moment of victory, we are mocked and insulted,' he said to the kitten.

'Tuf,' said Lysan from the head of the long table, 'what you suggest is impossible. We have explored Namor quite sufficiently in the century we have been here so as to be certain that no sentient races dwell upon it. There are no cities, no roads, no signs of any prior civilization or technology, no ruins or artifacts – *nothing*, neither above nor below the sea.'

'Moreover,' said another councillor, a beefy woman with a red face, 'the mud-pots cannot possibly be sentient. Agreed, they have brains the size of a human brain. But that is about all they have. They have no eyes, ears, noses, almost no sensory equipment whatever except for touch. They have only those feeble tendrils as manipulative organs, scarcely strong enough to lift a pebble. And in fact, the tendrils are only used to anchor them to their spot on the seabed. They are hermaphroditic and downright primitive, mobile only in the first month of life, before the shell hardens and grows heavy. Once they root on the bottom and cover themselves with mud, they never move again. They stay there for hundreds of years.'

'Thousands,' said Haviland Tuf. 'They are remarkably long-lived creatures. All that you say is undoubtedly correct. Nonetheless, your conclusions are in error. You have allowed yourself to be blinded by belligerence and fear. If you had removed yourself from the situation and paused long enough to think about it in depth, as I did, no doubt it would become obvious even to the military mind that your plight was no natural catastrophe. Only the machinations of some enemy intelligence could sufficiently explain the tragic course of events on Namor.'

'You don't expect us to believe—' someone began.

'Sir,' said Haviland Tuf, 'I expect you to listen. If you will refrain from interrupting me, I will explain all. Then you may choose to believe or not, as suits your peculiar fancy. I shall take my fee and depart.' Tuf looked at Dax. 'Idiots, Dax. Everywhere we are beset by idiots.' Turning his attention back to the Lords Guardian, he continued, 'As I have stated, intelligence was clearly at work here. The difficulty was in finding that intelligence. I perused the work of your Namorian biologists, living and dead, read much about your flora and fauna, recreated many of the native lifeforms aboard the *Ark*. No likely candidate for sentience was immediately forthcoming. The traditional hallmarks of intelligent life include a large brain, sophisticated biological sensors, mobility, and some sort of manipulative organ, such as an opposable thumb. Nowhere on Namor could I find a creature with all of these attributes. My hypothesis, however, was still correct. Therefore I must needs move on to unlikely candidates, as there were no likely ones.

'To this end I studied the history of your plight, and at once some things suggested themselves. You believed that your sea monsters emerged from the dark oceanic depths, but where did they first appear? In the offshore shallows – the areas where you practiced fishing and sea-farming. What did all these areas have in common? Certainly an abundance of life, that must be admitted. Yet not the same life. The fish that habituated the waters off New Atlantis did not frequent those of the Broken Hand. Yet I found two interesting exceptions, two species found virtually everywhere – the mud-pots, lying immobile in their great soft beds through the long slow centuries and, originally, the things you called Namorian men-of-war. The ancient native race has another term for those. They call them guardians.

'Once I had come this far, it was only a matter of working out the details and confirming my suspicions. I might have arrived at my conclusion much earlier, but for the rude interruptions of liaison officer Qay, who continually shattered my concentration and finally, most cruelly, forced me to waste much time sending forth gray krakens and razorwings and sundry other such creatures. In the future I shall spare myself such liaisons.

'Yet, in a way, the experiment was useful, since it confirmed my theory as to the true situation on Namor. Accordingly I pressed on. Geographic studies showed that all of the monsters were thickest near mud-pot beds. The heaviest fighting had been in those selfsame areas, my Lords Guardian. Clearly, these mud-pots you find so eminently edible were your mysterious foes. Yet how could that be? These creatures had large brains, to be sure, but lacked all the other traits we have come to associate with sentience, as we know it. And that was the very heart of it! Clearly they were sentient as we do not know it. What sort of intelligent being could live deep under the sea, immobile, blind, deaf, bereft of all input? I pondered that question. The answer, sirs, is obvious. Such an intelligence must interact with the world in ways we cannot, must have its own modes of sensing and communicating. Such an intelligence must be telepathic. Indeed. The more I considered it, the more obvious it became.

'Thereupon it was only a matter of testing my conclusions. To that end, I brought forth Dax. All cats have some small psionic ability, Lords Guardian. Yet long centuries ago, in the days of the Great War, the soldiers of the Federal Empire struggled against enemies with terrible psi powers; Hrangan Minds and *githyanki* soulsucks. To combat such formidable foes, the genetic engineers worked with felines, and vastly heightened and sharpened their psionic abilities, so they could esp in unison with mere humans. Dax is such a special animal.'

'You mean that thing is reading our minds?' Lysan said sharply.

'Insofar as you have minds to read,' said Haviland Tuf, 'yes. But more importantly, through Dax, I was able to reach that ancient people you have so ignominiously dubbed mud-pots. For they, you see, are entirely telepathic.

'For millennia beyond counting they have dwelled in tranquility and peace beneath the seas of this world. They are a slow, thoughtful, philosophic race, and they lived side by side in the billions, each linked with all the others, each an individual and each a part of the great racial whole. In a sense they were deathless, for all shared the experiences of each, and the death of one was as nothing. Experiences were few in the unchanging sea, however. For the most part their long lives are given over to abstract thought, to philosophy, to strange green dreams that neither you nor I can truly comprehend. They are silent musicians, one might say. Together they have woven great symphonies of dreams, and those songs go on and on.

'Before humanity came to Namor, they had had no real enemies for millions of years. Yet that had not always been the case. In the primordial beginnings of this wet world, the oceans teemed with creatures who relished the taste of the dreamers as much as you do. Even then, the race understood genetics, understood evolution. With their vast web of interwoven minds, they were able to manipulate the very stuff of life itself, more skillfully than any genetic engineers. And so they evolved their guardians, formidable predators with a biological imperative to protect those you call mud-pots. These were your men-of-war. From that time to this they guarded the beds, while the dreamers went back to their symphony of thought.

'Then you came, from Aquarius and Old Poseidon. Indeed you did. Lost in the reverie, the dreamers hardly noticed for many years, while you farmed and fished and discovered the taste of mud-pots. You must consider the shock you gave them, Lords Guardian. Each time you plunged one of them into boiling water, all of them shared the sensations. To the dreamers, it seemed as though some terrible new predator had evolved upon the landmass, a place of little interest to them. They had no inkling that you might be sentient, since they could no more conceive of a nontelepathic sentience than you could conceive of one blind, deaf, immobile, and edible. To them, things that moved and manipulated and ate flesh were animals, and could be nothing else.

'The rest you know, or can surmise. The dreamers are a slow people lost in their vast songs, and they were slow to respond. First they simply ignored you, in the belief that the ecosystem itself would shortly check your ravages. This did not appear to happen. To them it seemed you had no natural enemies. You bred and expanded constantly, and many thousands of minds fell silent. Finally they returned to the ancient, almost-forgotten ways of their dim past, and woke to protect themselves. They sped up the reproduction of their guardians until the seas above their beds teemed with their protectors, but the creatures that had once sufficed admirably against other enemies proved to be no match for you. Finally they were driven to new measures. Their minds broke off the great symphony and ranged out, and they sensed and understood. At last they began to fashion new guardians, guardians formidable enough to protect them against this great new nemesis. Thus it went. When I arrived upon the *Ark*, and Kefira Qay forced me to unleash many new threats to their peaceful dominion, the dreamers were initially taken aback. But the struggle had sharpened them and they responded more quickly now, and in only a very short time they were dreaming newer guardians still, and sending them forth to battle to oppose the creatures I had loosed upon them. Even as I speak to you in this most imposing tower of yours, many a terrible new lifeform is stirring beneath the waves, and soon will emerge to trouble your sleep in years to come – unless, of course, you come to a peace. That is entirely your decision. I am only a humble ecological engineer. I would not dream of dictating such matters to the likes of you. Yet I do suggest it, in the strongest possible terms. So here is the ambassador plucked from the sea – at great personal discomfort to myself, I might add. The dreamers are now in much turmoil, for when they felt Dax among them and through him touched me, their world increased a millionfold. They learned of the stars today, and learned moreover that they are not alone in this cosmos. I believe they will be reasonable, as they have no use for the land, nor any taste for fish. Here is Dax as well, and myself. Perhaps we might commence to talk?'

But when Haviland Tuf fell silent at last, no one spoke for quite a long time. The Lords Guardian were all ashen and numb. One by one they looked away from Tuf's impassive features, to the muddy shell on the table.

Finally Kefira Qay found her voice. 'What do they *want?*' she asked nervously.

'Chiefly,' said Haviland Tuf, 'they want you to stop eating them. This strikes me as an eminently sensible proposal. What is your reply?'

*

'Two million standards is insufficient,' Haviland Tuf said some time later, sitting in the communications room of the Ark. Dax rested calmly in his lap, having little of the frenetic energy of the other kittens. Elsewhere in the room Suspicion and Hostility were chasing each other hither and yon.

Up on the telescreen, Kefira Qay's features broke into a suspicious scowl. 'What do you mean? This was the price we agreed upon, Tuf. If you are trying to cheat us . . .'

'Cheat?' Tuf sighed. 'Did you hear her, Dax? After all we have done, such grim accusations are still flung at us willy-nilly. Yes. Willy-nilly indeed. An odd phrase, when one stops to mull on it.' He looked back at the telescreen. 'Guardian Qay, I am fully aware of the agreed-on price. For two million standards, I solved your difficulties. I analyzed and pondered and provided the insight and the translator you so sorely needed. I have even left you with twenty-five telepathic cats, each linked to one of your Lords Guardian, to facilitate further communications after my departure. That too is included within the terms of our initial agreement, since it was necessary to the solution of your problem. And, being at heart more a philanthropist than a businessman, and deeply sentimental as well, I have even allowed you to retain Foolishness, who took a liking to you for some reason that I am entirely unable to fathom. For that, too, there is no charge.'

'Then why are you demanding an additional three million standards?' demanded Kefira Qay.

'For unnecessary work which I was cruelly compelled to do,' Tuf replied. 'Would you care for an itemized accounting?'

'Yes, I would,' she said.

'Very well. For sharks. For barracuda. For giant squid. For orcas. For gray kraken. For blue kraken. For bloodlace. For waterjellies. Twenty thousand standards per item. For fortress-fish, fifty thousand standards. For the-weed-that-weeps-and-whispers, eight . . .' He went on for a long, long time.

When he was done, Kefira Qay set her lips sternly. 'I will submit your bill to the Council of Guardians,' she said. 'But I will tell you straight out that your demands are unfair and exorbitant, and our balance of trade is not sufficient to allow for such an outflow of hard standards. You can wait in orbit for a hundred years, Tuf, but you won't get any five million standards.'

Haviland Tuf raised his hands in surrender. 'Ah,' he said. 'So, because of my trusting nature, I must take a loss. I will not be paid, then?'

'Two million standards,' said the Guardian. 'As we agreed.'

'I suppose I might accept this cruel and unethical decision, and take it as one of life's hard lessons. Very well then. So be it.' He stroked Dax. 'It has been said that those who do not learn from history are doomed to repeat it. I can only blame myself for this wretched turn of events. Why, it was only a few scant months past that I chanced to view a historical drama on this very sort of situation. It was about a seedship such as my own that rid one small world of an annoying pest, only to have the ungrateful planetary government refuse payment. Had I been wiser, that would have taught me to demand my payment in advance.' He sighed. 'But I was not wise, and now I must suffer.' Tuf stroked Dax again, and paused. 'Perhaps your Council of Guardians might be interested in viewing this particular tape, purely for recreational purposes. It is holographic, fully dramatized, and well-acted, and moreover, it gives a fascinating insight into the workings and capabilities of a ship such as this one. Highly educational. The title is *Seedship of Hamelin*.'

*

They paid him, of course.

SEVEN
THE SIREN SONG OF HOLLYWOOD

THE SIREN SONG OF HOLLYWOOD

When I was in seventh grade *The Twilight Zone* was my favorite television show. I never dreamed that one day I'd be writing it.

Now, let us make it clear that we're talking about two different shows here. I must look one hell of a lot older than I think, because sometimes when I mention that I worked on *The Twilight Zone*, I get the response, 'Oh, I loved that show. What was it like to work with Rod Sterling?' (The clueless inevitably drop a 't' into Rod Serling's name.)

I loved that show too, but sad to say I never worked with Rod Sterling, or even Rod Serling. I did, however, work with Phil DeGuere, Jim Crocker, Alan Brennert, Rockne S. O'Bannon, and Michael Cassutt, as well as a host of terrific actors and directors, on the short-lived and much-lamented *Twilight Zone* revival of 1985–87. Call it *TZ-2*. (There have been two more incarnations since, *TZ-3* and *TZ-4*, but we prefer not to talk about them in polite company.)

It was *The Armageddon Rag* that sent me off to *The Twilight Zone*. Published by Poseidon Press in 1983, the *Rag* was supposed to be the breakout novel that would transform me into a bestselling author. I was proud of the book, and my agent and my editor were high on it as well. Poseidon paid me a whopping big advance for the rights, and I went right out and bought a larger house.

The *Rag* received some wonderful reviews. It was nominated for the World Fantasy Award, losing out to John M. Ford's superb *The Dragon Waiting*. And it died the death. It had all the hallmarks of a big bestseller save one. No one bought it. Far from building on the success of *Fevre Dream*, it sold badly in hardcover and miserably in paperback. The full extent of the disaster was not brought home to me until 1985, when Kirby tried to sell my unfinished fifth novel, *Black and White and Red All Over*, and found that neither Poseidon nor any other publisher was willing to make an offer.

Yet even as *The Armageddon Rag* slammed one door shut behind me, it was opening another. Dismal though its sales had been, the *Rag* did have its ardent fans. One was Phil DeGuere, the creator and executive producer of the hit television series *Simon & Simon*. DeGuere was a huge fan of rock music, especially the Grateful Dead. When our mutual agent Marvin Moss showed him my book, Phil saw a feature film in it, and optioned the movie rights. He intended to write and direct the film himself, and to shoot the huge concert sequences at Grateful Dead shows.

I'd sold other film options previously. My usual involvement was limited to signing the contract and cashing the check. Phil DeGuere was different. The ink was hardly dry on the deal before he flew me out to L.A. and put me up at a hotel for several days, so we could talk about the book and how best to adapt it. Phil went on to write several drafts of the screenplay, but was never able to get a studio to bite for the financing. No movie was made. During the course of this, however, he and I got to know each other a bit . . . enough so that, when he decided to revive *The Twilight Zone* for CBS in 1985, Phil phoned to ask me if I would like to try a script.

Surprisingly, I did not immediately leap at the chance. I had been weaned on television, sure, but I'd never written for it, had never *wanted* to write for it, knew nothing about scriptwriting, had never even seen a screenplay or a teleplay. Besides, all you ever heard about writing for Hollywood was the horror stories. I'd read Harlan Ellison's *Glass Teat*, after all. I'd even read *The Other Glass Teat*. I knew how crazy it was out there.

On the other hand, I liked Phil and respected him, and he had Alan Brennert on his staff, another writer whose work I had admired. DeGuere had brought Harlan Ellison aboard as well, as a writer and consultant. Maybe this new *Twilight Zone* would be different. And if truth be told, I needed the money. At the time I was madly writing Haviland Tuf stories to fill out *Tuf Voyaging* and keep my mortgage paid, but *Black and White and Red All Over* still had not sold, and my career as a novelist lay in ruins. I was still hesitating when Phil cinched the deal by promising my lady Parris backstage passes to all the Grateful Dead shows we cared to see. You couldn't say no to *that*.

He mailed me the show's bible and a stack of sample scripts, and I sent him a stack of tearsheets and xerox copies of stories I thought might make good *Twilight Zone* episodes. Since I had never done a teleplay before, I wanted to make things easier for myself by doing an adaptation rather than an original story. That way, I could concentrate on mastering the form, rather than having to come up with the plot and characters and dialogue as well. Adaptations did not pay as well as originals, but I was more concerned with not making an utter fool of myself than I was with making money.

DeGuere liked a number of the stories I sent them, and half a dozen would end up becoming episodes of *TZ-2*, some adapted by me, some by other hands. For my first outing, however, the tale that was chosen was 'Nackles,' a Christmas horror fable by a writer named Curt Clark. I'd found it in an obscure Terry Carr anthology.

Nackles was the sort of idea that makes you slap your head and cry, 'Why didn't *I* think of that?' Every god must have his devil. Nackles was the Anti-Santa. On Christmas Eve, while Santa Claus is flying around the world in his sled, sliding down chimneys to leave presents for good boys and girls, Nackles is moving through pitch dark tunnels beneath the earth in a railroad car pulled by a team of blind white goats, and crawling up through the furnace grate to stuff bad boys and girls in his big black sack.

I was delighted by Phil's choice. 'Nackles' seemed to me to be a perfect *Twilight Zone*, given a faithful adaptation. I also took a little pleasure imagining the thrill the sale would give Curt Clark, this obscure, forgotten little writer, who I pictured teaching English composition at some community college in Nowhere, North Dakota or Godforsaken, Georgia.

It turned out that 'Curt Clark' was a pseudonym for Donald E. Westlake, the bestselling author of the wonderful Dortmunder series and a hundred other mysteries and crime novels, half of which had been turned into feature films. It also turned out, once rights had been secured and I had signed my contract, that the guys at *Twilight Zone* did not want a faithful adaptation of Westlake's story. They liked the notion of the Anti-Santa, but not the rest of it: the abusive former football star who invents Nackles to terrorize his children, his wife and kids, the brother-in-law who narrates the story. All of that had to go, I was told. Before I could start my script, I would need to come up with a whole new story for Nackles and present it in a treatment.

(So much for adaptations being easier.)

I came up with half a dozen ways to handle 'Nackles.' The first one or two I wrote up as formal treatments, the later ones I pitched to Harlan over the phone. He didn't like any of them. After a month of this, I hit a wall. I had no more fresh ideas for 'Nackles,' and remained convinced that the best way to handle the material was the way Westlake handled it in his story. Harlan was growing as frustrated as I was, and I got the impression that Phil DeGuere was ready to pull the plug.

At that point Harlan came up with an idea. Another episode had also been giving trouble, an original called 'The Once and Future King,' about an Elvis impersonator who travels back in time and finds himself face-to-face with Elvis. A freelancer named Bryce Maritano had done several drafts of the script, but DeGuere and his team still felt it needed work. I was no stranger to rock'n roll, as *The Armageddon Rag* bore witness. Harlan suggested a switch. He would take over 'Nackles' himself, and I would move to the Maritano script. Phil thought that was worth a try, and the swap was made . . . with fateful consequences for all concerned.

The subsequent tale of 'Nackles' is as horrifying as Nackles himself. Harlan Ellison's approach to the story met with more approval than mine had, and his script was duly written and given the green light. Ed Asner was cast in the lead role, and Harlan himself was set to direct. He had added a new twist to the Westlake story, however, one that drew the ire of the network censors. In the midst of preproduction, 'Nackles' was brought to a screeching halt by

Standards and Practices. For those who are curious, all the grisly details of what followed can be found in Harlan's collection *Slippage* (Houghton Mifflin, 1998), along with Westlake's original story and Harlan's teleplay. Despite good faith efforts by Phil and Harlan to address the network's concerns, the CBS censors proved unrelenting. 'Nackles' was scrapped, and Harlan left the show.

Meanwhile, I was still at home in Santa Fe, a thousand miles away from the storms, reading up about the King. Elvis had shouldered Nackles aside. I wrote my treatment of 'The Once and Future King,' and when that was approved, I launched into the script. It was the first teleplay I had ever attempted, so it took me longer than it should have. I shot it off to *The Twilight Zone* with considerable trepidation. If Phil did not like what I'd done, I figured, my first teleplay would also be my last.

He did like it. Not well enough to shoot my first draft, mind you (I soon learned that in Hollywood no one ever likes a script *that* much) . . . but well enough to offer me a staff job after 'Nackles' blew up and Harlan's departure left the *Zone* shorthanded. Suddenly I was off to a land of both shadow and substance, of things and ideas, somewhere between the pit of man's fears and the summit of his knowledge: Studio City, California.

I joined the series near the end of its first season, as a lowly Staff Writer (you know the position is lowly if the title includes the word 'writer'). My first contract was for six weeks, and even that seemed optimistic. After a strong start, the ratings for *TZ-2* had slumped off steadily, and no one knew whether CBS would renew the series for a second season. I began my stint by doing several more drafts of 'The Once and Future King,' then moved on to new scripts, adaptations of Roger Zelazny's 'The Last Defender of Camelot' and Phyllis Eisenstein's 'Lost and Found.' Six weeks of talking story with DeGuere, Crocker, Brennert, and O'Bannon, reading scripts, giving and taking notes, sitting in on pitch meetings, and watching the show being filmed taught me more than I could have learned in six years back in Santa Fe. None of my own scripts went before the cameras until the very end, when 'The Last Defender of Camelot' was finally sent into production.

Casting, budgets, pre-production meetings, working with a director; all of it was new to me. My script was too long and too expensive. That would prove to be a hallmark of my career in film and television. *All* my scripts would be too long and too expensive. I tried to keep Roger Zelazny informed of all the changes we had to make, so he would not be too taken aback when he saw his story on the air. At one point, our line producer Harvey Frand came to me with a worried look on his face. 'You can have horses,' he told me, 'or you can have Stonehenge. But you can't have horses *and* Stonehenge.' That was a hard call, so I put the question to Roger. 'Stonehenge,' he said at once, and Stonehenge it was.

They built it on the sound stage behind my office, with wood and plaster and painted canvas. If there had been horses on the stage, Stonehenge would have trembled like a leaf every time one pounded by, but without horses, the fake rocks worked fine. Not so the stuntwork, alas. The director wanted to see Sir Lancelot's face during the climactic swordfight, which entailed removing the visor from Richard Kiley's helm . . . and that of his stunt double as well. All went well until someone zigged instead of zagging during the swordplay, and the stunt man's nose was cut off. 'Not the whole nose,' Harvey Frand explained to me, 'just the end bit.'

'The Last Defender of Camelot' was broadcast on April 11, 1986, as part of TZ-2's first season closer. After we wrapped I went home to Santa Fe, not knowing if there would be a second season. For all I knew, my brief stint in television was done.

But when the networks announced their fall schedules in May, it turned out that CBS had renewed The Twilight Zone after all. I was promoted from Staff Writer to Story Editor, and headed back to Studio City. Several new writers and producers joined us for that abbreviated second season, most notably Michael Cassutt, who took my place at the bottom of the food chain as the lowly Staff Writer. Cassutt had the office next to mine. Short, cynical, talented, funny, and wise in all the ways of Hollyweird, he showed me how to get a better office (come to work early and move in), and joined me in trying to teach Phil DeGuere's cockatoo to say, 'Stupid idea,' which we thought would enliven pitch meetings no end.

The second season of TZ-2 got off to a great start for me. Both of the my leftover season one scripts, 'Lost and Found' and 'The Once and Future King,' were put into production; the latter became our second season opener. As Story Editor, I did more duties, more rewrites, and had a bigger role in pitch meetings. I wrote two new teleplays as well. 'The Toys of Caliban' was another adaptation, this time of a story by Terry Matz. 'The Road Less Traveled,' which you'll find presented here, was my first (and last) original for the Zone. The idea was one that I'd come up with a few years earlier for an anthology about the War in Vietnam, but had never gotten around to writing.

On an anthology show like The Twilight Zone, the stories are the stars. We had no leads with fat weekly salaries, no recurring characters to service, no continuing storylines. As a result we could sometimes attract feature actors and directors who would never have consented to appear on an ordinary episodic drama. I got very lucky with 'The Road Less Traveled.' My script was sent to Wes Craven. He liked it, and agreed to direct.

We speak of television programs running an hour (most dramas) or a half-hour (all sitcoms), but of course the shows themselves are nowhere near that long, since commercials eat up a large amount of that time. In the mid '80s, an 'hour-long' drama was roughly forty-six minutes long, a 'half-hour' sitcom about twenty-three minutes.

Of course, when you shoot a script, it is very rare that you will get exactly as much film as you need. Most rough cuts run long, by anywhere from a few seconds to a few minutes. No problem. The show's editors, working with the director and the producers, simply take the tape into the editing room and trim, until they have forty-six or twenty-three minutes of footage, as required.

Rod Serling's original *Twilight Zone* was a half-hour program for most of its run. It is those episodes that most fans recall. The show actually expanded to a 'full hour' for one season, but those hours are seldom seen in syndication, since they will not fit into the same time slots as the rest of the series run. Whether an hour or a half-hour, however, Serling's *Twilight Zone* featured only one story per episode.

TZ-2 was an hour-long show, but it used the format of another Serling series, *The Night Gallery*, rather than that of the original *Zone*. Each hour was made up of two or three unconnected tales of varying length. It was seldom as neat as dividing one forty-six minute hour into two twenty-three minute half-hours. One week, the show might have a thirty-minute episode teamed with one that ran sixteen minutes; the next week, a twenty-one minute segment with a twenty-five; the week after an eighteen, a fifteen, and a thirteen. It did not matter how long the individual segments ran, so long as they added up to forty-six minutes after editing.

'The Road Less Traveled' was too long (and too expensive). But it was felt to be a strong script, and had a very strong director in Wes Craven, who shot some terrific film. When Wes turned in his director's cut, it was longer than all but a few of our previous segments, but it was also a powerful little film. The decision was made to make only minor trims to Wes Craven's cut. If the hour ran long, time could always be taken out of the other segment to get us down to the necessary forty-six minutes.

The show as finally assembled paired a thirty-six minute cut of 'The Road Less Traveled' with a ten-minute version of . . . well, to tell the truth, I no longer recall which second season episode I had drawn as my running mate. The show was edited, color-timed, scored. Effects were added, along with the opening and closing narrations. Around the office, Mike Cassutt and my other friends were congratulating me. There was talk of Emmy Awards for Wes Craven and Cliff DeYoung. The show was delivered to the network, locked and finished and ready for broadcast.

Then CBS took *The Twilight Zone* off the air.

It should not have come as a shock. Our ratings had been weak at the end of the first season, and had only gotten weaker during the second. Even so, the network was not canceling the show. Not quite. Instead they were taking us off the air for 'retooling'.

Gloom descended on the MTM lot as we sat around our offices waiting for the other shoe to drop. Soon enough it did. We were going back on the air, in a new time slot . . . as a *half-hour* show. The original *Twilight Zone* had enjoyed its greatest success as a half-hour, CBS reasoned; perhaps we could do the same. And by the way, no more of this two or three stories per show stuff. From now on each episode would be a single story, twenty-three minutes in length. As for those episodes already in the can, they would have to be re-edited to fit the new half-hour format.

'The Road Less Traveled' was broadcast on December 18, 1986, but it was not the show that I had been so proud of. A truncated, mutilated remnant aired instead. Thirteen minutes had been excised, more than a third of the episode's original length. The pacing was shot to hell, and much of the character development was gone.

If any of you chanced to catch 'The Road Less Traveled' in syndication, it was the butchered version you saw. The original thirty-six minute cut was never aired, and so far as I know only two copies of it still exist on tape. Wes Craven has one, I understand. I have the other. I would show it to you if I could, but I can't. All I can do is let you read my script.

For what it's worth, I can't really quarrel with the network's decision. *The Twilight Zone* was dying; CBS had to try something. The half-hour format was worth a shot. In hindsight, the series might have been better off if it had been a half-hour show right from the start. So I cannot fault the suits for making the change. I only wish they they had waited a week, until *after* 'The Road Less Traveled' had been aired.

Sad to say, ratings showed no notable improvement, and CBS finally pulled the plug halfway through the second season. A short time later, a third incarnation of *The Twilight Zone* arose from our ashes, and produced thirty cheap new half-hour shows which were bundled with our episodes to make a syndication package. *TZ-3* inherited our unproduced scripts and filmed a few of them (most notably Alan Brennert's fine adaptation of 'The Cold Equations'), but otherwise had no connection to its predecessor. Or to me.

The Twilight Zone was a unique show, the perfect series for someone like me. My first thought when it went off the air was that I was done with Hollywood. Hollywood was not done with me, however. The corpse of *TZ-2* had scarcely cooled before I found myself a writing treatment for *Max Headroom*. A few months after that one of my *TZ* scripts got into the hands of Ron Koslow, the creator and Executive Producer of a new urban fantasy series called *Beauty and the Beast* that would be making its premiere in the fall of 1987. I was not convinced I wanted to do another show, but when my agents sent me a tape of Koslow's *Beauty and the Beast* pilot, the quality of the writing, acting, and cinematography blew me away.

I joined the staff of *Beauty and the Beast* in June of 1987, and spent three years with the series, rising from Executive Story Consultant to Supervising Producer. It was a very different sort of show than *The Twilight Zone* had been, but once again I found myself working with some terrific actors, writers, and directors. The show was twice nominated for an Emmy Award as Best Dramatic Series. I wrote and produced thirteen episodes, did uncredited rewrites on a score of others, and had a finger in everything from casting and budgeting to post-production, learning a great deal in the process. By the time *Beauty and the Beast* died its premature death, I had the experience and the credits to dream about creating and running a show of my own.

Fast forward to the summer of 1991. I was back at home in Santa Fe (though I worked in Hollywood for ten years, I never actually moved to Los Angeles, and would flee back to New Mexico and Parris the moment my current project wrapped). Since the end of *Beauty and the Beast*, I had written the pilot for a medical show and the screenplay for a low-budget science fiction movie (it wasn't so low-budget after I got done with it). Neither had gone anywhere, and no new assignment was in the offing, so I started work on a new novel. *Avalon* was science fiction, a return to my old future history. The writing seemed to be going well, until one day a chapter came to me about a young boy who goes to see a man beheaded. It was not a part of *Avalon*, I knew. I knew I had to write it too, so I put the other book aside and began what would ultimately become *A Game of Thrones*.

When I was a hundred pages into the fantasy, however, my lovely and energetic Hollywood agent Jodi Levine called to report that she'd gotten pitch meetings for me at NBC, ABC, and Fox. (CBS, the network that had aired both *The Twilight Zone* and *Beauty and the Beast*, was the only network that did not want to hear my ideas. Go figure.) I had been telling Jodi that my werewolf novella 'The Skin Trade' would make a swell franchise for a series, and asking her to get me in to pitch it. Now she had. So I put *A Game of Thrones* in the same drawer with *Avalon* and flew out to L.A. to try and sell the networks on a buddy series about a hot young female private eye and an asthmatic hypochondriac werewolf.

It's always best to have more than one string to your bow when fiddling for networks, so I noodled with some other notions on the plane. Somewhere over Phoenix, the opening line of 'The Lonely Songs of Laren Dorr' came back to me. *There is a girl who goes between the worlds . . .*

By the time I got off the plane, that line had mutated into a concept for an alternate world series I called *Doors* (it was later changed to *Doorways*, to avoid confusion with Jim Morrison's band and Oliver Stone's film). It was *Doors* that ABC, NBC, and Fox all responded to, not 'The Skin Trade.' I flew home thinking that Fox was the most likely of the three to bite, but ABC was faster on the trigger. A few days later, I had a pilot.

Doorways became my life for the next two years. I took the project to Columbia Pictures Television, where my old *Twilight Zone* colleague Jim Crocker joined me as Executive Producer. The rest of 1991 I spent writing and rewriting the pilot. I did several story treatments and beat outlines before going to script. The toughest question I faced was deciding what sort of alternate world Tom and Cat should visit in the pilot. After long consultations with Jim Crocker and the execs at Columbia and ABC, I went with 'winter world,' a stark post-holocaust Earth locked in the throes of a nuclear winter. My first draft, as usual, was too long and too expensive, but Crocker seemed pleased with it, as was Columbia.

ABC was pleased as well . . . with the first half of the script. Unfortunately, the network guys had changed their minds about what should happen when Tom and Cat go through the first door. Winter world was too grim, they now decided. If we went to series, we could go there for an episode, certainly, but for the pilot ABC felt we needed a less depressing scenario.

It meant tearing up the entire second half of my script and doing it all over, but I gnashed my teeth, put in some late nights and long weekends, and got it done. In place of winter world, I sent Tom and Cat to a timeline where all the petroleum on Earth had been eaten some years earlier by a bioengineered virus designed to clean up oil spills. Needless to say, this caused a rather major . . . ah, *burp* . . . but civilization recovered after a fashion, and the resulting world was far less grim than winter world had been.

In January 1992, ABC gave us a production order for a ninety-minute pilot. To offset some of the projected budget deficits (my script was too long and too expensive), Columbia also decided to produce a two-hour version for European television. Academy Award winner Peter Werner was hired to direct, and pre-production began. Casting was a hell and a half, and actually caused us to delay the shoot (with fateful consequences further down the road), but we finally found our regulars. George Newbern was perfect as Tom, Rob Knepper made a splendid Thane, and Kurtwood Smith was so good in his dual role as Trager that we would have brought him back many times had we gone to series. For Cat, we had to go across the ocean to Paris, where we discovered a brilliant and beautiful young Breton stage actress named Anne LeGuernec. I remain convinced that if *Doorways* had gone to series, Anne would have become a huge star. There was no one like her on American television, then or now. We found some great people for our guest roles too, adding Hoyt Axton as Jake and Tisha Putman as Cissy. Finally we were go to roll.

When we screened the rough cut for ABC that summer, we got an enthusiastic reception and an order for six back-up scripts, so we would be ready to go into production as a mid-season replacement in 1993. I wrote one of the six scripts myself, hired some terrific writers to do the other five, and spent the remainder of 1992 and the first few months of 1993 doing rewrites, going over pattern budgets, and getting ready to go to series.

It never happened. ABC passed. The *why* of that remains a matter of conjecture, though I have my theories. Bad timing might have been a part of it. By the time we finally found our Tom and Cat, we had missed the development window for the '92 fall season. We seemed to be a lock for the fall of '93, but there was a shakeup at ABC before that decision day rolled around, and both of the execs who had supervised the pilot ended up leaving the network. We might also have made a mistake when we agreed to scrap winter world, which would have given the second half of the show a visual and visceral impact that no-oil world could not match. The test audiences and focus groups would have gotten a much different idea of the dramatic potential of the series from a world in more desperate straits.

Or maybe it was something else entirely. No one will ever know for certain. After ABC pulled the plug, Columbia screened the pilot for NBC, CBS, and Fox, but it is a rare thing for one network to pick up a project developed for another. Heinlein said it best: if you let them piss in the soup, they like the flavor better.

Doorways died. I mourned a while, and went on.

You don't forget, though. Ten years have passed, but it still makes me sad to think what might have been. It gives me great pleasure to include the script in this retrospective. No writer wants to see his children buried in an unmarked grave.

I debated a long time over which version of the script to use here. The later drafts are more polished, but in the end I decided to use the first draft, the one with winter world. The two-hour European cut of *Doorways* has been released on videotape everywhere but in the USA, and large crowds saw the rough cut of the ninety-minute version at the test screenings we did for MagiCon, the 1992 worldcon in Orlando, Florida. But no one has ever visited winter world till now. And what could be more appropriate for an alternate worlds story than to present an alternate version of the script?

Doorways will always be the great 'what if' of my career. I wrote other pilots – *Black Cluster*, *The Survivors*, *Starport* – but *Doorways* was the only one to get beyond the script stage, the only one to be filmed, the only one to come within a whisker of winning a spot on a network's primetime schedule. If it had, who knows? It might have run for two episodes, or for ten years. I might still be writing and producing the show today, or I might have been fired two months into the series. The only certainty is that I would be much, much richer than I am at present.

On the other hand, I would never have finished *A Game of Thrones*, or written the other volumes of *A Song of Ice and Fire*. So maybe it all turned out for the best after all.

The Twilight Zone:
'The Road Less Traveled'

FADE IN

INT. – LIVING ROOM – NIGHT

JEFF MCDOWELL and his wife DENISE, an attractive couple in their
late thirties, are cuddled together on their couch, watching TV. She's
sleepy but contented; he's rapt on the screen. The light of the TV plays
over their faces. The furnishings are eclectic, not expensive or terribly
chic, but comfortable. There's a fireplace, with bookshelves to either
side stuffed with magazines and plenty of well-read dog-eared
paperbacks.

O.S. we HEAR dialogue from the original version of The Thing: the
exchange 'What if it can read minds?' 'Then it'll be real mad when it
gets to me.' Jeff smiles. Behind them, we SEE their five-year-old
daughter, MEGAN, enter the room.

>   MEGAN
>   Daddy, I'm scared.

As Megan comes over to the couch, Denise sits up. The girl climbs up
into Jeff's lap.

>   JEFF
>   Hey, it's only a space carrot.
>   Vegetables are nothing to scared of.
>   (beat, smile)
>   What are you doing down here anyway?
>   Aren't you supposed to be in bed?

>   MEGAN
>   There's a man in my room.

Denise and Jeff exchange looks. Jeff hits the pause button.

>   DENISE
>   Honey, you were just having a bad dream.

>   MEGAN
>   (stubborn)
>   I was not! I saw him, Mommy.

>   JEFF
>   (to Denise)
>   My turn, I guess.

Jeff picks up his daughter, carries her toward the stairs.

>   JEFF
>   (cheerful, reassuring)
>   Well, we'll just have to see who's scaring my girl, huh?
>   (aside, to Denise)
>   If he reads minds, he'll be real mad when he gets to me.

>   CUT TO

INT. – MEGAN'S BEDROOM

as Jeff opens the door. A typical untidy five-year-old's room. Dolls,
toys, a small bed. A huge stuffed animal, fallen on its side, fills one
corner. The only light is a small nightlight in the shape of some
cartoon character. Megan points.

>   MEGAN
>   He was over there. He was watching me, Daddy.

JEFF'S POINT OF VIEW

as he looks. Under the window is a shape that does indeed look like a
man sitting in a chair, staring at them.

BACK TO THE SCENE

Jeff turns on the overhead light, and suddenly the man in the chair is
nothing but a pile of clothes.

JEFF

See. It's nothing, Megan.

MEGAN

It was a man, Daddy. He scared me.

Jeff musses his daughter's hair.

JEFF

Just a bad dream, Megan. My big girl isn't scared of a little nightmare, is she?

He carries her to bed, tucks her in. Megan looks uncertain about the whole thing; she sure doesn't want to left alone.

JEFF

Can you keep a secret?

Megan nods solemnly.

JEFF

(conspiratorially)

When I was a kid, I had <u>lots</u> of bad dreams. And monsters.

MEGAN

(wide-eyed)

Monsters?

JEFF

In the closet, under the bed, everywhere. Then my dad told me the secret. After that I wasn't scared any more.

(whispers in her ear)

Monsters can't get you if you hide under the blankets!

MEGAN

They can't?

JEFF

(solemn, definite)

Those are the rules. Even monsters have to obey the rules.

Megan pulls up her blankets and ducks underneath, giggling.

                            JEFF
        That's my girl.
                    (lifts blankets, tickles her)
        But blankets can't hide you from daddies.

They tussle playfully for a moment. Then Jeff kisses her, tucks her
back in.

                            JEFF
        Now go to sleep, you hear?

Megan nods, ducks under the blanket. Jeff smiles, goes to the door,
and pauses to look back before turning out the light.

JEFF'S POINT OF VIEW

Of the room, the bed, Megan's small form huddled under the blankets,
the scattered toys. He flicks the switch.

                                        SMASH CUT TO

INT. – HUT IN VIETNAM – NIGHT

Everything is the same; everything is grotesquely different. The walls
and roof are thatched, the floor is dirt. The arrangement of objects is a
distorted echo of Megan's room. Outside the window a nearby fire
illuminates the scene (instead of a streetlamp). In a dark corner, where
the stuffed animal lay in Megan's room, a body slumps instead. Every
toy, block, and object from Megan's room has a counterpart placed
identically; pots and pans, a rag doll, a gun, etc. The bed is a pile of
straw, and the blanket is ragged, but there's still a child's body
beneath. Only now there's a dark stain spreading on the cloth. We
HEAR Jeff's shocked gasp. The Vietnam shot should be held very
briefly, almost a subliminal. Then Jeff turns the light back on and we

                                        SMASH CUT TO

MEGAN'S ROOM

As before. Everything is normal.

CLOSE ON JEFF

Disoriented, confused, he stares for a beat, shakes his head.

BACK TO THE SCENE

Jeff turns off the light again. This time nothing happens. He closes the door softly, and we FOLLOW him downstairs.

LIVING ROOM

Denise is glancing over some legal briefs, oversized glasses on the end of her nose. She glances up at Jeff, and notices something in his expression that makes her put away the papers.

                    DENISE
          What's wrong? You look like death warmed over.

                    JEFF
                  (still shaken)
          It's nothing ... I thought ... ah, it's absurd. Like daughter
          like father, I guess.
                  (forced laugh)
          The 'man' was a chair full of clothes.

                    DENISE
          She's got your imagination.

                    JEFF
          I <u>wondered</u> who took it.

                    DENISE
          She's okay, though?

Jeff seats himself, picks up the remote control, turns the movie back on just in time for the 'Keep watching the skies' speech.

                    JEFF
          Sure.

CUT TO

MEGAN'S ROOM

The girl is huddled under the blankets in the soft glow of her
nightlight. We HEAR her soft, steady breathing. The camera MOVES
IN slowly, with the faint SOUND of a wheelchair moving across a
hardwood floor.

CLOSE ON MEGAN

As a shadow falls across her. She does not stir, not even when a man's
hand moves in from off camera, grasps the corner of her blanket, and
pulls it back with ominous slowness.

FADE OUT

FADE BACK IN

INT. – CLASSROOM – THE NEXT DAY

A college lecture hall. Twenty-odd students are watching and taking
notes while Jeff paces in front of the class, tossing a stub of chalk idly
as he lectures. On the blackboard is written NY JOURNAL – HEARST
and NY WORLD – PULITZER.

> JEFF
> —when Remington complained that he couldn't find a war,
> Hearst supposedly cabled him back and said, 'You provide the
> pictures. I'll provide the war.' Now, that anecdote is probably
> apocryphal, but the role the yellow press played in whipping
> up war fervor was beyond dispute.

A sullen dark-haired student with the look of a jock interrupts the
lecture before Jeff can proceed.

> JOCK
> At least they were on our side.

Jeff stops, looks at him, sits on the edge of his desk.

> JEFF
> You have a point to make, Mueller?

> JOCK
> (points at board)
> These guys, at least they were behind our boys. The real yellow
> journalists were the ones who ran down everything we did in
> Nam.

> JEFF
> (drily)
> Not every war can be as box office as Hearst's little shoot-em-
> up, I guess.

> JOCK
> Yeah, well at least we won that one. We could have won in
> Nam too.

> JEFF
> I wouldn't go that far, Mueller. You need to spend more time
> with your text and less with Rambo.

The class breaks into laughter, but the jock looks angry. Before Jeff can
resume his lecture, the class bell RINGS. The students begin to rise,
gather up their books, etc.

> JEFF
> Remember, chapter twelve of Emery is due by next week.

He puts down the chalk and begins to clear his papers into a briefcase
as the students file out. The jock lingers until he and Jeff are alone.
He steps up to the desk. Physically he is bigger than Jeff, who closes
the briefcase and looks up at him.

> JOCK
> So where were you during Nam, Mister McDowell?

The two men lock eyes for a long, solid beat. It is Jeff who breaks and
looks away first, his eyes averted as he replies.

> JEFF
> (brusquely)
> I was in school. Not that it's any of your business.

He brushes past, walking a little faster than necessary, while the jock watches him go.

                                                              CUT TO

EXT. – DAYCARE PARKING LOT – DAY

Denise and Megan emerge from a Day Care Center, and cross the
parking lot to her Volvo. Denise, on her way home from work, is
dressed in a chic tailored suit, carrying a briefcase. As she unlocks the
car, we HEAR the sound of a wheelchair.

ANGLE OVER VET'S SHOULDER AT DENISE

In f.g., we see a man's shoulder and the back of his head. Denise
backs out of the parking spot, turns toward the camera.

ANGLE ON CAR

As it passes we get a quick glimpse of a legless man in a wheelchair
(THE VET) turning to follow it with his eyes. He is long-haired,
bearded, his trousers pinned up at mid-thigh, wearing a shapeless olive
drab jacket without badges. We should not see his face clearly.

CLOSE ON MEGAN

staring out the car window, she SEES the Vet, follows him with her
eyes until they turn a corner.

                                                       TIME CUT TO

EXT. – MCDOWELL HOUSE – EVENING

Denise pulls up and parks the Volvo in the driveway, behind Jeff's
modest Datsun. The house is a two-story suburban tract home;
pleasant, respectable, in a decent neighborhood, but nothing too large
or expensive. A comfortable middle-class sort of house.

                                                              CUT TO

INT. – KITCHEN

Denise & Megan enter, to find Jeff tossing a salad. A small TV set sits on the counter, and Jeff watches the news from the corner of his eye. The newscaster is reading a story about El Salvador. An open bottle of wine and half-empty glass are close at hand. Jeff turns when they enter.

> JEFF
>
> Roast beef, baked potatoes, tossed salad, and wine.
>> (kisses Megan)
> Except for you. You get milk.
>> (to Denise)
> So how does that sound?

> DENISE
>
> Like paradise regained.
>> (to Megan)
> Go wash up, honey.

Megan rushes off upstairs.

> DENISE
>
> So what's wrong?

> JEFF
>
> Wrong? What makes you think something's wrong?

Denise gives him a rueful smile, picks up the wine bottle, sloshes it thoughtfully.

> DENISE
>
> Clues, Sherlock. The last time you served wine was the day your car got banged up in the school lot. What is it this time?

Jeff looks as though he's going to deny it, then stops, shrugs. She knows him too well.

> JEFF
>
> This morning in class, a student asked me where I was during Vietnam.
>> (beat, grimace)
> I told him I was in school.

                              DENISE
You were. I remember it distinctly. I was there with you,
remember?

                               JEFF
I left out the part about the school being in Canada.

                              DENISE
It's none of his business anyway.

                               JEFF
That's what I said. I just feel . . .
                          (beat, hesitant)
I don't know. Guilty. Like I did something wrong. Dumb, huh?

He opens the oven, pokes at the roast with a long fork.

                               JEFF
Well, it didn't moo. It think it's done.

                                                      CUT TO

INT. – DINING ROOM

Denise is filling bowls of salad as Jeff carries the roast out on a platter.
Megan has not yet reappeared. Denise goes to the stairs to call.

                              DENISE
Megan! Come on down, Hon, dinner's ready.

A beat, then a DOOR CLOSES upstairs and Megan comes down.
Denise takes her by the hand, frowns.

                              DENISE
Megan, you didn't wash up.

                              MEGAN
The man was upstairs, Mommy. He talked to me.

                              DENISE
                            (put upon)
Honestly. Come on, let's get you scrubbed up for dinner.

We TRACK with them as they go up the stairs and into the bathroom. Kneeling, Denise takes a facecloth and begins to wash a dirty spot off of Megan's face.

> DENISE
>
> Honey, it's okay to play pretend, but you shouldn't try to blame someone else when you forget to do something.

> MEGAN
>
> It's not pretend, Mommy.

> DENISE
>
> There, that's a little better.

She puts down the washcloth, looks at Megan's reflection in the mirror, smiles. We move in TIGHT on the mirror as Denise's eyes rise. Behind them, the open bathroom door is reflected, and outside in the hallway, sitting in his wheelchair, is the Vet. Denise spins around, and off her shocked reaction we

CUT TO

DINING ROOM

Jeff grabs a baked potato, winces as it burns his fingers, tosses it onto a plate, and then reacts as we HEAR Denise scream O.S. He's up like a shot, running for the stairs.

ANGLE ON JEFF

on the staircase, as he almost runs into Denise coming down.

> JEFF
>
> What's wrong?

> DENISE
> (frantic)
> Where is he? Did he come past you?

> JEFF
> (confused)
> What? Come past me? Who?

                              DENISE
The man in the wheelchair.
                    (impatient, off Jeff's confusion)
He was there, in the mirror . . . I mean, he was in the hall, but
I saw him in the mirror, and then . . . he <u>must</u> have come by
you!

                               JEFF
                             (baffled)
A man in a <u>wheelchair</u>?

He takes Denise by the shoulders, tries to calm her down.

                               JEFF
                           (continued)
I think I would have noticed a man in a wheelchair, honey.
Besides, how the hell could anyone get a chair down these
stairs?

Denise gapes at the narrow steps, realizes that Jeff is right. But she
knows she saw the Vet; she's totally lost.

                              DENISE
He was there, I tell you. If he didn't come down—
                    (whirls, scared he's still up there)

Megan appears at the top of the stairs, calm, unafraid.

                              MEGAN
He's gone, Mommy.

Denise wraps her in a tight hug.

                              MEGAN
Don't be scared, Mommy. He's a nice man.

ANGLE ON JEFF

as he watches wife and daughter embrace.

                               JEFF
There is <u>no way</u> anyone could have gotten out of this house.
What the hell is going on here?

> (starts up stairs)
Whatever it is, I'm going to find out.

JEFF'S POINT OF VIEW

As he moves upstairs, down the carpeted hall, slamming open doors, peering into the rooms, finding nothing. Bathroom, linen closet, Megan's room, the master bedroom and bath; all empty.

ANGLE ON JEFF

Standing in his bedroom, looking angry, disgusted. He starts back out into the hall, takes a few steps ... and stops dead outside the bathroom. He drops to one knee, reaches out.

CLOSE ON CARPET

As Jeff traces the clear, unmistakable track of a wheelchair tire in the thick shag carpet.

JEFF

What the ...

SMASH CUT TO

CLOSE ON MUDDY GROUND

Matching shot, the motion of Jeff's fingers CONTINUOUS from the last shot, but now the carpet is mud, the tracks are footprints, and Jeff's sleeve is an army uniform.

EXT. – JUNGLE TRAIL – DAY – JEFF'S POINT OF VIEW

Jeff looks up from the footprints. It's a jungle trail in Vietnam, narrow, overgrown, thick foliage all around. A black grunt stands a few feet away: a kid, no more than nineteen, his uniform dirty, a crude bandage wrapped around a head wound and soaked with blood. He's holding an M-16.

GRUNT

Hey man, what's wrong?

JEFF

As he staggers to his feet. It's Vietnam, he's in cammies, an M-16 slung over his shoulder. He can't believe any of it. He gapes – at himself, the trees, the gun, at everything.

                        GRUNT
                   (disgusted, scared)
            Don't freak on me, Spaceman. I need you, man.

Jeff backs away from him, shaking his head.

                         JEFF
            No. No way. This can't be—

He backs hard into a tree, stumbles. He's lost. When the grunt approaches, Jeff shrinks away from him.

                         JEFF
         Stay away from me!

                        GRUNT
                     (confused)
          What the hell's wrong? It's me, man!

He grabs Jeff by the shoulders, shakes him as Jeff struggles.

                        GRUNT
         Cut it out, man. It's me! Hey, Spaceman, it's only me.

CLOSE ON JEFF

As the grunt shakes him.

                      GRUNT (O.S.)
            It's me, man. It's me, it's me, it's me, it's me . . .

Off Jeff's SCREAM, we

                                                    SMASH CUT TO

INT. – HALLWAY

Where Denise has a hysterical Jeff by the shoulders, shaking him, shouting at him.

                              DENISE
     ... it's me, Jeff. It's only me! It's <u>me</u>!

Jeff suddenly realizes that he's back, wrenches free, staggers back away from her, panting.

                              JEFF
     I ... I ... where ... my god, what <u>happened</u> to me?

                              DENISE
     I heard you yelling. When I came up, you were on the floor. It was like you were terrified of me.

                              JEFF
     It's wasn't <u>you</u>!
                         (beat, confused)
     I mean ... I don't ... Denise, I was ... here, and then suddenly I wasn't ... I was in <u>Nam</u>!
                         (beat, continues off Denise's worried look)
     I know. It doesn't make sense. None of it makes sense.

                              DENISE
                         (timidly)
     Maybe ... I don't know ... maybe you had some kind of ... flashback or something?

                              JEFF
     How the hell can you flash back to a place you've never been?

                              DENISE
     Jeff, I'm scared.

Jeff takes her in his arms.

                              JEFF
     You're not the only one.

                                                      DISSOLVE TO

INT. – BEDROOM – LATE THAT NIGHT

Dinner's been reheated and eaten, Megan's been put to bed, but Jeff is
still shaken. Denise, in pajamas, sits up in bed, pillows propped up
against the headboard bookcase. Jeff, still dressed, stands by the
window, looking out, his back to her.

JEFF
(dully)

I have to go away.

DENISE

Go away? You're talking crazy, Jeff.

JEFF
(turns to face her)

Crazy? Tell me what's crazy! A man in a wheelchair who leaves
tracks in my carpet and vanishes into thin air, that's crazy.
One moment I'm in Megan's room and the next I'm in some
hut in Nam, that's crazy. But it's happening, all of it's
happening.
(beat, then earnestly)
Denise, don't you see? It's happening on account of me. I don't
know what's going on, but I'm the cause of it.

DENISE

You haven't done anything—

JEFF
(interrupts)

No? I can think of something I did. I was drafted, Denise. I
chose Canada instead. And now . . .
(beat, confused)
. . . now it's catching up with me, somehow. Maybe Nam was
my fate, maybe I was supposed to die there. Maybe this legless
ghost is the guy who went instead of me, or someone who
died because I wasn't there.

He turns away again, stares back out the window.

DENISE

That's your guilt talking, not you. And for what? You said no to a dirty little undeclared war. You helped to <u>stop</u> the war, damn it. You know that.

                    JEFF
All I know is that I've got to leave. If I go, maybe you and Megan will be safe.

Denise gets up from bed, walks over to the window, puts her arms around Jeff, hugs him. He does not turn.

                    DENISE
Jeff, <u>please</u>. Whatever is happening, we can face it together.

CLOSE ON JEFF

Worried, but softening. He doesn't want to go, not really.

                    JEFF
    Maybe you're right.

He turns toward her, to kiss her.

                                        SMASH CUT TO

INT. – BROTHEL – NIGHT

Jeff completes the turn to find himself standing in the bedroom of a brothel in Saigon, a young Vietnamese prostitute standing there with her arms around him, waiting for his kiss. The light flooding through the window is red, garish. Jeff CRIES OUT and thrusts the prostitute away roughly. She stumbles and falls.

                    JEFF
    No, <u>no</u>! Not again.

He backpedals, and runs from the room wildly as the woman gets back to her feet.

                                        CUT TO

EXT. – MCDOWELL HOUSE – NIGHT

As Jeff's Datsun revs up, backs out of the driveway, and screams off down the street, Denise comes running out of the house, a bathrobe flapping around her legs, shouting for him to stop.

DENISE

Jeff! Jeff! Wait!

The car screeches around a corner and Denise stands there, shaking, slumped in despair.

TIME CUT TO

INT. – DENISE'S OFFICE – THE NEXT DAY

A busy Legal Aid office. Denise is a staff attorney, with a private glass-walled cubicle. She's working on some briefs, although it's clear from her face that she's depressed, unhappy, worried. When her com line BUZZES, Denise lifts the phone.

DENISE

Yes, Susan.

SUSAN
(O.S.)

Your husband's on five.

DENISE

Thanks.
(pushes phone button, eager)
Jeff? Where have you been? I've been so worried.

We HEAR Jeff's voice over the phone. It has a hoarse, raspy tone; he sounds strained, uncertain.

JEFF (O.S.)

Denise? Is it you?

DENISE

Of course it's me. Where are you? Are you all right? You sound strange.

                         JEFF (O.S.)
Strange?
                          (beat)
I . . . I'm fine, Denny. How are you?

                          DENISE
Denny? You haven't called me Denny since high school. Jeff,
what's the matter?

                           JEFF
I just . . . need to see you, Denny. Just for a little while. I'm at
home, Denny. I need to see you.

                          DENISE
I'll be right there.

She HEARS the click as the phone is hung up. She rises, hurriedly
stuffs her briefcase, heads through the door into the outer office,
where she pauses by the receptionist's desk.

                          DENISE
Susan, I'm going home for the afternoon. Ask Fred to cover for
me.

                          SUSAN
Sure. I hope nothing's wrong.

Denise nods grimly, and exits.

                                               CUT TO

INT. – DENISE'S CAR

She has a worried look on her face as she drives home.

                                               CUT TO

LEGAL AID OFFICE

The outer office. Susan has just hung up the phone as Jeff comes
through the outer door, haggard and unshaven, wearing the same
clothes we saw him in the night before. Susan's obviously surprised to

see him.

                              JEFF
                        (weary, abashed)
        Hi, Susan. Denise in?

                              SUSAN
        She went home about five minutes ago. Right after you called.

                              JEFF
        Right after . . . I called? I never called.

                              SUSAN
        Of course you did. I put you through myself not ten minutes
        ago. I ought to know your voice by now.

                              JEFF
            (stares, with dawning apprehension and fear)
        My God!

He turns and runs from the office.

                                                          CUT TO

EXT. – MCDOWELL HOUSE – DAY

as Denise's car pulls up. She walks to the kitchen door.

INT. – KITCHEN

as Denise enters.

                              DENISE
                          (calls loudly)
        Jeff? I'm home.

There's no answer. Denise frowns. We TRACK with her as she walks
through the kitchen and into the living room.

                              DENISE
        Jeff? Are you there?

Silence for a long beat, and then, from upstairs, comes Jeff's voice . . . except that it's not quite his voice, it's a little harsher somehow, with a bitter edge to it, a rasp. And it's weak, a bit faint, as if talking was an effort.

> VET

Denny? I . . . I'm here, Denny.

Denise moves upstairs, down the hall.

> DENISE

Jeff?

> VET

Here. Back here.

The voice is coming from the bedroom. Denise enters. The drapes are pulled tight, the room is very dark.

> DENISE

Honey?

Silence. She crosses the room, pulls back the drapes, and as daylight floods the bedroom, the door SLAMS, Denise whirls.

DENISE'S POINT OF VIEW – WHAT SHE SEES

The Vet, legless, in fatigues, sits in his wheelchair, blocking the only exit from the room. We HOLD on him for a long beat, and for the first time we see that he is Jeff McDowell. A gaunt, hollow-cheeked Jeff McDowell, his scraggly beard doing little to disguise obvious ill-health. His speech patterns are rougher, cruder; this Jeff has been educated by Vietnam and VA hospitals, not colleges and universities. His eyes are deeply sunken; he looks at her like a starving man staring at a feast.

BACK TO THE SCENE

Denise is terrified for a beat, and then she recognizes him.

> DENISE
> (scared whisper)

Jeff?

The Vet smiles a tremulous, tentative smile. He looks almost as scared as she does.

> VET
> They call me Spaceman. I got the name in Nam, on account of the movies I liked.
> (beat)
> You're looking good, Denny. Even better than you did back ... back when we were together.

She backs away, shaking her head.

> DENISE
> This isn't happening ... Jeff ... what am I saying, you're not Jeff, you can't be Jeff.

The Vet rolls toward her.

CUT TO

EXT. – FREEWAY – DAY

Jeff's car is barreling through freeway traffic, cutting in and out, hurrying home. He comes down an exit ramp, speeds along a residential street.

INT. – JEFF'S CAR

Behind the wheel, he looks grim and intent, a little frightened.

CUT TO

THE BEDROOM

The Vet rolls forward as Denise backs away from him.

> VET
> You want to see my dogtags? I'm Jeff McDowell, just as much as he is. You want to test me? Go on, I know all the answers. We met in high school, working on the school paper. Your

parents are named Pete and Barbara. The first time we went all the way was on your couch, the night they went out for an anniversary dinner and I came over to watch War of the Worlds on your color TV. You've got a birthmark on the inside of your thigh, about an inch—

> DENISE
> (interrupting)
> My God . . . you are Jeff. What . . . What . . .

> VET
> (looks down at missing legs)
> What happened? Is that the question? Vietnam happened, Denny. Vietnam and the draft lottery and a mine.

> DENISE
> You didn't go to Vietnam. You went to Canada. We went to Canada, together, we got married up there. You taught up there until the amnesty.

> VET
> (bitter laugh)
> I'm still waiting for my amnesty.

> DENISE
> How . . . how did you get here? Where did you come from? And why? What do you want from us?

> VET
> I just want . . .

Before he can finish, they HEAR the sound of squealing brakes from outside.

CUT TO

EXT. – MCDOWELL HOUSE – DAY

Jeff's Datsun screeches up into the driveway, behind Denise's Volvo, He opens the door, rushes inside.

INT. – LIVING ROOM

as Jeff bursts in through the kitchen door.

                    JEFF
                  (wild, yells)
Denise! Where are you? <u>DENISE!</u>

He looks around the room, snatches up a fireplace poker.

                                              CUT TO

BEDROOM

where Denise hears him yelling.

                    DENISE
                  (shouts)
JEFF! Here, I'm up here.

                    VET
Denny, please. I don't have —

                    DENISE
                  (louder)
JEFF!

We HEAR Jeff's footsteps pounding up the stairs and a moment later
the door bursts open as he enters, brandishing the poker. The Vet
wheels his chair around and backs off.

                    JEFF
Stay away from her! Leave her alone—

Jeff stops dead, as the full realization hits him. He stares.

                    JEFF
                  (softly)
You're . . . me.

                    VET
                  (soft, weary)
Bingo.

                    JEFF
This isn't happening, this is some kind of—

                    VET
                (interrupts)
Dream? Yeah. But are you dreaming me or am I dreaming
you?
                (beat)
I don't give a damn either way. I think we're both real. I think
that back around 1971 we came to this fork in the road, and
you went one way, and I went the other, and we got to . . .
different places.

Jeff slowly lowers the fireplace poker. He's pale, scared.

                    JEFF
Then . . . those flashbacks I've been having . . . those are . . .

                    VET
                (hard smile)
Mine, brother. Part of the baggage. I guess they just come with
me. And you and me, we're the same person, right? I could
feel it happening . . . leaking. But I couldn't stop it. We just
got too close.

                    DENISE
Jeff—

Both of them turn to look at her.

                    DENISE
            (continues, with difficulty)
I mean . . . <u>Spaceman</u> . . . in your . . . road . . . what happened
to . . .

                    VET
To us, Denny? You and me?

Denise nods.

                    VET
You died in a motorcycle crash while I was in Nam. The guy

you were riding with didn't believe in helmets.

Denise looks sick, turns away. The Vet stares off into space,
remembering something, and when he continues his voice is dead,
hollow, full of pain.

> All the time I was over there, I knew I'd be coming back, I
> knew I'd find you again and make it right between us . . . and
> then your mother wrote me that letter.
> > (beat, with great difficulty)
> I was short, man. I was so short. I shoulda known better, but
> I wasn't thinking right, wasn't paying attention. You got to pay
> attention. I felt it when I stepped on it. It makes this sound,
> this little click.
> > (looks at them)
> That kind of mine . . . it don't go off when you step on it, you
> know. It's when you take your weight off. The rest of the guys
> just looked at me. I told them to get the hell away, and they
> backed off one by one, but they all kept looking at me, staring
> at the dead man who was standing there shouting at them.
> Even when they were all out of range, I couldn't move. But
> they were watching me, all of them watching me, and finally I
> couldn't take it no more. I jumped.
> > (bitter laugh)
> We never could jump very far, huh Jeffy?

CLOSE ON JEFF

For a beat, the silence is profound.

> > JEFF
> You saved them. You saved their lives.

BACK TO THE SCENE

> > VET
> Yeah. They gave me a medal.

> > JEFF
> You saved them.
> > (turns away)
> And I didn't. That's it, isn't it? I wasn't there.

He <u>flings</u> the poker away violently, and it smashes off a wall. Jeff turns back, angry.

> JEFF
> All right, then. Guilty, I'm guilty. I took . . . the other road. But whatever . . . retribution is due, it's mine. Denise and Megan have nothing to do with it. Whatever you have to do, leave them out of it.

ANGLE ON DENISE
as she listens to Jeff with fear, horror.

> DENISE
> No!
> (looks to Vet)
> I went with him to Canada. We decided together. I'm part of him, and everything that happens to him.

ANGLE ON THE VET

After a long beat, he smiles gently.

> VET
> I know. That's why I loved you, Denny.
> (to Jeff)
> You don't understand, man. You think I'd hurt <u>them</u>?
> (laughs)
> And they say us vets are crazy.

BACK TO THE SCENE

> JEFF
> Then . . . <u>why</u>? Why are you here?

> VET
> Good question.
> (grim smile)
> I'm dyin', man.

> DENISE
> My god . . .

VET

The doctors never tell you, but I feel it coming. And it's okay
... I lost everything important a long time ago ... my legs, my
girl, my future. Even Jeff. And Spaceman, he didn't have
nothing but some real nasty memories.
(beat)
I was in the VA ... waiting to get it over with ... and I kept
thinking about Denny, you know? Wondering how it would of
come out if I'd done it different. I guess I just ... <u>wondered</u>
myself here, huh?
(laughs)
I always liked ghosts, but I never thought I'd be one.

The Vet turns his wheelchair to face Jeff.

VET
(continues)
I just wanted ... to see them.
(beat, smile)
You did okay, McDowell.

Jeff shakes his head, obviously eaten up by guilt. He's sound and
whole, but he's the guy in the chair too, and his face is corroded by
self-doubt.

JEFF
You did okay. I wasn't there –

Unable to face his crippled counterpart, Jeff turns away.

VET
(softly)
I wasn't there either. Not for Denise. Not for Megan.

The Vet rolls himself over to a dresser, and picks up a framed
photograph of Megan, stares at it.

VET
(continues)
If you can hold your little girl in your arms and think for even
a second that you did anything wrong, then you're the
dumbest human being ever walked the face of the earth.

Believe me, Jeff. You didn't miss nothing.

ANGLE ON JEFF

As he turns back, reacting to what the Vet has said, to the obvious truth of it. He's choked up. Denise goes to him, wordlessly. They embrace.

> VET
> I think ... maybe it's time I went.

Denise turns to him.

> DENISE
> You don't have to. I mean, you can stay.

> VET
> (sadly)
> No. I can't. At least now I've got a few things to remember, huh?

Jeff reacts sharply; he's had a thought.

> JEFF
> The flashbacks—
> (beat)
> You and me, we're the same person. It has to work both ways.
> (beat, decisively)
> I've got memories too. Maybe if we touched, or—

He steps forward, but the Vet rolls backward, away from him.

> VET
> No! You don't know what you're talking about.

> JEFF
> (softly, with compassion)
> I'm talking about the day Denise and I got married. Our honeymoon. The day Megan was born.

> VET
> (bitterly)

It ain't one way, Jeff. Think of what you'll get in return. You'll
remember them dyin' around you. The hospitals, the years in
the chair.
                              (beat)
You'll remember standing there while they backed away from
you, watching you, all of them watching you. You won't sleep
so good, and sometimes you'll wake up screaming.

Jeff hesitates, looks to Denise. She nods. He kisses her, steps toward
the Vet.

                              JEFF
I'm not afraid of a few nightmares.
                              (wry smile)
I can always hide under the blankets, right?

He holds out his hand. The Vet stares up at him, then, very slowly,
reaches out and takes Jeff's hand in both of his. Jeff winces sharply,
as if in pain. The Vet closes his eyes. Tears begin to run down his
cheek.

CLOSE ON DENISE

as she watches.

ANGLE PAST DENISE ON SCENE

The two Jeff McDowells seem to glow with a strange blue-green light,
as ghostly afterimages flicker about each of them. Her Jeff, standing,
seems for a moment to be wearing a uniform, and then a long straggly
beard. The Vet appears to be dressed in a 60s-style tux, then in civilian
clothes; his trouser legs FILL OUT as LEGS shimmer into view,
spectral and glowing, but legs nonetheless. He opens his eyes, stares in
wonder, then RISES from the chair.

                              VET
I guess maybe we're both heroes, huh?

The Vet, now standing, EMBRACES Jeff, the strange light playing all
about them.

Then the two bodies seem to MELT into each other, to MERGE and become one. The light grows so intense that Denise shies away, covers her eyes.

When the glow fades, the wheelchair and the Vet are gone, and only the original Jeff McDowell remains. Denise runs to him, and they embrace, holding each other very tight and hard. We HOLD the shot as the NARRATOR'S voice comes up.

NARRATOR

We make our choices, and afterwards wonder what that other road was like. Jeff McDowell found out, and paid the toll. A lesson in courage and cartography, from the mapmakers of the Twilight Zone.

THE END

Doorways

FADE IN

EXT. – FREEWAY – NIGHT – AERIAL

Traffic is fast and heavy. Suddenly we hear a CRACK, as loud as a clap of thunder, as sharp as a sonic boom.

                    SMASH CUT TO TIGHT ON CAT

A girl stands trapped in the center of the freeway, as speeding traffic surges around her. Call her CAT. She's twenty. Her figure is lean, boyish, wiry-tough. Her hair is short, raggedly shorn. There is something wild about her, something quick and feral and not-quite-tamed. Her pants are leather, old, cracked, badly worn. She wears a loose black uniform shirt several sizes too big for her, unbuttoned, over a tight silver-gray undershirt. Her feet are bare. She looks lost, confused . . .

INTERCUT – CAT'S POV

HEADLIGHTS are coming at her from all directions, it seems, cars are missing her by inches.

RESUME CAT

She tries to dart toward the shoulder, misjudges the speed of traffic. A car almost hits her, its horn BLARING. Cat jumps back.

A second car SWERVES to avoid her. Brakes SQUEAL. More HORNS sound. Cat spins, searching for a way out. She takes a step in the other direction, jumps back as two cars SLAM TOGETHER. Metal CRUNCHES with impact. More HORNS. Off in the distance, we HEAR police SIRENS too.

CLOSE ON CAT

She covers her ears against the noise, draws herself in protectively, closes her eyes amidst the chaos . . .
Suddenly she is AWASH IN BLINDING LIGHT, and we hear the deep, terrifying sound of a big truck's AIR HORN. Her eyes snap open.

REVERSE ANGLE

A huge SEMI is bearing down on her.

RESUME CAT

She freezes, like a deer pinned by the truck's lights. Then the fear is replaced by defiance. From under her shirt, she pulls a WEAPON; sleek and strange, like no gun we have ever seen. Cat swings it up quickly, aims with both hands, and FIRES. The only sound is a soft PHUT of compressed air as the weapon spits out a needle.

ANGLE ON THE SEMI

One moment it is roaring forward at sixty miles an hour, its horn screaming, its headlights blinding. Then it EXPLODES. The cab blows apart, sending chunks of glass and metal flying in all directions. The huge truck careens wildly out of control, veers off to one side, and CRASHES. A second EXPLOSION rocks the truck as its gas tank blows, sending up a towering ball of flame.

CAT

is turning to make a break for the shoulder when a spinning piece of debris from the explosion comes flying at her. She ducks, but not fast enough. She catches a glancing blow on the forehead. The impact sends her sprawling.

PUSH IN TIGHT

Cat lies on the road, unconscious, bleeding from a cut over one eye. The weapon has slipped from her grasp, and the sleeve of her shirt has ridden up to reveal an ornate bracelet clasped around her right forearm. It's a strange piece, a Gigeresgue tangle of silvery metal inset with three parallel slashes of dark plastic, that coils around her arm like a nest of snakes.

OFF that image, we

FADE OUT

END OF TEASER

ACT I

FADE IN

EXT. – HOSPITAL – NIGHT

SIRENS scream through the night as an ambulance races down the freeway, closely followed by two POLICE CRUISERS with lights flashing.

CUT TO

INT. – EMERGENCY ROOM – NIGHT

An eight-year old BOY sits on an examination table, surrounded by his MOTHER, a young doctor (TOM), and a heavyset nurse (MADGE).

> TOM
> Not like that. Look at that mess. No, you have to keep your hand steady. It's a delicate operation. Mistakes can be fatal. Here, watch.

REVERSE ANGLE

Tom holds up his hand, palm down. He is twenty-seven, dark haired, rumpled, confident. The nameplate on his greens reads LAKE. He has a quarter between two fingers. He 'walks' it across his hand, flips it up in the air, catches it, opens his hand. He pulls it out from behind the boy's ear.

> TOM
> What did I tell you. Magic is easy. Diagnosis is hard.

He grins at the young patient, who LAUGHS with delight. The nurse and the mother smile fondly. In b.g., we HEAR the sound of SIRENS. Tom hears it too.

>TOM
>(to boy)
And for my next trick, I make you disappear.
>(to mother)
He'll be fine.

INT. – HOSPITAL – NIGHT

Two PARAMEDICS rush a gurney down a corridor to the Emergency Room. A pair of cops (CHAMBERS and SANCHEZ) follow close behind.

TRACKING WITH THE GURNEY

Tom falls in beside the gurney.

>TOM
What do we have?

>PARAMEDIC
Head injury, facial lacerations, maybe some internal. Her vitals are real strong, but she's non-responsive.

A gauze bandage covers Cat's cut; it's PINK with blood.

>SANCHEZ
She was playing tag out on the freeway. Blew the crap out of a semi with some weird gun.

INT. – EMERGENCY ROOM – CONTINUOUS

They push through a set of double doors into the ER.

>TOM
We'll take it from here. Madge, notify X-Ray I'm sending someone up. Tell them I'll need a full set of cranials.

The nurse scrawls a signature for the paramedics. They EXIT as Tom begins his examination of Cat. He feels gently around her neck, searching for breaks. Lifts the gauze pad to examine her head injury. When he pushes up her sleeve to take her pulse, he reveals her strange bracelet. He touches it.

TIGHT ON CAT

Her eyes snap open and Cat MOVES. She grabs Tom by the crotch and SQUEEZES. Tom GASPS in shock and pain.

RESUME

Cat rolls off as Tom collapses, on her feet with all the speed of her namesake. Chambers jumps her. Cat tries to punch him, but he grabs first one arm, then the other. He holds her by the wrists as she struggles.

> CHAMBERS
> You're under arrest, girly. You have the right to remain silent. You have the—

Cat throws herself right up against him, face to face, and BITES him on the nose. Chambers SCREAMS and grabs his face. BLOOD seeps between his fingers. Cat scrambles away.
Sanchez cuts off her exit. Tom is on his knees, unsteady, gasping for breath.

Cat backs off and SPITS a piece of the cop's nose onto the floor. There's a smear of blood around her mouth.

She snatches up a metal IV stand and holds it in front of her like a quarterstaff, ready for anyone.

Sanchez draws his gun.

> TOM

NO!
> (panting a little)

Put that ... put that away. This is ... a hospital.

> SANCHEZ
> She's psycho.

Tom pulls himself unsteadily to his feet.

> TOM
>
> She's scared. Look at her.

> CHAMBERS
>
> My nose . . .

> TOM
>
> It's around here somewhere. We can fix it. Madge, find the
> officer's nose.
>
> (to Cat)
>
> Don't be afraid. No one will hurt you. Promise.

She's watching him now, warily. She says nothing. Tom edges closer.
Cat gives a short, threatening swing of the pole.

> SANCHEZ
>
> I wouldn't go any closer if I was you. Doc.

> MADGE
>
> Tom, be careful. I don't think she understands English.

Tom keeps all his attention on Cat.

> TOM
>
> That's a nasty cut there.

Cat touches her face. Her fingers come away wet with blood.

> TOM
>
> Can I take a look at it? Put that down, why don't you? I won't
> hurt you.

TIGHT ON TOM AND CAT

A tense moment. He is right beside her now. He lifts a hand to her
face. No sudden movements. Cat is taut, poised. Tom turns her face to
one side to examine the gash.

> TOM
>
> Not as bad as it looks. Still, we better get an X-ray. Will you
> come with me?

Tom offers her his hand. Cat hesitates a long moment. Then she FLINGS AWAY the pole. It falls with a clatter.

> SANCHEZ
> Real good. We'll take her now, Doc.

Tom faces him down. The nurse is visible in E.G., on her hands and knees, searching for the missing bit of nose.

> TOM
> I'm admitting this patient overnight for observation.

> SANCHEZ
> She's under arrest. We'll observe her down in lockup.

> TOM
> You want the responsibility of removing her against medical advice?
> (off his hesitation)
> I didn't think so.

Madge triumphantly holds up something we cannot see.

> MADGE
> I found it!

> DISSOLVE TO

INT. – HOSPITAL ROOM – LATER THAT NIGHT A semi-private room with two beds.

CLOSE ON CAT

She stands by the window, dressed in a hospital gown now, looking out over the city lights like one entranced. The gash over her eye has been stitched and bandaged.

Cat pushes back her sleeve to expose the bracelet clasped around her forearm. She raises her arm, palm down, points it toward the window and the city beyond.

TIGHT ON CAT'S ARM

as she makes a fist. Inset deeply into the coiling metal are three matte
black SLASHES, roughly parallel, sinuous, suggestive.

Now those slashes begin to GLOW: very faint at first, a dim BLUE.
Slowly, deliberately, Cat moves her arm from right to left and back
again. The blue glow BRIGHTENS when she swings toward the east,
DIMS when her fist points west again.

CLOSE ON CAT

Her face solemn, her concentration fierce. She sweeps her arm back
and forth again; the glow BRIGHTENS and FADES.

She turns her arm over, opening her fingers.

TIGHT ON CAT'S HAND

As a HOLOGRAM springs to vivid life in her palm: a small, three-
dimensional EARTH, turning slowly. She holds a miniature world in
her hand. Strange swirling SYMBOLS run across its face, like stock
quotations on an electronic ticker.

Behind her, we HEAR the sound of a door OPENING.

RESUME CAT

She WHIRLS. The globe WINKS OUT at once.

REVERSE ANGLE – ON TOM

A uniformed POLICEMAN opens the door for him. Tom is carrying
her clothing, neatly folded. He can see how jumpy she is.

                                TOM
        Did I startle you? I'm sorry. I just wanted to see how you were
        doing.

He closes the door behind him. Cat seems to relax.

                                TOM
        I brought your clothes. We washed them for you.

Tom places the pile of clothing on the bed.

> TOM
> There's a new pair of jeans in there. Your pants were, ah,
> beyond salvage.

ANGLE ON CAT

Cat crosses the room and snatches up the clothing. She clutches it
tight against her chest.

ANGLE PAST CAT ON TOM

A little taken aback by the fierce possessiveness.

> TOM
> I know how you feel. My girlfriend is always throwing out my
> favorite shirts.

Cat slips out of the hospital gown, letting it puddle on the floor at
her
legs. She is naked underneath. We see her bare back as Cat starts to
dress.

She does it without a trace of self-consciousness or shame. Tom turns
his back, more embarrassed than she is.

She pulls on the silvery undershirt, SNIFFS at the jeans, steps into
them. Tom keeps up a stream of talk.

> TOM
> I didn't catch your name. I'm Dr Lake. Thomas.
> (nothing)
> We've got you down as a Jane Doe. For the paperwork. The
> office wants to know if you have any medical insurance, Jane.

CAT

is dressed now. She crosses the room to the door, tries to open it. It's
locked.

> TOM
>
> It's locked. I don't think the cops want you going anywhere right now.

Cat SLAMS a fist against the door.

> TOM
>
> Look, I know the food's not great, but there are worse places to spend the night.

Cat moves to the window. She looks down. She starts to push at the glass, looking for a way to open it.

> TOM
>
> Don't get any ideas. We're four floors up. Besides, this is a modern hospital. None of the windows open.

Cat gives up, turns away angrily.

CLOSE ON TOM

A dawning suspicion in his eyes.

RESUME

Cat retreats to a corner of the room, sinks down to the floor. Her stare is sullen, angry. Tom looks at her thoughtfully.

> TOM
>
> You knew what I was saying. About the window.

Cat watches him. Her face gives nothing away. Tom moves closer, smiling despite himself.

> TOM
>
> You little con artist. You hear me.

Cat turns her head away from him.

> TOM
>
> This would be a lot easier if you'd talk to me.

She ignores him.

                          TOM
      Come on. Say something. Anything. Name, rank, phone
      number, I don't care. What's your sign? What's your favorite
      color? You like anchovies on your pizza?
                          (nothing)
      Fine. I don't need to waste my time.

Scowling, Tom KNOCKS on the door.

ANGLE ON THE DOOR

The POLICEMAN opens the door from outside.

                       POLICEMAN
      All through in here, Dr Lake?

                          TOM
      I guess we are.

He is about to exit when . . .

                          CAT
                        (soft)
      Cat.

                          TOM
      She talks . . .
                        (to policeman)
      Maybe you better give us a few more minutes.

The policeman closes the door, leaving them alone.

                          TOM
      Did you say something?

                          CAT
                     (a beat, then:)
      Cat.

                          TOM
      Cat? Like in Catherine?

CAT

Cat. Name.

(shy smile)

Toe Mas.

Cat speaks with a slight ACCENT. Nothing we can easily put a finger on, nothing that suggests any known country or region, but a musical lilt to her words that hints that somehow she is a stranger in this place.

TOM

Bingo. Toe Mas. Toe Mas Lake.

(beat)

How about an address? Do you have a family? A boyfriend? Anyone we can contact?

(no response)

Where did you come from?

Cat gets up from the floor.

CAT

Earth.

TOM

That clarifies things. What part of Earth?

CAT

Angels.

TOM

Angels . . . you mean L.A.? Los Angeles? Here?

CAT

Not here. There. Angels.

TOM

Okay. How did you get from there to here?

CAT

Door.

Now it's his turn to look blank.

                          TOM
On the freeway? A car door?

                          CAT
Door between.
                       (impatient)
Leaving now, Toe Mas. Going now. Getting out.

She gets up, strides to the door, pulls at it. It's locked. She looks at
Tom, expecting him to help.

                          TOM
That door only opens for me right now. Sorry.

Firmly, but gently, he moves her away from the door, KNOCKS. The
policeman in the hall opens for him.

                          TOM
Look, my girlfriend's a lawyer. I'll talk to her. That's all I can
do for you right now.

                          CAT
Not knowing lawyer.

                          TOM
You really must be from another country.

He EXITS, the door closes, and Cat throws herself on the bed,
frustrated and trapped.

                                          DISSOLVE TO

EXT. – BEACHFRONT APARTMENT – NEAR DAWN

Tom's car, a little Mazda Miata, pulls up in front of a ramshackle old
wooden apartment building by the beach.

INT. – TOM'S BEDROOM – DAWN

A woman is asleep in a big brass bed, under a rumpled sheet. In b.g.
are lots of bookcases crammed with medical texts, law books, and
paperbacks. Right over the bed, very prominent, is Tom's framed
antique poster for a performance featuring HARRY HOUDINI.

The woman in the bed is in her late twenties, pretty, with long red hair. Her name is LAURA.

Tom sits on the bed beside her. He touches her shoulder, gently, Laura rolls over, muttering a protest. Tom shakes her a little harder. Her eyes open.

> LAURA
> (sleepy)
> Tom? Is that you? What time is it? You just get home?
> (glances at clock)
> Oh, god, it's too early. Go away. Leave me alone.

Laura rolls over and pulls the sheet back over her head. Tom gently tugs it down again.

> TOM
> Wake up. Coffee's on. Jump in the shower and put on your shyster hat. I need help.

Tom moves off. Laura SIGHS, stirs. She sits up in bed, grumpy but awake.

INT. – TOM'S KITCHEN – DAWN

Laura sits at the kitchen table. She has slipped into a terrycloth robe. Her hair is still tousled from sleep. She cradles a steaming mug of coffee and listens. Tom paces the kitchen floor, restless, angry.

> TOM
> I tell you, there's something very strange about this girl.

> LAURA
> She obviously made quite a first impression. Normally you don't get so involved with people who knee you in the groin.

> TOM
> It wasn't a knee. Look, can you help her?

> LAURA
> I'll see what I can do. Did she really bite off his nose?

                              TOM
                            (glumly)
    Just the end bit.

Laura can't help but smile.

                              LAURA
    That's something. If you bite off the whole nose they really
    throw the book at you.

She finishes her coffee and gets up. Tom grabs her, pulls her close for
a kiss.

                              TOM
    I'll owe you one.

TIGHT ON TOM AND LAURA

as he puts his arms around her.

                              LAURA
                            (playful)
    So, is she cute? Should I be jealous?

                              TOM
    What is this, cross-examination?

                              LAURA
    The witness is instructed to answer the question.

                              TOM
    Not guilty.

Their lips move together.

                              LAURA
    Good. Otherwise . . .

Laura changes direction. Instead of kissing, she snaps her teeth
together and lightly nips at the end of his nose. Tom breaks up. They
laugh together, then kiss.

                                                        CUT TO

EXT. – FREEWAY – DAWN

The burned wreckage of the semi still blocks part of one lane and spills across most of the shoulder. A road crew with a CRANE and a FLATBED TRUCK works to remove the wreck. The predawn traffic is light.

> WORKER
>
> Last year it was just freeway shootinqs. Now they're using missiles.

> FOREMAN
>
> From now on, I stick to surface streets.

Suddenly we hear a CRACK, as loud as a clap of thunder, as sharp as a sonic boom.

> FOREMAN
>
> What the hell . . .

The crane stops; its lights, its engine, everything. The big flatbed truck dies simultaneously. All the other lights in b.g. also go off: houses, cars, streetlamps.

ANGLE DOWN FREEWAY – FOREMAN'S POV

Only two or three cars are in sight. All of them are dead or dying: headlights out, engines giving up the ghost, slowly coasting to a halt, drivers climbing out.

RESUME

The worker is banging a big emergency flashlight against the heel of his hand, flicking the switch on and off.

> WORKER
>
> I don't get this, I just put in new batteries.

But the foreman isn't listening. We HEAR slow, ominous footsteps.

FOREMAN'S POV

Six figures fan out across the freeway. They were not there a moment
ago. Now they are. There are three men, three women. The women are
as lean and tough and hard-looking as the men. They wear high black
boots, black uniforms with silver metallic trim. Their hair is cropped
close to their skulls.

Behind them comes a strange vehicle, a PALANQUIN or open sedan
chair of black metal, as big as a Caddy, with long OUTRIDERS on
either side, as on an outrigger canoe. It FLOATS three feet above the
roadway, moving in utter silence, its line alien, suggestive, almost
organic. A single passenger rides inside, surrounded by a roiling
grayness: the DARKFIELD, a cloud that drinks light, making
everything within vague and mysterious, like shapes half-seen in fog.
All we can tell is that the passenger inside is hunched and massive,
altogether huge by human standards.

REVERSE ANGLE

The foreman and his road crew stare at these apparitions before them.
A few have the sense to be afraid.

REVERSE ANGLE – TIGHT ON THANE

The leader of the six on foot is THANE. His collar displays the insignia
of rank: a silver pin in the shape of a hound's head. He is in his
thirties, awesomely fit, with eyes like ice. A hunter's eyes. A warrior's
eyes.

His eyes meet the foreman's for a second.

One by one, the hunters step aboard the palanquin, taking up
position on the outriders like footmen on a carriage.

Thane boards last. The palanquin vanishes into the darkness.

THE ROAD CREW

stands in a stunned silence for a moment.

                         WORKER
             What the hell just happened?

FOREMAN
I don't think I want to know.

All at once, the power returns: headlights, streetlamps, flashlight, everything.

FADE OUT

END OF ACT I

ACT II

FADE IN

INT. – HOSPITAL CORRIDOR – AFTERNOON

Tom strides down the corridor, whistling. Then he notices something odd: no cop by Cat's door. He stops whistling, moves to the door, opens it.

ANGLE INTO ROOM – TOM'S POV

Cat's room is EMPTY, spotless, the bed freshly made. No one has been here for hours.

RESUME

People are coming and going: nurses, patients, a NUTRITIONIST with a food tray, an ORDERLY.

TOM
Pete, what happened to the girl in this room? Did they move her somewhere?

ORDERLY
Room was empty when I came on shift, man.

NUTRITIONIST
That patient was discharged last night, Doctor.

TOM
By who? I didn't authorize any discharge. Did anyone see the police leave?

Shrugs. No one knows, no one cares. Except one OLD WOMAN struggling down the hall, leaning on a walker.

> OLD WOMAN
> They took her. Men in suits. It was three in the morning. She woke me up, the way she was screaming and kicking.

> TOM
> God _damn_ it!

He goes striding off angrily.

> CUT TO

INT. – ER NURSE'S STATION – MOMENTS LATER

TIGHT ON TOM

He is on the phone, still furious. INTERCUT with shots of Laura, behind her desk in a legal office.

> TOM
> What do you mean she wasn't arrested?

> LAURA
> I mean there's no arrest report. No paper of any kind. Your little feline friend was never arraigned. The incident was never logged. Officers Sanchez and Chambers are mysteriously unavailable.

> TOM
> They can't just pretend it never happened. There must have been a hundred witnesses.

> LAURA
> You didn't happen to get the names of any, did you?

CLOSE ON A HAND

Before Tom can answer, a hand ENTERS FRAME and depresses the button on the receiver.

ANGLE PAST TOM

Still holding the dead phone, he turns to face an imposing man in a dark gray suit: TRAGER. About fifty, his suit impeccable, his hair carefully combed, Trager is a man of ice and iron.

> TRAGER
>
> Dr Thomas John Lake?

Tom just glares at him. Trager flashes a badge.

> TRAGER
>
> Special agent Trager, federal intelligence unit. Would you come with me, please?

Tom makes the connection. He's suspicious and angry.

> TOM
>
> Why?
>
> (beat)
>
> You removed a patient of mine from this hospital last night. Illegally. Who the hell do you think you are? What have you done with Cat?

> TRAGER
>
> Is that her name? She's in good care, Doctor. She'd like to see you.

> TOM
>
> I'm not going anywhere with you until I've talked to my lawyer.

Trager has had enough; his patience runs out.

> TRAGER
>
> Fine. You get one phone call. Tell her you're under arrest.

> TOM
>
> You can't do that!

> TRAGER
>
> You'd be astonished at what we can do, Doctor.
>
> (beat)
>
> On the other hand, if you'll give us your cooperation . . .

                              TOM
                        (reconsidering)
              I'll call someone to fill in for me.

CUT TO

EXT. – HOSPITAL – NIGHT

Trager escorts Tom out of the hospital. A long black limo with tinted windows waits by the curb. They get in.

INT. – LIMOUSINE – CONTINUOUS

Trager climbs in after Tom and closes the door. The car moves off without a word. A second man sits across from them: thirtyish, sandy-haired, muscular.

                            TRAGER
              This is agent Cameron.

Agent Cameron wears a blue suit and a large white BANDAGE over his nose that covers the center of his face. He looks unhappy.

                              TOM
              I see you've met Cat.

Cameron gives him a foul-tempered stare. Tom turns his head away and fakes a COUGH, covering his mouth to hide the smile he cannot quite suppress.

DISSOLVE TO

EXT. – DESERT BASE – NIGHT

The high desert of California. A uniformed GUARD waves the limo through a gate in a high chain link fence. On one side of the gate a sign says AUTHORIZED PERSONNEL ONLY; on the other DANGER HIGH VOLTAGE. Beyond the fence are the quonset huts and ugly cinder-block buildings of an abandoned army base.

INT. – DESERT BASE – NIGHT – TRACKING

Trager and Cameron escort Tom down a long windowless corridor. They pass one section where the wall has been BLOWN OUT; through a jagged blackened hole we glimpse a long interior room GUTTED by fire, its ceiling collapsed.

                    TOM
          You have a fire?

                    TRAGER
          Our shooting range. One of our bright boys decided to test fire
          your girlfriend's gun.

                    TOM
          She's not my girlfriend.

                    TRAGER
          Whatever. In here, please. There are some things I want you to
          see.

He opens a door. Tom steps through.

INT. – TRAGER'S OFFICE – NIGHT – TIGHT ON A WALL SAFE

A high tech, electronic safe with a card slot and numerical keyboard. Trager's HAND inserts a plastic security card into a slot. The keypad LIGHTS. Trager punches in a sequence of numbers. The safe swings open; Trager begins to remove the contents.

ANGLE DOWN ON DESK

as Trager spreads out Cat's weapon, her bracelet, three BLACK CYLINDERS. A hundred-odd BLACK PLASTIC NEEDLES are scattered across the desktop.

ANGLE UP

Trager and Tom have been joined by MATSUMOTO, a government scientist, Asian, forty, wearing a lab coat.

                    TOM
          She blew up a semi with that?

TRAGER

Correct. Go on, pick it up.

Tom lifts the weapon, sights down the barrel.

TOM

I used to have a water pistol that looked like this.

TRAGER

Close. Try a beebee gun.

MATSUMOTO

An air gun, more precisely. Quite sophisticated. I doubt we could duplicate it. It uses a high-velocity jet of pressurized air to spit out . . .

Matsumoto lifts a thin black needle with tweezers.

MATSUMOTO

. . . these.

TOM

Needles?

MATSUMOTO

Needles with the explosive power of a bazooka round.

TRAGER

This beebee gun has teeth.

Matsumoto picks up a cylinder: black, long as a finger.

MATSUMOTO

The police found three of these magazines in her pockets. Each one holds one hundred forty-four needles, and . . .

He pulls a cap off the back. Inside, built-in, is a POWER CELL; it pulses with RED LIGHT.

MATSUMOTO
(continuous)
. . . its own power cell. So you recharge every time you reload.

If Detroit had battery technology this good, we'd all be driving electric cars.

Tom is still hefting the weapon.

                    TOM
    Awkward grip. I can barely reach the trigger.

                  TRAGER
    The girl had to use both hands to fire it.

                    TOM
    Bad design . . .

                 MATSUMOTO
    Unless the gun was designed for someone with bigger hands.

                    TOM
    You'd need fingers like a squid.

Tom puts down the weapon, picks up the bracelet.

                    TOM
    She was wearing this when the paramedics brought her in.

                  TRAGER
    It seems to be very important to her.

                    TOM
    What is it?

                 MATSUMOTO
    The metal is a superconductive alloy. I've never seen anything like it. Inside it's solid microcircuitry. Very odd microcircuitry. Parts of it seem almost organic.

                    TOM
    But what does it do?

                 MATSUMOTO
    At a guess . . . it detects certain unusual subatomic particles.

Tom looks blankly over at Trager. He's lost.

                    TOM
    I don't understand any of this.

                    TRAGER
    Neither do we. That's why you're here. We need answers,
    Doctor. And the girl won't talk to anyone but you.

OFF Tom's silent, reluctant agreement, we

                                        CUT TO

INT. – CORRIDOR – NIGHT

A uniformed MATRON is seated outside a locked door, beside a
window of oneway glass. Cat is visible inside, curled up on a bed,
listless, in prison grays. The matron fans herself with a small HAND
FAN, its accordion folds alternately red and black.

                    TRAGER
    How's our guest?

                    MATRON
    Quiet. She just lays there, staring off. I don't blame her, in this
    heat.

                    TRAGER
    Let him in.

He gives the bracelet over to Tom.

                    TRAGER
    Your conversation will be monitored and recorded.

The matron unlocks the door. Tom enters.

INT. – CAT'S CELL – CONTINUOUS

Cat looks up slowly.

                    CAT
    Toe Mas.

Cat gets up. She sees the bracelet. Her eyes WIDEN. She moves across the room, reaching for it.

> CAT
>
> Mine! Give it, Toe Mas.

> TOM
>
> First we need to talk.

Cat doesn't take no for an answer. She reaches for the bracelet. Tom holds it out of her reach.

> CAT
>
> Give it now. Needing it now. Coming soon. Coming after.

> TOM
>
> Who is coming after?

> CAT
>
> Darklords! Manhounds! Give!

> TOM
>
> Tell me what it is and you can have it back.

Cat almost spits the word at him.

> CAT
>
> Geon. Give it now!

Tom TOSSES it to her. Cat snatches it out of the air, slides it back onto her arm. It seems to calm her.

> TOM
>
> What does it do, Cat? What's it for?

> CAT
>
> Finding doors. Doors between. Doors away.

Backing away from Tom, Cat extends her arm, hand tight in a fist. She turns in a slow circle, sweeping the room.

TOM

What kind of doors? Cat, what are you doing?

She ignores him, concentrating. The device can't find a reading in this enclosed place. It stays dark.

CAT

No good, no good, <u>no good</u>.

TOM

Cat, where did you get that? And the gun, the air gun . . .
(off her blank look)
The weapon, the . . .

Frustrated, Tom does a pantomime of lifting the gun with both hands, firing, with appropriate sound effects.

TOM

You know . . . phut . . . <u>BOOM!</u>

He shapes an EXPLOSION with his hands. Cat giggles.

CAT

Phut BOOM?

TOM

Right. The phut boom. Where did you get the phut boom?

She looks at him as though he were a moron.

CAT

Hand cannon, Toe Mas. Stealing it. Not-for-men, hand cannon.
(beat)
Needing it, taking it.

TOM

What did you need the hand cannon for?

CAT

Shooting. Killing.
(off his reaction)
Getting <u>away</u>, Toe Mas.

Cat is getting more and more agitated. She looks around the sealed room desperately, searching for a way out.

> CAT
>
> Lights <u>out!</u> Darklords coming soon.

> TOM
>
> The ... darklords. Is that a gang?

> CAT
>
> Darklords <u>masters.</u> Darklords <u>owners.</u>

> TOM
>
> And the ... manhounds?

> CAT
> (whisper)
>
> Thane ...

Tom can see the fear on her face now. This conversation is getting to her. She tries the door to the room. It's locked, of course. Cat spins away in frustration.

> TOM
>
> Hey, take it easy. I don't know who these people are, but they can't get to you here. You're safe.

Instead of calming her, that just drives her WILD. Grabbing up a CHAIR, she swings at the mirrored window with all her strength. It bounces off the glass. Cat swings it again and again. The mirror begins to BREAK. A spiderweb of CRACKS fissures out.

> CAT
> (screaming)
>
> Not safe! Not safe! Not safe!

The mirror SHATTERS, showering the hall outside with pieces of one-way glass. Cat is about to leap through the broken window when Tom grabs her, restrains her.

> TOM
>
> Cat, stop. Don't ...

He holds her tight, trying to comfort her, as the door opens and
Cameron and the Matron come running in.

DISSOLVE TO

EXT. – CANYONS – NIGHT

A densely wooded canyon outside Los Angeles. Thane stands on a
precipice, looking down at the city lights. His face is a mask. A woman
comes up beside him: DYANA. He senses her presence.

THANE
So many men, Dyana. Their lights go on forever.

DYANA
This is but a shadow of the trueworld, the master says.

THANE
Perhaps the masters of this world say the same thing of our
own.

Thane turns his head very slowly toward the east, as if he is listening
to something no one else can hear.

DYANA
What is it? Do you have a reading? Is she using the
geosyncronator?

When Thane speaks, it is not to Dyana.

THANE
I hear you, Cat. Even now, you call to me.

He turns sharply back to Dyana, all business.

THANE
East, northeast, three hundred hexes.

CUT TO

INT. TRAGER'S OFFICE – NIGHT

Trager behind a desk. Tom is pacing. Cameron sits in the visitor's chair, snapping a rubber band.

> CAMERON
>
> Pentathol.

> TOM
>
> No. She's my patient. I won't allow you to drug her.

> TRAGER
>
> We gave you a chance to do it your way, Doctor.

Tom leans over Trager's desk.

> TOM
>
> Give me one more shot at it. Let me hypnotize her.

Trager steeples his fingers, thinks, NODS.

CUT TO

INT. – TRAGER'S OFFICE – LATER

The lights have been turned down low. Cat sits in the visitor's chair, Tom close to her side. Trager is behind his desk, watching, Cameron stands.

> TOM
>
> ... deeper. You hear nothing but my voice now. There are no other sounds, no other voices. Only me. You are relaxed. So relaxed. Floating. All the fear has gone away.

Cat is deep in a trance.

> TOM
>
> Tell us your name. Your whole name.

> CAT

Cat.

Tom frowns. Trager and Cameron exchange glances.

> TOM
>
> All right. Cat, tell us about the place you come from.

                              CAT
All dark. Lights out.

                              TOM
Does it have a name?

                              CAT
Angels.

                              TOM
Where is it?

                              CAT
Behind. Other side.

                              TOM
The other side of . . . the door?

Cat NODS agreement. Tom continues, his voice gentle.

                              TOM
I am going to ask you something else now. You will not be
afraid. All the fear is gone.
                           (beat)
Cat, who are the darklords?

                              CAT
Owners. Masters.

                              TOM
What do they own?

                              CAT
Earths.

Behind him, Cameron ROLLS HIS EYES in scorn. Trager's face is
impassive, a mask. Only Tom picks up on the plural.

                              TOM
Earths . . . more than one Earth?

                              CAT
Not all. Some. Many.

TOM

And your world, from . . .

CAT

Darklords came. Long ago. Lights out. Mommy saying. No cars, no guns, no air-o-planes. Ashes, ashes. All fall down.

TOM

All fall down . . .

CAT

Cities. Soldier men. All fall down. Lights out. Long ago.

TOM

How long ago? How many years?

CAT

Before Cat.

TOM

Cat, where did the darklords come from?
(nothing)
From another country?
(no reply)
Another planet? Did they come in ships? Where?

CAT

The doors.

Silence. Trager leans forward.

TRAGER

Ask her about the weapon.

TOM

Cat, the hand cannon . . . you took that from your owner.

CAT
(vehement)
His owner. Owning Thane.

TOM

Thane. Thane was a . . . a manhound?

CAT
(echoing)

Let her live, saying. Give to me, saying. Served you well, saying. Little animal, wanting her, saying.

TOM

You were given to Thane . . .

CAT
(vehement denial)

Not his. Never his. Pretending. Watching. Listening. Knowing.

TOM

Learning . . .

CAT

Waiting. Long waiting. Then taking, running, killing.

TOM

Cat, who did you kill?

CAT

Darklord. Master.

TOM

You learned their secrets, stole the weapon, and escaped through a door, didn't you?

Cat NODS slowly. Cameron looks at Trager.

CAMERON

What the hell is he talking about?

Trager does not reply. He's listening, intent.

TOM

One last question, Cat.
(beat)

How many fingers do the darklords have?

Cat does not respond. Tom holds up a hand in front of her face, his fingers spread wide.

TOM

If this was a darklord's hand, how many fingers would you count?

TIGHT ON CAT – ANGLE THROUGH TOM'S FINGERS

Long hesitation. Finally Cat raises her hand, touching each of Tom's fingers as she counts, SLOWLY.

CAT

One. Two. Three. Four.
(beat)
Five.

'Five' is the thumb. There's a long beat. Cat is still staring at the hand, seeing something else, remembering. Just when we think she's done, her finger moves over PAST Tom's thumb, counting a 'finger' that is not there.

CAT

Six.

Now she is done. Tom closes his fingers into a FIST. In the strained silence that follows that moment, we

FADE OUT

END OF ACT II

ACT III

FADE IN

INT. – TRAGER'S OFFICE – NEAR DAWN

Trager leans forward, presses his intercom.

TRAGER

Griggs, summon the matron, and tell Matsumoto to prepare an injection of pentathol.
(to Tom)

Bring her out of it.

Trager heads for the door. Tom bolts after him.

> TOM
>
> You can't.

Trager EXITS, followed by Tom. Cameron remains with Cat.

CUT TO

INT. – CORRIDOR – CONTINUOUS

Tom catches Trager by the shoulder, spins him around.

> TOM
>
> What do you want from her?

> TRAGER
>
> A story that makes sense.

Matsumoto comes up to them in the hall. He's carrying an instrument case. Tom is still intent on Trager.

> TOM
>
> You refuse to see the truth when it's right in front of your face. How many fingers, Trager?

Tom holds up both hands, fingers spread.

> TRAGER
>
> What is it with you and fingers?

> TOM
>
> I learned to count on my fingers. So did you. It's universal. We have ten fingers, so we count in units of ten. One hundred is ten times ten. One thousand is ten times ten times ten.

> TRAGER
>
> What's your point?

                              TOM

That gun you took from Cat. Matsumoto said the magazines
hold one hundred forty-four rounds. Didn't that strike you as
an odd number?

In b.g., the matron approaches down the hall, FANNING herself,

                            TRAGER

  Maybe.

                              TOM

Twelve times twelve is one hundred forty-four.

Matsumoto gets it, even if Trager does not.

                          MATSUMOTO

Base twelve mathematics. Of course.

                              TOM

A race with <u>twelve</u> fingers would count in twelves, Trager. How
much evidence do you need? Face it. That woman in there is
<u>not</u> a twentieth century American.

                            TRAGER

What are you saying, that she came down from another
planet?

                          MATSUMOTO

Not likely. We've run DNA samples. Her genetic structure is
completely human.

                              TOM

She told you where she came from. Earth. But not our Earth.

                          MATSUMOTO

  A parallel world?

                              TOM

  Exactly.

The matron reaches them and stands fanning herself.

TRAGER

Excuse me?

MATSUMOTO

A neighbor universe. Certain mathematicians have theorized
about the existence of . . . well, a layman would call them
other dimensions. The proofs suggest that an infinite number
of these other timelines may coexist with our own.

TRAGER

What the hell is a timeline?

TOM

Remember the last World Series?

TRAGER

The Braves lost in seven. Cameron was out a week's pay.

TOM

Let me borrow that.
(grabs fan)
What if there was another world where the Braves won? Look,
we think of history as a straight line. Past leads to present.

He holds up the fan, folded: a straight line.

TOM

But if more than one result is possible . . . maybe they both
happen. New worlds are created at each nexus.

Tom unfolds the fan, just one notch. Now one red fold and one black
diverge from the axis pin.

TOM

So you have one world where the Braves won and one world
where the Twins won.
(opens the fan more)
Then you have the world where the Pirates and the Bluejays
played instead.

TOM

(still spreading)

The world where the Dodgers won the pennant. The world where the Dodgers are still in Brooklyn. The world where baseball was never invented and everybody bets on cricket in October.
> (the fan spreads wide)

An infinite numbers of worlds, embracing all the possibilities, all the alternatives. Not a universe. A multiverse.

Trager looks at the fan, then at Matsumoto.

TRAGER
And these other worlds exist?

MATSUMOTO
The math would seem to suggest that. Travel between universes, however, is flatly impossible.
> (shrugs)

In any case, it's all theory.

Trager scowls, takes the fan from Tom, folds it up.

TRAGER
Theory.
> (beat)

Here's a fact, Dr Lake. I'm sorry I ever involved you in this matter. It's time you went home. I'll arrange transport.
> (to matron)

Take her to a holding cell.

TOM
Trager, wait . . .

Tom GRASPS Trager by the arm, holds him for a moment.

TOM
At least give me a few moments alone with her. I want to say good-bye.

ECU – TOM'S OTHER HAND

While one hand is clutching Trager's arm, the other is dipping into his pocket and lifting his wallet.

RESUME

as Trager, unsuspecting, NODS his assent.

> ### TRAGER
> Five minutes. No more.

Trager walks off with Matsumoto. Tom artfully conceals the wallet he's
lifted.

CUT TO

INT. – TRAGER'S OFFICE – CONTINUOUS

Tom re-enters Trager's office. Cat is still in her trance. Cameron is
playing with his rubber band again.

> ### TOM
> Trager wants you.

> ### CAMERON
> (hesitant)
> Who's going to watch her?

> ### TOM
> Watch her do what? Sleep?

Cameron shrugs, and EXITS. Tom LOCKS the office door behind him,
sits beside Cat.

> ### TOM
> I'm going to count to five. When I reach five, you'll wake,
> refreshed, relaxed, unafraid. But you'll be very, very quiet. One.
> Two. Three. Four. Five.

Tom SNAPS his fingers. Cat's eyes open. He puts a finger to her lips.

> ### TOM
> No talking. Just nod.
> (she nods)

There's another door, isn't there? A door out. That's where you
want to go.

> CAT
> (softly)
> Time to go, Toe Mas. Leaving here now.

A long beat; Tom hesitates, his eyes search her face. He reaches a
decision, with vast reluctance.

> TOM
> I'm probably going to regret this, but ... watch the door, Cat.
> If anyone comes through, bite 'em.

Cat nods eagerly and scrambles to her feet. Tom moves to the wall
safe. He fishes the security card from Trager's wallet, inserts it into the
slot, punches some buttons.

> CUT TO

INT. – CORRIDOR – MOMENTS LATER

The matron waits by the door as Cameron and Trager come striding
up. Cameron tries the door. It's locked.

> CAMERON
> Open up in there. What the hell you trying to pull?

Trager motions him aside.

> TRAGER
> Doctor, this is very stupid.

He takes out his keys, unlocks the door, and enters the office with
Cameron right behind him.

TRAGER'S POV

He finds himself face-to-face with Tom ... and the hand cannon. Cat
is sliding the bracelet onto her arm. Trager keeps his cool.

                              TRAGER
You really don't want to do this, Dr Lake. If you fire that in
here, you'll kill all of us. Including your girlfriend.

                               TOM
She's not my girlfriend. We need a car.

                              TRAGER
Shall I tell you how many felonies you're committing?

                               TOM
I'd just as soon you didn't, thanks. That limo will do fine.

                              TRAGER
Cameron, bring the limousine around to the front.

                                                        CUT TO

INT. ENTRANCE – DAWN – ANGLE OUT THE DOOR

Trager stands at the exit with Tom and Cat. All the other guards are
face-down on the floor. Cameron pulls up in the limo.

                               TOM
Let her idle. Okay. Climb out nice and easy and back off.
That's it. A little more. Cat, make sure nobody's hiding in the
backseat.

Cat scrambles out to the limo, checks inside.

                               CAT
Not hiding, Toe Mas.

                               TOM
I didn't plan this, Trager. It's just happening. Don't take it
personally

Trager just looks at him. Tom makes his break for it.

INT. – LIMOUSINE – CONTINUOUS

Tom jumps in and slams the door. Cat is squirming anxiously beside
him in the passenger seat. He tosses the hand cannon into her lap as
he revs the engine, pops the clutch, and takes off.

The limo speeds across the compound. Tom drives with his left hand, fumbles in his pocket with his right, pulls out three black cylinders. He tosses those at Cat too.

> TOM
> Here. See if you can figure out how to load the phut-boom.

Cat GRINS at him, and slides one of the cylinders into the weapon with an audible CLICK.

> CAT
> Hand cannon, Toe Mas. Hand cannon.

Then the high electrified fence and the guardhouse loom up in front of them. Tom floors it.

> TOM
> Hold on. I was always wanted to see how fast one of these big mothers could go.

EXT. – DESERT BASE – CONTINUOUS

The guards leap out of the way as the limo CRASHES THROUGH the fence in a shower of SPARKS. They bring up their guns and FIRE as the car speeds off. To no effect ...

INT. – LIMOUSINE – CONTINUOUS

Tom turns the wheel hard. The limo fishtails, turns, and roars off down the road. Tom risks a quick look at Cat.

> TOM
> You know, if you turn out to be a runaway from Boise, I'm going to feel really stupid.
>> (smiles at Cat)
> We'll need to lose the limo soon. Every cop west of the Mississippi is going to be looking for it. Where are we going, anyway?

In answer, Cat lifts the bracelet, closes her hand into a fist. The insets GLOW BLUE once more. They are brightest when she points straight ahead: due east.

                              CAT
        That way, Toe Mas.

Tom is impressed.

                              TOM
        I guess you're not from Boise after all.

                                              DISSOLVE TO

EXT. – UNDERPASS – LATER THAT MORNING

Cat helps Tom roll the limo into a weed-choked underpass beneath the
highway. It's well hidden when they're done.

                              TOM
        That should do. They'll find it eventually. By then we should
        be long gone.

                              CAT
                           (echoing)
        Long gone.

She turns her hand up, opens her fingers. The HOLO appears; the
WORLD in her hand. Tom is suitably astonished.

                              TOM
        You know more tricks than Houdini.

TIGHT ON THE HOLO – TOM'S POV

The Earth turns slowly, a transparent ghost in brown and green and
blue, but down in what we would call southern New Mexico, a
WHITE LIGHT is FLASHING on and off.

                              CAT
        There, Toe Mas. Long gone.

RESUME

as Tom studies the display, makes sense of it.

                              TOM
     New Mexico. Eight hundred miles, at least. We can be there in
     a day.

Alien SYMBOLS crawl across the face of the globe. Cat understands
them, even if Tom does not.

                              CAT
     No good. Too late. Door opening, door closing. Quick quick. Be
     there sooner.
                         (glance at sun)
     Before new light. Before ...
                         (searching for word)
     ... before dawning.

                              TOM
     Tomorrow at dawn? What happens if we don't make it?

                              CAT
     No door.

                                                              CUT TO

EXT. – HIGHWAY – DAY

Tom tries to hitch a ride. The traffic shoots past, ignoring him.

                                                         DISSOLVE TO

EXT. – HIGHWAY – LATER

Tom coaching Cat on how to hold her thumb.

                                                         DISSOLVE TO

EXT. – HIGHWAY – STILL LATER
A car pulls over to pick her up. The DRIVER grins when Cat slides
into the passenger seat ... until Tom appears from nowhere and gets
in back.

                                                         DISSOLVE TO

EXT. – PICKUP TRUCK – SUNSET

Several rides and several hours later. Cat and Tom sit on a bale of
HAY in the back of a battered pick up, bouncing down a rough dirt
road. The sun is going down. Cat scans with the bracelet. The glow is
BRIGHTER now.

                          TOM
        It's brighter.

                          CAT
        Closer now.

Tom is in a pensive mood as he watches her scan.

                          TOM
        Cat . . . do you know where this door is going to take you?

                          CAT
        Some place.

She sits beside Tom. The bracelet goes dark again.

                          TOM
        Someplace worse, maybe. Can you come back?

                          CAT
        No coming back.

                          TOM
        The doors open only from one side, is that it?
                    (off her nod)
        And you'd go through, not knowing what might wait on the
        other side?

                          CAT
        Going through.

                          TOM
        You might not like where you wind up, Cat.

                              CAT
Is always a next door, Toe Mas.

                              TOM
You can't just keep running. What's the point?

Cat FROWNS, puzzled. The point seems obvious to her. She notices
the sunset: the gorgeous red and orange splendor of the evening sky.
She points.

                              CAT
    There.

Tom follows her finger, and seems to understand.

                                          DISSOLVE TO

EXT. – ROADSIDE DINER – NIGHT

A big rig slows with a HISS of air brakes on a dark mountain road,
Tom and Cat climb down from the cab in front of a roadside diner.
The truck rolls on.

INT. – ROADSIDE DINER – CONTINUOUS

Tom parks Cat in a booth, slides in opposite her. It's late. The place is
almost deserted. Signs over the counter advertise Mexican food
specials.

                           WAITRESS
    What can I get you?

                              TOM
    Let's have a couple of the cheeseburgers.

                              CAT
    Couple of cheeseburgers.

                           WAITRESS
    You want four cheeseburgers?

In b.g., a COWBOY in jeans and denim shirt enters the diner and
slides into a booth near the window.

                                  TOM
                                (firmly)
          Two. And two coffees.

                                  CAT
          Not knowing coffee.

                                  TOM
          Make that one coffee and one milk. You have a pay phone?

                               WAITRESS
          Over by the men's room.

          She goes off to place the order. Tom gets up.

                                  TOM
          I'll be right back. Don't bite anything but the food.

          Cat NODS. Her interest has been captured by a squeeze bottle of
          ketchup. She SNIFFS at it, squeezes a little on the back of her hand,
          tastes it, looks an inquiry at Tom.

                                  CAT
          Not knowing . . .

                                  TOM
          Ketchup. It's a kind of Republican vegetable. Eat all you want.

          He leaves Cat with the ketchup as he crosses to the phone.

          ANGLE ON THE PHONE

          The phone RINGS. We HEAR Laura's voice.

                                 LAURA
          Hello?

                                  TOM
          Laura? It's Tom. You're not going to believe—

LAURA

Don't say anything more. There are police here. They've been
questioning me about you.

TOM

Damn it. Is it Trager?

LAURA

No. They're very upset with you. Tom, what's this all about?

TOM

Cat. Listen, tell them I'll give myself up in . . .
                    (looks at watch)
. . . four hours. Just as soon as I get Cat to her door. I don't
care what they do to me then.

LAURA

I do.

TOM

It won't be so bad. I know a real good lawyer.
                    (beat)
I better get off before they trace this. I just wanted to hear
your voice. You okay?

LAURA

I will be once you're home.

TOM

Me too. I love you.

Tom HANGS UP. For a moment he seems sad and tired as he walks
back to the booth.

                                                    CUT TO

INT. – DINER – LATER

ANGLE ON THE REGISTER

The waitress is giving Tom his change.

                              TOM
Thanks. Hey, where are we? What town is this?

                            WAITRESS
        T-or-C.
                          (off his look)
        Truth or Consequences, New Mexico.

Tom pockets his change and GRINS.

                              TOM
        Yeah. Figures.

He EXITS, with Cat right behind him.

ANGLE ON THE COWBOY

Nursing a cup of coffee. He watches them through the window, then
produces a PALM-SIZED RADIO. He cups it, speaks into it in a
whisper.

                            COWBOY
        Subjects have just left the diner. Heading south along the road,
        on foot.

OFF his watchful eyes, we

                                                        CUT TO

EXT. – TWO-LANE ROAD – NIGHT

The night is warm and still. It's very late now, around three in the
morning. Cat and Tom walk slowly down the shoulder of a road on
the outskirts of T-or-C. There's no traffic at this hour, Cat raises her
arm to SCAN. The blue GLOW is VERY BRIGHT now.

                              TOM
        We must be close.

Cat brings her arm around in a slow SWEEP ... and the bracelet
begins to STROBE, the triple insets FLASHING on and off in

sequence, one two three, one two three, one two three, faster and faster.

CAT

There.

TOM

That?

REVERSE ANGLE – TOM'S POV

Cat is pointing at an old GAS STATION, a two-pump mom-and-pop operation that looks as though it's been shut for twenty years. The windows are boarded up, the pumps are gone.

Cat crosses the empty highway at a run. Tom comes after, slowly, She does another sweep. The silent STROBING indicates one particular door. Tom is bemused.

CAT

Door.

TOM

Of course. What else?

REVERSE ANGLE – ON THE DOOR

The Men's Room. It's BOARDED SHUT.

TOM

This one doesn't need Houdini.

Tom RIPS OFF the boards, tosses them aside. He opens the door cautiously, peeks inside.

TOM

I hate to tell you this, but it's a men's room.

CAT

Too soon.

TOM

So we wait.

                              CAT
                            (echoing)
So we wait.
                            (shyly)
Toe Mas . . . leaving here? Going with?

                              TOM
I'm sorry, Cat. This is as far as I go. Whatever's on the other
side of that door, it's not for me. I've got a life here. A career.
Friends, family.
                            (gently)
A woman I love.
                            (beat)
Do you understand?

Cat looks up, NODS briskly.
                              CAT
Understand.

She sits on the ground, crosses her legs. Her face gives nothing away.
After a moment, Tom sits beside her. Cat looks at him. Tom, feeling
awkward, says nothing. She moves closer, then curls up beside him,
and closes her eyes. Finally, Tom puts an arm around her. Cat stirs
faintly, and nuzzles closer.

                                      MATCH DISSOLVE TO

EXT. – GAS STATION – NEAR DAWN

Tom and Cat are both asleep.
Suddenly a BLINDING LIGHT hits them straight in the face. Cat
wakes instantaneously, Tom more groggily. He holds up a hand in
front of his face.

REVERSE ANGLE – TOM'S POV

He is staring into two sets of HEADLIGHTS. Dark figures move out in
front of the light, silhouetted in the glare. They have guns in hand.
Tom hears a familiar voice.

                            TRAGER
You're under arrest.

RESUME

Cat is not about to go meekly. She reaches for her weapon, Tom grabs
her arm before she can get it up.

> TOM
>> Cat, don't.

Cat won't fight Tom. He takes the hand cannon from her.

> TOM
>> Here. We're unarmed. Don't shoot.

> CAMERON
>> Smart move, Doctor.

Cameron relieves Tom of the weapon and slides it through his belt.
Behind him are Trager and two other agents, GRIGGS and
MONDRAGON.

> TOM
>> How did you find us?

> TRAGER
>> Please, doctor. We never lost you. We played out the line a
>> little to see where she'd go.

Cat struggles as Griggs and Mondragon pull her arms back, handcuff
her wrists. Cameron cuffs an unresisting Tom.

> TOM
>> Trager, please, don't do this.

Cat and Tom are forcibly walked toward the waiting cars.

> TOM
>> A few minutes, that's all I ask. The door is about to open.
>> What have you got to lose? For god's sakes, man—

They are about to force Tom inside the car when the headlights of
both cars suddenly GO OUT.

TIGHT ON CAT

She is the first to realize what it means. She goes wild, kicking and fighting, anything to be free.

RESUME

Trager has his first serious moments of doubt.

                         TRAGER
          Get her under control, damn it.

Tom, staring over Trager's shoulder, is the first to see them.

                          TOM
          Trager, we've got company.

REVERSE ANGLE

Silent as ghosts, three black-clad manhounds walk out of the predawn darkness: Thane, Dyana, ICE.

The palanquin appears a moment later, blocking out the moon. The other three manhounds are riding atop it, guarding their master. Its SHADOW drifts across the upturned faces of the agents, and the alien, distorted voice of the darklord booms down.

                       DARKLORD
          Give us the female.

                      MONDRAGON

          I'm not seeing this.

                        TRAGER

          Cat, who are these people?

                          TOM
          Look at them, Trager. You know who they are.

He does; but he still cannot admit it.

                        TRAGER
     The girl is a federal prisoner. What's your business with her?

Dyana and Ice move forward toward the feds.

                        CAMERON
          Hold it right there.

The manhounds keep coming. They're not even armed. Griggs lifts his
gun with both hands.

                        TRAGER
          Griggs, fire a warning shot.

Griggs squeezes off a round. The gun CLICKS. Then Dyana is on him.
She grabs his head on both sides. She TWISTS. We hear the SNAP as
his neck breaks. Then everything happens at once.

MONDRAGON

pulls the trigger. The gun CLICKS. Ice curls his hands into fists. Six-
inch STEEL CLAWS spring from his knuckles. He SLAMS his fist
hard into Mondragon's gut.

A BOLT OF ENERGY

crackles down from the palanquin, touching first one car, and then the
other. The vehicles EXPLODE and BURN.

THANE

strides through the carnage, straight for Cat. She backs up, looks
behind her. We see her REACT.

CAMERON

tries to face Dyana hand to hand. She blocks his karate blow, pulls
him off balance, and slams him down across her knee, snapping his
spine like a dry stick.

TRAGER

unlocks Tom's cuffs, gives him the keys.

> TRAGER
>
> Get her out of here.

Tom runs toward Cat. Trager turns, and . . .
A BOLT OF ENERGY

from the palanquin FRIES HIM where he stands.

ANGLE ON THE MEN'S ROOM

A pale blue GLOW shines through the crack beneath the men's room
door. Cat throws herself against the door. But with her hands cuffed,
she can't open it. Tom reaches her at a run. He has the keys.

> TOM
>
> Turn around. Hold still.
>   (unlocks cuffs)
> We've got to . . .

Too late. Thane is there. He grabs Tom contemptuously, and FLINGS
him aside like a child. Cat tries to claw out his eye. Thane catches her
hand, holds her prisoned by her wrist. She glares at him defiantly.

> THANE
>
> Look. Look at he who gave you mercy, and was repaid in
> shame.

Tom RABBIT PUNCHES Thane from behind.

> TOM
>
> Let go of her, you son of a—

Thane whirls, and tears into Tom, a brutal barehand attack. Blow after
blow drives Tom back across the lot, staggering.

ANGLE ON THE DOOR (SFX)

Cat OPENS the men's room door. Beyond is chaos, a portal of strobing
light. The light is a brilliant BLUE-WHITE. Somehow it hurts the eye
to look at it.

Within the light, images flicker past too fast to follow, almost
subliminal. For just an instant, the path is clear. Cat could step
through at will. But she hesitates ...

RESUME TOM

Thane is murdering him with his bare hands. Tom FALLS to his knees
beside Cameron's corpse. Thane grabs him by the hair, lifts his fist for
the killing blow ... and Cat comes hurtling through the air and lands
on his back, pummeling him with blows.

QUICK CUT – THE DOOR

The light has faded to a DEEP MIDNIGHT BLUE. We sense the
portal is closing.

RESUME

Thane pulls Cat off his back, and hits her a single terrible backhand
blow across the face. She falls.

TIGHT ON TOM

On the ground. Dazed. He wipes blood from his mouth. Then he sees
Cameron lying there, still and dead. He crawls to the body, fumbles in
the agent's jacket, and pulls out the hand cannon.

ANGLE ALONG THE HAND CANNON

Tom aims at Thane, but he's too close to Cat. Instead he swings the
cannon UP at the palanquin, and FIRES.

THE PALANQUIN

is rocked by a tremendous EXPLOSION. The darkfield protects the
rider, but we see one of the manhounds FALL, screaming, wreathed in
flame. A moment later, the massive palanquin itself CRASHES
DOWNWARD.

QUICK CUTS

The manhounds stare in horror.

Ice and Dyana are both directly under the palanquin. They look up in shock as it falls. Dyana drops and ROLLS out. Ice isn't quite quick enough. He SCREAMS as the palanquin crushes him.

Thane moves to help his master.

TOM

staggers over to Cat, sliding the cannon away. She is unconscious on the ground. Beyond her, the door has faded to a DEEP PURPLE GLOW. It's almost closed. Tom scoops up Cat in his arms, and RUNS.

THANE

sees, and comes after them. But too late. Tom LEAPS through the door. Thane lunges after him . . . and finds himself in a gas station men's room. Alone.

                                              SMASH CUT TO

EXT – BLIZZARD – DAY

as Tom emerges, cradling Cat, into knee-deep SNOW, in the midst of a HOWLING STORM.

                                                  FADE OUT

END OF ACT III

ACT IV

EXT. – BLIZZARD – DAY

Tom cradles Cat in his arms as the storm HOWLS around them. It's day, but the sky is DARK, the sun hidden from sight. The wind drives the snow into Tom's bruised, battered face. In b.g., we glimpse the mountains. Tom SHIVERS. He's not dressed for this kind of cold.

TOM'S POV

as he turns, slowly. The world is a stark white wilderness of ice and snow and rock, with no shelter in sight.

RESUME

Already frost is forming on Tom's eyebrows. He picks a direction at random, and begins to WALK, carrying Cat.

DISSOLVE TO

SERIES OF SHOTS – TIGHT ON TOM'S LEGS

as he struggles through knee-high snowdrifts, up ice-slick slopes, over rocks, sometimes staggering, fighting for every yard as the storm rages around him.

DISSOLVE TO

INT. – CAVE – DAY

As caves go, it isn't much: a hole, half hidden by an overhang of rock, a dead tree near its entrance. But it's shelter. Wearily, Tom carries Cat inside, lays her down on the hard-packed earth floor, out of the wind.

He's covered with caked snow, trembling. He picks up some fallen branches from the dead tree near the cave mouth, begins to gather wood for a fire.

DISSOLVE TO

INT. – CAVE – HOURS LATER

Flames crackle and dance near the mouth of the cave. Outside, the snow has finally stopped falling. Tom washes the blood off Cat's face with a handkerchief wet with melted snow.

ANGLE DOWN ON CAT – TOM'S POV

Cat's eyes are open. She's looking up at him.

TOM
Good morning. How's the head feel?

CAT
Hurts.

> TOM
Yeah. My face feels like chopmeat. Your friend Thane's got quite a punch.

> CAT
Not my friend.

She struggles to rise.

RESUME

Tom helps Cat to her feet. She crosses to the mouth of the cave, looks out. Beyond is a white wilderness of snow and ice. Cat SHIVERS, hugs herself.

> TOM
Grim, isn't it? You're sure the doors don't open in both directions?

> CAT
Sure.

> TOM
I was afraid you'd said that.
> (beat, weary)
Maybe I traded us a quick death for a slow one.

> CAT
Slow is better. More living.

> TOM
Even if it's only for a few days? A few hours?

> CAT
Even if.

She cocks her head sideways, regards him curiously.

> CAT
Why?

> TOM

The door was closing.

> CAT

Still. Why?

> TOM

Some things you have to do.

Cat thinks about that. Then she moves closer, HUGS him with all her strength.

We can see TEARS in her eyes. Tom can't.

CLOSE ON CAT

Her arms wrapped around Tom, holding him tight.

RESUME

Cat finally breaks the embrace, steps back. Tom looks as awkward as he feels. Maybe he doesn't know what that hug means. Maybe he's thinking of Laura.

> CAT

Some things you have to do.

That brings a SMILE to Tom's face.

> TOM

What we need to do is make plans. The firewood won't last long, and we're not dressed for skiing.

> CAT

Not knowing skiing.

> TOM

It's where you pay a lot of money to strap boards on your feet and slide down a mountain.

He moves to the cave mouth, studies the outside world. The black, overcast sky. The howling wind. The deep drifts of snow and overhangs of ice.

                              TOM
          I don't like the look of that sky. Darkness at—
                        (glances at watch)
          —ten twenty-seven. Blizzards in September.

ANGLE ON TOM

Tom moves away from the wind and the cold, picks up a stick, prods
the fire.

                              TOM
          Maybe there was a geographical shift. Maybe we're in
          Greenland ... Antarctica ...

                        SERGEANT (O.S.)
          Try Wyoming.

REVERSE ANGLE

as Tom whirls at the sound of the voice. Just inside the cave stand
FIVE ARMED SOLDIERS; gaunt, ragged men in ragged uniforms, ice
in their beards, hunger and fear in their eyes, snow caking their boots.
Their RIFLES cover Tom and Cat.

The SERGEANT is a tall black woman with a rough, earthy voice. She
warms her hands over the fire.

                           SERGEANT
          Nice. Warm. And you know, you can see it for miles.

ANGLE ON CAT

Backing up. She looks sideways at the hand cannon on the ground
nearby, tenses to make a dive for it.

RESUME

The sergeant knows exactly what she's doing.

                           SERGEANT
          Girl, if you're going to try for that gun over there, you're going
          to be real dead real soon.

Cat FREEZES.

SOLDIER

What are we going to do with them, Sarge?

SERGEANT

March them back to camp and let the Captain have a look.
(to Tom)
Gather up whatever food you've got and get into your snow gear.

TOM

We don't have any.

SERGEANT
(incredulous)
In that case, you two are going to have a long, cold walk.

OFF Tom's dismay, we

CUT TO

EXT. – BASE CAMP – THAT AFTERNOON – ESTABLISHING

A small military camp has been dug in against the side of a mountain. There are tents, crudely built hutches, a firepit in the center of camp. Around the perimeter, like snowbreaks, are an ancient yellow SCHOOL BUS, a JEEP and an ARMORED PERSONNEL CARRIER, all in sorry condition. More striking – and in better repair – are two larger and more futuristic vehicles: a huge HOVER TANK (designed to ride on a cushion of compressed air, it has no treads), and an even larger transport FLOATER, an eighteen-wheeler without the wheels.

ANGLE ON TOM AND CAT

The soldiers stare, curious, as the captives are marched in. Counting the squad that captured Cat and Tom, there are twenty of them. We glimpse a few women and three times as many men.

Their 'uniforms' are worn, much patched, and not very uniform. It looks as though they came from two or three different armies. A few have heavy, hooded parkas; one man wears a moth-eaten fur coat; the others bundle up under layers of clothing.

ANGLE ON THE JEEP

as Tom and Cat are marched past. A MACHINE GUN is mounted on the jeep. It's half in pieces now. WALSH, a private with a heavy dark beard wearing a fur-trimmed parka, is cleaning and repairing it. When he sees Cat, he stops, and jumps off the jeep to inspect her.

> WALSH
>
> Well, look at this. Maybe those snow patrols aren't useless after all.

He blocks Cat's path, touches her under the chin to raise her face, She stares at him impassively.

> WALSH
>
> You have a name, pretty thing?

> SERGEANT
>
> Knock it off, Walsh. And get back to work. You were supposed to have that gun cleaned and serviced an hour ago.

> WALSH
>
> I'd like to clean and service her.

> TOM
>
> I wouldn't touch her if I were you. She bites.

> SERGEANT
>
> Listen to the man. I want that gun back in one piece by mess.

Walsh turns on the sergeant, defiant.

> WALSH
>
> Why? You think it matters? What the hell we going to shoot? Snowmen?

> SERGEANT
>
> I gave you an order.

Other soldiers gather to watch the confrontation. Among the spectators is a woman, WHITMORE, very PREGNANT. A minority make it clear they agree with Walsh.

                    WALSH

Stuff your orders.

                    CRONY

You tell her, Walsh.

                    WALSH

All this patrolling and drilling and cleaning our guns, what
does it prove?

              THE CAPTAIN (O.S.)

It proves we can survive, Walsh.

REVERSE ANGLE – ON THE HUTCH

A tall, grim, powerful man has emerged from the command hutch.
THE CAPTAIN wears a heavy parka with a hood that shadows his
face.

              THE CAPTAIN

The snow is the enemy. The cold is the enemy. And despair is
the greatest enemy of all. Are you tired of living, Walsh?

CLOSE ON TOM

He is looking at the Captain hard, with a strange expression on his
face, almost as if he recognizes him.

RESUME

Walsh is cowed and a little frightened by the Captain.

                    WALSH

No, sir.

              THE CAPTAIN

Death is easy. Lie down in the snow, that's all it takes. Life is
harder.
It requires courage, work, discipline. Do you want to live?

                          WALSH
     Yes, sir.

                       THE CAPTAIN
     Then get back to work.

Walsh SALUTES and gets back into the jeep. The Captain turns to his
sergeant.

                       THE CAPTAIN
     Sergeant, who are these people?

                        SERGEANT
     We found them in a cave by the south ridge, Captain.

                       THE CAPTAIN
     Bring them inside.

                                                        CUT TO

INT. – CAPTAIN'S HUTCH – CONTINUOUS

The furniture is crude and well-worn. A wood-burning stove warms the
hutch to a comfortable temperature.

The sergeant and one of her men escort Tom and Cat into the hutch.
The Captain pulls down his hood. We see his face for the first time.
His hair is shoulder length, tangled, but the same iron gray color. He
sports a dark beard shot through with gray, but beneath it the face is
the same. Tom recognizes him; so does Cat.

                          TOM
                        (stunned)
     Trager.

CLOSE ON THE CAPTAIN

He frowns, off-balance for a second.

                       THE CAPTAIN
     Where did you hear that name?

                    TOM
I . . . knew you.

                THE CAPTAIN
Before the war?
                    (thoughtful)
No. You're not old enough.
                    (beat)
Names are for peacetime. I'm the Captain.
                    (to the sergeant)
Were they armed?

                  SERGEANT
We found these in the cave.

She deposits Cat's weapon and TWO spare magazines in front of the
Captain, who inspects them carefully.

                    CAT
Mine! Give it!

The soldiers restrain her as she starts forward.

                THE CAPTAIN
Curious. Is this what the enemy is carrying these days?

                    TOM
We're not the enemy.

                THE CAPTAIN
That remains to be seen.

                    TOM
Your sergeant said this was Wyoming.

That draws a long, curious stare from the Captain.

                THE CAPTAIN
This is the Mountain Free State. Or what remains of it.

                    TOM
The Mountain . . . Captain, what's <u>happened?</u>

Cat has figured it out; it's obvious.

                              CAT
        Warring.

                         THE CAPTAIN
        Twenty-nine years of it.

                              TOM
                           (shocked)
        Twenty-nine . . .

                         THE CAPTAIN
        You heard me.
                        (beat, brusque)
        My turn. I would like some answers. What's your purpose
        here? Where did you come from?

                              TOM
        Los Angeles.

                         THE CAPTAIN
        Do I look like a fool to you? There is no Los Angeles.
                         (to sergeant)
        Did you find their supplies?

                          SERGEANT
        The only clothing they've got is what they're wearing, and they
        had no food at all.

                         THE CAPTAIN
        How about a vehicle?

                              CAT
        Walked.

The Captain looks at Tom, who SHRUGS.

                              TOM
        Ah . . . I hate to say it, but we did.

THE CAPTAIN
(rising)
You're either a madman or a liar. We don't have food for
either. Sergeant, take this man and—

The Captain breaks off as a WOMAN SOLDIER bursts inside the
hutch, breathless and scared.

WOMAN SOLDIER
Captain, it's Barbara. She's gone into labor. Something's gone
wrong.

TOM
Take me there.
(no one moves)
I'm a doctor. I can help . . .

The Captain studies Tom a moment, uncertain. We hear a SCREAM. It
makes up his mind. He NODS. Tom rushes from the hutch with the
woman soldier.

CUT TO

INT. – WOMEN'S HUTCH – LATER

Candles and a smoking torch provide the only light. The hutch houses
the army's five women. On one cot, Whitmore shudders and pants in
the agony of labor.

The sergeant and the other women have gathered to help, but Tom is
the only man in the hutch. He kneels between Whitmore's legs. Cat
watches from the door, curious as her namesake.

WHITMORE
It hurts . . . oh, please . . . it hurts . . .

TOM
Bear down. That's it. Go on, scream if you have to.

She does. Tom ignores it, concentrating.

TOM
Barbara, listen to me. It's a breech birth. I'm going to have to

reach in and try and turn the baby around. It's going to hurt. Are you ready?

Biting her lip, face damp with sweat, Whitmore NODS.

                              TOM
          Here we go.

CLOSE ON CAT

Wide-eyed, watching. Whitmore's next scream is SHATTERING. Cat pales, whirls, and flees the hutch.

EXT. – WOMEN'S HUTCH – CONTINUOUS

In headlong flight, Cat runs right into the Captain, waiting with a few other men outside the hutch. The Captain catches her by her arms, holds her a moment.

                         THE CAPTAIN
          What's happening?

Cat shakes her head wildly; she's the wrong one to ask. She wrenches free of the Captain, and runs.

                                        DISSOLVE TO

EXT. – WOMEN'S HUTCH – LATER

The Captain and the other men are still waiting. It has grown quiet in the hutch. Finally the sergeant emerges.

                         SERGEANT
          It's a little girl.

The Captain nods. He shows no visible emotion.

                         THE CAPTAIN
          And Whitmore?

                         SERGEANT
          The doc says she'll make it. She wants to see you, Captain.

The Captain enters the hutch.

INT. – WOMEN'S HUTCH – CONTINUOUS

The mother is cradling a tiny newborn to her breast. She looks exhausted and weak, but happy. Tom is drying his hands.

> WHITMORE
> Look at her, John. Isn't she beautiful? Would you like to hold her?

The Captain looks uncomfortable. He doesn't know what to say. Whitmore pulls the child closer.

> WHITMORE
> She's going to be all right, isn't she?

> THE CAPTAIN
> She's going to be fine. We'll be going south as soon as the weather breaks. It's still warm down there south of Mexico. The oceans are full of fish, and there are green valleys where the food grows right out of the ground.

INTERCUT

with reaction shots from Tom, listening. The captain gently touches the baby's head as she nurses.

> THE CAPTAIN
> I promise you, Whitmore. She's going to grow up under blue skies. She's going to taste honey and ride a horse and play in the sun. I promise you.

CLOSE ON WHITMORE

There are tears in her eyes. Tears of joy, tears of sorrow? Maybe both. She bites her lips, and nods.

> WHITMORE
> I want to name her Eve. It will be a new world, won't it? And she's the first . . .

                    THE CAPTAIN
      It's a good name.

Whitemore SMILES.

RESUME

as the Captain gets up. He looks at Tom.

                    THE CAPTAIN
      Doctor, if I could have a word with you outside.

Tom follows him out.

EXT. – WOMEN'S HUTCH – CONTINUOUS

Outside the hutch, the Captain turns to face Tom. The sergeant,
standing nearby, listens to their exchange.

                    THE CAPTAIN
      So you really are a doctor.

                      TOM
      Not a liar or a madman?

Cat, hiding around the corner of the hutch, hears Tom's voice and
comes creeping back into view. She listens.

                    THE CAPTAIN
      Maybe all three. It doesn't matter.
                      (sees Cat, in hiding)
      Come out of there.

Cat emerges, shyly.

                      TOM
      Cat, are you all right? Why did you run away?

                      CAT
      Too much hurting. Dying.

                                TOM
Childbirth doesn't have to be fatal, Cat.

                                CAT
No dying?

                                TOM
No dying.

                            THE CAPTAIN
You had a lot to do with that, it seems. We need a doctor.
And we always need women. You're both drafted. Sergeant,
explain the terms of enlistment to our new recruits.

The Captain walks off. The sergeant takes over.

                            SERGEANT
Three articles. First, you obey orders. Second, you serve as long
as we want you. Third . . . the penalty for desertion is death.

OFF the look on Tom's face, we

                                                        FADE OUT

END OF ACT IV

ACT V

FADE IN

EXT. – FLOATER – DAY

Inside are crates of canned food, stacks of wood and faded yellow
newspaper, bundles of old clothing. The QUARTERMASTER, jowly
and unshaven, tosses down a bundle of clothing from the tailgate.

                            QUARTERMASTER
Here you go. You put on six, eight shirts, hey, who needs a
coat, right?

Cat pokes her finger through a hole, SNIFFS at the stain around the
hole.

                    QUARTERMASTER
That's good luck, you know. I mean, what's the odds on
another bullet hitting that same spot, right?

Cat starts pulling on the shirts, layer on layer. A little blood does not
bother her at all.

                         TOM
We need warm socks.

                    QUARTERMASTER
Try the five-and-dime.

The quartermaster hands down a couple of rifles.

                    QUARTERMASTER
This here is your rifle. Make sure you don't lose it. If the
enemy shows up, you can hit him with it.

Cat grabs her rifle eagerly, checking the action.

                         TOM
You mean there's no ammunition?

The quartermaster LAUGHS like that's the funniest thing he's heard in
years.

                         TOM
What good is a rifle without ammunition?

The sergeant gives him a wry, bemused smile.

                      SERGEANT
Good enough to capture you.

OFF Tom's reaction, we

                                          DISSOLVE TO

INT. – MESS TENT – EVENING

Tom and Cat, wearing their new 'uniforms' and looking as ragtag as

the rest of this army, accept tin plates of canned beans and mystery
meat from the COOK, and carry them to empty places on the mess
hall bench.

Cat picks up the meat with her fingers, tears at it with her teeth, She's
hungry.

                              CAT
                        (her mouth full)
            Good. Hot. Eat, Toe Mas.

There's a smear of GREASE around her lips as she grins at him over a
ragged piece of meat. She wipes it away with the back of her sleeve.
Tom holds up a FORK.

                              TOM
            Remind me to teach you how to use a fork.

He picks up his knife, tries to cut his meat. It's hard. Now it's Cat's
turn to grin.

                              CAT
            Use teeth. Better than forks.

Her smile fades as the quartermaster seats himself on the bench beside
her. She tries to ignore him.

                         QUARTERMASTER
            Your girlfriend's hungry.

                              TOM
            She's not my girlfriend.

                         QUARTERMASTER
            Your loss. Nice looking girl like her, nobody to keep her snug
            at night.
                          (to Cat)
            You come out and visit me tonight, I'll keep you nice and
            warm. Maybe I can even find you a pair of socks.

He slides close to Cat.

TIGHT ON CAT'S LEG

Under the bench. The quartermaster puts his hand on her knee, slides
it slowly up her thigh, his fingers groping.

ANGLE ON CAT

Her eyes flick sideways. That's all the warning he gets. He has one
hand on the table and the other under it.

> QUARTERMASTER
> I used to give roses to the girls. When there were roses. Hey,
> roses, socks, what's the difference? They both smell.

He starts to LAUGH at his own joke. Cat picks up a FORK and drives
it down brutally into the quartermaster's hand. The man SHRIEKS in
sudden agony, and leaps up, clutching his bleeding hand.

> QUARTERMASTER
> My hand . . .

Cat grins at Tom, her eyes sparkling.

> CAT
> Knowing how to use forks. See.

> QUARTERMASTER
> You filthy little . . .

> TOM
> (rising)
> Don't touch her.

The sergeant puts a hand on Tom to cool him.

> SERGEANT
> At ease, Lake. Timms, get back to the floater.

> QUARTERMASTER
> I was just trying to be nice to her.

The other soldiers don't have much sympathy.

WOMAN SOLDIER

Next time maybe she'll stick it between your legs.

The quartermaster GLARES at them all, and EXITS the mess tent, angry. Tom sits back down.

SERGEANT

He was a good man once.
(shrugs)
Things'll be better once we're moving again. Heading south.

Behind her, Walsh LAUGHS derisively.

WALSH

Yeah? When will that be, sarge? Tomorrow? Day after, you think?
(beat)
Face it. We're never moving south. We been here eighteen months. We'll die here.

WOMAN SOLDIER

The Captain says as soon as the weather breaks . . .

WALSH

Nothing's going to break around here but us. We're out of ammo, out of fuel, and sooner or later we're going to run out of food. We're all dead men.

He EXITS the mess tent, followed by two other men who obviously agree. A grim silence settles.

TOM

Your vehicles . . . that tank, the hovercraft . . .

SERGEANT
(wearily)
The big floater died eighteen months ago. That was the last. We have thousands of miles to go, and no transport.

CAT

Walk.

> SERGEANT

Even if we could make it through the blizzards on foot without freezing to death, there's no way to carry all the food we'd need.

No one has the heart to say anything more. The faces in the mess tent reflect resignation and despair. The sergeant gets to her feet.

> SERGEANT

Lake, you're on sentry duty tonight.

> TOM

How do you know I won't just run off?

> SERGEANT
> (bitter laugh)

And where the hell do you think you're going to run to?

DISSOLVE TO

EXT. – BASE CAMP – NIGHT

Tom, huddled up in his ragged clothes, rifle slung over a shoulder, walks his rounds as sentry. Tom's breath STEAMS in the chill night air. He looks cold, miserable, lonely.

The night is cold and still. The wind howls through the camp. Tom, gloveless, tries warming his hands in his armpits. It doesn't work. He fumbles in his pockets, takes out his wallet.

TIGHT ON TOM'S HAND

as he opens the wallet to a PHOTO of Laura.

RESUME

Tom looks at the photograph for a long time. He has come a long way, and there may be no way back. For the first time, Tom is thinking about that. We see the pain on his face.

Then we HEAR a noise. The sound of motion.

                        TOM
    Hello? Who goes there?

No answer. Hurriedly, he tucks away the photograph and unslings his
rifle.

TRACKING WITH TOM

as he moves in the direction of the noise. We HEAR it again. A
stealthy footfall, from the direction of the snowbound vehicles. Tom
creeps along past the old yellow school bus, stops. We HEAR a
MUFFLED THUD, a GROAN.

Tom screws up his courage, RUNS toward the cab of the big floater.
Outside, he finds the quartermaster lying in the snow, out cold. He
gapes at the unconscious man for a moment. Cat sticks her head out
of the cab.

                        CAT
    Quiet now, Toe Mas. Making noise loud. Too much.

                        TOM
                     (surprised)
        Cat, what are you—

She opens the door, grabs him, pulls him in.

                        CAT
        No talk. Inside now.

INT. – FLOATER CAB – CONTINUOUS

It looks like the cab of a semi. Cat slides down under the dash, lights
a MATCH. She's inspecting something.

                        TOM
                     (whisper)
        What are you doing here?

                        CAT
        Looking. Seeing.

She blows out the match, pulls herself up beside him.

                              CAT
      Leaving now.

Cat pushes up her sleeves, shirt after shirt, opens her hand.

The HOLOGRAM winks on. The world spins slowly between her
fingers; alien symbols squirm across the globe; a light flashes in
Montana.

                              TOM
      Another door? To where?

                              CAT
      Out.

                              TOM
                          (frustrated)
      Out. Out where? How do you know where it leads?

                              CAT
      Go through. Find out.

                              TOM
      Cat, is there a door that leads back the way we came? Can I
      get home again?

                              CAT
      Not knowing. Maybe. Maybe this door.

Tom studies the position of the light.

                              TOM
      That's got to be somewhere in Montana. When does it open?

She lowers her arm. The holo WINKS OUT.

                              CAT
      Two days. Going now.

                              TOM
                          (disappointed)

It's too far, Cat. A hundred miles, at least. We'll be lucky to make ten miles a day on foot.

                              CAT
Not feet. Taking this.

She touches the controls of the floater.

                              TOM
There's no power, remember?

                              CAT
Fixing it.

                              TOM
Who? You?

                              CAT
Knowing how. Thane teaching. Power cells.

It takes Tom a moment to comprehend. Then it hits him.

                              TOM
Power cells – god, yes!
                          (grins)
Cat, I could kiss you.

                              CAT
Not knowing <u>kiss</u>. Going now, kissing later.

                              TOM
                        (sudden doubt)
Wait a minute. The food . . .
                          (beat)
All the food is on the truck. If we take it, these people will die.

                              CAT
Dying anyway. Fast, slow. No matter.

                              TOM
That's not what you said back in the cave. Remember? You

thought life was worth something then, even if it was only a few more days, a few more hours . . .

Cat gets a stubborn look on her face. She doesn't like having her own words thrown back at her.

              CAT
Different then. Talking us then. Talking them now.

Tom stares at her, aghast, realizing maybe for the first time how strong her drive for survival is.

              TOM
They're people, Cat. Just like us. There's a baby in that camp not six hours old. A baby I delivered. I'm not going to sentence her to death.

Cat does not understand.

              CAT
Leaving now! Going fast!

              TOM
Then go.

              CAT
You too.

              TOM
I'm not going, Cat.

Cat is furious. Her mouth is set in a grim line.

              CAT

<u>Yes!</u>

              TOM
           (quiet but firm)
No.

They stare each other down. Finally Cat lowers her eyes.

                                   CAT
                              (surrender)
          Not going too.

                                                            CUT TO

EXT. – CAPTAIN'S HUTCH – NIGHT

Tom leads Cat inside the captain's hutch. The windows are all dark, as
if the captain were asleep.

INT. – CAPTAIN'S HUTCH – CONTINUOUS

The interior of the hutch is PITCH DARK. We can barely discern the
figures of Tom and Cat as they pass the windows. Cat is nervous.

                                   CAT
          Too dark.

                                   TOM
          Captain? Are you . . .

Behind him, a match FLARES to sudden light. The Captain is not
asleep. He is sitting up, behind his desk. He has a service revolver in
one hand. He lights a candle with the other. The hutch fills with
flickering light.

                              THE CAPTAIN
          Stay right there. I promise you, this gun is loaded.

                                   TOM
          We thought you were asleep.

                              THE CAPTAIN
          You thought wrong.

The Captain leans back in his chair. He keeps the pistol pointed at
Tom and Cat. Cat's hand cannon is on the table in front of him.

                              THE CAPTAIN
          You two. Odd. I had rather expected Walsh and his friends.

                    TOM

Expected Walsh to . . . ?

                THE CAPTAIN

To try and kill me, of course. The surest way to promotion.

                    TOM

We're not here to kill you. We want to talk.

                THE CAPTAIN

Yes. You strike me as the sort of man who is much better at
talking than at killing. Now your girlfriend here . . .

                    CAT

Not my girlfriend.

Tom is momentarily bemused by the echo.

                    TOM

Close, Cat. But we need to have a talk about pronouns.
                (to Captain)

Captain, is it true? About the warm place down south . . .

                THE CAPTAIN

I knew a man who knew a man who had seen it with his own
eyes.
                (shrugs)
A man needs hope if he wants to keep on living.

                    TOM

Can I show you something?

The Captain NODS. Tom crosses to the table, picks up one of the spare
cylinders, rips the cap off the end.

ANGLE ON TOM'S HAND

as he holds up the magazine for the Captain to see. Inside is the red
GLOW of the power cell, PULSING with energy. The Captain leans
forward, puzzled and curious.

THE CAPTAIN

What is it?

TOM

Hope . . .

The Captain looks at Tom's face. He puts down his gun.

THE CAPTAIN

I'm listening.

CUT TO

EXT. – THE MOUNTAINS – NIGHT

Black sky over still, silent snows. Nothing moves but the wind.
Suddenly we hear a CRACK, as loud as a clap of thunder, as sharp as
a sonic boom.

The darklord's palanquin is suddenly THERE, where there was nothing
an instant before. Three surviving manhounds – Thane, Dyana, and the
second woman, JAELE – cling to the battered vehicle. The palanquin is
visibly damaged.

Thane leaps down to the snow, light as a panther. The hunt has
resumed.

FADE OUT

END OF ACT V

ACT VI

FADE IN

EXT. – BASE CAMP – MORNING

The camp is feverish with activity. Soldiers are digging out the
snowbound bus, securing the load in the floater, cannibalizing parts
from the jeep and APC for the bus and the floater. A new animation
and energy seems to have taken possession of the Captain's listless
little army.

TIGHT ON CAT

Upside down under the raised hood of the floater, face and clothing covered with oil, cables running through her hands, her face as intent as a doctor in surgery. She holds out a hand, wordless. The woman soldier, assisting, puts a power cell in her palm. Cat solders it in place.

RESUME

The quartermaster, his head wrapped in a makeshift bandage to match the one on his hand, sticks his face out the driver's side window. He's excited.

> QUARTERMASTER
> She's showing a charge! Mother of god, look at it, the needle's halfway off the scale.

Cat climbs out, wipes her hands on a rag, NODS.

> SERGEANT
> Try the fans.
> (shouts)
> Stand clear! We're going to try and lift . . .

Soldiers SCRAMBLE out of the way. The quartermaster takes a deep breath, crosses himself, and turns the ignition. There's a high-pitched WHINE as the floater's electric turbines catch hold . . . and then the ROAR of the great fans under the floater as they start to turn.

LONG SHOT – THE FLOATER

The floater ROCKS back and forth for a moment. Snow comes SPRAYING out all around it, sending the spectators running. Then, slowly, majestically, the hovertruck begins to LIFT off the ground.

The soldiers break into a ragged CHEER.

CAT

All of a sudden, she's surrounded by people. They slap her on the back, grab her hand and pump it. She looks lost at first. Then she gets the idea and slowly begins to smile.

SERGEANT

One down. Now let's see what she can do with the tank.

CUT TO

EX. – SCHOOL BUS – HOURS LATER

The soldiers are filing aboard the school bus, carrying rifles and duffle bags. A crew is at work chaining the bus to the floater. Cat and Tom wait while the Captain talks to the sergeant.

THE CAPTAIN

Take the old interstate as far as you can, but stay well clear of Denver. It's still too hot for safety.

THE SERGEANT

Yes, sir.

THE CAPTAIN

I should catch up to you by Sunday at the latest. If I'm not at the rendezvous within the week, go on without me. Is that understood?

SERGEANT

Captain, we'd rather . . .

THE CAPTAIN

Is that understood?
(off her nod)
You keep on going. No matter what. Those turbines could burn out any time. You get as far south as you can.

Whitmore is about to board the school bus. Her little girl is cradled in her arms, swathed in layers of clothing. She stops to say good-bye.

WHITMORE

Doctor . . . thank you . . . for everything.

TOM

Take good care of her, you hear?

She KISSES him lightly. Cat watches, frowning.

> WHITMORE
>
> You too, Cat. Thank you.
> (to Captain)
> I ... I wish you were going with us.

> THE CAPTAIN
>
> I won't be long. The sergeant will get you through.

Whitmore nods. She seems awkward, shy. She turns to board the bus
... and the Captain speaks up.

> THE CAPTAIN
>
> Barbara ...
> (she stops)
> Could I ... hold her?

She gives him the baby. The Captain takes the infant tenderly, holds
her.

> WHITMORE
>
> She has your eyes.

The Captain gives her back the infant, and KISSES her. The kiss is
tender and affectionate; it lasts a long time. Cat stares openly,
curiously.

> TOM
>
> That's a kiss, Cat. They're kissing.

Whitmore is crying. Even the Captain's eyes are damp. They break
apart with an effort.

> THE CAPTAIN
>
> Take her someplace warm, love.

Choked up, unable to speak, Barbara NODS and boards the bus. Tears
are rolling down her face.

> CAT
>
> Kissing hurts.

TOM
(smiling)
Oh, I don't know about that

CUT TO

THE TOW CHAINS

The turbines WHINE. The fans ROAR. The floater lifts off the snow. The chains rattle and clank as the slack is pulled tight.

THE FLOATER

starts forward. Hovering a foot above the snow on a cushion of air, it begins the long journey south. The chains grow taut. For a moment, the bus refuses to move.

THE TIRES

of the bus are frozen into the snow, rimed in ice.

THE FLOATER

The whine of the turbines grows higher and faster as it strains against its load.

Nothing. Until finally

THE ICE ON THE TIRES

cracks, and the big tires begin to roll.

TOM AND CAT

watch as the vehicles start to move, very slowly. A window in the bus opens.

Walsh sticks his head out.

WALSH
Hey, Cat . . .
(off her glare)

You made a liar out of me, pretty lady. I owe you one.

He tosses his warm, heavy, fur-collared parka out of the window at Cat. She catches it, astonished.

WALSH

Keep it. It's warm where I'm going.

And then the bus is past. Cat stares after it.

TOM

Let's go. The Captain is waiting.

REVERSE ANGLE – OVER TOM'S SHOULDER

to where the huge, battle-scarred tank waits, its own turbines slowly starting to rev. They walk toward it, Cat shrugging into the parka as she goes.

MATCH DISSOLVE TO

EXT. – BASE CAMP – HOURS LATER

The empty hutches and abandoned vehicles sit forlorn in the snow, The floater, the school bus, and the tank are all gone. Dyana strides over a rise, to where the darklord waits in its palanquin, looking down over the camp. She bows her head to report. Jaele and a sullen Thane listen.

DYANA

A military encampment, my lord. Recently deserted. I found these.

CLOSE ON DYANA'S HAND

as she opens her fist. Inside are two black cylinders.

THANE

Cylinders from the hand cannon.

DYANA

They've been stripped of their power cells. Useless.

THANE

But they prove she was here.

RESUME

Within the shadowed darkfield, the alien STIRS angrily.

DARKLORD

And she is gone again!

DYANA

One group went north, another south.

THANE

The next door is north. Cat will run to it.

DARKLORD

Then those who went south are nothing to us. Dyana, take us north.

She BOWS her head in acknowledgment. Thane speaks up.

THANE

My lord, your vehicle is damaged. Travel will be slow. She may reach the door first.

DARKLORD

Pray that she does not, Thane, disgraced, twice-failed. I will have her, or I will have you in her stead.

THANE

Send me ahead, lord. She must go around the mountains. I can take a more direct road, and secure the door.

DARKLORD

Make it so. And do not harm her. She will serve my pleasure, not your empty human pride.

THANE

To hear is to obey.

Thane climbs onto the OUTRIDER on one side of the palanquin, straddling it like a motorcycle. He works a control. The front section of the outrider slides forward and DETACHES from the main vehicle.

> DARKLORD
>
> Be warned, dog. There must be no third failure. My mercy is not without limit.

Thane BOWS his head. The outrider takes off across the snow, swift and silent.

> CUT TO

EXT. – THE MOUNTAINS – DAY

The tank, hovering on its cushion of air, makes its way north over the wasteland of snow and ice toward the mountains.

INT. – THE TANK – DAY

The interior of the tank is cramped and cold. The vehicle is obviously in bad shape; in b.g. are circuit boards seared by fire, panels torn out, evidence of makeshift repair. The sound of the fans is loud.

The Captain drives. Tom is seated in the turret gunner's position, Cat huddled at his feet.

> TOM
>
> I've been thinking. You said it had been twenty-nine years. That would mean your war started in—

> THE CAPTAIN
>
> October, 1962. But it was never my war.

> TOM
> (figures it out)
> The Cuban missile crisis . . . the Soviets never backed down, did they?

The Captain gives a weary shake of his head.

> TOM
>
> How bad was it?

THE CAPTAIN

We lost a few cities. Boston, Denver, Washington . . . but we won. The new president – McNamara, I think it was – he said so. People were dancing in the streets. Flags flying everywhere, victory parades, the second baby boom . . . god, what fools we were.

TOM

Afterwards . . . the fallout.

THE CAPTAIN

Poison rains. Crop failures. The survivors swarmed out of the cities, starving. There was no place for them to go. The lights went out all over America.

CAT

Darklords . . .

TOM

Not here. They did it themselves here. Just men and women . . .

THE CAPTAIN

The food wars were the worst of it. Once they started there was no stopping them. And all the time the winters were getting longer and colder.

He shakes his head, as if to shake off the memories.

Then, suddenly, a CLAXON sounds. The tank SHAKES. Smoke starts to pour out of an instrument panel. Cat covers her ears against the noise.

The Captain grabs a fire extinguisher, rips off a panel cover, and starts to spray. The fans GRIND and fall silent, and the tank crashes to earth, jarringly. The smoke is thick.

THE CAPTAIN

Lake, pop the hatch. Move it! Before we all suffocate . . .

EXT. – THE TANK – CONTINUOUS

Smoke POURS from the open hatch as Tom climbs out. He pulls Cat

out after him. The Captain comes last, holding a cloth over his face
and COUGHING.

>   TOM

What happened?

>   CAT

Fire, Toe Mas.

>   TOM

I figured out that much.

>   THE CAPTAIN

Some kind of overload. This thing should have been put out of
its misery years ago.

>   TOM

Can we repair it?

The Captain looks around. There's nothing but mountains, as far as the
eye can see. Snow and ice everywhere.

>   THE CAPTAIN

Do we have a choice?

>   CUT TO

EXT. – ANOTHER PART OF THE MOUNTAINS – SIMULTANEOUS

Thane rides the outrider through the foothills. His face is grim and
implacable. He is moving very fast, eating up the miles. The mountains
loom large ahead of him.

>   DISSOLVE TO

EXT. – THE TANK – EVENING

The Captain has been working on the tank for hours. Cat sits perched
on top of the turret, their sentry. When the Captain emerges, she
comes vaulting down to hear.

                               TOM
         How does it look?

The Captain's face is grim.

                         THE CAPTAIN
         I can gerryrigg something to replace the burnt out
         circuitboards. The real problem is this.

He TOSSES something at Tom, who snatches it from the air.

TIGHT ON TOM'S HAND

He's holding a power cell. It's dead, blackened.

RESUME

Cat moves close. Tom gives her the dead power cell with a sour look
on his face.

                         THE CAPTAIN
         The faulty board caused an overload. We're going to need
         another power cell.

                               TOM
         We don't _have_ another power cell. There were only two spare
         cartridges.

Tom looks helplessly out over the barren winterscape.

                               TOM
         Where the hell is the Energizer bunny when you really need
         him?

                         THE CAPTAIN
         Excuse me?

                               TOM
         Never mind. What do we do now?

They look at each other helplessly.

                         THE CAPTAIN
         We die.

Tom is startled by the sudden despair in the Captain's tone. If this man is giving up, then the situation must be truly hopeless The Captain's voice is weary.

THE CAPTAIN

Funny way to end it, though. I always thought I'd die in battle. A soldier's death . . .
              (beat)
My father was a soldier, and his father before him. For them it was all about honor and courage, about defending your country from its enemies. Then the war came, and there was no more country, and the enemies I was killing one year turned out to be the people I'd been defending the year before.
              (beat)
Nothing was ever right in this war. Not even the dying.

Tom doesn't know what to say, but Cat does.

CAT

No dying now.

She draws the hand cannon, pops out the cartridge. The last cartridge. She offers it to the Captain. He takes it from her hand solemnly, realizing what it means.

THE CAPTAIN

Without this, your weapon is useless.

TOM

Cat, are you sure?

CAT

Sure.

THE CAPTAIN

You're leaving yourself defenseless. If your enemies find you . . . these darklords you've told me about . . . you'll have no way to fight them.

CAT

Lots of ways. Kicking. Biting. Throwing rocks.

The Captain draws his revolver from its holster, presses it into Cat's hand.

> THE CAPTAIN
> Here. There are only four bullets left, but it's something. Take it.

Cat takes the gun, examines it.

> CAT
> Something. Better than rocks.
> (tucks it away)
> Fixing now. Going now.

The Captain turns back to the tank to resume work.

DISSOLVE TO EXT. – CLIFF FACE – NIGHT – ANGLE DOWN

A bitter wind HOWLS across a sheer cliff of rock and ice. The ground is a long way down, the top of the precipice a long way up. A HAND enters frame, grabs a precarious finger hold. Then Thane pulls himself up into view. His fingers are BLOODY from clawing at the rock, and there is FROST on his face, yet he pushes himself on.

As Thane CLIMBS out of sight, we

> DISSOLVE TO

EXT. – MOUNTAIN PASS – THE NEXT DAY

The tank climbs slowly up a steep slope, and STOPS where a narrow pass opens between two high, ice-covered walls of stone. After a moment the hatch opens. Cat scrambles out first. Tom and the Captain are right behind.

Cat stands on top of the tank, exposes the bracelet, and SCANS. The BLUE GLOW is brightest when her fist points straight ahead, through the pass and up the mountain.

> CAT
> There. That way.

                        THE CAPTAIN
The pass is too narrow.

He glances up above them, at the looming mountains.

                        THE CAPTAIN
I don't like the look of that snow up there. If I try to get the
tank through, I could bring down half the mountain.

                            TOM
Cat, how close is the door?

                            CAT
Close. Two hex, three hex.

                            TOM
I think we can make it the rest of the way on foot.

                        THE CAPTAIN
Then this is it. I need to get back to my people.

                            TOM
You can come with us.

                        THE CAPTAIN
This is my world. Besides . . .
                        (smiling)
I still think you're mad.

Tom SMILES. They CLASP hands. Then Tom and Cat jump off into
the snow. Their feet drive DEEP FOOTPRINTS as they land. Tom slips
and goes down. Cat pulls him to his feet. The Captain watches them
walk off up the slope, then shuts the hatch.

                            MATCH DISSOLVE TO

THE SAME SPOT – AN HOUR LATER – ANGLE ON DYANA

She kneels beside the deep footprints that Cat and Tom left in the
snow. She stands.

THE PALANQUIN

floats close behind her. The creature in the darkfield leans forward eagerly.

> DYANA
> They left their vehicle here and continued on foot. Not more than an hour ago.

> DARKLORD
> Then she is ours.

> DYANA
> What will you do with her, my lord?

> DARKLORD
> To you, pain is as short and sharp as a scream. You cannot hear its music. But I can write a symphony with those notes, manhound.

Dyana doesn't want to hear any more. She vaults aboard the palanquin. They push on, through the pass.

CUT TO

EXT. – MINE ENTRANCE – DAY

Tom is breathing hard. Even Cat is flushed by the exertion of the climb, but when she sees the dark hole of the MINE ENTRANCE up ahead, she RUNS. Pushing up her sleeve, she exposes the bracelet, makes a fist. The insets begin to STROBE, one two three, one two three.

> TOM
> (breathing hard)
> Bingo. We found it.

Thane steps out of the darkness inside the mine.

> THANE
> So you did.

Cat SHRINKS back away from him. She whips out the battered old revolver the Captain gave her, swings it up with both hands, and

FIRES without a moment's hesitation.

The bullet catches Thane in the shoulder. He staggers, then straightens himself, smiling.

> THANE
> The child has a new toy to play with.

BLOOD is seeping from his shoulder wound, but Thane seems to feel very little pain. Tom is horrified.

> THANE
> That which does not kill me makes me stronger.

Cat SNARLS at him, and FIRES again. The second shot is a clean miss. We hear it RICOCHET off the rocks.

> THANE
> Afraid? You should be. She is coming, little animal. She is close now. Do you know what she will do with you?

Cat FIRES. The bullet catches Thane square in the stomach. He GRUNTS, bends, clutches at the wound – but only for a moment. Slowly, he straightens, his hands falling back to his sides.

> THANE
> That one almost hurt.

Only one shot left. Cat is about to use it when Tom catches her wrist.

> TOM
> Cat, enough.

> THANE
> Cat. Yes. I gave her that name, shadow man. Did she tell you that?
> (with mounting rage)
> I taught her to speak. To read. To use machines. I gave her life. Food. Honor. I took her as my mate.

> TOM
> (realizing)

You <u>loved</u> her . . .

(beat)

Let her <u>go</u>, Thane. What kind of man are you?

THANE

Not a man. A manhound.

Behind him, suddenly, the mine entrance LIGHTS with a BRILLIANT BLUE LIGHT as the door opens.

CAT

The door . . .

THANE

There it is. All you need to do is get past me.

At his sides, his hands coil into fists, and six-inch STEEL SPIKES slide from his knuckles. OFF that moment, we

CUT TO

EXT. – IN THE PASS – SIMULTANEOUS

The darklord drives the palanquin upward.

DARKLORD

Faster! Faster! The door is opening. She must not escape. <u>Faster!</u>

A half-mile in front of them, the HOVER TANK slowly lifts into view.

DARKLORD

What is that? That is a weapons system. Stop it.

The turret of the tank slowly swings around.

INT. – THE TANK

The Captain works the controls, a grim smile on his face.

THE CAPTAIN

Welcome to my world, you son of a bitch.

He presses the firing switch.

EXT. – THE TANK

The turret gun belches FLAME. The noise is a hammer blow.

THE PALANQUIN

veers off wildly as a shell EXPLODES directly underneath it. Both
manhounds are THROWN OFF. The darkfield absorbs most of the
damage, but the darklord SHRIEKS in fury, a torrent of unintelligible
alien sounds.

The palanquin returns fire. A LIGHTNING BOLT flies down the pass,
smashing into the tank. Then another. Another. The bolts CRACK
through the air, and the pass rolls with THUNDER.

INT. – THE TANK – TIGHT ON THE CAPTAIN

He's thrown sideways as the tank is hit. His lights go dark. The vehicle
loses power and CRASHES, jarring him.

> THE CAPTAIN
> Hit me again. Hit me again. Come on, <u>again</u>.
> (another hit)
> Yes!

Smoke is pouring from his bulkheads now, but the Captain SMILES.
He hears something else: a deep, ominous RUMBLING from above.

ANGLE THROUGH THE DARKFIELD

The darklord on her palanquin hears it too. Inside the darkfield, the
great distorted form twists in fear, and tries to shelter itself with its
arms.

> DARKLORD
> Nooooooo.

The word disintegrates into a SHRILL ALIEN SCREAM, and

AN AVALANCHE

thunders down and buries tank, palanquin, and all.

                                                    CUT TO

EXT. – MINE ENTRANCE – ON THANE

His head SNAPS sideways at the sound of the avalanche. In that brief
moment of distraction, Cat breaks free of Tom, snaps up the gun, and
FIRES her last shot.

The bullet catches Thane in the head, a grazing shot that bloodies his
temple. He spins and goes down. Cat flings away the empty gun and
scrambles past him to the door.

The BLUE GLOW of the door is fading, growing darker. Thane is
already moving, rolling over, hand on his bloody temple. Tom stands
frozen.

                          CAT
                        (to Tom)
              Coming on!

He doesn't need a second hint. Tom runs, jumping over Thane. Cat
takes him by the hand. Together, they LEAP through the door, and we

                                                SMASH CUT TO

EXT. – THE GREENWOOD – DAY

as Tom and Cat LAND in a pile of fallen leaves. The sky is a deep blue
overhead. They are in an autumn forest, the foliage brilliant all around.
In the distance, perched high on a mountain beside a glittering
waterfall, is a CASTLE. Tom stares at it.

An ARROW thunks into the tree trunk an inch from Tom's head, he
jerks back, and looks at Cat.

                          TOM
              Here we go again.

                          CAT
              Bingo.

And OFF Cat's GRIN, we

FADE OUT

THE END

EIGHT
DOING THE WILD
CARD SHUFFLE

DOING THE WILD CARD SHUFFLE

You can take the boy out of Bayonne, but you can't take Bayonne out of the boy. The same is true of funny books. I admit it. Cut me and I still bleed four-colored ink.

Maybe I don't know the name of the current Green Lantern, but I can still recite Hal Jordan's oath, and tell you how it differed from the one that Alan Scott once swore when he recharged his ring. I can name all of the Challengers of the Unknown for you and give you the original line-up of the Avengers, the X-Men, and the Justice League of America (do I really have to include Snapper Carr?). I have no doubt that in some alternate universe Marvel Comics *did* hire me when I applied in 1971, and right now in that world I am sitting at home muttering and gnawing at my wrists as I watch blockbuster movies based on my characters and stories rake in hundreds of millions of dollars while I receive exactly nothing.

In this world I was spared that fate. In this world I wrote short stories and novellas and novels instead of funny books, and later on screenplays and teleplays as well. Yet that love of superheroes never left me, even when I was well-established as a pro. I still had one more good 'text story' in me, I figured. Maybe more than one, but one for sure; a gritty, hard-nosed tale about what might befall a would-be superhero in the real world.

The germ of the notion went back years and years, but for most of that time it remained no more than a few lines in my files. A kid like me, raised on comic books, finds himself blessed (or is it cursed?) with an actual superpower. What would he do with it? Ignore it? Exploit it? Try to don a spandex costume and fight crime? How would it change his life? How would the real world react to someone who actually did possess powers and abilities far beyond those of mortal men?

(That was my working title: 'With Powers and Abilities Far Beyond Those of Mortal Men.' The phrase is from the old *Superman* TV show, of course, and I later learned that DC Comics had trademarked it, so it was just as well that I never used it).

Precisely what those powers and abilities should be I never did work out, which may be why I never wrote the story. For a long time I leaned toward pyrokinesis, until Stephen King came out with *Firestarter* in 1980. Not only did

King's novel feature a girl who could ignite fires with her mind, but it also gave her father a superpower of his own, a kind of mind control. Though my handling of the theme would have been very different, I could not help feeling as though King had beaten me to the punch.

My life was changing in more important ways in 1980, though. At the end of 1979, I had left my teaching job at Clarke College and moved from Iowa to New Mexico to try and make a go of it as a full time writer. My marriage had ended in the course of the move, so I arrived in the Land of Enchantment a single man again. Santa Fe has remained my home ever since. Though I ended up spending years in Los Angeles working in television and film, I never truly *moved* there. Instead I would rent a furnished apartment in one of the sprawling Oakwood complexes, or a guest house in someone's backyard, but the moment my current project wrapped I would be on the road again, headed home to New Mexico. Santa Fe was the place where I hung my hats and paid my taxes, the place where I kept my books and my funny books and the old double-breasted pinstriped mustard-yellow sports jacket that had not fit me for a decade.

And Santa Fe was where Parris was too, holding down the fort. We'd met at a convention in 1975, a few months before I entered into my ill-considered marriage. I knew I liked her the moment she told me that 'A Song for Lya' made her cry (well, she was a stone fox too, and we were both naked when we met, but never mind about that, it's none of your business). Parris and I stayed in touch after that con, exchanging occasional letters through all the years when I was teaching Catholic girls and she was selling sno-cones and shoveling elephant dung for Ringling Brothers. In 1981 we got together at another convention, and she came to Santa Fe to stay with me a while. That 'while' will have lasted twenty-two years by the time you read this. Now and again one of my readers will ask me why I don't write sad stories of unrequited love any longer, the way I did so often in the '70s. Parris is to blame for that. You can only write that stuff when your heart is broken.

When I first moved to Santa Fe in the wake of my divorce, I knew no one in the city but Roger Zelazny, and him only slightly. Roger took me under his wing. On the first Friday of every month we would drive down to Albuquerque to lunch with Tony Hillerman, Norm Zollinger, Fred Saberhagen, and the other New Mexico writers. I also dropped in on the Albuquerque SF club, where I met the local fans and still more writers and aspiring writers. Before very long, I found myself gaming with some of them.

Though I had been a serious chess player from seventh grade through college, and enjoyed *Risk* and *Diplomacy* and other board games, I had never played *Dungeons & Dragons* or any other role-playing game until I moved to New Mexico. Parris had, however, and she convinced me to give it a try. The bunch that we fell in with were mostly hardcore fans, and half of them were writers. At the time Parris and I joined the group, they were playing Chaosium's *Call of Cthulhu*, based on the works of H. P. Lovecraft, so I felt right at home. Since the rest of the party were all intrepid adventurers determined to save the world from the Cthulhu cults, I played a journalist who was yellow in both senses of the word. As my friends died screaming or went insane, I would run away to cable my story to the *Herald*. Our sessions were like some madcap improv theater, with shuggoths.

Before the year was out, I had become so enamored of gaming that I was running a *Call of Cthulhu* campaign of my own. I'd found that I enjoyed being a gamemaster even more than being a player.

Which brings us to September 1983, when Vic Milan presented me with a new game for my birthday. *SuperWorld* reawakened the frustrated comic book writer inside me, and soon replaced *Call of Cthulhu* as the group's favorite game. We played it obsessively for more than a year, two or three times a week, and no one became more obsessed than me. As gamemaster, I found myself dusting off old characters like Manta Ray and coming up with new ones, villains chiefly . . . plus one hero who floated around in an iron shell, and called himself the Great and Powerful Turtle. My players, half of whom were writers, created some unforgettable characters of their own; Yeoman, Crypt Kicker, Peregrine, Elephant Girl, Modular Man, Cap'n Trips, Straight Arrow, Black Shadow, Topper, and the Harlem Hammer were only a few of the strange and wondrous folks who first made their appearance in our *SuperWorld* sessions.

The tale of how *SuperWorld* ultimately begat *Wild Cards* is one that I've told numerous times before, most notably in my afterwords for the iBooks reissues of the early volumes of the series. I won't repeat myself here; the reissues are easily available, for those who would like to read the grisly details. Suffice it to say that a number of us fell in love with our characters, and began to think they might have possibilities beyond the game.

Shared worlds were all the rage in the early '80s, thanks to the tremendous success of the *Thieves World* anthologies edited by Bob Asprin and Lynn Abbey. The format was perfect for what we wanted to do with our *SuperWorld* characters, so I pitched the idea to my fellow gamers, filled out our ranks by recruiting Roger Zelazny, Howard Waldrop, Lew Shiner, Stephen Leigh, and half a dozen other writers from all across the country, and drew up a formal proposal for a three volume anthology series called *Wild Cards*. Shawna McCarthy bought it, her first day on the job as an editor at Bantam Books.

All shared worlds are collaborations, to a greater or a lesser extent. Looking over *Thieves World* and its imitators, I realized that the shared worlds that worked the best were those that shared the most, where the storylines and characters were the most tightly intertwined. Right from the first, therefore, we resolved that *Wild Cards* would be more than just a collection of loosely-connected stories set against a common background. We wanted to take the art of collaboration to a whole new level. To signal our intent, we called the books 'mosaic novels' rather than anthologies.

I do think we succeeded for the most part . . . but as with any new form, there were bumps in the road, and lessons that we had to learn the hard way. Editing the series, I often felt like the ringmaster at a nine-ring circus, trying to keep order with a whip made out of spaghetti. Some days it was fun and some days it was frustrating, but it was never ever tedious. When everything was going smoothly, I liked to compare us to a symphony orchestra, with me as the conductor, but a better metaphor might be a herd of cats. We all know how easy it is to herd cats, don't we?

So here's to all the members of the Wild Cards Consortium, as zany and talented a bunch of cats as any editor could ever hope to herd: Roger Zelazny, Howard Waldrop, Walter Jon Williams, Stephen Leigh, Gail Gerstner Miller, Lewis Shiner, John J. Miller, Victor Milan, Walton (Bud) Simons, Arthur Byron Cover, William F. Wu, Laura J. Mixon, Michael Cassutt, Sage Walker, Edward Bryant, Leanne C. Harper, Kevin Andrew Murphy, Steve Perrin, Parris, Royce Wideman, Pat Cadigan, Chris Claremont, Bob Wayne, and Daniel Abraham. And most of all, here's to Melinda M. Snodgrass, my tireless assistant editor, without whose diplomatic intercessions I would surely have killed and butchered at least four of the aforementioned.

Wild Cards was a hit right from the first, and not only by anthology standards. The sales of the first volume exceeded the sales of any of my novels to that date, save *Fevre Dream* alone, and the later books would be almost as successful. The reviews were excellent, by and large. Walter Jon Williams' story in the first book was a finalist for the Nebula, one of the few shared world stories ever accorded that honor, and the series as a whole was nominated for the Hugo Award, losing in 1988 at New Orleans to Alan Moore's splendid graphic novel *Watchmen*.

Bantam was only too pleased to make an offer for three more volumes after the first three had been delivered. Our advances rose and rose again. The series became a popular topic for worldcon panels, and two regional conventions chose Wild Cards themes, and brought all the authors in as Guests of Honor. Marvel Comics did a *Wild Cards* miniseries under its Epic imprint, and Steve Jackson Games issued a roleplaying game, bringing us full circle. Hollywood was heard from too. Disney Studios optioned the film rights to the books, and Melinda Snodgrass and I wrote several drafts of a *Wild Cards* screenplay in the early '90s.

The series began at virtually the same time as my association with *The Twilight Zone*, and continued my three seasons on *Beauty and the Beast*, through all my feature assignments and television pilots. That steady stream of books with my name on the covers undoubtedly helped to keep me alive in the worlds of science fiction and fantasy. Just as I had to return to Santa Fe from time to time during my Hollywood years, to remind myself of who I was and where I lived, I had to keep publishing books and short stories as well. If I hadn't . . . well, readers have short memories, I fear, and in recent years they have only grown shorter.

Given the long hours and high stress levels so typical of Hollywood, the last thing any television producer needs is a second job, but I had one, courtesy of *Wild Cards*. Not only did I edit the books, but I wrote for them, as often as I could find the time.

'Shell Games,' my principle contribution to volume one, had antecedents that went way back. The bones of the story were ones I'd been gnawing on for years before I ever heard of *SuperWorld*; this was 'With Powers and Abilities Far Beyond Those of Mortal Men,' reworked to fit our new shared universe. (Never throw anything away.) I'd intended to use pyrokinesis for my hero's power, until *Firestarter*, but telekinesis worked just as well. The Great and Powerful Turtle began life as a minor character in our *SuperWorld* campaign, but would soon become quite a major one in *Wild Cards*. Mind you, a story and a game have very different needs, and what works splendidly for one may not work at all for the other, so the Turtle changed quite a bit before he hit the page.

'Shell Games' was not his tale alone, though; he shared the stage with Dr Tachyon, a character created by Melinda Snodgrass. Working with other people's characters is one of the challenges of doing a shared world. It is often a lot of fun, and often a huge headache. Sometimes it is both at once. In her story 'Degradation Rites,' which preceded mine in *Wild Cards*, Melinda told how Dr Tachyon had inadvertently destroyed the mind of a woman he loved in an effort to protect the identity of his ace patients from HUAC. The experience had destroyed Dr Tachyon as well, and thereafter he had collapsed into a decade-long orgy of guilt, self-recrimination, and alcoholism. It was my job to drag him out of his funk in 'Shell Games,' and set him back on the path to recovery . . . while also introducing my own characters.

If you have read this far, you will soon realize that Thomas Tudbury is far and away the most autobiographical of all the characters I've ever created. That being said, there are important differences as well. Though I cannibalized many elements of my own childhood for Tom's, I also changed some crucial things. In real life I never had a friend like Junkyard Joey DiAngelis, though many was the time I wished for one. (Especially one like the Joey of the screenplay, who Melinda and I changed into a girl.) I had two terrific sisters, while Tom was an only child. Oh, and the real me never developed kickass telekinesis either, more's the pity.

Not all of the characters in *Wild Cards* had antecedents in our *SuperWorld*

campaigns. Many were entirely original. Among those were Howard Waldrop's Jetboy, Lew Shiner's heroic pimp Fortunato, Steve Leigh's sinister
Puppetman, and Roger Zelazny's Sleeper, Croyd Crenson, who drew the
wild card during a long walk home from school one day, and never learned
algebra. Jay Ackroyd (aka Popinjay), my other major character in the series,
was one of those as well. Jay was first mentioned in *Aces High*, our second
volume, but did not come on stage until the third, *Jokers Wild*, where he
teams up with Hiram Worchester for most of my storyline. As the series went
on, Ackroyd came more and more to the fore, and starred in several stories
of his own. By the end of our Bantam run, Jay had become almost as popular
as the Turtle.

Tom and Jay were not the only arrows in my quiver. From time to time I
would choose to tell a story from the viewpoint of one of my myriad lesser
characters. The focus of my interstitial narrative in *Aces High* was Jube the
Walrus, an alien in a Hawaiian shirt and pork-pie hat. In *Jokers Wild* my story
featured Hiram Worchester, the urbane and portly proprietor of the restaurant
atop the Empire State Building. For *Dealer's Choice* I used a character created
by Bud Simons, the bodysnatcher Zelda, to give the readers a better picture
of what the bad guys were up to on the Rox.

'The Journal of Xavier Desmond' is the story of another of my secondary
players, a joker activist who had first appeared in 'Shell Games' as the maitre
d' of the Funhouse. Des had risen in the world since then, and as the de facto
'mayor of Jokertown' he seemed a natural choice to become one of the joker
delegates on the global fact-finding tour that provided the spine for our fourth
volume, *Aces Abroad*. The Turtle could not very well go, since he never left
his shell. Nor was Jay Ackroyd likely to be invited. Hiram Worchester would
be, of course, and I could have chosen him to be my protagonist . . . but I
had just done Hiram in the third book, and I wanted to try a joker perspective.

The interstitial narrative was one of the toughest assignments in any *Wild
Cards* book. In a mosaic novel, you want the whole to be more than the sum
of its parts. If each story was a brick, the interstitial was the mortar that made
them a wall. Whoever wrote the interstitial had to wait until the other stories
were done, read the first drafts to see where the holes were, and then try to
patch them over . . . while also telling a good story of his own. If the
interstitial was just filler, the book would fall apart.

Later in the history of *Wild Cards*, other writers would step forward to do the
interstitials. Bud Simons took a crack at it, and Steve Leigh let himself be
drafted more than once. In the early volumes, however, the task usually fell
to me as editor. 'The Journal of Xavier Desmond' is my favorite of those
interstitial stories, and represents some of the best work I did for *Wild Cards*.
This is the first time it has been presented by itself, shorn of the stories it
originally wove around and through.

Nothing goes on forever. After a good long run the *Wild Cards* series began to lose steam. The books had gotten darker (and they had been pretty dark to begin with), and sales were declining with each volume, slowly but steadily. Some of our best writers had gone on to other projects; popular characters had died or retired. The books were still outselling most paperbacks by a healthy margin, but we were definitely on the downslope. When our contract came up for renewal, Bantam offered us the same terms for the next triad that we had received for the last two.

Foolishly, perhaps, we rejected that offer, and took the series to a smaller publisher for a substantial raise. It was a bad mistake. Though we got more money in the short run, our new publisher lacked both Bantam's resources and Bantam's commitment to the series. Without new titles in the pipeline, Bantam soon allowed the first twelve books go out of print, Not only did our backlist sales dry up, but new readers no longer had an easy entry to the world by the way of volume one. We tried to get around that by scrapping the old numbering and promoting volume thirteen as 'book one of a new series,' but *Card Sharks* remained a confusing read for readers not familiar with all that had gone before. Sales dropped precipitously, and after the publication of the fifteenth volume in 1995, we found ourselves without a publisher.

And that was the end of that.

Or was it? With strange aeons even death may die, said H. P. Lovecraft. As of 2001, *Wild Cards* returned with a brand new publisher, iBooks. After a seven-year hiatus, *Deuces Down*, the sixteenth volume in the series, was released in 2002 with all new stories. Our seventeenth volume is in the pipeline, and the old books are being re-released for a new generation of readers. Once more we're hearing talk of games and comic books and movie options.

Will any of this come to pass? Will there be an eighteenth book, a nineteenth, a twentieth? Damned if I know.

I wouldn't bet against us, though. There's a certain turtle that I know who has already had more lives than any cat.

Shell Games

When he'd moved into the dorm back in September, the first thing that Thomas Tudbury had done was tack up his signed photograph of President Kennedy, and the tattered 1944 *Time* cover with Jetboy as Man of the Year.

By November, the picture of Kennedy was riddled with holes from Rodney's darts. Rod had decorated his side of the room with a Confederate flag and a dozen *Playboy* centerfolds. He hated Jews, niggers, jokers, and Kennedy, and didn't like Tom much either. All through the fall semester, he had fun; covering Tom's bed with shaving cream, short-sheeting him, hiding his eyeglasses, filling his desk drawer with dog turds.

On the day that Kennedy was killed in Dallas, Tom came back to his room fighting to hold the tears. Rod had left him a present. He'd used a red pen. The whole top of Kennedy's head was dripping blood now, and over his eyes Rod had drawn little red *X*'s. His tongue was sticking out of the corner of his mouth.

Thomas Tudbury stared at that for a long, long time. He did not cry; he would not allow himself to cry. He began to pack his suitcases.

The freshman parking lot was halfway across campus. The trunk on his '54 Mercury had a broken lock, so he tossed the bags into the seat. He let the car warm up for a long time in the November chill. He must have looked funny sitting there; a short, overweight guy with a crew cut and horn-rim glasses, pressing his head against the top of the steering wheel like he was going to be sick.

As he was driving out of the lot, he spied Rodney's shiny Olds Cutlass.

Tom shifted to neutral and idled for a moment, considering. He looked around. There was no one in sight; everybody was inside watching the news. He licked his lips nervously, then looked back at the Oldsmobile. His knuckles whitened around the wheel. He stared hard, furrowed his brow, and *squeezed*.

The door panels gave first, bending inward slowly under the pressure. The headlights exploded with small pops, one after the other. Chrome trim clattered to the ground, and the rear windshield shattered suddenly, glass flying everywhere. Fenders buckled and collapsed, metal squealing in protest. Both rear tires blew at once, the side panels caved in, then the hood; the windshield disintegrated entirely. The crank-case gave, and then the walls of the gas tank; oil, gasoline, and transmission fluid pooled under the car. By then Tom Tudbury was more confident, and that made it easier. He imagined he had the Olds caught in a huge invisible fist, a *strong* fist, and he squeezed all the harder. The crunch of breaking glass and the scream of tortured metal filled the parking lot, but there was no one to hear. He methodically mashed the Oldsmobile into a ball of crushed metal.

When it was over, he shifted into gear and left college, Rodney, and childhood behind forever.

*

Somewhere a giant was crying.

Tachyon woke disoriented and sick, his hangover throbbing in time to the mammoth sobs. The shapes in the dark room were strange and unfamiliar. Had the assassins come in the night again, was the family under attack? He had to find his father. He lurched dizzily to his feet, head swimming, and put a hand against the wall to steady himself.

The wall was too close. These weren't his chambers, this was all wrong, the smell . . . and then the memories came back. He would have preferred the assassins.

He had dreamed of Takis again, he realized. His head hurt, and his throat was raw and dry. Fumbling in the darkness, he found the chain-pull for the overhead light. The bulb swung wildly when he yanked, making the shadows dance. He closed his eyes to still the lurching in his gut. There was a foul taste at the back of his mouth. His hair was matted and filthy, his clothing rumpled. And worst of all, the bottle was empty. Tachyon looked around helplessly. A six-by-ten on the second floor of a lodging house named ROOMS, on a street called the Bowery. Confusingly, the surrounding neighborhood had once been called the Bowery too – Angelface had told him that. But that was before; the area had a different name now. He went to the window, pulling up the shade. The yellow light of a streetlamp filled the room. Across the street, the giant was reaching for the moon, and weeping because he could not grasp it.

Tiny, they called him. Tachyon supposed that was human wit. Tiny would have been fourteen feet tall if only he could stand up. His face was unlined and innocent, crowned with a tangle of soft dark hair. His legs were slender, and perfectly proportioned. And that was the joke: slender, perfectly proportioned legs could not begin to support the weight of a fourteen-foot-tall man. Tiny sat in a wooden wheelchair, a great mechanized thing that rolled through the streets of Jokertown on four bald tires from a wrecked semi. When he saw Tach in the window, he screamed incoherently, almost as though he recognized him. Tachyon turned away from the window, shaking. It was another Jokertown night. He needed a drink.

His room smelled of mildew and vomit, and it was very cold. ROOMS was not as well heated as the hotels he had frequented in the old days. Unbidden, he remembered the Mayflower down in Washington, where he and Blythe ... but no, better not to think of that. What time was it anyway? Late enough. The sun was down, and Jokertown came to life at night.

He plucked his overcoat from the floor and slipped it on. Soiled as it was, it was still a marvelous coat, a lovely rich rose color, with fringed golden epaulets on the shoulders and loops of golden braid to fasten the long row of buttons. A musician's coat, the man at the Goodwill had told him. He sat on the edge of his sagging mattress to pull on his boots.

The washroom was down at the end of the hall. Steam rose from his urine as it splashed against the rim of the toilet; his hands shook so badly that he couldn't even aim right. He slapped cold, rust-colored water on his face, and dried his hands on a filthy towel.

Outside, Tach stood for a moment beneath the creaking ROOMS sign, staring at Tiny. He felt bitter and ashamed. And much too sober. There was nothing to be done about Tiny, but he could deal with his sobriety. He turned his back on the weeping giant, slid his hands deep into the pockets of his coat, and walked off briskly down the Bowery.

In the alleys, jokers and winos passed brown paper bags from hand to hand, and stared with dull eyes at the passersby. Taverns, pawnbrokers, and mask shops were all doing a brisk trade. The Famous Bowery Wild Card Dime Museum (they still called it that, but admission was a quarter now) was closing for the day. Tachyon had gone through it once, two years ago, on a day when he was feeling especially guilt-ridden; along with a half-dozen particularly freakish jokers, twenty jars of 'monstrous joker babies' floating in formaldehyde, and a sensational little newsreel about the Day of the Wild Card, the museum had a wax-works display whose dioramas featured Jetboy, the Four Aces, a Jokertown Orgy ... and him.

A tour bus rolled past, pink faces pressed to the windows. Beneath the neon light of a neighborhood pizza parlor, four youths in black leather jackets and rubber facemasks eyed Tachyon with open hostility. They made him uneasy. He averted his eyes and dipped into the mind of the nearest: *mincing pansy looka that hair dye-job fershure thinks he's inna marching band like to beat his fuckin' drums but no wait shit there's better we'll find us a good one tonight yeah wanna get one that squishes when we hit it.* Tach broke the contact with distaste and hurried on. It was old news, and a new sport:

come down to the Bowery, buy some masks, beat up a joker. The police didn't seem to care.

The Chaos Club and its famous All-Joker Revue had the usual big crowd. As Tachyon approached, a long gray limo pulled up to the curb. The doorman, wearing a black tuxedo over luxuriant white fur, opened the door with his tail and helped out a fat man in a dinner jacket. His date was a buxom teenager in a strapless evening gown and pearls, her blonde hair piled high in a bouffant hairdo.

A block farther on, a snake-lady called out a proposition from the top of a nearby stoop. Her scales were rainbow-colored, glistening. 'Don't be scared, Red,' she said, 'it's still soft inside.' He shook his head.

The Funhouse was housed in a long building with giant picture windows fronting the street, but the glass had been replaced with oneway mirrors. Randall stood out front, shivering in tails and domino. He looked perfectly normal – until you noticed that he never took his right hand out of his pocket. 'Hey, Tacky,' he called out. 'Whattaya make of Ruby?'

'Sorry, I don't know her,' Tachyon said.

Randall scowled. 'No, the guy who killed Oswald.'

'Oswald?' Tach said, confused. 'Oswald who?'

'Lee Oswald, the guy who shot Kennedy. He got killed on TV this afternoon.'

'Kennedy's dead?' Tachyon said. It was Kennedy who'd permitted his return to the United States, and Tach admired the Kennedys; they seemed almost Takisian. But assassination was part of leadership. 'His brothers will avenge him,' he said. Then he recalled that they didn't do things that way on earth, and besides, this man Ruby had already avenged him, it seemed. How strange that he had dreamed of assassins.

'They got Ruby in jail,' Randall was saying. 'If it was me, I'd give the fucker a medal.' He paused. 'He shook my hand once,' he added. 'When he was running against Nixon, he came through to give a speech at the Chaos Club. Afterward, when he was leaving, he was shaking hands with everybody.' The doorman took his right hand out of his pocket. It was hard and chitinous, insectile, and in the middle was a cluster of swollen blind eyes. 'He didn't even flinch,' Randall said. 'Smiled and said he hoped I'd remember to vote.'

Tachyon had known Randall for a year, but he had never seen his hand before. He wanted to do what Kennedy had done, to grasp that twisted claw, embrace it, shake it. He tried to slide his hand out of the pocket of his coat, but the bile rose in the back of his throat, and somehow all he could do was look away, and say, 'He was a good man.'

Randall hid his hand again. 'Go on inside, Tacky,' he said, not unkindly.

'Angelface had to go and see a man, but she told Des to keep your table open.'

Tachyon nodded and let Randall open the door for him. Inside, he gave his coat and shoes to the girl in the checkroom, a joker with a trim little body whose feathered owl mask concealed whatever the wild card had done to her face. Then he pushed through the interior doors, his stockinged feet sliding with smooth familiarity over the mirrored floor. When he looked down, another Tachyon was staring back up at him, framed by his feet; a grossly fat Tachyon with a head like a beach ball.

Suspended from the mirrored ceiling, a crystal chandelier glittered with a hundred pinpoint lights, its reflections sparkling off the floor tiles and walls and mirrored alcoves, the silvered goblets and mugs, and even the waiters' trays. Some of the mirrors reflected true; the others were distorting mirrors, funhouse mirrors. When you looked over your shoulder in the Funhouse, you could never tell what you'd find looking back. It was the only establishment in Jokertown that attracted jokers and normals in equal numbers. In the Funhouse the normals could see themselves twisted and malformed, and giggle, and play at being jokers; and a joker, if he was very lucky, might glance in the right mirror and see himself as he once had been.

'Your booth is waiting, Doctor Tachyon,' said Desmond, the maitre d'. Des was a large, florid man; his thick trunk, pink and wrinkled, curled around a wine list. He lifted it, and beckoned for Tachyon to follow with one of the fingers that dangled from its end. 'Will you be having your usual brand of cognac tonight?'

'Yes,' Tach said, wishing he had some money for a tip.

That night he had his first drink for Blythe, as always, but his second was for John Fitzgerald Kennedy.

The rest were for himself.

*

At the end of Hook Road, past the abandoned refinery and the import/export warehouses, past the railroad sidings with their forlorn red boxcars, beneath the highway underpass, past the empty lots full of weeds and garbage, past the huge soybean-oil tanks, Tom found his refuge. It was almost dark by the time he arrived, and the engine in the Merc was thumping ominously. But Joey would know what to do about that.

The junkyard stood hard on the oily polluted waters of New York Bay. Behind a ten-foot-high chain link fence topped with three curly strands of barbed wire, a pack of junkyard dogs kept pace with his car, barking a raucous welcome that would have terrified anyone who knew the dogs less well. The sunset gave a strange bronze cast to the mountains of shattered, twisted, rusted automobiles, the acres of scrap metal, the hills and valleys of junk and trash. Finally Tom came to the wide double gate. On one side a metal sign warned TRESPASSERS KEEP OUT; on the other side another sign told them to BEWARE OF THE DOGS. The gate was chained and locked.

Tom stopped and honked his horn.

Just beyond the fence he could see the four-room shack that Joey called home. A huge sign was mounted on top of the corrugated tin roof, with yellow spotlights stuck up there to illuminate the letters. It said DIANGELIS SCRAP METAL & AUTO PARTS. The paint was faded and blistered by two decades of sun and rain; the wood itself had cracked, and one of the spots had burned out. Next to the house was parked an ancient yellow dump truck, a tow truck, and Joey's pride and joy, a blood-red 1959 Cadillac coupe with tail fins like a shark and a monster of a hopped-up engine poking right up through its cutaway hood.

Tom honked again. This time he gave it their special signal, tooting out the *Here-he-comes-to-save-the-daaaay!* theme from the *Mighty Mouse* cartoons they'd watched as kids.

A square of yellow light spilled across the junkyard as Joey came out with a beer in either hand.

They were nothing alike, him and Joey. They came from different stock, lived in different worlds, but they'd been best friends since the day of the third-grade pet show. That was the day he'd found out that turtles couldn't fly; the day he realized what he was, and what he could do.

Stevie Bruder and Josh Jones had caught him out in the schoolyard. They played catch with his turtles, tossing them back and forth while Tommy ran between them, red-faced and crying. When they got bored, they bounced them off the punchball square chalked on the wall. Stevie's German shepherd ate one. When Tommy tried to grab the dog, Stevie laid into him and left him on the ground with broken glasses and a split lip.

They would have done worse, except for Junkyard Joey, a scrawny kid with shaggy black hair, two years older than his classmates, but he'd already been left back twice, couldn't hardly read, and they always said he smelled bad on account of his father, Dom, owned the junkyard. Joey wasn't as big as Stevie Bruder, but he didn't care, that day or any day. He just grabbed Stevie by the back of his shirt and yanked him around and kicked him in the balls. Then he kicked the dog too, and he would have kicked Josh Jones, except Josh ran away. As he fled, a dead turtle floated off the ground and flew across the schoolyard to smack him in the back of his fat red neck.

Joey had seen it happen. 'How'd you do that?' he said, astonished. Until that moment, even Tommy hadn't realized that *he* was the reason his turtles could fly.

It became their shared secret, the glue that held their odd friendship together. Tommy helped Joey with his homework and quizzed him for tests. Joey became Tommy's protector against the random brutality of playground and schoolyard. Tommy read comic books to Joey, until Joey's own reading got so much better that he didn't need Tommy. Dom, a grizzled man with salt-and-pepper hair, a beer belly, and a gentle heart, was proud of that; he couldn't read himself, not even Italian. The friendship lasted through grammar school and high school and Joey's dropping out. It survived their discovery of girls, weathered the death of Dom DiAngelis and Tom's family moving off to Perth Amboy. Joey DiAngelis was still the only one who knew what Tom was.

Joey popped the cap on another Rheingold with the church key that hung around his neck. Under his sleeveless white undershirt a beer belly like his father's was growing. 'You're too fucking smart to be doing shitwork in a TV repair shop,' he was saying.

'It's a job,' Tom said. 'I did it last summer, I can do it full time. It's not important what kind of job I have. What's important is what I do with my, uh, talent.'

'Talent?' Joey mocked.

'You know what I mean, you dumb wop.' Tom set his empty bottle down on the top of the orange crate next to the armchair. Most of Joey's furnishings weren't what you'd call lavish; he scavenged them from the junkyard. 'I been thinking about what Jetboy said at the end, trying to think what it meant. I figure he was saying that there were things he hadn't done yet. Well, shit, I haven't done *anything*. All the way back I asked what I could do for the country, y'know? Well, fuck, we both know the answer to that one.'

Joey rocked back in his chair, sucking on his Rheingold and shaking his head. Behind him, the wall was lined with the bookshelves that Dom had built for the kids almost ten years ago. The bottom row was all men's magazines. The rest were comic books. Their comic books. *Superman*s and *Batman*s, *Action Comics* and *Detective*, the *Classics Illustrated*s that Joey had mined for all his book reports, horror comics and crime comics and air-war comics, and best of all, their treasure – an almost complete run of *Jetboy Comics*.

Joey saw what he was looking at. 'Don't even think it,' he said, 'you're no fuckin' Jetboy, Tuds.'

'No,' said Tom, 'I'm more than he was. I'm—'

'A dork,' Joey suggested.

'An ace,' he said gravely. 'Like the Four Aces.'

'They were a colored doo-wop group, weren't they?'

Tom flushed. 'You dumb wop, they weren't singers, they—'

Joey cut him off with a sharp gesture. 'I know who the fuck they were, Tuds. Gimme a break. They were dumb shits, like you. They all went to jail or got shot or something, didn't they? Except for the fuckin' snitch, whatsisname.' He snapped his fingers. 'You know, the guy in *Tarzan*.'

'Jack Braun,' Tom said. He'd done a term paper on the Four Aces once. 'And I bet there are others, hiding out there. Like me. I've been hiding. But no more.'

'So you figure you're going to go to the *Bayonne Times* and give a fucking show? You asshole. You might as well tell 'em you're a commie. They'll make you move to Jokertown and they'll break all the goddamned windows in your dad's house. They might even draft you, asswipe.'

'No,' said Tom. 'I've got it scoped out. The Four Aces were easy targets. I'm not going to let them know who I am or where I live.' He used the beer bottle in his hand to gesture vaguely at the bookshelves. 'I'm going to keep my name secret, like in the comics.'

Joey laughed out loud. 'Fuckin' A. You gonna wear long johns too, you dumb shit?'

'Goddamn it,' Tom said. He was getting pissed off. 'Shut the fuck up.' Joey just sat there, rocking and laughing. 'Come on, big mouth,' Tom snapped, rising. 'Get off your fat ass and come outside, and I'll show just how dumb I am. C'mon, you know so damned much.'

Joey DiAngelis got to his feet. 'This I gotta see.'

Outside, Tom waited impatiently, shifting his weight from foot to foot, breath steaming in the cold November air, while Joey went to the big metal box on the side of the house and threw a switch. High atop their poles, the junkyard lights blazed to life. The dogs gathered around, sniffing, and followed them when they began to walk. Joey had a beer bottle poking out of a pocket of his black leather jacket.

It was only a junkyard, full of garbage and scrap metal and wrecked cars, but tonight it seemed as magical as when Tommy was ten. On a rise overlooking the black waters of New York Bay, an ancient white Packard loomed like a ghostly fort. That was just what it had been, when Joey and he had been kids; their sanctum, their stronghold, their cavalry outpost and space station and castle rolled all in one. It shone in the moonlight, and the waters beyond were full of promise as they lapped against the shore. Darkness and shadows lay heavy in the yard, changing the piles of trash and metal into mysterious black hills, with a maze of gray alleys between them. Tom led them into that labyrinth, past the big trash heap where they'd played king-of-the-mountain and dueled with scrap-iron swords, past the treasure troves where they'd found so many busted toys and hunks of colored glass and deposit bottles, and once even a whole cardboard carton full of comic books.

They walked between rows of twisted, rusty cars stacked one on another; Fords and Chevys, Hudsons and DeSotos, a Corvette with a shattered accordion hood, a litter of dead Beetles, a dignified black hearse as dead as the passengers it had carried. Tom looked at them all carefully. Finally he stopped. 'That one,' he said, pointing to the remains of a gutted old Studebaker Hawk. Its engine was gone, as were its tires; the windshield was a spiderweb of broken glass, and even in the darkness they could see where rust had chewed away at the fenders and side panels. 'Not worth anything, right?'

Joey opened his beer. 'Go ahead, it's all yours.'

Tom took a deep breath and faced the car. His hands became fists at his side. He stared hard, concentrating. The car rocked slightly. Its front grille lifted an unsteady couple of inches from the ground.

'Whooo-eeee,' Joey said derisively, punching Tom lightly in the shoulder. The Studebaker dropped with a clang, and a bumper fell off. 'Shit, I'm impressed,' Joey said.

'Damn it, keep quiet and leave me alone,' Tom said. 'I can do it, I'll show you, just shut your fuckin' mouth for a minute. I've been practicing, You don't know the things I can do.'

'Won't say a fuckin' word,' Joey promised, grinning. He took a swig of his beer.

Tom turned back to the Studebaker. He tried to blot out everything, forget about Joey, the dogs, the junkyard; the Studebaker filled his world. His stomach was a hard little ball. He told it to relax, took several deep breaths, let his fists uncurl. *Come on, come on, take it easy, don't get upset, do it, you've done more than this, this is easy, easy.*

The car rose slowly, drifting upward in a shower of rust. Tom turned it around and around, faster and faster. Then, with a triumphant smile, Tom threw it fifty feet across the junkyard. It crashed into a stack of dead Chevys and brought the whole thing down in an avalanche of metal.

Joey finished his Rheingold. 'Not bad. A few years ago, you could barely lift me over a fence.'

'I'm getting stronger all the time,' Tom said.

Joey DiAngelis nodded, and tossed his empty bottle to the side. 'Good,' he said, 'then you won't have any problem with me, willya?' He gave Tom a hard push with both hands.

Tom staggered back a step, frowning. 'Cut it out, Joey.'

'Make me,' Joey said. He shoved him again, harder. This time Tom almost lost his footing.

'Damn it, *stop* it,' Tom said. 'It's not funny, Joey.'

'No?' Joey said. He grinned. 'I think it's fuckin' hilarious. But hey, you can stop me, can't you? Use your damn power.' He moved right up in Tom's face and slapped him lightly across the cheek. 'Stop me, ace,' he said. He slapped him harder. 'C'mon, Jetboy, stop me.' The third slap was the hardest yet. 'Let's go, supes, whatcha waitin' for?' The fourth blow had a sharp sting; the fifth snapped Tom's head half around. Joey stopped smiling; Tom could smell the beer on his breath.

Tom tried to grab his hand, but Joey was too strong, too fast; he evaded Tom's grasp and landed another slap. 'You wanna box, ace? I'll turn you into fuckin' dogmeat. Dork. Asshole.' The slap almost tore Tom's head off, and brought stinging tears to his eyes. '*Stop me*, jagoff,' Joey screamed. He closed his hand, and buried his fist in Tom's stomach so hard it doubled him over and took his breath away.

Tom tried to summon his concentration, to grab and push, but it was the schoolyard all over again, Joey was everywhere, fists raining down on him, and it was all he could do to get his hands up and try to block the blows, and it was no good anyway, Joey was much stronger, he pounded him, pushed him, screaming all the while, and Tom couldn't think, couldn't focus, couldn't do anything but hurt, and he was retreating, staggering back, and Joey came after him, fists cocked, and caught him with an uppercut that landed right on his mouth with a crack that made his teeth hurt. All of a sudden Tom was lying on his back on the ground, with a mouth full of blood.

Joey stood over him frowning. 'Fuck,' he said. 'I didn't mean to bust your lip.' He reached down, took Tom by the hand, and yanked him roughly to his feet.

Tom wiped blood from his lip with the back of his hand. There was blood on the front of his shirt too. 'Look at me, I'm all messed up,' he said with disgust. He glared at Joey. 'That wasn't fair. You can't expect me to do anything when you're pounding on me, damn it.'

'Uh-huh,' Joey said. 'And while you're concentrating and squinting your eyes, you figure the fuckin' bad guys are just gonna leave you alone, right?' He clapped Tom across the back. 'They'll knock out all your fuckin' teeth. That's if you're lucky, if they don't just shoot you. You ain't no Jetboy, Tuds.' He shivered. 'C'mon. It's fuckin' cold out here.'

*

When he woke in warm darkness, Tach remembered only a little of the binge, but that was how he liked it. He struggled to sit up. The sheets he was lying on were satin, smooth and sensual, and beneath the odor of stale vomit he could still smell a faint trace of some flowery perfume.

Unsteady, he tossed off the bedclothes and pulled himself to the edge of the four-poster bed. The floor beneath his bare feet was carpeted. He was naked, the air uncomfortably warm on his bare skin. He reached out a hand, found the light switch, and whimpered a little at the brightness. The room was pink-and-white clutter with Victorian furnishings and thick, soundproofed walls. An oil painting of John F. Kennedy smiled down from above the hearth; in one corner stood a three-foot-tall plaster statue of the Virgin Mary.

Angelface was seated in a pink wingback chair by the cold fireplace, blinking at him sleepily and covering her yawn with the back of her hand.

Tach felt sick and ashamed. 'I put you out of your own bed again, didn't I?' he said.

'It's all right,' she replied. Her feet were resting on a tiny footstool. Her soles were ugly and bruised, black and swollen despite the special padded shoes she wore. Otherwise she was lovely. Unbound, her black hair fell to her waist, and her skin had a flushed, radiant quality to it, a warm glow of life. Her eyes were dark and liquid, but the most amazing thing, the thing that never failed to astonish Tachyon, was the warmth in them, the affection he felt so unworthy of. With all he had done to her, and to all the rest of them, somehow this woman called Angelface forgave, and cared.

Tach raised a hand to his temple. Someone with a buzzsaw was trying to remove the back of his skull. 'My head,' he groaned. 'At your prices, the least you could do is take the resins and poisons out of the drinks you sell. On Takis, we—'

'I know,' Angelface said. 'On Takis you've bred hangovers out of your wines. You told me that one already.'

Tachyon gave her a weary smile. She looked impossibly fresh, wearing nothing but a short satin tunic that left her legs bare to the thigh. It was a deep, wine red, lovely against her skin. But when she rose, he glimpsed the side of her face, where her cheek had rested against the chair as she slept. The bruise was darkening already, a purple blossom on her cheek. 'Angel . . .' he began.

'It's nothing,' she said. She pushed her hair forward to cover the blemish. 'Your clothes were filthy. Mal took them out to be cleaned. So you're my prisoner for a while.'

'How long have I slept?' Tachyon asked.

'All day,' Angelface replied. 'Don't worry about it. Once I had a customer get so drunk he slept for five months.' She sat down at her dressing table, lifted a phone, and ordered breakfast: toast and tea for herself, eggs and bacon and strong coffee with brandy for Tachyon. With aspirin on the side.

'No,' he protested. 'All that food. I'll get sick.'

'You have to eat. Even spacemen can't live on cognac alone.'

'Please . . .'

'If you want to drink, you'll eat,' she said brusquely. 'That's the deal, remember?'

The deal, yes. He remembered. Angelface provided him with rent money, food, and an unlimited bar tab, as much drink as he'd ever need to wash away his memories. All he had to do was eat and tell her stories. She loved to listen to him talk. He told her family anecdotes, lectured about Takisian customs, filled her with history and legends and romances, with tales of balls and intrigues and beauty far removed from the squalor of Jokertown.

Sometimes, after closing, he would dance for her, tracing the ancient, intricate pavanes of Takis across the nightclub's mirrored floors while she watched and urged him on. Once, when both of them had drunk far too much wine, she talked him into demonstrating the Wedding Pattern, an erotic ballet that most Takisians danced but once, on their wedding night. That was the only time she had ever danced with him, echoing the steps, hesitantly at first, and then faster and faster, swaying and spinning across the floor until her bare feet were raw and cracked and left wet red smears upon the mirror tiles. In the Wedding Pattern, the dancing couple came together at the end, collapsing into a long triumphant embrace. But that was on Takis; here, when the moment came, she broke the pattern and shied away from him, and he was reminded once again that Takis was far away.

Two years before, Desmond had found him unconscious and naked in a Jokertown alley. Someone had stolen his clothing while he slept, and he was fevered and delirious. Des had summoned help to carry him to the Funhouse. When he came to, he was lying on a cot in a back room, surrounded by beer kegs and wine racks. 'Do you know what you were drinking?' Angelface had asked him when they'd brought him to her office. He hadn't known; all he recalled was that he'd needed a drink so badly it was an ache inside him, and the old black man in the alley had generously offered to share. 'It's called Sterno,' Angelface told him. She had Des bring in a bottle of her finest brandy. 'If a man wants to drink, that's his business, but at least you can kill yourself with a little class.' The brandy spread thin tendrils of warmth through his chest and stopped his hands from shaking. When he'd emptied the snifter, Tach had thanked her effusively, but she drew back when he tried to touch her. He asked her why. 'I'll show you,' she had said, offering her hand. 'Lightly,' she told him. His kiss had been the merest brush of his lips, not on the back of her hand but against the inside of her wrist, to feel her pulse, the life current inside her, because she was so very lovely, and kind, and because he wanted her.

A moment later he'd watched with sick dismay as her skin darkened to purple and then black. *Another one of mine*, he'd thought.

Yet somehow they had become friends. Not lovers, of course, except sometimes in his dreams; her capillaries ruptured at the slightest pressure, and to her hypersensitive nervous system even the lightest touch was painful. A gentle caress turned her black and blue; lovemaking would probably kill her. But friends, yes. She never asked him for anything he could not give, and so he could never fail her.

Breakfast was served by a hunchbacked black woman named Ruth who had pale blue feathers instead of hair. 'The man brought this for you this morning,' she told Angelface after she'd set the table, handing across a thick, square packet wrapped in brown paper. Angelface accepted it without comment while Tachyon drank his brandy-laced coffee and lifted knife and fork to stare with sick dismay at the implacable bacon and eggs.

'Don't look so stricken,' Angelface said.

'I don't think I've told you about the time the Network starship came to Takis, and what my great-grandmother Amurath had to say to the Ly'bahr envoy,' he began.

'No,' she said. 'Go on. I like your great-grandmother.'

'That's one of us. She terrifies me,' Tachyon said, and launched into the story.

*

Tom woke well before dawn, while Joey was snoring in the back room. He brewed a pot of coffee in a battered percolator and popped a Thomas' English muffin into the toaster. While the coffee perked, he folded the hide-a-bed back into a couch. He covered his muffins with butter and strawberry preserves, and looked around for something to read. The comics beckoned.

He remembered the day they'd saved them. Most had been his, originally, including the run of *Jetboy* he got from his dad. He'd loved those comics. And then one day in 1954 he'd come home from school and found them gone, a full bookcase and two orange crates of funny books vanished. His mother said some women from the PTA had come by to tell her what awful things comic books were. They'd shown her a copy of a book by a Dr Wertham about how comics turned kids into juvenile delinquents and homos, and how they glorified aces and jokers, and so his mother had let them take Tom's collection. He screamed and yelled and threw a tantrum, but it did no good.

The PTA had gathered up comic books from every kid in school. They were going to burn them all Saturday, in the schoolyard. It was happening all over the country; there was even talk of a law banning comic books, or at least the kinds about horror and crime and people with strange powers.

Wertham and the PTA turned out to be right: that Friday night, on account of comic books, Tommy Tudbury and Joey DiAngelis became criminals.

Tom was nine; Joey was eleven, but he'd been driving his pop's truck since he was seven. In the middle of the night, he swiped the truck and Tom snuck out to meet him. When they got to the school, Joey jimmied open a window, and Tom climbed on his shoulders and looked into the dark classroom and concentrated and grabbed the carton with his collection in it and lifted it up and floated it out into the bed of the truck. Then he snatched four or five other cartons for good measure. The PTA never noticed; they still had plenty to burn. If Dom DiAngelis wondered where all the comics had come from, he never said a word; he just built the shelves to hold them, proud as punch of his son who could read. From that day on, it was their collection, jointly.

Setting his coffee and muffin on the orange crate, Tom went to the bookcase and took down a couple of issues of *Jetboy Comics*. He reread them as he ate, *Jetboy on Dinosaur Island, Jetboy and the Fourth Reich*, and his favorite, the final issue, the true one, *Jetboy and the Aliens*. Inside the cover, the title was 'Thirty Minutes Over Broadway.' Tom read it twice as he sipped his cooling coffee. He lingered over some of the best panels. On the last page, they had a picture of the alien, Tachyon, weeping. Tom didn't know if that had happened or not. He closed the comic book and finished his English muffin. For a long time he sat there thinking.

Jetboy was a hero. And what was he? Nothing. A wimp, a chickenshit. A fuck of a lot of good his wild card power did anybody. It was useless, just like him.

Dispiritedly, he shrugged into his coat and went outside. The junkyard looked raw and ugly in the dawn, and a cold wind was blowing. A few hundred yards to the east, the bay was green and choppy. Tom climbed up to the old Packard on its little hill. The door creaked when he yanked it open. Inside, the seats were cracked and smelled of rot, but at least he was out of that wind. Tom slouched back with his knees up against the dash, staring out at sunrise. He sat unmoving for a long time; across the yard, hubcaps and old tires floated up in the air and went screaming off to splash into the choppy green waters of New York Bay. He could see the Statue of Liberty on her island, and the hazy outlines of the towers of Manhattan off to the northeast.

It was nearly seven-thirty, his limbs were stiff, and he'd lost count of the number of hubcaps he'd flung, when Tom Tudbury sat up with a strange expression on his face. The icebox he'd been juggling forty feet from the ground came down with a crash. He ran his fingers through his hair and lifted the icebox again, moved it over twenty yards or so, and dropped it right on Joey's corrugated tin roof. Then he did the same with a tire, a twisted bicycle, six hubcaps, and a little red wagon.

The door to the house flew open with a bang, and Joey came charging out into the cold wearing nothing but boxer shorts and a sleeveless undershirt. He looked real pissed. Tom snatched his bare feet, pulled them out from under him, and dumped him on his butt, hard. Joey cursed.

Tom grabbed him and yanked him into the air, upside down. 'Where the fuck are you, Tudbury?' Joey screamed. 'Cut it out, you dork. Lemme down.'

Tom imagined two huge invisible hands, and tossed Joey from one to the other. 'When I get down, I'm going to punch you so fuckin' hard you'll eat through a straw for the rest of your life,' Joey promised.

The crank was stiff from years of disuse, but Tom finally managed to roll down the Packard's window. He stuck his head out. 'Hiya kids, hiya, hiya, hiya,' he croaked, chortling.

Suspended twelve feet from the ground, Joey dangled and made a fist. 'I'll pluck your fuckin' magic twanger, shithead,' he shouted. Tom yanked off his boxer shorts and hung them from a telephone pole. 'You're gonna die, Tudbury,' Joey said.

Tom took a big breath and set Joey on the ground, very gently. The moment of truth. Joey came running at him, screaming obscenities. Tom closed his eyes, put his hands on the steering wheel, and *lifted*. The Packard shifted beneath him. Sweat dotted his brow. He shut out the world, concentrated, counted to ten, slowly, backward.

When he finally opened his eyes, half expecting to see Joey's fist smashing into his nose, there was nothing to behold but a seagull perched on the hood of the Packard, its head cocked as it peered through the cracked windshield. He was floating. He was flying.

Tom stuck his head out of the window. Joey stood twenty feet below him, glaring, hands on his hips and a disgusted look on his face. 'Now,' Tom yelled down, smiling, 'what was it you were saying last night?'

'I hope you can stay up there all day, you son of a bitch,' Joey said. He made an ineffectual fist, and waved it. Lank black hair fell across his eyes. 'Ah, shit, what does this prove? If I had a gun, you'd still be dead meat.'

'If you had a gun, I wouldn't be sticking my head out the window,' Tom said. 'In fact, it'd be better if I didn't have a window.' He considered that for a second, but it was hard to think while he was up here. The Packard was heavy. 'I'm coming down,' he said to Joey. 'You, uh, you calmed down?'

Joey grinned. 'Try me and see, Tuds.'

'Move out of the way. I don't want to squash you with this damn thing.'

Joey shuffled to one side, bare-ass and goose-pimpled, and Tom let the Packard settle as gently as an autumn leaf on a still day. He had the door half open when Joey reached in, grabbed him, yanked him up, and pushed him back against the side of the car, his other hand cocked into a fist. 'I oughtta—' he began. Then he shook his head, snorted, and punched Tom lightly in the shoulder. 'Gimme back my fuckin' drawers, ace,' he said.

Back inside the house, Tom reheated the leftover coffee. 'I'll need you to do the work,' he said as he made himself some scrambled eggs and ham and a couple more English muffins. Using his teke always gave him quite an appetite. 'You took auto shop and welding and all that shit. I'll do the wiring.'

'Wiring?' Joey said, warming his hands over his cup. 'What the fuck for?'

'The lights and the TV cameras. I don't want any windows people can shoot through. I know where we can get some cameras cheap, and you got lots of old sets around here, I'll just fix them up.' He sat down and attacked his eggs wolfishly. 'I'll need loudspeakers too. Some kind of PA system. A generator. Wonder if I'll have room for a refrigerator in there?'

'That Packard's a big motherfucker,' Joey said. 'Take out the seats and you'll have room for three of the fuckers.'

'Not the Packard,' Tom said. 'I'll find a lighter car. We can cover up the windows with old body panels or something.'

Joey pushed hair out of his eyes. 'Fuck the body panels. I got armor plate. From the war. They scrapped a bunch of ships at the Navy base in '46 and '47, and Dom put in a bid for the metal, and bought us twenty goddamn tons. Fuckin' waste a money – who the fuck wants to buy battleship armor? I still got it all, sitting way out back rusting. You need a fuckin' sixteen-inch gun to punch through that shit, Tuds. You'll be safe as – fuck, I dunno. Safe, anyhow.'

Tom knew. 'Safe,' he said loudly, 'as a turtle in its shell!'

*

Only ten shopping days were left until Christmas, and Tach sat in one of the window alcoves, nursing an Irish coffee against the December cold and gazing through the one-way glass at the Bowery. The Funhouse wouldn't open for another hour yet, but the back door was always unlocked for Angelface's friends. Up on stage, a pair of joker jugglers who called themselves Cosmos and Chaos were tossing bowling balls around. Cosmos floated three feet above the stage in the lotus position, his eyeless face serene. He was totally blind, but he never missed a beat or dropped a ball. His partner, six-armed Chaos, capered around like a lunatic, chortling and telling bad jokes and keeping a cascade of flaming clubs going behind his back with two arms while the other four flung bowling balls at Cosmos. Tach spared them only a glance. As talented as they were, their deformities pained him.

Mal slid into his booth. 'How many of those you had?' the bouncer demanded, glaring at the Irish coffee. The tendrils that hung from his lower lip expanded and contracted in a blind wormlike pulsing, and his huge, malformed blue-black jaw gave his face a look of belligerent contempt.

'I don't see that it's any of your business.'

'You're no damn use at all, are you?'

'I never claimed I was.'

Mal grunted. 'You're worth 'bout as much as a sack of shit. I don't see why the hell Angel needs no damn pantywaist spaceman hanging round the place sopping up her booze . . .'

'She doesn't. I told her that.'

'You can't tell that woman nothin',' Mal agreed. He made a fist. A very large fist. Before the Day of the Wild Card, he'd been the eighth-ranked heavyweight contender. Afterward, he had climbed as high as third . . . until they'd banned wild cards from professional sports, and wiped out his dreams in a stroke. The measure was aimed at aces, they said, to keep the games competitive, but there had been no exceptions made for jokers. Mal was older now, sparse hair turned iron gray, but he still looked strong enough to break Floyd Patterson over his knee and mean enough to stare down Sonny Liston. 'Look at that,' he growled in disgust, glaring out the window. Tiny was outside in his chair. 'What the hell is he doing here? I told him not to come by here no more.' Mal started for the door.

'Can't you just leave him alone?' Tachyon called after him. 'He's harmless.'

'Harmless?' Mal rounded on him. 'His screamin' scares off all the fuckin' tourists, and who the hell's gonna pay for all your free booze?'

But then the door pushed open, and Desmond stood there, overcoat folded over one arm, his trunk half-raised. 'Let him be, Mal,' the maitre d'said wearily. 'Go on, now.' Muttering, Mal stalked off.

Desmond came over and seated himself in Tachyon's booth. 'Good morning, Doctor,' he said.

Tachyon nodded and finished his drink. The whiskey had all gone to the bottom of the cup, and it warmed him on the way down. He found himself staring at the face in the mirrored tabletop: a worn, dissipated, *coarse* face, eyes reddened and puffy, long red hair tangled and greasy, features distorted by alcoholic bloat. That wasn't him, that couldn't be him, he was handsome, clean-featured, distinguished, his face was—

Desmond's trunk snaked out, its fingers locking around his wrist roughly, yanking him forward. 'You haven't heard a word I've said, have you?' Des said, his voice low and urgent with anger. Blearily, Tach realized that Desmond had been talking to him. He began to mutter apologies.

'Never mind about that,' Des said, releasing his grip. 'Listen to me. I was asking for your help, Doctor. I may be a joker, but I'm not an uneducated man. I've read about you. You have certain – abilities, let us say.'

'No,' Tach interrupted. 'Not the way you're thinking.'

'Your powers are quite well documented,' Des said.

'I don't . . .' Tach began awkwardly. He spread his hands. 'That was then. I've lost – I mean, I can't, not anymore.' He stared down at his own wasted features, wanting to look Des in the eye, to make him understand, but unable to bear the sight of the joker's deformity.

'You mean you won't,' Des said. He stood up. 'I thought that if I spoke to you before we opened, I might actually find you sober. I see I was mistaken. Forget everything I said.'

'I'd help you if I could,' Tach began to say.

'I wasn't asking for me,' Des said sharply.

When he was gone, Tachyon went to the long silver-chrome bar and got down a full bottle of cognac. The first glass made him feel better; the second stopped his hands from shaking. By the third he had begun to weep. Mal came over and looked down at him in disgust. 'Never knew no man cried as much as you do,' he said, thrusting a dirty handkerchief at Tachyon roughly before he left to help them open.

*

He had been aloft for four and a half hours when the news of the fire came crackling over the police-band radio down by his right foot. Not very *far* aloft, true, only about six feet from the ground, but that was enough – six feet or sixty, it didn't make all that much difference, Tom had found. Four and a half hours, and he didn't feel the least bit tired yet. In fact, he felt *sensational*.

He was strapped securely into a bucket seat Joey had pulled from a mashed-up Triumph TR-3 and mounted on a low pivot right in the center of the VW. The only light was the wan phosphor glow from an array of mismatched television screens that surrounded him on all sides. Between the cameras and their tracking motors, the generator, the ventilation system, the sound equipment, the control panels, the spare box of vacuum tubes, and the little refrigerator, he hardly had space to swing around. But that was okay. Tom was more a claustrophile than a claustrophobe anyway; he liked it in here. Around the exterior of the gutted Beetle, Joey had mounted two overlapping layers of thick battleship armor. It was better than a goddamned tank. Joey had already pinged a few shots off it with the Luger that Dom had taken off a German officer during the war. A lucky shot might be able to take out one of his cameras or lights, but there was no way to get to Tom himself inside the shell. He was better than safe, he was *invulnerable*, and when he felt this secure and sure of himself, there was no limit on what he might be able to do.

The shell was heavier than the Packard by the time they'd gotten finished with it, but it didn't seem to matter. Four and a half hours, never touching ground, sliding around silently and almost effortlessly through the junkyard, and Tom hadn't even worked up a sweat.

When he heard the report over the radio, a jolt of excitement went through him. *This is it!* he thought. He ought to wait for Joey, but Joey had driven to Pompeii Pizza to pick up dinner (pepperoni, onion, and extra cheese) and there was no time to waste; this was his chance.

The ring of lights on the bottom of the shell threw stark shadows over the hills of twisted metal and trash as Tom pushed the shell higher into the air, eight feet up, ten, twelve. His eyes flicked nervously from one screen to the next, watching the ground recede. One set, its picture tube filched from an old Sylvania, began a slow vertical roll. Tom played with a knob and stopped it. His palms were sweaty. Fifteen feet up, he began to creep forward, until the shell reached the shoreline. In front of him was darkness; it was too thick a night to see New York, but he knew it was there, if he could reach it. On his small black-and-white screens, the waters of New York Bay seemed even darker than usual, an endless choppy ocean of ink looming before him. He'd have to grope his way across, until the city lights came into sight. And if he lost it out there, over the water, he'd be joining Jetboy and J.F.K. a lot sooner than he planned; even if he could unscrew the hatch quick enough to avoid drowning, he couldn't swim.

But he *wasn't* going to lose it, Tom thought suddenly. Why the fuck was he hesitating? He wasn't going to lose it ever again, was he? He had to believe that.

He pressed his lips together, pushed off with his mind, and the shell slid smoothly out over the water. The salt waves beneath him rose and fell. He'd never had to push against water before; it felt different. Tom had an instant of panic; the shell rocked and dropped three feet before he caught hold of himself and adjusted. He calmed himself with an effort, shoved upward, and rose. *High*, he thought, he'd come in high, he'd *fly* in, like Jetboy, like Black Eagle, like a fucking *ace*. The shell moved out, faster and faster, gliding across the bay with swift serenity as Tom gained confidence. He'd never felt so incredibly powerful, so good, so goddamned *right*.

The compass worked fine; in less than ten minutes, the lights of the

Battery and the Wall Street district loomed up before him. Tom pushed still higher, and floated uptown, hugging the shoreline of the Hudson. Jetboy's Tomb came and went beneath him. He'd stood in front of it a dozen times, gazing up at the face of the big metal statue out front. He wondered what that statue might think if it could look up and see him tonight.

He had a New York street map, but tonight he didn't need it; the flames could be seen almost a mile off. Even inside his armor Tom could feel the heat waves licking up at him when he made a pass overhead. He carefully began a descent. His fans whirred, and his cameras tracked at his command; below was chaos and cacophony, sirens and shouting, the crowd, the hurrying firemen, the police barricades and the ambulances, big hook-and-ladder trucks spraying water into the inferno. At first no one noticed him, hovering fifty feet above the sidewalk – until he came in low enough for his lights to play on the walls of the building. Then he saw them looking up, pointing; he felt giddy with excitement.

But he had only an instant to relish the feeling. Then, from the corner of an eye, he saw her in one of his screens. She appeared suddenly in a fifth-floor window, bent over and coughing, her dress already afire. Before he could act, the flames licked at her; she screamed and jumped.

He caught her in midair, without thinking, without hesitating, without wondering whether he could do it. He just *did* it, caught her and held her and lowered her gently to the ground. The firemen surrounded her, put out her dress, and hustled her into an ambulance. And now, Tom saw, *everyone* was looking up at him, at the strange dark shape floating high in the night, with its ring of shining lights. The police band was crackling; they were reporting him as a flying saucer, he heard. He grinned.

A cop climbed up on top of his police car, holding a bullhorn, and began to hail him. Tom turned off the radio to hear better over the roar of the flames. He was telling Tom to land and identify himself, asking who he was, what he was.

That was easy. Tom turned on his microphone. 'I'm the Turtle,' he said. The VW had no tires; in the wheel wells, Joey had rigged the most humongous speakers they could find, powered by the largest amp on the market. For the first time, the voice of the Turtle was heard in the land, a booming 'I'M THE TURTLE' echoing down the streets and alleys, a rolling thunder crackling with distortion. Except what he said didn't sound quite right. Tom cranked the volume up even higher, injected a little more bass into his voice. '*I AM THE GREAT AND POWERFUL TURTLE*,' he announced to them all.

Then he flew a block west, to the dark polluted waters of the Hudson, and imagined two huge invisible hands forty feet across. He lowered them

into the river, cupped them full, and lifted. Rivulets of water dribbled to
the street all the way back. When he dropped the first cascade on the
flames, a ragged cheering went up from the crowd below.

*

'Merry Christmas,' Tach declared drunkenly when the clock struck midnight
and the record Christmas Eve crowd began to whoop and shout and pound
on the tables. On stage, Humphrey Bogart cracked a lame joke in an
unfamiliar voice. All the lights in the house dimmed briefly; when they
came back up, Bogart had been replaced by a portly, round-faced man with
a red nose. 'Who is he now?' Tach asked the twin on his left.

'W. C. Fields,' she whispered. She slid her tongue around the inside of
his ear. The twin on the right was doing something even more interesting
under the table, where her hand had somehow found a way into his
trousers. The twins were his Christmas gift from Angelface. 'You can
pretend they're me,' she'd told him, though of course they were nothing
like her. Nice kids, both of them, buxom and cheerful and absolutely
uninhibited, if a bit simpleminded; they reminded him of Takisian sex
toys. The one on the right had drawn the wild card, but she wore her cat
mask even in bed, and there was no visible deformity to disturb the sweet
pleasure of his erection.

W. C. Fields, whoever he was, offered some cynical observation, about
Christmas and small children. The crowd hooted him off the stage. The
Projectionist had an astonishing array of faces, but he couldn't tell a joke.
Tach didn't mind; he had all the diversion he needed.

'Paper, Doc?' The vendor thrust a copy of the *Herald Tribune* across the
table with a thick three-fingered hand. His flesh was blue-black and oily
looking. 'All the Christmas news,' he said, shifting the clumsy stack of
papers under his arm. Two small curving tusks protruded from the corners
of his wide, grinning mouth. Beneath a porkpie hat, the great bulge of his
skull was covered with tufts of bristly red hair. On the streets they called
him the Walrus.

'No thank you, Jube,' Tach said with drunken dignity. 'I have no desire
to wallow in human folly tonight.'

'Hey, look,' said the twin on the right. 'The Turtle!'

Tachyon looked around, momentarily befuddled, wondering how that
huge armored shell could possibly have gotten inside the Funhouse, but of
course she was referring to the newspaper.

'You better buy it for her, Tacky,' the twin on the left said, giggling. 'If
you don't she'll pout.'

Tachyon sighed. 'I'll take one. But only if I don't have to listen to any of
your jokes, Jube.'

'Heard a new one about a joker, a Polack, and an Irishman stuck on a desert island, but just for that I'm not going to tell it,' the Walrus replied with a rubbery grin.

Tachyon dug for some coins, found nothing in his pockets but a small, feminine hand. Jube winked. 'I'll get it from Des,' he said. Tachyon spread the newspaper out on the table, while the club erupted in applause as Cosmos and Chaos made their entrance.

A grainy photograph of the Turtle was spread across two columns. Tachyon thought it looked like a flying pickle, a big lumpy dill covered with little bumps. The Turtle had apprehended a hit-and-run driver who had killed a nine-year-old boy in Harlem, intercepting his flight and lifting the car twenty feet off the ground, where it floated with its engine roaring and its tires spinning madly until the police finally caught up. In a related sidebar, the rumor that the shell was an experimental robot flying tank had been denied by an Air Force spokesman.

'You'd think they'd have found something more important to write about by now,' Tachyon said. It was the third big story about the Turtle this week. The letter columns, the editorial pages, everything was Turtle, Turtle, Turtle. Even television was rabid with Turtle speculation. Who was he? What was he? How did he do it?

One reporter had even sought out Tach to ask that question. 'Telekinesis,' Tachyon told him. 'It's nothing new. Almost common, in fact.' Teke had been the single ability most frequently manifested by virus victims back in '46. He'd seen a dozen patients who could move paper clips and pencils, and one woman who could lift her own body weight for ten minutes at a time. Even Earl Sanderson's flight had been telekinetic in origin. What he did not tell them was that teke on *this* scale was unprecedented. Of course, when the story ran, they got half of it wrong.

'He's a joker, you know,' whispered the twin on the right, the one in the silver-gray cat mask. She was leaning against his shoulder, reading about the Turtle.

'A joker?' Tach said.

'He hides inside a shell, doesn't he? Why would he do that unless he was really awful to look at?' She had taken her hand out of his trousers. 'Could I have that paper?'

Tach pushed it toward her. 'They're cheering him now,' he said sharply. 'They cheered the Four Aces too.'

'That was a colored group, right?' she said, turning her attention to the headlines.

'She's keeping a scrapbook,' her sister said. 'All the jokers think he's one of them. Stupid, huh? I bet it's just a machine, some kind of Air Force flying saucer.'

'He is not,' her twin said. 'It says so right here.' She pointed to the sidebar with a long, red-painted nail.

'Never mind about her,' the twin on the left said. She moved closer to Tachyon, nibbling on his neck as her hand went under the table. 'Hey, what's wrong? You're all soft.'

'My pardons,' Tachyon said gloomily. Cosmos and Chaos were flinging axes, machetes, and knives across the stage, the glittering cascade multiplied into infinity by the mirrors around them. He had a bottle of fine cognac at hand, and lovely, willing women on either side of him, but suddenly, for some reason he could not have named, it did not feel like such a good night after all. He filled his glass almost to the brim and inhaled the heady alcoholic fumes. 'Merry Christmas,' he muttered to no one in particular.

*

Consciousness returned with the angry tones of Mal's voice. Tach lifted his head groggily from the mirrored tabletop, blinking down at his puffy red reflection. The jugglers, the twins, and the crowd were long gone. His cheek was sticky from lying in a puddle of spilled liquor. The twins had jollied him and fondled him and one of them had even gone under the table, for all the good it did. Then Angelface had come to the tableside and sent them away. 'Go to sleep, Tacky,' she'd said. Mal had come up to ask if he should lug him back to bed. 'Not today,' she'd said, 'you know what day this is. Let him sleep it off here.' He couldn't recall when he'd gone to sleep.

His head was about to explode, and Mal's shouting wasn't making things any better. 'I don't give a flyin' fuck *what* you were promised, scumbag, you're not seeing her,' the bouncer yelled. A softer voice said something in reply. 'You'll get your fuckin' money, but that's all you'll get,' Mal snapped.

Tach raised his eyes. In the mirrors he saw their reflections darkly: odd twisted shapes outlined in the wan dawn light, reflections of reflections, hundreds of them, beautiful, monstrous, uncountable, his children, his heirs, the offspring of his failures, a living sea of jokers. The soft voice said something else. 'Ah, kiss my joker ass,' Mal said. He had a body like a twisted stick and a head like a pumpkin; it made Tach smile. Mal shoved someone and reached behind his back, groping for his gun.

The reflections and the reflections of the reflections, the gaunt shadows and the bloated ones, the round-faced ones and the knife-thin ones, the black and the white, they moved all at once, filling the club with noise; a hoarse shout from Mal, the crack of gunfire. Instinctively Tach dove for cover, cracking his forehead hard on the edge of the table as he slid down.

He blinked back tears of pain and lay curled up on the floor, peering out at the reflections of feet while the world disintegrated into a sharp-edged cacophony. Glass was shattering and falling, mirrors breaking on all sides, silvered knives flying through the air, too many for even Cosmos and Chaos to catch, dark splinters eating into the reflections, taking bites out of all the twisted shadow-shapes, blood spattering against the cracked mirrors.

It ended as suddenly as it had begun. The soft voice said something and there was the sound of footsteps, the crunch of glass underfoot. A moment later, a muffled scream from off behind him. Tach lay under the table, drunk and terrified. His finger hurt: bleeding, he saw, sliced open by a sliver of mirror. All he could think of were the stupid human superstitions about broken mirrors and bad luck. He cradled his head in his arms so the awful nightmare would go away. When he woke again, a policeman was shaking him roughly.

*

Mal was dead, one detective told him; they showed him a morgue photo of the bouncer lying in a pool of blood and a welter of broken glass. Ruth was dead too, and one of the janitors, a dim-witted cyclops who had never hurt anyone. They showed him a newspaper. The Santa Claus Slaughter, that was what they called it, and the lead was about three jokers who'd found death waiting under the tree on Christmas morning.

Miss Fascetti was gone, the other detective told him, did he know anything about that? Did he think she was involved? Was she a culprit or a victim? What could he tell them about her? He said he didn't know any such person, until they explained that they were asking about Angela Fascetti and maybe he knew her better as Angelface. She was gone and Mal was shot dead, and the most frightening thing of all was that Tach did not know where his next drink was coming from.

They held him for four days, questioning him relentlessly, going over the same ground again and again, until Tachyon was screaming at them, pleading with them, demanding his rights, demanding a lawyer, demanding a drink. They gave him only the lawyer. The lawyer said they couldn't hold him without charging him, so they charged him with being a material witness, with vagrancy, with resisting arrest, and questioned him again.

By the third day, his hands were shaking and he was having waking hallucinations. One of the detectives, the kindly one, promised him a bottle in return for his cooperation, but somehow his answers never quite satisfied them, and the bottle was not forthcoming. The bad-tempered one threatened to hold him forever unless he told the truth. I thought it was a nightmare, Tach told him, weeping. I was drunk, I'd been asleep. No, I couldn't see them, just the reflections, distorted, multiplied. I don't know how many there were. I don't know what it was about. No, she had no enemies, everyone loved Angelface. No, she didn't kill Mal, that didn't make sense, Mal loved her. One of them had a soft voice. No, I don't know which one. No, I can't remember what they said. No, I don't know if they were jokers or not, they looked like jokers, but the mirrors distort, some of them, not all of them, don't you see? No, I couldn't possibly pick them out of a lineup, I never really saw them. I had to hide under the table, do you see, the assassins had come, that's what my father always told me, there wasn't anything I could do.

When they realized that he was telling them all he knew, they dropped the charges and released him. To the dark streets of Jokertown and the cold of the night.

*

He walked down the Bowery alone, shivering. The Walrus was hawking the evening papers from his newsstand on the corner of Hester. 'Read all about it,' he called out. 'Turtle Terror in Jokertown.' Tachyon paused to stare dully at the headlines. POLICE SEEK TURTLE, the *Post* reported. TURTLE CHARGED WITH ASSAULT, announced the *World Telegram*. So the cheering had stopped already. He glanced at the text. The Turtle had been prowling Jokertown the past two nights, lifting people a hundred feet in the air to question them, threatening to drop them if he didn't like their answers. When police tried to make an arrest last night, the Turtle had deposited two of their black-and-whites on the roof of Freakers at Chatham Square. CURB THE TURTLE, the editorial in the *World-Telegram* said.

'You all right, Doc?' the Walrus asked.

'No,' said Tachyon, putting down the paper. He couldn't afford to pay for it anyway.

Police barriers blocked the entrance to the Funhouse, and a padlock secured the door. CLOSED INDEFINITELY, the sign said. He needed a drink, but the pockets of his bandleader's coat were empty. He thought of Des and Randall, and realized that he had no idea where they lived, or what their last names might be.

Trudging back to ROOMS, Tach climbed wearily up the stairs. When he stepped into the darkness, he had just enough time to notice that the room was frigidly cold; the window was open and a bitter wind was scouring out the old smells of urine, mildew, and drink. Had he done that? Confused, he stepped toward it, and someone came out from behind the door and grabbed him.

It happened so fast he scarcely had time to react. The forearm across his windpipe was an iron bar, choking off his scream, and a hand wrenched his right arm up behind his back, hard. He was choking, his arm close to breaking, and then he was being shoved toward the open window, running at it, and Tachyon could only thrash feebly in a grip much stronger than his own. The windowsill caught him square in the stomach, knocking the last of his breath right out of him, and suddenly he was falling, head over heels, locked helplessly in the steel embrace of his attacker, both of them plunging toward the sidewalk below.

They jerked to a stop five feet above the cement, with a wrench that elicited a grunt from the man behind him.

Tach had closed his eyes before the instant of impact. He opened them as they began to float upward. Above the yellow halo of the streetlamp was a ring of much brighter lights, set in a hovering darkness that blotted out the winter stars.

The arm across his throat had loosened enough for Tachyon to groan. 'You,' he said hoarsely, as they curved around the shell and came to rest gently on top of it. The metal was icy cold, its chill biting right through the fabric of Tachyon's pants. As the Turtle began to rise straight up into the night, Tachyon's captor released him. He drew in a shuddering breath of cold air, and rolled over to face a man in a zippered leather jacket, black dungarees, and a rubbery green frog mask. 'Who . . . ?' he gasped.

'I'm the Great and Powerful Turtle's mean-ass sidekick,' the man in the frog mask said, rather cheerfully.

'DOCTOR TACHYON, I PRESUME,' boomed the shell's speakers, far above the alleys of Jokertown. 'I'VE ALWAYS WANTED TO MEET YOU. I READ ABOUT YOU WHEN I WAS JUST A KID.'

'Turn it down,' Tach croaked weakly.

'OH. SURE. Is that better?' The volume diminished sharply. 'It's noisy in here, and behind all this armor I can't always tell how loud I sound. I'm sorry if we scared you, but we couldn't take the chance of you saying no. We need you.'

Tach stayed just where he was, shivering, shaken. 'What do you want?' he asked wearily.

'Help,' the Turtle declared. They were still rising; the lights of Manhattan spread out all around them, and the spires of the Empire State Building and the Chrysler Building rose uptown. They were higher than either. The wind was cold and gusting; Tach clung to the shell for dear life.

'Leave me alone,' Tachyon said. 'I have no help to give you. I have no help to give anybody.'

'Fuck, he's crying,' the man in the frog mask said.

'You don't understand,' the Turtle said. The shell began to drift west, its motion silent and steady. There was something awesome and eerie about the flight. 'You have to help. I've tried on my own, but I'm getting nowhere. But you, your powers, they can make the difference.'

Tachyon was lost in his own self-pity, too cold and exhausted and despairing to reply. 'I want a drink,' he said.

'Fuck it,' said Frog-face. 'Dumbo was right about this guy, he's nothing but a goddamned wino.'

'He doesn't understand,' said the Turtle. 'Once we explain, he'll come around. Doctor Tachyon, we're talking about your friend Angelface.'

He needed a drink so badly it hurt. 'She was good to me,' he said, remembering the sweet perfume of her satin sheets, and her bloody footprints on the mirror tiles. 'But there's nothing I can do. I told the police everything I know.'

'Chickenshit asshole,' said Frog-face.

'When I was a kid, I read about you in *Jetboy Comics*,' the Turtle said. '"Thirty Minutes Over Broadway," remember? You were supposed to be as smart as Einstein. I might be able to save your friend Angelface, but I can't without your powers.'

'I don't do that any longer. I *can't*. There was someone I hurt, someone I cared for, but I seized her mind, just for an instant, for a good reason, or at least I thought it was for a good reason, but it . . . destroyed her. I can't do it again.'

'Boo hoo,' said Frog-face mockingly. 'Let's toss 'im, Turtle, he's not worth a bucket of warm piss.' He took something out of one of the pockets of his leather jacket; Tach was astonished to see that it was a bottle of beer.

'Please,' Tachyon said, as the man popped off the cap with a bottle-opener hung round his neck. 'A sip,' Tach said. 'Just a sip.' He hated the taste of beer, but he needed something, anything. It had been days. 'Please.'

'Fuck off,' Frog-face said.

'Tachyon,' said the Turtle, 'you can make him.'

'No I can't,' Tach said. The man raised the bottle up to green rubber lips. 'I can't,' Tach repeated. Frog-face continued to drink. 'No.' He could hear it gurgling. 'Please, just a little.'

The man lowered the beer bottle, sloshed it thoughtfully. 'Just a swallow left,' he said.

'Please.' He reached out, hands trembling.

'Nah,' said Frog-face. He began to turn the bottle upside down. 'Course, if you're really thirsty, you could just grab my mind, right? *Make* me give you the fuckin' bottle.' He tipped the bottle a little more. 'Go on, I dare ya, try it.'

Tach watched the last mouthful of beer dribble down onto the Turtle's shell and run off into empty air.

'Fuck,' said the man in the frog mask. 'You got it bad, don't you?' He pulled another bottle from his pocket, opened it, and handed it across. Tach cradled it with both hands. The beer was cold and sour, but he had never tasted anything half so sweet. He drained it all in one long swallow.

'Got any other smart ideas?' Frog-face asked the Turtle.

Ahead of them was the blackness of the Hudson River, the lights of Jersey off to the west. They were descending. Beneath them, overlooking the Hudson, was a sprawling edifice of steel and glass and marble that Tachyon suddenly recognized, though he had never set foot inside it: Jetboy's Tomb. 'Where are we going?' he asked.

'We're going to see a man about a rescue,' the Turtle said.

Jetboy's Tomb filled the entire block, on the site where the pieces of his plane had come raining down. It filled Tom's screens too, as he sat in the warm darkness of his shell, bathed in a phosphor glow. Motors whirred as the cameras moved in their tracks. The huge flanged wings of the tomb curved upward, as if the building itself was about to take flight. Through tall, narrow windows, he could see glimpses of the full-size replica of the JB-1 suspended from the ceiling, its scarlet flanks aglow from hidden lights. Above the doors, the hero's last words had been carved, each letter chiseled into the black Italian marble and filled in stainless steel. The metal flashed as the shell's white-hot spots slid across the legend:

I CANT DIE YET,
I HAVEN'T SEEN *THE JOLSON STORY*

Tom brought the shell down in front of the monument, to hover five feet above the broad marble plaza at the top of the stairs. Nearby, a twenty-foot-tall steel Jetboy looked out over the West Side Highway and the Hudson beyond, his fists cocked. The metal used for the sculpture had come from the wreckage of crashed planes, Tom knew. He knew that statue's face better than he knew his father's.

The man they'd come to meet emerged from the shadows at the base of the statue, a chunky dark shape huddled in a thick overcoat, hands shoved deep into his pockets. Tom shone a light on him; a camera tracked to give him a better view. The joker was a portly man, round-shouldered and well-dressed. His coat had a fur collar and his fedora was pulled low. Instead of a nose, he had an elephant's trunk in the middle of his face. The end of it was fringed with fingers, snug in a little leather glove.

Dr Tachyon slid off the top of the shell, lost his footing and landed on his ass. Tom heard Joey laugh. Then Joey jumped down too and pulled Tachyon to his feet.

The joker glanced down at the alien. 'So you convinced him to come after all. I'm surprised.'

'We were real fuckin' persuasive,' Joey said.

'Des,' Tachyon said, sounding confused. 'What are you doing here? Do you know these people?'

Elephant-face twitched his trunk. 'Since the day before yesterday, yes, in a manner of speaking. They came to me. The hour was late, but a phone call from the Great and Powerful Turtle does pique one's interest. He offered his help, and I accepted. I even told them where you lived.'

Tachyon ran a hand through his tangled, filthy hair. 'I'm sorry about Mal. Do you know anything about Angelface? You know how much she meant to me.'

'In dollars and cents, I know quite precisely,' Des said.

Tachyon's mouth gaped open. He looked hurt. Tom felt sorry for him. 'I wanted to go to you,' he said. 'I didn't know where to find you.'

Joey laughed. 'He's listed in the fuckin' phone book, dork. Ain't that many guys named Xavier Desmond.' He looked at the shell. 'How the fuck is he gonna find the lady if he couldn't even find his buddy here?'

Desmond nodded. 'An excellent point. This isn't going to work. Just look at him!' His trunk pointed. 'What good is he? We're wasting precious time.'

'We did it your way,' Tom replied. 'We're getting nowhere. No one's talking. He can get the information we need.'

'I don't understand any of this,' Tachyon interrupted.

Joey made a disgusted sound. He had found a beer somewhere and was cracking the cap.

'What's happening?' Tach asked.

'If you had been the least bit interested in anything besides cognac and cheap tarts, you might know,' Des said icily.

'Tell him what you told us,' Tom commanded. When he knew, Tachyon would surely help, he thought. He *had* to.

Des gave a heavy sigh. 'Angelface had a heroin habit. She hurt, you know. Perhaps you noticed that from time to time, Doctor? The drug was the only thing that got her through the day. Without it, the pain would have driven her insane. Nor was hers an ordinary junkie's habit. She used uncut heroin in quantities that would have killed any normal user. You saw how minimally it affected her. The joker metabolism is a curious thing. Do you have any idea how expensive heroin is, Doctor Tachyon? Never mind, I see that you don't. Angelface made quite a bit of money from the Funhouse, but it was never enough. Her source gave her credit until she was in far over her head, then demanded . . . call it a promissory note. Or a Christmas present. She had no choice. It was that or be cut off. She hoped to come up with the money, being an eternal optimist. She failed. On Christmas morning her source came by to collect. Mal wasn't about to let them have her. They insisted.'

Tachyon was squinting in the glare of the lights. His image began to roll upward. 'Why didn't she tell me?' he said.

'I suppose she didn't want to burden you, Doctor. It might have taken the fun out of your self-pitying binges.'

'Have you told the police?'

'The police? Ah, yes. New York's finest. The ones who seem so curiously uninterested whenever a joker is beaten or killed, yet ever so diligent if a tourist is robbed. The ones who so regularly arrest, harass, and brutalize any joker who has the poor taste to live anywhere outside of Jokertown. Perhaps we might consult the officer who commented that raping a joker woman is more a lapse in taste than a crime.' Des snorted. 'Doctor Tachyon, where do you think Angelface bought her drugs? Do you think any ordinary street pusher would have access to uncut heroin in the quantities she needed? The police *were* her source. The head of the Jokertown narcotics squad, if you care to be precise. Oh, I'll grant you that it's unlikely the whole department is involved. Homicide may be conducting a legitimate investigation. What do you think they'd say if we told them that Bannister was the murderer? You think they'd arrest one of their own? On the strength of my testimony, or the testimony of any joker?'

'We'll make good her note,' Tachyon blurted. 'We'll give this man his money or the Funhouse or whatever it is he wants.'

'The promissory note,' Desmond said wearily, 'was not for the Funhouse.'

'Whatever it was, give it to him!'

'She promised him the only thing she still had that he wanted,' Desmond said. 'Herself. Her beauty and her pain. The word's out on the street, if you know how to listen. There's going to be a very special New Year's Eve party somewhere in the city. Invitation only. Expensive. A unique thrill. Bannister will have her first. He's wanted that for a long time. But the other guests will have their turn. Jokertown hospitality.'

Tachyon's mouth worked soundlessly for a moment. *'The police?'* he finally managed. He looked as shocked as Tom had been when Desmond told him and Joey.

'Do you think they love us, Doctor? We're freaks. We're *diseased*. Jokertown is a hell, a dead end, and the Jokertown police are the most brutal, corrupt, and incompetent in the city. I don't think anyone planned what happened at the Funhouse, but it happened, and Angelface knows too much. They can't let her live, so they're going to have some fun with the joker cunt.'

Tom Tudbury leaned toward his microphone. 'I can rescue her,' he said. 'These fuckers haven't seen anything like the Great and Powerful Turtle. But I can't *find* her.'

Des said, 'She has a lot of friends. But none of us can read minds, or make a man do something he doesn't want to.'

'I *can't*,' Tachyon protested. He seemed to shrink into himself, to edge away from them, and for an instant Tom thought the little man was going to run away. 'You don't understand.'

'What a fuckin' candy-ass,' Joey said loudly.

Watching Tachyon crumble on his screens, Tom Tudbury finally ran out of patience. 'If you fail, you fail,' he said. 'And if you don't try, you fail too, so what the fuck difference does it make? Jetboy failed, but at least he *tried*. He wasn't an ace, he wasn't a goddamned *Takisian*, he was just a guy with a jet, but he did what he could.'

'I want to. I . . . just . . . *can't*.'

Des trumpeted his disgust. Joey shrugged.

Inside his shell, Tom sat in stunned disbelief. He wasn't going to help. He hadn't believed it, not really. Joey had warned him, Desmond too, but Tom had insisted, he'd been sure, this was *Doctor Tachyon*, of course he'd help, maybe he was having some problems, but once they explained the situation to him, once they made it clear what was at stake and how much they needed him – he *had* to help. But he was saying no. It was the last goddamned straw.

He twisted the volume knob up all the way. 'YOU SON OF A BITCH,' he boomed, and the sound hammered out over the plaza. Tachyon flinched away. 'YOU NO-GOOD FUCKING LITTLE ALIEN CHICKENSHIT!' Tachyon stumbled backward down the stairs, but the Turtle drifted after him, loudspeakers blaring. 'IT WAS ALL A LIE, WASN'T IT? EVERYTHING IN THE COMIC BOOKS, EVERYTHING IN THE PAPERS, IT WAS ALL A STUPID LIE. ALL MY LIFE THEY BEAT ME UP AND THEY CALLED ME A FUCKING WIMP AND A COWARD BUT *YOU'RE* THE COWARD, YOU ASSHOLE, YOU SHITTY LITTLE WHINER, YOU WON'T EVEN TRY, YOU DON'T GIVE A DAMN ABOUT ANYBODY, ABOUT YOUR FRIEND ANGELFACE OR ABOUT KENNEDY OR JETBOY OR ANYBODY, YOU HAVE ALL THESE FUCKING POWERS AND YOU'RE *NOTHING*, YOU WON'T DO ANYTHING, YOU'RE WORSE THAN OSWALD OR BRAUN OR ANY OF THEM.' Tachyon staggered down the steps, hands over his ears, shouting something unintelligible, but Tom was past listening. His anger had a life of its own now. He lashed out, and the alien's head snapped around and reddened with the force of the slap. '*ASSHOLE!*' Tom was shrieking. '*YOU'RE THE ONE IN A SHELL.*' Invisible blows rained down on Tachyon in a fury. He reeled, fell, rolled a third of the way down the stairs, tried to get back to his feet, was bowled over again, and bounced down to the street head over heels. 'ASSHOLE!' the Turtle thundered. 'RUN, YOU SHITHEAD. GET OUT OF HERE, OR I'LL THROW YOU IN THE DAMNED RIVER! RUN, YOU LITTLE WIMP, BEFORE THE GREAT AND POWERFUL TURTLE REALLY GETS UPSET! RUN, DAMN IT! YOU'RE THE ONE IN THE SHELL! YOU'RE THE ONE IN THE SHELL!'

And he ran, dashing blindly from one streetlight to the next, until he was lost in the shadows. Tom Tudbury watched him vanish on the shell's array of television screens. He felt sick and beaten. His head was throbbing. He needed a beer, or an aspirin, or both. When he heard the sirens coming, he scooped up Joey and Desmond and set them on top of his shell, killed his lights, and rose straight up into the night, high, high up, into darkness and cold and silence.

*

That night Tach slept the sleep of the damned, thrashing about like a man in a fever dream, crying out, weeping, waking again and again from nightmares, only to drift back into them. He dreamt he was back on Takis, and his hated cousin Zabb was boasting about a new sex toy, but when he brought her out it was Blythe, and he raped her right there in front of him. Tach watched it all, powerless to intervene; her body writhed beneath his and blood flowed from her mouth and ears and vagina. She began to change, into a thousand joker shapes each more horrible than the last, and Zabb went right on raping them all as they screamed and struggled. But afterward, when Zabb rose from the corpse covered with blood, it wasn't his cousin's face at all, it was his own, worn and dissipated, a *coarse* face, eyes reddened and puffy, long red hair tangled and greasy, features distorted by alcoholic bloat or perhaps by a Funhouse mirror.

He woke around noon, to the terrible sound of Tiny weeping outside his window. It was more than he could stand. It was all more than he could stand. He stumbled to the window and threw it open and screamed at the giant to be quiet, to stop, to leave him alone, to give him peace, please, but Tiny went on and on, so much pain, so much guilt, so much shame, why couldn't they let him be, he couldn't take it anymore, no, shut up, shut up, *please shut up*, and suddenly Tach shrieked and reached out with his mind and plunged into Tiny's head and shut him up.

The silence was thunderous.

*

The nearest phone booth was in a candy store a block down. Vandals had ripped the phone book to shreds. He dialed information and got the listing for Xavier Desmond on Christie Street, only a short walk away. The apartment was a fourth-floor walkup above a mask shop. Tachyon was out of breath by the time he got to the top.

Des opened the door on the fifth knock. 'You,' he said.

'The Turtle,' Tach said. His throat was dry. 'Did he get anything last night?'

'No,' Desmond replied. His trunk twitched. 'The same story as before. They're wise to him now, they know he won't really drop them. They call his bluff. Short of actually killing someone, there's nothing to do.'

'Tell me who to ask,' Tach said.

'You?' Des said.

Tach could not look the joker in the eye. He nodded.

'Let me get my coat,' Des said. He emerged from the apartment bundled up for the cold, carrying a fur cap and a frayed beige raincoat. 'Put your hair up in the hat,' he told Tachyon, 'and leave that ridiculous coat here. You don't want to be recognized.' Tach did as he said. On the way out, Des went into the mask shop for the final touch.

'A chicken?' Tach said when Des handed him the mask. It had bright yellow feathers, a prominent orange beak, a floppy red coxcomb on top.

'I saw it and I knew it was you,' said Des. 'Put it on.'

A large crane was moving into position at Chatham Square, to get the police cars off Freakers' roof. The club was open. The doorman was a seven-foot-tall hairless joker with fangs. He grabbed Des by the arm as they tried to pass under the neon thighs of the six-breasted dancer who writhed on the marquee. 'No jokers allowed,' he said brusquely. 'Get lost, Tusker.'

Reach out and grab his mind, Tachyon thought. Once, before Blythe, he would have done it instinctively. But now he hesitated, and hesitating, he was lost.

Des reached into his back pocket, pulled out a wallet, extracted a fifty-dollar bill. 'You were watching them lower the police cars,' he said. 'You never saw me pass.'

'Oh, yeah,' the doorman said. The bill vanished in a clawed hand. 'Real interesting, them cranes.'

'Sometimes money is the most potent power of all,' Des said as they walked into the cavernous dimness within. A sparse noontime crowd sat eating the free lunch and watching a stripper gyrate down a long runway behind a barbed-wire barrier. She was covered with silky gray hair, except for her breasts, which had been shaved bare. Desmond scanned the booths along the far wall. He took Tach's elbow and led him to a dark corner, where a man in a peacoat was sitting with a stein of beer. 'They lettin'' jokers in here now?' the man asked gruffly as they approached. He was saturnine and pockmarked.

Tach went into his mind. *Fuck what's this now the elephant man's from the Funhouse who's the other one damned jokers anyhow gotta lotta nerve.*

'Where's Bannister keeping Angelface?' Des asked.

'Angelface is the slit at the Funhouse, right? Don't know no Bannister. Is this a game? Fuck off, joker, I ain't playing.' In his thoughts, images came tumbling: Tack saw mirrors shattering, silver knives flying through the air, felt Mal's shove and saw him reach for a gun, watched him shudder and spin as the bullets hit, heard Bannister's soft voice as he told them to kill Ruth, saw the warehouse over on the Hudson where they were keeping her, the livid bruises on her arm when they'd grabbed her, tasted the man's fear, fear of jokers, fear of discovery, fear of Bannister, the fear of *them.* Tach reached out and squeezed Desmond's arm.

Des turned to go. 'Hey, hold it right there,' the man with the pockmarked face said. He flashed a badge as he unfolded from the booth. 'Undercover narcotics,' he said, 'and you been using, mister, asking asshole junkie questions like that.' Des stood still as the man frisked him down. 'Well, looka this,' he said, producing a bag of white powder from one of Desmond's pockets. 'Wonder what this is? You're under arrest, freak-face.'

'That's not mine,' Desmond said calmly.

'The hell it ain't,' the man said, and in his mind the thoughts ran one after another *little accident resisting arrest what could i do huh? jokers'll scream but who listens to a fuckin' joker only whatymi gonna do with the other one?* and he glanced at Tachyon. *Jeez looka the chickenman's shaking maybe the fucker IS using that'd be great.*

Trembling, Tach realized the moment of truth was at hand.

He was not sure he could do it. It was different than with Tiny; that had been blind instinct, but he was awake now, and he knew what he was doing. It had been so easy once, as easy as using his hands. But now those hands trembled, and there was blood on them, and on his mind as well . . . he thought of Blythe and the way her mind had shattered under his touch, like the mirrors in the Funhouse, and for a terrible, long second nothing happened, until the fear was rank in his throat, and the familiar taste of failure filled his mouth.

Then the pockfaced man smiled an idiot's smile, sat back down in his booth, laid his head on the table, and went to sleep as sweetly as a child.

Des took it in stride. 'Your doing?'

Tachyon nodded.

'You're shaking,' Des asked. 'Are you all right, Doctor?'

'I think so,' Tachyon said. The policeman had begun to snore loudly. 'I think maybe I am all right, Des. For the first time in years.' He looked at the joker's face, looked past the deformity to the man beneath. 'I know where she is,' he said. They started toward the exit. In the cage, a full-breasted, bearded hermaphrodite had started into a bump-and-grind. 'We have to move quickly.'

'In an hour I can get together twenty men.'

'No,' Tachyon said. 'The place they're holding her isn't in Jokertown.'

Des stopped with his hand on the door. 'I see,' he said. 'And outside of Jokertown, jokers and masked men are rather conspicuous, aren't they?'

'Exactly,' Tach said. He did not voice his other fear, of the retribution that would surely be enacted should jokers dare to confront police, even police as corrupt as Bannister and his cohorts. He would take the risk himself, he had nothing left to lose, but he could not permit them to take it. 'Can you reach the Turtle?' he asked.

'I can take you to him,' Des replied. 'When?'

'Now,' Tach said. In an hour or two, the sleeping policeman would awaken and go straight to Bannister. And say what? That Des and a man in a chicken mask had been asking questions, that he'd been about to arrest them but suddenly he'd gotten very sleepy? Would he dare admit to that? If so, what would Bannister make of it? Enough to move Angelface? Enough to kill her? They could not chance it.

When they emerged from the dimness of Freakers, the crane had just lowered the second police car to the sidewalk. A cold wind was blowing, but behind his chicken feathers, Doctor Tachyon had begun to sweat.

*

Tom Tudbury woke to the dim, muffled sound of someone pounding on his shell.

He pushed aside the frayed blanket and bashed his head sitting up. 'Ow, goddamn it,' he cursed, fumbling in the darkness until he found the map light. The pounding continued, a hollow *boom boom boom* against the armor, echoing. Tom felt a stab of panic. The police, he thought, they've found me, they've come to drag me out and haul me up on charges. His head hurt. It was cold and stuffy in here. He turned on the space heater, the fans, the cameras. His screens came to life.

Outside was a bright cold December day, the sunlight painting every grimy brick with stark clarity. Joey had taken the train back to Bayonne, but Tom had remained; they were running out of time, he had no other choice. Des found him a safe place, an interior courtyard in the depths of Jokertown, surrounded by decaying five-story tenements, its cobblestones redolent with the smell of sewage, wholly hidden from the street. When he'd landed, just before dawn, lights had blinked on in a few of the dark windows, and faces had come to peer cautiously around the shades; wary, frightened, not-quite-human faces, briefly seen and gone as quickly, when they decided that the thing outside was none of their concern.

Yawning, Tom pulled himself into his seat and panned his cameras until he found the source of the commotion. Des was standing by an open cellar door, arms crossed, while Doctor Tachyon hammered on the shell with a length of broom handle.

Astonished, Tom flipped open his microphones. 'YOU.'

Tachyon winced. 'Please.'

He lowered the volume. 'Sorry. You took me by surprise. I never expected to see you again. After last night, I mean. I didn't hurt you, did I? I didn't mean to, I just—'

'I understand,' Tachyon said. 'But we've got no time for recriminations or apologies now.'

Des began to roll upward. Damn that vertical hold. 'We know where they have her,' the joker said as his image flipped. 'That is, if Doctor Tachyon can indeed read minds as advertised.'

'Where?' Tom said. Des continued to flip, flip, flip.

'A warehouse on the Hudson,' Tachyon replied. 'Near the foot of a pier. I can't tell you an address, but I saw it clearly in his thoughts. I'll recognize it.'

'Great!' Tom enthused. He gave up on his efforts to adjust the vertical hold and whapped the screen. The picture steadied. 'Then we've got them. Let's go.' The look on Tachyon's face took him aback. 'You are coming, aren't you?'

Tachyon swallowed. 'Yes,' he said. He had a mask in his hand. He slipped it on.

That was a relief, Tom thought; for a second there, he'd thought he'd have to go it alone. 'Climb on,' he said.

With a deep sigh of resignation, the alien scrambled on top of the shell, his boots scrabbling at the armor. Tom gripped his armrests tightly and pushed up. The shell rose as easily as a soap bubble. He felt elated. This was what he was meant to do, Tom thought; Jetboy must have felt like this.

Joey had installed a monster of a horn in the shell. Tom let it rip as they floated clear of the rooftops, startling a coop of pigeons, a few winos, and Tachyon with the distinctive blare of *Here-I-come-to-save-the-daaaaaay*.

'It might be wise to be a bit more subtle about this,' Tachyon said diplomatically.

Tom laughed. 'I don't believe it, I got a man from outer space who mostly dresses like Pinky Lee riding on my back, and he's telling me I ought to be subtle.' He laughed again as the streets of Jokertown spread out all around them.

*

They made their final approach through a maze of waterfront alleys. The last was a dead end, terminating in a brick wall scrawled over with the names of gangs and young lovers. The Turtle rose above it, and they emerged in the loading area behind the warehouse. A man in a short leather jacket sat on the edge of the loading dock. He jumped to his feet when they hove into view. His jump took him a lot higher than he'd anticipated, about ten feet higher. He opened his mouth, but before he could shout, Tach had him; he went to sleep in midair. The Turtle stashed him atop a nearby roof.

Four wide loading bays opened onto the dock, all chained and padlocked, their corrugated metal doors marked with wide brown streaks of rust. TRESPASSERS WILL BE PROSECUTED said the lettering on the narrow door to the side.

Tach hopped down, landing easily on the balls of his feet, his nerves tingling. 'I'll go through,' he told the Turtle. 'Give me a minute, and then follow.'

'A minute,' the speakers said. 'You got it.'

Tach pulled off his boots, opened the door just a crack, and slid into the warehouse on purple-stockinged feet, summoning up all the stealth and fluid grace they'd once taught him on Takis. Inside, bales of shredded paper, bound tightly in thin wire, were stacked twenty and thirty feet high. Tachyon crept down a crooked aisle toward the sound of voices. A huge yellow forklift blocked his path. He dropped flat and squirmed underneath it, to peer around one massive tire.

He counted five altogether. Two of them were playing cards, sitting in folding chairs and using a stack of coverless paperbacks for a table. A grossly fat man was adjusting a gigantic paper-shredding machine against the far wall. The last two stood over a long table, bags of white powder piled in neat rows in front of them. The tall man in the flannel shirt was weighing something on a small set of scales. Next to him, supervising, was a slender balding man in an expensive raincoat. He had a cigarette in his hand, and his voice was smooth and soft. Tachyon couldn't quite make out what he was saying. There was no sign of Angelface.

He dipped into the sewer that was Bannister's mind, and saw her. Between the shredder and the baling machine. He couldn't see it from under the forklift; the machinery blocked the line of sight, but she was there. A filthy mattress had been tossed on the concrete floor, and she lay atop it, her ankles swollen and raw where the handcuffs chafed against her skin.

*

'. . . fifty-eight hippopotami, fifty-nine hippopotami, *sixty* hippopotami,' Tom counted.

The loading bays were big enough. He squeezed, and the padlock disintegrated into shards of rust and twisted metal. The chains came clanking down, and the door rattled upward, rusty tracks screeching protest. Tom turned on all his lights as the shell slid forward. Inside, towering stacks of paper blocked his way. There wasn't room to go between them. He shoved them, *hard*, but even as they started to collapse, it occurred to him that he could go above them. He pushed up toward the ceiling.

*

'What the fuck,' one of the card players said, when they heard the loading gate screech open.

A heartbeat later, they were all moving. Both card players scrambled to their feet; one of them produced a gun. The man in the flannel shirt looked up from his scales. The fat man turned away from the shredder, shouting something, but it was impossible to make out what he was saying. Against the far wall, bales of paper came crashing down, knocking into neighboring stacks and sending them down too, in a chain reaction that spread across the warehouse.

Without an instant's hesitation, Bannister went for Angelface. Tach took his mind and stopped him in mid-stride, with his revolver half-drawn.

And then a dozen bales of shredded paper slammed down against the rear of the forklift. The vehicle shifted, just a little, crushing Tachyon's left hand under a huge black tire. He cried out in shock and pain, and lost Bannister.

*

Down below, two little men were shooting at him. The first shot startled him so badly that Tom lost his concentration for a split second, and the shell dropped four feet before he got it back. Then the bullets were *pinging* harmlessly off his armor and ricocheting around the warehouse. Tom smiled. 'I AM THE GREAT AND POWERFUL TURTLE,' he announced at full volume, as stacks of paper crashed down all around. 'YOU ASSHOLES ARE UP SHIT CREEK. SURRENDER NOW.'

The nearest asshole didn't surrender. He fired again, and one of Tom's screens went black. 'OH, FUCK,' Tom said, forgetting to kill his mike. He grabbed the guy's arm and pulled the gun away, and from the way the jerk screamed he'd probably dislocated his shoulder too, goddammit. He'd have to watch that. The other guy started running, jumping over a collapsed pile of paper. Tom caught him in mid-jump, took him straight up to the ceiling, and hung him from a rafter. His eyes flicked from screen to screen, but one screen was dark now and the damned vertical hold had gone again on the one next to it, so he couldn't make out a fucking thing to that side. He didn't have time to fix it. Some guy in a flannel shirt was loading bags into a suitcase, he saw on the big screen, and from the corner of his eye, he spied a fat guy climbing into a forklift . . .

*

His hand crushed beneath the tire, Tachyon writhed in excruciating pain and tried not to scream. Bannister – had to stop Bannister before he got to Angelface. He ground his teeth together and tried to will away the pain, to gather it into a ball and push it from him the way he'd been taught, but it was hard, he'd lost the discipline, he could feel the shattered bones in his hand, his eyes were blurry with tears, and then he heard the forklift's motor turn over, and suddenly it was surging forward, rolling right up his arm, coming straight at his head, the tread of the massive tire a black wall of death rushing toward him . . . and passing an inch over the top of his skull, as it took to the air.

*

The forklift flew nicely across the warehouse and embedded itself in the far wall, with a little push from the Great and Powerful Turtle. The fat man dove off in midair and landed on a pile of coverless paperbacks. It wasn't until then that Tom happened to notice Tachyon lying on the floor under the place the forklift had been. He was holding his hand funny and his chicken mask was all smashed up and dirty, Tom saw, and as he staggered to his feet he was shouting something. He went running across the floor, reeling, unsteady. Where the fuck was he going in such a hurry?

Frowning, Tom smacked the malfunctioning screen with the back of his hand, and the vertical roll stopped suddenly. For an instant, the image on the television was clear and sharp. A man in a raincoat stood over a woman on a mattress. She was real pretty, and there was a funny smile on her face, sad but almost accepting, as he pressed the revolver right up to her forehead.

*

Tach came reeling around the shredding machine, his ankles all rubber, the world a red blur, his shattered bones jabbing against each other with every step, and found them there, Bannister touching her lightly with his pistol, her skin already darkening where the bullet would go in, and through his tears and his fears and a haze of pain, he reached out for Bannister's mind and seized it . . . just in time to feel him squeeze the trigger, and wince as the gun kicked back in his mind. He heard the explosion from two sets of ears.

'*Noooooooooooooooooo!*' he shrieked. He closed his eyes, sunk to his knees. He made Bannister fling the gun away, for what good it would do, none at all, too late, again he'd come too late, *failed, failed*, again, Angelface, Blythe, his sister, everyone he loved, all of them gone. He doubled over on the floor, and his mind filled with images of broken mirrors, of the Wedding Pattern danced in blood and pain, and that was the last thing he knew before the darkness took him.

*

He woke to the astringent smell of a hospital room and the feel of a pillow under his head, the pillowcase crisp with starch. He opened his eyes. 'Des,' he said weakly. He tried to sit, but he was bound up somehow. The world was blurry and unfocused.

'You're in traction, Doctor,' Des said. 'Your right arm was broken in two places, and your hand is worse than that.'

'I'm sorry,' Tach said. He would have wept, but he had run out of tears. 'I'm so sorry. We tried, I . . . I'm so sorry, I—'

'Tacky,' she said in that soft, husky voice.

And she was there, standing over him, dressed in a hospital gown, black hair framing a wry smile. She had combed it forward to cover her forehead; beneath her bangs was a hideous purple-green bruise, and the skin around her eyes was red and raw. For a moment he thought he was dead, or mad, or dreaming. 'It's all right, Tacky. I'm okay. I'm here.'

He stared up at her numbly. 'You're dead,' he said dully. 'I was too late. I heard the shot, I had him by then but it was too late, I felt the gun recoil in his hand.'

'Did you feel it jerk?' she asked him.

'Jerk?'

'A couple of inches, no more. Just as he fired. Just enough. I got some nasty powder burns, but the bullet went into the mattress a foot from my head.'

'The Turtle,' Tach said hoarsely.

She nodded. 'He pushed aside the gun just as Bannister squeezed the trigger. And you made the son of a bitch throw away the revolver before he could get off a second shot.'

'You got them,' Des said. 'A couple of men escaped in the confusion, but the Turtle delivered three of them, including Bannister. Plus a suitcase packed with twenty pounds of pure heroin. And it turns out that warehouse is owned by the mafia.'

'The mafia?' Tachyon said.

'The mob,' Des explained. 'Criminals, Doctor Tachyon.'

'One of the men captured in the warehouse has already turned state's evidence,' Angelface said. 'He'll testify to everything – the bribes, the drug operation, the murders at the Funhouse.'

'Maybe we'll even get some decent police in Jokertown,' Des added.

The feelings that rushed through Tachyon went far beyond relief. He wanted to thank them, wanted to cry for them, but neither the tears nor the words would come. He was weak and happy. 'I didn't fail,' he managed at last.

'No,' Angelface said. She looked at Des. 'Would you wait outside?' When they were alone, she sat on the edge of the bed. 'I want to show you something. Something I wish I'd shown you a long time ago.' She held it up in front of him. It was a gold locket. 'Open it.'

It was hard to do with only one hand, but he managed. Inside was a small round photograph of an elderly woman in bed. Her limbs were skeletal and withered, sticks draped in mottled flesh, and her face was horribly twisted. 'What's wrong with her?' Tach asked, afraid of the answer. Another joker, he thought, another victim of his failures.

Angelface looked down at the twisted old woman, sighed, and closed the locket with a snap. 'When she was four, in Little Italy, she was run over while playing in the street. A horse stepped on her face, and the wagon wheel crushed her spine. That was in, oh, 1886. She was completely paralyzed, but she lived. If you could call it living. That little girl spent the next sixty years in a bed, being fed, washed and read to, with no company except the holy sisters. Sometimes all she wanted was to die. She dreamed about what it would be like to be beautiful, to be loved and desired, to be able to dance, to be able to *feel* things. Oh, how she wanted to *feel* things.' She smiled. 'I should have said thank you long ago, Tacky, but it's hard for me to show that picture to anyone. But I am grateful, and now I owe you doubly. You'll never pay for a drink at the Funhouse.'

He stared at her. 'I don't want a drink,' he said. 'No more. That's done.' And it was, he knew; if she could live with her pain, what excuse could he possibly have to waste his life and talents? 'Angelface,' he said suddenly, 'I can make you something better than heroin. I was . . . I *am* a biochemist, there are drugs on Takis, I can synthesize them, painkillers, nerve blocks. If you'll let me run some tests on you, maybe I can tailor something to your metabolism. I'll need a lab, of course. Setting things up will be expensive, but the drug could be made for pennies.'

'I'll have some money,' she said. 'I'm selling the Funhouse to Des. But what you're talking about is illegal.'

'To hell with their stupid laws,' Tach blazed. 'I won't tell if you won't.' Then words came tumbling out one after the other, a torrent: plans, dreams, hopes, all of the things he'd lost or drowned in cognac and Sterno, and Angelface was looking at him, astonished, smiling, and when the drugs they had given him finally began to wear off, and his arm began to throb again, Doctor Tachyon remembered the old disciplines and sent the pain away, and somehow it seemed as though part of his guilt and his grief went with it, and he was whole again, and alive.

*

The headline said TURTLE, TACHYON SMASH HEROIN RING. Tom was gluing the article into the scrapbook when Joey returned with the beers. 'They left out the Great and Powerful part,' Joey observed, setting down a bottle by Tom's elbow.

'At least I got first billing,' Tom said. He wiped thick white paste off his fingers with a napkin, and shoved the scrapbook aside. Underneath were some crude drawings he'd made of the shell. 'Now,' he said, 'where the fuck are we going to put the record player, huh?'

From the Journal of Xavier Desmond

NOVEMBER 30/JOKERTOWN:

My name is Xavier Desmond, and I am a joker.

Jokers are always strangers, even on the street where they were born, and this one is about to visit a number of strange lands. In the next five months I will see veldts and mountains, Rio and Cairo, the Khyber Pass and the Straits of Gibraltar, the Outback and the Champs-Élysées – all very far from home for a man who has often been called the mayor of Jokertown. Jokertown, of course, has no mayor. It is a neighborhood, a ghetto neighborhood at that, and not a city. Jokertown is more than a place though. It is a condition, a state of mind. Perhaps in that sense my title is not undeserved.

I have been a joker since the beginning. Forty years ago, when Jetboy died in the skies over Manhattan and loosed the wild card upon the world, I was twenty-nine years of age, an investment banker with a lovely wife, a two-year-old daughter, and a bright future ahead of me. A month later, when I was finally released from the hospital, I was a monstrosity with a pink elephantine trunk growing from the center of my face where my nose had been. There are seven perfectly functional fingers at the end of my trunk, and over the years I have become quite adept with this 'third hand.' Were I suddenly restored to so-called normal humanity, I believe it would be as traumatic as if one of my limbs were amputated. With my trunk I am ironically somewhat more than human ... and infinitely less.

My lovely wife left me within two weeks of my release from the hospital, at approximately the same time that Chase Manhattan informed me that my services would no longer be required. I moved to Jokertown nine months later, following my eviction from my Riverside Drive apartment for 'health reasons.' I last saw my daughter in 1948. She was married in June of 1964, divorced in 1969, remarried in June of 1972. She has a fondness for June weddings, it seems. I was invited to neither of them. The private detective I hired informs me that she and her husband now live in Salem, Oregon, and that I have two grandchildren, a boy and a girl, one from each marriage. I sincerely doubt that either knows that their grandfather is the mayor of Jokertown.

I am the founder and president emeritus of the Jokers' Anti-Defamation League, or JADL, the oldest and largest organization dedicated to the preservation of civil rights for the victims of the wild card virus. The JADL has had its failures, but overall it has accomplished great good. I am also a moderately successful businessman. I own one of New York's most storied and elegant nightclubs, the Funhouse, where jokers and nats and aces have enjoyed all the top joker cabaret acts for more than two decades. The Funhouse has been losing money steadily for the last five years, but no one knows that except me and my accountant. I keep it open because it is, after all, the Funhouse, and were it to close, Jokertown would seem a poorer place.

Next month I will be seventy years of age.

My doctor tells me that I will not live to be seventy-one. The cancer had already metastasized before it was diagnosed. Even jokers cling stubbornly to life, and I have been doing the chemotherapy and the radiation treatments for half a year now, but the cancer shows no sign of remission.

My doctor tells me the trip I am about to embark on will probably take months off my life. I have my prescriptions and will dutifully continue to take the pills, but when one is globe-hopping, radiation therapy must be forgone. I have accepted this.

Mary and I often talked of a trip around the world, in those days before the wild card when we were young and in love. I could never have dreamt that I would finally take that trip without her, in the twilight of my life, and at government expense, as a delegate on a fact-finding mission organized and funded by the Senate Committee on Ace Resources and Endeavors, under the official sponsorship of the United Nations and the World Health Organization. We will visit every continent but Antarctica and call upon thirty-nine different countries (some only for a few hours), and our official charge is to investigate the treatment of wild card victims in cultures around the world.

There are twenty-one delegates, only five of whom are jokers. I suppose my selection is a great honor, recognition of my achievements and my status as a community leader. I believe I have my good friend Dr Tachyon to thank for it.

But then, I have my good friend Dr Tachyon to thank for a great many things.

DECEMBER 1/NEW YORK CITY:

The journey is off to an inauspicious start. For the last hour we have been holding on the runway at Tomlin International, waiting for clearance for takeoff. The problem, we are informed, is not here, but down in Havana. So we wait.

Our plane is a custom 747 that the press has dubbed the *Stacked Deck*. The entire central cabin has been converted to our requirements, the seats replaced with a small medical laboratory, a press room for the print journalists, and a miniature television studio for their electronic counterparts. The newsmen themselves have been segregated in the tail. Already they've made it their own. I was back there twenty minutes ago and found a poker game in progress. The business-class cabin is full of aides, assistants, secretaries, publicists, and security personnel. First class is supposedly reserved exclusively for the delegates.

As there are only twenty-one delegates, we rattle around like peas in a pod. Even here the ghettoes persist – jokers tend to sit with jokers, nats with nats, aces with aces.

Hartmann is the only man aboard who seems entirely comfortable with all three groups. He greeted me warmly at the press conference and sat with Howard and myself for a few moments after boarding, talking earnestly about his hopes for the trip. It is difficult not to like the senator. Jokertown has delivered him huge majorities in each of his campaigns as far back as his term as mayor, and no wonder – no other politician has worked so long and hard to defend jokers' rights. Hartmann gives me hope; he's living proof that there can indeed be trust and mutual respect between joker and nat. He's a decent, honorable man, and in these days when fanatics such as Leo Barnett are inflaming the old hatreds and prejudices, jokers need all the friends they can get in the halls of power.

Dr Tachyon and Senator Hartmann co-chair the delegation. Tachyon arrived dressed like a foreign correspondent from some film noir classic, in a trench coat covered with belts, buttons, and epaulettes, a snap-brim fedora rakishly tilted to one side. The fedora sports a foot-long red feather, however, and I cannot begin to imagine where one goes to purchase a powder-blue crushed-velvet trench coat. A pity that those foreign-correspondent films were all in black and white.

Tachyon would like to think that he shares Hartmann's lack of prejudice toward jokers, but that's not strictly true. He labors unceasingly in his clinic, and one cannot doubt that he cares, and cares deeply . . . many jokers think of him as a saint, a hero . . . yet, when one has known the doctor as long as I have, deeper truths become apparent. On some unspoken level he thinks of his good works in Jokertown as a penance. He does his best to hide it, but even after all these years you can see the revulsion in his eyes. Dr Tachyon and I are 'friends,' we have known each other for decades now, and I believe with all my heart that he sincerely cares for me . . . but not for a second have I ever felt that he considers me an equal, as Hartmann does. The senator treats me like a man, even an important man, courting me as he might any political leader with votes to deliver. To Dr Tachyon, I will always be a joker.

Is that his tragedy, or mine?

Tachyon knows nothing of the cancer. A symptom that our friendship is as diseased as my body? Perhaps. He has not been my personal physician for many years now. My doctor is a joker, as are my accountant, my attorney, my broker, and even my banker – the world changed since the Chase dismissed me, and as mayor of Jokertown I am obliged to practice my own personal brand of affirmative action.

*

We have just been cleared for takeoff. The seat-hopping is over; people are belting themselves in. It seems I carry Jokertown with me wherever I go – Howard Mueller sits closest to me, his seat customized to accommodate his nine-foot tall form and the immense length of his arms. He's better known as Troll, and he works as chief of security at Tachyon's clinic, but I note that he does not sit with Tachyon among the aces. The other three joker delegates – Father Squid, Chrysalis, and the poet Dorian Wilde – are also here in the center section of first class. Is it coincidence, prejudice, or shame that puts us here, in the seats furthest from the windows? Being a joker makes one a tad paranoid about these things, I fear. The politicians, of both the domestic and UN varieties, have clustered to our right, the aces forward of us (aces up front, of course, of course) and to our left. Must stop now, the stewardess has asked me to put my tray table back up.

Airborne. New York and Robert Tomlin International Airport are far behind us, and Cuba waits ahead. From what I've heard, it will be an easy and pleasant first stop. Havana is almost as American as Las Vegas or Miami Beach, albeit considerably more decadent and wicked. I may actually have friends there – some of the top joker entertainers go on to the Havana casinos after getting their starts in the Funhouse and the Chaos Club. I must remind myself to stay away from the gaming tables, however; joker luck is notoriously bad.

*

As soon as the seat belt sign went off, a number of the aces ascended to the first-class lounge. I can hear their laughter drifting down the spiral stairway – Peregrine, pretty young Mistral – who looks just like the college student she is when not in her flying gear – boisterous Hiram Worchester, and Asta Lenser, the ballerina from the ABT whose ace name is Fantasy. Already they are a tight little clique, a 'fun bunch' for whom nothing could possibly go wrong. The golden people, and Tachyon very much in their midst. Is it the aces or the women that draw him? I wonder? Even my dear friend Angela, who still loves the man deeply after twenty-odd years, admits that Dr Tachyon thinks mainly with his penis where women are concerned.

Yet even among the aces there are the odd men out. Jones, the black strongman from Harlem (like Troll and Hiram W. and Peregrine, he requires a custom seat, in his case to support his extraordinary weight), is nursing a beer and reading a copy of *Sports Illustrated*. Radha O'Reilly is just as solitary, gazing out the window. She seems very quiet. Billy Ray and Joanne Jefferson, the two Justice Department aces who head up our security contingent, are not delegates and thus are seated back in the second section.

And then there is Jack Braun. The tensions that swirl around him are almost palpable. Most of the other delegates are polite to him, but no one is truly friendly, and he's being openly shunned by some, such as Hiram Worchester. For Dr Tachyon, clearly Braun does not even exist. I wonder whose idea it was to bring him on this trip? Certainly not Tachyon's, and it seems too politically dangerous for Hartmann to be responsible. A gesture to appease the conservatives on SCARE perhaps? Or are there ramifications that I have not considered?

Braun glances up at the stairway from time to time, as if he would love nothing so much as to join the happy group upstairs, but remains firmly in his seat. It is hard to credit that this smoothfaced, blond-haired boy in the tailored safari jacket is really the notorious Judas Ace of the fifties. He's my age or close to it, but he looks barely twenty . . . the kind of boy who might have taken pretty young Mistral to her senior prom a few years back and gotten her home well before midnight.

One of the reporters, a man named Downs from *Aces* magazine, was up here earlier, trying to get Braun to consent to an interview. He was persistent, but Braun's refusal was firm, and Downs finally gave up. Instead he handed out copies of the latest issue of *Aces* and then sauntered up to the lounge, no doubt to pester someone else. I am not a regular reader of *Aces*, but I accepted a copy and suggested to Downs that his publisher consider a companion periodical, to be called *Jokers*. He was not overly enthused about the idea.

The issue features a rather striking cover photograph of the Turtle's shell outlined against the oranges and reds of sunset, blurbed with 'The Turtle – Dead or Alive?' The Turtle has not been seen since Wild Card Day, back in September, when he was napalmed and crashed into the Hudson. Twisted and burnt pieces of his shell were found on the riverbed, though no body has ever been recovered. Several hundred people claim to have seen the Turtle near dawn the following day, flying an older shell in the sky over Jokertown, but since he has not reappeared since, some are putting that sighting down to hysteria and wishful thinking.

I have no opinion on the Turtle, though I would hate to think that he was truly dead. Many jokers believe that he is one of us, that his shell conceals some unspeakable joker deformity. Whether that is true or not, he has been a good friend to Jokertown for a long, long time.

There is, however, an aspect to this trip that no one ever speaks of, although Downs' article brings it to mind. Perhaps it falls to me to mention the unmentionable then. The truth is, all that laughter up in the lounge has a slightly nervous ring to it, and it is no coincidence that this junket, under discussion for so many years, was put together so swiftly in the past two months. They want to get us out of town for a while – not just the jokers, the aces too. The aces *especially*, one might even say.

This last Wild Card Day was a catastrophe for the city, and for every victim of the virus everywhere. The level of violence was shocking and made headlines across the nation. The still-unsolved murder of the Howler, the dismemberment of a child ace in the midst of a huge crowd at Jetboy's Tomb, the attack on Aces High, the destruction of the Turtle (or at least his shell), the wholesale slaughter at the Cloisters, where a dozen bodies were brought out in pieces, the predawn aerial battle that lit up the entire East Side . . . days and even weeks later the authorities were still not certain that they had an accurate death toll.

One old man was found literally embedded in a solid brick wall, and when they began to chip him out, they found they could not tell where his flesh ended and the wall began. The autopsy revealed a ghastly mess inside, where his internal organs were fused with the bricks that penetrated them.

A *Post* photographer snapped a picture of that old man trapped in his wall. He looks so gentle and sweet. The police subsequently announced that the old man was an ace himself, and moreover a notorious criminal, that he was responsible for the murders of Kid Dinosaur and the Howler, the attempted murder of the Turtle, the attack on Aces High, the battle over the East River, the ghastly blood rites performed at the Cloisters, and a whole range of lesser crimes. A number of aces came forward to support this explanation, but the public does not seem convinced. According to the polls, more people believe the conspiracy theory put forward in the *National Informer* – that the killings were independent, caused by powerful aces known and unknown carrying out personal vendettas, using their powers in utter disregard for law and public safety, and that afterward those aces conspired with each other and the police to cover up their atrocities, blaming everything on one crippled old man who happened to be conveniently dead, clearly at the hands of some ace.

Already several books have been announced, each purporting to explain what really happened – the immoral opportunism of the publishing industry knows no bounds. Koch, ever aware of the prevailing winds, has ordered several cases reopened and has instructed the IAD to investigate the police role.

Jokers are pitiful and loathed. Aces have great power, and for the first time in many years a sizable segment of the public has begun to distrust those aces and fear that power. No wonder that demagogues like Leo Barnett have swelled so vastly in the public mind of late.

So I'm convinced that our tour has a hidden agenda; to wash the blood with some 'good ink,' as they say, to defuse the fear, to win back trust and take everyone's mind off Wild Card Day.

I admit to mixed feelings about aces, some of whom definitely abuse their power. Nonetheless, as a joker, I find myself desperately hoping that we succeed . . . and desperately fearing the consequences if we do not.

DECEMBER 8, 1986/MEXICO CITY:

Another state dinner this evening, but I've begged off with a plea of illness. A few hours to relax in my hotel room and write in the journal are most welcome. And my regrets were anything but fabricated – the tight schedule and pressures of the trip have begun to take their toll, I fear. I have not been keeping down all of my meals, although I've done my utmost to see that my distress remains unnoticed. If Tachyon suspected, he would insist on an examination, and once the truth was discovered, I might be sent home.

I will not permit that. I wanted to see all the fabled, far-off lands that Mary and I had once dreamed of together, but already it is clear that what we are engaged in here is far more important than any pleasure trip. Cuba was no Miami Beach, not for anyone who cared to look outside Havana; there are more jokers dying in the cane fields than cavorting on cabaret stages. And Haiti and the Dominican Republic were infinitely worse, as I've already noted in these pages.

A joker presence, a strong joker voice – we desperately need these things if we are to accomplish any good at all. I will not allow myself to be disqualified on medical grounds. Already our numbers are down by one – Dorian Wilde returned to New York rather than continue on to Mexico. I confess to mixed feelings about that. When we began, I had little respect for the 'poet laureate of Jokertown,' whose title is as dubious as my own mayoralty, though his Pulitzer is not. He seems to get a perverse glee from waving those wet, slimy tendrils of his in people's faces, flaunting his deformity in a deliberate attempt to draw a reaction. I suspect this aggressive nonchalance is in fact motivated by the same self-loathing that makes so many jokers take to masks, and a few sad cases actually attempt to amputate the deformed parts of their bodies. Also, he dresses almost as badly as Tachyon with his ridiculous Edwardian affectation, and his unstated preference for perfume over baths makes his company a trial to anyone with a sense of smell. Mine, alas, is quite acute.

Were it not for the legitimacy conferred on him by the Pulitzer, I doubt that he would ever have been named for this tour, but there are very few jokers who have achieved that kind of worldly recognition. I find precious little to admire in his poetry either, and much that is repugnant in his endless mincing recitations.

All that being said, I confess to a certain admiration for his impromptu performance before the Duvaliers. I suspect he received a severe dressing down from the politicians. Hartmann had a long private conversation with 'The Divine Wilde' as we were leaving Haiti, and after that Dorian seemed much subdued.

While I don't agree with much that Wilde has to say, I do nonetheless think he ought to have the right to say it. He will be missed. I wish I knew why he was leaving. I asked him that very question and tried to convince him to go on for the benefit of all his fellow jokers. His reply was an offensive suggestion about the sexual uses of my trunk, couched in the form of a vile little poem. A curious man.

With Wilde gone, Father Squid and myself are the only true representatives of the joker point of view, I feel. Howard M. (Troll, to the world) is an imposing presence, nine feet tall, incredibly strong, his green-tinged skin as tough and hard as horn, and I also know him to be a profoundly decent and competent man, and a very intelligent one, but . . . he is by nature a follower, not a leader, and there is a shyness in him, a reticence, that prevents him from speaking out. His height makes it impossible for him to blend with the crowd, but sometimes I think that is what he desires most profoundly.

As for Chrysalis, she is none of those things, and she has her own unique charisma. I cannot deny that she is a respected community leader, one of the most visible (no pun intended) and powerful of jokers. Yet I have never much liked Chrysalis. Perhaps this is my own prejudice and self-interest. The rise of the Crystal Palace has had much to do with the decline of the Funhouse. But there are deeper issues. Chrysalis wields considerable power in Jokertown, but she has never used it to benefit anyone but herself. She has been aggressively apolitical, carefully distancing herself from the JADL and all joker rights agitation. When the times called for passion and commitment, she remained cool and uninvolved, hidden behind her cigarette holders, liqueurs, and upper-class British accent.

Chrysalis speaks only for Chrysalis, and Troll seldom speaks at all, which leaves it to Father Squid and myself to speak for the jokers. I would do it gladly, but I am so tired . . .

*

I fell asleep early and was wakened by the sounds of my fellow delegates returning from the dinner. It went rather well, I understand. Excellent. We need some triumphs. Howard tells me that Hartmann gave a splendid speech and seemed to captivate President de la Madrid Hurtado throughout the meal. Peregrine captivated all the other males in the room, according to reports. I wonder if the other women are envious. Mistral is quite pretty, Fantasy is mesmerizing when she dances, and Radha O'Reilly is arresting, her mixed Irish and Indian heritage giving her features a truly exotic cast. But Peregrine overshadows all of them. What do they make of her?

The male aces certainly approve. The *Stacked Deck* is close quarters, and gossip travels quickly up and down the aisles. Word is that Dr Tachyon and Jack Braun have both made passes and have been firmly rebuffed. If anything, Peregrine seems closest with her cameraman, a nat who travels back with the rest of the reporters. She's making a documentary of this trip. Hiram is also close to Peregrine, but while there's a certain flirtatiousness to their constant banter, their friendship is more platonic in nature. Worchester has only one true love, and that's food. To that, his commitment is extraordinary. He seems to know all the best restaurants in every city we visit. His privacy is constantly being invaded by local chefs, who sneak up to his hotel room at all hours, carrying their specialties and begging for just a moment, just a taste, just a little approval. Far from objecting, Hiram delights in it.

In Haiti he found a cook he liked so much that he hired him on the spot and prevailed upon Hartmann to make a few calls to the INS and expedite the visa and work permit. We saw the man briefly at the Port-au-Prince airport, struggling with a huge trunk full of cast-iron cookware. Hiram made the trunk light enough for his new employee (who speaks no English, but Hiram insists that spices are a universal language) to carry on one shoulder. At tonight's dinner, Howard tells me, Worchester insisted on visiting the kitchen to get the chef's recipe for *chicken mole*, but while he was back there he concocted some sort of flaming dessert in honor of our hosts.

By rights I ought to object to Hiram Worchester, who revels in his acedom more than any other man I know, but I find it hard to dislike anyone who enjoys life so much and brings such enjoyment to those around him. Besides, I am well aware of his various anonymous charities in Jokertown, though he does his best to conceal them. Hiram is no more comfortable around my kind than Tachyon is, but his heart is as large as the rest of him.

Tomorrow the group will fragment yet again. Senators Hartmann and Lyons, Congressman Rabinowitz, and Ericsson from WHO will meet with the leaders of the PRI, Mexico's ruling party, while Tachyon and our medical staff visit a clinic that has claimed extraordinary success in treating the virus with laetrile. Our aces are scheduled to lunch with three of their Mexican counterparts. I'm pleased to say that Troll has been invited to join them. In some quarters, at least, his superhuman strength and near invulnerability have qualified him as an ace. A small break-through, of course, but a breakthrough nonetheless.

The rest of us will be traveling down to Yucatan and the Quintana Roo to look at Mayan ruins and the sites of several reported antijoker atrocities. Rural Mexico, it seems, is not as enlightened as Mexico City. The others will join us in Chichén Itzá the following day, and our last day in Mexico will be given over to tourism.

And then it will be on to Guatemala . . . perhaps. The daily press has been full of reports on an insurrection down there, an Indian uprising against the central government, and several of our journalists have gone ahead already, sensing a bigger story than this tour. If the situation seems too unstable, we may be forced to skip that stop.

DECEMBER 15, 1986/EN ROUTE TO LIMA, PERU:

I have been dilatory about keeping up my journal – no entry yesterday or the day before. I can only plead exhaustion and a certain amount of despondence.

Guatemala took its toll on my spirit, I'm afraid. We are, of course, stringently neutral, but when I saw the televised news reports of the insurrection and heard some of the rhetoric being attributed to the Mayan revolutionaries, I dared to hope. When we actually met with the Indian leaders, I was even briefly elated. They considered my presence in the room an honor, an auspicious omen, seemed to treat me with the same sort of respect (or lack of respect) they gave Hartmann and Tachyon, and the way they treated their own jokers gave me heart.

Well, I am an old man – an old *joker* in fact – and I tend to clutch at straws. Now the Mayan revolutionaries have proclaimed a new nation, an Amerindian homeland, where their jokers will be welcomed and honored. The rest of us need not apply. Not that I would care much to live in the jungles of Guatemala – even an autonomous joker homeland down here would scarcely cause a ripple in Jokertown, let alone any kind of significant exodus. Still, there are so few places in the world where jokers are welcome, where we can make our homes in peace . . . the more we travel on, the more we see, the more I am forced to conclude that Jokertown is the best place for us, our only true home. I cannot express how much that conclusion saddens and terrifies me.

Why must we draw these lines, these fine distinctions, these labels and barriers that set us apart? Ace and nat and joker, capitalist and communist, Catholic and Protestant, Arab and Jew, Indian and Latino, and on and on everywhere, and of course true humanity is to be found only on *our* side of the line and we feel free to oppress and rape and kill the 'other,' whoever he might be.

There are those on the *Stacked Deck* who charge that the Guatemalans were engaged in conscious genocide against their own Indian populations, and who see this new nation as a very good thing. But I wonder.

*

The Mayas think jokers are touched by the gods, specially blessed. No doubt it is better to be honored than reviled for our various handicaps and deformities. No doubt.

But . . .

We have the Islamic nations still ahead of us . . . a third of the world, someone told me. Some Muslims are more tolerant than others, but virtually all of them consider deformity a sign of Allah's displeasure. The attitudes of the true fanatics such as the Shiites in Iran and the Nur sect in Syria are terrifying, Hitlerian. How many jokers were slaughtered when the Ayatollah displaced the Shah? To some Iranians the tolerance he extended to jokers and women was the Shah's greatest sin.

And are we so very much better in the enlightened USA, where fundamentalists like Leo Barnett preach that jokers are being punished for their sins? Oh, yes, there is a distinction; I must remember that. Barnett says he hates the sins but loves the sinners, and if we will only repent and have faith and love Jesus, surely we will be cured.

No, I'm afraid that ultimately Barnett and the Ayatollah and the Mayan priests are all preaching the same creed – that our bodies in some sense reflect our souls, that some divine being has taken a direct hand and twisted us into these shapes to signify his pleasure (the Mayas) or displeasure (Nur al-Allah, the Ayatollah, the Fire-breather). Most of all, each of them is saying that jokers are *different*.

My own creed is distressingly simple – I believe that jokers and aces and nats are all just men and women and ought to be treated as such. During my dark nights of the soul I wonder if I am the only one left who still believes this.

*

Still brooding about Guatemala and the Mayas. A point I failed to make earlier – I could not help noticing that this glorious idealistic revolution of theirs was led by two aces and a nat. Even down here, where jokers are supposedly kissed by the gods, the aces lead and the jokers follow.

A few days ago – it was during our visit to the Panama Canal, I believe – Digger Downs asked me if I thought the US would ever have a joker president. I told him I'd settle for a joker congressman (I'm afraid Nathan Rabinowitz, whose district includes Jokertown, heard the comment and took it for some sort of criticism of his representation). Then Digger wanted to know if I thought an ace could be elected president. A more interesting question, I must admit. Downs always looks half asleep, but he is sharper than he appears, though not in a class with some of the other reporters aboard the *Stacked Deck*, like Herrmann of the AP or Morgenstern of the *Washington Post*.

I told Downs that before this last Wild Card Day it might have been possible . . . barely. Certain aces, like the Turtle (still missing, the latest NY papers confirm), Peregrine, Cyclone, and a handful of others are first-rank celebrities, commanding considerable public affection. How much of that could translate to the public arena, and how well it might survive the rough give-and-take of a presidential campaign, that's a more difficult question. Heroism is a perishable commodity.

Jack Braun was standing close enough to hear Digger's question and my reply. Before I could conclude – I wanted to say that the whole equation had changed this September, that among the casualties of Wild Card Day was any faint chance that an ace might be a viable presidential candidate – Braun interrupted. 'They'd tear him apart,' he told us.

What if it was someone they loved? Digger wanted to know.

'They loved the Four Aces,' Braun said.

Braun is no longer quite the exile he was at the beginning of the tour. Tachyon still refuses to acknowledge his existence and Hiram is barely polite, but the other aces don't seem to know or care who he is. In Panama he was often in Fantasy's company, squiring her here and there, and I've heard rumors of a liaison between Golden Boy and Senator Lyons' press secretary, an attractive young blonde. Undoubtedly, of the male aces, Braun is by far the most attractive in the conventional sense, although Mordecai Jones has a certain brooding presence. Downs has been struck by those two also. The next issue of *Aces* will feature a piece comparing Golden Boy and the Harlem Hammer, he informs me.

DECEMBER 29, 1986/BUENOS AIRES:

Don't cry for Jack, Argentina . . .

Evita's bane has come back to Buenos Aires. When the musical first played Broadway, I wondered what Jack Braun must have thought, listening to Lupone sing of the Four Aces. Now that question has even more poignance. Braun has been very calm, almost stoic, in the face of his reception here, but what must he be feeling inside?

Peron is dead, Evita even deader, even Isabel just a memory, but the Peronistas are still very much a part of the Argentine political scene. They have not forgotten. Everywhere the signs taunt Braun and invite him to go home. He is the ultimate *gringo* (do they use that word in Argentina, I wonder), the ugly but awesomely powerful American who came to the Argentine uninvited and toppled a sovereign government because he disapproved of its politics. The United States has been doing such things for as long as there has been a Latin America, and I have no doubt that these same resentments fester in many other places. The United States and even the dread 'secret aces' of the CIA are abstract concepts, however, faceless and difficult to get a fix on – Golden Boy is flesh and blood, real and very visible, and *here*.

Someone inside the hotel leaked our room assignments, and when Jack stepped out onto his balcony the first day, he was showered with dung and rotten fruit. He has stayed inside ever since, except for official functions, but even there he is not safe. Last night as we stood in a receiving line at the Casa Rosada, the wife of a union official – a beautiful young woman, her small dark face framed by masses of lustrous black hair – stepped up to him with a sweet smile, looked straight into his eyes, and spit in his face.

It caused quite a stir, and Senators Hartmann and Lyons have filed some sort of protest, I believe. Braun himself was remarkably restrained, almost gallant. Digger was hounding him ruthlessly after the reception; he's cabling a write-up on the incident back to *Aces* and wanted a quote. Braun finally gave him something. 'I've done things I'm not proud of,' he said, 'but getting rid of Juan Peron isn't one of them.'

'Yeah, yeah,' I heard Digger tell him, 'but how did you feel when she spit on you?'

Jack just looked disgusted. 'I don't hit women,' he said. Then he walked off and sat by himself.

Downs turned to me when Braun was gone. 'I don't hit women,' he echoed in a singsong imitation of Golden Boy's voice, then added, 'What a weenie . . .'

The world is too ready to read cowardice and betrayal into anything Jack Braun says and does, but the truth, I suspect, is more complex. Given his youthful appearance, it's hard to recall at times how old the Golden Boy really is – his formative years were during the Depression and World War II, and he grew up listening to the NBC Blue Network, not MTV. No wonder some of his values seem quaintly old-fashioned.

In many ways the Judas Ace seems almost an innocent, a bit lost in a world that has grown too complicated for him. I think he is more troubled than he admits by his reception here in Argentina. Braun is the last representative of a lost dream that flourished briefly in the aftermath of World War II and died in Korea and the HUAC hearings and the Cold War. They thought they could reshape the world, Archibald Holmes and his Four Aces. They had no doubts, no more than their country did. Power existed to be used, and they were supremely confident in their ability to tell the good guys from the bad guys. Their own democratic ideals and the shining purity of their intentions were all the justification they needed. For those few early aces it must have been a golden age, and how appropriate that a golden boy be at its center.

Golden ages give way to dark ages, as any student of history knows, and as all of us are currently finding out.

Braun and his colleagues could do things no one else had ever done – they could fly and lift tanks and absorb a man's mind and memories, and so they bought the illusion that they could make a real difference on a global scale, and when that illusion dissolved beneath them, they fell a very long way indeed. Since then no other ace has dared to dream as big.

Even in the face of imprisonment, despair, insanity, disgrace, and death, the Four Aces had triumphs to cling to, and Argentina was perhaps the brightest of those triumphs. What a bitter homecoming this must be for Jack Braun.

As if this was not enough, our mail caught up with us just before we left Brazil, and the pouch included a dozen copies of the new issue of *Aces* with Digger's promised feature story. The cover has Jack Braun and Mordecai Jones in profile, scowling at each other – all cleverly doctored, of course. I don't believe the two had ever met before we all got together at Tomlin – over a blurb that reads, 'The Strongest Man in the World.'

The article itself is a lengthy discussion of the two men and their public careers, enlivened by numerous anecdotes about their feats of strength and much speculation about which of the two is, indeed, the strongest man in the world.

Both of the principals seem embarrassed by the piece, Braun perhaps more acutely. Neither much wants to discuss it, and they certainly don't seem likely to settle the matter anytime soon. I understand that there has been considerable argument and even wagering back in the press compartment since Digger's piece came out (for once, Downs seems to have had an impact on his journalistic colleagues), but the bets are likely to remain unresolved for a long time to come. I told Downs that the story was spurious and offensive as soon as I read it. He seemed startled. 'I don't get it,' he said to me. 'What's your beef?'

My beef, as I explained to him, was simple. Braun and Jones are scarcely the only people to manifest superhuman strength since the advent of the wild card; in fact, that particular power is a fairly common one, ranking close behind telekinesis and telepathy in Tachyon's incidence-of-occurrence charts. It has something to do with maximizing the contractile strength of the muscles, I believe. My point is, a number of prominent jokers display augmented strength as well – just off the top of my head, I cited Elmo (the dwarf bouncer at the Crystal Palace), Ernie of Ernie's Bar & Grill, the Oddity, Quasiman . . . and, most notably, Howard Mueller. The Troll's strength does not perhaps equal that of Golden Boy and the Harlem Hammer, but assuredly it approaches it. None of these jokers were so much as mentioned in passing in Digger's story, although the names of a dozen other superstrong aces were dropped here and there. Why was that? I wanted to know.

I can't claim to have made much of an impression unfortunately. When I was through, Downs simply rolled his eyes and said, 'You people are so damned *touchy*.' He tried to be accommodating by telling me that if this story went over big, maybe he'd write up a sequel on the strongest joker in the world, and he couldn't comprehend why that 'concession' made me even angrier. And they wonder why we people are touchy . . .

Howard thought the whole argument was vastly amusing. Sometimes I wonder about him.

Actually my fit of pique was nothing compared to the reaction the magazine drew from Billy Ray, our security chief. Ray was one of the other aces mentioned in passing, his strength dismissed as not being truly 'major league.' Afterward he could be heard the length of the plane, suggesting that maybe Downs would like to step outside with him, seeing as how he was so minor league. Digger declined the offer. From the smile on his face I doubt that Carnifex will be getting any good press in *Aces* anytime soon.

Since then, Ray has been grousing about the story to anyone who will listen. The crux of his argument is that strength isn't everything; he may not be as strong as Braun or Jones, but he's strong enough to take either of them in a fight, and he'd be glad to put his money where his mouth is.

Personally I have gotten a certain perverse satisfaction out of this tempest in a teapot. The irony is, they are arguing about who has the most of what is essentially a minor power. I seem to recall that there was some sort of demonstration in the early seventies, when the battleship *New Jersey* was being refitted at the Bayonne Naval Supply Center over in New Jersey. The Turtle lifted the battleship telekinetically, got it out of the water by several feet, and held it there for almost half a minute. Braun and Jones lift tanks and toss automobiles about, but neither could come remotely close to what the Turtle did that day.

The simple truth is, the contractile strength of the human musculature can be increased only so much. Physical limits apply. Dr Tachyon says there may also be limits to what the human mind can accomplish, but so far they have not been reached.

If the Turtle is indeed a joker, as many believe, I would find this irony especially satisfying.

I suppose I am, at base, as small a man as any.

JANUARY 16/ADDIS ABABA, ETHIOPIA:

A hard day in a stricken land. The local Red Cross representatives took some of us out to see some of their famine relief efforts. Of course we'd all been aware of the drought and the starvation long before we got here, but seeing it on television is one thing, and being here amidst it is quite another.

A day like this makes me acutely aware of my own failures and shortcomings. Since the cancer took hold of me, I've lost a good deal of weight (some unsuspecting friends have even told me how good I look), but moving among these people made me very self-conscious of the small paunch that remains. They were starving before my eyes, while our plane waited to take us back to Addis Ababa . . . to our hotel, another reception, and no doubt a gourmet Ethiopian meal. The guilt was overwhelming, as was the sense of helplessness.

I believe we all felt it. I cannot conceive of how Hiram Worchester must have felt. To his credit he looked sick as he moved among the victims, and at one point he was trembling so badly he had to sit in the shade for a while by himself. The sweat was just pouring off him. But he got up again afterward, his face white and grim, and used his gravity power to help them unload the relief provisions we had brought with us.

So many people have contributed so much and worked so hard for the relief effort, but here it seems like nothing. The only realities in the relief camps are the skeletal bodies with their massive swollen bellies, the dead eyes of the children, and the endless heat pouring down from above onto this baked, parched landscape.

Parts of this day will linger in my memory for a long time – or at least as long a time as I have left to me. Father Squid gave the last rites to a dying woman who had a Coptic cross around her neck. Peregrine and her cameraman recorded much of the scene on film for her documentary, but after a short time she had had enough and returned to the plane to wait for us. I've heard that she was so sick she lost her breakfast.

And there was a young mother, no more than seventeen or eighteen surely, so gaunt that you could count every rib, with eyes incredibly ancient. She was holding her baby to a withered, empty breast. The child had been dead long enough to begin to smell, but she would not let them take it from her. Dr Tachyon took control of her mind and held her still while he gently pried the child's body from her grasp and carried it away. He handed it to one of the relief workers and then sat on the ground and began to weep, his body shaking with each sob.

Mistral ended the day in tears as well. En route to the refugee camp, she had changed into her blue-and-white flying costume. The girl is young, an ace, and a powerful one; no doubt she thought she could help. When she called the winds to her, the huge cape she wears fastened at wrist and ankle ballooned out like a parachute and pulled her up into the sky. Even the strangeness of the jokers walking between them had not awakened much interest in the inward-looking eyes of the refugees, but when Mistral took flight, most of them – not all, but most – turned to watch, and their gaze followed her upward into that high, hot blueness until finally they sank back into the lethargy of despair. I think Mistral had dreamed that somehow her wind powers could push the clouds around and make the rains come to heal this land. And what a dutiful, vainglorious dream it was . . .

She flew for almost two hours, sometimes so high and far that she vanished from our sight, but for all her ace powers, all she could raise was a dust devil. When she gave up at last, she was exhausted, her sweet young face grimy with dust and sand, her eyes red and swollen.

Just before we left, an atrocity underscored the depth of the despair here. A tall youth with acne scars on his cheeks attacked a fellow refugee – went berserk, gouged out a woman's eye, and actually ate it while the people watched without comprehension. Ironically we'd met the boy briefly when we'd first arrived – he'd spent a year in a Christian school and had a few words of English. He seemed stronger and healthier than most of the others we saw. When Mistral flew, he jumped to his feet and called out after her. 'Jetboy!' he said in a very clear, strong voice. Father Squid and Senator Hartmann tried to talk to him, but his English-language skills were limited to a few nouns, including 'chocolate,' 'television,' and 'Jesus Christ.' Still, the boy was more alive than most – his eyes went wide at Father Squid, and he put out a hand and touched his facial tendrils wonderingly and actually smiled when the senator patted his shoulder and told him that we were here to help, though I don't think he understood a word. We were all shocked when we saw them carrying him away, still screaming, those gaunt brown cheeks smeared with blood.

A hideous day all around. This evening back in Addis Ababa our driver swung us by the docks, where relief shipments stand two stories high in some places. Hartmann was in a cold rage. If anyone can make this criminal government take action and feed its starving people, he is the one. I pray for him, or would, if I believed in a god ... but what kind of god would permit the obscenities we have seen on this trip ...

*

Africa is as beautiful a land as any on the face of the earth. I should write of all the beauty we have seen this past month. Victoria Falls, the snows of Kilimanjaro, a thousand zebra moving through the tall grass as if the wind had stripes. I've walked among the ruins of proud ancient kingdoms whose very names were unknown to me, held pygmy artifacts in my hand, seen the face of a bushman light up with curiosity instead of horror when he beheld me for the first time. Once during a visit to a game preserve I woke early, and when I looked out of my window at the dawn, I saw that two huge African elephants had come to the very building, and Radha stood between them, naked in the early morning light, while they touched her with their trunks. I turned away then; it seemed somehow a private moment.

Beauty, yes – in the land and in so many of the people, whose faces are full of warmth and compassion.

Still, for all that beauty, Africa has depressed and saddened me considerably, and I will be glad to leave. The camp was only part of it. Before Ethiopia there was Kenya and South Africa. It is the wrong time of year for Thanksgiving, but the scenes we have witnessed these past few weeks have put me more in the mood for giving thanks than I've ever felt during America's smug November celebration of football and gluttony. Even jokers have things to give thanks for. I knew that already, but Africa has brought it home to me forcefully.

South Africa was a grim way to begin this leg of the trip. The same hatreds and prejudices exist at home of course, but whatever our faults we are at least civilized enough to maintain a facade of tolerance, brotherhood, and equality under the law. Once I might have called that mere sophistry, but that was before I tasted the reality of Capetown and Pretoria, where all the ugliness is out in the open, enshrined by law, enforced by an iron fist whose velvet glove has grown thin and worn indeed. It is argued that at least South Africa hates openly, while America hides behind a hypocritical facade. Perhaps, perhaps ... but if so, I will take the hypocrisy and thank you for it.

I suppose that was Africa's first lesson, that there are worse places in the world than Jokertown. The second was that there are worse things than repression, and Kenya taught us that.

Like most of the other nations of Central and East Africa, Kenya was spared the worst of the wild card. Some spores would have reached these lands through airborne diffusion, more through the seaports, arriving via contaminated cargo in holds that had been poorly sterilized or never sterilized at all. CARE packages are looked on with deep suspicion in much of the world, and with good reason, and many captains have become quite adept at concealing the fact that their last port of call was New York City.

When one moves inland, wild card cases become almost nonexistent. There are those who say that the late Idi Amin was some kind of insane joker-ace, with strength as great as Troll or the Harlem Hammer, and the ability to transform into some kind of were-creature, a leopard or a lion or a hawk. Amin himself claimed to be able to ferret out his enemies telepathically, and those few enemies who survived say that he was a cannibal who felt human flesh was necessary to maintain his powers. All this is the stuff of rumor and propaganda, however, and whether Amin was a joker, an ace, or a pathetically deluded nat madman, he is assuredly dead, and in this corner of the world, documented cases of the wild card virus are vanishingly hard to locate.

But Kenya and the surrounding nations have their own viral nightmare. If the wild card is a chimera here, AIDS is an epidemic. While the president was hosting Senator Hartmann and most of the tour, a few of us were on an exhausting visit to a half-dozen clinics in rural Kenya, hopping from one village to another by helicopter. They assigned us only one battered chopper, and that at Tachyon's insistence. The government would have much preferred that we spend our time lecturing at the university, meeting with educators and political leaders, touring game preserves and museums.

Most of my fellow delegates were only too glad to comply. The wild card is forty years old, and we have grown used to it – but AIDS, that is a new terror in the world, and one that we have only begun to understand. At home it is thought of as a homosexual affliction, and I confess that I am guilty of thinking of it that way myself, but here in Africa, that belief is given the lie. Already there are more AIDS victims on this continent alone than have ever been infected by the Takisian xenovirus since its release over Manhattan forty years ago.

And AIDS seems a crueler demon somehow. The wild card kills ninety percent of those who draw it, often in ways that are terrible and painful, but the distance between ninety percent and one hundred is not insignificant if you are among the ten who live. It is the distance between life and death, between hope and despair. Some claim that it's better to die than to live as a joker, but you will not find me among their number. If my own life has not always been happy, nonetheless I have memories I cherish and accomplishments I am proud of. I am glad to have lived, and I do not want to die. I've accepted my death, but that does not mean I welcome it. I have too much unfinished business. Like Robert Tomlin, I have not yet seen *The Al Jolson Story*. None of us have.

In Kenya we saw whole villages that are dying. Alive, smiling, talking, capable of eating and defecating and making love and even babies, alive to all practical purposes – and yet dead. Those who draw the Black Queen may die in the agony of unspeakable transformations, but there are drugs for pain, and at least they die quickly. AIDS is less merciful.

We have much in common, jokers and AIDS victims. Before I left Jokertown, we had been planning for a JADL fund-raising benefit at the Funhouse in late May – a major event with as much big-name entertainment as we could book. After Kenya I cabled instructions back to New York to arrange for the proceeds of the benefit to be split with a suitable AIDS victims' group. We pariahs need to stick together. Perhaps I can still erect a few necessary bridges before my own Black Queen lies face up on the table.

JANUARY 30/JERUSALEM:

The open city of Jerusalem, they call it. An international metropolis, jointly governed by commissioners from Israel, Jordan, Palestine, and Great Britain under a United Nations mandate, sacred to three of the world's great religions.

Alas, the apt phrase is not 'open city' but 'open sore.' Jerusalem bleeds as it has for almost four decades. If this city is sacred, I should hate to visit one that was profane.

Senators Hartmann and Lyons and the other political delegates lunched with the city commissioners today, but the rest of us spent the afternoon touring this free international city in closed limousines with bulletproof windshields and special underbody armor to withstand bomb blasts. Jerusalem, it seems, likes to welcome distinguished international visitors by blowing them up. It does not seem to matter who the visitors are, where they come from, what religion they practice, how their politics lean – there are enough factions in this city so that everyone can count on being hated by someone.

Two days ago we were in Beirut. From Beirut to Jerusalem, that is a voyage from day to night. Lebanon is a beautiful country, and Beirut is so lovely and peaceful it seems almost serene. Its various regions appear to have solved the problem of living in comparative harmony, although there are of course incidents – nowhere in the Middle East (or the world, for that matter) is completely safe.

But Jerusalem – the outbreaks of violence have been endemic for thirty years, each worse than the one before. Entire blocks resemble nothing so much as London during the Blitz, and the population that remains has grown so used to the distant sound of machine-gun fire that they scarcely seem to pay it any mind.

We stopped briefly at what remains of the Wailing Wall (largely destroyed in 1967 by Palestinian terrorists in reprisal for the assassination of al-Haziz by Israeli terrorists the year before) and actually dared to get out of our vehicles. Hiram looked around fiercely and made a fist, as if daring anyone to start trouble. He has been in a strange state of late; irritable, quick to anger, moody. The things we witnessed in Africa have affected us all, however. One shard of the wall is still fairly imposing. I touched it and tried to feel the history. Instead I felt the pocks left in the stone by bullets.

Most of our party returned to the hotel afterward, but Father Squid and I took a detour to visit the Jokers' Quarter. I'm told that it is the second-largest joker community in the world, after Jokertown itself . . . a distant second, but second nonetheless. It does not surprise me. Islam does not view my people kindly, and so jokers come here from all over the Middle East for whatever meager protection is offered by UN sovereignty and a small, outmanned, outgunned, and demoralized international peacekeeping force.

The Quarter is unspeakably squalid, and the weight of human misery within its walls is almost palpable. Yet ironically the streets of the Quarter are reputed safer than any other place in Jerusalem. The Quarter has its own walls, built in living memory, originally to spare the feelings of decent people by hiding us living obscenities from their sight, but those same walls have given a measure of security to those who dwell within. Once inside I saw no nats at all, only jokers – jokers of all races and religions, all living in relative peace. Once they might have been Muslims or Jews or Christians, zealots or Zionists or followers of the Nur, but after their hand had been dealt, they were only jokers. The joker is the great equalizer, cutting through all other hatreds and prejudices, uniting all mankind in a new brotherhood of pain. A joker is a joker is a joker, and anything else he is, is unimportant.

Would that it worked the same way with aces.

The sect of Jesus Christ, Joker has a church in Jerusalem, and Father Squid took me there. The building looked more like a mosque than a Christian church, at least on the outside, but inside it was not so terribly different from the church I'd visited in Jokertown, though much older and in greater disrepair. Father Squid lit a candle and said a prayer, and then we went back to the cramped, tumbledown rectory where Father Squid conversed with the pastor in halting Latin while we shared a bottle of sour red wine. As they were talking, I heard the sound of automatic weaponry chattering off in the night somewhere a few blocks away. A typical Jerusalem evening, I suppose.

*

No one will read this book until after my death, by which time I will be safely immune from prosecution. I've thought long and hard about whether or not I should record what happened tonight, and finally decided that I should. The world needs to remember the lessons of 1976 and be reminded from time to time that the JADL does not speak for all jokers.

An old joker woman pressed a note into my hand as Father Squid and I were leaving the church. I suppose someone recognized me.

When I read the note, I begged off the official reception, pleading illness once again, but this time it was a ruse. I dined in my room with a wanted criminal, a man I can only describe as a notorious international joker terrorist, although he is a hero inside the Jokers' Quarter. I will not give his real name, even in these pages, since I understand that he still visits his family in Tel Aviv from time to time. He wears a black canine mask on his 'missions' and to the press, Interpol, and the sundry factions that police Jerusalem, he is variously known as the Black Dog and the Hound of Hell. Tonight he wore a completely different mask, a butterfly-shaped hood covered with silver glitter, and had no problem crossing the city.

'What you've got to remember,' he told me, 'is that nats are fundamentally stupid. You wear the same mask twice and let your picture get taken with it, and they start thinking it's your face.'

The Hound, as I'll call him, was born in Brooklyn but emigrated to Israel with his family at age nine and became an Israeli citizen. He was twenty when he became a joker. 'I traveled halfway around the world to draw the wild card,' he told me. 'I could have stayed in Brooklyn.'

We spent several hours discussing Jerusalem, the Middle East, and the politics of the wild card. The Hound heads what honesty forces me to call a joker terrorist organization, the Twisted Fists. They are illegal in both Israel and Palestine, no mean trick. He was evasive about how many members they had, but not at all shy about confessing that virtually all of their financial support comes from New York's Jokertown. 'You may not like us, Mr Mayor,' the Hound told me, 'but your people do.' He even hinted slyly that one of the joker delegates on our tour was among their supporters, although of course he refused to supply a name.

The Hound is convinced that war is coming to the Middle East, and soon. 'Is's overdue,' he said. 'Neither Israel or Palestine have ever had defensible borders, and neither one is an economically viable nation. Each is convinced that the other one is guilty of all sorts of terrorist atrocities, and they're both right. Israel wants the Negev and the West Bank, Palestine wants a port on the Mediterranean, and both countries are still full of refugees from the 1948 partition who want their homes back. Everyone wants Jerusalem except the UN, which has it. Shit, they *need* a good war. The Israelis looked like they were winning in '48 until the *Nasr* kicked their asses. I know that Bernadotte won the Nobel Peace Prize for the Treaty of Jerusalem, but just between you and me, it might have been better if they'd fought it out to the bitter end . . . any kind of end.'

I asked him about all the people who would have died, but he just shrugged. 'They'd be dead. But maybe if it was over, really *over*, some of the wounds would start to heal. Instead we got two pissed-off half-countries that share the same little desert and won't even recognize each other, we've got four decades of hatred and terrorism and fear, and we're still going to get the war, and soon. It beats me how Bernadotte pulled off the Peace of Jerusalem anyway, though I'm not surprised that he got assassinated for his troubles. The only ones who hate the terms worse than the Israelis are the Palestinians.'

I pointed out that, unpopular as it might be, the Peace of Jerusalem had lasted almost forty years. He dismissed that as 'a forty-year stalemate, not real peace. Mutual fear was what made it work. The Israelis have always had military superiority. But the Arabs had the Port Said aces, and you think the Israelis don't remember? Every time the Arabs put up a memorial to the *Nasr*, anywhere from Baghdad to Marrakesh, the Israelis blow it up. Believe me, they remember. Only now the whole thing's coming unbalanced. I got sources say Israel has been running its own wild card experiments on volunteers from their armed forces, and they've come up with a few aces of their own. Now that's fanaticism for you, to volunteer for the wild card. And on the Arab side, you've got Nur al-Allah, who calls Israel a "bastard joker nation" and has vowed to destroy it utterly. The Port Said aces were pussycats compared to his bunch, even old Khôf. No, it's coming, and soon.'

'And when it comes?' I asked him.

He was carrying a gun, some kind of small semiautomatic machine pistol with a long Russian name. He took it out and laid it on the table between us. 'When it comes,' he said, 'they can kill each other all they want, but they damn well better leave the Quarter alone, or they'll have us to deal with. We've already given the Nur a few lessons. Every time they kill a joker, we kill five of them. You'd think they'd get the idea, but the Nur's a slow learner.'

I told him that Senator Hartmann was hoping to set up a meeting with the Nur al-Allah to begin discussions that might lead to a peaceful solution to this area's problems. He laughed. We talked for a long time, about jokers and aces and nats, and violence and nonviolence and war and peace, about brotherhood and revenge and turning the other cheek and taking care of your own, and in the end we settled nothing. 'Why did you come?' I finally asked him.

'I thought we should meet. We could use your help. Your knowledge of Jokertown, your contacts in nat society, the money you could raise.'

'You won't get my help,' I told him. 'I've seen where your road leads. Tom Miller walked that road ten years ago.'

'Gimli?' He shrugged. 'First, Gimli was crazy as a bedbug, I'm not. Gimli wants the world to kiss it and make it all better. I just fight to protect my own. To protect you, Des. Pray that your Jokertown never needs the Twisted Fists, but if you do, we'll be there. I read *Time*'s cover story on Leo Barnett. Could be the Nur isn't the only slow learner. If that's how it is, maybe the Black Dog will go home and find that tree that grows in Brooklyn, right? I haven't been to a Dodgers game since I was eight.'

My heart stopped in my throat as I looked at the gun on the table, but I reached out and put my hand on the phone. 'I could call down to our security right now and make certain that won't happen, that you won't kill any more innocent people.'

'But you won't,' the Hound said. 'Because we have so much in common.'

I told him we had nothing in common.

'We're both jokers,' he said. 'What else matters?' Then he holstered his gun, adjusted his mask, and walked calmly from my room.

And God help me, I sat there alone for several endless minutes, until I heard the elevator doors open down the hall – and finally took my hand off the phone.

FEBRUARY 7/KABUL, AFGHANISTAN:

I am in a good deal of pain today. Most of the delegates have gone on a day trip to various historic sights, but I elected to stay at the hotel once again.

Our tour ... what can I say? Syria has made headlines around the world. Our press contingent has doubled in size, all of them eager to get the inside story of what happened out in the desert. For once, I am not unhappy to have been excluded. Peri has told me what it was like ...

Syria has touched all of us, myself included. Not all of my pain is caused by the cancer. There are times when I grow profoundly weary, looking back over my life and wondering whether I have done any good at all, or if all my life's work has been for nothing. I have tried to speak out on behalf of my people, to appeal to reason and decency and the common humanity that unites us all, and I have always been convinced that quiet strength, perseverance, and nonviolence would get us further in the long run. Syria makes me wonder ... how do you reason with a man like the Nur al-Allah, compromise with him, talk to him? How do you appeal to his humanity when he does not consider you human at all? If there is a God, I pray that he forgives me, but I find myself wishing they had killed the Nur.

Hiram has left the tour, albeit temporarily. He promises to rejoin in India, but by now he is back in New York City, after jetting from Damascus to Rome and then catching a Concorde back to America. He told us that an emergency had arisen at Aces High that demanded his personal attention, but I suspect the truth is that Syria shook him more than he cared to admit. The rumor has swept round the plane that Hiram lost control in the desert, that he hit General Sayyid with far more weight than was necessary to stop him. Billy Ray, of course, doesn't think Hiram went far enough. 'If it'd been me, I would have piled it on till he was just a brown and red stain on the floor,' he told me.

Worchester himself refused to talk about it and insisted that he was taking this brief leave of us simply because he was 'sick unto death of stuffed grape leaves,' but even as he made the joke, I noticed beads of sweat on his broad, bald forehead and a slight tremor in his hand. I hope a short respite restores him; the more we have traveled together, the more I have to come to respect Hiram Worchester.

If clouds do indeed have a silver lining, however, then perhaps one good did come out of the monstrous incident in Syria: Gregg Hartmann's stature seems to have been vastly enhanced by his near brush with death. For a decade now his political fortunes have been haunted by the specter of the Great Jokertown Riot in 1976, when he 'lost his head' in public. To me his reaction was only human – he had just witnessed a woman being torn to pieces by a mob, after all. But presidential candidates are not allowed to weep or grieve or rage like the rest of us, as Muskie proved in '72 and Hartmann confirmed in '76.

Syria may finally have put that tragic incident to rest. Everyone who was there agrees that Hartmann's behavior was exemplary – he was firm, cool-headed, courageous, a pillar of strength in the face of the Nur's barbarous threats. Every paper in America has run the AP photo that was taken as they pulled out: Hiram helping Tachyon into the helicopter in the background, while in the foreground Senator Hartmann waited, his face streaked with dust, yet still grim and strong, his blood soaking through the sleeve of his white shirt.

Gregg still claims that he is not going to be a presidential candidate in 1988, and indeed all the polls show that Gary Hart has an overwhelming lead for the Democratic nomination, but Syria and the photograph will surely do wonders for his name recognition and his standing. I find myself desperately hoping that he will reconsider. I have nothing against Gary Hart, but Gregg Hartmann is something special, and perhaps for those of us touched by the wild card, he is our last best hope.

If Hartmann fails, all my hopes fail with him, and then what choice will we have but to turn to the Black Dog?

*

I suppose I should write something about Afghanistan, but there is little to record. I don't have the strength to see what sights Kabul has to offer. The Soviets are much in evidence here, but they are being very correct and courteous. The war is being kept at arm's length for the duration of our short stopover. Two Afghan jokers have been produced for our approval, both of whom swear (through Soviet interpreters) that a joker's life is idyllic here. Somehow I am not convinced. If I understand correctly, they are the only two jokers in all of Afghanistan.

The *Stacked Deck* flew directly from Baghdad to Kabul. Iran was out of the question. The Ayatollah shares many of the Nur's views on wild cards, and he rules his nation in name as well as fact, so even the UN could not secure us permission to land. At least the Ayatollah makes no distinctions between aces and jokers – we are all the demon children of the Great Satan, according to him. Obviously he has not forgotten Jimmy Carter's ill-fated attempt to free the hostages, when a half-dozen government aces were sent in on a secret mission that turned into a horrid botch. The rumor is that Carnifex was one of the aces involved, but Billy Ray emphatically denies it. 'If I'd been along, we would have gotten our people out and kicked the old man's ass for good measure,' he says. His colleague from Justice, Lady Black, just pulls her black cloak more tightly about herself

and smiles enigmatically. Mistral's father, Cyclone, has often been linked
to that doomed mission as well, but it's not something she'll talk about.

Tomorrow morning we'll fly over the Khyber Pass and cross into India, a
different world entirely, a whole sprawling subcontinent, with the largest
joker population anywhere outside the United States.

FEBRUARY 12/CALCUTTA:

India is as strange and fabulous a land as any we have seen on this trip . . .
if indeed it is correct to call it a land at all. It seems more like a hundred
lands in one. I find it hard to connect the Himalayas and the palaces of the
Moguls to the slums of Calcutta and Bengali jungles. The Indians
themselves live in a dozen different worlds, from the aging Britishers who
try to pretend that the Viceroy still rules in their little enclaves of the Raj,
to the maharajas and nawabs who are kings in all but name, to the beggars
on the streets of this sprawling filthy city.

There is so *much* of India.

In Calcutta you see jokers on the streets everywhere you go. They are as
common as beggars, naked children, and corpses, and too frequently one
and the same. In this quasi-nation of Hindu and Muslim and Sikh, the
vast majority of jokers seems to be Hindu, but given Islam's attitudes, that
can hardly be a surprise. The orthodox Hindu has invented a new caste for
the joker, far below even the untouchable, but at least they are allowed to
live.

Interestingly enough, we have found no jokertowns in India. This
culture is sharply divided along racial and ethnic grounds, and the
enmities run very deep, as was clearly shown in the Calcutta wild card
riots of 1947, and the wholesale nationwide carnage that accompanied the
partition of the subcontinent that same year. Despite that, today you find
Hindu and Muslim and Sikh living side by side on the same street, and
jokers and nats and even a few pathetic deuces sharing the same hideous
slums. It does not seem to have made them love each other any more, alas.

India also boasts a number of native aces, including a few of
considerable power. Digger is having a grand time dashing about the
country interviewing them all, or as many as will consent to meet with
him.

Radha O'Reilly, on the other hand, is obviously very unhappy here. She
is Indian royalty herself, it appears, at least on her mother's side . . . her
father was some sort of Irish adventurer. Her people practice a variety of
Hinduism built around Ganesh, the elephant god, and the black mother
Kali, and to them her wild card ability makes her the destined bride of

Gonesh, or something along those lines. At any rate she seems firmly convinced that she is in imminent danger of being kidnapped and forcibly returned to her homeland, so except for the official receptions in New Delhi and Bombay, she has remained closely closeted in the various hotels, with Carnifex, Lady Black, and the rest of our security close at hand. I believe she will be very happy to leave India once again.

Dr Tachyon, Peregrine, Mistral, Fantasy, Troll, and the Harlem Hammer have just returned from a tiger hunt in the Bengal. Their host was one of the Indian aces, a maharaja blessed with a form of the Midas touch. I understand that the gold he creates is inherently unstable and reverts to its original state within twenty-four hours, although the process of transmutation is still sufficient to kill any living thing he touches. Still, his palace is reputed to be quite a spectacular place. He's solved the traditional mythic dilemma by having his servants feed him.

Tachyon returned from the expedition in as good a spirit as I've seen him since Syria, wearing a golden Nehru jacket and matching turban, fastened by a ruby the size of my thumb. The maharaja was lavish with his gifts, it seems. Even the prospect of the jacket and turban reverting to common cloth in a few hours does not seem to have dampened our alien's enthusiasm for the day's activities. The glittering pageant of the hunt, the splendors of the palace, and the maharaja's harem all seem to have reminded Tach of the pleasures and prerogatives he once enjoyed as a prince of the Ilkazam on his home world. He admitted that even on Takis there was no sight to compare to the end of the hunt, when the maneater had been brought to bay and the maharaja calmly approached it, removed one golden glove, and transmuted the huge beast to solid gold with a touch.

While our aces were accepting their presents of fairy gold and hunting tigers, I spent the day in humbler pursuits, in the unexpected company of Jack Braun, who was invited to the hunt with the others but declined. Instead Braun and I made our way across Calcutta to visit the monument the Indians erected to Earl Sanderson on the site where he saved Mahatma Gandhi from assassination.

The memorial resembles a Hindu temple and the statue inside looks more like some minor Indian deity than an American black who played football for Rutgers, but still . . . Sanderson has indeed become some sort of god to these people; various offerings left by worshipers were strewn about the feet of his statue. It was very crowded, and we had to wait for a long time before we were admitted. The Mahatma is still universally revered in India, and some of his popularity seems to have rubbed off on the memory of the American ace who stepped between him and an assassin's bullet.

Braun said very little when we were inside, just stared up at the statue as if somehow willing it to come to life. It was a moving visit, but not entirely a comfortable one. My obvious deformity drew hard looks from some of the higher-caste Hindus in the press of the people. And whenever someone brushed against Braun too tightly – as happened frequently among such a tightly packed mass of people – his biological force field would begin to shimmer, surrounding him with a ghostly golden glow. I'm afraid my nervousness got the better of me, and I interrupted Braun's reveries and got us out of there hastily. Perhaps I overreacted, but if even one person in that crowd had realized who Jack Braun was, it might have triggered a vastly ugly scene. Braun was very moody and quiet on the way back to our hotel.

Gandhi is a personal hero of mine, and for all my mixed feelings about aces I must admit that I am grateful to Earl Sanderson for the intervention that saved Gandhi's life. For the great prophet of nonviolence to die by an assassin's bullet would have been too grotesque, and I think India would have torn itself apart in the wake of such a death, in a fratricidal bloodbath the likes of which the world has never seen.

If Gandhi had not lived to lead the reunification of the subcontinent after the death of Jinnah in 1948, would that strange two-headed nation called Pakistan actually have endured? Would the All-India Congress have displaced all the petty rulers and absorbed their domains, as it threatened to do? The very shape of this decentralized, endlessly diverse patchwork country is an expression of the Mahatma's dreams. I find it inconceivable to imagine what course Indian history might have taken without him. So in that respect, at least, the Four Aces left a real mark on the world and perhaps demonstrated that one determined man can indeed change the course of history for the better.

I pointed all this out to Jack Braun on our ride home, when he seemed so withdrawn. I'm afraid it did not help much. He listened to me patiently and when I was finished, he said, 'It was Earl who saved him, not me,' and lapsed back into silence.

*

True to his promise, Hiram Worchester returned to the tour today, via Concorde from London. His brief sojourn in New York seems to have done him a world of good. His old ebullience was back, and he promptly convinced Tachyon, Mordecai Jones, and Fantasy to join him on an expedition to find the hottest vindaloo in Calcutta. He pressed Peregrine to join the foraging party as well, but the thought seemed to make her turn green.

Tomorrow morning Father Squid, Troll, and I will visit the Ganges, where legend has it a joker can bathe in the sacred waters and be cured of his afflictions. Our guides tell us there are hundreds of documented cases, but I am frankly dubious, although Father Squid insists that there have been miraculous joker cures in Lourdes as well. Perhaps I shall succumb and leap into the sacred waters after all. A man dying of cancer can ill afford the luxury of skepticism, I suppose.

Chrysalis was invited to join us, but declined. These days she seems most comfortable in the hotel bars, drinking amaretto and playing endless games of solitaire. She has become quite friendly with two of our reporters, Sara Morgenstern and the ubiquitous Digger Downs, and I've even heard talk that she and Digger are sleeping together.

Back from the Ganges. I must make my confession. I took off my shoe and sock, rolled up my pants legs, and put my foot in the sacred waters. Afterward, I was still a joker, alas . . . a joker with a wet foot.

The sacred waters are filthy, by the way, and while I was fishing for my miracle, someone stole my shoe.

MARCH 14/HONG KONG:

I have been feeling better of late, I'm pleased to say. Perhaps it was our brief sojourn in Australia and New Zealand. Coming close upon the heels of Singapore and Jakarta, Sydney seemed almost like home, and I was strangely taken with Auckland and the comparative prosperity and cleanliness of its little toy jokertown. Aside from a distressing tendency to call themselves 'uglies,' an even more offensive term than 'joker,' my Kiwi brethren seem to live as decently as any jokers anywhere. I was even able to purchase a week-old copy of the *Jokertown Cry* at my hotel. It did my soul good to read the news of home, even though too many of the headlines seem to be concerned with a gang war being fought in our streets.

Hong Kong has its jokertown too, as relentlessly mercantile as the rest of the city. I understand that mainland China dumps most of its jokers here, in the Crown Colony. In fact a delegation of leading joker merchants have invited Chrysalis and me to lunch with them tomorrow and discuss 'possible commercial ties between jokers in Hong Kong and New York City.' I'm looking forward to it.

Frankly it will be good to get away from my fellow delegates for a few hours. The mood aboard the *Stacked Deck* is testy at best at present, chiefly thanks to Thomas Downs and his rather overdeveloped journalistic instincts.

Our mail caught up with us in Christchurch, just as we were taking off for Hong Kong, and the packet included advance copies of the latest issue of *Aces*. Digger went up and down the aisles after we were airborne, distributing complimentary copies as is his wont. He ought to have read them first. He and his execrable magazine hit a new low this time out, I'm afraid.

The issue features his cover story of Peregrine's pregnancy. I was amused to note that the magazine obviously feels that Peri's baby is the big news of the trip, since they devoted twice as much space to it as they have to any of Digger's previous stories, even the hideous incident in Syria, though perhaps that was only to justify the glossy four-page footspread of Peregrine past and present, in various costumes and states of undress.

The whispers about her pregnancy started as early as India and were officially confirmed while we were in Thailand, so Digger could hardly be blamed for filing a story. It's just the sort of thing that *Aces* thrives on. Unfortunately for his own health and our sense of camaraderie aboard the *Stacked Deck*, Digger clearly did not agree with Peri that her 'delicate condition' was a private matter. Digger dug too far.

The cover asks, 'Who Fathered Peri's Baby?' Inside, the piece opens with a double-page spread illustrated by an artist's conception of Peregrine holding an infant in her arms, except that the child is a black silhouette with a question mark instead of a face. 'Daddy's an Ace, Tachyon Says,' reads the subhead, leading into a much larger orange banner that claims, 'Friends Beg Her to Abort Monstrous Joker Baby.' Gossip has it that Digger plied Tachyon with brandy while the two of them were inspecting the raunchier side of Singapore's nightlife, managing to elicit a few choice indiscretions. He did not get the name of the father of Peregrine's baby, but once drunk enough, Tachyon displayed no reticence in sounding off about all the reasons why he believes Peregrine ought to abort this child, the foremost of which is the nine percent chance that the baby will be born a joker.

I confess that reading the story filled me with a cold rage and made me doubly glad that Dr Tachyon is not my personal physician. It is at moments such as this that I find myself wondering how Tachyon can possibly pretend to be my friend, or the friend of any joker. *In vino veritas*, they say; Tachyon's comments make it quite clear that he thinks abortion is the only choice for any woman in Peregrine's position. The Takisians abhor deformity and customarily 'cull' (such a polite word) their own deformed children (very few in number, since they have not yet been blessed with the virus that they so generously decided to share with Earth) shortly after birth. Call me oversensitive if you will, but the clear implication of what Tachyon is saying is that death is preferable to jokerhood, that it is better that this child never live at all than live the life of a joker.

When I set the magazine aside I was so livid that I knew I could not possibly speak to Tachyon himself in any rational manner, so I got up and went back to the press compartment to give Downs a piece of my mind. At the very least I wanted to point out rather forcefully that it was grammatically permissible to omit the adjective 'monstrous' before the phrase 'joker baby,' though clearly the copy editors at *Aces* feel it compulsory.

Digger saw me coming, however, and met me halfway. I've managed to raise his consciousness at least enough so that he knew how upset I'd be, because he started right in with excuses. 'Hey, I just wrote the article,' he began. 'They do the headlines back in New York, that and the art, I've got no control over it. Look, Des, next time I'll talk to them—'

He never had a chance to finish whatever promise he was about to make, because just then Josh McCoy stepped up behind him and tapped him on the shoulder with a rolled-up copy of *Aces*. When Downs turned around, McCoy started swinging. The first punch broke Digger's nose with a sickening noise that made me feel rather faint. McCoy went on to split Digger's lips and loosen a few teeth. I grabbed McCoy with my arms and wrapped my trunk around his neck to try to hold him still, but he was crazy strong with rage and brushed me off easily, I'm afraid. I've never been the physical sort, and in my present condition I fear that I'm pitifully weak. Fortunately Billy Ray came along in time to break them up before McCoy could do serious damage.

Digger spent the rest of the flight back in the rear of the plane stoked up with painkillers. He managed to offend Billy Ray as well by dripping blood on the front of his white Carnifex costume. Billy is nothing if not obsessive about his appearance, and as he kept telling us, 'those fucking bloodstains don't come out.' McCoy went up front, where he helped Hiram, Mistral, and Mr Jayewardene console Peri, who was considerably upset by the story. While McCoy was assaulting Digger in the rear of the plane, she was tearing into Dr Tachyon up front. Their confrontation was less physical but equally dramatic, Howard tells me. Tachyon kept apologizing over and over again, but no amount of apologies seemed to stay Peregrine's fury. Howard says it was a good thing that her talons were packed away safely with the luggage.

Tachyon finished out the flight alone in the first-class lounge with a bottle of Remy Martin and the forlorn look of a puppy dog who has just piddled on the Persian rug. If I had been a crueler man, I might have gone upstairs and explained my own grievances to him, but I found that I did not have the heart. I find that very curious, but there is something about Dr Tachyon that makes it difficult to stay angry with him for very long, no matter how insensitive and egregious his behavior.

No matter. I am looking forward to this part of the trip. From Hong Kong we travel to the mainland, Canton and Shanghai and Peking and other stops equally exotic. I plan to walk upon the Great Wall and see the Forbidden City. During World War II I'd chosen to serve in the navy in hopes of seeing the world, and the Far East always had a special glamour for me, but I wound up assigned to a desk in Bayonne, New Jersey. Mary and I were going to make up for that afterward, when the baby was a little older and we had a little more in the way of financial security.

Well, we made our plans, and meanwhile the Takisians made theirs.

Over the years China came to represent all the things I'd never done, all the far places I meant to visit and never did, my own personal Jolson story. And now it looms on my horizon, at last. It's enough to make one believe the end is truly near.

MARCH 21/EN ROUTE TO SEOUL:

A face out of my past confronted me in Tokyo and has preyed on my mind ever since. Two days ago I decided that I would ignore him and the issues raised by his presence, that I would make no mention of him in this journal.

I've made plans to have this volume offered for publication after my death. I do not expect a bestseller, but I would think the number of celebrities aboard the *Stacked Deck* and the various newsworthy events we've generated will stir up at least a little interest in the great American public, so my volume may find its own audience. Whatever modest royalties it earns will be welcomed by the JADL, to which I've willed my entire estate.

Yet, even though I will be safely dead and buried before anyone reads these words, and therefore in no position to be harmed by any personal admissions I might make, I find myself reluctant to write of Fortunato. Call it cowardice, if you will. Jokers are notorious cowards, if one listens to the jests, the cruel sort that they do not allow on television. I can easily justify my decision to say nothing of Fortunato. My dealings with him over the years have been private matters, having little to do with politics or world affairs or the issues that I've tried to address in this journal, and nothing at all to do with this tour.

Yet I have felt free, in these pages, to repeat the gossip that has inevitably swirled about the airplane, to report on the various foibles and indiscretions of Dr Tachyon and Peregrine and Jack Braun and Digger Downs and all the rest. Can I truly pretend that their weaknesses are of public interest and my own are not? Perhaps I could . . . the public has always been fascinated by aces and repelled by jokers ... but I will not. I want this journal to be an honest one, a true one. And I want the readers to understand a little of what it has been like to live forty years a joker. And to do that I must talk of Fortunato, no matter how deeply it may shame me.

Fortunato now lives in Japan. He helped Hiram in some obscure way after Hiram had suddenly and quite mysteriously left the tour in Tokyo. I don't pretend to know the details of that; it was all carefully hushed up. Hiram seemed almost himself when he returned to us in Calcutta, but he has deteriorated rapidly again, and he looks worse every day. He has become volatile and unpleasant, and secretive. But this is not about Hiram, of whose woes I know nothing. The point is, Fortunato was embroiled in the business somehow and came to our hotel, where I spoke to him briefly in the corridor. That was all there was to it ... now. But in years past Fortunato and I have had other dealings.

*

Forgive me. This is hard. I am an old man and a joker, and age and deformity alike have made me sensitive. My dignity is all I have left, and I am about to surrender it.

I was writing about self-loathing.

This is a time for hard truths, and the first of those is that many nats are disgusted by jokers. Some of these are bigots, always ready to hate anything different. In that regard we jokers are no different from any other oppressed minority; we are all hated with the same honest venom by those predisposed to hate.

There are other normals, however, who are more predisposed to tolerance, who try to see beyond the surface to the human being beneath. People of good will, not haters, well-meaning generous people like ... well, like Dr Tachyon and Hiram Worchester to choose two examples close to hand. Both of these gentlemen have proven over the years that they care deeply about jokers in the abstract, Hiram through his anonymous charities, Tachyon through his work at the clinic. And yet both of them, I am convinced, are just as sickened by the simple physical deformity of most jokers as the Nur al-Allah or Leo Barnett. You can see it in their eyes, no matter how nonchalant and cosmopolitan they strive to be. Some of their best friends are jokers, but they wouldn't want their sister to marry one.

This is the first unspeakable truth of jokerhood.

How easy it would be to rail against this, to condemn men like Tach and Hiram for hypocrisy and 'formism' (a hideous word coined by a particularly moronic joker activist and taken up by Tom Miller's Jokers for a Just Society in their heyday). Easy, and wrong. They are decent men, but still only men, and cannot be thought less because they have normal human feelings.

Because, you see, the second unspeakable truth of jokerhood is that no matter how much jokers offend nats, we offend ourselves even more.

Self-loathing is the particular psychological pestilence of Jokertown, a disease that is often fatal. The leading cause of death among jokers under the age of fifty is, and always has been, suicide. This despite the fact that virtually every disease known to man is more serious when contracted by a joker, because our body chemistries and very shapes vary so widely and unpredictably that no course of treatment is truly safe.

In Jokertown you'll search long and hard before you'll find a place to buy a mirror, but there are mask shops on every block.

If that was not proof enough, consider the issue of names. Nick-flames, they call them. They are more than that. They are spotlights on the true depths of joker self-loathing.

If this journal is to be published, I intend to insist that it be titled The Journal of Xavier Desmond, not A Joker's Journal or any such variant. I am a man, a particular man, not just a generic joker. Names are important; they are more than just words, they shape and color the things they name. The feminists realized this long ago, but jokers still have not grasped it.

I have made it a point over the years to answer to no name but my own, yet I know a joker dentist who calls himself Fishface, an accomplished ragtime pianist who answers to Catbox, and a brilliant joker mathematician who signs his papers 'Slimer.' Even on this tour I find myself accompanied by three people named Chrysalis, Troll, and Father Squid.

We are, of course, not the first minority to experience this particular form of oppression. Certainly black people have been there – entire generations were raised with the belief that the 'prettiest' black girls were the ones with the lightest skins whose features most closely approximated the Caucasian ideal. Finally some of them saw through that lie and proclaimed that black was beautiful.

From time to time various well-meaning but foolish jokers have attempted to do the same thing. Freakers, one of the more debauched institutions of Jokertown, has what it calls a 'Twisted Miss' contest every year on Valentine's Day. However sincere or cynical these efforts are, they are surely misguided. Our friends the Takisians took care of that by putting a clever little twist on the prank they played on us.

The problem is, every joker is unique.

Even before my transformation I was never a handsome man. Even after the change I am by no means hideous. My 'nose' is a trunk, about two feet long, with fingers at its end. My experience has been that most people get used to the way I look if they are around me for a few days. I like to tell myself that after a week or so you scarcely notice that I'm any different, and maybe there's even a grain of truth in that.

If the virus had only been so kind as to give all jokers trunks where their noses had been, the adjustment might have been a good deal easier, and a 'Trunks Are Beautiful' campaign might have done some real good.

But to the best of my knowledge I am the only joker with a trunk. I might work very hard to disregard the aesthetics of the nat culture I live in, to convince myself that I am one handsome devil and that the rest of them are the funny-looking ones, but none of that will help the next time I find that pathetic creature they call Snotman sleeping in the dumpster behind the Funhouse. The horrible reality is, my stomach is as thoroughly turned by the more extreme cases of joker deformity as I imagine Dr Tachyon's must be – but if anything, I am even more guilty about it.

Which brings me, in a roundabout way, back to Fortunate. Fortunato is . . . or was at least . . . a procurer. He ran a high-priced call girl ring. All of his girls were exquisite; beautiful, sensual, skilled in every erotic art, and by and large pleasant people, as much a delight out of bed as in it. He called them geishas.

For more than two decades I was one of his best customers.

I believe he did a lot of business in Jokertown. I know for a fact that Chrysalis often trades information for sex, upstairs in her Crystal Palace, whenever a man who needs her services happens to strike her fancy. I know a handful of truly wealthy jokers, none of whom are married, but almost all of whom have nat mistresses. The hometown papers we've seen tell us that the Five Families and the Shadow Fists are warring in the streets, and I know why – because in Jokertown prostitution is big business, along with drugs and gambling.

The first thing a joker loses is his sexuality. Some lose it totally, becoming incapable or asexual. But even those whose genitalia and sexual drives remain unaffected by the wild card find themselves bereft of sexual identity. From the instant one stabilizes, one is no longer a man or a woman, only a joker.

A normal sex drive, abnormal self-loathing, and a yearning for the thing that's been lost . . . manhood, femininity, beauty, whatever. They are common demons in Jokertown, and I know them well. The onset of my cancer and the chemotherapy have combined to kill all my interest in sex, but my memories and my shame remain intact. It shames me to be reminded of Fortunato. Not because I patronized a prostitute or broke their silly laws – I have contempt for those laws. It shames me because, try as I did over the years, I could never find it in me to desire a joker woman. I knew several who were worthy of love; kind, gentle, caring women, who needed commitment and tenderness and yes, sex, as much as I did. Some of them became my cherished friends. Yet I could never respond to them sexually. They remained as unattractive in my eyes as I must have been in theirs.

So it goes, in Jokertown.

The seat belt light has just come on, and I'm not feeling very well at present, so I will sign off here.

APRIL 10/STOCKHOLM:

Very tired. I fear my doctor was correct – this trip may have been a drastic mistake, insofar as my health is concerned. I feel I held up remarkably well during the first few months, when everything was fresh and new and exciting, but during this last month a cumulative exhaustion has set in, and the day-to-day grind has become almost unbearable. The flights, the dinners, the endless receiving lines, the visits to hospitals and joker ghettos and research institutions, it is all threatening to become one great blur of dignitaries and airports and translators and buses and hotel dining rooms.

I am not keeping my food down well, and I know I have lost weight. The cancer, the strain of travel, my age . . . who can say? All of these, I suspect.

Fortunately the trip is almost over now. We are scheduled to return to Tomlin on April 29, and only a handful of stops remain. I confess that I am looking forward to my return home, and I do not think I am alone in that. We are all tired.

Still, despite the toll it has taken, I would not have forfeited this trip for anything. I have seen the Pyramids and the Great Wall, walked the streets of Rio and Marrakesh and Moscow, and soon will add Rome and Paris and London to that list. I have seen and experienced the stuff of dreams and nightmares, and I have learned much, I think. I can only pray that I survive long enough to use some of that knowledge.

Sweden is a bracing change from the Soviet Union and the other Warsaw Pact nations we have visited. I have no strong feelings about socialism one way or the other, but grew very weary of the model joker 'medical hostels' we were constantly being shown and the model jokers who occupied them. Socialist medicine and socialist science would undoubtedly conquer the wild card, and great strides were already being made, we were repeatedly told, but even if one credits these claims, the price is a lifetime of 'treatment' for the handful of jokers the Soviets admit to having.

Billy Ray insists that the Russians actually have thousands of jokers locked away safely out of sight in huge gray 'joker warehouses,' nominally hospitals but actually prisons in all but name, staffed by a lot of guards and precious few doctors and nurses. Ray also says there are a dozen Soviet aces, all of them secretly employed by the government, the military, the police, or the party. If these things exist – the Soviet Union denies all such allegations, of course – we got nowhere close to any of them, with Intourist and the KGB carefully managing every aspect of our visit, despite the government's assurance to the United Nations that this UN-sanctioned tour would receive 'every cooperation.'

To say that Dr Tachyon did not get along well with his socialist colleagues would be a considerable understatement. His disdain for Soviet medicine is exceeded only by Hiram's disdain for Soviet cooking. Both of them do seem to approve of Soviet vodka, however, and have consumed a great deal of it.

There was an amusing little debate in the Winter Palace, when one of our hosts explained the dialectic of history to Dr Tachyon, telling him feudalism must inevitably give way to capitalism, and capitalism to socialism, as a civilization matures. Tachyon listened with remarkable politeness and then said, 'My dear man, there are two great star-faring civilizations in this small sector of the galaxy. My own people, by your lights, must be considered feudal, and the Network is a form of capitalism more rapacious and virulent than than anything you've ever dreamed of. Neither of us show any signs of maturing into socialism, thank you.' Then he paused for a moment and added, 'Although, if you think of it in the right light, perhaps the Swarm might be considered communist, though scarcely civilized.'

It was a clever little speech, I must admit, although I think it might have impressed the Soviets more if Tachyon had not been dressed in full cossack regalia when he delivered it. Where does he get these outfits?

*

Of the other Warsaw Bloc nations there is little to report. Yugoslavia was the warmest, Poland the grimmest, Czechoslovakia seemed the most like home. Downs wrote a marvelously engrossing piece for *Aces*, speculating that the widespread peasant accounts of active contemporary vampires in Hungary and Romania were actually manifestations of the wild card. It was his best work, actually, some really excellent writing, and all the more remarkable when you consider that he based the whole thing on a five-minute conversation with a pastry chef in Budapest. We found a small joker ghetto in Warsaw and a widespread belief in a hidden 'solidarity ace' who will shortly come forth to lead that outlawed trade union to victory. He did not, alas, come forth during our two days in Poland. Senator Hartmann, with greatest difficulty, managed to arrange a meeting with

Lech Walesa, and I believe that the AP news photo of their meeting has enhanced his stature back home. Hiram left us briefly in Hungary – another 'emergency' back in New York, he said – and returned just as we arrived in Sweden, in somewhat better spirits.

Stockholm is a most congenial city, after many of the places we have been. Virtually all the Swedes we have met speak excellent English, we are free to come and go as we please (within the confines of our merciless schedule, of course), and the king was gracious to all of us. Jokers are quite rare here, this far north, but he greeted us with complete equanimity, as if he'd been hosting jokers all of his life.

Still, as enjoyable as our brief visit has been, there is only one incident that is worth recording for posterity. I believe we have unearthed something that will make the historians around the world sit up and take notice, a hitherto-unknown fact that puts much of recent Middle Eastern history into a new and startling perspective.

It occurred during an otherwise unremarkable afternoon a number of the delegates spent with the Nobel trustees. I believe it was Senator Hartmann they actually wanted to meet. Although it ended in violence, his attempt to meet and negotiate with the Nur al-Allah in Syria is correctly seen here for what it was – a sincere and courageous effort on behalf of peace and understanding, and one that makes him to my mind a legitimate candidate for next year's Nobel Peace Prize.

At any rate, several of the other delegates accompanied Gregg to the meeting, which was cordial but hardly stimulating. One of our hosts, it turned out, had been a secretary to Count Folke Bernadotte when he negotiated the Peace of Jerusalem, and sadly enough had also been with Bernadotte when he was gunned down by Israeli terrorists two years later. He told us several fascinating anecdotes about Bernadotte, for whom he clearly had great admiration, and also showed us some of his personal memorabilia of those difficult negotiations. Among the notes, journals, and interim drafts was a photo book.

I gave the book a cursory glance and then passed it on, as did most of my companions. Dr Tachyon, who was seated beside me on the couch, seemed bored by the proceedings and leafed through the photographs with rather more care. Bernadotte figured in most of them, of course – standing with his negotiating team, talking with David Ben-Gurion in one photo and King Faisal in the next. The various aides, including our host, were seen in less formal poses, shaking hands with Israeli soldiers, eating with a tentful of Bedouin, and so on. The usual sort of thing. By far the single most interesting picture showed Bernadotte surrounded by the *Nasr*, the Port Said aces who so dramatically reversed the tide of battle when they joined with Jordan's crack Arab Legion. Khôf sits beside Bernadotte in the center of the photograph, all in black, looking like death incarnate, surrounded by the younger aces. Ironically enough, of all the faces in that photo, only three are still alive, the ageless Khôf among them. Even an undeclared war takes its toll.

That was not the photograph that caught Tachyon's attention, however. It was another, a very informal snapshot, showing Bernadotte and various members of his team in some hotel room, the table in front of them littered with papers. In one corner of the photograph was a young man I had not noticed in any of the other pictures – slim, dark-haired, with a certain intense look around the eyes, and a rather ingratiating grin. He was pouring a cup of coffee. All very innocent, but Tachyon stared at the photograph for a long time and then called our host over and said to him privately, 'Forgive me if I tax your memory, but I would be very interested to know if you remember this man.' He pointed him out. 'Was he a member of your team?'

Our Swedish friend leaned over, studied the photograph, and chuckled. 'Oh, him,' he said in excellent English. 'He was . . . what is the slang word you use, for a boy who runs errands and does odd jobs? An animal of some sort . . .'

'A gofer,' I supplied.

'Yes, he was a *gopher*, as you put it. Actually a young journalism student. Joshua, that was his name. Joshua . . . something. He said he wanted to observe the negotiations from within so he could write about them afterward. Bernadotte thought the idea was ridiculous when it was first put to him, rejected it out of hand in fact, but the young man was persistent. He finally managed to corner the count and put his case to him personally, and somehow he talked him around. So he was not officially a member of the team, but he was with us constantly from that point through the end. He was not a very efficient gopher, as I recall, but he was such a pleasant young man that everyone liked him regardless. I don't believe he ever wrote his article.'

'No,' Tachyon said. 'He wouldn't have. He was a chess player, not a writer.'

Our host lit up with remembrance. 'Why, yes! He played incessantly, now that I recall. He was quite good. Do you know him, Dr Tachyon? I've often wondered whatever became of him.'

'So have I,' Tachyon replied very simply and very sadly. Then he closed the book and changed the topic.

I have known Dr Tachyon for more years than I care to contemplate. That evening, spurred by my own curiosity, I managed to seat myself near to Jack Braun and ask him a few innocent questions while we ate. I'm certain that he suspected nothing, but he was willing enough to reminisce

about the Four Aces, the things they did and tried to do, the places they
went, and more importantly, the places they did not go. At least not
officially.

Afterward, I found Dr Tachyon drinking alone in his room. He invited
me in, and it was clear that he was feeling quite morose, lost in his
damnable memories. He lives as much in the past as any man I have ever
known. I asked him who the young man in the photograph had been.

'No one,' Tachyon said. 'Just a boy I used to play chess with.' I'm not
sure why he felt he had to lie to me.

'His name was not Joshua,' I told him, and he seemed startled. I
wonder, does he think my deformity affects my mind, my memory? 'His
name was David, and he was not supposed to be there. The Four Aces were
never officially involved in the Mideast, and Jack Braun says that by late
1948 the members of the group had gone their own ways. Braun was
making movies.'

'Bad movies,' Tachyon said with a certain venom.

'Meanwhile,' I said, 'the Envoy was making peace.'

'He was gone for two months. He told Blythe and me that he was going
on a vacation. I remember. It never occurred to me that he was involved.'

No more has it ever occurred to the rest of the world, though perhaps it
should have. David Harstein was not particularly religious, from what little
I know of him, but he was Jewish, and when the Port Said aces and the
Arab armies threatened the very existence of the new state of Israel, he
acted all on his own.

His was a power for peace, not war; not fear or sandstorms or lightning
from a clear sky, but pheromones that made people like him and want
desperately to please him and agree with him, that made the mere
presence of the ace called Envoy a virtual guarantee of a successful
negotiation. But those who knew who and what he was showed a
distressing tendency to repudiate their agreements once Harstein and his
pheromones had left their presence. He must have pondered that, and
with the stakes so high, he must have decided to find out what might
happen if his role in the process was carefully kept secret. The Peace of
Jerusalem was his answer.

I wonder if even Folke Bernadotte knew who his gopher really was. I
wonder where Harstein is now, and what he thinks of the peace that he so
carefully and secretly wrought. And I find myself reflecting on what the
Black Dog said in Jerusalem.

What would it do to the fragile Peace of Jerusalem if its origins were
revealed to the world? The more I reflect on that, the more certain I grow
that I ought tear these pages from my journal before I offer it for

publication. If no one gets Dr Tachyon drunk, perhaps this secret can even be kept.

Did he ever do it again, I wonder? After HUAC, after prison and disgrace and his celebrated conscription and equally celebrated disappearance, did the Envoy ever sit in on any other negotiations with the world's being none the wiser? I wonder if we'll ever know.

I think it unlikely and wish it were not. From what I have seen on this tour, in Guatemala and South Africa, in Ethiopia and Syria and Jerusalem, in India and Indonesia and Poland, the world today needs the Envoy more than ever.

APRIL 27/SOMEWHERE OVER THE ATLANTIC:

The interior lights were turned out several hours ago, and most of my fellow travelers are long asleep, but the pain has kept me awake. I've taken some pills, and they are helping, but still I cannot sleep. Nonetheless, I feel curiously elated ... almost serene. The end of my journey is near, in both the larger and smaller senses. I've come a long way, yes, and for once I feel good about it.

We still have one more stop – a brief sojourn in Canada, whirlwind visits to Montreal and Toronto, a government reception in Ottawa. And then home. Tomlin International, Manhattan, Jokertown. It will be good to see the Funhouse again.

I wish I could say that the tour had accomplished everything we set out to do, but that's scarcely the case. We began well, perhaps, but the violence in Syria, West Germany, and France undid our unspoken dream of making the public forget the carnage of Wild Card Day. I can only hope that the majority will realize that terrorism is a bleak and ugly part of the world we live in, that it would exist with or without the wild card. The bloodbath in Berlin was instigated by a group that included jokers, aces, and nats, and we would do well to remember that and remind the world of it forcefully. To lay that carnage at the door of Gimli and his pathetic followers, or the two fugitive aces still being sought by the German police, is to play into the hands of men like Leo Barnett and the Nur al-Allah. Even if the Takisians had never brought their curse to us, the world would have no shortage of desperate, insane, and evil men.

For me, there is a grim irony in the fact that it was Gregg's courage and compassion that put his life at risk, and hatred that saved him, by turning his captors against each other in that fratricidal holocaust.

Truly, this is a strange world.

I pray that we have seen the last of Gimli, but meanwhile I can rejoice.

After Syria it seems unlikely that anyone could still doubt Gregg Hartmann's coolness under fire, but if that was indeed the case, surely all such fears have now been firmly laid to rest by Berlin. After Sara Morgenstern's exclusive interview was published in the Post, I understand Hartmann shot up ten points in the polls. He's almost neck and neck with Hart now. The feeling aboard the plane is that Gregg is definitely going to run.

I said as much to Digger back in Dublin, over a Guinness and some fine Irish soda bread in our hotel, and he agreed. In fact, he went further and predicted that Hartmann would get the nomination. I wasn't quite so certain and reminded him that Gary Hart still seems a formidable obstacle, but Downs grinned in that maddeningly cryptic way of his beneath his broken nose and said, 'Yeah, well, I got this hunch that Gary is going to fuck up and do something really stupid, don't ask me why.'

If my health permits, I will do everything I can to rally Jokertown behind a Hartmann candidacy. I don't think I'm alone in my commitment either. After the things we have seen, both at home and abroad, a growing number of prominent aces and jokers are likely to throw their weight behind the senator. Hiram Worchester, Peregrine, Mistral, Father Squid, Jack Braun . . . perhaps even Dr Tachyon, despite his notorious distaste for politics and politicians.

Terrorism and bloodshed notwithstanding, I do believe we accomplished some good on this journey. Our report will open some official eyes, I can only hope, and the press spotlight that has shone on us everywhere has greatly increased public awareness of the plight of jokers in the Third World.

On a more personal level, Jack Braun did much to redeem himself and even buried his thirty-year emnity with Tachyon; Peri seems positively radiant in her pregnancy; and we did manage, however belatedly, to free poor Jeremiah Strauss from twenty years of simian bondage. I remember Strauss from the old days, when Angela owned the Funhouse and I was only the maitre d', and I offered him a booking if and when he resumes his theatrical career as the Projectionist. He was appreciative, but noncommittal. I don't envy him his period of adjustment. For all practical purposes, he is a time traveler.

And Dr Tachyon . . . well, his new punk haircut is ugly in the extreme, he still favors his wounded leg, and by now the entire plane knows of his sexual dysfunction, but none of this seems to bother him since young Blaise came aboard in France. Tachyon has been evasive about the boy in his public statements, but of course everyone knows the truth. The years he spent in Paris are scarcely a state secret, and if the boy's hair was not a sufficient clue, his mind control power makes his lineage abundantly clear.

Blaise is a strange child. He seemed a little awed by the jokers when he first joined us, particularly Chrysalis, whose transparent skin clearly fascinated him. On the other hand, he has all of the natural cruelty of an unschooled child (and believe me, any joker knows how cruel a child can be). One day in London, Tachyon got a phone call and had to leave for a few hours. While he was gone, Blaise grew bored, and to amuse himself he seized control of Mordecai Jones and made him climb onto a table and recite 'I'm a Little Teapot,' which Blaise had just learned as part of an English lesson. The table collapsed under the Hammer's weight, and I don't think Jones is likely to forget the humiliation. He didn't much like Dr Tachyon to begin with.

Of course not everyone will look back on this tour fondly. The trip was very hard on a number of us, there's no gainsaying that. Sara Morgenstern has filed several major stories and done some of the best writing of her career, but nonetheless the woman is edgier and more neurotic with every passing day. As for her colleagues in the back of the plane, Josh McCoy seems alternately madly in love with Peregrine and absolutely furious with her, and it cannot be easy for him with the whole world knowing that he is not the father of her child. Meanwhile, Digger's profile will never be the same.

Downs is, at least, as irrepressible as he is irresponsible. Just the other day he was telling Tachyon that if he got an exclusive on Blaise, maybe he would be able to keep Tach's impotence off-the-record. This gambit was not well received. Digger has also been thick as thieves with Chrysalis of late. I overheard them having a very curious conversation in the bar one night in London. 'I know he is,' Digger was saying. Chrysalis told him that knowing it and proving it were two different things. Digger said something about how they smelled different to him, how he'd known ever since they met, and Chrysalis just laughed and said that was fine, but smells that no one else could detect weren't much good as proof, and even if they were, he'd have to blow his own cover to go public. They were still going at it when I left the bar.

I think even Chrysalis will be delighted to return to Jokertown. Clearly she loved England, but given her Anglophile tendencies, that was hardly a surprise. There was one tense moment when she was introduced to Churchill during a reception, and he gruffly inquired as to exactly what she was trying to prove with her affected British accent. It is quite difficult to read expressions on her unique features, but for a moment I was sure she was going to kill the old man right there in front of the Queen, Prime Minister, and a dozen British aces. Thankfully she gritted her teeth and put it down to Lord Winston's advanced age. Even when he was younger, he was never precisely reticent about expressing his thoughts.

Hiram Worchester has perhaps suffered more on this trip than any of us. Whatever reserves of strength were left to him burned out in Germany, and since then he has seemed exhausted. He shattered his special custom seat as we were leaving Paris – some sort of miscalculation with his gravity control, I believe, but it delayed us nearly three hours while repairs were made. His temper has been fraying too. During the business with the seat, Billy Ray made one too many fat jokes, and Hiram finally snapped and turned on him in a white rage, calling him (among other things) an 'incompetent little guttermouth.' That was all it took. Carnifex just grinned that ugly little grin of his, said, 'For that you get your ass kicked, fat man,' and started to get out of his seat. 'I didn't say you could get up,' Hiram replied; he made a fist and trebled Billy's weight, slamming him right back into the seat cushion. Billy was still straining to get up and Hiram was making him heavier and heavier, and I don't know where it might have ended if Dr Tachyon hadn't broken it up by putting both of them to sleep with his mind control.

I don't know whether to be disgusted or amused when I see these world-famous aces squabbling like petty children, but Hiram at least has the excuse of ill health. He looks terrible these days: white-faced, puffy, perspiring, short of breath. He has a huge, hideous scab on his neck, just below the collar line, that he picks at when he thinks no one is watching. I would strongly advise him to seek out medical attention, but he is so surly of late that I doubt my counsel would be welcomed. His short visits to New York during the tour always seemed to do him a world of good, however, so we can only hope that homecoming restores his health and spirits.

*

And lastly, me.

Observing and commenting on my fellow travelers and what they've gained or lost, that's the easy part. Summing up my own experience is harder. I'm older and, I hope, wiser than when we left Tomlin International, and undeniably I am five months closer to death.

Whether this journal is published or not after my passing, Mr Ackroyd assures me that he will personally deliver copies to my grandchildren and do everything in his power to make sure that they are read. So perhaps it is to them that I write these last, concluding words . . . to them, and all the others like them . . .

Robert, Cassie . . . we never met, you and I, and the blame for that falls as much on me as on your mother and your grandmother. If you wonder why, remember what I wrote about self-loathing and please understand that I was not exempt. Don't think too harshly of me . . . or of your mother or grandmother. Joanna was far too young to understand what was happening when her daddy changed, and as for Mary . . . we loved each other once, and I cannot go to my grave hating her. The truth is, had our roles been reversed, I might well have done the same thing. We're all only human, and we do the best we can with the hand that fate has dealt us.

Your grandfather was a joker, yes. But I hope as you read this book you'll realize that he was something else as well – that he accomplished a few things, spoke up for his people, did some good. The JADL is perhaps as good a legacy as most men leave behind them, a better monument to my mind than the Pyramids, the Taj Mahal, or Jetboy's Tomb. All in all, I haven't done so badly. I'll leave behind some friends who loved me, many treasured memories, much unfinished business. I've wet my foot in the Ganges, heard Big Ben sound the hour, and walked on the Great Wall of China. I've seen my daughter born and held her in my arms, and I've dined with aces and TV stars, with presidents and kings.

Most important, I think I leave the world a slightly better place for my having been in it. And that's really all that can be asked of any of us.

Remember me to your children, if you will.

My name was Xavier Desmond, and I was a man.

NINE
THE HEART IN CONFLICT

THE HEART IN CONFLICT

Oldtimers and truefen still cherish their memories of Bat Durston, that fearless scourge of the spaceways whose adventures appeared so often in *Galaxy* in the early '50s.

Bat always got the cover in those days. The *back* cover. Under the legend 'YOU'LL NEVER SEE IT IN GALAXY' ran twin columns:

Hoofs drumming, Bat Durston came galloping down through the narrow pass at Eagle Gulch, a tiny gold colony 400 miles north of Tombstone. He spurred hard for a low overhang of rimrock . . . and at that point, a tall, lean wrangler stepped out from behind a high boulder, six-shooter in a sun-tanned hand. 'Rear back and dismount, Bat Durston,' the stranger lipped thinly. 'You don't know it, but this is your last saddle-jaunt through these here parts.'

Jets blasting, Bat Durston came screeching down through the atmosphere of Bbllzznaj, a tiny planet seven billion light-years from Sol. He cut out his superhyper-drive for the landing . . . and at that point a tall, lean spaceman stepped out of the tail assembly, proton gun blaster in a space-tanned hand. 'Get back from those controls, Bat Durston,' the tall stranger lipped thinly. 'You don't know it, but this is your last space trip through this particular section of the universe.'

'Sound alike?' editor H. L. Gold would write, beneath the twin columns. 'They should – one is merely a western transplanted to some alien and impossible planet. If this is your idea of science fiction, you're welcome to it. YOU'LL NEVER FIND IT IN GALAXY! What you will find in *Galaxy* is the finest science fiction . . . authentic, plausible, thoughtful . . . written by authors who do not automatically switch over from crime waves to earth invasions; by people who know and love science fiction . . . for people who also know and love it.'

The ad appeared on the premiere issue of *Galaxy* in September, 1950, and turned up again on many subsequent issues. This was back when I was a wee lad of two (I have pictures to prove it). Even *Rocky Jones* was in my future at that point (Rocky and Bat had surely palled around in space ranger school), along with Heinlein, Howard, Tolkien, Lovecraft, and the Fantastic Four.

By the time I reached the point where I writing SF myself, *Galaxy* was well past its H. L. Golden age. Gold gave up the reins (the helm? the starship controls?) in 1961 after an auto accident, and Frederik Pohl stepped in for a distinguished stint as editor. Toward the end of the decade Ejler Jakobsson succeeded Pohl and hired Gardner Dozois to read his slush. The rest is history, as you know if you've read my earlier commentaries.

I never sold another story to *Galaxy* while Jakobsson was editor, though I did come close once or twice. I did sell many more stories to Ted White, though after 'Exit to San Breta' most of my stuff appeared in *Amazing*, not *Fantastic*. But the market where I made my reputation, where all my early award nominees appeared, and ultimately my first Hugo winner, was *Analog*, the leading magazine in the field, which for decades had come to epitomize 'hard science fiction' under its legendary editor, John W. Campbell, Jr.

JWC passed away just as I was breaking in, and Ben Bova succeeded him at *Analog*. Campbell is rightly regarded as a great editor. He remade the field when he took over *Astounding* in the '30s, and gave science fiction its Golden Age. He was famous for developing new writers as well, but somehow I doubt that he would have responded as favorably as Bova did to the melancholy, romantic, downbeat stories I was writing in the early '70s. Had Campbell lived for another ten years, my career would have taken a much different path, I suspect, along with many other careers.

Bova came to the editor's chair as a science fiction writer of impeccable credentials. Ben was known for hard SF, *real* SF, and that was important in those vanished days of yesteryear, when the war between the Old Wave and the New Wave still raged. Nonetheless, the moment he was enthroned, Ben began to open up the magazine, and stories soon appeared within the hallowed pages of *Analog* that would never have appeared under JWC . . . mine own among them.

This was not an entirely painless process, as a glance at any letter column of that period would tell you. Every new issue contained one or two 'cancel my subscription' letters from old subscribers outraged at the appearance of a profane word, a sex scene, or a less-than-competent man. Fortunately, they were a minority. The reborn *Analog* became the best short fiction market of the '70s, and Ben Bova won the Hugo for Best Editor five years in a row from 1973 to 1977, and once again in 1979.

The first sale I made to Bova – my third sale overall, and the first one that wasn't lost before being bought – was actually a 'science fact' article about computer chess. I had been captain of my college chess team at Northwestern, where some friends of mine had written a chess-playing program for the big campus mainframe, a giant CDC 6400 that lived in its own sealed, temperature controlled building. When Chess 4.0 defeated rival programs from a half-dozen other colleges to win the world's first computer chess championship, I knew I had an article, and indeed I did.

It was the only science fact article I ever sold to *Analog*, the only one I ever *wrote*. I was a journalist, not a scientist. But once I'd sold a science fact article to *Analog*, no one could question my bona fides, the way they were then questioning all those squishy-soft New Wave writers who were selling to *Orbit* and *New Dimensions*. Though Bova had broadened *Analog*'s horizons, the magazine still had the reputation of being hard-nosed, steel-clad, scientifically rigorous, and perhaps a bit puritanical. Gardner Dozois once told a woman I was chasing that there was no point in going to bed with me, since when you sold to *Analog* a white van pulled up in front of your house, and two guys in silver jumpsuits confiscated your penis. (I will not comment on the truth of this, except to note that Gardner himself later sold to *Analog*, and presently shares an office with its editor. I have never asked to see what it is in the large locked cabinet behind Stan Schmidt's desk.)

'The Computer Was a Fish,' my science fact article about David Slate and his champion chess-playing program, was shortly followed by 'With Morning Comes Mistfall' and 'The Second Kind of Loneliness' and 'A Song for Lya' and all the rest. I had other markets besides *Analog*, of course. Ted White bought as many stories from me as did Bova; *Amazing* and *Fantastic* under White were terrific magazines. I also sold to *The Magazine of Fantasy and Science Fiction*, and managed to hit many of the original anthologies series of the day.

But I got my share of rejections as well. No writer likes being rejected, though it comes with the territory, and you need to get used to it. A few of mine were especially galling, though. Those were the ones where the editors had no problems with my plot or characterization or style, and even went out of their way to say that they'd enjoyed reading the stories. They rejected them nonetheless . . . because *they weren't real science fiction*.

'Night Shift' was about the night shift at a busy spaceport, as the spaceships come and go. They could have just as easily been trucks, an editor said. Another said that 'With Morning Comes Mistfall' put him in mind of attempts to find the Loch Ness monster. Even 'Second Kind of Loneliness' took its lumps. This could be a story about a lighthouse keeper, one rejection said. The focus is not on the star ring or the nullspace vortex so much as on the 'rather pathetic' protagonist, with his hopes and dreams and fears.

I mean, really. What were these guys trying to tell me? I was an *Analog* writer, I'd sold a science fact article . . . *and they were claiming that I wrote Bat Durston stories!*

Of course, it was true that I had based 'Night Shift' on my father's experiences as a longshoreman and a few weeks I once spent working in a truck dispatch office . . .

And it was true that the seed for 'With Morning Comes Mistfall' had been planted when I read an article in the paper about a scientist who was taking a fleet of sonar-equipped boats to Loch Ness, intending to flush out Nessie or disprove him . . .

And it was true that 'Second Kind of Loneliness' was peopled by my own personal demons, and based on incidents and characters from my own life, as was 'A Song for Lya.'

And even 'Sandkings,' a few years later, started with that guy I knew in college and his aquarium of piranha.

But so what? When I wrote the stories I moved them to other planets, and put aliens in them, and spaceships. How much more bloody science-fictional could they get?

All those years when I'd been growing up and reading fantasy and horror and science fiction, I'd never once worried about which was what and what was which or where the boundaries were drawn or whether this was *real* science fiction and *real* fantasy and *real* horror. My staple fare in the '50s was made up of paperbacks and comic books. I knew the SF magazines were out there somewhere, but seldom saw one, so I remained blissfully unaware of Bat Durston and Horace Gold's fulminations against him. As a kid I did not even know the proper names for all the genres and subgenres. To me they were monster stories and space stuff and sword & sorcery. Or 'weird stuff.' That was my father's term for all of it. He liked westerns, you see, but his son liked 'weird stuff.'

But now that I was a published professional writer, and an *Analog* writer at that (with penis, thank you very much), it behooved me to find out what *real* science fiction was. So I reread Damon Knight's *In Search of Wonder*, James Blish's *The Issue At Hand*, and L. Sprague de Camp's *Science Fiction Handbook*, and looked into *Locus* and *Science Fiction Review*. I paid careful attention to Alexei Panshin's 'SF in Dimension' columns in *Amazing*. I followed the debate between the Old Wave and New Wave with interest, since that New Wave crap wasn't real SF science fiction either, according to the Old Wave guys. And of course I paid careful attention to the various definitions of science fiction.

There were a lot of those about, many of them mutually contradictory. L. Sprague de Camp defined SF in *The Science Fiction Handbook*, and Kingsley Amis defined it differently in *New Maps of Hell*. Ted Sturgeon had a definition, Fred Pohl had a definition, Reginald Bretnor had a definition, David G. Hartwell had a definition, Alexei Panshin had a definition, and over in the corner stood Damon Knight pointing at something. The Old Wave and the New Wave each championed its own view of what the genre ought to be. H.

L. Gold must surely have had a definition, since he knew Bat Durston did not fit it. I absorbed all of this as best I could, and finally discerned the shape of a *real* science fiction story, as opposed to the stuff that I was writing.

The ultimate template for the True Science Fiction Story was Isaac Asimov's first sale, 'Marooned Off Vesta,' published in *Amazing* in 1939. Asimov would later write more famous stories, and better stories – well, to tell the truth, pretty much *everything* he wrote after that was a better story – but 'Marooned Off Vesta' was sure-enough pure-quill science fiction, in which everything hinges on the fact that water boils at a lower temperature in vacuum.

This was a sobering realization for me. For although I had pages of scribbled notes for the stories I wanted to tell next year and the year after and the year after that, not one of them had anything to do with the boiling point of water. If truth be told, it seemed to me that Asimov had said just about all there was to say on that particular subject, leaving nothing for the rest of us except, well . . . Bat Durston.

The thing is, though, the more I considered old Bat, and Asimov, and Heinlein and Campbell, and Wells and Verne, and Vance and Anderson and Le Guin and Brackett and Williamson and deCamp and Kuttner and Moore and Cordwainer Smith and Doc Smith and George O. Smith and Northwest Smith, and all the rest of the Smiths and the Joneses too, the more I realized something that H. L. Gold did not.

Boys and girls, they're *all* Bat Durston stories.

All of mine, and all of yours, and all of his, and all of hers. The *Space Merchants* (which Gold serialized in *Galaxy* as *Gravy Planet*) is about Madison Avenue in the '50s, *The Forever War* is about Vietnam, *Neuromancer* is a caper novel tricked up in fancy prose, and Asimov's Galactic Empire bears a suspicious likeness to one the Romans had a while back. Why else would Bel Riose remind us so much of this guy Belisarius? And when you look really really hard at 'Marooned Off Vesta,' it turns out that it's not about the boiling point of water after all. It's about some desperate men trying to survive.

Step back and squint hard at the back cover of that first issue of *Galaxy*, if you will, and you will realize how easily those two columns might have been reversed. The same advertisement could just as well have been run on a western magazine, with only minor changes. 'YOU'LL NEVER SEE IT IN SIX-GUN STORIES,' the editor might well have trumpeted. 'Sound alike? They should – one is merely a sci-fi story transplanted to the range. If this is your idea of western fiction, you're welcome to it. YOU'LL NEVER FIND IT IN SIX-GUN STORIES! What you will find here is the finest western fiction . . . authentic, plausible, thoughtful . . . written by people who know and love the Old West . . . for people who also know and love it.'

So I will see your Bat Durston, Mr Gold. And I'll raise you William Faulkner, *Casablanca*, and the Bard.

In the film *The Goodbye Girl* Richard Dreyfess plays an actor forced to portray Richard III as a lisping effiminate poof by a 'genius' director. These days that no longer seems quite as much like a parody as it once did. The London stage has given us Derek Jarman's notorious modern dress version of Marlowe's *Edward II*, wherein Piers Gaveston's chief item of wardrobe is a studded leather jock strap. When I was last in the West End, they were presenting a *Coriolanus* set against the Terror of Revolutionary France. The most recent filmed version of *Romeo and Juliet* made it a tale of warring urban street gangs, complete with automobiles, helicopters, and television reporters. And if you have not seen Ian McClellan's film of *Richard III*, set in a fascist England during the 1930s, you've missed some fabulous art direction and cinematography, and a mesmerizing performance by McClellan, whose portrayal of Dickie Crookback is equal to Olivier's.

One might argue that *Richard III* is rightfully about the Wars of the Roses, not the fascist movements of the '30s. One might also insist that *Coriolanus* should be set in Rome, not Paris. One might point out rather forcefully that Mercutio was *not*, in fact, a black drag queen. All that is true, as far as it goes.

And yet . . . sometimes . . . more often than not . . . the Bard's plays still work, no matter how bizarrely the genius directors decide to trick them out. Once in the while, as in Ian McClellan's film of *Richard III*, they work rather magnificently.

And for that matter, my favorite science fiction film of all time is not *2001: A Space Odyssey* or *Alien*, or *Star Wars*, or *Bladerunner*, or (ugh) *The Matrix*, but rather *Forbidden Planet*, better known to us cognoscenti as *The Tempest on Altair-4*, and starring Leslie Nielsen, Anne Francis, Walter Pidgeon, and Bat Durston.

But how could this be? How could critics and theatre-goers and Shakespeareans possibly applaud these Bat Durston productions, ripp'd untimely as they are from their natural and proper settings?

The answer is simple. Motor cars or horses, tricorns or togas, ray-guns or six-shooters, none of it matters, so long as the people remain. Sometimes we get so busy drawing boundaries and making labels that we lose track of that truth.

Casablanca put it most succinctly. 'It's still the same old story, a fight for love and glory, a case of do or die.'

William Faulkner said much the same thing while accepting the Nobel Prize for Literature, when he spoke of 'the old verities and truths of the heart, the universal truths lacking which any story is ephemeral and doomed – love and honor and pity and pride and compassion and sacrifice.' The 'human heart in conflict with itself,' Faulkner said, 'alone can make good writing, because only that is worth writing about.'

We can make up all the definitions of science fiction and fantasy and horror that we want. We can draw our boundaries and make our labels, but in the end it's still the same old story, the one about the human heart in conflict with itself.

The rest, my friends, is furniture.

The House of Fantasy is built of stone and wood and furnished in High Medieval. Its people travel by horse and galley, fight with sword and spell and battleaxe, communicate by palantir or raven, and break bread with elves and dragons.

The House of Science Fiction is built of duralloy and plastic and furnished in Faux Future. Its people travel by starship and aircar, fight with nukes and tailored germs, communicate by ansible and laser, and break protein bars with aliens.

The House of Horror is built of bone and cobwebs and furnished in Ghastly Gothick. Its people travel only by night, fight with anything that will kill messily, communicate in screams and shrieks and gibbers, and sip blood with vampires and werewolves.

The Furniture Rule, I call it.

Forget the definitions. Furniture Rules.

Ask Phyllis Eisenstein, who has written a series of fine stories about a minstrel named Alaric, traveling through a medieval realm she never names . . . but if you corner her at a con she may whisper the name of this far kingdom. 'Germany.' The only fantastic element in the Alaric stories is teleportation, a psi ability generally classed as a trope of SF. Ah, but Alaric carries a lute, and sleeps in castles, and around him are lords with swords, so ninety-nine readers out of every hundred, and most publishers as well, see the series as fantasy. The Furniture Rules.

Ask Walter Jon Williams. In *Metropolitan* and *City on Fire* he gives us a secondary world as fully imagined as Tolkien's Middle Earth, a world powered entirely by magic, which Walter calls 'plasm.' But because the world is a single huge decaying city, rife with corrupt politics and racial tensions, and the plasm is piped and metered by the plasm authority, and the sorcerers live in high rises instead of castles, critics and reviewers and readers alike keep calling the books science fiction. The Furniture Rules.

Peter Nicholls writes, '. . . SF and fantasy, if genres at all, are impure genres . . . their fruit may be SF, but the roots are fantasy, and the flowers and leaves perhaps something else again.' If anything, Nicholls does not go far enough, for westerns and mysteries and romances and historicals and all the rest are impure as well. What we really have, when we get right down to the nitty gritty, are *stories*. Just stories.

And that's what we have in this final section of the book. Some stories that I wrote. A little of this with a little of that. Weird stuff, folks, just weird stuff.

'Under Siege,' for instance. It's a time travel story. By definition that makes it science fiction (though, come to think of it, isn't time travel actually a rather unscientific fantasy?), yet it began life as a mainstream historical. If you started reading this book at the beginning *(as you should have!)* and didn't skip over my juvenilia, certain aspects of this story will seem oddly familiar to you. Yes indeed, it's our old friend 'The Fortress,' which earned me an A and my first rejection, courtesy of Franklin D. Scott and Erik J. Friis. In 1968 'The Fortress' went into the drawer to hibernate. In 1984 I took it out again, added a dwarf and some time travel, called it 'Under Siege,' and sold it to Ellen Datlow for *Omni*. (Never throw *anything* away.)

Then there's 'The Skin Trade,' the first (and only) story in my series about PI Randi Wade and Willie the werewolf collection agent. I wrote that one for the 1988 installment of Dark Harvest's annual horror anthology, while I was out in L.A. working on *Beauty and the Beast*. I shared *Night Visions 5* with Stephen King and Dan Simmons. To play on the same field as those two, I knew I'd need to bring my game. Hunched over my computer at the old Seward offices of *Beauty and the Beast* long after everyone else had left, I would drink whole pots of coffee to keep myself awake, and stagger home so wired that I *couldn't* sleep even when I tumbled into bed. It is a wonder that Willie Flambeaux didn't come out talking like Vincent, or vice versa. My deadline came and went, and on I wrote, months after King and Simmons had delivered. I have no doubt that Paul Mikol of Dark Harvest was sorely tempted to give my place to someone faster. But when I finally got the story in, Paul wrote to say, 'All right, it kills me, but it was worth the wait.' In 1989 'The Skin Trade' won the World Fantasy Award for Best Novella, and I took home one of Gahan Wilson's wonderfully gloomy busts of H. P. Lovecraft to adorn my mantel. Sometimes I put a little hat on him.

'Unsound Variations' is my chess story. It's got some time travel too, sure, but mostly it's my chess story. Not long after moving to Santa Fe, I had this swell idea for an anthology of science fiction and fantasy stories about chess. I could reprint 'Midnight By the Morphy Watch' by Fritz Leiber, 'The Marvelous Brass Chessplaying Automaton' by Gene Wolfe, and 'Von Goom's Gambit,' a wonderfully weird Lovecraftian short originally published in *Chess Review*. The rest of the book I would fill out with originals. I knew lots of writers who loved chess.

Fred Saberhagen was one of them. Unfortunately, when I wrote him about my book, he wrote back to tell me he'd just sold a chess anthology to Ace, and would be reprinting 'Midnight by the Morphy Watch' and 'The Marvelous Brass Chessplaying Automaton' and 'Von Goom's Gambit.' So instead of him writing a story for my anthology, I wrote a story for his *Pawn to Infinity*, drawing on my experiences as the captain of Northwestern's chess team. The story is fiction, to be sure, and any resemblance to actual persons living or dead is coincidental . . . but I would like to point out that I myself once actually fielded six teams for the Pan-American Intercollegiate Team Championships, a record that endured for close to thirty years.

'The Glass Flower' has a sadder distinction. It marked the last time I ever returned to my old SF future history. Kleronomas was one of the touchstone names of that history, along with Stephan Cobalt Northstar, Erika Stormjones, and Tomo and Walberg. I thought it was past time that I brought one of my mythic figures onto the stage. 'The Glass Flower' appeared in *Asimov's* in September, 1986. Except for *Avalon*, the abortive novel I began before getting caught up by *A Game of Thrones* and *Doorways*, I have not since visited any of my thousand worlds. Will I ever return to them? I make no promises. Maybe. That's the best that I can do. Definitely maybe.

'The Hedge Knight' is a prequel to my epic fantasy series *A Song of Ice and Fire*, set amongst the Seven Kingdoms of Westeros about ninety years prior to *A Game of Thrones*. Since the epic itself is far from finished, it would never have occured to me to write a prequel had not Robert Silverberg phoned me to invite me to contribute to *Legends*, his gigantic new fantasy anthology. Big fantasy anthologies had been done before, of course, but Silverberg had put together an all-star roster of contributors for *Legends*, including Stephen King, Terry Pratchett, Ursula K. Le Guin, and most of the world's other leading fantasists. It was plain that this book was going to be huge, and I knew I had to be a part of it. I did not want to give away anything about the end of *A Song of Ice and Fire* or the fate of its principal characters, so a prequel seemed the way to go. (Several of the other *Legends* contributors took the same route, as it turned out.)

'The Hedge Knight' is high fantasy, nothing could be plainer. Or could it? Doesn't fantasy require, well . . . *magic*? I have dragons in 'The Hedge Knight,' yes indeed . . . on helmet crests and banners. Plus one stuffed with sawdust, dancing on its strings. Oh, and Dunk remembers old Ser Arlan talking about seeing a real live dragon once, perhaps that should suffice. If not, well . . . you can say 'The Hedge Knight' is more of a historical adventure than a true fantasy, except that all the history is imaginary. So what does that make it? Don't ask me, I just wrote it. I have since written a sequel, 'The Sworn Sword.' Look for it come Christmas, in Silverberg's *LEGENDS II*. More tales of Dunk and Egg will follow in the years to come, unless I'm run down by a bus or a better idea.

The last story in the book is 'Portraits of His Children,' a novelette for which I won the Nebula and lost the Hugo back in 1986. This is a story about writing, and the price we writers pay when we mine our dreams and fears and memories. Back when 'Portraits' was nominated for those awards, there was some spirited debate about whether or not it should actually be eligible. Is it a fantasy story, or just a tale of madness? Is it neither, is it both? You be the judge. So long as it's a good story, that's enough for me.

Stories of the human heart in conflict with itself transcend time, place, and setting. So long as love and honor and pity and pride and compassion and sacrifice are present, it matters not a whit whether that tall, lean stranger has a proton pistol or a six-shooter in his hand. Or a sword—

> Armor clinking, Lord Durston rode toward the crumbling old castle, hard by the waters of the Dire Lake, a drear land a thousand leagues beyond the realms of men. He reined up as he drew near . . . and at that point a tall, lean elven lord stepped out from the mouth of a cave, a glowing longsword in one moon-pale hand. 'Throw down your blade, Lord Durston,' the tall stranger lipped thinly. 'You know it not, but you shall ride no more through the land of faery.'

Fantasy? Science fiction? Horror?
I say it's a story, and I say the hell with it.

Under Siege

On the high ramparts of Vargön, Colonel Bengt Anttonen stood alone and watched phantasms race across the ice.

The world was snow and wind and bitter, burning cold. The winter sea had frozen hard around Helsinki, and in its icy grip it held the six island citadels of the great fortress called Sveaborg. The wind was a knife drawn from a sheath of ice. It cut through Anttonen's uniform, chafed at his cheeks, brought tears to his eyes and froze them as they trickled down his face. The wind howled around the towering gray granite walls, forced its way through doors and cracks and gun emplacements, insinuated itself everywhere. Out upon the frozen sea, it snapped and shrieked at the Russian artillery, and sent puffs of snow from the drifts running and swirling over the ice like strange white beasts, ghostly animals all asparkle, wearing first one shape and then another, changing constantly as they ran.

They were creatures as malleable as Anttonen's thoughts. He wondered what form they would take next and where they were running to so swiftly, these misty children of snow and wind. Perhaps they could be taught to attack the Russians. He smiled, savoring the fancy of the snow beasts unleashed upon the enemy. It was a strange, wild thought. Colonel Bengt Anttonen had never been an imaginative man before, but of late his mind had often been taken by such whimsies.

Anttonen turned his face into the wind again, welcoming the chill, the numbing cold. He wanted it to cool his fury, to cut into the heart of him and freeze the passions that seethed there. He wanted to be numb. The cold had turned even the turbulent sea into still and silent ice; now let it conquer the turbulence within Bengt Anttonen. He opened his mouth, exhaled a long plume of breath that rose from his reddened cheeks like steam, inhaled a draught of frigid air that went down like liquid oxygen.

But panic came in the wake of that thought. Again, it was happening again. What was liquid oxygen? Cold, he knew somehow; colder than the ice, colder than this wind. Liquid oxygen was bitter and white, and it steamed and flowed. He knew it, knew it as certainly as he knew his own name. But *how?*

Anttonen turned from the ramparts. He walked with long swift strides, his hand touching the hilt of his sword as if it could provide some protection against the demons that had invaded his mind. The other officers were right; he was going mad, surely. He had proved it this afternoon at the staff meeting.

The meeting had gone very badly, as they all had of late. As always, Anttonen had raised his voice against the others, hopelessly, stupidly. He was right, he *knew* that. Yet he knew also that he could not convince them, and that each word further undermined his status, further damaged his career.

Jägerhorn had brought it on once again. Colonel F. A. Jägerhorn was everything that Anttonen was not; dark and handsome, polished and politic, an aristocrat with an aristocrat's control. Jägerhorn had important connections, had influential relatives, had a charmed career. And, most importantly, Jägerhorn had the confidence of Vice-Admiral Carl Olof Cronstedt, commandant of Sveaborg.

At the meeting, Jägerhorn had had a sheaf of reports.

'The reports are wrong,' Anttonen had insisted. 'The Russians do not outnumber us. And they have barely forty guns, sir. Sveaborg mounts ten times that number.'

Cronstedt seemed shocked by Anttonen's tone, his certainty, his insistence. Jägerhorn simply smiled. 'Might I ask how you come by this intelligence, Colonel Anttonen?' he asked.

That was the question Bengt Anttonen could never answer. 'I know,' he said stubbornly.

Jägerhorn rattled the papers in his hand. 'My own intelligence comes from Lieutenant Klick, who is in Helsinki and has direct access to reliable reports of enemy plans, movements, and numbers.' He looked to Vice-Admiral Cronstedt. 'I submit, sir, that this information is a good deal more reliable than Colonel Anttonen's mysterious certainties. According to Klick, the Russians outnumber us already, and General Suchtelen will soon be receiving sufficient reinforcements to enable him to launch a major assault. Furthermore, they have a formidable amount of artillery on hand. Certainly more than the forty pieces that Colonel Anttonen would have us believe the extent of their armament.'

Cronstedt was nodding, agreeing. Even then Anttonen could not be silent. 'Sir,' he insisted, 'Klick's reports must be discounted. The man cannot be trusted. Either he is in the pay of the enemy or they are deluding him.'

Cronstedt frowned. 'That is a grave charge, Colonel.'

'Klick is a fool and a damned Anjala traitor!'

Jägerhorn bristled at that, and Cronstedt and a number of junior officers looked plainly aghast. 'Colonel,' the commandant said, 'it is well known that Colonel Jägerhorn has relatives in the Anjala League. Your comments are offensive. Our situation here is perilous enough without my officers fighting among themselves over petty political differences. You will offer an apology at once.'

Given no choice, Anttonen had tendered an awkward apology. Jägerhorn accepted with a patronizing nod.

Cronstedt went back to the papers. 'Very persuasive,' he said, 'and very alarming. It is as I have feared. We have come to a hard place.' Plainly his mind was made up. It was futile to argue further. It was at times like this that Bengt Anttonen most wondered what madness had possessed him. He would go to staff meetings determined to be circumspect and politic, and no sooner would he be seated than a strange arrogance would seize him. He argued long past the point of wisdom; he denied obvious facts, confirmed in written reports from reliable sources; he spoke out of turn and made enemies on every side.

'No, sir,' he said, 'I beg of you, disregard Klick's intelligence. Sveaborg is vital to the spring counteroffensive. We have nothing to fear if we can hold out until the ice melts. Once the sea lanes are open, Sweden will send help.'

Vice-Admiral Cronstedt's face was drawn and weary, an old man's face. 'How many times must we go over this? I grow tired of your argumentative attitude, and I am quite aware of Sveaborg's importance to the spring offensive. The facts are plain. Our defenses are flawed, and the ice makes our walls accessible from all sides. Sweden's armies are being routed—'

'We know that only from the newspapers the Russians allow us, sir,' Anttonen blurted. 'French and Russian papers. Such news is unreliable.'

Cronstedt's patience was exhausted. 'Quiet!' he said, slapping the table with an open palm. 'I have had enough of your intransigence, Colonel Anttonen. I respect your patriotic fervor, but not your judgment. In the future, when I require your opinion, I shall ask for it. Is that clear?'

'Yes, sir,' Anttonen had said.

Jägerhorn smiled. 'If I may proceed?'

The rebuke had been as smarting as the cold winter wind. It was no wonder Anttonen had felt driven to the cold solitude of the battlements afterwards.

By the time he returned to his quarters, Bengt Anttonen's mood was bleak and confused. Darkness was falling, he knew. Over the frozen sea, over Sveaborg, over Sweden and Finland. And over America, he thought. Yet the afterthought left him sick and dizzy. He sat heavily on his cot, cradling his head in his hands. America, America, what madness was that, what possible difference could the struggle between Sweden and Russia make to that infant nation so far away?

Rising, he lit a lamp, as if light would drive the troubling thoughts away, and splashed some stale water on his face from the basin atop the modest dresser. Behind the basin was the mirror he used for shaving; slightly warped and dulled by corrosion, but serviceable. As he dried his big, bony hands, he found himself staring at his own face, the features at once so familiar and so oddly, frighteningly strange. He had unruly graying hair, dark gray eyes, a narrow straight nose, slightly sunken cheeks, a square chin. He was too thin, almost gaunt. It was a stubborn, common, plain face. The face he had worn all his life. Long ago, Bengt Anttonen had grown resigned to the way he looked. Until recently, he scarcely gave his appearance any thought. Yet now he stared at himself, unblinking, and felt a disturbing fascination welling up inside him, a sense of satisfaction, a pleasure in the cast of his image that was alien and troubling.

Such vanity was sick, unmanly, another sign of madness. Anttonen wrenched his gaze from the mirror. He lay himself down with a will.

For long moments he could not sleep. Fancies and visions danced against his closed eyelids, sights as fantastic as the phantom animals fashioned by the wind: flags he did not recognize, walls of polished metal, great storms of fire, men and women as hideous as demons asleep in beds of burning liquid. And then, suddenly, the thoughts were gone, peeled off like a layer of burned skin. Bengt Anttonen sighed uneasily, and turned in his sleep . . .

*

. . . before the awareness is always the pain, and the pain comes first, the only reality in a still quiet empty world beyond sensation. For a second, an hour I do not know where I am and I am afraid. And then the knowledge comes to me; returning, I am returning, in the return is always pain, I do not want to return, but I must. I want the sweet clean purity of ice and snow, the bracing touch of the winter wind, the healthy lines of Bengt's face. But it fades, fades though I scream and clutch for it, crying, wailing. It fades, fades, and then is gone.

I sense motion, a stirring all around me as the immersion fluid ebbs away. My face is exposed first. I suck in air through my wide nostrils, spit the tubes out of my bleeding mouth. When the fluid falls below by ears, I hear a gurgling, a greedy sucking sound. The vampire machines feed on the juices of my womb, the black blood of my second life. The cold touch of air on my skin pains me. I try not to scream, manage to hold the noise down to a whimper.

Above, the top of my tank is coated by a thin ebony film that has clung to the polished metal. I can see my reflection. I'm a stirring sight, nostril hairs aquiver on my noseless face, my right cheek bulging with a swollen greenish tumor. Such a handsome devil. I smile, showing a triple row of rotten teeth, fresh new incisors pushing up among them like sharpened stakes in a field of yellow toadstools. I wait for release. The tank is too damned small, a coffin. I am buried alive, and the fear is a palpable weight upon me. They do not like me. What if they just leave me in here to suffocate and die? 'Out!' I whisper, but no one hears.

Finally the lid lifts and the orderlies are there. Rafael and Slim. Big strapping fellows, blurred white colossi with flags sewn above the pockets of their uniforms. I cannot focus on their faces. My eyes are not so good at the best of times, and especially bad just after a return. I know the dark one is Rafe, though, and it is he who reaches down and unhooks the IV tubes and the telemetry, while Slim gives me my injection. Ahhh. Good. The hurt fades. I force my hands to grasp the sides of the tank. The metal feels strange; the motion is clumsy, deliberate, my body slow to respond. 'What took you so long?' I ask.

'Emergency,' says Slim. 'Rollins.' He is a testy, laconic sort, and he doesn't like me. To learn more, I would have to ask question after question. I don't have the strength. I concentrate instead on pulling myself to a sitting position. The room is awash with a bright blue-white fluorescent light. My eyes water after so long in darkness. Maybe the orderlies think I'm crying with joy to be back. They're big but not too bright. The air has an astringent, sanitized smell and the hard coolness of air conditioning. Rafe lifts me up from the coffin, the fifth silvery casket in a row of six, each hooked up to the computer banks that loom around us. The other coffins are all empty now. I am the last vampire to rise this night, I think. Then I remember. Four of them are gone, have been gone for a long time. There is only Rollins and myself, and something has happened to Rollins.

They set me in my chair and Slim moves behind me, rolls me past the empty caskets and up the ramps to debriefing. 'Rollins,' I ask him.

'We lost him.'

I didn't like Rollins. He was even uglier than me, a wizened little homunculus with a swollen, oversized cranium and a distorted torso without arms or legs. He had real big eyes, lidless, so he could never close them.

Even asleep, he looked like he was staring at you. And he had no sense of humor. No goddamned sense of humor at all. When you're a geek, you got to have a sense of humor. But whatever his faults, Rollins was the only one left, besides me. Gone now. I feel no grief, only a numbness.

The debriefing room is cluttered but somehow impersonal. They wait for me on the other side of the table. The orderlies roll me up opposite them and depart. The table is a long Formica barrier between me and my superiors, maybe a *cordon sanitaire*. They cannot let me get too close, after all, I might be contagious. They are normals. I am ... what am I? When they conscripted me, I was classified as a HM$_3$. Human Mutation, third category. Or a hum-three, in the vernacular. The hum-ones are the nonviables, stillborns and infant deaths and living veggies. We got millions of 'em. The hum-twos are viable but useless, all the guys with extra toes and webbed hands and funny eyes. Got thousands of them. But us hum-threes are a fucking *elite*, so they tell us. That's when they draft us. Down here, inside the Graham Project bunker, we get new names. Old Charlie Graham himself used to call us his 'timeriders' before he croaked, but that's too romantic for Major Salazar. Salazar prefers the official government term: G. C., for Graham Chrononaut. The orderlies and grunts turned G. C. into 'geek,' of course, and we turned it right back on 'em, me and Nan and Creeper, when they were still with us. *They* had a terrific sense of humor, now. The killer geeks, we called ourselves. Six little killer geeks riding the timestream biting the heads off vast chickens of probability. Heigh-ho.

And then there was one.

Salazar is pushing papers around on the table. He looks sick. Under his dark complexion I can see an unhealthy greenish tinge, and the blood vessels in his nose have burst beneath the skin. None of us are in good shape down here, but Salazar looks worse than most. He's been gaining weight, and it looks bad on him. His uniforms are all too tight now, and there won't be any fresh ones. They've closed down the commissaries and the mills, and in a few years we'll all be wearing rags. I've told Salazar he ought to diet, but no one will listen to a geek, except when the subject is chickens. 'Well,' Salazar says to me, his voice snapping. A hell of a way to start a debriefing. Three years ago, when it began, he was full of starch and vinegar, very correct and military, but even the Maje has no time left for decorum now.

'What happened to Rollins?' I ask.

Doctor Veronica Jacobi is seated next to Salazar. She used to be chief headshrinker down here, but since Graham Crackers went and expired she's been heading up the whole scientific side of the show. 'Death trauma,' she says, professionally. 'Most likely, his host was killed in action.'

I nod. Old story. Sometimes the chickens bite back. 'He accomplish anything?'

'Not that we've noticed,' Salazar says glumly.

The answer I expected. Rollins had gotten rapport with some ignorant grunt of a footsoldier in the army of Charles XII. I had this droll mental picture of him marching the guy up to his loon of a teenaged king and trying to tell the boy to stay away from Poltava. Charles probably hanged him on the spot – though, come to think of it, it had to be something quicker, or else Rollins would have had time to disengage.

'Your report,' prompts Salazar.

'Right, Maje,' I say lazily. He hates to be called Maje, though not so much as he hated Sally, which was what Creeper used to call him. Us killer geeks are an insolent lot. 'It's no good,' I tell them. 'Cronstedt is going to meet with General Suchtelen and negotiate for surrender. Nothing Bengt says sways him one damned bit. I been pushing too hard. Bengt thinks he's going crazy. I'm afraid he may crack.'

'All timeriders take that risk,' Jacobi says. 'The longer you stay in rapport, the stronger your influence grows on the host, and the more likely it becomes that your presence will be felt. Few hosts can deal with that perception.' Ronnie has a nice voice, and she's always polite to me. Well-scrubbed and tall and calm and even friendly, and above all ineffably polite. I wonder if she'd be as polite if she knew that she'd figured prominently in my masturbation fantasies ever since we'd been down here? They only put five women into the Cracker Box, with thirty-two men and six geeks, and she's by far the most pleasant to contemplate.

Creeper liked to contemplate her, too. He even bugged her bedroom, to watch her in action. She never knew. Creeper had a talent for that stuff, and he'd rig up these tiny little audio-video units on his workbench and plant them everywhere. He said that if he couldn't live life, at least he was going to watch it. One night he invited me into his room, when Ronnie was entertaining big, red-haired Captain Halliburton, the head of the base security, and her fella in those early days. I watched, yeah; got to confess that I watched. But afterward I got angry. Told Creeper he had no right to spy on Ronnie, or on any of them. 'They make us spy on our hosts,' he said, 'right inside their fucking *heads*, you geek. Turnabout is fair play.' I told him it was different, but I got so mad I couldn't explain why.

It was the only fight Creeper and me ever had. In the long run, it didn't mean much. He went on watching, without me. They never caught the little sneak, but it didn't matter, one day he went timeriding and didn't come back. Big strong Captain Halliburton died too, caught too many rads on those security sweeps, I guess. As far as I know, Creeper's hookup is still in place; from time to time I've thought about going in and taking a peek, to see if Ronnie has herself a new lover. But I haven't. I really don't want to know. Leave me with my fantasies and my wet dreams; they're a lot better anyway.

Salazar's fat fingers drum upon the table. 'Give us a full report on your activities,' he says curtly.

I sigh and give them what they want, everything in boring detail. When

I'm done, I say, 'Jägerhorn is the key to the problem. He's got Cronstedt's ear. Anttonen don't.'

Salazar is frowning. 'If only you could establish rapport with Jägerhorn,' he grumbles. What a futile whiner. He knows that's impossible.

'You takes what you gets,' I tell him. 'If you're going to wish impossible wishes, why stop at Jägerhorn? Why not Cronstedt? Hell, why not the goddamned *Czar?*'

'He's right, Major,' Veronica says. 'We ought to be grateful that we've got a link with Anttonen. At least he's a colonel. That's better than we did in any of the other target periods.'

Salazar is still unhappy. He's a military historian by trade. He thought this would be easy when they transferred him out from West Point, or what was left of it. 'Anttonen is peripheral,' he declares. 'We must reach the key figures. Your chrononauts are giving me footnotes, bystanders, the wrong men in the wrong place at the wrong time. It is impossible.'

'You knew the job was dangerous when you took it,' I say. A killer geek quoting Superchicken; I'd get thrown out of the union if they knew. 'We don't get to pick and choose.'

The Maje scowls at me. I yawn. 'I'm tired of this,' I say. 'I want something to eat. Some ice cream. I want some rocky road ice cream. Seems funny, don't it? All that goddamned ice, and I come back wanting ice cream.' There is no ice cream, of course. There hasn't been any ice cream for half a generation, anywhere in the godforsaken mess they call a world. But Nan used to tell me about it. Nan was the oldest geek, the only one born before the big crash, and she had lots of stories about the way things used to be. I liked it best when she talked about ice cream. It was smooth and cold and sweet, she said. It melted on your tongue, and filled your mouth with liquid, delicious cold. Sometimes she would recite the flavors for us, as solemnly as Chaplain Todd reading his Bible: vanilla and strawberry and chocolate, fudge swirl and praline, rum raisin and heavenly hash, banana and orange sherbet and mint chocolate chip, pistachio and butterscotch and coffee and cinnamon and butter pecan. Creeper used to make up flavors to poke fun at her, but there was no getting to Nan. She just added his inventions to her list, and spoke fondly thereafter of anchovy almond and liver chip and radiation ripple, until I couldn't tell the real flavors from the made-up ones any more, and didn't really care.

Nan was the first we lost. Did they have ice cream in St Petersburg back in 1917? I hope they did. I hope she got a bowl or two before she died.

Major Salazar is still talking, I realize. He has been talking for some time, '. . . our last chance now,' he is saying. He begins to babble about Sveaborg, about the importance of what we are doing here, about the urgent need to *change* something somehow, to prevent the Soviet Union from ever coming into existence, and thus forestall the war that has laid the world to waste. I've heard it all before, I know it all by heart. The Maje has terminal verbal diarrhea, and I'm not so dumb as I look.

It was all Graham Cracker's idea, the last chance to win the war or maybe just save ourselves from the plagues and bombs and the poisoned winds. But the Maje was the historian, so he got to pick all the targets, when the computers had done their probability analysis. He had six geeks and he got six tries. 'Nexus points,' he called 'em. Critical points in history. Of course, some were better than others. Rollins got the Great Northern War, Nan got the Revolution, Creeper got to go all the way back to Ivan the Terrible, and I got Sveaborg. Impregnable, invincible Sveaborg. Gibraltar of the North.

'There is no reason for Sveaborg to surrender,' the Maje is saying. It is his own ice cream litany. History and tactics give him the sort of comfort that butter brickle gave to Nan. 'The garrison is seven thousand strong, vastly outnumbering the besieging Russians. The artillery inside the fortress is much superior. There is plenty of ammunition, plenty of food. If Sveaborg only holds out until the sea lanes are open, Sweden will launch its counteroffensive and the siege will be broken easily. The entire course of the war may change! You must make Cronstedt listen to reason.'

'If I could just lug back a history text and let him read what they say about him, I'm sure he'd jump through flaming hoops,' I say. I've had enough of this. 'I'm tired,' I announce. 'I want some food.' Suddenly, for no apparent reason, I feel like crying. 'I want something to eat, damn it, I don't want to talk anymore, you hear, I want *something to eat.*'

Salazar glares, but Veronica hears the stress in my voice, and she is up and moving around the table. 'Easy enough to arrange,' she says to me, and to the Maje, 'We've accomplished all we can for now. Let me get him some food.' Salazar grunts, but he dares not object. Veronica wheels me away, toward the commissary.

Over stale coffee and a plate of mystery meat and overcooked vegetables, she consoles me. She's not half bad at it; a pro, after all. Maybe, in the old days, she wouldn't have been considered especially striking – I've seen the old magazines, after all, even down here we have our old *Playboys,* our old video tapes, our old novels, our old record albums, our old funny books, nothing *new* of course, nothing recent, but lots and lots of the old junk. I ought to know, I practically mainline the stuff; when I'm not flailing around inside Bengt's cranium, I'm planted in front of my tube, running some old TV show or a movie, maybe reading a paperback at the same time, trying to imagine what it would be like to live back then, before they screwed up everything. So I know all about the old standards, and maybe it's true that Ronnie ain't up to, say, Bo or Marilyn or Brigitte or Garbo.

Still, she's nicer to look at than anybody else down in this damned septic tank. And the rest of us don't quite measure up either. Creeper wasn't no Groucho, no matter how hard he tried; me, I look just like Jimmy Cagney, but the big green tumor and all the extra yellow teeth and the want of a nose spoil the effect, just a little.

I push my fork away with the meal half-eaten. 'It has no taste. Back then, food had *taste*.'

Veronica laughs. 'You're lucky. You get to taste it. For the rest of us, this is all there is.'

'Lucky? Ha-ha. I know the difference, Ronnie. You don't. Can you miss something you never had?' I'm sick of talking about it, though; I'm sick of it all. 'You want to play chess?'

She smiles and gets up in search of our set. An hour later, she's won the first game and we're starting the second. There are about a dozen chess players down here in the Cracker Box; now that Graham and Creeper are gone, I can beat all of them except Ronnie. The funny thing is, back in 1808 I could probably be world champion. Chess has come a long way in the last two hundred years, and I've memorized openings that those old guys never even dreamed of.

'There's more to the game than book openings,' Veronica says, and I realize I've been talking aloud.

'I'd still win,' I insist. 'Hell, those guys have been dead for centuries, how much fight can they put up?'

She smiles, and moves a knight. 'Check,' she says.

I realize that I've lost again. 'Some day I've got to learn to play this game,' I say. 'Some world champion.'

Veronica begins to put the pieces back in the box. 'This Sveaborg business is a kind of chess game too,' she says conversationally, 'a chess game across time, us and the Swedes against the Russians and the Finnish nationalists. What move do you think we should make against Cronstedt?'

'Why did I know that the conversation was going to come back to that?' I say. 'Damned if I know. I suppose the Maje has an idea.'

She nods. Her face is serious now. Pale soft face, framed by dark hair. 'A desperate idea. These are desperate times.'

What would it be like if I did succeed, I wonder? If I changed something? What would happen to Veronica and the Maje and Rafe and Slim and all the rest of them? What would happen to *me*, lying there in my coffin full of darkness? There are theories, of course, but no one really knows. 'I'm a desperate man, ma'am,' I say to her, 'ready for any desperate measures. Being subtle sure hasn't done diddly-squat. Let's hear it. What do I gotta get Bengt to do now? Invent the machine gun? Defect to the Russkis? Expose his privates on the battlements? What?'

She tells me.

I'm dubious. 'Maybe it'll work,' I say. 'More likely, it'll get Bengt slung into the deepest goddamned dungeon that place has. They'll really think he's nuts. Jägerhorn might just shoot him outright.'

'No,' she says. 'In his own way, Jägerhorn is an idealist. A man of principle. I agree, it is a chancy move. But you don't win chess games without taking chances. Will you do it?'

She has such a nice smile; I think she likes me. I shrug. 'Might as well,' I say. 'Can't dance.'

*

'. . . shall be allowed to dispatch two couriers to the King, the one by the northern, the other by the southern road. They shall be furnished with passports and safeguards, and every possible facility shall be given them for accomplishing their journey. Done at the island of Lonan, 6 April, 1808.'

The droning voice of the officer reading the agreement stopped suddenly, and the staff meeting was deathly quiet. A few of the Swedish officers stirred uneasily in their seats, but no one spoke.

Vice-Admiral Cronstedt rose slowly. 'This is the agreement,' he said. 'In view of our perilous position, it is better than we could have hoped for. We have used a third of our powder already, our defenses are exposed to attack from all sides because of the ice, we are outnumbered and forced to support a large number of fugitives who rapidly consume our provisions. General Suchtelen might have demanded our immediate surrender. By the grace of God, he did not. Instead we have been allowed to retain three of Sveaborg's six islands, and will regain two of the others, should five Swedish ships-of-the-line arrive to aid us before the third of May. If Sweden fails us, we must surrender. Yet the fleet shall be restored to Sweden at the conclusion of the war, and this immediate truce will prevent any further loss of life.'

Cronstedt sat down. At his side, Colonel Jägerhorn came crisply to his feet. 'In the event the Swedish ships do not arrive on time, we must make plans for an orderly surrender of the garrison.' He launched into a discussion of the details.

Bengt Anttonen sat quietly. He had expected the news, had somehow known it was coming, but it was no less dismaying for all that. Cronstedt and Jägerhorn had negotiated a disaster. It was foolish. It was craven. It was hopelessly doomed. Immediate surrender of Wester-Svartö, Langorn, and Oster-Lilla-Svartö, the rest of the garrison to come later, capitulation deferred for a meaningless month. History would revile them. School children would curse their names. And he was helpless.

When the meeting at last ended, the others rose to depart. Anttonen rose with them, determined to be silent, to leave the room quietly for once, to let them sell Sveaborg for thirty pieces of silver if they would. But as he tried to turn, the compulsion seized him, and he went instead to where Cronstedt and Jägerhorn lingered. They both watched him approach. In their eyes, Anttonen thought he could see a weary resignation.

'You must not do this,' he said heavily.

'It is done,' Cronstedt replied. 'The subject is not open for further discussion, Colonel. You have been warned. Go about your duties.' He climbed to his feet, turned to go.

'The Russians are cheating you,' Anttonen blurted.

Cronstedt stopped and looked at him.

'Admiral, please, you must listen to me. This provision, this agreement that we will retain the fortress if five ships-of-the-line reach us by the third of May, it is a fraud. The ice will not have melted by the third of May. No ship will be able to reach us. The armistice agreement provides that the ships must have entered Sveaborg's harbor by noon on the third of May. General Suchtelen will use the time afforded by the truce to move his guns and gain control of the sea approaches. Any ship attempting to reach Sveaborg will come under heavy attack. And there is more. The messengers you are sending to the King, sir, they—' Cronstedt's face was ice and granite. He held up a hand. 'I have heard enough. Colonel Jägerhorn, arrest this madman.' He gathered up his papers, refusing to look Anttonen in the face, and strode angrily from the room.

'Colonel Anttonen, you are under arrest,' Jägerhorn said, with surprising gentleness in his voice. 'Don't resist, I warn you, that will only make it worse.'

Anttonen turned to face the other colonel. His heart was sick. 'You will not listen. None of you will listen. Do you know what you are doing?'

'I think I do,' Jägerhorn said.

Anttonen reached out and grabbed him by the front of his uniform. 'You do *not*. You think I don't know what you are, Jägerhorn? You're a nationalist, damn you. This is the great age of nationalism. You and your Anjala League, your damned Finnlander noblemen, you're all Finnish nationalists. You resent Sweden's domination. The Czar has promised you that Finland will be an autonomous state under his protection, so you have thrown off your loyalty to the Swedish crown.'

Colonel F. A. Jägerhorn blinked. A strange expression flickered across his face before he regained his composure. 'You cannot know that,' he said. 'No one knows the terms – I—'

Anttonen shook him bodily. 'History is going to laugh at you, Jägerhorn. Sweden will lose this war, because of you, because of Sveaborg's surrender, and you'll get your wish, Finland will become an autonomous state under the Czar. But it will be no freer than it is now, under Sweden. You'll swap your King like a secondhand chair at a flea market, for the butchers of the Great Wrath, and gain nothing by the transaction.'

'Like a . . . a market for fleas? What is that?'

Anttonen scowled. 'A flea market, a flea . . . I don't know,' he said. He released Jägerhorn, turned away. 'Dear God, I do know. It is a place where . . . where things are sold and traded. A fair. It has nothing to do with fleas, but it is full of strange machines, strange smells.' He ran his fingers through his hair, fighting not to scream. 'Jägerhorn, my head is full of demons. Dear God, I must confess. Voices, I hear voices day and night, even as the French girl, Joan, the warrior maid. I know things that will come to pass.' He looked into Jägerhorn's eyes, saw the fear there, and held his hands up, entreating now. 'It is no choice of mine, you must believe that. I pray for silence, for release, but the whispering continues, and these strange fits seize me. They are not of my doing, yet they must be sent for a reason, they must be true, or why would God torture me so? Have mercy, Jägerhorn. Have mercy on me, and listen!'

Colonel Jägerhorn looked past Anttonen, his eyes searching for help, but the two of them were quite alone. 'Yes,' he said. 'Voices, like the French girl. I did not understand.'

Anttonen shook his head. 'You hear, but you will not believe. You are a patriot, you dream you will be a hero. You will be no hero. The common folk of Finland do not share your dreams. They remember the Great Wrath. They know the Russians only as ancient enemies, and they hate. They will hate you as well. And Cronstedt, ah, poor Admiral Cronstedt. He will be reviled by every Finn, every Swede, for generations to come. He will live out his life in this new Grand Duchy of Finland, on a Russian stipend, and he will die a broken man on April 7, 1820, twelve years and one day after he met with Suchtelen on Lonan and gave Sveaborg to Russia. Later, years later, a man named Runeberg will write a series of poems about this war. Do you know what he will say of Cronstedt?'

'No,' Jägerhorn said. He smiled uneasily. 'Have your voices told you?'

'They have taught me the words by heart,' said Bengt Anttonen. He recited:

> Call him the arm we trusted in,
> that shrank in time of stress,
> call him Affliction, Scorn, and Sin,
> and Death and Bitterness,
> but mention not his former name,
> lest they should blush who bear the same.

'That is the glory you and Cronstedt are winning here, Jägerhorn,' Anttonen said bitterly. 'That is your place in history. Do you like it?'

Colonel Jägerhorn had been carefully edging around Anttonen; there was a clear path between him and the door. But now he hesitated. 'You are speaking madness,' he said. 'And yet – and yet – how could you have known of the Czar's promises? You would almost have me believe you. Voices? Like the French girl? The voice of God, you say?'

Anttonen sighed. 'God? I do not know. Voices, Jägerhorn, that is all I hear. Perhaps I am mad.'

Jägerhorn grimaced. 'They will revile us, you say? They will call us traitors and denounce us in poems?'

Anttonen said nothing. The madness had ebbed; he was filled with a helpless despair.

'No,' Jägerhorn insisted. 'It is too late. The agreement is signed. We have staked our honor on it. And Vice-Admiral Cronstedt, he is so uncertain. His family is here, and he fears for them. Suchtelen has played him masterfully and we have done our part. It cannot be undone. I do not believe this madness of yours, yet even if I believed, there is no hope for it, nothing to be done. The ships will not come in time. Sveaborg must yield, and the war must end with Sweden's defeat. How could it be otherwise? The Czar is allied with Bonaparte himself, he cannot be resisted!'

'The alliance will not last,' Anttonen said, with a rueful smile. 'The French will march on Moscow and it will destroy them as it destroyed Charles XII. The winter will be their Poltava. All of this will come too late for Finland, too late for Sveaborg.'

'It is too late even now,' Jägerhorn said. 'Nothing can be changed.'

For the first time, Bengt Anttonen felt the tiniest glimmer of hope. 'It is not too late.'

'What course do you urge upon us, then? Cronstedt has made his decision. Should we mutiny?'

'There will be a mutiny in Sveaborg, whether we take part or not. It will fail.'

'What then?'

Bengt Anttonen lifted his head, stared Jägerhorn in the eyes. 'The agreement stipulates that we may send two couriers to the King, to inform him of the terms, so the Swedish ships may be dispatched on time.'

'Yes. Cronstedt will choose our couriers tonight, and they will leave tomorrow, with papers and safe passage furnished by Suchtelen.'

'You have Cronstedt's ear. See that I am chosen as one of the couriers.'

'You?' Jägerhorn looked doubtful. 'What good will that serve?' He frowned. 'Perhaps this voice you hear is the voice of your own fear.

Perhaps you have been under siege too long, and it has broken you, and now you hope to run free.'

'I can prove my voices speak true,' Anttonen said.

'How?' snapped Jägerhorn.

'I will meet you tomorrow at dawn at Ehrensvard's tomb, and I will tell you the names of the couriers that Cronstedt has chosen. If I am right, you will convince him to send me in the place of one of those chosen. He will agree, gladly. He is anxious to be rid of me.'

Colonel Jägerhorn rubbed his jaw, considering. 'No one could know the choices but Cronstedt. It is a fair test.' He put out his hand. 'Done.'

They shook. Jägerhorn turned to go. But at the doorway he turned back. 'Colonel Anttonen,' he said, 'I have forgotten my duty. You are in my custody. Go to your own quarters and remain there, until the dawn.'

'Gladly,' said Anttonen. 'At dawn, you will see that I am right.'

'Perhaps,' said Jägerhorn, 'but for all our sakes, I shall hope very much that you are wrong.'

*

. . . and the machines suck away the liquid night that enfolds me, and I'm screaming, screaming so loudly that Slim draws back, a wary look on his face. I give him a broad geekish smile, rows on rows of yellow rotten teeth. 'Get me out of here, turkey,' I shout. The pain is a web around me, but this time it doesn't seem as bad, this time I can almost stand it, this time the pain is *for* something.

They give me my shot, and lift me into my chair, but this time I'm eager for the debriefing. I grab the wheels and give myself a push, breaking free of Rafe, rolling down the corridors like I used to do in the old days, when Creeper was around to race me. There's a bit of a problem with one ramp, and they catch me there, the strong silent guys in their ice cream suits (that's what Nan called 'em, anyhow), but I scream at them to leave me alone. They do. Surprises the hell out of me.

The Maje is a little startled when I come rolling into the room all by my lonesome. He starts to get up. 'Are you . . .'

'Sit down, Sally,' I say. 'It's good news. Bengt psyched out Jägerhorn good. I thought the kid was gonna wet his pants, believe me. I think we got it socked. I'm meeting Jägerhorn tomorrow at dawn to clinch the sale.' I'm grinning, listening to myself. Tomorrow, hey, I'm talking about 1808, but tomorrow is how it feels. 'Now here's the sixty-four thousand dollar question. I need to know the names of the two guys that Cronstedt is going to try and send to the Swedish king. Proof, y'know?

'Jägerhorn says he'll get me sent if I can convince him. So you look up those names for me, Maje, and once I say the magic words, the duck will come down and give us Sveaborg.'

'This is very obscure information,' Salazar complains. 'The couriers were detained for weeks, and did not even arrive in Stockholm until the day of the surrender. Their names may be lost to history.' What a whiner, I'm thinking; the man is never satisfied.

Ronnie speaks up for me, though. 'Major Salazar, those names had better not be lost to history, or to us. You were our military historian. It was your job to research each of the target periods *thoroughly*.' The way she's talking to him, you'd never guess he was the boss. 'The Graham Project has every priority. You have our computer files, our dossiers on the personnel of Sveaborg, and you have access to the war college at New West Point. Maybe you can even get through to someone in what remains of Sweden. I don't care how you do it, but it must be done. The entire project could rest on this piece of information. The entire world. Our past and our future. I shouldn't need to tell you that.' She turns to me. I applaud. She smiles. 'You've done well,' she says. 'Would you give us the details.'

'Sure,' I say. 'It was a piece of cake. With ice cream on top. What'd they used to call that?'

'A la mode.'

'Sveaborg a la mode,' I say, and I serve it up to them. I talk and talk. When I finally finish, even the Maje looks grudgingly pleased.

Pretty damn good for a geek, I think. 'OK,' I say when I'm done with the report. 'What's next? Bengt gets the courier job, right? And I get the message through somehow. Avoid Suchtelen, don't get detained, the Swedes send in the cavalry.'

'Cavalry?' Sally looks confused.

'It's a figure of speech,' I say, with unusual patience.

The Maje nods. 'No,' he says. 'The couriers – it's true that General Suchtelen lied, and held them up as an extra form of insurance. The ice might have melted, after all. The ships might have come through in time. But it was an unnecessary precaution. That year, the ice around Helsinki did not melt until well after the deadline date.' He gives me a solemn stare. He has never looked sicker, and the greenish tinge of his skin undermines the effect he's trying to achieve. 'We must make a bold stroke. You will be sent out as a courier, under the terms of the truce. You and the other courier will be brought before General Suchtelen to receive your safe conducts through Russian lines. That is the point at which you will strike. The affair is settled, and war in those days was an honorable affair. No one will expect treachery.'

'Treachery?' I say. I don't like the sound of what I'm hearing.

For a second, the Maje's smile looks almost genuine; he's finally lit on something that pleases him. 'Kill Suchtelen,' he says.

'Kill Suchtelen?' I repeat.

'Use Anttonen. Fill him with rage. Have him draw his weapon. Kill Suchtelen.'

I see. A new move in our crosstime chess game. The geek gambit.

'They'll kill Bengt,' I say.

'You can disengage,' Salazar says.

'Maybe they'll kill him fast,' I point out. 'Right there, on the spot, y'know.'

'You take that risk. Other men have given their lives for our nation. This is war.' The Maje frowns. 'Your success may doom us all. When you change the past, the present as it now exists may simply cease to exist, and us with it. But our nation will live, and millions we have lost will be restored to us. Healthier, happier versions of ourselves will enjoy the rich lives that were denied us. You yourself will be born whole, without sickness or deformity.'

'Or talent,' I say. 'In which case I won't be able to go back to do this, in which case the past stays unchanged.'

'The paradox does not apply. You have been briefed on this. The past and the present and future are not co-temporaneous. And it will be Anttonen who affects the change, not yourself. He is of that time.' The Maje is impatient. His thick, dark fingers drum on the tabletop. 'Are you a coward?'

'Fuck you and the horse you rode in on,' I tell him. 'You don't get it. I couldn't give a shit about me. I'm better off dead. But they'll kill *Bengt*.'

He frowns. 'What of it?'

Veronica has been listening intently. Now she leans across the table and touches my hand, gently. 'I understand. You identify with him, don't you?'

'He's a good man,' I say. Do I sound defensive? Very well, then; I *am* defensive. 'I feel bad enough that I'm driving him around the bend, I don't want to get him killed. I'm a freak, a geek, I've lived my whole life under siege and I'm going to die here, but Bengt has people who love him, a life ahead of him. Once he gets out of Sveaborg, there's a whole world out there.'

'He has been dead for almost two centuries,' Salazar says.

'I was inside his head this afternoon,' I snap.

'He will be a casualty of war,' the Maje says. 'In war, soldiers die. It is a fact of life, then as now.'

Something else is bothering me. 'Yeah, maybe, he's a soldier, I'll buy that. He knew the job was dangerous when he took it. But he cares about *honor*, Sally. A little thing we've forgotten. To die in battle sure, but you want me to make him a goddamned *assassin*, have him violate a flag of truce. He's an honorable man. They'll revile him.'

'The ends justify the means,' says Salazar bluntly. 'Kill Suchtelen, kill him under the flag of truce, yes. It will kill the truce as well. Suchtelen's second-in-command is far less wily, more prone to outbursts of temper, more eager for a spectacular victory. You will tell him that Cronstedt *ordered* you to cut down Suchtelen. He will shatter the truce, will launch a furious attack against the fortress, an attack that Sveaborg, impregnable as it is, will easily repulse. Russian casualties will be heavy, and Swedish determination will be fired by what they will see as Russian treachery. Jägerhorn, with proof before him that the Russian promises are meaningless, will change sides. Cronstedt, the hero of Ruotsinsalmi, will become the hero of Sveaborg as well. The fortress will hold. With the spring the Swedish fleet will land an army at Sveaborg, behind Russian lines, while a second Swedish army sweeps down from the north. The entire course of the war will change. When Napoleon marches on Moscow, a Swedish army will already hold St Petersburg. The Czar will be caught in Moscow, deposed, executed. Napoleon will install a puppet government, and when his retreat comes, it will be north, to link up with his Swedish allies at St Petersburg. The new Russian regime will not survive Bonaparte's fall, but the Czarist restoration will be as short-lived as the French restoration, and Russia will evolve toward a liberal parliamentary democracy. The Soviet Union will never come into being to war against the United States.' He emphasizes his final words by pounding his fist on the conference table.

'Sez you,' I say mildly.

Salazar gets red in the face. 'That is the computer projection,' he insists. He looks away from me, though. Just a quick little averting of the eyes, but I catch it. Funny. He can't look me in the eyes.

Veronica squeezes my hand. 'The projection may be off,' she admits. 'A little or a lot. But it is all we have. And this is our last chance. I understand your concern for Anttonen, really I do. It's only natural. You've been part of him for months now, living his life, sharing his thoughts and feelings. Your reservations do you credit. But now millions of lives are in the balance, against the life of this one man. This one, dead man. It's your decision. The most important decision in all of human history, perhaps, and it rests with you alone.' She smiles. 'Think about it carefully, at least.'

When she puts it like that, and holds my little hand all the while, I'm powerless to resist. Ah, Bengt. I look away from them, sigh. 'Break out the booze tonight,' I say wearily to Salazar, 'the last of that old prewar stuff you been saving.'

The Maje looks startled, discomfited; the jerk thought his little cache of prewar Glenlivet and Irish Mist and Remy Martin was a well-kept secret.

And so it was until Creeper planted one of his little bugs, heigh-ho. 'I do not think drunken revelry is in order,' Sally says. Defending his treasure. He's homely and mean-spirited, but nobody ever said he wasn't selfish.

'Shut up and come across,' I say. Tonight I ain't gonna be denied. I'm giving up Bengt, the Maje can give up some booze. 'I want to get shit-faced,' I tell them. 'It's time to drink to the goddamned dead and toast the living, past and present. It's in the rules, damn you. The geek always gets a bottle before he goes out to meet the chickens.'

*

Within the central courtyard of the Vargön citadel, Bengt Anttonen waited in the predawn chill. Behind him stood Ehrensvard's tomb, the final resting place of the man who had built Sveaborg, and now slept securely within the bosom of his creation, his bones safe behind her guns and her thick granite walls, guarded by all her daunting might. He had built her impregnable, and impregnable she stood, so none would come to disturb his rest. But now they wanted to give her away.

The wind was blowing. It came howling down out of a black empty sky, stirred the barren branches of the trees that stood in the empty courtyard, and cut through Anttonen's warmest coat. Or perhaps it was another sort of chill that lay upon him; the chill of fear. Dawn was almost at hand. Above, the stars were fading. And his head was empty, echoing, mocking. Light would soon break over the horizon, and with the light would come Colonel Jägerhorn, hard-faced, imperious, demanding, and Anttonen would have nothing to say to him.

He heard footsteps. Jägerhorn's boots rang on the stones. Anttonen turned to face him, watching him climb the few small steps up to Ehrensvard's memorial. They stood a foot apart, conspirators huddled against the cold and darkness. Jägerhorn gave him a curt, short nod. 'I have met with Cronstedt.'

Anttonen opened his mouth. His breath steamed in the frigid air. And just as he was about to succumb to the emptiness, about to admit that his voices had failed him, something whispered deep inside him. He spoke two names.

There was such a long silence that Anttonen once again began to fear. Was it madness after all, and not the voice of God? Had he been wrong? But then Jägerhorn looked down, frowning, and clapped his gloved hands together in a gesture that spoke of finality. 'God help us all,' he said, 'but I believe you.'

'I will be the courier?'

'I have already broached the subject with Vice-Admiral Cronstedt.' Jägerhorn said. 'I have reminded him of your years of service, your excellent record. You are a good soldier and a man of honor, damaged only by your own patriotism and the pressure of the siege. You are that sort of warrior who cannot bear inaction, who must always be doing something. You deserve more than arrest and disgrace, I have argued. As a courier, you will redeem yourself, I have told him I have no doubt of it. And by removing you from Sveaborg, we will remove also a source of tension and dissent around which mutiny might grow. The Vice-Admiral is well aware that a good many of the men are most unwilling to honor our pact with Suchtelen. He is convinced.' Jägerhorn smiled wanly. 'I am nothing if not convincing, Anttonen. I can marshal an argument as Bonaparte marshals his armies. So this victory is ours. You are named courier.'

'Good,' said Anttonen. Why did he feel so sick at heart? He should have been full of jubilation.

'What will you do?' Jägerhorn asked. 'For what purpose do we conspire?'

'I will not burden you with that knowledge,' Anttonen replied. It was knowledge he lacked himself. He must be the courier, he had known that since yesterday, but the why of it still eluded him, and the future was cold as the stone of Ehrensvard's tomb, as misty as Jägerhorn's breath. He was full of a strange foreboding, a sense of approaching doom.

'Very well,' said Jägerhorn. 'I pray that I have acted wisely in this.' He removed his glove, offered his hand. 'I will count on you, on your wisdom and your honor.'

'My honor,' Bengt repeated. Slowly, too slowly, he took off his own glove to shake the hand of the dead man standing there before him. Dead man? He was no dead man; he was live, warm flesh. But it was frigid there under those bare trees, and when Anttonen clasped Jägerhorn's hand, the other's skin felt cold to the touch.

'We have had our differences,' said Jägerhorn, 'but we are both Finns, after all, and patriots, and men of honor, and now too we are friends.'

'Friends,' Anttonen repeated. And in his head, louder than it had ever been before, so clear and strong it seemed almost as if someone had spoken behind him, came a whisper, sad somehow, and bitter. *C'mon, Chicken Little*, it said, *shake hands with your pal, the geek.*

*

Gather ye Four Roses while ye may, for time is still aflying, and this same geek what smiles today tomorrow may be dying. Heigh-ho, drunk again, second night inna row, chugging all the Maje's good booze, but what does it matter, he won't be needing it. After this next little timeride, he won't even exist, or that's what they tell me. In fact, he'll never have existed, which is a real weird thought. Old Major Sally Salazar, his big thick fingers, his greenish tinge, the endearing way he had of whining and bitching, he sure seemed real this afternoon at that last debriefing, but now it turns out there never was any such person. Never was a Creeper, never a Rafe or a Slim, Nan never ever told us about ice cream and reeled off the names of all those flavors, butter pecan and rum raisin are one with Nineveh and Tyre, heigh-ho. Never happened, nope, and I slug down another shot, drinking alone, in my room, in my cubicle, the savior at this last liquid supper, where the hell are all my fucking apostles? Ah, drinking, drinking, but not with me.

They ain't s'posed to know, nobody's s'posed to know but me and the Maje and Ronnie, but the word's out, yes it is, and out there in the corridors it's turned into a big wild party, boozing and singing and fighting, a little bit of screwing for those lucky enough to have a partner, of which number I am not one, alas. I want to go out and join in, hoist a few with the boys, but no, the Maje says no, too dangerous, one of the motley horde might decide that even this kind of has-been life is better than a never-was nonlife, and therefore off the geek, ruining everybody's plans for a good time. So here I sit on geek row, in my little room boozing alone, surrounded by five other little rooms, and down at the end of the corridor is a most surly guard, pissed off that he isn't out there getting a last taste, who's got to keep me in and the rest of them out.

I was sort of hoping Ronnie might come by, you know, to share a final drink and beat me in one last game of chess and maybe even play a little kissy-face, which is a ridiculous fantasy on the face of it, but somehow I don't wanna die a virgin, even though I'm not really going to die, since once the trick is done, I won't ever have lived at all. It's goddamned noble of me if you ask me and you got to 'cause there ain't nobody else around to ask. Another drink now but the bottle's almost empty, I'll have to ring the Maje and ask for another. Why won't Ronnie come by? I'll never be seeing her again, after tomorrow, tomorrow-tomorrow and two-hundred-years-ago-tomorrow. I could refuse to go, stay here and keep the happy lil' family alive, but I don't think she'd like that. She's a lot more sure than me. I asked her this afternoon if Sally's projections could tell us about the side effects. I mean, we're changing this war, and we're keeping Sveaborg and (we hope) losing the Czar and (we hope) losing the Soviet Union and (we sure as hell hope) maybe losing the big war and all, the bombs and the rads and the plagues and all that good stuff, even radiation ripple ice cream which was the Creeper's favorite flavor, but what if we lose other stuff? I mean, with Russia so changed and all, are we going to lose Alaska? Are we gonna lose vodka? Are we going to lose George Orwell? Are we going to lose Karl Marx? We tried to lose Karl Marx, actually, one of the other geeks, Blind Jeffey, he went back to take care of Karlie, but it didn't work out. Maybe vision was too damn much for him. So we got to keep Karl, although come to think of it, who cares about Karl Marx, are we gonna lose Groucho? No Groucho, no Groucho ever, I don't like that concept, last night I shot a geek in my pajamas and how he got in my pajamas I'll never know, but maybe, who the hell knows how us geeks get anyplace, all these damn dominoes falling every which way, knocking over other dominoes, dominoes was never my game, I'm a chess player, world chess champion in temporal exile, that's me, dominoes is a dumb damn game. What if it don't work, I asked Ronnie, what if we take out Russia, and, well, Hitler wins World War II so we wind up swapping missiles and germs and biotoxins with Nazi Germany? Or England? Or fucking Austria-Hungary, maybe, who can say? The superpower Austria-Hungary, what a thought, last night I shot a Hapsburg in my pajamas, the geeks put him there, heigh-ho.

Ronnie didn't make me no promises, kiddies. Best she could do was shrug and tell me this story about a horse. This guy was going to get his head cut off by some old-timey king, y'see, so he pipes up and tells the king that if he's given a year, he'll teach the king's horse to talk. The king likes this idea, for some reason, maybe he's a Mister Ed fan, I dunno, but he gives the guy a year. And afterwards, the guy's friends say, hey, what is this, you can't get no horse to talk. So the guy says, well, I got a year now, that's a long time, all kinds of things could happen. Maybe the king will die. Maybe I'll die. Maybe the horse will die. Or maybe the horse will talk.

I'm too damn drunk, I am I am, and my head's full of geeks and talking horses and falling dominoes and unrequited love, and all of a sudden I got to see her. I set down the bottle, oh so carefully, even though it's empty, don't want no broken glass on geek row, and I wheel myself out into the corridor, going slow, I'm not too coordinated right now. The guard is at the end of the hall, looking wistful. I know him a little bit. Security guy, big black fellow, name of Dex. 'Hey, Dex,' I say as I come wheeling up, 'screw this shit, let's us go party, I want to see lil' Ronnie.' He just looks at me, shakes his head. 'C'mon,' I say. I bat my baby-blues at him. Does he let me by? Does the Pope shit in the woods? Hell no, old Dex says, 'I got my orders, you stay right here.' All of a sudden I'm mad as hell, this ain't fair, I want to see Ronnie. I gather up all my strength and try to wheel right by him. No cigar; Dex turns, blocks my way, grabs the wheelchair and pushes. I go backwards fast, spin around when a wheel jams, flip over and out of the chair. It hurts. Goddamn it hurts. If I had a nose, I woulda bloodied it, I bet. 'You stay where you are, you fucking freak,' Dex tells me. I start to cry, damn him anyhow, and he watches me as I get my chair upright and pull myself into it. I sit there staring at him. He stands there staring at me. 'Please,' I say finally. He shakes his head. 'Go get her then,' I say. 'Tell her I want to see her.' Dex grins. 'She's busy,' he tells me. 'Her and Major Salazar. She don't want to see you.'

I stare at him some more. A real withering, intimidating stare. He doesn't wither or look intimidated. It can't be, can it? Her and the Maje? Her and old Sally Greenface? No way, he's not her type, she's got better taste than that, I know she has. Say it ain't so, Joe. I turn around, start back to my cubicle. Dex looks away. Heigh-ho, fooled him.

Creeper's room is the one beyond mine, the last one at the end of the hall. Everything's just like he left it. I turn on the set, play with the damn switches, trying to figure out how it works. My mind isn't at its sharpest right at this particular minute, it takes me a while, but finally I get it, and I jump from scene to scene down in the Cracker Box, savoring all these little vignettes of life in these United States as served up by Creeper's clever ghost. Each scene has its own individual charm. There's a gang bang going on in the commissary, right on top of one of the tables where Ronnie and I used to play chess. Two huge security men are fighting up in the airlock area; they've been at it a long time, their faces are so bloody I can't tell who the hell they are, but they keep at it, staggering at each other blindly, swinging huge awkward fists, grunting, while a few others stand around and egg them on. Slim and Rafe are sharing a joint, leaning up against my coffin. Slim thinks they ought to rip out all the wires, fuck up everything so I can't go timeriding. Rafe thinks it'd be easier to just bash my head in. Somehow I don't think he loves me no more. Maybe I'll cross him off my Christmas list. Fortunately for the geek, both of them are too stoned and screwed up to do anything at all. I watch a half-dozen other scenes, and finally, a little reluctantly, I go to Ronnie's room, where I watch her screwing Major Salazar.

Heigh-ho, as Creeper would say, what'd you expect, really?

I could not love thee, dear, so much, loved I not honor more. She walks in beauty like the night. But she's not so pretty, not really, back in 1808 there were lovelier women, and Bengt's just the man to land 'em too, although Jägerhorn probably does even better. My Veronica's just the queen bee of a corrupt poisoned hive, that's all. They're done now. They're talking. Or rather the Maje is talking, bless his soul, he's into his ice cream litany, he's just been making love to Ronnie and now he's lying there in bed talking about Sveaborg, damn him. ' . . . only a thirty percent chance that the massacre will take place,' he's saying, 'the fortress is very strong, formidably strong, but the Russians have the numbers, and if they do bring up sufficient reinforcements, Cronstedt's fears may prove to be substantial. But even that will work out. The assassination, well, the rules will be suspended, they'll slaughter everyone inside, but Sveaborg will become a sort of Swedish Alamo, and the branching paths ought to come

together again. Good probability. The end results will be the same.' Ronnie
isn't listening to him, though; there's a look on her face I've never seen,
drunken, hungry, scared, and now she's moving lower on him and doing
something I've only seen in my fantasies, and now I don't want to watch
anymore, no, oh no, no, oh no.

*

General Suchtelen had established his command post on the outskirts of
Helsinki, another clever ploy. When Sveaborg turned its cannon on him,
every third shot told upon the city the fortress was supposed to protect,
until Cronstedt finally ordered the firing stopped. Suchtelen took advantage of that concession as he had all the rest. His apartments were large and
comfortable; from his windows, across the white expanse of ice and snow,
the gray form of Sveaborg loomed large. Colonel Bengt Anttonen stared at
it morosely as he waited in the anteroom with Cronstedt's other courier
and the Russians who had escorted them to Suchtelen. Finally the inner
doors opened and the dark Russian captain emerged. 'The general will see
you now,' he said.

    General Suchtelen sat behind a wide wooden desk. An aide stood by his
right arm. A guard was posted at the door, and the captain entered with
the Swedish couriers. On the broad, bare expanse of the desk was an
inkwell, a blotter, and two signed safe conducts, the passes that would
take them through the Russian lines to Stockholm and the Swedish king,
one by the southern and the other by the northern route. Suchtelen said
something, in Russian; the aide provided a translation. Horses had been
provided, and fresh mounts would be available for them along the way,
orders had been given. Anttonen listened to the discussion with a
curiously empty feeling and a vague sense of disorientation. Suchtelen was
going to let them go. Why did that surprise him? Those were the terms of
the agreement, after all, those were the conditions of the truce. As the
translator droned on, Anttonen felt increasingly lost and listless. He had
conspired to get himself here, the voices had told him to, and now here he
was, and he did not know why, nor did he know what he was to do.

    They handed him one of the safe conducts, placed it in his outstretched
hand. Perhaps it was the touch of the paper; perhaps it was something
else. A sudden red rage filled him, an anger so fierce and blind and all-
consuming that for an instant the world seemed to flicker and vanish and
he was somewhere else, seeing naked bodies twining in a room whose
walls were made of pale green blocks. And then he was back, the rage still
hot within him, but cooling now, cooling quickly. They were staring at
him, all of them. With a sudden start, Anttonen realized that he had let
the safe conduct fall to the floor, that his hand had gone to the hilt of his

sword instead, and the blade was now half-drawn, the metal shining dully in the sunlight that streamed through Suchtelen's window. Had they acted more quickly, they might have stopped him, but he had caught them all by surprise. Suchtelen began to rise from his chair, moving as if in slow motion. Slow motion, Bengt wondered briefly, what was that? But he knew, he knew. The sword was all the way out now. He heard the captain shout something behind him, the aide began to go for his pistol, but Quick Draw McGraw he wasn't, Bengt had the drop on them all, heigh-ho. He grinned, spun the sword in his hand, and offered it, hilt first, to General Suchtelen.

'My sword, sir, and Colonel Jägerhorn's compliments,' Bengt Anttonen heard himself say with something approaching awe. 'The fortress is in your grasp. Colonel Jägerhorn suggests that you hold up our passage for a month. I concur. Detain us here, and you are certain of victory. Let us go, and who knows what chance misfortune might occur to bring the Swedish fleet? It is a long time until the third of May. In such a time, the king might die, or the horse might die, or you or I might die. Or the horse might talk.'

The translator put away his pistol and began to translate; the other courier began to protest, ineffectually. Bengt Anttonen found himself possessed of an eloquence that even his good friend might envy. He spoke on and on. He had one moment of strange weakness, when his stomach churned and his head swam, but somehow he knew it was nothing to be alarmed at, it was just the pills taking effect, it was just a monster dying far away in a metal coffin full of night, and then there were none, heigh-ho, one siege was ending and another would go on and on, and what did it matter to Bengt, the world was a big, crisp, cold, jeweled oyster. He thought this was the beginning of a beautiful friendship, and what the hell, maybe he'd save their asses after all, if he happened to feel like it, but he'd do it his way.

After a time, General Suchtelen, nodding, reached out and accepted the proffered sword.

*

Colonel Bengt Anttonen reached Stockholm on the third of May, in the Year of Our Lord Eighteen-Hundred-and-Eight, with a message for Gustavus IV Adolphus, King of Sweden. On the same date, Sveaborg, impregnable Sveaborg, Gibraltar of the North, surrendered to the inferior Russian forces.

At the conclusion of hostilities, Colonel Anttonen resigned his commission in the Swedish army and became an émigré, first to England, and later to America. He took up residence in New York City, where he married, fathered nine children, and became a well-known and influential journalist, widely respected for his canny ability to sense coming trends. When events proved him wrong, as happened infrequently, Anttonen was always surprised. He was a founder of the Republican Party, and his writings were instrumental in the election of John Charles Fremont to the Presidency in 1856.

In 1857, a year before his death, Anttonen played Paul Morphy in a New York chess tournament, and lost a celebrated game. Afterward, his only comment was, 'I could have beat him at dominoes,' a phrase that Morphy's biographers are fond of quoting.

The Skin Trade

Willie smelled the blood a block away from her apartment.

He hesitated and sniffed at the cool night air again. It was autumn, with the wind off the river and the smell of rain in the air, but the scent, *that* scent, was copper and spice and fire, unmistakable. He knew the smell of human blood.

A jogger bounced past, his orange sweats bright under the light of the full moon. Willie moved deeper into the shadows. What kind of fool ran at this hour of the night? *Asshole*, Willie thought, and the sentiment emerged in a low growl. The man looked around, startled. Willie crept back further into the foliage. After a long moment, the jogger continued up the bicycle path, moving a little faster now.

Taking a chance, Willie moved to the edge of the park, where he could stare down her street from the bushes. Two police cruisers were parked outside her building, lights flashing. What the hell had she gone and done?

When he heard the distant sirens and saw another set of lights approaching, flashing red and blue, Willie felt close to panic. The blood scent was heavy in the air and set his skull to pounding. It was too much. He turned and ran deep into the park, for once not caring who might see him, anxious only to get away. He ran south, swift and silent, until he was panting for breath, his tongue lolling out of his mouth. He wasn't in shape for this kind of shit. He yearned for the safety of his own apartment, for his La-Z-Boy and a good shot of Primatene Mist.

Down near the riverfront, he finally came to a stop, wheezing and trembling, half-drunk with blood and fear. He crouched near a bridge abutment, staring at the headlights of passing cars and listening to the sound of traffic to soothe his ragged nerves.

Finally, when he was feeling a little stronger, he ran down a squirrel. The blood was hot and rich in his mouth, and the flesh made him feel ever so much stronger, but afterwards he got a hairball from all the goddamned fur.

*

'Willie,' Randi Wade said suspiciously, 'if this is just some crazy scheme to get into my pants, it's not going to work.'

The small man studied his reflection in the antique oval mirror over her couch, tried out several faces until he found a wounded look he seemed to like, then turned back to let her see it. 'You'd think that? You'd think that of *me?* I come to you, I need your help, and what do I get, cheap sexual innuendo. You ought to know me better than that, Wade, I mean, Jesus, how long we been friends?'

'Nearly as long as you've been trying to get into my pants,' Randi said. 'Face it, Flambeaux, you're a horny little bastard.'

Willie deftly changed the subject. 'It's very amateur hour, you know, doing business out of your apartment.'

He sat in one of her red velvet wingback chairs. 'I mean, it's a nice place, don't get me wrong, I love this Victorian stuff, can't wait to see the bedroom, but isn't a private eye supposed to have a sleazy little office in the bad part of town? You know, frosted glass on the door, a bottle in the drawer, lots of dust on the filing cabinets . . . '

Randi smiled. 'You know what they charge for those sleazy little offices in the bad part of town? I've got a phone machine, I'm listed in the Yellow Pages . . . '

'AAA-Wade Investigations,' Willie said sourly. 'How do you expect people to find you? Wade, it should be under W, if God had meant everybody to be listed under A, he wouldn't have invented all those other letters.' He coughed. 'I'm coming down with something,' he complained, as if it were her fault. 'Are you going to help me, or what?'

'Not until you tell me what this is all about,' Randi said, but she'd already decided to do it. She liked Willie, and she owed him. He'd given her work when she needed it, with his friendship thrown into the bargain. Even his constant, futile attempts to jump her bones were somehow endearing, although she'd never admit it to Willie. 'You want to hear about my rates?'

'Rates?' Willie sounded pained. 'What about friendship? What about old times' sake? What about all the times I bought you lunch?'

'You never bought me lunch,' Randi said accusingly.

'Is it my fault you kept turning me down?'

'Taking a bucket of Popeye's extra spicy to an adult motel for a snack and a quickie does not constitute a lunch invitation in my book,' Randi said.

Willie had a long, morose face, with broad rubbery features capable of an astonishing variety of expressions. Right now he looked as though someone had just run over his puppy. 'It would not have been a quickie,' he said with vast wounded dignity. He coughed, and pushed himself back in the chair, looking oddly childlike against the red velvet cushions. 'Randi,' he said, his voice suddenly gone scared and weary, 'this is for real.'

She'd first met Willie Flambeaux when his collection agency had come after her for the unpaid bills left by her ex. She'd been out of work, broke, and desperate, and Willie had taken pity on her and given her work at the agency. As much as she'd hated hassling people for money, the job had been a godsend, and she'd stayed long enough to wipe out her debt. Willie's lopsided smile, endless propositions, and mordant intelligence had somehow kept her sane. They'd kept in touch, off and on, even after Randi had left the hounds of hell, as Willie liked to call the collection agency.

All that time, Randi had never heard him sound scared, not even when discoursing on the prospect of imminent death from one of his many grisly and undiagnosed maladies. She sat down on the couch. 'Then I'm listening,' she said. 'What's the problem?'

'You see this morning's *Courier?*' he asked. 'The woman that was murdered over on Parkway?'

'I glanced at it.' Randi said.

'She was a friend of mine.'

'Oh, Jesus.' Suddenly Randi felt guilty for giving him a hard time. 'Willie, I'm so sorry.'

'She was just a kid,' Willie said. 'Twenty-three. You would have liked her. Lots of spunk. Bright too. She'd been in a wheelchair since high school. The night of her senior prom, her date drank too much and got pissed when she wouldn't go all the way. On the way home he floored it and ran head-on into a semi. Really showed her. The boy was killed instantly. Joanie lived through it, but her spine was severed, she was paralyzed from the waist down. She never let it stop her. She went on to college and graduated with honors, had a good job.'

'You knew her through all this?'

Willie shook his head. 'Nah. Met her about a year ago. She'd been a little overenthusiastic with her credit cards, you know the tune. So I showed up on her doorstep one day, introduced her to Mr Scissors, one thing led to another and we got to be friends. Like you and me, kind of.' He looked up into her eyes. 'The body was mutilated. Who'd do something like that? Bad enough to kill her, but . . . ' Willie was beginning to wheeze. His asthma. He stopped, took a deep breath. 'And what the fuck does it mean? *Mutilated*, Jesus, what a nasty word, but mutilated *how?* I mean, are we talking Jack the Ripper here?'

'I don't know. Does it matter?'

'It matters to me.' He wet his lips. 'I phoned the cops today, tried to get more details. It was a draw. I wouldn't tell them my name and they wouldn't give me any information. I tried the funeral home too. A closed casket wake, then the body is going to be cremated. Sounds to me like something getting covered up.'

'Like what?' she said.

Willie sighed. 'You're going to think this is real weird, but what if . . .' He ran his fingers through his hair. He looked very agitated. 'What if Joanie was . . . well, savaged . . . ripped up, maybe even . . . well, partially eaten . . . you know, like by . . . some kind of animal.'

Willie was going on, but Randi was no longer listening.

A coldness settled over her. It was old and gray, full of fear, and suddenly she was twelve years old again, standing in the kitchen door listening to her mother make that sound, that terrible high thin wailing sound. The men were still trying to talk to her, to make her understand . . . *some kind of animal*, one of them said. Her mother didn't seem to hear or understand, but Randi did. She'd repeated the words aloud, and all the eyes had gone to her, and one of the cops had said, *Jesus, the kid*, and they'd all stared until her mother had finally gotten up and put her to bed. She began to weep uncontrollably as she tucked in the sheets . . . her mother, not Randi. Randi hadn't cried. Not then, not at the funeral, not ever in all the years since.

'Hey. Hey! Are you okay?' Willie was asking.

'I'm fine,' she said sharply.

'Jesus, don't scare me like that, I got problems of my own, you know? You looked like . . . hell, I don't know what you looked like, but I wouldn't want to meet it in a dark alley.'

Randi gave him a hard look. 'The paper said Joan Sorenson was murdered. An animal attack isn't murder.'

'Don't get legal on me, Wade. I don't know, I don't even know that an animal was involved, maybe I'm just nuts, paranoid, you name it. The paper left out the grisly details. The fucking paper left out a lot.' Willie was breathing rapidly, twisting around in his chair, his fingers drumming on the arm.

'Willie, I'll do whatever I can, but the police are going to go all out on something like this, I don't know how much I'll be able to add.'

'The police,' he said in a morose tone. 'I don't trust the police.' He shook his head. 'Randi, if the cops go through her things, my name will come up, you know, on her Rolodex and stuff.'

'So you're afraid you might be a suspect, is that it?'

'Hell, I don't know, maybe so.'

'You have an alibi?'

Willie looked very unhappy. 'No. Not really. I mean, not anything you could use in court. I was supposed to . . . to see her that night. Shit, I mean, she might have written my name on her fucking *calendar* for all I know. I just don't want them nosing around, you know?'

'Why not?'

He made a face. 'Even us turnip-squeezers have our dirty little secrets. Hell, they might find all those nude photos of you.' She didn't laugh. Willie shook his head. 'I mean, god, you'd think the cops would have better things to do than go around solving murders – I haven't gotten a parking ticket in over a year. Makes you wonder what the hell this town is coming to.' He had begun to wheeze again. 'Now I'm getting too worked up again, damn it. It's you, Wade. I'll bet you're wearing crotchless panties under those jeans, right?' Glaring at her accusingly, Willie pulled a bottle of Primatene Mist from his coat pocket, stuck the plastic snout in his mouth, and gave himself a blast, sucking it down greedily.

'You must be feeling better,' Randi said.

'When you said you'd do anything you could to help, did that include taking off all of your clothes?' Willie said hopefully.

'No,' Randi said firmly. 'But I'll take the case.'

*

River Street was not exactly a prestige address, but Willie liked it just fine. The rich folks up on the bluffs had 'river views' from the gables and widow's walks of their old Victorian houses, but Willie had the river itself flowing by just beneath his windows. He had the sound of it, night and day, the slap of water against the pilings, the foghorns when the mists grew thick, the shouts of pleasure-boaters on sunny afternoons. He had moonlight on the black water, and his very own rotting pier to sit on, any midnight when he had a taste for solitude. He had eleven rooms that used to be offices, a men's room (with urinal) *and* a ladies' room (with Tampax dispenser), hardwood floors, lovely old skylights, and if he ever got that loan, he was definitely going to put in a kitchen. He also had an abandoned brewery down on the ground floor, should he ever decide to make his own beer. The drafty red brick building had been built a hundred years ago, which was about how long the flats had been considered the bad part of town. These days what wasn't boarded up was industrial, so Willie didn't have many neighbors, and that was the best part of all.

Parking was no problem either. Willie had a monstrous old lime-green Cadillac, all chrome and fins, that he left by the foot of the pier, two feet from his door. It took him five minutes to undo all his locks. Willie believed in locks, especially on River Street. The brewery was dark and quiet. He locked and bolted the doors behind him and trudged upstairs to his living quarters.

He was more scared than he'd let on to Randi. He'd been upset enough last night, when he'd caught the scent of blood and figured that Joanie had done something really dumb, but when he'd gotten the morning paper and read that she'd been the victim, that she'd been tortured and killed and mutilated . . . *mutilated*, dear god, what the hell did that *mean*, had one of the others . . . no, he couldn't even think about that, it made him sick.

His living room had been the president's office back when the brewery was a going concern. It fronted on the river, and Willie thought it was nicely furnished, all things considered. None of it matched, but that was all right. He'd picked it up piece by piece over the years, the new stuff usually straight repossession deals, the antiques taken in lieu of cash on hopeless and long-overdue debts. Willie nearly always managed to get *something*, even on the accounts that everyone else had written off as a dead loss. If it was something he liked, he paid off the client out of his own pocket, ten or twenty cents on the dollar, and kept the furniture. He got some great bargains that way.

He had just started to boil some water on his hotplate when the phone began to ring.

Willie turned and stared at it, frowning. He was almost afraid to answer. It could be the police . . . but it could be Randi or some other friend, something totally innocent. Grimacing, he went over and picked it up 'Hello.'

'Good evening, William.' Willie felt as though someone was running a cold finger up his spine. Jonathon Harmon's voice was rich and mellow; it gave him the creeps. 'We've been trying to reach you.'

I'll bet you have, Willie thought, but what he said was, 'Yeah, well, I been out.'

'You've heard about the crippled girl, of course.'

'*Joan*,' Willie said sharply. 'Her name was Joan. Yeah, I heard. All I know is what I read in the paper.'

'I own the paper,' Jonathan reminded him. 'William, some of us are getting together at Blackstone to talk. Zoe and Amy are here right now, and I'm expecting Michael any moment. Steven drove down to pick up Lawrence. He can swing by for you as well, if you're free.'

'No,' Willie blurted. 'I may be cheap, but I'm never free.' His laugh was edged with panic.

'William, your life may be at stake.'

'Yeah, I'll bet, you son of a bitch. Is that a threat? Let me tell you, I wrote down everything I know, *everything*, and gave copies to a couple of friends of mine.' He hadn't, but come to think of it, it sounded like a good idea. 'If I wind up like Joanie, they'll make sure those letters get to the police, you hear me?'

He almost expected Jonathan to say, calmly, '*I own* the police,' but there was only silence and static on the line, then a sigh. 'I realize you're upset about Joan—'

'Shut the fuck up about Joanie,' Willie interrupted. 'You got no right to say jack shit about her; I know how you felt about her. You listen up good, Harmon, if it turns out that you or that twisted kid of yours had anything to do with what happened, I'm going to come up to Blackstone one night and kill you myself, see if I don't. She was a good kid, she ... she ...' Suddenly, for the first time since it had happened, his mind was full of her – her face, her laugh, the smell of her when she was hot and bothered, the graceful way her muscles moved when she ran beside him, the noises she made when their bodies joined together. They all came back to him, and Willie felt tears on his face. There was a tightness in his chest as if iron bands were closing around his lungs. Jonathan was saying something, but Willie slammed down the receiver without bothering to listen, then pulled the jack. His water was boiling merrily away on the hotplate. He fumbled in his pocket and gave himself a good belt of his inhaler, then stuck his head in the steam until he could breathe again. The tears dried up, but not the pain.

Afterwards he thought about the things he'd said, the threats he made, and he got so shaky that he went back downstairs to double-check all his locks.

*

Courier Square was far gone in decay. The big department stores had moved to suburban malls, the grandiose old movie palaces had been chopped up into multi-screens or given over to porno, once-fashionable storefronts now housed palm readers and adult bookstores. If Randi had really wanted a seedy little office in the bad part of town, she could find one on Courier Square. What little vitality the Square had left came from the newspaper.

The Courier Building was a legacy of another time, when downtown was still the heart of the city and the newspaper its soul. Old Douglas Harmon, who'd liked to tell anyone who'd listen that he was cut from the same cloth as Hearst and Pulitzer, had always viewed journalism as something akin to a religious vocation, and the 'gothic deco' edifice he built to house his newspaper looked like the result of some unfortunate mating between the Chrysler Building and some especially grotesque cathedral. Five decades of smog had blackened its granite facade and acid rain had eaten away at the wolf's head gargoyles that snarled down from its walls, but you could still set your watch by the monstrous old presses in the basement and a Harmon still looked down on the city from the publisher's office high atop the Iron Spire. It gave a certain sense of continuity to the square, and the city.

The black marble floors in the lobby were slick and wet when Randi came in out of the rain, wearing a Burberry raincoat a couple sizes too big for her, a souvenir of her final fight with her ex-husband. She'd paid for it, so she was damn well going to wear it. A security guard sat behind the big horseshoe-shaped reception desk, beneath a wall of clocks that once had given the time all over the world. Most were broken now, hands frozen into a chronological cacophony. The lobby was a gloomy place on a dark afternoon like this, full of drafts as cold as the guard's face. Randi took off her hat, shook out her hair, and gave him a nice smile. 'I'm here to see Barry Schumacher.'

'Editorial. Third floor.' The guard barely gave her a glance before he went back to the bondage magazine spread across his lap. Randi grimaced and walked past, heels clicking against the marble.

The elevator was an open grillework of black iron; it rattled and shook and took forever to deliver her to the city room on the third floor. She found Schumacher alone at his desk, smoking and staring out his window at the rain-slick streets. 'Look at that,' he said when Randi came up behind him. A streetwalker in a leather miniskirt was standing under the darkened marquee of the Castle. The rain had soaked her thin white blouse and plastered it to her breasts. 'She might as well be topless,' Barry said. 'Right in front of the Castle too. First theater in the state to show *Gone with the Wind*, you know that? All the big movies used to open there.' He grimaced, swung his chair around, ground out his cigarette. 'Hell of a thing,' he said.

'I cried when Bambi's mother died,' Randi said.

'In the Castle?'

She nodded. 'My father took me, but he didn't cry. I only saw him cry once, but that was later, much later, and it wasn't a movie that did it.'

'Frank was a good man,' Schumacher said dutifully. He was pushing retirement age, overweight and balding, but he still dressed impeccably, and Randi remembered a young dandy of a reporter who'd been quite a rake in his day. He'd been a regular in her father's Wednesday night poker game for years. He used to pretend that she was his girlfriend, that he was waiting for her to grow up so they could get married. It always made her giggle. But that had been a different Barry Schumacher; this one looked as if he hadn't laughed since Kennedy was president. 'So what can I do for you?' he asked.

'You can tell me everything that got left out of the story on that Parkway murder,' she said. She sat down across from him.

Barry hardly reacted. She hadn't seen him much since her father died;

each time she did, he seemed grayer and more exhausted, like a man who'd been bled dry of passion, laughter, anger, everything. 'What makes you think anything was left out?'

'My father was a cop, remember? I know how this city works. Sometimes the cops ask you to leave something out.'

'They ask,' Barry agreed. 'Them asking and us doing, that's two different things. Once in a while we'll omit a key piece of evidence, to help them weed out fake confessions. You know the routine.' He paused to light another cigarette.

'How about this time?'

Barry shrugged. 'Hell of a thing. Ugly. But we printed it, didn't we?'

'Your story said the victim was mutilated. What does that mean, exactly?'

'We got a dictionary over by the copyeditors' desk, you want to look it up.'

'I don't want to look it up,' Randi said, a little too sharply. Barry was being an asshole; she hadn't expected that. 'I know what the word means.'

'So you are saying we should have printed all the juicy details?' Barry leaned back, took a long drag on his cigarette. 'You know what Jack the Ripper did to his last victim? Among other things, he cut off her breasts. Sliced them up neat as you please, like he was carving white meat off a turkey, and piled the slices on top of each other, beside the bed. He was very tidy, put the nipples on top and everything.' He exhaled smoke. 'Is that the sort of detail you want? You know how many kids read the *Courier* every day?'

'I don't care what you print in the *Courier*,' Randi said. 'I just want to know the truth. Am I supposed to infer that Joan Sorenson's breasts were cut off?'

'I didn't say that,' Schumacher said.

'No. You didn't say much of anything. Was she killed by some kind of animal?'

That did draw a reaction. Schumacher looked up, his eyes met hers, and for a moment she saw a hint of the friend he had been in those tired eyes behind their wire-rim glasses. 'An animal?' he said softly. 'Is that what you think? This isn't about Joan Sorenson at all, is it? This is about your father.' Barry got up and came around his desk. He put his hands on her shoulders and looked into her eyes. 'Randi, honey, let go of it. I loved Frank too, but he's dead, he's been dead for . . . hell, it's almost twenty years now. The coroner said he got killed by some kind of rabid dog, and that's all there is to it.'

'There was no trace of rabies, you know that as well as I do. My father emptied his gun. What kind of rabid dog takes six shots from a police .38 and keeps on coming, huh?'

'Maybe he missed,' Barry said.

'*He didn't miss*!' Randi said sharply. She turned away from him. 'We couldn't even have an open casket, too much of the body had been . . .' Even now, it was hard to say without gagging, but she was a big girl now and she forced it out. '. . . eaten,' she finished softly. 'No animal was ever found.'

'Frank must have put some bullets in it, and after it killed him the damned thing crawled off somewhere and died,' Barry said. His voice was not unkind. He turned her around to face him again. 'Maybe that's how it was and maybe not. It was a hell of a thing, but it happened eighteen years ago, honey, and it's got nothing to do with Joan Sorenson.'

'Then tell me what happened to her,' Randi said.

'Look, I'm not supposed to . . .' He hesitated, and the tip of his tongue flicked nervously across his lips. 'It was a knife,' he said softly. 'She was killed with a knife, it's all in the police report, just some psycho with a sharp knife.' He sat down on the edge of his desk, and his voice took on its familiar cynicism again. 'Some weirdo seen too many of those damn sick holiday movies, you know the sort, *Halloween*, *Friday the 13th*, they got one for every holiday.'

'All right.' She could tell from his tone that she wouldn't be getting any more out of him. 'Thanks.'

He nodded, not looking at her. 'I don't know where these rumors come from. All we need, folks thinking there's some kind of wild animal running around, killing people.' He patted her shoulder. 'Don't be such a stranger, you hear? Come by for dinner some night. Adele is always asking about you.'

'Give her my best.' She paused at the door. 'Barry.' He looked up, forced a smile. 'When they found the body, there wasn't anything missing?'

He hesitated briefly. 'No,' he said.

Barry had always been the big loser at her father's poker games. He wasn't a bad player, she recalled her father saying, but his eyes gave him away when he tried to bluff . . . like they gave him away right now.

Barry Schumacher was lying.

*

The doorbell was broken, so he had to knock. No one answered, but Willie didn't buy that for a minute. 'I know you're there, Mrs Juddiker,' he shouted through the window. 'I could hear the TV a block off. You turned it off when you saw me coming up the walk. Gimme a break, okay?' He knocked again. 'Open up, I'm not going away.'

Inside, a child started to say something, and was quickly shushed. Willie sighed. He hated this. Why did they always put him through this? He took out a credit card, opened the door, and stepped into a darkened living room, half-expecting a scream. Instead he got shocked silence.

They were gaping at him, the woman and two kids. The shades had been pulled down and the curtains drawn. The woman wore a white terry cloth robe, and she looked even younger than she'd sounded on the phone. 'You can't just walk in here,' she said.

'I just did,' Willie said. When he shut the door, the room was awfully dark. It made him nervous. 'Mind if I put on a light?' She didn't say anything, so he did. The furniture was all ratty Salvation Army stuff, except for the gigantic big-screen projection TV in the far corner of the room. The oldest child, a little girl who looked about four, stood in front of it protectively. Willie smiled at her. She didn't smile back.

He turned back to her mother. She looked maybe twenty, maybe younger, dark, maybe ten pounds overweight but still pretty. She had a spray of brown freckles across the bridge of her nose. 'Get yourself a chain for the door and use it,' Willie told her. 'And don't try the no one's-home game on us hounds of hell, okay?' He sat down in a black vinyl recliner held together by electrical tape. 'I'd love a drink. Coke, juice, milk, anything, it's been one of those days.' No one moved, no one spoke. 'Aw, come on,' Willie said, 'cut it out. I'm not going to make you sell the kids for medical experiments, I just want to talk about the money you owe, okay?'

'You're going to take the television,' the mother said.

Willie glanced at the monstrosity and shuddered. 'It's a year old and it weighs a million pounds. How'm I going to move something like that, with my bad back? I've got asthma too.' He took the inhaler out of his pocket, showed it to her. 'You want to kill me, making me take the damned TV would do the trick.'

That seemed to help a little. 'Bobby, get him a can of soda,' the mother said. The boy ran off. She held the front of her robe closed as she sat down on the couch, and Willie could see that she wasn't wearing anything underneath. He wondered if she had freckles on her breasts too; sometimes they did. 'I told you on the phone, we don't have no money. My husband run off. He was out of work anyway, ever since the pack shut down.'

'I know,' Willie said. The pack was short for meatpacking plant, which is what everyone liked to call the south side slaughterhouse that had been the city's largest employer until it shut its doors two years back. Willie took a notepad out of his pocket, flipped a few pages. 'Okay, you bought the thing on time, made two payments, then moved, left no forwarding address. You still owe two thousand eight hundred-sixteen dollars. And thirty-one cents. We'll forget the interest and late charges.' Bobby returned and handed him a can of Diet Chocolate Ginger Beer. Willie repressed a shudder and cracked the pop-top.

'Go play in the backyard,' she said to the children. 'Us grown-ups have to talk.' She didn't sound very grown-up after they had left, however; Willie was half-afraid she was going to cry. He hated it when they cried. 'It was Ed bought the set,' she said, her voice trembling. 'It wasn't his fault. The card came in the mail.'

Willie knew that tune. A credit card comes in the mail, so the next day you run right out and buy the biggest item you can find. 'Look, I can see you got plenty of troubles. You tell me where to find Ed, and I'll get the money out of him.'

She laughed bitterly. 'You don't know Ed. He used to lug around those big sides of beef at the pack, you ought to see the arms on him. You go bother him and he'll just rip your face off and shove it up your asshole, mister.'

'What a lovely turn of phrase,' Willie said. 'I can't wait to make his acquaintance.'

'You won't tell him it was me that told you where to find him?' she asked nervously.

'Scout's honor,' Willie said. He raised his right hand in a gesture that he thought was vaguely Boy Scoutish, although the can of Diet Chocolate Ginger Beer spoiled the effect a little.

'Were you a Scout?' she asked.

'No,' he admitted. 'But there was one troop that used to beat me up regularly when I was young.'

That actually got a smile out of her. 'It's your funeral. He's living with some slut now, I don't know where. But weekends he tends bar down at Squeaky's.'

'I know the place.'

'It's not real work,' she added thoughtfully. 'He don't report it or nothing. That way he still gets the unemployment. You think he ever sends anything over for the kids? No way!'

'How much you figure he owes you?' Willie said.

'Plenty,' she said.

Willie got up. 'Look, none of my business, but it is my business, if you know what I mean. You want, after I've talked to Ed about this television, I'll see what I can collect for you. Strictly professional, I mean, I'll take a little cut off the top, give the rest to you. It may not be much, but a little bit is better than nothing, right?'

She stared at him, astonished. 'You'd do that?'

'Shit, yeah. Why not?' He took out his wallet, found a twenty. 'Here,' he said. 'An advance payment. Ed will pay me back.' She looked at him incredulously, but did not refuse the bill. Willie fumbled in the pocket of his coat. 'I want you to meet someone,' he said. He always carried a few cheap pairs of scissors in the pocket of his coat. He found one and put it in her hand. 'Here, this is Mr Scissors. From now on, he's your best friend.'

She looked at him like he'd gone insane.

'Introduce Mr Scissors to the next credit card that comes in the mail,' Willie told her, 'and then you won't have to deal with assholes like me.'

He was opening the door when she caught up to him. 'Hey, what did you say your name was?'

'Willie,' he told her.

'I'm Betsy.' She leaned forward to kiss him on the cheek, and the white robe opened just enough to give him a quick peek at her small breasts. Her chest was lightly freckled, her nipples wide and brown. She closed the robe tight again as she stepped back. 'You're no asshole, Willie,' she said as she closed the door.

He went down the walk feeling almost human, better than he'd felt since Joanie's death. His Caddy was waiting at the curb, the ragtop up to keep out the off-again on-again rain that had been following him around the city all morning. Willie got in and started her, then glanced into the rearview mirror just as the man in the back seat sat up.

The eyes in the mirror were pale blue. Sometimes, after the spring runoff was over and the river had settled back between its banks, you could find stagnant pools along the shore, backwaters cut off from the flow, foul-smelling places, still and cold, and you wondered how deep they were and whether there was anything living down there in that darkness. Those were the kind of eyes he had, deep-set in a dark, hollow-cheeked face and framed by brown hair that fell long and straight to his shoulders.

Willie swiveled around to face him. 'What the hell were you doing back there, catching forty winks? Hate to point this out, Steven, but this vehicle is actually one of the few things in the city that the Harmons do not own. Guess you got confused, huh? Or did you just mistake it for a bench in the park? Tell you what, no hard feelings, I'll drive you to the park, even buy you a newspaper to keep you warm while you finish your little nap.'

'Jonathan wants to see you,' Steven said, in that flat, chill tone of his. His voice, like his face, was still and dead.

'Yeah, good for him, but maybe I don't want to see Jonathan, you ever think of that?' He was dogmeat, Willie thought; he had to suppress the urge to bolt and run.

'Jonathan wants to see you,' Steven repeated, as if Willie hadn't understood. He reached forward. A hand closed on Willie's shoulder.

Steven had a woman's fingers, long and delicate, his skin pale and fine. But his palm was crisscrossed by burn scars that lay across the flesh like brands, and his fingertips were bloody and scabbed, the flesh red and raw. The fingers dug into Willie's shoulder with ferocious, inhuman strength. 'Drive,' he said, and Willie drove.

*

'I'm sorry,' the police receptionist said. 'The chief has a full calendar today. I can give you an appointment on Thursday.'

'I don't want to see him on Thursday. I want to see him now.' Randi hated the cophouse. It was always full of cops. As far as she was concerned, cops came in three flavors: those who saw an attractive woman they could hit on, those who saw a private investigator and resented her, and the old ones who saw Frank Wade's little girl and felt sorry for her. Types one and two annoyed her; the third kind really pissed her off.

The receptionist pressed her lips together, disapproving. 'As I've explained, that simply isn't possible.'

'Just tell him I'm here,' Randi said. 'He'll see me.'

'He's with someone at the moment, and I'm quite sure that he doesn't want to be interrupted.'

Randi had about had it. The day was pretty well shot, and she'd found out next to nothing. 'Why don't I just see for myself?' she said sweetly. She walked briskly around the desk, and pushed through the waist-high wooden gate.

'You can't go in there!' the receptionist squeaked in outrage, but by then Randi was opening the door. Police Chief Joseph Urquhart sat behind an old wooden desk cluttered with files, talking to the coroner. Both of them looked up when the door opened. Urquhart was a tall, powerful man in his early sixties. His hair had thinned considerably, but what remained of it was still red, though his eyebrows had gone completely gray. 'What the hell—' he started.

'Sorry to barge in, but Miss Congeniality wouldn't give me the time of day,' Randi said as the receptionist came rushing up behind her.

'Young lady, this is the police department, and I'm going to throw you out on your ass,' Urquhart said gruffly as he stood up and came around the desk, 'unless you come over here right now and give your Uncle Joe a big hug.'

Smiling, Randi crossed the bearskin rug, wrapped her arms around him, and laid her head against his chest as the chief tried to crush her. The door closed behind them, too loudly. Randi broke the embrace. 'I miss you,' she said.

'Sure you do,' he said, in a faintly chiding tone. 'That's why we see so much of you.'

Joe Urquhart had been her father's partner for years, back when they were both in uniform. They'd been tight, and the Urquharts had been like an aunt and uncle to her. His older daughter had babysat for her, and Randi had returned the favor for the younger girl. After her father's death, Joe had looked out for them, helped her mother through the funeral and all the legalities, made sure the pension fund got Randi through college. Still, it hadn't been the same, and the families drifted apart, even more so after her mother had finally passed away. These days Randi saw him only once or twice a year, and felt guilty about it. 'I'm sorry,' she said. 'You know I mean to keep in touch, but—'

'There's never enough time, is there?' he said.

The coroner cleared her throat. Sylvia Cooney was a local institution, a big brusque woman of indeterminate age, built like a cement mixer, her iron-gray hair tied in a tight bun at the back of her smooth, square face. She'd been coroner as long as Randi could remember. 'Maybe I should excuse myself,' she said.

Randi stopped her. 'I need to ask you about Joan Sorenson. When will autopsy results be available?'

Cooney's eyes went quickly to the chief, then back to Randi. 'Nothing I can tell you,' she said. She left the office and closed the door with a soft click behind her.

'That hasn't been released to the public yet,' Joe Urquhart said. He walked back behind his desk, gestured 'Sit down.'

Randi settled into a seat, let her gaze wander around the office. One wall was covered by commendations, certificates, and framed photographs. She saw her father there with Joe, both of them looking so achingly young, two grinning kids in uniform standing in front of their black-and-white. A moose head was mounted above the photographs, peering down at her with its glassy eyes. More trophies hung from the other walls. 'Do you still hunt?' she asked him.

'Not in years,' Urquhart said. 'No time. Your dad used to kid me about it all the time. Always said that if I ever killed anyone on duty, I'd want the head stuffed and mounted. Then one day it happened, and the joke wasn't so funny anymore.' He frowned. 'What's your interest in Joan Sorenson?'

'Professional,' Randi said.

'Little out of your line, isn't it?'

Randi shrugged. 'I don't pick my cases.'

'You're too good to waste your life snooping around motels,' Urquhart said. It was a sore point between them. 'It's not too late to join the force.'

'No,' Randi said. She didn't try to explain; she knew from past experience that there was no way to make him understand. 'I went out to the precinct house this morning to look at the report on Sorenson. It's missing from the file; no one knows where it is. I got the names of the cops who were at the scene, but none of them had time to talk to me. Now I'm told the autopsy results aren't being made public either. You mind telling me what's going on?'

Joe glanced out the windows behind him. The panes were wet with rain. 'This is a sensitive case,' he said. 'I don't want the media blowing this thing all out of proportion.'

'I'm not the media,' Randi said.

Urquhart swiveled back around. 'You're not a cop either. That's your choice. Randi, I don't want you involved in this, do you hear?'

'I'm involved whether you like it or not,' she said. She didn't give him time to argue. 'How did Joan Sorenson die? Was it an animal attack?'

'No,' he said. 'It was not. And that's the last question I'm going to answer.' He sighed. 'Randi,' he said, 'I know how hard you got hit by Frank's death. It was pretty rough on me too, remember? He phoned me for backup. I didn't get there in time. You think I'll ever forget that?' He shook his head. 'Put it behind you. Stop imagining things.'

'I'm not imagining anything,' Randi snapped. 'Most of the time I don't even think about it. This is different.'

'Have it your way,' Joe said. There was a small stack of files on the corner of the desk near Randi. Urquhart leaned forward and picked them up, tapped them against his blotter to straighten them. 'I wish I could help you.' He slid open a drawer, put the file folders away. Randi caught a glimpse of the name on the top folder: *Helander*. 'I'm sorry,' Joe was saying. He started to rise. 'Now, if you'll excuse—'

'Are you just rereading the Helander file for old times' sake, or is there some connection to Sorenson?' Randi asked.

Urquhart sat back down. 'Shit,' he said.

'Or maybe I just imagined that was the name on the file.'

Joe looked pained. 'We have reason to think the Helander boy might be back in the city.'

'Hardly a boy any more,' Randi said. 'Roy Helander was three years older than me. You're looking at him for Sorenson?'

'We have to, with his history. The state released him two months ago, it turns out. The shrinks said he was cured.' Urquhart made a face. 'Maybe, maybe not. Anyway, he's just a name. We're looking at a hundred names.'

'Where is he?'

'I wouldn't tell you if I knew. He's a bad piece of business, like the rest of his family. I don't like you getting mixed up with his sort, Randi. Your father wouldn't either.'

Randi stood up. 'My father's dead,' she said, 'and I'm a big girl now.'

*

Willie parked the car where 13th Street dead-ended, at the foot of the bluffs. Blackstone sat high above the river, surrounded by a ten-foot high wrought iron fence with a row of forbidding spikes along its top. You could drive to the gatehouse easily enough, but you had to go all the way down Central, past downtown, then around on Grandview and Harmon Drive, up and down the hills and all along the bluffs where aging steamboat Gothic mansions stood like so many dowagers staring out over the flats and river beyond, remembering better days. It was a long, tiresome drive.

Back before the automobile, it had been even longer and more tiresome. Faced with having to travel to Courier Square on a daily basis, Douglas Harmon made things easy for himself. He built a private cable car: a two-car funicular railway that crept up the gray stone face of the bluffs from the foot of 13th below to Blackstone above.

Internal combustion, limousines, chauffeurs, and paved roads had all conspired to wean the Harmons away from Douglas' folly, making the cable car something of a back door in more recent years, but that suited Willie well enough. Jonathan Harmon always made him feel like he ought to come in by the servant's entrance anyway.

Willie climbed out of the Caddy and stuck his hands in the sagging pockets of his raincoat. He looked up. The incline was precipitous, the rock wet and dark. Steven took his elbow roughly and propelled him forward. The cable car was wooden, badly in need of a whitewash, with bench space for six. Steven pulled the bell cord; the car jerked as they began to ascend. The second car came down to meet them, and they crossed halfway up the bluff. The car shook and Willie spotted rust on the rails. Even here at the gate of Blackstone, things were falling apart.

Near the top of the bluff, they passed through a gap in the wrought iron fence, and the New House came into view, gabled and turreted and covered with Victorian gingerbread. The Harmons had lived there for almost a century, but it was still the New House, and always would be. Behind the house the estate was densely forested, the narrow driveway winding through thick stands of old growth. Where the other founding families had long ago sold off or parceled out their lands to developers, the Harmons had held tight, and Blackstone remained intact, a piece of the forest primeval in the middle of the city.

Against the western sky, Willie glimpsed the broken silhouette of the tower, part of the Old House whose soot-dark stone walls gave Blackstone its name. The house was set well back among the trees, its lawns and courts overgrown, but even when you couldn't see it you knew it was there somehow. The tower was a jagged black presence outlined against the red-stained gray of the western horizon, crooked and forbidding. It had been Douglas Harmon, the journalist and builder of funicular railways, who had erected the New House and closed the Old, immense and gloomy even by Victorian standards; but neither Douglas, his son Thomas, nor his grandson Jonathan had ever found the will to tear it down. Local legend said the Old House was haunted. Willie could just about believe it. Blackstone, like its owner, gave him the creeps.

The cable car shuddered to a stop, and they climbed out onto a wooden deck, its paint weathered and peeling. A pair of wide French doors led into the New House. Jonathan Harmon was waiting for them, leaning on a walking stick, his gaunt figure outlined by the light that spilled through the door. 'Hello, William,' he said. Harmon was barely past sixty, Willie knew, but long snow-white hair and a body wracked by arthritis made him look much older. 'I'm so glad that you could join us,' he said.

'Yeah, well, I was in the neighborhood, just thought I'd drop by,' Willie said. 'Only thing is, I just remembered, I left the windows open in the brewery. I better run home and close them, or my dust bunnies are going to get soaked.'

'No,' said Jonathan Harmon. 'I don't think so.'

Willie felt the bands constricting across his chest. He wheezed, found his inhaler, and took two long hits. He figured he'd need it. 'Okay, you talked me into it, I'll stay,' he told Harmon, 'but I damn well better get a drink out of it. My mouth still tastes like Diet Chocolate Ginger Beer.'

'Steven, be a good boy and get our friend William a snifter of Remy Martin, if you'd be so kind. I'll join him. The chill is on my bones.' Steven, silent as ever, went inside to do as he was told. Willie made to follow, but Jonathan touched his arm lightly. 'A moment,' he said. He gestured. 'Look.'

Willie turned and looked. He wasn't quite so frightened anymore. If Jonathan wanted him dead, Steven would have tried already, and maybe succeeded. Steven was a dreadful mistake by his father's standards, but there was a freakish strength in those scarred hands. No, this was some other kind of deal.

They looked east over the city and the river. Dusk had begun to settle, and the streetlights were coming on down below, strings of luminescent pearls that spread out in all directions as far as the eye could see and leapt across the river on three great bridges. The clouds were gone to the east, and the horizon was a deep cobalt blue. The moon had begun to rise.

'There were no lights out there when the foundations of the Old House were dug,' Jonathan Harmon said. 'This was all wilderness. A wild river coursing through the forest primeval, and if you stood on high at dusk, it must have seemed as though the blackness went on forever. The water was pure, the air was clean, and the woods were thick with game . . . deer, beaver, bear . . . but no people, or at least no white men. John Harmon and his son James both wrote of seeing Indian camp-fires from the tower from time to time, but the tribes avoided this place, especially after John had begun to build the Old House.'

'Maybe the Indians weren't so dumb after all,' Willie said.

Jonathan glanced at Willie, and his mouth twitched. 'We built this city out of nothing,' he said. 'Blood and iron built this city, blood and iron nurtured it and fed its people. The old families knew the power of blood and iron, they knew how to make this city great. The Rochmonts hammered and shaped the metal in smithies and foundries and steel mills, the Anders family moved it on their flatboats and steamers and railroads, and your own people found it and pried it from the earth. You come from iron stock, William Flambeaux, but we Harmons were always blood. We had the stockyards and the slaughterhouse, but long before that, before this city or this nation existed, the Old House was a center of the skin trade. Trappers and hunters would come here every season with furs and skins and beaver pelts to sell the Harmons, and from here the skins would move downriver. On rafts, at first, and then on flatboats. Steam came later, much later.'

'Is there going to be a pop quiz on this?' Willie asked.

'We've fallen a long way,' he said, looking pointedly at Willie. 'We need to remember how we started. Black iron and red, red blood. You need to remember. Your grandfather had the Flambeaux blood, the old pure strain.'

Willie knew when he was being insulted. 'And my mother was a Pankowski,' he said, 'which makes me half-frog, half-Polack, and all mongrel. Not that I give a shit. I mean, it's terrific that my great-grandfather owned half the state, but the mines gave out around the turn of the century, the Depression took the rest, my father was a drunk, and I'm in collections, if that's okay with you.' He was feeling pissed off and rash by then. 'Did you have any particular reason for sending Steven to kidnap me, or was it just a yen to discuss the French and Indian War?'

Jonathan said, 'Come. We'll be more comfortable inside, the wind is cold.' The words were polite enough, but his tone had lost all faint trace of warmth. He led Willie inside, walking slowly, leaning heavily on the cane. 'You must forgive me,' he said. 'It's the damp. It aggravates the arthritis, inflames my old war wounds.' He looked back at Willie. 'You were unconscionably rude to hang up on me. Granted, we have our differences, but simple respect for my position—'

'I been having a lot of trouble with my phone lately,' Willie said. 'Ever since they deregulated, service has turned to shit.' Jonathan led him into a small sitting room. There was a fire burning in the hearth; the heat felt good after a long day tramping through the cold and the rain. The furnishings were antique, or maybe just old; Willie wasn't too clear on the difference.

Steven had preceded them. Two brandy snifters, half-full of amber liquid, sat on a low table. Steven squatted by the fire, his tall, lean body folded up like a jackknife. He looked up as they entered and stared at Willie a moment too long, as if he'd suddenly forgotten who he was or what he was doing there. Then his flat blue eyes went back to the fire, and he took no more notice of them or their conversation.

Willie looked around for the most comfortable chair and sat in it. The style reminded him of Randi Wade, but that just made him feel guilty. He picked up his cognac. Willie was couth enough to know that he was supposed to sip but cold and tired and pissed-off enough so that he didn't care. He emptied it in one long swallow, put it down on the floor, and relaxed back into the chair as the heat spread through his chest.

Jonathan, obviously in some pain, lowered himself carefully onto the edge of the couch, his hands closed round the head of his walking stick. Willie found himself staring. Jonathan noticed. 'A wolf's head,' he said. He moved his hands aside to give Willie a clear view. The firelight reflected off the rich yellow metal. The beast was snarling, snapping.

Its eyes were red. 'Garnets?' Willie guessed.

Jonathan smiled the way you might smile at a particularly doltish child. 'Rubies,' he said, 'set in 18-karat gold.' His hands, large and heavily veined, twisted by arthritis, closed round the stick again, hiding the wolf from sight.

'Stupid,' Willie said. 'There's guys in this city would kill you as soon as look at you for a stick like that.'

Jonathan's smile was humorless. 'I will not die on account of gold, William.' He glanced at the window. The moon was well above the horizon. 'A good hunter's moon,' he said. He looked back at Willie. 'Last night you all but accused me of complicity in the death of the crippled girl.' His voice was dangerously soft. 'Why would you say such a thing?'

'I can't imagine,' Willie said. He felt light-headed. The brandy had rushed right to his mouth. 'Maybe the fact that you can't remember her name had something to do with it. Or maybe it was because you always hated Joanie, right from the moment you heard about her. My pathetic little mongrel bitch, I believe that was what you called her. Isn't it funny the way that little turns of phrase stick in the mind? I don't know, maybe it was just me, but somehow I got this impression that you didn't exactly wish her well. I haven't even mentioned Steven yet.'

'Please don't,' Jonathan said icily. 'You've said quite enough. Look at me, William. Tell me what you see.'

'You,' said Willie. He wasn't in the mood for asshole games, but Jonathan Harmon did things at his own pace.

'An old man,' Jonathan corrected. 'Perhaps not so old in years alone, but old nonetheless. The arthritis grows worse every year, and there are days when the pain is so bad I can scarcely move. My family is all gone but for Steven, and Steven, let us be frank, is not all that I might have hoped for in a son.' He spoke in firm, crisp tones, but Steven did not even look up from the flames. 'I'm tired, William. It's true, I did not approve of your crippled girl, or even particularly of you. We live in a time of corruption and degeneracy, when the old truths of blood and iron have been forgotten. Nonetheless, however much I may have loathed your Joan Sorenson and what she represented, I had no taste of her blood. All I want is to live out my last years in peace.'

Willie stood up. 'Do me a favor and spare me the old sick man act. Yeah, I know all about your arthritis and your war wounds. I also know who you are and what you're capable of. Okay, you didn't kill Joanie. So who did? Him?' He jerked a thumb toward Steven.

'Steven was here with me.'

'Maybe he was and maybe he wasn't,' Willie said.

'Don't flatter yourself, Flambeaux, you're not important enough for me to lie to you. Even if your suspicion was correct, my son is not capable of such an act. Must I remind you that Steven is crippled as well, in his own way?'

Willie gave Steven a quick glance. 'I remember once when I was just a kid, my father had to come see you, and he brought me along. I used to love to ride your little cable car. Him and you went inside to talk, but it was a nice day, so you let me play outside. I found Steven in the woods, playing with some poor sick mutt that had gotten past your fence. He was holding it down with his foot, and pulling off its legs, one by one, just ripping them out with his bare hands like a normal kid might pull petals off a flower. When I walked up behind him, he had two off and was working on the third. There was blood all over his face. He couldn't have been more than eight.'

Jonathan Harmon sighed. 'My son is . . . disturbed. We both know that, so there is no sense in my denying it. He is also dysfunctional, as you know full well. And whatever residual strength remains is controlled by his medication. He has not had a truly violent episode in years. Have you, Steven?'

Steven Harmon looked back at them. The silence went on too long as he stared, unblinking, at Willie. 'No,' he finally said.

Jonathan nodded with satisfaction, as if something had been settled. 'So you see, William, you do us a great injustice. What you took for a threat was only an offer of protection. I was going to suggest that you move to one of our guest rooms for a time. I've made the same suggestion to Zoe and Amy.'

Willie laughed. 'I'll bet. Do I have to fuck Steven too or is that just for the girls?'

Jonathan flushed, but kept his temper. His futile efforts to marry off Steven to one of the Anders sisters was a sore spot. 'I regret to say they declined my offer. I hope you will not be so unwise. Blackstone has certain . . . protections . . . but I cannot vouch for your safety beyond these walls.'

'Safety?' Willie said. 'From what?'

'I do not know, but I can tell you this – in the dark of night, there are things that hunt the hunters.'

'Things that hunt the hunters,' Willie repeated. 'That's good, has a nice beat, but can you dance to it?' He'd had enough. He started for the door. 'Thanks but no thanks. I'll take my chances behind my own walls.' Steven made no move to stop him.

Jonathan Harmon leaned more heavily on his cane. 'I can tell you how she was really killed,' he said quietly.

Willie stopped and stared into the old man's eyes. Then he sat back down.

*

It was on the south side in a neighborhood that made the flats look classy, on an elbow of land between the river and that old canal that ran past the pack. Algae and raw sewage choked the canal and gave off a smell that drifted for blocks. The houses were single-story clapboard affairs, hardly more than shacks. Randi hadn't been down here since the pack had closed its doors. Every third house had a sign on the lawn, flapping forlornly in the wind, advertising a property for sale or for rent, and at least half of those were dark. Weeds grew waist-high around the weathered rural mailboxes, and they saw at least two burned-out lots.

Years had passed, and Randi didn't remember the number, but it was the last house on the left, she knew, next to a Sinclair station on the corner. The cabbie cruised until they found it. The gas station was boarded up; even the pumps were gone, but the house stood there much as she recalled. It had a For Rent sign on the lawn, but she saw a light moving around inside. A flashlight, maybe? It was gone before she could be sure.

The cabbie offered to wait. 'No,' she said. 'I don't know how long I'll be.' After he was gone, she stood on the barren lawn for a long time, staring at the front door, before she finally went up the walk.

She'd decided not to knock, but the door opened as she was reaching for the knob. 'Can I help you, miss?'

He loomed over her, a big man, thick-bodied but muscular. His face was unfamiliar, but he was no Helander. They'd been a short, wiry family, all with the same limp, dirty blond hair. This one had hair black as wrought iron, and shaggier than the department usually liked. Five o'clock shadow gave his jaw a distinct blue-black cast. His hands were large, with short blunt fingers. Everything about him said cop.

'I was looking for the people who used to live here.'

'The family moved away when the pack closed,' he told her. 'Why don't you come inside?' He opened the door wider. Randi saw bare floors, dust, and his partner, a beer-bellied black man standing by the door to the kitchen.

'I don't think so,' she said.

'I insist,' he replied. He showed her a gold badge pinned to the inside of his cheap gray suit.

'Does that mean I'm under arrest?'

He looked taken aback. 'No. Of course not. We'd just like to ask you a few questions.' He tried to sound friendlier. 'I'm Rogoff.'

'Homicide,' she said.

His eyes narrowed. 'How—?'

'You're in charge of the Sorenson investigation,' she said. She'd been given his name at the cophouse that morning. 'You must not have much of a case if you've got nothing better to do than hang around here waiting for Roy Helander to show.'

'We were just leaving. Thought maybe he'd get nostalgic, hole up at the old house, but there's no sign of it.' He looked at her hard and frowned. 'Mind telling me your name?'

'Why?' she asked. 'Is this a bust or a come-on?'

He smiled. 'I haven't decided yet.'

'I'm Randi Wade.' She showed him her license.

'Private detective,' he said, his tone carefully neutral. He handed the license back to her. 'You working?'

She nodded.

'Interesting. I don't suppose you'd care to tell me the name of your client.'

'No.'

'I could haul you into court, make you tell the judge. You can get that license lifted, you know. Obstructing an ongoing police investigation, withholding evidence.'

'Professional privilege,' she said.

Rogoff shook his head. 'PIs don't have privilege. Not in this state.'

'This one does,' Randi said. 'Attorney-client relationship. I've got a law degree too.' She smiled at him sweetly. 'Leave my client out of it. I know a few interesting things about Roy Helander I might be willing to share.'

Rogoff digested that. 'I'm listening.'

Randi shook her head. 'Not here. You know the automat on Courier Square?' He nodded. 'Eight o'clock,' she told him. 'Come alone. Bring a copy of the coroner's report on Sorenson.'

'Most girls want candy or flowers,' he said.

'The coroner's report,' she repeated firmly. 'They still keep the old case records downtown?'

'Yeah,' he said. 'Basement of the courthouse.'

'Good. You can stop by and do a little remedial reading on the way. It was eighteen years ago. Some kids had been turning up missing. One of them was Roy's little sister. There were others – Stanski, Jones, I forget all the names. A cop named Frank Wade was in charge of the investigation. A gold badge, like you. He died.'

'You saying there's a connection?'

'You're the cop. You decide.' She left him standing in the doorway and walked briskly down the block.

*

Steven didn't bother to see him down to the foot of the bluffs. Willie rode the little funicular railway alone, morose and lost in thought. His joints ached like nobody's business and his nose was running. Every time he got upset his body fell to pieces, and Jonathan Harmon had certainly upset him. That was probably better than killing him, which he'd half expected when he found Steven in his car, but still . . .

He was driving home along 13th Street when he saw the bar's neon sign on his right. Without thinking, he pulled over and parked. Maybe Harmon was right and maybe Harmon had his ass screwed on backwards, but in any case Willie still had to make a living. He locked up the Caddy and went inside.

It was a slow Tuesday night, and Squeaky's was empty. It was a workingman's tavern. Two pool tables, a shuffleboard machine in back, booths along one wall. Willie took a bar stool. The bartender was an old guy, hard and dry as a stick of wood. He looked mean. Willie considered ordering a banana daiquiri, just to see what the guy would say, but one look at that sour, twisted old face cured the impulse, and he asked for a boilermaker instead. 'Ed working tonight?' he asked when the bartender brought the drinks.

'Only works weekends,' the man said, 'but he comes in most nights, plays a little pool.'

'I'll wait,' Willie said. The shot made his eyes water. He chased it down with a gulp of beer. He saw a pay phone back by the men's room. When the bartender gave him his change, he walked back, put in a quarter, and dialed Randi. She wasn't home; he got her damned machine. Willie hated phone machines. They'd made life a hell of a lot more difficult for collection agents, that was for sure. He waited for the tone, left Randi an obscene message, and hung up.

The men's room had a condom dispenser mounted over the urinals. Willie read the instructions as he took a leak. The condoms were intended for prevention of disease only, of course, even though the one dispensed by the left-hand slot was a French tickler. Maybe he ought to install one of these at home, he thought. He zipped up, flushed, washed his hands.

When he walked back out into the taproom, two new customers stood over the pool table, chalking up cues. Willie looked at the bartender, who nodded. 'One of you Ed Juddiker?' Willie asked.

Ed wasn't the biggest – his buddy was as large and pale as Moby Dick – but he was big enough, with a real stupid-mean look on his face. 'Yeah?'

'We need to talk about some money you owe.' Willie offered him one of his cards.

Ed looked at the hand, but made no effort to take the card. He laughed. 'Get lost,' he said. He turned back to the pool table. Moby Dick racked up the balls and Ed broke.

That was all right, if that was the way he wanted to play it. Willie sat back on the bar stool and ordered another beer. He'd get his money one way or the other. Sooner or later Ed would have to leave, and then it would be his turn.

*

Willie still wasn't answering his phone. Randi hung up the pay phone and frowned. He didn't have an answering machine either, not Willie Flambeaux, that would be too sensible. She knew she shouldn't worry. The hounds of hell don't punch time clocks, as he'd told her more than once. He was probably out running down some deadbeat. She'd try again when she got home. If he still didn't answer, then she'd start to worry.

The automat was almost empty. Her heels made hollow clicks on the old linoleum as she walked back to her booth and sat down. Her coffee had gone cold. She looked idly out the window. The digital clock on the State National Bank said 8:13. Randi decided to give him ten more minutes.

The red vinyl of the booth was old and cracking, but she felt strangely comfortable here, sipping her cold coffee and staring off at the Iron Spire across the square. The automat had been her favorite restaurant when she was a little girl. Every year on her birthday she would demand a movie at the Castle and dinner at the automat, and every year her father would laugh and oblige. She loved to put the nickels in the coin slots and make the windows pop open, and fill her father's cup out of the old brass coffee machine with all its knobs and levers.

Sometimes you could see disembodied hands through the glass, sticking a sandwich or a piece of pie into one of the slots, like something from an old horror movie. You never saw any people working at the automat, just hands; the hands of people who hadn't paid their bills, her father once told her, teasing. That gave her the shivers, but somehow made her annual visits even more delicious, in a creepy kind of way. The truth, when she learned it, was much less interesting. Of course, that was true of most everything in life.

These days, the automat was always empty, which made Randi wonder how the floor could possibly stay so filthy, and you had to put quarters into the coin slots beside the little windows instead of nickels. But the banana cream pie was still the best she'd ever had, and the coffee that came out of those worn brass spigots was better than anything she'd ever brewed at home.

She was thinking of getting a fresh cup when the door opened and Rogoff finally came in out of the rain. He wore a heavy wool coat. His hair was wet. Randi looked out at the clock as he approached the booth. It said 8:17. 'You're late,' she said.

'I'm a slow reader,' he said. He excused himself and went to get some food. Randi watched him as he fed dollar bills into the change machine. He wasn't bad-looking if you liked the type, she decided, but the type was definitely cop.

Rogoff returned with a cup of coffee, the hot beef sandwich with mashed potatoes, gravy, and overcooked carrots, and a big slice of apple pie.

'The banana cream is better,' Randi told him as he slid in opposite her.

'I like apple,' he said, shaking out a paper napkin.

'Did you bring the coroner's report?'

'In my pocket.' He started cutting up the sandwich. He was very methodical, slicing the whole thing into small bite-sized portions before he took his first taste. 'I'm sorry about your father.'

'So was I. It was a long time ago. Can I see the report?'

'Maybe. Tell me something I don't already know about Roy Helander.'

Randi sat back. 'We were kids together. He was older, but he'd been left back a couple of times, till he wound up in my class. He was a bad kid from the wrong side of the tracks and I was a cop's daughter, so we didn't have much in common . . . until his little sister disappeared.'

'He was with her,' Rogoff said.

'Yes he was. No one disputed that, least of all Roy. He was fifteen, she was eight. They were walking the tracks. They went off together, and Roy came back alone. He had blood on his dungarees and all over his hands. His sister's blood.'

Rogoff nodded. 'All that's in the file. They found blood on the tracks too.'

'Three kids had already vanished. Jessie Helander made four. The way most people looked at it, Roy had always been a little strange. He was solitary, inarticulate, used to hook school and run off to some secret hideout he had in the woods. He liked to play with the younger kids instead of boys his own age. A degenerate from a bad family, a child molester who had actually raped and killed his own sister, that was what they said. They gave him all kinds of tests, decided he was deeply disturbed, and sent him away to some kiddy snakepit. He was still a juvenile, after all. Case closed, and the city breathed easier.'

'If you don't have any more than that, the coroner's report stays in my pocket,' Rogoff said.

'Roy said he didn't do it. He cried and screamed a lot, and his story wasn't coherent, but he stuck to it. He said he was walking along ten feet or so behind his sister, balancing on the rails and listening for a train when a monster came out of a drainage culvert and attacked her.'

'A monster,' Rogoff said.

'Some kind of big shaggy dog, that was what Roy said. He was describing a wolf. Everybody knew it.'

'There hasn't been a wolf in this part of the country for over a century.'

'He described how Jessie screamed as the thing began to rip her apart. He said he grabbed her leg, tried to pull her out of its jaws, which would explain why he had her blood all over him. The wolf turned and looked at him and growled. It had red eyes, burning red eyes, Roy said, and he was real scared, so he let go. By then Jessie was almost certainly dead. It gave him one last snarl and ran off, carrying the body in its jaws.' Randi paused, took a sip of coffee. 'That was his story. He told it over and over, to his mother, the police, the psychologists, the judge, everyone. No one ever believed him.'

'Not even you?'

'Not even me. We all whispered about Roy in school, about what he'd done to his sister and those other kids. We couldn't quite imagine it, but we knew it had to be horrible. The only thing was, my father never quite bought it.'

'Why not?'

She shrugged. 'Instincts, maybe. He was always talking about how a cop had to go with his instincts. It was his case, he'd spent more time with Roy than anyone else, and something about the way the boy told the story had affected him. But it was nothing that could be proved. The evidence was overwhelming. So Roy was locked up.' She watched his eyes as she told him. 'A month later, Eileen Stanski vanished. She was six.'

Rogoff paused with a forkful of the mashed potatoes, and studied her thoughtfully. 'Inconvenient,' he said.

'Dad wanted Roy released, but no one supported him. The official line was that the Stanski girl was unconnected to the others. Roy had done four, and some other child molester had done the fifth.'

'It's possible.'

'It's bullshit,' Randi said. 'Dad knew it and he said it. That didn't make him any friends in the department, but he didn't care. He could be a very stubborn man. You read the file on his death?'

Rogoff nodded. He looked uncomfortable.

'My father was savaged by an animal. A dog, the coroner said. If you want to believe that, go ahead.' This was the hard part. She'd picked at it like an old scab for years, and then she'd tried to forget it, but nothing ever made it easier. 'He got a phone call in the middle of the night, some kind of lead about the missing kids. Before he left he phoned Joe Urquhart to ask for backup.'

'Chief Urquhart?'

Randi nodded. 'He wasn't chief then. Joe had been his partner when he was still in uniform. He said Dad told him he had a hot tip, but not the details, not even the name of the caller.'

'Maybe he didn't know the name.'

'He knew. My father wasn't the kind of cop who goes off alone in the middle of the night on an anonymous tip. He drove down to the stockyards by himself. It was waiting for him there. Whatever it was took six rounds and kept coming. It tore out his throat, and after he was dead it ate him. What was left by the time Urquhart got there . . . Joe testified that when he first found the body he wasn't even sure it was human.'

She told the story in a cool, steady voice, but her stomach was churning. When she finished Rogoff was staring at her. He set down his fork and pushed his plate away. 'Suddenly I'm not very hungry anymore.'

Randi's smile was humorless. 'I love our local press. There was a case a few years ago when a woman was kidnapped by a gang, held for two weeks. She was beaten, tortured, sodomized, raped hundreds of times. When the story broke, the paper said she'd been quote *assaulted* unquote. It said my father's body had been mutilated. It said the same thing about Joan Sorenson. I've been told her body was intact.' She leaned forward, looked hard into his dark brown eyes. 'That's a lie.'

'Yes,' he admitted. He took a sheet of paper from his breast pocket, unfolded it, passed it across to her. 'But it's not the way you think.'

Randi snatched the coroner's report from his hand, and scanned quickly down the page. The words blurred, refused to register. It wasn't adding up the way it was supposed to.

Cause of death: exsanguination.

Somewhere far away, Rogoff was talking. 'It's a security building, her apartment's on the fourteenth floor. No balconies, no fire escapes, and the doorman didn't see a thing. The door was locked. It was a cheap spring lock, easy to jimmy, but there was no sign of forced entry.'

The instrument of death was a blade at least twelve inches long, extremely sharp, slender and flexible, perhaps a surgical instrument.

'Her clothing was all over the apartment, just ripped to hell, in tatters. In her condition, you wouldn't think she'd put up much of a struggle, but it looks like she did. None of the neighbors heard anything, of course. The killer chained her to her bed, naked, and went to work. He worked fast, knew what he was doing, but it still must have taken her a long time to die. The bed was soaked with her blood, through the sheets and mattress, right down to the box spring.'

Randi looked back up at him, and the coroner's report slid from her fingers onto the Formica table. Rogoff reached over and took her hand.

'Joan Sorenson wasn't devoured by any animal, Miss Wade. She was flayed alive, and left to bleed to death. And the part of her that's missing is her skin.'

*

It was a quarter past midnight when Willie got home. He parked the Caddy by the pier. Ed Juddiker's wallet was on the seat beside him. Willie opened it, took out the money, counted. Seventy-nine bucks. Not much, but it was a start. He'd give half to Betsy this first time, credit the rest to Ed's account. Willie pocketed the money and locked the empty wallet in the glovebox. Ed might need the driver's license. He'd bring it by Squeaky's over the weekend, when Ed was on, and talk to him about a payment schedule.

Willie locked up the car and trudged wearily across the rain-slick cobbles to his front door. The sky above the river was dark and starless. The moon was up by now, he knew, hidden somewhere behind those black cotton clouds. He fumbled for his keys, buried down under his inhaler, his pillbox, a half-dozen pairs of scissors, a handkerchief, and the miscellaneous other junk that made his coat pocket sag. After a long minute, he tried his pants pocket, found them, and started in on his locks. He slid the first key into his double deadbolt.

The door opened slowly, silently.

The pale yellow light from a streetlamp filtered through the brewery's high, dusty windows, patterning the floor with faint squares and twisted lines. The hulks of rusting machines crouched in the dimness like great dark beasts. Willie stood in the doorway, keys in hand, his heart pounding like a triphammer. He put the keys in his pocket, found his Primatene, took a hit. The hiss of the inhaler seemed obscenely loud in the stillness.

He thought of Joanie, of what happened to her.

He could run, he thought. The Cadillac was only a few feet behind him, just a few steps; whatever was waiting in there couldn't possibly be fast enough to get him before he reached the car. Yeah, hit the road, drive all night, he had enough gas to make Chicago, it wouldn't follow him there. Willie took the first step back, then stopped, and giggled nervously. He had a sudden picture of himself sitting behind the wheel of his big lime-green chromeboat, grinding the ignition, grinding and grinding and flooding the engine as something dark and terrible emerged from inside the brewery and crossed the cobblestones behind him. That was silly; it was only in bad horror movies that the ignition didn't turn over, wasn't it? Wasn't it?

Maybe he had just forgotten to lock up when he'd left for work that morning. He'd had a lot on his mind, a full day's work ahead of him and a night of bad dreams behind; maybe he'd just closed the fucking door behind him and forgotten about his locks.

He never forgot about his locks.

But maybe he had, just this once.

Willie thought about changing. Then he remembered Joanie, and put the thought aside. He stood on one leg, pulled off his shoe. Then the other. Water soaked through his socks. He edged forward, took a deep breath, moved into the darkened brewery as silently as he could, pulling the door shut behind him. Nothing moved. Willie reached down into his pocket, pulled out Mr Scissors. It wasn't much, but it was better than bare hands. Hugging the thick shadows along the wall, he crossed the room and began to creep upstairs on stockinged feet.

The streetlight shone through the window at the end of the hall. Willie paused on the steps when his head came up to the level of the second-story landing. He could look up and down the hallway. All the office doors were shut. No light leaking underneath or through the frosted-glass transoms. Whatever waited for him waited in darkness.

He could feel his chest constricting again. In another moment he'd need his inhaler. Suddenly he just wanted to get it over with. He climbed the final steps and crossed the hall in two long strides, threw open the door to his living room, and slammed on the lights.

Randi Wade was sitting in his beanbag chair. She looked up blinking as he hit the lights. 'You startled me,' she said.

'I startled *you!*' Willie crossed the room and collapsed into his La-Z-Boy. The scissors fell from his sweaty palm and bounced on the hardwood floor. 'Jesus H. Christ on a crutch, you almost made me lose control of my personal hygiene. What the hell are you doing here? Did I forget to lock the door?'

Randi smiled. 'You locked the door and you locked the door and then you locked the door some more. You're world class when it comes to locking doors, Flambeaux. It took me twenty minutes to get in.'

Willie massaged his throbbing temples. 'Yeah, well, with all the women who want this body, I got to have some protection, don't I?' He noticed his wet socks, pulled one off, grimaced. 'Look at this,' he said. 'My shoes are out in the street getting rained on, and my feet are soaking. If I get pneumonia, you get the doctor bills, Wade. You could have waited.'

'It was raining,' she pointed out. 'You wouldn't have wanted me to wait in the rain, Willie. It would have pissed me off, and I'm in a foul mood already.'

Something in her voice made Willie stop rubbing his toes to look up at her. The rain had plastered loose strands of light brown hair across her forehead, and her eyes were grim. 'You look like a mess,' he admitted.

'I tried to make myself presentable, but the mirror in your ladies' room is missing.'

'It broke. There's one in the men's room.'

'I'm not that kind of a girl,' Randi said. Her voice was hard and flat. 'Willie, your friend Joan wasn't killed by an animal. She was flayed. The killer took her skin.'

'I know,' Willie said, without thinking.

Her eyes narrowed. They were gray-green, large and pretty, but right now they looked as cold as marbles. 'You *know?*' she echoed. Her voice had gone very soft, almost to a whisper, and Willie knew he was in trouble. 'You give me some bullshit story and send me running all around town, and you *know?* Do you know what happened to my father too, is that it? It was just your clever little way of getting my attention?'

Willie gaped at her. His second sock was in his hand. He let it drop to the floor. 'Hey, Randi, gimme a break, okay? It wasn't like that at all. I just found out a few hours ago, honest. How could I know? I wasn't there, it wasn't in the paper.' He was feeling confused and guilty. 'What the hell am I supposed to know about your father? I don't know jack shit about your father. All the time you worked for me, you mentioned your family maybe twice.'

Her eyes searched his face for signs of deception. Willie tried to give his warmest, most trustworthy smile. Randi grimaced. 'Stop it,' she said wearily. 'You look like a used car salesman. All right, you didn't know about my father. I'm sorry. I'm a little wrought up right now, and I thought . . .' She paused thoughtfully. 'Who told you about Sorenson?'

Willie hesitated. 'I can't tell you,' he said. 'I wish I could, I really do. I can't. You wouldn't believe me anyway.' Randi looked very unhappy. Willie kept talking. 'Did you find out whether I'm a suspect? The police haven't called.'

'They've probably been calling all day. By now they may have an APB out on you. If you won't get a machine, you ought to try coming home occasionally.' She frowned. 'I talked to Rogoff from Homicide.' Willie's heart stopped, but she saw the look on his face and held up a hand. 'No, your name wasn't mentioned. By either of us. They'll be calling everyone who knew her, probably, but it's just routine questioning. I don't think they'll be singling you out.'

'Good,' Willie said. 'Well, look, I owe you one, but there's no reason for you to go on with this. I know it's not paying the rent, so—'

'So what?' Randi was looking at him suspiciously. 'Are you trying to get rid of me now? After you got me involved in the first place?' She frowned. 'Are you holding out on me?'

'I think you've got that reversed,' Willie said lightly. Maybe he could joke his way out of it. 'You're the one who gets bent out of shape whenever I offer to help you shop for lingerie.'

'Cut the shit,' Randi said sharply. She was not amused in the least, he could see that. 'We're talking about the torture and murder of a girl who was supposed to be a friend of yours. Or has that slipped your mind somehow?'

'No,' he said, abashed. Willie was very uncomfortable. He got up and crossed the room, plugged in the hotplate. 'Hey, listen, you want a cup of tea? I got Earl Grey, Red Zinger, Morning Thunder—'

'The police think they have a suspect,' Randi said.

Willie turned to look at her. 'Who?'

'Roy Helander,' Randi said.

'Oh, boy,' Willie said. He'd been a PFC in Hamburg when the Helander thing went down, but he'd had a subscription to the *Courier* to keep up on the old hometown, and the headlines had made him ill. 'Are you sure?'

'No,' she said. 'They're just rounding up the usual suspects. Roy was a great scapegoat last time, why not use him again? First they have to find him, though. No one's really sure that he's still in the state, let alone the city.'

Willie turned away, busied himself with hotplate and kettle. All of a sudden he found it difficult to look Randi in the eye. 'You don't think Helander was the one who grabbed those kids.'

'Including his own sister? Hell no. Jessie was the last person he'd ever have hurt, she actually *liked* him. Not to mention that he was safely locked away when number five disappeared. I knew Roy Helander. He had bad teeth and he didn't bathe often enough, but that doesn't make him a child molester. He hung out with younger kids because the older ones made fun of him. I don't think he had any friends. He had some kind of secret place in the woods where he'd go to hide when things got too rough, he—'

She stopped suddenly, and Willie turned toward her, a teabag dangling from his fingers. 'You thinking what I'm thinking?'

The kettle began to scream.

*

Randi tossed and turned for over an hour after she got home, but there was no way she could sleep. Every time she closed her eyes she would see her father's face, or imagine poor Joan Sorenson, tied to that bed as the killer came closer, knife in hand. She kept coming back to Roy Helander, to Roy Helander and his secret refuge. In her mind, Roy was still the gawky adolescent she remembered, his blond hair lank and unwashed, his eyes frightened and confused as they made him tell the story over and over again. She wondered what had become of that secret place of his during all the years he'd been locked up and drugged in the state mental home, and she wondered if maybe sometimes he hadn't dreamt of it as he lay there in his cell. She thought maybe he had. If Roy Helander had indeed come home, Randi figured she knew just where he was.

Knowing about it and finding it were two different things, however. She and Willie had kicked it around without narrowing it down any. Randi tried to remember, but it had been so long ago, a whispered conversation in the schoolyard. A secret place in the woods, he'd said, a place where no one ever came that was his and his alone, hidden and full of magic. That could be anything, a cave by the river, a treehouse, even something as simple as a cardboard lean-to. But where were these woods? Outside the city were suburbs and industrial parks and farms; the nearest state forest was forty miles north along the river road. If this secret place was in one of the city parks, you'd think someone would have stumbled on it years ago. Without more to go on, Randi didn't have a prayer of finding it. But her mind worried it like a pit bull with a small child.

Finally her digital alarm clock read 2:13, and Randi gave up on sleep altogether. She got out of bed, turned on the light, and went back to the kitchen. The refrigerator was pretty dismal, but she found a couple of

bottles of Pabst. Maybe a beer would help put her to sleep. She opened a
bottle and carried it back to bed.

Her bedroom furnishings were a hodgepodge. The carpet was a remnant,
the blond chest-of-drawers was boring and functional, and the four-
poster queen-sized bed was a replica, but she did own a few genuine
antiques – the massive oak wardrobe, the full-length clawfoot dressing
mirror in its ornate wooden frame, and the cedar chest at the foot of the
bed. Her mother always used to call it a hope chest. Did little girls still keep
hope chests? She didn't think so, at least not around here. Maybe there
were still places where hope didn't seem so terribly unrealistic, but this
city wasn't one of them.

Randi sat on the floor, put the beer on the carpet, and opened the chest.

Hope chests were where you kept your future, all the little things that
were part of the dreams they taught you to dream when you were a child.
She hadn't been a child since she was twelve, since the night her mother
woke her with that terrible inhuman sound. Her chest was full of
memories now.

She took them out, one by one. Yearbooks from high school and college,
bundles of love letters from old boyfriends and even that asshole she'd
married, her school ring and her wedding ring, her diplomas, the letters
she'd won in track and girls' softball, a framed picture of her and her date
at the senior prom.

Way, way down at the bottom, buried under all the other layers of her
life, was a police .38. Her father's gun, the gun he emptied the night he
died. Randi took it out and carefully put it aside. Beneath it was the book,
an old three-ring binder with a blue cloth cover. She opened it across her
lap.

The yellowed *Courier* story on her father's death was Scotch-taped to the
first sheet of paper, and Randi stared at that familiar photograph for a long
time before she flipped the page. There were other clippings: stories about
the missing children that she'd torn furtively from *Courier* back issues in
the public library, magazine articles about animal attacks, serial killers,
and monsters, all sandwiched between the lined pages she'd filled with
her meticulous twelve-year-old's script. The handwriting grew broader and
sloppier as she turned the pages; she'd kept up the book for years, until
she'd gone away to college and tried to forget. She'd thought she'd done a
pretty good job of that, but now, turning the pages, she knew that was a
lie. You never forget. She only had to glance at the headlines, and it all
came back to her in a sickening rush.

Eileen Stanski, Jessie Helander, Diane Jones, Gregory Torio, Erwin
Weiss. None of them had ever been found, not so much as a bone or a
piece of clothing. The police said her father's death was accidental,

unrelated to the case he was working on. They'd all accepted that, the chief, the mayor, the newspaper, even her mother, who only wanted to get it all behind them and go on with their lives. Barry Schumacher and Joe Urquhart were the last to buy in, but in the end even they came around, and Randi was the only one left. Mere mention of the subject upset her mother so much that she finally stopped talking about it, but she didn't forget. She just asked her questions quietly, kept up her binder, and hid it every night at the bottom of the hope chest.

For all the good it had done.

The last twenty-odd pages in the back of the binder were still blank, the blue lines on the paper faint with age. The pages were stiff as she turned them. When she reached the final page, she hesitated. Maybe it wouldn't be there, she thought. Maybe she had just imagined it. It made no sense anyway. He would have known about her father, yes, but their mail was censored, wasn't it? They'd never let him send such a thing.

Randi turned the last page. It was there, just as she'd known it would be.

She'd been a junior in college when it arrived. She'd put it all behind her. Her father had been dead for seven years, and she hadn't even looked at her binder for three. She was busy with her classes and her sorority and her boyfriends, and sometimes she had bad dreams but mostly it was okay, she'd grown up, she'd gotten real. If she thought about it at all, she thought that maybe the adults had been right all along, it had just been some kind of an animal.

. . . some kind of animal . . .

Then one day the letter had come. She'd opened it on the way to class, read it with her friends chattering beside her, laughed and made a joke and stuck it away, all very grown-up. But that night, when her roommate had gone to sleep, she took it out and turned on her Tensor to read it again, and felt sick. She was going to throw it away, she remembered. It was just trash, a twisted product of a sick mind.

Instead she'd put it in the binder.

The Scotch tape had turned yellow and brittle, but the envelope was still white, with the name of the institution printed neatly in the left-hand corner. Someone had probably smuggled it out for him. The letter itself was scrawled on a sheet of cheap typing paper in block letters. It wasn't signed, but she'd known who it was from.

Randi slid the letter out of the envelope, hesitated for a moment, and opened it.

IT WAS A WEREWOLF

She looked at it and looked at it and looked at it, and suddenly she didn't feel very grown up any more. When the phone rang she nearly jumped a foot.

Her heart was pounding in her chest. She folded up the letter and stared at the phone, feeling strangely guilty, as if she'd been caught doing something shameful. It was 2:53 in the morning. Who the hell would be calling now? If it was Roy Helander, she thought she might just scream. She let the phone ring.

On the fourth ring, her machine cut in. 'This is AAA-Wade Investigations, Randi Wade speaking. I can't talk right now, but you can leave a message at the tone, and I'll get back to you.'

The tone sounded. 'Uh, hello,' said a deep male voice that was definitely not Roy Helander.

Randi put down the binder, snatched up the receiver. 'Rogoff? Is that you?'

'Yeah,' he said. 'Sorry if I woke you. Listen, this isn't by the book and I can't figure out a good excuse for why I'm calling you, except that I thought you ought to know.'

Cold fingers crept down Randi's spine. 'Know what?'

'We've got another one,' he said.

*

Willie woke in a cold sweat.

What was that?

A noise, he thought. Somewhere down the hall.

Or maybe just a dream? Willie sat up in bed and tried to get a grip on himself. The night was full of noises. It could have been a towboat on the river, a car passing by underneath his windows, anything. He still felt sheepish about the way he'd let his fear take over when he found his door open. He was just lucky he hadn't stabbed Randi with those scissors. He couldn't let his imagination eat him alive. He slid back down under the covers, rolled over on his stomach, closed his eyes.

Down the hall, a door opened and closed.

His eyes opened wide. He lay very still, listening. He'd locked all the locks, he told himself, he'd walked Randi to the door and locked all his locks, the springlock, the chain, the double deadbolt, he'd even lowered the police bar. No one could get in once the bar was in place, it could only be lifted from inside, the door was solid steel. And the back door might as well be welded shut, it was so corroded and unmovable. If they broke a window he would have heard the noise, there was no way, no way. He was just dreaming.

The knob on his bedroom door turned slowly, clicked. There was a small metallic rattle as someone pushed at the door. The lock held. The second push was slightly harder, the noise louder.

By then Willie was out of bed. It was a cold night, his jockey shorts and undershirt small protection against the chill, but Willie had other things on his mind. He could see the key still sticking out of the keyhole. An antique key for a hundred-year-old lock. The office keyholes were big enough to peek through. Willie kept the keys inside them, just to plug up the drafts, but he never turned them . . . except tonight. Tonight for some reason he'd turned that key before he went to bed and somehow felt a little more secure when he heard the tumblers click. And now that was all that stood between him and whatever was out there.

He backed up against the window, glanced out at the cobbled alley behind the brewery. The shadows lay thick and black beneath him. He seemed to recall a big green metal dumpster down below, directly under the window, but it was too dark to make it out.

Something hammered at the door. The room shook.

Willie couldn't breathe. His inhaler was on the dresser across the room, over by the door. He was caught in a giant's fist and it was squeezing all the breath right out of him. He sucked at the air.

The thing outside hit the door again. The wood began to splinter. Solid wood, a hundred years old, but it split like one of your cheap-ass hollow core modern doors.

Willie was starting to get dizzy. It was going to be real pissed off, he thought giddily, when it finally got in here and found that his asthma had already killed him. Willie peeled off his undershirt, dropped it to the floor, hooked a thumb in the elastic of his shorts.

The door shook and shattered, falling half away from its hinges. The next blow snapped it in two. His head swam from lack of oxygen. Willie forgot all about his shorts and gave himself over to the change.

Bones and flesh and muscles shrieked in the agony of transformation, but the oxygen rushed into his lungs, sweet and cold, and he could breathe again. Relief shuddered through him and he threw back his head and gave it voice. It was a sound to chill the blood, but the dark shape picking its way through the splinters of his door did not hesitate, and neither did Willie. He gathered his feet up under him, and leapt. Glass shattered all around him as he threw himself through the window, and the shards spun outward into the darkness. Willie missed the dumpster, landed on all fours, lost his footing, and slid three feet across the cobbles.

When he looked up, he could see the shape above him, filling his window. Its hands moved, and he caught the terrible glint of silver, and that was all it took. Willie was on his feet again, running down the street faster than he had ever run before.

*

The cab let her off two houses down. Police barricades had gone up all around the house, a dignified old Victorian manor badly in need of fresh paint. Curious neighbors, heavy coats thrown on over pajamas and bathrobes, lined Grandview, whispering to each other and glancing back at the house. The flashers on the police cars lent a morbid avidity to their faces.

Randi walked past them briskly. A patrolman she didn't know stopped her at the police barrier. 'I'm Randi Wade,' she told him. 'Rogoff asked me to come down.'

'Oh,' he said. He jerked a thumb back at the house. 'He's inside, talking to the sister.'

Randi found them in the living room. Rogoff saw her, nodded, waved her off, and went back to his questioning.

The other cops looked at her curiously, but no one said anything. The sister was a young looking forty, slender and dark, with pale skin and a wild mane of black hair that fell half down her back. She sat on the edge of a sectional in a white silk teddy that left little to the imagination, seemingly just as indifferent to the cold air coming through the open door as she was to the lingering glances of the policemen.

One of the cops was taking some fingerprints off a shiny black grand piano in the corner of the room. Randi wandered over as he finished. The top of the piano was covered with framed photographs. One was a summer scene, taken somewhere along the river, two pretty girls in matching bikinis standing on either side of an intense young man. The girls were dappled with moisture, laughing for the photographer, long black hair hanging wetly down across wide smiles. The man, or boy, or whatever he was, was in a swimsuit, but you could tell he was bone dry. He was gaunt and sallow, and his blue eyes stared into the lens with a vacancy that was oddly disturbing. The girls could have been as young as eighteen or as old as twenty. One of them was the woman Rogoff was questioning, but Randi could not have told you which one. Twins. She glanced at the other photos, half-afraid she'd find a picture of Willie. Most of the faces she didn't recognize, but she was still looking them over when Rogoff came up behind her.

'Coroner's upstairs with the body,' he said. 'You can come up if you've got the stomach.'

Randi turned away from the piano and nodded. 'You learn anything from the sister?'

'She had a nightmare,' he said. He started up the narrow staircase, Randi close behind him. 'She says that as far back as she can remember, whenever she had bad dreams, she'd just cross the hall and crawl in bed with Zoe.' They reached the landing. Rogoff put his hand on a glass doorknob, then paused. 'What she found when she crossed the hall this time is going to keep her in nightmares for years to come.'

He opened the door. Randi followed him inside.

The only light was a small bedside lamp, but the police photographer was moving around the room, snapping pictures of the red twisted thing on the bed. The light of his flash made the shadows leap and writhe, and Randi's stomach writhed with them. The smell of blood was overwhelming. She remembered summers long ago, hot July days when the wind blew from the south and the stink of the slaughterhouse settled over the city. But this was a thousand times worse.

The photographer was moving, flashing, moving, flashing. The world went from gray to red, then back to gray again. The coroner was bent over the corpse, her motions turned jerky and unreal by the strobing of the big flash gun. The white light blazed off the ceiling, and Randi looked up and saw the mirrors there. The dead woman's mouth gaped open, round and wide in a silent scream. He'd cut off her lips with her skin, and the inside of her mouth was no redder than the outside. Her face was gone, nothing left but the glistening wet ropes of muscle and here and there the pale glint of bone, but he'd left her her eyes. Large dark eyes, pretty eyes, sensuous, like her sister's downstairs. They were wide open, staring up in terror at the mirror on the ceiling. She'd been able to see every detail of what was being done to her. What had she found in the eyes of her reflection? Pain, terror, despair? A twin all her life, perhaps she'd found some strange comfort in her mirror image, even as her face and her flesh and her humanity had been cut away from her.

The flash went off again, and Randi caught the glint of metal at wrist and ankle. She closed her eyes for a second, steadied her breathing, and moved to the foot of the bed, where Rogoff was talking to the coroner.

'Same kind of chains?' he asked.

'You got it. And look at this.' Coroner Cooney took the unlit cigar out of her mouth and pointed.

The chain looped tightly around the victim's ankle. When the flash went off again, Randi saw the other circles, dark, black lines, scored across the raw flesh and exposed nerves. It made her hurt just to look.

'She struggled,' Rogoff suggested. 'The chain chafed against her flesh.'

'Chafing leaves you raw and bloody,' Cooney replied. 'What was done to her, you'd never notice chafing. That's a burn, Rogoff, a third-degree burn. Both wrists, both ankles, wherever the metal touched her. Sorenson had the same burn marks. Like the killer heated the chains until they were white hot. Only the metal is cold now. Go on, touch it.'

'No thanks,' Rogoff said. 'I'll take your word for it.'

'Wait a minute,' Randi said.

The coroner seemed to notice her for the first time. 'What's she doing here?' she asked.

'It's a long story,' Rogoff replied. 'Randi, this is official police business, you'd better keep—'

Randi ignored him. 'Joan Sorenson had the same kind of burn marks?' she asked Cooney. 'At wrist and ankle, where the chains touched her skin?'

'That's right,' Cooney said. 'So what?'

'What are you trying to say?' Rogoff asked her.

She looked at him. 'Joan Sorenson was a cripple. She had no use of her legs, no sensation at all below the waist. So why bother to chain her ankles?'

Rogoff stared at her for a long moment, then shook his head. He looked over to Cooney. The coroner shrugged. 'Yeah. So. An interesting point, but what does it mean?'

She had no answer for them. She looked away, back at the bed, at the skinned, twisted, mutilated thing that had once been a pretty woman.

The photographer moved to a different angle, pressed his shutter. The flash went off again. The chain glittered in the light. Softly, Randi brushed a fingertip across the metal. She felt no heat. Only the cold, pale touch of silver.

*

The night was full of sounds and smells.

Willie had run wildly, blindly, a gray shadow streaking down black rain-slick streets, pushing himself harder and faster than he had ever pushed before, paying no attention to where he went, anywhere, nowhere, everywhere, just so it was far away from his apartment and the thing that waited there with death shining bright in its hand. He darted along grimy alleys, under loading docks, bounded over low chain-link fences. There was a cinder-block wall somewhere that almost stopped him, three leaps and he failed to clear it, but on the fourth try he got his front paws over the top, and his back legs kicked and scrabbled and pushed him over. He fell onto damp grass, rolled in the dirt, and then he was up and running again. The streets were almost empty of traffic, but as he streaked across one wide boulevard, a pickup truck appeared out of nowhere, speeding, and caught him in its lights. The sudden glare startled him; he froze for a long instant in the center of the street, and saw shock and terror on the driver's face. A horn blared as the pickup began to brake, went into a skid, and fishtailed across the divider.

By then Willie was gone.

He was moving through a residential section now, down quiet streets lined by neat two-story houses. Parked cars filled the narrow driveways, realtor's signs flapped in the wind, but the only lights were the streetlamps . . . and sometimes, when the clouds parted for a second, the pale circle of the moon. He caught the scent of dogs from some of the backyards, and from time to time he heard a wild, frenzied barking, and knew that they had smelled him too. Sometimes the barking woke owners and neighbors, and then lights would come on in the silent houses, and doors would open in the backyards, but by then Willie would be blocks away, still running.

Finally, when his legs were aching and his heart was thundering and his tongue lolled redly from his mouth, Willie crossed the railroad tracks, climbed a steep embankment, and came hard up against a ten-foot chain-link fence with barbed wire strung along the top. Beyond the fence was a wide, empty yard and a low brick building, windowless and vast, dark beneath the light of the moon. The smell of old blood was faint but unmistakable, and abruptly Willie knew where he was.

The old slaughterhouse. The pack, they'd called it, bankrupt and abandoned now for almost two years. He'd run a long way. At last he let himself stop and catch his breath. He was panting, and as he dropped to the ground by the fence, he began to shiver, cold despite his ragged coat of fur.

He was still wearing jockey shorts, Willie noticed after he'd rested a moment. He would have laughed, if he'd had the throat for it. He thought of the man in the pickup and wondered what he'd thought when Willie appeared in his headlights, a gaunt gray specter in a pair of white briefs, with glowing eyes as red as the pits of hell.

Willie twisted himself around and caught the elastic in his jaws. He tore at them, growling low in his throat, and after a brief struggle managed to rip them away. He slung them aside and lowered himself to the damp ground, his legs resting on his paws, his mouth half-open, his eyes wary, watchful. He let himself rest. He could hear distant traffic, a dog barking wildly a half-mile away, could smell rust and mold, the stench of diesel fumes, the cold scent of metal. Under it all was the slaughterhouse smell, faded but not gone, lingering, whispering to him of blood and death. It woke things inside him that were better left sleeping, and Willie could feel the hunger churning in his gut.

He could not ignore it, not wholly, but tonight he had other concerns, fears that were more important than his hunger. Dawn was only a few hours away, and he had nowhere to go. He could not go home, not until he knew it was safe again, until he had taken steps to protect himself. Without keys and clothes and money, the agency was closed to him too. He had to go somewhere, trust someone.

He thought of Blackstone, thought of Jonathan Harmon sitting by his fire, of Steven's dead blue eyes and scarred hands, of the old tower jutting up like a rotten black stake. Jonathan might be able to protect him, Jonathan with his strong walls and his spiked fence and all his talk of blood and iron.

But when he saw Jonathan in his mind's eye, the long white hair, the gold wolf's head cane, the veined arthritic hands twisting and grasping, then the growl rose unbidden in Willie's throat, and he knew Blackstone was not the answer.

Joanie was dead, and he did not know the others well enough, hardly knew all their names, didn't want to know them better.

So, in the end, like it or not, there was only Randi.

Willie got to his feet, weary now, unsteady. The wind shifted, sweeping across the yards and the runs, whispering to him of blood until his nostrils quivered. Willie threw back his head and howled, a long shuddering lonely call that rose and fell and went out through the cold night air until the dogs began to bark for blocks around. Then, once again, he began to run.

*

Rogoff gave her a lift home. Dawn was just starting to break when he pulled his old black Ford up to the front of her six-flat. As she opened the door, he shifted into neutral and looked over at her. 'I'm not going to insist right now,' he said, 'but it might be that I need to know the name of your client. Sleep on it. Maybe you'll decide to tell me.'

'Maybe I can't,' Randi said. 'Attorney-client privilege, remember?'

Rogoff gave her a tired smile. 'When you sent me to the courthouse, I had a look at your file too. You never went to law school.'

'No?' She smiled back. 'Well, I meant to. Doesn't that count for something?' She shrugged. 'I'll sleep on it, we can talk tomorrow.' She got out, closed the door, moved away from the car. Rogoff shifted into drive, but Randi turned back before he could pull away. 'Hey, Rogoff, you have a first name?'

'Mike,' he said.

'See you tomorrow, Mike.'

He nodded and pulled away just as the streetlamps began to go out. Randi walked up the stoop, fumbling for her key.

'*Randi!*'

She stopped, looked around. 'Who's there?'

'Willie.' The voice was louder this time. 'Down here by the garbage cans.'

Randi leaned over the stoop and saw him. He was crouched down low, surrounded by trash bins, shivering in the morning chill. 'You're naked,' she said.

'Somebody tried to kill me last night. I made it out. My clothes didn't. I've been here an hour, not that I'm complaining mind you, but I think I have pneumonia and my balls are frozen solid. I'll never be able to have children now. Where the fuck have you been?'

'There was another murder. Same m.o.'

Willie shook so violently that the garbage cans rattled together. 'Jesus,' he said, his voice gone weak. 'Who?'

'Her name was Zoe Anders.'

Willie flinched. 'Fuck fuck fuck,' he said. He looked back up at Randi. She could see the fear in his eyes, but he asked anyway. 'What about Amy?'

'Her sister?' Randi said. He nodded. 'In shock, but fine. She had a nightmare.' She paused a moment. 'So you knew Zoe too. Like Sorenson?'

'No. Not like Joanie.' He looked at her wearily. 'Can we go in?'

She nodded and opened the door. Willie looked so grateful she thought he was about to lick her hand.

*

The underwear was her ex-husband's, and it was too big. The pink bathrobe was Randi's, and it was too small. But the coffee was just right, and it was warm in here, and Willie felt bone-tired and nervous but glad to be alive, especially when Randi put the plate down in front of him. She'd scrambled the eggs up with cheddar cheese and onion and done up a rasher of bacon on the side, and it smelled like nirvana. He fell to eagerly.

'I think I've figured out something,' she said. She sat down across from him.

'Good,' he said. 'The eggs, I mean. That is, whatever you figured out, that's good too, but Jesus, I *needed* these eggs. You wouldn't believe how hungry you get—' He stopped suddenly, stared down at the scrambled eggs, and reflected on what an idiot he was, but Randi hadn't noticed. Willie reached for a slice of bacon, bit off the end. 'Crisp,' he said. 'Good.'

'I'm going to tell you,' Randi said, as if he hadn't spoken at all. 'I've got to tell somebody, and you've known me long enough so I don't think you'll have me committed. You may laugh.' She scowled at him. 'If you laugh, you're back out in the street, minus the boxer shorts and the bathrobe.'

'I won't laugh,' Willie said. He didn't think he'd have much difficulty not laughing. He felt rather apprehensive. He stopped eating.

Randi took a deep breath and looked him in the eye. She had very lovely eyes, Willie thought. 'I think my father was killed by a werewolf,' she said seriously, without blinking.

'Oh, Jesus,' Willie said. He didn't laugh. A very large invisible anaconda wrapped itself around his chest and began to squeeze. 'I,' he said, 'I, I, I.'

Nothing was coming in or out. He pushed back from the table, knocking over the chair, and ran for the bathroom. He locked himself in and turned on the shower full blast, twisting the hot tap all the way around. The bathroom began to fill up with steam. It wasn't nearly as good as a blast from his inhaler, but it did beat suffocating. By the time the steam was really going good, Willie was on his knees, gasping like a man trying to suck an elephant through a straw. Finally he began to breathe again.

He stayed on his knees for a long time, until the spray from the shower had soaked through his robe and his underwear and his face was flushed and red. Then he crawled across the tiled floor, turned off the shower, and got unsteadily to his feet. The mirror above the sink was all fogged up. Willie wiped it off with a towel and peered in at himself. He looked like shit. Wet shit. Hot wet shit. He felt worse. He tried to dry himself off, but the steam and the shower spray had gone everywhere and the towels were as damp as he was. He heard Randi moving around outside, opening and closing drawers. He wanted to go out and face her, but not like this. A man has to have some pride. For a moment he just wanted to be home in bed with his Primatene on the end table, until he remembered that his bedroom had been occupied the last time he'd been there.

'Are you ever coming out?' Randi asked.

'Yeah,' Willie said, but it was so weak that he doubted she heard him. He straightened and adjusted the frilly pink robe. Underneath the undershirt looked as though he'd been competing in a wet T-shirt contest. He sighed, unlocked the door, and exited. The cold air gave him goose pimples.

Randi was seated at the table again. Willie went back to his place. 'Sorry,' he said. 'Asthma attack.'

'I noticed,' Randi replied. 'Stress related, aren't they?'

'Sometimes.'

'Finish your eggs,' she urged. 'They're getting cold.'

'Yeah,' Willie said, figuring he might as well, since it would give him something to do while he figured out what to tell her. He picked up his fork.

It was like the time he'd grabbed a dirty pot that had been sitting on top of his hotplate since the night before and realized too late that he'd never turned the hotplate off. Willie shrieked and the fork clattered to the table and bounced, once, twice, three times. It landed in front of Randi. He sucked on his fingers. They were already starting to turn red. Randi looked at him very calmly and picked up the fork. She held it, stroked it with her thumb, touched its prongs thoughtfully to her lip. 'I brought out the good silver while you were in the bathroom,' she said. 'Solid sterling. It's been in the family for generations.'

His fingers hurt like hell. 'Oh, Jesus. You got any butter? Oleo, lard, I don't care, anything will . . .' He stopped when her hand went under the table and came out again holding a gun. From where Willie sat, it looked like a very big gun.

'Pay attention, Willie. Your fingers are the least of your worries. I realize you're in pain, so I'll give you a minute or two to collect your thoughts and try to tell me why I shouldn't blow off your fucking head right here and now.' She cocked the hammer with her thumb.

Willie just stared at her. He looked pathetic, like a half-drowned puppy. For one terrible moment Randi thought he was going to have another asthma attack. She felt curiously calm, not angry or afraid or even nervous, but she didn't think she had it in her to shoot a man in the back as he ran for the bathroom, even if he was a werewolf.

Thankfully, Willie spared her that decision. 'You don't want to shoot me,' he said, with remarkable aplomb under the circumstances. 'It's bad manners to shoot your friends. You'll make a hole in the bathrobe.'

'I never liked that bathrobe anyway. I hate pink.'

'If you're really so hot to kill me, you'd stand a better chance with the fork,' Willie said.

'So you admit that you're a werewolf?'

'A lycanthrope,' Willie corrected. He sucked at his burnt fingers again and looked at her sideways. 'So sue me. It's a medical condition. I got allergies, I got asthma, I got a bad back, and I got lycanthropy, is it my fault? I didn't kill your father. I never killed anyone. I ate half a pit bull once, but can you blame me?' His voice turned querulous. 'If you want to shoot me, go ahead and try. Since when do you carry a gun anyway? I thought all that shit about private eyes stuffing heat was strictly television.'

'The phrase is *packing* heat, and it is. I only bring mine out for special occasions. My father was carrying it when he died.'

'Didn't do him much good, did it?' Willie said softly.

Randi considered that for a moment. 'What would happen if I pulled the trigger?' The gun was getting heavy, but her hand was steady.

'I'd try to change. I don't think I'd make it, but I'd have to try. A couple bullets in the head at this range, while I'm still human, yeah, that'd probably do the job. But you don't want to miss and you *really* don't want to wound me. Once I'm changed, it's a whole different ball game.'

'My father emptied his gun on the night he was killed,' Randi said thoughtfully.

Willie studied his hand and winced. 'Oh fuck,' he said. 'I'm getting a blister.'

Randi put the gun on the table and went to the kitchen to get him a stick of butter. He accepted it from her gratefully. She glanced toward the window as he treated his burns. 'The sun's up,' she said, 'I thought werewolves only changed at night, during the full moon?'

'Lycanthropes,' Willie said. He flexed his fingers, sighed. 'That full moon shit was all invented by some screenwriter for Universal, go look at your literature, we change at will, day, night, full moon, new moon, makes no difference. Sometimes I *feel* more like changing during the full moon, some kind of hormonal thing, but more like getting horny than going on the rag, if you know what I mean.' He grabbed his coffee. It was cold by now, but that didn't stop Willie from emptying the cup. 'I shouldn't be telling you all this, fuck, Randi, I like you, you're a friend, I care about you, you should only forget this whole morning, believe me, it's healthier.'

Why?' she said bluntly. She wasn't about to forget anything. 'What's going to happen to me if I don't? Are you going to rip my throat out? Should I forget Joan Sorenson and Zoe Anders too? How about Roy Helander and all those missing kids? *Am I supposed to forget what happened to my father?*' She stopped for a moment, lowered her voice. 'You came to me for help, Willie, and pardon, but you sure as hell look as though you still need it.'

Willie looked at her across the table with a morose hangdog expression on his long face. 'I don't know whether I want to kiss you or slap you,' he finally admitted. 'Shit, you're right, you know too much already.' He stood up. 'I got to get into my own clothes, this wet underwear is giving me pneumonia. Call a cab, we'll go check out my place, talk. You got a coat?'

'Take the Burberry,' Randi said. 'It's in the closet.' The coat was even bigger on him than it had been on Randi, but it beat the pink bathrobe. He looked almost human as he emerged from the closet, fussing with the belt. Randi was rummaging in the silver drawer. She found a large carving knife, the one her grandfather used to use on Thanksgiving, and slid it through the belt of her jeans. Willie looked at it nervously. 'Good idea,' he finally said, 'but take the gun too.'

*

The cab driver was the quiet type. The drive across town passed in awkward silence. Randi paid him while Willie climbed out to check the doors. It was a blustery overcast day, and the river looked gray and choppy as it slapped against the pier.

Willie kicked his front door in a fit of pique, and vanished down the alley. Randi waited by the pier and watched the cab drive off. A few minutes later Willie was back, looking disgusted. 'This is ridiculous,' he said. 'The back door hasn't been opened in years, you'd need a hammer and chisel just to knock through the rust. The loading docks are bolted down and chained with the mother of all padlocks on the chains. And the front door . . . there's a spare set of keys in my car, but even if we got those the police bar can only be lifted from inside. So how the hell did it get in, I ask you?'

Randi looked at the brewery's weathered brick walls appraisingly. They looked pretty solid to her, and the second floor windows were a good twenty feet off street level. She walked around the side to take a look down the alley. 'There's a window broken,' she said.

'That was me getting out,' Willie said, 'not my nocturnal caller getting in.'

Randi had already figured out that much from the broken glass all over the cobblestones. 'Right now I'm more concerned about how *we're* going to get in.' She pointed. 'If we move that dumpster a few feet to the left and climb on top, and you climb on my shoulders, I think you might be able to hoist yourself in.'

Willie considered that. 'What if it's still in there?'

'What?' Randi said.

'Whatever was after me last night. If I hadn't jumped through that window, it'd be me without a skin this morning, and believe me, I'm cold enough as is.' He looked at the window, at the dumpster, and back at the window. 'Fuck,' he said, 'we can't stand here all day. But I've got a better idea. Help me roll the dumpster away from the wall a little.'

Randi didn't understand, but she did as Willie suggested. They left the dumpster in the center of the alley, directly opposite the broken window. Willie nodded and began unbelting the coat she'd lent him. 'Turn around,' he told her. 'I don't want you freaking out. I've got to get naked and your carnal appetites might get the best of you.'

Randi turned around. The temptation to glance over her shoulder was irresistible. She heard the coat fall to the ground. Then she heard something else . . . soft padding steps, like a dog. She turned. He'd circled all the way down to the end of the alley. Her ex-husband's old underwear lay puddled across the cobblestones atop the Burberry coat. Willie came streaking back toward the brewery building speed. He was, Randi noticed, not a very prepossessing wolf. His fur was a dirty gray-brown color, kind of mangy, his rear looked too large and his legs too thin, and there was something ungainly about the way he ran. He put on a final burst of speed, leapt on top of the dumpster, bounded off the metal lid, and flew through the shattered window, breaking more glass as he went. Randi heard a loud *thump* from inside the bedroom.

She went around to the front. A few moments later, the locks began to unlock, one by one, and Willie opened the heavy steel door. He was wearing his own bathrobe, a red tartan flannel, and his hand was full of keys. 'Come on,' he said. 'No sign of night visitors. I put on some water for tea.'

*

'The fucker must have crawled out of the toilet,' Willie said. 'I don't see any other way he could have gotten in.'

Randi stood in front of what remained of his bedroom door. She studied the shattered wood, ran her finger lightly across one long, jagged splinter, then knelt to look at the floor. 'Whatever it was, it was strong. Look at these gouges in the wood, look at how sharp and clean they are. You don't do that with a fist. Claws, maybe. More likely some kind of knife. And take a look at this.' She gestured toward the brass door-knob, which lay on the floor amidst a bunch of kindling.

Willie bent to pick it up.

'Don't touch,' she said, grabbing his arm. 'Just look.'

He got down on one knee. At first he didn't notice anything. But when he leaned close, he saw how the brass was scored and scraped.

'Something sharp,' Randi said, 'and hard.' She stood. 'When you first heard the sounds, what direction were they coming from?'

Willie thought for a moment. 'It was hard to tell,' he said. 'Toward the back, I think.'

Randi walked back. All along the hall, the doors were closed. She studied the banister at the top of the stairs, then moved on, and began opening and closing doors. 'Come here,' she said, at the fourth door.

Willie trotted down the hall. Randi had the door ajar. The knob on the hall side was fine; the knob on the inside displayed the same kind of scoring they'd seen on his bedroom door. Willie was aghast. 'But this is the *men's room*,' he said. 'You mean it *did* come out of the toilet? I'll never shit again.'

'It came out of this room,' Randi said. 'I don't know about the toilet.' She went in and looked around. There wasn't much to look at. Two toilet stalls, two urinals, two sinks with a long mirror above them and antique brass soap dispensers beside the water taps, a paper towel dispenser, Willie's towels and toiletries. No window. Not even a small frosted-glass window. No window at all.

Down the hall the teakettle began to whistle. Randi looked thoughtful as they walked back to the living room.

'Joan Sorenson died behind a locked door, and the killer got to Zoe Anders without waking her sister right across the hall.'

'The fucking thing can come and go as it pleases,' Willie said. The idea gave him the creeps. He glanced around nervously as he got out the teabags, but there was nobody there but him and Randi.

'Except it can't,' Randi said. 'With Sorenson and Anders, there was no damage, no sign of a break-in, nothing but a corpse. But with you, the killer was stopped by something as simple as a locked door.'

'Not stopped,' Willie said, 'just slowed down a little.' He repressed a shudder and brought the tea over to his coffee table.

'Did he get the right Anders sister?' she asked.

Willie stood there stupidly for a moment holding the kettle poised over the cups. 'What do you mean?'

'You've got identical twins sharing the same house. Let's presume it's a house the killer's never visited before. Somehow he gains entry, and he chains, murders, and flays only *one* of them, without even waking the other.' Randi smiled up at him sweetly. 'You can't tell them apart by sight, he probably didn't know which room was which, so the question is, did he get the werewolf?'

It was nice to know that she wasn't infallible. 'Yes,' he said, 'and no. They were twins, Randi. Both lycanthropes.' She looked honestly surprised. 'How did you know?' he asked her.

'Oh, the chains,' she said negligently. Her mind was far away, gnawing at the puzzle. 'Silver chains. She was burned wherever they'd touched her flesh. And Joan Sorenson was a werewolf too, of course. She was crippled, yes . . . but only as a human, not after her transformation. That's why her legs were chained, to hold her if she changed.' She looked at Willie with a baffled expression on her face. 'It doesn't make sense, to kill one and leave the other untouched. Are you sure that Amy Anders is a werewolf too?'

'A lycanthrope,' he said. 'Yes. Definitely. They were even harder to tell apart as wolves. At least when they were human they dressed differently. Amy likes white lace, frills, that kind of stuff, and Zoe was into leather.' There was a cut-glass ashtray in the center of the coffee table filled with Willie's private party mix: aspirin, Allerest, and Tums. He took a handful of pills and swallowed them.

'Look, before we go on with this, I want one card on the table,' Randi said.

For once he was ahead of her. 'If I knew who killed your father, I'd tell you, but I don't, I was in the service, overseas. I vaguely remember something in the *Courier*, but to tell the truth I'd forgotten all about it until you threw it at me last night. What can I tell you?' He shrugged.

'Don't bullshit me, Willie. My father was killed by a werewolf. You're a werewolf. You must know something.'

'Hey, try substituting *Jew* or *diabetic* or *bald man* for werewolf in that statement, and see how much sense it makes. I'm not saying you're wrong about your father because you're not; it fits, it all fits, everything from the condition of the body to the empty gun, but even if you buy that much, then you got to ask *which* werewolf.'

'How many of you *are* there,' Randi asked incredulously.

'Damned if I know,' Willie said. 'What do you think, we get together for a lodge meeting every time the moon is full? The purebloods, hell, not many, the pack's been getting pretty thin these last few generations. But there's lots of mongrels like me, half-breeds, quarter-breeds, what have you, the old families had their share of bastards. Some can work the change, some can't. I've heard of a few who change one day and never do manage to change back. And that's just from the old bloodlines, never mind the ones like Joanie.'

'You mean Joanie was different?'

Willie gave her a reluctant nod. 'You've seen the movies. You get bitten by a werewolf, you turn into a werewolf; that is, assuming there's enough of you left to turn into anything except a cadaver.' She nodded, and he went on. 'Well, that part's true, or partly true, it doesn't happen as often as it once did. Guy gets bit nowadays, he runs to a doctor, gets the wound cleaned and treated with antiseptic, gets his rabies shots and his tetanus shots and his penicillin and fuck-all knows what else, and he's fine. The wonders of modern medicine.'

Willie hesitated briefly, looking in her eyes, those lovely eyes, wondering if she'd understand, and finally he plunged ahead. 'Joanie was such a good kid, it broke my heart to see her in that chair. One night she told me that the hardest thing of all was realizing that she'd never know what it felt like to make love. She'd been a virgin when they hit that truck. We'd had a few drinks, she was crying, and . . . well, I couldn't take it. I told her what I was and what I could do for her, she didn't believe a word of it, so I had to show her. I bit her leg, she couldn't feel a damned thing down there anyway, I bit her and I held the bite for a long time, worried it around good. Afterwards I nursed her myself. No doctors, no antiseptic, no rabies vaccine. We're talking major league infection here, there was a day or two when her fever was running so high I thought maybe I'd killed her; her leg had turned nearly black, you could see the stuff going up her veins. I got to admit it was pretty gross, I'm in no hurry to try it again, but it worked. The fever broke and Joanie changed.'

'You weren't just friends,' Randi said with certainty. 'You were lovers.'

'Yeah,' he said. 'As wolves. I guess I look sexier in fur. I couldn't even begin to keep up with her, though. Joanie was a pretty active wolf. We're talking almost every night here.'

'As a human, she was still crippled,' Randi said.

Willie nodded, held up his hand. 'See.' The burns were still there, and a blood blister had formed on his index finger. 'Once or twice the change has saved my life, when my asthma got so bad I thought I was going to suffocate. That kind of thing doesn't cross over, but it's sure as hell waiting for you when you cross back. Sometimes you even get nasty surprises. Catch a bullet as a wolf and it's nothing, a sting and a slap, heals up right away, but you can pay for it when you change into human form, especially if you change too soon and the damn thing gets infected. And silver will burn the shit out of you no matter what form you're in. LBJ was my favorite president, just *loved* them cupro-nickel-sandwich quarters.'

Randi stood up. 'This is all a little overwhelming. Do you *like* being a werewolf?'

'A lycanthrope.' Willie shrugged. 'I don't know, do you like being a woman? It's what I am.'

Randi crossed the room and stared out his window at the river. 'I'm very confused,' she said. 'I look at you and you're my friend Willie. I've known you for years. Only you're a werewolf too. I've been telling myself that werewolves don't exist since I was twelve, and now I find out the city is full of them. Only someone or something is killing them, flaying them. Should I care? Why should I care?' She ran a hand through her tangled hair. 'We both know that Roy Helander didn't kill those kids. My father knew it too. He kept pressing, and one night he was lured to the stockyards and some kind of animal tore out his throat. Every time I think of that I think maybe I ought to find this werewolf killer and sign up to help him. Then I look at you again.' She turned and looked at him. 'And damn it, you're *still* my friend.'

She looked as though she was going to cry. Willie had never seen her cry and he didn't want to. He hated it when they cried. 'Remember when I first offered you a job, and you wouldn't take it, because you thought all collection agents were pricks?'

She nodded.

'Lycanthropes are skinchangers. We turn into wolves. Yeah, we're carnivores, you got it, you don't meet many vegetarians in the pack, but there's meat and there's meat. You won't find nearly as many rats around here as you will in other cities this size. What I'm saying is the skin may change, but what you do is still up to the person inside. So stop thinking about werewolves and werewolf-killers and start thinking about murderers, 'cause that's what we're talking about.'

Randi crossed the room and sat back down. 'I hate to admit it, but you're making sense.'

'I'm good in bed too,' Willie said with a grin. The ghost of a smile crossed her face.

'Fuck you.'

'Exactly my suggestion. What kind of underwear are you wearing?'

'Never mind my underwear,' she said. 'Do you have any ideas about these murderers? Past *or* present?'

Sometimes Randi had a one track mind, Willie thought; unfortunately, it never seemed to be the track that led under the sheets. 'Jonathan told me about an old legend,' he said.

'Jonathan?' she said.

'Jonathan Harmon, yeah, that one, old blood and iron, the *Courier*, Blackstone, the pack, the founding family, all of it.'

'Wait a minute. He's a were – a lycanthrope?'

Willie nodded. 'Yeah, leader of the pack, he—'

Randi leapt ahead of him. 'And it's hereditary?'

He saw where she was going. 'Yes, but—'

'Steven Harmon is mentally disturbed,' Randi interrupted. 'His family keeps it out of the papers, but they can't stop the whispering. Violent episodes, strange doctors coming and going at Blackstone, shock treatments. He's some kind of pain freak, isn't he?'

Willie sighed. 'Yeah. Ever see his hands? The palms and fingers are covered with silver burns. Once I saw him close his hand around a silver cartwheel and hold it there until smoke started to come out between his fingers. It burned a big round hole right in the center of his palm.' He shuddered. 'Yeah, Steven's a freak all right, and he's strong enough to rip your arm out of your socket and beat you to death with it, but he didn't kill your father, he couldn't have.'

'Says you,' she said.

'He didn't kill Joanie or Zoe either. They weren't just murdered, Randi. They were skinned. That's where the legend comes in. The word is *skinchangers*, remember? What if the power was *in* the skin? So you catch a werewolf, flay it, slip into the bloody skin . . . and change.'

Randi was staring at him with a sick look on her face. 'Does it really work that way?'

'Someone thinks so.'

'Who?'

'Someone who's been thinking about werewolves for a long time. Someone who's gone way past obsession into full-fledged psychopathy. Someone who thinks he saw a werewolf once, who thinks werewolves done him wrong, who hates them, wants to hurt them, wants revenge . . . but maybe also, down deep, someone who wants to know what's it like.'

'Roy Helander,' she said.

'Maybe if we could find this damned secret hideout in the woods, we'd know for sure.'

Randi stood up. 'I racked my brains for hours. We could poke around a few of the city parks some, but I'm not sanguine on our prospects. No. I want to know more about these legends, and I want to look at Steven with my own eyes. Get your car, Willie. We're going to pay a visit to Blackstone.'

He'd been afraid she was going to say something like that. He reached out and grabbed another handful of his party mix. 'Oh, Jesus,' he said, crunching down on a mouthful of pills. 'This isn't the Addams Family, you know. Jonathan is for real.'

'So am I,' said Randi, and Willie knew the cause was lost.

*

It was raining again by the time they reached Courier Square. Willie waited in the car while Randi went inside the gunsmith's. Twenty minutes later, when she came back out, she found him snoring behind the wheel. At least he'd had the sense to lock the doors of his mammoth old Cadillac. She tapped on the glass, and he sat right up and stared at her for a moment without recognition. Then he woke up, leaned over, and unlocked the door on the passenger side. Randi slid beside him.

'How'd it go?'

'They don't get much call for silver bullets, but they know someone upstate who does custom work for collectors,' Randi said in a disgusted tone of voice.

'You don't sound too happy about it.'

'I'm not. You wouldn't believe what they're going to charge me for a box of silver bullets, never mind that it's going to take two weeks. It was going to take a month, but I raised the ante.' She looked glumly out the rain-streaked window. A torrent of gray water rushed down the gutter, carrying its flotilla of cigarette butts and scraps of yesterday's newspaper.

'Two weeks?' Willie turned the ignition and put the barge in gear. 'Hell, we'll both probably be dead in two weeks. Just as well, the whole idea of silver bullets makes me nervous.'

They crossed the square, past the Castle marquee and the Courier Building, and headed up Central, the windshield wipers clicking back and forth rhythmically. Willie hung a left on 13th and headed toward the bluff while Randi took out her father's revolver, opened the cylinder, and checked to see that it was fully loaded. Willie watched her out of the corner of his eye as he drove. 'Waste of time,' he said. 'Guns don't kill werewolves, werewolves kill werewolves.'

'Lycanthropes,' Randi reminded him.

He grinned and for a moment looked almost like the man she'd shared an office with, a long time ago.

Both of them grew visibly more intense as they drove down 13th, the Caddy's big wheels splashing through the puddles. They were still a block away when she saw the little car crawling down the bluff, white against the dark stone. A moment later, she saw the lights, flashing red-and-blue.

Willie saw them too. He slammed on the brakes, lost traction, and had to steer wildly to avoid slamming into a parked car as he fish-tailed. His forehead was beading with sweat when he finally brought the car to a stop, and Randi didn't think it was from the near collision. 'Oh, Jesus,' he said, 'oh, Jesus, not Harmon too, I don't *believe* it.' He began to wheeze, and fumbled in his pocket for an inhaler.

'Wait here, I'll check it out,' Randi told him. She got out, turned up the collar of her coat, and walked the rest of the way, to where 13th dead-ended flush against the bluff. The coroner's wagon was parked amidst three police cruisers. Randi arrived at the same time as the cable car. Rogoff was the first one out. Behind him she saw Cooney, the police photographer, and two uniforms carrying a body bag. It must have gotten pretty crowded on the way down.

'You.' Rogoff seemed surprised to see her. Strands of black hair were plastered to his forehead by the rain.

'Me,' Randi agreed. The plastic of the body bag was wet, and the uniforms were having trouble with it. One of them lost his footing as he stepped down, and Randi thought she saw something shift inside the bag. 'It doesn't fit the pattern,' she said to Rogoff. 'The other killings have all been at night.'

Rogoff took her by the arm and drew her away, gently but firmly. 'You don't want to look at this one, Randi.'

There was something in his tone that made her look at him hard. 'Why not? It can't be any worse than Zoe Anders, can it? Who's in the bag, Rogoff? The father or the son?'

'Neither one,' he said. He glanced back behind them, up toward the top of the bluff, and Randi found herself following his gaze. Nothing was visible of Blackstone but the high wrought iron fence that surrounded the estate. 'This time his luck ran out on him. The dogs got to him first. Cooney says the scent of blood off of . . . of what he was wearing . . . well, it must have driven them wild. They tore him to pieces, Randi.' He put his hand on her shoulder, as if to comfort her.

'No,' Randi said. She felt numb, dazed.

'Yes,' he insisted. 'It's over. And believe me, it's not something you want to see.'

She backed away from him. They were loading the body in the rear of the coroner's wagon while Sylvia Cooney supervised the operation, smoking her cigar in the rain. Rogoff tried to touch her again, but she whirled away from him, and ran to the wagon. 'Hey!' Cooney said.

The body was on the tailgate, half-in and half-out of the wagon. Randi reached for the zipper on the body bag. One of the cops grabbed her arm. She shoved him aside and unzipped the bag. His face was half gone. His right cheek and ear and part of his jaw had been torn away, devoured right down to the bone. What features he had left were obscured by blood.

Someone tried to pull her away from the tailgate. She spun and kicked him in the balls, then turned back to the body and grabbed it under the arms and pulled. The inside of the body bag was slick with blood. The corpse slid loose of the plastic sheath like a banana squirting out of its skin and fell into the street. Rain washed down over it, and the runoff in the gutter turned pink, then red. A hand, or part of a hand, fell out of the bag almost like an afterthought. Most of the arm was gone, and Randi could see bones peeking through, and places where huge hunks of flesh had been torn out of his thigh, shoulder, and torso. He was naked, but between his legs was nothing but a raw red wound where his genitalia had been.

Something was fastened around his neck, and knotted beneath his chin. Randi leaned forward to touch it, and drew back when she saw his face. The rain had washed it clean. He had one eye left, a green eye, open and staring. The rain pooled in the socket and ran down his cheek. Roy had grown gaunt to the point of emaciation, with a week's growth of beard, but his long hair was still the same color, the color he'd shared with all his brothers and sisters, that muddy Helander blond.

Something was knotted under his chin, a long twisted cloak of some kind; it had gotten all tangled when he fell. Randi was trying to straighten it when they caught her by both arms and dragged her away bodily. 'No,' she said wildly. 'What was he wearing? What was he wearing, damn you! I have to see!' No one answered. Rogoff had her right arm prisoned in a grip that felt like steel. She fought him wildly, kicking and shouting, but he held her until the hysteria had passed, and then held her some more as she leaned against his chest, sobbing.

She didn't quite know when Willie had come up, but suddenly there he was. He took her away from Rogoff and led her back to his Cadillac, and they sat inside, silent, as first the coroner's wagon and then the police cruisers drove off one by one. She was covered with blood. Willie gave her some aspirin from a bottle he kept in his glove compartment. She tried to swallow it, but her throat was raw and she wound up gagging it back up. 'It's all right,' he told her, over and over. 'It wasn't your father, Randi. Listen to me, please, it *wasn't your father!*'

'It was Roy Helander,' Randi said to him at last. 'And he was wearing Joanie's skin.'

*

Willie drove her home; she was in no shape to confront Jonathan Harmon or anybody. She'd calmed down, but the hysteria was still there, just under the surface, he could see it in the eyes, hear it in her voice. If that wasn't enough, she kept telling him the same thing, over and over. 'It was Roy Helander,' she'd say, like he didn't know, 'and he was wearing Joanie's skin.'

Willie found her keys and helped her upstairs to her apartment. Inside, he made her take a couple of sleeping pills from the all-purpose pharmaceutical in his glove box, then turned down the bed and undressed her. He figured if anything would snap her back to herself, it would be his fingers on the buttons of her blouse, but she just smiled at him, vacant and dreamy, and told him that it was Roy Helander and he was wearing Joanie's skin. The big silver knife jammed through her belt loops gave him pause. He finally unzipped her fly, undid her buckle, and yanked off the jeans, knife and all. She didn't wear panties. He'd always suspected as much.

When Randi was finally in bed asleep, Willie went back to her bathroom and threw up.

Afterward he made himself a gin-and-tonic to wash the taste of vomit out of his mouth, and went and sat alone in her living room in one of her red velvet chairs. He'd had even less sleep than Randi these past few nights, and he felt as though he might drift off at any moment, but he knew somehow that it was important not to. It was Roy Helander and he was wearing Joanie's skin. So it was over, he was safe.

He remembered the way his door shook last night, a solid wood door, and it split like so much cheap paneling. Behind it was something dark and powerful, something that left scars on brass doorknobs and showed up in places it had no right to be. Willie didn't know what had been on the other side of his door, but somehow he didn't think that the gaunt, wasted, half-eaten travesty of a man he'd seen on 13th Street quite fit the bill. He'd believe that his nocturnal visitor had been Roy Helander, with or without Joanie's skin, about the same time he'd believe that the man had been eaten by dogs. *Dogs!* How long did Jonathan expect to get away with that shit? Still, he couldn't blame him, not with Zoe and Joanie dead, and Helander trying to sneak into Blackstone dressed in a human skin.

. . . there are things that hunt the hunters.

Willie picked up the phone and dialed Blackstone.

'Hello.' The voice was flat, affectless, the voice of someone who cared about nothing and no one, not even himself.

'Hello, Steven,' Willie said quietly. He was about to ask for Jonathan when a strange sort of madness took hold of him, and he heard himself say, 'Did you watch? Did you see what Jonathan did to him, Steven? Did it get you off?'

The silence on the other end of the line went on for ages. Sometimes Steven Harmon simply forgot how to talk. But not this time. 'Jonathan didn't do him. I did. It was easy. I could smell him coming through the woods. He never even saw me. I came around behind him and pinned him down and bit off his ear. He wasn't very strong at all. After a while he changed into a man, and then he was all slippery, but it didn't matter, I—'

Someone took the phone away. 'Hello, who is this?' Jonathan's voice said from the receiver.

Willie hung up. He could always call back later. Let Jonathan sweat awhile, wondering who it had been on the other end of the line. 'After a while he changed into a man,' Willie repeated aloud. Steven did it himself. Steven couldn't do it himself. Could he? 'Oh Jesus,' Willie said.

*

Somewhere far away, a phone was ringing.

Randi rolled over in her bed. 'Joanie's skin,' she muttered groggily in low, half-intelligible syllables. She was naked, with the blankets tangled around her. The room was pitch dark. The phone rang again. She sat up, a sheet curled around her neck. The room was cold, and her head pounded. She ripped loose the sheet, threw it aside. Why was she naked? What the hell was going on? The phone rang again and her machine cut in. 'This is AAA-Wade Investigations, Randi Wade speaking. I can't talk right now, but you can leave a message at the tone, and I'll get back to you.'

Randi reached out and speared the phone just in time for the *beep* to sound in her ear. She winced. 'It's me,' she said. 'I'm here. What time is it? Who's this?'

'Randi, are you all right? It's Uncle Joe.' Joe Urquhart's gruff voice was a welcome relief. 'Rogoff told me what happened, and I was very concerned about you. I've been trying to reach you for hours.'

'Hours?' She looked at the clock. It was past midnight. 'I've been asleep. I think.' The last she remembered, it had been daylight and she and Willie had been driving down 13th on their way to Blackstone to . . .

It was Roy Helander and he was wearing Joanie's skin.

'Randi, what's wrong? You sure you're okay? You sound wretched. Damn it, *say* something.'

'I'm here,' she said. She pushed hair back out of her eyes. Someone had opened her window, and the air was frigid on her bare skin. 'I'm fine,' she said. 'I just . . . I was asleep. It shook me up, that's all. I'll be fine.'

'If you say so.' Urquhart sounded dubious.

Willie must have brought her home and put her to bed, she thought. So where was he? She couldn't imagine that he'd just dump her and then take off, that wasn't like Willie.

'Pay attention,' Urquhart said gruffly. 'Have you heard a word I've said?'

She hadn't. 'I'm sorry. I'm just . . . disoriented, that's all. It's been a strange day.'

'I need to see you,' Urquhart said. His voice had taken on a sudden urgency. 'Right away. I've been going over the reports on Roy Helander and his victims. There's something out of place, something disturbing. And the more I look at these case files and Cooney's autopsy report, the more I keep thinking about Frank, about what happened that night.' He hesitated. 'I don't know how to say this. All these years . . . I only wanted the best for you, but I wasn't . . . wasn't completely honest with you.'

'Tell me,' she said. Suddenly she was a lot more awake.

'Not over the phone. I need to see you face to face, to show it to you. I'll swing by and get you. Can you be ready in fifteen minutes?'

'Ten,' Randi said.

She hung up, hopped out of bed and opened the bedroom door. 'Willie?' she called out. There was no answer. 'Willie!' she repeated more loudly. Nothing. She turned on the lights, padded barefoot down the hall, expecting to find him snoring away on her sofa. But the living room was empty.

Her hands were sandpaper dry, and when she looked down she saw that they were covered with old blood. Her stomach heaved. She found the clothes she'd been wearing in a heap on the bedroom floor. They were brown and crusty with dried blood as well. Randi started the shower and stood under the water for a good five minutes, running it so hot that it burned the way that silver fork must have burned in Willie's hand. The blood washed off, the water turning faintly pink as it whirled away and down. She toweled off thoroughly, and found a warm flannel shirt and a fresh pair of jeans. She didn't bother with her hair; the rain would wet it down again soon enough. But she made a point of finding her father's gun and sliding the long silver carving knife through the belt loop of her jeans.

As she bent to pick up the knife, Randi saw the square of white paper on the floor by her end table. She must have knocked it off when she'd reached for the phone.

She picked it up, opened it. It was covered with Willie's familiar scrawl, a page of hurried, dense scribbling. *I got to go, you're in no condition*, it began. *Don't go anywhere or talk to anyone. Roy Helander wasn't sneaking in to kill Harmon, I finally figured it out. The damned Harmon family secret that's no secret at all, I should have twigged, Steven—*

That was as far as she'd gotten when the doorbell rang.

*

Willie hugged the ground two-thirds of the way up the bluff, the rain coming down around him and his heart pounding in his chest as he clung to the tracks. Somehow the grade didn't seem nearly as steep when you were riding the cable car as it did now. He glanced behind him, and saw 13th Street far below. It made him dizzy. He wouldn't even have gotten this far if it hadn't been for the tracks. Where the slope grew almost vertical, he'd been able to scrabble up from tie to tie, using them like rungs on a ladder. His hands were full of splinters, but it beat trying to crawl up the wet rock, clinging to ferns for dear life.

Of course, he could have changed, and bounded up the tracks in no time at all. But somehow he didn't think that would have been such a good idea. *I could smell him coming*, Steven had said. The human scent was fainter, in a city full of people. He had to hope that Steven and Jonathan were inside the New House, locked up for the night. But if they were out prowling around, at least this way Willie thought he had a ghost of a chance.

He'd rested long enough. He craned his head back, looking up at the high black iron fence that ran along the top of the bluff, trying to measure how much further he had to go. Then he took a good long shot off his inhaler, gritted his teeth, and scrambled for the next tie up.

*

The windshield wipers swept back and forth almost silently as the long dark car nosed through the night. The windows were tinted a gray so dark it was almost black. Urquhart was in civvies, a red-and-black lumberjack shirt, dark woolen slacks, and bulky down jacket. His police cap was his only concession to uniform. He stared straight out into the darkness as he drove. 'You look terrible,' she told him.

'I feel worse.' They swept under an overpass and around a long ramp onto the river road. 'I feel old, Randi. Like this city. This whole damn city is old and rotten.'

'Where are we going?' she asked him. At this hour of night, there was no other traffic on the road. The river was a black emptiness off to their left. Streetlamps swam in haloes of rain to the right as they sailed past block after cold, empty block stretching away toward the bluffs.

'To the pack,' Urquhart said. 'To where it happened.'

The car's heater was pouring out a steady blast of warm air, but suddenly Randi felt deathly cold. Her hand went inside her coat, and closed around the hilt of the knife. The silver felt comfortable and comforting. 'All right,' she said. She slid the knife out of her belt and put it on the seat between them.

Urquhart glanced over. She watched him carefully 'What's that?' he said.

'Silver,' Randi said. 'Pick it up.'

He looked at her. 'What?'

'You heard me,' she said. 'Pick it up.'

He looked at the road, at her face, back out at the road. He made no move to touch the knife.

'I'm not kidding,' Randi said. She slid away from him, to the far side of the seat, and braced her back against the door. When Urquhart looked over again, she had the gun out, aimed right between his eyes. 'Pick it up,' she said very clearly.

The color left his face. He started to say something, but Randi shook her head curtly. Urquhart licked his lips, took his hand off the wheel, and picked up the knife. 'There,' he said, holding it up awkwardly while he drove with one hand. 'I picked it up. Now what am I supposed to do with it?'

Randi slumped back against the seat. 'Put it down,' she said with relief.

Joe looked at her.

*

He rested for a long time in the shrubs on top of the bluff, listening to the rain fall around him and dreading what other sounds he might hear. He kept imagining soft footfalls stealing up behind him, and once he thought he heard a low growl somewhere off to his right. He could feel his hackles rise, and until that moment he hadn't even known he *had* hackles, but it was nothing, just his nerves working on him; Willie had always had bad nerves. The night was cold and black and empty.

When he finally had his breath back, Willie began to edge past the New House, keeping to the bushes as much as he could, well away from the windows. There were a few lights on, but no other sign of life. Maybe they'd all gone to bed. He hoped so.

He moved slowly and carefully, trying to be as quiet as possible. He watched where his feet came down, and every few steps he'd stop, look around, listen. He could change in an instant if he heard anyone . . . or any*thing* . . . coming toward him. He didn't know how much good that would do, but maybe, just maybe, it would give him a chance.

His raincoat dragged at him, a water-logged second skin as heavy as lead. His shoes had soaked through, and the leather squished when he moved. Willie pushed away from the house, further back into the trees, until a bend in the road hid the lights from view. Only then, after a careful glance in both directions to make sure nothing was coming, did he dare risk a dash across the road.

Once across he plunged deeper into the woods, moving faster now, a little more heedless. He wondered where Roy Helander had been when

Steven had caught him. Somewhere around here, Willie thought, some-where in this dark primal forest, surrounded by old growth, with centuries of leaves and moss and dead things rotting in the earth beneath his feet.

As he moved away from the bluff and the city, the forest grew denser, until finally the trees pressed so close together that he lost sight of the sky, and the raindrops stopped pounding against his head. It was almost dry here. Overhead, the rain drummed relentlessly against a canopy of leaves. Willie's skin felt clammy, and for a moment he was lost, as if he'd wandered into some terrible cavern far beneath the earth, a dismal cold place where no light ever shone.

Then he stumbled between two huge, twisted old oaks, and felt air and rain against his face again, and raised his head, and there it was ahead of him, broken windows gaping down like so many blind eyes from walls carved from rock that shone like midnight and drank all light and hope. The tower loomed up to his right, some monstrous erection against the storm clouds, leaning crazily.

Willie stopped breathing, groped for his inhaler, found it, dropped it, picked it up. The mouthpiece was slimy with humus. He cleaned it on his sleeve, shoved it in his mouth, took a hit, two, three, and finally his throat opened up again.

He glanced around, heard only the rain, saw nothing. He stepped forward toward the tower. Toward Roy Helander's secret refuge.

*

The big double gate in the high chain-link fence had been padlocked for two years, but it was open tonight, and Urquhart drove straight through. Randi wondered if the gate had been opened for her father as well. She thought maybe it had.

Joe pulled up near one of the loading docks, in the shadow of the old brick slaughterhouse. The building gave them some shelter from the rain, but Randi still trembled in the cold as she climbed out. 'Here?' she asked. 'This is where you found him?'

Urquhart was staring off into the stockyard. It was a huge area, subdivided into a dozen pens along the railroad siding. There was a maze of chest-high fencing they called the 'runs' between the slaughterhouse and the pens, to force the cows into a single line and herd them along inside, where a man in a blood-splattered apron waited with a hammer in his hand. 'Here,' Joe said, without looking back at her.

There was a long silence. Somewhere far off, Randi thought she heard a faint, wild howl, but maybe that was just the wind and the rain. 'Do you believe in ghosts?' she asked Joe.

'Ghosts?' The chief sounded distracted.

She shivered. 'It's like . . . I can feel him, Joe. Like he's still here, after all this time, still watching over me.'

Joe Urquhart turned toward her. His face was wet with rain or maybe tears. 'I watched over you,' he said. 'He asked me to watch over you, and I did, I did my best.'

Randi heard a sound somewhere off in the night. She turned her head, frowning, listening. Tires crunched across gravel and she saw headlights outside the fence. Another car coming.

'You and your father, you're a lot alike,' Joe said wearily. 'Stubborn. Won't listen to nobody. I took good care of you, didn't I take good care of you? I got my own kids, you know, but you never wanted nothing, did you? So why the hell didn't you listen to me?'

By then Randi knew. She wasn't surprised. Somehow she felt as though she'd known for a long time. 'There was only one phone call that night,' she said. 'You were the one who phoned for backup, not Dad.'

Urquhart nodded. He was caught for a moment in the headlights of the oncoming car, and Randi saw the way his jaw trembled as he worked to get out the words. 'Look in the glove box,' he said.

Randi opened the car door, sat on the edge of the seat, and did as he said. The glove compartment was unlocked. Inside was a bottle of aspirin, a tire pressure gauge, some maps, and a box of cartridges. Randi opened the box and poured some bullets out into her palm. They glimmered pale and cold in the car's faint dome light. She left the box on the seat, climbed out, kicked the door shut. 'My silver bullets,' she said. 'I hadn't expected them quite so soon.'

'Those are the ones Frank ordered made up, eighteen years ago,' Joe said. 'After he was buried, I went by the gunsmith and picked them up. Like I said, you and him you were a lot alike.'

The second car pulled to a stop, pinning her in its high beams. Randi threw a hand across her eyes against the glare. She heard a car door opening and closing.

Urquhart's voice was anguished. 'I told you to stay away from this thing, damn it. I *told* you! Don't you understand? They *own* this city!'

'He's right. You should have listened,' Rogoff said, as he stepped into the light.

*

Willie groped his way down the long dark hall with one hand on the wall, placing each foot carefully in front of the last. The stone was so thick that even the sound of the rain did not reach him. There was only the echo of his careful footsteps, and the rush of blood inside his ears. The silence within the Old House was profound and unnerving, and there was something about the walls that bothered him as well. It was cold, but the stones under his fingers were moist and curiously warm to the touch, and Willie was glad for the darkness.

Finally he reached the base of the tower, where shafts of dim light fell across crabbed, narrow stone steps that spiraled up and up and up. Willie began to climb. He counted the steps at first, but somewhere around two hundred he lost the count, and the rest was a grim ordeal that he endured in silence. More than once he thought of changing. He resisted the impulse.

His legs ached from the effort when he reached the top. He sat down on the steps for a moment, his back to a slick stone wall. He was breathing hard, but when he groped for his inhaler, it was gone. He'd probably lost it in the woods. He could feel his lungs constricting in panic, but there was no help for it.

Willie got up.

The room smelled of blood and urine and something else, a scent he did not place, but somehow it made him tremble. There was no roof. Willie realized that the rain had stopped while he'd been inside. He looked up as the clouds parted, and a pale white moon stared down.

And all around other moons shimmered into life, reflected in the tall empty mirrors that lined the chamber. They reflected the sky above and each other, moon after moon after moon, until the room swam in silvered moonlight and reflections of reflections of reflections.

Willie turned around in a slow circle and a dozen other Willies turned with him. The moonstruck mirrors were streaked with dried blood, and above them a ring of cruel iron hooks curved up from the stone walls. A human skin hung from one of them, twisting slowly in some wind he could not feel, and as the moonlight hit it, it seemed to writhe and change, from woman to wolf to woman, both and neither.

That was when Willie heard the footsteps on the stairs.

*

'The silver bullets were a bad idea,' Rogoff said. 'We have a local ordinance here. The police get immediate notice any time someone places an order for custom ammunition. Your father made the same mistake. The pack takes a dim view of silver bullets.'

Randi felt strangely relieved. For a moment she'd been afraid that Willie had betrayed her, that he'd been one of them after all, and that thought had been like poison in her soul. Her fingers were still curled tight around a dozen of the bullets. She glanced down at them, so close and yet so far.

'Even if they're still good, you'll never get them loaded in time,' Rogoff said.

'You don't need the bullets,' Urquhart told her. 'He just wants to talk. They promised me, honey, no one needs to get hurt.'

Randi opened her hand. The bullets fell to the ground. She turned to Joe Urquhart. 'You were my father's best friend. He said you had more guts than any man he ever knew.'

'They don't give you any choice,' Urquhart said. 'I had kids of my own. They said if Roy Helander took the fall, no more kids would vanish, they promised they'd take care of it, but if we kept pressing, one of my kids would be the next to go. That's how it works in this town. Everything would have been all right, but Frank just wouldn't let it alone.'

'We only kill in self-defense,' Rogoff said. 'There's a sweetness to human flesh, yes, a power that's undeniable, but it's not worth the risk.'

'What about the children?' Randi said. 'Did you kill them in self-defense too?'

'That was a long time ago,' Rogoff said.

Joe stood with his head downcast. He was beaten, Randi saw, and she realized that he'd been beaten for a long time. All those trophies on his walls, but somehow she knew that he had given up hunting forever on the night her father died 'It was his son.' Joe muttered quietly, in a voice full of shame. 'Steven's never been right in the head, everyone knows that, he was the one who killed the kids, *ate* them. It was horrible, Harmon told me so himself, but he still wasn't going to let us have Steven. He said he'd . . . he'd control Steven's . . . appetites . . . if we closed the case. He was good as his word too, he put Steven on medication, and it stopped, the murders stopped.'

She ought to hate Joe Urquhart, she realized, but instead she pitied him. After all this time, he still didn't understand. 'Joe, he lied. It was never Steven.'

'It was Steven,' Joe insisted, 'it had to be, he's insane. The rest of them . . . you can do business with them, Randi, listen to me now, you can talk to them.'

'Like you did,' she said. 'Like Barry Schumacher.'

Urquhart nodded. 'That's right. They're just like us, they got some crazies, but not all of them are bad. You can't blame them for taking care of their own, we do the same thing, don't we? Look at Mike here, he's a good cop.'

'A good cop who's going to change into a wolf in a minute or two and tear out my throat,' Randi said.

'Randi, honey, listen to me,' Urquhart said. 'It doesn't have to be like that. You can walk out of here, just say the word. I'll get you onto the force, you can work with us, help us to . . . to keep the peace. Your father's dead, you won't bring him back, and the Helander boy, he deserved what he got, he was *killing* them, skinning them alive; it was self-defense. Steven is sick, he's always been sick—'

Rogoff was watching her from beneath his tangle of black hair. 'He still doesn't get it,' she said. She turned back to Joe. 'Steven is sicker than you think. Something is missing. Too inbred, maybe. Think about it. Anders and Rochmonts, Flambeauxes and Harmons, the four great founding families, all werewolves, marrying each other generation after generation to keep the lines pure, for how many centuries? They kept the lines pure all right. They bred themselves Steven. He didn't kill those children. Roy Helander saw a *wolf* carry off his sister, and Steven can't change into a wolf. He got the bloodlust, he got inhuman strength, he burns at the touch of silver, but that's all. The last of the purebloods *can't work the change!*'

'She's right,' Rogoff said quietly.

'Why do you think you never found any remains?' Randi put in. 'Steven didn't kill those kids. His father carried them off, up to Blackstone.'

'The old man had some crazy idea that if Steven ate enough human flesh, it might fix him, make him whole,' Rogoff said.

'It didn't work,' Randi said. She took Willie's note out of her pocket, let the pages flutter to the ground. It was all there. She'd finished reading it before she'd gone down to meet Joe. Frank Wade's little girl was nobody's fool.

'It didn't work,' Rogoff echoed, 'but by then Jonathan had got the taste. Once you get started, it's hard to stop.' He looked at Randi for a long time, as if he were weighing something. Then he began . . .

*

. . . to change. Sweet cold air filled his lungs, and his muscles and bones ran with fire as the transformation took hold. He'd shrugged out of pants and coat, and he heard the rest of his clothing ripping apart as his body writhed, his flesh ran like hot wax, and he reformed, born anew.

Now he could see and hear and smell. The tower room shimmered with moonlight, every detail clear and sharp as noon, and the night was alive with sound, the wind and the rain and the rustle of bats in the forest around them, and traffic sounds and sirens from the city beyond. He was alive and full of power, and something was coming up the steps. It climbed slowly, untiring, and its smells filled the air. The scent of blood hung all around it, and beneath he sensed an aftershave that masked an unwashed body, sweat and dried semen on its skin, a heavy tang of wood smoke in its hair, and under it all the scent of sickness, sweetly rotten as a grave.

Willie backed all the way across the room, staring at the arched door, the growl rising in his throat. He bared long yellowed teeth, and slaver ran between them.

Steven stopped in the doorway and looked at him. He was naked. The wolf's hot red eyes met his cold blue ones, and it was hard to tell which were more inhuman. For a moment Willie thought that Steven didn't quite comprehend. Until he smiled and reached for the skin that twisted above him, on an iron hook.

Willie leapt.

He took Steven high in the back and bore him down, with his hand still clutched around Zoe's skin. For a second Willie had a clear shot at his throat, but he hesitated and the moment passed. Steven caught Willie's foreleg in a pale scarred fist, and snapped it in half like a normal man might break a stick. The pain was excruciating. Then Steven was lifting him, flinging him away. He smashed up hard against one of the mirrors, and felt it shatter at the impact. Jagged shards of glass flew like knives, and one of them lanced through his side.

Willie rolled away; the glass spear broke under him, and he whimpered. Across the room, Steven was getting to his feet. He put out a hand to steady himself.

Willie scrambled up. His broken leg was knitting already, though it hurt when he put his weight on it. Glass fragments clawed inside him with every step. He could barely move. Some fucking werewolf he turned out to be.

Steven was adjusting his ghastly cloak, pulling flaps of skin down over his own face. The skin trade, Willie thought giddily, yeah, that was it, and in a moment Steven would use that damn flayed skin to do what he could never manage on his own, he would *change*, and then Willie would be meat.

Willie came at him, jaws gaping, but too slow. Steven's foot pistoned down, caught him hard enough to take his breath away, pinned him to the floor. Willie tried to squirm free, but Steven was too strong. He was bearing down, crushing him. All of a sudden Willie remembered that dog, so many years ago.

Willie bent himself almost double and took a bite out of the back of Steven's calf.

The blood filled his mouth, exploding inside him. Steven reeled back. Willie jumped up, darted forward, bit him again. This time he sank his teeth in good and held, worrying at the flesh. The pounding in his head was thunderous. He was full of power, he could feel it swelling within him. Suddenly he knew that he could tear Steven apart; he could taste the fine sweet flesh close to the bone, could hear the music of his screams, could imagine the way it would feel when he held him in his jaws and shook him like a rag doll and felt the life go out of him in a sudden giddy rush. It swept over him, and Willie bit and bit and bit again, ripping away chunks of meat, drunk on blood.

And then, dimly, he heard Steven screaming, screaming in a high shrill thin voice, a little boy's voice. 'No, Daddy,' he was whining, over and over again. 'No, please, don't bite me, Daddy, don't bite me any more.'

Willie let him go and backed away.

Steven sat on the floor, sobbing. He was bleeding like a son of a bitch. Pieces were missing from thigh, calf, shoulder, and foot. His legs were drenched in blood. Three fingers were gone off his right hand. His cheeks were slimy with gore.

Suddenly Willie was scared.

For a moment he didn't understand. Steven was beaten, he could see that; he could rip out his throat or let him live, it didn't matter, it was over. But something was wrong, something was terribly, sickeningly wrong. It felt as though the temperature had dropped a hundred degrees, and every hair on his body was prickling and standing on end. What the hell was going on? He growled low in his throat and backed away, toward the door, keeping a careful eye on Steven.

Steven giggled. 'You'll get it now,' he said. 'You called it. You got blood on the mirrors. You called it back again.'

The room seemed to spin. Moonlight ran from mirror to mirror to mirror, dizzyingly. Or maybe it wasn't moonlight.

Willie looked into the mirrors.

The reflections were gone. Willie, Steven, the moon, all gone. There was blood on the mirrors and they were full of fog, a silvery pale fog that shimmered as it moved.

Something was moving through the fog, sliding from mirror to mirror to mirror, around and around. Something hungry that wanted to get out.

He saw it, lost it, saw it again. It was in front of him, behind him, off to the side. It was a hound, gaunt and terrible; it was a snake, scaled and foul; it was a man, with eyes like pits and knives for its fingers. It wouldn't hold still, every time he looked its shape seemed to change, and each shape was worse than the last, more twisted and obscene. Everything about it was lean and cruel. Its fingers were sharp, so sharp, and he looked at them and felt their caress sliding beneath his skin, tingling along the nerves, pain and blood and fire trailing behind them. It was black, blacker than black, a black that drank all light forever, and it was all shining silver too. It was a nightmare that lived in a funhouse mirror, the thing that hunts the hunters.

He could feel the evil throbbing through the glass.

'Skinner,' Steven called.

The surface of the mirrors seemed to ripple and bulge, like a wave

cresting on some quicksilver sea. The fog was thinning, Willie realized with
sudden terror; he could see it clearer now, and he knew it could see him.
And suddenly Willie Flambeaux knew what was happening, knew that
when the fog cleared the mirrors wouldn't be mirrors anymore; they'd be
doors, *doors*, and the skinner would come . . .

*

. . . sliding forward, through the ruins of his clothing, slitted eyes glowing
like embers from a muzzle black as coal. He was half again as large as
Willie had been, his fur thick and black and shaggy, and when he opened
his mouth, his teeth gleamed like ivory daggers.

Randi edged backward, along the side of the car. The knife was in her
hand, moonlight running off the silver blade, but somehow it didn't seem
like very much. The huge black wolf advanced on her, his tongue lolling
between his teeth, and she put her back up against the car door and braced
herself for his leap.

Joe Urquhart stepped between them.

'No,' he said. 'Not her too, you owe me, talk to her, give her a chance, I'll
make her see how it is.'

The wolf growled a warning.

Urquhart stood his ground, and all of a sudden he had his revolver out,
and he was holding it in two shaky hands, drawing a bead. 'Stop. I mean
it. She didn't have time to load the goddamned silver bullets, but I've had
eighteen fucking years. I'm the fucking police chief in this fucking city,
and you're under arrest.'

Randi put her hand on the door handle, eased it open. For a moment the
wolf stood frozen, baleful red eyes fixed on Joe, and she thought it was
actually going to work. She remembered her father's old Wednesday night
poker games; he'd always said Joe, unlike Barry Schumacher, ran one hell
of a bluff.

Then the wolf threw back his head and howled, and all the blood went
out of her. She knew that sound. She'd heard it in her dreams a thousand
times. It was in her blood, that sound, an echo from far off and long ago,
when the world had been a forest and humans had run naked in fear
before the hunting pack. It echoed off the side of the old slaughterhouse
and trembled out over the city, and they must have heard it all over the
flats, heard it and glanced outside nervously and checked their locks before
they turned up the volumes on their TVs.

Randi opened the door wider and slid one leg inside the car as the wolf
leapt.

She heard Urquhart fire, and fire again, and then the wolf slammed into
his chest and smashed him back against the car door. Randi was half into

the car, but the door swung shut hard, crunching down on her left foot with awful force. She heard a bone break under the impact, and shrieked at the sudden flare of pain. Outside Urquhart fired again, and then he was screaming. There were ripping sounds and more screams and something wet spattered against her ankle.

Her foot was trapped, and the struggle outside slammed her open door against it again and again and again. Each impact was a small explosion as the shattered bones grated together and ripped against raw nerves. Joe was screaming and droplets of blood covered the tinted window like rain. Her head swam, and for a moment Randi thought she'd faint from the pain, but she threw all her weight against the door and moved it just enough and drew her foot inside and when the next impact came it slapped the door shut *hard* and Randi pressed the lock.

She leaned against the wheel and almost threw up. Joe had stopped screaming, but she could hear the wolf tearing at him, ripping off chunks of flesh. *Once you get started it's hard to stop,* she thought hysterically. She got out the .38, cracked the cylinder with shaking hands, flicked out the shells. Then she was fumbling around on the front seat. She found the box, tipped it over, snatched up a handful of silver.

It was silent outside. Randi stopped, looked up.

He was on the hood of the car.

*

Willie *changed*.

He was running on instinct now; he didn't know why he did it, he just did. The pain was there waiting for him along with his humanity, as he'd known it would be. It shrieked through him like a gale wind, and sent him whimpering to the floor. He could feel the glass shard under his ribs, dangerously close to a lung, and his left arm bent sickeningly downward at a place it was never meant to bend, and when he tried to move it, he screamed and bit his tongue and felt his mouth fill with blood.

The fog was a pale thin haze now, and the mirror closest to him bulged outward, throbbing like something alive.

Steven sat against the wall, his blue eyes bright and avid, sucking his own blood from the stumps of his fingers. 'Changing won't help,' he said in that weird flat tone of his. 'Skinner don't care. It knows what you are. Once it's called, it's got to have a skin.' Willie's vision was blurry with tears, but he saw it again then, in the mirror behind Steven, pushing at the fading fog, pushing, pushing, trying to get through.

He staggered to his feet. Pain roared through his head. He cradled his broken arm against his body, took a step toward the stairs, and felt broken glass grind against his bare feet. He looked down. Pieces of the shattered mirror were everywhere.

Willie's head snapped up. He looked around wildly, dizzy, counting. Six, seven, eight, nine . . . the tenth was broken. Nine then. He threw himself forward, slammed all his body weight into the nearest mirror. It shattered under the impact, disintegrated into a thousand pieces. Willie crunched the biggest shards underfoot, stamped on them until his heels ran wet with blood. He was moving without thought. He caromed around the room, using his own body as a weapon, hearing the sweet tinkling music of breaking glass. The world turned into a red fog of pain and a thousand little knives sliced at him everywhere, and he wondered, if the skinner came through and got him, whether he'd even be able to tell the difference.

Then he was staggering away from another mirror, and white hot needles were stabbing through his feet with every step, turning into fire as they lanced up his calves. He stumbled and fell, hard. Flying glass had cut his face to ribbons, and the blood ran down into his eyes.

Willie blinked, and wiped the blood away with his good hand. His old raincoat was underneath him, blood-soaked and covered with ground glass and shards of mirror. Steven stood over him, staring down. Behind him was a mirror. Or was it a door?

'You missed one,' Steven said flatly.

Something hard was digging into his gut, Willie realized. His hand fumbled around beneath him, slid into the pocket of his raincoat, closed on cold metal.

'Skinner's coming for you now,' Steven said.

Willie couldn't see. The blood had filled his eyes again. But he could still feel. He got his fingers through the loops and rolled and brought his hand up fast and hard, with all the strength he had left, and put Mr Scissors right through the meat of Steven's groin.

The last thing he heard was a scream, and the sound of breaking glass.

*

Calm, Randi thought, *calm*, but the dread that filled her was more than simple fear. Blood matted his jaws, and his eyes stared at her through the windshield, glowing that hideous baleful red. She looked away quickly, tried to chamber a bullet. Her hands shook, and it slid out of her grip, onto the floor of the car. She ignored it, tried again.

The wolf howled, turned, fled. For a moment she lost sight of him. Randi craned her head around, peering nervously out through the darkness. She glanced into the rearview mirror, but it was fogged up, useless. She shivered, as much from cold as from fear. *Where was he?* she thought wildly.

Then she saw him, running toward the car.

Randi looked down, chambered a bullet, and had a second in her fingers when he came flying over the hood and smashed against the glass. Cracks spiderwebbed out from the center of the windshield. The wolf snarled at her. Slaver and blood smeared the glass. Then he hit the glass again. Again. Again. Randi jumped with every impact. The windshield cracked and cracked again, then a big section in the center went milky and opaque.

She had the second bullet in the cylinder. She slid in a third. Her hands were shaking as much from cold as from fear. It was freezing inside the car. She looked out into the darkness through a haze of cracks and blood smears, loaded a fourth bullet, and was closing the cylinder when he hit the windshield again and it all caved in on her.

One moment she had the gun and the next it was gone. The weight was on her chest and the safety glass, broken into a million milky pieces but still clinging together, fell across her face like a shroud. Then it ripped away, and the blood-soaked jaws and hot red eyes were right there in front of her.

The wolf opened his mouth and she was feeling the furnace heat of his breath, smelling awful carnivore stench.

'You fucker!' she screamed, and almost laughed, because it wasn't much as last words go.

Something sharp and silvery bright came sliding down through the back of his throat.

It went so quickly Randi didn't understand what was happening, no more than he did. Suddenly the bloodlust went out of the dark red eyes, and they were full of pain and shock and finally fear, and she saw more silver knives sliding through his throat before his mouth filled with blood. And then the great black-furred body shuddered, and struggled, as something pulled it back off her, front paws beating a tattoo against the seat. There was a smell of burning hair in the air. When the wolf began to scream, it sounded almost human.

Randi choked back her own pain, slammed her shoulder against the door, and knocked what was left of Joe Urquhart aside. Halfway out the door, she glanced back.

The hand was twisted and cruel, and its fingers were long bright silver razors, pale and cold and sharp as sin. Like five long jointed knives the fingers had sunk through the back of the wolf's neck, and grabbed hold, and pulled, and the blood was coming out between his teeth in great gouts now and his legs were kicking feebly. It yanked at him then, and she heard a sickening wet *crunching* as the thing began to *pull* the wolf through the rearview mirror with inexorable, unimaginable force, to whatever was on the other side. The great black-furred body seemed to waver and shift for a second, and the wolf's face took on an almost human cast.

When his eyes met hers, the red light had gone out of them; there was nothing there but pain and pleading.

His first *name was Mike,* she remembered.

Randi looked down. Her gun was on the floor.

She picked it up, checked the cylinder, closed it, jammed the barrel up against his head, and fired four times.

When she got out of the car and put her weight on her ankle, the pain washed over her in great waves. Randi collapsed to her hands and knees. She was throwing up when she heard the sirens.

*

'. . . some kind of animal,' she said.

The detective gave her a long, sour look, and closed his notebook. 'That's all you can tell me?' he said. 'That Chief Urquhart was killed by some kind of animal?'

Randi wanted to say something sharp, but she was all fucked up on painkillers. They'd had to put two pins in her and it still hurt like hell, and the doctors said she'd have to stay another week. 'What do you want me to tell you?' she said weakly. 'That's what I saw, some kind of animal. A wolf.'

The detective shook his head. 'Fine. So the chief was killed by some kind of animal, probably a wolf. So where's Rogoff? His car was there, his blood was all over the inside of the chief's car, so tell me . . . *where the fuck is Rogoff?'*

Randi closed her eyes, and pretended it was the pain. 'I don't know,' she said.

'I'll be back,' the detective said when he left.

She lay with her eyes closed for a moment, thinking maybe she could drift back to sleep, until she heard the door open and close. 'He won't be,' a soft voice told her. 'We'll see to it.'

Randi opened her eyes. At the foot of the bed was an old man with long white hair leaning on a gold wolf's head cane. He wore a black suit, a mourning suit, and his hair fell to his shoulders. 'My name is Jonathan Harmon,' he said.

'I've seen your picture. I know who you are. And what you are.' Her voice was hoarse. 'A lycanthrope.'

'Please,' he said. 'A werewolf.'

'Willie . . . what happened to Willie?'

'Steven is dead,' Jonathan Harmon said.

'Good,' Randi spat. 'Steven and Roy, they were doing it together, Willie said. For the skins. Steven hated the others, because they could work the change and he couldn't. But once your son had his skin, he didn't need Helander anymore, did he?'

'I can't say I will mourn greatly. To be frank, Steven was never the sort of heir I might have wished for.' He went to the window, opened the curtains, and looked out. 'This was once a great city, you know, a city of blood and iron. Now it's all turned to rust.'

'Fuck your city,' Randi said. 'What about Willie?'

'It was a pity about Zoe, but once the skinner has been summoned, it keeps hunting until it takes a skin, from mirror to mirror to mirror. It knows our scent, but it doesn't like to wander far from its gates. I don't know how your mongrel friend managed to evade it twice, but he did . . . to Zoe's misfortune, and Michael's.' He turned and looked at her. 'You will not be so lucky. Don't congratulate yourself too vigorously, child. The pack takes care of its own. The doctor who writes your next prescription, the pharmacist who fills it, the boy who delivers it . . . any of them could be one of us. We don't forget our enemies, Miss Wade. Your family would do well to remember that.'

'You were the one,' she said with a certainty. 'In the stockyards, the night my father . . .'

Jonathan nodded curtly. 'He was a crack shot, I'll grant him that. He put six bullets in me. My war wounds, I call them. They still show up on X-rays, but my doctors have learned not to be curious.'

'I'll kill you,' Randi said.

'I think not.' He leaned over the bed. 'Perhaps I'll come for you myself some night. You ought to see me, Miss Wade. My fur is white now, pale as snow, but the stature, the majesty, the power, those have not left me. Michael was a half-breed, and your Willie, he was hardly more than a dog. The pureblood is rather more. We are the dire wolves, the nightmares who haunt your racial memories, the dark shapes circling endlessly beyond the light of your fires.'

He smiled down at her, then turned and walked away. At the door he paused. 'Sleep well,' he said.

Randi did not sleep at all, not even when night fell and the nurse came in and turned out the lights, despite all her pleading. She lay there in the dark staring up at the ceiling, feeling more alone than she'd ever been. He was dead, she thought. Willie was dead and she'd better start getting used to the idea. Very softly, alone in the darkness of the private room, she began to cry.

She cried for a long time, for Willie and Joan Sorenson and Joe Urquhart and finally, after all this time, for Frank Wade. She ran out of tears and kept crying, her body shaking with dry sobs. She was still shaking when the door opened softly, and a thin knife of light from the hall cut across the room.

'Who's there?' she said hoarsely. 'Answer, or I'll scream.'

The door closed quietly. 'Ssssh. Quiet, or they'll hear.' It was a woman's voice, young, a little scared. 'The nurse said I couldn't come in, that it was after visiting hours, but he told me to get to you right away.' She moved close to the bed.

Randi turned on her reading light. Her visitor looked nervously toward the door. She was dark, pretty, no more than twenty, with a spray of freckles across her nose. 'I'm Betsy Juddiker,' she whispered. 'Willie said I was to give you a message, but it's all crazy stuff . . .'

Randi's heart skipped a beat. 'Willie . . . tell me! I don't care how crazy it sounds, just tell me.'

'He said that he couldn't phone you hisself because the pack might be listening in, that he got hurt bad but he's okay, that he's up north, and he's found this vet who's taking care of him good. I know, it sounds funny, but that's what he said, a vet.'

'Go on.'

Betsy nodded. 'He sounded hurt on the phone, and he said he couldn't . . . couldn't *change* right now, except for a few minutes to call, because he was hurt and the pain was always waiting for him, but to say that the vet had gotten most of the glass out and set his leg and he was going to be fine. And then he said that on the night he'd gone, he'd come by *my* house and left something for you, and I was to find it and bring it here.' She opened her purse and rummaged around. 'It was in the bushes by the mailbox, my little boy found it.' She gave it over.

It was a piece of some broken mirror, Randi saw, a shard as long and slender as her finger. She held it in her hand for a moment, confused and uncertain. The glass was cold to the touch, and it seemed to grow colder as she held it.

'Careful, it's real sharp,' Betsy said. 'There was one more thing, I don't understand it at all, but Willie said it was important. He said to tell you that there were no mirrors where he was, not a one, but last he'd seen, there were plenty up in Blackstone.'

Randi nodded, not quite grasping it, not yet. She ran a finger thoughtfully along the shiny sliver of glass.

'Oh, look,' Betsy said. 'I told you. Now you've gone and cut yourself.'

Unsound Variations

A fter they swung off the interstate, the road became a narrow two-lane that wound a tortuous path through the mountains in a series of switchbacks, each steeper than the last. Peaks rose all around them, pine-covered and crowned by snow and ice, while swift cold waterfalls flashed by, barely seen, on either side. The sky was a bright and brilliant blue. It was exhilarating scenery, but it did nothing to lighten Peter's mood. He concentrated blindly on the road, losing himself in the mindless reflexes of driving.

As the mountains grew higher, the radio reception grew poorer, stations fading in and out with every twist in the road, until at last they could get nothing at all. Kathy went from one end of the band to the other, searching, and then back again. Finally she snapped off the radio in disgust. 'I guess you'll just have to talk to me,' she said.

Peter didn't need to look at her to hear the sharpness in her tone, the bitter edge of sarcasm that had long ago replaced fondness in her voice. She was looking for an argument, he knew. She was angry about the radio, and she resented him dragging her on this trip, and most of all she resented being married to him. At times, when he was feeling very sorry for himself, he did not even blame her. He had not turned out to be much of a bargain as a husband; a failed writer, failed journalist, failing businessman, depressed and depressing. He was still a lively sparring partner, however. Perhaps that was why she tried to provoke fights so often. After all the blood had been let, one or both of them would start crying, and then they would usually make love, and life would be pleasant for an hour or two. It was about all they had left.

Not today, though. Peter lacked the energy, and his mind was on other things. 'What do you want to talk about?' he asked her. He kept his tone amicable and his eyes on the road.

'Tell me about these clowns we're going to visit,' she said.

'I did. They were my teammates on the chess team, back when I was at Northwestern.'

'Since when is chess a team sport anyway?' Kathy said. 'What'd you do, vote on each move?'

'No. In chess, a team match is really a bunch of individual matches. Usually four or five boards, at least in college play. There's no consultation or anything. The team that wins the most individual games wins the match point. The way it works—'

'I get it,' she said sharply. 'I may not be a chess player, but I'm not stupid. So you and these other three were the Northwestern team?'

'Yes and no,' Peter said. The Toyota was straining; it wasn't used to grades this steep, and it hadn't been adjusted for altitude before they took off from Chicago. He drove carefully. They were up high enough now to come across icy patches, and snow drifting across the road.

'Yes and no,' Kathy said sarcastically. 'What does that mean?'

'Northwestern had a big chess club back then. We played in a lot of tournaments – local, state, national. Sometimes we fielded more than one team, so the line-up was a bit different every tournament. It depended on who could play and who couldn't, who had a midterm, who'd played in the last match – lots of things. We four were Northwestern's B team in the North American Intercollegiate Team Championships, ten years ago this week. Northwestern hosted that tournament, and I ran it, as well as playing.'

'What do you mean *B team?*'

Peter cleared his throat and eased the Toyota around a sharp curve, gravel rattling against the underside of the car as one wheel brushed the shoulder. 'A school wasn't limited to just one team,' he said. 'If you had the money and a lot of people who wanted to play, you could enter several. Your best four players would make up your A team, the real contender. The second four would be the B team, and so on.' He paused briefly, and continued with a faint note of pride in his voice. 'The nationals at Northwestern were the biggest ever held, up to that time, although of course that record has since been broken. We set a second record, though, that still stands. Since the tournament was on our home grounds, we had lots of players on hand. We entered six teams. No other school has ever had more than four in the nationals, before or after.' The record still brought a smile to his face. Maybe it wasn't much of a record, but it was the only one he had, and it was *his.* Some people lived and died without ever setting a record of any kind, he reflected silently. Maybe he ought to tell Kathy to put his on his tombstone: HERE LIES PETER K. NORTEN. HE FIELDED SIX TEAMS. He chuckled.

'What's so funny?'

'Nothing.'

She didn't pursue it. 'So you ran this tournament, you say?'

'I was the club president and the chairman of the local committee. I didn't direct, but I put together the bid that brought the nationals to

Evanston, made all the preliminary arrangements. And I organized all six of our teams, decided who would play on each one, appointed the team captains. But during the tournament itself I was only the captain of the B team.'

She laughed. 'So you were a big deal on the second-string. It figures. The story of your life.'

Peter bit back a sharp reply, and said nothing. The Toyota swerved around another hairpin, and a vast Colorado mountain panorama opened up in front of them. It left him strangely unmoved.

After a while Kathy said, 'When did you stop playing chess?'

'I sort of gave it up after college. Not a conscious decision, really. I just kind of drifted out of it. I haven't played a game of tournament chess in almost nine years. I'm probably pretty rusty by now. But back then I was fairly good.'

'How good is fairly good?'

'I was rated as a Class A player, like everyone else on our B team.'

'What does that mean?'

'It means my USCF rating was substantially higher than that of the vast majority of tournament chess players in the country,' he said. 'And the tournament players are generally much better than the unrated wood-pushers you encounter in bars and coffeehouses. The ratings went all the way down to Class E. Above Class A you had Experts, and Masters, and Senior Masters at the top, but there weren't many of them.'

'Three classes above you?'

'Yes.'

'So you might say, at your very best, you were a fourth-class chess player.'

At that Peter did look over at her. She was leaning back in her seat, a faint smirk on her face. 'Bitch,' he said. He was suddenly angry.

'Keep your eyes on the road!' Kathy snapped.

He wrenched the car around the next turn hard as he could, and pressed down on the gas. She hated it when he drove fast. 'I don't know why the hell I try to talk to you,' he said.

'My husband, the big deal,' she said. She laughed. 'A fourth-class chess player playing on the junior varsity team. And a fifth-rate driver too.'

'Shut up,' Peter said furiously. 'You don't know what the hell you're talking about. Maybe we were only the B team, but we were good. We finished better than anyone had any right to expect, only a half-point behind Northwestern A. And we almost scored one of the biggest upsets in history.'

'Do tell.'

Peter hesitated, already regretting his words. The memory was important to him, almost as important as his silly little record. *He* knew what it
meant, how close they had come. But she'd never understand; it would
only be another failure for her to laugh at. He should never have
mentioned it.

'Well?' she prodded. 'What about this great upset, dear? Tell me.'

It was too late, Peter realized. She'd never let him drop it now. She'd
needle him and needle him until he told her. He sighed and said, 'It was
ten years ago this week. The nationals were always held between
Christmas and New Year's, when everyone was on break. An eight-round
team tournament, two rounds a day. All of our teams did moderately well.
Our A team finished seventh overall.'

'You were on the B team, sweetie.'

Peter grimaced. 'Yes. And we were doing best of all, up to a point. Scored
a couple nice upsets late in the tournament. It put us in a strange position.
Going into the last round, the University of Chicago was in first place,
alone, with a 6–1 match record. They'd beaten our A team, among their
other victims, and they were defending national champions. Behind them
were three other schools at $5\frac{1}{2}$–$\frac{1}{2}$. Berkeley, the University of Massachusetts,
and – I don't know, someone else, it doesn't matter. What mattered was
that all three of those teams had already played U of C. Then you had a
whole bunch of teams at 5–2, including both Northwestern A and B. One
of the 5–2 teams had to be paired up against Chicago in the final round. By
some freak, it turned out to be us. Everyone thought that cinched the
tournament for them.

'It was really a mismatch. They were the defending champions, and they
had an awesome team. Three Masters and an Expert, if I recall. They
outrated us by hundreds of points on every board. It should have been
easy. It wasn't.

'It was never easy between U of C and Northwestern. All through my
college years, we were the two big Midwestern chess powers, and we were
archrivals. The Chicago captain, Hal Winslow, became a good friend of
mine, but I gave him a lot of headaches. Chicago *always* had a stronger
team than we did, but we gave them fits nonetheless. We met in the
Chicago Intercollegiate League, in state tournaments, in regional tournaments, and several times in the nationals. Chicago won most of those, but
not all. We took the city championship away from them once, and racked
up a couple other big upsets too. And that year, in the nationals, we came
this close' – he held up two fingers, barely apart – 'to the biggest upset of
all.' He put his hand and back on the wheel, and scowled.

'Go on,' she said. 'I'm breathless to know what comes next.'

Peter ignored the sarcasm. 'An hour into the match, we had half the tournament gathered around our tables, watching. Everyone could see that Chicago was in trouble. We clearly had superior positions on two boards, and we were even on the other two.

'It got better. I was playing Hal Winslow on third board. We had a dull, even position, and we agreed to a draw. And on fourth board, E.C. gradually got outplayed and finally resigned in a dead lost position.'

'E.C.?'

'Edward Colin Stuart. We all called him E.C. Quite a character. You'll meet him up at Bunnish's place.'

'He lost?'

'Yes.'

'This doesn't sound like such a thrilling upset to me,' she said drily. 'Though maybe by your standards, it's a triumph.'

'E.C. lost,' Peter said, 'but by that time, Delmario had clearly busted his man on board two. The guy dragged it out, but finally we got the point, which tied the score at $1\frac{1}{2}$–$1\frac{1}{2}$, with one game in progress. And we were winning that one. It was incredible. Bruce Bunnish was our first board. A real turkey, but a half-decent player. He was another A player, but he had a trick memory. Photographic. Knew every opening backwards and forwards. He was playing Chicago's big man.' Peter smiled wryly. 'In more ways than one. A Master name of Robinson Vesselere. Damn strong chess player, but he must have weighed four hundred pounds. He'd sit there absolutely immobile as you played him, his hands folded on top of his stomach, little eyes squinting at the board. And he'd crush you. He should have crushed Bunnish easily. Hell, he was rated four hundred points higher. But that wasn't what had gone down. With that trick memory of his, Bunnish had somehow outplayed Vesselere in an obscure variation of the Sicilian. He was swarming all over him. An incredible attack. The position was as complicated as anything I'd ever seen, very sharp and tactical. Vesselere was counterattacking on the queenside, and he had some pressure, but nothing like the threats Bunnish had on the kingside. It was a won game. We were all sure of that.'

'So you almost won the championship?'

'No,' Peter said. 'No, it wasn't that. If we'd won the match, we would have tied Chicago and a few other teams at 6–2, but the championship would have gone to someone else, some team with $6\frac{1}{2}$ match points. Berkeley maybe, or Mass. It was just the upset itself we wanted. It would have been *incredible*. They were the best college chess team in the country. We weren't even the best at our school. If we had beaten them, it would have caused a sensation. And we came so close.'

'What happened?'

'Bunnish blew it,' Peter said sourly. 'There was a critical position.

Bunnish had a sac. A sacrifice, you know? A double piece sac. Very sharp, but it would have busted up Vesselere's kingside and driven his king out into the open. But Bunnish was too timid for that. Instead he kept looking at Vesselere's queenside attack, and finally he made some feeble defensive move. Vesselere shifted another piece to the queenside, and Bunnish defended again. Instead of following up his advantage, he made a whole series of cautious little adjustments to the position, and before long his attack had dissipated. After that, of course, Vesselere overwhelmed him.' Even now, after ten years, Peter felt the disappointment building inside him as he spoke. 'We lost the match $2\frac{1}{2}$–$1\frac{1}{2}$, and Chicago won another national championship. Afterwards, even Vesselere admitted that he was busted if Brucie had played knight takes pawn at the critical point. Damn.'

'You lost. That's what this amounts to. You lost.'

'We came close.'

'Close only counts in horseshoes and grenades,' Kathy said. 'You lost. Even then you were a loser, dear. I wish I'd known.'

'Bunnish lost, damn it,' Peter said. 'It was just like him. He had a Class A rating, and that trick memory, but as a team player he was worthless. You don't know how many matches he blew for us. When the pressure was on, we could always count on Bunnish to fold. But that time was the worst, that game against Vesselere. I could have killed him. He was an arrogant asshole, too.'

Kathy laughed. 'Isn't this arrogant asshole the one we are now speeding to visit?'

'It's been ten years. Maybe he's changed. Even if he hasn't, well, he's a multimillionaire asshole now. Electronics. Besides, I want to see E.C. and Steve again, and Bunnish said they'd be there.'

'Delightful,' said Kathy. 'Well, rush on, then. I wouldn't want to miss this. It might be my only opportunity to spend four days with an asshole millionaire and three losers.'

Peter said nothing, but he pressed down on the accelerator, and the Toyota plunged down the mountain road, faster and faster, rattling as it picked up speed. Down and down, he thought, down and down. Just like my goddamned life.

*

Four miles up Bunnish's private road, they finally came within sight of the house. Peter, who still dreamed of buying his own house after a decade of living in cheap apartments, took one look and knew he was gazing at a three million dollar piece of property. There were three levels, all blending into the mountainside so well you hardly noticed them, built of natural wood and native stone and tinted glass. A huge solar greenhouse was the most conspicuous feature. Beneath the house, a four-car garage was sunk right into the mountain itself.

Peter pulled into the last empty spot, between a brand new silver Cadillac Seville that was obviously Bunnish's and an ancient rusted VW Beetle that was obviously not. As he pulled the key from the ignition, the garage doors shut automatically behind them, blocking out daylight and the gorgeous mountain vistas. The door closed with a resounding metallic clang.

'Someone knows we're here,' Kathy observed.

'Get the suitcases,' Peter snapped.

To the rear of the garage they found the elevator, and Peter jabbed the topmost of the two buttons. When the elevator doors opened again, it was on a huge living room. Peter stepped out and stared at a wilderness of potted plants beneath a vaulting skylight, at thick brown carpets, fine wood paneling, bookcases packed with leatherbound volumes, a large fireplace, and Edward Colin Stuart, who rose from a leather-clad armchair across the room when the elevator arrived.

'E.C,' Peter said, setting down his suitcase. He smiled.

'Hello, Peter,' E.C. said, coming toward them quickly. They shook hands.

'You haven't changed a goddamned bit in ten years,' Peter said. It was true. E.C. was still slender and compact, with a bushy head of sandy blonde hair and a magnificent handlebar mustache. He was wearing jeans and a tapered purple shirt with a black vest, and he seemed just as he had a decade ago: brisk, trim, efficient. 'Not a damn bit,' Peter repeated.

'More's the pity,' E.C. said. 'One is supposed to change, I believe.' His blue eyes were as unreadable as ever. He turned to Kathy, and said, 'I'm E.C. Stuart.'

'Oh, pardon,' Peter said. 'This is my wife, Kathy.'

'Delighted,' she said, taking his hand and smiling at him.

'Where's Steve?' Peter asked. 'I saw his VW down in the garage. Gave me a start. How long has he been driving that thing now? Fifteen years?'

'Not quite,' E.C. said. 'He's around somewhere, probably having a drink.' His mouth shifted subtly when he said it, telling Peter a good deal more than his words did.

'And Bunnish?'

'Brucie has not yet made his appearance. I think he was waiting for you to arrive. You probably want to settle in to your rooms.'

'How do we find them, if our host is missing?' Kathy asked drily.

'Ah,' said E.C, 'you haven't been acquainted with the wonders of Bunnishland yet. Look.' He pointed to the fireplace.

Peter would have sworn that there had been a painting above the mantle when they had entered, some sort of surreal landscape. Now there was a large rectangular screen, with words on it, vivid red against black WELCOME, PETER. WELCOME, KATHY. YOUR SUITE IS ON THE SECOND LEVEL, FIRST DOOR. PLEASE MAKE YOURSELF COMFORTABLE.

Peter turned. 'How . . . ?'

'No doubt triggered by the elevator,' E.C. said. 'I was greeted the same way. Brucie is an electronics genius, remember. The house is full of gadgets and toys. I've explored a bit.' He shrugged. 'Why don't you two unpack and then wander back? I won't go anywhere.'

They found their rooms easily enough. The huge, tiled bath featured an outside patio with a hot tub, and the suite had its own sitting room and fireplace. Above it was an abstract painting, but when Kathy closed the room door it faded away and was replaced by another message: I HOPE YOU FIND THIS SATISFACTORY.

'Cute guy, this host of ours,' Kathy said, sitting on the edge of the bed. 'Those TV screens or whatever they are better not be two-way. I don't intend to put on any show for any electronic voyeur.'

Peter frowned. 'Wouldn't be surprised if the house was bugged. Bunnish was always a strange sort.'

'How strange?'

'He was hard to like,' Peter said. 'Boastful, always bragging about how good he was as a chess player, how smart he was, that sort of thing. No one really believed him. His grades were good, I guess, but the rest of the time he seemed close to dense. E.C. has a wicked way with hoaxes and practical jokes, and Bunnish was his favorite victim. I don't know how many laughs we had at his expense. Bunnish was kind of a goon in person, too. Pudgy, round-faced with big cheeks like some kind of chipmunk, wore his hair in a crew cut. He was in ROTC. I've never seen anyone who looked more ridiculous in a uniform. He never dated.'

'Gay?'

'No, not hardly. Asexual is closer to it.' Peter looked around the room and shook his head. 'I can't imagine how Bunnish made it this big. Him of all people.' He sighed, opened his suitcase, and started to unpack. 'I might have believed it of Delmario,' he continued. 'Steve and Bunnish were both in Tech, but Steve always seemed much brighter. We all thought he was a real whiz-kid. Bunnish just seemed like an arrogant mediocrity.'

'Fooled you,' Kathy said. She smiled sweetly. 'Of course, he's not the only one to fool you, is he? Though perhaps he was the first.'

'Enough,' Peter said, hanging the last of his shirts in the closet. 'Come on, let's get back downstairs. I want to talk to E.C.'

They had no sooner stepped out of their suite when a voice hailed them. 'Pete?'

Peter turned, and the big man standing in the doorway down the hall smiled a blurry smile at him. 'Don't you recognize me, Peter?'

'Steve?' Peter said wonderingly.

'Sure, hey, who'd you think?' He stepped out of his own room, a bit unsteadily, and closed the door behind him. 'This must be the wife, eh? Am I right?'

'Yes,' Peter said. 'Kathy, this is Steve Delmario. Steve, Kathy.' Delmario came over and pumped her hand enthusiastically, after clapping Peter roundly on the back. Peter found himself staring. If E.C. had scarcely changed at all in the past ten years, Steve had made up for it. Peter would never have recognized his old teammate on the street.

The old Steve Delmario had lived for chess and electronics. He was a fierce competitor, and he loved to tinker things together, but he was frustratingly uninterested in anything outside his narrow passions. He had been a tall, gaunt youth with incredibly intense eyes held captive behind Coke-bottle lenses in heavy black frames. His black hair had always been either ruffled and unkempt or – when he treated himself to one of his do-it-yourself haircuts – grotesquely butchered. He was equally careless about his clothing, most of which was Salvation Army chic minus the chic: baggy brown pants with cuffs, ten-year-old shirts with frayed collars, a zippered and shapeless gray sweater he wore everywhere. Once E.C. had observed that Steve Delmario looked like the last man left alive on earth after a nuclear holocaust, and for almost a semester thereafter the whole club had called Delmario, 'the last man on earth.' He took it with good humor. For all his quirks, Delmario had been well liked.

The years had been cruel to him, however. The Coke-bottle glasses in the black frames were the same, and the clothes were equally haphazard – shabby brown cords, a short-sleeved white shirt with three felt-tip pens in the pocket, a faded sweater-vest with every button buttoned, scuffed hush puppies – but the rest had all changed. Steve had gained about fifty pounds, and he had a bloated, puffy look about him. He was almost entirely bald, nothing left of the wild black hair but a few sickly strands around his ears. And his eyes had lost their feverish intensity, and were filled instead with a fuzziness that Peter found terribly disturbing. Most shocking of all was the smell of alcohol on his breath. E.C. had hinted at it, but Peter still found it difficult to accept. In college, Steve Delmario had never touched anything but an infrequent beer.

'It is good to see you again,' Peter said, though he was no longer quite sure that was true. 'Shall we go on downstairs? E.C. is waiting.'

Delmario nodded. 'Sure, sure, let's do it.' He clapped Peter on the back again. 'Have you seen Bunnish yet? Damn, this is some place he's got, isn't it? You seen those message screens? Clever, real clever. Never would have figured Bunnish to go as far as this, not our old Funny Bunny, eh?' He chuckled. 'I've looked at some of his patents over the years, you know. Real ingenious. Real fine work. And from *Bunnish*. I guess you just never know, do you?'

The living room was awash with classical music when they descended the spiral stair. Peter didn't recognize the composition; his own tastes had always run to rock. But classical music had been one of E.C.'s passions, and he was sitting in an armchair now, eyes closed, listening.

'Drinks,' Delmario was saying. 'I'll fix us all some drinks. You folks must be thirsty. Bunny's got a wet bar right behind the stair here. What do you want?'

'What are the choices?' Kathy asked.

'Hell, he's got anything you could think of,' said Delmario.

'A Beefeater martini, then,' she said. 'Very dry.'

Delmario nodded. 'Pete?'

'Oh,' said Peter. He shrugged. 'A beer, I guess.'

Delmario went behind the stair to fix up their drinks, and Kathy arched her eyebrows at him. 'Such refined tastes,' she said. '*A beer!*'

Peter ignored her and went over to sit beside E.C. Stuart. 'How the hell did you find the stereo?' he asked. 'I don't see it anywhere.' The music seemed to be coming right out of the walls.

E.C. opened his eyes, gave a quirkish little smile, and brushed one end of his mustache with a finger. 'The message screen blabbed the secret to me,' he said. 'The controls are built into the wall back over there,' nodding, 'and the whole system is concealed. It's voice activated, too. Computerized. I *told* it what album I wanted to hear.'

'Impressive,' Peter admitted. He scratched his head. 'Didn't Steve put together a voice-activated stereo back in college?'

'Your beer,' Delmario said. He was standing over them, holding out a cold bottle of Heineken. Peter took it, and Delmario – with a drink in hand – seated himself on the ornate tiled coffee table. 'I had a system,' he said. 'Real crude, though. Remember, you guys used to kid me about it.'

'You bought a good cartridge, as I recall,' E.C. said, 'but you had it held by a tone-arm you made out of a bent coat hanger.'

'It worked,' Delmario protested. 'It was voice-activated too, like you said, but real primitive. Just on and off, that's all, and you had to speak real loud. I figured I could improve on it after I got out of school, but I never did.' He shrugged. 'Nothing like this. This is real sophisticated.'

'I've noticed,' E.C. said. He craned up his head slightly and said, in a very loud clear voice, 'I've had enough music now, thank you.' The silence that followed was briefly startling. Peter couldn't think of a thing to say.

Finally E.C. turned to him and said, all seriously, 'How did Bunnish get you here, Peter?'

Peter was puzzled. 'Get me here? He just invited us. What do you mean?'

'He paid Steve's way, you know,' E.C. said. 'As for me, I turned down this invitation. Brucie was never one of my favorite people, you know that. He pulled strings to change my mind. I'm with an ad agency in New York. He dangled a big account in front of them, and I was told to come here or lose my job. Interesting, eh?'

Kathy had been sitting on the sofa, sipping her martini and looking bored. 'It sounds as though this reunion is important to him,' she observed.

E.C. stood up. 'Come here,' he said. 'I want to show you something.' The rest of them rose obediently, and followed him across the room. In a shadowy corner surrounded by bookcases, a chessboard had been set up, with a game in progress. The board was made of squares of light and dark wood, painstakingly inlaid into a gorgeous Victorian table. The pieces were ivory and onyx. 'Take a look at that,' E.C. said.

'That's a beautiful set,' Peter said, admiringly. He reached down to lift the Black queen for a closer inspection, and grunted in surprise. The piece wouldn't move.

'Tug away,' E.C. said. 'It won't do you any good. I've tried. The pieces are glued into position. Every one of them.'

Steve Delmario moved around the board, his eyes blinking behind his thick glasses. He set his drink on the table and sank into the chair behind the White pieces. 'The position,' he said, his voice a bit blurry with drink. 'I know it.'

E.C. Stuart smiled thinly and brushed his mustache. 'Peter,' he said, nodding toward the chessboard. 'Take a good look.'

Peter stared, and all of a sudden it came clear to him, the position on the board became as familiar as his own features in a mirror. 'The game,' he said. 'From the nationals. This is the critical position from Bunnish's game with Vesselere.'

E.C. nodded. 'I thought so. I wasn't sure.'

'Oh, *I'm* sure,' Delmario said loudly. 'How the hell could I *not* be sure? This is right where Bunny blew it, remember? He played king to knight one, instead of the sac. Cost us the match. Me, I was sitting right next to him, playing the best damned game of chess I ever played. Beat a Master, and what good did it do? Not a damn bit of good, thanks to Bunnish.' He looked at the board and glowered. 'Knight takes pawn, that's all he's got to play, busts Vesselere wide open. Check, check, check, check, got to be a mate there somewhere.'

'You were never able to find it, though, Delmario,' Bruce Bunnish said from behind them.

None of them had heard him enter. Peter started like a burglar surprised while copping the family silver.

Their host stood in the doorway a few yards distant. Bunnish had changed, too. He had lost weight since college, and his body looked hard and fit now, though he still had the big round cheeks that Peter remembered. His crew cut had grown out into a healthy head of brown hair, carefully styled and blow-dried. He wore large, tinted glasses and expensive clothes. But he was still Bunnish. His voice was loud and grating, just as Peter remembered it.

Bunnish strolled over to the chessboard almost casually. 'You analyzed that position for weeks afterward, Delmario,' he said. 'You never found the mate.'

Delmario stood up. 'I found a dozen mates,' he said.

'Yes,' Bunnish said, 'but none of them were forced. Vesselere was a Master. He wouldn't have played into any of your so-called mating lines.'

Delmario frowned and took a drink. He was going to say something else – Peter could see him fumbling for the words – but E.C. stood up and took away his chance. 'Bruce,' he said, holding out his hand. 'Good to see you again. How long has it been?'

Bunnish turned and smiled superciliously. 'Is that another of your jokes, E.C.? You know how long it has been, and I know how long it has been, so why do you ask? Norten knows, and Delmario knows. Maybe you're asking for Mrs Norten.' He looked at Kathy. 'Do you know how long it has been?'

She laughed. 'I've heard.'

'Ah,' said Bunnish. He swung back to face E.C. 'Then we all know, so it must be another of your jokes, and I'm not going to answer. Do you remember how you used to phone me at three in the morning, and ask me what time it was? Then I'd tell you, and you'd ask me what I was doing calling you at that hour?'

E.C. frowned and lowered his hand.

'Well,' said Bunnish, into the awkward silence that followed, 'no sense standing here around this stupid chessboard. Why don't we all go sit down by the fireplace, and talk.' He gestured. 'Please.'

But when they were seated, the silence fell again. Peter took a swallow of beer and realized that he was more than just ill-at-ease. A palpable tension hung in the air. 'Nice place you've got here, Bruce,' he said, hoping to lighten the atmosphere.

Bunnish looked around smugly. 'I know,' he said. 'I've done awfully well, you know. Awfully well. You wouldn't believe how much money I have. I hardly know what to do with it all.' He smiled broadly and fatuously. 'And how about you, my friends? Here I am boasting once again, when I ought to be listening to all of you recount your own triumphs.' Bunnish looked at Peter. 'You first, Norten. You're the captain, after all. How have you done?'

'All right,' Peter said, uncomfortably. 'I've done fine. I own a bookstore.'

'A *bookstore!* How wonderful! I recall that you always wanted to be in publishing, though I rather thought you'd be writing books instead of selling them. Whatever happened to those novels you were going to write, Peter? Your literary career?'

Peter's mouth was very dry. 'I . . . things change, Bruce. I haven't had much time for writing.' It sounded so feeble, Peter thought. All at once, he was desperately wishing he was elsewhere.

'No time for writing,' echoed Bunnish. 'A pity, Norten. You had such promise.'

'He's still promising,' Kathy put in sharply. 'You ought to hear him promise. He's been promising as long as I've known him. He never writes, but he does promise.'

Bunnish laughed. 'Your wife is very witty,' he said to Peter. 'She's almost as funny as E.C. was, back in college. You must enjoy being married to her a great deal. I recall how fond you were of E.C.'s little jokes.' He looked at E.C. 'Are you still a funny man, Stuart?'

E.C. looked annoyed. 'I'm hysterical,' he said, in a flat voice.

'Good,' said Bunnish. He turned to Kathy and said, 'I don't know if Peter has told you all the stories about old E.C., but he really played some amazing pranks. Hilarious man, that's our E.C. Stuart. Once, when our chess team had won the city championship, he had a girlfriend of his call up Peter and pretend to be an AP reporter. She interviewed him for an hour before he caught on.'

Kathy laughed. 'Peter is sometimes a bit slow,' she said.

'Oh, that was nothing. Normally I was the one E.C. liked to play tricks on. I didn't go out much, you know. Deathly afraid of girls. But E.C. had a hundred girlfriends, all of them gorgeous. One time he took pity on me and offered to fix me up on a blind date. I accepted eagerly, and when the girl arrived on the corner where we were supposed to meet, she was wearing dark glasses and carrying a cane. Tapping. You know.'

Steve Delmario guffawed, tried to stifle his laughter, and nearly choked on his drink. 'Sorry,' he wheezed, 'sorry.'

Bunnish waved casually. 'Oh, go ahead, laugh. It *was* funny. The girl wasn't really blind, you know, she was a drama student who was rehearsing a part in a play. But it took me all night to find that out. I was such a fool. And that was only one joke. There were hundreds of others.'

E.C. looked somber. 'That was a long time ago. We were kids. It's all behind us now, Bruce.'

'Bruce?' Bunnish sounded surprised. 'Why, Stuart, that's the first time you've ever called me *Bruce*. You *have* changed. You were the one who started calling me Brucie. God, how I hated that name! Brucie, Brucie, Brucie, I *loathed* it. How many times did I ask you to call me Bruce? How many times? Why, I don't recall. I do recall, though, that after three years you finally came up to me at one meeting and said that you'd thought it over, and now you agreed that I was right, that Brucie was not an appropriate name for a Class A chess player, a twenty-year old, an officer in ROTC. Your exact words. I remember the whole speech, E.C. It took me so by surprise that I didn't know what to say, so I said, *"Good, it's about time!"* And then you grinned, and said that Brucie was out, that you'd never call me Brucie again. From now on, you said, you'd call me *Bunny*.'

Kathy laughed, and Delmario choked down an explosive outburst, but Peter only felt cold all over. Bunnish's smile was genial enough, but his tone was pure iced venom as he recounted the incident. E.C. did not look amused either. Peter took a swallow of his beer, casting about for some ploy to get the conversation onto a different track. 'Do any of you still play?' he heard himself blurt out.

They all looked at him. Delmario seemed almost befuddled. 'Play?' he said. He blinked down at his empty glass.

'Help yourself to a refill,' Bunnish told him. 'You know where it is.' He smiled at Peter as Delmario moved off to the bar. 'You mean chess, of course.'

'Chess,' Peter said. 'You remember chess. Odd little pastime played with black and white pieces and lots of two-faced clocks.' He looked around. 'Don't tell me we've *all* given it up?'

E.C. shrugged. 'I'm too busy. I haven't played a rated game since college.'

Delmario had returned, ice cubes clinking softly in a tumbler full of bourbon. 'I played a little after college,' he said, 'but not for the last five years.' He sat down heavily, and stared into the cold fireplace. 'Those were my bad years. Wife left me, I lost a couple jobs. Bunny here was way ahead of me. Every goddamn idea I came up with, he had a patent on it already. Got so I was useless. That was when I started to drink.' He smiled, and took a sip. 'Yeah,' he said. 'Just then. And I stopped playing chess. It all comes out, you know, it all comes out over the board. I was losing, losing lots. To all these *fish*, god, I tell you, I couldn't take it. Rating went down to Class B.' Delmario took another drink, and looked at Peter. 'You need something to play good chess, you know what I'm saying? A kind of . . . hell, I don't know . . . a kind of arrogance. Self-confidence. It's all wrapped up with ego, that kind of stuff, and I didn't have it any more, whatever it was. I used to have it, but I lost it all. I had bad luck, and I looked around one day and it was gone, and my chess was gone with it. So I quit.' He lifted the tumbler to his lips, hesitated, and drained it all. Then he smiled for them. 'Quit,' he repeated. 'Gave it up. Chucked it away. Bailed out.' He chuckled, and stood up, and went off to the bar again.

'I play,' Bunnish said forcefully. 'I'm a Master now.'

Delmario stopped in midstride, and fixed Bunnish with such a look of total loathing that it could have killed. Peter saw that Steve's hand was shaking.

'I'm very happy for you, Bruce,' E.C. Stuart said. 'Please do enjoy your Mastership, and your money, and Bunnishland.' He stood and straightened his vest, frowning. 'Meanwhile, I'm going to be going.'

'Going?' said Bunnish. 'Really, E.C., so soon? Must you?'

'Bunnish,' E.C. said, 'you can spend the next four days playing your little ego games with Steve and Peter, if you like, but I'm afraid I am not amused. You always were a pimple-brain, and I have better things to do with my life than to sit here and watch you squeeze out ten-year-old pus. Am I making myself clear?'

'Oh, perfectly,' Bunnish said.

'Good,' said E.C. He looked at the others. 'Kathy, it was nice meeting you. I'm sorry it wasn't under better circumstances. Peter, Steve, if either of you comes to New York in the near future, I hope you'll look me up. I'm in the book.'

'E.C., don't you . . .' Peter began, but he knew it was useless. Even in the old days, E.C. Stuart was headstrong. You could never talk him into or out of anything.

'Good-bye,' he said, interrupting Peter. He went briskly to the elevator, and they watched the wood-paneled doors close on him.

'He'll be back,' Bunnish said after the elevator had gone.

'I don't think so,' Peter replied.

Bunnish got up, smiling broadly. Deep dimples appeared in his large, round cheeks. 'Oh, but he will, Norten. You see, it's my turn to play the little jokes now, and E.C. will soon find that out.'

'What?' Delmario said.

'Don't you fret about it, you'll understand soon enough,' Bunnish said. 'Meanwhile, please do excuse me. I have to see about dinner. You all must be ravenous. I'm making dinner myself, you know. I sent my servants away, so we could have a nice private reunion.' He looked at his watch, a heavy gold Swiss. 'Let's all meet in the dining room in, say, an hour. Everything should be ready by then. We can talk some more. About life. About chess.' He smiled, and left.

Kathy was smiling too. 'Well,' she said to Peter after Bunnish had left the room, 'this is all vastly more entertaining than I would have imagined. I feel as if I just walked into a Harold Pinter play.'

'Who's that?' Delmario asked, resuming his seat.

Peter ignored him. 'I don't like any of this,' he said. 'What the hell did Bunnish mean about playing a joke on us?'

He didn't have to wait long for an answer. While Kathy went to fix herself another martini, they heard the elevator again, and turned expectantly toward the doors. E.C. stepped out frowning. 'Where is he?' he said in a hard voice.

'He went to cook dinner,' Peter said. 'What is it? He said something about a joke . . .'

'Those garage doors won't open,' E.C. said. 'I can't get my car out. There's no place to go without it. We must be fifty miles from the nearest civilization.'

'I'll go down and ram out with my VW,' Delmario said helpfully. 'Like in the movies.'

'Don't be absurd,' E.C. said. 'That door is stainless steel. There's no way you're going to batter it down.' He scowled and brushed back one end of his mustache. 'Battering down Brucie, however, is a much more viable proposition. Where the hell is the kitchen?'

Peter sighed. 'I wouldn't if I were you, E.C,' he said. 'From the way he's been acting, he'd just love a chance to clap you in jail. If you touch him, it's assault, you know that.'

'Phone the police,' Kathy suggested.

Peter looked around. 'Now that you mention it, I don't see a phone anywhere in this room. Do you?' Silence. 'There was no phone in our suite, either, that I recall.'

'Hey!' Delmario said. 'That's right, Pete, you're right.'

E.C. sat down. 'He appears to have us checkmated,' he said.

'The exact word,' said Peter. 'Bunnish is playing some kind of game with us. He said so himself. A joke.'

'Ha, ha,' said E.C. 'What do you suggest we do, then? Laugh?'

Peter shrugged. 'Eat dinner, talk, have our reunion, find out what the hell Bunnish wants with us.'

'Win the game, guys, that's what we do,' Delmario said.

E.C. stared at him. 'What the hell does that mean?'

Delmario sipped his bourbon and grinned. 'Peter said Bunny was playing some kind of game with us, right? OK, fine. Let's play. Let's beat him at this goddamned game, whatever the hell it is.' He chuckled. 'Hell, guys, this is the Funny Bunny we're playing. Maybe he is a Master, I don't give a good goddamn, he'll still find a way to blow it in the end. You know how it was. Bunnish *always* lost the big games. He'll lose this one, too.'

'I wonder,' said Peter. 'I wonder.'

*

Peter brought another bottle of Heineken back to the suite with him, and sat in a deck chair on the patio drinking it while Kathy tried out the hot tub.

'This is nice,' she said from the tub. 'Relaxing. Sensuous, even. Why don't you come on in?'

'No, thanks,' Peter said.

'We ought to get one of these.'

'Right. We could put it in our living room. The people in the apartment downstairs would love it.' He took a swallow of beer and shook his head.

'What are you thinking about?' Kathy asked.

Peter smiled grimly. 'Chess, believe it or not.'

'Oh? Do tell.'

'Life is a lot like chess,' he said.

She laughed. 'Really? I'd never noticed, somehow.'

Peter refused to let her needling get to him. 'All a matter of choices. Every move you face choices, and every choice leads to different variations. It branches and then branches again, and sometimes the variation you pick isn't as good as it looked, isn't sound at all. But you don't know that until your game is over.'

'I hope you'll repeat this when I'm out of the tub,' Kathy said. 'I want to write it all down for posterity.'

'I remember, back in college, how many possibilities life seemed to hold. Variations. I knew, of course, that I'd only live one of my fantasy lives, but for a few years there, I had them all, all the branches, all the variations. One day I could dream of being a novelist, one day I would be a journalist covering Washington, the next – oh, I don't know, a politician, a teacher, whatever. My dream lives. Full of dream wealth and dream women. All the things I was going to do, all the places I was going to live. They were mutually exclusive, of course, but since I didn't have any of them, in a sense I had them all. Like when you sit down at a chessboard to begin a game, and you don't know what the opening will be. Maybe it will be a Sicilian, or a French, or a Ruy Lopez. They all coexist, all the variations, until you start making the moves. You always dream of winning, no matter what line you choose, but the variations are still . . . different.' He drank some more beer. 'Once the game begins, the possibilities narrow and narrow and narrow, the other variations fade, and you're left with what you've got – a position half of your own making, and half chance, as embodied by that stranger across the board. Maybe you've got a good game, or maybe you're in trouble, but in any case there's just that one position to work from. The might-have-beens are gone.'

Kathy climbed out of the hot tub and began toweling herself off. Steam rose from the water, and moved gently around her. Peter found himself looking at her almost with tenderness, something he had not felt in a long time. Then she spoke, and ruined it. 'You missed your calling,' she said, rubbing briskly with the towel. 'You should have taken up poster-writing. You have a knack for poster profundity. You know, like, *I am not in this world to live up to your expect—*'

'Enough,' Peter said. 'How much blood do you have to draw, damn it?'

Kathy stopped and looked at him. She frowned. 'You're really down aren't you?' she said.

Peter stared off at the mountains, and did not bother to reply.

The concern left her voice as quickly as it had come. 'Another depression, huh? Drink another beer, why don't you? Feel sorry for yourself some more. By midnight you'll have worked yourself up to a good crying jag. Go on.'

'I keep thinking of that match,' Peter said.

'Match?'

'In the nationals,' he said. 'Against Chicago. It's weird, but I keep having this funny feeling, like . . . like it was right there that it all started to go bad. We had a chance to do something big, something special. But it slipped away from us, and nothing has been right since. A losing variation, Kathy. We picked a losing variation, and we've been losing ever since. All of us.'

Kathy sat down on the edge of the tub. 'All of you?'

Peter nodded. 'Look at us. I failed as a novelist, failed as a journalist, and now I've got a failing bookstore. Not to mention a bitch wife. Steve is a drunk who couldn't even get together enough money to pay his way out here. E.C. is an aging account executive with an indifferent track record, going nowhere. Losers. You said it, in the car.'

She smiled. 'Ah, but what about our host? Bunnish lost bigger than any of you, and he seems to have won everything since.'

'Hmmmm,' said Peter. He sipped thoughtfully at his beer. 'I wonder. Oh, he's rich enough, I'll give you that. But he's got a chessboard in his living room with the pieces glued into position, so he can stare every day at the place he went wrong in a game played ten years ago. That doesn't sound like a winner to me.'

She stood up, and shook loose her hair. It was long and auburn and it fell around her shoulders gorgeously, and Peter remembered the sweet lady he had married eight years ago, when he was a bright young writer working hard on his first novel. He smiled. 'You look nice,' he said.

Kathy seemed startled. 'You *are* feeling morose,' she said. 'Are you sure you don't have a fever?'

'No fever. Just a memory, and a lot of regrets.'

'Ah,' she said. She walked back toward their bedroom, and snapped the towel at him in passing. 'C'mon, captain. Your team is going to be waiting, and all this heavy philosophy has given me quite an appetite.'

*

The food was fine, but the dinner was awful.

They ate thick slabs of rare prime rib, with big baked potatoes and lots of fresh vegetables. The wine looked expensive and tasted wonderful. Afterwards, they had their choice of three desserts, plus fresh-ground coffee and several delicious liqueurs. Yet the meal was strained and unpleasant, Peter thought. Steve Delmario was in pretty bad shape even before he came to the table, and while he was there he drank wine as if it were water, getting louder and fuzzier in the process. E.C. Stuart was coldly quiet, his fury barely held in check behind an icy, aloof demeanor. And Bunnish thwarted every one of Peter's attempts to move conversation to safe neutral ground.

His genial expansiveness was a poor mask for gloating, and he insisted on opening old wounds from their college years. Every time Peter recounted an anecdote that was amusing or harmless, Bunnish smiled and countered with one that stank of hurt and rejection.

Finally, over coffee, E.C. could stand no more of it. 'Pus,' he said loudly, interrupting Bunnish. It was about the third word he'd permitted himself the entire meal. 'Pus and more pus. Bunnish, what's the point? You've brought us here. You've got us trapped here, with you. Why? So you can prove that we treated you shabbily back in college? Is that the idea? If so, fine. You've made your point. You were treated shabbily. I am ashamed, I am guilty. Mea culpa, mea culpa, mea maxima culpa. Now let's end it. It's over.'

'Over?' said Bunnish, smiling. 'Perhaps it is. But you've changed, E.C. Back when I was the butt of your jokes, you'd recount them for weeks. *Over* wasn't so final then, was it? And what about my game with Vesselere in the nationals? When that was over, did we forget it? Oh, no, we did not. That game was played in December, you'll recall. I heard about it until I graduated in May. At every meeting. That game was *never* over for me. Delmario liked to show me a different checkmate every time I saw him. Our dear captain refrained from playing me in any league matches for the rest of the year. And you, E.C., you liked to greet me with, "Say, Bunny, lost any big ones lately?" You even reprinted that game in the club newsletter, and mailed it in to *Chess Life*. No doubt all this seems like ancient history to you. I have this trick memory, though. I can't forget things quite so easily. I remember it all. I remember the way Vesselere sat there, with his hands folded on his stomach, never moving, staring at me out of those itty bitty eyes of his. I remember the way he moved his pieces, very carefully, very daintily, lifting each one between thumb and forefinger. I remember wandering into the halls between moves, to get a drink of water, and seeing Norten over by the wall charts, talking to Mavora from the A team. You know what he was saying? He was gesturing with his hands, all worked up, and he was telling him, *He's going to blow it, damn it, he's going to blow it!* Isn't that right, Peter? And Les looked over at me as I passed, and said, *Lose this one and your ass is grass, Bunny!* He was another endearing soul. I remember all the people who kept coming to look at my game. I remember Norten standing in the corner with Hal Winslow, the two mighty captains, talking heatedly. Winslow was all rumpled and needed a shave and he had his clipboard, and he was trying to figure out who'd finish where if we won, or tied, or lost. I remember how it felt when I tipped over my king, too. I remember the way Delmario started kicking the wall, the way E.C. shrugged and glanced up at the ceiling, and the way Peter came over and just said *Bunnish!* and shook his head. You see? My trick memory is as tricky as ever, and I haven't forgotten a thing. And especially I haven't forgotten that game. I can recite all the moves to you right now, if you'd like.'

'Shit,' said Steve Delmario. 'Only one important move to recite, Bunny. Knight takes pawn, that's the move you ought to recite. The sac, the winning sac, the one you didn't play. I forget what kind of feeble thing you did instead.'

Bunnish smiled. 'My move was king to knight one,' he said. 'To protect my rook pawn. I'd castled long, and Vesselere was threatening to snatch it.'

'Pawn, shmawn,' said Delmario. 'You had him busted. The sac would have gutted that whale like nobody's goddamned business. What a laugh that would have been. The bunny rabbit beating the whale. Old Hal Winslow would have been so shocked he would have dropped his clipboard. But you blew it, guarding some diddlysquat little pawn. You blew it.'

'So you told me,' said Bunnish. 'And told me, and told me.'

'Look,' Peter said, 'I don't see the sense in rehashing all of this. Steve is drunk, Bruce. You can see that. He doesn't know what he's saying.'

'He knows exactly what he's saying, Norten,' Bunnish replied. He smiled thinly and removed his glasses. Peter was startled by his eyes. The hatred there was almost tangible, and there was something else as well, something old and bitter and somehow *trapped*. The eyes passed lightly over Kathy, who was sitting quietly amidst all the old hostility, and touched Steve Delmario, Peter Norten, and E.C. Stuart each in turn, with vast loathing and vast amusement.

'Enough,' Peter said, almost pleadingly.

'*NO!*' said Delmario. The drink had made him belligerent. 'It's not enough, it'll never be enough, goddamn it. Get out a set, Bunny! I dare you! We'll analyze it right now, go over the whole thing again, I'll show you how you pissed it all away.' He pulled himself to his feet.

'I have a better idea,' said Bunnish. 'Sit down, Delmario.'

Delmario blinked uncertainly, and then fell back into his chair.

'Good,' said Bunnish. 'We'll get to my idea in a moment, but first I'm going to tell you all a story. As Archie Bunker once said, revenge is the best way to get even. But it isn't revenge unless the victim knows. So I'm going to tell you. I'm going to tell you exactly how I've ruined your lives.'

'Oh, come off it!' E.C. said.

'You never did like stories, E.C.,' Bunnish said. 'Know why? Because when someone tells a story, they become the center of attention. And you always needed to be the center of attention, wherever you were. Now you're not the center of anything, though. How does it feel to be insignificant?'

E.C. gave a disgusted shake of his head and poured himself more coffee. 'Go on, Bunnish,' he said. 'Tell your story. You have a captive audience.'

'I do, don't I?' Bunnish smiled. 'All right. It all begins with that game. Me and Vesselere. I did *not* blow that game. It was never won.'

Delmario made a rude noise.

'I know,' Bunnish continued, unperturbed, 'now, but I did not know then. I thought that you were right. I'd thrown it all away, I thought. It ate at me. For years and years, more years than you would believe. Every night I went to sleep replaying that game in my head. That game blighted my entire life. It became an obsession. I wanted only one thing – another chance. I wanted to go back, somehow, to choose another line, to make different moves, to come out a winner. I'd picked the wrong variation, that was all. I knew that if I had another chance, I'd do better. For more than fifty years, I worked toward that end, and that end alone.'

Peter swallowed a mouthful of cold coffee hastily and said, 'What? Fifty years? You mean five, don't you?'

'Fifty,' Bunnish repeated.

'You are insane,' said E.C.

'No,' said Bunnish. 'I am a genius. Have you ever heard of time travel, any of you?'

'It doesn't exist,' said Peter. 'The paradoxes . . .'

Bunnish waved him quiet. 'You're right and you're wrong, Norten. It exists, but only in a sort of limited fashion. Yet that is enough. I won't bore you with mathematics none of you can understand. Analogy is easier. Time is said to be the fourth dimension, but it differs from the other three in one conspicuous way – our consciousness moves along it. From past to present only, alas. Time itself does not flow, no more than, say, width can flow. Our minds flicker from one instant of time to the next. This analogy was my starting point. I reasoned that if consciousness can move in one direction, it can move in the other direction as well. It took me fifty years to work out the details, however, and make what I call a *flashback* possible.

'That was in my first life, gentlemen, a life of failure and ridicule and poverty. I tended my obsession and did what I had to so as to keep myself fed. And I hated you, each of you, for every moment of those fifty years. My bitterness was inflamed as I watched each of you succeed, while I struggled and failed. I met Norten once, twenty years after college, at an autographing party. You were so patronizing. It was then that I determined to ruin you, all of you.

'And I did. What is there to say? I perfected my device at the age of seventy-one. There is no way to move matter through time, but *mind*, mind is a different issue. My device would send my mind back to any point in my own lifetime that I chose, superimpose my consciousness with all of its memories on the consciousness of my earlier self. I could take nothing with me, of course.' Bunnish smiled and tapped his temple significantly. 'But I still had my photographic memory. It was more than enough. I memorized things I would need to know in my new life, and I flashed back to my youth. I was given another chance, a chance to make some different moves in the game of life. I did.'

Steve Delmario blinked. 'Your body,' he said blurrily. 'What happened to your body, huh?'

'An interesting question. The kick of the flashback kills the would-be time-traveler. The body, that is. The timeline itself goes on, however. At least my equations indicate that it should. I've never been around to witness it. Meanwhile, changes in the past create a new, variant timeline.'

'Oh, alternate tracks,' Delmario said. He nodded. 'Yeah.'

Kathy laughed. 'I can't believe I'm sitting here listening to all this,' she said. 'And that *he*' – she pointed to Delmario – 'is taking it seriously.'

E.C. Stuart had been looking idly at the ceiling, with a disdainful, faintly tolerant smile on his face. Now he straightened. 'I agree,' he said to Kathy. 'I am not so gullible as you were, Bruce,' he told Bunnish, 'and if you are trying to get some laughs by having us swallow this crock of shit, it isn't going to work.'

Bunnish turned to Peter. 'Captain, what's your vote?'

'Well,' said Peter carefully, 'all this is a little hard to credit, Bruce. You spoke of the game becoming an obsession with you, and I think that's true. I think you ought to be talking to a professional about this, not to us.'

'A professional what?' Bunnish said.

Peter fidgeted uncomfortably. 'You know. A shrink or a counselor.'

Bunnish chuckled. 'Failure hasn't made you any less patronizing,' he said. 'You were just as bad in the bookstore, in that line where you turned out to be a successful novelist.'

Peter sighed, 'Bruce, can't you see how pathetic these delusions of yours are? I mean, you've obviously been quite a success, and none of us have done as well, but even that wasn't enough for you, so you've constructed all these elaborate fantasies about how *you* have been the one behind our various failures. Vicarious, imaginary revenge.'

'Neither vicarious nor imaginary, Norten,' Bunnish snapped. 'I can tell you exactly how I did it.'

'Let him tell his stories, Peter,' E.C. said. 'Then maybe he'll let us out of this funny farm.'

'Why thank you, E.C,' Bunnish said. He looked around the table with smug satisfaction, like a man about to live out a dream he has cherished for a long, long time. Finally he fastened on Steve Delmario. 'I'll start with you,' he said, 'because in fact, I *did* start with you. You were easy to destroy, Delmario, because you were always so limited. In the original timeline, you were as wealthy as I am in this one. While I spent my life perfecting my flashback device, you made vast fortunes in the wide world out there. Electronic games at first, later more basic stuff, home computers, that sort of thing. You were born for that, and you were the best in the business, inspired and ingenious.

'When I flashed back, I simply took your place. Before using my device, I studied all your early little games, your cleverest ideas, the basic patents that came later and made you so rich. And I memorized all of them, along with the dates on which you'd come up with each and every one. Back in the past, armed with all this foreknowledge, it was child's play to beat you to the punch. Again and again. In those early years, Delmario, didn't it ever strike you as strange the way I anticipated every one of your small brainstorms? I'm living *your* life, Delmario.'

Delmario's hand had begun to tremble as he listened. His face looked dead. 'God damn you,' he said. 'God *damn* you.'

'Don't let him get to you, Steve,' E.C. put in. 'He's just making this up to see us squirm. It's all too absurd for words.'

'But it's *true*,' Delmario wailed, looking from E.C. to Bunnish and then, helpless, at Peter. Behind the thick lenses his eyes seemed wild. 'Peter, what he said – all my ideas – he was always ahead of me, he, he, I *told* you, he—'

'Yes,' Peter said firmly, 'and you told Bruce too, when we were talking earlier. Now he's just using your fears against you.'

Delmario opened his mouth, but no words came out.

'Have another drink,' Bunnish suggested.

Delmario stared at Bunnish as if he were about to leap up and strangle him. Peter tensed himself to intervene. But then, instead, Delmario reached out for a half-empty wine bottle, and filled his glass sloppily.

'This is contemptible, Bruce,' E.C. said.

Bunnish turned to face him. 'Delmario's ruin was easy and dramatic,' he said. 'You were more difficult, Stuart. He had nothing to live for but his work, you see, and when I took that away from him, he just collapsed. I only had to anticipate him a half-dozen times before all of his belief in himself was gone, and he did the rest himself. But you, E.C., you had more resources.'

'Go on with the fairy tale, Bunnish,' E.C. said in a put-upon tone.

'Delmario's ideas had made me rich,' Bunnish said. 'I used the money against you. Your fall was less satisfying and less resounding than Delmario's. He went from the heights to the pits. You were only a moderate success to begin with, and I had to settle for turning you into a moderate failure. But I managed. I pulled strings behind the scenes to lose you a number of large accounts. When you were with Foote, Cone I made sure another agency hired away a copywriter named Allerd, just before he came up with a campaign that would have rebounded to your credit. And remember when you left that position to take a better-paying slot at a brand new agency? Remember how quickly that agency folded, leaving you without an income? That was me. I've given your career twenty or thirty little shoves like that. Haven't you ever wondered at how infallibly wrong most of your professional moves have been, Stuart? At your bad luck?'

'No,' said E.C. 'I'm doing well enough, thank you.'

Bunnish smiled. 'I played one other little joke on you, too. You can thank me for that case of herpes you picked up last year. The lady who gave it to you was well paid. I had to search for her for a good number of years until I found the right combination – an out-of-work actress who was young and gorgeous and precisely your type, yet sufficiently desperate to do just about anything, and gifted with an incurable venereal disease as well. How did you like her, Stuart? It's your fault, you know. I just put her in your path, you did the rest yourself. And I thought it was so fitting, after my blind date and all.'

E.C.'s expression did not change. 'If you think this is going to break me down or make me believe you, you're way off base. All this proves is that you've had me investigated, and managed to dig up some dirt on my life.'

'Oh,' said Bunnish. 'Always so skeptical, Stuart. Scared that if you believe, you'll wind up looking foolish. Tsk.' He turned toward Peter. 'And you, Norten. You. Our fearless leader. You were the most difficult of all.'

Peter met Bunnish's eyes and said nothing.

'I read your novel, you know,' Bunnish said casually.

'I've never published a novel.'

'Oh, but you have! In the original timeline, that is. Quite a success too. The critics loved it, and it even appeared briefly on the bottom of the *Time* bestseller list.'

Peter was not amused. 'This is so obvious and pathetic,' he said.

'It was called *Beasts in a Cage*, I believe,' Bunnish said.

Peter had been sitting and listening with contempt, humoring a sick, sad man. Now, suddenly, he sat upright as if slapped.

He heard Kathy suck in her breath. 'My god,' she said.

E.C. seemed puzzled. 'Peter? What is it? You look . . .'

'No one knows about that book,' Peter said. 'How the hell did you find out? My old agent, you must have gotten the title from him. Yes. That's it, isn't it?'

'No,' said Bunnish, smiling complacently.

'You're lying!'

'Peter, what is it?' said E.C. 'Why are you so upset?'

Peter looked at him. 'My book,' he said. 'I . . . *Beasts in a Cage* was . . .'

'There was such a book?'

'Yes,' Peter said. He swallowed nervously, feeling confused and angry. 'Yes, there was. I . . . after college. My first novel.' He gave a nervous laugh. 'I thought it would be the first. I had . . . had a lot of hopes. It was ambitious. A serious book, but I thought it had commercial possibilities as well. The circus. It was about the circus, you know how I was always fascinated by the circus. A metaphor for life, I thought, a kind of life, but very colorful too, and dying, a dying institution. I thought I could write the great circus novel. After college, I traveled with Ringling Brothers' Blue Show for a year, doing research. I was a butcher, I . . . that's what they call the vendors in the stands, you see. A year of research, and I took two years to write the novel. The central character was a boy who worked with the big cats. I finally finished it and sent it off to my agent, and less than three weeks after I'd gotten it into the mail, I, I . . .' He couldn't finish.

But E.C. understood. He frowned. 'That circus bestseller? What was the title?'

'*Blue Show*,' Peter said, the words bitter in his mouth. 'By Donald Hastings Sullivan, some old hack who'd written fifty gothics and a dozen formula westerns, all under pen names. Such a book, from such a writer. No one could believe it. E.C., *I* couldn't believe it. It was *my* book, under a different title. Oh, it wasn't word-for-word. *Beasts in a Cage* was a lot better written. But the story, the background, the incidents, even a few of the character names . . . it was frightening. My agent never marketed my book. He said it was too much like *Blue Show* to be publishable, that no one would touch it. And even if I did get it published, he warned me, I would be labeled derivative at best, and a plagiarist at worst. It looked like a rip-off, he said. Three years of my life, and he called it a rip-off. We had words. He fired me, and I couldn't get another agent to take me on. I never wrote another book. The first one had taken too much out of me.' Peter turned to Bunnish. 'I destroyed my manuscript, burned every copy. No one knew about that book except my agent, me, and Kathy. How did you find out?'

'I told you,' said Bunnish. 'I read it.'

'*You damned liar!*' Peter said. He scooped up a glass in a white rage, and flung it down the table at Bunnish's smiling face, wanting to obliterate that complacent grin, to see it dissolve into blood and ruin. But Bunnish ducked and the glass shattered against a wall.

'Easy, Peter,' E.C. said. Delmario was blinking in owlish stupidity, lost in an alcoholic haze. Kathy was gripping the edge of the table. Her knuckles had gone white.

'Methinks our captain doth protest too much,' Bunnish said, his dimples showing. 'You know I'm telling the truth, Norten. I read your novel. I can recite the whole plot to prove it.' He shrugged. 'In fact, I did recite the whole plot. To Donald Hastings Sullivan, who wrote *Blue Show* while in my employ. I would have done it myself, but I had no aptitude for writing. Sully was glad for the chance. He got a handsome flat fee and we split the royalties, which were considerable.'

'You son of a bitch,' Peter said, but he said it without force. He felt his rage ebbing away, leaving behind it only a terrible sickly feeling, the certainty of defeat. He felt cheated and helpless and, all of a sudden, he realized that he believed Bunnish, believed every word of his preposterous story. 'It's true, isn't it?' he said. 'It is really true. You did it to me. You. You stole my words, my dreams, all of it.'

Bunnish said nothing.

'And the rest of it,' Peter said, 'the other failures, those were all you too, weren't they? After *Blue Show*, when I went into journalism . . . that big story that evaporated on me, all my sources suddenly denying everything or vanishing, so it looked like I'd made it all up. The assignments that evaporated, all those lawsuits, plagiarism, invasion of privacy, libel, every time I turned around I was being sued. Two years, and they just about ran me out of the profession. But it wasn't bad luck, was it? It was you. You stole my *life*.'

'You ought to be complimented, Norten. I had to break you twice. The first time I managed to kill your literary career with *Blue Show*, but then while my back was turned you managed to become a terribly popular journalist. Prizewinning, well known, all of it, and by then it was too late to do anything. I had to flash back once more to get you, do everything all over.'

'I ought to kill you, Bunnish,' Peter heard himself say.

E.C. shook his head. 'Peter,' he said, in the tone of a man explaining something to a high-grade moron, 'this is all an elaborate hoax. Don't take Bunny seriously.'

Peter stared at his old teammate. 'No, E.C. It's true. It's all true. Stop worrying about being the butt of a joke, and think about it. It makes sense. It explains everything that has happened to us.'

E.C. Stuart made a disgusted noise, frowned, and fingered the end of his mustache.

'Listen to your captain, Stuart,' Bunnish said.

Peter turned back to him. 'Why? That's what I want to know. *Why?* Because we played jokes on you? Kidded you? Maybe we were rotten, I don't know, it didn't seem to be so terrible at the time. You brought a lot of it on yourself. But whatever we might have done to you, we never deserved this. We were your teammates, your friends.'

Bunnish's smile curdled, and the dimples disappeared. 'You were *never* my friends.'

Steve Delmario nodded vigorously at that. 'You're no friend of mine, Funny Bunny, I tell you that. Know what you are? A *wimp*. You were always a goddamn wimp, that's why nobody ever liked you, you were just a damn wimp loser with a crew cut. Hell, you think you were the only one ever got kidded? What about me, the ol' last man on earth, huh, what about that? What about the jokes E.C. played on Pete, on Les, on all the others?' He took a drink. 'Bringing us here like this, that's another damn wimp thing to do. You're the same Bunny you always were. Wasn't enough to *do* something, you had to brag about it, let everybody know. And if somethin' went wrong, was never your fault, was it? You only lost 'cause the room was too noisy, or the lighting was bad, whatever.' Delmario stood up. 'You make me sick. Well, you screwed up all our lives maybe, and now you told us about it. Good for you. You had your damn wimp fun. Now let us out of here.'

'I second that motion,' said E.C.

'Why, I wouldn't think of it,' Bunnish replied. 'Not just yet. We haven't played any chess yet. A few games for old times' sake.'

Delmario blinked, and moved slightly as he stood holding the back of his chair. 'The *game*,' he said, suddenly reminded of his challenge to Bunnish of a few minutes ago. 'We were goin' to play over the game.'

Bunnish folded his hands neatly in front of him on the table. 'We can do better than that,' he said. 'I am a very fair man, you see. None of you ever gave me a chance, but I'll give one to you, to each of you. I've stolen your lives. Wasn't that what you said, Norten? Well, *friends*, I'll give you a shot at winning those lives back. We'll play a little chess. We'll replay the game, from the critical position. I'll take Vesselere's side and you can have mine. The three of you can consult, if you like, or I'll play you one by one. I don't care. All you have to do is beat me. Win the game you say I should have won, and I'll let you go, and give you anything you like. Money, property, a job, whatever.'

'Go t'hell, wimp,' Delmario said. 'I'm not interested in your damn money.'

Bunnish picked up his glasses from the table and donned them, smiling widely. 'Or,' he said, 'if you prefer, you can win a chance to use my flashback device. You can go back then, anticipate me, do it all over, live the lives you were destined to live before I dealt myself in. Just think of it. It's the best opportunity you'll ever have, any of you, and I'm making it so *easy*. All you have to do is win a won game.'

'Winning a won game is one of the hardest things in chess,' Peter said sullenly. But even as he said it, his mind was racing, excitement stirring deep in his gut. It was a chance, he thought, a chance to reshape the ruins of his life, to make it come out right. To obliterate the wrong turnings, to taste the wine of success instead of the wormwood of failure, to avoid the mockery that his marriage to Kathy had become. Dead hopes rose like ghosts to dance again in the graveyard of his dreams. He had to take the shot, he knew. He *had* to.

Steve Delmario was there before him. 'I can win that goddamned game,' he boomed drunkenly. 'I could win it with my eyes shut. You're on, Bunny. Get out a set, damn you!'

Bunnish laughed and stood up, putting his big hands flat on the tabletop and using them to push himself to his feet. 'Oh no, Delmario. You're not going to have the excuse of being drunk when you lose. I'm going to crush you when you are cold stone sober. Tomorrow. I'll play you tomorrow.'

Delmario blinked furiously. 'Tomorrow,' he echoed.

*

Later, when they were alone in their room, Kathy turned on him. 'Peter,' she said, 'let's get out of here. Tonight. Now.'

Peter was sitting before the fire. He had found a small chess set in the top drawer of his bedside table, and had set up the critical position from Vesselere-Bunnish to study it. He scowled at the distraction and said, 'Get out? How the hell do you propose we do that, with our car locked up in that garage?'

'There's got to be a phone here somewhere. We could search, find it, call for help. Or just walk.'

'It's December, and we're in the mountains miles from anywhere. We try to walk out of here and we could freeze to death. No.' He turned his attention back to the chessboard and tried to concentrate.

'*Peter,*' she said angrily.

He looked up again. 'What?' he snapped. 'Can't you see I'm busy?'

'We have to do *something*. This whole scene is insane. Bunnish needs to be locked up.'

'He was telling the truth,' Peter said.

Kathy's expression softened, and for an instant there was something like sorrow on her face. 'I know,' she said softly.

'You know,' Peter mimicked savagely. 'You know, do you? Well, do you know how it *feels?* That bastard is going to pay. He's responsible for every rotten thing that has happened to me. For all I know, he's probably responsible for you.'

Kathy's lips moved only slightly, and her eyes moved not at all, but suddenly the sorrow and sympathy were gone from her face, and instead Peter saw familiar pity, well-honed contempt. 'He's just going to crush you again,' she said coldly. 'He wants you to lust after this chance, because he intends to deny it to you. He's going to beat you, Peter. How are you going to like that? How are you going to live with it, afterwards?'

Peter looked down at the chess pieces. 'That's what he intends, yeah. But he's a moron. This is a *won* position. It's only a matter of finding the winning line, the right variation. And we've got three shots at it. Steve goes first. If he loses, E.C. and I will be able to learn from his mistakes. I won't lose. I've lost everything else, maybe, but not this. This time I'm going to be a winner. You'll see.'

'I'll see, all right,' Kathy said. 'You pitiful bastard.'

Peter ignored her, and moved a piece. Knight takes pawn.

*

Kathy remained in the suite the next morning. 'Go play your damn games if you like,' she told Peter. 'I'm going to soak in the hot tub, and read. I want no part of this.'

'Suit yourself,' Peter said. He slammed the door behind him, and thought once again what a bitch he'd married.

Downstairs, in the huge living room, Bunnish was setting up the board. The set he'd chosen was not ornate and expensive like the one in the corner, with its pieces glued into place. Sets like that looked good for decorative purposes, but were useless in serious play. Instead Bunnish had shifted a plain wooden table to the center of the room, and fetched out a standard tournament set: a vinyl board in green and white that he unrolled carefully, a well-worn set of Drueke pieces of standard Staunton design, cast in black and white plastic with lead weights in the bases, beneath the felt, to give them a nice heft. He placed each piece into position from memory, without once looking at the game frozen on the expensive inlaid board across the room. Then he began to set a double-faced chess clock. 'Can't play without the clock, you know,' he said, smiling. 'I'll set it exactly the same as it stood that day in Evanston.'

When everything was finished, Bunnish surveyed the board with satisfaction and seated himself behind Vesselere's Black pieces. 'Ready?' he asked.

Steve Delmario sat down opposite him, looking pale and terribly hung over. He was holding a big tumbler full of orange juice, and behind his thick glasses his eyes moved nervously. 'Yeah,' he said. 'Go on.'

Bunnish pushed the button that started Delmario's clock.

Very quickly, Delmario reached out, played knight takes pawn – the pieces clicked together softly as he made the capture – and used the pawn he'd taken to punch the clock, stopping his own timer and starting Bunnish's.

'The sac,' said Bunnish. 'What a surprise.' He took the knight.

Delmario played bishop takes pawn, saccing another piece. Bunnish was forced to capture with his king. He seemed unperturbed. He was smiling faintly, his dimples faint creases in his big cheeks, his eyes clear and sharp and cheerful behind his tinted eyeglasses.

Steve Delmario was leaning forward over the board, his dark eyes sweeping back and forth over the position, back and forth, over and over again as if double-checking that everything was really where he thought it was. He crossed and uncrossed his legs. Peter, standing just behind him, could almost feel the tension beating off Delmario in waves, twisting him. Even E.C. Stuart, seated a few feet distant in a big comfortable armchair, was staring at the game intently. The clock ticked softly. Delmario lifted his hand to move his queen, but hesitated with his fingers poised above it. His hand trembled.

'What's the matter, Steve?' Bunnish asked. He steepled his hands just beneath his chin, and smiled when Delmario looked up at him. 'You hesitate. Don't you know? He who hesitates is lost. Uncertain, all of a sudden? Surely that can't be. You were always so certain before. How many mates did you show me? How many?'

Delmario blinked, frowned. 'I'm going to show you one more, Bunny,' he said furiously. His fingers closed on his queen, shifted it across the board. 'Check.'

'Ah,' said Bunnish. Peter studied the position. The double sac had cleared away the pawns in front of the Black king, and the queen check permitted no retreat. Bunnish marched his king up a square, toward the center of the board, toward the waiting White army. Surely he was lost now. His own defenders were all over on the queenside, and the enemy was all around him. But Bunnish did not seem worried.

Delmario's clock was ticking as he examined the position. He sipped his juice, shifted restlessly in his seat. Bunnish yawned, and grinned tauntingly. 'You were the winner that day, Delmario. Beat a Master. The only winner. Can't you find the win now? Where are all those mates, eh?'

'There's so many I don't know which one to go with, Bunny,' Steve said. 'Now shut up, damn you. I'm trying to think.'

'Oh,' said Bunnish. 'Pardon.'

Delmario consumed ten minutes on his clock before he reached out and moved his remaining knight. 'Check.'

Bunnish advanced his king again.

Delmario licked his lips, slid his queen forward a square. 'Check.'

Bunnish's king went sideways, toward the safety of the queenside.

Delmario flicked a pawn forward. 'Check.'

Bunnish had to take. He removed the offending pawn with his king, smiling complacently.

With the file open, Delmario could bring his rooks into play. He shifted one over. 'Check.'

Bunnish's harried king moved again.

Now Delmario moved the rook forward, sliding it right up the file to confront the enemy king face to face. 'Check!' he said loudly.

Peter sucked in his breath sharply, without meaning to. The rook was hanging! Bunnish could just snatch it off. He stared at the position over Delmario's shoulder. Bunnish could take the rook with his king, all right, but then the other rook came over, the king had to go back, then if the queen shifted just one square . . . yes . . . too many mate threats in that variation. Black had lots of resources, but they all ended in disaster. But if Bunnish took with his knight instead of his king, he left that square unguarded . . . hmmm . . . queen check, king up, bishop comes in . . . no, mate was even quicker that way.

Delmario drained his orange juice and set the empty tumbler down with self-satisfied firmness.

Bunnish moved his king diagonally forward. The only possible move, Peter thought. Delmario leaned forward. Behind him, Peter leaned forward too. The White pieces were swarming around Black's isolated king now, but how to tighten the mating net? Steve had three different checks, Peter thought. No, four, he could do that too. He watched and analyzed in silence. The rook check was no good, the king just retreated, and further checks simply drove him to safety. The bishop? No, Bunnish could trade off, take with his rook – he was two pieces up, after all. Several subvariations branched off from the two queen checks. Peter was still trying to figure out where they led, when Delmario reached out suddenly, grabbed a pawn from in front of his king, and moved it up two squares. He slammed it down solidly, and slapped the clock. Then he sat back and crossed his arms. 'Your move, Bunny,' he said.

Peter studied the board. Delmario's last move didn't give check, but the pawn advance cut off an important escape square. Now that threatened rook check was no longer innocuous. Instead of being chased back to safety, the Black king got mated in three. Of course, Bunnish had a tempo now, it was his move, he could bring up a defender. His queen now, could ... no, then queen check, king back, rook check, and the Black queen fell ... bishop maybe ... no, check there and mate in one, unstoppable. The longer Peter looked at the position, the fewer defensive resources he saw for Black. Bunnish could delay the loss, but he couldn't stop it. He was smashed!

Bunnish did not look smashed. Very calmly he picked up a knight and moved it to queen's knight six. 'Check,' he said quietly.

Delmario stared. Peter stared. E.C. Stuart got up out of his chair and drifted closer, his finger brushing back his mustache as he considered the game. The check was only a time-waster, Peter thought. Delmario could capture the knight with either of two pawns, or he could simply move his king. Except ... Peter scowled ... if White took with the bishop pawn, queen came up with check, king moved to the second, queen takes rook pawn with check, king ... no, that was no good. White got mated by force. The other way seemed to bring on the mate even faster, after the queen checked from the eighth rank.

Delmario moved his king up.

Bunnish slid a bishop out along a diagonal. 'Check.'

There was only one move. Steve moved his king forward again. He was being harassed, but his mating net was still intact, once the checks had run their course.

Bunnish flicked his knight backward, with another check.

Delmario was blinking and twisting his legs beneath the table. Peter saw that if he brought his king back, Bunnish had a forced series of checks leading to mate . . . but the Black knight hung now, to both rook and queen, and . . . Delmario captured it with the rook.

Bunnish grabbed White's advanced pawn with his queen, removing the cornerstone of the mating net. Now Delmario could play queen takes queen, but then he lost his queen to a fork, and after the tradeoffs that followed he'd be hopelessly busted. Instead he retreated his king.

Bunnish made a *tsk*ing noise and captured the White knight with his queen, again daring Delmario to take it. With knight and pawn both gone, Delmario's mating threats had all dissipated, and if White snatched that Black queen, there was a check, a pin, take, take, take, and . . . Peter gritted his teeth together . . . and White would suddenly be in the endgame down a piece, hopelessly lost. No. There had to be something better. The position still had a lot of play in it. Peter stared, and analyzed.

Steve Delmario stared too, while his clock ticked. The clock was one of those fancy jobs, with a move counter. It showed that he had to make seven more moves to reach time control. He had just under fifteen minutes remaining. Some time pressure, but nothing serious.

Except that Delmario sat and sat, eyes flicking back and forth across the board, blinking. He took off his thick glasses and cleaned them methodically on his shirttail. When he slid them back on, the position had not changed. He stared at the Black king fixedly, as if he were willing it to fall. Finally he started to get up. 'I need a drink,' he said.

'I'll get it,' Peter snapped. 'Sit down. You've only got eight minutes left.'

'Yeah,' Delmario said. He sat down again. Peter went to the bar and made him a screwdriver. Steve drained half of it in a gulp, never taking his eyes from the chessboard.

Peter happened to glance at E.C. Stuart. E.C. shook his head and cast his eyes up toward the ceiling. Not a word was spoken, but Peter heard the message: *forget it.*

Steve Delmario sat there, growing more and more agitated. With three minutes remaining on his clock, he reached out his hand, thought better of it, and pulled back. He shifted in his seat, gathered his legs up under him, leaned closer to the board, his nose a bare couple inches above the chessmen. His clock ticked.

He was still staring at the board when Bunnish smiled and said, 'Your flag is down, Delmario.'

Delmario looked up, blinking. His mouth hung open. 'Time,' he said urgently. 'I just need time to find the win, got to be here someplace, got to, all those checks . . .'

Bunnish rose. 'You're out of time, Delmario. Doesn't matter anyway. You're dead lost.'

'NO! No I'm not, damn you, there's a win . . .'

Peter put a hand on Steve's shoulder. 'Steve, take it easy,' he said. 'I'm sorry. Bruce is right. You're busted here.'

'No,' Delmario insisted. 'I *know* there's a winning combo, I just got to . . . got to . . . only . . .' His right hand, out over the board, began to shake, and he knocked over his own king.

Bunnish showed his dimples. 'Listen to your captain, winner-boy,' he said. Then he looked away from Delmario, to where E.C. stood scowling. 'You're next, Stuart. Tomorrow. Same time, same place.'

'And if I don't care to play?' E.C. said disdainfully.

Bunnish shrugged. 'Suit yourself,' he said. 'I'll be here, and the game will be here. I'll start your clock on time. You can lose over the board or lose by forfeit. You lose either way.'

'And me?' Peter said.

'Why, captain,' said Bunnish. 'I'm saving *you* for last.'

*

Steve Delmario was a wreck. He refused to leave the chessboard except to mix himself fresh drinks. For the rest of the morning and most of the afternoon he remained glued to his seat, drinking like a fish and flicking the chess pieces around like a man possessed, playing and replaying the game. Delmario wolfed down a couple sandwiches that Peter made up for him around lunchtime, but there was no talking to him, no calming him. Peter tried. In an hour or so, Delmario would be passed out from the booze he was downing in such alarming quantities.

Finally he and E.C. left Delmario alone, and went upstairs to his suite. Peter knocked on the door. 'You decent, Kathy? E.C. is with me.'

She opened the door. She had on jeans and a T-shirt. 'Decent as I ever get,' she said. 'Come on in. How did the great game come out?'

'Delmario lost,' Peter said. 'It was a close thing, though. I thought we had him for a moment.'

Kathy snorted.

'So what now?' E.C. said.

'You going to play tomorrow?'

E.C. shrugged. 'Might as well. I've got nothing to lose.'

'Good,' Peter said. 'You can beat him. Steve almost won, and we both know the shape he's in. We've got to analyze, figure out where he went wrong.'

E.C. fingered his mustache. He looked cool and thoughtful. 'That pawn move,' he suggested. 'The one that didn't give check. It left White open for that counterattack.'

'It also set up the mating net,' Peter said. He looked over his shoulder, saw Kathy standing with her arms crossed. 'Could you get the chessboard from the bedroom?' he asked her. When she left, Peter turned back to E.C. 'I think Steve was already lost by the time he made that pawn move. That was his only good shot – lots of threats there. Everything else just petered out after a few checks. He went wrong before that, I think.'

'All those checks,' E.C. said. 'One too many, maybe?'

'Exactly,' said Peter. 'Instead of driving him into a checkmate, Steve drove him into safety. You've got to vary somewhere in there.'

'Agreed.'

Kathy arrived with the chess set and placed it on the low table between them. As Peter swiftly set up the critical position, she folded her legs beneath her and sat on the floor. But she grew bored very quickly when they began to analyze, and it wasn't long before she got to her feet again with a disgusted noise. 'Both of you are crazy,' she said. 'I'm going to get something to eat.'

'Bring us back something, will you?' Peter asked. 'And a couple of beers?' But he hardly noticed it when she placed the tray beside them.

They stayed at it well into the night. Kathy was the only one who went down to dine with Bunnish. When she returned, she said, 'That man is *disgusting*,' so emphatically that it actually distracted Peter from the game. But only for an instant.

'Here, try this,' E.C. said, moving a knight, and Peter looked back quickly.

*

'I see you decided to play, Stuart,' Bunnish said the next morning.

E.C., looking trim and fresh, his sandy hair carefully combed and brushed, a steaming mug of black coffee in hand, nodded briskly. 'You're as sharp as ever, Brucie.'

Bunnish chuckled.

'One point, however,' E.C. said, holding up a finger. 'I still don't believe your cock-and-bull story about time-travel. We'll play this out, alright, but we'll play for money, not for one of your flashbacks. Understood?'

'You jokers are such suspicious types,' Bunnish said. He sighed. 'Anything you say, of course. You want money. Fine.'

'One million dollars.'

Bunnish smiled broadly. 'Small change,' he said. 'But I agree. Beat me, and you'll leave here with one million. You'll take a check, I hope?'

'A certified check.' E.C. turned to Peter. 'You're my witness,' he said, and Peter nodded. The three of them were alone this morning. Kathy was firm in her disinterest, and Delmario was in his room sleeping off his binge.

'Ready?' Bunnish asked.

'Go on.'

Bunnish started the clock. E.C. reached out and played the sacrifice. Knight takes pawn. His motions were crisp and economical. Bunnish captured, and E.C. played the bishop sac without a second's hesitation. Bunnish captured again, pushed the clock.

E.C. Stuart brushed back his mustache, reached down, and moved a pawn. No check.

'Ah,' Bunnish said. 'An improvement. You have something up your sleeve, don't you? Of course you do. E.C. Stuart always has something up his sleeve. The hilarious, unpredictable E.C. Stuart. Such a joker. So imaginative.'

'Play chess, Brucie,' snapped E.C.

'Of course.' Peter drifted closer to the board while Bunnish studied the position. They had gone over and over the game last night, and had finally decided that the queen check that Delmario had played following the double sac was unsound. There were several other checks in the position, all tempting, but after hours of analysis he and E.C. had discarded those as well. Each of them offered plenty of traps and checkmates should Black err, but each of them seemed to fail against correct play, and they had to assume Bunnish would play correctly.

E.C.'s pawn move was a more promising line. Subtler. Sounder. It opened lines for White's pieces, and interposed another barrier between Black's king and the safety of the queenside. Suddenly White had threats everywhere. Bunnish had serious troubles to chew on now.

He did not chew on them nearly as long as Peter would have expected. After studying the position for a bare couple minutes, he picked up his queen and snatched off White's queen rook pawn, which was undefended. Bunnish cupped the pawn in his hand, yawned, and slouched back in his chair, looking lazy and unperturbed.

E.C. Stuart permitted himself a brief scowl as he looked over the position. Peter felt uneasy as well. That move ought to have disturbed Bunnish more than it had, he thought. White had so many threats . . . last night they had analyzed the possibilities exhaustively, playing and replaying every variation and subvariation until they were sure that they had found the win. Peter had gone to sleep feeling almost jubilant. Bunnish had a dozen feasible defenses to their pawn thrust. They'd had no way of knowing which one he would choose, so they had satisfied themselves that each and every one ultimately ended in failure.

Only now Bunnish had fooled them. He hadn't played *any* of the likely defenses. He had just ignored E.C.'s mating threats, and gone pawn-snatching as blithely as the rankest patzer. Had they missed something? While E.C. considered the best reply, Peter drew up a chair to the side of the board so he could analyze in comfort.

There was nothing, he thought, nothing. Bunnish had a check next move, if he wanted it, by pushing his queen to the eighth rank. But it was meaningless. E.C. hadn't weakened his queenside the way Steve had yesterday, in his haste to find a mate. If Bunnish checked, all Stuart had to do was move his king up to queen two. Then the Black queen would be under attack by a rook, and forced to retreat or grab another worthless pawn. Meanwhile, Bunnish would be getting checkmated in the middle of the board. The more Peter went over the variations, the more convinced he became that there was no way Bunnish could possibly work up the kind of counterattack he had used to smash Steve Delmario.

E.C., after a long and cautious appraisal of the board, seemed to reach the same conclusion. He reached out coolly and moved his knight, hemming in Bunnish's lonely king once and for all. Now he threatened a queen check that would lead to mate in one. Bunnish could capture the dominating knight, but then E.C. just recaptured with a rook, and checkmate followed soon thereafter, no matter how Bunnish might wriggle on the hook.

Bunnish smiled across the board at his opponent, and lazily shoved his queen forward a square to the last rank. 'Check,' he said.

E.C. brushed back his moustache, shrugged, and played his king up. He punched the clock with a flourish. 'You're lost,' he said flatly.

Peter was inclined to agree. That last check had accomplished nothing; in fact, it seemed to have worsened Black's plight. The mate threats were still there, as unstoppable as ever, and now Black's queen was under attack as well. He could pull it back, of course, but not in time to help with the defense. Bunnish ought to be frantic and miserable.

Instead his smile was so broad that his fat cheeks were threatening to crack in two. 'Lost?' he said. 'Ah, Stuart, this time the joke is on you!' He giggled like a teenage girl, and brought his queen down the rank to grab off White's rook. 'Check!'

Peter Norten had not played a game of tournament chess in a long, long time, but he still remembered the way it had felt when an opponent suddenly made an unexpected move that changed the whole complexion of a game: the brief initial confusion, the *what is that?* feeling, followed by panic when you realized the strength of the unanticipated move, and then the awful swelling gloom that built and built as you followed through one losing variation after another in your head. There was no worse moment in the game of chess.

That was how Peter felt now.

They had missed it totally. Bunnish was giving up his queen for a rook, normally an unthinkable sacrifice, but not in this position. E.C. *had* to take the offered queen. But if he captured with his king, Peter saw with sudden awful clarity, Black had a combination that won the farm, which meant he had to use the other rook, pulling it off its crucial defense of the central knight . . . and then . . . oh, *shit!*

E.C. tried to find another alternative for more than fifteen minutes, but there was no alternative to be found. He played rook takes queen. Bunnish quickly seized his own rook and captured the knight that had moved so menacingly into position only two moves before. With ruthless precision, Bunnish then forced the tradeoff of one piece after another, simplifying every danger off the board. All of a sudden they were in the endgame. E.C. had a queen and five pawns; Bunnish had a rook, two bishops, a knight, and four pawns, and – ironically – his once-imperiled king now occupied a powerful position in the center of the board.

Play went on for hours, as E.C. gamely gave check after check with his rogue queen, fighting to pick up a loose piece or perhaps draw by repetition. But Bunnish was too skilled for such desperation tactics. It was only a matter of technique.

Finally E.C. tipped over his king.

'I thought we looked at every possible defense,' Peter said numbly.

'Why, captain,' said Bunnish cheerfully. 'Every attempt to defend loses. The defending pieces block off escape routes or get in the way. Why should I help mate myself? I'd rather let you try to do that.'

'I *will* do that,' Peter promised angrily. 'Tomorrow.'

Bunnish rubbed his hands together. 'I can scarcely wait!'

*

That night the postmortem was held in E.C.'s suite; Kathy – who had greeted their glum news with an 'I told you so' and a contemptuous smile – had insisted that she didn't want them staying up half the night over a chessboard in *her* presence. She told Peter he was behaving like a child, and they had angry words before he stormed out.

Steve Delmario was going over the morning's loss with E.C. when Peter joined them. Delmario's eyes looked awfully bloodshot, but otherwise he appeared sober, if haggard. He was drinking coffee. 'How does it look?' Peter asked when he pulled up a seat.

'Bad,' E.C. said.

Delmario nodded. 'Hell, worse'n bad, it's starting to look like that damn sac is unsound after all. I can't believe it, I just can't, it all looks so promising, got to be something there. *Got* to. But I'm damned if I can find it.'

E.C. added, 'The surprise he pulled today is a threat in a number of variations. Don't forget, we gave up two pieces to get to this position. Unfortunately, that means that Brucie can easily afford to give some of that material back to get out of the fix. He still comes out ahead, and wins the endgame. We've found a few improvements on my play this morning—'

'That knight doesn't have to drop,' interjected Delmario.

'. . . but nothing convincing,' E.C. concluded.

'You ever think,' Delmario said, 'that maybe the Funny Bunny was *right*? That maybe the sac don't work, maybe the game was never won at all?' His voice had a note of glum disbelief in it.

'There's one thing wrong with that,' Peter said.

'Oh?'

'Ten years ago, after Bunnish had blown the game and the match, Robinson Vesselere *admitted* that he had been lost.'

E.C. looked thoughtful. 'That's true. I'd forgotten that.'

'Vesselere was almost a Senior Master. He had to know what he was talking about. The win is there. I mean to find it.'

Delmario clapped his hands together and whooped gleefully. 'Hell yes, Pete, you're right! Let's go!'

*

'At last the prodigal spouse returns,' Kathy said pointedly when Peter came in. 'Do you have any idea what time it is?'

She was seated in a chair by the fireplace, though the fire had burned down to ashes and embers. She wore a dark robe, and the end of the cigarette she was smoking was a bright point in the darkness. Peter had come in smiling, but now he frowned. Kathy had once been a heavy smoker, but she'd given it up years ago. Now she only lit a cigarette when she was very upset. When she lit up, it usually meant they were headed for a vicious row.

'It's late,' Peter said. 'I don't know how late. What does it matter?' He'd spent most of the night with E.C. and Steve, but it had been worth it. They'd found what they had been looking for. Peter had returned tired but elated, expecting to find his wife asleep. He was in no mood for grief. 'Never mind about the time,' he said to her, trying to placate. 'We've *got* it, Kath.'

She crushed out her cigarette methodically. 'Got what? Some new move you think is going to defeat our psychopathic host? Don't you understand that I don't give a damn about this stupid game of yours? Don't you listen to a thing I say? I've been waiting up half the night, Peter. It's almost three in the morning. I want to talk.'

'Yeah?' Peter snapped. Her tone had gotten his back up. 'Did you ever think that maybe I didn't want to listen? Well, think it. I have a big game tomorrow. I need my sleep. I can't afford to stay up till dawn screaming at you. Understand? Why the hell are you so hot to talk anyway? What could you possibly have to say that I haven't heard before, huh?'

Kathy laughed nastily. 'I could tell you a few things about your old friend Bunnish that you haven't heard before.'

'I doubt it.'

'Do you? Well, did you know that he's been trying to get me into bed for the past two days?'

She said it tauntingly, throwing it at him. Peter felt as if he had been struck. *'What?'*

'Sit down,' she snapped, 'and listen.'

Numbly, he did as she bid him. 'Did you?' he asked, staring at her silhouette in the darkness, the vaguely ominous shape that was his wife.

'Did I? Sleep with him, you mean? Jesus, Peter, how can you ask that? Do you loathe me that much? I'd sooner sleep with a roach. That's what he reminds me of anyway.' She gave a rueful chuckle. 'He isn't exactly a sophisticated seducer, either. He actually offered me money.'

'Why are you telling me this?'

'To knock some goddamned sense into you! Can't you see that Bunnish is trying to destroy you, all of you, any way he can? He didn't want me. He just wanted to get at you. And you, you and your moron teammates, are playing right into his hands. You're becoming as obsessed with that idiot chess game as *he* is.' She leaned forward. Dimly, Peter could make out the lines of her face. 'Peter,' she said almost imploringly, 'don't play him. He's going to beat you, love, just like he beat the others.'

'I don't think so, *love,*' Peter said from between clenched teeth. The endearment became an epithet as he hurled it back at her. 'Why the hell are you always so ready to predict defeat for me, huh? Can't you ever be supportive, not even for a goddamned minute? If you won't help, why don't you just bug off? I've had all I can stand of you, damn it. Always belittling me, mocking. You've never believed in me. I don't know why the hell you married me, if all you wanted to do was make my life a hell. *Just leave me alone!'*

For a long moment after Peter's outburst there was silence. Sitting there in the darkened room, he could almost feel her rage building – any instant now he expected to hear her start screaming. Then he would scream back, and she would get up and break something, and he would grab her, and then the knives would come out in earnest. He closed his eyes, trembling, feeling close to tears. He didn't want this, he thought. He really didn't.

But Kathy fooled him. When she spoke, her voice was surprisingly gentle. 'Oh, Peter,' she said. 'I never meant to hurt you. Please. I love you.'

He was stunned. 'Love me?' he said wonderingly.

'Please listen. If there is anything at all left between us, please just listen to me for a few minutes. Please.'

'All right,' he said.

'Peter, *I did* believe in you once. Surely you must remember how good things were in the beginning? I was supportive then, wasn't I? The first few years, when you were writing your novel? I worked, I kept food on the table, I gave you the time to write.'

'Oh, yes,' he said, anger creeping back into his tone. Kathy had thrown that at him before, had reminded him forcefully of how she'd supported them for two years while he wrote a book that turned out to be so much wastepaper. 'Spare me your reproaches, huh? It wasn't my fault I couldn't sell the book. You heard what Bunnish said.'

'I wasn't reproaching you, damn it!' she snapped. 'Why are you always so ready to read criticism into every word I say?' She shook her head, and got her voice back under control. 'Please, Peter, don't make this harder than it is. We have so many years of pain to overcome, so many wounds to bind up. Just hear me out.

'I was trying to say that I did believe in you. Even after the book, after you burned it . . . even then. You made it hard, though. I didn't think you were a failure, but *you* did, and it changed you, Peter. You let it get to you. You gave up writing, instead of just gritting your teeth and doing another book.'

'I wasn't tough enough, I know,' he said. 'The loser. The weakling.'

'*Shut up!*' she said in exasperation. 'I didn't say that, *you* did. Then you went into journalism. I still believed. But everything kept going wrong. You got fired, you got sued, you became a disgrace. Our friends started drifting away. And all the time you insisted that none of it was your fault. You lost all the rest of your self-confidence. You didn't dream any more. You whined, bitterly and incessantly, about your bad luck.'

'You never helped.'

'Maybe not,' Kathy admitted. 'I tried to, at the start, but it just got worse and worse and I couldn't deal with it. You weren't the dreamer I'd married. It was hard to remember how I'd admired you, how I'd respected you. Peter, you loathed yourself so much that there was no way to keep the loathing from rubbing off on me.'

'So?' Peter said. 'What's the point, Kathy?'

'I never left you, Peter,' she said. 'I could have, you know. I wanted to. I stayed, through all of it, all the failures and all the self-pity. Doesn't that say anything to you?'

'It says you're a masochist,' he snapped. 'Or maybe a sadist.'

That was too much for her. She started to reply, and her voice broke, and she began to weep. Peter sat where he was and listened to her cry. Finally the tears ran out, and she said, quietly, 'Damn you. Damn you. I hate you.'

'I thought you loved me. Make up your mind.'

'You ass. You insensitive creep. Don't you understand, Peter?'

'Understand *what?*' he said impatiently. 'You said listen, so I've been listening, and all you've been doing is rehashing all the same old stuff, recounting all my inadequacies. I heard it all before.'

'Peter, can't you see that this week has changed *everything?* If you'd only stop hating, stop loathing me and yourself, maybe you could see it. We have a chance again, Peter. If we try. Please.'

'I don't see that anything has changed. I'm going to play a big chess game tomorrow, and you know how much it means to me and my self-respect, and you don't care. You don't care if I win or lose. You keep telling me I'm *going* to lose. You're *helping* me to lose by making me argue when I should be sleeping. What the hell has changed? You're the same damn bitch you've been for years.'

'I will tell you what has changed,' she said. 'Peter, up until a few days ago, both of us thought you were a failure. But you aren't! *It hasn't been your fault*. None of it. Not bad luck, like you kept saying, and not personal inadequacy either, like you really thought. Bunnish has done it all. Can't you see what a difference that makes? You've never had a chance, Peter, but you have one now. There's no reason you shouldn't believe in yourself. We *know* you can do great things! Bunnish admitted it. We can leave here, you and I, and start all over again. You could write another book, write plays, do anything you want. You have the talent. You've never lacked it. We can dream again, believe again, love each other again. Don't you see? Bunnish had to gloat to complete his revenge, but by gloating he's *freed* you!'

Peter sat very still in the dark room, his hand clenching and unclenching on the arm of the chair as Kathy's words sunk in. He had been so wrapped up in the chess game, so obsessed with Bunnish's obsession, that he had never seen it, never considered it. *It wasn't me*, he thought wonderingly. *All those years, it was never me*. 'It's true,' he said in a small voice.

'Peter?' she said, concerned.

He heard the concern, heard more than that, heard love in her voice. So many people, he thought, make such grand promises, promise better or worse, promise rich or poorer, and bail out as soon as things turn the least bit sour in a relationship. But she had stayed, through all of it, the failures, the disgrace, the cruel words and the poisonous thoughts, the weekly fights, the poverty. She had stayed.

'Kathy,' he said. The next words were very hard. 'I love you, too.' He started to get up and move toward her, and began to cry.

*

They arrived late the next morning. They showered together, and Peter dressed with unusual care. For some reason, he felt it was important to look his best. It was a new beginning, after all. Kathy came with him. They entered the living room holding hands. Bunnish was already behind the board, and Peter's clock was ticking. The others were there too. E.C. was seated patiently in a chair. Delmario was pacing. 'Hurry up,' he said when Peter came down the stairs. 'You've lost five minutes already.'

Peter smiled. 'Easy, Steve,' he said. He went over and took his seat behind the White pieces. Kathy stood behind him. She looked gorgeous this morning, Peter thought.

'It's your move, captain,' Bunnish said, with an unpleasant smile.

'I know,' Peter said. He made no effort to move, scarcely even looked at the board. 'Bruce, why do you hate me? I've been thinking about that, and I'd like to know the answer. I can understand about Steve and E.C. Steve had the presumption to win when you lost, and he rubbed your nose in that defeat afterwards. E.C. made you the butt of his jokes. But why me? What did I ever do to you?'

Bunnish looked briefly confused. Then his face grew hard. 'You. You were the worst of them all.'

Peter was startled. 'I never . . .'

'The big captain,' Bunnish said sarcastically. 'That day ten years ago, you never even *tried*. You took a quick grandmaster draw with your old friend Hal Winslow. You could have tried for a win, played on, but you didn't. Oh, no. You never cared how much more pressure you put on the rest of us. And when we lost, you didn't take any of the blame, not a bit of it, even though you gave up half a point. It was all *my* fault. And that wasn't all of it, either. Why was *I* on first board, Norten? All of us on the B team had approximately the same rating. How did I get the honor of being board one?'

Peter thought for a minute, trying to recall the strategies that had motivated him ten years before. Finally he nodded. 'You always lost the big games, Bruce. It made sense to put you up on board one, where you'd face the other teams' big guns, the ones who'd probably beat whoever we played there. That way the lower boards would be manned by more reliable players, the ones we could count on in the clutch.'

'In other words,' Bunnish said, 'I was a write-off. You expected me to lose, while you won matches on the lower boards.'

'Yes,' Peter admitted. 'I'm sorry.'

'Sorry,' mocked Bunnish. 'You *made* me lose, expected me to lose, and then tormented me for losing, and now you're sorry. You didn't play chess that day. You never played chess. You were playing a bigger game, a game that lasted for years, between you and Winslow of U.C. And the team members were your pieces and your pawns. Me, I was a sac. A gambit. That was all. And it didn't work anyway. Winslow beat you. You *lost*.'

'You're right,' Peter admitted. 'I lost. I think I understand now. Why you did all the things you've done.'

'You're going to lose again now,' Bunnish said. '*Move*, before your clock runs out.' He nodded down at the checkered wasteland that lay between them, at the complex jumble of Black and White pieces.

Peter glanced at the board with disinterest. 'We analyzed until three in the morning last night, the three of us. I had a new variation all set. A single sacrifice, instead of the double sac. I play knight takes pawn, but I hold back from the bishop sac, swing my queen over instead. That was the idea. It looked pretty good. But it's unsound, isn't it?'

Bunnish stared at him. 'Play it, and we'll find out!'

'No,' said Peter. 'I don't want to play.'

'*Pete!*' Steve Delmario said in consternation. 'You got to, what are you saying, beat this damn bastard.'

Peter looked at him. 'It's no good, Steve.'

There was a silence. Finally Bunnish said, 'You're a coward, Norten. A coward and a failure and a weakling. Play the game out.'

'I'm not interested in the game, Bruce. Just tell me. The variation is unsound.'

Bunnish made a disgusted noise. 'Yes, yes,' he snapped. 'It's unsound. There's a countersac, I give up a rook to break up your mating threats, but I win a piece back a few moves later.'

'All the variations are unsound, aren't they?' Peter said.

Bunnish smiled thinly.

'White doesn't have a won game at all,' Peter said. 'We were wrong, all those years. You never blew the win. You never *had* a win. Just a position that looked good superficially, but led nowhere.'

'Wisdom, at last,' Bunnish said. 'I've had computers print out every possible variation. They take forever, but I've had lifetimes. When I flashed back – you have no idea how many times I have flashed back, trying one new idea after another – that is always my target point, that day in Evanston, the game with Vesselere. I've tried every move there is to be tried in that position, every wild idea. It makes no difference. Vesselere always beats me. All the variations are unsound.'

'But,' Delmario protested, looking bewildered, 'Vesselere *said* he was lost. He *said* so!'

Bunnish looked at him with contempt. 'I had made him sweat a lot in a game he should have won easily. He was just getting back. He was a vindictive man, and he knew that by saying that he'd make the loss that much more painful.' He smirked. 'I've taken care of *him* too, you know.'

E.C. Stuart rose up from his chair and straightened his vest. 'If we're done now, Brucie, maybe you would be so kind as to let us out of Bunnishland?'

'*You* can go,' Bunnish said. 'And that drunk, too. But not Peter.' He showed his dimples. 'Why, Peter has almost won, in a sense. So I'm going to be generous. You know what I'm going to do for you, Captain? I'm going to let you use my flashback device.'

'No thank you,' Peter said.

Bunnish stared, befuddled. 'What do you mean, no? Don't you understand what I'm giving you? You can wipe out all your failures, try again, make some different moves. Be a success in another timeline.'

'I know. Of course, that would leave Kathy with a dead body in *this* timeline, wouldn't it? And you with the satisfaction of driving me to something that uncannily resembles suicide. No. I'll take my chances with the future instead of the past. With Kathy.'

Bunnish let his mouth droop open. 'What do you care about her? She hates you anyway. She'll be better off with you dead. She'll get the insurance money and you'll get somebody better, somebody who cares about you.'

'But I do care about him,' Kathy said. She put a hand on Peter's shoulder. He reached up and touched it, and smiled.

'Then you're a fool too,' Bunnish cried. 'He's nothing, he'll *never* be anything. I'll see to that.'

Peter stood up. 'I don't think so, somehow. I don't think you can hurt us anymore. Any of us.' He looked at the others. 'What do you think, guys?'

E.C. cocked his head thoughtfully, and ran a finger along the underside of his mustache. 'You know,' he said, 'I think you're right.'

Delmario just seemed baffled, until all of a sudden the light broke across his face, and he grinned. 'You can't steal ideas I haven't come up with yet, can you?' he said to Bunnish. 'Not in this timeline, anyhow.' He made a loud whooping sound and stepped up to the chessboard. Reaching down, he stopped the clock. 'Checkmate,' he said. 'Checkmate, checkmate, *checkmate!*'

*

Less than two weeks later, Kathy knocked softly on the door of the study. 'Wait a sec!' Peter shouted. He typed out another sentence, then flicked off the typewriter and swiveled in his chair. 'C'mon in.'

She opened the door and smiled at him. 'I made some tuna salad, if you want to take a break for lunch. How's the book coming?'

'Good,' Peter said. 'I should finish the second chapter today, if I keep at it.' She was holding a newspaper, he noticed. 'What's that?'

'I thought you ought to see this,' she replied, handing it over.

She'd folded it open to the obits. Peter took it and read. Millionaire electronics genius Bruce Bunnish had been found dead in his Colorado home, hooked up to a strange device that had seemingly electrocuted him. Peter sighed.

'He's going to try again, isn't he?' Kathy said.

Peter put down the newspaper. 'The poor bastard. He can't see it.'

'See what?'

Peter took her hand and squeezed it. 'All the variations are unsound,' he said. It made him sad. But after lunch, he soon forgot about it, and went back to work.

The Glass Flower

Once, when I was just a girl in the first flush of my true youth, a young boy gave me a glass flower as a token of his love.

He was a rare and precious boy, though I confess that I have long forgotten his name. So too was the flower he gave me. On the steel and plastic worlds where I have spent my lives, the ancient glassblower's art is lost and forgotten, but the unknown artisan who had fashioned my flower remembered it well. My flower has a long and delicate stem, curved and graceful, all of fine thin glass, and from that frail support the bloom explodes, as large as my fist, impossibly exact. Every detail is there, caught, frozen in crystal for eternity; petals large and small crowding each other, bursting from the center of the blossom in a slow transparent riot, surrounded by a crown of six wide drooping leaves, each with its tracery of veins intact, each unique. It was as if an alchemist had been wandering through a garden one day, and in a moment of idle play had transmuted an especially large and beautiful flower into glass.

All that it lacks is life.

I kept that flower with me for near two hundred years, long after I had left the boy who gave it to me and the world where he had done the giving. Through all the varied chapters of my lives, the glass flower was always close at hand. It amused me to keep it in a vase of polished wood and set it near a window. Sometimes the leaves and petals would catch the sun and flash brilliantly for an incandescent instant; at other times they would filter and fracture the light, scattering blurred rainbows on my floor. Often towards dusk, when the world was dimmer, the flower would seem to fade entirely from view, and I might sit staring at an empty vase. Yet, when the morning came, the flower would be back again. It never failed me.

The glass flower was terribly fragile, but no harm ever came to it. I cared for it well; better, perhaps, than I have ever cared for anything, or anyone. It outlasted a dozen lovers, more than a dozen professions, and more worlds and friends than I can name. It was with me in my youth on Ash and Erikan and Shamdizar, and later on Rogue's Hope and Vagabond, and still later when I had grown old on Dam Tullian and Lilith and Gulliver.

And when I finally left human space entirely, put all my lives and all the worlds of men behind me, and grew young again, the glass flower was still at my side.

And, at very long last, in my castle built on stilts, in my house of pain and rebirth where the game of mind is played, amid the swamps and stinks of Croan'dhenni, far from all humanity save those few lost souls who seek us out – it was there too, my glass flower.

On the day Kleronomas arrived.

*

'Joachim Kleronomas,' I said.

'Yes.'

There are cyborgs and then there are cyborgs. So many worlds, so many different cultures, so many sets of values and levels of technologies. Some cyberjacks are half organic, some more, some less; some sport only a single metal hand, the rest of their cyberhalves cleverly concealed beneath the flesh. Some cyborgs wear synthaflesh that is indistinguishable from human skin, though that is no great feat, given the variety of skin to be seen among the thousand worlds. Some hide the metal and flaunt the flesh; with others the reverse is true.

The man who called himself Kleronomas had no flesh to hide or flaunt. A cyborg he called himself, and a cyborg he was in the legends that had grown up around his name, but as he stood before me, he seemed more a robot, insufficiently organic to pass even as android.

He was naked, if a thing of metal and plastic can be naked. His chest was jet; some shining black alloy or smooth plastic, I could not tell. His arms and legs were transparent plasteel. Beneath that false skin, I could see the dark metal of his duralloy bones, the power-bars and flexors that were muscles and tendons, the micromotors and sensing computers, the intricate pattern of lights racing up and down his superconductive neurosystem. His fingers were steel. On his right hand, long silver claws sprang rakishly from his knuckles when he made a fist.

He was looking at me. His eyes were crystalline lenses set in metal sockets, moving back and forth in some green translucent gel. They had no visible pupils; behind each implacable crimson iris burned a dim light that gave his stare an ominous red glow. 'Am I that fascinating?' he asked me. His voice was surprisingly natural; deep and resonant, with no metallic echoes to corrode the humanity of his inflections.

'Kleronomas,' I said. 'Your name is fascinating, certainly. A very long time ago, there was another man of that name, a cyborg, a legend. You know that, of course. He of the Kleronomas Survey. The founder of the

Academy of Human Knowledge on Avalon. Your ancestor? Perhaps metal runs in your family.'

'No,' said the cyborg. 'Myself. I am Joachim Kleronomas.'

I smiled for him. 'And I'm Jesus Christ. Would you care to meet my Apostles?'

'You doubt me, Wisdom?'

'Kleronomas died on Avalon a thousand years ago.'

'No,' he said. 'He stands before you now.'

'Cyborg,' I said, 'this is Croan'dhenni. You would not have come here unless you sought rebirth, unless you sought to win new life in the game of mind. So be warned. In the game of mind, your lies will be stripped away from you. Your flesh and your metal and your illusions, we will take them all, and in the end there will be only you, more naked and alone than you can ever imagine. So do not waste my time. It is the most precious thing I have, time. It is the most precious thing any of us have. Who are you, cyborg?'

'Kleronomas,' he said. Was there a mocking note in his voice? I could not tell. His face was not built for smiling. 'Do you have a name?' he asked me.

'Several,' I said.

'Which do you use?'

'My players call me Wisdom.'

'That is a title, not a name,' he said.

I smiled. 'You are traveled, then. Like the real Kleronomas. Good. My birth name was Cyrain. I suppose, of all my names, I am most used to that one. I wore it for the first fifty years of my life, until I came to Dam Tullian and studied to be a Wisdom and took a new name with the title.'

'Cyrain,' he repeated. 'That alone?'

'Yes.'

'On what world were you born, then?'

'Ash.'

'Cyrain of Ash,' he said. 'How old are you?'

'In standard years?'

'Of course.'

I shrugged. 'Close to two hundred. I've lost count.'

'You look like a child, like a girl close to puberty, no more.'

'I am older than my body,' I said.

'As am I,' he said. 'The curse of the cyborg, Wisdom, is that parts can be replaced.'

'Then you're immortal?' I challenged him.

'In one crude sense, yes.'

'Interesting,' I said. 'Contradictory. You come here to me, to

Croan'dhenni and its Artifact, to the game of mind. Why? This is a place where the dying come, cyborg, in hopes of winning life. We don't get many immortals.'

'I seek a different prize,' the cyborg said.

'Yes?' I prompted.

'Death,' he told me. 'Life. Death. Life.'

'Two different things,' I said. 'Opposites. Enemies.'

'No,' said the cyborg. 'They are the same.'

*

Six hundred standard years ago, a creature known in legend as The White landed among the Croan'dhenni in the first starship they had ever seen. If the descriptions in Croan'dhic folklore can be trusted, then The White was of no race I have ever encountered, nor heard of, though I am widely traveled. This does not surprise me. The manrealm and its thousand worlds (perhaps there are twice that number, perhaps less, but who can keep count?), the scattered empires of Fyndii and Damoosh and g'vhern and N'or Talush, and all the other sentients who are known to us or rumored of, all this together, all those lands and stars and lives colored by passion and blood and history, sprawling proudly across the light-years, across the black gulfs that only the *volcryn* ever truly know, all of this, all of our little universe . . . it is only an island of light surrounded by a vastly greater area of grayness and myth that fades ultimately into the black of ignorance. And *this* only in one small galaxy, whose uttermost reaches we shall never know, should we endure a billion years. Ultimately, the sheer size of things will defeat us, however we may strive or scream; that truth I am sure of.

But I do not defeat easily. That is my pride, my last and only pride; it is not much to face the darkness with, but it is something. When the end comes, I will meet it raging.

The White was like me in that. It was a frog from a pond beyond ours, a place lost in the gray where our little lights have not yet shone on the dark waters. Whatever sort of creature it might have been, whatever burdens of history and evolution it carried in its genes, it was nonetheless my kin. Both of us were angry mayflies, moving restlessly from star to star because we, alone among our fellows, knew how short our day. Both of us found a destiny of sorts in these swamps of Croan'dhenni.

The White came utterly alone to this place, set down its little starship (I have seen the remains: a toy, that ship, a trinket, but with lines that are utterly alien to me, and deliciously chilling), and, exploring, found something.

Something older than itself, and stranger.

The Artifact.

Whatever strange instruments it had, whatever secret alien knowledge it possessed, whatever instinct bid it enter; all lost now, and none of it matters. The White knew, knew something the native sentients had never guessed, knew the purpose of the Artifact, knew how it might be activated. For the first time in – a thousand years? A million? For the first time in a long while, the game of mind was played. And The White changed, emerged from the Artifact as something else, as the first. The first mindlord. The first master of life and death. The first painlord. The first lifelord. The titles are born, worn, discarded, forgotten, and none of them matter.

Whatever I am, The White was the first.

*

Had the cyborg asked to meet my Apostles, I would not have disappointed him. I gathered them when he left me. 'The new player,' I told them, 'calls himself Kleronomas. I want to know who he is, what he is, and what he hopes to gain. Find out for me.'

I could feel their greed and fear. The Apostles are a useful tool, but loyalty is not for them. I have gathered to me twelve Judas Iscariots, each of them hungry for that kiss.

'I'll have a full scan worked up,' suggested Doctor Lyman, pale weak eyes considering me, flatterer's smile trembling.

'Will he consent to an interface?' asked Deish Green-9, my own cyberjack. His right hand, sunburned red-black flesh, was balled into a fist; his left was a silver ball that cracked open to exude a nest of writhing metallic tendrils. Beneath his heavy beetling brow, where he should have had eyes, a seamless strip of mirrorglass was set into his skull. He had chromed his teeth. His smile was very bright.

'We'll find out,' I said.

Sebastian Cayle floated in his tank, a twisted embryo with a massive monstrous head, flippers moving vaguely, huge blind eyes regarding me through turgid greenish fluids as bubbles rose all around his pale naked flesh. *He is a Liar* came the whisper in my head. *I will find the truth for you, Wisdom.*

'Good,' I told him.

Tr'k'nn'r, my Fyndii mindmute, sang to me in a high shrill voice at the edge of human hearing. He loomed above them all like a stickman in a child's crude drawing, a stickman three meters tall, excessively jointed, bending in all the wrong places at all the wrong angles, assembled of old bones turned gray as ash by some ancient fire. But the crystalline eyes beneath his brow ridge were fervid as he sang, and fragrant black fluids ran from the bottom of his lipless vertical mouth. His song was of pain and screaming and nerves set afire, of secrets revealed, of truth dragged steaming and raw from all its hidden crevasses.

'No,' I said to him. 'He is a cyborg. If he feels pain it is only because he wills it. He would shut down his receptors and turn you off, loneling, and your song would turn to silence.'

The neurowhore Shayalla Loethen smiled with resignation. 'Then there's nothing for me to work on either, Wisdom?'

'I'm not sure,' I admitted. 'He has no obvious genitalia, but if there's anything organic left inside him, his pleasure centers might be intact. He claims to have been male. The instincts might still be viable. Find out.'

She nodded. Her body was soft and white as snow, and sometimes as cold, when she wanted cold, and sometimes white hot, when that was her desire. Those lips that curled upwards now with anticipation were crimson and alive. The garments that swirled around her changed shape and color even as I watched, and sparks began to play along her fingertips, arcing across her long, painted nails.

'Drugs?' asked Braje, biomed, gengineer, poisoner. She sat thinking, chewing some tranq of her own devising, her swollen body as damp and soft as the swamps outside. 'Truetell? Agonine? Esperon?'

'I doubt it,' I said.

'Disease,' she offered. 'Manthrax or gangrene. The slow plague, and we've got the cure?' She giggled.

'No,' I said curtly.

And the rest, and on and on. They all had their suggestions, their ways of finding out things I wanted to know, of making themselves useful to me, of earning my gratitude. Such are my Apostles. I listened to them, let myself be carried along by the babble of voices, weighed, considered, handed out orders, and finally I sent them all away, all but one.

Khar Dorian will be the one to kiss me when that day finally comes. I do not have to be a Wisdom to know that truth.

The rest of them want something of me. When they get it, they will be gone. Khar got his desire long ago, and still he comes back and back and back, to my world and my bed. It is not love of me that brings him back, nor the beauty of the young body I wear, nor anything as simple as the riches he earns. He has grander things in mind.

'He rode with you,' I said. 'All the way from Lilith. Who is he?'

'A player,' Dorian said, grinning at me crookedly, taunting me. He is breathtakingly beautiful. Lean and hard and well fit, with the arrogance and rough-hewn masculine sexuality of a thirty-year-old, flush with health and power and hormones. His hair is blond and long and unkempt. His jaw is clean and strong, his nose straight and unbroken, his eyes a hale, vibrant blue. But there is something old living behind those eyes, something old and cynical and sinister.

'Dorian,' I warned him, 'don't try games with me. He is more than just a player. Who is he?'

Khar Dorian got up, stretched lazily, yawned, grinned. 'Who he says he is,' my slaver told me. 'Kleronomas.'

*

Morality is a closely knit garment that binds tightly when it binds at all, but the vastnesses that lie between the stars are prone to unraveling it, to plucking it apart into so many loose threads, each brightly colored, but forming no discernible pattern. The fashionable Vagabonder is a rustic-spectacular on Cathaday, the Ymirian swelters on Vess, the Vessman freezes on Ymir, and the shifting lights the Fellanei wear instead of cloth provoke rape, riot, and murder on half a dozen worlds. So it is with morals. Good is no more constant than the cut of a lapel; the decision to take a sentient life weighs no more heavily than the decision to bare one's breasts, or hide them.

There are worlds on which I am a monster. I stopped caring a long time ago. I came to Croan'dhenni with my own fashion sense, and no concern for the aesthetic judgments of others.

Khar Dorian calls himself a slaver, and points out to me that we do, indeed, deal in human flesh. He can call himself what he likes. I am no slaver; the charge offends me. A slaver sells his clients into bondage and servitude, deprives them of freedom, mobility, and time, all precious commodities. I do no such thing. I am only a thief. Khar and his underlings bring them to me from the swollen cities of Lilith, from the harsh mountains and cold wastes of Dam Tullian, from the rotting tenements along the canals of Vess, from spaceport bars on Fellanora and Cymeranth and Shrike, from wherever he can find them, he takes them and brings them to me, and I steal from them and set them free.

A lot of them refuse to go.

They cluster outside my castle walls in the city they have built, toss gifts to me as I pass, call out my name, beg favors of me. I have left them freedom, mobility, and time, and they squander it all in futility, hoping to win back the one thing I have stolen.

I steal their bodies, but they lose their souls themselves.

And perhaps I am unduly harsh to call myself a thief. These victims Khar brings me are unwilling players in the game of mind, but no less players for all that. Others pay so very dearly and risk so very much for the same privilege. Some we call players and some we call prizes, but when the pain comes and the game of mind begins, we are all the same, all naked and alone without riches or health or status, armed with only the strength that lies within us. Win or lose, live or die, it is up to us and us alone.

I give them a chance. A few have even won. Very few, true, but how many thieves give their victims any chance at all?

The Steel Angels, whose worlds lie far from Croan'dhenni on the other side of human space, teach their children that strength is the only virtue and weakness the only sin, and preach that the truth of their faith is written large on the universe itself. It is a difficult point to argue. By their creed, I have every moral right to the bodies I take, because I am stronger and therefore better and more holy than those born to that flesh.

The little girl born in my present body was not a Steel Angel, unfortunately.

*

'And baby makes three,' I said, 'even if baby is made of metal and plastic and names himself a legend.'

'Eh?' Rannar looked at me blankly. He is not as widely traveled as me, and the reference, something I have dredged up from my forgotten youth on some world he's never walked, escapes him entirely. His long, sour face wore a look of patient bafflement.

'We have three players now,' I told him carefully. 'We can play the game of mind.'

That much Rannar understood. 'Ah yes, of course. I'll see to it at once, Wisdom.'

Craimur Delhune was the first. An ancient thing, almost as old as me, though he had done all of his living in the same small body. No wonder it was worn out. He was hairless and shriveled, a wheezing half-blind travesty, his flesh full of alloplas and metal implants that labored day and night just to keep him alive. It was not something they could do much longer, but Craimur Delhune had not had enough living yet, and so he had come to Croan'dhenni to pay for the flesh and begin all over again. He had been waiting nearly half a standard year.

Rieseen Jay was a stranger case. She was under fifty and in decent health, though her flesh bore its own scars. Rieseen was jaded. She had sampled every pleasure Lilith offered, and Lilith offers a good many pleasures. She had tasted every food, flowed with every drug, sexed with males, females, aliens, and animals, risked her life skiing the glaciers, baiting pit-dragons, fighting in the soar-wars for the delectation of holofans everywhere. She thought a new body would be just the thing to add spice to life. Maybe a male body, she thought, or an alien's off-color flesh. We get a few like her.

And Joachim Kleronomas made three.

In the game of mind, there are seats for seven. Three players, three prizes, and me.

Rannar offered me a thick portfolio, full of photographs and reports on the prizes newly arrived on Khar Dorian's ships, on the *Bright Phoenix* and the *Second Chance* and the *New Deal* and the *Fleshpot* (Khar has always had a certain black sense of humor). The majordomo hovered at my elbow, solicitous and helpful, as I turned the pages and made my selections. 'She's delicious,' he said once, at a picture of a slim Vessgirl with frightened yellow eyes that hinted at a hybrid gene-mix. 'Very strong and healthy, that one,' he said later, as I considered a hugely muscled youth with green eyes and waist-long braided black hair. I ignored him. I always ignore him.

'Him,' I said, taking out the file of a boy as slender as a stiletto, his ruddy skin covered with tattoos. Khar had purchased him from the authorities on Shrike, where he'd been convicted of killing another sixteen-year-old. On most worlds, Khar Dorian, the infamous free trader, smuggler, raider, and slaver, had a name synonymous with evil; parents threatened their children with him. On Shrike he was a solid citizen who did the community great service by buying up the garbage in the prisons.

'Her,' I said, setting aside a second photograph, of a pudgy young woman of about thirty standard whose wide green eyes betrayed a certain vacancy. From Cymeranth, her file said. Khar had dropped one of his raiders into a coldsleep facility for the mentally damaged and helped himself to some young, healthy, attractive bodies. This one was soft and fat, but that would change once an active mind wore the flesh again. The original owner had sucked up too much dreamdust.

'And it,' I said. The third file was that of a g'vhern hatchling, a grim looking individual with fierce magenta eye-crests and huge, leathery batwings that glistened with iridescent oils. It was for Rieseen Jay, who thought she might like to try a nonhuman body. If she could win it.

'Very good, Wisdom,' said Rannar approvingly. He was always approving. When he had come to Croan'dhenni, his body was grotesque; he'd been caught in bed with the daughter of his employer, a V'lador knight of the blood, and the punishment was extensive ritual mutilation. He did not have the price of a game. But I'd had two players waiting for almost a year, one of whom was dying of manthrax, so when Rannar offered me ten years of faithful service to make up the difference, I accepted.

Sometimes I had my regrets. I could feel his eyes on my body, could sense his mind stripping away the soft armor of my clothes to fasten, leechlike, on my small, budding breasts. The girl he'd been found with was not much younger than the flesh I now wore.

*

My castle is built of obsidian.

North of here, far north, in the smoky polar wastelands where eternal
fires burn against a purple sky, the black volcanic glass lies upon the
ground like common stone. It took thousands of Croan'dhic miners nine
standard years to find enough for my purposes and drag it all back to the
swamps, over all those barren kilometers. It took hundreds of artisans
another six years to cut and polish it and fit it all together into the dark
shimmering mosaic that is my home. I judged the effort worthwhile.

My castle stands on four great jagged pillars high up above the smells
and damp of the Croan'dhic swampland, ablaze with colored lights whose
ghosts glimmer within the black glass. My castle gleams; a thing of beauty,
austere and forbidding, supreme and apart from the shantytown that has
grown up around it, where the losers and discards and dispossessed
huddle hopelessly in floating reed-huts, festering treehouses, and hovels
on half-rotted wooden stilts. The obsidian appeals to my aesthetic sense,
and I find its symbolism appropriate to this house of pain and rebirth. Life
is born in the heat of sexual passion as obsidian is born in volcanic fire. The
clean truth of light can sometimes flow through its blackness, beauty seen
dimly through darkness, and like life, it is terribly fragile, with edges that
can be dangerously sharp.

Inside my castle are rooms on rooms, some paneled over with fragrant
native woods and covered with furs and thick carpets, some left bare and
black, ceremonial chambers where dark reflections move through glass
walls and footsteps click brittle against glass floors. In the center, at the
very apex, rises an onion-shaped obsidian tower, braced by steel. Within
the dome, a single chamber.

I ordered the castle built, replacing an older and much shabbier
structure, and to that single tower chamber, I caused the Artifact to be
moved.

It is there that the game of mind is played.

My own suite is at the base of the tower. The reasons for that were
symbolic as well. None achieve rebirth without first passing through me.

I was breaking fast in bed, on butterfruit and raw fish and strong black
coffee, with Khar Dorian stretched out languid and insolent beside me,
when my scholar Apostle, Alta-k-Nahr, came to me with her report.

She stood at the foot of my bed, her back twisted like a great question
mark by her disease, her long features permanently set in a grimace of
distaste, her skin shot through with swollen veins like great blue worms,
and she told me of her researches on the historical Kleronomas in a voice
unnecessarily soft.

'His full name was Joachim Charle Kleronomas,' she said, 'and he was native to New Alexandria, a first generation colony less than seventy light years from Old Earth. Records of his birthdate, childhood, and adolescence are fragmentary and contradictory. The most popular legends indicate his mother was a high-ranking officer on a warship of the 13th Human Fleet, under Stephen Cobalt Northstar, and that Kleronomas met her only twice. He was gestated in a hireling host-mother and reared by his father, a minor scholar at a library on New Alexandria. My opinion is that this tale of his origin explains, a bit too neatly, how Kleronomas came to combine both the scholastic and martial traditions; therefore I question its reliability.

'More certain is the fact that he joined the military at a very early age, in those last days of the Thousand Years War. He served initially as systems tech on a screamer-class raider with the 17th Human Fleet, distinguished himself in deepspace actions off El Dorado and Arturius and in the raids on Hrag Druun, after which he was promoted to cadet and given command training. By the time the 17th was shifted from its original base on Fenris to a minor sector capital called Avalon, Kleronomas had earned further distinction, and was the third-in-command of the dropship *Hannibal*. But in the raids on Hruun-Fourteen, the *Hannibal* took heavy damage from Hrangan defenders, and was finally abandoned. The screamer in which Kleronomas escaped was disabled by enemy fire and crashed planetside, killing everyone aboard. He was the sole survivor. Another screamer picked up what was left of him, but he was so near dead and horribly maimed that they shoved him into cryostorage at once. He was taken back to Avalon, but resources were few and demands many, and they had no time to bother reviving him. They kept him under for years.

'Meanwhile, the Collapse was in progress. It had been in progress all of his lifetime, actually, but communications across the width of the old Federal Empire were so slow that no one knew it. But a single decade saw the revolt on Thor, the total disintegration of the 15th Human Fleet, and Old Earth's attempt to remove Stephen Cobalt Northstar from command of the 13th, which led inevitably to the secession of Newholme and most of the other first generation colonies, to Northstar's obliteration of Wellington, to civil war, breakaway colonies, lost worlds, the fourth great expansion, the hellfleet legend, and ultimately the sealing of Old Earth and the effective cessation of commercial starflight for a generation. Longer than that, far far longer, on some more remote worlds, many of which devolved to near-savagery or developed odd variant cultures.

'Out on the front, Avalon had its own first-hand experience of the Collapse when Rajeen Tober, commanding the 17th Fleet, refused to submit to the civil authorities and took his ships deep into the Tempter's Veil to found his own personal empire safe from both Hrangan and human retaliation. The departure of the 17th left Avalon essentially defenseless. The only warships still in the sector were the ancient hulks of the 5th Human Fleet, which had last seen combat nearly seven centuries earlier, when Avalon was a very distant strikebase against the Hrangans. About a dozen capital-class ships and thirty-odd smaller craft of the 5th remained in orbit around Avalon, most needing extensive repairs, all functionally obsolete. But they were the only defenders left to a frightened world, so Avalon determined to refit and restore them. To crew these museum pieces, Avalon turned to its cryonic wards, and began to thaw every combat veteran on hand, including Joachim Kleronomas. The damage he had sustained was extensive, but Avalon needed every last body. Kleronomas returned more machine than man. A cyborg.'

I leaned forward to interrupt Alta's recitation. 'Are there any pictures of him as he was then?' I asked her.

'Yes. Both before and after. Kleronomas was a big man, with blue-black skin, a heavy outthrust jaw, gray eyes, long pure white hair. After the operation, the jaw and the bottom half of his face were gone entirely, replaced with seamless metal. No mouth, no nose. He took nourishment intravenously. One eye was lost, replaced by a crystal sensor with IR/UV range. His right arm and the entire right half of his chest was cybered, steel plate, duralloy mesh, plastic. A third of his inner organs were synthetic. And they gave him a jack, of course, and built in a small computer. From the beginning, Kleronomas disdained cosmetics; he looked exactly like what he was.'

I smiled. 'But what he was, that was still a good deal more fleshy than our new guest?'

'True,' said my scholar. 'The rest of the history is more well known. There weren't many officers among the revived. Kleronomas was given his own command, a small courier-class ship. He served for a decade, pursuing the scholarly studies in history and anthropology that were his private passion, and rising higher and higher in the ranks while Avalon waited for ships that never came and built more and more ships of its own. There were no trades, no raids; the interregnum had come.

'Finally, a bolder civil leadership decided to risk a few of its ships and find out how the rest of human civilization had fared. Six of the ancient 5th Fleet dreadnaughts were refitted as science survey craft and sent out. Kleronomas was given command of one of them. Of those survey ships, two were lost on their missions, and three others returned within two years carrying minimal information on a handful of the closest systems, prompting the Avalonians to reinitiate starflight on a very limited local basis. Kleronomas was thought lost.

'He was not lost. When the small, limited goals of the original survey were completed, he decided to continue rather than return to Avalon. He became obsessed with the next star, and the next after that, and the next after that. He took his ship on and on. There were mutinies, desertions, dangers to be faced and fought, and Kleronomas dealt with them all. As a cyborg, he was immensely long-lived. The legends say he became ever more metallic as the voyage went on, and on Eris discovered the matrix crystal and expanded his intellectual abilities by orders of magnitude through the addition of the first crystal matrix computer. That particular story fits his character; he was obsessed not only with the acquisition of knowledge, but with its retention. Altered so, he would never forget.

'When he finally returned to Avalon, more than a hundred standard years had passed. Of the men and women who had left Avalon with him, Kleronomas alone survived; his ship was manned by the descendants of its original crew, plus those recruits he had gathered on the worlds he visited. But he had surveyed four hundred and forty-nine planets, and more asteroids, comets, and satellites than anyone would have dreamed possible. The information he brought back became the foundation upon which the Academy of Human Knowledge was built, and the crystal samples, incorporated into existing systems, became the medium in which that knowledge was stored, eventually evolving into the academy's vast Artificial Intelligences and the fabled crystal towers of Avalon. The resumption of large-scale starflight soon thereafter was the real end of the interregnum. Kleronomas himself served as the first academy administrator until his death, which supposedly came on Avalon in ai-42, that is, forty-two standard years after the day of his return.'

I laughed. 'Excellent,' I told Alta-k-Nahr. 'He's a fraud, then. Dead at least seven hundred years.' I looked at Khar Dorian, whose long fine hair was spread across the pillow as he nibbled on a heel of mead bread. 'You are slipping, Khar. He fooled you.'

Khar swallowed, grinned. 'Whatever you say, Wisdom,' he said, in a tone that told me he was anything but contrite. 'Shall I kill him for you?'

'No,' I said. 'He is a player. In the game of mind, there are no imposters. Let him play. Let him play.'

*

Days later, when the game had been scheduled, I called the cyborg to me. I saw him in my office, a large room with deep scarlet carpeting, where my glass flower sits by the great window that overlooks my battlements and the swamp town below.

His face was without expression. Of course, of course. 'You summoned me, Cyrain of Ash.'

'The game is set,' I told him. 'Four days from today.'

'I am pleased,' he said.

'Would you like to see the prizes?' I offered him the files; the boy, the girl, the hatchling.

He glanced at them briefly, without interest.

'I am told,' I said to him, 'that you have spent a lot of time wandering these past days. Inside my castle, and outside in the town and the swamps.'

'True,' he said. 'I do not sleep. Knowledge is my diversion, my addiction. I was curious to learn what sort of place this was.'

Smiling, I said, 'And what sort of place is it, cyborg?'

He could not smile, nor frown. His tone was even, polite. 'A vile place,' he said. 'A place of despair and degradation.'

'A place of eternal, undying hope,' I said.

'A place of sickness, of the body and the soul.'

'A place where the sick grow well,' I countered.

'And where the well grow sick,' the cyborg said. 'A place of death.'

'A place of life,' I said. 'Isn't that why you came? For life?'

'And death,' he said. 'I have told you, they are the same.'

I leaned forward. 'And I have told you, they are very different. You make harsh judgments, cyborg. Rigidity is to be expected in a machine, but this fine, precious moral sensitivity is not.'

'Only my body is machine,' he said.

I picked up his file. 'That is not my understanding,' I said. 'Where is your morality in regard to lying? Especially so transparent a lie?' I opened the file flat on my desk. 'I've had a few interesting reports from my Apostles. You've been extraordinarily cooperative.'

'If you wish to play the game of mind, you cannot offend the painlord,' he said.

I smiled. 'I'm not as easily offended as you might think.' I searched through the reports. 'Doctor Lyman did a full scan on you. He finds you an ingenious construct. And made entirely of plastic and metal. There is nothing organic left inside you, cyborg. Or should I call you robot? Can computers play the game of mind, I wonder? We will certainly find out. You have three of them, I see. A small one in what should be your brain case that attends to motor functions, sensory input and internal monitoring, a much larger library unit occupying most of your lower torso, and a crystal matrix in your chest.' I looked up. 'Your heart, cyborg?'

'My mind,' he said. 'Ask your Doctor Lyman, and he will tell of other cases like mine. What is a human mind? Memories. Memories are data. Character, personality, individual volition. Those are programming. It is possible to imprint the whole of a human mind upon a crystal matrix computer.'

'And trap the soul in the crystal?' I said. 'Do you believe in souls?'

'Do you?' he asked.

'I must. I am mistress of the game of mind. It would seem to be required of me.' I turned to the other reports my Apostles had assembled on this construct who called himself Kleronomas. 'Deish Green-9 interfaced with you. He says you have a system of incredible sophistication, that the speed of your circuitry greatly exceeds human thought, that your library contains far more accessible information than any single organic brain could retain even were it able to make full use of its capacity, and that the mind and memories locked within that crystal matrix are that of one Joachim Kleronomas. He swears to that.'

The cyborg said nothing. Perhaps he might have smiled then, had he the capacity.

'On the other hand,' I said, 'my scholar Alta-k-Nahr assures me that Kleronomas is dead seven hundred years. Who am I to believe?'

'Whomever you choose,' he said indifferently.

'I might hold you here and send to Avalon for confirmation,' I said. I grinned. 'A thirty year voyage in, thirty more years back out. Say a year to research the question. Can you wait sixty-one years to play, cyborg?'

'As long as necessary,' he said.

'Shayalla says you are thoroughly asexual.'

'That capacity was lost from the day they remade me,' he said. 'My interest in the subject lingered for some centuries afterwards, but finally that too faded. If I choose, I have access to a full range of erotic memories of the days when I wore organic flesh. They remain as fresh as the day there were entered into my computer. Once locked in crystal, memories cannot fade, as with a human brain. They are there, waiting to be tapped. But for centuries now, I have had no inclination to recall them.'

I was intrigued. 'You cannot forget,' I said.

'I can erase,' he said. 'I can choose not to remember.'

'If you are among the winners in our little game of mind, you will regain your sexuality.'

'I am aware of that. It will be an interesting experience. Perhaps then I will choose to tap those ancient memories.'

'Yes,' I said, delighted. 'You'll begin to use them, and at precisely the same instant you will begin to forget them. There is a loss there, cyborg, as sharp as your gain.'

'Gain or loss. Living and dying. I have told you, Cyrain, they cannot be separated.'

'I don't accept that,' I said. It was at issue with all I believe, all I am; his repetition of the lie annoyed me. 'Braje says you cannot be affected by drugs or disease. Obvious. You could be dismantled, though. Several of my

Apostles have offered to dispose of you, at my command. My aliens are especially bloodthirsty, it seems.'

'I have no blood,' he said. Sardonic? Or was it all the power of suggestion?

'Your lubricants might suffice,' I said drily. 'Tr'k'nn'r would test your capacity for pain. AanTerg Moonscorer, my g'vhern aerialist, has offered to drop you from a great height.'

'That would be an unconscionable crime by nest standards.'

'Yes and no,' I said. 'A nestborn g'vhern would be aghast at the suggestion that flight be thus perverted. My Apostle, on the other hand, would be more aghast at the suggestion of birth control. Flapping those oily leather wings you'll find the mind of a half-sane cripple from New Rome. This is Croan'dhenni. We are not as we seem.'

'So it appears.'

'Jonas has offered to destroy you too, in a less dramatic but equally effective fashion. He's my largest Apostle. Deformed by runaway glands. The patron saint of advanced automatic weaponry, and my chief of security.'

'Obviously you have declined these offers,' the cyborg said.

I leaned back. 'Obviously,' I said, 'though I always reserve the right to change my mind.'

'I am a player,' he said. 'I have paid Khar Dorian, have bribed the Croan'dhic port-guards, have paid your majordomo and yourself. Inwards, on Lilith and Cymeranth and Shrike and other worlds where they speak of this black palace and its half-mythical mistress, they say that your players are treated fairly.'

'Wrong,' I said. 'I am never fair, cyborg. Sometimes I am just. When the whim takes me.'

'Do you threaten all your players as you have threatened me?' he asked.

'No,' I admitted. 'I'm making a special exception in your case.'

'Why?' he asked.

'Because you're dangerous,' I said, smiling. We had come to the heart of it at last. I shuffled through all my Apostolic bulls, and extracted the last of them, the most important. 'At least one of my Apostles you have never met, but he knows you, cyborg, knows you better than you would dream.'

The cyborg said nothing.

'My pet telepath,' I said. 'Sebastian Cayle. He's blind and twisted and I keep him in a big jar, but he has his uses. He can probe through walls. He has stroked the crystals of your mind, friend, and tripped the binary synapses of your id. His report is a bit cryptic, but admirably terse.' I slid it across the desk for the cyborg to read.

A haunted labyrinth of thought. The steel ghost. The truth within the lie, life in death and death in life. He will take everything from you if he can. Kill him now.

'You are ignoring his advice,' the cyborg said.

'I am,' I told him.

'Why?'

'Because you're a mystery, one I plan to solve when we play the game of mind. Because you're a challenge, and it has been a long time since I was challenged. Because you dare to judge me and dream of destroying me, and it has been ages since anyone found the courage to do either of those things.'

*

Obsidian makes a dark, distorted mirror, but one that suits me. We take our reflections for granted all our lives, until the hour comes when our eyes search for the familiar features and find instead the image of a stranger. You cannot know the meaning of horror or of fascination until you take that first long gaze from a stranger's eyes, and raise an unfamiliar hand to touch the other's cheek, and feel those fingers, light and cool and afraid, brush against your skin.

I was already a stranger when I came to Croan'dhenni more than a century ago. I knew my face, as well I should, having worn it nearly ninety years. It was the face of a woman who was both hard and strong, with deep lines around her gray eyes from squinting into alien suns, a wide mouth not without its generosity, a nose once broken that had not healed straight, short brown hair in perpetual disarray. A comfortable face, and one that I had a certain affection for. But I lost it somewhere, perhaps during my years on Gulliver, lost it when I was too busy to notice. By the time I reached Lilith, the first stranger had begun to haunt my mirrors. She was an old woman, old and wrinkled. Her eyes were gray and rheumy and starting to dim, her hair white and thin, with patches of pinkish scalp showing through; the edge of her mouth trembled, there were broken capillaries in her nose, and beneath her chin lay several folds of soft gray flesh like the wattles of a hen. Her skin was soft and loose, where mine had always been taut and flush with health, and there was another thing, a thing you could not see in the mirror – a smell of sickness that enveloped her like the cheap perfume of an aged courtesan, a pheromone for death.

I did not know her, this old sick thing, nor did I cherish her company. They say that age and sickness come slowly on worlds like Avalon and Newholme and Prometheus; legends claim death no longer comes at all on Old Earth behind its shining walls. But Avalon and Newholme and

Prometheus were far away, and Old Earth is sealed and lost to us, and I was alone on Lilith with a stranger in my mirror. And so I took myself beyond the manrealm, past the furthest reach of human arms, to the wet dimness of Croan'dhenni, where whispers said a new life could be found. I wanted to look into a mirror once more, and find the old friend that I had lost.

Instead I found more strangers.

The first was the painlord itself; mindlord, lifelord, master of life and death. Before my coming, it had ruled here forty-odd standard years. It was Croand'hic, a native, a great bulbous thing with swollen eyes and mottled blue-green skin, a grotesque parody of a toad with slender, double-jointed arms and three long vertical maws like wet black wounds in its fragrant flesh. When I looked upon it, I could taste its weakness; it was vastly fat, a sea of spreading blubber with an odor like rotten eggs, where the Croand'hic guards and servants were well-muscled and hard. But to topple the mindlord, you must become the mindlord. When we played the game of mind I took its life, and woke in that vile body.

It is no easy thing for a human mind to wear an alien skin; for a day and a night I was lost inside that hideous flesh, sorting through sights and sounds and smells that made no more sense than the images in a nightmare, screaming, clawing for control and sanity. I survived. A triumph of spirit over flesh. When I was ready, another game of mind was called, and this time I emerged with the body of my choice.

She was a human. Thirty-nine years of age by her reckoning, healthy, plain of face but strong of body, a professional gambler who had come to Croan'dhenni for the ultimate game. She had long red-brown hair and eyes whose blue-green color reminded me of the seas of Gulliver. She had some strength, but not enough. In those distant days, before the coming of Khar Dorian and his slavers' fleet, few humans found their way to Croan'dhenni. My choice was limited. I took her.

That night I looked into the mirror again. It was still a stranger's face, hair too long, eyes of the wrong hue, a nose as straight as the blade of a knife, a careful guarded mouth that had done too little smiling.

Years afterward, when that body began to cough blood from some infernal pestilence out of the Croan'dhic swamps, I built a room of obsidian mirrors to meet each new stranger. Years pass more swiftly than I care to think while that room remains sealed and inviolate, but always, finally, the day comes when I know I will be visiting it once more, and then my servants climb the stairs and polish the black mirrors to a fine dark sheen, and when the game of mind is done I ascend alone and strip off my clothing and stand and turn in solitude, slow dancing with the images of others.

High, sharp cheekbones and dark eyes sunk in deep hollows beneath her brow. A face shaped like a heart, surrounded by a nimbus of wild black hair, large pale breasts tipped with brown.

Taut lean muscles moving beneath oiled red-brown skin, long finger-nails sharp as claws, a narrow pointed chin, brown hair like wire bristles cut in a thin high stripe across her scalp and halfway down her back, the hot scent of rut heavy between her thighs. My thighs? On a thousand worlds, humanity changes in a thousand different ways.

Massive bony head looking down at the world from near three meters height, beard and hair blending into one leonine mane as bright as beaten gold, strength written large in every bone and sinew, the broad flat chest with its useless red nipples, the strangeness of the long, soft penis between my legs. Too much strangeness for me; the penis stayed soft all the months I wore that body, and that year my mirrored room was opened twice.

A face very like the one that I remember. But how well do I remember? A century was gone to dust, and I kept no likenesses of the faces I had worn. From my first youth long ago, only the glass flower remained. But she had short brown hair, a smile, gray-green eyes. Her neck was too long, her breasts too small, perhaps. But she was close, close, until she grew old, and the day came when I glimpsed another stranger walking beside me inside the castle walls.

And now the haunted child. In the mirrors she looks like a daughter of dreams, the daughter I might have birthed had I been far lovelier than I ever was. Khar brought her to me, a gift he said, a most beautiful gift, to repay me in kind after I had found him gray and impotent, hoarse of voice and scarred of face, and made him young and handsome.

She is perhaps eleven years old, perhaps twelve. Her body is gaunt and awkward, but the beauty is there, locked inside, just beginning to blossom. Her breasts are budding now, and her blood first came less than half a year ago. Her hair is silver-gold, long and straight, a glittering cascade that falls nearly to her heels. Her eyes are large in her small face, and they are the deepest, purest violet. Her face is something sculpted. She was bred to be thus, no doubt of that; genetic tailoring has made the Shrikan trade-lords and the wealthy of Lilith and Fellanora a breathtakingly beautiful folk.

When Khar brought her to me, she was shy of seven, her mind already gone, a whimpering animal thing screaming in a dark locked room within her skull. Khar says she was that way when he bought her, the dispossessed daughter of a Fellanei robber baron toppled and executed for political crimes, his family and friends and retainers slain with him or turned into mindless sexual playthings for his victorious enemies. That is what Khar says. Most of the time I even believe him.

She is younger and prettier than I can ever remember being, even in my lost first youth on Ash, where a nameless boy gave me a glass flower. I hope to wear this sweet flesh for as many years as I wore the body I was born to. If I dwell here long enough, perhaps the day will come when I can look into a dark mirror and see my own face again.

*

One by one they ascended unto me; through Wisdom to rebirth, or so they hoped.

High above the swamps, locked within my tower, I prepared for them in the changing chamber, hard by my unimpressive throne. The Artifact is not prepossessing; a rudely-shaped bowl of some soft alien alloy, charcoal gray in color and faintly warm to the touch, with six niches spaced evenly around the rim. They are seats; cramped, hard, uncomfortable seats, designed for obviously nonhuman physiognomies, but seats nonetheless. From the floor of the bowl rises a slender column that blossoms into another seat, the awkward cup that enthrones . . . choose the title you like best. Painlord, mindlord, lifelord, giver and taker, operator, trigger, master. All of them are me. And others before me, the chain rattling back to The White and perhaps earlier, to the makers, the unknowns who fashioned this machine in the dimness of distant eons.

If the chamber has its drama, that is my doing. The walls and ceiling are curved, and fashioned laboriously of a thousand individual pieces of polished obsidian. Some shards are cut very thin, so the gray light of the Croan'dhic sun can force its way through. Some shards are so thick as to be almost opaque. The room is one color, but a thousand shades, and for those who have the wit to see it, it forms a great mosaic of life and death, dreams and nightmares, pain and ecstasy, excess and emptiness, everything and nothing, blending one into the other, around and around unending, a circle, a cycle, the worm that eats its own tail forever, each piece individual and fragile and razor-edged and each part of a greater picture that is vast and black and brittle.

I stripped and handed my clothing to Rannar, who folded each garment neatly. The cup is topless and egg-shaped. I climbed inside and folded my legs beneath me in a lotus, the best possible compromise between the lines of the Artifact and the human physique. The interior walls of the machine began to bleed; glistening red-black fluid beading on the gray metal of the egg, each globule swelling fatter and heavier until it burst. Streams trickled down the smooth, curved walls, and the moisture began to collect at the bottom. My bare skin burned where the fluid touched me. The flow came faster and heavier, the fire creeping up my body, until I was half immersed.

'Send them in,' I told Rannar. How many times have I said those words? I have lost count.

The prizes were led in first. Khar Dorian came with the tattooed boy. 'There,' Khar said offhandedly, gesturing to a seat while smiling lasciviously for me, and the hard youth, this killer, this wild bloody tough, shrank away from his escort and took the place assigned to him. Braje, my biomed, brought the woman. They too are of a kind; pallid, overweight, soft. Braje giggled as she fastened the manacles about her complaisant charge. The hatchling fought, its lean muscles writhing, its great wings beating together in a dramatic but ultimately ineffectual thunderclap as huge, glowering Jonas and his men forced it down into its niche. As they manacled it into place, Khar Dorian grinned and the g'vhern made a high, thin whistling sound that hurt the ears.

Craimur Delhune had to be carried in by his aides and hirelings. 'There,' I told them, pointing, and they propped him awkwardly into one of the niches. His shrunken, wizened face stared at me, half-blind eyes darting around the chamber like small, feral beasts, his mouth sucking greedily, as if his rebirth was done and he sought a mother's breast. He was blind to the mosaic; for him, it was only a dark room with black glass walls.

Rieseen Jay swaggered in, bored by my chamber before she even entered it. She saw the mosaic but gave it only a cursory glance, as something beneath her notice, too tiresome to study. Instead she made a slow circuit of the niches, inspecting each of the prizes like a butcher examining the meat. She lingered longest in front of the hatchling, seeming to delight in its struggles, its obvious fear, the way it hissed and whistled at her and glared from those fierce, bright eyes. She reached out to touch a wing, and leapt back, laughing, when the hatchling bit at her. Finally she took herself to a seat, where she sprawled languidly, waiting for the game to begin.

Finally Kleronomas.

He saw the mosaic at once, stopped, stared up at it, his crystalline eyes scanning slowly around the room, halting here and there again to study some fine detail. He paused so long that Rieseen Jay grew impatient, and snapped at him to take a seat. The cyborg studied her, metal face unreadable. 'Quiet,' I said.

He finished his study of the dome, taking his own time, and only then seated himself in the final empty niche. The way he took his place was as if all the seats had been vacant and this was his choice, selected by him alone.

'Clear the room,' I commanded. Rannar bowed and gestured them out, Jonas and Braje and the others. Khar Dorian went last, and made a gesture at me as he took his leave. Meaning what? Good luck? Perhaps. I heard Rannar seal the door.

'Well?' demanded Rieseen Jay.

I gave her a look that silenced her. 'You are all seated in the Siege Perilous,' I said. I always began with those words. No one ever understood. This time . . . Kleronomas, perhaps. I watched the mask that was his face. Within the crystal of his eyes, I saw a slight shifting motion, and tried to find a meaning in it. 'There are no rules in the game of mind. But I have rules, for when it is over, when you are back in my domain.

'Those of you who are here unwillingly, if you are strong enough to hold the flesh you wear, it is yours forever. I give it to you freely. No prize plays more than once. Hold fast to your birthflesh and when it is done, Khar Dorian will take you back to the world he found you on and set you loose with a thousand standards and your freedom.

'Those players who find rebirth this day, who rise in strange flesh when this game is ended, remember that what you have won or lost is your own doing, and spare me your regrets and recriminations. If you are dissatisfied with the outcome of this gaming, you may of course play again. If you have the price.

'One last warning. For all of you. This is going to hurt. This is going to hurt more than anything you ever imagined.'

So saying, I began the game of mind.

Once more.

*

What can you say about pain?

Words can trace only the shadow of the thing itself. The reality of hard, sharp physical pain is like nothing else, and it is beyond language. The world is too much with us, day and night, but when we hurt, when we really hurt, the world melts and fades and becomes a ghost, a dim memory, a silly unimportant thing. Whatever ideals, dreams, loves, fears, and thoughts we might have had become ultimately unimportant. We are alone with our pain, it is the only force in the cosmos, the only thing of substance, the only thing that matters, and if the pain is bad enough and lasts long enough, if it is the sort of agony that goes on and on, then all the things that are our humanity melt before it and the proud sophisticated computer that is the human brain becomes capable of but a single thought:

Make it stop, make it STOP!

And if the pain does eventually stop, afterwards, with the passage of time, even the mind that has experienced it becomes unable to compre-hend it, unable to remember how bad it truly was, unable to describe it so as to even approach the terrible truth of what it felt like when it was happening.

In the game of mind, the agony of the painfield is like no other pain, like nothing I have ever experienced.

The painfield does no harm to the body, leaves no marks, no scars, no injuries, no signs to mark its passing. It touches the mind directly with an agony beyond my power to express. How long does it last? A question for relativists. It lasts but the smallest part of a microsecond, and it lasts forever.

The Wisdoms of Dam Tullian are masters of a hundred different disciplines of mind and body, and they teach their acolytes a technique for isolating pain, dissociating from it, pushing it away and thus transcending it. I had been a Wisdom for half my life when I first played the game of mind. I used all I had been taught, all the tricks and truths I had mastered and learned to rely on. They were utterly useless. This was a pain that did not touch the body, a pain that did not race along the nerve paths, a pain that filled the mind so completely and so shatteringly that not even the smallest part of you was free to think or plan or meditate. The pain was you, and you were the pain. There was nothing to dissociate from, no cool sanctum of thought where you might retreat.

The painfield was infinite and eternal, and from that ceaseless and unthinkable agony there was only one sure surcease. It was the old one, the true one, the same balm that has been succor to billions of men and women, and even the smallest of the beasts of the field, since the beginning of time. Pain's dark lord. My enemy, my lover. Again, yet again, wanting only an end to suffering, I rushed to his black embrace.

Death took me, and the pain ended.

On a vast, echoey plain in a place beyond life, I waited for the others.

*

Dim shadows taking form from the mists. Four, five, yes. Have we lost some of them? It would not surprise me. In three games out of four, a player finds his truth in death and seeks no further. This time? No. I see the sixth shape striding out of the writhing fog, we are all here, I look around myself once more, count three, four, five, six, seven, and me, eight.

Eight?

That's wrong, that's very wrong. I am dizzy, disoriented. Nearby someone is screaming. A little girl, sweet-faced, innocent, dressed in pastels and pretty gems. She does not know how she got here, she does not understand, her eyes are lost and childish and far too trusting, and the pain has woken her from a dreamdust languor to a strange land full of fear.

I raise a small, strong hand, gaze at the thick brown fingers, the patch of callus by my thumb, the blunt wide nails trimmed to the quick. I make a fist, a familiar gesture, and in my hand a mirror takes shape from the iron of my will and the quicksilver of my desire. Within its glittering depths I see a face. It is the face of a woman who is both hard and strong, with deep lines around her gray eyes from squinting into alien suns, a wide mouth not without its generosity, a nose once broken that has not healed straight, short brown hair in perpetual disarray. A comfortable face. It gives me comfort now.

The mirror dissolves into smoke. The land, the sky, everything is shifting and uncertain. The sweet little girl is still screaming for her daddy. Some of the others are staring at me, lost. There is a young man, plain of face, his black hair swept back straight and feathered with color in a style that has not been the fashion on Gulliver for a century. His body looks soft, but in his eyes I see a hard edge that reminds me of Khar Dorian. Rieseen Jay seems stunned, wary, frightened, but still she is recognizably Rieseen Jay; whatever else might be said of her, she has a strong sense of who she is. Perhaps that will even be enough. The g'vhern looms near her, far larger here than it seemed before, its body glistening with oil as it spreads demonic wings and begins to whip the fog into long gray ribbons. In the game of mind, it wears no manacles; Rieseen Jay looks long, and cowers away from it. So too does another player, a wisty gray shape covered by a blaze of tattoos, his face a pale blur with neither purpose nor definition. The little girl screams on and on. I turn away from them, leave them to their own devices, and face the final player.

A big man, his skin the color of polished ebony with a dark blue undertone where his long muscles flex as he stretches. He is naked. His jaw is square and heavy, jutting sharply forward. Long hair surrounds his face and falls past his shoulders, hair as white and crisp as fresh bedsheets, as white as the untouched snow of a world that men have never walked. As I watch him, his thick, dark penis stirs against his leg, swells, grows erect. He smiles at me. 'Wisdom,' he says.

Suddenly I'm naked too.

I frown, and now I wear an ornate suit of armor, overlapping plates of gilded duralloy, filigreed with forbidding runes, and beneath my arm is a matching antique helmet, festooned with a plume of bright feathers. 'Joachim Kleronomas,' I say. His penis grows and thickens until it is an absurd fat staff that presses hard against the flatness of his stomach. I cover it, and him, in a uniform from a history text, all black and silver, with the blue-green globe of Old Earth sewn on his right sleeve and twin silver galaxies swirling on his collar.

'No', he says, amused, 'I never reached that rank,' and the galaxies are gone, replaced by a circle of six silver stars. 'And for most of my time, Wisdom, my allegiance was to Avalon, not Earth.' His uniform is less martial, more functional, a simple gray-green jumpsuit with a black fabric belt and a pocket heavy with pens. Only the silver circle of stars remains. 'There,' he says.

'Wrong,' I tell him. 'Wrong still.' And when I am done talking, only the uniform remains. Inside the cloth the flesh is gone, replaced by silver-metal mockery, a shining empty thing with a toaster for a head. But only for an instant. Then the man is back, frowning, unhappy. 'Cruel,' he says to me. The hardness of his penis strains at the fabric of his crotch.

Behind him, the eighth man, the ghost who ought not be here, the misplaced phantom, makes a soft whispery sound, a sound like the rustling of dry dead leaves in a cold autumn wind.

He is a thin, shadowy thing, this intruder. I must look at him very hard to see him at all. He is much smaller than Kleronomas, and he gives the impression of being old and frail, though his flesh is so wispy, so insubstantial, that it is hard to be sure. He is a vision suggested by the random drift of the fog, perhaps, an echo dressed in faded white, but his eyes glow and shimmer and they are trapped and afraid. He reaches out to me. The flesh of his hand is translucent, pulled tightly over gray ancient bones.

I back away, uncertain. In the game of mind, the lightest touch can have a terrible reality.

Behind me I hear more screaming, the terrible wild sound of someone in an ecstasy of fear. I turn.

It has begun in earnest now. The players are seeking their prey. Craimur Delhune, young and vital and far more muscular than he was a moment ago, stands with a flaming sword in one hand, swinging it easily at the tattooed boy. The boy is on his knees, shrieking, trying to cover himself with upraised arms, but Delhune's bright blade passes through the gray shadowflesh unimpeded, and slices at the shining tattoos. He removes them from the boy surgically, swing by swing, and they drift upwards in the misty air, shining images of life cut free of the gray skin on which they were imprisoned. Delhune snatches them as they float by and swallows them whole. Smoke drifts from his nostrils and his open mouth. The boy screams and cringes. Soon there will be nothing left but shadow.

The hatchling has taken to the air. It circles above us, keening at us in its high, thin voice as its wings thunder.

Rieseen Jay has had second thoughts, it seems. She stands above the whimpering little girl, who grows less little with each passing moment. Jay is changing her. She is older now, fatter, her eyes just as frightened but far more vacant. Wherever she turns her head, mirrors appear and sing taunts at her with fat wet lips. Her flesh swells and swells, tearing free of her poor, frayed clothing; thin lines of spittle run down her chin, She wipes at it, crying, but it only flows faster, and now it turns pink with blood. She is enormous, gross, revolting. 'That's you,' the mirrors say. 'Don't look away. Look at yourself. You're not a little girl. Look, look, look. Aren't you pretty? Aren't you sweet? Look at you, look at you.' Rieseen Jay folds her arms, smiles with satisfaction.

Kleronomas looks at me with cold judgment on his face. A band of black cloth wraps itself about my eyes. I blink, vanish it, glare at him. 'I'm not blind,' I say. 'I see them. It is not my fight.'

The fat woman is as large as a truck, as pale and soft as a maggot. She is naked and immense and with each blink of Jay's eye she grows more monstrous. Huge white breasts burst forth from her face, hands, thighs, and the brown meaty nipples open gaping mouths and began to sing. A thick green penis appears above her vagina, curls down, enters her. Cancers blossom on her skin like a field of dark flowers. And everywhere are the mirrors, blinking in and out, reflecting and distorting and enlarging, relentlessly showing her everything she is, documenting every grotesque fancy that Jay inflicts upon her. The fat woman is hardly human. From a mouth the size of my head, gumless and bleeding, she issues forth a sound like the wailing of the damned. Her flesh begins to smoke and tremble.

The cyborg points. All the mirrors explode.

The mist is full of daggers, shards of silvered glass flying everywhere. One comes at me and I make it gone. But the others, the others . . . they curve like smart missiles, become an aerial flotilla, attack. Rieseen Jay is pierced in a thousand places, and the blood drips from her eyes, her breasts, her open mouth. The monster is a little girl again, crying.

'A moralist,' I say to Kleronomas.

He ignores me, turns to look at Craimur Delhune and the shadow boy. Tattoos flame to new life upon the youth's skin, and in his hand a sword appears and takes fire. Delhune takes a step back, unnerved. The boy touches his flesh, mouths some silent oath, rises warily.

'An altruist,' I say. 'Giving succor to the weak.'

Kleronomas turns. 'I hold no brief with slaughter.'

I laugh at him. 'Maybe you're just saving them for yourself, cyborg. If not, you had better grow wings fast, before your prize flies away.'

His face is cold. 'My prize is in front of me,' he says.

'Somehow I knew that,' I reply, donning my plumed helmet. My armor is alive with golden highlights; my sword is a spear of light.

My armor is as black as the pit, and the designs worked upon it, black on black, are of spiders and snakes and human skulls and faces awrithe with pain. My long straight silver sword turns to obsidian, and twists into a grotesquerie of barbs and hooks and cruel spikes. He has a sense of drama, this damned cyborg. 'No,' I say. 'I will not be cast as evil.' I am gold and silver once more, shining, and my plumes are red and blue. 'Wear the suit yourself if you like it so much.'

It stands before me, black and hideous, the helmet open on a grinning skull. Kleronomas sends it away. 'I need no props,' he says. His gray-and-white ghost flitters at his side, plucking at him. Who is that? I wonder yet again.

'Fine,' I say. 'Then we'll dispense with the symbols.'

My armor is gone.

I hold out my bare, open hand. 'Touch me,' I say. 'Touch me, cyborg.'

As his hand reaches out to mine, metal creeps up his long dark fingers.

*

In the game of mind, even more than in life, image and metaphor are everything.

The place beyond time, the endless fog-shrouded plain, the cold sky and the uncertain earth beneath us, even that is illusion. It is mine, all of it, a setting – however unearthly, however surreal – against which the players may act out their tawdry dramas of dominance and submission, conquest and despair, death and rebirth, rape and mind-rape. Without my shaping, my vision and the visions of all the other painlords through the eons, they would have no ground below, no sky above, no place to set their feet, no feet to set. The reality offers not even the scant comfort of the barren landscape I give them. The reality is chaos, unendurable, outside of space and time, bereft of matter or energy, without measurement and therefore frighteningly infinite and suffocatingly claustrophobic, terribly eternal and achingly brief. In that reality the players are trapped; seven minds locked into a telepathic gestalt, into a congress so intimate it cannot be borne by most. And therefore they shrink away, and the very first things we create, in a place where we are gods (or devils, or both), are the bodies we have left behind. Within these walls of flesh we take our refuge and try to order chaos.

The blood has the taste of salt; but there is no blood, only illusion. The cup holds a black and bitter drink; but there is no cup, only an image. The wounds are open and raw, dripping anguish; but there are no wounds, no body to be wounded, only metaphor, symbol, conjuring. Nothing is real, and everything can hurt, can kill, can evoke a lasting madness.

To survive, the players must be resilient, disciplined, stable, and ruthless; they must possess a ready imagination, an extensive vocabulary of symbols, a certain amount of psychological insight. They must find the weakness in their opponent, and hide their own phobias thoroughly. The rules are simple. Believe in everything; believe in nothing. Hold tight to yourself and your sanity.

Even when they kill you, it has no meaning, unless you believe that you have died.

Upon this plain of illusion where these all-too-mutable bodies whirl and feint in a trite pavane that I have seen a thousand times before, plucking swords and mirrors and monsters from the air to throw at one another like jugglers gone mad, the most frightening thing of all is a simple touch.

The symbolism is direct, the meaning clear. Flesh upon flesh. Stripped of metaphor, stripped of protection, stripped of masks. Mind upon mind. When we touch, the walls are down.

Even time is illusory in the game of mind; it runs as fast, or as slow, as we desire.

I am Cyrain, I tell myself, born of Ash, far-traveled, a Wisdom of Dam Tullian, master of the game of mind, mistress of the obsidian castle, ruler of Croan'dhenni, mindlord, painlord, lifelord, whole and immortal and invulnerable. Enter me.

His fingers are cool and hard.

*

I have played the game of mind before, have clasped hands with others who thought themselves strong. In their minds, in their souls, in them, I have seen things. In dark gray tunnels I have traced the graffiti of their ancient scars. The quicksand of their insecurities has clutched at my boots. I have smelled the rank odor of their fears, great swollen beasts who dwell in a palpable living darkness. I have burned my fingers on the hot flesh of lusts who will not speak a name. I have ripped the cloaks from their still, quiet secrets. And then I have taken it all, been them, lived their lives, drunk the cold draught of their knowledge, rummaged through their memories. I have been born a dozen times, have suckled at a dozen teats, have lost a dozen virginities, male and female.

Kleronomas was different.

I stood in a great cavern, alive with lights. The walls and floor and ceiling were translucent crystal, and all around me spires and cones and twisted ribbons rose bright and red and hard, cold to the touch yet alive, the soulsparks moving through them everywhere. A crystalline fairy city in a cave. I touched the nearest outcropping, and the memory flooded into me, the knowledge as clear and sharp and certain as the day it had been etched there. I turned and looked around with new eyes, now discerning rigid order where initially I had perceived only chaotic beauty. It was clean. It took my breath away. I looked everywhere for the vulnerability, the door of gangrenous flesh, the pool of blood, the place of weeping, the shuffling unclean thing that must live deep inside him, and I found nothing, nothing, nothing, only perfection, only the clean sharp crystal, so very red, glowing from within, growing, changing, yet eternal. I touched it once again, wrapping my hand about an outcropping that rose in front of me like a stalagmite. The knowledge was mine. I began to walk, touching, touching, drinking everywhere. Glass flowers bloomed on every side, fantastic scarlet blooms, fragile and beautiful. I took one and sniffed at it, but it had no scent. The perfection was daunting. Where was his weakness? Where was the hidden flaw in this diamond that would enable me to crack it with a single sharp blow?

Here within him there was no decay.

Here there was no place for death.

Here nothing lived.

It felt like home.

And then in front of me the ghost took form, gray and gaunt and unsteady. His bare feet sent up thin tendrils of smoke as they trod lightly on the gleaming crystals underneath, and I caught the scent of burning meat. And I smiled. The specter haunted the crystal maze, but every touch meant pain and destruction. 'Come here,' I said. He looked at me. I could see the lights on the far side of the cavern through the haze of his uncertain flesh. He moved to me and I opened my arms to him, entered him, possessed him.

*

I seated myself upon a balcony in the highest tower of my castle, and drank from a small cup of fragrant black coffee laced with brandy. The swamps were gone; instead I gazed upon mountains, hard and cold and clean. They rose blue-white all around me, and from the highest peak flew a plume of snow crystals caught in a steady endless wind. The wind cut through me, but I scarcely felt it. I was alone and at peace, and the coffee tasted good, and death was far away.

He walked out upon the balcony, and seated himself upon one of the parapets. His pose was casual, insolent, confident. 'I know you,' he said. It was the ultimate threat.

I was not afraid. 'I know you,' I said. 'Shall I conjure up your ghost?'

'He will be here soon enough. He is never far from me.'

'No,' I said. I sipped my coffee, and let him wait. 'I am stronger than you,' I told him finally. 'I can win the game, cyborg. You were wrong to challenge me.'

He said nothing.

I set down my cup, drained and empty, passed my hand across it, smiled as my glass flower grew and spread its colorless transparent petals. A broken rainbow crawled across the table.

He frowned. Color crept into my flower. It softened and drooped, the rainbow was banished. 'The other was not real,' he said. 'A glass flower is not alive.'

I held up his rose, pointed at the broken stem. 'This flower is dying,' I said. In my hands, it became glass once again. 'A glass flower lasts forever.'

He transmuted the glass back to living tissue. He was stubborn, I will say that for him. 'Even dying, it lives.'

'Look at its imperfections,' I said. I pointed them out, one by one. 'Here an insect has gnawed upon it. Here a petal has grown malformed, here, these dark splotches, those are blight, here the wind has bent it. And look what I can do.' I took the largest, prettiest petal between thumb and forefinger, ripped it off, fed it to the wind. 'Beauty is no protection. Life is terribly vulnerable. And ultimately, all of it ends like this.' In my hand, the flower turned brown and shriveled and began to rot. Worms festered upon it briefly, and foul black fluids ran from it, and then it was dust. I crumpled it, blew it away, and from behind his ear I plucked another flower. Glass.

'Glass is hard,' he said, 'and cold.'

'Warmth is a byproduct of decay, the stepchild of entropy.' I told him.

Perhaps he would have replied, but we were no longer alone. Over the crenellated edge of the parapets the ghost came crawling, pulling himself up with frail gray-white hands that left bloody stains upon the purity of my stone. He stared at us wordlessly, a half-transparent whispering in white. Kleronomas averted his eyes.

'Who is he?' I asked.

The cyborg could not answer.

'Do you even remember his name?' I asked him. He replied with silence, and I laughed at them both. 'Cyborg, you judged me, found my morality suspect, my actions tainted, but whatever I might be, I am nothing to you. I steal their bodies. You've taken his mind. Haven't you? *Haven't you?*'

'I never meant to,' he said.

'Joachim Kleronomas died on Avalon seven hundred years ago, just as they say he did. Steel and plastic he might wear, but inside he was still rotting flesh, even at the end, and with all flesh there comes a time when the cells die. A thin flat line on a machine, glowing in the darkness, and an empty metal shell. The end of a legend. What did they do then? Scoop out the brain and bury it beneath some oversized monument? No doubt.' The coffee was strong and sweet; here it never grew lukewarm, because my will did not permit it. 'But they did not bury the machine, did they? That expensive, sophisticated cybernetic organism, the library computer with its wealth of knowledge, the crystal matrix with all its frozen memories. All that was too valuable to discard. The good scientists of Avalon kept it in an interface with the Academy's main system, correct? How many centuries passed before one of them decided to don that cyborg body again, and keep his own death at bay?'

'Less than one,' the cyborg said. 'Less than fifty standard years.'

'He should have erased you,' I said. 'But why? His brain would be riding the machine, after all. Why deny himself access to all that marvelous knowledge, why destroy those crystallized memories? Why, when he could savor them instead? How much better to have a whole second lifetime at his disposal, to be able to access wisdom he had never earned, recollect places he had never been and people he had never met.' I shrugged, and looked at the ghost. 'Poor stupid thing. If you'd ever played the game of mind, you might have understood.'

What can the mind be made of, if not memories? Who are we, after all? Only who we think we are, no more, no less.

Etch your memories on diamond, or on a block of rancid meat, those are the choices. Bit by bit the flesh must die, and give way to steel and metal. Only the diamond memories survive to drive the body. In the end no flesh remains, and the echoes of lost memories are ghostly scratchings on the crystal.

'He forgot who he was,' the cyborg said. 'I forgot who I was, rather. I began to think . . . he began to think he was me.' He looked up at me, his eyes locked on mine. They were red crystal, those eyes, and behind them I could see a glow. His skin was taking on a hard, polished sheen, silvering as I watched. And this time he was doing it himself. 'You have your own weaknesses,' he said, pointing.

Where it curls about the handle of my coffee cup, my hand has grown black, and spotted with corruption. I could smell the decay. Flesh began to flake off, and beneath I saw the bloody bone, bleaching to grim whiteness. Death crept up my bare arm, inexorably. I suppose it was meant to fill me with horror. It only filled me with disgust.

'No,' I said. My arm was whole and healthy. 'No,' I repeated, and now I was metal, silver-bright and undying, eyes like opals, glass flowers twined through platinum hair. I could see my reflection gleaming upon the polished jet of his chest; I was beautiful. Perhaps he could see himself as well, mirrored in my chrome, for just then he turned his head away.

He seemed so strong, but on Croan'dhenni, in my castle of obsidian, in this house of pain and rebirth where the game of mind is played, things are not always as they seem.

'Cyborg,' I said to him, 'you are lost.'

'The other players,' he began.

'No.' I pointed. 'He will stand between you and any victim you might choose. Your ghost. Your guilt. He will not allow it. You will not allow it.'

The cyborg could not look at me. 'Yes,' in a voice tainted by metal and corroded by despair.

'You will live forever,' I said.

'No. I will go on forever. It is different, Wisdom. I can tell you the precise temperature reading of any environment, but I cannot feel heat or cold. I can see into the infrared and the ultraviolet, can magnify my sensors to count every pore on your skin, but I am blind to what I think must be your beauty. I desire life, real life, with the seed of death growing inexorably within it, and therefore giving it meaning.'

'Good,' I said, satisfied.

He finally looked at me. Trapped in that shining metal face were two pale, lost, human eyes. 'Good?'

'I make my own meaning, cyborg, and life is the enemy of death, not its mother. Congratulations. You've won. And so have I.' I rose and reached across the table, plunged my hand through the cold black chest, and ripped the crystal heart from his breast. I held it up and it shone, brighter and brighter, its scarlet rays dancing brilliantly upon the cold dark mountains of my mind.

*

I opened my eyes.

No, incorrect; I activated my sensors once again, and the scene in the chamber of change came into focus with a clarity and sharpness I had never experienced. My obsidian mosaic, black against black, was now a hundred different shades, each distinct from the others, the pattern crisp and clear. I was seated in a niche along the rim; in the center cup, the child-woman stirred and blinked large violet eyes. The door opened and they came to her, Rannar solicitous, Khar Dorian aloof, trying to conceal his curiosity, Braje giggling as she gave her shots.

'No,' I announced to them. My voice was too deep, too male. I adjusted it. 'No, here,' I said, sounding more like myself.

Their stares were like the cracking of whips.

*

In the game of mind, there are winners and there are losers.

The cyborg's interference had its effects, perhaps. Or perhaps not, perhaps before the game was over, the pattern would have been the same. Craimur Delhune is dead; they gave his corpse to the swamps last evening. But the vacancy is gone from the eyes of the pudgy young dreamduster, and she is dieting and exercising even now, and when Khar Dorian leaves, he will take her back to Delhune's estates on Gulliver.

Rieseen Jay complains that she was cheated. I believe she will linger here, outside, in the city of the damned. No doubt that will cure her boredom. The g'hvern struggles to speak, and has painted elaborate symbols on its wings. The tattooed boy leapt from the castle battlements a few hours after his return, and impaled himself upon the jagged obsidian spikes far below, flapping his arms until the last instant. Wings and fierce eyes do not equate with strength.

A new mindlord has begun to reign. She has commanded them to start on a new castle, a structure shaped from living woods, its foundations rooted deep in the swamps, its exterior covered with vines and flowers and other living things. 'You will get insects,' I have warned her, 'parasites and stinging flies, miner-worms in the wood, blight in your foundation, rot in your walls. You will have to sleep with netting over your bed. You will have to kill, constantly, day and night. Your wooden castle will swim in a miasma of little deaths, and in a few years the ghosts of a million insects will swarm your halls by night.'

'Nonetheless,' she says, 'my home will be warm and alive, where yours was cold and brittle.'

We all have our symbols, I suppose.

And our fears.

'Erase him,' she has warned me. 'Blank the crystal, or in time he will consume you, and you will become another ghost in the machine.'

'Erase him?' I might have laughed, if the mechanism permitted laughter. I can see right through her. Her soul is scrawled upon that soft, fragile face. I can count her pores and note each flicker of doubt in the pupils of those violet eyes. 'Erase me, you mean. The crystal is home to us both, child. Besides, I do not fear him. You miss the point. Kleronomas was crystal, the ghost organic meat, the outcome inevitable. My case is different. I am as crystalline as he is, and just as eternal.'

'Wisdom—' she began.

'Wrong,' I said.

'Cyrain, if you prefer—'

'Wrong again. Call me Kleronomas.' I have been many things through my long and varied lives, but I have never been a legend. It has a certain cachet.

The little girl looked at me. 'I am Kleronomas,' she said in a high sweet voice, her eyes baffled.

'Yes,' I said, 'and no. Today we are both Kleronomas. We have lived the same lives, done the same things, stored the same memories. But from this day on, we walk different paths. I am steel and crystal, and you are childflesh. You wanted life, you said. Embrace it, it's yours, and all that goes with it. Your body is young and healthy, just beginning to blossom, your years will be long and full. Today you think you are still Kleronomas. And tomorrow?

'Tomorrow you will learn about lust again, and open your little thighs to Khar Dorian, and shudder and cry out as he rides you to orgasm. Tomorrow you will bear children in blood and pain, and watch them grow and age and bear children of their own, and die. Tomorrow you will ride through the swamps and the dispossessed will toss you gifts, and curse you, and praise you, and pray to you. Tomorrow new players will arrive, begging for bodies, for rebirth, for another chance, and tomorrow Khar's ships will land with a new load of prizes, and all your moral certainties will be tested, and tested again, and twisted to new shapes. Tomorrow Khar and Jonas or Sebastian Cayle will decide that they have waited long enough, and you'll taste the honeyed treason of their kiss, and perhaps you'll win, or perhaps you'll lose. There's no certainty to it. But there's one sure thing I can promise. On the day after tomorrow, long years from now, though they will not seem long once passed, death will begin to grow inside you. The seed is already planted. Perhaps it will be some disease blooming in one of those small sweet breasts Rannar would so dearly love to suckle, perhaps a fine thin wire pulled tight across your throat as you sleep, perhaps a sudden solar flare that will burn this planet clean. It will come, though, and sooner than you think.'

'I accept it,' she said. She smiled as she spoke; I think she really meant it. 'All of it, every part. Life and death. I have been without it for a long time, Wis – Kleronomas.'

'Already you're forgetting things,' I observed. 'Every day you will lose more. Today we both remember. We remember the crystal caverns of Eris, the first ship we ever served on, the lines of our father's face. We remember what Tomas Chung said when we decided not to turn back to Avalon, and the other words he said as he lay dying. We remember the last woman we ever made love to, the shape and smell of her, the taste of her breasts, the noises she made when we pleasured her. She's been dead and gone eight hundred years, but she lives in our memories. But she's dying in yours, isn't she? Today you are Kleronomas. Yet I am him as well, and I am Cyrain of Ash, and a small part of me is still our ghost, poor sad man. But when tomorrow comes, I'll hold tight to all I am, and you, you'll be the mindlord, or perhaps just a sex-slave in some perfumed brothel on Cymeranth, or a scholar on Avalon, but in any case a different person than you are now.'

She understood; she accepted. 'So you'll play the game of mind forever,' she said, 'and I will never die.'

'You will die,' I pointed out. 'Most certainly. Kleronomas is immortal.'
'And Cyrain of Ash.'
'Her too. Yes.'
'What will you do?' she asked me.

I went to the window. The glass flower was there, in its simple wooden vase, its petals refracting the light. I looked up at the source of that light, the brilliant sun of Croan'dhenni burning in the clear midday sky. I could look straight into it now, could focus on the sunspots and the flaming towers of its prominences. I made a small conscious adjustment to the crystal lenses of my eyes, and the empty sky was full of stars, more stars than I had ever seen before, more stars than I could possibly have imagined.

'Do?' I said, still gazing up at those secret starfields, visible to me alone. They brought to mind my obsidian mosaic. 'There are worlds I've never been to,' I told my sister-twin, father, daughter, enemy, mirror-image, whatever she was. 'There are things I don't yet know, stars that even now I cannot see. What will I do? Everything. To begin with, everything.'

As I spoke, a fat striped insect flew through the open window on six gossamer wings that trilled the air too fast for human sight, though I could count every languid beat if I so chose. It landed briefly on my glass flower, found neither scent nor pollen, and slipped back outside. I watched it go, growing smaller and smaller, dwindling in the distance, until at last I had telescoped my vision to the maximum, and the small dying bug was lost among the swamps and stars.

The Hedge Knight

A TALE OF THE SEVEN KINGDOMS

The spring rains had softened the ground, so Dunk had no trouble digging the grave. He chose a spot on the western slope of a low hill, for the old man had always loved to watch the sunset. 'Another day done,' he would sigh, 'and who knows what the morrow will bring us, eh, Dunk?'

Well, one morrow had brought rains that soaked them to the bones, and the one after had brought wet gusty winds, and the next a chill. By the fourth day the old man was too weak to ride. And now he was gone. Only a few days past, he had been singing as they rode, the old song about going to Gulltown to see a fair maid, but instead of Gulltown he'd sung of Ashford. *Off to Ashford to see the fair maid, heigh-ho, heigh-ho,* Dunk thought miserably as he dug.

When the hole was deep enough, he lifted the old man's body in his arms and carried him there. He had been a small man, and slim; stripped of hauberk, helm, and sword belt, he seemed to weigh no more than a bag of leaves. Dunk was hugely tall for his age, a shambling, shaggy, big-boned boy of sixteen or seventeen years (no one was quite certain which) who stood closer to seven feet than to six, and had only just begun to fill out his frame. The old man had often praised his strength. He had always been generous in his praise. It was all he had to give.

He laid him out in the bottom of the grave and stood over him for a time. The smell of rain was in the air again, and he knew he ought to fill the hole before the rain broke, but it was hard to throw dirt down on that tired old face. *There ought to be a septon here, to say some prayers over him, but he only has me.* The old man had taught Dunk all he knew of swords and shields and lances, but had never been much good at teaching him words.

'I'd leave your sword, but it would rust in the ground,' he said at last, apologetic. 'The gods will give you a new one, I guess. I wish you didn't die, ser.' He paused, uncertain what else needed to be said. He didn't know any prayers, not all the way through; the old man had never been much for praying. 'You were a true knight, and you never beat me when I didn't deserve it,' he finally managed, 'except that one time in Maidenpool. It was the inn boy who ate the widow woman's pie, not me, I told you. It don't matter now. The gods keep you, ser.' He kicked dirt in the hole, then began to fill it methodically, never looking at the thing at the bottom. *He had a long life*, Dunk thought. *He must have been closer to sixty than to fifty, and how many men can say that?* At least he had lived to see another spring.

The sun was westering as he fed the horses. There were three; his swaybacked stot, the old man's palfrey, and Thunder, his warhorse, who was ridden only in tourney and battle. The big brown stallion was not as swift or strong as he had once been, but he still had his bright eye and fierce spirit, and he was more valuable than everything else Dunk owned. *If I sold Thunder and old Chestnut, and the saddles and bridles too, I'd come away with enough silver to . . .* Dunk frowned. The only life he knew was the life of a hedge knight, riding from keep to keep, taking service with this lord and that lord, fighting in their battles and eating in their halls until the war was done, then moving on. There were tourneys from time to time as well, though less often, and he knew that some hedge knights turned robber during lean winters, though the old man never had.

I could find another hedge knight in need of a squire to tend his animals and clean his mail, he thought, *or might be I could go to some city, to Lannisport or King's Landing, and join the City Watch. Or else . . .*

He had piled the old man's things under an oak. The cloth purse contained three silver stags, nineteen copper pennies, and a chipped garnet; as with most hedge knights, the greatest part of his worldly wealth had been tied up in his horses and weapons. Dunk now owned a chain-mail hauberk that he had scoured the rust off a thousand times. An iron halfhelm with a broad nasal and a dent on the left temple. A sword belt of cracked brown leather, and a longsword in a wood-and-leather scabbard. A dagger, a razor, a whetstone. Greaves and gorget, an eight-foot war lance of turned ash topped by a cruel iron point, and an oaken shield with a scarred metal rim, bearing the sigil of Ser Arlan of Pennytree: a winged chalice, silver on brown.

Dunk looked at the shield, scooped up the sword belt, and looked at the shield again. The belt was made for the old man's skinny hips. It would never do for him, no more than the hauberk would. He tied the scabbard to a length of hempen rope, knotted it around his waist, and drew the longsword.

The blade was straight and heavy, good castle-forged steel, the grip soft leather wrapped over wood, the pommel a smooth polished black stone. Plain as it was, the sword felt good in his hand, and Dunk knew how sharp it was, having worked it with whetstone and oilcloth many a night before they went to sleep. *It fits my grip as well as it ever fit his*, he thought to himself, *and there is a tourney at Ashford Meadow.*

*

Sweetfoot had an easier gait than old Chestnut, but Dunk was still sore and tired when he spied the inn ahead, a tall daub-and-timber building beside a stream. The warm yellow light spilling from its windows looked so inviting that he could not pass it by. *I have three silvers*, he told himself, *enough for a good meal and as much ale as I care to drink.*

As he dismounted, a naked boy emerged dripping from the stream and began to dry himself on a roughspun brown cloak. 'Are you the stableboy?' Dunk asked him. The lad looked to be no more than eight or nine, a pasty-faced skinny thing, his bare feet caked in mud up to the ankle. His hair was the queerest thing about him. He had none. 'I'll want my palfrey rubbed down. And oats for all three. Can you tend to them?'

The boy looked at him brazenly. 'I could. If I wanted.'

Dunk frowned. 'I'll have none of that. I am a knight, I'll have you know.'

'You don't look to be a knight.'

'Do all knights look the same?'

'No, but they don't look like you, either. Your sword belt's made of rope.'

'So long as it holds my scabbard, it serves. Now see to my horses. You'll get a copper if you do well, and a clout in the ear if you don't.' He did not wait to see how the stableboy took that, but turned away and shouldered through the door.

At this hour, he would have expected the inn to be crowded, but the common room was almost empty. A young lordling in a fine damask mantle was passed out at one table, snoring softly into a pool of spilled wine. Otherwise there was no one. Dunk looked around uncertainly until a stout, short, whey-faced woman emerged from the kitchens and said, 'Sit where you like. Is it ale you want, or food?'

'Both.' Dunk took a chair by the window, well away from the sleeping man.

'There's good lamb, roasted with a crust of herbs, and some ducks my son shot down. Which will you have?'

He had not eaten at an inn in half a year or more. 'Both.'

The woman laughed. 'Well, you're big enough for it.' She drew a tankard of ale and brought it to his table. 'Will you be wanting a room for the night as well?'

'No.' Dunk would have liked nothing better than a soft straw mattress and a roof above his head, but he needed to be careful with his coin. The ground would serve. 'Some food, some ale, and it's on to Ashford for me. How much farther is it?'

'A day's ride. Bear north when the road forks at the burned mill. Is my boy seeing to your horses, or has he run off again?'

'No, he's there,' said Dunk. 'You seem to have no custom.'

'Half the town's gone to see the tourney. My own would as well, if I allowed it. They'll have this inn when I go, but the boy would sooner swagger about with soldiers, and the girl turns to sighs and giggles every time a knight rides by. I swear I couldn't tell you why. Knights are built the same as other men, and I never knew a joust to change the price of eggs.' She eyed Dunk curiously; his sword and shield told her one thing, his rope belt and roughspun tunic quite another. 'You're bound for the tourney yourself?'

He took a sip of the ale before he answered. A nut brown color it was, and thick on the tongue, the way he liked it. 'Aye,' he said. 'I mean to be a champion.'

'Do you, now?' the innkeep answered, polite enough.

Across the room, the lordling raised his head from the wine puddle. His face had a sallow, unhealthy cast to it beneath a rat's nest of sandy brown hair, and blonde stubble crusted his chin. He rubbed his mouth, blinked at Dunk, and said, 'I dreamed of you.' His hand trembled as he pointed a finger. 'You stay away from me, do you hear? You stay well away.'

Dunk stared at him uncertainly. 'My lord?'

The innkeep leaned close. 'Never you mind that one, ser. All he does is drink and talk about his dreams. I'll see about that food.' She bustled off.

'Food?' The lordling made the word an obscenity. He staggered to his feet, one hand on the table to keep himself from falling. 'I'm going to be sick,' he announced. The front of his tunic was crusty red with old wine stains. 'I wanted a whore, but there's none to be found here. All gone to Ashford Meadow. Gods be good, I need some wine.' He lurched unsteadily from the common room, and Dunk heard him climbing steps, singing under his breath.

A sad creature, thought Dunk. *But why did he think he knew me?* He pondered that a moment over his ale.

The lamb was as good as any he had ever eaten, and the duck was even better, cooked with cherries and lemons and not near as greasy as most. The innkeep brought buttered pease as well, and oaten bread still hot from her oven. *This is what it means to be a knight*, he told himself as he sucked the last bit of meat off the bone. *Good food, and ale whenever I want it, and no one to clout me in the head*. He had a second tankard of ale with the meal, a third to wash it down, and a fourth because there was no one to tell him he couldn't, and when he was done he paid the woman with a silver stag and still got back a fistful of coppers.

It was full dark by the time Dunk emerged. His stomach was full and his purse was a little lighter, but he felt good as he walked to the stables. Ahead, he heard a horse whicker. 'Easy, lad,' a boy's voice said. Dunk quickened his step, frowning.

He found the stableboy mounted on Thunder and wearing the old man's armor. The hauberk was longer than he was, and he'd had to tilt the helm back on his bald head or else it would have covered his eyes. He looked utterly intent, and utterly absurd. Dunk stopped in the stable door and laughed.

The boy looked up, flushed, vaulted to the ground. 'My lord, I did not mean—'

'Thief,' Dunk said, trying to sound stern. 'Take off that armor, and be glad that Thunder didn't kick you in that fool head. He's a warhorse, not a boy's pony.'

The boy took off the helm and flung it to the straw. 'I could ride him as well as you,' he said, bold as you please.

'Close your mouth, I want none of your insolence. The hauberk too, take it off. What did you think you were doing?'

'How can I tell you, with my mouth closed?' The boy squirmed out of the chain mail and let it fall.

'You can open your mouth to answer,' said Dunk. 'Now pick up that mail, shake off the dirt, and put it back where you found it. And the halfhelm too. Did you feed the horses, as I told you? And rub down Sweetfoot?'

'Yes,' the boy said, as he shook straw from the mail. 'You're going to Ashford, aren't you? Take me with you, ser.'

The innkeep had warned him of this. 'And what might your mother say to that?'

'My mother?' The boy wrinkled up his face. 'My mother's dead, she wouldn't say anything.'

He was surprised. Wasn't the innkeep his mother? Perhaps he was only 'prenticed to her. Dunk's head was a little fuzzy from the ale. 'Are you an orphan boy?' he asked uncertainly.

'Are you?' the boy threw back.

'I was once,' Dunk admitted. *Till the old man took me in.*

'If you took me, I could squire for you.'

'I have no need of a squire,' he said.

'Every knight needs a squire,' the boy said. 'You look as though you need one more than most.'

Dunk raised a hand threateningly. 'And you look as though you need a clout in the ear, it seems to me. Fill me a sack of oats. I'm off for Ashford . . . alone.'

If the boy was frightened, he hid it well. For a moment he stood there defiant, his arms crossed, but just as Dunk was about to give up on him the lad turned and went for the oats.

Dunk was relieved. *A pity I couldn't . . . but he has a good life here at the inn, a better one than he'd have squiring for a hedge knight. Taking him would be no kindness.*

He could still feel the lad's disappointment, though. As he mounted Sweetfoot and took up Thunder's lead, Dunk decided that a copper penny might cheer him. 'Here, lad, for your help.' He flipped the coin down at him with a smile, but the stableboy made no attempt to catch it. It fell in the dirt between his bare feet, and there he let it lie.

He'll scoop it up as soon as I am gone, Dunk told himself. He turned the palfrey and rode from the inn, leading the other two horses. The trees were bright with moonlight, and the sky was cloudless and speckled with stars. Yet as he headed down the road he could feel the stableboy watching his back, sullen and silent.

*

The shadows of the afternoon were growing long when Dunk reined up on the edge of broad Ashford Meadow. Three score pavilions had already risen on the grassy field. Some were small, some large; some square, some round; some of sailcloth, some of linen, some of silk; but all were brightly colored, with long banners streaming from their center poles, brighter than a field of wildflowers with rich reds and sunny yellows, countless shades of green and blue, deep blacks and grays and purples.

The old man had ridden with some of these knights; others Dunk knew from tales told in common rooms and round campfires. Though he had never learned the magic of reading or writing, the old man had been relentless when it came to teaching him heraldry, often drilling him as they rode. The nightingales belonged to Lord Caron of the Marches, as skilled with the high harp as he was with a lance. The crowned stag was for Ser Lyonel Baratheon, the Laughing Storm. Dunk picked out the Tarly huntsman, House Dondarrion's purple lightning, the red apple of the Fossoways. There roared the lion of Lannister gold on crimson, and there the dark green sea turtle of the Estermonts swam across a pale green field. The brown tent beneath red stallion could only belong to Ser Otho Bracken, who was called the Brute of Bracken since slaying Lord Quentyn Blackwood three years past during a tourney at King's Landing. Dunk heard that Ser Otho struck so hard with the blunted longaxe that he stove in the visor of Lord Blackwood's helm and the face beneath it. He saw some Blackwood banners as well, on the west edge of the meadow, as distant from Ser Otho as they could be. Marbrand, Mallister, Cargyll, Westerling, Swann, Mullendore, Hightower, Florent, Frey, Penrose, Stokeworth, Darry, Parren, Wylde; it seemed as though every lordly house of the west and south had sent a knight or three to Ashford to see the fair maid and brave the lists in her honor.

Yet however fine their pavilions were to look upon, he knew there was no place there for him. A threadbare wool cloak would be all the shelter he had tonight. While the lords and great knights dined on capons and suckling pigs, Dunk's supper would be a hard, stringy piece of salt beef. He knew full well that if he made his camp upon that gaudy field, he would need to suffer both silent scorn and open mockery. A few perhaps would treat him kindly, yet in a way that was almost worse.

A hedge knight must hold tight to his pride. Without it, he was no more than a sellsword. *I must earn my place in that company. If I fight well, some lord may take me into his household. I will ride in noble company then, and eat fresh meat every night in a castle hall, and raise my own pavilion at tourneys. But first I must do well.* Reluctantly, he turned his back on the tourney grounds and led his horses into the trees.

On the outskirts of the great meadow a good half mile from town and castle he found a place where a bend in a brook had formed a deep pool. Reeds grew thick along its edge, and a tall leafy elm presided over all. The spring grass there was as green as any knight's banner and soft to the touch. It was a pretty spot, and no one had yet laid claim to it. *This will be my pavilion*, Dunk told himself, *a pavilion fed with leaves, greener even than the banners of the Tyrells and the Estermonts.* His horses came first. After they had been tended, he stripped and led into the pool to wash away the dust of travel. 'A true knight is cleanly as well as godly,' the old man always said, insisting that they wash themselves head to heels every time the moon turned, whether they smelled sour or not. Now that he was a knight, Dunk vowed he would do the same.

He sat naked under the elm while he dried, enjoying the warmth of spring air on his skin as he watched a dragonfly move lazily among the reeds. *Why would they name it a dragonfly?* he wondered. *It looks nothing like a dragon.* Not that Dunk had ever seen a dragon. The old man had, though. Dunk had heard the story half a hundred times, how Ser Arlan had been just a little boy when his grandfather had taken him to King's Landing, and how they'd seen the last dragon there the year before it died. She'd been a green female, small and stunted, her wings withered. None of her eggs had ever hatched. 'Some say King Aegon poisoned her,' the old man would tell. 'The third Aegon that would be, not King Daeron's father, but the one they named Dragon-bane, or Aegon the Unlucky. He was afraid of dragons, for he'd seen his uncle's beast devour his own mother. The summers have been shorter since the last dragon died, and the winters longer and crueler.'

The air began to cool as the sun dipped below the tops of the trees. When Dunk felt gooseflesh prickling his arms, he beat his tunic and breeches against the trunk of the elm to knock off the worst of the dirt, and donned them once again. On the morrow he could seek out the master of the games and enroll his name, but he had other matters he ought to look into tonight if he hoped to challenge.

He did not need to study his reflection in the water to know that he did not look much a knight, so he slung Ser Arlan's shield across his back to display the sigil. Hobbling the horses, Dunk left them to crop the thick green grass beneath the elm as he set out on foot for the tourney grounds.

*

In normal times the meadow served as a commons for the folk of Ashford town across the river, but now it was transformed. A second town had sprung up overnight, a town of silk instead of stone, larger and fairer than its elder sister. Dozens of merchants had erected their stalls along the edge of the field, selling felts and fruits, belts and boots, hides and hawks, earthenware, gemstones, pewterwork, spices, feathers, and all manner of other goods. Jugglers, puppeteers, and magicians wandered among the crowds plying their trades . . . as did the whores and cutpurses. Dunk kept a wary hand on his coin.

When he caught the smell of sausages sizzling over a smoky fire, his mouth began to water. He bought one with a copper from his pouch, and a horn of ale to wash it down. As he ate he watched a painted wooden knight battle a painted wooden dragon. The puppeteer who worked the dragon was good to watch too; a tall drink of water, with the olive skin and black hair of Dorne. She was slim as a lance with no breasts to speak of, but Dunk liked her face and the way her fingers made the dragon snap and slither at the end of its strings. He would have tossed the girl a copper if he'd had one to spare, but just now he needed every coin.

There were armorers among the merchants, as he had hoped. A Tyroshi with a forked blue beard was selling ornate helms, gorgeous fantastical things wrought in the shapes of birds and beasts and chased with gold and silver. Elsewhere he found a swordmaker hawking cheap steel blades, and another whose work was much finer, but it was not a sword he lacked.

The man he needed was all the way down at the end of the row, a shirt of fine chain mail and a pair of lobstered steel gauntlets displayed on the table before him. Dunk inspected them closely. 'You do good work,' he said.

'None better.' A stumpy man, the smith was no more than five feet tall, yet wide as Dunk about the chest and arms. He had a black beard, huge hands, and no trace of humility.

'I need armor for the tourney,' Dunk told him. 'A suit of good mail, with gorget, greaves, and greathelm.' The old man's halfhelm would fit his head, but he wanted more protection for his face than a nasal bar alone could provide.

The armorer looked him up and down. 'You're a big one, but I've armored bigger.' He came out from behind the table. 'Kneel, I want to measure those shoulders. Aye, and that thick neck o' yours.' Dunk knelt. The armorer laid a length of knotted rawhide along his shoulders, grunted, slipped it about his throat, grunted again. 'Lift your arm. No, the right.' He grunted a third time. 'Now you can stand.' The inside of a leg, the thickness of his calf, and the size of his waist elicited further grunts. 'I have some pieces in me wagon that might do for you,' the man said when he was done. 'Nothing prettied up with gold nor silver, mind you, just good steel, strong and plain. I make helms that look like helms, not winged pigs and queer foreign fruits, but mine will serve you better if you take a lance in the face.'

'That's all I want,' said Dunk. 'How much?'

'Eight hundred stags, for I'm feeling kindly.'

'*Eight hundred?*' It was more than he had expected. 'I . . . I could trade you some old armor, made for a smaller man . . . a halfhelm, a mail hauberk . . .'

'Steely Pate sells only his own work,' the man declared, 'but it might be I could make use of the metal. If it's not too rusted, I'll take it and armor you for six hundred.'

Dunk could beseech Pate to give him the armor on trust, but he knew what sort of answer that request would likely get. He had traveled with the old man long enough to learn that merchants were notoriously mistrustful of hedge knights, some of whom were little better than robbers. 'I'll give you two silvers now, and the armor and the rest of the coin on the morrow.'

The armorer studied him a moment. 'Two silvers buys you a day. After that, I sell me work to the next man.'

Dunk scooped the stags out of his pouch and placed them in the armorer's callused hand. 'You'll get it all. I mean to be a champion here.'

'Do you?' Pate bit one of the coins. 'And these others, I suppose they all came just to cheer you on?'

*

The moon was well up by the time he turned his steps back toward his elm. Behind him, Ashford Meadow was ablaze with torchlight. The sounds of song and laughter drifted across the grass, but his own mood was somber. He could think of only one way to raise the coin for his armor. And if he should be defeated . . . 'One victory is all I need,' he muttered aloud. 'That's not so much to hope for.'

Even so, the old man would never have hoped for it. Ser Arlan had not ridden a tilt since the day he had been unhorsed by the Prince of Dragonstone in a tourney at Storm's End, many years before. 'It is not every man who can boast that he broke seven lances against the finest knight in the Seven Kingdoms,' he would say. 'I could never hope to do better, so why should I try?'

Dunk had suspected that Ser Arlan's age had more to do with it than the Prince of Dragonstone did, but he never dared say as much. The old man had his pride, even at the last. *I am quick and strong, he always said so, what was true for him need not be true for me*, he told himself stubbornly.

He was moving through a patch of weed, chewing over his chances in his head, when he saw the flicker of firelight through the bushes. *What is this?* Dunk did not stop to think. Suddenly his sword was in his hand and he was crashing through the grass.

He burst out roaring and cursing, only to jerk to a sudden halt at the sight of the boy beside the campfire. 'You!' He lowered the sword. 'What are you doing here?'

'Cooking a fish,' said the bald boy. 'Do you want some?'

'I meant, how did you *get* here? Did you steal a horse?'

'I rode in the back of a cart, with a man who was bringing some lambs to the castle for my lord of Ashford's table.'

'Well, you'd best see if he's gone yet, or find another cart. I won't have you here.'

'You can't make me go,' the boy said, impertinent. 'I'd had enough of that inn.'

'I'll have no more insolence from you,' Dunk warned. 'I should throw you over my horse right now and take you home.'

'You'd need to ride all the way to King's Landing,' said the boy. 'You'd miss the tourney.'

King's Landing. For a moment Dunk wondered if he was being mocked, but the boy had no way of knowing that he had been born in King's Landing as well. *Another wretch from Flea Bottom, like as not, and who can blame him for wanting out of that place?*

He felt foolish standing there with sword in hand over an eight-year-old orphan. He sheathed it, glowering so the boy would see that he would suffer no nonsense. *I ought to give him a good beating at the least*, he thought, but the child looked so pitiful he could not bring himself to hit him. He glanced around the camp. The fire was burning merrily within a neat circle of rocks. The horses had been brushed, and clothes were hanging from the elm, drying above the flames. 'What are those doing there?'

'I washed them,' the boy said. 'And I groomed the horses, made the fire, and caught this fish. I would have raised your pavilion, but I couldn't find one.'

'There's my pavilion.' Dunk swept a hand above his head, at the ranches of the tall elm that loomed above them.

'That's a tree,' the boy said, unimpressed.

'It's all the pavilion a true knight needs. I would sooner sleep under the stars than in some smoky tent.'

'What if it rains?'

'The tree will shelter me.'

'Trees leak.'

Dunk laughed. 'So they do. Well, if truth be told, I lack the coin for a pavilion. And you'd best turn that fish, or it will be burned on the bottom and raw on the top. You'd never make a kitchen boy.'

'I would if I wanted,' the boy said, but he turned the fish.

'What happened to your hair?' Dunk asked of him.

'The maesters shaved it off.' Suddenly self-conscious, the boy pulled up the hood of his dark brown cloak, covering his head.

Dunk had heard that they did that sometimes, to treat lice or root-worms or certain sicknesses. 'Are you ill?'

'No,' said the boy. 'What's your name?'

'Dunk,' he said.

The wretched boy laughed aloud, as if that was the funniest thing he'd ever heard. '*Dunk?*' he said. 'Ser Dunk? That's no name for a knight. Is it short for Duncan?'

Was it? The old man had called him just Dunk for as long as he could recall, and he did not remember much of his life before. 'Duncan, yes,' he said. 'Ser Duncan of . . . ' Dunk had no other name, nor any house; Ser Arlan had found him living wild in the stews and alleys of Flea Bottom. He had never known his father or mother. What was he to say? 'Ser Duncan of Flea Bottom' did not sound very knightly. He could take Pennytree, but what if they asked him where it was? Dunk had never been to Pennytree, nor had the old man talked much about it. He frowned for a moment, and then blurted out, 'Ser Duncan the Tall.' He *was* tall, no one could dispute that, and it sounded puissant.

Though the little sneak did not seem to think so. 'I have never heard of any Ser Duncan the Tall.'

'Do you know every knight in the Seven Kingdoms, then?'

The boy looked at him boldly. 'The good ones.'

'I'm as good as any. After the tourney, they'll all know that. Do you have a name, thief?'

The boy hesitated. 'Egg,' he said.

Dunk did not laugh. *His head does look like an egg. Small boys can be cruel, and grown men as well.* 'Egg,' he said, 'I should beat you bloody and send you on your way, but the truth is, I have no pavilion and I have no squire either. If you'll swear to do as you're told, I'll let you serve me for the tourney. After that, well, we'll see. If I decide you're worth your keep, you'll have clothes on your back and food in your belly. The clothes might be roughspun and the food salt beef and salt fish, and maybe some venison from time to time where there are no foresters about, but you won't go hungry. And I promise not to beat you except when you deserve it.'

Egg smiled. 'Yes, my lord.'

'*Ser*,' Dunk corrected. 'I am only a hedge knight.' He wondered if the old man was looking down on him. *I will teach him the arts of battle, the same as you taught me, ser. He seems a likely lad, might be one day he'll make a knight.*

The fish was still a little raw on the inside when they ate it, and the boy had not removed all the bones, but it still tasted a world better than hard salt beef.

Egg soon fell asleep beside the dying fire. Dunk lay on his back nearby, his big hands behind his head, gazing up at the night sky. He could hear distant music from the tourney grounds, half a mile away. The stars were everywhere, thousands and thousands of them. One fell as he was watching, a bright green streak that flashed across the black and then was gone.

A falling star brings luck to him who sees it, Dunk thought. *But the rest of them are all in their pavilions by now, staring up at silk instead of sky. So the luck is mine alone.*

*

In the morning, he woke to the sound of a cock crowing. Egg was still there, curled up beneath the old man's second-best cloak. *Well, the boy did not run off during the night, that's a start*. He prodded him awake with his foot. 'Up. There's work to do.' The boy rose quick enough, rubbing his eyes. 'Help me saddle Sweetfoot,' Dunk told him.

'What about breakfast?'

'There's salt beef. *After* we're done.'

'I'd sooner eat the horse,' Egg said. 'Ser.'

'You'll eat my fist if you don't do as you're told. Get the brushes. They're in the saddle sack. Yes, that one.'

Together they brushed out the palfrey's sorrel coat, hefted Ser Arlan's best saddle over her back, and cinched it tight. Egg was a good worker once he put his mind to it, Dunk saw.

'I expect I'll be gone most of the day,' he told the boy as he mounted. 'You're to stay here and put the camp in order. Make sure no *other* thieves come nosing about.'

'Can I have a sword to run them off with?' Egg asked. He had blue eyes, Dunk saw, very dark, almost purple. His bald head made them seem huge, somehow.

'No,' said Dunk. 'A knife's enough. And you had best be here when I come back, do you hear me? Rob me and run off and I'll hunt you down, I swear I will. With dogs.'

'You don't have any dogs,' Egg pointed out.

'I'll get some,' said Dunk. 'Just for you.' He turned Sweetfoot's head toward the meadow and moved off at a brisk trot, hoping the threat would be enough to keep the boy honest. Save for the clothes on his back, the armor in his sack, and the horse beneath him, everything Dunk owned in the world was back at that camp. *I am a great fool to trust the boy so far, but it is no more than the old man did for me, he reflected. The Mother must have sent him to me so that I could pay my debt.*

As he crossed the field, he heard the ring of hammers from the riverside, where carpenters were nailing together jousting barriers and raising a lofty viewing stand. A few new pavilions were going up as well, while the knights who had come earlier slept off last night's revels or sat to break their fasts. Dunk could smell woodsmoke, and bacon as well.

To the north of the meadow flowed the river Cockleswent, a vassal stream to the mighty Mander. Beyond the shallow ford lay town and castle. Dunk had seen many a market town during his journeys with the old man. This was prettier than most; the whitewashed houses with their thatched roofs had an inviting aspect to them. When he was smaller, he used to wonder what it would be like to live in such a place; to sleep every night with a roof over your head, and wake every morning with the same walls wrapped around you. *It may be that soon I'll know. Aye, and Egg too. It could happen. Stranger things happened every day.*

Ashford Castle was a stone structure built in the shape of a triangle, with round towers rising thirty feet tall at each point and thick crenellated walls running between. Orange banners flew from its battlements, displaying the white sun-and-chevron sigil of its lord. Men-at-arms in orange-and-white livery stood outside the gates with halberds, watching people come and go, seemingly more intent on joking with a pretty milkmaid than in keeping anyone out. Dunk reined up in front of the short, bearded man he took for their captain and asked for the master of the games.

'It's Plummer you want, he's steward here. I'll show you.'

Inside the yard, a stableboy took Sweetfoot for him. Dunk slung Ser Arlan's battered shield over a shoulder and followed the guards captain back of the stables to a turret built into an angle of the curtain wall. Steep stone steps led up to the wallwalk. 'Come to enter your master's name for the lists?' the captain asked as they climbed.

'It's my own name I'll be putting in.'

'Is it now?'

Was the man smirking? Dunk was not certain. 'That door there. I'll leave you to it and get back to my post.'

When Dunk pushed open the door, the steward was sitting at a trestle table, scratching on a piece of parchment with a quill. He had thinning gray hair and a narrow pinched face. 'Yes?' he said, looking up. 'What do you want, man?'

Dunk pulled shut the door. 'Are you Plummer the steward? I came for the tourney. To enter the lists.'

Plummer pursed his lips. 'My lord's tourney is a contest for knights. Are you a knight?'

He nodded, wondering if his ears were red.

'A knight with a name, mayhaps?'

'Dunk.' Why had he said *that*? 'Ser Duncan. The Tall.'

'And where might you be from, Ser Duncan the Tall?'

'Everyplace. I was squire to Ser Arlan of Pennytree since I was five or six. This is his shield.' He showed it to the steward. 'He was coming to the tourney, but he caught a chill and died, so I came in his stead. He knighted me before he passed, with his own sword.' Dunk drew the longsword and laid it on the scarred wooden table between them.

The master of the lists gave the blade no more than a glance. 'A sword it is, for a certainty. I have never heard of this Arlan of Pennytree, however. You were his squire, you say?'

'He always said he meant for me to be a knight, as he was. When he was dying he called for his longsword and bade me kneel. He touched me once on my right shoulder and once on my left, and said some words, and when I got up he said I was a knight.'

'Hmpf.' The man Plummer rubbed his nose. 'Any knight can make a knight, it is true, though it is more customary to stand a vigil and be anointed by a septon before taking your vows. Were there any witnesses to your dubbing?'

'Only a robin, up in a thorn tree. I heard it as the old man was saying the words. He charged me to be a good knight and true, to obey the seven gods, defend the weak and innocent, serve my lord faithfully and defend the realm with all my might, and I swore that I would.'

'No doubt.' Plummer did not deign to call him *ser*, Dunk could not help but notice. 'I shall need to consult with Lord Ashford. Will you or your late master be known to any of the good knights here assembled?'

Dunk thought a moment. 'There was a pavilion flying the banner of House Dondarrion? The black, with purple lightning?'

'That would be Ser Manfred, of that House.'

'Ser Arlan served his lord father in Dorne, three years past. Ser Manfred might remember me.'

'I would advise you to speak to him. If he will vouch for you, bring him here with you on the morrow, at this same time.'

'As you say, m'lord.' He started for the door.

'Ser Duncan,' the steward called after him.

Dunk turned back.

'You are aware,' the man said, 'that those vanquished in tourney forfeit their arms, armor, and horse to the victors, and must needs ransom them back?'

'I know.'

'And do you have the coin to pay such ransom?'

Now he *knew* his ears were red. 'I won't have need of coin,' he said, praying it was true. *All I need is one victory. If I win my first tilt, I'll have the loser's armor and horse, or his gold, and I can stand a loss myself.*

He walked slowly down the steps, reluctant to get on with what he must do next. In the yard, he collared one of the stableboys. 'I must speak with Lord Ashford's master of horse.'

'I'll find him for you.'

It was cool and dim in the stables. An unruly gray stallion snapped at him as he passed, but Sweetfoot only whickered softly and nuzzled his hand when he raised it to her nose. 'You're a good girl, aren't you?' he murmured. The old man always said that a knight should never love a horse, since more than a few were like to die under him, but he never heeded his own counsel either. Dunk had often seen him spend his last copper on an apple for old Chestnut or some oats for Sweetfoot and Thunder. The palfrey had been Ser Arlan's riding horse, and she had borne him tirelessly over thousands of miles, all up and down the Seven Kingdoms. Dunk felt as though he were betraying an old friend, but what choice did he have? Chestnut was too old to be worth much of anything, and Thunder must carry him in the lists.

Some time passed before the master of horse deigned to appear. As he waited, Dunk heard a blare of trumpets from the walls, and a voice in the yard. Curious, he led Sweetfoot to the stable door to see what was happening. A large party of knights and mounted archers poured through the gates, a hundred men at least, riding some of the most splendid horses that Dunk had ever seen. *Some great lord has come.* He grabbed the arm of a stableboy as he ran past. 'Who are they?'

The boy looked at him queerly. 'Can't you see the banners?' He wrenched free and hurried off.

The banners . . . As Dunk turned his head, a gust of wind lifted the black silk pennon atop the tall staff, and the fierce three-headed dragon of House Targaryen seemed to spread its wings, breathing scarlet fire. The banner-bearer was a tall knight in white scale armor chased with gold, a pure white cloak streaming from his shoulders. Two of the other riders were armored in white from head to heel as well. *Kingsguard knights with the royal banner.* Small wonder Lord Ashford and his sons came hurrying out the doors of the keep, and the fair maid too, a short girl with yellow hair and a round pink face. *She does not seem so fair to me,* Dunk thought. The puppet girl was prettier.

'Boy, let go of that nag and see to my horse.'

A rider had dismounted in front of the stables. *He is talking to me,* Dunk realized. 'I am not a stableboy, m'lord.'

'Not clever enough?' The speaker wore a black cloak bordered in scarlet satin, but underneath was raiment bright as flame, all reds and yellows and golds. Slim and straight as a dirk, though only of middling height, he was near Dunk's own age. Curls of silver-gold hair framed a face sculpted and imperious; high brow and sharp cheekbones, straight nose, pale smooth skin without blemish. His eyes were a deep violet color. 'If you cannot manage a horse, fetch me some wine and a pretty wench.'

'I . . . m'lord, pardons, I'm no serving man either. I have the honor to be a knight.'

'Knighthood has fallen on sad days,' said the princeling, but then one of the stableboys came rushing up, and he turned away to hand him the reins of his palfrey, a splendid blood bay. Dunk was forgotten in an instant. Relieved, he slunk back inside the stables to wait for the master of horse. He felt ill-at-ease enough around the lords in their pavilions, he had no business speaking to princes.

That the beautiful stripling was a prince he had no doubt. The Targaryens were the blood of lost Valyria across the seas, and their silver-gold hair and violet eyes set them apart from common men. Dunk knew Prince Baelor was older, but the youth might well have been one of his sons: Valarr, who was often called 'the Young Prince' to set him apart from his father, or Matarys, 'the Even Younger Prince,' as old Lord Swann's fool had named him once. There were other princelings as well, cousins to Valarr and Matarys. Good King Daeron had four grown sons, three with sons of their own. The line of the dragonkings had almost died out during his father's day, but it was commonly said that Daeron II and his sons had left it secure for all time.

'You. Man. You asked for me.' Lord Ashford's master of horse had a red face made redder by his orange livery, and a brusque manner of speaking. 'What is it? I have no time for—'

'I want to sell this palfrey,' Dunk broke in quickly, before the man could dismiss him. 'She's a good horse, sure of foot—'

'I have no time, I tell you.' The man gave Sweetfoot no more than a glance. 'My lord of Ashford has no need of such. Take her to the town, perhaps Henly will give you a silver or three.' That quick, he was turning away.

'Thank you, m'lord,' Dunk said before he could go. 'M'lord, has the king come?'

The master of horse laughed at him. 'No, thank the gods. This infestation of princes is trial enough. Where am I going to find the stalls for all these animals? And fodder?' He strode off shouting at his stableboys.

By the time Dunk left the stable, Lord Ashford had escorted his princely guests into the hall, but two of the Kingsguard knights in their white armor and snowy cloaks still lingered in the yard, talking with the captain of the guard. Dunk halted before them. 'M'lords, I am Ser Duncan the Tall.'

'Well met, Ser Duncan,' answered the bigger of the white knights. 'I am Ser Roland Crakehall, and this is my Sworn Brother, Ser Donnel of Duskendale.'

The seven champions of the Kingsguard were the most puissant warriors in all the Seven Kingdoms, saving only perhaps the crown prince, Baelor Breakspear himself. 'Have you come to enter the lists?' Dunk asked anxiously.

'It would not be fitting for us to ride against those we are sworn to protect,' answered Ser Donnel, red of hair and beard.

'Prince Valarr has the honor to be one of Lady Ashford's champions,' explained Ser Roland, 'and two of his cousins mean to challenge. The rest of us have come only to watch.'

Relieved, Dunk thanked the white knights for their kindness, and rode out through the castle gates before another prince should think to accost him. *Three princelings*, he pondered as he turned the palfrey toward the streets of Ashford town. Valarr was the eldest son of Prince Baelor, second in line to the Iron Throne, but Dunk did not know how much of his father's fabled prowess with lance and sword he might have inherited. About the other Targaryen princes he knew even less. *What will I do if I have to ride against a prince? Will I even be allowed to challenge one so highborn?* He did not know the answer. The old man had often said he was thick as a castle wall, and just now he felt it.

Henly liked the look of Sweetfoot well enough until he heard Dunk wanted to sell her. Then all the stableman could see in her were faults. He offered three hundred silvers. Dunk said he must have three thousand. After much arguing and cursing, they settled at seven hundred fifty silver stags. That was a deal closer to Henly's starting price than to Dunk's, which made him feel the loser in the tilt, but the stableman would go no higher, so in the end he had no choice but to yield. A second argument began when Dunk declared that the price did not include the saddle, and Henly insisted that it had.

Finally it was all settled. As Henly left to fetch his coin, Dunk stroked Sweetfoot's mane and told her to be brave. 'If I win, I'll come back and buy you again, I promise.' He had no doubt that all the palfrey's flaws would vanish in the intervening days, and she would be worth twice what she was today.

The stableman gave him three gold pieces and the rest in silver. Dunk bit one of the gold coins and smiled. He had never tasted gold before, nor handled it. 'Dragons,' men called the coins, since they were stamped with the three-headed dragon of House Targaryen on one side. The other bore the likeness of the king. Two of the coins Henly gave him had King Daeron's face; the third was older, well worn, and showed a different man. His name was there under his head, but Dunk could not read the letters. Gold had been shaved off its edges too, he saw. He pointed this out to Henly, and loudly. The stableman grumbled, but handed over another few silvers and a fistful of coppers to make up the weight. Dunk handed a few of the coppers right back, and nodded at Sweetfoot. 'That's for her,' he said. 'See that she has some oats tonight. Aye, and an apple too.'

With the shield on his arm and the sack of old armor slung over his shoulder, Dunk set out on foot through the sunny streets of Ashford town. The heft of all that coin in his pouch made him feel queer; almost giddy on one hand, and anxious on the other. The old man had never trusted him with more than a coin or two at a time. He could live a year on this much money. *And what will I do when it's gone, sell Thunder?* That road ended in beggary or outlawry. *This chance will never come again; I must risk all.*

By the time he splashed back across the ford to the south bank of the Cockleswent, the morning was almost done and the tourney grounds had come to life once more. The winesellers and sausage makers were doing a brisk trade, a dancing bear was shuffling along to his master's playing as a singer sang 'The Bear, the Bear, and the Maiden Fair,' jugglers were juggling, and the puppeteers were just finishing another fight.

Dunk stopped to watch the wooden dragon slain. When the puppet knight cut its head off and the red sawdust spilled out onto the grass, he laughed aloud and threw the girl two coppers. 'One for last night,' he called. She caught the coins in the air and threw him back a smile as sweet as any he had ever seen.

Is it me she smiles at, or the coins? Dunk had never been with a girl, and they made him nervous. Once, three years past, when the old man's purse was full after half a year in the service of blind Lord Florent, he'd told Dunk the time had come to take him to a brothel and make him a man. He'd been drunk, though, and when he was sober he did not remember. Dunk had been too embarrassed to remind him. He was not certain he wanted a whore anyway. If he could not have a highborn maiden like a proper knight, he wanted one who at least liked him more than his silver.

'Will you drink a horn of ale?' he asked the puppet girl as she was scooping the sawdust blood back into her dragon. 'With me, I mean? Or a sausage? I had a sausage last night, and it was good. They're made with pork, I think.'

'I thank you, m'lord, but we have another show.' The girl rose, and ran off to the fierce fat Dornishwoman who worked the puppet knight while Dunk stood there feeling stupid. He liked the way she ran, though. *A pretty girl, and tall. I would not have to kneel to kiss that one.* He knew how to kiss. A tavern girl had showed him one night in Lannisport, a year ago, but she'd been so short she had to sit on the table to reach his lips. The memory made his ears burn. What a great fool he was. It was jousting he should be thinking about, not kissing.

Lord Ashford's carpenters were whitewashing the waist-high wooden barriers that would separate the jousters. Dunk watched them work awhile. There were five lanes, arrayed north to south so none of the competitors would ride with the sun in his eyes. A three-tiered viewing stand had been raised on the eastern side of the lists, with an orange canopy to shield the lords and ladies from rain and sun. Most would sit on benches, but four high-backed chairs had been erected in the center of the platform, for Lord Ashford, the fair maid, and the visiting princes.

On the eastern verge of the meadow, a quintain had been set up and a dozen knights were tilting at it, sending the pole arm spinning every time they struck the splintered shield suspended from one end. Dunk watched the Brute of Bracken take his turn, and then Lord Caron of the Marches. *I do not have as good a seat as any of them,* he thought uneasily.

Elsewhere, men were training afoot, going at each other with wooden swords while their squires stood shouting ribald advice. Dunk watched a stocky youth try to hold off a muscular knight who seemed lithe and quick as a mountain cat. Both had the red apple of the Fossoways painted on their shields, but the younger man's was soon hacked and chipped to pieces. 'Here's an apple that's not ripe yet,' the older said as he slammed the other's helm. The younger Fossoway was bruised and bloody by the time he yielded, but his foe was hardly winded. He raised his visor, looked about, saw Dunk, and said, 'You there. Yes, you, the big one. Knight of the winged chalice. Is that a longsword you wear?'

'It is mine by rights,' Dunk said defensively. 'I am Ser Duncan the Tall.'

'And I Ser Steffon Fossoway. Would you care try me, Ser Duncan the Tall? It would be good to have someone new to cross swords with. My cousin's not ripe yet, as you've seen.'

'Do it, Ser Duncan,' urged the beaten Fossoway as he removed his helm. 'I may not be ripe, but my good cousin is rotten to the core. Knock the seeds out of him.'

Dunk shook his head. Why were these lordlings involving him in their quarrel? He wanted no part of it. 'I thank you, ser, but I have matters to attend.' He was uncomfortable carrying so much coin. The sooner he paid Steely Pate and got his armor, the happier he would be.

Ser Steffon looked at him scornfully. 'The hedge knight has matters.' He glanced about and found another likely opponent loitering nearby. 'Ser Grance, well met. Come try me. I know every feeble trick my cousin Raymun has mastered, and it seems that Ser Duncan needs to return to the hedges. Come, come.'

Dunk stalked away red-faced. He did not have many tricks himself, feeble or otherwise, and he did not want anyone to see him fight until the tourney. The old man always said that the better you knew your foe, the easier it was to best him. Knights like Ser Steffon had sharp eyes to find a man's weakness at a glance. Dunk was strong and quick, and his weight and reach were in his favor, but he did not believe for a moment that his skills were the equal of these others. Ser Arlan had taught him as best he could, but the old man had never been the greatest of knights even when young. Great knights did not live their lives in the hedges, or die by the side of a muddy road. That will not happen to me, Dunk vowed. *I will show them that I can be more than a hedge knight.*

'Ser Duncan.' The younger Fossoway hurried to catch him. 'I should not have urged you to try my cousin. I was angry with his arrogance, and you are so large, I thought . . . well, it was wrong of me. You wear no armor. He would have broken your hand if he could, or a knee. He likes to batter men in the training yard, so they will be bruised and vulnerable later, should he meet them in the lists.'

'He did not break you.'

'No, but I am his own blood, though his is the senior branch of the apple tree, as he never ceases to remind me. I am Raymun Fossoway.'

'Well met. Will you and your cousin ride in the tourney?'

'He will, for a certainty. As to me, would that I could. I am only a squire as yet. My cousin has promised to knight me, but insists that I am not ripe yet.' Raymun had a square face, a pug nose, and short woolly hair, but his smile was engaging. 'You have the look of a challenger, it seems to me. Whose shield do you mean to strike?'

'It makes no difference,' said Dunk. That was what you were supposed to say, though it made all the difference in the world. 'I will not enter the lists until the third day.'

'And by then some of the champions will have fallen, yes,' Raymun said. 'Well, may the Warrior smile on you, ser.'

'And you.' *If he is only a squire, what business do I have being a knight? One of us is a fool.* The silver in Dunk's pouch clinked with every step, but he could lose it all in a heartbeat, he knew. Even the rules of this tourney worked against him, making it very unlikely that he would face a green or feeble foe.

There were a dozen different forms a tourney might follow, according to the whim of the lord who hosted it. Some were mock battles between teams of knights, others wild melees where the glory went to the last fighter left standing. Where individual combats were the rule, pairings were sometimes determined by lot, and sometimes by the master of the games.

Lord Ashford was staging this tourney to celebrate his daughter's thirteenth nameday. The fair maid would sit by her father's side as the reigning Queen of Love and Beauty. Five champions wearing her favors would defend her. All others must perforce be challengers, but any man who could defeat one of the champions would take his place and stand as a champion himself, until such time as another challenger unseated him. At the end of three days of jousting, the five who remained would determine whether the fair maid would retain the crown of Love and Beauty, or whether another would wear it in her place.

Dunk stared at the grassy lists and the empty chairs on the viewing stand and pondered his chances. One victory was all he needed; then he could name himself one of the champions of Ashford Meadow, if only for an hour. The old man had lived nigh on sixty years and had never been a champion. *It is not too much to hope for, if the gods are good.* He thought back on all the songs he had heard, songs of blind Symeon Star-Eyes and noble Serwyn of the Mirror Shield, of Prince Aemon the Dragonknight, Ser Ryam Redwyne, and Florian the Fool. They had all won victories against foes far more terrible than any he would face. *But they were great heroes, brave men of noble birth, except for Florian. And what am I? Dunk of Flea Bottom? Or Ser Duncan the Tall?*

He supposed he would learn the truth of that soon enough. He hefted the sack of armor and turned his feet toward the merchants' stalls, in search of Steely Pate.

*

Egg had worked manfully at the campsite. Dunk was pleased; he had been half afraid his squire would run off again. 'Did you get a good price for your palfrey?' the boy asked.

'How did you know I'd sold her?'

'You rode off and walked back, and if robbers had stolen her you'd be more angry than you are.'

'I got enough for this.' Dunk took out his new armor to show the boy. 'If you're ever to be a knight, you'll need to know good steel from bad. Look here, this is fine work. This mail is double-chain, each link bound to two others, see? It gives more protection than single-chain. And the helm, Pate's rounded the top, see how it curves? A sword or an axe will slide off, where they might bite through a flat-topped helm.' Dunk lowered the greathelm over his head. 'How does it look?'

'There's no visor,' Egg pointed out.

'There's air holes. Visors are points of weakness.' Steely Pate had said as much. 'If you knew how many knights have taken an arrow in the eye as they lifted their visor for a suck o' cool air, you'd never want one,' he'd told Dunk.

'There's no crest either,' said Egg. 'It's just plain.'

Dunk lifted off the helm. 'Plain is fine for the likes of me. See how bright the steel is? It will be your task to keep it that way. You know how to scour mail?'

'In a barrel of sand,' said the boy, 'but you don't have a barrel. Did you buy a pavilion too, ser?'

'I didn't get that good a price.' *The boy is too bold for his own good, I ought to beat that out of him.* He knew he would not, though. He liked the boldness. He needed to be bolder himself. *My squire is braver than I am, and more clever.* 'You did well here, Egg,' Dunk told him. 'On the morrow, you'll come with me. Have a look at the tourney grounds. We'll buy oats for the horses and fresh bread for ourselves. Maybe a bit of cheese as well; they were selling good cheese at one of the stalls.'

'I won't need to go into the castle, will I?'

'Why not? One day, I mean to live in a castle. I hope to win a place above the salt before I'm done.'

The boy said nothing. *Perhaps he fears to enter a lord's hall,* Dunk reflected. *That's no more than might be expected. He will grow out of it in time.* He went back to admiring his armor, and wondering how long he would wear it.

*

Ser Manfred was a thin man with a sour look on his face. He wore a black surcoat slashed with the purple lightning of House Dondarrion, but Dunk would have remembered him anyway by his unruly mane of red-gold hair. 'Ser Arlan served your lord father when he and Lord Caron burned the Vulture King out of the Red Mountains, ser,' he said from one knee. 'I was only a boy then, but I squired for him. Ser Arlan of Pennytree.'

Ser Manfred scowled. 'No. I know him not. Nor you, boy.'

Dunk showed him the old man's shield. 'This was his sigil, the winged chalice.'

'My lord father took eight hundred knights and near four thousand foot into the mountains. I cannot be expected to remember every one of them, nor what shields they carried. It may be that you were with us, but . . .' Ser Manfred shrugged.

Dunk was struck speechless for an instant. *The old man took a wound in your father's service, how can you have forgotten him?* 'They will not allow me to challenge unless some knight or lord will vouch for me.'

'And what is that to me?' said Ser Manfred. 'I have given you enough of my time, ser.'

If he went back to the castle without Ser Manfred, he was lost. Dunk eyed the purple lightning embroidered across the black wool of Ser Manfred's surcoat and said, 'I remember your father telling the camp how your house got its sigil. One stormy night, as the first of your line bore a message across the Dornish Marches, an arrow killed his horse beneath him and spilled him on the ground. Two Dornishmen came out of the darkness in ring mail and crested helms. His sword had broken beneath him when he fell. When he saw that, he thought he was doomed. But as the Dornishmen closed to cut him down, lightning cracked from the sky. It was a bright burning purple, and it split, striking the Dornishmen in their steel and killing them both where they stood. The message gave the Storm King victory over the Dornish, and in thanks he raised the messenger to lordship. He was the first Lord Dondarrion, so he took for his arms a forked purple lightning bolt, on a black field powdered with stars.'

If Dunk thought the tale would impress Ser Manfred, he could not have been more wrong. 'Every pot boy and groom who has ever served my father hears that story soon or late. Knowing it does not make you a knight. Begone with you, ser.'

*

It was with a leaden heart that Dunk returned to Ashford Castle, wondering what he might say so that Plummer would grant him the right of challenge. The steward was not in his turret chamber, however. A guard told him he might be found in the Great Hall. 'Shall I wait here?' Dunk asked. 'How long will he be?'

'How should I know? Do what you please.'

The Great Hall was not so great, as halls went, but Ashford was a small castle. Dunk entered through a side door, and spied the steward at once. He was standing with Lord Ashford and a dozen other men at the top of the hall. He walked toward them, beneath a wall hung with wool tapestries of fruits and flowers.

'—more concerned if they were *your* sons, I'll wager,' an angry man was saying as Dunk approached. His straight hair and square-cut beard were so fair they seemed white in the dimness of the hall, but as he got closer he saw that they were in truth a pale silvery color touched with gold.

'Daeron has done this before,' another replied. Plummer was standing so as to block Dunk's view of the speaker. 'You should never have commanded him to enter the lists. He belongs on a tourney field no more than Aerys does, or Rhaegel.'

'By which you mean he'd sooner ride a whore than a horse,' the first man said. Thickly built and powerful, the prince – he was surely a prince – wore a leather brigandine covered with silver studs beneath a heavy black cloak trimmed with ermine. Pox scars marked his cheeks, only partly concealed by his silvery beard. 'I do not need to be reminded of my son's failings, brother. He has only eighteen years. He can change. He *will* change, gods be damned, or I swear I'll see him dead.'

'Don't be an utter fool. Daeron is what he is, but he is still your blood and mine. I have no doubt Ser Roland will turn him up, and Aegon with him.'

'When the tourney is over, perhaps.'

'Aerion is here. He is a better lance than Daeron in any case, if it is the tourney that concerns you.' Dunk could see the speaker now. He was seated in the high seat, a sheaf of parchments in one hand, Lord Ashford hovering at his shoulder. Even seated, he looked to be a head taller than the other, to judge from the long straight legs stretched out before him. His short-cropped hair was dark and peppered with gray, his strong jaw clean-shaven. His nose looked as though it had been broken more than once. Though he was dressed very plainly, in green doublet, brown mantle, and scuffed boots, there was a weight to him, a sense of power and certainty.

It came to Dunk that he had walked in on something that he ought never have heard. I had best go and come back later, when they are done, he decided. But it was already too late. The prince with the silvery beard suddenly took note of him. 'Who are you, and what do you mean by bursting in on us?' he demanded harshly.

'He is the knight that our good steward was expecting,' the seated man said, smiling at Dunk in a way that suggested he had been aware of him all the time. 'You and I are the intruders here, brother. Come closer, ser.'

Dunk edged forward, uncertain what was expected of him. He looked at Plummer, but got no help there. The pinch-faced steward who had been so forceful yesterday now stood silent, studying the stones of the floor. 'My lords,' he said, 'I asked Ser Manfred Dondarrion to vouch for me so I might enter the lists, but he refuses. He says he knows me not. Ser Arlan served him, though, I swear it. I have his sword and shield, I—'

'A shield and a sword do not make a knight,' declared Lord Ashford, a big bald man with a round red face. 'Plummer has spoken to me of you. Even if we accept that these arms belonged to this Ser Arlan of Pennytree, it may well be that you found him dead and stole them. Unless you have some better proof of what you say, some writing or—'

'I remember Ser Arlan of Pennytree,' the man in the high seat said quietly. 'He never won a tourney that I know, but he never shamed himself either. At King's Landing sixteen years ago, he overthrew Lord Stokeworth and the Bastard of Harrenhal in the melee, and many years before at Lannisport he unhorsed the Grey Lion himself. The lion was not so gray then, to be sure.'

'He told me about that, many a time,' said Dunk.

The tall man studied him. 'Then you will remember the Grey Lion's true name, I have no doubt.'

For a moment there was nothing in Dunk's head at all. A thousand times the old man had told that tale, a thousand times, the lion, the lion, his name, his name, his name . . . He was near despair when suddenly it came. 'Ser Damon Lannister!' he shouted. 'The Grey Lion! He's Lord of easterly Rock now.'

'So he is,' said the tall man pleasantly, 'and he enters the lists on the morrow.' He rattled the sheaf of papers in his hand.

'How can you possibly remember some insignificant hedge knight who chanced to unhorse Damon Lannister sixteen years ago?' said the prince with the silver beard, frowning.

'I make it a practice to learn all I can of my foes.'

'Why would you deign to joust with a hedge knight?'

'It was nine years past, at Storm's End. Lord Baratheon held a hastilude to celebrate the birth of a grandson. The lots made Ser Arlan my opponent in the first tilt. We broke four lances before I finally unhorsed him.'

'Seven,' insisted Dunk, 'and that was against the Prince of Dragonstone!' No sooner were the words out than he wanted them back. *Dunk the lunk, thick as a castle wall*, he could hear the old man chiding.

'So it was.' The prince with the broken nose smiled gently. 'Tales grow in the telling, I know. Do not think ill of your old master, but it was four lances only, I fear.'

Dunk was grateful that the hall was dim; he knew his ears were red. 'My lord.' No, that's wrong too. 'Your Grace.' He fell to his knees and lowered his head. 'As you say, four, I meant no ... I never ... The old man, Ser Arlan, he used to say I was thick as a castle wall and slow as an aurochs.'

'And strong as an aurochs, by the look of you,' said Baelor Breakspear. 'No harm was done, ser. Rise.'

Dunk got to his feet, wondering if he should keep his head down or if he was allowed to look a prince in the face. *I am speaking with Baelor Targaryen, Prince of Dragonstone, Hand of the King, and heir apparent to the Iron Throne of Aegon the Conqueror. What could a hedge knight dare say to such a person?* 'Y-you gave him back his horse and armor and took no ransom, I remember,' he stammered. 'The old – Ser Arlan, he told me you were the soul of chivalry, and that one day the Seven Kingdoms would be safe in your hands.'

'Not for many a year still, I pray,' Prince Baelor said.

'No,' said Dunk, horrified. He almost said, *I didn't mean that the king should die*, but stopped himself in time. 'I am sorry, m'lord. Your Grace, I mean.'

Belatedly he recalled that the stocky man with the silver beard had addressed Prince Baelor as brother. *He is blood of the dragon as well, damn me for a fool.* He could only be Prince Maekar, the youngest of King Daeron's four sons. Prince Aerys was bookish and Prince Rhaegel mad, meek, and sickly. Neither was like to cross half the realm to attend a tourney, but Maekar was said to be a redoubtable warrior in his own right, though ever in the shadow of his eldest brother.

'You wish to enter the lists, is that it?' asked Prince Baelor. 'That decision rests with the master of the games, but I see no reason to deny you.'

The steward inclined his head. 'As you say, my lord.'

Dunk tried to stammer out thanks, but Prince Maekar cut him off. 'Very well, ser, you are grateful. Now be off with you.'

'You must forgive my noble brother, ser,' said Prince Baelor. 'Two of his sons have gone astray on their way here, and he fears for them.'

'The spring rains have swollen many of the streams,' said Dunk. 'Perhaps the princes are only delayed.'

'I did not come here to take counsel from a hedge knight,' Prince Maekar declared to his brother.

'You may go, ser,' Prince Baelor told Dunk, not unkindly.

'Yes, my lord.' He bowed and turned.

But before he could get away, the prince called after him. 'Ser. One thing more. You are not of Ser Arlan's blood?'

'Yes, m'lord. I mean, no. I'm not.'

The prince nodded at the battered shield Dunk carried, and the winged chalice upon its face. 'By law, only a trueborn son is entitled to inherit a knight's arms. You must needs find a new device, ser, a sigil of your own.'

'I will,' said Dunk. 'Thank you again, Your Grace. I will fight bravely, you'll see.' *As brave as Baelor Breakspear*, the old man would often say.

*

The winesellers and sausage makers were doing a brisk trade, and whores walked brazenly among the stalls and pavilions. Some were pretty enough, one red-haired girl in particular. He could not help staring at her breasts, the way they moved under her loose shift as she sauntered past. He thought of the silver in his pouch. *I could have her, if I liked. She'd like the clink of my coin well enough, I could take her back to my camp and have her, all night if I wanted.* He had never lain with a woman, and for all he knew he might die in his first tilt. Tourneys could be dangerous . . . but whores could be dangerous too, the old man had warned him of that. *She might rob me while I slept, and what would I do then?* When the red-haired girl glanced back over her shoulder at him, Dunk shook his head and walked away.

He found Egg at the puppet show, sitting cross-legged on the ground with the hood of his cloak pulled all the way forward to hide his baldness. The boy had been afraid to enter the castle, which Dunk put down to equal parts shyness and shame. *He does not think himself worthy to mingle with lords and ladies, let alone great princes.* It had been the same with him when he was little. The world beyond Flea Bottom had seemed as frightening as it was exciting. *Egg needs time, that's all.* For the present, it seemed kinder to give the lad a few coppers and let him enjoy himself among the stalls than to drag him along unwilling into the castle.

This morning the puppeteers were doing the tale of Florian and Jonquil. The fat Dornishwoman was working Florian in his armor made of motley, while the tall girl held Jonquil's strings. 'You are no knight,' she was saying as the puppet's mouth moved up and down. 'I know you. You are Florian the Fool.'

'I am, my lady,' the other puppet answered, kneeling. 'As great a fool as ever lived, and as great a knight as well.'

'A fool and a knight?' said Jonquil. 'I have never heard of such a thing.'

'Sweet lady,' said Florian, 'all men are fools, and all men are knights, where women are concerned.'

It was a good show, sad and sweet both, with a sprightly swordfight at the end, and a nicely painted giant. When it was over, the fat woman went among the crowd to collect coins while the girl packed away the puppets.

Dunk collected Egg and went up to her.

'M'lord?' she said, with a sideways glance and a half-smile. She was a head shorter than he was, but still taller than any other girl he had ever seen.

'That was good,' Egg enthused. 'I like how you make them move, Jonquil and the dragon and all. I saw a puppet show last year, but they moved all jerky. Yours are more smooth.'

'Thank you,' she told the boy politely.

Dunk said, 'Your figures are well carved too. The dragon, especially. A fearsome beast. You make them yourself?'

She nodded. 'My uncle does the carving. I paint them.'

'Could you paint something for me? I have the coin to pay.' He slipped the shield off his shoulder and turned it to show her. 'I need to paint something over the chalice.'

The girl glanced at the shield, and then at him. 'What would you want painted?'

Dunk had not considered that. If not the old man's winged chalice, what? His head was empty. *Dunk the lunk, thick as a castle wall.* 'I don't . . . I'm not certain.' His ears were turning red, he realized miserably. 'You must think me an utter fool.'

She smiled. 'All men are fools, and all men are knights.'

'What color paint do you have?' he asked, hoping that might give him an idea.

'I can mix paints to make any color you want.'

The old man's brown had always seemed drab to Dunk. 'The field should be the color of sunset,' he said suddenly. 'The old man liked sunsets. And the device . . .'

'An elm tree,' said Egg. 'A big elm tree, like the one by the pool, with a brown trunk and green branches.'

'Yes,' Dunk said. 'That would serve. An elm tree . . . but with a shooting star above. Could you do that?'

The girl nodded. 'Give me the shield. I'll paint it this very night, and have it back to you on the morrow.'

Dunk handed it over. 'I am called Ser Duncan the Tall.'

'I'm Tanselle,' she laughed. 'Tanselle Too-Tall, the boys used to call me.'

'You're not too tall,' Dunk blurted out. 'You're just right for . . .' He realized what he had been about to say, and blushed furiously.

'For?' said Tanselle, cocking her head inquisitively.

'Puppets,' he finished lamely.

*

The first day of the tourney dawned bright and clear. Dunk bought a sackful of foodstuffs, so they were able to break their fast on goose eggs, fried bread, and bacon, but when the food was cooked he found he had no appetite. His belly felt hard as a rock, even though he knew he would not ride today. The right of first challenge would go to knights of higher birth and greater renown, to lords and their sons and champions from other tourneys.

Egg chattered all though their breakfast, talking of this man and that man and how they might fare. *He was not japing me when he said he knew every good knight in the Seven Kingdoms,* Dunk thought ruefully. He found it humbling to listen so intently to the words of a scrawny orphan boy, but Egg's knowledge might serve him should he face one of these men in a tilt.

The meadow was a churning mass of people, all trying to elbow their way closer for a better view. Dunk was as good an elbower as any, and bigger than most. He squirmed forward to a rise six yards from the fence. When Egg complained that all he could see were arses, Dunk sat the boy on his shoulders. Across the field, the viewing stand was filling up with highborn lords and ladies, a few rich townfolk, and a score of knights who had decided not to compete today. Of Prince Maekar he saw no sign, but he recognized Prince Baelor at Lord Ashford's side. Sunlight flashed golden off the shoulder clasp that held his cloak and the slim coronet about his temples, but otherwise he dressed far more simply than most of the other lords. *He does not look a Targaryen in truth, with that dark hair.* Dunk said as much to Egg.

'It's said he favors his mother,' the boy reminded him. 'She was a Dornish princess.'

The five champions had raised their pavilions at the north end of the lists with the river behind them. The smallest two were orange, and the shields hung outside their doors displayed the white sun-and-chevron. Those would be Lord Ashford's sons Androw and Robert, brothers to the fair maid. Dunk had never heard other knights speak of their prowess, which meant they would likely be the first to fall.

Beside the orange pavilions stood one of deep-dyed green, much larger. The golden rose of Highgarden flapped above it, and the same device was emblazoned on the great green shield outside the door. 'That's Leo Tyrell, Lord of Highgarden,' said Egg.

'I knew that,' said Dunk, irritated. 'The old man and I served at Highgarden before you were ever born.' He hardly remembered that year himself, but Ser Arlan had often spoken of Leo Longthorn, as he was sometimes called; a peerless jouster, for all the silver in his hair. 'That must be Lord Leo beside the tent, the slender graybeard in green and gold.'

'Yes,' said Egg. 'I saw him at King's Landing once. He's not one you'll want to challenge, ser.'

'Boy, I do not require your counsel on who to challenge.'

The fourth pavilion was sewn together from diamond-shaped pieces of cloth, alternating red and white. Dunk did not know the colors, but Egg said they belonged to a knight from the Vale of Arryn named Ser Humfrey Hardyng. 'He won a great melee at Maidenpool last year, ser, and overthrew Ser Donnel of Duskendale and the Lords Arryn and Royce in the lists.'

The last pavilion was Prince Valarr's. Of black silk it was, with a line of pointed scarlet pennons hanging from its roof like long red flames. The shield on its stand was glossy black, emblazoned with the three-headed dragon of House Targaryen. One of the Kingsguard knights stood beside it, his shining white armor stark against the black of the tentcloth. Seeing him there, Dunk wondered whether any of the challengers would dare to touch the dragon shield. Valarr was the king's grandson, after all, and son to Baelor Breakspear.

He need not have worried. When the horns blew to summon the challengers, all five of the maid's champions were called forth to defend her. Dunk could hear the murmur of excitement in the crowd as the challengers appeared one by one at the south end of the lists. Heralds boomed out the name of each knight in turn. They paused before the viewing stand to dip their lances in salute to Lord Ashford, Prince Baelor, and the fair maid, then circled to the north end of the field to select their opponents. The Grey Lion of easterly Rock struck the shield of Lord Tyrell, while his golden-haired heir Ser Tybolt Lannister challenged Lord Ashford's eldest son. Lord Tully of Riverrun tapped the diamond-patterned shield of Ser Humfrey Hardyng, Ser Abelar Hightower knocked upon Valarr's, and the younger Ashford was called out by Ser Lyonel Baratheon, the knight they called the Laughing Storm.

The challengers trotted back to the south end of the lists to await their foes: Ser Abelar in silver and smoke colors, a stone watchtower on his shield, crowned with fire; the two Lannisters all crimson, bearing the golden lion of easterly Rock; the Laughing Storm shining in cloth-of-gold, with a black stag on breast and shield and a rack of iron antlers on his helm; Lord Tully wearing a striped blue-and-red cloak clasped with a silver trout at each shoulder. They pointed their twelve-foot lances skyward, the gusty winds snapping and tugging at the pennons.

At the north end of the field, squires held brightly barded destriers for the champions to mount. They donned their helms and took up lance and shield, in splendor the equal of their foes: the Ashfords' billowing orange silks, Ser Humfrey's red-and-white diamonds, Lord Leo on his white charger with green satin trappings patterned with golden roses, and of course Valarr Targaryen. The Young Prince's horse was black as night, to match the color of his armor, lance, shield, and trappings. Atop his helm was a gleaming three-headed dragon, wings spread, enameled in a rich red; its twin was painted upon the glossy black surface of his shield. Each of the defenders had a wisp of orange silk knotted about an arm, a favor bestowed by the fair maid.

As the champions trotted into position, Ashford Meadow grew almost still. Then a horn sounded, and stillness turned to tumult in half a heartbeat. Ten pairs of gilded spurs drove into the flanks of ten great warhorses, a thousand voices began to scream and shout, forty iron-shod hooves pounded and tore the grass, ten lances dipped and steadied, the field seemed almost to shake, and champions and challengers came together in a rending crash of wood and steel. In an instant, the riders were beyond each other, wheeling about for another pass. Lord Tully reeled in his saddle but managed to keep his seat. When the commons realized that all ten of the lances had broken, a great roar of approval went up. It was a splendid omen for the success of the tourney, and a testament to the skill of the competitors.

Squires handed fresh lances to the jousters to replace the broken ones they cast aside, and once more the spurs dug deep. Dunk could feel the earth trembling beneath the soles of his feet. Atop his shoulders, Egg shouted happily and waved his pipestem arms. The Young Prince passed nearest to them. Dunk saw the point of his black lance kiss the watchtower on his foe's shield and slide off to slam into his chest, even as Ser Abelar's own lance burst into splinters against Valarr's breastplate. The gray stallion in the silver-and-smoke trappings reared with the force of the impact, and Ser Abelar Hightower was lifted from his stirrups and dashed violently to the ground.

Lord Tully was down as well, unhorsed by Ser Humfrey Hardyng, but he sprang up at once and drew his longsword, and Ser Humfrey cast aside his lance – unbroken – and dismounted to continue their fight afoot. Ser Abelar was not so sprightly. His squire ran out, loosened his helm, and called for help, and two servingmen lifted the dazed knight by the arms to help him back to his pavilion. Elsewhere on the field, the six knights who had remained ahorse were riding their third course. More lances shattered, and this time Lord Leo Tyrell aimed his point so expertly he ripped the Grey Lion's helm cleanly off his head. Barefaced, the Lord of Casterly Rock raised his hand in salute and dismounted, yielding the match. By then Ser Humfrey had beaten Lord Tully into surrender, showing himself as skilled with a sword as he was with a lance.

Tybolt Lannister and Androw Ashford rode against each other thrice more before Ser Androw finally lost shield, seat, and match all at once. The younger Ashford lasted even longer, breaking no less than nine lances against Ser Lyonel Baratheon, the Laughing Storm. Champion and challenger both lost their saddles on their tenth course, only to rise together to fight on, sword against mace. Finally a battered Ser Robert Ashford admitted defeat, but on the viewing stand his father looked anything but dejected. Both Lord Ashford's sons had been ushered from the ranks of the champions, it was true, but they had acquitted themselves nobly against two of the finest knights in the Seven Kingdoms.

I must do even better, though, Dunk thought as he watched victor and vanquished embrace and walk together from the field. *It is not enough for me to fight well and lose. I must win at least the first challenge, or I lose all.*

Ser Tybolt Lannister and the Laughing Storm would now take their places among the champions, replacing the men they had defeated. Already the orange pavilions were coming down. A few feet away, the Young Prince sat at his ease in a raised camp chair before his great black tent. His helm was off. He had dark hair like his father, but a bright streak ran through it. A servingman brought him a silver goblet and he took a sip. *Water, if he is wise,* Dunk thought, *wine if not.* He found himself wondering if Valarr had indeed inherited a measure of his father's prowess, or whether it had only been that he had drawn the weakest opponent.

A fanfare of trumpets announced that three new challengers had entered the lists. The heralds shouted their names. 'Ser Pearse of House Caron, Lord of the Marches.' He had a silver harp emblazoned on his shield, though his surcoat was patterned with nightingales. 'Ser Joseth of House Mallister, from Seagard.' Ser Joseth sported a winged helm; on his shield, a silver eagle flew across an indigo sky. 'Ser Gawen of House Swann, Lord of Stonehelm on the Cape of Wrath.' A pair of swans, one black and one white, fought furiously on his arms. Lord Gawen's armor, cloak, and horse bardings were a riot of black and white as well, down to the stripes on his scabbard and lance.

Lord Caron, harper and singer and knight of renown, touched the point of his lance to Lord Tyrell's rose. Ser Joseth thumped on Ser Humfrey Hardyng's diamonds. And the black-and-white knight, Lord Gawen Swann, challenged the black prince with the white guardian. Dunk rubbed his chin. Lord Gawen was even older than the old man, and the old man was dead. 'Egg, who is the least dangerous of these challengers?' he asked the boy on his shoulders, who seemed to know so much of these knights.

'Lord Gawen,' the boy said at once. 'Valarr's foe.'

'*Prince* Valarr,' he corrected. 'A squire must keep a courteous tongue, boy.'

The three challengers took their places as the three champions mounted up. Men were making wagers all around them and calling out encouragement to their choices, but Dunk had eyes only for the prince. On the first pass he struck Lord Gawen's shield a glancing blow, the blunted point of the lance sliding aside just as it had with Ser Abelar Hightower, only this time it was deflected the other way, into empty air. Lord Gawen's own lance broke clean against the prince's chest, and Valarr seemed about to fall for an instant before he recovered his seat.

The second time through the lists, Valarr swung his lance left, aiming for his foe's breast, but struck his shoulder instead. Even so, the blow was enough to make the older knight lose his lance. One arm flailed for balance and Lord Gawen fell. The Young Prince swung from the saddle and drew his sword, but the fallen man waved him off and raised his visor. 'I yield, Your Grace,' he called. 'Well fought.' The lords in the viewing stand echoed him, shouting, *'Well fought! Well fought!'* as Valarr knelt to help the gray-haired lord to his feet.

'It was not either,' Egg complained.

'Be quiet, or you can go back to camp.'

Farther away, Ser Joseth Mallister was being carried off the field unconscious, while the harp lord and the rose lord were going at each other lustily with blunted longaxes, to the delight of the roaring crowd. Dunk was so intent on Valarr Targaryen that he scarcely saw them. *He is a fair knight, but no more than that,* he found himself thinking. *I would have a chance against him. If the gods were good, I might even unhorse him, and once afoot my weight and strength would tell.*

'Get him!' Egg shouted merrily, shifting his seat on Dunk's back in his excitement. 'Get him! Hit him! Yes! He's right there, he's right there!' It seemed to be Lord Caron he was cheering on. The harper was playing a different sort of music now, driving Lord Leo back and back as steel sang on steel. The crowd seemed almost equally divided between them, so cheers and curses mingled freely in the morning air. Chips of wood and paint were flying from Lord Leo's shield as Lord Pearse's axe knocked the petals off his golden rose, one by one, until the shield finally shattered and split. But as it did, the axehead hung up for an instant in the wood . . . and Lord Leo's own axe crashed down on the haft of his foe's weapon, breaking it off not a foot from his hand. He cast aside his broken shield, and suddenly he was the one on the attack. Within moments, the harper knight was on one knee, singing his surrender.

For the rest of the morning and well into the afternoon, it was more of the same, as challengers took the field in twos and threes, and sometimes five together. Trumpets blew, the heralds called out names, warhorses charged, the crowd cheered, lances snapped like twigs, and swords rang against helms and mail. It was, smallfolk and high lord alike agreed, a splendid day of jousting. Ser Humfrey Hardyng and Ser Humfrey Beesbury, a bold young knight in yellow and black stripes with three beehives on his shield, splintered no less than a dozen lances apiece in an epic struggle the smallfolk soon began calling 'the Battle of Humfrey.' Ser

Tybolt Lannister was unhorsed by Ser Jon Penrose and broke his sword in his fall, but fought back with shield alone to win the bout and remain a champion. One-eyed Ser Robyn Rhysling, a grizzled old knight with a salt-and-pepper beard, lost his helm to Lord Leo's lance in their first course, yet refused to yield. Three times more they rode at each other, the wind whipping Ser Robyn's hair while the shards of broken lances flew round his bare face like wooden knives, which Dunk thought all the more wondrous when Egg told him that Ser Robyn had lost his eye to a splinter from a broken lance not five years earlier. Leo Tyrell was too chivalrous to aim another lance at Ser Robyn's unprotected head, but even so Rhysling's stubborn courage (or was it folly?) left Dunk astounded. Finally the Lord of Highgarden struck Ser Robyn's breastplate a solid thump right over the heart and sent him cartwheeling to the earth.

Ser Lyonel Baratheon also fought several notable matches. Against lesser foes, he would often break into booming laughter the moment they touched his shield, and laugh all the time he was mounting and charging and knocking them from their stirrups. If his challengers wore any sort of crest on their helm, Ser Lyonel would strike it off and fling it into the crowd. The crests were ornate things, made of carved wood or shaped leather, and sometimes gilded and enameled or even wrought in pure silver, so the men he beat did not appreciate this habit, though it made him a great favorite of the commons. Before long, only crestless men were choosing him. As loud and often as Ser Lyonel laughed down a challenger, though, Dunk thought the day's honors should go to Ser Humfrey Hardyng, who humbled fourteen knights, each one of them formidable.

Meanwhile the Young Prince sat outside his black pavilion, drinking from his silver goblet and rising from time to time to mount his horse and vanquish yet another undistinguished foe. He had won nine victories, but it seemed to Dunk that every one was hollow. *He is beating old men and upjumped squires, and a few lords of high birth and low skill. The truly dangerous men are riding past his shield as if they do not see it.*

Late in the day, a brazen fanfare announced the entry of a new challenger to the lists. He rode in on a great red charger whose black bardings were slashed to reveal glimpses of yellow, crimson, and orange beneath. As he approached the viewing stand to make his salute, Dunk saw the face beneath the raised visor, and recognized the prince he'd met in Lord Ashford's stables.

Egg's legs tightened around his neck. 'Stop that,' Dunk snapped, yanking them apart. 'Do you mean to choke me?'

'*Prince Aerion Brightflame,*' a herald called, '*of the Red Keep of King's Landing, son of Maekar Prince of Summerhall of House Targaryen, grandson to Daeron the*

Good, the Second of His Name, King of the Andals, the Rhoynar, and the First Men, and Lord of the Seven Kingdoms.'

Aerion bore a three-headed dragon on his shield, but it was rendered in colors much more vivid than Valarr's; one head was orange, one yellow, one red, and the flames they breathed had the sheen of gold leaf. His surcoat was a swirl of smoke and fire woven together, and his blackened helm was surmounted by a crest of red enamel flames.

After a pause to dip his lance to Prince Baelor, a pause so brief that it was almost perfunctory, he galloped to the north end of the field, past Lord Leo's pavilion and the Laughing Storm's, slowing only when he approached Prince Valarr's tent. The Young Prince rose and stood stiffly beside his shield, and for a moment Dunk was certain that Aerion meant to strike it . . . but then he laughed and trotted past, and banged his point hard against Ser Humfrey Hardyng's diamonds.

'Come out, come out, little knight,' he sang in a loud clear voice, 'it's time you faced the dragon.'

Ser Humfrey inclined his head stiffly to his foe as his destrier was brought out, and then ignored him while he mounted, fastened his helm, and took up lance and shield. The spectators grew quiet as the two knights took their places. Dunk heard the *clang* of Prince Aerion dropping his visor. The horn blew.

Ser Humfrey broke slowly, building speed, but his foe raked the red charger hard with both spurs, coming hard. Egg's legs tightened again. '*Kill him!*' he shouted suddenly. '*Kill him, he's right there, kill him, kill him, kill him!*' Dunk was not certain which of the knights he was shouting to.

Prince Aerion's lance, gold-tipped and painted in stripes of red, orange, and yellow, swung down across the barrier. *Low, too low,* thought Dunk the moment he saw it. *He'll miss the rider and strike Ser Humfrey's horse, he needs to bring it up.* Then, with dawning horror, he began to suspect that Aerion intended no such thing. *He cannot mean to . . .*

At the last possible instant, Ser Humfrey's stallion reared away from the oncoming point, eyes rolling in terror, but too late. Aerion's lance took the animal just above the armor that protected his breastbone, and exploded out of the back of his neck in a gout of bright blood. Screaming, the horse crashed sideways, knocking the wooden barrier to pieces as he fell. Ser Humfrey tried to leap free, but a foot caught in a stirrup and they heard his shriek as his leg was crushed between the splintered fence and falling horse.

All of Ashford Meadow was shouting. Men ran onto the field to extricate Ser Humfrey, but the stallion, dying in agony, kicked at them as they approached. Aerion, having raced blithely around the carnage to the end of the lists, wheeled his horse and came galloping back. He was shouting too, though Dunk could not make out the words over the almost human screams of the dying horse. Vaulting from the saddle, Aerion drew his sword and advanced on his fallen foe. His own squires and one of Ser Humfrey's had to pull him back. Egg squirmed on Dunk's shoulders. 'Let me down,' the boy said. 'The poor horse, *let me down.*'

Dunk felt sick himself. *What would I do if such a fate befell Thunder?* A man-at-arms with a poleaxe dispatched Ser Humfrey's stallion, ending the hideous screams. Dunk turned and forced his way through the press. When he came to open ground, he lifted Egg off his shoulders. The boy's hood had fallen back and his eyes were red. 'A terrible sight, aye,' he told the lad, 'but a squire must needs be strong. You'll see worse mishaps at other tourneys, I fear.'

'It was no mishap,' Egg said, mouth trembling. 'Aerion meant to do it. You saw.'

Dunk frowned. It had looked that way to him as well, but it was hard to accept that any knight could be so unchivalrous, least of all one who was blood of the dragon. 'I saw a knight green as summer grass lose control of his lance,' he said stubbornly, 'and I'll hear no more of it. The jousting is done for the day, I think. Come, lad.'

*

He was right about the end of the day's contests. By the time the chaos had been set to rights, the sun was low in the west, and Lord Ashford had called a halt. As the shadows of evening crept across the meadow, a hundred torches were lit along the merchants' row. Dunk bought a horn of ale for himself and half a horn for the boy, to cheer him. They wandered for a time, listening to a sprightly air on pipes and drums and watching a puppet show about Nymeria, the warrior queen with the ten thousand ships. The puppeteers had only two ships, but managed a rousing sea battle all same. Dunk wanted to ask the girl Tanselle if she had finished painting his shield, but he could see that she was busy. *I'll wait until she is done for the night*, he resolved. *Perhaps she'll have a thirst then.*

'Ser Duncan,' a voice called behind him. And then again, 'Ser Duncan.' Suddenly Dunk remembered that was him. 'I saw you among the smallfolk today, with this boy on your shoulders,' said Raymun Fossoway as he came up, smiling. 'Indeed, the two of you were hard to miss.'

'The boy is my squire. Egg, this is Raymun Fossoway.' Dunk had to pull the boy forward, and even then Egg lowered his head and stared at Raymun's boots as he mumbled a greeting.

'Well met, lad,' Raymun said easily. 'Ser Duncan, why not watch from the viewing gallery? All knights are welcome there.'

Dunk was at ease among smallfolk and servants; the idea of claiming a place among the lords, ladies, and landed knights made him uncomfortable. 'I would not have wanted any closer view of that last tilt.'

Raymun grimaced. 'Nor I. Lord Ashford declared Ser Humfrey the victor and awarded him Prince Aerion's courser, but even so, he will not be able to continue. His leg was broken in two places. Prince Baelor sent his own maester to tend him.'

'Will there be another champion in Ser Humfrey's place?'

'Lord Ashford had a mind to grant the place to Lord Caron, or perhaps the other Ser Humfrey, the one who gave Hardyng such a splendid match, but Prince Baelor told him that it would not be seemly to remove Ser Humfrey's shield and pavilion under the circumstances. I believe they will continue with four champions in place of five.'

Four champions, Dunk thought. *Leo Tyrell, Lyonel Baratheon, Tybolt Lannister, and Prince Valarr.* He had seen enough this first day to know how little chance he would stand against the first three. Which left only . . .

A hedge knight cannot challenge a prince. Valarr is second in line to the Iron Throne. He is Baelor Breakspear's son, and his blood is the blood of Aegon the Conqueror and the Young Dragon and Prince Aemon the Dragonknight, and I am some boy the old man found behind a pot shop in Flea Bottom.

His head hurt just thinking about it. 'Who does your cousin mean to challenge?' he asked Raymun.

'Ser Tybolt, all things being equal. They are well matched. My cousin keeps a sharp watch on every tilt, though. Should any man be wounded on the morrow, or show signs of exhaustion or weakness, Steffon will be quick to knock on his shield, you may count on it. No one has ever accused him of an excess of chivalry.' He laughed, as if to take the sting from his words. 'Ser Duncan, will you join me for a cup of wine?'

'I have a matter I must attend to,' said Dunk, uncomfortable with the notion of accepting hospitality he could not return.

'I could wait here and bring your shield when the puppet show is over, ser,' said Egg. 'They're going to do Symeon Star-Eyes later, and make the dragon fight again as well.'

'There, you see, your matter is attended to, and the wine awaits,' said Raymun. 'It's an Arbor vintage, too. How can you refuse me?'

Bereft of excuses, Dunk had no choice but to follow, leaving Egg at the puppet show. The apple of House Fossoway flew above the gold-colored pavilion where Raymun attended his cousin. Behind it, two servants were basting a goat with honey and herbs over a small cookfire. 'There's food as well, if you're hungry,' Raymun said negligently as he held the flap for Dunk. A brazier of coals lit the interior and made the air pleasantly warm. Raymun filled two cups with wine. 'They say Aerion is in a rage at Lord Ashford for awarding his charger to Ser Humfrey,' he commented as he poured, 'but I'll wager it was his uncle who counseled it.' He handed Dunk a wine cup.

'Prince Baelor is an honorable man.'

'As the Bright Prince is not?' Raymun laughed. 'Don't look so anxious, Ser Duncan, there's none here but us. It is no secret that Aerion is a bad piece of work. Thank the gods that he is well down in the order of succession.'

'You truly believe he meant to kill the horse?'

'Is there any doubt of it? If Prince Maekar had been here, it would have gone differently, I promise you. Aerion is all smiles and chivalry so long as his father is watching, if the tales be true, but when he's not . . .'

'I saw that Prince Maekar's chair was empty.'

'He's left Ashford to search for his sons, along with Roland Crakehall of the Kingsguard. There's a wild tale of robber knights going about, but I'll wager the prince is just off drunk again.'

The wine was fine and fruity, as good a cup as he had ever tasted. He rolled it in his mouth, swallowed, and said, 'Which prince is this now?'

'Maekar's heir. Daeron, he's named, after the king. They call him Daeron the Drunken, though not in his father's hearing. The youngest boy was with him as well. They left Summerhall together but never reached Ashford.' Raymun drained his cup and set it aside. 'Poor Maekar.'

'Poor?' said Dunk, startled. 'The king's son?'

'The king's *fourth* son,' said Raymun, 'not quite as bold as Prince Baelor, nor as clever as Prince Aerys, nor as gentle as Prince Rhaegel. And now he must suffer seeing his own sons overshadowed by his brother's. Daeron is a sot, Aerion is vain and cruel, the third son was so unpromising they gave him to the Citadel to make a maester of him, and the youngest—'

'*Ser! Ser Duncan!*' Egg burst in panting. His hood had fallen back, and the light from the brazier shone in his big dark eyes. 'You have to run, he's hurting her!'

Dunk lurched to his feet, confused. 'Hurting? Who?'

'*Aerion!*' the boy shouting. 'He's *hurting* her. The puppet girl. Hurry.' Whirling, he darted back out into the night.

Dunk made to follow, but Raymun caught his arm. 'Ser Duncan. Aerion, he said. A prince of the blood. Be careful.'

It was good counsel, he knew. The old man would have said the same. But he could not listen. He wrenched free of Raymun's hand and shouldered his way out of the pavilion. He could hear shouting off in the direction of the merchants' row. Egg was almost out of sight. Dunk ran after him. His legs were long and the boy's short; he quickly closed the distance.

A wall of watchers had gathered around the puppeteers. Dunk

shouldered through them, ignoring their curses. A man-at-arms in the royal livery stepped up to block him. Dunk put a big hand on his chest and shoved, sending the man flailing backward to sprawl on his arse in the dirt.

The puppeteer's stall had been knocked on its side. The fat Dornishwoman was on the ground weeping. One man-at-arms was dangling the puppets of Florian and Jonquil from his hands as another set them afire with a torch. Three more men were opening chests, spilling more puppets on the ground and stamping on them. The dragon puppet was scattered all about them, a broken wing here, its head there, its tail in three pieces. And in the midst of it all stood Prince Aerion, resplendent in a red velvet doublet with long dagged sleeves, twisting Tanselle's arm in both hands. She was on her knees, pleading with him. Aerion ignored her. He forced open her hand and seized one of her fingers. Dunk stood there stupidly, not quite believing what he saw. Then he heard a *crack*, and Tanselle screamed.

One of Aerion's men tried to grab him, and went flying. Three long strides, then Dunk grabbed the prince's shoulder and wrenched him around hard. His sword and dagger were forgotten, along with everything the old man had ever taught him. His fist knocked Aerion off his feet, and the toe of his boot slammed into the prince's belly. When Aerion went for his knife, Dunk stepped on his wrist and then kicked him again, right in the mouth. He might have kicked him to death right then and there, but the princeling's men swarmed over him. He had a man on each arm and another pounding him across the back. No sooner had he wrestled free of one than two more were on him.

Finally they shoved him down and pinned his arms and legs. Aerion was on his feet again. The prince's mouth was bloody. He pushed inside it with a finger. 'You've loosened one of my teeth,' he complained, 'so we'll start by breaking all of yours.' He pushed his hair from his eyes. 'You look familiar.'

'You took me for a stableboy.'

Aerion smiled redly. 'I recall. You refused to take my horse. Why did you throw your life away? For this whore?' Tanselle was curled up on the ground, cradling her maimed hand. He gave her a shove with the toe of his boot. 'She's scarcely worth it. A traitor. The dragon ought never to lose.'

He is mad, thought Dunk, *but he is still a prince's son, and he means to kill me*. He might have prayed then, if he had known a prayer all the way through, but there was no time. There was hardly even time to be afraid.

'Nothing more to say?' said Aerion. 'You bore me, ser.' He poked at his bloody mouth again. 'Get a hammer and break all his teeth out, Wate,' he commanded, 'and then let's cut him open and show him the color of his entrails.'

'No!' a boy's voice said. 'Don't hurt him!'

Gods be good, the boy, the brave foolish boy, Dunk thought. He fought against the arms restraining him, but it was no good. 'Hold your tongue, you stupid boy. Run away. They'll hurt you!'

'No they won't.' Egg moved closer. 'If they do, they'll answer to my father. And my uncle as well. Let go of him, I said. Wate, Yorkel, you know me. Do as I say.'

The hands holding his left arm were gone, and then the others. Dunk did not understand what was happening. The men-at-arms were backing away. One even knelt. Then the crowd parted for Raymun Fossoway. He had donned mail and helm, and his hand was on his sword. His cousin Ser Steffon, just behind him, had already bared his blade, and with them were a half-dozen men-at-arms with the red apple badge sewn on their breasts.

Prince Aerion paid them no mind.' Impudent little wretch,' he said to Egg, spitting a mouthful of blood at the boy's feet. 'What happened to your hair?'

'I cut it off, brother,' said Egg. 'I didn't want to look like you.'

*

The second day of the tourney was overcast, with a gusty wind blowing from the west. *The crowds should be less on a day like this,* Dunk thought. *It would have been easier for them to find a spot near the fence to see the jousting up close. Egg might have sat on the rail, while I stood behind him.*

Instead Egg would have a seat in the viewing box, dressed in silks and furs, while Dunk's view would be limited to the four walls of the tower cell where Lord Ashford's men had confined him. The chamber had a window, but it faced in the wrong direction. Even so, Dunk crammed himself into the window seat as the sun came up, and stared gloomily off across town and field and forest. They had taken his hempen sword belt, and his sword and dagger with it, and they had taken his silver as well. He hoped Egg or Raymun would remember Chestnut and Thunder.

'Egg,' he muttered low under his breath. His squire, a poor lad plucked from the streets of King's Landing. Had ever a knight been made such a fool? *Dunk the lunk, thick as a castle wall and slow as an aurochs.*

He had not been permitted to speak to Egg since Lord Ashford's soldiers had scooped them all up at the puppet show. Nor Raymun, nor Tanselle, nor anyone, not even Lord Ashford himself. He wondered if he would ever see any of them again. For all he knew, they meant to keep him in this small room until he died. *What did I think would happen?* he asked himself bitterly. *I knocked down a prince's son and kicked him in the face.*

Beneath these gray skies, the flowing finery of the highborn lords and great champions would not seem quite so splendid as it had the day before. The sun, walled behind the clouds, would not brush their steel helms with brilliance, nor make their gold and silver chasings glitter and flash, but even so, Dunk wished he were in the crowd to watch the jousting. It would be a good day for hedge knights, for men in plain mail on unbarded horses.

He could *hear* them, at least. The horns of the heralds carried well, and from time to time a roar from the crowd told him that someone had fallen, or risen, or done something especially bold. He heard faint hoofbeats too, and once in a great while the clash of swords or the *snap* of a lance. Dunk winced whenever he heard that last; it reminded him of the noise Tanselle's finger had made when Aerion broke it. There were other sounds too, closer at hand: footfalls in the hall outside his door, the stamp of hooves in the yard below, shouts and voices from the castle walls. Sometimes they drowned out the tourney. Dunk supposed that was just as well.

'A hedge knight is the truest kind of knight, Dunk,' the old man had told him, a long long time ago. 'Other knights serve the lords who keep them, or from whom they hold their lands, but we serve where we will, for men whose causes we believe in. Every knight swears to protect the weak and innocent, but we keep the vow best, I think.' Queer how strong that memory seemed. Dunk had quite forgotten those words. And perhaps the old man had as well, toward the end.

The morning turned to afternoon. The distant sounds of the tourney began to dwindle and die. Dusk began to seep into the cell, but Dunk still sat in the window seat, looking out on the gathering dark and trying to ignore his empty belly.

And then he heard footsteps and a jangling of iron keys. He uncoiled and rose to his feet as the door opened. Two guards pushed in, one bearing an oil lamp. A servingman followed with a tray of food. Behind came Egg. 'Leave the lamp and the food and go,' the boy told them.

They did as he commanded, though Dunk noticed that they left the heavy wooden door ajar. The smell of the food made him realize how ravenous he was. There was hot bread and honey, a bowl of pease porridge, a skewer of roast onions and well-charred meat. He sat by the tray, pulled apart the bread with his hands, and stuffed some into his mouth. 'There's no knife,' he observed. 'Did they think I'd stab you, boy?'

'They didn't tell me what they thought.' Egg wore a close-fitting black wool doublet with a tucked waist and long sleeves lined with red satin. Across his chest was sewn the three-headed dragon of House Targaryen. 'My uncle says I must humbly beg your forgiveness for deceiving you.'

'Your uncle,' said Dunk. 'That would be Prince Baelor.'

The boy looked miserable. 'I never meant to lie.'

'But you did. About everything. Starting with your name. I never heard of a Prince Egg.'

'It's short for Aegon. My brother Aemon named me Egg. He's off at the Citadel now, learning to be a maester. And Daeron sometimes calls me Egg as well, and so do my sisters.'

Dunk lifted the skewer and bit into a chunk of meat. Goat, flavored with some lordly spice he'd never tasted before. Grease ran down his chin. 'Aegon,' he repeated. 'Of course it would be Aegon. Like Aegon the Dragon. How many Aegons have been king?'

'Four,' the boy said. 'Four Aegons.'

Dunk chewed, swallowed, and tore off some more bread. 'Why did you do it? Was it some jape, to make a fool of the stupid hedge knight?'

'No.' The boy's eyes filled with tears, but he stood there manfully. 'I was supposed to squire for Daeron. He's my oldest brother. I learned everything I had to learn to be a good squire, but Daeron isn't a very good knight. He didn't want to ride in the tourney, so after we left Summerhall he stole away from our escort, only instead of doubling back he went straight on toward Ashford, thinking they'd never look for us that way. It was him shaved my head. He knew my father would send men hunting us. Daeron has common hair, sort of a pale brown, nothing special, but mine is like Aerion's and my father's.'

'The blood of the dragon,' Dunk said. 'Silver-gold hair and purple eyes, everyone knows that.' *Thick as a castle wall, Dunk.*

'Yes. So Daeron shaved it off. He meant for us to hide until the tourney was over. Only then you took me for a stableboy, and . . .' He lowered his eyes. 'I didn't care if Daeron fought or not, but I wanted to be somebody's squire. I'm sorry, ser. I truly am.'

Dunk looked at him thoughtfully. He knew what it was like to want something so badly that you would tell a monstrous lie just to get near it. 'I thought you were like me,' he said. 'Might be you are. Only not the way I thought.'

'We're both from King's Landing still,' the boy said hopefully.

Dunk had to laugh. 'Yes, you from the top of Aegon's Hill and me from the bottom.'

'That's not so far, ser.'

Dunk took a bite from an onion. 'Do I need to call you *m'lord* or *Your Grace* or something?'

'At court,' the boy admitted, 'but other times you can keep on calling me Egg if you like. Ser.'

'What will they do with me, Egg?'

'My uncle wants to see you. After you're done eating, ser.'

Dunk shoved the platter aside, and stood. 'I'm done now, then. I've already kicked one prince in the mouth, I don't mean to keep another waiting.'

*

Lord Ashford had turned his own chambers over to Prince Baelor for the duration of his stay, so it was to the lord's solar that Egg – no, *Aegon*, he would have to get used to that – conducted him. Baelor sat reading by the light of beeswax candle. Dunk knelt before him. 'Rise,' the prince said. 'Would you care for wine?'

'As it please you, Your Grace.'

'Pour Ser Duncan a cup of the sweet Dornish red, Aegon,' the prince commanded. 'Try not to spill it on him, you've done him sufficient ill already.'

'The boy won't spill, Your Grace,' said Dunk. 'He's a good boy. A good squire. And he meant no harm to me, I know.'

'One need not intend harm to do it. Aegon should have come to me when he saw what his brother was doing to those puppeteers. Instead he ran to you. That was no kindness. What you did, ser . . . well, I might have done the same in your place, but I am a prince of the realm, not a hedge knight. It is never wise to strike a king's grandson in anger, no matter the cause.'

Dunk nodded grimly. Egg offered him a silver goblet, brimming with wine. He accepted it and took a long swallow.

'I *hate* Aerion,' Egg said with vehemence. 'And I had to run for Ser Duncan, uncle, the castle was too far.'

'Aerion is your brother,' the prince said firmly, 'and the septons say we must love our brothers. Aegon, leave us now, I would speak with Ser Duncan privately.'

The boy put down the flagon of wine and bowed stiffly. 'As you will, Your Grace.' He went to the door of the solar and closed it softly behind him.

Baelor Breakspear studied Dunk's eyes for a long moment. 'Ser Duncan, let me ask you this – how good a knight are you, truly? How skilled at arms?'

Dunk did not know what to say. 'Ser Arlan taught me sword and shield, and how to tilt at rings and quintains.'

Prince Baelor seemed troubled by that answer. 'My brother Maekar returned to the castle a few hours ago. He found his heir drunk in an inn a day's ride to the south. Maekar would never admit as much, but I believe it was his secret hope that his sons might outshine mine in this tourney.

Instead they have both shamed him, but what is he to do? They are blood of his blood. Maekar is angry, and must needs have a target for his wrath. He has chosen you.'

'Me?' Dunk said miserably.

'Aerion has already filled his father's ear. And Daeron has not helped you either. To excuse his own cowardice, he told my brother that a huge robber knight, chance met on the road, made off with Aegon. I fear you have been cast as this robber knight, ser. In Daeron's tale, he has spent all these days pursuing you hither and yon, to win back his brother.'

'But Egg will tell him the truth. Aegon, I mean.'

'Egg *will* tell him, I have no doubt,' said Prince Baelor, 'but the boy has been known to lie too, as you have good reason to recall. Which son will my brother believe? As for the matter of these puppeteers, by the time Aerion is done twisting the tale it will be high treason. The dragon is the sigil of the royal House. To portray one being slain, sawdust blood spilling from its neck . . . well, it was doubtless innocent, but it was far from wise. Aerion calls it a veiled attack on House Targaryen, an incitement to revolt. Maekar will likely agree. My brother has a prickly nature, and he has placed all his best hopes on Aerion, since Daeron has been such a grave disappointment to him.' The prince took a sip of wine, then set the goblet aside. 'Whatever my brother believes or fails to believe, one truth is beyond dispute. You laid hands upon the blood of the dragon. For that offense, you must be tried, and judged, and punished.'

'Punished?' Dunk did not like the sound of that.

'Aerion would like your head, with or without teeth. He will not have it, I promise you, but I cannot deny him a trial. As my royal father is hundreds of leagues away, my brother and I must sit in judgment of you, along with Lord Ashford, whose domains these are, and Lord Tyrell of Highgarden, his liege lord. The last time a man was found guilty of striking one of royal blood, it was decreed that he should lose the offending hand.'

'My *hand*?' said Dunk, aghast.

'And your foot. You kicked him too, did you not?'

Dunk could not speak.

'To be sure, I will urge my fellow judges to be merciful. I am the King's Hand and the heir to the throne, my word carries some weight. But so does my brother's. The risk is there.'

'I,' said Dunk, 'I . . . Your Grace, I . . .' *They meant no treason, it was only a wooden dragon, it was never meant to be a royal prince,* he wanted to say, but his words had deserted him once and all. He had never been any good with words.

'You have another choice, though,' Prince Baelor said quietly. 'Whether it is a better choice or a worse one, I cannot say, but I remind you that any knight accused of a crime has the right to demand trial by combat. So I ask you once again, Ser Duncan the Tall – how good a knight are you? Truly?'

*

'A trial of seven,' said Prince Aerion, smiling. 'That is my right, I do believe.'

Prince Baelor drummed his fingers on the table, frowning. To his left, Lord Ashford nodded slowly.

'Why?' Prince Maekar demanded, leaning forward toward his son. 'Are you afraid to face this hedge knight alone, and let the gods decide the truth of your accusations?'

'Afraid?' said Aerion. 'Of such as this? Don't be absurd, Father. My thought is for my beloved brother. Daeron has been wronged by this Ser Duncan as well, and has first claim to his blood. A trial of seven allows both of us to face him.'

'Do me no favors, brother,' muttered Daeron Targaryen. The eldest son of Prince Maekar looked even worse than he had when Dunk had encountered him in the inn. He seemed to be sober this time, his red-and-black doublet unstained by wine, but his eyes were bloodshot, and a fine sheen of sweat covered his brow. 'I am content to cheer you on as you slay the rogue.'

'You are too kind, sweet brother,' said Prince Aerion, all smiles, 'but it would be selfish of me to deny you the right to prove the truth of your words at the hazard of your body. I must insist upon a trial of seven.'

Dunk was lost. 'Your Graces, my lords,' he said to the dais. 'I do not understand. What is this *trial of seven?*'

Prince Baelor shifted uncomfortably in his seat. 'It is another form of trial by combat. Ancient, seldom invoked. It came across the narrow sea with the Andals and their seven gods. In any trial by combat, the accuser and accused are asking the gods to decide the issue between them. The Andals believed that if the seven champions fought on each side, the gods, being thus honored, would be more like to take a hand and see that a just result was achieved.'

'Or mayhap they simply had a taste for swordplay,' said Lord Leo Tyrell, a cynical smile touching his lips. 'Regardless, Ser Aerion is within his rights. A trial of seven it must be.'

'I must fight *seven men*, then?' Dunk asked hopelessly.

'Not alone, ser,' Prince Maekar said impatiently. 'Don't play the fool, it will not serve. It must be seven against seven. You must needs find six other knights to fight beside you.'

Six knights, Dunk thought. They might as well have told him to find six thousand. He had no brothers, no cousins, no old comrades who had stood beside him in battle. Why would six strangers risk their own lives to defend a hedge knight against two royal princelings? 'Your Graces, my lords,' he said, 'what if no one will take my part?'

Maekar Targaryen looked down on him coldly. 'If a cause is just, good men will fight for it. If you can find no champions, ser, it will be because you are guilty. Could anything be more plain?'

*

Dunk had never felt so alone as he did when he walked out the gates of Ashford Castle and heard the portcullis rattle down behind him. A soft rain was falling, light as dew on his skin, and yet he shivered at the touch of it. Across the river, colored rings haloed the scant few pavilions where fires still burned. The night was half gone, he guessed. Dawn would be on him in few hours. *And with dawn comes death.*

They had given him back his sword and silver, yet as he waded across the ford, his thoughts were bleak. He wondered if they expected him to saddle a horse and flee. He could, if he wished. That would be the end of his knighthood, to be sure; he would be no more than an outlaw henceforth, until the day some lord took him and struck off his head. *Better to die a knight than live like that*, he told himself stubbornly. Wet to the knee, he trudged past the empty lists. Most of the pavilions were dark, their owners long asleep, but here and there a few candles still burned. Dunk heard soft moans and cries of pleasure coming from within one tent. It made him wonder whether he would die without ever having known a maid.

Then he heard the snort of a horse, a snort he somehow knew for Thunder's. He turned his steps and ran, and there he was, tied up with Chestnut outside a round pavilion lit from within by a vague golden glow. On its center pole the banner hung sodden, but Dunk could still make out the dark curve of the Fossoway apple. It looked like hope.

'A trial by combat,' Raymun said heavily. 'Gods be good, Duncan, that means lances of war, morningstars, battle-axes . . . the swords won't be blunted, do you understand that?'

'Raymun the Reluctant,' mocked his cousin Ser Steffon. An apple made of gold and garnets fastened his cloak of yellow wool. 'You need not fear, cousin, this is a knightly combat. As you are no knight, your skin is not at risk. Ser Duncan, you have one Fossoway at least. The ripe one. I saw what Aerion did to those puppeteers. I am for you.'

'And I,' snapped Raymun angrily. 'I only meant—'

His cousin cut him off. 'Who else fights with us, Ser Duncan?'

Dunk spread his hands hopelessly. 'I know no one else. Well, except for

Ser Manfred Dondarrion. He wouldn't even vouch that I was a knight, he'll never risk his life for me.'

Ser Steffon seemed little perturbed. 'Then we need five more good men. Fortunately, I have more than five friends. Leo Longthorn, the Laughing Storm, Lord Caron, the Lannisters, Ser Otho Bracken . . . aye, and the Blackwoods as well, though you will never get Blackwood and Bracken on the same side of a melee. I shall go and speak with some of them.'

'They won't be happy at being woken,' his cousin objected.

'Excellent,' declared Ser Steffon. 'If they are angry, they'll fight all the more fiercely. You may rely on me, Ser Duncan. Cousin, if I do not return before dawn, bring my armor and see that Wrath is saddled and barded for me. I shall meet you both in the challengers' paddock.' He laughed. 'This will be a day long remembered, I think.' When he strode from the tent, he looked almost happy.

Not so Raymun. 'Five knights,' he said glumly after his cousin had gone. 'Duncan, I am loath to dash your hopes, but . . .'

'If your cousin can bring the men he speaks of . . .'

'Leo Longthorn? The Brute of Bracken? The Laughing Storm?' Raymun stood. 'He knows all of them, I have no doubt, but I would be less certain that any of them know him. Steffon sees this as a chance for glory, but it means your life. You should find your own men. I'll help. Better you have too many champions than too few.' A noise outside made Raymun turn his head. 'Who goes there?' he demanded, as a boy ducked through the flap, followed by a thin man in a rain-sodden black cloak.

'Egg?' Dunk got to his feet. 'What are you doing here?'

'I'm your squire,' the boy said. 'You'll need someone to arm you, ser.'

'Does your lord father know you've left the castle?'

'Gods be good, I hope not.' Daeron Targaryen undid the clasp of his cloak and let it slide from his thin shoulders.

'*You*? Are you mad, coming here?' Dunk pulled his knife from his sheath. 'I ought to shove this through your belly.'

'Probably,' Prince Daeron admitted. 'Though I'd sooner you poured me a cup of wine. Look at my hands.' He held one out and let them all see how it shook.

Dunk stepped toward him, glowering. 'I don't care about your hands. You lied about me.'

'I had to say *something* when my father demanded to know where my little brother had gotten to,' the prince replied. He seated himself, ignoring Dunk and his knife. 'If truth be told, I hadn't even realized Egg was gone. He wasn't at the bottom of my wine cup, and I hadn't looked anywhere else, so . . .' He sighed.

'Ser, my father is going to join the seven accusers,' Egg broke in. 'I begged him not to, but he won't listen. He says it is the only way to redeem Aerion's honor, and Daeron's.'

'Not that I ever asked to have my honor redeemed,' said Prince Daeron sourly. 'Whoever has it can keep it, so far as I'm concerned. Still, here we are. For what it's worth, Ser Duncan, you have little to fear from me. The only thing I like less than horses are swords. Heavy things, and beastly sharp. I'll do my best to look gallant in the first charge, but after that . . . well, perhaps you could strike me a nice blow to the side of the helm. Make it ring, but not *too* loud, if you take my meaning. My brothers have my measure when it comes to fighting and dancing and thinking and reading books, but none of them is half my equal at lying insensible in the mud.'

Dunk could only stare at him, and wonder whether the princeling was trying to play him for a fool. 'Why did you come?'

'To warn you of what you face,' Daeron said. 'My father has commanded the Kingsguard to fight with him.'

'The Kingsguard?' said Dunk, appalled.

'Well, the three who are here. Thank the gods Uncle Baelor left the other four at King's Landing with our royal grandfather.'

Egg supplied the names. 'Ser Roland Crakehall, Ser Donnel of Dusken-dale, and Ser Willem Wylde.'

'They have small choice in the matter,' said Daeron. 'They are sworn to protect the lives of the king and royal family, and my brothers and I are blood of the dragon, gods help us.'

Dunk counted on his fingers. 'That makes six. Who is the seventh man?'

Prince Daeron shrugged. 'Aerion will find someone. If need be, he will buy a champion. He has no lack of gold.'

'Who do you have?' Egg asked.

'Raymun's cousin Ser Steffon.'

Daeron winced. 'Only one?'

'Ser Steffon has gone to some of his friends.'

'I can bring people,' said Egg. 'Knights. I can.'

'Egg,' said Dunk, 'I will be fighting your own brothers.'

'You won't hurt Daeron, though,' the boy said. 'He told you he'd fall down. And Aerion . . . I remember, when I was little, he used to come into my bedchamber at night and put his knife between my legs. He had too many brothers, he'd say, maybe one night he'd make me his sister, then he could marry me. He threw my cat in the well too. He says he didn't, but he always lies.'

Prince Daeron gave a weary shrug. 'Egg has the truth of it. Aerion's quite the monster. He thinks he's a dragon in human form, you know. That's why he was so wroth at that puppet show. A pity he wasn't born a

Fossoway, then he'd think himself an apple and we'd all be a deal safer, but there you are.' Bending, he scooped up his fallen cloak and shook the rain from it. 'I must steal back to the castle before my father wonders why I'm taking so long to sharpen my sword, but before I go, I would like a private word, Ser Duncan. Will you walk with me?'

Dunk looked at the princeling suspiciously a moment. 'As you wish. Your Grace.' He sheathed his dagger. 'I need to get my shield too.'

'Egg and I will look for knights,' promised Raymun.

Prince Daeron knotted his cloak around his neck and pulled up the hood. Dunk followed him back out into the soft rain. They walked toward the merchants' wagons.

'I dreamed of you,' said the prince.

'You said that at the inn.'

'Did I? Well, it's so. My dreams are not like yours, Ser Duncan. Mine are true. They frighten me. *You* frighten me. I dreamed of you and a dead dragon, you see. A great beast, huge, with wings so large they could cover this meadow. It had fallen on top of you, but you were alive and the dragon was dead.'

'Did I kill it?'

'That I could not say, but you were there, and so was the dragon. We were the masters of dragons once, we Targaryens. Now they are all gone, but we remain. I don't care to die today. The gods alone know why, but I don't. So do me a kindness if you would, and make certain it is my brother Aerion you slay.'

'I don't care to die either,' said Dunk.

'Well, I shan't kill you, ser. I'll withdraw my accusation as well, but it won't serve unless Aerion withdraws his.' He sighed. 'It may be that I've killed you with my lie. If so, I am sorry. I'm doomed to some hell, I know. Likely one without wine.' He shuddered, and on that they parted, there in the cool soft rain.

*

The merchants had drawn up their wagons on the western verge of the meadow, beneath a stand of birch and ash. Dunk stood under the trees and looked helplessly at the empty place where the puppeteers' wagon had been. Gone. He had feared they might be. *I would flee as well, if I were not thick as a castle wall.* He wondered what he would do for a shield now. He had the silver to buy one, he supposed, if he could find one for sale . . .

'Ser Duncan,' a voice called out of the dark. Dunk turned to find Steely Pate standing behind him, holding an iron lantern. Under a short leather cloak, the armorer was bare from the waist up, his broad chest and thick arms covered with coarse black hair. 'If you are come for your shield, she left it with me.' He looked Dunk up and down. 'Two hands and two feet, I count. So it's to be trial by combat, is it?'

'A trial of seven. How did you know?'

'Well, they might have kissed you and made you a lord, but it didn't seem likely, and if it went t'other way, you'd be short some parts. Now follow me.'

His wagon was easy to distinguish by the sword and anvil painted on its side. Dunk followed Pate inside. The armorer hung the lantern on a hook, shrugged out of his wet cloak, and pulled a roughspun tunic down over his head. A hinged board dropped down from one wall to make a table. 'Sit,' he said, shoving a low stool toward him.

Dunk sat. 'Where did she go?'

'They make for Dorne. The girl's uncle, there's a wise man. Well gone is well forgot. Stay and be seen, and belike the dragon remembers. Besides, he did not think she ought see you die.' Pate went to the far end of the wagon, rummaged about in the shadows a moment, and returned with the shield. 'Your rim was old cheap steel, brittle and rusted,' he said. 'I've made you a new one, twice as thick, and put some bands across the back. It will be heavier now, but stronger too. The girl did the paint.'

She had made a better job of it than he could ever have hoped for. Even by lantern light, the sunset colors were rich and bright, the tree tall and strong and noble. The falling star was a bright slash of paint across the oaken sky. Yet now that Dunk held it in his hands, it seemed all wrong. The star was *falling*, what sort of sigil was that? Would he fall just as fast? And sunset heralds night. 'I should have stayed with the chalice,' he said miserably. 'It had wings, at least, to fly away, and Ser Arlan said the cup was full of faith and fellowship and good things to drink. This shield is all painted up like death.'

'The elm's alive,' Pate pointed out. 'See how green the leaves are? Summer leaves, for certain. And I've seen shields blazoned with skulls and wolves and ravens, even hanged men and bloody heads. They served well enough, and so will this. You know the old shield rhyme? *Oak and iron, guard me well ...* '

'*... or else I'm dead, and doomed to hell*,' Dunk finished. He had not thought of that rhyme in years. The old man had taught it to him, a long time ago. 'How much do you want for the new rim and all?' he asked Pate.

'From you?' Pate scratched his beard. 'A copper.'

*

The rain had all but stopped as the first wan light suffused the eastern sky, but it had done its work. Lord Ashford's men had removed the barriers, and the tourney field was one great morass of gray-brown mud and torn grass. Tendrils of fog were writhing along the ground like pale white snakes as Dunk made his way back toward the lists. Steely Pate walked with him.

The viewing stand had already begun to fill, the lords and ladies clutching their cloaks tight about them against the morning chill. Smallfolk were drifting toward the field as well, and hundreds of them already stood along the fence. *So many come to see me die*, thought Dunk bitterly, but he wronged them. A few steps farther on, a woman called out, 'Good fortune to you.' An old man stepped up to take his hand and said, 'May the gods give you strength, ser.' Then a begging brother in a tattered brown robe said a blessing on his sword, and a maid kissed his cheek. *They are for me.* 'Why?' he asked Pate. 'What am I to them?'

'A knight who remembered his vows,' the smith said.

They found Raymun outside the challengers' paddock at the south end of the lists, waiting with his cousin's horse and Dunk's. Thunder tossed restlessly beneath the weight of chinet, chamfron, and blanket of heavy mail. Pate inspected the armor and pronounced it good work, even though someone else had forged it. Wherever the armor had come from, Dunk was grateful.

Then he saw the others: the one-eyed man with the salt-and-pepper beard, the young knight in the striped yellow-and-black surcoat with the beehives on the shield. *Robyn Rhysling and Humfrey Beesbury*, he thought in astonishment. *And Ser Humfrey Hardyng as well.* Hardyng was mounted on Aerion's red charger, now barded in his red-and-white diamonds.

He went to them. 'Sers, I am in your debt.'

'The debt is Aerion's,' Ser Humfrey Hardyng replied, 'and we mean to collect it.'

'I had heard your leg was broken.'

'You heard the truth,' Hardyng said. 'I cannot walk. But so long as I can sit a horse, I can fight.'

Raymun took Dunk aside. 'I hoped Hardyng would want another chance at Aerion, and he did. As it happens, the other Humfrey is his brother by marriage. Egg is responsible for Ser Robyn, whom he knew from other tourneys. So you are five.'

'Six,' said Dunk in wonder, pointing. A knight was entering the paddock, his squire leading his charger behind him. 'The Laughing Storm.' A head taller than Ser Raymun and almost of a height with Dunk, Ser Lyonel wore a cloth-of-gold surcoat bearing the crowned stag of House Baratheon, and carried his antlered helm under his arm. Dunk reached for his hand. 'Ser Lyonel, I cannot thank you enough for coming, nor Ser Steffon for bringing you.'

'Ser Steffon?' Ser Lyonel gave him a puzzled look. 'It was your squire who came to me. The boy, Aegon. My own lad tried to chase him off, but he slipped between his legs and turned a flagon of wine over my head.' He laughed. 'There has not been a trial of seven for more than a hundred years, do you know that? I was not about to miss a chance to fight the Kingsguard knights, and tweak Prince Maekar's nose in the bargain.'

'Six,' Dunk said hopefully to Raymun Fossoway as Ser Lyonel joined the others. 'Your cousin will bring the last, surely.'

A roar went up from the crowd. At the north end of the meadow, a column of knights came trotting out of the river mist. The three Kingsguard came first, like ghosts in their gleaming white enamel armor, long white cloaks trailing behind them. Even their shields were white, blank and clean as a field of new-fallen snow. Behind rode Prince Maekar and his sons. Aerion was mounted on a dapple gray, orange and red flickering through the slashes in the horse's caparison at each stride. His brother's destrier was a smaller bay, armored in overlapping black and gold scales. A green silk plume trailed from Daeron's helm. It was their father who made the most fearsome appearance, however. Black curved dragon teeth ran across his shoulders, along the crest of his helm, and down his back, and the huge spiked mace strapped to his saddle was as deadly-looking a weapon as any Dunk had ever seen.

'Six,' Raymun exclaimed suddenly. 'They are only six.'

It was true, Dunk saw. *Three black knights and three white. They are a man short as well.* Was it possible that Aerion had not been able to find a seventh man? What would that mean? Would they fight six against six if neither found a seventh?

Egg slipped up beside him as he was trying to puzzle it out. 'Ser, it's time you donned your armor.'

'Thank you, squire. If you would be so good?'

Steely Pate lent the lad a hand. Hauberk and gorget, greaves and gauntlet, coif and codpiece, they turned him into steel, checking each buckle and each clasp thrice. Ser Lyonel sat sharpening his sword on a whetstone while the Humfreys talked quietly, Ser Robyn prayed, and Raymun Fossoway paced back and forth, wondering where his cousin had got to.

Dunk was fully armored by the time Ser Steffon finally appeared. 'Raymun,' he called, 'my mail, if you please.' He had changed into a padded doublet to wear beneath his steel.

'Ser Steffon,' said Dunk, 'what of your friends? We need another knight to make our seven.'

'You need two, I fear,' Ser Steffon said. Raymun laced up the back of the hauberk.

'M'lord?' Dunk did not understand. 'Two?'

Ser Steffon picked up a gauntlet of fine lobstered steel and slid his left hand into it, flexing his fingers. 'I see five here,' he said while Raymun fastened his sword belt. 'Beesbury, Rhysling, Hardyng, Baratheon, and yourself.'

'And you,' said Dunk. 'You're the sixth.'

'I am the seventh,' said Ser Steffon, smiling, 'but for the other side. I fight with Prince Aerion and the accusers.'

Raymun had been about to hand his cousin his helm. He stopped as if struck. 'No.'

'Yes.' Ser Steffon shrugged. 'Ser Duncan understands, I am sure. I have a duty to my prince.'

'You told him to rely on you.' Raymun had gone pale.

'Did I?' He took the helm from his cousin's hands. 'No doubt I was sincere at the time. Bring me my horse.'

'Get him yourself,' said Raymun angrily. 'If you think I wish any part of this, you're as thick as you are vile.'

'Vile?' Ser Steffon tsked. 'Guard your tongue, Raymun. We're both apples from the same tree. And you are my squire. Or have you forgotten your vows?'

'No. Have you forgotten yours? You swore to be a knight.'

'I shall be more than a knight before this day is done. *Lord* Fossoway. I like the sound of that.' Smiling, he pulled on his other gauntlet, turned away, and crossed the paddock to his horse. Though the other defenders stared at him with contemptuous eyes, no one made a move to stop him.

Dunk watched Ser Steffon lead his destrier back across the field. His hands coiled into fists, but his throat felt too raw for speech. *No words would move the likes of him anyway.*

'Knight me.' Raymun put a hand on Dunk's shoulder and turned him. 'I will take my cousin's place. Ser Duncan, knight me.' He went to one knee.

Frowning, Dunk moved a hand to the hilt of his longsword, then hesitated. 'Raymun, I . . . I should not.'

'You must. Without me, you are only five.'

'The lad has the truth of it,' said Ser Lyonel Baratheon. 'Do it, Ser Duncan. Any knight can make a knight.'

'Do you doubt my courage?' Raymun asked.

'No,' said Dunk. 'Not that, but . . .' Still he hesitated.

A fanfare of trumpets cut the misty morning air. Egg came running up to them. 'Ser, Lord Ashford summons you.'

The Laughing Storm gave an impatient shake of the head. 'Go to him, Ser Duncan. I'll give squire Raymun his knighthood.' He slid his sword out of his sheath and shouldered Dunk aside. 'Raymun of House Fossoway,' he began solemnly, touching the blade to the squire's right shoulder, 'in the name of the Warrior I charge you to be brave.' The sword moved from his right shoulder to his left. 'In the name of the Father I charge you to be just.' Back to the right. 'In the name of the Mother I charge you to defend the young and innocent.' The left. 'In the name of the Maid I charge you to protect all women . . .'

Dunk left them there, feeling as relieved as he was guilty. *We are still one short*, he thought as Egg held Thunder for him. *Where will I find another man?* He turned the horse and rode slowly toward the viewing stand, where Lord Ashford stood waiting. From the north end of the lists, Prince Aerion advanced to meet him. 'Ser Duncan,' he said cheerfully, 'it would seem you have only five champions.'

'Six,' said Dunk. 'Ser Lyonel is knighting Raymun Fossoway. We will fight you six against seven.' Men had won at far worse odds, he knew.

But Lord Ashford shook his head. 'That is not permitted, ser. If you cannot find another knight to take your side, you must be declared guilty of the crimes of which you stand accused.'

Guilty, thought Dunk. *Guilty of loosening a tooth, and for that I must die.* 'M'lord, I beg a moment.'

'You have it.'

Dunk rode slowly along the fence. The viewing stand was crowded with knights. *'M'lords,'* he called to them, *'do none of you remember Ser Arlan of Pennytree? I was his squire. We served many of you. Ate at your tables and slept in your halls.'* He saw Manfred Dondarrion seated in the highest tier. *'Ser Arlan took a wound in your lord father's service.'* The knight said something to the lady beside him, paying no heed. Dunk was forced to move on. *'Lord Lannister, Ser Arlan unhorsed you once in tourney.'* The Grey Lion examined his gloved hands, studiedly refusing to raise his eyes. *'He was a good man, and he taught me how to be a knight. Not only sword and lance, but honor. A knight defends the innocent, he said. That's all I did. I need one more knight to fight beside me. One, that's all. Lord Caron? Lord Swann?'* Lord Swann laughed softly as Lord Caron whispered in his ear.

Dunk reined up before Ser Otho Bracken, lowering his voice. 'Ser Otho, all know you for a great champion. Join us, I beg you. In the names of the old gods and the new. My cause is just.'

'That may be,' said the Brute of Bracken, who had at least the grace to reply, 'but it is your cause, not mine. I know you not, boy.'

Heartsick, Dunk wheeled Thunder and raced back and forth before the tiers of pale cold men. Despair made him shout. *'ARE THERE NO TRUE KNIGHTS AMONG YOU?'*

Only silence answered.

Across the field, Prince Aerion laughed. 'The dragon is not mocked,' he called out.

Then came a voice. 'I will take Ser Duncan's side.'

A black stallion emerged from out of the river mists, a black knight on his back. Dunk saw the dragon shield, and the red enamel crest upon his helm with its three roaring heads. *The Young Prince. Gods be good, it is truly him?*

Lord Ashford made the same mistake. 'Prince Valarr?'

'No.' The black knight lifted the visor of his helm. 'I did not think to enter the lists at Ashford, my lord, so I brought no armor. My son was good enough to lend me his.' Prince Baelor smiled almost sadly.

The accusers were thrown into confusion, Dunk could see. Prince Maekar spurred his mount forward. 'Brother, have you taken leave of your senses?' He pointed a mailed finger at Dunk. 'This man attacked my son.'

'This man protected the weak, as every true knight must,' replied Prince Baelor. 'Let the gods determine if he was right or wrong.' He gave a tug on his reins, turned Valarr's huge black destrier, and trotted to the south end of the field.

Dunk brought Thunder up beside him, and the other defenders gathered round them; Robyn Rhysling and Ser Lyonel, the Humfreys. *Good men all, but are they good enough?* 'Where is Raymun?'

'*Ser* Raymun, if you please.' He cantered up, a grim smile lighting his face beneath his plumed helm. 'My pardons, ser. I needed to make a small change to my sigil, lest I be mistaken for my dishonorable cousin.' He showed them all his shield. The polished golden field remained the same, and the Fossoway apple, but this apple was green instead of red. 'I fear I am still not ripe . . . but better green than wormy, eh?'

Ser Lyonel laughed, and Dunk grinned despite himself. Even Prince Baelor seemed to approve.

Lord Ashford's septon had come to the front of the viewing stand and raised his crystal to call the throng to prayer.

'Attend me, all of you,' Baelor said quietly. 'The accusers will be armed with heavy war lances for the first charge. Lances of ash, eight feet long, banded against splitting and tipped with a steel point sharp enough to drive through plate with the weight of a warhorse behind it.'

'We shall use the same,' said Ser Humfrey Beesbury. Behind him, the septon was calling on the Seven to look down and judge this dispute, and grant victory to the men whose cause was just.

'No,' Baelor said. 'We will arm ourselves with tourney lances instead.'

'Tourney lances are made to break,' objected Raymun.

'They are also made twelve feet long. If our points strike home, theirs cannot touch us. Aim for helm or chest. In a tourney it is a gallant thing to break your lance against a foe's shield, but here it may well mean death. If we can unhorse them and keep our own saddles, the advantage is ours.' He glanced to Dunk. 'If Ser Duncan is killed, it is considered that the gods have judged him guilty, and the contest is over. If both of his accusers are slain, or withdraw their accusations, the same is true. Elsewise, all seven of one side or the other must perish or yield for the trial to end.'

'Prince Daeron will not fight,' Dunk said.

'Not well, anyway,' laughed Ser Lyonel. 'Against that, we have three of the White Swords to contend with.'

Baelor took that calmly. 'My brother erred when he demanded that the Kingsguard fight for his son. Their oath forbids them to harm a prince of the blood. Fortunately, I am such.' He gave them a faint smile. 'Keep the others off me long enough, and I shall deal with the Kingsguard.'

'My prince, is that chivalrous?' asked Ser Lyonel Baratheon as the septon was finishing his invocation.

'The gods will let us know,' said Baelor Breakspear.

A deep expectant silence had fallen across Ashford Meadow.

Eighty yards away, Aerion's gray stallion trumpeted with impatience and pawed the muddy ground. Thunder was very still by comparison; he was an older horse, veteran of half a hundred fights, and he knew what was expected of him. Egg handed Dunk up his shield. 'May the gods be with you, ser,' the boy said.

The sight of his elm tree and shooting star gave him heart. Dunk slid his left arm through the strap and tightened his fingers around the grip. *Oak and iron, guard me well, or else I'm dead and doomed to hell.* Steely Pate brought his lance to him, but Egg insisted that it must be he who put it into Dunk's hand.

To either side, his companions took up their own lances and spread out in a long line. Prince Baelor was to his right and Ser Lyonel to his left, but the narrow eye slit of the greathelm limited Dunk's vision to what was directly ahead of him. The viewing stand was gone, and likewise the smallfolk crowding the fence; there was only the muddy field, the pale blowing mist, the river, town, and castle to the north, and the princeling on his gray charger with flames on his helm and a dragon on his shield. Dunk watched Aerion's squire hand him a war lance, eight feet long and black as night. *He will put that through my heart if he can.*

A horn sounded.

For a heartbeat Dunk sat as still as a fly in amber, though all the horses were moving. A stab of panic went through him. *I have forgotten,* he thought wildly, *I have forgotten all, I will shame myself, I will lose everything.*

Thunder saved him. The big brown stallion knew what to do, even if his rider did not. He broke into a slow trot. Dunk's training took over then. He gave the warhorse a light touch of spur and couched his lance. At the same time he swung his shield until it covered most of the left side of his body.

He held it at an angle, to deflect blows away from him. *Oak and iron guard me well, or else I'm dead and doomed to hell.*

The noise of the crowd was no more than the crash of distant waves. Thunder slid into a gallop. Dunk's teeth jarred together with the violence of the pace. He pressed his heels down, tightening his legs with all his strength and letting his body become part of the motion of the horse beneath. *I am Thunder and Thunder is me, we are one beast, we are joined, we are one.* The air inside his helm was already so hot he could scarce breathe.

In a tourney joust, his foe would be to his left across the tilting barrier, and he would need to swing his lance across Thunder's neck. The angle made it more likely that the wood would split on impact. But this was a deadlier game they played today. With no barriers dividing them, the destriers charged straight at one another. Prince Baelor's huge black was much faster than Thunder, and Dunk glimpsed him pounding ahead through the corner of his eye slit. He sensed more than saw the others. *They do not matter, only Aerion matters, only him.*

He watched the dragon come. Spatters of mud sprayed back from the hooves of Prince Aerion's gray, and Dunk could see the horse's nostrils flaring. The black lance still angled upward. A knight who holds his lance high and brings it on line at the last moment always risks lowering it too far, the old man had told him. He brought his own point to bear on the center of the princeling's chest. *My lance is part of my arm*, he told himself. *It's my finger, a wooden finger. All I need do is touch him with my long wooden finger.*

He tried not to see the sharp iron point at the end of Aerion's black lance, growing larger with every stride. *The dragon, look at the dragon*, he thought. The great three-headed beast covered the prince's shield, red wings and gold fire. *No, look only where you mean to strike*, he remembered suddenly, but his lance had already begun to slide offline. Dunk tried to correct, but it was too late. He saw his point strike Aerion's shield, taking the dragon between two of its heads, gouging into a gout of painted flame. At the muffled *crack*, he felt Thunder recoil under him, trembling with the force of the impact, and half a heartbeat later something smashed into his side with awful force. The horses slammed together violently, armor crashing and clanging as Thunder stumbled and Dunk's lance fell from his hand. Then he was past his foe, clutching at his saddle in a desperate effort to keep his seat. Thunder lurched sideways in the sloppy mud and Dunk felt his rear legs slip out from under. They were sliding, spinning, and then the stallion's hindquarters slapped down hard. *'Up!'* Dunk roared, lashing out with his spurs. *'Up, Thunder!'* And somehow the old warhorse found his feet again.

He could feel a sharp pain under his rib, and his left arm was being pulled down. Aerion had driven his lance through oak, wool, and steel; three feet of splintered ash and sharp iron stuck from his side. Dunk reached over with his right hand, grasped the lance just below the head, clenched his teeth, and pulled it out of him with one savage yank. Blood followed, seeping through the rings of his mail to redden his surcoat. The world swam and he almost fell. Dimly, through the pain, he could hear voices calling his name. His beautiful shield was useless now. He tossed it aside, elm tree, shooting star, broken lance, and all, and drew his sword, but he hurt so much he did not think he could swing it.

Turning Thunder in a tight circle, he tried to get a sense of what was happening elsewhere on the field. Ser Humfrey Hardyng clung to the neck of his mount, obviously wounded. The other Ser Humfrey lay motionless in a lake of bloodstained mud, a broken lance protruding from his groin. He saw Prince Baelor gallop past, lance still intact, and drive one of the Kingsguard from his saddle. Another of the white knights was already down, and Maekar had been unhorsed as well. The third of the Kingsguard was fending off Ser Robyn Rhysling.

Aerion, where is Aerion? The sound of drumming hooves behind him made Dunk turn his head sharply. Thunder bugled and reared, hooves lashing out futilely as Aerion's gray stallion barreled into him at full gallop.

This time there was no hope of recovery. His longsword went spinning from his grasp, and the ground rose up to meet him. He landed with a bruising impact that jarred him to the bone. Pain stabbed through him, so sharp he sobbed. For a moment it was all he could do to lie there. The taste of blood filled his mouth. *Dunk the lunk, thought he could be a knight.* He knew he had to find his feet again, or die. Groaning, he forced himself to hands and knees. He could not breathe, nor could he see. The eye slit of his helm was packed with mud. Lurching blindly to his feet, Dunk scraped at the mud with a mailed finger. *There, that's . . .*

Through his fingers, he glimpsed a dragon flying, and a spiked morningstar whirling on the end of a chain. Then his head seemed to burst to pieces.

When his eyes opened he was on the ground again, sprawled on his back. The mud had all been knocked from his helm, but now one eye was closed by blood. Above was nothing but dark gray sky. His face throbbed, and he could feel cold wet metal pressing in against cheek and temple. *He broke my head, and I'm dying.* What was worse was the others who would die with him, Raymun and Prince Baelor and the rest. *I've failed them. I am no champion. I'm not even a hedge knight. I am nothing.* He remembered Prince Daeron boasting that no one could lie insensible in the mud as well as he did. *He never saw Dunk the lunk, though, did he?* The shame was worse than the pain.

The dragon appeared above him.

Three heads it had, and wings bright as flame, red and yellow and orange. It was laughing. 'Are you dead yet, hedge knight?' it asked. 'Cry for quarter and admit your guilt, and perhaps I'll only claim a hand and a foot. Oh, and those teeth, but what are a few teeth? A man like you can live years on pease porridge.' The dragon laughed again. 'No? Eat *this,* then.' The spiked ball whirled round and round the sky, and fell toward his head as fast as a shooting star.

Dunk rolled.

Where he found the strength he did not know, but he found it. He rolled into Aerion's legs, threw a steel-clad arm around his thigh, dragged him cursing into the mud, and rolled on top of him. *Let him swing his bloody morningstar now.* The prince tried forcing the lip of his shield up at Dunk's head, but his battered helm took the brunt of the impact. Aerion was strong, but Dunk was stronger, and larger and heavier as well. He grabbed hold of the shield with both hands and twisted until the straps broke. Then he brought it down on the top of the princeling's helm, again and again and again, smashing the enameled flames of his crest. The shield was thicker than Dunk's had been, solid oak banded with iron. A flame broke off. Then another. The prince ran out of flames long before Dunk ran out of blows.

Aerion finally let go the handle of his useless morningstar and clawed for the poniard at his hip. He got it free of its sheath, but when Dunk whanged his hand with the shield the knife sailed off into the mud.

He could vanquish Ser Duncan the Tall, but not Dunk of Flea Bottom. The old man had taught him jousting and swordplay, but this sort of fighting he had learned earlier, in shadowy wynds and crooked alleys behind the city's winesinks. Dunk flung the battered shield away and wrenched up the visor of Aerion's helm.

A visor is a weak point, he remembered Steely Pate saying. The prince had all but ceased to struggle. His eyes were purple and full of terror. Dunk had a sudden urge to grab one and pop it like a grape between two steel fingers, but that would not be knightly. 'YIELD!' he shouted.

'I yield,' the dragon whispered, pale lips barely moving. Dunk blinked down at him. For a moment he could not credit what his ears had heard. *Is it done, then?* He turned his head slowly from side to side, trying to see. His vision slit was partly closed by the blow that had smashed in the left side of his face. He glimpsed Prince Maekar, mace in hand, trying to fight his way to his son's side. Baelor Breakspear was holding him off.

Dunk lurched to his feet and pulled Prince Aerion up after him. Fumbling at the lacings of his helm, he tore it off and flung it away. At once he was drowned in sights and sounds; grunts and curses, the shouts of the crowd, one stallion screaming while another raced riderless across the field. Everywhere steel rang on steel. Raymun and his cousin were slashing at each other in front of the viewing stand, both afoot. Their shields were splintered ruins, the green apple and the red both hacked to tinder. One of the Kingsguard knights was carrying a wounded brother from the field. They both looked alike in their white armor and white cloaks. The third of the white knights was down, and the Laughing Storm had joined Prince Baelor against Prince Maekar. Mace, battle-axe, and longsword clashed and clanged, ringing against helm and shield. Maekar was taking three blows for every one he landed, and Dunk could see that it would be over soon. *I must make an end to it before more of us are killed.*

Prince Aerion made a sudden dive for his morningstar. Dunk kicked him in the back and knocked him facedown, then grabbed hold of one of his legs and dragged him across the field. By the time he reached the viewing stand where Lord Ashford sat, the Bright Prince was brown as a privy. Dunk hauled him onto his feet and rattled him, shaking some of the mud onto Lord Ashford and the fair maid. 'Tell him!'

Aerion Brightflame spit out a mouthful of grass and dirt. 'I withdraw my accusation.'

*

Afterward Dunk could not have said whether he walked from the field under his own power or had required help. He hurt everywhere, and some places worse than others. *I am a knight now in truth?* he remembered wondering. *Am I a champion?*

Egg helped him remove his greaves and gorget, and Raymun as well, and even Steely Pate. He was too dazed to tell them apart. They were fingers and thumbs and voices. Pate was the one complaining, Dunk knew. 'Look what he's done to me armor,' he said. 'All dinted and banged and scratched. Aye, I ask you, why do I bother? I'll have to cut that mail off him, I fear.'

'Raymun,' Dunk said urgently, clutching at his friend's hands. 'The others. How did they fare?' He had to know. 'Has anyone died?'

'Beesbury,' Raymun said. 'Slain by Donnel of Duskendale in the first charge. Ser Humfrey is gravely wounded as well. The rest of us are bruised and bloody, no more. Save for you.'

'And them? The accusers?'

'Ser Willem Wylde of the Kingsguard was carried from the field insensate, and I think I cracked a few of my cousin's ribs. At least I hope so.'

'And Prince Daeron?' Dunk blurted. 'Did he survive?'

'Once Ser Robyn unhorsed him, he lay where he fell. He may have a broken foot. His own horse trod on him while running loose about the field.'

Dazed and confused as he was, Dunk felt a huge sense of relief. 'His dream was wrong, then. The dead dragon. Unless Aerion died. He didn't though, did he?'

'No,' said Egg. 'You spared him. Don't you remember?'

'I suppose.' Already his memories of the fight were becoming confused and vague. 'One moment I feel drunk. The next it hurts so bad I know I'm dying.'

They made him lie down on his back and talked over him as he gazed up into the roiling gray sky. It seemed to Dunk that it was still morning. He wondered how long the fight had taken.

'Gods be good, the lance point drove the rings deep into his flesh,' he heard Raymun saying. 'It will mortify unless . . .'

'Get him drunk and pour some boiling oil into it,' someone suggested. 'That's how the maesters do it.'

'Wine.' The voice had a hollow metallic ring to it. '*Not* oil, that will kill him, boiling wine. I'll send Maester Yormwell to have a look at him when he's done tending my brother.'

A tall knight stood above him, in black armor dinted and scarred by many blows. *Prince Baelor.* The scarlet dragon on his helm had lost a head, both wings, and most of its tail. 'Your Grace,' Dunk said, 'I am your man. Please. Your man.'

'My man.' The black knight put a hand on Raymun's shoulder to steady himself. 'I need good men, Ser Duncan. The realm . . .' His voice sounded oddly slurred. Perhaps he'd bit his tongue.

Dunk was very tired. It was hard to stay awake. 'Your man,' he murmured once more.

The prince moved his head slowly from side to side. 'Ser Raymun . . . my helm, if you'd be so kind. Visor . . . visor's cracked, and my fingers . . . fingers feel like wood . . .'

'At once, Your Grace.' Raymun took the prince's helm in both hands and grunted. 'Goodman Pate, a hand.'

Steely Pate dragged over a mounting stool. 'It's crushed down at the back, Your Grace, toward the left side. Smashed into the gorget. Good steel, this, to stop such a blow.'

'Brother's mace, most like,' Baelor said thickly. 'He's strong.' He winced. 'That . . . feels queer, I . . .'

'Here it comes.' Pate lifted the battered helm away. 'Gods be good. *Oh gods oh gods oh gods preserve . . .*'

Dunk saw something red and wet fall out of the helm. Someone was screaming, high and terrible. Against the bleak gray sky swayed a tall prince in black armor with only half a skull. He could see red blood and pale bone beneath and something else, something blue-gray and pulpy. A queer troubled look passed across Baelor Breakspear's face, like a cloud passing before a sun. He raised his hand and touched the back of his head with two fingers, oh so lightly. And then he fell.

Dunk caught him. 'Up,' they say he said, just as he had with Thunder in the melee, 'up, up.' But he never remembered that afterward, and the prince did not rise.

*

Baelor of House Targaryen, Prince of Dragonstone, Hand of the King, Protector of the Realm, and heir apparent to the Iron Throne of the Seven Kingdoms of Westeros, went to the fire in the yard of Ashford Castle on the north bank of River Cockleswent. Other great houses might choose to bury their dead in the dark earth or sink them in the cold green sea, but the Targaryens were the blood of the dragon, and their ends were writ in flame.

He had been the finest knight of his age, and some argued that he should have gone to face the dark clad in mail and plate, a sword in his hand. In the end, though, his royal father's wishes prevailed, and Daeron II had a peaceable nature. When Dunk shuffled past Baelor's bier, the prince wore a black velvet tunic with the three-headed dragon picked out in scarlet thread upon his breast. Around his throat was a heavy gold chain. His sword was sheathed by his side, but he did wear a helm, a thin golden helm with an open visor so men could see his face.

Valarr, the Young Prince, stood vigil at the foot of the bier while his father lay in state. He was a shorter, slimmer, handsomer version of his sire, without the twice-broken nose that had made Baelor seem more human than royal. Valarr's hair was brown, but a bright streak of silver-gold ran through it. The sight of it reminded Dunk of Aerion, but he knew that was not fair. Egg's hair was growing back as bright as his brother's, and Egg was a decent enough lad, for a prince.

When he stopped to offer awkward sympathies, well larded with thanks, Prince Valarr blinked cool blue eyes at him and said, 'My father was only nine-and-thirty. He had it in him to be a great king, the greatest since Aegon the Dragon. Why would the gods take him, and leave *you?*' He shook his head. 'Begone with you, Ser Duncan. Begone.'

Wordless, Dunk limped from the castle, down to the camp by the green pool. He had no answer for Valarr. Nor for the questions he asked himself. The maesters and the boiling wine had done their work, and his wound was healing cleanly, though there would be a deep puckered scar between his left arm and his nipple. He could not see the wound without thinking of Baelor. *He saved me once with his sword, and once with a word, even though he was a dead man as he stood there.* The world made no sense when a great prince died so a hedge knight might live. Dunk sat beneath his elm and stared morosely at his foot.

*

When four guardsmen in the royal livery appeared in his camp late one day, he was sure they had come to kill him after all. Too weak and weary to reach for a sword, he sat with his back to the elm, waiting.

'Our prince begs the favor of a private word.'

'Which prince?' asked Dunk, wary.

'This prince,' a brusque voice said before the captain could answer. Maekar Targaryen walked out from behind the elm.

Dunk got slowly to his feet. *What would he have of me now?*

Maekar motioned, and the guards vanished as suddenly as they had appeared. The prince studied him a long moment, then turned and paced away from him to stand beside the pool, gazing down at his reflection in the water. 'I have sent Aerion to Lys,' he announced abruptly. 'A few years in the Free Cities may change him for the better.'

Dunk had never been to the Free Cities, so he did not know what to say to that. He was pleased that Aerion was gone from the Seven Kingdoms, and hoped he never came back, but that was not a thing you told a father of his son. He stood silent.

Prince Maekar turned to face him. 'Some men will say I meant to kill my brother. The gods know it is a lie, but I will hear the whispers till the day I die. And it was my mace that dealt the fatal blow, I have no doubt. The only other foes he faced in the melee were three Kingsguard, whose vows forbade them to do any more than defend themselves. So it was me. Strange to say, I do not recall the blow that broke his skull. Is that a mercy or a curse? Some of both, I think.'

From the way he looked at Dunk, it seemed the prince wanted an answer. 'I could not say, Your Grace.' Perhaps he should have hated Maekar, but instead he felt a queer sympathy for the man. 'You swung the mace, m'lord, but it was for me Prince Baelor died. So I killed him too, as much as you.'

'Yes,' the prince admitted. 'You'll hear them whisper as well. The king is old. When he dies, Valarr will climb the Iron Throne in place of his father. Each time a battle is lost or a crop fails, the fools will say, "Baelor would not have let it happen, but the hedge knight killed him."'

Dunk could see the truth in that. 'If I had not fought, you would have had my hand off. And my foot. Sometimes I sit under that tree there and look at my feet and ask if I couldn't have spared one. How could my foot be worth a prince's life? And the other two as well, the Humfreys, they were good men too.' Ser Humfrey Hardyng had succumbed to his wounds only last night.

'And what answer does your tree give you?'

'None that I can hear. But the old man, Ser Arlan, every day at evenfall he'd say, "I wonder what the morrow will bring." He never knew, no more than we do. Well, mighten it be that some morrow will come when I'll have need of that foot? When the realm will need that foot, even more than a prince's life?'

Maekar chewed on that a time, mouth clenched beneath the silvery-pale beard that made his face seem so square. 'It's not bloody likely,' he said harshly. 'The *realm* has as many hedge knights as hedges, and all of them have feet.'

'If Your Grace has a better answer, I'd want to hear it.'

Maekar frowned. 'It may be that the gods have a taste for cruel japes. Or perhaps there are no gods. Perhaps none of this had any meaning. I'd ask the High Septon, but the last time I went to him he told me that no man can truly understand the workings of the gods. Perhaps he should try sleeping under a tree.' He grimaced. 'My youngest son seems to have grown fond of you, ser. It is time he was a squire, but he tells me he will serve no knight but you. He is an unruly boy, as you will have noticed. Will you have him?'

'Me?' Dunk's mouth opened and closed and opened again. 'Egg . . . Aegon, I mean . . . he is a good lad, but, Your Grace, I know you honor me, but . . . I am only a hedge knight.'

'That can be changed,' said Maekar. 'Aegon is to return to my castle at Summerhall. There is a place there for you, if you wish. A knight of my household. You'll swear your sword to me, and Aegon can squire for you. While you train him, my master-at-arms will finish your own training.' The prince gave him a shrewd look. 'Your Ser Arlan did all he could for you, I have no doubt, but you still have much to learn.'

'I know, m'lord.' Dunk looked about him. At the green grass and the reeds, the tall elm, the ripples dancing across the surface of the sunlit pool. Another dragonfly was moving across the water, or perhaps it was the same one. *What shall it be, Dunk?* he asked himself. *Dragonflies or dragons?* A few days ago he would have answered at once. It was all he had ever dreamed, but now that the prospect was at hand it frightened him. 'Just before Prince Baelor died, I swore to be his man.'

'Presumptuous of you,' said Maekar. 'What did he say?'

'That the realm needed good men.'

'That's true enough. What of it?'

'I will take your son as squire, Your Grace, but not at Summerhall. Not for a year or two. He's seen sufficient of castles, I would judge. I'll have him only if I can take him on the road with me.' He pointed to old Chestnut. 'He'll ride my steed, wear my old cloak, and he'll keep my sword sharp and my mail scoured. We'll sleep in inns and stables, and now and again in the halls of some landed knight or lesser lordling, and maybe under trees when we must.'

Prince Maekar gave him an incredulous look. 'Did the trial addle your wits, man? Aegon is a prince of the realm. The blood of the dragon. Princes are not made for sleeping in ditches and eating hard salt beef.' He saw Dunk hesitate. 'What is it you're afraid to tell me? Say what you will, ser.'

'Daeron never slept in a ditch, I'll wager,' Dunk said, very quietly, 'and all the beef that Aerion ever ate was thick and rare and bloody, like as not.'

Maekar Targaryen, Prince of Summerhall, regarded Dunk of Flea Bottom for a long time, his jaw working silently beneath his silvery beard. Finally he turned and walked away, never speaking a word. Dunk heard him riding off with his men. When they were gone, there was no sound but the faint thrum of the dragonfly's wings as it skimmed across the water.

The boy came the next morning, just as the sun was coming up. He wore old boots, brown breeches, a brown wool tunic, and an old traveler's cloak 'My lord father says I am to serve you.'

'Serve you, *ser*,' Dunk reminded him. 'You can start by saddling the horses. Chestnut is yours, treat her kindly. I don't want to find you on Thunder unless I put you there.'

Egg went to get the saddles. 'Where are we going, ser?'

Dunk thought for a moment. 'I have never been over the Red Mountains. Would you like to have a look at Dorne?'

Egg grinned. 'I hear they have good puppet shows,' he said.

Portraits of His Children

Richard Cantling found the package leaning up against his front door, one evening in late October when he was setting out for his walk. It annoyed him. He had told his postman repeatedly to ring the bell when delivering anything too big to fit through the mail slot, yet the man persisted in abandoning the packages on the porch, where any passerby could simply walk off with them. Although, to be fair, Cantling's house was rather isolated, sitting on the river bluffs at the end of a cul-de-sac, and the trees effectively screened it off from the street. Still, there was always the possibility of damage from rain or wind or snow.

Cantling's displeasure lasted only an instant. Wrapped in heavy brown paper and carefully sealed with tape, the package had a shape that told all. Obviously a painting. And the hand that had block-printed his address in heavy green marker was unmistakably Michelle's. Another self-portrait then. She must be feeling repentant.

He was more surprised than he cared to admit, even to himself. He had always been a stubborn man. He could hold grudges for years, even decades, and he had the greatest difficulty admitting any wrong. And Michelle, being his only child, seemed to take after him in all of that. He hadn't expected this kind of gesture from her. It was . . . well, sweet.

He set aside his walking stick to lug the package inside, where he could unwrap it out of the damp and the blustery October wind. It was about three feet tall, and unexpectedly heavy. He carried it awkwardly, shutting the door with his foot and struggling down the long foyer toward his den. The brown drapes were tightly closed; the room was dark and heavy with the smell of dust. Cantling had to set down the package to fumble for the light.

He hadn't used his den much since that night, two months ago, when Michelle had gone storming out. Her self-portrait was still sitting up above the wide slate mantel. Below, the fireplace badly wanted cleaning, and on the built-in bookshelves his novels, all bound in handsome dark leather, stood dusty and disarrayed. Cantling looked at the old painting and felt a brief wash of anger return to him, followed by depression. It had been such a nasty thing for her to do. The portrait had been quite good, really.

Much more to his taste than the tortured abstractions that Michelle liked to paint for her own pleasure, or the trite paperback covers she did to make her living. She had done it when she was twenty, as a birthday gift for him. He'd always been fond of it. It captured her as no photograph had ever done, not just the lines of her face, the high angular cheekbones and blue eyes and tangled ash-blonde hair, but the personality inside. She looked so young and fresh and confident, and her smile reminded him so much of Helen and the way she had smiled on their wedding day. He'd told Michelle more than once how much he'd liked that smile.

And so, of course, it had been the smile that she'd started on. She used an antique dagger from his collection, chopped out the mouth with four jagged slashes. She'd gouged out the wide blue eyes next, as if intent on blinding the portrait, and when he came bursting in after her, she'd been slicing the canvas into ribbons with long angry crooked cuts. Cantling couldn't forget that moment. So ugly. And to do something like that to her own work, he couldn't imagine it. He had tried to picture himself mutilating one of his books, tried to comprehend what might drive one to such an act, and he had failed utterly. It was unthinkable, beyond even imagination.

The mutilated portrait still hung in its place. He'd been too stubborn to take it down, and yet he could not bear to look at it. So he had taken to avoiding his den. It wasn't hard. The old house was a huge, rambling place, with more rooms than he could possibly need or want, living alone as he did. It had been built a century ago, when Perrot had been a thriving river town, and they said that a succession of steamer captains had lived there. Certainly the steamboat gothic architecture and all the gingerbread called up visions of the glory days of the river, and he had a fine view of the Mississippi from the third-story windows and the widow's walk. After the incident, Cantling had moved his desk and his typewriter to one of the unused bedrooms and settled in there, determined to let the den remain as Michelle had left it until she came back with an apology.

He had not expected that apology quite so soon, however, nor in quite this form. A tearful phone call, yes – but not another portrait. Still, this was nicer somehow, more personal. And it was a gesture, the first step toward a reconciliation. Richard Cantling knew too well that he was incapable of taking that step himself, no matter how lonely he might become. He had left all his New York friends behind when he moved out to this Iowa river town, and had formed no local friendships to replace them. That was nothing new. He had never been an outgoing sort. He had a certain shyness that kept him apart, even from those few friends he did make. Even from his family, really. Helen had often accused him of caring more for his characters than for real people, an accusation that Michelle had picked up on by the time she was in her teens. Helen was gone too. They'd divorced ten years ago, and she'd been dead for five. Michelle, infuriating as she could be, was really all he had left. He had missed her, missed even the arguments.

He thought about Michelle as he tore open the plain brown paper. He would call her, of course. He would call her and tell her how good the new portrait was, how much he liked it. He would tell her that he'd missed her, invite her to come out for Thanksgiving. Yes, that would be the way to handle it. No mention of their argument, he didn't want to start it all up again, and neither he nor Michelle was the kind to back down gracefully. A family trait, that stubborn willful pride, as ingrained as the high cheekbones and squarish jaw. The Cantling heritage.

It was an antique frame, he saw. Wooden, elaborately carved, very heavy, just the sort of thing he liked. It would mesh with his Victorian decor much better than the thin brass frame on the old portrait. Cantling pulled the wrapping paper away, eager to see what his daughter had done. She was nearly thirty now – or was she past thirty already? He never could keep track of her age, or even her birthdays. Anyway, she was a much better painter than she'd been at twenty. The new portrait ought to be striking. He ripped away the last of the wrappings and turned it around.

His first reaction was that it was a fine, fine piece of work, maybe the best thing that Michelle Cantling had ever done.

Then, belatedly, the admiration washed away, and was replaced by anger. It wasn't her. It wasn't Michelle. Which meant it wasn't a replacement for the portrait she had so willfully vandalized. It was . . . something else.

Someone else.

It was a face he had never before laid eyes on. But it was a face he recognized as readily as if he had looked on it a thousand times. Oh yes.

The man in the portrait was young. Twenty, maybe even younger, though his curly brown hair was already well-streaked with gray. It was unruly hair, disarrayed as if the man had just come from sleep, falling forward into his eyes. Those eyes were a bright green, lazy eyes somehow, shining with some secret amusement. He had high Cantling cheekbones, but the jaw line was all wrong for a relative. Beneath a wide, flat nose, he wore a sardonic smile; his whole posture was somehow insolent. The portrait showed him dressed in faded dungarees and a raveled YMCA Good Guy sweatshirt, with a half-eaten raw onion in one hand. The background was a brick wall covered with graffiti.

Cantling had created him.

Edward Donohue. Dunnahoo, that's what they'd called him, his friends and peers. The other characters in Richard Cantling's first novel, *Hangin'*

Out. Dunnahoo had been the protagonist. A wise guy, a smart mouth, too damn bright for his own good. Looking down at the portrait, Cantling felt as if he'd known him for half his life. As indeed he had, in a way. Known him and, yes, cherished him, in the peculiar way a writer can cherish one of his characters.

Michelle had captured him true. Cantling stared at the painting and it all came back to him, all the events he had bled over so long ago, all the people he had fashioned and described with such loving care. He remembered Jocko, and the Squid, and Nancy, and Ricci's Pizzeria where so much of the book's action had taken place (he could see it vividly in his mind's eye), and the business with Arthur and the motorcycle, and the climactic pizza fight. And Dunnahoo. Dunnahoo especially. Smarting off, fooling around, hanging out, coming of age. 'Fuck 'em if they can't take a joke,' he said. A dozen times or so. It was the book's closing line.

For a moment, Richard Cantling felt a vast, strange affection well up inside him, as if he had just been reunited with an old, lost friend.

And then, almost as an afterthought, he remembered all the ugly words that he and Michelle had flung at each other that night, and suddenly it made sense. Cantling's face went hard. 'Bitch,' he said aloud. He turned away in fury, helpless without a target for his anger 'Bitch,' he said again, as he slammed the door of the den behind him.

*

'Bitch,' he had called her.

She turned around with the knife in her hand. Her eyes were raw and red from crying. She had the smile in her hand. She balled it up and threw it at him. 'Here, you bastard, you like the damned smile so much, here it is.'

It bounced off his cheek. His face was reddening. 'You're just like your mother,' he said. 'She was always breaking things too.'

'You gave her good reason, didn't you?'

Cantling ignored that. 'What the hell is wrong with you? What the hell do you think you're going to accomplish with this stupid melodramatic gesture? That's all it is, you know. Bad melodrama. Who the hell do you think you are, some character in a Tennessee Williams play? Come off it, Michelle. If I wrote a scene like this in one of my books, they'd laugh at me.'

'*This isn't one of your goddamned books!*' she screamed. 'This is real life. My life. I'm a real person, you son of a bitch, not a character in some damned book.' She whirled, raised the knife, slashed and slashed again.

Cantling folded his arms against his chest as he stood watching. 'I hope you're enjoying this pointless exercise.'

'I'm enjoying the hell out of it,' Michelle yelled back.

'Good. I'd hate to think it was for nothing. This is all very revealing, you know. That's your own face you're working on. I didn't think you had that much self-hate in you.'

'If I do, we know who put it there, don't we?' She was finished. She turned back to him, and threw down the knife. She had begun to cry again, and her breath was coming hard. 'I'm leaving. Bastard. I hope you're ever so fucking happy here, really I do.'

'I haven't done anything to deserve this,' Cantling said awkwardly. It was not much of an apology, not much of a bridge back to understanding, but it was the best he could do. Apologies had never come easily to Richard Cantling.

'You deserve a thousand times worse,' Michelle had screamed back at him. She was such a pretty girl, and she looked so ugly. All that nonsense about anger making people beautiful was a dreadful cliché, and wrong as well; Cantling was glad he'd never used it. 'You're supposed to be my father,' Michelle said. 'You're supposed to love me. You're supposed to be my father, and you *raped me*, you bastard.'

*

Cantling was a light sleeper. He woke in the middle of the night, and sat up in bed shivering, with the feeling that something was wrong.

The bedroom seemed dark and quiet. What was it? A noise? He was very sensitive to noise. Cantling slid out from under the covers and donned his slippers. The fire he'd enjoyed before retiring for the night had burned down to embers, and the room was chilly. He felt for his tartan robe, hanging from the foot of the big antique four-poster, slipped into it, cinched the belt, and moved quietly to the bedroom door. The door creaked a little at times, so he opened it very slowly, very cautiously. He listened.

Someone was downstairs. He could hear them moving around.

Fear coiled in the pit of his stomach. He had no gun up here, nothing like that. He didn't believe in that. Besides, he was supposed to be safe. This wasn't New York. He was supposed to be safe here in quaint old Perrot, Iowa. And now he had a prowler in his house, something he had never faced in all of his years in Manhattan. What the hell was he supposed to do?

The police, he thought. He'd lock the door and call the police. He moved back to the bedside, and reached for the phone.

It rang.

Richard Cantling stared at the telephone. He had two lines; a business number hooked up to his recording machine, and an unlisted personal number that he gave only to very close friends. Both lights were lit. It was his private number ringing. He hesitated, then scooped up the receiver. 'Hello.'

'The man himself,' the voice said. 'Don't get weird on me, Dad. You were going to call the cops, right? Stupid. It's only me. Come down and talk.'

Cantling's throat felt raw and constricted. He had never heard that voice before, but he knew it, he knew it. 'Who is this?' he demanded.

'Silly question,' the caller replied. 'You know who it is.'

He did. But he said, 'Who?'

'Not who. Dunnahoo.' Cantling had written that line.

'You're not real.'

'There were a couple of reviewers who said that too. I seem to remember how it pissed you off, back then.'

'You're not *real*,' Cantling insisted.

'I'm cut to the goddamned quick,' Dunnahoo said. 'If I'm not real, it's your fault. So quit getting on my case about it, OK? Just get your ass in gear and hustle it downstairs so we can hang out together.' He hung up.

The lights went out on the telephone. Richard Cantling sat down on the edge of his bed, stunned. What was he supposed to make of this? A dream? It was no dream. What could he do?

He went downstairs.

Dunnahoo had built a fire in the living room fireplace, and was settled into Cantling's big leather recliner, drinking Pabst Blue Ribbon from a bottle. He smiled lazily when Cantling appeared under the entry arch. 'The man,' he said. 'Well, don't you look half-dead. Want a beer?'

'Who the hell are you?' Cantling demanded.

'Hey, we been round that block already. Don't bore me. Grab a beer and park your ass by the fire.'

'An actor,' Cantling said. 'You're some kind of goddamned actor. Michelle put you up to this, right?'

Dunnahoo grinned. 'An actor? Well, that's fuckin' unlikely, ain't it? Tell me, would you stick something that weird in one of your novels? No way, Jose. You'd never do it yourself and if somebody else did it, in one of them workshops or a book you were reviewing, you'd rip his fuckin' liver out.'

Richard Cantling moved slowly into the room, staring at the young man sprawled in his recliner. It was no actor. It was Dunnahoo, the kid from his book, the face from the portrait. Cantling settled into a high, overstuffed armchair, still staring. 'This makes no sense,' he said. 'This is like something out of Dickens.'

Dunnahoo laughed. 'This ain't no fucking Christmas Carol, old man, and I sure ain't no ghost of Christmas past.'

Cantling frowned; whoever he was, that line was out of character.

'That's wrong,' he snapped. 'Dunnahoo didn't read Dickens. Batman and Robin, yes, but not Dickens.'

'I saw the movie, Dad,' Dunnahoo said. He raised the beer bottle to his lips and had a swallow.

'Why do you keep calling me dad?' Cantling said. 'That's wrong too. Anachronistic. Dunnahoo was a street kid, not a beatnik.'

'You're telling me? Like I don't know or something?' He laughed. 'Shit man, what the hell else should I call you?' He ran his fingers through his hair, pushing it back out of his eyes. 'After all, I'm still your fuckin' first-born.'

*

She wanted to name it Edward, if it turned out to be boy. 'Don't be ridiculous, Helen,' he told her.

'I thought you liked the name Edward,' she said.

He didn't know what she was doing in his office anyway. He was working, or trying to work. He'd told her never to come into his office when he was at the typewriter. When they were first married, Helen was very good about that, but there had been no dealing with her since she'd gotten pregnant. 'I do like the name Edward,' he told her, trying hard to keep his voice calm. He hated being interrupted. 'I like the name Edward a lot. I love the goddamned name Edward. That's why I'm using it for my protagonist. Edward, that's his name. Edward Donohue. So we can't use it for the baby because I've already used it. How many times do I have to explain that?'

'But you never *call* him Edward in the book,' Helen protested.

Cantling frowned. 'Have you been reading the book again? Damn it, Helen, I *told* you I don't want you messing around with the manuscript until it's done.'

She refused to be distracted. 'You never call him Edward,' she repeated.

'No,' he said. 'That's right. I never call him Edward. I call him Dunnahoo, because he's a street kid, and because that's his street name, and he doesn't like to be called Edward. Only it's still his name, you see. Edward is his name. He doesn't like it, but it's his fucking *name*, and at the end he tells someone that his name is Edward, and that's real damned important. So we can't name the kid Edward, because *he's* named Edward, and I'm tired of this discussion. If it's a boy, we can name it Lawrence, after my grandfather.'

'But I don't *want* to name him Lawrence,' she whined. 'It's so old-fashioned, and then people will call him Larry, and I hate the name Larry. Why can't you call the character in your book Lawrence?'

'Because his name is Edward.'

'This is our baby I'm carrying,' she said. She put a hand on her swollen stomach, as if Cantling needed a visual reminder.

He was tired of arguing. He was tired of discussing. He was tired of being interrupted. He leaned back in his chair. 'How long have you been carrying the baby?'

Helen look baffled. 'You know. Seven months now. And a week.'

Cantling leaned forward and slapped the stack of manuscript pages piled up beside his typewriter. 'Well, I've been carrying *this* baby for three damned years now. This is the fourth fucking draft, and the last one. He was named Edward on the first draft, and on the second draft, and on the third draft, and he's damn well going to be named Edward when the goddamned novel comes out. He'd been named Edward for *years* before that night of fond memory when you decided to surprise me by throwing away your diaphragm, and thereby got yourself knocked up.'

'It's not fair,' she complained. 'He's only a character. This is our baby.'

'Fair? You want fair? OK. I'll make it fair. Our first-born son will get named Edward. How's that for fair?'

Helen's face softened. She smiled shyly.

He held up a hand before she had a chance to say anything. 'Of course, I figure I'm only about a month away from finishing this damn thing, if you ever stop interrupting me. You've got a little further to go. But that's as fair as I can make it. You pop before I type THE END and you got the name. Otherwise, my baby here' – he slapped the manuscript again – 'is first-born.'

'You can't,' she started.

Cantling resumed his typing.

'My first-born,' Richard Cantling said.

*

'In the flesh,' Dunnahoo said. He raised his beer bottle in salute, and said, 'To fathers and sons, hey!' He drained it with one long swallow and flipped the bottle across the room end over end. It smashed in the fireplace.

'This is a dream,' Cantling said.

Dunnahoo gave him a raspberry. 'Look, old man, face it, I'm here.' He jumped to his feet. 'The prodigal returns,' he said, bowing. 'So where the fuck is the fatted calf and all that shit? Least you coulda done was order a pizza.'

'I'll play the game,' Cantling said. 'What do you want from me?'

Dunnahoo grinned. 'Want? Who, me? Who the fuck knows? I never knew what I wanted, you know that. Nobody in the whole fucking book knew what they wanted.'

'That was the point,' Cantling said.

'Oh, I get it,' Dunnahoo said. 'I'm not dumb. Old Dicky Cantling's boy is anything but dumb, right?' He wandered off toward the kitchen. 'There's more beer in the fridge. Want one?'

'Why not?' Cantling asked. 'It's not every day my oldest son comes to visit. Dos Equis with a slice of lime, please.'

'Drinking fancy Spic beer now, huh? Shit. What ever happened to Piels? You could suck up Piels with the best of them, once upon a time.' He vanished through the kitchen door. When he returned he was carrying two bottles of Dos Equis, holding them by the necks with his fingers jammed down into the open mouths. In his other hand he had a raw onion. The bottles clanked together as he carried them. He gave one to Cantling. 'Here. I'll suck up a little culture myself.'

'You forgot the lime,' Cantling said.

'Get your own fuckin' lime,' Dunnahoo said. 'Whatcha gonna do, cut off my allowance?' He grinned, tossed the onion lightly into the air, caught it, and took a big bite. 'Onions,' he said. 'I owe you for that one, Dad. Bad enough I have to eat raw onions, I mean, shit, but you fixed it so I don't even *like* the fucking things. You even said so in the damned book.'

'Of course,' Cantling said. 'The onion had a dual function. On one level, you did it just to prove how tough you were. It was something none of the others hanging out at Ricci's could manage. It gave you a certain status. But on a deeper level, when you bit into an onion you were making a symbolic statement about your appetite for life, your hunger for it all, the bitter and the sharp parts as well the sweet.'

Dunnahoo took another bite of onion. 'Horseshit,' he said. 'I ought to make you eat a fucking onion, see how you like it.'

Cantling sipped at his beer. 'I was young. It was my first book. It seemed like a nice touch at the time.'

'Eat it raw,' Dunnahoo said. He finished the onion.

Richard Cantling decided this cozy domestic scene had gone on long enough. 'You know, Dunnahoo or whoever you are,' he said in a conversational tone, 'you're not what I expected.'

'What did you expect, old man?'

Cantling shrugged. 'I made you with my mind instead of my sperm, so you've got more of me in you than any child of my flesh could ever have. You're me.'

'Hey,' said Dunnahoo, 'not fucking guilty. I wouldn't be you on a bet.'

'You have no choice. Your story was built from my own adolescence. First novels are like that. Ricci's was really Pompeii Pizza in Newark. Your friends were my friends. And you were me.'

'That so?' Dunnahoo replied, grinning.

Richard Cantling nodded.

Dunnahoo laughed. 'You should be so fuckin' lucky, Dad.'

'What does that mean?' Cantling snapped.

'You live in a dream world, old man, you know that? Maybe you like to pretend you were like me, but there ain't no way it's true. I was the big man at Ricci's. At Pompeii, you were the four-eyes hanging out back by the pinball machine. You had me balling my fuckin' brains out at sixteen. You never even got bare tit till you were past twenty, off in that college of yours. It took you weeks to come up with the wisecracks you had me tossing off every fuckin' time I turned around. All those wild crazy things I did in that book, some of them happened to Dutch and some of them happened to Joey and some of them never happened at all, but none of them happened to you, old man, so don't make me laugh.'

Cantling flushed a little. 'I was writing fiction. Yes, I was a bit of a misfit in my youth, but . . .'

'A nerd,' Dunnahoo said. 'Don't fancy it up.'

'I was not a nerd,' Cantling said, stung. *'Hangin' Out* told the truth. It made sense to use a protagonist who was more central to the action than I'd been in real life. Art draws on life but it has to shape it, rearrange it, give it structure, it can't simply replicate it. That's what I did.'

'Nah. What *you* did was to suck off Dutch and Joey and the rest. You helped yourself to their lives, man, and took credit for it all yourself. You even got this weird fuckin' idea that I was based on you, and you been thinking that so long you believe it. You're a leech, Dad. You're a goddamned thief.'

Richard Cantling was furious. 'Get out of here!' he said.

Dunnahoo stood up, stretched. 'I'm fuckin' wounded. Throwing your baby boy out into the cold Ioway night, old man? What's wrong? You liked me well enough when I was in your damn book, when you could control every thing I did and said, right? Don't like it so well now that I'm real, though. That's your problem. You never did like real life half as well as you liked books.'

'I like life just fine, thank you,' Cantling snapped.

Dunnahoo smiled. Standing there, he suddenly looked washed out, insubstantial. 'Yeah?' he said. His voice seemed weaker than it had been.

'Yeah!' Cantling replied.

Now Dunnahoo was fading visibly. All the color had drained from his body, and he looked almost transparent. 'Prove it,' he said. 'Go into your kitchen, old man, and take a great big bite out of your fuckin' raw onion of life.' He tossed back his hair, and laughed, and laughed, and laughed, until he was quite gone.

Richard Cantling stood staring at the place where he had been for a long time. Finally, very tired, he climbed upstairs to bed.

*

He made himself a big breakfast the next morning: orange juice and fresh-brewed coffee, English muffins with lots of butter and blackberry preserves, a cheese omelet, six strips of thick-sliced bacon. The cooking and the eating were supposed to distract him. It didn't work. He thought of Dunnahoo all the while. A dream, yes, some crazy sort of dream. He had no ready explanation for the broken glass in the fireplace or the empty beer bottles in his living room, but finally he found one. He had experienced some sort of insane drunken somnambulist episode, Cantling decided. It was the stress of the ongoing quarrel with Michelle, of course, triggered by the portrait she'd sent him. Perhaps he ought to see someone about it, a doctor or a psychologist or someone.

After breakfast, Cantling went straight to his den, determined to confront the problem directly and resolve it. Michelle's mutilated portrait still hung above the fireplace. A festering wound, he thought; it had infected him, and the time had come to get rid of it. Cantling built a fire. When it was going good, he took down the ruined painting, dismantled the metal frame – he was a thrifty man, after all – and burned the torn, disfigured canvas. The oily smoke made him feel clean again.

Next there was the portrait of Dunnahoo to deal with. Cantling turned to consider it. A good piece of work, really. She had captured the character. He could burn it, but that would be playing Michelle's own destructive game. Art should never be destroyed. He had made his mark in the world by creation, not destruction, and he was too old to change. The portrait of Dunnahoo had been intended as a cruel taunt, but Cantling decided to throw it back in his daughter's teeth, to make a splendid celebration of it. He would hang it, and hang it prominently. He knew just the place for it.

Up at the top of the stairs was a long landing; an ornate wooden banister overlooked the first floor foyer and entry hall. The landing was fifteen feet long, and the back wall was entirely blank. It would make a splendid portrait gallery, Cantling decided. The painting would be visible to anyone entering the house, and you would pass right by it on the way to any of the second floor rooms. He found a hammer and some nails and hung Dunnahoo in a place of honor. When Michelle came back to make peace, she would see him there, and no doubt leap to the conclusion that Cantling had totally missed the point of her gift. He'd have to remember to thank her effusively for it.

Richard Cantling was feeling much better. Last night's conversation was receding into a bad memory. He put it firmly out of his mind and spent the rest of the day writing letters to his agent and publisher. In the late afternoon, pleasantly weary, he enjoyed a cup of coffee and some butter streusel he'd hidden away in the refrigerator. Then he went out on his daily walk, and spent a good ninety minutes hiking along the river bluffs with a fresh, cold wind in his face.

When he returned, a large square package was waiting on his porch.

*

He leaned it up against an armchair, and settled into his recliner to study it. It made him uneasy. It had an effect, no doubt of it. He could feel an erection stirring against his leg, pressing uncomfortably against his trousers.

The portrait was . . . well, frankly erotic.

She was in bed, a big old antique four-poster, much like his own. She was naked. She was half-turned in the painting, looking back over her right shoulder; you saw the smooth line of her backbone, the curve of her right breast. It was a large, shapely, and very pretty breast; the aureole was pale pink and very large, and her nipple was erect. She was clutching a rumpled sheet up to her chin, but it did little to conceal her. Her hair was red-gold, her eyes green, her smile playful. Her smooth young skin had a flush to it, as if she had just risen from a bout of lovemaking. She had a peace symbol tattooed high on the right cheek of her ass. She was obviously very young. Richard Cantling knew just how young: she was eighteen, a child-woman, caught in that precious time between innocence and experience when sex is just a wonderfully exciting new toy. Oh yes, he knew a lot about her. He knew her well.

Cissy.

He hung her portrait next to Dunnahoo.

*

Dead Flowers was Cantling's title for the book. His editor changed it to *Black Roses*; more evocative, he said, more romantic, more upbeat. Cantling fought the change on artistic grounds, and lost. Afterwards, when the novel made the bestseller lists, he managed to work up the grace to admit that he'd been wrong. He sent Brian a bottle of his favorite wine.

It was his fourth novel, and his last chance. *Hangin' Out* had gotten excellent reviews and had sold decently, but his next two books had been panned by the critics and ignored by the readers. He had to do something different, and he did. *Black Roses* turned out to be highly controversial. Some reviewers loved it, some loathed it. But it sold and sold and sold, and the paperback sale and the film option (they never made the movie) relieved him of financial worries for the first time in his life. They were finally able to afford a down payment on a house, transfer Michelle to a private school and get her those braces; the rest of the money Cantling invested as shrewdly as he was able. He was proud of *Black Roses* and pleased by its success. It made his reputation.

Helen hated the book with a passion.

On the day the novel finally fell off the last of the lists, she couldn't quite conceal her satisfaction. 'I knew it wouldn't last forever,' she said.

Cantling slapped down the newspaper angrily. 'It lasted long enough. What the hell's wrong with you? You didn't like it before, when we were barely scraping by. The kid needs braces, the kid needs a better school, the kid shouldn't have to eat goddamn peanut butter and jelly sandwiches every day. Well, that's all behind us. And you're more pissed off than ever. Give me a little credit. Did you like being married to a failure?'

'I don't like being married to a pornographer,' Helen snapped at him.

'Fuck you,' Cantling said.

She gave him a nasty smile. 'When? You haven't touched me in weeks. You'd rather be fucking your Cissy.'

Cantling stared at her. 'Are you crazy, or what? She's a character in a book I wrote. That's all.'

'Oh go to hell,' Helen said furiously. 'You treat me like I'm a goddamned idiot. You think I can't read? You think I don't know? I read your shitty book. I'm not stupid. The wife, Marsha, dull ignorant boring Marsha, cud-chewing mousy Marsha, that cow, that nag, that royal pain-in-the-ass, that's me. You think I can't tell? I can tell, and so can my friends. They're all very sorry for me. You love me as much as Richardson loved Marsha. Cissy's just a character, right, like hell, like bloody hell.' She was crying now. 'You're in love with her, damn you. She's your own little wet dream. If she walked in the door right now you'd dump me as fast as Richardson dumped good old Marsha. Deny it. Go on, deny it, I dare you!'

Cantling regarded his wife incredulously. 'I don't believe you. You're jealous of a character in my book. You're jealous of someone who doesn't exist.'

'She exists in your head, and that's the only place that matters with you. Of course you want to fuck her. Of course your damned book was a big seller. You think it was because of your writing? It was on account of the sex, on account of *her!*'

'Sex is an important part of life,' Cantling said defensively. 'It's a perfectly legitimate subject for art. You want me to pull down a curtain every time my characters go to bed, is that it? Coming to terms with sexuality, that's what *Black Roses* is all about. Of course it had to be written explicitly. If you weren't such a damned prude you'd realize that.'

'I'm not a prude!' Helen screamed at him. 'Don't you dare call me one, either.' She picked up one of the breakfast plates and threw it at him.

Cantling ducked; the plate shattered on the wall behind him. 'Just because I don't like your goddamned filthy book doesn't make me a prude.'

'The novel has nothing to do with it,' Cantling said. He folded his arms against his chest but kept his voice calm. 'You're a prude because of the things you do in bed. Or should I say the things you won't do?' He smiled.

Helen's face was red; beet red, Cantling thought, and rejected it, too old, too trite. 'Oh, yes, but she'll do them, won't she?' Her voice was pure acid. 'Cissy, your cute little Cissy. She'll get a sexy little tattoo on her ass if you ask her to, right? She'll do it outdoors, she'll do it in all kinds of strange places, with people all around. She'll wear kinky underwear, she thinks it's fun. She'll let you come in her mouth whenever you like. She's always ready and she doesn't have any stretch marks and she has eighteen-year-old tits, and she'll always have eighteen-year-old tits, won't she? How the hell do I compete with that, huh? How? How? *HOW?*'

Richard Cantling's own anger was a cold, controlled, sarcastic thing. He stood up in the face of her fury and smiled sweetly. 'Read the book,' he said. 'Take notes.'

*

He woke suddenly, in darkness, to the light touch of skin against his foot.

Cissy was perched on top of the footboard, a red satin sheet wrapped around her, a long slim leg exploring under his blankets. She was playing footsie with him, and smiling mischievously. 'Hi, Daddy,' she said.

Cantling had been afraid of this. It had been in his mind all evening. Sleep had not come easily. He pulled his foot away and struggled to a sitting position.

Cissy pouted. 'Don't you want to play?' she asked.

'I,' he said, 'I don't believe this. This can't be real.'

'It can still be fun,' she said.

'What the hell is Michelle doing to me? How can this be happening?'

She shrugged. The sheet slipped a little; one perfect red-tipped eighteen-year-old breast peeked out.

'You still have eighteen-year-old tits,' Cantling said numbly. 'You'll always have eighteen-year-old tits.'

Cissy laughed. 'Sure. You can borrow them, if you like, Daddy. I'll bet you can think of something interesting to do with them.'

'Stop calling me Daddy,' Cantling said.

'Oh, but you *are* my daddy,' Cissy said in her little-girl voice.

'Stop that!' Cantling said.

'Why? You want to, Daddy, you want to play with your little girl, don't you?' She winked. 'Vice is nice but incest is best. The families that play together stay together.' She looked around. 'I like four-posters. You want to tie me up, Daddy? I'd like that.'

'No,' Cantling said. He pushed back the covers, got out of bed, found his slippers and robe. His erection throbbed against his leg. He had to get away, he had to put some distance between him and Cissy, otherwise . . . he didn't want to think about otherwise. He busied himself making a fire.

'I like that,' Cissy said when he got it going. 'Fires are so romantic.'

Cantling turned around to face her again. 'Why you?' he asked, trying to stay calm. 'Richardson was the protagonist of *Black Roses*, not you. And why skip to my fourth book? Why not somebody from *Family Tree* or *Rain?*'

'Those gobblers?' Cissy said. 'Nobody real there. You didn't really want Richardson, did you? I'm a lot more fun.' She stood up and let go of the satin sheet. It puddled about her ankles, the flames reflected off its shiny folds. Her body was soft and sweet and young. She kicked free of the sheet and padded toward him.

'Cut it out, Cissy,' Cantling barked.

'I won't bite,' Cissy said. She giggled. 'Unless you want me to. Maybe I should tie *you* up, huh?' She put her arms around him, gave him a hug, turned up her face for a kiss.

'Let go of me,' he said, said weakly. Her arms felt good. She felt good as she pressed up against him. It had been a long time since Richard Cantling had held a woman in his arms; he didn't like to think about how long. And he had never had a woman like Cissy, never, never. But he was frightened. 'I can't do this,' he said. 'I can't. I don't want to.'

Cissy reached through the folds of his robe, shoved her hand inside his briefs, squeezed him gently. 'Liar,' she said. 'You want me. You've always wanted me. I'll bet you used to stop and jack off when you were writing the sex scenes.'

'No,' Cantling said. 'Never.'

'Never?' She pouted. Her hand moved up and down. 'Well, I bet you wanted to. I bet you got hard, anyway. I bet you got hard every time you described me.'

'I,' he said. The denial would not come. 'Cissy, please.'

'Please,' she murmured. Her hand was busy. 'Yes, please.' She tugged at his briefs and they fluttered to the floor. 'Please,' she said. She untied his robe and helped him out of it. 'Please.' Her hand moved along his side, played with his nipples; she stepped closer, and her breasts pressed lightly against his chest. 'Please,' she said, and she looked up at him. Her tongue moved between her lips.

Richard Cantling groaned and took her in his trembling arms.

She was like no woman he had ever had. Her touch was fire and satin, electric, and her secret places were sweet as honey.

*

In the morning she was gone.

Cantling woke late, too exhausted to make himself breakfast. Instead he dressed and walked into town, to a small café in a quaint hundred-year-old brick building at the foot of the bluffs. He tried to sort things out over coffee and blueberry pancakes.

None of it made any sense. It could not be happening, but it was; denial accomplished nothing. Cantling forked down a mouthful of homemade blueberry pancake, but the only taste in his mouth was fear. He was afraid for his sanity. He was afraid because he did not understand, did not want to understand. And there was another, deeper, more basic fear.

He was afraid of what would come next. Richard Cantling had published nine novels.

He thought of Michelle. He could phone her, beg her to call it off before he went mad. She was his daughter, his flesh and blood, surely she would listen to him. She loved him. Of course she did. And he loved her too, no matter what she might think. Cantling knew his faults. He had examined himself countless times, under various guises, in the pages of his books. He was impossibly stubborn, willful, opinionated. He could be rigid and unbending. He could be cold. Still, he thought of himself as a decent man. Michelle . . . she had inherited some of his perversity, she was furious at him, hate was so very close to love, but surely she did not mean to do him serious harm.

Yes, he could phone Michelle, ask her to stop. Would she? If he begged her forgiveness, perhaps. That day, that terrible day, she'd told him that she would never forgive him, never, but she couldn't have meant that. She was his only child. The only child of his flesh, at any rate.

Cantling pushed away his empty plate and sat back. His mouth was set in a hard rigid line. Beg for mercy? He did not like that. What had he done, after all? Why couldn't they understand? Helen had never understood and Michelle was as blind as her mother. A writer must live for his work. What had he done that was so terrible? What had he done that required forgiveness? Michelle ought to be the one phoning him.

The hell with it, Cantling thought. He refused to be cowed. He was right; she was wrong. Let Michelle call him if she wanted a rapprochement. She was not going to terrify him into submission. What was he so afraid of, anyway? Let her send her portraits, all the portraits she wanted to paint. He'd hang them up on his walls, display the paintings proudly (they were really a homage to his work, after all), and if the damned things came alive at night and prowled through his house, so be it. He'd enjoy their visits. Cantling smiled. He'd certainly enjoyed Cissy, no doubt of that. Part of him hoped she'd come back. And even Dunnahoo, well, he was an insolent kid, but there was no real harm in him, he just liked to mouth off.

Why, now that he stopped to consider it, Cantling found that the possibilities had a certain intoxicating charm. He was uniquely privileged. Scott Fitzgerald never attended one of Gatsby's fabulous parties, Conan Doyle could never really sit down with Holmes and Watson, Nabokov never actually tumbled Lolita. What would they have said to the idea?

The more he considered things, the more cheerful he became. Michelle was trying to rebuke him, to frighten him, but she was really giving him a delicious experience. He could play chess with Sergei Tederenko, the cynical émigré hustler from *En Passant*. He could argue politics with Frank Corwin, the union organizer from his Depression novel, *Times Are Hard*. He might flirt with beautiful Beth McKenzie, go dancing with crazy old Miss Aggie, seduce the Danzinger twins and fulfill the one sexual fantasy that Cissy had left untouched, yes, certainly, what the hell had he been afraid of? There were his own creations, his characters, his friends and family.

Of course, there was the new book to consider. Cantling frowned. That was a disturbing thought. But Michelle was his daughter, she loved him, surely she wouldn't go that far. No, of course not. He put the idea firmly aside and picked up his check.

*

He expected it. He was almost looking forward to it. And when he returned from his evening constitutional, his cheeks red from the wind, his heart beating just a little faster in anticipation, it was there waiting for him, the familiar rectangle wrapped in plain brown paper. Richard Cantling carried it inside carefully. He made himself a cup of coffee before he unwrapped it, deliberately prolonging the suspense to savor the moment, delighting in the thought of how deftly he'd turned Michelle's cruel little plan on its head.

He drank his coffee, poured a refill, drank that. The package stood a few feet away. Cantling played a little game with himself, trying to guess whose portrait might be within. Cissy had said something about none of the characters from *Family Tree* or *Rain* being real enough. Cantling mentally reviewed his life's work, trying to decide which characters seemed most real. It was a pleasant speculation, but he could reach no firm conclusions. Finally he shoved his coffee cup aside and moved to undo the wrappings. And there it was.

Barry Leighton.

Again, the painting itself was superb. Leighton was seated in a newspaper city room, his elbow resting on the gray metal case of an old manual typewriter. He wore a rumpled brown suit and his white shirt was

open at the collar and plastered to his body by perspiration. His nose had
been broken more than once, and was spread all across his wide, homely,
somehow comfortable face. His eyes were sleepy. Leighton was overweight
and jowly and rapidly losing his hair. He'd given up smoking but not
cigarettes; an unlit Camel dangled from one corner of his mouth. 'As long
as you don't light the damned things, you're safe,' he'd said more than
once in Cantling's novel *Byeline*.

The book hadn't done very well. It was a depressing book, all about the
last week of a grand old newspaper that had fallen on bad times. It was
more than that, though. Cantling was interested in people, not newspapers; he had used the failing paper as a metaphor for failing lives. His
editor had wanted to work in some kind of strong, sensational subplot,
have Leighton and the others on the trail of some huge story that offered
the promise of redemption, but Cantling had rejected that idea. He wanted
to tell a story about small people being ground down inexorably by time
and age, about the inevitability of loneliness and defeat. He produced a
novel as gray and brittle as newsprint. He was very proud of it.

No one read it.

Cantling lifted the portrait and carried it upstairs, to hang beside those
of Dunnahoo and Cissy. Tonight should be interesting, he thought. Barry
Leighton was no kid, like the others; he was a man of Cantling's own
years. Very intelligent, mature. There was a bitterness in Leighton,
Cantling knew very well; a disappointment that life had, after all, yielded
so little, that all his bylines and big stories were forgotten the day after
they ran. But the reporter kept his sense of humor through all of it, kept
off the demons with nothing but a mordant wit and an unlit Camel.
Cantling admired him, would enjoy talking to him. Tonight, he decided, he
wouldn't bother going to bed. He'd make a big pot of strong black coffee,
lay in some Seagram's 7, and wait.

*

It was past midnight and Cantling was rereading the leather-bound copy
of *Byeline* when he heard ice cubes clinking together in the kitchen. 'Help
yourself, Barry,' he called out.

Leighton came through the swinging door, tumbler in hand. 'I did,' he
said. He looked at Cantling through heavily-lidded eyes, and gave a little
snort. 'You look old enough to be my father,' he said. 'I didn't think
anybody could look that old.'

Cantling closed the book and set it aside. 'Sit down,' he said. 'As I recall,
your feet hurt.'

'My feet always hurt,' Leighton said. He settled himself into an armchair
and swallowed a mouthful of whiskey. 'Ah,' he said, 'that's better.'

Cantling tapped the novel with a fingertip. 'My eighth book,' he said. 'Michelle skipped right over three novels. A pity. I would have liked to meet some of those people.'

'Maybe she wants to get to the point,' Leighton suggested.

'And what is the point?'

Leighton shrugged. 'Damned if I know. I'm only a newspaperman. Five Ws and an H. You're the novelist. You tell me the point.'

'My ninth novel,' Cantling suggested. 'The new one.'

'The last one?' said Leighton.

'Of course not. Only the most recent. I'm working on something new right now.'

Leighton smiled. 'That's not what my sources tell me.'

'Oh? What do your sources say?'

'That you're an old man waiting to die,' Leighton said. 'And that you're going to die alone.'

'I'm fifty-two,' Cantling said crisply. 'Hardly old.'

'When your birthday cake has got more candles than you can blow out, you're old,' said Leighton drily. 'Helen was younger than you, and she died five years ago. It's in the mind, Cantling. I've seen young octogenarians and old adolescents. And you, you had liver spots on your brain before you had hair on your balls.'

'That's unfair,' Cantling protested.

Leighton drank his Seagram's. 'Fair?' he said. 'You're too old to believe in fair, Cantling. Young people live life. Old people sit and watch it. You were born old. You're a watcher, not a liver.' He frowned. 'Not a liver, jeez, what a figure of speech. Better a liver than a gall bladder, I guess. You were never a gall bladder either. You've been full of piss for years, but you don't have any gall at all. Maybe you're a kidney.'

'You're reaching, Barry,' Cantling said. 'I'm a writer. I've always been a writer. That's my life. Writers observe life, they report on life. It's in the job description. You ought to know.'

'I do know,' Leighton said. 'I'm a reporter, remember? I've spent a lot of long gray years writing up other peoples' stories. I've got no story of my own. You know that, Cantling. Look what you did to me in *Byline*. The *Courier* croaks and I decide to write my memoirs and what happens?'

Cantling remembered. 'You blocked. You rewrote your old stories, twenty-year-old stories, thirty-year-old stories. You had that incredible memory. You could recall all the people you'd ever reported on, the dates, the details, the quotes. You could recite the first story you'd had bylined word for word, but you couldn't remember the name of the first girl you'd been to bed with, couldn't remember your ex-wife's phone number, you couldn't ... you couldn't ...' His voice failed.

'I couldn't remember my daughter's birthday,' Leighton said. 'Where do you get those crazy ideas, Cantling?'

Cantling was silent.

'From life, maybe?' Leighton said gently. 'I was a good reporter. That was about all you could say about me. You, well, maybe you're a good novelist. That's for the critics to judge, and I'm just a sweaty newspaperman whose feet hurt. But even if you are a good novelist, even if you're one of the great ones, you were a lousy husband, and a miserable father.'

'No,' Cantling said. It was a weak protest.

Leighton swirled his tumbler; the ice cubes clinked and clattered. 'When did Helen leave you?' he asked.

'I don't . . . ten years ago, something like that. I was in the middle of the final draft of *En Passant*.'

'When was the divorce final?'

'Oh, a year later. We tried reconciliation, but it didn't take. Michelle was in school, I remember. I was writing *Times Are Hard*.'

'You remember her third grade play?'

'Was that the one I missed?'

'The one you missed? You sound like Nixon saying, "Was that the time I lied?" That was the one Michelle had the lead in. Cantling.'

'I couldn't help that,' Cantling said. 'I wanted to come. They were giving me an award. You don't skip the National Literary League dinner. You can't.'

'Of course not,' said Leighton. 'When was it that Helen died?'

'I was writing *Byeline*,' Cantling said.

'Interesting system of dating you've got there. You ought to put out a calendar.' He swallowed some whiskey.

'All right,' Cantling said. 'I'm not going to deny that my work is important to me. Maybe too important, I don't know. Yes, the writing has been the biggest part of my life. But I'm a decent man, Leighton, and I've always done my best. It hasn't all been like you're implying. Helen and I had good years. We loved each other once. And Michelle . . . I loved Michelle. When she was a little girl, I used to write stories just for her. Funny animals, space pirates, silly poems. I'd write them up in my spare time and read them to her at bedtime. They were something I did just for Michelle, for love.'

'Yeah,' Leighton said cynically. 'You never even thought about getting them published.'

Cantling grimaced. 'That . . . you're implying . . . that's a distortion. Michelle loved the stories so much, I thought maybe other kids might like them too. It was just an idea. I never did anything about it.'

'Never?'

Cantling hesitated. 'Look, Bert was my friend as well as my agent. He had a little girl of his own. I showed him the stories once. Once!'

'I can't be pregnant,' Leighton said. 'I only let him fuck me once. Once!'

'He didn't even like them,' Cantling said.

'Pity,' replied Leighton.

'You're laying this on me with a trowel, and I'm not guilty. No, I wasn't father of the year, but I wasn't an ogre either. I changed her diaper plenty of times. Before *Black Roses*, Helen had to work, and I took care of the baby every day, from nine to five.'

'You hated it when she cried and you had to leave your typewriter.'

'Yes,' Cantling said. 'Yes, I hated being interrupted, I've always hated being interrupted, I don't care if it was Helen or Michelle or my mother or my roommate in college, when I'm writing I don't like to be interrupted. Is that a fucking capital crime? Does that make me inhuman? When she cried, I went to her. I didn't like it, I hated it, I resented it, but I *went to her.*'

'When you heard her,' said Leighton. 'When you weren't in bed with Cissy, dancing with Miss Aggie, beating up scabs with Frank Corwin, when your head wasn't full of their voices, yeah, sometimes you heard, and when you heard you went. Congratulations, Cantling.'

'I taught her to read,' Cantling said. 'I read her *Treasure Island* and *Wind in the Willows* and *The Hobbit* and *Tom Sawyer*, all kinds of things.'

'All books you wanted to reread anyway,' said Leighton. 'Helen did the real teaching, with *Dick and Jane*.'

'I hate *Dick and Jane*!' Cantling shouted.

'So?'

'You don't know what you're talking about,' Richard Cantling said. 'You weren't there. Michelle was there. She loved me, she still loves me. Whenever she got hurt, scraped her knee or got her nose bloodied, whatever it was, it was me she'd run to, never Helen. She'd come crying to me and I'd hug her and dry her tears and I'd tell her . . . I used to tell her . . .' But he couldn't go on. He was close to tears himself; he could feel them hiding in the corners of his eyes.

'I know what you used to tell her,' said Barry Leighton in a sad, gentle voice.

'She remembered it,' Cantling said. 'She remembered it all those years. Helen got custody, they moved away, I didn't see her much, but Michelle always remembered, and when she was all grown up, after Helen was gone and Michelle was on her own, there was this time she got hurt, and I . . . I . . .'

'Yes,' said Leighton. 'I know.'

*

The police were the ones that phoned him. Detective Joyce Brennan, that
was her name, he would never forget that name. 'Mister Cantling?' she
said.

'Yes?'

'Mister Richard Cantling?'

'Yes,' he said. 'Richard Cantling the writer.' He had gotten strange calls
before. 'What can I do for you?'

She identified herself. 'You'll have to come down to the hospital,' she
said to him. 'It's your daughter, Mister Cantling. I'm afraid she's been
assaulted.'

He hated evasion, hated euphemism. Cantling's characters never passed
away, they died; they never broke wind, they farted. And Richard
Cantling's daughter ... 'Assaulted?' he said. 'Do you mean she's been
assaulted or do you mean she's been raped?'

There was a silence on the other end of the line. 'Raped,' she said at last.
'She's been raped, Mister Cantling.'

'I'll be right down,' he said.

She had in fact been raped repeatedly and brutally. Michelle had been as
stubborn as Helen, as stubborn as Cantling himself. She wouldn't take his
money, wouldn't take his advice, wouldn't take the help he offered her
through his contacts in publishing. She was going to make it on her own.
She waitressed in a coffee house in the Village, and lived in a large, drafty,
and rundown warehouse loft down by the docks. It was a terrible
neighborhood, a dangerous neighborhood, and Cantling had told her so a
hundred times, but Michelle would not listen. She would not even let him
pay to install good locks and a security system. It had been very bad. The
man had broken in before dawn on a Friday morning. Michelle was alone.
He had ripped the phone from the wall and held her prisoner there
through Monday night. Finally one of the busboys from the coffeehouse
had gotten worried and come by, and the rapist had left by the fire escape.

When they let him see her, her face was a huge purple bruise. She had
burn marks all over her, where the man had used his cigarette, and three
of her ribs were broken. She was far beyond hysteria. She screamed when
they tried to touch her; doctors, nurses, it didn't matter, she screamed as
soon as they got near. But she let Cantling sit on the edge of the bed, and
take her in his arms, and hold her. She cried for hours, cried until there
were no more tears in her. Once she called him 'Daddy,' in a choked sob. It
was the only word she spoke; she seemed to have lost the capacity for
speech. Finally they tranquilized her to get her to sleep.

Michelle was in the hospital for two weeks, in a deep state of shock. Her
hysteria waned day by day, and she finally became docile, so they were

able to fluff her pillows and lead her to the bathroom. But she still would not, or could not, speak. The psychologist told Cantling that she might never speak again. 'I don't accept that,' he said. He arranged Michelle's discharge. Simultaneously he decided to get them both out of this filthy hellhole of a city. She had always loved big old spooky houses, he remembered, and she used to love the water, the sea, the river, the lake. Cantling consulted realtors, considered a big place on the coast of Maine, and finally settled on an old steamboat gothic mansion high on the bluffs of Perrot, Iowa. He supervised every detail of the move.

Little by little, recovery began.

She was like a small child again, curious, restless, full of sudden energy. She did not talk, but she explored everything, went everywhere. In spring she spent hours up on the widow's walk, watching the big towboats go by on the Mississippi far below. Every evening they would walk together on the bluffs, and she would hold his hand. One day she turned and kissed him suddenly, impulsively, on his cheek. 'I love you, Daddy,' she said, and she ran away from him, and as Cantling watched her run, he saw a lovely, wounded woman in her mid-twenties, and saw too the gangling, coltish tomboy she had been.

The dam was broken after that day. Michelle began to talk again. Short, childlike sentences at first, full of childish fears and childish naïveté. But she matured rapidly, and in no time at all she was talking politics with him, talking books, talking art. They had many a fine conversation on their evening walks. She never talked about the rape, though; never once, not so much as a word.

In six months she was cooking, writing letters to friends back in New York, helping with the household chores, doing lovely things in the garden. In eight months she had started to paint again. That was very good for her; now she seemed to blossom daily, to grow more and more radiant. Richard Cantling didn't really understand the abstractions his daughter liked to paint, he preferred representational art, and best of all he loved the self-portrait she had done for him when she was still an art major in college. But he could feel the pain in these new canvasses of hers, he could sense that she was engaged in an exorcism of sorts, trying to squeeze the pus from some wound deep inside, and he approved. His writing had been a balm for his own wounds more than once. He envied her now, in a way. Richard Cantling had not written a word for more than three years. The crashing commercial failure of *Byeline*, his best novel, had left him blocked and impotent. He'd thought perhaps the change of scene might restore him as well as Michelle, but that had been a vain hope. At least one of them was busy.

Finally, late one night after Cantling had gone to bed, his door opened and Michelle came quietly into his bedroom and sat on the edge of his bed. She was barefoot, dressed in a flannel nightgown covered with tiny pink flowers. 'Daddy,' she said, in a slurred voice.

Cantling had woken when the door opened. He sat up and smiled for her. 'Hi,' he said. 'You've been drinking.'

Michelle nodded. 'I'm going back,' she said. 'Needed some courage, so's I could tell you.'

'Going back?' Cantling said. 'You don't mean to New York? You can't be serious!'

'I got to,' she said. 'Don't be mad. I'm better now.'

'Stay here. Stay with me. New York is uninhabitable, Michelle.'

'I don't want to go back. It scares me. But I got to. My friends are there. My work is there. My life is back there, Daddy. My friend Jimmy, you remember Jimmy, he's art director for this little paperback house, he can get me some cover assignments, he says. He wrote. I won't have to wait tables any more.'

'I don't believe I'm hearing this,' Richard Cantling said. 'How can you go back to that damned city after what happened to you there?'

'That's why I have to go back,' Michelle insisted. 'That guy, what he did ... what he did to me ...' Her voice caught in her throat. She drew in her breath, got hold of herself. 'If I don't go back, it's like he ran me out of town, took my whole life away from me, my friends, my art, everything. I can't let him get away with that, can't let him scare me off. I got to go back and take up what's mine, prove that I'm not afraid.'

Richard Cantling looked at his daughter helplessly. He reached out, gently touched her long, soft hair. She had finally said something that made sense in his terms. He would do the same thing, he knew. 'I understand,' he said. 'It's going to be lonely here without you, but I understand, I do.'

'I'm scared,' Michelle said. 'I bought plane tickets. For tomorrow.'

'So soon?'

'I want to do it quickly, before I lose my nerve,' she said. 'I don't think I've ever been this scared. Not even ... not even when it was happening. Funny, huh?'

'No,' said Cantling. 'It makes sense.'

'Daddy, hold me,' Michelle said. She pressed herself into his arms.

He hugged her and felt her body tremble.

'You're shaking,' he said.

She wouldn't let go of him. 'You remember, when I was real little, I used to have those nightmares, and I'd come bawling into your bedroom in the middle of the night and crawl into bed between you and Mommy.'

Cantling smiled. 'I remember,' he said.

'I want to stay here tonight,' Michelle said, hugging him even more tightly. 'Tomorrow I'll be back there, alone. I don't want to be alone tonight. Can I, Daddy?'

Cantling disengaged gently, looked her in the eyes. 'Are you sure?'

She nodded; a tiny, quick, shy nod. A child's nod.

He threw back the covers and she crept in next to him. 'Don't go away,' she said. 'Don't even go to the bathroom, okay? Just stay right here with me.'

'I'm here,' he said. He put his arms around her, and Michelle curled up under the covers with her head on his shoulder. They lay together that way for a long time. He could feel her heart beating inside her chest. It was a soothing sound; soon Cantling began to drift back to sleep.

'Daddy?' she whispered against his chest.

He opened his eyes. 'Michelle?'

'Daddy, I have to get rid of it. It's inside me and it's poison. I don't want to take it back with me. I have to get rid of it.'

Cantling stroked her hair, long slow steady motions, saying nothing.

'When I was little, you remember, whenever I fell down or got in a fight, I'd come running to you, all teary, and show you my booboo. That's what I used to call it when I got hurt, remember, I'd say I had a booboo.'

'I remember,' Cantling said.

'And you, you'd always hug me and you'd say, "Show me where it hurts," and I would and you'd kiss it and make it better, you remember that? Show me where it hurts?'

Cantling nodded. 'Yes,' he said softly.

Michelle was crying quietly. He could feel the wetness soaking through the top of his pajamas. 'I can't take it back with me, Daddy. I want to show you where it hurts. Please. Please.'

He kissed the top of her head. 'Go on.'

She started at the beginning, in a halting whisper.

When dawn light broke through the bedroom windows, she was still talking. They never slept. She cried a lot, screamed once or twice, shivered frequently despite the weight of the blankets; Richard Cantling never let go of her, not once, not for a single moment. She showed him where it hurt.

*

Barry Leighton sighed. 'It was a far, far better thing you did than you had ever done,' he said. 'Now if you'd only gone off to that far, far better rest right then and there, that very moment, everything would have been fine.' He shook his head. 'You never did know when to write Thirty, Cantling.'

'Why?' Cantling demanded. 'You're a good man, Leighton, tell me. Why is this happening. Why?'

The reporter shrugged. He was beginning to fade now. 'That was the W that always gave me the most trouble,' he said wearily. 'Pick the story, and let me loose, and I could tell you the who and the what and the when and the where and even the how. But the why . . . ah, Cantling, you're the novelist, the whys are your province, not mine. The only Y that I ever really got on speaking terms with was the one goes with MCA.'

Like the Cheshire cat, his smile lingered long after the rest of him was gone. Richard Cantling sat staring at the empty chair, at the abandoned tumbler, watching the whiskey-soaked ice cubes melt slowly.

*

He did not remember falling asleep. He spent the night in the chair, and woke stiff and achy and cold. His dreams had been dark and shapeless and full of fear. He had slept well into the afternoon; half the day was gone. He made himself a tasteless breakfast in a kind of fog. He seemed distant from his own body, and every motion was slow and clumsy. When the coffee was ready, he poured a cup, picked it up, dropped it. The mug broke into a dozen pieces. Cantling stared down at it stupidly, watching rivulets of hot brown liquid run between the tiles. He did not have the energy to clean it up. He got a fresh mug, poured more coffee, managed to get down a few swallows.

The bacon was too salty; the eggs were runny, disgusting. Cantling pushed the meal away half-eaten, and drank more of the black, bitter coffee. He felt hung over, but he knew that booze was not the problem.

Today, he thought. It will end today, one way or the other. She will not go back. *Byeline* was his eighth novel, the next to the last. Today the final portrait would arrive. A character from his ninth novel, his last novel. And then it would be over.

Or maybe just beginning.

How much did Michelle hate him? How badly had he wronged her? Cantling's hand shook; coffee slopped over the top of the mug, burning his fingers. He winced, cried out. Pain was so inarticulate. Burning. He thought of smoldering cigarettes, their tips like small red eyes. His stomach heaved. Cantling lurched to his feet, rushed to the bathroom. He got there just in time, gave his breakfast to the bowl. Afterwards he was too weak to move. He lay slumped against the cold white porcelain, his head swimming. He imagined somebody coming up behind him, taking him by the hair, forcing his face down into the water, flushing, flushing, laughing all the while, saying dirty, dirty, I'll get you clean, you're so dirty, flushing, flushing so the toilet ran and ran, holding his face down so the water and the vomit filled his mouth, his nostrils, until he could hardly breathe, until the world was almost black, until it was almost over, and then up again, laughing while he sucked in air, and then pushing him down again, flushing again, and again and again and again. But it was only his imagination. There was no one there. No one. Cantling was alone in the bathroom.

He forced himself to stand. In the mirror his face was gray and ancient, his hair filthy and unkempt. Behind him, leering over his shoulder, was another face. A man's face, pale and drawn, with black hair parted in the middle and slicked back. Behind a pair of small round glasses were eyes the color of dirty ice, eyes that moved constantly, frenetically, wild animals caught in a trap. They would chew off their own limbs to be free, those eyes. Cantling blinked and the face was gone. He turned on the cold tap, plunged his cupped hands under the stream, splashed water on his face. He could feel the stubble of his beard. He needed to shave. But there wasn't time, it wasn't important, he had to . . . he had to . . .

He had to do something. Get out of there. Get away, get to someplace safe, somewhere his children couldn't find him.

But there was nowhere safe, he knew.

He had to reach Michelle, talk to her, explain, plead. She loved him. She *would* forgive him, she had to. She would call it off, she would tell him what to do.

Frantic, Cantling rushed back to the living room, snatched up the phone. He couldn't remember Michelle's number. He searched around, found his address book, flipped through it wildly. There, there; he punched in the numbers.

The phone rang four times. Then someone picked it up.

'Michelle—' he started.

'Hi,' she said. 'This is Michelle Cantling, but I'm not in right now. If you'll leave your name and number when you hear the tone, I'll get back to you, unless you're selling something.'

The beep sounded. 'Michelle, are you there?' Cantling said. 'I know you hide behind the machine sometimes, when you don't want to talk. It's me. Please pick up. Please.'

Nothing.

'Call me back, then,' he said. He wanted to get it all in; his words tumbled over each other in their haste to get out. 'I, you, you can't do it, please, let me explain, I never meant, I never meant, please . . .' There was the beep again, and then a dial tone. Cantling stared at the phone, hung up slowly. She would call him back. She had to, she was his daughter, they loved each other, she had to give him the chance to explain. Of course, he had tried to explain before.

*

His doorbell was the old-fashioned kind, a brass key that projected out of the door. You had to turn it by hand, and when you did it produced a loud, impatient metallic rasp. Someone was turning it furiously, turning it and turning it and turning it. Cantling rushed to the door, utterly baffled. He had never made friends easily, and it was even harder now that he had become so set in his ways. He had no real friends in Perrot, a few acquaintances perhaps, but no one who would come calling so unexpectedly, and twist the bell with such energetic determination.

He undid his chain and flung the door open, wrenching the bell key out of Michelle's fingers.

She was dressed in a belted raincoat, a knitted ski cap, a matching scarf. The scarf and a few loose strands of hair were caught in the wind, moving restlessly. She was wearing high, fashionable boots and carrying a big leather shoulder bag. She looked good. It had been almost a year since Cantling had seen her, on his last Christmas visit to New York. It had been two years since she'd moved back east.

'Michelle,' Cantling said. 'I didn't . . . this is quite a surprise. All the way from New York and you didn't even tell me you were coming?'

'No,' she snapped. There was something wrong with her voice, her eyes. 'I didn't want to give you any warning, you bastard. You didn't give me any warning.'

'You're upset,' Cantling said. 'Come in, let's talk.'

'I'll come in all right.' She pushed past him, kicked the door shut behind her with so much force that the buzzer sounded again. Out of the wind, her face got even harder. 'You want to know why I came? I am going to tell you what I think of you. Then I'm going to turn around and leave, I'm going to walk right out of this house and out of your fucking life, just like mom did. She was the smart one, not me. I was dumb enough to think you loved me, crazy enough to think you cared.'

'Michelle, don't,' Cantling said. 'You don't understand. I do love you. You're my little girl, you—'

'Don't you *dare!*' she screamed at him. She reached into her shoulder bag. 'You call this *love*, you rotten bastard!' She pulled it out and flung it at him.

Cantling was not as quick as he'd been. He tried to duck, but it caught him on the side of his neck, and it hurt. Michelle had thrown it hard, and it was a big, thick, heavy hardcover, not some flimsy paperback. The pages fluttered as it tumbled to the carpet; Cantling stared down at his own photograph on the back of the dust-wrapper. 'You're just like your mother,' he said, rubbing his neck where the book had hit. 'She always threw things too. Only you aim better.' He smiled weakly.

'I'm not interested in your jokes,' Michelle said. 'I'll never forgive you. Never. Never ever. All I want to know is how you can do this to me, that's all. You tell me. You tell me now.'

'I,' Cantling said. He held his hands out helplessly. 'Look, I . . . you're upset now, why don't we have some coffee or something, and talk about it when you calm down a little. I don't want a big fight.'

'I don't give a fuck what you want,' Michelle screamed. 'I want to talk about it right now!' She kicked the fallen book.

Richard Cantling felt his own anger building. It wasn't right for her to yell at him like that, he didn't deserve this attack, he hadn't done anything. He tried not to say anything for fear of saying the wrong thing and escalating the situation. He knelt and picked up his book. Without thinking, he brushed it off, turned it over almost tenderly. The title glared up at him; stark, twisted red letters against a black background, the distorted face of a pretty young woman, mouth open in a scream. *Show Me Where It Hurts*.

'I was afraid you'd take it the wrong way,' Cantling said.

'The *wrong way!*' Michelle said. A look of incredulity passed across her face. 'Did you think I'd *like* it?'

'I, I wasn't sure,' said Cantling. 'I hoped . . . I mean, I was uncertain of your reaction, and so I thought it would be better not to mention what I was working on, until, well . . .'

'Until the fucking thing was in the bookstore windows,' Michelle finished for him.

Cantling flipped past the title page. 'Look,' he said, holding it out, 'I dedicated it to you.' He showed her:

To Michelle, who knew the pain.

Michelle swung at it, knocked it out of Cantling's hands. 'You bastard,' she said. 'You think that makes it better? You think your stinking dedication excuses what you did? Nothing excuses it. I'll never forgive you.'

Cantling edged back a step, retreating in the face of her fury. 'I didn't do anything,' he said stubbornly. 'I wrote a book. A novel. Is that a crime?'

'You're my *father*,' she shrieked. 'You knew . . . you knew, you bastard, you knew I couldn't bear to talk about it, to talk about what happened. Not to my lovers or my friends or even my therapist, I can't, I just can't, I can't even think about it, you knew. I told you, I told only you, because you were my daddy and I trusted you and I had to get it out, and I told you, it was private, it was just between us, you knew, but what did you do? You wrote it all up in a goddamned book and *published* it for millions of people to read! Damn you, damn you. Were you planning to do that all along, you son of a bitch? Were you? That night in bed, were you memorizing every word?'

'I,' said Cantling. 'No, I didn't memorize anything, I just, well, I just remembered it. You're taking it all wrong, Michelle. The book's not about what happened to you. Yes, it's inspired by that, that was the starting point, but it's fiction, I changed things, it's just a novel.'

'Oh yeah, Daddy, you changed things all right. Instead of Michelle Cantling it's all about Nicole Mitchell, and she's a fashion designer instead of an artist, and she's also kind of stupid, isn't she? Was that a change or is that what you think, that I was stupid to live there, stupid to let him in like that? It's all fiction, yeah. It's just a coincidence that it's about this girl that gets held prisoner and raped and tortured and terrorized and raped some more, and that you've got a daughter who was held prisoner and raped and tortured and terrorized and raped some more, right, just a fucking coincidence!'

'You don't understand,' Cantling said helplessly.

'No, *you* don't understand. You don't understand what it's like. This is your biggest book in years, right? Number one bestseller, you've never been number one before, haven't even been on the lists since *Times Are Hard*, or was it *Black Roses?* And why not, why not number one, this isn't no boring story about a has-been newspaper, this is *rape*, hey, what could be hotter? Lots of sex and violence, torture and fucking and terror, and doncha know, *it really happened*, yeah.' Her mouth twisted and trembled. 'It was the worst thing that ever happened to me. It was all the nightmares that have ever been. I still wake up screaming sometimes, but I was getting better, it was behind me. And now it's there in every bookstore window, and all my friends know, everybody knows, strangers come up to me at parties and tell me how sorry they are.' She choked back a sob; she was halfway between anger and tears. 'And I pick up your book, your fucking no-good book, and there it is again, in black and white, all written down. You're such a fucking *good* writer, Daddy, you make it all so real. A book you can't put down. Well, I put it down but it didn't help, it's all there, now it will always be there, won't it? Every day somebody in the world will pick up your book and read it and I'll get raped again. That's what you did. You finished the job for him, Daddy. You violated me, took me without my consent, just like he did. You raped me. You're my own father and you raped me!'

'You're not being fair,' Cantling said. 'I never meant to hurt you. The book . . . Nicole is strong and smart. It's the man who's the monster. He uses all those different names because fear has a thousand names, but only one face, you see. He's not just a man, he's the darkness made flesh, the mindless violence that waits out there for all of us, the gods that play with us like flies, he's a symbol of all—'

'He's the man who raped me! He's not a symbol!'

She screamed it so loudly that Richard Cantling had to retreat in the face of her fury. 'No,' he said. 'He's just a character. He's . . . Michelle, I know it hurts, but what you went through, it's something people should know about, should think about, it's a part of life. Telling about life, making sense of it, that's the job of literature, that's my job. Someone had to tell your story. I tried to make it true, tried to do my—'

His daughter's face, red and wet with tears, seemed almost feral for a moment, unrecognizable, inhuman. Then a curious calm passed across her features. 'You got one thing right,' she said. 'Nicole didn't have a father. When I was a little kid I'd come to you crying and my daddy would say show me where it hurts, and it was a private thing, a special thing, but in the book Nicole doesn't have a father, he says it, you gave it to him, he says show me where it hurts, he says it all the time. You're so ironic. You're so clever. The way he said it, it made him so real, more real than when he was real. And when you wrote it, you were right. That's what the monster says. Show me where it hurts. That's the monster's line. Nicole doesn't have a father, he's dead, yes, that was right too. I don't have a father. No I don't.'

'Don't you talk to me like that,' Richard Cantling said. It was terror inside him; it was shame. But it came out anger. 'I won't have that, no matter what you've been through. I'm your father.'

'No,' Michelle said, grinning crazy now, backing away from him. 'No, I don't have a father, and you don't have any children, no, unless it's in your books. Those are your children, your only children. Your books, your damned fucking books, those are your children, those are your children, those are your children.' Then she turned and ran past him, down the foyer. She stopped at the door to his den. Cantling was afraid of what she might do. He ran after her.

When he reached the den, Michelle had already found the knife and set to work.

*

Richard Cantling sat by his silent phone and watched his grandfather clock tick off the hours toward darkness.

He tried Michelle's number at three o'clock, at four, at five. The machine, always the machine, speaking in a mockery of her voice. His messages grew more desperate. It was growing dim outside. His light was fading.

Cantling heard no steps on his porch, no knock on his door, no rasping summons from his old brass bell. It was an afternoon as silent as the grave.

But by the time evening had fallen, he knew it was out there. A big square package, wrapped in brown paper, addressed in a hand he had known well. Inside a portrait.

He had not understood, not really, and so she was teaching him.

The clock ticked. The darkness grew thicker. The sense of a waiting presence beyond his door seemed to fill the house. His fear had been growing for hours. He sat in the armchair with his legs pulled up under him, his mouth hanging open, thinking, remembering. Heard cruel laughter. Saw the dim red tips of cigarettes in the shadows, moving, circling. Imagined their small hot kisses on his skin. Tasted urine, blood, tears. Knew violence, knew violation, of every sort there was. His hands, his voice, his face, his face, his face. The character with a dozen names, but fear had only a single face. The youngest of his children. His baby. His monstrous baby.

He had been blocked for so long, Cantling thought. If only he could make her understand. It was a kind of impotence, not writing. He had been a writer, but that was over. He had been a husband, but his wife was dead. He had been a father, but she got better, went back to New York. She left him alone, but that last night, wrapped in his arms, she told him the story, she showed him where it hurt, she gave him all that pain. What was he to do with it?

Afterwards he could not forget. He thought of it constantly. He began to reshape it in his head, began to grope for the words, the scenes, the symbols that would make sense of it. It was hideous, but it was life, raw strong life, the grist for Cantling's mill, the very thing he needed. She had showed him where it hurt; he could show them all. He did resist, he did try. He began a short story, an essay, finished some reviews. But it returned. It was with him every night. It would not be denied.

He wrote it.

'Guilty,' Cantling said in the darkened room. And when he spoke the word, a kind of acceptance seemed to settle over him, banishing the terror. He was guilty. He had done it. He would accept the punishment, then. It was only right.

Richard Cantling stood and went to his door.

The package was there.

He lugged it inside, still wrapped, carried it up the stairs. He would hang him beside the others, beside Dunnahoo and Cissy and Barry Leighton, all in a row, yes. He went for his hammer, measured carefully, drove the nail. Only then did he unwrap the portrait, and look at the face within.

It captured her as no other artist had ever done, not just the lines of her face, the high angular cheekbones and blue eyes and tangled ash-blonde hair, but the personality inside. She looked so young and fresh and confident, and he could see the strength there, the courage, the stubbornness.

But best of all he liked her smile. It was a lovely smile, a smile that illuminated her whole face. The smile seemed to remind him of someone he had known once. He couldn't remember who.

Richard Cantling felt a strange, brief sense of relief, followed by an even greater sense of loss, a loss so terrible and final and total that he knew it was beyond the power of the words he worshipped.

Then the feeling was gone.

Cantling stepped back, folded his arms, studied the four portraits. Such excellent work; looking at the paintings, he could almost feel their presence in his house.

Dunnahoo, his first-born, the boy he wished he'd been.

Cissy, his true love.

Barry Leighton, his wise and tired alter-ego.

Nicole, the daughter he'd never had.

His people. His characters. His children.

*

A week later, another, much smaller, package arrived. Inside the carton were copies of four of his novels, a bill, and a polite note from the artist inquiring if there would be any more commissions.

Richard Cantling said no, and paid the bill by check.

George R. R. Martin

A RRETROSPECTIVE FICTION CHECKLIST

As of 31 December 2002

By Leslie Kay Swigart

University Library, California State University, Long Beach

This retrospective checklist of the professionally published fiction of George R. R. Martin is the initial issue of a larger project which is to be as complete and thorough a bibliography of the work by and about George R. R. Martin as may be created by diligence, persistence, and sheer dogged research. In this future bibliography I hope to provide meticulously detailed bibliographic descriptions of all known editions, versions, adaptations, and translations of all books, scripts, short fiction, and nonfiction by Mr Martin, as well as an annotated bibliography of all known reviews, interviews, articles, and biographical works about Mr Martin and his work.

This retrospective checklist is a much more modest effort. The focus of this listing is on the first English-language professional print publications of his books, the books he has edited, and his short fiction. For the books, only the first American and British English language editions are given, with no attempt to track the reprintings of these or other editions. There is a note of those foreign languages and nonprint formats into which they are known to have been translated. The short fiction and scripts are listed chronologically by year, then alphabetically by title, with the first publication or first air dates given, along with appearances in his collections, and any translations or nonprint formats.

This project began, although I was then unaware of it, one late June weekend in 1973 in Dallas, Texas. I was attending D-Con '73, a comics- and science fiction-oriented convention, as the author of *Harlan Ellison: A Bibliographical Checklist*, which was being published that weekend by the convention chairman, Joe Bob Williams, in honor of the con's guest of honor, Harlan Ellison. In attendance at the con was a group of young writers, most of whom knew each other through their SF or comics connections. Among these writers were Howard Waldrop, Steve Utley, and George R. R. Martin.

As far as any evidence exists, I next ran into George at the Science Fiction Writers of America's Nebula Awards weekend in spring 1974 where George took a photo of a very young and startled looking me which I still have. By DisCon II (32nd World Science Fiction Convention, Washington, D.C., 1974), our acquaintance was off and running (literally!). Over the years there have been many conversations, mail and email exchanged, and meals shared, as well as the occasional convention.

After a while, as George's writing career continued to prosper, there were thoughts and desultory discussion about my doing a bibliography of George's work along the lines of the one I'd done on Ellison. Then, while attending a party at ConJose (60th World SF Convention, San Jose, California) in 2002, George asked me if I'd be interested in doing a modest bibliography for the collection of his work that was being proposed for publication in time for his Guest of Honor gig at Torcon III (61st World SF Convention in Toronto) the next year. If so, he would broach the subject with his publisher, William Schafer of Subterranean Press. Then, in late September an email arrived with the subject line of 'wanna do my bibliography?' Schafer was interested. Emails were exchanged. Et voilà!

Leslie Kay Swigart
Los Angeles and Long Beach, California
January 2003

The sources of this checklist are as follows:

My own collection, which has been generously supplemented over the years by gifts of books, especially foreign editions, from George. Thanks George!

Stephensen-Payne, Phil. *George R. R. Martin: The Ace from New Jersey; A Working Bibliography*. 2nd rev. edn. [Leeds, England; Albuquerque, NM]: Galactic Central [1989]. The original edition (1987) of this bibliography was the first separately published bibliography of Martin's work.

Marano, Lydia C. 'George R(aymond) R(ichard) Martin: Bibliography.' Manuscript bibliography, dated 31 May 1994, prepared for an unrealized publication.

Miller, John J. 'Collecting George R. R. Martin.' *Firsts: The Book Collector's Magazine*, 11 (9), November 2001: 36–45. Provides valuation ranges for first editions.

WorldCat [OCLC; accessed 2002–08–19]

Index Translationum, 1971-date. [print: 1971–1977; electronic: 1978-date, http://databases.unesco.org/xtrans/; last accessed: 2003–01–06]

'George R. R. Martin – Bibliography Summary.' The Internet Speculative Fiction Database, [http://www.sfsite.com; accessed: 2002–09–30; currently at: http://www.isfdb.com]

'George R. R. Martin Bibliography' [and] 'George R. R. Martin Cover Art Gallery.' George R. R. Martin Official Website. [http://www.georgerrmartin.com; last accessed: 2003–01–23]

Order of information and Abbreviations used in this checklist:

For Books and Books Edited:
Title of Book [type of book]
a. [Hardcover, paperback or trade paper indicator] Place of publication: publisher name, year of publication. Price in country of publication (additional prices if given). Note: Only first American and British editions are given, with the occasional limited edition where that edition is not the first.
b. Foreign languages, adaptations, and nonprint formats into which book is known to have been translated.
c. Contents of collections are given based on the first publication.

For scripts:
a. [TV scripts] 'Episode title.' *Series title*, first airdate.
b. [Film scripts] **Title**. Producing company, year of first release.

Order of information (when known) for short fiction:

For short fiction in periodicals:
a. 'Title of story.' *Periodical title*, volume number (issue number; whole issue number). [Abbreviations for appearances in Martin's own collections]
b. Foreign languages, adaptations, and nonprint formats into which book is known to have been translated.

For short fiction in books:
a. 'Title of story.' Place of publication: publisher name, year of publication. [Abbreviations for appearances in Martin's collections]
b. Foreign languages, adaptations, and nonprint formats into which book is known to have been translated.

General notes: Slight variations in titles from edition to edition are not usually noted. Subsequent reprints at variant prices are not noted.

Abbreviations for Martin collections in which the publication also appears:

SLya =　　　　*A Song for Lya and Other Stories* [1976]
SongS&S =　　*Songs of Stars and Shadows* [1977]
Wind =　　　　*Windhaven* [1981; novel based on previously published stories]
Sks =　　　　　*Sandkings* [1981]
SongsDMS =　*Songs the Dead Men Sing* [1983]
Nflyrs =　　　*Nightflyers* [the collection; 1985]
TufV =　　　　*Tuf Voyaging* [1986]
Portraits =　　*Portraits of His Children* [1987]
Quartet =　　　*Quartet* [2001]

General Abbreviations:

E-text =　　　electronic-based text
Ed. =　　　　Edited
HC =　　　　　hardcover edition
Ltd =　　　　limited edition
PB =　　　　　mass market paperback edition
TPB =　　　　trade paperback edition

BOOKS BY:

A Song for Lya and Other Stories [Short Story Collection]
[PB] New York: Avon, 1976; $1.25
[PB] Sevenoaks [UK]: Coronet, 1978
Other forms: French; German; Italian; Spanish.
Contents: With Morning Comes Mistfall. The Second Kind of Loneliness. Override. Dark, Dark Were the Tunnels. The Hero. fta. Run to Starlight. The Exit to San Breta. Slide Show. A Song for Lya.

Songs of Stars and Shadows [Short Story Collection]
[PB] New York: Pocket Books, 1977; $1.75

Other forms: French; German; Italian; Spanish.

Contents: Introduction. This Tower of Ashes. Patrick Henry, Jupiter, and the Little Red Brick Spaceship. Men of Greywater Station [written with Howard Waldrop]. The Lonely Songs of Laren Dorr. Night of the Vampyres. The Runners. Night Shift. '. . . for a single yesterday.' And Seven Times Never Kill Man.

Dying of the Light [Novel]

[HC] New York: Simon and Schuster, 1977; $9.95

[HC] London: Victor Gollancz, 1978

Other forms: French; German; Italian; Russian; Spanish; Audiorecording for the blind and physically handicapped.

Hugo Awards nominee.

Windhaven. Written with Lisa Tuttle. [Novel based on previously published stories]

[HC] New York: Timescape Books, 1981; $13.95

[PB] London: New English Library, 1982

Other forms: Croatian; Czech; Dutch; French; German; Italian; Japanese; Polish; Russian; Spanish.

Contents: Novel based on previously published stories: Storms [original title: The Storms of Windhaven]. One-Wing. The Fall (published contemporaneously in *Amazing*).

Nightflyers. [Novella expanded from the originally published story]

[PB; with: *True Names*, by Vernor Vinge.] New York: Dell, 1981 (*Binary Star* #5); $2.50

Other forms: French.

Hugo Awards nominee.

Sandkings [Short Story Collection]

[PB] New York: Pocket Books, 1981; $2.75

[PB] London: Futura, 1983; £2.25 ($6.95 Australia)

Other forms: Czech; German; Japanese; Polish.

Contents: The Way of Cross and Dragon. Bitterblooms. In the House of the Worm. Fast-Friend. The Stone City. Starlady. Sandkings.

Fevre Dream [Novel]

[HC] New York: Poseidon Press, 1982; $14.95

[HC] London: Victor Gollancz, 1983

Other forms: German; Italian; Japanese; Spanish; Audiorecording for the blind and physically handicapped.

World Fantasy Awards nominee.

Songs the Dead Men Sing [Short Story Collection]

[HC Ltd] Niles, Illinois: Dark Harvest, 1983; $35.00 [for 500 for sale copies] [Limitation statement: 'The First Edition of *Songs the Dead Men Sing* is limited to five hundred individually signed and numbered copies.' Marano notes that there were also 50 presentation copies, and six proofs.]

[HC] London: Victor Gollancz, 1985; £9.95

Other forms: Spanish.

Contents: George R. R. Martin, Dark Harbinger [introduction; by A. J. Budrys; omitted from British editions]. The Monkey Treatment. ' . . . for a single yesterday.' In the House of the Worm [omitted from British editions]. The Needle Men. Meathouse Man. Sandkings. This Tower of Ashes [omitted from British editions]. Nightflyers [expanded version]. Remembering Melody.

The Armageddon Rag: A Stereophonic Long-Playing Novel [Novel]

[HC] New York: Poseidon Press, 1983; $15.95

[HC Ltd] Omaha [and] Kansas City: Nemo Press, 1983; $50.00 [for 500 for sale copies] [Limitation statement: 'This special collector's first edition is limited to 540 signed and slipcased copies, of which 500 are for sale, 14 are specially marked and numbered as review copies, and the remaining 26, marked A through Z are reserved for the Press, having been designated as presentation copies. Six of these presentation copies are hand-bound in leather and are personalized with foil stamping'.]

[PB] Sevenoaks [UK]: New English Library, 1984; £2.95

Other forms: Croatian; French; German; Swedish; Braille edition.

World Fantasy Awards nominee.

Nightflyers [Short Story Collection]

[TPB] New York: Bluejay Books, 1985; $8.95

Other forms: Russian.

Contents: Nightflyers [expanded version]. Override. Weekend in a War Zone. And Seven Times Never Kill Man. Nor the Many-Colored Fires of a Star Ring. A Song for Lya.

Tuf Voyaging [Short Story Collection]

[HC] New York: Baen Books, 1986; $15.95

[HC] London: Victor Gollancz, 1987; £10.95

Contents: Prologue. The Plague Star. Loaves and Fishes. Guardians. Second Helpings. A Beast for Norn [rewritten version]. Call Him Moses. Manna from Heaven.

Other forms: Bulgarian; Czech; Lithuanian; Polish; Romanian; Russian; Spanish.

Portraits of His Children [Short Story Collection]

[HC Ltd] Arlington Hts., Illinois: Dark Harvest, 1987; $150.00 [52 copies lettered, signed, boxed]; $39.95 [Limitation statement: 'This deluxe first edition of Portraits of His Children is limited to four hundred-fifty individually signed and numbered copies.'] [Note: Marano says: 75 presentation copies and 24 proofs also.]

[HC] Arlington Hts., Illinois: Dark Harvest, 1987; $18.95 [2500 copies]

Other forms: Czech.

Contents: A Sketch of Their Fathers [introduction by Roger Zelazny]. With Morning Comes Mistfall. The Second Kind of Loneliness. The Last Super Bowl. The Lonely Songs of Laren Dorr. The Ice Dragon. In the Lost Lands. Unsound Variations. Closing Time. Under Siege. The Glass Flower. Portraits of His Children.

Dead Man's Hand [Novel; written with John J. Miller; *Wild Cards, 7*]
See below: Books Edited By GRRM.

The Pear-Shaped Man [separately published short story]

[PB] Eugene [Oregon]: Pulphouse, 1991 (Short Story Paperback, #37); $1.95

[HC] Eugene [Oregon]: Pulphouse, 1991 (Short Story Hardback, #24); $20.00 [Limitation statement: 'Short Story Hardback Issue Twenty-Four: The Pear-Shaped Man by George R. R. Martin has been published in a limited edition of 100 copies. 100 limited, signed, and numbered 1–100.']

The Way of Cross and Dragon; [Russian title transliterated:] *Put' kresta i drakona* [Russian language 'Short Story Collection; no English language equivalent]

[HC] Moscow: AST, 1996

Contents: A Song for Lya. The Stone City. The Glass Flower. Sandkings. The Way of Cross and Dragon. With Morning Comes Mistfall. Unsound Variations. Closing Time. Portraits of His Children.

A Game of Thrones [Novel; *A Song of Ice and Fire, NBI1*]

[The opening chapters published as in a paperback as a 'preview edition.'] London: HarperCollins, 1996; £0.99

[HC] New York: Bantam Books, 1996; $21.95 ($29.95 Canada)

[HC] London: HarperCollins, 1996

[HC Ltd] Atlanta [Georgia]: Meisha Merlin, 2000 [Limitation Statement: 'This edition of *A Game of Thrones* is limited to 500 copies, 52 lettered and 448 numbered.']

Other forms: Chinese; Czech; Dutch; French; German; Hebrew; Italian; Polish; Swedish; Audiorecording for the blind and physically handicapped.

Nebula Awards nominee; World Fantasy Awards nominee.

A Clash of Kings [Novel; *A Song of Ice and Fire, 2*]
[HC] London: HarperCollins, 1998; £17.99
[HC] New York: Bantam Books, 1999; $25.95
Other forms: Czech; Dutch; French; German; Hebrew; Italian; Polish;
Russian; Audiorecording for the blind and physically handicapped.
Nebula Awards nominee.

A Storm of Swords [Novel; *A Song of Ice and Fire, 3*]
[HC] London: HarperCollins, 2000
[HC] New York: Bantam Books, 2000; $26.95 ($39.95 Canada)
Other forms: Czech; Dutch; French; German; Hebrew; Italian; Audiore-
cording for the blind and physically handicapped.
Nebula Awards nominee; Hugo Awards nominee.

Quartet: Four Tales from the Crossroads [Collection; edited by Christine
Carpenito]
[IIC Ltd] Framingham [Massachusetts]: NESFA Press, 2001 [Limitation
statement: '*Quartet* was printed in an edition of 1200 numbered
hardcover books, of which the first 200 were signed by the author and
artist, bound with special endpapers and slipcased. Of these 200 copies,
the first 10 are lettered A through J and the remainder are numbered 1
through 190. The trade copies are numbered 191 through 1190.']
[HC] Framingham [Massachusetts]: NESFA Press, 2001; $25.00
[TPB] Framingham [Massachusetts]: NESFA Press, 2001; $15.00
Contents: Introduction. Black and White and Red All Over. Skin Trade.
StarPort. Blood of the Dragon.

A Feast for Crows [Novel; *A Song of Ice and Fire, 4*] forthcoming.

BOOKS EDITED BY:

New Voices in Science Fiction: Stories by Campbell Award Nominees.
[Anthology; edited by George R. R. Martin]
[HC] New York: Macmillan, 1977; $8.95
Other forms: German.
Contents: Bova, Ben: Introduction. Tuttle, Lisa: The Family Monkey.
Thurston, Robert: Kingmakers. Martin, George R. R.: The Stone City.
Berman, Ruth: To Ceremark. Effinger, George Alec: Mom's Differentials.
Pournelle, Jerry: Silent Leges.

New Voices II. [Anthology; edited by George R. R. Martin]
[PB] New York: Jove/HBJ, 1979; $1.75
Other forms: German.
Contents: Martin, George R. R.: Preface. Sturgeon, Theodore: Introduction. Tuttle, Lisa: The Hollow Man. Snyder, Guy: Lady of Ice. Monteleone, Thomas F.: The Dancer in the Darkness. Miller, Jesse: Twilight Lives. Robinson, Spider: Satan's Children.

New Voices III: The Campbell Award Nominees. [Anthology; edited by George R. R. Martin]
[PB] New York: Berkley, 1980; $1.95
Contents: Martin, George R. R.: Preface. Asimov, Isaac: Introduction. Varley, John: Beatnik Bayou. Pearce, Brenda: Haute Falaisc Bay. Charnas, Suzy McKee: Scorched Supper on New Niger. Brennert, Alan: Stage Whisper. Brennert, Alan: Queen of the Magic Kingdom. Gotschalk, Felix: The Wishes of Maidens. Plauger, P. J.: Virtual Image.

New Voices 4: The John W. Campbell Award Nominees. [Anthology; edited by George R. R. Martin]
[PB] New York: Berkley, 1981; $2.25
Contents: Martin, George R. R.: Preface. van Vogt, A. E.: Introduction. Varley, John: Blue Champagne. Foster, M. A.: Entertainment. Darnay, Arsen: The Pilgrimage of Ishten Telen Haragosh. Vinge, Joan D.: Psiren. Reamy, Tom: M Is for the Million Things. Budrys, Algis: Afterword: Tom Reamy.

The Science Fiction Weight-Loss Book. [Anthology; edited by Isaac Asimov, George R. R. Martin. and Martin H. Greenberg]
[HC] New York: Crown, 1983; $12.95
Contents: Asimov, Isaac: Introduction: Fat! Aandahl, Vance: Sylvester's Revenge. Card, Orson Scott: Fat Farm. Merwin, Sam, Jr.: The Stretch. Lafferty, R. A.: Camels and Dromedaries, Clem. Boyle, T. Coraghessan: The Champ. Wells, H. G.: The Truth about Pyecraft. Silverberg, Robert: The Iron Chancellor. Pohl, Frederik: The Man Who Ate the World. West, John Anthony: Gladys' Gregory. Vance, Jack: Abercrombie Station. Morrison, William: Shipping Clerk. Tenn, William: The Malted Milk Monster. Reed, Kit: The Food Farm. Sanders, Scott: The Artist of Hunger. King, Stephen: Quitters, Inc.

The John W. Campbell Awards, Volume 5. [Anthology; edited by George R. R. Martin]
[TPB] New York: Bluejay Books, 1984; $7.95
Contents: Martin, George R. R.: Preface. Anderson, Poul: Introduction. Chalker, Jack L.: In the Dowaii Chambers. Foster, M. A.: Dreams. Scholz,

Carter: A Catastrophe Machine. Cherryh, C. J.: The Dark King. Cherryh, C. J.: Companions.

Night Visions 3. [Anthology; edited by George R. R. Martin]
[HC Ltd] Niles, Illinois: Dark Harvest, 1986; $49.00 [Limitation statement: 'The deluxe first edition of *Night Visions 3* is limited to four hundred individually signed and numbered copies.' In slipcase.]
[HC] Niles, Illinois: Dark Harvest, 1986; $18.00
[HC] London: Victor Gollancz, 1987
Other forms: Dutch.
Contents: Martin, George R. R.: Introduction: The Horror, The Horror. Campbell, Ramsey: In the Trees; This Time; Missed Conection; Root Cause; Looking Out; Bedtime Story; Beyond Words. Tuttle, Lisa: Riding the Nightmare; From Another Country; The Dragon's Bride. Barker, Clive: The Hellbound Heart.
World Fantasy Awards nominee.

Wild Cards: A Mosaic Novel [Mosaic novel; ***Wild Cards, 1***; edited by George R. R. Martin]
[PB] Toronto [and] New York: Bantam, 1997 $3.95; ($4.95 Canada)
[PB] London: Titan Books, 1989; £3.95
Other forms: German; Japanese; E-text.
Contents: Martin, George R. R.: Prologue. Waldrop, Howard: Thirty Minutes Over Broadway! Zelazny, Roger: The Sleeper. Williams, Walter Jon: Witness. Melinda M. Snodgrass: Degradation Rites. Martin, George R. R.: Interlude One. Martin, George R. R.: Shell Games. Martin, George R. R.: Interlude Two. Shiner, Lewis: The Long, Dark Night of Fortunato. Milán, Victor: Transfigurations. Martin, George R. R.: Interlude Three. Bryant, Edward and Harper, Leanne C.: Down Deep. Martin, George R. R.: Interlude Four. Leigh, Stephen: Strings. Martin, George R. R.: Interlude Five. Miller, John J.: Comes a Hunter. Shiner, Lewis: Epilogue: Third Generation. Milán, Victor: Appendix. [2001 ibooks edition adds:] Wild Cards: A Mike Zeck Gallery. Martin, George R. R.: Afterword.
The Wild Cards series was a Hugo Awards nominee in 1988.

Aces High. [Mosaic novel; ***Wild Cards, 2***; edited by George R. R. Martin]
[PB] Toronto [and] New York: Bantam Books, 1987; $3.95 ($4.95 Canada)
[PB] London: Titan Books, 1989; £3.95
Other forms: German; Japanese.
Contents. Shiner, Lewis: Pennies From Heaven. Martin, George R. R.: Jube: One. Williams, Walter Jon: Unto the Sixth Generation: Prologue. Martin, George R. R.: Jube: Two. Zelazny, Roger: Ashes to Ashes. Williams, Walter Jon: Unto the Sixth Generation: Part One. Williams,

Walter Jon: Unto the Sixth Generation: Part Two. Martin, George R. R.: Jube: Three. Simons, Walton: If Looks Could Kill. Martin, George R. R.: Jube: Four. Williams, Walter Jon: Unto the Sixth Generation: Epilog. Martin, George R. R.: Winter's Chill. Martin, George R. R.: Jube: Five. Snodgrass, Melinda M.: Relative Difficulties. Milán, Victor: With a Little Help from His Friends. Martin, George R. R.: Jube: Six. Cadigan, Pat: By Lost Ways. Williams, Walter Jon: Mr Koyama's Comet. Miller, John J.: Half Past Dead. Martin, George R. R.: Jube: Seven. [2001 ibooks edition adds:] Wild Cards: The Floyd Hughes Gallery. Martin, George R. R.: Afterword.

Jokers Wild: A Wild Cards Mosaic Novel*. [Mosaic novel; **Wild Cards, 3**; edited by George R. R. Martin]
[PB] Toronto [and] New York: Bantam, 1987; $4.50 ($5.50 Canada)
[PB] London: Titan Books, 1989; £3.95
Other forms: German; Japanese; E-text.
Contents: This mosaic novel was collectively written by Edward Bryant, Leanne C. Harper, George R. R. Martin, John J. Miller, Lewis Shiner, Walton Simons, and Melinda M. Snodgrass, but responsibility for the individual parts is not identified. [2002 ibooks edition adds:] Wild Cards: The Tom Palmer Gallery. Martin, George R. R.: Afterword.

Aces Abroad: A Wild Cards Mosaic Novel*. [Mosaic novel; **Wild Cards, 4**; edited by George R. R. Martin; assistant editor: Melinda M. Snodgrass]
[PB] Toronto [and] New York: Bantam, 1988; $4.50 ($5.50 Canada)
[PB] London: Titan Books,1990; £3.95
Other forms: E-text.
Contents: Leigh, Stephen: The Tint of Hatred. Martin, George R. R.: The Journal of Xavier Desmond. Miller, John J.: Beasts of Burden. Harper, Leanne C.: Blood Rights. Gerstner-Miller, Gail: Down by the Nile. Simons, Walton: The Teardrop of India. Bryant, Edward: Down in the Dreamtime. Shiner, Lewis: Zero Hour. Milán, Victor: Puppets. Snodgrass, Melinda M.: Mirror of the Soul. Cassutt, Michael: Legends. [2002 ibooks edition adds:] Illustrations by Tom Mandrake. Martin, George R. R.: Afterword.

Down & Dirty: A Wild Cards Mosaic Novel*. [Mosaic novel; **Wild Cards, 5**; edited by George R. R. Martin; assistant editor: Melinda M. Snodgrass]
[PB] Toronto [and] New York: Bantam, 1988; $4.50 ($5.50 Canada)
[PB] London: Titan Books,1990; £3.99
Other forms: German.

Contents: Miller, John J.: Only the Dead Know Jokertown. Martin, George R. R.: All the King's Horses. Zelazny, Roger: Conterto for Siren and Serotonin. Harper, Leanne C: Breakdown. Cover, Arthur Byron: Jesus Was an Ace. Snodgrass, Melinda M.: Blood Ties. Bryant, Edward: The Second Coming of Buddy Holly. Leigh, Stephen: The Hue of a Mind. Cadigan, Pat: Addicted to Love. Williams, Walter Jon: Mortality. Harper, Leanne C: 'What Rough Beast . . .' [2002 ibooks edition adds:] Illustrations by Timothy Truman. Martin, George R. R.: Afterword.

Ace in the Hole: A Wild Cards Mosaic Novel. [Mosaic novel; *Wild Cards, 6*; edited by George R. R. Martin, assisted by Melinda M. Snodgrass]
[PB] New York [and] Toronto: Bantam, 1990; $4.50 ($5.50 Canada)
[PB] London: Titan Books,1990; £3.99
Other forms: German.
Contents: This mosaic novel was collectively written by Stephen Leigh, Victor Milán, Walton Simons, Melinda M. Snodgrass, and Walter Jon Williams, but responsibility for the individual parts is not identified.

Dead Man's Hand: A Wild Card Novel [Mosaic novel; *Wild Cards, 7*; edited by George R R Martin; assistant editor: Melinda M. Snodgrass]
[PB] New York [and] Toronto: Bantam Books, 1990; $4.50 ($5.50 Canada)
Contents: This novel was written by George R. R. Martin and John J. Miller.

One-Eyed Jacks: A Wild Card Mosaic Novel [Mosaic novel; *Wild Cards, 8*; edited by George R. R. Martin; assistant editor: Melinda M. Snodgrass]
[PB] New York [and] Toronto: Bantam Books, 1991; $4.95 ($5.95 Canada)
Contents: Simons, Walton: Nobody's Girl. Claremont, Chris: Luck Be a Lady. Simons, Walton: Nobody Knows Me Like My Baby. Shiner, Lewis: Horses. Simons, Walton: Mr Nobody Goes to Town. Wu, William F.: Snow Dragon. Simons, Walton: Nobody Knows the Trouble I've Seen. Milán, Victor: Nowadays Clancy Can't Even Sing. Simons, Walton: You're Nobody till Somebody Loves You. Leigh, Stephen: Sixteen Candles. Simons, Walton: My Name Is Nobody. Snodgrass, Melinda M.: The Devil's Triangle. Simons, Walton: Nobody's Home. Miller, John J.: Dead Heart Beating. Simons, Walton: Nobody Gets Out Alive.

Jokertown Shuffle: A Wild Cards Mosaic Novel [Mosaic novel; *Wild Cards, 9*; edited by George R. R. Martin; assistant editor: Melinda M. Snodgrass]
[PB] New York [and] Toronto: Bantam Books, 1991; $4.99 ($5.99 Canada)
Contents: Leigh, Stephen: The Temptation of Hieronymous Bloat. Miller,

John J.: And Hope to Die. Snodgrass, Melinda M.: Lovers. Milán, Victor: Madman across the Water. Williams, Walter Jon: While Night's Black Agents to Their Preys Do Rouse. Shiner, Lewis: Riders. Simons, Walton: Nobody Does It Alone.

Double Solitaire: A Wild Cards Mosaic Novel [Mosaic novel; **Wild Cards, 10**; edited by George R. R. Martin]
[PB] New York [and] Toronto: Bantam Books, 1992; $5.50 ($6.50 Canada)
Contents: This novel was written by Melinda M. Snodgrass.

Dealer's Choice: A Wild Cards Mosaic Novel [Mosaic novel; **Wild Cards, 11**; edited by George R. R. Martin; assistant editor: Melinda M. Snodgrass]
[PB] New York [and] Toronto: Bantam Books, 1992; $5.99 ($6.99 Canada)
Contents: This mosaic novel was collectively written by Edward Bryant, Stephen Leigh, John J. Miller, George R. R. Martin, and Walter Jon Williams, but responsibility for the individual parts is not identified.

Turn of the Cards: A Wild Cards Novel [Mosaic novel; **Wild Cards, 12**; edited by George R. R. Martin]
[PB] New York [and] Toronto: Bantam Books, 1993; $5.99 ($6.99)
Contents: This novel was written by Victor Milán.

Card Sharks: A Wild Cards Mosaic Novel [Mosaic novel; **Wild Cards, 13; Wild Cards, A New Cycle, 1**; edited by George R. R. Martin; assistant editor: Melinda M. Snodgrass]
[PB] Riverdale, NY: Baen, 1993; $5.99 ($6.99 Canada)
Contents: Leigh, Stephen: The Ashes of Memory. Wu, William F: Till I Kissed You. Snodgrass Melinda M.: The Crooked Man. Cassutt, Michael: A Method of Reaching Extreme Altitudes. Milán, Victor: A Wind from Khorasan: The Narrative of J. Robert Belew. Zelazny, Roger: The Long Sleep. Murphy, Kevin Andrew: Cursum Perficio. Mixon, Laura J.: The Lamia's Tale.

Marked Card: A Wild Card Mosaic Novel [Mosaic novel; **Wild Cards, 14; Wild Cards, A New Cycle, 2**; edited by George R. R. Martin; assistant editor: Melinda M. Snodgrass]
[PB] Riverdale, NY: Baen, 1994; $5.99 ($7.50 Canada)
Contents: Leigh, Stephen: The Color of His Skin. Simons, Walton: Two of a Kind. Milán, Victor: My Sweet Lord. Harper, Leanne C: Paths of Silence and of Night. Williams, Walter Jon: Feeding Frenzy. Walker, Sage: A Breath of Life. Mixon, Laura J. and Snodgrass, Melinda M.: A Dose of Reality.

Black Trump: A Wild Card Mosaic Novel [Mosaic novel; **Wild Cards 15; Wild Cards, A New Cycle, 3**; edited by George R. R. Martin; assistant editor: Melinda M. Snodgrass]
[PB] Riverdale, NY: Baen, 1995; $5.99
Contents: This mosaic novel was collectively written by Geroge R. R. Martin, Stephen Leigh, Victor Milán, John J. Miller, and Sage Walker, but responsibility for the individual parts is not identified.

Deuces Down: A Mosaic Novel [Mosaic novel; **Wild Cards, 16**; edited by George R. R. Martin; assistant editor: Melinda M. Snodgrass]
[HC] New York: ibooks, 2002; $23.00 ($35.00 Canada; £12.99 UK)
Other forms: E-book.
Contents: Simons, Walton: Introduction. Cassutt, Michael: Storming Space. Miller, John J.: Four Days in October. Simons, Walton: Walking the Floor over You. Snodgrass, Melinda M.: A Face for the Cutting Room Floor. Abraham, Daniel: Father Henry's Little Miracle. Leigh, Stephen: Promises. Murphy, Kevin Andrew: With a Flourish and a Flair.

SCRIPTS BY:

The Last Defender of Camelot. Based on the short story by Roger Zelazny. *Twilight Zone*, 11 April 1986.
Writers Guild of America Award, for Best Teleplay/Anthology nominee.

The Once and Future King. Based on a story by Bryce Maritano, *Twilight Zone*, 27 September 1986.

Lost and Found. Based on the short story Phyllis Eisenstein, *Twilight Zone*, 18 October 1986.

The Toys of Caliban. Based on a story by Terry Matz, *Twilight Zone*, 4 December 1986.

The Road Less Traveled. *Twilight Zone*, 18 December 1986.

Terrible Savior. *Beauty and the Beast*, 2 October 1987.
Other forms: Videocassette.

Masques. *Beauty and the Beast*, 30 October 1987.
Other forms: Videocassette.

Shades of Grey. Written with David Peckinpah. *Beauty and the Beast*, 8 January 1988.

Other forms: Videocassette.

Promises of Someday. *Beauty and the Beast*, 12 February 1988.
Other forms: Videocassette.

Ozymandias. *Beauty and the Beast*, 1 April 1988.
Other forms: Videocassette.

Dead of Winter. *Beauty and the Beast*, 9 December 1988.

Brothers. *Beauty and the Beast*, 3 February 1989.

When the Blue Bird Sings. Written with Robert John Guttke. *Beauty and the Beast*, 31 March 1989.

A Kingdom by the Sea. *Beauty and the Beast*, 28 April 1989.

Ceremony of Innocence. Based on a story by Alex Gansa, Howard Gordon, and GRRM. *Beauty and the Beast*, 19 May 1989.

Snow. *Beauty and the Beast*, 27 December 1989.

Beggar's Comet. *Beauty and the Beast*, 3 January 1990.

Invictus. *Beauty and the Beast*, 24 January 1990.

Doorways. Columbia Pictures, 1992. [Note: Originally a pilot for a TV series.]

Other forms: Videocassette.

Starport. [Note: Originally a two-hour pilot for a TV series (1994); not produced.]
[*Quartet*].

SCRIPTS BY OTHERS, BASED ON STORIES BY GRRM:

Remembering Melody. Scriptwriter unknown. *The Hitchhiker*. Home Box Office, 27 November 1984.

Nightflyers [feature film]. Screenplay by Robert Jaffe. Directed by Robert Collector. Vista Films, 1987.
Other forms: Videocassette.

Sandkings. Teleplay by Melinda M. Snodgrass. *The Outer Limits*. Showtime, 26 March 1995. Two-hour TV movie.
Other forms: Videocassette; videodisc.

STORIES BY:

1971

The Hero. *Galaxy*, 31 (3), February 1971. [*SLya*]
Other forms: Czech; French.

1972

The Exit to San Breta. *Fantastic*, 21 (3), February 1972. [*SLya*]
Other forms: French; Japanese.

The Second Kind of Loneliness. *Analog*, 90 (4), December 1972. [*SLya, Portraits*]
Other forms: French; Italian.

1973

Dark, Dark Were the Tunnels. *Vertex*, 1 (5), December 1973. [*SLya*]
Other forms: French.

Night Shift. *Amazing*, 46 (5), January 1973. [*SongsS&S*]
Other forms: Italian.

Override. *Analog*, 92 (1), September 1973. [*SLya, Nflyrs*]
Other forms: French.

A Peripheral Affair. *The Magazine of Fantasy and Science Fiction*, 44 (1; whole #260), January 1973.
Other forms: E-text.

Slide Show. *Omega*. Ed. by Roger Elwood. New York: Walker, 1973. [*SLya*]
Other forms: French.

With Morning Comes Mistfall. *Analog*, 93 [sic, 91] (3), May 1973: [98]–114. [*SLya; Portraits*]
Other forms: French; Italian; Japanese; Russian.
Nebula Awards nominee; Hugo Awards nominee.

1974

fta. *Analog*, 93 (3), May 1974. [*SLya*]
Other forms: French; Italian; Japanese.

Run to Starlight. *Amazing*, 48 (4), December 1974. [*SLya*]

A Song for Lya. *Analog*, 93 (4), June 1974. [*SLya, Nflyrs*]
Other forms: French; Italian; Japanese; Russian.
Nebula Awards nominee; Hugo Awards winner.

1975

And Seven Times Never Kill Man. *Analog*, 95 (7), July 1975. [*SongsS&S; Nflyrs*]
Other forms: Greek; Italian; Japanese.
Hugo Awards nominee.

The Last Super Bowl Game [short version]. *Gallery*, 3 (1), February 1975; [longer version first published in:] *Run to Starlight: Sports through Science Fiction*. Ed. by Martin H. Greenberg, Joseph D. Olander, Patricia Warrick. New York: Delacorte, 1975 [unknown]: [9]–36. [longer version in: *Portraits*]

Night of the Vampyres. *Amazing*, 48 (6), May 1975. [*SongsS&S*]
Other forms: Italian.

The Runners. *The Magazine of Fantasy and Science Fiction*, 49 (3; whole #292), September 1975. [*SongsS&S*]
Other forms: Italian; Japanese.

The Storms of Windhaven. Written with Lisa Turtle. *Analog*, 95 (5), May 1975. [*Wind*]
Other forms: Italian.
Nebula Awards nominee.

1976

A Beast for Norn. *Andromeda 1*. Ed. by Peter Weston. London: Futura, 1976. [Revised version in: *TufV*]
Other forms: German.

The Computer Cried Charge! *Amazing*, 49 (4), January 1976.

Fast-Friend. *Faster than Light*. Ed. by Jack Dann and George Zebrowski. New York: Harper & Row, 1976. [*Sks*]
Other forms: German; Japanese.

'. . . for a single yesterday.' *Epoch*. Ed. by Roger Elwood & Robert Silverberg. New York: Berkley, 1976. [*SongsS&S; SongsDMS*]
Other forms: Italian; Japanese.

In the House of the Worm. *Ides of Tomorrow*. Ed. by Terry Carr. New York: Little Brown, 1976. [*Sks; SongsDMS*]

Other forms: German; Japanese; Spanish.

The Lonely Songs of Laren Dorr. *Fantastic*, 25 (3), May 1976. [*SongsS&S, Portraits*]
Other forms: French; Greek; Italian.

Meathouse Man. *Orbit 18*. Ed. by Damon Knight. New York: Harper & Row, 1976. [*SongsDMS*]
Other forms: Italian.

Men of Greywater Station. Written with Howard Waldrop. *Amazing*, 49 (5), March 1976. [*SongsS&S*]
Other forms: Greek; Italian.

Nobody Leaves New Pittsburg. *Amazing*, 50 (2), September 1976.

Nor the Many-Colored Fires of a Star Ring. *Faster than Light*. Ed. by Jack Dann & George Zebrowski. New York: Harper & Row, 1976. [*Nflyrs*]

Patrick Henry, Jupiter, and the Little Red Brick Spaceship. *Amazing*, 50 (3), December 1976. [*SongsS&S*]
Other forms: Italian.

Starlady. *Science Fiction Discoveries*. Ed. by Carol and Frederik Pohl. New York: Bantam, 1976. [*Sks*]
Other forms: German; Italian; Japanese.

This Tower of Ashes. *Analog Annual*. Ed. by Ben Bova. New York: Pyramid, 1976. [*SongsS&S; Songs DMS*]
Other forms: Italian; Japanese; Spanish.

1977

After the Festival. [Part One of Four Parts] *Analog*, 97 (4), April 1977; [Part II] *Analog*, 97 (5), May 1977; [Part III] *Analog*, 97 (6), June 1977; [Part IV] *Analog*, 97 (7), July 1977.

Bitterblooms. *Cosmos*, 1 (4), November 1977. [*Sks*]
Other forms: German; Japanese.

The Stone City. *New Voices in Science Fiction: Stories by Campbell Award Nominees*. Ed. by George R. R. Martin. New York: Macmillan, 1977. [*Sks*]
Other forms: German; Japanese; Russian; E-text.
Nebula Awards nominee.

Weekend in a War Zone. *Future Pastimes*. Ed. by Scott Edelstein. Nashville, Tennessee: Aurora Publishers, 1977. [*Nflyrs*]

1978

Call Him Moses. *Analog*, 98 (2), February 1978. [*TufV*]
Other forms: Japanese; Russian.

1979

Sandkings. *Omni*, 1 (11), August 1979. [*Sks; SongsDMS*]
Other forms: German; Italian; Japanese; Russian; Spanish; Graphic novel;
TV adaptation; Audiorecording; E-text.
Nebula Awards winner; Hugo Awards winner.

Warship. Written with George Florance-Guthridge. *The Magazine of Fantasy and Science Fiction*, 56; (4; whole #335), April 1979.

The Way of Cross and Dragon. *Omni*, 1 (9), June 1979. [*Sks*]
Other forms: German; Italian; Japanese; Russian.
Nebula Awards nominee; Hugo Awards winner.

1980

The Ice Dragon. *Dragons of Light*. Ed. by Orson Scott Card. New York: Ace,
1980. [*Portraits*]
Other forms: Italian; E-text.

Nightflyers. *Analog*, 100 (4), April 1980. [Expanded version in: *Nightflyers* (Dell, 1981); *Nflyrs, SongsDMS*]
Other forms: Italian; Japanese; Film adaptation; Audiorecording.
Hugo Awards nominee.

One-Wing. Written with Lisa Tuttle. [Part One of Two Parts] *Analog*, 100 (1), January 1980; [Part II] *Analog*, 100 (2), February 1980. [*Wind*]
Other forms: Italian.

1981

The Fall. Written with Lisa Tuttle. *Amazing*, 27 (12), May 1981. [*Wind*]
Other forms: Italian.

Guardians. *Analog*, 101 (11), October 12, 1981. [*TufV*]
Other forms: French.
Hugo Awards nominee.

The Needle Men. *The Magazine of Fantasy and Science Fiction*, 61 (4; whole #365), October 1981. [*SongsDMS*]

Other forms: Japanese; Spanish.

Remembering Melody. *The Twilight Zone Magazine*, 1 (1), April 1981. [*SongsDMS*]
Other forms: Japanese; Spanish; TV adaptation.

1982

Closing Time. *Isaac Asimov's Science Fiction Magazine*, 6 (11; whole #58), November 1982. [*Portraits*]
Other forms: Italian; Russian.

Fevre Dream [excerpt]. *Science Fiction Digest*, [1 (4), September-October 1982].

In the Lost Lands. *Amazons II*. Ed. by Jessica Amanda Salmonson. New York: DAW, 1982. [*Portraits*]
Other forms: Italian.

Unsound Variations. *Amazing*, 28 (4), January 1982. [*Portraits*]
Other forms: German; Russian.
Nebula Awards nominee; Hugo Awards nominee.

1983

The Monkey Treatment. *The Magazine of Fantasy and Science Fiction*, 65 (1; whole #386), July 1983. [*SongsDMS*]
Other forms: Japanese; Spanish.
Nebula Awards nominee; Hugo Awards nominee.

1985

Loaves and Fishes. *Analog*, 105 (10), October 1985. [*TufV*]

Manna from Heaven. *Analog*, 105 (13), Mid-December 1985. [*TufV*]
Other forms: Italian.

The Plague Star. [Part One of Two] *Analog*, 105 (1), January 1985; [Conclusion] *Analog*, 105 (2), February 1985. [*TufV*]

Portraits of His Children. *Isaac Asimov's Science Fiction Magazine*, 9 (11; whole #97), November 1985. [*Portraits*]
Other forms: Italian; Russian; Braille.
Nebula Awards winner; Hugo Awards nominee.

Second Helpings. *Analog*, 105 (11), November 1985. [*TufV*]
Other forms: Italian.

Under Siege. *Omni*, 8 (1), October 1985. [*Portraits*]
Other forms: Audiorecording.

1986

The Glass Flower. *Isaac Asimov's Science Fiction*, 10 (10 [sic, 9]; whole #109 [sic, #108]), September 1986. [*Portraits*]
Other forms: Russian.

1987

Interlude[s] One-Five. *Wild Cards*. Ed. by George R. R. Martin. Toronto [and] New York: Bantam, 1987.
Other forms: German; Japanese; E-text.

Jube: One [through] Jube: Seven. *Aces High*. Ed. by George R. R. Martin. Toronto [and] New York: Bantam, 1987.
Other forms: German; Japanese.

The Pear-Shaped Man. *Omni*, 10 (1), October 1987. [*The Pear-Shaped Man (book)*]
Other forms: E-text.
World Fantasy Awards nominee.

Shell Games. *Wild Cards*. Ed. by George R. R. Martin. Toronto [and] New York: Bantam, 1987.
Other forms: German; Japanese; E-text.

Winter's Chill. *Aces High*. Ed. by George R. R. Martin. Toronto [and] New York: Bantam, 1987.
Other forms: German; Japanese.

1988

All the King's Horses. *Down and Dirty*. Ed. by George R. R. Martin; assistant editor: Melinda M. Snodgrass. New York: Bantam, 1988.
Other forms: German.

The Journal of Xavier Desmond. *Aces Abroad*. Ed. by George R. R. Martin; assistant editor: Melinda M. Snodgrass. New York: Bantam, 1988.
Other forms: E-text.

The Skin Trade. *Night Visions 5*. Ed. by Douglas E. Winter. Arlington Hts, Illinois: Dark Harvest, 1988. [*Quartet*]
Other forms: Czech; German; Italian; Japanese; Audiorecording.
World Fantasy Awards winner.

1996

Blood of the Dragon [Excerpted from *A Game of Thrones*.] *Asimov's Science Fiction*, 20 (7; whole #247), July 1996. [*Quartet*]
Other forms: Italian.
Nebula Awards nominee; World Fantasy Awards nominee; Hugo Awards winner.

1998

The Hedge Knight. [Set in the cycle of *A Song of Ice and Fire*.] *Legends: Short Novels by the Masters of Modern Fantasy*. Ed by Robert Silverberg. New York: Tor Fantasy; A Tom Doherty Associates Book, 1998.
Other forms: German; Hebrew; Italian; Japanese; Audiorecording.
World Fantasy Awards nominee.

2000

Path of the Dragon. [Set in the cycle of *A Song of Ice and Fire*.] *Asimov's Science Fiction*, 24 (12; whole #299), December 2000.

2001

Black and White and Red All Over [novel fragment]. [*Quartet*]